CO 2 73 44848 X1

GHOST

100 STORIES
TO READ WITH
THE LIGHTS ON

CHOSEN BY
LOUISE WELSH

HEAD
of ZEUS

To my niece, Sophie Sinclair

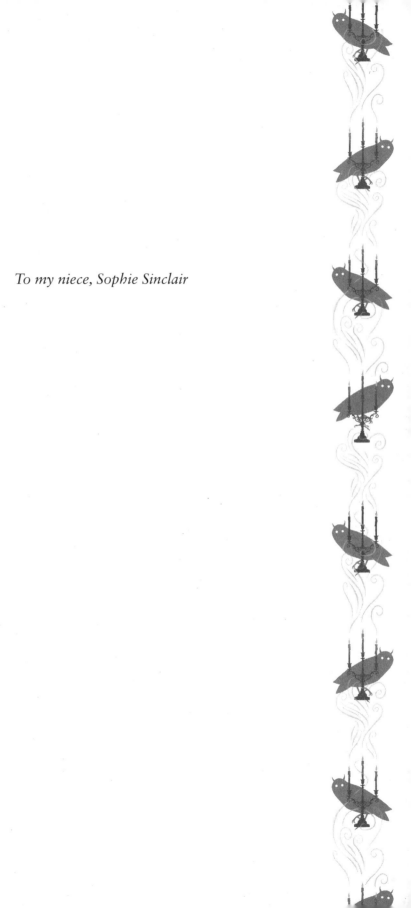

CONTENTS

Introduction

INTRODUCTION

. . . The time has been
That, when the brains were out, the man would die,
And there an end. But now they rise again

Macbeth, William Shakespeare

We love and miss our dead, but few of us would like them to return.

'For God's sake don't let it in,' cries the old man in W.W. Jacob's 'The Monkey's Paw' (1895), when the mangled son he has wished back to life comes knocking at the cottage door. Resurrection is a tricky business. It goes against the laws of nature and we would rather graves remain undisturbed, tombs locked and bolted.

Every civilisation has its ghosts. I imagine my ancient ancestors, clustered together around a smoky fire in some dank cave, casting nervous looks into the darkness beyond. One of them picks up a stick and pokes it into the flames, and then she begins to weave a story. A tale of ghosties, ghoulies, bogles and spunkies; substituted bairns and the disappeared who return aeons later, as young as they were, but strangely changed.

The endurance and plasticity of ghost stories remind us that we are drawn from the same stock as our ancestors and people of other nations and other cultures. Love, fear and mortality are common to us all. They are also at the heart of ghostly tales.

'A great number of people nowadays are beginning broadly to insinuate that there are no such things as ghosts, or spiritual beings visible to mortal sight,' James Hogg asserts in 'The Mysterious Bride' (1830). I am among the naysayers. I do not believe in ghosts, but it is still possible to be disquieted by things we do not believe in. The libraries of disturbing tales I read while assembling this collection of one hundred haunting stories have resulted in bad dreams and broken nights. My selection begins circa 113 AD with Pliny the Younger's 'Haunted House' and

finishes in 2014 with James Robertson's 'The Ghost'. It includes spine-chillers from Edith Wharton, Robert Louis Stevenson and Nathaniel Hawthorne; weird tales from H.P. Lovecraft, J.G. Ballard and Ray Bradbury. No collection of ghost stories would be complete without the walking dead, and so vampires are represented by Jewelle Gomez and Bram Stoker. Some ghosts are less frightening than others. Oscar Wilde, P.G. Wodehouse and Richmal Crompton are amongst those who invite us to laugh at our superstitions.

A few of the stories I have chosen are not stories at all. Kazuo Ishiguro has contributed a film script, Robert Burns a narrative poem, Mary Shelley a fragment of a novel. The collection contains classics of the genre from M.R. James, Charles Dickens and Sir Walter Scott. It also includes lesser known and recently published tales. Some stories hold no trace of the supernatural. Does Truman Capote's 'A Beautiful Child' (1979) featuring a very alive Marilyn Monroe, belong here? When I read it I feel that I am in the company of a dead woman walking; a ghost. But I will leave it for you to decide.

———

Ghost stories express fears that go beyond a glimpse of a ghoul draped in a white sheet. Many, such as the death of a child, are common to all peoples, all eras.

Toshiko, in Yukio Mishima's 'Swaddling Clothes' (1955) worries too much. She looks, 'more like a transparent picture than a creature of flesh and blood'. When we meet her she is upset by the contempt a doctor showed for her maid's unexpected and illegitimate child, born earlier that evening on the living room floor. What kind of future will a child swaddled in old newspapers have? Guilt can open the door to strange spectres and Toshiko discovers the answer to her question sooner than expected.

In Elizabeth Gaskell's 'The Old Nurse's Story' (1852), a ghost child tries to lure a living one out into the snow. Some phantoms are angry, but this dead child is lonely. Like Rosemary Timperley's 'Harry'(1955), it seeks a playmate to keep it company. We do not want to think of the dead as being left adrift, but we dread the idea that they might return to take us with them.

Governess tales were a popular nineteenth century genre. Neither gentry nor servant, governesses occupied a liminal space in the household. Like ghosts they existed on the threshold of different worlds. Lonely, sexually frustrated and at risk to flights of fancy, their impressions were not necessarily to be trusted, even by themselves. Female servants' precarious place in the world also made them vulnerable to other dangers, as the unfortunate Florence discovers in Elizabeth Taylor's 'Poor Girl' (1958), a story that owes a debt to Henry James's masterpiece, *The Turn of the Screw* (1898).

Newly engaged lady's maid Alice Hartley is wise to the pitfalls of her position, in 'The Lady's Maid's Bell' (1914) by Edith Wharton. When her employee's husband looks her up and down she tells us:

> I knew what the look meant, from having experienced it once or twice in my former places . . . The typhoid had served me well enough in one way: it kept that kind of gentleman at arm's-length.

A reminder of the fate that might yet await Alice flits along the corridors of the servants' quarters by night, the ghost of her predecessor.

It is notable how many of the late-nineteenth and early-twentieth century writers included in *Ghost* were supporters of the women's suffrage movement and other feminist and equal rights campaigns. Governesses and lady's maids were not the only people to be constricted and marginalised. Other classes had their trials too.

Charlotte Perkins Gilman's 'The Yellow Wallpaper' (1892) is narrated by a woman who is confined to bed and mentally unravelling. The story was inspired by treatment Gilman received for postpartum depression. Her doctor advised her to, 'Live as domestic a life as possible. Have your child with you all the time . . . Lie down an hour after each meal. Have but two hours' intellectual life a day. And never touch pen, brush or pencil as long as you live.' The cure turned out to be worse than the illness and Gilman eventually healed herself by quitting domesticity altogether.

The twenty-first century offers many of us a range of choices that would have been unimaginable to our forebears, but it seems that freedoms do not banish ghosts. The alternative lives we might have led can also inspire hauntings. In Jackie Kay's 'The White Cot' (2009) Dionne is on holiday with her girlfriend Sam. 'That wallpaper would drive me mad,' she says, in a nod to 'The Yellow Wallpaper', but it is not the furnishings that are playing with her mind.

Madness is a recurring theme in ghost stories and gothic tales: '. . . nervous – very, very dreadfully nervous I had been and am; but why will you say that I am mad?' asks Edgar Allan Poe's narrator in 'The Tell-Tale Heart' (1843). The story resonates with nerves strung tight to snapping point. Ghost stories place us on slip-changing sands where we are uncertain of our footing. A mad narrator is, of course, an unreliable narrator. But you do not have to be mad to be unreliable. Hilton is only seven years old in Tananarive Due's 'Prologue, 1963' (1995). Children have limited experience and vast imaginations, so we are not necessarily inclined to believe Hilton when he tells us that his Nana is a dead woman. The old lady walks, talks and gets on with her household duties but her flesh is, 'as cold as just-drawn well water. As cold as December'.

Weather can turn our thoughts to the supernatural as Robert Burns's

'Tam O'Shanter' (1791) discovers when 'roaring fou' he at last makes his way home across the Ayrshire countryside in the dead of a stormy night.

> The wind blew as 'twad blawn its last;
> The rattling show'rs rose on the blast;
> The speedy gleams the darkness swallow'd;
> Loud, deep, and lang the thunder bellowed:
> That night, a child might understand,
> The deil had business on his hand.

Tam has been supping ale all day with his friend Souter Johnny, and a drunk man is many more times likely to come across devil worshiping witches in Alloway Kirkyard than a sober man. But his horse's missing tail is evidence that her master's unlikely story may be true.

Tam O'Shanter is a trial to his wife Kate, but he's a cheerful, sociable drunk who we root for against the witches. The drunken man in Dylan Thomas's 'The Vest' (1939) is of another stamp. He is the danger we should run from, a man who might bring death into the cheeriest of public houses.

In 'The Tooth' (1948) by Shirley Jackson it is pain that alters Clara Spencer's perceptions and shifts her into a parallel world, where beguiling Jim is waiting to take care of her. Is it just 'the dope' that has made the world surreal: 'All that codeine and the whiskey, and nothing to eat all day'? Is Clara hallucinating or is she truly away with the fairies? Ghost stories invite us to question existence itself. Perhaps death is the most altering experience of all; or perhaps, as Jean Rhys's 'I Used to Live Here Once' (1976) suggests, it makes very little difference to our impressions.

'It's better to know you're dead,' says Tiny in Stevie Smith's 'Is There a Life Beyond the Gravy?' (1947) '"We're all dead" cried the children in a loud shrill chorus . . . "we've been dead for ages." . . . "We rather like it,"' Tiny adds. But adjusting to their new state is not always easy for the newly departed and some of them, such as Emma Jeffries in Mary Austin's 'The Readjustment' (1909) and Marianne in Kate Atkinson's 'Temporal Anomaly' (2002), feel a compulsion to linger in the land of the living. Marianne has carelessly caused the fatal car crash every driver fears. Her skull is fractured, her hair matted with blood and what might be brain matter, but she is not yet ready for the grave: 'She felt fucking awful but she didn't feel dead.'

Death is not the only taboo ghost stories give us permission to explore. This is a genre where nothing is off-limits. Robert Nye's 'Randal' (1976) contains quiet intimations of incest, and madness. Mark Twain's 'Cannibalism in the Cars' (1868) features a reminiscence about eating human flesh. Jewelle Gomez's 'The Gilda Stories' (1991) star a lesbian vampire and Louise Eldrich's 'Fleur' (1986) is subjected to sexual violence.

Joanne Rush's 'Guests' (2013) includes victims of the Bosnian war who begin to congregate in a lonely young woman's apartment: '"Motherfucking Chetnik!" "Sisterfucking Turk!"'

Sex can also be considered taboo. E. Nesbit's 'John Charrington's Wedding' (1891) and Elizabeth Bowen's 'The Demon Lover' (1945) both involve fiancés who return from the dead. 'Alive or dead, I mean to be married on Thursday!' John Charrington vows. Nesbit's tale, with its unspoken shades of necrophilia, expresses some of the nervous dread a Victorian bride might have felt as her wedding night approached. May Foster loves John Charrington but, much as she will mourn him, she does not want to be the bride of a corpse.

Elizabeth Bowen's 'The Demon Lover', first published at the end of World War II, suggests that for some women, the telegram informing them that their lover was 'missing presumed dead' came as a relief. 'You need do nothing but wait,' Kathleen's fiancé tells her before he leaves for war, '"I shall be with you . . . sooner or later" . . . She could not have plighted a more sinister troth.'

Love and lust are powerful forces and both young men refuse to lie easy without their true love. Of course in sex, as in everything else, personal tastes apply. In 'The Nature of the Evidence' (1923) by May Sinclair, Marston's beautiful young wife Rosamond returns from the dead after he has married sexy vamp Pauline. Marston ends up in a rather thrilling tug of love, but after a night in the library with the phantasm there is no doubt which woman he prefers.

Ghost stories remain in the literary lexicon regardless of changes in fashions. The form is both fundamental and flexible and pertains as much to life as it does to death.

'My death ship lost its way, a wrong turn of the wheel, a moment's absence of mind on the pilot's part, the distraction of my lovely native country, I cannot tell what it was . . .' Franz Kafka's 'The Hunter Gracchus', written in 1917, but not published until 1931, could belong to a much earlier, or a much later age. There is no sense of fear in the story. It is permeated instead by an atmosphere of loneliness familiar to anyone who has ever lost their way in life.

'The Singing Bone' is included in the Grimm brothers' *Children's and Household Tales*. The collection of folk tales was published in 1812, but it is impossible to date the individual stories. 'The Singing Bone' may be ancient, but its theme – the use of human remains to help track down a killer – continues to feature in twenty-first century murder mysteries.

Bones are central, too, in Zora Neale Hurston's 'High Walker and Bloody Bones', published in 1935 but again, as a folk tale, difficult to accurately date. Hurston faithfully reproduces the words and speech patterns of the people who originally told her their stories. Hurston's contemporaries

sometimes criticised her for this technique, but it enables us to hear the voices of earlier storytellers across the ages, an effect which adds vitality and expression to a simple tale.

Ghost stories cross ethnicities, cultures and continents. This collection is predominately European, but includes stories from Africa, Japan, Scandinavia, America and from writers of Native American and African American heritage. Jewelle Gomez's *The Gilda Stories* (1991) and Phyllis Alesia Perry's 'Stigmata' (1998) both draw on the slavery era in America.

Gomez's Gilda is transformed into a vampire while enslaved on a plantation. *The Gilda Stories* (represented in this collection by 'Off-Broadway: 1971') follow the eponymous heroine across two hundred years. As a vampire of colour, her history is also the history of social and political attitudes towards people of colour in the United States. Gomez's vampire has her own moral code; the people whose blood she drinks remain unharmed. Indeed the process enables Gilda to perceive their stories and to plant suggestions as to how their lives might be improved. The vampire's ethics may seem in danger of removing all tension from the plot; until we remember the danger her ethnicity regularly places her in across centuries.

'Our white nightgowns fly out from our legs, making us winged spirits.' Perry's 'Stigmata' depicts Ruth and Lizzie running through the night. Lizzie is a young African American woman coming of age in the 1960s, but this image would not be out of place in one of Mrs Radcliffe's eighteenth century gothic novels. Lizzie has begun to experience strange episodes. Her skin is bruised and tender for no reason, she sees visions and 'the line between dreaming and waking has become hard to see with the naked eye'. Is she in the grip of some psychosis, or are her enslaved African ancestors somehow reaching out to her across the centuries? This extract from a novel draws on classic ghost story iconography while also acknowledging the ongoing legacy of slavery.

Colonies and colonialism are fertile material for ghost stories. It is easier to imagine supernatural happenings taking place elsewhere, in a land where the gods are different and the customs mysterious. The sergeant-major who introduces the monkey's paw in W.W. Jacob's story presumably came across the evil charm while serving in India. He tells the old man that it is reputed to have 'had a spell put on it by an old fakir'.

'The other' is often a source of anxiety – especially for colonists who suspect the indigenous population might one day take back what has been stolen from them. Rudyard Kipling's 'My Own True Ghost Story' (1888) is set in India where he spent much of his life. It begins rather like a travelogue:

There are, in this land, ghosts who take the form of fat, cold, pobby corpses, and hide in trees near the roadside till a traveller passes. Then they drop upon his neck and remain. There are also terrible ghosts of women who have died in child-bed. These wander along the pathways at dusk, or hide in the crops near a village, and call seductively. But to answer their call is death in this world and the next. Their feet are turned backward that all sober men may recognize them. There are ghosts of little children who have been thrown into wells. These haunt well curbs and the fringes of jungles, and wail under the stars, or catch women by the wrist and beg to be taken up and carried . . .

He adds, tongue firmly in his cheek, 'No native ghost has yet been authentically reported to have frightened an Englishman'. The account takes the form of a reminiscence in which Kipling shows himself to be as susceptible to atmosphere as any khansamah. But he distinguishes himself from 'the natives', whose dishonesty is treated as childish and inevitable, by showing that his English good sense and persistence banishes the 'ghosts' who kept him awake all night.

Robert Morrison, 'A Man From Glasgow' (1944), is a long way from his rainy homeland. He meets Somerset Maugham's narrator in Algeciras in Southern Spain, on his way home from Ecija where he has been managing some olive groves. Once again the indigenous population is considered undependable. 'I couldn't get a trustworthy man to be at Ecija so last year I went there myself.' The summer proved hotter than anything he had experienced before. 'That blasted sun beat down and the glare was so awful, you felt your eyes would shoot out of your head.' Morrison reports that it was not long before he began to hear ghostly laughter coming from a deserted house on the other side of the grove.

'A Man from Glasgow' relies on a slow, creeping sense of dread for its effect. Maugham makes a point of stating that Robert Morrison seemed 'perfectly sober', but his face is marked by chronic alcoholism which, combined with the searing heat and isolation, may have sent the man temporarily mad. The atmosphere builds gradually as Morrison describes his increasing terror. The effect replicates similar sensations in the reader and encourages us to think that the Glaswegian may not be entirely wrong in his belief that something lays awake, waiting for him in the olive groves.

Kipling and Maugham both give their stories locations whose atmosphere helps build tension. Place is often crucial to the success of ghostly tales, and what is more ghostly than a haunted house? The illustrator in Tove Jansson's homage to Edward Gorey, 'Black-White' (1971) finds he cannot produce the right shade of black while living in his wife's beautifully designed modern home, 'an enormous openwork of glass and unpainted wood'. Instead he decides to work in a tall, narrow, abandoned house that merges with a hill in the shadow of the pines. 'No one can depict desolation who hasn't inhabited desolation,' he writes to his wife. 'Things condemned have a terrible beauty.'

Not all ghost stories are set in gloomy locations. Extreme landscapes perk the senses and both Ambrose Bierce and Annie Proulx find inspiration for their respective stories – 'The Stranger' (1909) and 'The Sagebrush Kid' (2008) – in desert landscapes more usually associated with Westerns.

Endlessly adaptable, ghost stories can cross genres. Science fiction is also inclined to allegories and encounters with frightening beings from different worlds, so it is unsurprising that the forms frequently overlap. In Ray Bradbury's 'Mars is Heaven' (1948) the crew of a rocket ship land safely on the red planet, where they are amazed to encounter their dead loved ones. The experience is so wonderful that, to their cost, the astronauts neglect to interrogate possible reasons for the phenomenon.

J.G. Ballard's 'The Dead Astronaut' (1976) has no supernatural aspect to its plot, but Judith, Philip and the relic hunters of Cape Kennedy are haunted by the returning dead. The ghostly form of Robert Hamilton has been orbiting the earth, in his burnt out capsule, for more than fifteen years. Now he is coming home and Judith is determined to receive his remains. Her obsession leads to her receiving more than she expected.

'I was the slave, not the master, of an impulse, which I detested, yet could not disobey.' The creature in Mary Wollstonecraft Shelley's *Frankenstein* or *The Modern Prometheus* (1818) is made from recycled body parts dug up from a graveyard in the dead of night. The central premise of the novel is that the monster is alive, but he is an unnatural being that, by the end of the book, is locked into a terrible cycle of hunting and haunting with his creator Dr Frankenstein: '. . . the fallen angel becomes a malignant devil. Yet even that enemy of God and man had friends and associates in his desolation; I am alone.'

It is tempting to imagine ghosts as always being alone, but in Fyodor Dostoyevsky's 'Bobok' (1873) the bodies buried in the graveyard are engaged in a spirited conversation, full of the petty snobberies that characterised them in life. Adam Marek's 'Dinner of the Dead Alumni' (2010) and Helen Simpson's 'The Festival of the Immortals' (2013) also depict ghosts as part of a busy throng. 'The streets of Cambridge are crawling with dead alumni' as Marek's ghosts take part in a reunion. Simpson's ghosts are possibly even more distinguished, though subject to prurient questions. They are dead, out-of-copyright writers, taking part in an unusual literary festival. Charlotte Brontë will read from *Villette*, her sister Emily is scheduled to take part in a session entitled 'TB and Me' and Shakespeare has half promised to give a creative writing workshop. The afterlife may not be as desolate as some fear.

———

I have arranged my selection in order of year of publication. Inevitably there were some stories I wanted desperately to include, but which had to be excluded for reasons of copyright or length. They included E.T.A. Hoffman's 'The Sandman', Henry James's *The Turn of the Screw* and Karen Blixen's 'The Supper at Elsinore'. Each of these texts is readily available. If you have not read them before then you are in for a series of disturbing treats.

I began this introduction by stating that few of us want the dead to return. That is untrue. Sometimes it is what we want most of all. Ghost stories disturb, entertain and enlighten us about the world we live in. They also occasionally grant us a glimpse of those who have gone before. As Tim O'Brien writes in 'The Lives of the Dead' (1989) 'in a story, which is a kind of dreaming, the dead sometimes smile and sit up and return to the world.'

Happy hauntings.

Louise Welsh

Glasgow
July 2015

THE HAUNTED HOUSE

Pliny the Younger

Gaius Plinius (c.AD 61–c.113) was born in Como in northern Italy to a wealthy landowner, Lucius Caecilius, and Plinia Marcella, sister of Pliny the Elder. His father died young and he was adopted by his uncle. Pliny the Younger is best known for his letters (*Epistulae*), nine books of which were published between AD 99 and 109. He practised law and later entered the senate where he became Praetor in AD 93 and Consul in AD 100.

There was at Athens a mansion, spacious and commodious, but of evil repute and dangerous to health. In the dead of night there was a noise as of iron, and, if you listened more closely, a clanking of chains was heard, first of all from a distance, and afterwards hard by. Presently a spectre used to appear, an ancient man sinking with emaciation and squalor, with a long beard and bristly hair, wearing shackles on his legs and fetters on his hands, and shaking them.

Hence the inmates, by reason of their fears, passed miserable and horrible nights in sleeplessness. This want of sleep was followed by disease, and, their terrors increasing, by death. For in the daytime as well, though the apparition had departed, yet a reminiscence of it flitted before their eyes, and their dread outlived its cause.

The mansion was accordingly deserted and, condemned to solitude, was entirely abandoned to the dreadful ghost. However, it was advertised, on the chance of some one, ignorant of the fearful curse attached to it, being willing to buy or to rent it.

Athenodorus the philosopher came to Athens and read the advertisement. When he had been informed of the terms, which were so low as to appear suspicious, he made inquiries, and learned the whole of the particulars. Yet none the less on that account, nay, all the more readily, did he rent the house.

As evening began to draw on, he ordered a sofa to be set for himself in the front part of the house, and called for his notebooks, writing implements, and a light. All his servants he dismissed to the interior apartments, and for himself applied his soul, eyes, and hand to composition, that his mind might not, from want of occupation, picture to itself the phantoms of which he had heard, or any empty terrors.

At the commencement there was the universal silence of night. Soon the shaking of irons and the clanking of chains was heard, yet he never raised his eyes nor slackened his pen, but hardened his soul and deadened his ears by its help.

The noise grey and approached: now it seemed to be heard at the door, and next inside the door.

He looked round, beheld and recognised the figure he had been told of. It was standing and signalling to him with its finger, as though inviting him. He, in reply, made a sign with his hand that it should wait a moment, and applied himself afresh to his tablets and pen. Upon this the figure kept rattling its chains over his head as he wrote.

On looking round again, he saw it making the same signal as before, and without delay took up a light and followed it. It moved with a slow step, as though oppressed by its chains, and, after turning into the courtyard of the house, vanished suddenly and left his company.

On being thus left to himself, he marked the spot with some grass and leaves which he plucked. Next day he applied to the magistrates, and urged them to have the spot in question dug up. There were found there some bones attached to and intermingled with fetters; the body to which they had belonged, rotted away by time and the soil, had abandoned them thus naked and corroded to the chains. They were collected and interred at the public expense, and the house was ever afterwards free from the spirit, which had obtained due sepulture.

The above story I believe on the strength of those who affirm it. What follows I am myself in a position to affirm to others. I have a freedman, who is not without some knowledge of letters. A younger brother of his was sleeping with him in the same bed. The latter dreamed he saw some one sitting on the couch, who approached a pair of scissors to his head, and even cut the hair from the crown of it. When day dawned he was found to be cropped round the crown, and his locks were discovered lying about. A very short time afterwards a fresh occurrence of the same kind confirmed the truth of the former one. A lad of mine was sleeping, in company with several others, in the pages' apartment. There came through the windows (so he tells the story) two figures in white tunics, who cut his hair as he lay, and departed the way they came. In his case, too, daylight exhibited him shorn, and his locks scattered around. Nothing remarkable followed, except, perhaps, this, that I was not brought under accusation, as I should have been, if Domitian (in whose reign these events happened) had lived longer. For in his desk was found an information against me which had been presented by Carus; from which circumstance it may be conjectured – inasmuch as it is the custom of accused persons to let their hair grow – that the cutting off of my slaves' hair was a sign of the danger which threatened me being averted.

I beg, then, that you will apply your great learning to this subject. The matter is one which deserves long and deep consideration on your part; nor am I, for my part, undeserving of having the fruits of your wisdom imparted to me. You may even argue on both sides (as your way is), provided you argue more forcibly on one side than the other, so as not to dismiss me in suspense and anxiety, when the very cause of my consulting you has been to have my doubts ended.

DANIEL CROWLEY AND THE GHOSTS

Anon.

I have no idea who wrote 'Daniel Crowley and the Ghosts'. My instinct is that this story was the product of many voices and imaginations, developed and embellished over numerous tellings until eventually someone committed it to paper.

There lived a man in Cork whose name was Daniel Crowley. He was a coffin-maker by trade, and had a deal of coffins laid by, so that his apprentice might sell them when himself was not at home.

A messenger came to Daniel Crowley's shop one day and told him that there was a man dead at the end of the town, and to send up a coffin for him, or to make one.

Daniel Crowley took down a coffin, put it on a donkey cart, drove to the wake house, went in and told the people of the house that the coffin was there for them. The corpse was laid out on a table in a room next to the kitchen. Five or six women were keeping watch around it; many people were in the kitchen. Daniel Crowley was asked to sit down and commence to shorten the night: that is, to tell stories, amuse himself and others. A tumbler of punch was brought, and he promised to do the best he could.

He began to tell stories and shorten the night. A second glass of punch was brought to him, and he went on telling tales. There was a man at the wake who sang a song: after him another was found, and then another. Then the people asked Daniel Crowley to sing, and he did. The song that he sang was of another nation. He sang about the good people, the fairies. The song pleased the company, they desired him to sing again, and he did not refuse.

Daniel Crowley pleased the company so much with his two songs that a woman who had three daughters wanted to make a match for one of them, and get Daniel Crowley as a husband for her. Crowley was a bachelor, well on in years, and had never thought of marrying.

The mother spoke of the match to a woman sitting next to her. The woman shook her head, but the mother said: "If he takes one of my daughters I'll be glad, for he has money laid by. Do you go and speak to him, but say nothing of me at first."

The woman went to Daniel Crowley then, and told him that she had a fine, beautiful girl in view, and that now was his time to get a good wife; he'd never have such a chance again.

Crowley rose up in great anger. "There isn't a woman wearing clothes that I'd marry," said he. "There isn't a woman born that could bring me to make two halves of my loaf for her."

The mother was insulted now and forgot herself. She began to abuse Crowley.

"Bad luck to you, you hairy little scoundrel," said she, "you might be a grandfather to my child. You are not fit to clean the shoes on her feet. You have only dead people for company day and night; 'tis by them you make your living."

"Oh, then," said Daniel Crowley, "I'd prefer the dead to the living any day if all the living were like you. Besides, I have nothing against the dead. I am getting employment by them and not by the living, for 'tis the dead that want coffins."

"Bad luck to you, 'tis with the dead you ought to be and not with the living; 'twould be fitter for you to go out of this altogether and go to your dead people."

"I'd go if I knew how to go to them," said Crowley.

"Why not invite them to supper?" retorted the woman.

He rose up then, went out, and called: "Men, women, children, soldiers, sailors, all people that I have ever made coffins for, I invite you to-night to my house, and I'll spend what is needed in giving a feast."

The people who were watching the dead man on the table saw him smile when he heard the invitation. They ran out of the room in a fright and out of the kitchen, and Daniel Crowley hurried away to his shop as fast as ever his donkey could carry him. On the way he came to a public-house and, going in, bought a pint bottle of whiskey, put it in his pocket, and drove on.

The workshop was locked and the shutters down when he left that evening, but when he came near he saw that all the windows were shining with light, and he was in dread that the building was burning or that robbers were in it. When right there Crowley slipped into a corner of the building opposite, to know could he see what was happening, and soon he saw crowds of men, women, and children walking toward his shop and going in, but none coming out. He was hiding some time when a man tapped him on the shoulder and asked, "Is it here you are, and we waiting for you? 'Tis a shame to treat company this way. Come now."

Crowley went with the man to the shop, and as he passed the threshold he saw a great gathering of people. Some were neighbours, people he had known in the past. All were dancing, singing, amusing themselves. He was not long looking on when a man came up to him and said: "You seem not to know me, Daniel Crowley."

"I don't know you," said Crowley. "How could I?"

"You might then, and you ought to know me, for I am the first man you made a coffin for, and 'twas I gave you the first start in business."

Soon another came up, a lame man: "Do you know me, Daniel Crowley?"

"I do not."

"I am your cousin, and it isn't long since I died."

"Oh, now I know you well, for you are lame. In God's name," said Crowley to the cousin, "how am I to get these people out o' this. What time is it?"

"Tis early yet, it's hardly eleven o'clock, man."

Crowley wondered that it was so early.

"Receive them kindly," said the cousin; "be good to them, make merriment as you can."

"I have no money with me to get food or drink for them; 'tis night now, and all places are closed," answered Crowley.

"Well, do the best you can," said the cousin.

The fun and dancing went on, and while Daniel Crowley was looking around, examining everything, he saw a woman in the far-off corner. She took no part in the amusement, but seemed very shy in herself.

"Why is that woman so shy – she seems to be afraid?" asked he of the cousin. "And why doesn't she dance and make merry like others?"

"Oh, 'tis not long since she died, and you gave the coffin, as she had no means of paying for it. She is in dread you'll ask her for the money, or let the company know that she didn't pay," said the cousin.

The best dancer they had was a piper by the name of John Reardon from the city of Cork. The fiddler was one John Healy. Healy brought no fiddle with him, but he made one, and the way he made it was to take off what flesh he had on his body. He rubbed up and down on his own ribs, each rib having a different note, and he made the loveliest music that Daniel Crowley had ever heard. After that the whole company followed his example. All threw off what flesh they had on them and began to dance jigs and hornpipes in their bare bones. When by chance they struck against one another in dancing, you'd think it was Brandon Mountain that was striking Mount Eagle, with the noise that was in it.

Daniel Crowley plucked up all his courage to know could he live through the night, but still he thought daylight would never come. There was one man, John Sullivan, that he noticed especially. This man had married twice in his life, and with him came the two women. Crowley saw him taking out the second wife to dance a breakdown, and the two danced so well that the company were delighted, and all the skeletons had their mouths open, laughing. He danced and knocked so much merriment out of them all that his first wife, who was at the end of the house, became jealous and very mad altogether. She ran down to where he was and told him she had a better right to dance with him than the second wife; "That's not the truth for you," said the second wife; "I have a better right than you. When he married me you were a dead woman and he was free, and, besides, I'm a better dancer than what you are, and I will dance with him whether you like it or not."

"Hold your tongue!" screamed the first wife. "Sure, you couldn't come to this feast tonight at all but for the loan of another woman's shinbones."

Sullivan looked at his two wives, and asked the second one: "Isn't it your own shinbones you have?"

"No, they are borrowed. I borrowed a neighbouring woman's shins from her, and 'tis those I have with me tonight."

"Who is the owner of the shinbones you have under you?" asked the husband.

"They belong to one Catherine Murray. She hadn't a very good name in life."

"But why didn't you come on your own feet?"

"Oh, I wasn't good myself in life, and I was put under a penalty, and the penalty is that whenever there is a feast or a ball I cannot go to it unless I am able to borrow a pair of shins."

Sullivan was raging when he found that the shinbones he had been dancing with belonged to a third woman, and she not the best, and he gave a slap to the wife that sent her spinning into a corner.

The woman had relations among the skeletons present, and they were angry when they saw the man strike their friend. "We'll never let that go with him," said they. "We must knock satisfaction out of Sullivan!"

The woman's friends rose up, and, as there were no clubs or weapons, they pulled off their left arms and began to slash and strike with them in terrible fashion. There was an awful battle in one minute.

While this was going on Daniel Crowley was standing below at the end of the room, cold and hungry, not knowing but he'd be killed. As Sullivan was trying to dodge the blows sent against him, he got as far as Daniel Crowley and stepped on his toe without knowing it; Crowley got vexed and gave Sullivan a blow with his fist that drove the head from him and sent it flying to the opposite corner.

When Sullivan saw his head flying off from the blow, he ran, and, catching it, aimed a blow at Daniel Crowley with the head, and aimed so truly that he knocked him under the bench; then, having him at a disadvantage, Sullivan hurried to the bench and began to strangle him. He squeezed his throat and held him so firmly between the bench and the floor that the man lost his senses, and couldn't remember a thing more.

When Daniel Crowley came to himself in the morning, his apprentice found him stretched under the bench with an empty bottle under his arm. He was bruised and pounded. His throat was sore where Sullivan had squeezed it; he didn't know how the company broke up, nor when his guests went away.

TAM O'SHANTER

Robert Burns

Robert Burns (1759–1796) was born in Alloway, Ayrshire and spent his early life working on a series of barely profitable tenant farms. He was considering decamping for the West Indies when his first collection, *Poems, Chiefly in the Scottish Dialect* was published in 1786. Burns was often in conflict with the kirk. His poems reflect a love of nature, the opposite sex, carousing and a desire for social equality. His birthday is celebrated on the 25th January each year at Burns Suppers across the world.

When chapman billies leave the street,
And drouthy neebors, neebors meet,
As market-days are wearing late,
An' folk begin to tak the gate;
While we sit bousing at the nappy,
An' getting fou and unco happy,
We think na on the lang Scots miles,
The mosses, waters, slaps, and styles,
That lie between us and our hame,
Whar sits our sulky sullen dame,
Gathering her brows like gathering storm,
Nursing her wrath to keep it warm.

This truth fand honest Tam o' Shanter,
As he frae Ayr ae night did canter
(Auld Ayr wham ne'er a town surpasses
For honest men and bonny lasses).

O Tam! hadst thou but been sae wise,
As ta'en thy ain wife Kate's advice!
She tauld thee weel thou was a skellum,
A blethering, blustering, drunken blellum;
That frae November till October,
Ae market-day thou was nae sober;
That lika melder, wi' the miller,
Thou sat as lang as thou had siller;
That ev'ry naig was ca'd a shoe on,
The smith and thee gat roaring fou on;

That at the L – d's house, ev'n on Sunday,
Thou drank wi' Kirton Jean till Monday.
She prophesy'd that late or soon,
Thou would be found deep drown'd in Doon;
Or catch'd wi' warlocks in the mirk,
By Alloway's auld haunted kirk.

The landlady and Tam grew gracious.
The landlady and Tam grew gracious.
Ah, gentle dames! it gars me greet,
To think how mony counsels sweet,
How mony lengthen'd sage advices,
The husband frae the wife despises!

But to our tale: Ae market night,
Tam had got planted unco right;
Fast by an ingle, bleezing finely,
Wi' reaming swats, that drank divinely;
And at his elbow, Souter Johnny,
His ancient, trusty, drouthy crony;
Tam lo'ed him like a vera brither;
They had been fou for weeks thegither.
The night drave on wi' sangs an' clatter;
And ay the ale was growing better:
The landlady and Tam grew gracious,
Wi' favors, secret, sweet, and precious:
The Souter tauld his queerest stories;
The landlord's laugh was ready chorus:
The storm without might rair and rustle,
Tam did na mind the storm a whistle.

Care, mad to see a man sae happy,
E'en drown'd himself amang the nappy,
As bees flee hame wi' lades o' treasure,
The minutes wing'd their way wi' pleasure:
Kings may be blest, but Tam was glorious,
O'er a' the ills o' life victorious!

But pleasures are like poppies spread,
You seize the flow'r, its bloom is shed;
Or like the snow-falls in the river,
A moment white – then melt forever;
Or like the borealis race,
That flit ere you can point their place;
Or like the rainbow's lovely form
Evanishing amid the storm. –
Nae man can tether time or tide;

The hour approaches Tam maun ride;
That hour, o' night's black arch the key-stane,
That dreary hour he mounts his beast in,
And sic a night he taks the road in;
As ne'er poor sinner was abroad in.

Well mounted on his grey mare, Meg.
Well mounted on his grey mare, Meg.
The wind blew as 'twad blawn its last;
The rattling show'rs rose on the blast;
The speedy gleams the darkness swallow'd;
Loud, deep, and lang the thunder bellowed:
That night, a child might understand,
The deil had business on his hand.

Weel mounted on his grey mare, Meg,
A better never lifted leg,
Tam skelpit on thro' dub and mire,
Despising wind, and rain, and fire;
Whiles holding fast his gude blue bonnet;
Whiles crooning o'er some auld Scots sonnet;
Whiles glow'ring round wi' prudent cares,
Lest bogles catch him unawares:
Kirk-Alloway was drawing nigh,
Whare ghaists and houlets nightly cry. –

By this time he was cross the ford,
Whare in the snaw the chapman smoor'd;
And past the birks and meikie stane,
Whare drunken Charlie brak's neck-bane;
And thro' the whins, and by the cairn,
Whare hunters fand the murder'd bairn;
And near the thorn, aboon the well,
Whare Mungo's mither hang'd hersel. –
Before him Doon pours all his floods;
The doubling storm roars thro' the woods;
The lightnings flash from pole to pole;
Near and more near the thunders roll:
When, glimmering thro' the groaning trees,
Kirk-Alloway seem'd in a bleeze;
Thro' ilka bore the beams were glancing;
And loud resounded mirth and dancing. –

Inspiring bold John Barleycorn!
What dangers thou canst make us scorn;
Wi' tippenny, we fear nae evil;
Wi' usquabae we'll face the devil! –

The swats sae ream'd in Tammie's noddle,
Fair play, he car'd na deils a boddle.
But Maggie stood right sair astonish'd,
Till, by the heel and hand admonish'd,
She ventur'd forward on the light:
And, vow! Tam saw an unco sight!
Warlocks and witches in a dance;
Nae cotillion brent new frae France,
But hornpipes, jigs, strathspeys, and reels,
Put life and mettle in their heels.
A winnock-bunker in the east,
There sat auld Nick, in shape o' beast;
A towzie tyke, black, grim, and large,
To gie them music was his charge;
He screw'd the pipes and gart them skirl,
Till roof and rafters a' did dirl. –
Coffins stood round, like open presses,
That shaw'd the dead in their last dresses;
And by some devilish cantrip slight,
Each in its cauld hand held a light. –
By which heroic Tam was able
To note upon the haly table,
A murderer's banes in gibbet airns;
Twa span-lang, wee, unchristen'd bairns;
A thief, new-cutted frae a rape,
Wi' his last gasp his gab did gape;
Five tomahawks, wi' blude red-rusted;
Five scymitars, wi' murder crusted;
A garter, which a babe had strangled;
A knife, a father's throat had mangled,
Whom his ain son o' life bereft,
The gray hairs yet stack to the heft:
Wi' mair o' horrible and awfu',
Which ev'n to name wad be unlawfu'.

The dancers quick and quicker flew.
The dancers quick and quicker flew.
As Tammie glowr'd, amaz'd, and curious,
The mirth and fun grew fast and furious:
The piper loud and louder blew:
The dancers quick and quicker flew;
They reel'd, they set, they cross'd, they cleekit,
Till ilka carlin swat and reekit,
And coost her duddies to the wark,
And linket at it in her sark!
Now Tam, O Tam! had thae been queans
A' plump and strapping, in their teens:

Their sarks, instead o' creeshie flannen,
Been snaw-white seventeen hunder linen!
Thir breeks o' mine, my only pair,
That ance were plush, o' gude blue hair,
I wad hae gi'en them off my hurdies,
For ae blink o' the bonnie burdies!

But wither'd beldams, auld and droll,
Rigwoodie hags wad spean a foal,
Lowping an' flinging on a crummock,
I wonder didna turn thy stomach.

But Tam kend what was what fu' brawlie,
There was ae winsome wench and walie,
That night enlisted in the core
(Lang after kend on Carrick shore;
For mony a beast to dead she shot,
And perish'd mony a bonnie boat,
And shook baith meikle corn and bear,
And kept the country-side in fear),
Her cutty sark, o' Paisley harn,
That while a lassie she had worn,
In longitude tho' sorely scanty,
It was her best, and she was vauntie. –
Ah! little kend thy reverend grannie,
That sark she coft for her wee Nannie,
Wi' twa pund Scots ('twas a' her riches),
Wad ever grac'd a dance of witches!

But here my muse her wing maun cour;
Sic flights are far beyond her pow'r;
To sing how Nannie lap and flang
(A souple jade she was and strang),
And how Tam stood like ane bewitch'd,
And thought his very een enrich'd;
Even Satan glowr'd, and fidg'd fu' fain,
And hotch'd and blew wi' might and main:
Till first ae caper, syne anither,
Tam tint his reason a' thegither,
And roars out, "Weel done, Cutty-sark!"
And in an instant all was dark;
And scarcely had he Maggie rallied,
When out the hellish legion sallied.

As bees bizz out wi' angry fyke,
When plundering herds assail their byke;
As open pussie's mortal foes,

When, pop! she starts before their nose;
As eager runs the market-crowd,
When "Catch the thief!" resounds aloud;
So Maggie runs, the witches follow,
Wi' mony an eldritch skreech and hollow.

Ah, Tam! Ah, Tam! thou'll get thy fairin!
In hell they'll roast thee like a herrin!
In vain thy Kate awaits thy coming!
Kate soon will be a woefu' woman!
Now, do thy speedy utmost, Meg,
An win the key-stane[A] of the brig;
There at them thou thy tail may toss,
A running stream they dare na cross.
But ere the key-stane she could make,
The fient a tail she had to shake!
For Nannie, far before the rest,
Hard upon noble Maggie prest,
And flew at Tam wi' furious ettle;
But little wist she Maggie's mettle –
Ae spring brought off her master hale,
But left behind her ain gray tail:
The carlin claught her by the rump,
And left poor Maggie scarce a stump.

Now, wha this tale o' truth shall read,
Ilk man and mother's son, take heed;
Whene'er to drink you are inclin'd,
Or cutty-sarks run in your mind,
Think, ye may buy the joys o'er dear,
Remember Tam o' Shanter's mare.

THE SINGING BONE

Brothers Grimm

Brothers **Jacob** and **Wilhelm Grimm** (1785–1863 / 1786–1859) were born in Hanau, Germany. The brothers began collecting folk tales while attending the University of Marburg. Their careers were remarkably parallel. Both served together as librarians in Kassel, Göttingen and Berlin. Volume I of *Children's and Household Tales* appeared in 1812. Volume II followed three years later. The collection, popularly known as Grimm's Tales, has attracted controversy due to the violent, erotic and disturbing nature of some of the stories.

In a certain country there was once great lamentation over a wild boar that laid waste the farmers' fields, killed the cattle, and ripped up people's bodies with his tusks. The King promised a large reward to anyone who would free the land from this plague; but the beast was so big and strong that no one dared to go near the forest in which it lived. At last the King gave notice that whosoever should capture or kill the wild boar should have his only daughter to wife.

Now there lived in the country two brothers, sons of a poor man, who declared themselves willing to undertake the hazardous enterprise; the elder, who was crafty and shrewd, out of pride; the younger, who was innocent and simple, from a kind heart. The King said: "In order that you may be the more sure of finding the beast, you must go into the forest from opposite sides." So the elder went in on the west side, and the younger on the east.

When the younger had gone a short way, a little man stepped up to him. He held in his hand a black spear and said: "I give you this spear because your heart is pure and good; with this you can boldly attack the wild boar, and it will do you no harm."

He thanked the little man, shouldered the spear, and went on fearlessly.

Before long he saw the beast, which rushed at him; but he held the spear towards it, and in its blind fury it ran so swiftly against it that its heart was cloven in twain. Then he took the monster on his back and went homewards with it to the King.

As he came out at the other side of the wood, there stood at the entrance a house where people were making merry with wine and dancing. His elder brother had gone in here, and, thinking that after all the boar would not run away from him, was going to drink until he felt brave. But when he saw his young brother coming out of the wood laden with his booty, his envious, evil heart gave him no peace. He called out to him: "Come in, dear brother, rest and refresh yourself with a cup of wine."

The youth, who suspected no evil, went in and told him about the good little man who had given him the spear where with he had slain the boar.

The elder brother kept him there until the evening, and then they went away together, and when in the darkness they came to a bridge over a brook, the elder brother let the other go first; and when he was half-way across he gave him such a blow from behind that he fell down dead. He buried him beneath the bridge, took the boar, and carried it to the King, pretending that he had killed it; whereupon he obtained the King's daughter in marriage. And when his younger brother did not come back he said: "The boar must have ripped up his body," and every one believed it.

But as nothing remains hidden from God, so this black deed also was to come to light.

Years afterwards a shepherd was driving his herd across the bridge, and saw lying in the sand beneath, a snow-white little bone. He thought that it would make a good mouth-piece, so he clambered down, picked it up, and cut out of it a mouth-piece for his horn. But when he blew through it for the first time, to his great astonishment, the bone began of its own accord to sing:

> "Ah, friend, thou blowest upon my bone!
> Long have I lain beside the water;
> My brother slew me for the boar,
> And took for his wife the King's young daughter."

"What a wonderful horn!" said the shepherd; "it sings by itself; I must take it to my lord the King." And when he came with it to the King the horn again began to sing its little song. The King understood it all, and caused the ground below the bridge to be dug up, and then the whole skeleton of the murdered man came to light. The wicked brother could not deny the deed, and was sewn up in a sack and drowned. But the bones of the murdered man were laid to rest in a beautiful tomb in the churchyard.

CAPTAIN WALTON'S FINAL LETTER

Mary Wollstonecraft Shelley

Mary Wollstonecraft Shelley's (1797–1851) life was punctuated by tragic early deaths. Her mother, Mary Wollstonecraft, author of *A Vindication of the Rights of Women*, died of a placental infection when Mary was eleven days old. In 1814 Mary eloped to Switzerland with the already married poet Percy Bysshe Shelley. Mary lost three children before the birth of her surviving son Percy. She published *Frankenstein* at the age of twenty-one and was widowed at twenty-four. Percy Shelley drowned in 1822 when his yacht sank during a storm near Viareggio.

September 9th, the ice began to move, and roarings like thunder were heard at a distance, as the islands split and cracked in every direction. We were in the most imminent peril; but, as we could only remain passive, my chief attention was occupied by my unfortunate guest, whose illness increased in such a degree, that he was entirely confined to his bed. The ice cracked behind us, and was driven with force towards the north; a breeze sprung from the west, and on the 11th the passage towards the south became perfectly free. When the sailors saw this, and that their return to their native country was apparently assured, a shout of tumultuous joy broke from them, loud and long-continued. Frankenstein, who was dozing, awoke, and asked the cause of the tumult. "They shout," I said, "because they will soon return to England."

"Do you then really return?"

"Alas! yes; I cannot withstand their demands. I cannot lead them unwillingly to danger, and I must return."

"Do so, if you will; but I will not. You may give up your purpose, but mine is assigned to me by Heaven, and I dare not. I am weak; but surely the spirits who assist my vengeance will endow me with sufficient strength." Saying this, he endeavoured to spring from the bed, but the exertion was too great for him; he fell back, and fainted.

It was long before he was restored; and I often thought that life was entirely extinct. At length he opened his eyes; he breathed with difficulty, and was unable to speak. The surgeon gave him a composing draught, and ordered us to leave him undisturbed. In the mean time he told me, that my friend had certainly not many hours to live.

His sentence was pronounced; and I could only grieve, and be patient. I sat by his bed, watching him; his eyes were closed, and I thought he slept; but presently he called to me in a feeble voice, and, bidding me come near, said – "Alas! the strength I relied on is gone; I feel that I shall soon die, and he, my enemy and persecutor, may still be in being. Think not, Walton, that in the last moments of my existence I feel that burning hatred, and ardent desire of revenge, I once expressed; but I feel myself justified in desiring the death of my adversary. During these last days I have been occupied in examining my past conduct; nor do I find it blamable. In a fit of enthusiastic madness I created a rational creature, and was bound towards him, to assure, as far as was in my power, his happiness and well-being. This was my duty; but there was another still paramount to that. My duties towards the beings of my own species had greater claims to my attention, because they included a greater proportion of happiness or misery. Urged by this view, I refused, and I did right in refusing, to create a companion for the first creature. He showed unparalleled malignity and selfishness, in evil: he destroyed my friends; he devoted to destruction beings who possessed exquisite sensations, happiness, and wisdom; nor do I know where this thirst for vengeance may end. Miserable himself, that he may render no other wretched, he ought to die. The task of his destruction was mine, but I have failed. When actuated by selfish and vicious motives, I asked you to undertake my unfinished work; and I renew this request now, when I am only induced by reason and virtue.

"Yet I cannot ask you to renounce your country and friends, to fulfil this task; and now, that you are returning to England, you will have little chance of meeting with him. But the consideration of these points, and the well balancing of what you may esteem your duties, I leave to you; my judgment and ideas are already disturbed by the near approach of death. I dare not ask you to do what I think right, for I may still be misled by passion.

"That he should live to be an instrument of mischief disturbs me; in other respects, this hour, when I momentarily expect my release, is the only happy one which I have enjoyed for several years. The forms of the beloved dead flit before me, and I hasten to their arms. Farewell, Walton! Seek happiness in tranquillity, and avoid ambition, even if it be only the apparently innocent one of distinguishing yourself in science and discoveries. Yet why do I say this? I have myself been blasted in these hopes, yet another may succeed."

His voice became fainter as he spoke; and at length, exhausted by his effort, he sunk into silence. About half an hour afterwards he attempted again to speak, but was unable; he pressed my hand feebly, and his eyes closed for ever, while the irradiation of a gentle smile passed away from his lips.

Margaret, what comment can I make on the untimely extinction of this glorious spirit? What can I say, that will enable you to understand the depth of my sorrow? All that I should express would be inadequate and feeble. My tears flow; my mind is overshadowed by a cloud of disappointment. But I journey towards England, and I may there find consolation.

I am interrupted. What do these sounds portend? It is midnight; the breeze blows fairly, and the watch on deck scarcely stir. Again; there is a sound as of a human voice, but hoarser; it comes from the cabin where the remains of Frankenstein still lie. I must arise, and examine. Good night, my sister.

Great God! what a scene has just taken place! I am yet dizzy with the remembrance of it. I hardly know whether I shall have the power to detail it; yet the tale which I have recorded would be incomplete without this final and wonderful catastrophe.

I entered the cabin, where lay the remains of my ill-fated and admirable friend. Over him hung a form which I cannot find words to describe; gigantic in stature, yet uncouth and distorted in its proportions. As he hung over the coffin, his face was concealed by long locks of ragged hair; but one vast hand was extended, in colour and apparent texture like that of a mummy. When he heard the sound of my approach, he ceased to utter exclamations of grief and horror, and sprung towards the window. Never did I behold a vision so horrible as his face, of such loathsome, yet appalling hideousness. I shut my eyes involuntarily, and endeavoured to recollect what were my duties with regard to this destroyer. I called on him to stay.

He paused, looking on me with wonder; and, again turning towards the lifeless form of his creator, he seemed to forget my presence, and every feature and gesture seemed instigated by the wildest rage of some uncontrollable passion.

"That is also my victim!" he exclaimed: "in his murder my crimes are consummated; the miserable series of my being is wound to its close! Oh, Frankenstein! generous and self-devoted being! what does it avail that I now ask thee to pardon me? I, who irretrievably destroyed thee by destroying all thou lovedst. Alas! he is cold, he cannot answer me."

His voice seemed suffocated; and my first impulses, which had suggested to me the duty of obeying the dying request of my friend, in destroying his enemy, were now suspended by a mixture of curiosity and compassion. I approached this tremendous being; I dared not again raise my eyes to his face, there was something so scaring and unearthly in his ugliness. I attempted to speak, but the words died away on my lips. The monster continued to utter wild and incoherent self-reproaches. At length I gathered resolution to address him in a pause of the tempest of his passion: "Your repentance," I said, "is now superfluous. If you had listened to the voice of conscience, and heeded the stings of remorse, before you had urged your diabolical vengeance to this extremity, Frankenstein would yet have lived.

"And do you dream?" said the dæmon; "do you think that I was then dead to agony and remorse? – He," he continued, pointing to the corpse, "he suffered not in the consummation of the deed – oh! not the ten-thousandth portion of the anguish that was mine during the lingering detail of its execution. A frightful selfishness hurried me on, while my heart was poisoned with remorse. Think you that the groans of Clerval were music to my ears? My heart was fashioned to be susceptible of love and sympathy; and, when wrenched by misery to vice and hatred, it did not endure the violence of the change, without torture such as you cannot even imagine.

"After the murder of Clerval, I returned to Switzerland, heart-broken and overcome. I pitied Frankenstein; my pity amounted to horror: I abhorred myself. But when I discovered that he, the author at once of my existence and of its unspeakable torments, dared to hope for happiness; that while he accumulated wretchedness and despair upon me, he sought his own enjoyment in feelings and passions from the indulgence of which I was for ever barred, then impotent envy and bitter indignation filled me with an insatiable thirst for vengeance. I recollected my threat, and resolved that it should be accomplished. I knew that I was preparing for myself a deadly torture; but I was the slave, not the master, of an impulse, which I detested, yet could not disobey. Yet when she died! – nay, then I was not miserable. I had cast off all feeling, subdued all anguish, to riot in the excess of my despair. Evil thenceforth became my good. Urged thus far, I had no choice but to adapt my nature to an element which I had willingly chosen. The completion of my demoniacal design became an insatiable passion. And now it is ended; there is my last victim!"

I was at first touched by the expressions of his misery; yet, when I called to mind what Frankenstein had said of his powers of eloquence and persuasion, and when I again cast my eyes on the lifeless form of my friend, indignation was rekindled within me. "Wretch!" I said, "it is well that you come here to whine over the desolation that you have made. You throw a torch into a pile of buildings; and, when they are consumed, you sit among the ruins, and lament the fall. Hypocritical fiend! if he whom you mourn still lived, still would he be the object, again would he become the prey, of your accursed vengeance. It is not pity that you feel; you lament only because the victim of your malignity is withdrawn from your power."

"Oh, it is not thus – not thus," interrupted the being; "yet such must be the impression conveyed to you by what appears to be the purport of my actions. Yet I seek not a fellow-feeling in my misery. No sympathy may I ever find. When I first sought it, it was the love of virtue, the feelings of happiness and affection with which my whole being overflowed, that I wished to be participated. But now, that virtue has become to me a shadow, and that happiness and affection are turned into bitter and loathing despair, in what should I seek for sympathy? I am content to suffer alone, while my sufferings shall endure: when I die, I am well satisfied that abhorrence and opprobrium should load my memory. Once my fancy was soothed with dreams of virtue, of fame, and of enjoyment. Once I falsely hoped to meet with beings, who, pardoning my outward form, would love me for the excellent qualities which I was capable of unfolding. I was nourished with high thoughts of honour and devotion. But now crime has degraded me beneath the meanest animal. No guilt, no mischief, no malignity, no misery, can be found comparable to mine. When I run over the frightful catalogue of my sins, I cannot believe that I am the same creature whose thoughts were once filled with sublime and transcendent visions of the beauty and the majesty of goodness. But it is even so; the fallen angel becomes a malignant devil. Yet even that enemy of God and man had friends and associates in his desolation; I am alone.

"You, who call Frankenstein your friend, seem to have a knowledge of my crimes and his misfortunes. But, in the detail which he gave you of them, he could not sum up the hours and months of misery which I endured, wasting in impotent passions. For while I destroyed his hopes, I did not satisfy my own desires. They were for ever ardent and craving; still I desired love and fellowship, and I was still spurned. Was there no injustice in this? Am I to be thought the only criminal, when all human kind sinned against me? Why do you not hate Felix, who drove his friend from his door with contumely? Why do you not execrate the rustic who sought to destroy the saviour of his child? Nay, these are virtuous and immaculate beings! I, the miserable and the abandoned, am an abortion, to be spurned at, and kicked, and trampled on. Even now my blood boils at the recollection of this injustice.

"But it is true that I am a wretch. I have murdered the lovely and the helpless; I have strangled the innocent as they slept, and grasped to death his throat who never injured me or any other living thing. I have devoted my creator, the select specimen of all that is worthy of love and admiration among men, to misery; I have pursued him even to that irremediable ruin. There he lies, white and cold in death. You hate me; but your abhorrence cannot equal that with which I regard myself. I look on the hands which executed the deed; I think on the heart in which the imagination of it was conceived, and long for the moment when these hands will meet my eyes, when that imagination will haunt my thoughts no more.

"Fear not that I shall be the instrument of future mischief. My work is nearly complete. Neither yours nor any man's death is needed to consummate the series of my being, and accomplish that which must be done; but it requires my own. Do not think that I shall be slow to perform this sacrifice. I shall quit your vessel on the ice-raft which brought me thither, and shall seek the most northern extremity of the globe; I shall collect my funeral pile, and consume to ashes this miserable frame, that its remains may afford no light to any curious and unhallowed wretch, who would create such another as I have been. I shall die. I shall no longer feel the agonies which now consume me, or be the prey of feelings unsatisfied, yet unquenched. He is dead who called me into being; and when I shall be no more, the very remembrance of us both will speedily vanish. I shall no longer see the sun or stars, or feel the winds play on my cheeks. Light, feeling, and sense will pass away; and in this condition must I find my happiness. Some years ago, when the images which this world affords first opened upon me, when I felt the cheering warmth of summer, and heard the rustling of the leaves and the warbling of the birds, and these were all to me, I should have wept to die; now it is my only consolation. Polluted by crimes, and torn by the bitterest remorse, where can I find rest but in death?

"Farewell! I leave you, and in you the last of human kind whom these eyes will ever behold. Farewell, Frankenstein! If thou wert yet alive, and yet cherished a desire of revenge against me, it would be better satiated in my life than in my destruction. But it was not so; thou didst seek my extinction, that I might not cause greater wretchedness; and if yet, in some mode unknown to me, thou hadst not ceased to think and feel, thou wouldst not desire against me a vengeance greater than that which I feel. Blasted as thou wert, my agony was still superior to thine; for the bitter sting of remorse will not cease to rankle in my wounds until death shall close them for ever.

"But soon," he cried, with sad and solemn enthusiasm, "I shall die, and what I now feel be no longer felt. Soon these burning miseries will be extinct. I shall ascend my funeral pile triumphantly, and exult in the agony of the torturing flames. The light of that conflagration will fade away; my ashes will be swept into the sea by the winds. My spirit will sleep in peace; or if it thinks, it will not surely think thus. Farewell."

He sprung from the cabin-window, as he said this, upon the ice-raft which lay close to the vessel. He was soon borne away by the waves, and lost in darkness and distance. .

WANDERING WILLIE'S TALE

Sir Walter Scott

Sir Walter Scott (1771–1832) was born in Edinburgh and read classics at Edinburgh University. He suffered from polio as a child and spent time recuperating at his grandfather's farm in the Scottish Borders. There he encountered the Jacobite oral culture which would influence much of his later work. Scott was phenomenally popular in his own lifetime, but was financially ruined when his publisher Constable and printers Ballantyne collapsed. The strain of writing to repay his debts contributed to his early death.

"Honest folks like me! How do ye ken whether I am honest, or what I am? I may be the deevil himsell for what ye ken, for he has power to come disguised like an angel of light; and, besides, he is a prime fiddler. He played a sonata to Corelli, ye ken."

There was something odd in this speech, and the tone in which it was said. It seemed as if my companion was not always in his constant mind, or that he was willing to try if he could frighten me. I laughed at the extravagance of his language, however, and asked him in reply if he was fool enough to believe that the foul fiend would play so silly a masquerade.

"Ye ken little about it – little about it," said the old man, shaking his head and beard, and knitting his brows. "I could tell ye something about that."

What his wife mentioned of his being a tale-teller as well as a musician now occurred to me; and as, you know, I like tales of superstition, I begged to have a specimen of his talent as we went along.

"It is very true," said the blind man, "that when I am tired of scraping thairm or singing ballants I whiles make a tale serve the turn among the country bodies; and I have some fearsome anes, that make the auld carlines shake on the settle, and the bits o' bairns skirl on their minnies out frae their beds. But this that I am going to tell you was a thing that befell in our ain house in my father's time – that is, my father was then a hafflins callant; and I tell it to you, that it may be a lesson to you that are but a young thoughtless chap, wha ye draw up wi' on a lonely road; for muckle was the dool and care that came o' 't to my gudesire."

He commenced his tale accordingly, in a distinct narrative tone of voice, which he raised and depressed with considerable skill; at times sinking almost into a whisper, and turning his clear but sightless eyeballs upon my face, as if it had been possible for him to witness the impression which his narrative made upon my features. I will not spare a syllable of it, although it be of the longest; so I make a dash – and begin: –

Ye maun have heard of Sir Robert Redgauntlet of that ilk, who lived in these parts before the dear years. The country will lang mind him; and our fathers used to draw breath thick if ever they heard him named. He was out wi' the Hielandmen in Montrose's time; and again he was in the hills wi' Glencairn in the saxteen hundred and fifty-twa; and sae when King Charles the Second came in, wha was in sic favor as the laird of Redgauntlet? He was knighted at Lonon Court, wi' the king's ain sword; and being a red-hot prelatist, he came down here, rampauging like a lion, with commissions of lieutenancy (and of lunacy, for what I ken), to put down a' the Whigs and Covenanters in the country. Wild wark they made of it; for the Whigs were as dour as the Cavaliers were fierce, and it was which should first tire the other. Redgauntlet was aye for the strong hand; and his name is kend as wide in the country as Claver-house's or Tam Dalyell's. Glen, nor dargle, nor mountain, nor cave could hide the puir hill-folk when Redgauntlet was out with bugle and bloodhound after them, as if they had been sae mony deer. And, troth, when they fand them, they didna make muckle mair ceremony than a Hielandman wi' a roebuck. It was just, "Will ye tak' the test?" If not – "Make ready – present – fire!" and there lay the recusant.

Far and wide was Sir Robert hated and feared. Men thought he had a direct compact with Satan; that he was proof against steel, and that bullets happed aff his buff-coat like hailstanes from a hearth; that he had a mear that would turn a hare on the side of Carrifragauns; and muckle to the same purpose, of whilk mair anon. The best blessing they wared on him was, "Deil scowp wi' Redgauntlet!" He wasna a bad master to his ain folk, though, and was weel aneugh liked by his tenants; and as for the lackeys and troopers that rade out wi' him to the persecutions, as the Whigs caa'd those killing-times, they wad hae drunken themsells blind to his health at ony time.

Now you are to ken that my gudesire lived on Redgauntlet's grund – they ca' the place Primrose Knowe. We had lived on the grund, and under the Redgauntlets, since the riding days, and lang before. It was a pleasant bit; and I think the air is callerer and fresher there than onywhere else in the country. It's a' deserted now; and I sat on the broken doorcheek three days since, and was glad I couldna see the plight the place was in – but that's a' wide o' the mark. There dwelt my gudesire, Steenie Steenson; a rambling, rattling chiel' he had been in his young days, and could play weel on the pipes; he was famous at "hoopers and girders," a' Cumberland couldna touch him at "Jockie Lattin," and he had the finest finger for the back-lilt between Berwick and Carlisle. The like o' Steenie wasna the sort that they made Whigs o'. And so he became a Tory, as they ca' it, which we now ca' Jacobites, just out of a kind of needcessity, that he might belang to some side or other. He had nae ill-will to the Whig bodies, and liked little to see the blude rin, though, being obliged to follow Sir Robert in hunting and hoisting, watching and warding, he saw muckle mischief, and maybe did some that he couldna avoid.

Now Steenie was a kind of favorite with his master, and kend a' the folk about the castle, and was often sent for to play the pipes when they were at their merriment. Auld Dougal MacCallum, the butler, that had followed Sir Robert through gude and ill, thick and thin, pool and stream, was specially fond of the pipes, and aye gae my gudesire his gude word wi' the laird; for Dougal could turn his master round his finger.

Weel, round came the Revolution, and it had like to hae broken the hearts baith of Dougal and his master. But the change was not a'thegether sae great as they feared and other folk thought for. The Whigs made an unco crawing what they wad do with their auld enemies, and in special wi' Sir Robert Redgauntlet. But there were owermony great folks dipped in the same doings to make a spick-and-span new warld. So Parliament passed it a' ower easy; and Sir Robert, bating that he was held to hunting foxes instead of Covenanters, remained just the man he was. His revel was as loud, and his hall as weel lighted, as ever it had been, though maybe he lacked the fines of the nonconformists, that used to come to stock his larder and cellar; for it is certain he began to be keener about the rents than his tenants used to find him before, and they behooved to be prompt to the rent day, or else the laird wasna pleased. And he was sic an awsome body that naebody cared to anger him; for the oaths he swore, and the rage that he used to get into, and the looks that he put on made men sometimes think him a devil incarnate.

Weel, my gudesire was nae manager – no that he was a very great misguider – but he hadna the saving gift, and he got twa terms' rent in arrear. He got the first brash at Whitsunday put ower wi' fan word and piping; but when Martinmas came there was a summons from the grund officer to come wi' the rent on a day preceese, or else Steenie behooved to flit. Sair wark he had to get the siller; but he was weel freended, and at last he got the haill scraped thegether – a thousand merks. The maist of it was from a neighbor they caa'd Laurie Lapraik – a sly tod. Laurie had wealth o' gear, could hunt wi' the hound and rin wi' the hare, and be Whig or Tory, saunt or sinner, as the wind stood. He was a professor in this Revolution warld, but he liked an orra sough of this warld, and a tune on the pipes, weel aneugh at a by-time; and, bune a', he thought he had gude security for the siller he len my gudesire ower the stocking at Primrose Knowe.

Away trots my gudesire to Redgauntlet Castle wi' a heavy purse and a light heart, glad to be out of the laird's danger. Weel, the first thing he learned at the castle was that Sir Robert had fretted himsell into a fit of the gout because he did no appear before twelve o'clock. It wasna a'thegether for sake of the money, Dougal thought, but because he didna like to part wi' my gudesire aff the grund. Dougal was glad to see Steenie, and brought him into the great oak parlor; and there sat the laird his leesome lane, excepting thar he had beside him a great, ill-favored jackanape that was a special pet of his. A cankered beast it was, and mony an ill-natured trick it played; ill to please it was, and easily angered – ran about the haill castle, chattering and rowling, and pinching and biting folk, specially before ill weather, or disturbance in the state. Sir Robert caa'd it Major Weir, after the warlock that was burnt; and few folk liked either the name or the conditions of the creature – they thought there was something in it by ordinar – and my gudesire was not just easy in mind when the door shut on him, and he saw himsell in the room wi' naebody but the laird, Dougal MacCullum, and the major – a thing that hadna chanced to him before.

Sir Robert sat, or, I should say, lay, in a great armchair, wi' his grand velvet gown, and his feet on a cradle; for he had baith gout and gravel, and his face looked as gash and ghastly as Satan's. Major Weir sat opposite to him, in a red-laced coat, and the laird's wig on his head; and aye as Sir Robert girned wi' pain, the jackanape girned too, like a sheep's head between a pair of tangs – an ill-faur'ed, fearsome couple they were. The laird's buff-coat was hung on a pin behind him, and his broadsword and his pistols within reach; for he keep it up the auld fashion of having the weapons ready, and a horse saddled day and night, just as he used to do when he was able to loup on horseback, and sway after ony of the hill-folk he could get speerings of. Some said it was for fear of the Whigs taking vengence, but I judge it was just his auld custom – he wasna gine not fear onything. The rental book, wi' its black cover and brass clasps, was lying beside him; and a book of sculduddery sangs was put betwixt the leaves, to keep it open at the place where it bore evidence against the goodman of Primrose Knowe, as behind the hand with his mails and duties. Sir Robert gave my gudesire a look, as if he would have withered his heart in his bosom. Ye maun ken he had a way of bending his brows that men saw the visible mark of a horseshoe in his forehead, deep-dinted, as if it had been stamped there.

"Are ye come light-handed, ye son of a toom whistle?" said Sir Robert. "Zounds! if you are – "

My gudesire, with as gude a countenance as he could put on, made a leg, and placed the bag of money on the table wi' a dash, like a man that does something clever. The laird drew it to him hastily. "Is all here, Steenie, man?"

"Your honor will find it right," said my gudesire.

"Here, Dougal," said the laird, "gie Steenie a tass of brandy, till I count the siller and write the receipt."

But they werena weel out of the room when Sir Robert gied a yelloch that garr'd the castle rock. Back ran Dougal; in flew the liverymen; yell on yell gied the laird, ilk ane mair awfu' than the ither. My gudesire knew not whether to stand or flee, but he ventured back into the parlor, where a' was gaun hirdie-girdie – naebody to say "come in" or "gae out." Terribly the laird roared for cauld water to his feet, and wine to cool his throat; and "Hell, hell, hell, and its flames," was aye the word in his mouth. They brought him water, and when they plunged his swoln feet into the tub, he cried out it was burning; and folks say that it did bubble and sparkle like a seething caldron. He flung the cup at Dougal's head and said he had given him blood instead of Burgundy; and, sure aneugh, the lass washed clotted blood aff the carpet the neist day. The jackanape they caa'd Major Weir, it jibbered and cried as if it was mocking its master. My gudesire's head was like to turn; he forgot baith siller and receipt, and downstairs he banged; but, as he ran, the shrieks came fainter and fainter; there was a deep-drawn shivering groan, and word gaed through the castle that the laird was dead.

Weel, away came my gudesire wi' his finger in his mouth, and his best hope was that Dougal had seen the money bag and heard the laird speak of writing the receipt. The young laird, now Sir John, came from Edinburgh to see things put to rights. Sir John and his father never 'greed weel. Sir John had been bred an advocate, and afterward sat in the last Scots Parliament and voted for the Union, having gotten, it was thought, a rug of the compensations – if his father could have come out of his grave he would have brained him for it on his awn hearthstane. Some thought it was easier counting with the auld rough knight than the fair-spoken young ane – but mair of that anon.

Dougal MacCallum, poor body, neither grat nor graned, but gaed about the house looking like a corpse, but directing, as was his duty, a' the order of the grand funeral. Now Dougal looked aye waur and waur when night was coming, and was aye the last to gang to his bed, whilk was in a little round just opposite the chamber of dais, whilk his master occupied while he was living, and where he now lay in state, as they caa'd it, weeladay! The night before the funeral Dougal could keep his awn counsel nae longer; he came doun wi' his proud spirit, and fairly asked auld Hutcheon to sit in his room with him for an hour. When they were in the round, Dougal took a tass of brandy to himsell, and gave another to Hutcheon, and wished him all health and lang life, and said that, for himsell, he wasna lang for this world; for that every night since Sir Robert's death his silver call had sounded from the state chamber just as it used to do at nights in his life-time to call Dougal to help to turn him in his bed. Dougal said that, being alone with the dead on that floor of the tower (for naebody cared to wake Sir Robert Redgauntlet like another corpse), he had never daured to answer the call, but that now his conscience checked him for neglecting his duty; for, "though death breaks service," said MacCallum, "it shall never weak my service to Sir Robert; and I will answer his next whistle, so be you will stand by me, Hutcheon."

Hutcheon had nae will to the wark, but he had stood by Dougal in battle and broil, and he wad not fail him at this pinch; so doun the carles sat ower a stoup of brandy, and Hutcheon, who was something of a clerk, would have read a chapter of the Bible; but Dougal would hear naething but a blaud of Davie Lindsay, whilk was the waur preparation.

When midnight came, and the house was quiet as the grave, sure enough the silver whistle sounded as sharp and shrill as if Sir Robert was blowing it; and up got the twa auld serving men, and tottered into the room where the dead man lay. Hutcheon saw aneugh at the first glance; for there were torches in the room, which showed him the foul fiend, in his ain shape, sitting on the laird's coffin! Ower he couped as if he had been dead. He could not tell how lang he lay in a trance at the door, but when he gathered himsell he cried on his neighbor, and getting nae answer raised the house, when Dougal was found lying dead within twa steps of the bed where his master's coffin was placed. As for the whistle, it was gane anes and aye; but mony a time was it heard at the top of the house on the bartizan, and amang the auld chimneys and turrets where the howlets have their nests. Sir John hushed the matter up, and the funeral passed over without mair bogie wark.

But when a' was ower, and the laird was beginning to settle his affairs, every tenant was called up for his arrears, and my gudesire for the full sum that stood against him in the rental book. Weel, away he trots to the castle to tell his story, and there he is introduced to Sir John, sitting in his father's chair, in deep mourn-ing, with weepers and hanging cravat, and a small walking rapier by his side, instead of the auld broadsword that had a hunderweight of steel about it, what with blade, chape, and basket hilt. I have heard their communings so often tauld ower that I almost think I was there mysell, though I couldna be born at the time. (In fact, Alan, my companion, mimicked, with a good deal of humor, the flattering, conciliating tone of the tenant's address and the hypocritical melancholy of the laird's reply. His grandfather, he said, had, while he spoke, his eye fixed on the rental book, as if it were a mastiff dog that he was afraid would spring up and bite him.)

"I wuss ye joy, sir, of the head seat and the white loaf and the brid lairdship. Your father was a kind man to freends and followers; muckle grace to you, Sir John, to fill his shoon – his boots, I suld say, for he seldom wore shoon, unless it were muils when he had the gout.

"Aye, Steenie," quoth the laird, sighing deeply, and putting his napkin to his een, "his was a sudden call, and he will be missed in the country; no time to set his house in order – weel prepared Godward, no doubt, which is the root of the matter; but left us behind a tangled hesp to wind, Steenie. Hem! hem! We maun go to business, Steenie; much to do, and little time to do it in."

Here he opened the fatal volume. I have heard of a thing they call Dooms-day-book – I am clear it has been a rental of back-ganging tenants.

"Stephen," said Sir John, still in the same soft, sleekit tone of voice – "Stephen Stephenson, or Steenson, ye are down here for a year's rent behind the hand – due at last term."

Stephen. Please your honor, Sir John, I paid it to your father.

Sir John. Ye took a receipt, then, doubtless, Stephen, and can produce it?

Stephen. Indeed, I hadna time, and it like your honor; for nae sooner had I set doun the siller, and just as his honor, Sir Robert, that's gaen, drew it till him to count it and write out the receipt, he was ta'en wi' the pains that removed him.

"That was unlucky," said Sir John, after a pause. "But ye maybe paid it in the presence of somebody. I want but a talis qualis evidence, Stephen. I would go ower-strictly to work with no poor man."

Stephen. Troth, Sir John, there was naebody in the room but Dougal Mac Callum, the butler. But, as your honor kens, he has e'en followed his auld master.

"Very unlucky again, Stephen," said Sir John, without altering his voice a single note. "The man to whom ye paid the money is dead, and the man who witnessed the payment is dead, too; and the siller, which should have been to the fore, is neither seen nor heard tell of in the repositories. How am I to believe a' this?"

Stephen. I dinna ken, your honor; but there is a bit memorandum note of the very coins, for, God help me! I had to borrow out of twenty purses; and I am sure that ilka man there set down will take his grit oath for what purpose I borrowed the money.

Sir John. I have little doubt ye borrowed the money, Steenie. It is the payment that I want to have proof of.

Stephen. The siller maun be about the house, Sir John. And since your honor never got it, and his honor that was canna have ta'en it wi' him, maybe some of the family may hae seen it.

Sir John. We will examine the servants, Stephen; that is but reasonable.

But lackey and lass, and page and groom, all denied stoutly that they had ever seen such a bag of money as my gudesire described. What saw waur, he had un-luckily not mentioned to any living soul of them his purpose of paying his rent. Ae quean had noticed something under his arm, but she took it for the pipes.

Sir John Redgauntlet ordered the servants out of the room, and then said to my gudesire: "Now, Steenie, ye see ye have fair play; and, as I have little doubt ye ken better where to find the siller than ony other body, I beg in fair terms, and for your own sake, that you will end this fasherie; for, Stephen, ye maun pay or flit."

"The Lord forgie your opinion," said Stephen, driven almost to his wit's end – "I am an honest man."

"So am I, Stephen," said his honor; "and so are all the folks in this house, I hope. But if there be a knave among us, it must be he that tells the story he can-not prove." He paused, and then added, mair sternly: "If I understand your trick, sir, you want to take advantage of some malicious reports concerning things in this family, and particularly respecting my father's sudden death, thereby to cheat me out of the money, and perhaps take away my character by insinuating that I have received the rent I am demanding. Where do you suppose this money to be? I insist upon knowing."

My gudesire saw everything look so muckle against him that he grew nearly desperate. However, he shifted from one foot to another, looked to every corner of the room, and made no answer.

"Speak out, sirrah," said the laird, assuming a look of his father's, a very particular ane, which he had when he was angry – it seemed as if the wrinkles of his frown made that self same fearful shape of a horse's shoe in the middle of his brow; "speak out, sir! I will know your thoughts; do you suppose that I have this money?"

"Far be it frae me to say so," said Stephen.

"Do you charge any of my people with having taken it?"

"I wad be laith to charge them that may be innocent," said my gudesire; "and if there be any one that is guilty, I have nae proof."

"Somewhere the money must be, if there is a word of truth in your story," said Sir John; "I ask where you think it is – and demand a correct answer!"

"In hell, if you will have my thoughts of it," said my gudesire, driven to extremity – "in hell! with your father, his jackanape, and his silver whistle."

Down the stairs he ran (for the parlor was nae place for him after such a word) and he heard the laird swearing blood and wounds behind him, as fast as ever did Sir Robert, and roaring for the bailie and the baron-officer.

Away rode my gudesire to his chief creditor (him they caa'd Laurie Lapraik), to try if he could make onything out of him; but when he tauld his story, he got but the worst word in his wame – thief, beggar, and dyvour were the saftest terms; and to the boot of these hard terms, Laurie brought up the auld story of dipping his hand in the blood of God's saunts, just as if a tenant could have helped riding with the laird, and that a laird like Sir Robert Redgauntlet. My gudesire was, by this time, far beyond the bounds of patience, and, while he and Laurie were at deil speed the liars, he was wanchancie aneugh to abuse Lapraik's doctrine as weel as the man, and said things that garr'd folks' flesh grue that heard them – he wasna just himsell, and he had lived wi' a wild set in his day.

At last they parted, and my gudesire was to ride hame through the wood of Pitmurkie, that is a' fou of black firs, as they say. I ken the wood, but the firs may be black or white for what I can tell. At the entry of the wood there is a wild common, and on the edge of the common a little lonely change house, that was keepit then by an hostler wife – they suld hae caa'd her Tibbie Faw – and there puir Steenie cried for a mutchkin of brandy, for he had had no refreshment the haill day. Tibbie was earnest wi' him to take a bite of meat, but he couldna think o' 't, nor would he take his foot out of the stirrup, and took off the brandy wholely at twa draughts, and named a toast at each. The first was, the memory of Sir Robert Redgauntlet, and may he never lie quiet in his grave till he had righted his poor bond tenant; and the second was, a health to Man's Enemy, if he would but get him back the pock of siller, or tell him what came o' 't, for he saw the haill world was like to regard him as a thief and a cheat, and he took that waur than even the ruin of his house and hauld.

On he rode, little caring where. It was a dark night turned, and the trees made it yet darker, and he let the beast take its ain road through the wood; when all of a sudden, from tired and wearied that it was before, the nag began to spring and flee and stend, that my gudesire could hardly keep the saddle. Upon the whilk, a horseman, suddenly riding up beside him, said, "That's a mettle beast of yours, freend; will you sell him?" So saying, he touched the horse's neck with his riding wand, and it fell into its auld heigh-ho of a stumbling trot. "But his spunk's soon out of him, I think," continued the stranger, "and that is like mony a man's courage, that thinks he wad do great things."

My gudesire scarce listened to this, but spurred his horse, with "Gude-e'en to you, freend."

But it's like the stranger was ane that doesna lightly yield his point; for, ride as Steenie liked, he was aye beside him at the selfsame pace. At last my gudesire, Steenie Steenson, grew half angry, and, to say the truth, half feard.

"What is it that you want with me, freend?" he said. "If ye be a robber, I have nae money; if ye be a leal man, wanting company, I have nae heart to mirth or speaking; and if ye want to ken the road, I scarce ken it mysell."

"If you will tell me your grief," said the stranger, "I am one that, though I have been sair miscaa'd in the world, am the only hand for helping my freends."

So my gudesire, to ease his ain heart, mair than from any hope of help, told him the story from beginning to end.

"It's a hard pinch," said the stranger; "but I think I can help you."

"If you could lend the money, sir, and take a lang day – I ken nae other help on earth," said my gudesire.

"But there may be some under the earth," said the stranger. "Come, I'll be frank wi' you; I could lend you the money on bond, but you would maybe scruple my terms. Now I can tell you that your auld laird is disturbed in his grave by your curses and the wailing of your family, and if ye daur venture to go to see him, he will give you the receipt."

My gudesire's hair stood on end at this proposal, but he thought his companion might be some humorsome chield that was trying to frighten him, and might end with lending him the money. Besides, he was bauld wi' brandy, and desperate wi' distress; and he said he had courage to go to the gate of hell, and a step farther, for that receipt. The stranger laughed.

Weel, they rode on through the thickest of the wood, when, all of a sudden, the horse stopped at the door of a great house; and, but that he knew the place was ten miles off, my father would have thought he was at Redgauntlet

Castle. They rode into the outer courtyard, through the muckle faulding yetts, and aneath the auld portcullis; and the whole front of the house was lighted, and there were pipes and fiddles, and as much dancing and deray within as used to be at Sir Robert's house at Pace and Yule, and such high seasons. They lap off, and my gudesire, as seemed to him, fastened his horse to the very ring he had tied him to that morning when he gaed to wait on the young Sir John.

"God!" said my gudesire, "if Sir Robert's death be but a dream!"

He knocked at the ha' door just as he was wont, and his auld acquaintance, Dougal MacCallum – just after his wont, too – came to open the door, and said, "Piper Steenie, are ye there, lad? Sir Robert has been crying for you."

My gudesire was like a man in a dream – he looked for the stranger, but he was gane for the time. At last he just tried to say: "Ha! Dougal Driveower, are you living? I thought ye had been dead."[66]

"Never fash yoursell wi' me," said Dougal, "but look to yourself; and see ye tak' naething frae onybody here, neither meat, drink, or siller, except the receipt that is your ain."

So saying, he led the way out through halls and trances that were weel kend to my gudesire, and into the auld oak parlor; and there was as much singing of profane sangs, and birling of red wine, and blasphemy sculduddery as had ever been in Redgauntlet Castle when it was at the blythest.

But Lord take us in keeping! what a set of ghastly revelers there were that sat around that table! My gudesire kend mony that had long before gane to their place, for often had he piped to the most part in the hall of Redgauntlet. There was the fierce Middleton, and the dissolute Rothes, and the crafty Lauderdale; and Dalyell, with his bald head and a beard to his girdle; and Earlshall, with Cameron's blude on his hand; and wild Bonshaw, that tied blessed Mr. Cargill's limbs till the blude sprung; and Dumbarton Douglas, the twice-turned traitor baith to country and king. There was the Bludy Advocate MacKenzie, who, for his worldly wit and wisdom, had been to the rest as a god. And there was Claver-house, as beautiful as when he lived, with his long, dark, curled locks streaming down over his laced buff-coat, and with his left hand always on his right spule-blade, to hide the wound that the silver bullet had made. He sat apart from them all, and looked at them with a melancholy, haughty countenance; while the rest hallooed and sang and laughed, and the room rang. But their smiles were fearful-ly contorted from time to time; and their laughter passed into such wild sounds as made my gudesire's very nails grow blue, and chilled the marrow in his banes.

They that waited at the table were just the wicked serving men and troop-ers that had done their work and cruel bidding on earth. There was the Lang Lad of the Nethertown, that helped to take Argyle; and the bishop's summoner, that they called the Deil's Rattlebag; and the wicked guardsmen in their laced coats; and the savage Highland Amorites, that shed blood like water; and mony a proud serving man, haughty of heart and bloody of hand, cringing to the rich, and making them wickeder than they would be; grinding the poor to powder when the rich had broken them to fragments. And mony, mony mair were com-ing and ganging, a' as busy in their vocation as if they had been alive.

Sir Robert Redgauntlet, in the midst of a' this fearful riot, cried, wi' a voice like thunder, on Steenie Piper to come to the board-head where he was sitting, his legs stretched out before him, and swathed up with flannel, with his holster pistols aside him, while the great broadsword rested against his chair, just as my gudesire had seen him the last time upon earth; the very cushion for the jacka-nape was close to him; but the creature itsell was not there – it wasna its hour, it's likely; for he heard them say, as he came forward, "Is not the major come yet?" And another answered, "The jackanape will be here betimes the morn." And when my gudesire came forward, Sir Robert, or his ghaist, or the deevil in his likeness, said, "Weel, piper, hae ye settled wi' my son for the year's rent?"

With much ado my father gat breath to say that Sir John would not settle without his honor's receipt.

"Ye shall hae that for a tune of the pipes, Steenie," said the appearance of Sir Robert – "play us up Weel Hoddled, Luckie."

Now this was a tune my gudesire learned frae a warlock, that heard it when they were worshiping Satan at their meetings; and my gudesire had sometimes played it at the ranting suppers in Redgauntlet Castle, but never very willingly; and now he grew cauld at the very name of it, and said, for excuse, he hadna his pipes wi' him.

"MacCallum, ye limb of Beelzebub," said the fearfu' Sir Robert, "bring Stee-nie the pipes that I am keeping for him!"

MacCallum brought a pair of pipes might have served the piper of Donald of the Isles. But he gave my gudesire a nudge as he offered them; and looking secretly and closely, Steenie saw that the chanter was of steel, and heated to a white heat; so he had fair warning not to trust his fingers with it. So he excused himsell again, and said he was faint and frightened, and had not wind aneugh to fill the bag.

"Then ye maun eat and drink, Steenie," said the figure; "for we do little else here; and it's ill speaking between a fou man and a fasting." Now these were the very words that the bloody Earl of Douglas said to keep the king's messenger in hand while he cut the head off MacLellan of Bombie, at the Threave Castle; and that put Steenie mair and mair on his guard. So he spoke up like a man, and said he came neither to eat nor drink, nor make minstrelsy; but simply for his ain – to ken what was come o' the money he had paid, and to get a discharge for it; and he was so stout-hearted by this time that he charged Sir Robert for conscience' sake (he had no power to say the holy name), and as he hoped for peace and rest, to spread no snares for him, but just to give him his ain.

The appearance gnashed its teeth and laughed, but it took from a large pock-et-book the receipt, and handed it to Steenie. "There is your receipt, ye pitiful cur; and for the money, my dog-whelp of a son may go look for it in the Cat's Cradle."

My gudesire uttered mony thanks, and was about to retire, when Sir Robert roared aloud: "Stop, though, thou sack-doudling son of a – ! I am not done with thee. HERE we do nothing for nothing; and you must return on this very day twelvemonth to pay your master the homage that you owe me for my protection."

My father's tongue was loosed of a suddenty, and he said aloud, "I refer myself to God's pleasure, and not to yours."

He had no sooner uttered the word than all was dark around him; and he sank on the earth with such a sudden shock that he lost both breath and sense.

How lang Steenie lay there he could not tell; but when he came to himsell he was lying in the auld kirkyard of Redgauntlet parochine, just at the door of the family aisle, and the scutcheon of the auld knight, Sir Robert, hanging over his head. There was a deep morning fog on grass and gravestane around him, and his horse was feeding quietly beside the ministers twa cows. Steenie would have thought the whole was a dream, but he had the receipt in his hand fairly written and signed by the auld laird; only the last letters of his name were a little disorderly, written like one seized with sudden pain.

Sorely troubled in his mind, he left that dreary place, rode through the mist to Redgauntlet Castle, and with much ado he got speech of the laird.

"Well, you dyvour bankrupt," was the first word, "have you brought me my rent?"

"No," answered my gudesire, "I have not; but I have brought your honor Sir Robert's receipt for it."

"How, sirrah? Sir Robert's receipt! You told me he had not given you one."

"Will your honor please to see if that bit line is right?"

Sir John looked at every line, and at every letter, with much attention; and at last at the date, which my gudesire had not observed – "From my appointed place," he read, "this twenty-fifth of November."

"What! That is yesterday! Villain, thou must have gone to hell for this!"

"I got it from your honor's father; whether he be in heaven or hell, I know not," said Steenie.

"I will debate you for a warlock to the Privy Council!" said Sir John. "I will send you to your master, the devil, with the help of a tar barrel and a torch!"

"I intend to debate mysell to the Presbytery," said Steenie, "and tell them all I have seen last night, whilk are things fitter for them to judge of than a borrel man like me."

Sir John paused, composed himself, and desired to hear the full history; and my gudesire told it him from point to point, as I have told it you – neither more nor less.

Sir John was silent again for a long time, and at last he said, very composedly: "Steenie, this story of yours concerns the honor of many a noble family besides mine; and if it be a leasing-making, to keep yoursell out of my danger, the least you can expect is to have a red-hot iron driven through your tongue, and that will be as bad as scaulding your fingers wi' a red-hot chanter. But yet it may be true, Steenie; and if the money cast up, I shall not know what to think of it. But where shall we find the Cat's Cradle? There are cats enough about the old house, but I think they kitten without the ceremony of bed or cradle."

"We were best ask Hutcheon," said my gudesire; "he kens a' the odd corners about as weel as – another serving man that is now gane, and that I wad not like to name."

Aweel, Hutcheon, when he was asked, told them that a ruinous turret lang disused, next to the clock house, only accessible by a ladder, for the opening was on the outside, above the battlements, was called of old the Cat's Cradle.

"There will I go immediately," said Sir John; and he took – with what purpose Heaven kens – one of his father's pistols from the hall table, where they had lain since the night he died, and hastened to the battlements.

It was a dangerous place to climb, for the ladder was auld and frail, and wanted ane or twa rounds. However, up got Sir John, and entered at the turret door, where his body stopped the only little light that was in the bit turret. Something flees at him wi' a vengeance, maist dang him back ower – bang! gaed the knight's pistol, and Hutcheon, that held the ladder, and my gudesire, that stood beside him, hears a loud skelloch. A minute after, Sir John flings the body of the jackanape down to them, and cries that the siller is fund, and that they should come up and help him. And there was the bag of siller sure aneugh, and mony orra thing besides, that had been missing for mony a day. And Sir John, when he had riped the turret weel, led my gudesire into the dining-parlor, and took him by the hand, and spoke kindly to him, and said he was sorry he should have doubted his word, and that he would hereafter be a good master to him, to make amends.

"And now, Steenie," said Sir John, "although this vision of yours tends, on the whole, to my father's credit as an honest man, that he should, even after his death, desire to see justice done to a poor man like you, yet you are sensible that ill-dispositioned men might make bad constructions upon it concerning his soul's health. So, I think, we had better lay the haill dirdum on that ill-deedie creature, Major Weir, and say naething about your dream in the wood of Pitmurkie. You had taen ower-muckle brandy to be very certain about onything; and, Steenie, this receipt" – his hand shook while he held it out – "it's but a queer kind of document, and we will do best, I think, to put it quietly in the fire."

"Od, but for as queer as it is, it's a' the voucher I have for my rent," said my gudesire, who was afraid, it may be, of losing the benefit of Sir Robert's discharge.

"I will bear the contents to your credit in the rental book, and give you a discharge under my own hand," said Sir John, "and that on the spot. And, Steenie, if you can hold your tongue about this matter, you shall sit, from this time downward, at an easier rent."

"Mony thanks to your honor," said Steenie, who saw easily in what corner the wind was; "doubtless I will be conformable to all your honor's commands; only I would willingly speak wi' some powerful minister on the subject, for I do not like the sort of soumons of appointment whilk your honor's father – "

"Do not call the phantom my father!" said Sir John, interrupting him.

"Well, then, the thing that was so like him," said my gudesire; "he spoke of my coming back to see him this time twelvemonth, and it's a weight on my conscience."

"Aweel, then," said Sir John, "if you be so much distressed in mind, you may speak to our minister of the parish; he is a douce man, regards the honor of our family, and the mair that he may look for some patronage from me."

Wi' that, my father readily agreed that the receipt should be burned; and the laird threw it into the chimney with his ain hand. Burn it would not for them, though; but away it flew up the lum, wi' a lang train of sparks at its tail, and a hissing noise like a squib.

My gudesire gaed down to the manse, and the minister, when he had heard the story, said it was his real opinion that, though my gudesire had gane very far in tampering with dangerous matters, yet as he had refused the devil's arles (for such was the offer of meat and drink), and had refused to do homage by piping at his bidding, he hoped that, if he held a circumspect walk hereafter, Satan could take little advantage by what was come and gane. And, indeed, my gudesire, of his ain accord, lang forswore baith the pipes and the brandy – it was not even till the year was out, and the fatal day past, that he would so much as take the fiddle or drink usquebaugh or tippenny.

Sir John made up his story about the jackanape as he liked himsell; and some believe till this day there was no more in the matter than the filching nature of the brute. Indeed, ye'll no hinder some to thread that it was nane o' the auld Enemy that Dougal and Hutcheon saw in the laird's room, but only that wanchancie creature the major, capering on the coffin; and that, as to the blawing on the laird's whistle that was heard after he was dead, the filthy brute could do that as weel as the laird himself, if not better. But Heaven kens the truth, whilk first came out by the minister's wife, after Sir John and her ain gudeman were baith in the molds. And then my gudesire, wha was failed in his limbs, but not in his judgment or memory – at least nothing to speak of – was obliged to tell the real narrative to his freends, for the credit of his good name. He might else have been charged for a warlock.

The shades of evening were growing thicker around us as my conductor finished his long narrative with this moral: "You see, birkie, it is nae chancy thing to tak' a stranger traveler for a guide when you are in an uncouth land."

"I should not have made that inference," said I. "Your grandfather's adventure was fortunate for himself, whom it saved from ruin and distress; and fortunate for his landlord."

"Aye, but they had baith to sup the sauce o' 't sooner or later," said Wandering Willie; "what was fristed wasna forgiven. Sir John died before he was much over threescore; and it was just like of a moment's illness. And for my gudesire, though he departed in fullness of life, yet there was my father, a yauld man of forty-five, fell down betwixt the stilts of his plow, and rase never again, and left nae bairn but me, a puir, sightless, fatherless, motherless creature, could neither work nor want. Things gaed weel aneugh at first; for Sir Regwald Redgauntlet, the only son of Sir John and the oye of auld Sir Robert, and, wae 's me! the last of the honorable house, took the farm aff our hands, and brought me into his household to have care of me. My head never settled since I lost him; and if I say another word about it, deil a bar will I have the heart to play the night. Look out, my gentle chap," he resumed, in a different tone; "ye should see the lights at Brokenburn Glen by this time."

THE MYSTERIOUS BRIDE

James Hogg

James Hogg (1770–1835) was born in Ettrick. His mother was a collector
of Scottish ballads and his grandfather Will o' Phawhope was reputed to
be the last man in the Borders to have spoken with the fairies. Hogg was
apprenticed at the age of seven as a cowherd, for a half-yearly wage of
a ewe-lamb and a pair of shoes. He wrote in Scots and English. Hogg's
novel, *The Private Memoirs and Confessions of a Justified Sinner*, is a
classic of Scottish literature.

A great number of people now-a-days are beginning broadly to insinuate
that there are no such things as ghosts, or spiritual beings visible to mortal sight. Even Sir Walter Scott is turned renegade, and, with his stories
made up of half-and-half, like Nathaniel Gow's toddy, is trying to throw cold
water on the most certain, though most impalpable, phenomena of human nature. The bodies are daft. Heavenmend their wits! Before they had ventured to
assert such things, Iwish they had been where I have often been; or, in particular,
where the Laird of Birkendelly was on St. Lawrence's Eve, in the year 1777, and
sundry times subsequent to that.

Be it known, then, to every reader of this relation of facts that happened in my
own remembrance, that the road from Birkendelly to the great muckle village
of Balmawhapple, (commonly called the muckle town, in opposition to the little
town that stood on the other side of the burn) – that road, I say, lay between
two thorn hedges, so well kept by the Laird's hedger, so close, and so high, that a
rabbit could not have escaped from the highway into any of the adjoining fields.
Along this road was the Laird riding on the Eve of St. Lawrence, in a careless,
indifferent manner, with his hat to one side, and his cane dancing a horn-pipe
on the curtch of the saddle before him. He was, moreover, chanting a song to
himself, and I have heard people tell what song it was too. There was once a
certain, or rather uncertain, bard, ycleped Robert Burns, who made a number of
good songs; but this that the Laird sang was an amorous song of great antiquity,
which, like all the said bard's best songs, was sung one hundred and fifty years
before he was born. It began thus:

"I am the Laird of Windy-wa's,
I cam nae here without a cause,
An' I hac gotten forty fa's
   In coming o'er the knowe, joe!

The night it is baith wind and weet;
The morn it will be snaw and sleet;
My shoon are frozen to my feet;
   O, rise an' let me in, joe!
     Let me in this ae night," etc.

This song was the Laird singing, while, at the same time, he was smudging and laughing at the catastrophe, when, ere ever aware, he beheld, a short way before him, an uncommonly elegant and beautiful girl walking in the same direction with him. "Aye," said the Laird to himself, "here is something very attractive indeed! Where the deuce can she have sprung from? She must have risen out of the earth, for I never saw her till this breath. Well, I declare I have not seen such a female figure – I wish I had such an assignation with her as the Laird of Windy-wa's had with his sweetheart."

As the Laird was half-thinking, half-speaking this to himself, the enchanting creature looked back at him with a motion of intelligence that she knew what he was half-saying, half-thinking, and then vanished over the summit of the rising ground before him, called the Birky Brow. "Aye, go your ways!" said the Laird; "I see by you, you'll not be very hard to overtake. You cannot get off the road, and I'll have a chat with you before you make the Deer's Den."

The Laird jogged on. He did not sing the "Laird of Windy-wa's" any more, for he felt a sort of stifling about his heart; but he often repeated to himself, "She's a very fine woman! – a very fine woman indeed! – and to be walking here by herself! I cannot comprehend it."

When he reached the summit of the Birky Brow he did not see her, although he had a longer view of the road than before. He thought this very singular, and began to suspect that she wanted to escape him, although apparently rather lingering on him before. "I shall have another look at her, however," thought the Laird; and off he set at a flying trot. No. He came first to one turn, then another. There was nothing of the young lady to be seen. "Unless she take wings and fly away, I shall be up with her," quoth the Laird, and off he set at the full gallop.

In the middle of his career he met with Mr. M'Murdie, of Aulton, who hailed him with, "Hilloa! Birkendelly! where the deuce are you flying at that rate?"

"I was riding after a woman," said the Laird, with great simplicity, reining in his steed.

"Then I am sure no woman on earth can long escape you, unless she be in an air balloon."

"I don't know that. Is she far gone?"

"In which way do you mean?"

"In this."

"Aha-ha-ha! Hee-hee-hee!" nichered M'Murdie, misconstruing the Laird's meaning.

"What do you laugh at, my dear sir? Do you know her, then?"

"Ho-ho-ho! Hee-hee-hee! How should I, or how can I, know her, Birkendelly, unless you inform me who she is?"

"Why, that is the very thing I want to know of you. I mean the young lady whom you met just now."

"You are raving, Birkendelly. I met no young lady, nor is there a single person on the road I have come by, while you know, that for a mile and a half forward your way she could not get out of it."

"I know that," said the Laird, biting his lip, and looking greatly puzzled. "But confound me if I understand this; for I was within speech of her just now on the top of the Birky Brow there; and, when I think of it, she could not have been even thus far as yet. She had on a pure white gauze frock, a small green bonnet and feathers, and a green veil, which, flung back over her left shoulder, hung below her waist, and was altogether such an engaging figure that no man could have passed her on the road without taking some note of her. – Are you not making game of me? Did you not really meet with her?"

"On my word of truth and honour, I did not. Come, ride back with me, and we shall meet her still, depend on it. She has given you the go-by on the road. Let us go; I am only going to call at the mill about some barley for the distillery, and will return with you to the big town."

Birkendelly returned with his friend. The sun was not yet set, yet M'Murdie could not help observing that the Laird looked thoughtful and confused, and not a word could he speak about anything save this lovely apparition with the white frock and the green veil; and lo, when they reached the top of Birky Brow, there was the maiden again before them, and exactly at the same spot where the Laird first saw her before, only walking in the contrary direction.

"Well, this is the most extraordinary thing that I ever knew!" exclaimed the Laird.

"What is it, sir?" said M'Murdie.

"How that young lady could have eluded me," returned the Laird. "See, here she is still!"

"I beg your pardon, sir, I don't see her. Where is she?"

"There, on the other side of the angle; but you are short sighted. See, there she is ascending the other eminence in her white frock and green veil, as I told you – What a lovely creature!"

"Well, well, we have her fairly before us now, and shall see what she is like at all events," said M'Murdie.

Between the Birky Brow and this other slight eminence, there is an obtuse angle of the road at the part where it is lowest, and, in passing this, the two friends necessarily lost sight of the object of their curiosity. They pushed on at a quick pace – cleared the low angle – the maiden was not there! They rode full speed to the top of the eminence from whence a long extent of road was visible before them – there was no human creature in view! M'Murdie laughed aloud; but the Laird turned pale as death and bit his lip. His friend asked him, good-humouredly, why he was so much affected. He said, because he could not comprehend the meaning of this singular apparition or illusion, and it troubled him the more, as he now remembered a dream of the same nature which he had had, and which terminated in a dreadful manner.

"Why, man, you are dreaming still," said M'Murdie; "but never mind. It is quite common for men of your complexion to dream of beautiful maidens with white frocks, and green veils, bonnets, feathers, and slender waists. It is a lovely image, the creation of your own sanguine imagination, and you may worship it without any blame. Were her shoes black or green? – And her stockings, did you note them? The symmetry of the limbs, I am sure you did! Good-bye; I see you are not disposed to leave the spot. Perhaps she will appear to you again."

So saying, McMurdie rode on towards the mill, and Birkendelly, after musing for some time, turned his beast's head slowly round, and began to move towards the great muckle village.

The Laird's feelings were now in terrible commotion. He was taken beyond measure with the beauty and elegance of the figure he had seen; but he remembered, with a mixture of admiration and horror, that a dream of the same enchanting object had haunted his slumbers all the days of his life; yet, how singular that he should never have recollected the circumstance till now! But farther, with the dream there were connected some painful circumstances, which, though terrible in their issue, he could not recollect, so as to form them into any degree of arrangement.

As he was considering deeply of these things, and riding slowly down the declivity, neither dancing his cane, nor singing the "Laird of Windy-wa's," he lifted up his eyes, and there was the girl on the same spot where he saw her first, walking deliberately up the Birky Brow. The sun was down; but it was the month of August and a fine evening, and the Laird, seized with an unconquerable desire to see and speak with that incomparable creature, could restrain himself no longer, but shouted out to her to stop till he came up. She beckoned acquiescence, and slackened her pace into a slow movement. The Laird turned the corner quickly, but when he had rounded it, the maiden was still there, though on the summit of the Brow. She turned round, and, with an ineffable smile and curtsy, saluted him, and again moved slowly on. She vanished gradually beyond the summit, and while the green feathers were still nodding in view and so nigh, that the Laird could have touched them with a fishing-rod, he reached the top of the Brow himself. There was no living soul there, nor onward, as far as his view reached. He now trembled every limb, and, without knowing what he did, rode straight on to the big town, not daring well to return and see what he had seen for three several times; and, certain he would see it again when the shades of evening were deepening, he deemed it proper and prudent to decline the pursuit of such a phantom any farther.

He alighted at the Queen's Head, called for some brandy and water, quite forgot what was his errand to the great muckle town that afternoon, there being nothing visible to his mental sight but lovely fairy images, with white gauze frocks and green veils. His friend, M'Murdie, joined him; they drank deep, bantered, reasoned, got angry, reasoned themselves calm again, and still all would not do. The Laird was conscious that he had seen the beautiful apparition, and, moreover, that she was the very maiden, or the resemblance of her, who, in the irrevocable decrees of Providence, was destined to be his. It was in vain that M'Murdie reasoned of impressions on the imagination, and

> "Of fancy moulding in the mind,
> Light visions on the passing wind."

Vain also was a story that he told him of a relation of his own, who was greatly harassed by the apparition of an officer in a red uniform, that haunted him day and night, and had very nigh put him quite distracted several times; till at length his physician found out the nature of this illusion so well that he knew, from the state of his pulse, to an hour when the ghost of the officer would appear, and by bleeding, low diet, and emollients, contrived to keep the apparition away altogether.

The Laird admitted the singularity of this incident, but not that it was one in point; for the one, he said, was imaginary, and the other real; and that no conclusions could convince him in opposition to the authority of his own senses. He accepted of an invitation to spend a few days with M'Murdie and his family, but they all acknowledged afterwards that the Laird was very much like one bewitched.

As soon as he reached home, he went straight to the Birky Brow, certain of seeing once more the angelic phantom; but she was not there. He took each of his former positions again and again, but the desired vision would in nowise make its appearance. He tried every day, and every hour of the day, all with the same effect, till he grew absolutely desperate, and had the audacity to kneel on the spot and entreat of Heaven to see her. Yes, he called on Heaven to see her once more, whatever she was, whether a being of earth, heaven, or hell!

He was now in such a state of excitement that he could not exist; he grew listless, impatient, and sickly; took to his bed, and sent for M'Murdie and the doctor; and the issue of the consultation was, that Birkendelly consented to leave the country for a season, on a visit to his only sister in Ireland, whither we must now accompany him for a short space.

His sister was married to Captain Bryan, younger of Scoresby, and they two lived in a cottage on the estate, and the Captain's parents and sisters at Scoresby Hall. Great was the stir and preparation when the gallant young Laird of Birkendelly arrived at the cottage, it never being doubted that he had come to forward a second bond of connexion with the family, which still contained seven dashing sisters, all unmarried, and all alike willing to change that solitary and helpless state for the envied one of matrimony – a state highly popular among the young women of Ireland. Some of the Misses Bryan had now reached the years of womanhood, several of them scarcely; but these small disqualifications made no difference in the estimation of the young ladies themselves; each and all of them brushed up for the competition with high hopes and unflinching resolutions. True, the elder ones tried to check the younger in their good-natured, forthright Irish way; but they retorted, and persisted in their superior pretensions. Then there was such shopping in the county-town! It was so boundless that the credit of the Hall was finally exhausted, and the old Squire was driven to remark that "Och, and to be sure it was a dreadful and tirrabell concussion, to be put upon the equipment of seven daughters all at the same moment, as if the young gentleman could marry them all! Och, then, poor dear shoul, he would be after finding that one was sufficient, if not one too many. And therefore there was no occasion, none at all, at all, and that there was not, for any of them to rig out more than one."

It was hinted that the Laird had some reason for complaint at this time, but as the lady sided with her daughters, he had no chance. One of the items of his account was thirty-seven buckling-combs, then greatly in vogue. There were black combs, pale combs, yellow combs, and gilt ones, all to suit or set off various complexions; and if other articles bore any proportion at all to these, it had been better for the Laird and all his family that Birkendelly had never set foot in Ireland.

The plan was all concocted. There was to be a grand dinner at the Hall, at which the damsels were to appear in all their finery. A ball to follow, and note be taken which of the young ladies was their guest's choice, and measures taken accordingly. The dinner and the ball took place; and what a pity I may not describe that entertainment, the dresses, and the dancers, for they were all exquisite in their way, and *outré* beyond measure. But such details only serve to derange a winter's evening tale such as this.

Birkendelly having at this time but one model for his choice among womankind, all that ever he did while in the presence of ladies was to look out for some resemblance to her, the angel of his fancy; and it so happened that in one of old Bryan's daughters named Luna, or, more familiarly, Loony, he perceived, or thought he perceived, some imaginary similarity in form and air to the lovely apparition. This was the sole reason why he was incapable of taking his eyes off from her the whole of that night; and this incident settled the point, not only with the old people, but even the young ladies were forced, after every exertion on their own parts, to "yild the pint to their sister Loony, who certainly was nit the mist genteelest, nor mist handsomest of that guid-lucking fimily."

The next day Lady Luna was dispatched off to the cottage in grand style, there to live hand in glove with her supposed lover. There was no standing all this. There were the two parrocked together, like a ewe and a lamb, early and late; and though the Laird really appeared to have, and probably had, some delight in her company, it was only in contemplating that certain indefinable air of resemblance which she bore to the sole image impressed on his heart. He bought her a white gauze frock, a green bonnet and feather, with a veil, which she was obliged to wear thrown over her left shoulder, and every day after, six times a day, was she obliged to walk over a certain eminence at a certain distance before her lover. She was delighted to oblige him; but still when he came up, he looked disappointed, and never said, "Luna, I love you; when are we to be married?" No, he never said any such thing, for all her looks and expressions of fondest love; for, alas, in all this dalliance, he was only feeding a mysterious flame, that preyed upon his vitals, and proved too severe for the powers either of reason or religion to extinguish. Still, time flew lighter and lighter by, his health was restored, the bloom of his cheek returned, and the frank and simple confidence of Luna had a certain charm with it, that reconciled him to his sister's Irish economy. But a strange incident now happened to him which deranged all his immediate plans.

He was returning from angling one evening, a little before sunset, when he saw Lady Luna awaiting him on his way home. But instead of rushing up to meet him as usual, she turned, and walked up the rising ground before him. "Poor sweet girl! how condescending she is," said he to himself, "and how like she is in reality to the angelic being whose form and features are so deeply impressed on my heart! I now see it is no fond or fancied resemblance. It is real! real! real! How I long to clasp her in my arms, and tell her how I love her; for, after all, that is the girl that is to be mine, and the former a vision to impress this the more on my heart."

He posted up the ascent to overtake her. When at the top she turned, smiled, and curtsied. Good heavens! it was the identical lady of his fondest adoration herself, but lovelier, far lovelier, than ever. He expected every moment that she would vanish, as was her wont; but she did not – she awaited him, and received his embraces with open arms. She was a being of real flesh and blood, courteous, elegant, and affectionate. He kissed her hand, he kissed her glowing cheek, and blessed all the powers of love who had thus restored her to him again, after undergoing pangs of love such as man never suffered.

"But, dearest heart, here we are standing in the middle of the highway," said he; "suffer me to conduct you to my sister's house, where you shall have an apartment with a child of nature having some slight resemblance to yourself." She smiled, and said, "No, I will not sleep with Lady Luna to-night. Will you please to look round you, and see where you are." He did so, and behold they were standing on the Birky Brow, on the only spot where he had ever seen her. She smiled at his embarrassed look, and asked if he did not remember aught of his coming over from Ireland. He said he thought he did remember something of it, but love with him had long absorbed every other sense. He then asked her to his own house, which she declined, saying she could only meet him on that spot till after their marriage, which could not be before St. Lawrence's Eve come three years. "And now," said she, "we must part. My name is Jane Ogilvie, and you were betrothed to me before you were born. But I am come to release you this evening, if you have the slightest objection."

He declared he had none; and, kneeling, swore the most solemn oath to be hers forever, and to meet her there on St. Lawrence's Eve next, and every St. Lawrence's Eve until that blessed day on which she had consented to make him happy, by becoming his own forever. She then asked him affectionately to change rings with her, in pledge of their faith and truth, in which he joyfully acquiesced; for she could not have then asked any conditions which, in the fulness of his heart's love, he would not have granted; and after one fond and affectionate kiss, and repeating all their engagements over again, they parted.

Birkendelly's heart was now melted within him, and all his senses overpowered by one overwhelming passion. On leaving his fair and kind one, he got bewildered, and could not find the road to his own house, believing sometimes that he was going there, and sometimes to his sister's, till at length he came, as he thought, upon the Liffey, at its junction with Loch Allan; and there, in attempting to call for a boat, he awoke from a profound sleep, and found himself lying in his bed within his sister's house, and the day sky just breaking.

If he was puzzled to account for some things in the course of his dream, he was much more puzzled to account for them now that he was wide awake. He was sensible that he had met his love, had embraced, kissed, and exchanged vows and rings with her, and, in token of the truth and reality of all these, her emerald ring was on his finger, and his own away; so there was no doubt that they had met, – by what means it was beyond the power of man to calculate.

There was then living with Mrs Bryan an old Scotswoman, commonly styled Lucky Black. She had nursed Birkendelly's mother, and been dry-nurse to himself and sister; and having more than a mother's attachment for the latter, when she was married, old Lucky left her country, to spend the last of her days in the house of her beloved young lady. When the Laird entered the breakfast-parlor that morning she was sitting in her black velvet hood, as usual, reading "The Fourfold State of Man," and, being paralytic and somewhat deaf, she seldom regarded those who went or came in. But chancing to hear him say something about the ninth of August, she quitted reading, turned round her head to listen, and then asked, in a hoarse tremulous voice: "What's that he's saying? What's the unlucky callant saying about the 9th of August? Aih? To be sure it is St. Lawrence's Eve, although the tenth be his day. It's ower true, ower true! ower true for him an' a' his kin, poor man! Aih? What was he saying then?"

The men smiled at her incoherent earnestness, but the lady, with true feminine condescension, informed her, in a loud voice, that Allan had an engagement in Scotland on St. Lawrence's Eve. She then started up, extended her shrivelled hands, that shook like the aspen, and panted out: "Aih, aih? Lord preserve us! Whaten an engagement has he on St. Lawrence's Eve? Bind him! bind him! Shackle him wi' bands of steel, and of brass, and of iron! – O may He whose blessed will was pleased to leave him an orphan sae soon, preserve him from the fate which I tremble to think on!"

She then tottered round the table, as with supernatural energy, and seizing the Laird's right hand, she drew it close to her unstable eyes, and then perceiving the emerald ring chased in blood, she threw up her arms with a jerk, opened her skinny jaws with a fearful gape, and uttering a shriek that made all the house yell, and every one within it to tremble, she fell back lifeless and rigid on the floor. The gentlemen both fled, out of sheer terror; but a woman never deserts her friends in extremity. The lady called her maids about her, had her old nurse conveyed to bed, where every means were used to restore animation. But, alas! life was extinct! The vital spark had fled forever, which filled all their hearts with grief, disappointment, and horror, as some dreadful tale of mystery was now sealed up from their knowledge, which, in all likelihood, no other could reveal. But to say the truth, the Laird did not seem greatly disposed to probe it to the bottom.

Not all the arguments of Captain Bryan and his lady, nor the simple entreaties of Lady Luna, could induce Birkendelly to put off his engagement to meet his love on the Birky Brow on the evening of the 9th of August; but he promised soon to return, pretending that some business of the utmost importance called him away. Before he went, however, he asked his sister if ever she had heard of such a lady in Scotland as Jane Ogilvie. Mrs Bryan repeated the name many times to herself, and said that name undoubtedly was once familiar to her, although she thought not for good, but at that moment she did not recollect one single individual of the name. He then showed her the emerald ring that had been the death of Lucky Black; but the moment the lady looked at it, she made a grasp at it to take it off by force, which she had very nearly effected. "Oh, burn it! burn it!" cried she; "it is not a right ring! Burn it!"

"My dear sister, what fault is in the ring?" said he. "It is a very pretty ring, and one that I set great value by."

"O, for Heaven's sake, burn it, and renounce the giver!" cried she. "If you have any regard for your peace here or your soul's welfare hereafter, burn that ring! If you saw with your own eyes, you would easily perceive that that is not a ring befitting a Christian to wear."

This speech confounded Birkendelly a good deal. He retired by himself and examined the ring, and could see nothing in it unbecoming a Christian to wear. It was a chased gold ring, with a bright emerald, which last had a red foil, in some lights giving it a purple gleam, and inside was engraven "*Elegit*," much defaced, but that his sister could not see; therefore he could not comprehend her vehement injunctions concerning it. But that it might no more give her offence, or any other, he sewed it within his vest, opposite his heart, judging that there was something in it which his eyes were withholden from discerning.

Thus he left Ireland with his mind in great confusion, groping his way, as it were, in a hole of mystery, yet with the passion that preyed on his heart and vitals more intense than ever. He seems to have had an impression all his life that some mysterious fate awaited him, which the correspondence of his dreams and day visions tended to confirm. And though he gave himself wholly up to the sway of one overpowering passion, it was not without some yearnings of soul, manifestations of terror, and so much earthly shame, that he never more mentioned his love, or his engagements, to any human being, not even to his friend M'Murdie, whose company he forthwith shunned.

It is on this account that I am unable to relate what passed between the lovers thenceforward. It is certain they met at the Birky Brow that St. Lawrence's Eve, for they were seen in company together; but of the engagements, vows, or dalliance that passed between them I can say nothing; nor of all their future meetings, until the beginning of August, 1781, when the Laird began decidedly to make preparations for his approaching marriage; yet not as if he and his betrothed had been to reside at Birkendelly, all his provisions rather bespeaking a meditated journey.

On the morning of the 9th he wrote to his sister, and then arraying himself in his new wedding suit, and putting the emerald ring on his finger, he appeared all impatience, until towards evening, when he sallied out on horseback to his appointment. It seems that his mysterious inamorata had met him, for he was seen riding through the big town before sunset, with a young lady behind him, dressed in white and green, and the villagers affirmed that they were riding at the rate of fifty miles an hour! They were seen to pass a cottage called Mosskilt, ten miles farther on, where there was no highway, at the same tremendous speed; and I could never hear that they were any more seen, until the following morning, when Birkendelly's fine bay horse was found lying dead at his own stable door; and shortly after his master was likewise discovered lying a blackened corpse on the Birky Brow, at the very spot where the mysterious, but lovely dame, had always appeared to him. There was neither wound, bruise, nor dislocation in his whole frame; but his skin was of a livid colour, and his features terribly distorted.

This woful catastrophe struck the neighborhood with great consternation, so that nothing else was talked of. Every ancient tradition and modern incident were raked together, compared, and combined; and certainly a most rare concatenation of misfortunes was elicited. It was authenticated that his father had died on the same spot that day twenty years, and his grandfather that day forty years, the former, as was supposed, by a fall from his horse when in liquor, and the latter, nobody knew how; and now this Allan was the last of his race, for Mrs Bryan had no children.

It was moreover now remembered by many, and among the rest, the Rev.

Joseph Taylor, that he had frequently observed a young lady, in white and green, sauntering about the spot on a St. Lawrence's Eve.

When Captain Bryan and his lady arrived to take possession of the premises, they instituted a strict inquiry into every circumstance; but nothing further than what was related to them by Mr. M'Murdie could be learned of this Mysterious Bride, besides what the Laird's own letter bore. It ran thus: –

Dearest Sister,

I shall before this time to-morrow be the most happy, or most miserable, of mankind, having solemnly engaged myself this night to wed a young and beautiful lady, named Jane Ogilvie, to whom it seems I was betrothed before I was born. Our correspondence has been of a most private and mysterious nature; but my troth is pledged, and my resolution fixed. We set out on a far journey to the place of her abode on the nuptial eve, so that it will be long before I see you again.

Yours till death,
Allan George Sandison
Birkendelly, August 8th, 1781

That very same year, an old woman, named Marion Haw, was returned upon that, her native parish, from Glasgow. She had led a migratory life with her son – who was what he called a bell-hanger, but in fact a tinker of the worst grade – for many years, and was at last returned to the muckle town in a state of great destitution. She gave the parishioners a history of the Mysterious Bride, so plausibly correct, but withal so romantic, that everybody said of it (as is often said of my narratives, with the same narrow-minded prejudice and in-justice,) that it was *a made story*. There were, however, some strong testimonies of its veracity.

She said the first Allan Sandison, who married the great heiress of Birkendelly, was previously engaged to a beautiful young lady named Jane Ogilvie, to whom he gave anything but fair play; and, as she believed, either murdered her, or caused her to be murdered, in the midst of a thicket of birch and broom, at a spot which she mentioned; and she had good reasons for believ-ing so, as she had seen the red blood and the new grave, when she was a little girl, and ran home and mentioned it to her grandfather, who charged her as she valued her life never to mention that again, as it was only the nombles and hide of a deer, which he himself had buried there. But when, twenty years subsequent to that, the wicked and unhappy Allan Sandison was found dead on that very spot, and lying across the green mound, then nearly level with the surface, which she had once seen a new grave, she then for the first time ever thought of a Divine Providence; and she added, "For my grandfather, Neddy Haw, he dee'd too; there's naebody kens how, nor ever shall."

As they were quite incapable of conceiving, from Marion's description any-thing of the spot, Mr. M'Murdie caused her to be taken out to the Birky Brow in a cart, accompanied by Mr Taylor, and some hundreds of the town's folks; but whenever she saw it, she said, "Aha, birkies! the haill kintra's altered now. There was nae road here then; it gaed straight ower the tap o' the hill. An' let me see – there's the thorn where the cushats biggit; an' there's the auld birk that I ance fell aff an' left my shoe sticking i' the cleft. I can tell ye, birkies, either the deer's grave or bonny Jane Ogilvie's is no twa yards off the place where that horse's hind-feet are standin'; sae ye may howk, an' see if there be ony remains."

The minister and M'Murdie, and all the people, stared at one another, for they had purposely caused the horse to stand still on the very spot where both the father and son had been found dead. They digged, and deep, deep below the road, they found part of the slender bones and skull of a young female, which they deposited decently in the church-yard. The family of the Sandisons is extinct – the Mysterious Bride appears no more on the Eve of St. Lawrence – and the wicked people of the great muckle village have got a lesson on Divine justice written to them in lines of blood.

NAPOLEON AND THE SPECTRE

Charlotte Brontë

Charlotte Brontë's (1816–1855) life was marked by the early death of her siblings. Two sisters died in childhood. Her brother Branwell and remaining sisters, the writers Anne and Emily Brontë, died within eight months of each other. Charlotte wrote under the name Currer Bell in an attempt to avoid prejudice against women writers. She was pregnant with her first child when she died.

Well, as I was saying, the Emperor got into bed.

"Chevalier," says he to his valet, "let down those window-curtains, and shut the casement before you leave the room."

Chevalier did as he was told, and then, taking up his candlestick, departed.

In a few minutes the Emperor felt his pillow becoming rather hard, and he got up to shake it. As he did so a slight rustling noise was heard near the bed-head. His Majesty listened, but all was silent as he lay down again.

Scarcely had he settled into a peaceful attitude of repose, when he was disturbed by a sensation of thirst. Lifting himself on his elbow, he took a glass of lemonade from the small stand which was placed beside him. He refreshed himself by a deep draught. As he returned the goblet to its station a deep groan burst from a kind of closet in one corner of the apartment.

"Who's there?" cried the Emperor, seizing his pistols. "Speak, or I'll blow your brains out."

This threat produced no other effect than a short, sharp laugh, and a dead silence followed.

The Emperor started from his couch, and, hastily throwing on a robe-de-chambre which hung over the back of a chair, stepped courageously to the haunted closet. As he opened the door something rustled. He sprang forward sword in hand. No soul or even substance appeared, and the rustling, it was evident, proceeded from the falling of a cloak, which had been suspended by a peg from the door.

Half ashamed of himself he returned to bed.

Just as he was about once more to close his eyes, the light of the three wax tapers, which burned in a silver branch over the mantlepiece, was suddenly darkened. He looked up. A black, opaque shadow obscured it. Sweating with terror, the Emperor put out his hand to seize the bell-rope, but some invisible being snatched it rudely from his grasp, and at the same instant the ominous shade vanished.

"Pooh!" exclaimed Napoleon, "it was but an ocular delusion."

"Was it?" whispered a hollow voice, in deep mysterious tones, close to his ear. "Was it a delusion, Emperor of France? No! All thou hast heard and seen is sad forewarning reality. Rise, lifter of the Eagle Standard! Awake, swayer of the Lily Sceptre! Follow me, Napoleon, and thou shalt see more."

As the voice ceased, a form dawned on his astonished sight. It was that of a tall, thin man, dressed in a blue surtout edged with gold lace. It wore a black cravat very tightly round its neck, and confined by two little sticks placed behind each ear. The countenance was livid; the tongue protruded from between the teeth, and the eyes all glazed and bloodshot started with frightful prominence from their sockets.

"Mon Dieu!" exclaimed the Emperor, "what do I see? Spectre, whence cometh thou?"

The apparition spoke not, but gliding forward beckoned Napoleon with up-lifted finger to follow.

Controlled by a mysterious influence, which deprived him of the capability of either thinking or acting for himself, he obeyed in silence.

The solid wall of the apartment fell open as they approached, and, when both had passed through, it closed behind them with a noise like thunder.

They would now have been in total darkness had it not been for a dim light which shone round the ghost and revealed the damp walls of a long, vaulted passage. Down this they proceeded with mute rapidity. Ere long a cool, refreshing breeze, which rushed wailing up the vault and caused the Emperor to wrap his loose nightdress closer round, announced their approach to the open air.

This they soon reached, and Nap found himself in one of the principal streets of Paris.

"Worthy Spirit," said he, shivering in the chill night air, "permit me to return and put on some additional clothing. I will be with you again presently."

"Forward," replied his companion sternly.

He felt compelled, in spite of the rising indignation which almost choked him, to obey.

On they went through the deserted streets till they arrived at a lofty house built on the banks of the Seine. Here the Spectre stopped, the gates rolled back to receive them, and they entered a large marble hall which was partly concealed by a curtain drawn across, through the half transparent folds of which a bright light might be seen burning with dazzling lustre. A row of fine female figures, richly attired, stood before this screen. They wore on their heads garlands of the most beautiful flowers, but their faces were concealed by ghastly masks representing death's-heads.

"What is all this mummery?" cried the Emperor, making an effort to shake off the mental shackles by which he was so unwillingly restrained, "Where am I, and why have I been brought here?"

"Silence," said the guide, lolling out still further his black and bloody tongue. "Silence, if thou wouldst escape instant death."

The Emperor would have replied, his natural courage overcoming the temporary awe to which he had at first been subjected, but just then a strain of wild, supernatural music swelled behind the huge curtain, which waved to and fro, and bellied slowly out as if agitated by some internal commotion or battle of waving winds. At the same moment an overpowering mixture of the scents of mortal corruption, blent with the richest Eastern odours, stole through the haunted hall.

A murmur of many voices was now heard at a distance, and something grasped his arm eagerly from behind.

He turned hastily round. His eyes met the well-known countenance of Marie Louise.

"What! Are you in this infernal place, too?" said he. "What has brought you here?"

"Will your Majesty permit me to ask the same question of yourself?" said the Empress, smiling.

He made no reply; astonishment prevented him.

No curtain now intervened between him and the light. It had been removed as if by magic, and a splendid chandelier appeared suspended over his head. Throngs of ladies, richly dressed, but without death's-head masks, stood round, and a due proportion of gay cavaliers was mingled with them. Music was still sounding, but it was seen to proceed from a band of mortal musicians stationed in an orchestra near at hand. The air was yet redolent of incense, but it was incense unblended with stench.

"Mon dieu!" cried the Emperor, "how is all this come about? Where in the world is Piche?"

"Piche?" replied the Empress. "What does your Majesty mean? Had you not better leave the apartment and retire to rest?"

"Leave the apartment? Why, where am I?"

"In my private drawing-room, surrounded by a few particular persons of the Court whom I had invited this evening to a ball. You entered a few minutes since in your nightdress with your eyes fixed and wide open. I suppose from the astonishment you now testify that you were walking in your sleep."

The Emperor immediately fell into a fit of catalepsy, in which he continued during the whole of that night and the greater part of the next day.

THE MINISTER'S BLACK VEIL

Nathaniel Hawthorne

Nathaniel Hawthorne (1804–1864) wrote for children and adults. He was born into a prominent puritan family in Salem, Massachusetts and was a descendent of John Hawthorne, a judge at the Salem witchcraft trials of 1692. Hawthorne's puritan background influenced his fiction, notably his most famous novel, *The Scarlet Letter* (1850).

The sexton stood in the porch of Milford meeting-house pulling lustily at the bell-rope. The old people of the village came stooping along the street. Children with bright faces tripped merrily beside their parents or mimicked a graver gait in the conscious dignity of their Sunday clothes. Spruce bachelors looked sidelong at the pretty maidens, and fancied that the Sabbath sunshine made them prettier than on week-days. When the throng had mostly streamed into the porch, the sexton began to toll the bell, keeping his eye on the Reverend Mr. Hooper's door. The first glimpse of the clergyman's figure was the signal for the bell to cease its summons.

"But what has good Parson Hooper got upon his face?" cried the sexton in astonishment.

All within hearing immediately turned about, and beheld the semblance of Mr. Hooper, pacing slowly his meditative way toward the meeting-house. With one accord they started, expressing more wonder than if some strange minister were coming to dust the cushions of Mr. Hooper's pulpit.

"Are you sure it is our parson?" inquired Goodman Gray of the sexton.

"Of a certainty it is good Mr. Hooper," replied the sexton. "He was to have exchanged pulpits with Parson Shute of Westbury; but Parson Shute sent to excuse himself yesterday, being to preach a funeral sermon."

The cause of so much amazement may appear sufficiently slight. Mr. Hooper, a gentlemanly person of about thirty, though still a bachelor, was dressed with due clerical neatness, as if a careful wife had starched his band and brushed the weekly dust from his Sunday's garb. There was but one thing remarkable in his appearance. Swathed about his forehead and hanging down over his face, so low as to be shaken by his breath, Mr. Hooper had on a black veil. On a nearer view it seemed to consist of two folds of crape, which entirely concealed his features except the mouth and chin, but probably did not intercept his sight further than to give a darkened aspect to all living and inanimate things. With this gloomy shade before him good Mr. Hooper walked onward at a slow and quiet pace, stooping somewhat and looking on the ground, as is customary with abstracted men, yet nodding kindly to those of his parishioners who still waited on the meeting-house steps. But so wonder-struck were they, that his greeting hardly met with a return.

"I can't really feel as if good Mr. Hooper's face was behind that piece of crape," said the sexton.

"I don't like it," muttered an old woman as she hobbled into the meeting-house. "He has changed himself into something awful only by hiding his face."

"Our parson has gone mad!" cried Goodman Gray, following him across the threshold.

A rumor of some unaccountable phenomenon had preceded Mr. Hooper into the meeting-house and set all the congregation astir. Few could refrain from twisting their heads toward the door; many stood upright and turned directly about; while several little boys clambered upon the seats, and came down again with a terrible racket. There was a general bustle, a rustling of the women's gowns and shuffling of the men's feet, greatly at variance with that hushed repose which should attend the entrance of the minister. But Mr. Hooper appeared not to notice the perturbation of his people. He entered with an almost noiseless step, bent his head mildly to the pews on each side and bowed as he passed his oldest parishioner, a white-haired great-grandsire, who occupied an arm-chair in the centre of the aisle. It was strange to observe how slowly this venerable man became conscious of something singular in the appearance of his pastor. He seemed not fully to partake of the prevailing wonder till Mr. Hooper had ascended the stairs and showed himself in the pulpit, face to face with his congregation except for the black veil. That mysterious emblem was never once withdrawn. It shook with his measured breath as he gave out the psalm, it threw its obscurity between him and the holy page as he read the Scriptures, and while he prayed the veil lay heavily on his uplifted countenance. Did he seek to hide it from the dread Being whom he was addressing?

Such was the effect of this simple piece of crape that more than one woman of delicate nerves was forced to leave the meeting-house. Yet perhaps the pale-faced congregation was almost as fearful a sight to the minister as his black veil to them.

Mr. Hooper had the reputation of a good preacher, but not an energetic one: he strove to win his people heavenward, by mild, persuasive influences rather than to drive them thither, by the thunders of the word. The sermon which he now delivered was marked by the same characteristics of style and manner as the general series of his pulpit oratory, but there was something either in the sentiment of the discourse itself or in the imagination of the auditors which made it greatly the most powerful effort that they had ever heard from their pastor's lips. It was tinged rather more darkly than usual with the gentle gloom of Mr. Hooper's temperament. The subject had reference to secret sin and those sad mysteries which we hide from our nearest and dearest, and would fain conceal from our own consciousness, even forgetting that the Omniscient can detect them. A subtle power was breathed into his words. Each member of the congregation, the most innocent girl and the man of hardened breast, felt as if the preacher had crept upon them behind his awful veil and discovered their hoarded iniquity of deed or thought. Many spread their clasped hands on their bosoms. There was nothing terrible in what Mr. Hooper said; at least, no violence; and yet with every tremor of his melancholy voice the hearers quaked. An unsought pathos came hand in hand with awe. So sensible were the audience of some unwonted attribute in their minister that they longed for a breath of wind to blow aside the veil, almost believing that a stranger's visage would be discovered, though the form, gesture and voice were those of Mr. Hooper.

At the close of the services the people hurried out with indecorous confusion, eager to communicate their pent-up amazement, and conscious of lighter spirits the moment they lost sight of the black veil. Some gathered in little circles, huddled closely together, with their mouths all whispering in the centre; some went homeward alone, wrapped in silent meditation; some talked loudly and profaned the Sabbath-day with ostentatious laughter. A few shook their sagacious heads, intimating that they could penetrate the mystery, while one or two affirmed that there was no mystery at all, but only that Mr. Hooper's eyes were so weakened by the midnight lamp as to require a shade.

After a brief interval forth came good Mr. Hooper also, in the rear of his flock. Turning his veiled face from one group to another, he paid due reverence to the hoary heads, saluted the middle-aged with kind dignity as their friend and spiritual guide, greeted the young with mingled authority and love, and laid his hands on the little children's heads to bless them. Such was always his custom on the Sabbath-day. Strange and bewildered looks repaid him for his courtesy. None, as on former occasions, aspired to the honor of walking by their pastor's side. Old Squire Saunders, doubtless by an accidental lapse of memory, neglected to invite Mr. Hooper to his table, where the good clergyman had been wont to bless the food almost every Sunday since his settlement. He returned, therefore, to the parsonage, and at the moment of closing the door was observed to look back upon the people, all of whom had their eyes fixed upon the minister. A sad smile gleamed faintly from beneath the black veil and flickered about his mouth, glimmering as he disappeared.

"How strange," said a lady, "that a simple black veil, such as any woman might wear on her bonnet, should become such a terrible thing on Mr. Hooper's face!"

"Something must surely be amiss with Mr. Hooper's intellects," observed her husband, the physician of the village. "But the strangest part of the affair is the effect of this vagary, even on a sober-minded man like myself. The black veil, though it covers only our pastor's face, throws its influence over his whole person and makes him ghost-like from head to foot. Do you not feel it so?"

"Truly do I," replied the lady; "and I would not be alone with him for the world. I wonder he is not afraid to be alone with himself."

"Men sometimes are so," said her husband.

The afternoon service was attended with similar circumstances. At its conclusion the bell tolled for the funeral of a young lady. The relatives and friends were assembled in the house and the more distant acquaintances stood about the door, speaking of the good qualities of the deceased, when their talk was interrupted by the appearance of Mr. Hooper, still covered with his black veil. It was now an appropriate emblem. The clergyman stepped into the room where the corpse was laid, and bent over the coffin to take a last farewell of his deceased parishioner. As he stooped the veil hung straight down from his forehead, so that, if her eye-lids had not been closed for ever, the dead maiden might have seen his face. Could

Mr. Hooper be fearful of her glance, that he so hastily caught back the black veil? A person who watched the interview between the dead and living scrupled not to affirm that at the instant when the clergyman's features were disclosed the corpse had slightly shuddered, rustling the shroud and muslin cap, though the countenance retained the composure of death. A superstitious old woman was the only witness of this prodigy. From the coffin Mr. Hooper passed into the chamber of the mourners, and thence to the head of the staircase, to make the funeral prayer. It was a tender and heart-dissolving prayer, full of sorrow, yet so imbued with celestial hopes that the music of a heavenly harp swept by the fingers of the dead seemed faintly to be heard among the saddest accents of the minister. The people trembled, though they but darkly understood him, when he prayed that they and himself, and all of mortal race, might be ready, as he trusted this young maiden had been, for the dreadful hour that should snatch the veil from their faces. The bearers went heavily forth and the mourners followed, saddening all the street, with the dead before them and Mr. Hooper in his black veil behind.

"Why do you look back?" said one in the procession to his partner.

"I had a fancy," replied she, "that the minister and the maiden's spirit were walking hand in hand."

"And so had I, at the same moment," said the other.

That night the handsomest couple in Milford village were to be joined in wedlock. Though reckoned a melancholy man, Mr. Hooper had a placid cheerfulness for such occasions which often excited a sympathetic smile where livelier merriment would have been thrown away. There was no quality of his disposition which made him more beloved than this. The company at the wedding awaited his arrival with impatience, trusting that the strange awe which had gathered over him throughout the day would now be dispelled. But such was not the result. When Mr. Hooper came, the first thing that their eyes rested on was the same horrible black veil which had added deeper gloom to the funeral and could portend nothing but evil to the wedding. Such was its immediate effect on the guests that a cloud seemed to have rolled duskily from beneath the black crape and dimmed the light of the candles. The bridal pair stood up before the minister, but the bride's cold fingers quivered in the tremulous hand of the bridegroom, and her death-like paleness caused a whisper that the maiden who had been buried a few hours before was come from her grave to be married. If ever another wedding were so dismal, it was that famous one where they tolled the wedding-knell. After performing the ceremony Mr. Hooper raised a glass of wine to his lips, wishing happiness to the new-married couple in a strain of mild pleasantry that ought to have brightened the features of the guests like a cheerful gleam from the hearth. At that instant, catching a glimpse of his figure in the looking-glass, the black veil involved his own spirit in the horror with which it overwhelmed all others. His frame shuddered – his lips grew white – he spilt the untasted wine upon the carpet – and rushed forth into the darkness. For the Earth, too, had on her Black Veil.

The next day the whole village of Milford talked of little else than Parson Hooper's black veil. That, and the mystery concealed behind it, supplied a topic for discussion between acquaintances meeting in the street and good women gossiping at their open windows. It was the first item of news that the tavernkeeper told to his guests. The children babbled of it on their way to school. One imitative little imp covered his face with an old black handkerchief, thereby so affrighting his playmates that the panic seized himself and he well nigh lost his wits by his own waggery.

It was remarkable that, of all the busybodies and impertinent people in the parish, not one ventured to put the plain question to Mr. Hooper wherefore he did this thing. Hitherto, whenever there appeared the slightest call for such interference, he had never lacked advisers nor shown himself averse to be guided by their judgment. If he erred at all, it was by so painful a degree of self-distrust that even the mildest censure would lead him to consider an indifferent action as a crime. Yet, though so well acquainted with this amiable weakness, no individual among his parishioners chose to make the black veil a subject of friendly remonstrance. There was a feeling of dread, neither plainly confessed nor carefully concealed, which caused each to shift the responsibility upon another, till at length it was found expedient to send a deputation of the church, in order to deal with Mr. Hooper about the mystery before it should grow into a scandal. Never did an embassy so ill discharge its duties. The minister received them with friendly courtesy, but became silent after they were seated, leaving to his visitors the whole burden of introducing their important business. The topic, it might be supposed, was obvious enough. There was the black veil swathed round Mr. Hooper's forehead and concealing every feature above his placid mouth, on which, at times, they could perceive the glimmering of a melancholy smile. But that piece of crape, to their imagination, seemed to hang down before his heart, the symbol of a fearful secret between him and them. Were the veil but cast aside, they might speak freely of it, but not till then. Thus they sat a considerable time, speechless, confused and shrinking uneasily from Mr. Hooper's eye, which they felt to be fixed upon them with an invisible glance. Finally, the deputies returned abashed to their constituents, pronouncing the matter too weighty to be handled except by a council of the churches, if, indeed, it might not require a General Synod.

But there was one person in the village unappalled by the awe with which the black veil had impressed all beside herself. When the deputies returned without an explanation, or even venturing to demand one, she, with the calm energy of her character determined to chase away the strange cloud that appeared to be settling round Mr. Hooper every moment more darkly than before. As his plighted wife it should be her privilege to know what the black veil concealed. At the minister's first visit, therefore, she entered upon the subject with a direct simplicity which made the task easier both for him and her. After he had seated himself she fixed her eyes steadfastly upon the veil, but could discern nothing of the dreadful gloom that had so overawed the multitude; it was but a double fold of crape hanging down from his forehead to his mouth and slightly stirring with his breath.

"No," said she, aloud, and smiling, "there is nothing terrible in this piece of crape, except that it hides a face which I am always glad to look upon. Come, good sir; let the sun shine from behind the cloud. First lay aside your black veil, then tell me why you put it on."

Mr. Hooper's smile glimmered faintly.

"There is an hour to come," said he, "when all of us shall cast aside our veils.

Take it not amiss, beloved friend, if I wear this piece of crape till then."

"Your words are a mystery too," returned the young lady. "Take away the veil from them, at least."

"Elizabeth, I will," said he, "so far as my vow may suffer me. Know, then, this veil is a type and a symbol, and I am bound to wear it ever, both in light and darkness, in solitude and before the gaze of multitudes, and as with strangers, so with my familiar friends. No mortal eye will see it withdrawn. This dismal shade must separate me from the world; even you, Elizabeth, can never come behind it."

"What grievous affliction hath befallen you," she earnestly inquired, "that you should thus darken your eyes for ever?"

"If it be a sign of mourning," replied Mr. Hooper, "I, perhaps, like most other mortals, have sorrows dark enough to be typified by a black veil."

"But what if the world will not believe that it is the type of an innocent sorrow?" urged Elizabeth. "Beloved and respected as you are, there may be whispers that you hide your face under the consciousness of secret sin. For the sake of your holy office do away this scandal."

The color rose into her cheeks as she intimated the nature of the rumors that were already abroad in the village. But Mr. Hooper's mildness did not forsake him. He even smiled again – that same sad smile which always appeared like a faint glimmering of light proceeding from the obscurity beneath the veil.

"If I hide my face for sorrow, there is cause enough," he merely replied; "and if I cover it for secret sin, what mortal might not do the same?"

And with this gentle but unconquerable obstinacy did he resist all her entreaties. At length Elizabeth sat silent. For a few moments she appeared lost in thought, considering, probably, what new methods might be tried, to withdraw her lover from so dark a fantasy, which, if it had no other meaning, was perhaps a symptom of mental disease. Though of a firmer character than his own, the tears rolled down her cheeks. But in an instant, as it were, a new feeling took the place of sorrow: her eyes were fixed insensibly on the black veil, when like a sudden twilight in the air its terrors fell around her. She arose and stood trembling before him.

"And do you feel it, then, at last?" said he, mournfully.

She made no reply, but covered her eyes with her hand and turned to leave the room. He rushed forward and caught her arm.

"Have patience with me, Elizabeth!" cried he, passionately. "Do not desert me though this veil must be between us here on earth. Be mine, and hereafter there shall be no veil over my face, no darkness between our souls! It is but a mortal veil; it is not for eternity! Oh, you know not how lonely I am, and how frightened to be alone behind my black veil. Do not leave me in this miserable obscurity for ever!"

"Lift the veil but once, and look me in the face," said she.

"Never! It cannot be!" replied Mr. Hooper.

"Then farewell!" said Elizabeth.

She withdrew her arm from his grasp and slowly departed, pausing at the door to give one long, shuddering gaze that seemed almost to penetrate the mystery of the black veil. But even amid his grief Mr. Hooper smiled to think that only a material emblem had separated him from happiness, though the horrors which it shadowed forth must be drawn darkly between the fondest of lovers.

From that time no attempts were made to remove Mr. Hooper's black veil, or, by a direct appeal, to discover the secret which it was supposed to hide. By persons who claimed a superiority to popular prejudice, it was reckoned merely an eccentric whim, such as often mingles with the sober actions of men otherwise rational, and tinges them all with its own semblance of insanity. But with the multitude, good Mr. Hooper was irreparably a bugbear. He could not walk the street with any peace of mind, so conscious was he that the gentle and timid would turn aside to avoid him, and that others would make it a point of hardihood to throw themselves in his way. The impertinence of the latter class compelled him to give up his customary walk, at sunset, to the burial-ground; for when he leaned pensively over the gate, there would always be faces behind the gravestones, peeping at his black veil. A fable went the rounds, that the stare of the dead people drove him thence. It grieved him, to the very depth of his kind heart, to observe how the children fled from his approach, breaking up their merriest sports, while his melancholy figure was yet afar off. Their instinctive dread caused him to feel more strongly than aught else, that a preternatural horror was interwoven with the threads of the black crape. In truth, his own antipathy to the veil was known to be so great that he never willingly passed before a mirror, nor stooped to drink at a still fountain, lest, in its peaceful bosom he should be affrighted by himself. This was what gave plausibility to the whispers that Mr. Hooper's conscience tortured him for some great crime, too horrible to be entirely concealed, or otherwise than so obscurely intimated. Thus, from beneath the black veil, there rolled a cloud into the sunshine, an ambiguity of sin or sorrow, which enveloped the poor minister, so that love or sympathy could never reach him. It was said that ghost and fiend consorted with him there. With self-shudderings and outward terrors he walked continually in its shadow, groping darkly within his own soul or gazing through a medium that saddened the whole world. Even the lawless wind, it was believed, respected his dreadful secret and never blew aside the veil. But still good Mr. Hooper sadly smiled at the pale visages of the worldly throng as he passed by.

Among all its bad influences, the black veil had the one desirable effect of making its wearer a very efficient clergyman. By the aid of his mysterious emblem – for there was no other apparent cause – he became a man of awful power over souls that were in agony for sin. His converts always regarded him with a dread peculiar to themselves, affirming, though but figuratively, that before he brought them to celestial light they had been with him behind the black veil. Its gloom, indeed, enabled him to sympathize with all dark affections. Dying sinners cried aloud for Mr. Hooper and would not yield their breath till he appeared, though ever, as he stooped to whisper consolation, they shuddered at the veiled face so near their own. Such were the terrors of the black veil even when Death had bared his visage. Strangers came long distances to attend service at his church with the mere idle purpose of gazing at his figure because it was forbidden them to behold his face. But many were made to quake ere they departed! Once, during Governor Belcher's administration, Mr. Hooper was appointed to preach the election sermon. Covered with his black veil, he stood before the chief magistrate, the council and the representatives, and wrought so deep an impression that the legislative measures of that year were characterized by all the gloom and piety of our earliest ancestral sway.

In this manner Mr. Hooper spent a long life, irreproachable in outward act, yet shrouded in dismal suspicions; kind and loving, though unloved and dimly feared; a man apart from men, shunned in their health and joy, but ever summoned to their aid in mortal anguish. As years wore on, shedding their snows above his sable veil, he acquired a name throughout the New England churches, and they called him Father Hooper. Nearly all his parishioners, who were of mature age when he was settled, had been borne away by many a funeral: he had one congregation in the church, and a more crowded one in the churchyard; and, having wrought so late into the evening and done his work so well, it was now good Father Hooper's turn to rest.

Several persons were visible by the shaded candlelight in the death-chamber of the old clergyman. Natural connections he had none. But there was the decorously grave, though unmoved physician, seeking only to mitigate the last pangs of the patient whom he could not save. There were the deacons, and other eminently pious members of his church. There, also, was the Reverend Mr. Clark, of Westbury, a young and zealous divine, who had ridden in haste to pray by the bedside of the expiring minister. There was the nurse – no hired handmaiden of death, but one whose calm affection had endured thus long in secrecy, in solitude, amid the chill of age, and would not perish, even at the dying-hour. Who, but Elizabeth! And there lay the hoary head of good Father Hooper upon the death-pillow with the black veil still swathed about his brow and reaching down over his face, so that each more difficult gasp of his faint breath caused it to stir. All through life that piece of crape had hung between him and the world: it had separated him from cheerful brotherhood and woman's love, and kept him in that saddest of all prisons, his own heart; and still it lay upon his face, as if to deepen the gloom of his darksome chamber and shade him from the sunshine of eternity.

For some time previous, his mind had been confused, wavering doubtfully between the past and the present, and hovering forward, as it were, at intervals, into the indistinctness of the world to come. There had been feverish turns, which tossed him from side to side and wore away what little strength he had. But in his most convulsive struggles, and in the wildest vagaries of his intellect, when no other thought retained its sober influence, he still showed an awful solicitude lest the black veil should slip aside. Even if his bewildered soul could have forgotten, there was a faithful woman at his pillow who with averted eyes would have covered that aged face which she had last beheld in the comeliness of manhood. At length the death-stricken old man lay quietly in the torpor of mental and bodily exhaustion, with an imperceptible pulse, and breath that grew fainter and fainter, except when a long, deep, and irregular inspiration seemed to prelude the flight of his spirit.

The minister of Westbury approached the bedside.

"Venerable Father Hooper," said he, "the moment of your release is at hand. Are you ready for the lifting of the veil, that shuts in time from eternity?"

Father Hooper at first replied merely by a feeble motion of his head; then, apprehensive, perhaps, that his meaning might be doubtful, he exerted himself to speak.

"Yea," said he, in faint accents; "my soul hath a patient weariness until that veil be lifted."

"And is it fitting," resumed the Reverend Mr. Clark, "that a man so given to prayer, of such a blameless example, holy in deed and thought, so far as mortal judgment may pronounce; is it fitting that a father in the Church should leave a shadow on his memory that may seem to blacken a life so pure? I pray you, my venerable brother, let not this thing be! Suffer us to be gladdened by your triumphant aspect, as you go to your reward. Before the veil of eternity be lifted let me cast aside this black veil from your face!"

And, thus speaking, the Reverend Mr. Clark bent forward to reveal the mystery of so many years.

But, exerting a sudden energy that made all the beholders stand aghast, Father Hooper snatched both his hands from beneath the bedclothes and pressed them strongly on the black veil, resolute to struggle if the minister of Westbury would contend with a dying man.

"Never!" cried the veiled clergyman. "On earth, never!"

"Dark old man," exclaimed the affrighted minister, "with what horrible crime upon your soul are you now passing to the judgment?"

Father Hooper's breath heaved: it rattled in his throat; but, with a mighty effort grasping forward with his hands, he caught hold of life and held it back till he should speak. He even raised himself in bed, and there he sat shivering with the arms of Death around him, while the black veil hung down, awful at that last moment in the gathered terrors of a lifetime. And yet the faint, sad smile so often there now seemed to glimmer from its obscurity and linger on Father Hooper's lips.

"Why do you tremble at me alone?" cried he, turning his veiled face round the circle of pale spectators. "Tremble also at each other. Have men avoided me and women shown no pity and children screamed and fled only for my black veil? What but the mystery which it obscurely typifies has made this piece of crape so awful? When the friend shows his inmost heart to his friend; the lover to his best-beloved; when man does not vainly shrink from the eye of his Creator, loathsomely treasuring up the secret of his sin; then deem me a monster for the symbol beneath which I have lived and die! I look around me, and, lo! on every visage a black veil!"

While his auditors shrank from one another in mutual affright, Father Hooper fell back upon his pillow, a veiled corpse with a faint smile lingering on the lips. Still veiled, they laid him in his coffin, and a veiled corpse they bore him to the grave. The grass of many years has sprung up and withered on that grave, the burial-stone is moss-grown, and good Mr. Hooper's face is dust; but awful is still the thought that it mouldered beneath the black veil.

THE TELL-TALE HEART

Edgar Allan Poe

It is tempting to ascribe **Edgar Allan Poe**'s (1809–1849) gothic tendencies to his often miserable life. He was born in Boston to itinerant actors, his father abandoned the family when Poe was a year old. His mother died young, leaving him alone at the age of two. Poe was rarely solvent and tried to make his living variously as a soldier, critic, writer and editor. He married his cousin Virginia when she was thirteen. They were married for eleven years until Virginia's early death. Perhaps unsurprisingly Poe struggled with alcoholism and depression.

True! – nervous – very, very dreadfully nervous I had been and am; but why will you say that I am mad? The disease had sharpened my senses – not destroyed – not dulled them. Above all was the sense of hearing acute. I heard all things in the heaven and in the earth. I heard many things in hell. How, then, am I mad? Hearken! and observe how healthily – how calmly I can tell you the whole story.

It is impossible to say how first the idea entered my brain; but once conceived, it haunted me day and night. Object there was none. Passion there was none. I loved the old man. He had never wronged me. He had never given me insult. For his gold I had no desire. I think it was his eye! yes, it was this! He had the eye of a vulture – a pale blue eye, with a film over it. Whenever it fell upon me, my blood ran cold; and so by degrees – very gradually – I made up my mind to take the life of the old man, and thus rid myself of the eye forever.

Now this is the point. You fancy me mad. Madmen know nothing. But you should have seen me. You should have seen how wisely I proceeded – with what caution – with what foresight – with what dissimulation I went to work! I was never kinder to the old man than during the whole week before I killed him. And every night, about midnight, I turned the latch of his door and opened it – oh so gently! And then, when I had made an opening sufficient for my head, I put in a dark lantern, all closed, closed, that no light shone out, and then I thrust in my head. Oh, you would have laughed to see how cunningly I thrust it in! I moved it slowly – very, very slowly, so that I might not disturb the old man's sleep. It took me an hour to place my whole head within the opening so far that I could see him as he lay upon his bed. Ha! would a madman have been so wise as this, And then, when my head was well in the room, I undid the lantern cautiously-oh, so cautiously – cautiously (for the hinges creaked) – I undid it just so much that a single thin ray fell upon the vulture eye. And this I did for seven long nights – every night just at midnight – but I found the eye always closed; and so it was impossible to do the work; for it was not the old man who vexed me, but his Evil Eye. And every morning, when the day broke, I went boldly into the chamber, and spoke courageously to him, calling him by name in a hearty tone, and inquiring how he has passed the night. So you see he would have been a very profound old man, indeed, to suspect that every night, just at twelve, I looked in upon him while he slept.

Upon the eighth night I was more than usually cautious in opening the door. A watch's minute hand moves more quickly than did mine. Never before that night had I felt the extent of my own powers – of my sagacity. I could scarcely contain my feelings of triumph. To think that there I was, opening the door, little by little, and he not even to dream of my secret deeds or thoughts. I fairly chuckled at the idea; and perhaps he heard me; for he moved on the bed suddenly, as if startled. Now you may think that I drew back – but no. His room was as black as pitch with the thick darkness, (for the shutters were close fastened, through fear of robbers,) and so I knew that he could not see the opening of the door, and I kept pushing it on steadily, steadily.

I had my head in, and was about to open the lantern, when my thumb slipped upon the tin fastening, and the old man sprang up in bed, crying out – "Who's there?"

I kept quite still and said nothing. For a whole hour I did not move a muscle, and in the meantime I did not hear him lie down. He was still sitting up in the bed listening; – just as I have done, night after night, hearkening to the death watches in the wall.

Presently I heard a slight groan, and I knew it was the groan of mortal terror. It was not a groan of pain or of grief – oh, no! – it was the low stifled sound that arises from the bottom of the soul when overcharged with awe. I knew the sound well. Many a night, just at midnight, when all the world slept, it has welled up from my own bosom, deepening, with its dreadful echo, the terrors that distracted me. I say I knew it well. I knew what the old man felt, and pitied him, although I chuckled at heart. I knew that he had been lying awake ever since the first slight noise, when he had turned in the bed. His fears had been ever since growing upon him. He had been trying to fancy them causeless, but could not. He had been saying to himself – "It is nothing but the wind in the chimney – it is only a mouse crossing the floor," or "It is merely a cricket which has made a single chirp." Yes, he had been trying to comfort himself with these suppositions: but he had found all in vain. All in vain; because Death, in approaching him had stalked with his black shadow before him, and enveloped the victim. And it was the mournful influence of the unperceived shadow that caused him to feel – although he neither saw nor heard – to feel the presence of my head within the room.

When I had waited a long time, very patiently, without hearing him lie down, I resolved to open a little – a very, very little crevice in the lantern. So I opened it – you cannot imagine how stealthily, stealthily – until, at length a simple dim ray, like the thread of the spider, shot from out the crevice and fell full upon the vulture eye.

It was open – wide, wide open – and I grew furious as I gazed upon it. I saw it with perfect distinctness – all a dull blue, with a hideous veil over it that chilled the very marrow in my bones; but I could see nothing else of the old man's face or person: for I had directed the ray as if by instinct, precisely upon the damned spot.

And have I not told you that what you mistake for madness is but over-acuteness of the sense? – now, I say, there came to my ears a low, dull, quick sound, such as a watch makes when enveloped in cotton. I knew that sound well, too. It was the beating of the old man's heart. It increased my fury, as the beating of a drum stimulates the soldier into courage.

But even yet I refrained and kept still. I scarcely breathed. I held the lantern motionless. I tried how steadily I could maintain the ray upon the eve. Meantime the hellish tattoo of the heart increased. It grew quicker and quicker, and louder and louder every instant. The old man's terror must have been extreme! It grew louder, I say, louder every moment! – do you mark me well I have told you that I am nervous: so I am. And now at the dead hour of the night, amid the dreadful silence of that old house, so strange a noise as this excited me to uncontrollable terror. Yet, for some minutes longer I refrained and stood still. But the beating grew louder, louder! I thought the heart must burst. And now a new anxiety seized me – the sound would be heard by a neighbour! The old man's hour had come! With a loud yell, I threw open the lantern and leaped into the room. He shrieked once – once only. In an instant I dragged him to the floor, and pulled the heavy bed over him. I then smiled gaily, to find the deed so far done. But, for many minutes, the heart beat on with a muffled sound. This, however, did not vex me; it would not be heard through the wall. At length it ceased. The old man was dead. I removed the bed and examined the corpse. Yes, he was stone, stone dead. I placed my hand upon the heart and held it there many minutes. There was no pulsation. He was stone dead. His eve would trouble me no more.

If still you think me mad, you will think so no longer when I describe the wise precautions I took for the concealment of the body. The night waned, and I worked hastily, but in silence. First of all I dismembered the corpse. I cut off the head and the arms and the legs.

I then took up three planks from the flooring of the chamber, and deposited all between the scantlings. I then replaced the boards so cleverly, so cunningly, that no human eye – not even his – could have detected any thing wrong. There was nothing to wash out – no stain of any kind – no blood-spot whatever. I had been too wary for that. A tub had caught all – ha! ha!

When I had made an end of these labors, it was four o'clock – still dark as midnight. As the bell sounded the hour, there came a knocking at the street door. I went down to open it with a light heart, – for what had I now to fear? There entered three men, who introduced themselves, with perfect suavity, as officers of the police. A shriek had been heard by a neighbour during the night; suspicion of foul play had been aroused; information had been lodged at the police office, and they (the officers) had been deputed to search the premises.

I smiled, – for what had I to fear? I bade the gentlemen welcome. The shriek, I said, was my own in a dream. The old man, I mentioned, was absent in the country. I took my visitors all over the house. I bade them search – search well. I led them, at length, to his chamber. I showed them his treasures, secure, undisturbed. In the enthusiasm of my confidence, I brought chairs into the room, and desired them here to rest from their fatigues, while I myself, in the wild audacity of my perfect triumph, placed my own seat upon the very spot beneath which reposed the corpse of the victim.

The officers were satisfied. My manner had convinced them. I was singularly at ease. They sat, and while I answered cheerily, they chatted of familiar things. But, ere long, I felt myself getting pale and wished them gone. My head ached, and I fancied a ringing in my ears: but still they sat and still chatted. The ringing became more distinct: – It continued and became more distinct: I talked more freely to get rid of the feeling: but it continued and gained definiteness – until, at length, I found that the noise was not within my ears.

No doubt I now grew very pale; – but I talked more fluently, and with a heightened voice. Yet the sound increased – and what could I do? It was a low, dull, quick sound – much such a sound as a watch makes when enveloped in cotton. I gasped for breath – and yet the officers heard it not. I talked more quickly – more vehemently; but the noise steadily increased. I arose and argued about trifles, in a high key and with violent gesticulations; but the noise steadily increased. Why would they not be gone? I paced the floor to and fro with heavy strides, as if excited to fury by the observations of the men – but the noise steadily increased. Oh God! what could I do? I foamed – I raved – I swore! I swung the chair upon which I had been sitting, and grated it upon the boards, but the noise arose over all and continually increased. It grew louder – louder – louder! And still the men chatted pleasantly, and smiled. Was it possible they heard not? Almighty God! – no, no! They heard! – they suspected! – they knew! – they were making a mockery of my horror! – this I thought, and this I think. But anything was better than this agony! Anything was more tolerable than this derision! I could bear those hypocritical smiles no longer! I felt that I must scream or die! and now – again! – hark! louder! louder! louder! louder!

"Villains!" I shrieked, "dissemble no more! I admit the deed! – tear up the planks! here, here! – It is the beating of his hideous heart!"

CHRISTMAS GHOSTS

Charles Dickens

Charles Dickens (1812–1870) was born in Portsmouth. His father's finances were often precarious, and in 1824 the Dickens family (with the exception of Charles, who was working in a blacking factory, and his sister Fanny) spent some months in Marshalsea debtors' prison. Despite becoming the most popular writer of his era, Dickens never forgot his early experiences of poverty. He was an influential social commentator campaigning for children's rights and other reforms.

I like to come home at Christmas. We all do, or we all *should*. We all come home, or ought to come home, for a short holiday – the longer, the better – from the great boarding-school, where we are for ever working at our arithmetical slates, to take, and give a rest. As to going a-visiting, where can we not go, if we will; where have we not been, when we would; starting our fancy from our Christmas Tree!

Away into the winter prospect. There are many such upon the tree! On, by low-lying misty grounds, through fens and fogs, up long hills, winding dark as caverns between thick plantations, almost shutting out the sparkling stars; so, out on broad heights, until we stop at last, with sudden silence, at an avenue. The gate-bell has a deep, half-awful sound in the frosty air; the gate swings open on its hinges; and, as we drive up to a great house, the glancing lights grow larger in the windows, and the opposing rows of trees seem to fall solemnly back on either side, to give us place. At intervals, all day, a frightened hare has shot across this whitened turf; or the distant clatter of a herd of deer trampling the hard frost, has, for the minute, crushed the silence too. Their watchful eyes beneath the fern may be shining now, if we could see them, like the icy dewdrops on the leaves; but they are still, and all is still. And so, the lights growing larger, and the trees falling back before us, and closing up again behind us, as if to forbid retreat, we come to the house.

There is probably a smell of roasted chestnuts and other good comfortable things all the time, for we are telling Winter Stories – Ghost Stories, or more shame for us – round the Christmas fire; and we have never stirred, except to draw a little nearer to it. But, no matter for that. We come to the house, and it is an old house, full of great chimneys where wood is burnt on ancient dogs upon the hearth, and grim portraits (some of them with grim legends, too) lour distrustfully from the oaken panels of the walls. We are a middle-aged nobleman, and we make a generous supper with our host and hostess and their guests – it being Christmas-time, and the old house full of company – and then we go to bed. Our room is a very old room. It is hung with tapestry. We don't like the portrait of a cavalier in green, over the fireplace. There are great black beams in the ceiling, and there is a great black bedstead, supported at the foot by two great black figures, who seem to have come off a couple of tombs in the old baronial church in the park, for our particular accommodation. But, we are not a superstitious nobleman, and we don't mind. Well! we dismiss our servant, lock the door, and sit before the fire in our dressing-gown, musing about a great many things. At length we go to bed. Well! we can't sleep. We toss and tumble, and can't sleep. The embers on the hearth burn fitfully and make the room look ghostly. We can't help peeping out over the counterpane at the two black figures and the cavalier – that wicked looking cavalier – in green. In the flickering light they seem to advance and retire: which, though we are not by any means a superstitious nobleman, is not agreeable. Well! we get nervous – more and more nervous. We say, "This is very foolish, but we can't stand this; we'll pretend to be ill, and knock up somebody." Well! we are just going to do it, when the locked door opens, and there comes in a young woman, deadly pale, and with long fair hair, who glides to the fire, and sits down in the chair we have left there, wringing her hands. Then, we notice that her clothes are wet. Our tongue cleaves to the roof of our mouth, and we can't speak; but, we observe her accurately. Her clothes are wet; her long hair is dabbled with moist mud; she is dressed in the fashion of two hundred years ago; and she has at her girdle a bunch of rusty keys. Well! there she sits, and we can't even faint, we are in such a state about it. Presently she gets up, and tries all of the locks in the room with the rusty keys, which won't fit one of them; then, she fixes her eyes on the portrait of the cavalier in green, and says, in a low, terrible voice, "The stags know it!" After that, she wrings her hands again, passes the bedside, and goes out at the door. We hurry on our dressing-gown, seize our pistols (we always travel with pistols), and are following, when we find the door locked. We turn the key, look out into the dark gallery; no one there. We wander away, and try to find our servant. Can't be done. We pace the gallery till daybreak; then return to our deserted room, fall asleep, and are awakened by our servant (nothing ever haunts him) and the shining sun. Well! we make a wretched breakfast, and all the company say we look queer. After breakfast, we go over the house with our host, and then we take him to the portrait of the cavalier in green, and then it all comes out. He was false to a young housekeeper once attached to that family, and famous for her beauty, who drowned herself in a pond, and whose body was discovered, after a long time, because the stags refused to drink of the water. Since which, it has been whispered that she traverses the house at midnight (but goes especially to that room where the cavalier in green was wont to sleep), trying the old locks with the rusty keys. Well! we tell our host of what we have seen, and a shade comes over his features, and he begs it may be hushed up; and so it is. But, it's all true; and we said so, before we died (we are dead now) to many responsible people.

There is no end to the old houses, with resounding galleries, and dismal state-bedchambers, and haunted wings shut up for many years, through which we may ramble, with an agreeable creeping up our back, and encounter any number of ghosts, but (it is worthy of remark perhaps) reducible to a very few general types and classes; for, ghosts have little originality, and "walk" in a beaten track. Thus, it comes to pass, that a certain room in a certain old hall, where a certain bad lord, baronet, knight, or gentleman, shot himself, has certain planks in the floor from which the blood *will not* be taken out. You may scrape and scrape, as the present owner has done, or plane and plane, as his father did, or scrub and scrub, as his grandfather did, or burn and burn with strong acids, as his great-grandfather did, but, there the blood will still be – no redder and no paler – no more and no less – always just the same. Thus, in such another house there is a haunted door, that never will keep open; or another door that never will keep shut, or a haunted sound of a spinning-wheel, or a hammer, or a foot-step, or a cry, or a sigh, or a horse's tramp, or the rattling of a chain. Or else, there is a turret-clock, which, at the midnight hour, strikes thirteen when the head of the family is going to die; or a shadowy, immovable black carriage which at such a time is always seen by somebody, waiting near the great gates in the stable-yard. Or thus, it came to pass how Lady Mary went to pay a visit at a large wild house in the Scottish Highlands, and, being fatigued with her long journey, retired to bed early, and innocently said, next morning, at the breakfast-table, "How odd, to have so late a party last night, in this remote place, and not to tell me of it, before I went to bed!" Then, everyone asked Lady Mary what she meant? Then, Lady Mary replied, "Why, all night long, the carriages were driving round and round the terrace, underneath my window!" Then, the owner of the house turned pale, and so did his Lady, and Charles Macdoodle of Macdoodle signed to Lady Mary to say no more, and everyone was silent. After breakfast, Charles Macdoodle told Lady Mary that it was a tradition in the family that those rumbling carriages on the terrace betokened death. And so it proved, for, two months afterwards, the Lady of the mansion died. And Lady Mary, who was Maid of Honour at Court, often told this story to the old Queen Charlotte; by this token that the old King always said, "Eh, eh? What, what? Ghosts, ghosts? No such thing, no such thing!" And never left off saying so, until he went to bed.

Or, a friend of somebody's whom most of us know, when he was a young man at college, had a particular friend, with whom he made the compact that, if it were possible for the Spirit to return to this earth after its separation from the body, he of the twain who first died, should reappear to the other. In course of time, this compact was forgotten by our friend; the two young men having pro-gressed in life, and taken diverging paths that were wide asunder. But, one night, many years afterwards, our friend being in the North of England, and staying for the night in an inn, on the Yorkshire Moors, happened to look out of bed; and there, in the moonlight, leaning on a bureau near the window, steadfastly regarding him, saw his old college friend! The appearance being solemnly ad-dressed, replied, in a kind of whisper, but very audibly, "Do not come near me. I am dead. I am here to redeem my promise. I come from another world, but may not disclose its secrets!" Then, the whole form becoming paler, melted, as it were, into the moonlight, and faded away.

Or, there was the daughter of the first occupier of the picturesque Elizabethan house, so famous in our neighbourhood. You have heard about her? No! Why, *she* went out one summer evening at twilight, when she was a beautiful girl, just seventeen years of age, to gather flowers in the garden; and presently cam running, terrified, into the hall to her father, saying, "Oh, dear father, I have met myself!" He took her in his arms and told her it was fancy, but she said, "Oh no! I met myself in the broad walk, and I was pale and gathering withered flowers, and I turned my head, and held them up!" And, that night, she died; and a picture of her story was begun, though never finished, and they say it is somewhere in the house to this day, with its face to the wall.

Or, the uncle of my brother's wife was riding home on horseback, one mellow evening at sunset, when, in a green lane close to his own house, he saw a man standing before him, in the very centre of a narrow way. "Why does that man in the cloak stand there!" he thought. "Does he want me to ride over him?" But the figure never moved. He felt a strange sensation at seeing it so still, but slackened his trot and rode forward. When he was so close to it, as almost to touch it with his stirrup, his horse shied, and the figure glided up the ban, in a curious, unearthly manner – backward and without seeming to use its feet – and was gone. The uncle of my brother's wife, exclaiming, "Good Heaven! It's my cousin Harry, from Bombay!" put spears to his horse, which was suddenly in a profuse sweat, and, wondering at such strange behaviour, dashed round to the front of his house. There, he saw the same figure, just passing in at the long French window of the drawing-room, opening on the ground. He threw his bridle to a servant, and hastened in after it. His sister was sitting there, alone. "Alice, where's my cousin Harry?" "Your cousin Harry, John?" "Yes. From Bombay. I met him in the lane just now, and saw him enter here, this instant." Not a creature had been seen by anyone; and in that hour and minute, as it afterwards appeared, this cousin died in India.

Or, it was a certain sensible old maiden lady, who died at ninety-nine, and retained her faculties to the last, who really did see the Orphan Boy; a story which has often been incorrectly told, but, of which the real truth is this – because it is, in fact, a story belonging to our family – and she was a connection of our family. When she was about forty years of age, and still an uncommonly fine woman (her lover died young, which was the reason why she never married, though she had many offers), she went to stay at a place in Kent, which her brother, an Indian-Merchant, had newly bought. There was a story that this place had once been held in trust by the guardian of a young boy; who was himself the next heir, and who killed the young boy by harsh and cruel treatment. She knew nothing of that. It has been said that there was a cage in her bedroom in which the guardian used to put the boy. There was no such thing. There was only a closet. She went to bed, made no alarm whatever in the night, and in the morning said composedly to her maid when she came in, "Who is the pretty forlorn-looking child who has been peeping out of that closet all night? The maid replied by giving a loud scream and instantly decamping. She was surprised; but she was a woman of remarkable strength of mind, and she dressed herself and went downstairs, and closeted herself with her brother. "Now, Walter," she said, "I have been disturbed all night by a pretty, forlorn-looking boy, who has been constantly peeping out of that closet in my room, which I can't open. This is some trick." "I am afraid not, Charlotte," said he, "for it is the legend of the house. It is the Orphan Boy. What did he do?" "He opened the door softly," said she, "and peeped out. Sometimes, he came a step or two into the room. Then, I called to him, to encourage him, and he shrank, and shuddered, and crept in again, and shut the door." "The closet has no communication, Charlotte," said her brother, "with any other part of the house, and it's nailed up." This was undeniably true, and it took two carpenters a whole forenoon to get it open, for examination. Then, she was satisfied that she had seen the Orphan Boy. But the wild and terrible part of the story is that he was also seen by three of her brother's sons, in succession, who all died young. On the occasion of each child being taken ill, he came home in a heat, twelve hours before, and said, Oh, mamma, he had been playing under a particular oak tree, in a certain meadow, with a strange boy – a pretty, forlorn-looking boy, who was very timid, and made signs! From fatal experience, the parents came to know that this was the Orphan Boy, and that the course of the child whom he chose for his little playmate was surely run.

A TERRIBLY STRANGE BED

Wilkie Collins

William Wilkie Collins (1824–1889) was an English novelist, playwright and author of short stories. A close friend of Charles Dickens, Collins enjoyed international success in his lifetime. He suffered terribly from gout and developed an addiction to opium later in life He died of a paralytic stroke and is buried in Kensal Green Cemetary.

Shortly after my education at college was finished, I happened to be staying at Paris with an English friend. We were both young men then, and lived, I am afraid, rather a wild life, in the delightful city of our sojourn. One night we were idling about the neighbourhood of the Palais Royal, doubtful to what amusement we should next betake ourselves. My friend proposed a visit to Frascati's; but his suggestion was not to my taste. I knew Frascati's, as the French saying is, by heart; had lost and won plenty of five-franc pieces there, merely for amusement's sake, until it was amusement no longer, and was thoroughly tired, in fact, of all the ghastly respectabilities of such a social anomaly as a respectable gambling-house. "For Heaven's sake," said I to my friend, "let us go somewhere where we can see a little genuine, blackguard, poverty-stricken gaming with no false gingerbread glitter thrown over it all. Let us get away from fashionable Frascati's, to a house where they don't mind letting in a man with a ragged coat, or a man with no coat, ragged or otherwise." "Very well," said my friend, "we needn't go out of the Palais Royal to find the sort of company you want. Here's the place just before us; as blackguard a place, by all report, as you could possibly wish to see." In another minute we arrived at the door and entered the house.

When we got upstairs, and had left our hats and sticks with the doorkeeper, we were admitted into the chief gambling-room. We did not find many people assembled there. But, few as the men were who looked up at us on our entrance, they were all types – lamentably true types – of their respective classes.

We had come to see blackguards; but these men were something worse. There is a comic side, more or less appreciable, in all blackguardism – here there was nothing but tragedy – mute, weird tragedy. The quiet in the room was horrible. The thin, haggard, long-haired young man, whose sunken eyes fiercely watched the turning up of the cards, never spoke; the flabby, fat-faced, pimply player, who pricked his piece of pasteboard perseveringly, to register how often black won, and how often red – never spoke; the dirty, wrinkled old man, with the vulture eyes and the darned great-coat, who had lost his last *sou*, and still looked on desperately, after he could play no longer- – never spoke. Even the voice of the croupier sounded as if it were strangely dulled and thickened in the atmosphere of the room. I had entered the place to laugh, but the spectacle before me was something to weep over. I soon found it necessary to take refuge in excitement from the depression of spirits which was fast stealing on me. Unfortunately I sought the nearest excitement, by going to the table and beginning to play. Still more unfortunately, as the event will show, I won – won prodigiously; won incredibly; won at such a rate that the regular players at the table crowded round me; and staring at my stakes with hungry, superstitious eyes, whispered to one another that the English stranger was going to break the bank.

The game was *Rouge et Noir*. I had played at it in every city in Europe, without, however, the care or the wish to study the Theory of Chances – that philosopher's stone of all gamblers! And a gambler, in the strict sense of the word, I had never been. I was heart-whole from the corroding passion for play. My gaming was a mere idle amusement. I never resorted to it by necessity, because I never knew what it was to want money. I never practised it so incessantly as to lose more than I could afford, or to gain more than I could coolly pocket without being thrown off my balance by my good luck. In short, I had hitherto frequented gambling-tables – just as I frequented ball-rooms and opera-houses – because they amused me, and because I had nothing better to do with my leisure hours.

But on this occasion it was very different – now, for the first time in my life, I felt what the passion for play really was. My success first bewildered, and then, in the most literal meaning of the word, intoxicated me. Incredible as it may appear, it is nevertheless true, that I only lost when I attempted to estimate chances, and played according to previous calculation. If I left everything to luck, and staked without any care or consideration, I was sure to win – to win in the face of every recognized probability in favour of the bank. At first some of the men present ventured their money safely enough on my colour; but I speedily increased my stakes to sums which they dared not risk. One after another they left off playing, and breathlessly looked on at my game.

Still, time after time, I staked higher and higher, and still won. The excitement in the room rose to fever pitch. The silence was interrupted by a deep-muttered chorus of oaths and exclamations in different languages, every time the gold was shovelled across to my side of the table--even the imperturbable croupier dashed his rake on the floor in a (French) fury of astonishment at my success. But one man present preserved his self-possession, and that man was my friend. He came to my side, and whispering in English, begged me to leave the place, satisfied with what I had already gained. I must do him the justice to say that he repeated his warnings and entreaties several times, and only left me and went away after I had rejected his advice (I was to all intents and purposes gambling drunk) in terms which rendered it impossible for him to address me again that night.

Shortly after he had gone, a hoarse voice behind me cried: "Permit me, my dear sir – permit me to restore to their proper place two napoleons which you have dropped. Wonderful luck, sir! I pledge you my word of honour, as an old soldier, in the course of my long experience in this sort of thing, I never saw such luck as yours – never! Go on, sir--*Sacre mille bombes*! Go on boldly, and break the bank!"

I turned round and saw, nodding and smiling at me with inveterate civility, a tall man, dressed in a frogged and braided surtout. If I had been in my senses, I should have considered him, personally, as being rather a suspicious specimen of an old soldier. He had goggling bloodshot eyes, mangy moustaches, and a broken nose. His voice betrayed a barrack-room intonation of the worst order, and he had the dirtiest pair of hands I ever saw – even in France. These little personal peculiarities exercised, however, no repelling influence on me. In the mad excitement, the reckless triumph of that moment, I was ready to "fraternize" with anybody who encouraged me in my game. I accepted the old soldier's offered pinch of snuff; clapped him on the back, and swore he was the honestest fellow in the world--the most glorious relic of the Grand Army that I had ever met with. "Go on!" cried my military friend, snapping his fingers in ecstasy – "Go on, and win! Break the bank – *Mille tonnerres*! My gallant English comrade, break the bank!"

And I *did* go on – went on at such a rate, that in another quarter of an hour the croupier called out, "Gentlemen, the bank has discontinued for to-night." All the notes, and all the gold in that "bank" now lay in a heap under my hands; the whole floating capital of the gambling-house was waiting to pour into my pockets!

"Tie up the money in your pocket-handkerchief, my worthy sir," said the old soldier, as I wildly plunged my hands into my heap of gold. "Tie it up, as we used to tie up a bit of dinner in the Grand Army; your winnings are too heavy for any breeches-pockets that ever were sewed. There! That's it – shovel them in, notes and all! *Credie*! What luck! Stop! Another napoleon on the floor! Ah! *Sacre petit polisson de Napoleon*! Have I found thee at last? Now then, sir – two tight double knots each way with your honourable permission, and the money's safe. Feel it! Feel it, fortunate sir! Hard and round as a cannon-ball – *Ah, bah*! If they had only fired such cannon-balls at us at Austerlitz – *nom d'une pipe*! If they only had! And now, as an ancient grenadier, as an ex-brave of the French army, what remains for me to do? I ask what? Simply this: to entreat my valued English friend to drink a bottle of champagne with me, and toast the goddess Fortune in foaming goblets before we part!"

"Excellent ex-brave! Convivial ancient grenadier! Champagne by all means! An English cheer for an old soldier! Hurrah! hurrah! Another English cheer for the goddess Fortune! Hurrah! Hurrah! Hurrah!"

"Bravo! the Englishman; the amiable, gracious Englishman, in whose veins circulates the vivacious blood of France! Another glass? *Ah, bah*! – the bottle is empty! Never mind! Vive le vin! I, the old soldier, order another bottle, and half a pound of *bonbons* with it!"

"No, no, ex-brave; never – ancient grenadier! Your bottle last time; my bottle this. Behold it! Toast away! The French Army! The great Napoleon! The present company! The croupier! The honest croupier's wife and daughters – if he has any! The Ladies generally! Everybody in the world!"

By the time the second bottle of champagne was emptied, I felt as if I had been drinking liquid fire – my brain seemed all aflame. No excess in wine had ever had this effect on me before in my life. Was it the result of a stimulant acting upon my system when I was in a highly excited state? Was my stomach in a particularly disordered condition? Or was the champagne amazingly strong?

"Ex-brave of the French Army!" cried I, in a mad state of exhilaration, "I am on fire! how are you? You have set me on fire. Do you hear, my hero of Austerlitz? Let us have a third bottle of champagne to put the flame out!"

The old soldier wagged his head, rolled his goggle-eyes, until I expected to see them slip out of their sockets; placed his dirty forefinger by the side of his broken nose; solemnly ejaculated "Coffee!" and immediately ran off into an inner room.

The word pronounced by the eccentric veteran seemed to have a magical effect on the rest of the company present. With one accord they all rose to depart. Probably they had expected to profit by my intoxication; but finding that my new friend was benevolently bent on preventing me from getting dead drunk, had now abandoned all hope of thriving pleasantly on my winnings. Whatever their motive might be, at any rate they went away in a body. When the old soldier returned, and sat down again opposite to me at the table, we had the room to ourselves. I could see the croupier, in a sort of vestibule which opened out of it, eating his supper in solitude. The silence was now deeper than ever.

A sudden change, too, had come over the "ex-brave". He assumed a portentously solemn look; and when he spoke to me again, his speech was ornamented by no oaths, enforced by no finger-snapping, enlivened by no apostrophes or exclamations.

"Listen, my dear sir," said he, in mysteriously confidential tones – "listen to an old soldier's advice. I have been to the mistress of the house (a very charming woman, with a genius for cookery!) to impress on her the necessity of making us some particularly strong and good coffee. You must drink this coffee in order to get rid of your little amiable exaltation of spirits before you think of going home – you must, my good and gracious friend! With all that money to take home to-night, it is a sacred duty to yourself to have your wits about you. You are known to be a winner to an enormous extent by several gentlemen present to-night, who, in a certain point of view, are very worthy and excellent fellows; but they are mortal men, my dear sir, and they have their amiable weaknesses. Need I say more? Ah, no, no! You understand me! Now, this is what you must do – send for a cabriolet when you feel quite well again – draw up all the windows when you get into it – and tell the driver to take you home only through the large and well-lighted thoroughfares. Do this; and you and your money will be safe. Do this; and to-morrow you will thank an old soldier for giving you a word of honest advice."

Just as the ex-brave ended his oration in very lachrymose tones, the coffee came in, ready poured out in two cups. My attentive friend handed me one of the cups with a bow. I was parched with thirst, and drank it off at a draught. Almost instantly afterwards, I was seized with a fit of giddiness, and felt more completely intoxicated than ever. The room whirled round and round furiously; the old soldier seemed to be regularly bobbing up and down before me like the piston of a steam-engine. I was half deafened by a violent singing in my ears; a feeling of utter bewilderment, helplessness, idiocy, overcame me. I rose from my chair, holding on by the table to keep my balance; and stammered out that I felt dreadfully unwell – so unwell that I did not know how I was to get home.

"My dear friend," answered the old soldier – and even his voice seemed to be bobbing up and down as he spoke – "my dear friend, it would be madness to go home in your state; you would be sure to lose your money; you might be robbed and murdered with the greatest ease. I am going to sleep here; do you sleep here, too – they make up capital beds in this house – take one; sleep off the effects of the wine, and go home safely with your winnings to-morrow – to-morrow, in broad daylight."

I had but two ideas left: one, that I must never let go hold of my handkerchief full of money; the other, that I must lie down somewhere immediately, and fall off into a comfortable sleep. So I agreed to the proposal about the bed, and took the offered arm of the old soldier, carrying my money with my disengaged hand. Preceded by the croupier, we passed along some passages and up a flight of stairs into the bedroom which I was to occupy. The ex-brave shook me warmly by the hand, proposed that we should breakfast together, and then, followed by the croupier, left me for the night.

I ran to the wash-hand stand; drank some of the water in my jug; poured the rest out, and plunged my face into it; then sat down in a chair and tried to compose myself. I soon felt better. The change for my lungs, from the fetid atmosphere of the gambling-room to the cool air of the apartment I now occupied, the almost equally refreshing change for my eyes, from the glaring gaslights of the "salon" to the dim, quiet flicker of one bedroom candle, aided wonderfully the restorative effects of cold water. The giddiness left me, and I began to feel a little like a reasonable being again. My first thought was of the risk of sleeping all night in a gambling-house; my second, of the still greater risk of trying to get out after the house was closed, and of going home alone at night through the streets of Paris with a large sum of money about me. I had slept in worse places than this on my travels; so I determined to lock, bolt, and barricade my door, and take my chance till the next morning.

Accordingly, I secured myself against all intrusion; looked under the bed, and into the cupboard; tried the fastening of the window; and then, satisfied that I had taken every proper precaution, pulled off my upper clothing, put my light, which was a dim one, on the hearth among a feathery litter of wood-ashes, and got into bed, with the handkerchief full of money under my pillow.

I soon felt not only that I could not go to sleep, but that I could not even close my eyes. I was wide awake, and in a high fever. Every nerve in my body trembled – every one of my senses seemed to be preternaturally sharpened. I tossed and rolled, and tried every kind of position, and perseveringly sought out the cold corners of the bed, and all to no purpose. Now I thrust my arms over the clothes; now I poked them under the clothes; now I violently shot my legs straight out down to the bottom of the bed; now I convulsively coiled them up as near my chin as they would go; now I shook out my crumpled pillow, changed it to the cool side, patted it flat, and lay down quietly on my back; now I fiercely doubled it in two, set it up on end, thrust it against the board of the bed, and tried a sitting posture. Every effort was in vain; I groaned with vexation as I felt that I was in for a sleepless night.

What could I do? I had no book to read. And yet, unless I found out some method of diverting my mind, I felt certain that I was in the condition to imagine all sorts of horrors; to rack my brain with forebodings of every possible and impossible danger; in short, to pass the night in suffering all conceivable varieties of nervous terror.

I raised myself on my elbow, and looked about the room – which was brightened by a lovely moonlight pouring straight through the window – to see if it contained any pictures or ornaments that I could at all clearly distinguish. While my eyes wandered from wall to wall, a remembrance of Le Maistre's delightful little book, *Voyage autour de ma Chambre*, occurred to me. I resolved to imitate the French author, and find occupation and amusement enough to relieve the tedium of my wakefulness, by making a mental inventory of every article of furniture I could see, and by following up to their sources the multitude of associations which even a chair, a table, or a wash-hand stand may be made to call forth.

In the nervous unsettled state of my mind at that moment, I found it much easier to make my inventory than to make my reflections, and thereupon soon gave up all hope of thinking in Le Maistre's fanciful track – or, indeed, of thinking at all. I looked about the room at the different articles of furniture, and did nothing more.

There was, first, the bed I was lying in; a four-post bed, of all things in the world to meet with in Paris – yes, a thoroughly clumsy British four-poster, with the regular top lined with chintz – the regular fringed valance all round – the regular stifling, unwholesome curtains, which I remembered having mechanically drawn back against the posts without particularly noticing the bed when I first got into the room. Then there was the marble-topped wash-hand stand, from which the water I had spilled, in my hurry to pour it out, was still dripping, slowly and more slowly, on to the brick floor. Then two small chairs, with my coat, waistcoat, and trousers flung on them. Then a large elbow-chair covered with dirty-white dimity, with my cravat and shirt collar thrown over the back. Then a chest of drawers with two of the brass handles off, and a tawdry, broken china inkstand placed on it by way of ornament for the top. Then the dressing-table, adorned by a very small looking-glass, and a very large pincushion. Then the window – an unusually large window. Then a dark old picture, which the feeble candle dimly showed me. It was a picture of a fellow in a high Spanish hat, crowned with a plume of towering feathers. A swarthy, sinister ruffian, looking upward, shading his eyes with his hand, and looking intently upward – it might be at some tall gallows at which he was going to be hanged. At any rate, he had the appearance of thoroughly deserving it.

This picture put a kind of constraint upon me to look upward too – at the top of the bed. It was a gloomy and not an interesting object, and I looked back at the picture. I counted the feathers in the man's hat – they stood out in relief – three white, two green. I observed the crown of his hat, which was of conical shape, according to the fashion supposed to have been favoured by Guido Fawkes. I wondered what he was looking up at. It couldn't be at the stars; such a desperado was neither astrologer nor astronomer. It must be at the high gallows, and he was going to be hanged presently. Would the executioner come into possession of his conical crowned hat and plume of feathers? I counted the feathers again – three white, two green.

While I still lingered over this very improving and intellectual employment, my thoughts insensibly began to wander. The moonlight shining into the room reminded me of a certain moonlight night in England – the night after a picnic party in a Welsh valley. Every incident of the drive homeward, through lovely scenery, which the moonlight made lovelier than ever, came back to my remembrance, though I had never given the picnic a thought for years; though, if

I had tried to recollect it, I could certainly have recalled little or nothing of that scene long past. Of all the wonderful faculties that help to tell us we are immortal, which speaks the sublime truth more eloquently than memory? Here was I, in a strange house of the most suspicious character, in a situation of uncertainty, and even of peril, which might seem to make the cool exercise of my recollection almost out of the question; nevertheless, remembering, quite involuntarily, places, people, conversations, minute circumstances of every kind, which I had thought forgotten for ever; which I could not possibly have recalled at will, even under the most favourable auspices. And what cause had produced in a moment the whole of this strange, complicated, mysterious effect? Nothing but some rays of moonlight shining in at my bedroom window.

I was still thinking of the picnic – of our merriment on the drive home – of the sentimental young lady who would quote "Childe Harold" because it was moonlight. I was absorbed by these past scenes and past amusements, when, in an instant, the thread on which my memories hung snapped asunder; my attention immediately came back to present things more vividly than ever, and I found myself, I neither knew why nor wherefore, looking hard at the picture again.

Looking for what?

Good God! The man had pulled his hat down on his brows! No! The hat itself was gone! Where was the conical crown? Where the feathers – three white, two green? Not there! In place of the hat and feathers, what dusky object was it that now hid his forehead, his eyes, his shading hand?

Was the bed moving?

I turned on my back and looked up. Was I mad? Drunk? Dreaming? Giddy again? Or was the top of the bed really moving down – sinking slowly, regularly, silently, horribly, right down throughout the whole of its length and breadth – right down upon me, as I lay underneath?

My blood seemed to stand still. A deadly paralysing coldness stole all over me as I turned my head round on the pillow and determined to test whether the bedtop was really moving or not, by keeping my eye on the man in the picture.

The next look in that direction was enough. The dull, black, frowzy outline of the valance above me was within an inch of being parallel with his waist. I still looked breathlessly. And steadily and slowly – very slowly – I saw the figure, and the line of frame below the figure, vanish, as the valance moved down before it.

I am, constitutionally, anything but timid. I have been on more than one occasion in peril of my life, and have not lost my self-possession for an instant; but when the conviction first settled on my mind that the bed-top was really moving, was steadily and continuously sinking down upon me, I looked up shuddering, helpless, panic-stricken, beneath the hideous machinery for murder, which was advancing closer and closer to suffocate me where I lay.

I looked up, motionless, speechless, breathless. The candle, fully spent, went out; but the moonlight still brightened the room. Down and down, without pausing and without sounding, came the bedtop, and still my panic terror seemed to bind me faster and faster to the mattress on which I lay – down and down it sank, till the dusty odour from the lining of the canopy came stealing into my nostrils.

At that final moment the instinct of self-preservation startled me out of my trance, and I moved at last. There was just room for me to roll myself sideways off the bed. As I dropped noiselessly to the floor, the edge of the murderous canopy touched me on the shoulder.

Without stopping to draw my breath, without wiping the cold sweat from my face, I rose instantly on my knees to watch the bedtop. I was literally spellbound by it. If I had heard footsteps behind me, I could not have turned round; if a means of escape had been miraculously provided for me, I could not have moved to take advantage of it. The whole life in me was, at that moment, concentrated in my eyes.

It descended – the whole canopy, with the fringe round it, came down – down – close down; so close that there was not room now to squeeze my finger between the bedtop and the bed. I felt at the sides, and discovered that what had appeared to me from beneath to be the ordinary light canopy of a four-post bed was in reality a thick, broad mattress, the substance of which was concealed by the valance and its fringe. I looked up and saw the four posts rising hideously bare. In the middle of the bedtop was a huge wooden screw that had evidently worked it down through a hole in the ceiling, just as ordinary presses are worked down on the substance selected for compression. The frightful apparatus moved without making the faintest noise. There had been no creaking as it came down; there was now not the faintest sound from the room above. Amid a dead and awful silence I beheld before me – in the nineteenth century, and in the civilized capital of France – such a machine for secret murder by suffocation as might have existed in the worst days of the Inquisition, in the lonely inns among the Harz Mountains, in the mysterious tribunals of Westphalia! Still, as I looked on it, I could not move, I could hardly breathe, but I began to recover the power of thinking, and in a moment I discovered the murderous conspiracy framed against me in all its horror.

My cup of coffee had been drugged, and drugged too strongly. I had been saved from being smothered by having taken an overdose of some narcotic. How I had chafed and fretted at the fever-fit which had preserved my life by keeping me awake! How recklessly I had confided myself to the two wretches who had led me into this room, determined, for the sake of my winnings, to kill me in my sleep by the surest and most horrible contrivance for secretly accomplishing my destruction! How many men, winners like me, had slept, as I had proposed to sleep, in that bed, and had never been seen or heard of more! I shuddered at the bare idea of it.

But, ere long, all thought was again suspended by the sight of the murderous canopy moving once more. After it had remained on the bed – as nearly as I could guess – about ten minutes, it began to move up again. The villains who worked it from above evidently believed that their purpose was now accomplished. Slowly and silently, as it had descended, that horrible bedtop rose towards its former place. When it reached the upper extremities of the four posts, it reached the ceiling, too. Neither hole nor screw could be seen; the bed became in appearance an ordinary bed again – the canopy an ordinary canopy – even to the most suspicious eyes.

Now, for the first time, I was able to move – to rise from my knees – to dress myself in my upper clothing – and to consider of how I should escape. If

I betrayed by the smallest noise that the attempt to suffocate me had failed, I was certain to be murdered. Had I made any noise already? I listened intently, looking towards the door.

No! No footsteps in the passage outside – no sound of a tread, light or heavy, in the room above – absolute silence everywhere. Besides locking and bolting my door, I had moved an old wooden chest against it, which I had found under the bed. To remove this chest (my blood ran cold as I thought of what its contents might be!) without making some disturbance was impossible; and, moreover, to think of escaping through the house, now barred up for the night, was sheer insanity. Only one chance was left me – the window. I stole to it on tiptoe.

My bedroom was on the first floor, above an *entresol*, and looked into a back street. I raised my hand to open the window, knowing that on that action hung, by the merest hairbreadth, my chance of safety. They keep vigilant watch in a house of murder. If any part of the frame cracked, if the hinge creaked, I was a lost man! It must have occupied me at least five minutes, reckoning by time – five hours, reckoning by suspense--to open that window. I succeeded in doing it silently – in doing it with all the dexterity of a house-breaker – and then looked down into the street. To leap the distance beneath me would be almost certain destruction! Next, I looked round at the sides of the house. Down the left side ran a thick water-pipe – it passed close by the outer edge of the window. The moment I saw the pipe I knew I was saved. My breath came and went freely for the first time since I had seen the canopy of the bed moving down upon me!

To some men the means of escape which I had discovered might have seemed difficult and dangerous enough – to me the prospect of slipping down the pipe into the street did not suggest even a thought of peril. I had always been accustomed, by the practice of gymnastics, to keep up my school-boy powers as a daring and expert climber; and knew that my head, hands, and feet would serve me faithfully in any hazards of ascent or descent. I had already got one leg over the window-sill, when I remembered the handkerchief filled with money under my pillow. I could well have afforded to leave it behind me, but I was revengefully determined that the miscreants of the gambling-house should miss their plunder as well as their victim. So I went back to the bed and tied the heavy handkerchief at my back by my cravat.

Just as I had made it tight and fixed it in a comfortable place, I thought I heard a sound of breathing outside the door. The chill feeling of horror ran through me again as I listened. No! Dead silence still in the passage – I had only heard the night air blowing softly into the room. The next moment I was on the window-sill, and the next I had a firm grip on the water-pipe with my hands and knees.

I slid down into the street easily and quietly, as I thought I should, and immediately set off at the top of my speed to a branch "prefecture" of Police, which I knew was situated in the immediate neighbourhood. A "subprefect," and several picked men among his subordinates, happened to be up, maturing, I believe, some scheme for discovering the perpetrator of a mysterious murder which all Paris was talking of just then. When I began my story, in a breathless hurry and in very bad French, I could see that the subprefect suspected me of being a drunken Englishman who had robbed somebody; but he soon altered his opinion as I went on, and before I had anything like concluded, he shoved all the papers before him into a drawer, put on his hat, supplied me with another (for I was bareheaded), ordered a file of soldiers, desired his expert followers to get ready all sorts of tools for breaking open doors and ripping up brick flooring, and took my arm, in the most friendly and familiar manner possible, to lead me with him out of the house. I will venture to say that when the subprefect was a little boy, and was taken for the first time to the play, he was not half as much pleased as he was now at the job in prospect for him at the gambling-house!

Away we went through the streets, the subprefect cross-examining and congratulating me in the same breath as we marched at the head of our formidable *posse comitatus*. Sentinels were placed at the back and front of the house the moment we got to it; a tremendous battery of knocks was directed against the door; a light appeared at a window; I was told to conceal myself behind the police; then came more knocks and a cry of "Open in the name of the law!" At that terrible summons bolts and locks gave way before an invisible hand, and the moment after the subprefect was in the passage, confronting a waiter half dressed and ghastly pale. This was the short dialogue which immediately took place:

"We want to see the Englishman who is sleeping in this house."

"He went away hours ago."

"He did no such thing. His friend went away; he remained. Show us to his bedroom!"

"I swear to you, Monsieur le Sous-prefet, he is not here! he—"

"I swear to you, Monsieur le Garcon, he is. He slept here; he didn't find your bed comfortable; he came to us to complain of it; here he is among my men; and here am I ready to look for a flea or two in his bedstead. Renaudin!" (calling to one of the subordinates, and pointing to the waiter), "collar that man, and tie his hands behind him. Now then, gentlemen, let us walk upstairs!"

Every man and woman in the house was secured – the "old soldier" the first. Then I identified the bed in which I had slept, and then we went into the room above.

No object that was at all extraordinary appeared in any part of it. The subprefect looked round the place, commanded everybody to be silent, stamped twice on the floor, called for a candle, looked attentively at the spot he had stamped on, and ordered the flooring there to be carefully taken up. This was done in no time. Lights were produced, and we saw a deep raftered cavity between the floor of this room and the ceiling of the room beneath. Through this cavity there ran perpendicularly a sort of case of iron, thickly greased; and inside the case appeared the screw, which communicated with the bedtop below. Extra lengths of screw, freshly oiled; levers covered with felt; all the complete upper works of a heavy press – constructed with infernal ingenuity so as to join the fixtures below, and when taken to pieces again to go into the smallest possible compass – were next discovered and pulled out on the floor. After some little difficulty the subprefect succeeded in putting the machinery together, and, leaving his men to work it, descended with me to the bedroom. The smothering canopy was then lowered, but not so noiselessly as I had seen it lowered. When I mentioned this to the subprefect, his answer, simple as it was, had a terrible significance. "My men," said he, "are working down the bedtop for the first time; the men whose money you won were in better practice."

We left the house in the sole possession of two police agents, every one of the inmates being removed to prison on the spot. The subprefect, after taking down my *proces verbal* in his office, returned with me to my hotel to get my passport. "Do you think," I asked, as I gave it to him, "that any men have really been smothered in that bed, as they tried to smother me?"

"I have seen dozens of drowned men laid out at the morgue," answered the subprefect, "in whose pocket-books were found letters stating that they had committed suicide in the Seine, because they had lost everything at the gaming-table. Do I know how many of those men entered the same gambling-house that youentered? won as you won? took that bed as you took it? slept in it? were smothered in it? and were privately thrown into the river, with a letter of explanation written by the murderers and placed in their pocket-books? No man can say how many or how few have suffered the fate from which you have escaped. The people of the gambling-house kept their bedstead machinery a secret from us – even from the police! The dead kept the rest of the secret for them. Goodnight, or rather good-morning, Monsieur Faulkner! Be at my office again at nine o'clock; in the meantime, *au revoir*!"

The rest of my story is soon told. I was examined and reexamined; the gambling-house was strictly searched all through from top to bottom; the prisoners were separately interrogated, and two of the less guilty among them made a confession. I discovered that the old soldier was master of the gambling-house – justice discovered that he had been drummed out of the army as a vagabond years ago; that he had been guilty of all sorts of villainies since; that he was in possession of stolen property, which the owners identified; and that he, the croupier, another accomplice, and the woman who had made my cup of coffee were all in the secret of the bedstead. There appeared some reason to doubt whether the inferior persons attached to the house knew anything of the suffocating machinery; and they received the benefit of that doubt, by being treated simply as thieves and vagabonds. As for the old soldier and his two head myrmidons, they went to the galleys; the woman who had drugged my coffee was imprisoned for I forget how many years; the regular attendants at the gambling-house were considered "suspicious," and placed under "surveillance"; and I became, for one whole week (which is a long time), the head "lion" in Parisian society. My adventure was dramatised by three illustrious play-makers, but never saw theatrical daylight; for the censorship forbade the introduction on the stage of a correct copy of the gambling-house bedstead.

One good result was produced by my adventure, which any censorship must have approved: it cured me of ever again trying rouge-et-noir as an amusement. The sight of a green cloth, with packs of cards and heaps of money on it, will henceforth be for ever associated in my mind with the sight of a bed canopy descending to suffocate me in the silence and darkness of the night.

THE OLD NURSE'S STORY

Elizabeth Gaskell

Elizabeth Gaskell's (1810–1865) mother died when she was one year old. She married William Gaskell, a junior Unitarian minister in 1832. The couple both came from the dissenting tradition. Gaskell spent most of her adult life in Manchester and the lives of the working-class people of that city provide much of the inspiration for her work. Her first novel, *Mary Barton*, was published anonymously in 1848. She was a close friend of Charlotte Brontë, of whom she wrote an acclaimed biography.

You know, my dears, that your mother was an orphan, and an only child; and I dare say you have heard that your grandfather was a clergyman up in Westmoreland, where I come from. I was just a girl in the village school, when, one day, your grandmother came in to ask the mistress if there was any scholar there who would do for a nurse-maid; and mighty proud I was, I can tell ye, when the mistress called me up, and spoke to my being a good girl at my needle, and a steady honest girl, and one whose parents were very respectable, though they might be poor. I thought I should like nothing better than to serve the pretty young lady, who was blushing as deep as I was, as she spoke of the coming baby, and what I should have to do with it. However, I see you don't care so much for this part of my story, as for what you think is to come, so I'll tell you at once. I was engaged and settled at the parsonage before Miss Rosamond (that was the baby, who is now your mother) was born. To be sure, I had little enough to do with her when she came, for she was never out of her mother's arms, and slept by her all night long; and proud enough was I sometimes when missis trusted her to me. There never was such a baby before or since, though you've all of you been fine enough in your turns; but for sweet, winning ways, you've none of you come up to your mother. She took after her mother, who was a real lady born; a Miss Furnivall, a grand-daughter of Lord Furnivall's, in Northumberland. I believe she had neither brother nor sister, and had been brought up in my lord's family till she had married your grandfather, who was just a curate, son to a shopkeeper in Carlisle – but a clever, fine gentleman as ever was – and one who was a right-down hard worker in his parish, which was very wide, and scattered all abroad over the Westmoreland Fells. When your mother, little Miss Rosamond, was about four or five years old, both her parents died in a fortnight – one after the other. Ah! that was a sad time. My pretty young mistress and me was looking for another baby, when my master came home from one of his long rides, wet and tired, and took the fever he died of; and then she never held up her head again, but just lived to see her dead baby, and have it laid on her breast, before she sighed away her life. My mistress had asked me, on her death-bed, never to leave Miss Rosamond; but if she had never spoken a word, I would have gone with the little child to the end of the world.

The next thing, and before we had well stilled our sobs, the executors and guardians came to settle the affairs. They were my poor young mistress's own cousin, Lord Furnivall, and Mr. Esthwaite, my master's brother, a shopkeeper in Manchester; not so well to do then, as he was afterwards, and with a large family rising about him. Well! I don't know if it were their settling, or because of a letter my mistress wrote on her death-bed to her cousin, my lord; but somehow it was settled that Miss Rosamond and me were to go to Furnivall Manor House, in Northumberland, and my lord spoke as if it had been her mother's wish that she should live with his family, and as if he had no objections, for that one or two more or less could make no difference in so grand a household. So, though that was not the way in which I should have wished the coming of my bright and pretty pet to have been looked at – who was like a sunbeam in any family, be it never so grand – I was well pleased that all the folks in the Dale should stare and admire, when they heard I was going to be young lady's maid at my Lord Furnivall's at Furnivall Manor.

But I made a mistake in thinking we were to go and live where my lord did. It turned out that the family had left Furnivall Manor House fifty years or more. I could not hear that my poor young mistress had ever been there, though she had been brought up in the family; and I was sorry for that, for I should have liked Miss Rosamond's youth to have passed where her mother's had been.

My lord's gentleman, from whom I asked as many questions as I durst, said that the Manor House was at the foot of the Cumberland Fells, and a very grand place; that an old Miss Furnivall, a great-aunt of my lord's, lived there, with only a few servants; but that it was a very healthy place, and my lord had thought that it would suit Miss Rosamond very well for a few years, and that her being there might perhaps amuse his old aunt.

I was bidden by my lord to have Miss Rosamond's things ready by a certain day. He was a stern proud man, as they say all the Lords Furnivall were; and he never spoke a word more than was necessary. Folk did say he had loved my young mistress; but that, because she knew that his father would object, she would never listen to him, and married Mr. Esthwaite; but I don't know. He never married at any rate. But he never took much notice of Miss Rosamond; which I thought he might have done if he had cared for her dead mother. He sent his gentleman with us to the Manor House, telling him to join him at Newcastle that same evening; so there was no great length of time for him to make us known to all the strangers before he, too, shook us off; and we were left, two lonely young things (I was not eighteen) in the great old Manor House. It seems like yesterday that we drove there. We had left our own dear parsonage very early, and we had both cried as if our hearts would break, though we were travelling in my lord's carriage, which I thought so much of once. And now it was long past noon on a September day, and we stopped to change horses for the last time at a little smoky town, all full of colliers and miners. Miss Rosamond had fallen asleep, but Mr. Henry told me to waken her, that she might see the park and the Manor House as we drove up. I thought it rather a pity; but I did what he bade me, for fear he should complain of me to my lord. We had left all signs of a town, or even a village, and were then inside the gates of a large wild park – not like the parks here in the south, but with rocks, and the noise of running water, and gnarled thorn-trees, and old oaks, all white and peeled with age.

The road went up about two miles, and then we saw a great and stately house, with many trees close around it, so close that in some places their branches dragged against the walls when the wind blew; and some hung broken down; for no one seemed to take much charge of the place; – to lop the wood, or to keep the moss-covered carriage-way in order. Only in front of the house all was clear. The great oval drive was without a weed; and neither tree nor creeper was allowed to grow over the long, many-windowed front; at both sides of which a wing projected, which were each the ends of other side fronts; for the house, although it was so desolate, was even grander than I expected. Behind it rose the Fells, which seemed unenclosed and bare enough; and on the left hand of the house, as you stood facing it, was a little, old-fashioned flower-garden, as I found out afterwards. A door opened out upon it from the west front; it had been scooped out of the thick dark wood for some old Lady Furnivall; but the branches of the great forest-trees had grown and overshadowed it again, and there were very few flowers that would live there at that time.

When we drove up to the great front entrance, and went into the hall I thought we would be lost – it was so large, and vast, and grand. There was a chandelier all of bronze, hung down from the middle of the ceiling; and I had never seen one before, and looked at it all in amaze. Then, at one end of the hall, was a great fire-place, as large as the sides of the houses in my country, with massy andirons and dogs to hold the wood; and by it were heavy old-fashioned sofas. At the opposite end of the hall, to the left as you went in – on the western side – was an organ built into the wall, and so large that it filled up the best part of that end. Beyond it, on the same side, was a door; and opposite, on each side of the fire-place, were also doors leading to the east front; but those I never went through as long as I stayed in the house, so I can't tell you what lay beyond.

The afternoon was closing in and the hall, which had no fire lighted in it, looked dark and gloomy, but we did not stay there a moment. The old servant, who had opened the door for us bowed to Mr. Henry, and took us in through the door at the further side of the great organ, and led us through several smaller halls and passages into the west drawing-room, where he said that Miss Furnivall was sitting. Poor little Miss Rosamond held very tight to me, as if she were scared and lost in that great place, and as for myself, I was not much better. The west drawing-room was very cheerful-looking, with a warm fire in it, and plenty of good, comfortable furniture about. Miss Furnivall was an old lady not far from eighty, I should think, but I do not know. She was thin and tall, and had a face as full of fine wrinkles as if they had been drawn all over it with a needle's point. Her eyes were very watchful to make up, I suppose, for her being so deaf as to be obliged to use a trumpet. Sitting with her, working at the same great piece of tapestry, was Mrs. Stark, her maid and companion, and almost as old as she was. She had lived with Miss Furnivall ever since they both were young, and now she seemed more like a friend than a servant; she looked so cold and grey, and stony, as if she had never loved or cared for any one; and I don't suppose she did care for any one, except her mistress; and, owing to the great deafness of the latter, Mrs. Stark treated her very much as if she were a child. Mr. Henry gave some message from my lord, and then he bowed good-by to us all, – taking no notice of my sweet little Miss Rosamond's out-stretched hand – and left us standing there, being looked at by the two old ladies through their spectacles.

I was right glad when they rung for the old footman who had shown us in at first, and told him to take us to our rooms. So we went out of that great drawing-room, and into another sitting-room, and out of that, and then up a great flight of stairs, and along a broad gallery – which was something like a library, having books all down one side, and windows and writing-tables all down the other – till we came to our rooms, which I was not sorry to hear were just over the kitchens; for I began to think I should be lost in that wilderness of a house. There was an old nursery, that had been used for all the little lords and ladies long ago, with a pleasant fire burning in the grate, and the kettle boiling on the hob, and tea things spread out on the table; and out of that room was the night-nursery, with a little crib for Miss Rosamond close to my bed. And old James called up Dorothy, his wife, to bid us welcome; and both he and she were so hospitable and kind, that by and by Miss Rosamond and me felt quite at home; and by the time tea was over, she was sitting on Dorothy's knee, and chattering away as fast as her little tongue could go. I soon found out that Dorothy was from Westmoreland, and that bound her and me together, as it were; and I would never wish to meet with kinder people than were old James and his wife. James had lived pretty nearly all his life in my lord's family, and thought there was no one so grand as they. He even looked down a little on his wife; because, till he had married her, she had never lived in any but a farmer's household. But he was very fond of her, as well he might be. They had one servant under them, to do all the rough work. Agnes they called her; and she and me, and James and Dorothy, with Miss Furnivall and Mrs. Stark, made up the family; always remembering my sweet little Miss Rosamond! I used to wonder what they had done before she came, they thought so much of her now. Kitchen and drawing-room, it was all the same. The hard, sad Miss Furnivall, and the cold Mrs. Stark, looked pleased when she came fluttering in like a bird, playing and pranking hither and thither, with a continual murmur, and pretty prattle of gladness. I am sure, they were sorry many a time when she flitted away into the kitchen, though they were too proud to ask her to stay with them, and were a little surprised at her taste; though to be sure, as Mrs. Stark said, it was not to be wondered at, remembering what stock her father had come of. The great, old rambling house was a famous place for little Miss Rosamond. She made expeditions all over it, with me at her heels; all, except the east wing, which was never opened, and whither we never thought of going. But in the western and northern part was many a pleasant room; full of things that were curiosities to us, though they might not have been to people who had seen more. The windows were darkened by the sweeping boughs of the trees, and the ivy which had overgrown them: but, in the green gloom, we could manage to see old China jars and carved ivory boxes, and great heavy books, and, above all, the old pictures!

Once, I remember, my darling would have Dorothy go with us to tell us who they all were; for they were all portraits of some of my lord's family, though Dorothy could not tell us the names of every one. We had gone through most of the rooms, when we came to the old state drawing-room over the hall, and there was a picture of Miss Furnivall; or, as she was called in those days, Miss Grace, for she was the younger sister. Such a beauty she must have been! but with such a set, proud look, and such scorn looking out of her handsome eyes, with her eyebrows just a little raised, as if she wondered how anyone could have the impertinence to look at her; and her lip curled at us, as we stood there gazing. She had a dress on, the like of which I had never seen before, but it was all the fashion when she was young; a hat of some soft white stuff like beaver, pulled a little over her brows, and a beautiful plume of feathers sweeping round it on one side; and her gown of blue satin was open in front to a quilted white stomacher.

"Well, to be sure!" said I, when I had gazed my fill. "Flesh is grass, they do say; but who would have thought that Miss Furnivall had been such an out-and-out beauty, to see her now."

"Yes," said Dorothy. "Folks change sadly. But if what my master's father used to say was true, Miss Furnivall, the elder sister, was handsomer than Miss Grace. Her picture is here somewhere; but, if I show it you, you must never let on, even to James, that you have seen it. Can the little lady hold her tongue, think you?" asked she.

I was not so sure, for she was such a little sweet, bold, open-spoken child, so I set her to hide herself; and then I helped Dorothy to turn a great picture, that leaned with its face towards the wall, and was not hung up as the others were. To be sure, it beat Miss Grace for beauty; and, I think, for scornful pride, too, though in that matter it might be hard to choose. I could have looked at it an hour, but Dorothy seemed half frightened at having shown it to me, and hurried it back again, and bade me run and find Miss Rosamond, for that there were some ugly places about the house, where she should like ill for the child to go. I was a brave, high-spirited girl, and thought little of what the old woman said, for I liked hide-and-seek as well as any child in the parish; so off I ran to find my little one.

As winter drew on, and the days grew shorter, I was sometimes almost certain that I heard a noise as if some one was playing on the great organ in the hall. I did not hear it every evening; but, certainly, I did very often; usually when I was sitting with Miss Rosamond, after I had put her to bed, and keeping quite still and silent in the bed-room. Then I used to hear it booming and swelling away in the distance. The first night, when I went down to my supper, I asked Dorothy who had been playing music, and James said very shortly that I was a gowk to take the wind soughing among the trees for music: but I saw Dorothy look at him very fearfully, and Bessy, the kitchen-maid, said something beneath her breath, and went quite white. I saw they did not like my question, so I held my peace till I was with Dorothy alone, when I knew I could get a good deal out of her. So, the next day, I watched my time, and I coaxed and asked her who it was that played the organ; for I knew that it was the organ and not the wind well enough, for all I had kept silence before James. But Dorothy had had her lesson I'll warrant, and never a word could I get from her. So then I tried Bessy, though I had always held my head rather above her, as I was evened to James and Dorothy, and she was little better than their servant. So she said I must never, never tell; and if ever I told, I was never to say *she* had told me; but it was a very strange noise, and she had heard it many a time, but most of all on winter nights, and before storms; and folks did say it was the old lord playing on the great organ in the hall, just as he used to do when he was alive; but who the old lord was, or why he played, and why he played on stormy winter evenings in particular, she either could not or would not tell me. Well! I told you I had a brave heart; and I thought it was rather pleasant to have that grand music rolling about the house, let who would be the player; for now it rose above the great gusts of wind, and wailed and triumphed just like a living creature, and then it fell to a softness most complete, only it was always music, and tunes, so it was nonsense to call it the wind. I thought at first, that it might be Miss Furnivall who played, unknown to Bessy; but, one day, when I was in the hall by myself, I opened the organ and peeped all about it and around it, as I had done to the organ in Crosthwaite church once before, and I saw it was all broken and destroyed inside, though it looked so brave and fine; and then, though it was noon-day, my flesh began to creep a little, and I shut it up, and run away pretty quickly to my own bright nursery; and I did not like hearing the music for some time after that, any more than James and Dorothy did. All this time Miss Rosamond was making herself more, and more beloved. The old ladies liked her to dine with them at their early dinner. James stood behind Miss Furnivall's chair, and I behind Miss Rosamond's all in state; and, after dinner, she would play about in a corner of the great drawing-room, as still as any mouse, while Miss Furnivall slept, and I had my dinner in the kitchen. But she was glad enough to come to me in the nursery afterwards; for, as she said, Miss Furnivall was so sad, and Mrs. Stark so dull; but she and I were merry enough; and, by-and-by, I got not to care for that weird rolling music, which did one no harm, if we did not know where it came from.

That winter was very cold. In the middle of October the frosts began, and lasted many, many weeks. I remember, one day at dinner, Miss Furnivall lifted up her sad, heavy eyes, and said to Mrs. Stark, "I am afraid we shall have a terrible winter," in a strange kind of meaning way. But Mrs. Stark pretended not to hear, and talked very loud of something else. My little lady, and I did not care for the frost; not we! As long as it was dry, we climbed up the steep brows, behind the house, and went up on the Fells, which were bleak, and bare enough, and there we ran races in the fresh, sharp air; and once we came down by a new path that took us past the two old gnarled holly-trees, which grew about half-way down by the east side of the house. But the days grew shorter, and shorter, and the old lord, if it was he, played away more, and more stormily and sadly on the great organ. One Sunday afternoon – it must have been towards the end of November – I asked Dorothy to take charge of little missy when she came out of the drawing-room, after Miss Furnivall had had her nap; for it was too cold to take her with me to church, and yet I wanted to go. And Dorothy was glad enough to promise, and was so fond of the child that all seemed well; and Bessy and I set off very briskly, though the sky hung heavy and black over the white earth, as if the night had never fully gone away; and the air, though still, was very biting and keen.

"We shall have a fall of snow," said Bessy to me. And sure enough, even while we were in church, it came down thick, in great large flakes, so thick it almost darkened the windows. It had stopped snowing before we came out, but it lay soft, thick and deep beneath our feet, as we tramped home. Before we got to the hall the moon rose, and I think it was lighter then – what with the moon, and what with the white dazzling snow – than it had been when we went to church, between two and three o'clock. I have not told you that Miss Furnivall and Mrs. Stark never went to church; they used to read the prayers together, in their quiet gloomy way; they seemed to feel the Sunday very long without their tapestry-work to be busy at. So when I went to Dorothy in the kitchen, to fetch Miss Rosamond and take her up-stairs with me, I did not much wonder when the old woman told me that the ladies had kept the child with them, and that she had never come to the kitchen, as I had bidden her, when she was tired of behaving pretty in the drawing-room. So I took off my things and went to find her, and bring her to her supper in the nursery. But when I went into the best drawing-room, there sat the two old ladies, very still and quiet, dropping out a word now and then, but looking as if nothing so bright and merry as Miss Rosamond had ever been near them. Still I thought she might be hiding from me; it was one of her pretty ways; and that she had persuaded them to look as if they knew nothing about her; so I went softly peeping under this sofa, and behind that chair, making believe I was sadly frightened at not finding her.

"What's the matter, Hester?" said Mrs. Stark, sharply. I don't know if Miss Furnivall had seen me, for, as I told you, she was very deaf, and she sat quite still, idly staring into the fire, with her hopeless face. "I'm only looking for my little Rosy-Posy," replied I, still thinking that the child was there, and near me, though I could not see her.

"Miss Rosamond is not here," said Mrs. Stark. "She went away, more than an hour ago to find Dorothy." And she too turned and went on looking into the fire.

My heart sank at this, and I began to wish I had never left my darling. I went back to Dorothy and told her. James was gone out for the day, but she, and me, and Bessy took lights and went up into the nursery first; and then we roamed over the great large house, calling and entreating Miss Rosamond to come out of her hiding place, and not frighten us to death in that way. But there was no answer; no sound.

"Oh!" said I at last, "can she have got into the east wing and hidden there?"

But Dorothy said it was not possible, for that she herself had never been in there; that the doors were always locked, and my lord's steward had the keys, she believed; at any rate, neither she nor James had ever seen them: so, I said I would go back and see if, after all, she was not hidden in the drawing-room, unknown to the old ladies; and if I found her there, I said, I would whip her well for the fright she had given me; but I never meant to do it. Well, I went back to the west drawing-room, and I told Mrs. Stark we could not find her anywhere, and asked for leave to look all about the furniture there, for I thought now, that she might have fallen asleep in some warm hidden corner; but no! we looked, Miss Furnivall got up and looked, trembling all over – and she was nowhere there; then we set off again, every one in the house, and looked in all the places we had searched before, but we could not find her. Miss Furnivall shivered and shook so much, that Mrs. Stark took her back into the warm drawing-room; but not before they had made me promise to bring her to them when she was found. Well-a-day! I began to think she never would be found, when I bethought me to look into the great front court, all covered with snow. I was up-stairs when I looked out; but, it was such clear moonlight, I could see quite plain two little footprints, which might be traced from the hall-door, and round the corner of the east wing. I don't know how I got down, but I tugged open the great, stiff hall-door, and, throwing the skirt of my gown over my head for a cloak, I ran out. I turned the east corner, and there a black shadow fell on the snow; but when I came again into the moonlight, there were the little footmarks going up – up to the Fells. It was bitter cold; so cold that the air almost took the skin off my face as I ran, but I ran on, crying to think how my poor little darling must be perished, and frightened. I was within sight of the holly-trees, when I saw a shepherd coming down the hill, bearing something in his arms wrapped in his maud. He shouted to me, and asked me if I had lost a bairn; and, when I could not speak for crying, he bore towards me, and I saw my wee bairnie, lying still, and white, and stiff, in his arms, as if she had been dead. He told me he had been up the Fells to gather in his sheep, before the deep cold of night came on, and that under the holly-trees (black marks on the hill-side, where no other bush was for miles around) he had found my little lady – my lamb – my queen – my darling – stiff, and cold, in the terrible sleep which is frost-begotten. Oh! the joy, and the tears of having her in my arms once again! for I would not let him carry her; but took her, maud and all, into my own arms, and held her near my own warm neck, and heart, and felt the life stealing slowly back again into her little gentle limbs. But she was still insensible when we reached the hall, and I had no breath for speech. We went in by the kitchen-door.

"Bring the warming-pan," said I; and I carried her up-stairs and began un-dressing her by the nursery fire, which Bessy had kept up. I called my little lam-mie all the sweet and playful names I could think of, – even while my eyes were blinded by my tears; and at last, oh! at length she opened her large blue eyes. Then I put her into her warm bed, and sent Dorothy down to tell Miss Furnivall that all was well; and I made up my mind to sit by my darling's bedside the live-long night. She fell away into a soft sleep as soon as her pretty head had touched the pillow, and I watched by her till morning light; when she wakened up bright and clear – or so I thought at first – and, my dears, so I think now.

She said, that she had fancied that she should like to go to Dorothy, for that both the old ladies were asleep, and it was very dull in the drawing-room; and that, as she was going through the west lobby, she saw the snow through the high window falling – falling – soft and steady; but she wanted to see it lying pretty and white on the ground; so she made her way into the great hall; and then, go-ing to the window, she saw it bright and soft upon the drive; but while she stood there, she saw a little girl, not so old as she was, "but so pretty," said my darling, "and this little girl beckoned to me to come out; and oh, she was so pretty and so sweet, I could not choose but go." And then this other little girl had taken her by the hand, and side by side the two had gone round the east corner.

"Now you are a naughty little girl, and telling stories," said I. "What would your good mamma, that is in heaven, and never told a story in her life, say to her little Rosamond, if she heard her – and I daresay she does – telling stories!"

"Indeed, Hester," sobbed out my child, "I'm telling you true. Indeed I am."

"Don't tell me!" said I, very stern. "I tracked you by your foot-marks through the snow; there were only yours to be seen: and if you had had a little girl to go hand-in-hand with you up the hill, don't you think the footprints would have gone along with yours?"

"I can't help it, dear, dear Hester," said she, crying, "if they did not; I never looked at her feet, but she held my hand fast and tight in her little one, and it was very, very cold. She took me up the Fell-path, up to the holly-trees; and there I saw a lady weeping and crying; but when she saw me, she hushed her weeping, and smiled very proud and grand, and took me on her knee, and began to lull me to sleep; and that's all, Hester – but that is true; and my dear mamma knows it is," said she, crying. So I thought the child was in a fever, and pretended to believe her, as she went over her story – over and over again, and always the same. At last Dorothy knocked at the door with Miss Rosamond's breakfast; and she told me the old ladies were down in the eating parlour, and that they wanted to speak to me. They had both been into the night-nursery the evening before, but it was after Miss Rosamond was asleep; so they had only looked at her – not asked me any questions.

"I shall catch it," thought I to myself, as I went along the north gallery. "And yet," I thought, taking courage, "it was in their charge I left her; and it's they that's to blame for letting her steal away unknown and unwatched." So I went in boldly, and told my story. I told it all to Miss Furnivall, shouting it close to her ear; but when I came to the mention of the other little girl out in the snow, coaxing and tempting her out, and willing her up to the grand and beautiful lady by the holly-tree, she threw her arms up – her old and withered arms – and cried aloud, "Oh! Heaven, forgive! Have mercy!"

Mrs. Stark took hold of her; roughly enough, I thought; but she was past Mrs. Stark's management, and spoke to me, in a kind of wild warning and authority.

"Hester! keep her from that child! It will lure her to her death! That evil child! Tell her it is a wicked, naughty child." Then, Mrs. Stark hurried me out of the room; where, indeed, I was glad enough to go; but Miss Furnivall kept shrieking out, "Oh, have mercy! Wilt Thou never forgive! It is many a long year ago – "

I was very uneasy in my mind after that. I durst never leave Miss Rosamond, night or day, for fear lest she might slip off again, after some fancy or other; and all the more, because I thought I could make out that Miss Furnivall was crazy, from their odd ways about her; and I was afraid lest something of the same kind (which might be in the family, you know) hung over my darling. And the great frost never ceased all this time; and, whenever it was a more stormy night than usual, between the gusts, and through the wind, we heard the old lord playing on the great organ. But, old lord, or not, wherever Miss Rosamond went, there I followed; for my love for her, pretty helpless orphan, was stronger than my fear for the grand and terrible sound. Besides, it rested with me to keep her cheerful and merry, as beseemed her age. So we played together, and wandered together, here and there, and everywhere; for I never dared to lose sight of her again in that large and rambling house. And so it happened, that one afternoon, not long before Christmas day, we were playing together on the billiard-table in the great hall (not that we knew the right way of playing, but she liked to roll the smooth ivory balls with her pretty hands, and I liked to do whatever she did); and, by-and-by, without our noticing it, it grew dusk indoors, though it was still light in the open air, and I was thinking of taking her back into the nursery, when, all of a sudden, she cried out,

"Look, Hester! look! there is my poor little girl out in the snow!"

I turned towards the long narrow windows, and there, sure enough, I saw a little girl, less than my Miss Rosamond – dressed all unfit to be out-of-doors such a bitter night – crying, and beating against the window-panes, as if she wanted to be let in. She seemed to sob and wail, till Miss Rosamond could bear it no longer, and was flying to the door to open it, when, all of a sudden, and close upon us, the great organ pealed out so loud and thundering, it fairly made me tremble; and all the more, when I remembered me that, even in the stillness of that dead-cold weather, I had heard no sound of little battering hands upon the window-glass, although the Phantom Child had seemed to put forth all its force; and, although I had seen it wail and cry, no faintest touch of sound had fallen upon my ears. Whether I remembered all this at the very moment, I do not know; the great organ sound had so stunned me into terror; but this I know, I caught up Miss Rosamond before she got the hall-door opened, and clutched her, and carried her away, kicking and screaming, into the large, bright kitchen, where Dorothy and Agnes were busy with their mince-pies.

"What is the matter with my sweet one?" cried Dorothy, as I bore in Miss Rosamond, who was sobbing as if her heart would break.

"She won't let me open the door for my little girl to come in; and she'll die if she is out on the Fells all night. Cruel, naughty Hester," she said, slapping me; but she might have struck harder, for I had seen a look of ghastly terror on Dorothy's face, which made my very blood run cold.

"Shut the back kitchen door fast, and bolt it well," said she to Agnes. She said no more; she gave me raisins and almonds to quiet Miss Rosamond; but she sobbed about the little girl in the snow, and would not touch any of the good things. I was thankful when she cried herself to sleep in bed. Then I stole down to the kitchen, and told Dorothy I had made up my mind. I would carry my darling back to my father's house in Applethwaite; where, if we lived humbly, we lived at peace. I said I had been frightened enough with the old lord's organ-playing; but now that I had seen for myself this little moaning child, all decked out as no child in the neighbourhood could be, beating and battering to get in, yet always without any sound or noise – with the dark wound on its right shoulder; and that Miss Rosamond had known it again for the phantom that had nearly lured her to her death (which Dorothy knew was true); I would stand it no longer.

I saw Dorothy change colour once or twice. When I had done, she told me she did not think I could take Miss Rosamond with me, for that she was my lord's ward, and I had no right over her; and she asked me would I leave the child that I was so fond of just for sounds and sights that could do me no harm; and that they had all had to get used to in their turns? I was all in a hot, trembling passion; and I said it was very well for her to talk; that knew what these sights and noises betokened, and that had, perhaps, had something to do with the Spectre-Child while it was alive. And I taunted her so, that she told me all she knew, at last; and then I wished I had never been told, for it only made me more afraid than ever.

She said she had heard the tale from old neighbours, that were alive when she was first married; when folks used to come to the hall sometimes, before it had got such a bad name on the country side: it might not be true, or it might, what she had been told.

The old lord was Miss Furnivall's father – Miss Grace, as Dorothy called her, for Miss Maude was the elder, and Miss Furnivall by rights. The old lord was eaten up with pride. Such a proud man was never seen or heard of; and his daughters were like him. No one was good enough to wed them, although they had choice enough; for they were the great beauties of their day, as I had seen by their portraits, where they hung in the state drawing-room. But, as the old saying is, "Pride will have a fall;" and these two haughty beauties fell in love with the same man, and he no better than a foreign musician, whom their father had down from London to play music with him at the Manor House. For, above all things, next to his pride, the old lord loved music. He could play on nearly every instrument that ever was heard of, and it was a strange thing it did not soften him; but he was a fierce dour old man, and had broken his poor wife's heart with his cruelty, they said. He was mad after music, and would pay any money for it. So he got this foreigner to come; who made such beautiful music, that they said the very birds on the trees stopped their singing to listen. And, by degrees, this foreign gentleman got such a hold over the old lord, that nothing would serve him but that he must come every year; and it was he that had the great organ brought from Holland, and built up in the hall, where it stood now. He taught the old lord to play on it; but many and many a time, when Lord Furnivall was thinking of nothing but his fine organ, and his finer music, the dark foreigner was walking abroad in the woods with one of the young ladies; now Miss Maude, and then Miss Grace.

Miss Maude won the day and carried off the prize, such as it was; and he and she were married, all unknown to any one; and before he made his next yearly visit, she had been confined of a little girl at a farm-house on the Moors, while her father and Miss Grace thought she was away at Doncaster Races. But though she was a wife and a mother, she was not a bit softened, but as haughty and as passionate as ever; and perhaps more so, for she was jealous of Miss Grace, to whom her foreign husband paid a deal of court – by way of blinding her – as he told his wife. But Miss Grace triumphed over Miss Maude, and Miss Maude grew fiercer and fiercer, both with her husband and with her sister; and the former – who could easily shake off what was disagreeable, and hide himself in foreign countries – went away a month before his usual time that summer, and half-threatened that he would never come back again. Meanwhile, the little girl was left at the farm-house, and her mother used to have her horse saddled and gallop wildly over the hills to see her once every week, at the very least – for where she loved, she loved; and where she hated, she hated. And the old lord went on playing – playing on his organ; and the servants thought the sweet music he made had soothed down his awful temper, of which (Dorothy said) some terrible tales could be told. He grew infirm too, and had to walk with a crutch; and his son – that was the present Lord Furnivall's father – was with the army in America, and the other son at sea; so Miss Maude had it pretty much her own way, and she and Miss Grace grew colder and bitterer to each other every day; till at last they hardly ever spoke, except when the old lord was by. The foreign musician came again the next summer, but it was for the last time; for they led him such a life with their jealousy and their passions, that he grew weary, and went away, and never was heard of again. And Miss Maude, who had always meant to have her marriage acknowledged when her father should be dead, was left now a deserted wife, whom nobody knew to have been married, with a child that she dared not own, although she loved it to distraction; living with a father whom she feared, and a sister whom she hated. When the next summer passed over, and the dark foreigner never came, both Miss Maude and Miss Grace grew gloomy and sad; they had a haggard look about them, though they looked handsome as ever. But, by-and-by, Maude brightened; for her father grew more and more infirm, and more than ever carried away by his music; and she and Miss Grace lived almost entirely apart, having separate rooms, the one on the west side, Miss Maude on the east – those very rooms which were now shut up. So she thought she might have her little girl with her, and no one need ever know except those who dared not speak about it, and were bound to believe that it was, as she said, a cottager's child she had taken a fancy to. All this, Dorothy said, was pretty well known; but what came afterwards no one knew, except Miss Grace and Mrs. Stark, who was even then her maid, and much more of a friend to her than ever her sister had been. But the servants supposed, from words that were dropped, that Miss Maude had triumphed over Miss Grace, and told her that all the time the dark foreigner had been mocking her with pretended love – he was her own husband. The colour left Miss Grace's cheek and lips that very day for ever, and she was heard to say many a time that sooner or later she would have her revenge; and Mrs. Stark was for ever spying about the east rooms.

One fearful night, just after the New Year had come in, when the snow was lying thick and deep; and the flakes were still falling – fast enough to blind any one who might be out and abroad – there was a great and violent noise heard, and the old lord's voice above all, cursing and swearing awfully, – and the cries of a little child, – and the proud defiance of a fierce woman, – and the sound of a blow, – and a dead stillness, – and moans and wailings dying away on the hillside! Then the old lord summoned all his servants, and told them, with terrible oaths, and words more terrible, that his daughter had disgraced herself, and that he had turned her out of doors – her, and her child – and that if ever they gave her help, or food, or shelter, he prayed that they might never enter heaven. And, all the while, Miss Grace stood by him, white and still as any stone; and when he had ended she heaved a great sigh, as much as to say her work was done, and her end was accomplished. But the old lord never touched his organ again, and died within the year; and no wonder! for, on the morrow of that wild and fearful night, the shepherds, coming down the Fell side, found Miss Maude sitting, all crazy and smiling, under the holly-trees, nursing a dead child, with a terrible mark on its right shoulder. "But that was not what killed it," said Dorothy: "it was the frost and the cold; – every wild creature was in its hole, and every beast in its fold, – while the child and its mother were turned out to wander on the Fells! And now you know all! and I wonder if you are less frightened now?"

I was more frightened than ever; but I said I was not. I wished Miss Rosamond and myself well out of that dreadful house for ever; but I would not leave her, and I dared not take her away. But oh! how I watched her, and guarded her! We bolted the doors, and shut the window-shutters fast, an hour or more before dark, rather than leave them open five minutes too late. But my little lady still heard the weird child crying and mourning; and not all we could do or say could keep her from wanting to go to her, and let her in from the cruel wind and the snow. All this time I kept away from Miss Furnivall and Mrs. Stark, as much as ever I could; for I feared them – I knew no good could be about them, with their grey, hard faces, and their dreamy eyes, looking back into the ghastly years that were gone. But, even in my fear, I had a kind of pity for Miss Furnivall, at least. Those gone down to the pit can hardly have a more hopeless look than that which was ever on her face. At last I even got so sorry for her – who never said a word but what was quite forced from her – that I prayed for her; and I taught Miss Rosamond to pray for one who had done a deadly sin; but often when she came to those words, she would listen, and start up from her knees, and say, "I hear my little girl plaining and crying very sad – Oh! let her in, or she will die!"

One night – just after New Year's Day had come at last, and the long winter had taken a turn, as I hoped – I heard the west drawing-room bell ring three times, which was the signal for me. I would not leave Miss Rosamond alone, for all she was asleep – for the old lord had been playing wilder than ever – and I feared lest my darling should waken to hear the spectre child; see her I knew she could not. I had fastened the windows too well for that. So I took her out of her bed, and wrapped her up in such outer clothes as were most handy, and carried her down to the drawing-room, where the old ladies sat at their tapestry-work as usual. They looked up when I came in, and Mrs. Stark asked, quite astounded, "Why did I bring Miss Rosamond there, out of her warm bed?" I had begun to whisper, "Because I was afraid of her being tempted out while I was away, by the wild child in the snow," when she stopped me short (with a glance at Miss Furnivall), and said Miss Furnivall wanted me to undo some work she had done wrong, and which neither of them could see to unpick. So I laid my pretty dear on the sofa, and sat down on a stool by them, and hardened my heart against them, as I heard the wind rising and howling.

Miss Rosamond slept on sound, for all the wind blew so; and Miss Furnivall said never a word, nor looked round when the gusts shook the windows. All at once she started up to her full height, and put up one hand, as if to bid us to listen.

"I hear voices!" said she. "I hear terrible screams – I hear my father's voice!"

Just at that moment, my darling wakened with a sudden start: "My little girl is crying, oh, how she is crying!" and she tried to get up and go to her, but she got her feet entangled in the blanket, and I caught her up; for my flesh had begun to creep at these noises, which they heard while we could catch no sound. In a minute or two the noises came, and gathered fast, and filled our ears; we, too, heard voices and screams, and no longer heard the winter's wind that raged abroad. Mrs. Stark looked at me, and I at her, but we dared not speak. Suddenly Miss Furnivall went towards the door, out into the ante-room, through the west lobby, and opened the door into the great hall. Mrs. Stark followed, and I durst not be left, though my heart almost stopped beating for fear. I wrapped my darling tight in my arms, and went out with them. In the hall the screams were louder than ever; they seemed to come from the east wing – nearer and nearer – close on the other side of the locked-up doors – close behind them. Then I noticed that the great bronze chandelier seemed all alight, though the hall was dim, and that a fire was blazing in the vast hearth-place, though it gave no heat; and I shuddered up with terror, and folded my darling closer to me. But as I did so the east door shook, and she, suddenly struggling to get free from me, cried, "Hester! I must go. My little girl is there! I hear her; she is coming! Hester, I must go!"

I held her tight with all my strength; with a set will, I held her. If I had died, my hands would have grasped her still, I was so resolved in my mind. Miss Furnivall stood listening, and paid no regard to my darling, who had got down to the ground, and whom I, upon my knees now, was holding with both my arms clasped round her neck; she still striving and crying to get free.

All at once, the east door gave way with a thundering crash, as if torn open in a violent passion, and there came into that broad and mysterious light, the figure of a tall old man, with grey hair and gleaming eyes. He drove before him, with many a relentless gesture of abhorrence, a stern and beautiful woman, with a little child clinging to her dress.

"Oh, Hester! Hester!" cried Miss Rosamond; "it's the lady! the lady below the holly-trees; and my little girl is with her. Hester! Hester! let me go to her; they are drawing me to them. I feel them – I feel them. I must go!"

Again she was almost convulsed by her efforts to get away; but I held her tighter and tighter, till I feared I should do her a hurt; but rather that than let her go towards those terrible phantoms. They passed along towards the great hall-door, where the winds howled and ravened for their prey; but before they reached that, the lady turned; and I could see that she defied the old man with a fierce and proud defiance; but then she quailed – and then she threw up her arms wildly and piteously to save her child – her little child – from a blow from his uplifted crutch.

And Miss Rosamond was torn as by a power stronger than mine and writhed in my arms, and sobbed (for by this time the poor darling was growing faint).

"They want me to go with them on to the Fells – they are drawing me to them. Oh, my little girl! I would come, but cruel, wicked Hester holds me very tight." But when she saw the uplifted crutch, she swooned away, and I thanked God for it. Just at this moment – when the tall old man, his hair streaming as in the blast of a furnace, was going to strike the little shrinking child – Miss Furnivall, the old woman by my side, cried out, "Oh father! father! spare the little innocent child!" But just then I saw – we all saw – another phantom shape itself, and grow clear out of the blue and misty light that filled the hall; we had not seen her till now, for it was another lady who stood by the old man, with a look of relentless hate and triumphant scorn. That figure was very beautiful to look upon, with a soft, white hat drawn down over the proud brows, and a red and curling lip. It was dressed in an open robe of blue satin. I had seen that figure before. It was the likeness of Miss Furnivall in her youth; and the terrible phantoms moved on, regardless of old Miss Furnivall's wild entreaty, – and the uplifted crutch fell on the right shoulder of the little child, and the younger sister looked on, stony, and deadly serene. But at that moment, the dim lights, and the fire that gave no heat, went out of themselves, and Miss Furnivall lay at our feet stricken down by the palsy – death-stricken.

Yes! she was carried to her bed that night never to rise again. She lay with her face to the wall, muttering low, but muttering always: "Alas! alas! what is done in youth can never be undone in age! What is done in youth can never be undone in age!"

CANNIBALISM IN THE CARS

Mark Twain

> **Mark Twain** (1835–1910) was one of the first American writers to employ colloquial language in his writings. His novels, *The Adventures of Tom Sawyer* (1876) and *Adventures of Huckleberry Finn* (1884), are classics of American literature. Twain grew up in the busy Mississippi port town of Hannibal and was forced to leave school at the age of twelve after the death of his father. He worked as a journeyman printer, a riverboat pilot and a miner before finding success as a writer.

I visited St. Louis lately, and on my way West, after changing cars at Terre Haute, Indiana, a mild, benevolent-looking gentleman of about forty-five, or maybe fifty, came in at one of the way-stations and sat down beside me. We talked together pleasantly on various subjects for an hour, perhaps, and I found him exceedingly intelligent and entertaining. When he learned that I was from Washington, he immediately began to ask questions about various public men, and about Congressional affairs; and I saw very shortly that I was conversing with a man who was perfectly familiar with the ins and outs of political life at the Capital, even to the ways and manners, and customs of procedure of Senators and Representatives in the Chambers of the national Legislature. Presently two men halted near us for a single moment, and one said to the other:

"Harris, if you'll do that for me, I'll never forget you, my boy."

My new comrade's eye lighted pleasantly. The words had touched upon a happy memory, I thought. Then his face settled into thoughtfulness – almost into gloom. He turned to me and said,

"Let me tell you a story; let me give you a secret chapter of my life – a chapter that has never been referred to by me since its events transpired. Listen patiently, and promise that you will not interrupt me."

I said I would not, and he related the following strange adventure, speaking sometimes with animation, sometimes with melancholy, but always with feeling and earnestness.

The Stranger's Narrative

"On the 19th of December, 1853, I started from St. Louis on the evening train bound for Chicago. There were only twenty-four passengers, all told. There were no ladies and no children. We were in excellent spirits, and pleasant acquaintanceships were soon formed. The journey bade fair to be a happy one; and no individual in the party, I think, had even the vaguest presentiment of the horrors we were soon to undergo.

"At 11 P.M. it began to snow hard. Shortly after leaving the small village of Welden, we entered upon that tremendous prairie solitude that stretches its leagues on leagues of houseless dreariness far away toward the Jubilee Settlements. The winds, unobstructed by trees or hills, or even vagrant rocks, whistled fiercely across the level desert, driving the falling snow before it like spray from the crested waves of a stormy sea. The snow was deepening fast; and we knew, by the diminished speed of the train, that the engine was plowing through it with steadily increasing difficulty. Indeed, it almost came to a dead halt sometimes, in the midst of great drifts that piled themselves like colossal graves across the track. Conversation began to flag. Cheerfulness gave place to grave concern. The possibility of being imprisoned in the snow, on the bleak prairie, fifty miles from any house, presented itself to every mind, and extended its depressing influence over every spirit.

"At two o'clock in the morning I was aroused out of an uneasy slumber by the ceasing of all motion about me. The appalling truth flashed upon me instantly – we were captives in a snow-drift! 'All hands to the rescue!' Every man sprang to obey. Out into the wild night, the pitchy darkness, the billowy snow, the driving storm, every soul leaped, with the consciousness that a moment lost now might bring destruction to us all. Shovels, hands, boards – anything, everything that could displace snow, was brought into instant requisition. It was a weird picture, that small company of frantic men fighting the banking snows, half in the blackest shadow and half in the angry light of the locomotive's reflector.

"One short hour sufficed to prove the utter uselessness of our efforts. The storm barricaded the track with a dozen drifts while we dug one away. And worse than this, it was discovered that the last grand charge the engine had made upon the enemy had broken the fore-and-aft shaft of the driving-wheel! With a free track before us we should still have been helpless. We entered the car wearied with labor, and very sorrowful. We gathered about the stoves, and gravely canvassed our situation. We had no provisions whatever – in this lay our chief distress. We could not freeze, for there was a good supply of wood in the tender. This was our only comfort. The discussion ended at last in accepting the disheartening decision of the conductor, viz., that it would be death for any man to attempt to travel fifty miles on foot through snow like that. We could not send for help, and even if we could it would not come. We must submit, and await, as patiently as we might, succor or starvation! I think the stoutest heart there felt a momentary chill when those words were uttered.

"Within the hour conversation subsided to a low murmur here and there about the car, caught fitfully between the rising and falling of the blast; the lamps grew dim; and the majority of the castaways settled themselves among the flickering shadows to think – to forget the present, if they could – to sleep, if they might.

"The eternal night – it surely seemed eternal to us – wore its lagging hours away at last, and the cold gray dawn broke in the east. As the light grew stronger the passengers began to stir and give signs of life, one after another, and each in turn pushed his slouched hat up from his forehead, stretched his stiffened limbs, and glanced out of the windows upon the cheerless prospect. It was cheer less, indeed! – not a living thing visible anywhere, not a human habitation; nothing but a vast white desert; uplifted sheets of snow drifting hither and thither before the wind – a world of eddying flakes shutting out the firmament above.

"All day we moped about the cars, saying little, thinking much. Another lingering dreary night – and hunger.

"Another dawning – another day of silence, sadness, wasting hunger, hopeless watching for succor that could not come. A night of restless slumber, filled with dreams of feasting – wakings distressed with the gnawings of hunger.

"The fourth day came and went – and the fifth! Five days of dreadful imprisonment! A savage hunger looked out at every eye. There was in it a sign of awful import – the foreshadowing of a something that was vaguely shaping itself in every heart – a something which no tongue dared yet to frame into words.

"The sixth day passed – the seventh dawned upon as gaunt and haggard and hopeless a company of men as ever stood in the shadow of death. It must out now! That thing which had been growing up in every heart was ready to leap from every lip at last! Nature had been taxed to the utmost – she must yield. RICHARD H. GASTON of Minnesota, tall, cadaverous, and pale, rose up. All knew what was coming. All prepared – every emotion, every semblance of excitement – was smothered – only a calm, thoughtful seriousness appeared in the eyes that were lately so wild.

"'Gentlemen: It cannot be delayed longer! The time is at hand! We must determine which of us shall die to furnish food for the rest!'

"MR. JOHN J. WILLIAMS of Illinois rose and said: 'Gentlemen – I nominate the Rev. James Sawyer of Tennessee.'

"MR. Wm. R. ADAMS of Indiana said: 'I nominate Mr. Daniel Slote of New York.'

"MR. CHARLES J. LANGDON: 'I nominate Mr. Samuel A. Bowen of St. Louis.'

"MR. SLOTE: 'Gentlemen – I desire to decline in favor of Mr. John A. Van Nostrand, Jun., of New Jersey.'

"MR. GASTON: 'If there be no objection, the gentleman's desire will be acceded to.'

"MR. VAN NOSTRAND objecting, the resignation of Mr. Slote was rejected. The resignations of Messrs. Sawyer and Bowen were also offered, and refused upon the same grounds.

"MR. A. L. BASCOM of Ohio: 'I move that the nominations now close, and that the House proceed to an election by ballot.'

"MR. SAWYER: 'Gentlemen – I protest earnestly against these proceedings. They are, in every way, irregular and unbecoming. I must beg to move that they be dropped at once, and that we elect a chairman of the meeting and proper officers to assist him, and then we can go on with the business before us understandingly.'

"MR. BELL of Iowa: 'Gentlemen – I object. This is no time to stand upon forms and ceremonious observances. For more than seven days we have been without food. Every moment we lose in idle discussion increases our distress. I am satisfied with the nominations that have been made – every gentleman present is, I believe – and I, for one, do not see why we should not proceed at once to elect one or more of them. I wish to offer a resolution – '

"MR. GASTON: 'It would be objected to, and have to lie over one day under the rules, thus bringing about the very delay you wish to avoid. The gentleman from New Jersey – '

"MR. VAN NOSTRAND: 'Gentlemen – I am a stranger among you; I have not sought the distinction that has been conferred upon me, and I feel a delicacy – '

"MR. MORGAN Of Alabama (interrupting): 'I move the previous question.'

"The motion was carried, and further debate shut off, of course. The motion to elect officers was passed, and under it Mr. Gaston was chosen chairman, Mr. Blake, secretary, Messrs. Holcomb, Dyer, and Baldwin a committee on nominations, and Mr. R. M. Howland, purveyor, to assist the committee in making selections.

"A recess of half an hour was then taken, and some little caucusing followed. At the sound of the gavel the meeting reassembled, and the committee reported in favor of Messrs. George Ferguson of Kentucky, Lucien Herrman of Louisiana, and W. Messick of Colorado as candidates. The report was accepted.

"MR. ROGERS of Missouri: 'Mr. President – The report being properly before the House now, I move to amend it by substituting for the name of Mr. Herrman that of Mr. Lucius Harris of St. Louis, who is well and honorably known to us all. I do not wish to be understood as casting the least reflection upon the high character and standing of the gentleman from Louisiana – far from it. I respect and esteem him as much as any gentleman here present possibly can; but none of us can be blind to the fact that he has lost more flesh during the week that we have lain here than any among us – none of us can be blind to the fact that the committee has been derelict in its duty, either through negligence or a graver fault, in thus offering for our suffrages a gentleman who, however pure his own motives may be, has really less nutriment in him – '

"THE CHAIR: 'The gentleman from Missouri will take his seat. The Chair cannot allow the integrity of the committee to be questioned save by the regular course, under the rules. What action will the House take upon the gentleman's motion?'

"MR. HALLIDAY of Virginia: 'I move to further amend the report by substituting Mr. Harvey Davis of Oregon for Mr. Messick. It may be urged by gentlemen that the hardships and privations of a frontier life have rendered Mr. Davis tough; but, gentlemen, is this a time to cavil at toughness? Is this a time to be fastidious concerning trifles? Is this a time to dispute about matters of paltry significance? No, gentlemen, bulk is what we desire – substance, weight, bulk – these are the supreme requisites now – not talent, not genius, not education. I insist upon my motion.'

"MR. MORGAN (excitedly): 'Mr. Chairman – I do most strenuously object to this amendment. The gentleman from Oregon is old, and furthermore is bulky only in bone – not in flesh. I ask the gentleman from Virginia if it is soup we want instead of solid sustenance? if he would delude us with shadows? if he would mock our suffering with an Oregonian specter? I ask him if he can look upon the anxious faces around him, if he can gaze into our sad eyes, if he can listen to the beating of our expectant hearts, and still thrust this famine-stricken fraud upon us? I ask him if he can think of our desolate state, of our past sorrows, of our dark future, and still unpityingly foist upon us this wreck, this ruin, this tottering swindle, this gnarled and blighted and sapless vagabond from Oregon's inhospitable shores? Never!' [Applause.]

"The amendment was put to vote, after a fiery debate, and lost. Mr. Harris was substituted on the first amendment. The balloting then began. Five ballots were held without a choice. On the sixth, Mr. Harris was elected, all voting for him but himself. It was then moved that his election should be ratified by acclamation, which was lost, in consequence of his again voting against himself.

"MR. RADWAY moved that the House now take up the remaining candidates, and go into an election for breakfast. This was carried.

"On the first ballot there was a tie, half the members favoring one candidate on account of his youth, and half favoring the other on account of his superior size. The President gave the casting vote for the latter, Mr. Messick. This decision created considerable dissatisfaction among the friends of Mr. Ferguson, the defeated candidate, and there was some talk of demanding a new ballot; but in the midst of it a motion to adjourn was carried, and the meeting broke up at once.

"The preparations for supper diverted the attention of the Ferguson faction from the discussion of their grievance for a long time, and then, when they would have taken it up again, the happy announcement that Mr. Harris was ready drove all thought of it to the winds.

"We improvised tables by propping up the backs of car-seats, and sat down with hearts full of gratitude to the finest supper that had blessed our vision for seven torturing days. How changed we were from what we had been a few short hours before! Hopeless, sad-eyed misery, hunger, feverish anxiety, desperation, then; thankfulness, serenity, joy too deep for utterance now. That I know was the cheeriest hour of my eventful life. The winds howled, and blew the snow wildly about our prison house, but they were powerless to distress us any more. I liked Harris. He might have been better done, perhaps, but I am free to say that no man ever agreed with me better than Harris, or afforded me so large a degree of satisfaction. Messick was very well, though rather high-flavored, but for genuine nutritiousness and delicacy of fiber, give me Harris. Messick had his good points – I will not attempt to deny it, nor do I wish to do it – but he was no more fitted for breakfast than a mummy would be, sir – not a bit. Lean? – why, bless me! – and tough? Ah, he was very tough! You could not imagine it – you could never imagine anything like it."

"Do you mean to tell me that – "

"Do not interrupt me, please. After breakfast we elected a man by the name of Walker, from Detroit, for supper. He was very good. I wrote his wife so afterward. He was worthy of all praise. I shall always remember Walker. He was a little rare, but very good. And then the next morning we had Morgan of Alabama for breakfast. He was one of the finest men I ever sat down to – handsome, educated, refined, spoke several languages fluently – a perfect gentleman – he was a perfect gentleman, and singularly juicy. For supper we had that Oregon patriarch, and he was a fraud, there is no question about it – old, scraggy, tough, nobody can picture the reality. I finally said, gentlemen, you can do as you like, but I will wait for another election. And Grimes of Illinois said, 'Gentlemen, I will wait also. When you elect a man that has something to recommend him, I shall be glad to join you again.' It soon became evident that there was general dissatisfaction with Davis of Oregon, and so, to preserve the good will that had prevailed so pleasantly since we had had Harris, an election was called, and the result of it was that Baker of Georgia was chosen. He was splendid! Well, well – after that we had Doolittle, and Hawkins, and McElroy (there was some complaint about McElroy, because he was uncommonly short and thin), and Penrod, and two Smiths, and Bailey (Bailey had a wooden leg, which was clear loss, but he was otherwise good), and an Indian boy, and an organ-grinder, and a gentleman by the name of Buckminster – a poor stick of a vagabond that wasn't any good for company and no account for break- fast. We were glad we got him elected before relief came."

"And so the blessed relief did come at last?"

"Yes, it came one bright, sunny morning, just after election. John Murphy was the choice, and there never was a better, I am willing to testify; but John Murphy came home with us, in the train that came to succor us, and lived to marry the widow Harris – "

"Relict of – "

"Relict of our first choice. He married her, and is happy and respected and prosperous yet. Ah, it was like a novel, sir – it was like a romance. This is my stopping-place, sir; I must bid you goodby. Any time that you can make it con- venient to tarry a day or two with me, I shall be glad to have you. I like you, sir; I have conceived an affection for you. I could like you as well as I liked Harris himself, sir. Good day, sir, and a pleasant journey."

He was gone. I never felt so stunned, so distressed, so bewildered in my life. But in my soul I was glad he was gone. With all his gentleness of manner and his soft voice, I shuddered whenever he turned his hungry eye upon me; and when I heard that I had achieved his perilous affection, and that I stood almost with the late Harris in his esteem, my heart fairly stood still!

I was bewildered beyond description. I did not doubt his word; I could not question a single item in a statement so stamped with the earnestness of truth as his; but its dreadful details overpowered me, and threw my thoughts into hope- less confusion. I saw the conductor looking at me. I said, "Who is that man?"

"He was a member of Congress once, and a good one. But he got caught in a snow-drift in the cars, and like to have been starved to death. He got so frost- bitten and frozen up generally, and used up for want of something to eat, that he was sick and out of his head two or three months afterward. He is all right now, only he is a monomaniac, and when he gets on that old subject he never stops till he has eat up that whole car-load of people he talks about. He would have fin- ished the crowd by this time, only he had to get out here. He has got their names as pat as A B C. When he gets them all eat up but himself, he always says: 'Then the hour for the usual election for breakfast having arrived, and there being no opposition, I was duly elected, after which, there being no objections offered, I resigned. Thus I am here.'"

I felt inexpressibly relieved to know that I had only been listening to the harm- less vagaries of a madman instead of the genuine experiences of a bloodthirsty cannibal.

MADAM CROWL'S GHOST

Sheridan Le Fanu

Joseph Thomas Sheridan Le Fanu (1814–1873) was born in Dublin. He attended Trinity College and afterwards studied law at King's Inns. His first short stories appeared in *Dublin University Magazine*. His wife Susanna's sudden and early death in 1858, which left him alone with four children and mounting debts, prompted a religious crisis. After Susanna's death Sheridan Le Fanu largely withdrew from public life. He became proprietor of the *Dublin Evening Mail* and *Dublin University Magazine* in 1861.

"I'm an old woman now, and I was but thirteen, my last birthday, the night I came to Applewale House. My aunt was the housekeeper there, and a sort o' one-horse carriage was down at Lexhoe waitin' to take me and my box up to Applewale.

"I was a bit frightened by the time I got to Lexhoe, and when I saw the carriage and horse, I wished myself back again with my mother at Hazelden. I was crying when I got into the 'shay' – that's what we used to call it – and old John Mulbery that drove it, and was a good-natured fellow, bought me a handful of apples at the Golden Lion to cheer me up a bit; and he told me that there was a currant-cake, and tea, and pork-chops, waiting for me, all hot, in my aunt's room at the great house. It was a fine moonlight night, and I eat the apples, lookin' out o' the shay winda.

"It's a shame for gentlemen to frighten a poor foolish child like I was. I sometimes think it might be tricks. There was two on 'em on the tap o' the coach beside me. And they began to question me after nightfall, when the moon rose, where I was going to. Well, I told them it was to wait on Dame Arabella Crowl, of Applewale House, near by Lexhoe.

"'Ho, then,' says one of them, 'you'll not be long there!'

"And I looked at him as much as to say 'Why not?' for I had spoken out when I told them where I was goin', as if 'twas something clever I hed to say.

"'Because,' says he, 'and don't you for your life tell no one, only watch her and see – she's possessed by the devil, and more an half a ghost. Have you got a Bible?'

"'Yes, sir,' says I. For my mother put my little Bible in my box, and I knew it was there: and by the same token, though the print's too small for my ald eyes, I have it in my press to this hour.

"As I looked up at him saying 'Yes, sir,' I thought I saw him winkin' at his friend; but I could not be sure.

"'Well,' says he, 'be sure you put it under your bolster every night, it will keep the ald girl's claws aff ye.'

"And I got such a fright when he said that, you wouldn't fancy! And I'd a liked to ask him a lot about the ald lady, but I was too shy, and he and his friend began talkin' together about their own consarns, and dowly enough I got down, as I told ye, at Lexhoe. My heart sank as I drove into the dark avenue. The trees stand very thick and big, as ald as the ald house almost, and four people, with their arms out and finger-tips touchin', barely girds round some of them.

"Well my neck was stretched out o' the winda, looking for the first view o' the great house; and all at once we pulled up in front of it.

"A great white-and-black house it is, wi' great black beams across and right up it, and gables lookin' out, as white as a sheet, to the moon, and the shadows o' the trees, two or three up and down in front, you could count the leaves on them, and all the little diamond-shaped winda-panes, glimmering on the great hall winda, and great shutters, in the old fashion, hinged on the wall outside, boulted across all the rest o' the windas in front, for there was but three or four servants, and the old lady in the house, and most o' t' rooms was locked up.

"My heart was in my mouth when I sid the journey was over, and this the great house afoore me, and I sa near my aunt that I never sid till noo, and Dame Crowl, that I was come to wait upon, and was afeard on already.

"My aunt kissed me in the hall, and brought me to her room. She was tall and thin, wi' a pale face and black eyes, and long thin hands wi' black mittins on. She was past fifty, and her word was short; but her word was law. I hev no complaints to make of her; but she was a hard woman, and I think she would hev bin kinder to me if I had bin her sister's child in place of her brother's. But all that's o' no consequence noo.

"The squire – his name was Mr. Chevenix Crowl, he was Dame Crowl's grandson – came down there, by way of seeing that the old lady was well treated, about twice or thrice in the year. I sid him but twice all the time I was at Applewale House.

"I can't say but she was well taken care of, notwithstanding; but that was because my aunt and Meg Wyvern, that was her maid, had a conscience, and did their duty by her.

"Mrs. Wyvern – Meg Wyvern my aunt called her to herself, and Mrs. Wyvern to me – was a fat, jolly lass of fifty, a good height and a good breadth, always good-humoured and walked slow. She had fine wages, but she was a bit stingy, and kept all her fine clothes under lock and key, and wore, mostly, a twilled chocolate cotton, wi' red, and yellow, and green sprigs and balls on it, and it lasted wonderful.

"She never gave me nout, not the vally o' a brass thimble, all the time I was there; but she was good-humoured, and always laughin', and she talked no end o' proas over her tea; and, seeing me sa sackless and dowly, she roused me up wi' her laughin' and stories; and I think I liked her better than my aunt – children is so taken wi' a bit o' fun or a story – though my aunt was very good to me, but a hard woman about some things, and silent always.

"My aunt took me into her bed-chamber, that I might rest myself a bit while she was settin' the tea in her room. But first, she patted me on the shouther, and said I was a tall lass o' my years, and had spired up well, and asked me if I could do plain work and stitchin'; and she looked in my face, and said I was like my father, her brother, that was dead and gone, and she hoped I was a better Christian, and wad na du a' that lids (would not do anything of that sort).

"It was a hard sayin' the first time I set foot in her room, I thought.

"When I went into the next room, the housekeeper's room – very comfortable, yak (oak) all round – there was a fine fire blazin' away, wi' coal, and peat, and wood, all in a low together, and tea on the table, and hot cake, and smokin' meat; and there was Mrs. Wyvern, fat, jolly, and talkin' away, more in an hour than my aunt would in a year.

"While I was still at my tea my aunt went up-stairs to see Madam Crowl.

"'She's agone up to see that old Judith Squailes is awake,' says Mrs. Wyvern. 'Judith sits with Madam Crowl when me and Mrs. Shutters' – that was my aunt's name – 'is away. She's a troublesome old lady. Ye'll hev to be sharp wi' her, or she'll be into the fire, or out o' t' winda. She goes on wires, she does, old though she be.'

"'How old, ma'am?' says I.

"'Ninety-three her last birthday, and that's eight months gone,' says she; and she laughed. 'And don't be askin' questions about her before your aunt – mind, I tell ye; just take her as you find her, and that's all.'

"'And what's to be my business about her, please, ma'am?' says I.

"'About the old lady? Well,' says she, 'your aunt, Mrs. Shutters, will tell you that; but I suppose you'll hev to sit in the room with your work, and see she's at no mischief, and let her amuse herself with her things on the table, and get her her food or drink as she calls for it, and keep her out o' mischief, and ring the bell hard if she's troublesome.'

"'Is she deaf, ma'am?'

"'No, nor blind,' says she; 'as sharp as a needle, but she's gone quite aupy, and can't remember nout rightly; and Jack the Giant Killer, or Goody Twoshoes will please her as well as the king's court, or the affairs of the nation.'

"'And what did the little girl go away for, ma'am, that went on Friday last? My aunt wrote to my mother she was to go.'

"'Yes; she's gone.'

"'What for?' says I again.

"'She didn't answer Mrs. Shutters, I do suppose,' says she. 'I don't know. Don't be talkin'; your aunt can't abide a talkin' child.'

"'And please, ma'am, is the old lady well in health?' says I.

"'It ain't no harm to ask that,' says she. 'She's torflin a bit lately, but better this week past, and I dare say she'll last out her hundred years yet. Hish! Here's your aunt coming down the passage.'

"In comes my aunt, and begins talkin' to Mrs. Wyvern, and I, beginnin' to feel more comfortable and at home like, was walkin' about the room lookin' at this thing and at that. There was pretty old china things on the cupboard, and pictures again the wall; and there was a door open in the wainscot, and I sees a queer old leathern jacket, wi' straps and buckles to it, and sleeves as long as the bed-post hangin' up inside.

"'What's that you're at, child?' says my aunt, sharp enough, turning about when I thought she least minded. 'What's that in your hand?'

"'This, ma'am?' says I, turning about with the leathern jacket. 'I don't know what it is, ma'am.'

"Pale as she was, the red came up in her cheeks, and her eyes flashed wi' anger, and I think only she had half a dozen steps to take, between her and me, she'd a gev me a sizzup. But she did gie me a shake by the shouther, and she plucked the thing out o' my hand, and says she, 'While ever you stay here, don't ye meddle wi' nout that don't belong to ye', and she hung it up on the pin that was there, and shut the door wi' a bang and locked it fast.

"Mrs. Wyvern was liftin' up her hands and laughin' all this time, quietly, in her chair, rolling herself a bit in it, as she used when she was kinkin'.

"The tears was in my eyes, and she winked at my aunt, and says she, dryin' her own eyes that was wet wi' the laughin', 'Tut, the child meant no harm – come here to me, child. It's only a pair o' crutches for lame ducks, and ask us no questions mind, and we'll tell ye no lies; and come here and sit down, and drink a mug o' beer before ye go to your bed.'

"My room, mind ye, was upstairs, next to the old lady's, and Mrs. Wyvern's bed was near hers in her room, and I was to be ready at call, if need should be.

"The old lady was in one of her tantrums that night and part of the day before. She used to take fits o' the sulks. Sometimes she would not let them dress her, and at other times she would not let them take her clothes off. She was a great beauty, they said, in her day. But there was no one about Applewale that remembered her in her prime. And she was dreadful fond o' dress, and had thick silks, and stiff satins, and velvets, and laces, and all sorts, enough to set up seven shops at the least. All her dresses was old-fashioned and queer, but worth a fortune.

"Well, I went to my bed. I lay for a while awake; for a' things was new to me; and I think the tea was in my nerves, too, for I wasn't used to it, except now and then on a holiday, or the like. And I heard Mrs. Wyvern talkin', and I listened with my hand to my ear; but I could not hear Mrs. Crowl, and I don't think she said a word.

"There was great care took of her. The people at Applewale knew that when she died they would every one get the sack; and their situations was well paid and easy.

"The doctor came twice a week to see the old lady, and you may be sure they all did as he bid them. One thing was the same every time; they were never to cross or frump her, any way, but to humour and please her in everything.

"So she lay in her clothes all that night, and next day, not a word she said, and I was at my needlework all that day, in my own room, except when I went down to my dinner.

"I would a liked to see the ald lady, and even to hear her speak. But she might as well a' bin in Lunnon a' the time for me.

"When I had my dinner my aunt sent me out for a walk for an hour. I was glad when I came back, the trees was so big, and the place so dark and lonesome, and 'twas a cloudy day, and I cried a deal, thinkin' of home, while I was walkin' alone there. That evening, the candles bein' alight, I was sittin' in my room, and the door was open into Madam Crowl's chamber, where my aunt was. It was, then, for the first time I heard what I suppose was the ald lady talking.

"It was a queer noise like, I couldn't well say which, a bird, or a beast, only it had a bleatin' sound in it, and was very small.

"I pricked my ears to hear all I could. But I could not make out one word she said. And my aunt answered:

" 'The evil one can't hurt no one, ma'am, bout the Lord permits.'

"Then the same queer voice from the bed says something more that I couldn't make head nor tail on.

"And my aunt med answer again: 'Let them pull faces, ma'am, and say what they will; if the Lord be for us, who can be against us?'

"I kept listenin' with my ear turned to the door, holdin' my breath, but not another word or sound came in from the room. In about twenty minutes, as I was sittin' by the table, lookin' at the pictures in the old Aesop's Fables, I was aware o' something moving at the door, and lookin' up I sid my aunt's face lookin' in at the door, and her hand raised.

" 'Hish!' says she, very soft, and comes over to me on tiptoe, and she says in a whisper: 'Thank God, she's asleep at last, and don't ye make no noise till I come back, for I'm goin' down to take my cup o' tea, and I'll be back i' noo – me and Mrs. Wyvern, and she'll be sleepin' in the room, and you can run down when we come up, and Judith will gie ye yaur supper in my room.'

"And with that she goes.

"I kep' looking at the picture-book, as before, listenin' every noo and then, but there was no sound, not a breath, that I could hear; an' I began whisperin' to the pictures and talkin' to myself to keep my heart up, for I was growin' feared in that big room.

"And at last up I got, and began walkin' about the room, lookin' at this and peepin' at that, to amuse my mind, ye'll understand. And at last what sud I do but peeps into Madam Crowl's bedchamber.

"A grand chamber it was, wi' a great four-poster, wi' flowered silk curtains as tall as the ceilin', and foldin' down on the floor, and drawn close all round. There was a lookin'-glass, the biggest I ever sid before, and the room was a blaze o' light. I counted twenty-two wax candles, all alight. Such was her fancy, and no one dared say her nay.

"I listened at the door, and gaped and wondered all round. When I heard there was not a breath, and did not see so much as a stir in the curtains, I took heart, and walked into the room on tiptoe, and looked round again. Then I takes a keek at myself in the big glass; and at last it came in my head, 'Why couldn't I ha' a keek at the ald lady herself in the bed?

"Ye'd think me a fule if ye knew half how I longed to see Dame Crowl, and I thought to myself if I didn't peep now I might wait many a day before I got so gude a chance again.

"Well, my dear, I came to the side o' the bed, the curtains bein' close, and my heart a'most failed me. But I took courage, and I slips my finger in between the thick curtains, and then my hand. So I waits a bit, but all was still as death. So, softly, softly I draws the curtain, and there, sure enough, I sid before me, stretched out like the painted lady on the tomb-stean in Lexhoe Church, the famous Dame

Crowl, of Applewale House. There she was, dressed out. You never sid the like in they days. Satin and silk, and scarlet and green, and gold and pint lace; by Jen! 'twas a sight! A big powdered wig, half as high as herself, was a-top o' her head, and, wow! – was ever such wrinkles? – and her old baggy throat all powdered white, and her cheeks rouged, and mouse-skin eyebrows, that Mrs. Wyvern used to stick on, and there she lay proud and stark, wi' a pair o' clocked silk hose on, and heels to her shoon as tall as nine-pins. Lawk! But her nose was crooked and thin, and half the whites o' her eyes was open. She used to stand, dressed as she was, gigglin' and dribblin' before the lookin'-glass, wi' a fan in her hand and a big nosegay in her bodice. Her wrinkled little hands was stretched down by her sides, and such long nails, all cut into points, I never sid in my days. Could it even a bin the fashion for grit fowk to wear their fingernails so?

"Well, I think ye'd a-bin frightened yourself if ye'd a sid such a sight. I couldn't let go the curtain, nor move an inch, nor take my eyes off her; my very heart stood still. And in an instant she opens her eyes and up she sits, and spins herself round, and down wi' her, wi' a clack on her two tall heels on the floor, facin' me, ogglin' in my face wi' her two great glassy eyes, and a wicked simper wi' her wrinkled lips, and lang fause teeth.

"Well, a corpse is a natural thing; but this was the dreadfullest sight I ever sid. She had her fingers straight out pointin' at me, and her back was crooked, round again wi' age. Says she:

"'Ye little limb! what for did ye say I killed the boy? I'll tickle ye till ye're stiff!'

"If I'd a thought an instant, I'd a turned about and run. But I couldn't take my eyes off her, and I backed from her as soon as I could; and she came clatterin' after like a thing on wires, with her fingers pointing to my throat, and she makin' all the time a sound with her tongue like zizz-zizz-zizz.

"I kept backin' and backin' as quick as I could, and her fingers was only a few inches away from my throat, and I felt I'd lose my wits if she touched me.

"I went back this way, right into the corner, and I gev a yellock, ye'd think saul and body was partin', and that minute my aunt, from the door, calls out wi' a blare, and the ald lady turns round on her, and I turns about, and ran through my room, and down the stairs, as hard as my legs could carry me.

"I cried hearty, I can tell you, when I got down to the housekeeper's room. Mrs. Wyvern laughed a deal when I told her what happened. But she changed her key when she heard the ald lady's words.

"'Say them again,' says she.

"So I told her.

"'Ye little limb! What for did ye say I killed the boy? I'll tickle ye till ye're stiff.'

"'And did ye say she killed a boy?' says she.

"'Not I, ma'am,' says I.

"Judith was always up with me, after that, when the two elder women was away from her. I would a jumped out at winda, rather than stay alone in the same room wi' her.

"It was about a week after, as well as I can remember, Mrs. Wyvern, one day when me and her was alone, told me a thing about Madam Crowl that I did not know before.

"She being young and a great beauty, full seventy year before, had married

Squire Crowl, of Applewale. But he was a widower, and had a son about nine years old.

"There never was tale or tidings of this boy after one mornin'. No one could say where he went to. He was allowed too much liberty, and used to be off in the morning, one day, to the keeper's cottage and breakfast wi' him, and away to the warren, and not home, mayhap, till evening; and another time down to the lake, and bathe there, and spend the day fishin' there, or paddlin' about in the boat. Well, no one could say what was gone wi' him; only this, that his hat was found by the lake, under a haathorn that grows thar to this day, and 'twas thought he was drowned bathin'. And the squire's son, by his second marriage, with this Madam Crowl that lived sa dreadful lang, came in far the estates. It was his son, the ald lady's grandson, Squire Chevenix Crowl, that owned the estates at the time I came to Applewale.

"There was a deal o' talk lang before my aunt's time about it; and 'twas said the step-mother knew more than she was like to let out. And she managed her husband, the ald squire, wi' her white-heft and flatteries. And as the boy was never seen more, in course of time the thing died out of fowks' minds.

"I'm goin' to tell ye noo about what I sid wi' my own een.

"I was not there six months, and it was winter time, when the ald lady took her last sickness.

"The doctor was afeard she might a took a fit o' madness, as she did fifteen years befoore, and was buckled up, many a time, in a strait-waistcoat, which was the very leathern jerkin I sid in the closet, off my aunt's room.

"Well, she didn't. She pined, and windered, and went off, torflin', torflin', quiet enough, till a day or two before her flittin', and then she took to rabblin', and sometimes skirlin' in the bed, ye'd think a robber had a knife to her throat, and she used to work out o' the bed, and not being strong enough, then, to walk or stand, she'd fall on the flure, wi' her ald wizened hands stretched before her face, and skirlin' still for mercy.

"Ye may guess I didn't go into the room, and I used to be shiverin' in my bed wi' fear, at her skirlin' and scrafflin' on the flure, and blarin' out words that id make your skin turn blue.

"My aunt, and Mrs. Wyvern, and Judith Squailes, and a woman from Lexhoe, was always about her. At last she took fits, and they wore her out.

"T' sir was there, and prayed for her; but she was past praying with. I suppose it was right, but none could think there was much good in it, and sa at lang last she made her flittin', and a' was over, and old Dame Crowl was shrouded and coffined, and Squire Chevenix was wrote for. But he was away in France, and the delay was sa lang, that t' sir and doctor both agreed it would not du to keep her langer out o' her place, and no one cared but just them two, and my aunt and the rest o' us, from Applewale, to go to the buryin'. So the old lady of Applewale was laid in the vault under Lexhoe Church; and we lived up at the great house till such time as the squire should come to tell his will about us, and pay off such as he chose to discharge.

"I was put into another room, two doors away from what was Dame Crowl's chamber, after her death, and this thing happened the night before Squire Chevenix came to Applewale.

"The room I was in now was a large square chamber, covered wi' yak pannels, but unfurnished except for my bed, which had no curtains to it, and a chair and a table, or so, that looked nothing at all in such a big room. And the big looking-glass, that the old lady used to keek into and admire herself from head to heel, now that there was na mair o' that wark, was put out of the way, and stood against the wall in my room, for there was shiftin' o' many things in her chamber ye may suppose, when she came to be coffined.

"The news had come that day that the squire was to be down next morning at Applewale; and not sorry was I, for I thought I was sure to be sent home again to my mother. And right glad was I, and I was thinkin' of a' at hame, and my sister Janet, and the kitten and the pymag, and Trimmer the tike, and all the rest, and I got sa fidgetty, I couldn't sleep, and the clock struck twelve, and me wide awake, and the room as dark as pick. My back was turned to the door, and my eyes toward the wall opposite.

"Well, it could na be a full quarter past twelve, when I sees a lightin' on the wall befoore me, as if something took fire behind, and the shadas o' the bed, and the chair, and my gown, that was hangin' from the wall, was dancin' up and down on the ceilin' beams and the yak pannels; and I turns my head ower my shouther quick, thinkin' something must a gone a' fire.

"And what sud I see, by Jen! but the likeness o' the ald beldame, bedizened out in her satins and velvets, on her dead body, simperin', wi' her eyes as wide as saucers, and her face like the fiend himself. 'Twas a red light that rose about her in a fuffin low, as if her dress round her feet was blazin'. She was drivin' on right for me, wi' her ald shrivelled hands crooked as if she was goin' to claw me. I could not stir, but she passed me straight by, wi' a blast o' cald air, and I sid her, at the wall, in the alcove as my aunt used to call it, which was a recess where the state bed used to stand in ald times wi' a door open wide, and her hands gropin' in at somethin' was there. I never sid that door befoore. And she turned round to me, like a thing on a pivot, flyrin', and all at once the room was dark, and I standin' at the far side o' the bed; I don't know how I got there, and I found my tongue at last, and if I did na blare a yellock, rennin' down the gallery and almost pulled Mrs. Wyvern's door off t' hooks, and frighted her half out o' wits.

"Ye may guess I did na sleep that night; and wi' the first light, down wi' me to my aunt, as fast as my two legs cud carry me.

"Well my aunt did na frump or flite me, as I thought she would, but she held me by the hand, and looked hard in my face all the time. And she telt me not to be feared; and says she:

"'Hed the appearance a key in its hand?'

"'Yes,' says I, bringin' it to mind, 'a big key in a queer brass handle.'

"'Stop a bit,' says she, lettin' go ma hand, and openin' the cupboard-door. 'Was it like this?' says she, takin' one out in her fingers, and showing it to me, with a dark look in my face.

"'That was it,' says I, quick enough.

"'Are ye sure?' she says, turnin' it round.

"'Sart,' says I, and I felt like I was gain' to faint when I sid it.

"'Well, that will do, child,' says she, saftly thinkin', and she locked it up again.

"'The squire himself will be here today, before twelve o'clock, and ye must tell him all about it,' says she, thinkin', 'and I suppose I'll be leavin' soon, and so the best thing for the present is, that ye should go home this afternoon, and I'll look out another place for you when I can.'

"Fain was I, ye may guess, at that word.

"My aunt packed up my things for me, and the three pounds that was due to me, to bring home, and Squire Crowl himself came down to Applewale that day, a handsome man, about thirty years ald. It was the second time I sid him. But this was the first time he spoke to me.

"My aunt talked wi' him in the housekeeper's room, and I don't know what they said. I was a bit feared on the squire, he bein' a great gentleman down in Lexhoe, and I darn't go near till I was called. And says he, smilin':

"'What's a' this ye a sen, child? it mun be a dream, for ye know there's na sic a thing as a bo or a freet in a' the world. But whatever it was, ma little maid, sit ye down and tell all about it from first to last.'

"Well, so soon as I made an end, he thought a bit, and says he to my aunt:

"'I mind the place well. In old Sir Olivur's time lame Wyndel told me there was a door in that recess, to the left, where the lassie dreamed she saw my grandmother open it. He was past eighty when he told me that, and I but a boy. It's twenty year sen. The plate and jewels used to be kept there, long ago, before the iron closet was made in the arras chamber, and he told me the key had a brass handle, and this ye say was found in the bottom o' the kist where she kept her old fans. Now, would not it be a queer thing if we found some spoons or diamonds forgot there? Ye mun come up wi' us, lassie, and point to the very spot.'

"Loth was I, and my heart in my mouth, and fast I held by my aunt's hand as I stept into that awsome room, and showed them both how she came and passed me by, and the spot where she stood, and where the door seemed to open.

"There was an ald empty press against the wall then, and shoving it aside, sure enough there was the tracing of a door in the wainscot, and a keyhole stopped with wood, and planed across as smooth as the rest, and the joining of the door all stopped wi' putty the colour o' yak, and, but for the hinges that showed a bit when the press was shoved aside, ye would not consayt there was a door there at all.

"'Ha!' says he, wi' a queer smile, 'this looks like it.'

"It took some minutes wi' a small chisel and hammer to pick the bit o' wood out o' the keyhole. The key fitted, sure enough, and, wi' a strang twist and a lang skreak, the boult went back and he pulled the door open.

"There was another door inside, stranger than the first, but the lacks was gone, and it opened easy. Inside was a narrow floor and walls and vault o' brick; we could not see what was in it, for 'twas dark as pick.

"When my aunt had lighted the candle, the squire held it up and stept in.

"My aunt stood on tiptoe tryin' to look over his shouther, and I did na see nout.

"'Ha! ha!' says the squire, steppin' backward. 'What's that? Gi' ma the poker – quick!' says he to my aunt. And as she went to the hearth I peeps beside his arm, and I sid squat down in the far corner a monkey or a flayin' on the chest, or else the maist shrivelled up, wizzened ald wife that ever was sen on yearth.

"'By Jen!' says my aunt, as puttin' the poker in his hand, she keeked by his shouther, and sid the ill-favoured thing, 'hae a care, sir, what ye're doin'. Back wi' ye, and shut to the door!'

"But in place o' that he steps in saftly, wi' the poker pointed like a swoord, and he gies it a poke, and down it a' tumbles together, head and a', in a heap o' bayans and dust, little meyar an' a hatful.

"'Twas the bayans o' a child; a' the rest went to dust at a touch. They said nout for a while, but he turns round the skull, as it lay on the floor.

"Young as I was, I consayted I knew well enough what they was thinkin' on.

"'A dead cat!' says he, pushin' back and blowin' out the can'le, and shuttin' to the door. 'We'll come back, you and me, Mrs. Shutters, and look on the shelves by-and-bye. I've other matters first to speak to ye about; and this little girl's goin' hame, ye say. She has her wages, and I mun mak' her a present,' says he, pattin' my shouther wi' his hand.

"And he did gimma a goud pound and I went aff to Lexhoe about an hour after, and sa hame by the stage-coach, and fain was I to be at hame again; and I never sid Dame Crowl o' Applewale, God be thanked, either in appearance or in dream, at-efter. But when I was grown to be a woman, my aunt spent a day and night wi' me at Littleham, and she telt me there was no doubt it was the poor little boy that was missing sa lang sen, that was shut up to die thar in the dark by that wicked beldame, whar his skirls, or his prayers, or his thumpin' cud na be heard, and his hat was left by the water's edge, whoever did it, to mak' belief he was drowned. The clothes, at the first touch, a' ran into a snuff o' dust in the cell whar the bayans was found. But there was a handful o' jet buttons, and a knife with a green heft, together wi' a couple o' pennies the poor little fella had in his pocket, I suppose, when he was decoyed in thar, and sid his last o' the light. And there was, amang the squire's papers, a copy o' the notice that was prented after he was lost, when the ald squire thought he might 'a run away, or bin took by gipsies, and it said he had a green-hefted knife wi' him, and that his buttons were o' cut jet. Sa that is a' I hev to say consarnin' ald Dame Crowl, o' Applewale House."

BOBOK: FROM SOMEBODY'S DIARY

Fyodor Dostoyevsky

Fyodor Dostoyevsky (1821–1881) had a difficult relationship with his father, who was rumoured to have been murdered by his own serfs in 1839. He graduated from the St Petersburg Military Engineering Academy as junior lieutenant, but shortly afterwards abandoned a military career to become a writer. In 1849 Dostoyevsky was arrested for being a member of the Petrashevsky circle and subjected to a mock-execution. He was subsequently sent to Siberia, an experience which profoundly affected his philosophy and his development as a writer.

Semyon Ardalyonovitch said to me all of a sudden the day before yesterday: "Why, will you ever be sober, Ivan Ivanovitch? Tell me that, pray."

A strange requirement. I did not resent it, I am a timid man; but here they have actually made me out mad. An artist painted my portrait as it happened: "After all, you are a literary man," he said. I submitted, he exhibited it. I read: "Go and look at that morbid face suggesting insanity."

It may be so, but think of putting it so bluntly into print. In print everything ought to be decorous; there ought to be ideals, while instead of that. . .

Say it indirectly, at least; that's what you have style for. But no, he doesn't care to do it indirectly. Nowadays humour and a fine style have disappeared, and abuse is accepted as wit. I do not resent it: but God knows I am not enough of a literary man to go out of my mind. I have written a novel, it has not been published. I have written articles – they have been refused. Those articles I took about from one editor to another; everywhere they refused them: you have no salt they told me. "What sort of salt do you want?" I asked with a jeer. "Attic salt?"

They did not even understand. For the most part I translate from the French for the booksellers. I write advertisements for shopkeepers too: "Unique opportunity! Fine tea, from our own plantations. . ." I made a nice little sum over a panegyric on his deceased excellency Pyotr Matveyitch. I compiled the "Art of pleasing the ladies," a commission from a bookseller. I have brought out some six little works of this kind in the course of my life. I am thinking of making a collection of the bon mots of Voltaire, but am afraid it may seem a little flat to our people. Voltaire's no good now; nowadays we want a cudgel, not Voltaire. We knock each other's last teeth out nowadays. Well, so that's the whole extent of my literary activity. Though indeed I do send round letters to the editors gratis and fully signed. I give them all sorts of counsels and admonitions, criticise and point out the true path. The letter I sent last week to an editor's office was the fortieth I had sent in the last two years. I have wasted four roubles over stamps alone for them. My temper is at the bottom of it all.

I believe that the artist who painted me did so not for the sake of literature, but for the sake of two symmetrical warts on my forehead, a natural phenomenon, he would say. They have no ideas, so now they are out for phenomena. And didn't he succeed in getting my warts in his portrait – to the life. That is what they call realism.

And as to madness, a great many people were put down as mad among us last year. And in such language! "With such original talent" . . . "and yet, after all, it appears" . . . "however, one ought to have foreseen it long ago." That is rather artful; so that from the point of view of pure art one may really commend it. Well, but after all, these so-called madmen have turned out cleverer than ever. So it seems the critics can call them mad, but they cannot produce any one better.

The wisest of all, in my opinion, is he who can, if only once a month, call himself a fool – a faculty unheard of nowadays. In old days, once a year at any rate a fool would recognise that he was a fool, but nowadays not a bit of it. And they have so muddled things up that there is no telling a fool from a wise man. They have done that on purpose.

I remember a witty Spaniard saying when, two hundred and fifty years ago, the French built their first madhouses: "They have shut up all their fools in a house apart, to make sure that they are wise men themselves." Just so: you don't show your own wisdom by shutting some one else in a madhouse. "K. has gone out of his mind, means that we are sane now." No, it doesn't mean that yet.

Hang it though, why am I maundering on? I go on grumbling and grumbling. Even my maidservant is sick of me. Yesterday a friend came to see me. "Your style is changing," he said; "it is choppy: you chop and chop – and then a parenthesis, then a parenthesis in the parenthesis, then you stick in something else in brackets, then you begin chopping and chopping again."

The friend is right. Something strange is happening to me. My character is changing and my head aches. I am beginning to see and hear strange things, not voices exactly, but as though some one beside me were muttering, "*bobok, bobok, bobok*!"

What's the meaning of this bobok? I must divert my mind.

I went out in search of diversion, I hit upon a funeral. A distant relation – a collegiate counsellor, however. A widow and five daughters, all marriageable young ladies. What must it come to even to keep them in slippers. Their father managed it, but now there is only a little pension. They will have to eat humble pie. They have always received me ungraciously. And indeed I should not have gone to the funeral now had it not been for a peculiar circumstance. I followed the procession to the cemetery with the rest; they were stuck-up and held aloof from me. My uniform was certainly rather shabby. It's five-and-twenty years, I believe, since I was at the cemetery; what a wretched place!

To begin with the smell. There were fifteen hearses, with palls varying in expensiveness; there were actually two catafalques. One was a general's and one some lady's. There were many mourners, a great deal of feigned mourning and a great deal of open gaiety. The clergy have nothing to complain of; it brings them a good income. But the smell, the smell. I should not like to be one of the clergy here.

I kept glancing at the faces of the dead cautiously, distrusting my impressionability. Some had a mild expression, some looked unpleasant. As a rule the smiles were disagreeable, and in some cases very much so. I don't like them; they haunt one's dreams.

During the service I went out of the church into the air: it was a grey day, but dry. It was cold too, but then it was October. I walked about among the tombs. They are of different grades. The third grade cost thirty roubles; it's decent and not so very dear. The first two grades are tombs in the church and under the porch; they cost a pretty penny. On this occasion they were burying in tombs of the third grade six persons, among them the general and the lady.

I looked into the graves – and it was horrible: water and such water! Absolutely green, and . . . but there, why talk of it! The gravedigger was baling it out every minute. I went out while the service was going on and strolled outside the gates. Close by was an almshouse, and a little further off there was a restaurant. It was not a bad little restaurant: there was lunch and everything. There were lots of the mourners here. I noticed a great deal of gaiety and genuine heartiness. I had something to eat and drink.

Then I took part in the bearing of the coffin from the church to the grave. Why is it that corpses in their coffins are so heavy? They say it is due to some sort of inertia, that the body is no longer directed by its owner . . . or some nonsense of that sort, in opposition to the laws of mechanics and common sense. I don't like to hear people who have nothing but a general education venture to solve the problems that require special knowledge; and with us that's done continually. Civilians love to pass opinions about subjects that are the province of the soldier and even of the field-marshal; while men who have been educated as engineers prefer discussing philosophy and political economy.

I did not go to the requiem service. I have some pride, and if I am only received owing to some special necessity, why force myself on their dinners, even if it be a funeral dinner. The only thing I don't understand is why I stayed at the cemetery; I sat on a tombstone and sank into appropriate reflections.

I began with the Moscow exhibition and ended with reflecting upon astonishment in the abstract. My deductions about astonishment were these:

"To be surprised at everything is stupid of course, and to be astonished at nothing is a great deal more becoming and for some reason accepted as good form. But that is not really true. To my mind to be astonished at nothing is much more stupid than to be astonished at everything. And, moreover, to be astonished at nothing is almost the same as feeling respect for nothing. And indeed a stupid man is incapable of feeling respect."

"But what I desire most of all is to feel respect. I thirst to feel respect," one of my acquaintances said to me the other day.

He thirsts to feel respect! Goodness, I thought, what would happen to you if you dared to print that nowadays?

At that point I sank into forgetfulness. I don't like reading the epitaphs of tombstones: they are everlastingly the same. An unfinished sandwich was lying on the tombstone near me; stupid and inappropriate. I threw it on the ground, as it was not bread but only a sandwich. Though I believe it is not a sin to throw bread on the earth, but only on the floor. I must look it up in Suvorin's calendar.

I suppose I sat there a long time – too long a time, in fact; I must have lain down on a long stone which was of the shape of a marble coffin. And how it happened I don't know, but I began to hear things of all sorts being said. At first I did not pay attention to it, but treated it with contempt. But the conversation went on. I heard muffled sounds as though the speakers' mouths were covered with a pillow, and at the same time they were distinct and very near. I came to myself, sat up and began listening attentively.

"Your Excellency, it's utterly impossible. You led hearts, I return your lead, and here you play the seven of diamonds. You ought to have given me a hint about diamonds."

"What, play by hard and fast rules? Where is the charm of that?"

"You must, your Excellency. One can't do anything without something to go upon. We must play with dummy, let one hand not be turned up."

"Well, you won't find a dummy here."

What conceited words! And it was queer and unexpected. One was such a ponderous, dignified voice, the other softly suave; I should not have believed it if I had not heard it myself. I had not been to the requiem dinner, I believe. And yet how could they be playing preference here and what general was this? That the sounds came from under the tombstones of that there could be no doubt. I bent down and read on the tomb:

"Here lies the body of Major-General Pervoyedov . . . a cavalier of such and such orders." Hm! "Passed away in August of this year . . . fifty-seven. . . Rest, beloved ashes, till the joyful dawn!"

Hm, dash it, it really is a general! There was no monument on the grave from which the obsequious voice came, there was only a tombstone. He must have been a fresh arrival. From his voice he was a lower court councillor.

"Oh-ho-ho-ho!" I heard in a new voice a dozen yards from the general's resting-place, coming from quite a fresh grave. The voice belonged to a man and a plebeian, mawkish with its affectation of religious fervour. "Oh-ho-ho-ho!"

"Oh, here he is hiccupping again!" cried the haughty and disdainful voice of an irritated lady, apparently of the highest society. "It is an affliction to be by this shopkeeper!"

"I didn't hiccup; why, I've had nothing to eat. It's simply my nature. Really, madam, you don't seem able to get rid of your caprices here."

"Then why did you come and lie down here?"

"They put me here, my wife and little children put me here, I did not lie down here of myself. The mystery of death! And I would not have lain down beside you not for any money; I lie here as befitting my fortune, judging by the price. For we can always do that – pay for a tomb of the third grade."

"You made money, I suppose? You fleeced people?"

"Fleece you, indeed! We haven't seen the colour of your money since January. There's a little bill against you at the shop."

"Well, that's really stupid; to try and recover debts here is too stupid, to my thinking! Go to the surface. Ask my niece – she is my heiress."

"There's no asking any one now, and no going anywhere. We have both reached our limit and, before the judgment-seat of God, are equal in our sins."

"In our sins," the lady mimicked him contemptuously. "Don't dare to speak to me."

"Oh-ho-ho-ho!"

"You see, the shopkeeper obeys the lady, your Excellency."

"Why shouldn't he?"

"Why, your Excellency, because, as we all know, things are different here."

"Different? How?"

"We are dead, so to speak, your Excellency."

"Oh, yes! But still. . ."

Well, this is an entertainment, it is a fine show, I must say! If it has come to this down here, what can one expect on the surface? But what a queer business! I went on listening, however, though with extreme indignation.

"Yes, I should like a taste of life! Yes, you know. . . I should like a taste of life." I heard a new voice suddenly somewhere in the space between the general and the irritable lady.

"Do you hear, your Excellency, our friend is at the same game again. For three days at a time he says nothing, and then he bursts out with 'I should like a taste of life, yes, a taste of life!' And with such appetite, he-he!"

"And such frivolity."

"It gets hold of him, your Excellency, and do you know, he is growing sleepy, quite sleepy – he has been here since April; and then all of a sudden 'I should like a taste of life!'"

"It is rather dull, though," observed his Excellency.

"It is, your Excellency. Shall we tease Avdotya Ignatyevna again, he-he?"

"No, spare me, please. I can't endure that quarrelsome virago."

"And I can't endure either of you," cried the virago disdainfully. "You are both of you bores and can't tell me anything ideal. I know one little story about you, your Excellency – don't turn up your nose, please – how a man-servant swept you out from under a married couple's bed one morning."

"Nasty woman," the general muttered through his teeth.

"Avdotya Ignatyevna, ma'am," the shopkeeper wailed suddenly again, "my dear lady, don't be angry, but tell me, am I going through the ordeal by torment now, or is it something else?"

"Ah, he is at it again, as I expected! For there's a smell from him which means he is turning round!"

"I am not turning round, ma'am, and there's no particular smell from me, for I've kept my body whole as it should be, while you're regularly high. For the smell is really horrible even for a place like this. I don't speak of it, merely from politeness."

"Ah, you horrid, insulting wretch! He positively stinks and talks about me."

"Oh-ho-ho-ho! If only the time for my requiem would come quickly: I should hear their tearful voices over my head, my wife's lament and my children's soft weeping!. . ."

"Well, that's a thing to fret for! They'll stuff themselves with funeral rice and go home. . . Oh, I wish somebody would wake up!"

"Avdotya Ignatyevna," said the insinuating government clerk, "wait a bit, the new arrivals will speak."

"And are there any young people among them?"

"Yes, there are, Avdotya Ignatyevna. There are some not more than lads."

"Oh, how welcome that would be!"

"Haven't they begun yet?" inquired his Excellency.

"Even those who came the day before yesterday haven't awakened yet, your Excellency. As you know, they sometimes don't speak for a week. It's a good job that to-day and yesterday and the day before they brought a whole lot. As it is, they are all last year's for seventy feet round."

"Yes, it will be interesting."

"Yes, your Excellency, they buried Tarasevitch, the privy councillor, to-day. I knew it from the voices. I know his nephew, he helped to lower the coffin just now."

"Hm, where is he, then?"

"Five steps from you, your Excellency, on the left. . . Almost at your feet. You should make his acquaintance, your Excellency."

"Hm, no – it's not for me to make advances."

"Oh, he will begin of himself, your Excellency. He will be flattered. Leave it to me, your Excellency, and I. . ."

"Oh, oh!. . . What is happening to me?" croaked the frightened voice of a new arrival.

"A new arrival, your Excellency, a new arrival, thank God! And how quick he's been! Sometimes they don't say a word for a week."

"Oh, I believe it's a young man!" Avdotya Ignatyevna cried shrilly.

"I . . . I . . . it was a complication, and so sudden!" faltered the young man again. "Only the evening before, Schultz said to me, 'There's a complication,' and I died suddenly before morning. Oh! Oh!"

"Well, there's no help for it, young man," the general observed graciously, evidently pleased at a new arrival. "You must be comforted. You are kindly welcome to our Vale of Jehoshaphat, so to call it. We are kind-hearted people, you will come to know us and appreciate us. Major-General Vassili Vassilitch Pervoyedov, at your service."

"Oh, no, no! Certainly not! I was at Schultz's; I had a complication, you know, at first it was my chest and a cough, and then I caught a cold: my lungs and influenza . . . and all of a sudden, quite unexpectedly . . . the worst of all was its being so unexpected."

"You say it began with the chest," the government clerk put in suavely, as though he wished to reassure the new arrival.

"Yes, my chest and catarrh and then no catarrh, but still the chest, and I couldn't breathe . . . and you know. . ."

"I know, I know. But if it was the chest you ought to have gone to Ecke and not to Schultz."

"You know, I kept meaning to go to Botkin's, and all at once . . ."

"Botkin is quite prohibitive," observed the general.

"Oh, no, he is not forbidding at all; I've heard he is so attentive and foretells everything beforehand."

"His Excellency was referring to his fees," the government clerk corrected him.

"Oh, not at all, he only asks three roubles, and he makes such an examination, and gives you a prescription . . . and I was very anxious to see him, for I have been told. . . Well, gentlemen, had I better go to Ecke or to Botkin?"

"What? To whom?" The general's corpse shook with agreeable laughter. The government clerk echoed it in falsetto.

"Dear boy, dear, delightful boy, how I love you!" Avdotya Ignatyevna squealed ecstatically. "I wish they had put some one like you next to me."

No, that was too much! And these were the dead of our times! Still, I ought to listen to more and not be in too great a hurry to draw conclusions. That snivelling new arrival – I remember him just now in his coffin – had the expression of a frightened chicken, the most revolting expression in the world! However, let us wait and see.

But what happened next was such a Bedlam that I could not keep it all in my memory. For a great many woke up at once; an official – a civil councillor – woke up, and began discussing at once the project of a new sub-committee in a government department and of the probable transfer of various functionaries in connection with the sub-committee – which very greatly interested the general. I must confess I learnt a great deal that was new myself, so much so that I marvelled at the channels by which one may sometimes in the metropolis learn government news. Then an engineer half woke up, but for a long time muttered absolute nonsense, so that our friends left off worrying him and let him lie till he was ready. At last the distinguished lady who had been buried in the morning under the catafalque showed symptoms of the reanimation of the tomb. Lebeziatnikov (for the obsequious lower court councillor whom I detested and who lay beside General Pervoyedov was called, it appears, Lebeziatnikov) became much excited, and surprised that they were all waking up so soon this time. I must own I was surprised too; though some of those who woke had been buried for three days, as, for instance, a very young girl of sixteen who kept giggling . . . giggling in a horrible and predatory way.

"Your Excellency, privy councillor Tarasevitch is waking!" Lebeziatnikov announced with extreme fussiness.

"Eh? What?" the privy councillor, waking up suddenly, mumbled, with a lisp of disgust. There was a note of ill-humoured peremptoriness in the sound of his voice.

I listened with curiosity – for during the last few days I had heard something about Tarasevitch – shocking and upsetting in the extreme.

"It's I, your Excellency, so far only I."

"What is your petition? What do you want?"

"Merely to inquire after your Excellency's health; in these unaccustomed surroundings every one feels at first, as it were, oppressed. . . General Pervoyedov wishes to have the honour of making your Excellency's acquaintance, and hopes. . ."

"I've never heard of him."

"Surely, your Excellency! General Pervoyedov, Vassili Vassilitch. . ."

"Are you General Pervoyedov?"

"No, your Excellency, I am only the lower court councillor Lebeziatnikov, at your service, but General Pervoyedov. . ."

"Nonsense! And I beg you to leave me alone."

"Let him be." General Pervoyedov at last himself checked with dignity the disgusting officiousness of his sycophant in the grave.

"He is not fully awake, your Excellency, you must consider that; it's the novelty of it all. When he is fully awake he will take it differently."

"Let him be," repeated the general.

"Vassili Vassilitch! Hey, your Excellency!" a perfectly new voice shouted loudly and aggressively from close beside Avdotya Ignatyevna. It was a voice of gentlemanly insolence, with the languid pronunciation now fashionable and an arrogant drawl. "I've been watching you all for the last two hours. Do you remember me, Vassili Vassilitch? My name is Klinevitch, we met at the Volokonskys' where you, too, were received as a guest, I am sure I don't know why."

"What, Count Pyotr Petrovitch?. . . Can it be really you . . . and at such an early age? How sorry I am to hear it."

"Oh, I am sorry myself, though I really don't mind, and I want to amuse myself as far as I can everywhere. And I am not a count but a baron, only a baron. We are only a set of scurvy barons, risen from being flunkeys, but why I don't know and I don't care. I am only a scoundrel of the pseudo-aristocratic society, and I am regarded as 'a charming polisson.' My father is a wretched little general, and my mother was at one time received en haut lieu. With the help of the Jew Zifel I forged fifty thousand rouble notes last year and then I informed against him, while Julie Charpentier de Lusignan carried off the money to Bordeaux. And only fancy, I was engaged to be married – to a girl still at school, three months under sixteen, with a dowry of ninety thousand. Avdotya Ignatyevna, do you remember how you seduced me fifteen years ago when I was a boy of fourteen in the Corps des Pages?"

"Ah, that's you, you rascal! Well, you are a godsend, anyway, for here. . ."

"You were mistaken in suspecting your neighbour, the business gentleman, of unpleasant fragrance. . . I said nothing, but I laughed. The stench came from me: they had to bury me in a nailed-up coffin."

"Ugh, you horrid creature! Still, I am glad you are here; you can't imagine the lack of life and wit here."

"Quite so, quite so, and I intend to start here something original. Your Excellency – I don't mean you, Pervoyedov – your Excellency the other one, Tarasevitch, the privy councillor! Answer! I am Klinevitch, who took you to Mlle. Furie in Lent, do you hear?"

"I do, Klinevitch, and I am delighted, and trust me. . ."

"I wouldn't trust you with a halfpenny, and I don't care. I simply want to kiss you, dear old man, but luckily I can't. Do you know, gentlemen, what this grandpère's little game was? He died three or four days ago, and would you believe it, he left a deficit of four hundred thousand government money from the fund for widows and orphans. He was the sole person in control of it for some reason, so that his accounts were not audited for the last eight years. I can fancy what long faces they all have now, and what they call him. It's a delectable thought, isn't it? I have been wondering for the last year how a wretched old man of seventy, gouty and rheumatic, succeeded in preserving the physical energy for his debaucheries – and now the riddle is solved! Those widows and orphans – the very thought of them must have egged him on! I knew about it long ago, I was the only one who did know; it was Julie told me, and as soon as I discovered it, I attacked him in a friendly way at once in Easter week: 'Give me twenty-five thousand, if you don't they'll look into your accounts to-morrow.' And just fancy, he had only thirteen thousand left then, so it seems it was very apropos his dying now. Grand-père, grand-père, do you hear?"

"Cher Klinevitch, I quite agree with you, and there was no need for you . . . to go into such details. Life is so full of suffering and torment and so little to make up for it . . . that I wanted at last to be at rest, and so far as I can see I hope to get all I can from here too."

"I bet that he has already sniffed Katiche Berestov!"

"Who? What Katiche?" There was a rapacious quiver in the old man's voice.

"A-ah, what Katiche? Why, here on the left, five paces from me and ten from you. She has been here for five days, and if only you knew, grand-père, what a little wretch she is! Of good family and breeding and a monster, a regular monster! I did not introduce her to any one there, I was the only one who knew her . . . Katiche, answer!"

"He-he-he!" the girl responded with a jangling laugh, in which there was a note of something as sharp as the prick of a needle. "He-he-he!"

"And a little blonde?" the grand-père faltered, drawling out the syllables.

"He-he-he!"

"I . . . have long . . . I have long," the old man faltered breathlessly, "cherished the dream of a little fair thing of fifteen and just in such surroundings."

"Ach, the monster!" cried Avdotya Ignatyevna.

"Enough!" Klinevitch decided. "I see there is excellent material. We shall soon arrange things better. The great thing is to spend the rest of our time cheerfully; but what time? Hey, you, government clerk, Lebeziatnikov or whatever it is, I hear that's your name!"

"Semyon Yevseitch Lebeziatnikov, lower court councillor, at your service, very, very, very much delighted to meet you."

"I don't care whether you are delighted or not, but you seem to know everything here. Tell me first of all how it is we can talk? I've been wondering ever since yesterday. We are dead and yet we are talking and seem to be moving – and yet we are not talking and not moving. What jugglery is this?"

"If you want an explanation, baron, Platon Nikolaevitch could give you one better than I."

"What Platon Nikolaevitch is that? To the point. Don't beat about the bush."

"Platon Nikolaevitch is our home-grown philosopher, scientist and Master of Arts. He has brought out several philosophical works, but for the last three months he has been getting quite drowsy, and there is no stirring him up now. Once a week he mutters something utterly irrelevant."

"To the point, to the point!"

"He explains all this by the simplest fact, namely, that when we were living on the surface we mistakenly thought that death there was death. The body revives, as it were, here, the remains of life are concentrated, but only in consciousness.

I don't know how to express it, but life goes on, as it were, by inertia. In his opinion everything is concentrated somewhere in consciousness and goes on for two or three months . . . sometimes even for half a year. . . There is one here, for instance, who is almost completely decomposed, but once every six weeks he suddenly utters one word, quite senseless of course, about some bobok, 'Bobok, bobok,' but you see that an imperceptible speck of life is still warm within him."

"It's rather stupid. Well, and how is it I have no sense of smell and yet I feel there's a stench?"

"That . . . he-he. . . Well, on that point our philosopher is a bit foggy. It's apropos of smell, he said, that the stench one perceives here is, so to speak, moral – he-he! It's the stench of the soul, he says, that in these two or three months it may have time to recover itself . . . and this is, so to speak, the last mercy. . . Only, I think, baron, that these are mystic ravings very excusable in his position. . ."

"Enough; all the rest of it, I am sure, is nonsense. The great thing is that we have two or three months more of life and then – bobok! I propose to spend these two months as agreeably as possible, and so to arrange everything on a new basis. Gentlemen! I propose to cast aside all shame."

"Ah, let us cast aside all shame, let us!" many voices could be heard saying; and strange to say, several new voices were audible, which must have belonged to others newly awakened. The engineer, now fully awake, boomed out his agreement with peculiar delight. The girl Katiche giggled gleefully.

"Oh, how I long to cast off all shame!" Avdotya Ignatyevna exclaimed rapturously.

"I say, if Avdotya Ignatyevna wants to cast off all shame. . ."

"No, no, no, Klinevitch, I was ashamed up there all the same, but here I should like to cast off shame, I should like it awfully."

"I understand, Klinevitch," boomed the engineer, "that you want to rearrange life here on new and rational principles."

"Oh, I don't care a hang about that! For that we'll wait for Kudeyarov who was brought here yesterday. When he wakes he'll tell you all about it. He is such a personality, such a titanic personality! To-morrow they'll bring along another natural scientist, I believe, an officer for certain, and three or four days later a journalist, and, I believe, his editor with him. But deuce take them all, there will be a little group of us anyway, and things will arrange themselves. Though meanwhile I don't want us to be telling lies. That's all I care about, for that is one thing that matters. One cannot exist on the surface without lying, for life and lying are synonymous, but here we will amuse ourselves by not lying. Hang it all, the grave has some value after all! We'll all tell our stories aloud, and we won't be ashamed of anything. First of all I'll tell you about myself. I am one of the predatory kind, you know. All that was bound and held in check by rotten cords up there on the surface. Away with cords and let us spend these two months in shameless truthfulness! Let us strip and be naked!"

"Let us be naked, let us be naked!" cried all the voices.

"I long to be naked, I long to be," Avdotya Ignatyevna shrilled.

"Ah . . . ah, I see we shall have fun here; I don't want Ecke after all."

"No, I tell you. Give me a taste of life!"

"He-he-he!" giggled Katiche.

"The great thing is that no one can interfere with us, and though I see Pervoyedov is in a temper, he can't reach me with his hand. Grand-père, do you agree?"

"I fully agree, fully, and with the utmost satisfaction, but on condition that Katiche is the first to give us her biography."

"I protest! I protest with all my heart!" General Pervoyedov brought out firmly.

"Your Excellency!" the scoundrel Lebeziatnikov persuaded him in a murmur of fussy excitement, "your Excellency, it will be to our advantage to agree. Here, you see, there's this girl's . . . and all their little affairs."

"There's the girl, it's true, but. . ."

"It's to our advantage, your Excellency, upon my word it is! If only as an experiment, let us try it. . ."

"Even in the grave they won't let us rest in peace."

"In the first place, General, you were playing preference in the grave, and in the second we don't care a hang about you," drawled Klinevitch.

"Sir, I beg you not to forget yourself."

"What? Why, you can't get at me, and I can tease you from here as though you were Julie's lapdog. And another thing, gentlemen, how is he a general here? He was a general there, but here is mere refuse."

"No, not mere refuse. . . Even here. . ."

"Here you will rot in the grave and six brass buttons will be all that will be left of you."

"Bravo, Klinevitch, ha-ha-ha!" roared voices.

"I have served my sovereign. . . I have the sword. . ."

"Your sword is only fit to prick mice, and you never drew it even for that."

"That makes no difference; I formed a part of the whole."

"There are all sorts of parts in a whole."

"Bravo, Klinevitch, bravo! Ha-ha-ha!"

"I don't understand what the sword stands for," boomed the engineer.

"We shall run away from the Prussians like mice, they'll crush us to powder!" cried a voice in the distance that was unfamiliar to me, that was positively spluttering with glee.

"The sword, sir, is an honour," the general cried, but only I heard him. There arose a prolonged and furious roar, clamour, and hubbub, and only the hysterically impatient squeals of Avdotya Ignatyevna were audible.

"But do let us make haste! Ah, when are we going to begin to cast off all shame!"

"Oh-ho-ho!. . . The soul does in truth pass through torments!" exclaimed the voice of the plebeian, "and . . ."

And here I suddenly sneezed. It happened suddenly and unintentionally, but the effect was striking: all became as silent as one expects it to be in a churchyard, it all vanished like a dream. A real silence of the tomb set in. I don't believe they were ashamed on account of my presence: they had made up their minds to cast off all shame! I waited five minutes – not a word, not a sound. It cannot be supposed that they were afraid of my informing the police; for what could the police do to them? I must conclude that they had some secret unknown to the living, which they carefully concealed from every mortal.

"Well, my dears," I thought, "I shall visit you again." And with those words, I left the cemetery.

No, that I cannot admit; no, I really cannot! The bobok case does not trouble me (so that is what that bobok signified!).

Depravity in such a place, depravity of the last aspirations, depravity of sodden and rotten corpses – and not even sparing the last moments of consciousness! Those moments have been granted, vouchsafed to them, and . . . and, worst of all, in such a place! No, that I cannot admit.

I shall go to other tombs, I shall listen everywhere. Certainly one ought to listen everywhere and not merely at one spot in order to form an idea. Perhaps one may come across something reassuring.

But I shall certainly go back to those. They promised their biographies and anecdotes of all sorts. Tfoo! But I shall go, I shall certainly go; it is a question of conscience!

I shall take it to the *Citizen*; the editor there has had his portrait exhibited too. Maybe he will print it.

THE VERY IMAGE

Auguste Villiers de l'Isle-Adam

Jean-Marie-Mathias-Philippe-Auguste, Comte de Villiers de l'Isle-Adam (1838–1889) was born into an aristocratic family who had been left impoverished by the French Revolution. He moved to Paris at the age of eighteen where he met Baudelaire who introduced him to the works of Edgar Allan Poe and encouraged his interest in the occult. Villiers de l'Isle-Adam was embraced by the decadent movement and is mentioned in Huysmans' *A Rebours*.

Darting their dark eyes everywhere.

– C. Baudelaire

One grey November morning I was hurrying along the embankments. The air was damp with a cold drizzle. Black-clad passers-by, sheltering under shapeless umbrellas, came and went.

The yellow Seine swept its merchant vessels along as if they were outsize cockchafers. On the bridges, the wind kept snatching at hats whose owners fought with space to save them, with those convulsive gestures which are always such a painful sight for artists' eyes.

My ideas were pale and misty; the thought of a business appointment, arranged the day before, was nagging at my mind. Time was pressing; and I decided to shelter under the porch of a doorway, from where it would be easier for me to signal a cab.

At that very moment I noticed, right beside me, the entrance of a square, solid-looking building.

It had reared up in the mist like a stone apparition, and, despite its rigid architecture, despite the dismal, eerie vapour in which it was enveloped, I recognized a certain cordial air of hospitality about it which reassured me.

"The people who live here," I said to myself, "must surely be sedentary folk. This threshold has an inviting look: isn't the door open?"

So, in the politest possible way, with a contented air, hat in hand, and even planning a complimentary speech to make to the mistress of the house, I went smilingly in, and promptly found myself before a room with a glass roof through which a ghastly light was falling.

There were pillars on which clothes, mufflers, and hats had been hung.

Marble tables were installed on all sides.

Some people were there with legs outstretched, heads raised, staring eyes, and matter-of-fact expressions, who appeared to be meditating.

And their gaze was devoid of thought, their faces the colour of the weather.

There were portfolios lying open and papers spread out beside each one of them.

And then I realized that the mistress of the house, on whose courteous welcome I had been counting, was none other than Death.

I looked at my hosts.

It was obvious that, in order to escape from the worries of a harassing life, most of them had murdered their bodies, hoping in that way to obtain a little more comfort.

As I was listening to the noise of the brass taps fastened to the wall and intended for the daily refreshment of those mortal remains, I heard the rumbling of a cab. It was stopping outside the establishment. I reflected that my businessmen were waiting, and turned round to take advantage of my good luck.

The cab had, in fact, just disgorged, on the threshold of the building, some students on the spree who needed to see death to believe in it.

I looked at the empty carriage and said to the driver:

"The Passage de l'Opéra!"

A little later, on the boulevards, the weather struck me as duller than ever, on account of the absence of any horizon. The skeletal trees looked as if, with the tips of their black branches, they were vaguely pointing out pedestrians to the sleepy policemen.

The carriage sped along.

The passers-by, seen through the window, gave me the impression of flowing water.

On arriving at my destination, I jumped out on to the pavement and plunged into the arcade, which was full of care-worn faces.

At the end I noticed, right in front of me, the entrance to a café – since burnt down in a famous fire (for life is a dream). It was tucked away at the back of a sort of shed, under a square, sinister archway.

"It is there," I thought, "that my businessmen are waiting for me, glass in hand, their shining eyes defying Fate."

I accordingly turned the handle of the door and promptly found myself in a room into which a ghastly light was filtering through the windows.

There were pillars on which clothes, mufflers, and hats had been hung.

Marble tables were installed on all sides.

Some people were there with legs outstretched, heads raised, staring eyes, and matter-of-fact expressions, who appeared to be meditating.

And their faces were the colour of the weather, their gaze devoid of thought.

There were portfolios lying open and spread out beside each one of them.

I looked at those men.

It was obvious that, in order to escape from the obsessions of an unbearable conscience, most of them had long ago murdered their "souls," hoping in that way to obtain a little more comfort.

As I was listening to the noise of the brass taps fastened to the wall and intended for the daily refreshment of those mortal remains, the memory of the rumbling cab came back to my mind.

"That driver," I said to myself, "must have been afflicted in the course of time by a sort of coma, to have brought me back, after so many circumconvolutions, to my starting-point. All the same, I must admit (if there has been a mistake) that *the second glimpse is more sinister than the first!*"

I therefore silently shut the glass door and went home, firmly resolved – despite the force of example and whatever might become of me – never to do any business.

DRACULA'S GUEST

Bram Stoker

Abraham Stoker (1847–1912) was born in Dublin. He was an invalid as a child and did not learn how to walk until he was seven years old. A trained lawyer, Stoker worked for most of his life as a theatre administrator for the actor-manager Henry Irving, who may have helped to inspire the character of Dracula. Stoker's literary output was prodigious, but *Dracula* remains his most influential novel. In 1878 he married Florence Balcombe, who had previously been courted by Oscar Wilde.

When we started for our drive the sun was shining brightly on Munich, and the air was full of the joyousness of early summer. Just as we were about to depart, Herr Delbrück (the maître d'hôtel of the Quatre Saisons, where I was staying) came down, bareheaded, to the carriage and, after wishing me a pleasant drive, said to the coachman, still holding his hand on the handle of the carriage door:

"Remember you are back by nightfall. The sky looks bright but there is a shiver in the north wind that says there may be a sudden storm. But I am sure you will not be late." Here he smiled, and added, "for you know what night it is."

Johann answered with an emphatic, "Ja, mein Herr," and, touching his hat, drove off quickly. When we had cleared the town, I said, after signalling to him to stop:

"Tell me, Johann, what is tonight?"

He crossed himself, as he answered laconically: "Walpurgis nacht." Then he took out his watch, a great, old-fashioned German silver thing as big as a turnip, and looked at it, with his eyebrows gathered together and a little impatient shrug of his shoulders. I realised that this was his way of respectfully protesting against the unnecessary delay, and sank back in the carriage, merely motioning him to proceed. He started off rapidly, as if to make up for lost time. Every now and then the horses seemed to throw up their heads and sniffed the air suspiciously. On such occasions I often looked round in alarm. The road was pretty bleak, for we were traversing a sort of high, wind-swept plateau. As we drove, I saw a road that looked but little used, and which seemed to dip through a little, winding valley. It looked so inviting that, even at the risk of offending him, I called Johann to stop – and when he had pulled up, I told him I would like to drive down that road. He made all sorts of excuses, and frequently crossed himself as he spoke. This somewhat piqued my curiosity, so I asked him various questions. He answered fencingly, and repeatedly looked at his watch in protest. Finally I said:

"Well, Johann, I want to go down this road. I shall not ask you to come unless you like; but tell me why you do not like to go, that is all I ask." For answer he seemed to throw himself off the box, so quickly did he reach the ground. Then he stretched out his hands appealingly to me, and implored me not to go. There was just enough of English mixed with the German for me to understand the drift of his talk. He seemed always just about to tell me something – the very idea of which evidently frightened him; but each time he pulled himself up, saying, as he crossed himself: "Walpurgis-Nacht!"

I tried to argue with him, but it was difficult to argue with a man when I did not know his language. The advantage certainly rested with him, for although he began to speak in English, of a very crude and broken kind, he always got excited and broke into his native tongue – and every time he did so, he looked at his watch. Then the horses became restless and sniffed the air. At this he grew very pale, and, looking around in a frightened way, he suddenly jumped forward, took them by the bridles and led them on some twenty feet. I followed, and asked why he had done this. For answer he crossed himself, pointed to the spot we had left and drew his carriage in the direction of the other road, indicating a cross, and said, first in German, then in English: "Buried him – him what killed themselves."

I remembered the old custom of burying suicides at cross-roads: "Ah! I see, a suicide. How interesting!" But for the life of me I could not make out why the horses were frightened.

Whilst we were talking, we heard a sort of sound between a yelp and a bark. It was far away; but the horses got very restless, and it took Johann all his time to quiet them. He was pale, and said, "It sounds like a wolf – but yet there are no wolves here now."

"No?" I said, questioning him; "isn't it long since the wolves were so near the city?"

"Long, long," he answered, "in the spring and summer; but with the snow the wolves have been here not so long."

Whilst he was petting the horses and trying to quiet them, dark clouds drifted rapidly across the sky. The sunshine passed away, and a breath of cold wind seemed to drift past us. It was only a breath, however, and more in the nature of a warning than a fact, for the sun came out brightly again. Johann looked under his lifted hand at the horizon and said:

"The storm of snow, he comes before long time." Then he looked at his watch again, and, straightway holding his reins firmly – for the horses were still pawing the ground restlessly and shaking their heads – he climbed to his box as though the time had come for proceeding on our journey.

I felt a little obstinate and did not at once get into the carriage.

"Tell me," I said, "about this place where the road leads," and I pointed down.

Again he crossed himself and mumbled a prayer, before he answered, "It is unholy."

"What is unholy?" I enquired.

"The village."

"Then there is a village?"

"No, no. No one lives there hundreds of years." My curiosity was piqued, "But you said there was a village."

"There was."

"Where is it now?"

Whereupon he burst out into a long story in German and English, so mixed up that I could not quite understand exactly what he said, but roughly I gathered that long ago, hundreds of years, men had died there and been buried in their graves; and sounds were heard under the clay, and when the graves were opened, men and women were found rosy with life, and their mouths red with blood. And so, in haste to save their lives (aye, and their souls! – and here he crossed himself) those who were left fled away to other places, where the living lived, and the dead were dead and not – not something. He was evidently afraid to speak the last words. As he proceeded with his narration, he grew more and more excited. It seemed as if his imagination had got hold of him, and he ended in a perfect paroxysm of fear – white-faced, perspiring, trembling and looking round him, as if expecting that some dreadful presence would manifest itself there in the bright sunshine on the open plain. Finally, in an agony of desperation, he cried:

"Walpurgis nacht!" and pointed to the carriage for me to get in. All my English blood rose at this, and, standing back, I said:

"You are afraid, Johann – you are afraid. Go home; I shall return alone; the walk will do me good." The carriage door was open. I took from the seat my oak walking-stick – which I always carry on my holiday excursions – and closed the door, pointing back to Munich, and said, "Go home, Johann – Walpurgis-nacht doesn't concern Englishmen."

The horses were now more restive than ever, and Johann was trying to hold them in, while excitedly imploring me not to do anything so foolish. I pitied the poor fellow, he was deeply in earnest; but all the same I could not help laughing. His English was quite gone now. In his anxiety he had forgotten that his only means of making me understand was to talk my language, so he jabbered away in his native German. It began to be a little tedious. After giving the direction, "Home!" I turned to go down the cross-road into the valley.

With a despairing gesture, Johann turned his horses towards Munich. I leaned on my stick and looked after him. He went slowly along the road for a while: then there came over the crest of the hill a man tall and thin. I could see so much in the distance. When he drew near the horses, they began to jump and kick about, then to scream with terror. Johann could not hold them in; they bolted down the road, running away madly. I watched them out of sight, then looked for the stranger, but I found that he, too, was gone.

With a light heart I turned down the side road through the deepening valley to which Johann had objected. There was not the slightest reason, that I could see, for his objection; and I daresay I tramped for a couple of hours without thinking of time or distance, and certainly without seeing a person or a house. So far as the place was concerned, it was desolation itself. But I did not notice this particularly till, on turning a bend in the road, I came upon a scattered fringe of wood; then I recognised that I had been impressed unconsciously by the desolation of the region through which I had passed.

I sat down to rest myself, and began to look around. It struck me that it was considerably colder than it had been at the commencement of my walk – a sort of sighing sound seemed to be around me, with, now and then, high overhead, a sort of muffled roar. Looking upwards I noticed that great thick clouds were drifting rapidly across the sky from North to South at a great height. There were signs of coming storm in some lofty stratum of the air. I was a little chilly, and, thinking that it was the sitting still after the exercise of walking, I resumed my journey.

The ground I passed over was now much more picturesque. There were no striking objects that the eye might single out; but in all there was a charm of beauty. I took little heed of time and it was only when the deepening twilight forced itself upon me that I began to think of how I should find my way home. The brightness of the day had gone. The air was cold, and the drifting of clouds high overhead was more marked. They were accompanied by a sort of far-away rushing sound, through which seemed to come at intervals that mysterious cry which the driver had said came from a wolf. For a while I hesitated. I had said I would see the deserted village, so on I went, and presently came on a wide stretch of open country, shut in by hills all around. Their sides were covered with trees which spread down to the plain, dotting, in clumps, the gentler slopes and hollows which showed here and there. I followed with my eye the winding of the road, and saw that it curved close to one of the densest of these clumps and was lost behind it.

As I looked there came a cold shiver in the air, and the snow began to fall. I thought of the miles and miles of bleak country I had passed, and then hurried on to seek the shelter of the wood in front. Darker and darker grew the sky, and faster and heavier fell the snow, till the earth before and around me was a glistening white carpet the further edge of which was lost in misty vagueness. The road was here but crude, and when on the level its boundaries were not so marked, as when it passed through the cuttings; and in a little while I found that I must have strayed from it, for I missed underfoot the hard surface, and my feet sank deeper in the grass and moss. Then the wind grew stronger and blew with ever increasing force, till I was fain to run before it. The air became icy-cold, and in spite of my exercise I began to suffer. The snow was now falling so thickly and whirling around me in such rapid eddies that I could hardly keep my eyes open. Every now and then the heavens were torn asunder by vivid lightning, and in the flashes I could see ahead of me a great mass of trees, chiefly yew and cypress all heavily coated with snow.

I was soon amongst the shelter of the trees, and there, in comparative silence, I could hear the rush of the wind high overhead. Presently the blackness of the storm had become merged in the darkness of the night. By-and-by the storm seemed to be passing away: it now only came in fierce puffs or blasts. At such moments the weird sound of the wolf appeared to be echoed by many similar sounds around me.

Now and again, through the black mass of drifting cloud, came a straggling ray of moonlight, which lit up the expanse, and showed me that I was at the edge of a dense mass of cypress and yew trees. As the snow had ceased to fall, I walked out from the shelter and began to investigate more closely. It appeared to me that, amongst so many old foundations as I had passed, there might be still standing a house in which, though in ruins, I could find some sort of shelter for a while. As I skirted the edge of the copse, I found that a low wall encircled it, and following this I presently found an opening. Here the cypresses formed an alley leading up to a square mass of some kind of building. Just as I caught sight of this, however, the drifting clouds obscured the moon, and I passed up the path in darkness. The wind must have grown colder, for I felt myself shiver as I walked; but there was hope of shelter, and I groped my way blindly on.

I stopped, for there was a sudden stillness. The storm had passed; and, perhaps in sympathy with nature's silence, my heart seemed to cease to beat. But this was only momentarily; for suddenly the moonlight broke through the clouds, showing me that I was in a graveyard, and that the square object before me was a great massive tomb of marble, as white as the snow that lay on and all around it. With the moonlight there came a fierce sigh of the storm, which appeared to resume its course with a long, low howl, as of many dogs or wolves. I was awed and shocked, and felt the cold perceptibly grow upon me till it seemed to grip me by the heart. Then while the flood of moonlight still fell on the marble tomb, the storm gave further evidence of renewing, as though it was returning on its track. Impelled by some sort of fascination, I approached the sepulchre to see what it was, and why such a thing stood alone in such a place. I walked around it, and read, over the Doric door, in German:

COUNTESS DOLINGEN OF GRATZ
IN STYRIA
SOUGHT AND FOUND DEATH
1801

On the top of the tomb, seemingly driven through the solid marble – for the structure was composed of a few vast blocks of stone – was a great iron spike or stake. On going to the back I saw, graven in great Russian letters:

"The dead travel fast."

There was something so weird and uncanny about the whole thing that it gave me a turn and made me feel quite faint. I began to wish, for the first time, that I had taken Johann's advice. Here a thought struck me, which came under almost mysterious circumstances and with a terrible shock. This was Walpurgis Night!

Walpurgis Night, when, according to the belief of millions of people, the devil was abroad – when the graves were opened and the dead came forth and walked. When all evil things of earth and air and water held revel. This very place the driver had specially shunned. This was the depopulated village of centuries ago. This was where the suicide lay; and this was the place where I was alone – un-manned, shivering with cold in a shroud of snow with a wild storm gathering again upon me! It took all my philosophy, all the religion I had been taught, all my courage, not to collapse in a paroxysm of fright.

And now a perfect tornado burst upon me. The ground shook as though thou-sands of horses thundered across it; and this time the storm bore on its icy wings, not snow, but great hailstones which drove with such violence that they might have come from the thongs of Balearic slingers – hailstones that beat down leaf and branch and made the shelter of the cypresses of no more avail than though their stems were standing-corn. At the first I had rushed to the nearest tree; but I was soon fain to leave it and seek the only spot that seemed to afford refuge, the deep Doric doorway of the marble tomb. There, crouching against the massive bronze door, I gained a certain amount of protection from the beating of the hailstones, for now they only drove against me as they ricocheted from the ground and the side of the marble.

As I leaned against the door, it moved slightly and opened inwards. The shelter of even a tomb was welcome in that pitiless tempest, and I was about to enter it when there came a flash of forked-lightning that lit up the whole expanse of the heavens. In the instant, as I am a living man, I saw, as my eyes were turned into the darkness of the tomb, a beautiful woman, with rounded cheeks and red lips, seemingly sleeping on a bier. As the thunder broke overhead, I was grasped as by the hand of a giant and hurled out into the storm. The whole thing was so sudden that, before I could realise the shock, moral as well as physical, I found the hailstones beating me down. At the same time I had a strange, dominating feeling that I was not alone. I looked towards the tomb. Just then there came another blinding flash, which seemed to strike the iron stake that surmounted the tomb and to pour through to the earth, blasting and crumbling the marble, as in a burst of flame. The dead woman rose for a moment of agony, while she was lapped in the flame, and her bitter scream of pain was drowned in the thundercrash. The last thing I heard was this mingling of dreadful sound, as again I was seized in the giant-grasp and dragged away, while the hailstones beat on me, and the air around seemed reverberant with the howling of wolves. The last sight that I remembered was a vague, white, moving mass, as if all the graves around me had sent out the phantoms of their sheeted-dead, and that they were closing in on me through the white cloudiness of the driving hail.

Gradually there came a sort of vague beginning of consciousness; then a sense of weariness that was dreadful. For a time I remembered nothing; but slowly my senses returned. My feet seemed positively racked with pain, yet I could not move them. They seemed to be numbed. There was an icy feeling at the back of my neck and all down my spine, and my ears, like my feet, were dead, yet in torment; but there was in my breast a sense of warmth which was, by comparison, delicious. It was as a nightmare – a physical nightmare, if one may use such an expression; for some heavy weight on my chest made it difficult for me to breathe.

This period of semi-lethargy seemed to remain a long time, and as it faded away I must have slept or swooned. Then came a sort of loathing, like the first stage of sea-sickness, and a wild desire to be free from something – I knew not what. A vast stillness enveloped me, as though all the world were asleep or dead – only broken by the low panting as of some animal close to me. I felt a warm rasping at my throat, then came a consciousness of the awful truth, which chilled me to the heart and sent the blood surging up through my brain. Some great animal was lying on me and now licking my throat. I feared to stir, for some instinct of prudence bade me lie still; but the brute seemed to realise that there was now some change in me, for it raised its head. Through my eyelashes I saw above me the two great flaming eyes of a gigantic wolf. Its sharp white teeth gleamed in the gaping red mouth, and I could feel its hot breath fierce and acrid upon me.

For another spell of time I remembered no more. Then I became conscious of a low growl, followed by a yelp, renewed again and again. Then, seemingly very far away, I heard a "Holloa! holloa!" as of many voices calling in unison. Cautiously I raised my head and looked in the direction whence the sound came; but the cemetery blocked my view. The wolf still continued to yelp in a strange way, and a red glare began to move round the grove of cypresses, as though following the sound. As the voices drew closer, the wolf yelped faster and louder. I feared to make either sound or motion. Nearer came the red glow, over the white pall which stretched into the darkness around me. Then all at once from beyond the trees there came at a trot a troop of horsemen bearing torches. The wolf rose from my breast and made for the cemetery. I saw one of the horsemen (soldiers by their caps and their long military cloaks) raise his carbine and take aim. A companion knocked up his arm, and I heard the ball whizz over my head. He had evidently taken my body for that of the wolf. Another sighted the animal as it slunk away, and a shot followed. Then, at a gallop, the troop rode forward – some towards me, others following the wolf as it disappeared amongst the snow-clad cypresses.

As they drew nearer I tried to move, but was powerless, although I could see and hear all that went on around me. Two or three of the soldiers jumped from their horses and knelt beside me. One of them raised my head, and placed his hand over my heart.

"Good news, comrades!" he cried. "His heart still beats!"

Then some brandy was poured down my throat; it put vigour into me, and I was able to open my eyes fully and look around. Lights and shadows were moving among the trees, and I heard men call to one another. They drew together, uttering frightened exclamations; and the lights flashed as the others came pouring out of the cemetery pell-mell, like men possessed. When the further ones came close to us, those who were around me asked them eagerly:

"Well, have you found him?"

The reply rang out hurriedly:

"No! no! Come away quick – quick! This is no place to stay, and on this of all nights!"

"What was it?" was the question, asked in all manner of keys. The answer came variously and all indefinitely as though the men were moved by some common impulse to speak, yet were restrained by some common fear from giving their thoughts.

"It – it – indeed!" gibbered one, whose wits had plainly given out for the moment.

"A wolf – and yet not a wolf!" another put in shudderingly.

"No use trying for him without the sacred bullet," a third remarked in a more ordinary manner.

"Serve us right for coming out on this night! Truly we have earned our thousand marks!" were the ejaculations of a fourth.

"There was blood on the broken marble," another said after a pause – "the lightning never brought that there. And for him – is he safe? Look at his throat! See, comrades, the wolf has been lying on him and keeping his blood warm."

The officer looked at my throat and replied:

"He is all right; the skin is not pierced. What does it all mean? We should never have found him but for the yelping of the wolf."

"What became of it?" asked the man who was holding up my head, and who seemed the least panic-stricken of the party, for his hands were steady and without tremor. On his sleeve was the chevron of a petty officer.

"It went to its home," answered the man, whose long face was pallid, and who actually shook with terror as he glanced around him fearfully. "There are graves enough there in which it may lie. Come, comrades – come quickly! Let us leave this cursed spot."

The officer raised me to a sitting posture, as he uttered a word of command; then several men placed me upon a horse. He sprang to the saddle behind me, took me in his arms, gave the word to advance; and, turning our faces away from the cypresses, we rode away in swift, military order.

As yet my tongue refused its office, and I was perforce silent. I must have fallen asleep; for the next thing I remembered was finding myself standing up, supported by a soldier on each side of me. It was almost broad daylight, and to the north a red streak of sunlight was reflected, like a path of blood, over the waste of snow. The officer was telling the men to say nothing of what they had seen, except that they found an English stranger, guarded by a large dog.

"Dog! that was no dog," cut in the man who had exhibited such fear. "I think I know a wolf when I see one."

The young officer answered calmly: "I said a dog."

"Dog!" reiterated the other ironically. It was evident that his courage was rising with the sun; and, pointing to me, he said, "Look at his throat. Is that the work of a dog, master?"

Instinctively I raised my hand to my throat, and as I touched it I cried out in pain. The men crowded round to look, some stooping down from their saddles; and again there came the calm voice of the young officer:

"A dog, as I said. If aught else were said we should only be laughed at."

I was then mounted behind a trooper, and we rode on into the suburbs of Munich. Here we came across a stray carriage, into which I was lifted, and it was driven off to the Quatre Saisons – the young officer accompanying me, whilst a trooper followed with his horse, and the others rode off to their barracks.

When we arrived, Herr Delbrück rushed so quickly down the steps to meet me, that it was apparent he had been watching within. Taking me by both hands he solicitously led me in. The officer saluted me and was turning to withdraw, when I recognised his purpose, and insisted that he should come to my rooms. Over a glass of wine I warmly thanked him and his brave comrades for saving me. He replied simply that he was more than glad, and that Herr Delbrück had at the first taken steps to make all the searching party pleased; at which ambiguous utterance the maître d'hôtel smiled, while the officer pleaded duty and withdrew.

"But Herr Delbrück," I enquired, "how and why was it that the soldiers searched for me?"

He shrugged his shoulders, as if in depreciation of his own deed, as he replied:

"I was so fortunate as to obtain leave from the commander of the regiment in which I served, to ask for volunteers."

"But how did you know I was lost?" I asked.

"The driver came hither with the remains of his carriage, which had been upset when the horses ran away."

"But surely you would not send a search-party of soldiers merely on this account?"

"Oh, no!" he answered; "but even before the coachman arrived, I had this telegram from the Boyar whose guest you are," and he took from his pocket a telegram which he handed to me, and I read:

> Bistritz. Be careful of my guest – his safety is most precious to me. Should aught happen to him, or if he be missed, spare nothing to find him and ensure his safety. He is English and therefore adventurous. There are often dangers from snow and wolves and night. Lose not a moment if you suspect harm to him. I answer your zeal with my fortune. – Dracula.

As I held the telegram in my hand, the room seemed to whirl around me; and, if the attentive maître d'hôtel had not caught me, I think I should have fallen. There was something so strange in all this, something so weird and impossible to imagine, that there grew on me a sense of my being in some way the sport of opposite forces – the mere vague idea of which seemed in a way to paralyse me. I was certainly under some form of mysterious protection. From a distant country had come, in the very nick of time, a message that took me out of the danger of the snow-sleep and the jaws of the wolf.

THE ROMANCE OF CERTAIN OLD CLOTHES

Henry James

Henry James (1843–1916) was an American who spent much of his life in Britain, finally becoming a British citizen a year before his death. His novels often explore the experience of upper-class Americans encountering Europe. James is the author of one of the best short ghost novels in the English language, *The Turn of the Screw*. He was the brother of the psychologist William James and the diarist Alice James.

Towards the middle of the eighteenth century, there lived in the Province of Massachusetts a widowed gentlewoman, the mother of three children. Her name is of little account: I shall take the liberty of calling her Mrs Willoughby – a name, like her own, of a highly respectable sound. She had been left a widow after some six years of marriage, and had devoted herself to the care of her progeny. These young persons grew up in a manner to reward her zeal and to gratify her fondest hopes. The first-born was a son, whom she had called Bernard, after his father. The others were daughters – born at an interval of three years apart. Good looks were traditional in the family, and this youthful trio were not likely to allow the tradition to perish. The boy was of that fair and ruddy complexion and of that athletic mould which in those days (as in these) were the sign of genuine English blood – a frank, affectionate young fellow, a deferential son, a patronising brother, and a steadfast friend. Clever, however, he was not; the wit of the family had been apportioned chiefly to his sisters. Mr Willoughby had been a great reader of Shakespeare, at a time when this pursuit implied more liberality of taste than at the present day, and in a community where it required much courage to patronise the drama even in the closet; and he had wished to record his admiration of the great poet by calling his daughters out of his favourite plays. Upon the elder he had bestowed the romantic name of Viola; and upon the younger, the more serious one of Perdita,[1] in memory of a little girl born between them, who had lived but a few weeks.

When Bernard Willoughby came to his sixteenth year, his mother put a brave face upon it, and prepared to execute her husband's last request. This had been an earnest entreaty that, at the proper age, his son should be sent out to England, to complete his education at the University of Oxford, which had been the seat of his own studies. Mrs Willoughby fancied that the lad's equal was not to be found in the two hemispheres, but she had the antique wifely submissiveness. She swallowed her sobs, and made up her boy's trunk and his simple provincial outfit, and sent him on his way across the seas. Bernard was entered at his father's college, and spent five years in England, without great honour, indeed, but with a vast deal of pleasure and no discredit. On leaving the University, he made the journey to France. In his twenty-third year, he took ship for home, prepared to find poor little New England (New England was very small in those days) an utterly intolerable place of abode. But there had been changes at home, as well as in Mr Bernard's opinions. He found his mother's house quite habitable, and his sisters grown into two very charming young ladies, with all the accomplishments and graces of the young women of Britain, and a certain native-grown gentle *brusquerie*[2] and wildness, which, if it was not an accomplishment, was certainly a grace the more. Bernard privately assured his mother that his sisters were fully a match for the most genteel young women in England; whereupon poor Mrs Willoughby you may be sure, bade them hold up their heads. Such was Bernard's opinion, and such, in a tenfold higher degree, was the opinion of Mr Arthur Lloyd. This gentleman, I hasten to add, was a college-mate of Mr Bernard, a young man of reputable family, of a good person and a handsome inheritance, which latter appurtenance he proposed to invest in trade in this country. He and Bernard were warm friends; they had crossed the ocean together, and the young American had lost no time in presenting him at his mother's house, where he had made quite as good an impression as that which he had received, and of which I have just given a hint.

The two sisters were at this time in all the freshness of their youthful bloom; each wearing, of course, this natural brilliancy in the manner that became her best. They were equally dissimilar in appearance and character. Viola, the elder – now in her twenty-second year – was tall and fair, with calm grey eyes and auburn tresses; a very faint likeness to the Viola of Shakespeare's comedy, whom I imagine as a brunette (if you will), but a slender, airy creature, full of the softest and finest emotions. Miss Willoughby, with her candid complexion, her fine arms, her majestic height, and her slow utterance, was not cut out for adventures. She would never have put on a man's jacket and hose; and, indeed, being a very plump beauty, it is perhaps as well that she would not. Perdita, too, might very well have exchanged the sweet melancholy of her name against something more in consonance with her aspect and disposition. She was a positive brunette, short of stature, light of foot, with a vivid dark brown eye. She had been from her childhood a creature of smiles and gaiety; and so far from making you wait for an answer to your speech, as her handsome sister was wont to do (while she gazed at you with her somewhat cold grey eyes), she had given you the choice of half a dozen, suggested by the successive clauses of your proposition, before you had got to the end of it.

The young girls were very glad to see their brother once more; but they found themselves quite able to maintain a reserve of goodwill for their brother's friend. Among the young men their friends and neighbours, the *belle jeunesse*[3] of the Colony, there were many excellent fellows, several devoted swains, and some two or three who enjoyed the reputation of universal charmers and conquerors. But the homebred arts and the somewhat boisterous gallantry of those honest young colonists were completely eclipsed by the good looks, the fine clothes, the punctilious courtesy, the perfect elegance, the immense information, of Mr

Arthur Lloyd. He was in reality no paragon; he was an honest, resolute, intelligent young man rich in pounds sterling, in his health and comfortable hopes, and his little capital of uninvested affections. But he was a gentleman; he had a handsome face; he had studied and travelled; he spoke French, he played on the flute, and he read verses aloud with very great taste. There were a dozen reasons why Miss Willoughby and her sister should forthwith have been rendered fastidious in the choice of their male acquaintance. The imagination of woman is especially adapted to the various small conventions and mysteries of polite society. Mr Lloyd's talk told our little New England maidens a vast deal more of the ways and means of people of fashion in European capitals than he had any idea of doing. It was delightful to sit by and hear him and Bernard discourse upon the fine people and fine things they had seen. They would all gather round the fire after tea, in the little wainscoted parlour – quite innocent then of any intention of being picturesque or of being anything else, indeed, than economical, and saving an outlay in stamped papers and tapestries – and the two young men would remind each other, across the rug, of this, that, and the other adventure. Viola and Perdita would often have given their ears to know exactly what adventure it was, and where it happened, and who was there, and what the ladies had on; but in those days a well-bred young woman was not expected to break into the conversation of her own movement or to ask too many questions; and the poor girls used therefore to sit fluttering behind the more languid – or more discreet – curiosity of their mother.

That they were both very fine girls Arthur Lloyd was not slow to discover; but it took him some time to satisfy himself as to the apportionment of their charms. He had a strong presentiment – an emotion of a nature entirely too cheerful to be called a foreboding – that he was destined to marry one of them; yet he was unable to arrive at a preference, and for such a consummation a preference was certainly indispensable, inasmuch as Lloyd was quite too gallant a fellow to make a choice by lot and be cheated of the heavenly delight of falling in love. He resolved to take things easily, and to let his heart speak. Meanwhile, he was on a very pleasant footing. Mrs Willoughby showed a dignified indifference to his "intentions", equally remote from a carelessness of her daughters' honour and from that odious alacrity to make him commit himself, which, in his quality of a young man of property, he had but too often encountered in the venerable dames of his native islands. As for Bernard, all that he asked was that his friend should take his sisters as his own; and as for the poor girls themselves, however each may have secretly longed for the monopoly of Mr Lloyd's attentions, they observed a very decent and modest and contented demeanour.

Towards each other, however, they were somewhat more on the offensive. They were good sisterly friends, betwixt whom it would take more than a day for the seeds of jealousy to sprout and bear fruit; but the young girls felt that the seeds had been sown on the day that Mr Lloyd came into the house. Each made up her mind that, if she should be slighted, she would bear her grief in silence, and that no one should be any the wiser; for if they had a great deal of love, they had also a great deal of pride. But each prayed in secret, nevertheless, that upon *her* the glory might fall. They had need of a vast deal of patience, of self-control, and of dissimulation. In those days, a young girl of decent breeding could make no advances whatever, and barely respond, indeed, to those that were made. She was expected to sit still in her chair with her eyes on the carpet, watching the spot where the mystic handkerchief should fall. Poor Arthur Lloyd was obliged to undertake his wooing in the little wainscoted parlour, before the eyes of Mrs Willoughby, her son, and his prospective sister-in-law. But youth and love are so cunning that a hundred signs and tokens might travel to and fro, and not one of these three pair of eyes detect them in their passage. The young girls had but one chamber and one bed between them, and for long hours together they were under each other's direct inspection. That each knew that she was being watched, however, made not a grain of difference in those little offices which they mutually rendered, or in the various household tasks which they performed in common. Neither flinched nor fluttered beneath the silent batteries of her sister's eyes. The only apparent change in their habits was that they had less to say to each other. It was impossible to talk about Mr Lloyd, and it was ridiculous to talk about anything else. By tacit agreement, they began to wear all their choice finery, and to devise such little implements of coquetry, in the way of ribbons and topknots and furbelows as were sanctioned by indubitable modesty. They executed in the same inarticulate fashion an agreement of sincerity on these delicate matters. "Is it better so?" Viola would ask, tying a bunch of ribbons on her bosom, and turning about from her glass to her sister. Perdita would look up gravely from her work and examine the decoration. "I think you had better give it another loop," she would say, with great solemnity, looking hard at her sister with eyes that added, "upon my honour!" So they were forever stitching and trimming their petticoats, and pressing out their muslins, and contriving washes and ointments and cosmetics, like the ladies in the household of the Vicar of Wakefield.[4] Some three or four months went by; it grew to be mid-winter, and as yet Viola knew that if Perdita had nothing more to boast of than she, there was not much to be feared from her rivalry. But Perdita by this time, the charming Perdita, felt that her secret had grown to be tenfold more precious than her sister's.

One afternoon, Miss Willoughby sat alone before her toilet-glass combing out her long hair. It was getting too dark to see; she lit the two candles in their sockets on the frame of her mirror, and then went to the window to draw her curtains. It was a grey December evening; the landscape was bare and bleak, and the sky heavy with snow-clouds. At the end of the long garden into which her window looked was a wall with a little postern door, opening into a lane. The door stood ajar, as she could vaguely see in the gathering darkness, and moved slowly to and fro, as if someone were swaying it from the lane without. It was doubtless a servant-maid. But as she was about to drop her curtain, Viola saw her sister step within the garden and hurry along the path towards the house. She dropped the curtain, all save a little crevice for her eyes. As Perdita came up the path, she seemed to be examining something in her hand, holding it close to her eyes. When she reached the house, she stopped a moment, looked intently at the object, and pressed it to her lips.

Poor Viola slowly came back to her chair, and sat down before her glass, where, if she had looked at it less abstractedly, she would have seen her handsome features sadly disfigured by jealousy. A moment afterwards the door opened behind her, and her sister came into the room, out of breath, and her cheeks aglow with the chilly air.

Perdita started. "Ah," said she, "I thought you were with our mother." The ladies were to go to a tea party, and on such occasions it was the habit of one of the young girls to help their mother to dress. Instead of coming in, Perdita lingered at the door.

"Come in, come in," said Viola. "We've more than an hour yet. I should like you very much to give a few strokes to my hair." She knew her sister wished to retreat, and that she could see in the glass all her movements in the room. "Nay, just help me with my hair," she said, "and I'll go to mamma."

Perdita came reluctantly, and took the brush. She saw her sister's eyes, in the glass, fastened hard upon her hands. She had not made three passes, when Viola clapped her own right hand upon her sister's left, and started out of her chair. "Whose ring is that?" she cried passionately, drawing her towards the light.

On the young girl's third finger glistened a little gold ring, adorned with a couple of small rubies. Perdita felt that she need no longer keep her secret, yet that she must put a bold face on her avowal. "It's mine," she said proudly.

"Who gave it to you?" cried the other.

Perdita hesitated a moment. "Mr Lloyd."

"Mr Lloyd is generous, all of a sudden."

"Ah no," cried Perdita, with spirit, "not all of a sudden. He offered it to me a month ago."

"And you needed a month's begging to take it?" said Viola, looking at the little trinket; which indeed was not especially elegant, although it was the best that the jeweller of the Province could furnish. "I shouldn't have taken it in less than two."

"It isn't the ring," said Perdita, "it's what it means!"

"It means that you're not a modest girl," cried Viola. "Pray does your mother know of your conduct? does Bernard?"

"My mother has approved my "conduct", as you call it. Mr Lloyd has asked my hand, and mamma has given it. Would you have had him apply to you, sister?"

Viola gave her sister a long look, full of passionate envy and sorrow. Then she dropped her lashes on her pale cheeks and turned away. Perdita felt that it had not been a pretty scene; but it was her sister's fault. But the elder girl rapidly called back her pride, and turned herself about again. "You have my very best wishes," she said, with a low curtsey. "I wish you every happiness, and a very long life."

Perdita gave a bitter laugh. "Don't speak in that tone," she cried. "I'd rather you cursed me outright. Come, sister," she added, "he couldn't marry both of us."

"I wish you very great joy," Viola repeated mechanically, sitting down to her glass again, "and a very long life, and plenty of children."

There was something in the sound of these words not at all to Perdita's taste. "Will you give me a year, at least?" she said. "In a year I can have one little boy – or one little girl at least. If you'll give me your brush again I'll do your hair."

"Thank you," said Viola. "You had better go to mamma. It isn't becoming that a young lady with a promised husband should wait on a girl with none."

"Nay," said Perdita, good-humouredly, "I have Arthur to wait upon me. You need my service more than I need yours."

But her sister motioned her away, and she left the room. When she had gone, poor Viola fell on her knees before her dressing-table, buried her head in her arms, and poured out a flood of tears and sobs. She felt very much better for this effusion of sorrow. When her sister came back, she insisted upon helping her to dress, and upon her wearing her prettiest things. She forced upon her acceptance a bit of lace of her own, and declared that now that she was to be married she should do her best to appear worthy of her lover's choice. She discharged these offices in stern silence; but, such as they were, they had to do duty as an apology and an atonement; she never made any other.

Now that Lloyd was received by the family as an accepted suitor, nothing remained but to fix the wedding day. It was appointed for the following April, and in the interval preparations were diligently made for the marriage. Lloyd, on his side, was busy with his commercial arrangements, and with establishing a correspondence with the great mercantile house to which he had attached himself in England. He was therefore not so frequent a visitor at Mrs Willoughby's as during the months of his diffidence and irresolution, and poor Viola had less to suffer than she had feared from the sight of the mutual endearments of the young lovers. Touching his future sister-in-law, Lloyd had a perfectly clear conscience. There had not been a particle of sentiment uttered between them, and he had not the slightest suspicion that she coveted anything more than his fraternal regard. He was quite at his ease; life promised so well, both domestically and financially. The lurid clouds of revolution were as yet twenty years beneath the horizon, and that his connubial felicity should take a tragic turn it was absurd, it was blasphemous, to apprehend. Meanwhile at Mrs Willoughby's there was a greater rustling of silks, a more rapid clicking of scissors and flying of needles, than ever. Mrs Willoughby had determined that her daughter should carry from home the most elegant outfit that her money could buy, or that the country could furnish. All the sage women in the county were convened, and their united taste was brought to bear on Perdita's wardrobe. Viola's situation, at this moment, was assuredly not to be envied. The poor girl had an inordinate love of dress, and the very best taste in the world, as her sister perfectly well knew. Viola was tall, she was stately and sweeping, she was made to carry stiff brocade and masses of heavy lace, such as belong to the toilet of a rich man's wife. But Viola sat aloof, with her beautiful arms folded and her head averted, while her mother and sister and the venerable women aforesaid worried and wondered over their materials, oppressed by the multitude of their resources. One day, there came in a beautiful piece of white silk, brocaded with celestial blue and silver, sent by the bridegroom himself – it not being thought amiss in those days that the husband-elect should contribute to the bride's trousseau.[5] Perdita was quite at a loss to imagine a fashion which should do sufficient honour to the splendour of the material.

"Blue's your colour, sister, more than mine," she said, with appealing eyes. "It's a pity it's not for you. You'd know what to do with it."

Viola got up from her place and looked at the great shining fabric as it lay spread over the back of a chair. Then she took it up in her hands and felt it – lovingly, as Perdita could see – and turned about towards the mirror with it. She let it roll down to her feet, and flung the other end over her shoulder, gathering it in about her waist with her white arm bare to the elbow. She threw back her head, and looked at her image, and a hanging tress of her auburn hair fell upon the gorgeous surface of the silk. It made a dazzling picture. The women standing about uttered a little "Ah!" of admiration. "Yes, indeed," said Viola, quietly, "blue is my colour." But Perdita could see that her fancy had been stirred, and that she would now fall to work and solve all their silken riddles. And indeed she behaved very well, as Perdita, knowing her insatiable love of millinery, was quite ready to declare. Innumerable yards of lustrous silk and satin, of muslin, velvet, and lace, passed through her cunning hands, without a word of envy coming from her lips. Thanks to her industry, when the wedding day came, Perdita was prepared to espouse more of the vanities of life than any fluttering young bride who had yet challenged the sacramental blessing of a New England divine.

It had been arranged that the young couple should go out and spend the first days of their wedded life at the country house of an English gentleman – a man of rank and a very kind friend to Lloyd. He was an unmarried man; he professed himself delighted to withdraw and leave them for a week to their billing and cooing. After the ceremony at church – it had been performed by an English parson – young Mrs Lloyd hastened back to her mother's house to change her wedding gear for a riding-dress. Viola helped her to effect the change, in the little old room in which they had been fond sisters together. Perdita then hurried off to bid farewell to her mother, leaving Viola to follow. The parting was short; the horses were at the door and Arthur impatient to start. But Viola had not followed, and Perdita hastened back to her room, opening the door abruptly. Viola, as usual, was before the glass, but in a position which caused the other to stand still, amazed. She had dressed herself in Perdita's cast-off wedding veil and wreath, and on her neck she had hung the heavy string of pearls which the young girl had received from her husband as a wedding gift. These things had been hastily laid aside, to await their possessor's disposal on her return from the country. Bedizened in this unnatural garb, Viola stood at the mirror, plunging a long look into its depths, and reading Heaven knows what audacious visions. Perdita was horrified. It was a hideous image of their old rivalry come to life again. She made a step towards her sister, as if to pull off the veil and the flowers. But catching her eyes in the glass, she stopped.

"Farewell, Viola," she said. "You might at least have waited till I had got out of the house." And she hurried away from the room.

Mr Lloyd had purchased in Boston a house which, in the taste of those days, was considered a marvel of elegance and comfort; and here he very soon established himself with his young wife. He was thus separated by a distance of twenty miles from the residence of his mother-in-law. Twenty miles, in that primitive era of roads and conveyances, were as serious a matter as a hundred at the present day, and Mrs Willoughby saw but little of her daughter during the first twelvemonth of her marriage. She suffered in no small degree from her absence; and her affliction was not diminished by the fact that Viola had fallen into terribly low spirits and was not to be roused or cheered but by change of air and circumstances. The real cause of the young girl's dejection the reader will not be slow to suspect. Mrs Willoughby and her gossips, however, deemed her complaint a purely physical one, and doubted not that she would obtain relief from the remedy just mentioned. Her mother accordingly proposed on her behalf a visit to certain relatives on the paternal side, established in New York, who had long complained that they were able to see so little of their New England cousins. Viola was despatched to these good people, under a suitable escort, and remained with them for several months. In the interval, her brother Bernard, who had begun the practice of the law, made up his mind to take a wife. Viola came home to the wedding, apparently cured of her heartache, with honest roses and lilies in her face, and a proud smile on her lips. Arthur Lloyd came over from Boston to see his brother-in-law married, but without his wife, who was expecting shortly to present him with an heir. It was nearly a year since Viola had seen him. She was glad – she hardly knew why – that Perdita had stayed at home. Arthur looked happy, but he was more grave and solemn than before his marriage. She thought he looked "interesting", – for although the word in its modern sense was not then invented, we may be sure that the idea was. The truth is, he was simply preoccupied with his wife's condition. Nevertheless, he by no means failed to observe Viola's beauty and splendour, and how she quite effaced the poor little bride. The allowance that Perdita had enjoyed for her dress had now been transferred to her sister, who turned it to prodigious account. On the morning after the wedding, he had a lady's saddle put on the horse of the servant who had come with him from town, and went out with the young girl for a ride. It was a keen, clear morning in January; the ground was bare and hard, and the horses in good condition – to say nothing of Viola, who was charming in her hat and plume, and her dark blue riding-coat, trimmed with fur. They rode all the morning, they lost their way, and were obliged to stop for dinner at a farmhouse. The early winter dusk had fallen when they got home. Mrs Willoughby met them with a long face. A messenger had arrived at noon from Mrs Lloyd; she was beginning to be ill, and desired her husband's immediate return. The young man, at the thought that he had lost several hours, and that by hard riding he might already have been with his wife, uttered a passionate oath. He barely consented to stop for a mouthful of supper, but mounted the messenger's horse and started off at a gallop.

He reached home at midnight. His wife had been delivered of a little girl. "Ah, why weren't you with me?" she said, as he came to her bedside.

"I was out of the house when the man came. I was with Viola," said Lloyd, innocently.

Mrs Lloyd made a little moan, and turned about. But she continued to do very well, and for a week her improvement was uninterrupted. Finally, however, through some indiscretion in the way of diet or of exposure, it was checked, and the poor lady grew rapidly worse. Lloyd was in despair. It very soon became evident that she was breathing her last. Mrs Lloyd came to a sense of her approaching end, and declared that she was reconciled with death. On the third evening after the change took place, she told her husband that she felt she would not outlast the night. She dismissed her servants, and also requested her mother to withdraw – Mrs Willoughby having arrived on the preceding day. She had had her infant placed on the bed beside her, and she lay on her side, with the child against her breast, holding her husband's hands. The night-lamp was hidden behind the heavy curtains of the bed, but the room was illumined with a red glow from the immense fire of logs on the hearth.

"It seems strange to die by such a fire as that," the young woman said, feebly trying to smile. "If I had but a little of such fire in my veins! But I've given it all to this little spark of mortality." And she dropped her eyes on her child. Then raising them she looked at her husband with a long penetrating gaze. The last feeling which lingered in her heart was one of mistrust. She had not recovered from the shock which Arthur had given her by telling her that in the hour of her agony he had been with Viola. She trusted her husband very nearly as well as she loved him; but now that she was called away forever, she felt a cold horror of her sister. She felt in her soul that Viola had never ceased to envy her good fortune; and a year of happy security had not effaced the young girl's image, dressed in her wedding garments, and smiling with coveted triumph. Now that Arthur was to be alone, what might not Viola do? She was beautiful, she was engaging; what arts might she not use, what impression might she not make upon the young man's melancholy heart? Mrs Lloyd looked at her husband in silence. It seemed hard, after all, to doubt of his constancy. His fine eyes were filled with tears; his face was convulsed with weeping; the clasp of his hands was warm and passionate. How noble he looked, how tender, how faithful and devoted! "Nay," thought Perdita, "he's not for such as Viola. He'll never forget me. Nor does Viola truly care for him; she cares only for vanities and finery and jewels." And she dropped her eyes on her white hands, which her husband's liberality had covered with rings, and on the lace ruffles which trimmed the edge of her nightdress. "She covets my rings and my laces more than she covets my husband."

At this moment, the thought of her sister's rapacity seemed to cast a dark shadow between her and the helpless figure of her little girl. "Arthur," she said, "you must take off my rings. I shall not be buried in them. One of these days my daughter shall wear them – my rings and my laces and silks. I had them all brought out and shown me today. It's a great wardrobe – there's not such another in the Province; I can say it without vanity now that I've done with it. It will be a great inheritance for my daughter, when she grows into a young woman. There are things there that a man never buys twice, and if they're lost you'll never again see the like. So you'll watch them well. Some dozen things I've left to Viola; I've named them to my mother. I've given her that blue and silver; it was meant for her; I wore it only once, I looked ill in it. But the rest are to be sacredly kept for this little innocent. It's such a providence that she should be my colour; she can wear my gowns; she has her mother's eyes. You know the same fashions come back every twenty years. She can wear my gowns as they are. They'll lie there quietly waiting till she grows into them – wrapped in camphor and rose-leaves, and keeping their colours in the sweet-scented darkness. She shall have black hair, she shall wear my carnation satin. Do you promise me, Arthur?"

"Promise you what, dearest?"

"Promise me to keep your poor little wife's old gowns."

"Are you afraid I'll sell them?"

"No, but that they may get scattered. My mother will have them properly wrapped up, and you shall lay them away under a double-lock. Do you know the great chest in the attic, with the iron bands? There's no end to what it will hold. You can lay them all there. My mother and the housekeeper will do it, and give you the key. And you'll keep the key in your secretary, and never give it to anyone but your child. Do you promise me?"

"Ah, yes, I promise you," said Lloyd, puzzled at the intensity with which his wife appeared to cling to this idea.

"Will you swear?" repeated Perdita.

"Yes, I swear."

"Well – I trust you – I trust you," said the poor lady, looking into his eyes with eyes in which, if he had suspected her vague apprehensions, he might have read an appeal quite as much as an assurance.

Lloyd bore his bereavement soberly and manfully. A month after his wife's death, in the course of commerce, circumstances arose which offered him an opportunity of going to England. He embraced it as a diversion from gloomy thoughts. He was absent nearly a year, during which his little girl was tenderly nursed and cherished by her grandmother. On his return he had his house again thrown open, and announced his intention of keeping the same state as during his wife's lifetime. It very soon came to be predicted that he would marry again, and there were at least a dozen young women of whom one may say that it was by no fault of theirs that, for six months after his return, the prediction did not come true. During this interval, he still left his little daughter in Mrs Willoughby's hands, the latter assuring him that a change of residence at so tender an age was perilous to her health. Finally, however, he declared that his heart longed for his daughter's presence, and that she must be brought up to town. He sent his coach and his housekeeper to fetch her home. Mrs Willoughby was in terror lest something should befall her on the road; and, in accordance with this feeling, Viola offered to ride along with her. She could return the next day. So she went up to town with her little niece, and Mr Lloyd met her on the threshold of his house, overcome with her kindness and with gratitude. Instead of returning the next day, Viola stayed out the week; and when at last she reappeared, she had come only for her clothes. Arthur would not hear of her coming home, nor would the baby. She cried and moaned if Viola left her; and at the sight of her grief, Arthur lost his wits, and swore that she was going to die. In fine, nothing would suit them but that Viola should remain until the poor child had grown used to strange faces.

It took two months to bring this consummation about; for it was not until this period had elapsed that Viola took leave of her brother-in-law. Mrs Willoughby had shaken her head over her daughter's absence; she declared it was not becoming, and that it was the talk of the town. She had reconciled herself to it only because, during the young girl's visit, the household enjoyed an unwonted term of peace. Bernard Willoughby had brought his wife home to live, between whom and her sister-in-law there existed a bitter hostility. Viola was perhaps no angel; but in the daily practice of life she was a sufficiently good-natured girl, and if she quarrelled with Mrs Bernard, it was not without provocation. Quarrel, however, she did, to the great annoyance not only of her antagonist, but of the two spectators of these constant altercations. Her stay in the household of her brother-in-law, therefore, would have been delightful, if only because it removed her from contact with the object of her antipathy at home. It was doubly – it was ten times

– delightful, in that it kept her near the object of her old passion. Mrs Lloyd's poignant mistrust had fallen very far short of the truth. Viola's sentiment had been a passion at first, and a passion it remained – a passion of whose radiant heat, tempered to the delicate state of his feelings, Mr Lloyd very soon felt the influence. Lloyd, as I have hinted, was not a modern Petrarch;[6] it was not in his nature to practise an ideal constancy. He had not been many days in the house with his sister-in-law before he began to assure himself that she was, in the language of that day, a devilish fine woman. Whether Viola really practised those insidious arts that her sister had been tempted to impute to her, it is needless to inquire. It is enough to say that she found means to appear to the very best advantage. She used to seat herself every morning before the great fireplace in the dining-room, at work upon a piece of tapestry, with her little niece disporting herself on the carpet at her feet, or on the train of her dress, and playing with her woollens balls. Lloyd would have been a very stupid fellow if he had remained insensible to the rich suggestions of this charming picture. He was prodigiously fond of his little girl, and was never weary of taking her in his arms and tossing her up and down, and making her crow with delight. Very often, however, he would venture upon greater liberties than the young lady was yet prepared to allow, and she would suddenly vociferate her displeasure. Viola would then drop her tapestry, and put out her handsome hands with the serious smile of the young girl whose virgin fancy has revealed to her all a mother's healing arts. Lloyd would give up the child, their eyes would meet, their hands would touch, and Viola would extinguish the little girl's sobs upon the snowy folds of the kerchief that crossed her bosom. Her dignity was perfect, and nothing could be more discreet than the manner in which she accepted her brother-in-law's hospitality. It may be almost said, perhaps, that there was something harsh in her reserve. Lloyd had a provoking feeling that she was in the house, and yet that she was unapproachable. Half an hour after supper, at the very outset of the long winter evenings, she would light her candle, and make the young man a most respectful curtsey, and march off to bed. If these were arts, Viola was a great artist. But their effect was so gentle, so gradual, they were calculated to work upon the young widower's fancy with such a finely shaded *crescendo*, that, as the reader has seen, several weeks elapsed before Viola began to feel sure that her return would cover her outlay. When this became morally certain, she packed up her trunk, and returned to her mother's house. For three days she waited; on the fourth, Mr Lloyd made his appearance – a respectful but ardent suitor. Viola heard him out with great humility, and accepted him with infinite modesty. It is hard to imagine that Mrs Lloyd should have forgiven her husband; but if anything might have disarmed her resentment, it would have been the ceremonious continence of this interview. Viola imposed upon her lover but a short probation. They were married, as was becoming, with great privacy – almost with secrecy – in the hope perhaps, as was waggishly remarked at the time, that the late Mrs Lloyd wouldn't hear of it.

The marriage was to all appearance a happy one, and each party obtained what each had desired – Lloyd "a devilish fine woman," and Viola – but Viola's desires, as the reader will have observed, have remained a good deal of a mystery. There were, indeed, two blots upon their felicity; but time would, perhaps, efface them. During the first three years of her marriage, Mrs Lloyd failed to become a mother, and her husband on his side suffered heavy losses of money. This latter circumstance compelled a material retrenchment in his expenditure, and Viola was perforce less of a great lady than her sister had been. She contrived, however, to sustain with unbroken consistency the part of an elegant woman, although it must be confessed that it required the exercise of more ingenuity than belongs to your real aristocratic repose. She had long since ascertained that her sister's immense wardrobe had been sequestrated for the benefit of her daughter, and that it lay languishing in thankless gloom in the dusty attic. It was a revolting thought that these exquisite fabrics should await the commands of a little girl who sat in a high chair and ate bread-and-milk with a wooden spoon. Viola had the good taste, however, to say nothing about the matter until several months had expired. Then, at last, she timidly broached it to her husband. Was it not a pity that so much finery should be lost? – for lost it would be, what with colours fading, and moths eating it up, and the change of fashions. But Lloyd gave so abrupt and peremptory a negative to her inquiry, that she saw that for the present her attempt was vain. Six months went by, however, and brought with them new needs and new fancies. Viola's thoughts hovered lovingly about her sister's relics. She went up and looked at the chest in which they lay imprisoned. There was a sullen defiance in its three great padlocks and its iron bands, which only quickened her desires. There was something exasperating in its incorruptible immobility. It was like a grim and grizzled old household servant, who locks his jaws over a family secret. And then there was a look of capacity in its vast extent, and a sound as of dense fullness, when Viola knocked its side with the toe of her little slipper, which caused her to flush with baffled longing. "It's absurd," she cried; "it's improper, it's wicked"; and she forthwith resolved upon another attack upon her husband. On the following day, after dinner, when he had had his wine, she bravely began it. But he cut her short with great sternness.

"Once and for all, Viola," said he, "it's out of the question. I shall be gravely displeased if you return to the matter."

"Very good," said Viola. "I'm glad to learn the value at which I'm held. Great Heaven!" she cried, "I'm a happy woman. It's an agreeable thing to feel one's self sacrificed to a caprice!" And her eyes filled with tears of anger and disappointment.

Lloyd had a good-natured man's horror of a woman's sobs, and he attempted – I may say he condescended – to explain. "It's not a caprice, dear, it's a promise," he said – "an oath."

"An oath? It's a pretty matter for oaths! and to whom, pray?"

"To Perdita," said the young man, raising his eyes for an instant, but immediately dropping them.

"Perdita – ah, Perdita!" and Viola's tears broke forth. Her bosom heaved with stormy sobs – sobs which were the long-deferred counterpart of the violent fit of weeping in which she had indulged herself on the night when she discovered her sister's betrothal. She had hoped, in her better moments, that she had done with her jealousy; but her temper, on that occasion, had taken an ineffaceable fold. "And pray, what right," she cried, "had Perdita to dispose of my future? What right had she to bind you to meanness and cruelty? Ah, I occupy a dignified place, and I make a very fine figure! I'm welcome to what Perdita has left! And what has she left? I never knew till now how little! Nothing, nothing, nothing."

This was very poor logic, but it was very good passion. Lloyd put his arm around his wife's waist and tried to kiss her, but she shook him off with magnificent scorn. Poor fellow, he had coveted a "devilish fine woman", and he had got one! Her scorn was intolerable. He walked away with his ears tingling – irresolute, distracted. Before him was his secretary, and in it the sacred key which with his own hand he had turned in the triple lock. He marched up and opened it, and took the key from a secret drawer, wrapped in a little packet which he had sealed with his own honest bit of blazonry. *Teneo*, said the motto – "I hold". But he was ashamed to put it back. He flung it upon the table beside his wife.

"Keep it!" she cried. "I want it not. I hate it!"

"I wash my hands of it," cried her husband. "God forgive me!"

Mrs Lloyd gave an indignant shrug of her shoulders, and swept out of the room, while the young man retreated by another door. Ten minutes later, Mrs Lloyd returned, and found the room occupied by her little step-daughter and the nursery-maid. The key was not on the table. She glanced at the child. The child was perched on a chair with the packet in her hands. She had broken the seal with her own little fingers. Mrs Lloyd hastily took possession of the key.

At the habitual supper-hour, Arthur Lloyd came back from his counting-room. It was the month of June, and supper was served by daylight. The meal was placed on the table, but Mrs Lloyd failed to make her appearance. The servant whom his master sent to call her came back with the assurance that her room was empty, and that the women informed him that she had not been seen since dinner. They had in truth observed her to have been in tears, and, supposing her to be shut up in her chamber, had not disturbed her. Her husband called her name in various parts of the house, but without response. At last it occurred to him that he might find her by taking the way to the attic. The thought gave him a strange feeling of discomfort, and he bade his servants remain behind, wishing no witness in his quest. He reached the foot of the staircase leading to the topmost flat, and stood with his hand on the banisters, pronouncing his wife's name. His voice trembled. He called again, louder and more firmly. The only sound which disturbed the absolute silence was a faint echo of his own tones, repeating his question under the great eaves. He nevertheless felt irresistibly moved to ascend the staircase. It opened upon a wide hall, lined with wooden closets, and terminating in a window which looked westward, and admitted the last rays of the sun. Before the window stood the great chest. Before the chest, on her knees, the young man saw with amazement and horror the figure of his wife. In an instant he crossed the interval between them, bereft of utterance. The lid of the chest stood open, exposing, amid their perfumed napkins, its treasure of stuffs and jewels. Viola had fallen backwards from a kneeling posture, with one hand supporting her on the floor and the other pressed to her heart. On her limbs was the stiffness of death, and on her face, in the fading light of the sun, the terror of something more than death. Her lips were parted in entreaty, in dismay, in agony; and on her bloodless brow and cheeks there glowed the marks of ten hideous wounds from two vengeful ghostly hands.

A BAD BUSINESS

Anton Chekhov

Anton Chekhov (1860–1904) was the grandson of a serf who bought his own freedom. His father was a religious fanatic who went bankrupt in 1875. Eviction and homelessness are recurring themes in Chekhov's work. He initially wrote short stories to support himself while studying to become a doctor. His plays continue to be performed around the world. Chekhov suffered from tuberculosis and his final words (after a glass of the stuff) were: 'It's a long time since I drank champagne.'

"Who goes there?"

No answer. The watchman sees nothing, but through the roar of the wind and the trees distinctly hears someone walking along the avenue ahead of him. A March night, cloudy and foggy, envelopes the earth, and it seems to the watchman that the earth, the sky, and he himself with his thoughts are all merged together into something vast and impenetrably black. He can only grope his way.

"Who goes there?" the watchman repeats, and he begins to fancy that he hears whispering and smothered laughter. "Who's there?"

"It's I, friend . . ." answers an old man's voice.

"But who are you?"

"I . . . a traveller."

"What sort of traveller?" the watchman cries angrily, trying to disguise his terror by shouting. "What the devil do you want here? You go prowling about the graveyard at night, you ruffian!"

"You don't say it's a graveyard here?"

"Why, what else? Of course it's the graveyard! Don't you see it is?"

"O-o-oh . . . Queen of Heaven!" there is a sound of an old man sighing. "I see nothing, my good soul, nothing. Oh the darkness, the darkness! You can't see your hand before your face, it is dark, friend. O-o-oh . . ."

"But who are you?"

"I am a pilgrim, friend, a wandering man."

"The devils, the nightbirds. . . Nice sort of pilgrims! They are drunkards . . ." mutters the watchman, reassured by the tone and sighs of the stranger. "One's tempted to sin by you. They drink the day away and prowl about at night. But I fancy I heard you were not alone; it sounded like two or three of you."

"I am alone, friend, alone. Quite alone. O-o-oh our sins. . ."

The watchman stumbles up against the man and stops.

"How did you get here?" he asks.

"I have lost my way, good man. I was walking to the Mitrievsky Mill and I lost my way."

"Whew! Is this the road to Mitrievsky Mill? You sheepshead! For the Mitrievsky Mill you must keep much more to the left, straight out of the town along the high road. You have been drinking and have gone a couple of miles out of your way. You must have had a drop in the town."

"I did, friend . . . Truly I did; I won't hide my sins. But how am I to go now?"

"Go straight on and on along this avenue till you can go no farther, and then turn at once to the left and go till you have crossed the whole graveyard right to the gate. There will be a gate there. . . Open it and go with God's blessing. Mind you don't fall into the ditch. And when you are out of the graveyard you go all the way by the fields till you come out on the main road."

"God give you health, friend. May the Queen of Heaven save you and have mercy on you. You might take me along, good man! Be merciful! Lead me to the gate."

"As though I had the time to waste! Go by yourself!"

"Be merciful! I'll pray for you. I can't see anything; one can't see one's hand before one's face, friend. . . It's so dark, so dark! Show me the way, sir!"

"As though I had the time to take you about; if I were to play the nurse to everyone I should never have done."

"For Christ's sake, take me! I can't see, and I am afraid to go alone through the graveyard. It's terrifying, friend, it's terrifying; I am afraid, good man."

"There's no getting rid of you," sighs the watchman. "All right then, come along."

The watchman and the traveller go on together. They walk shoulder to shoulder in silence. A damp, cutting wind blows straight into their faces and the unseen trees murmuring and rustling scatter big drops upon them. . . . . The path is almost entirely covered with puddles.

"There is one thing passes my understanding," says the watchman after a prolonged silence – "how you got here. The gate's locked. Did you climb over the wall? If you did climb over the wall, that's the last thing you would expect of an old man."

"I don't know, friend, I don't know. I can't say myself how I got here. It's a visitation. A chastisement of the Lord. Truly a visitation, the evil one confounded me. So you are a watchman here, friend?"

"Yes."

"The only one for the whole graveyard?"

There is such a violent gust of wind that both stop for a minute.

Waiting till the violence of the wind abates, the watchman answers: "There are three of us, but one is lying ill in a fever and the other's asleep. He and I take turns about."

"Ah, to be sure, friend. What a wind! The dead must hear it! It howls like a wild beast! O-o-oh."

"And where do you come from?"

"From a distance, friend. I am from Vologda, a long way off. I go from one holy place to another and pray for people. Save me and have mercy upon me, O Lord."

The watchman stops for a minute to light his pipe. He stoops down behind the traveller's back and lights several matches. The gleam of the first match lights up for one instant a bit of the avenue on the right, a white tombstone with an angel, and a dark cross; the light of the second match, flaring up brightly and extinguished by the wind, flashes like lightning on the left side, and from the darkness nothing stands out but the angle of some sort of trellis; the third match throws light to right and to left, revealing the white tombstone, the dark cross, and the trellis round a child's grave.

"The departed sleep; the dear ones sleep!" the stranger mutters, sighing loudly. "They all sleep alike, rich and poor, wise and foolish, good and wicked. They are of the same value now. And they will sleep till the last trump. The Kingdom of Heaven and peace eternal be theirs."

"Here we are walking along now, but the time will come when we shall be lying here ourselves," says the watchman.

"To be sure, to be sure, we shall all. There is no man who will not die. O-o-oh. Our doings are wicked, our thoughts are deceitful! Sins, sins! My soul accursed, ever covetous, my belly greedy and lustful! I have angered the Lord and there is no salvation for me in this world and the next. I am deep in sins like a worm in the earth."

"Yes, and you have to die."

"You are right there."

"Death is easier for a pilgrim than for fellows like us," says the watchman.

"There are pilgrims of different sorts. There are the real ones who are God-fearing men and watch over their own souls, and there are such as stray about the graveyard at night and are a delight to the devils . . . Ye-es! There's one who is a pilgrim could give you a crack on the pate with an axe if he liked and knock the breath out of you."

"What are you talking like that for?"

"Oh, nothing . . . Why, I fancy here's the gate. Yes, it is. Open it, good man."

The watchman, feeling his way, opens the gate, leads the pilgrim out by the sleeve, and says:

"Here's the end of the graveyard. Now you must keep on through the open fields till you get to the main road. Only close here there will be the boundary ditch – don't fall in. . . And when you come out on to the road, turn to the right, and keep on till you reach the mill. . ."

"O-o-oh!" sighs the pilgrim after a pause, "and now I am thinking that I have no cause to go to Mitrievsky Mill. . . Why the devil should I go there? I had better stay a bit with you here, sir. . ."

"What do you want to stay with me for?"

"Oh . . . it's merrier with you! . . ."

"So you've found a merry companion, have you? You, pilgrim, are fond of a joke I see. . ."

"To be sure I am," says the stranger, with a hoarse chuckle. "Ah, my dear good man, I bet you will remember the pilgrim many a long year!"

"Why should I remember you?"

"Why I've got round you so smartly. . . Am I a pilgrim? I am not a pilgrim at all."

"What are you then?"

"A dead man. . . . I've only just got out of my coffin. . . Do you remember Gubaryev, the locksmith, who hanged himself in carnival week? Well, I am Gubaryev himself! . . ."

"Tell us something else!"

The watchman does not believe him, but he feels all over such a cold, oppressive terror that he starts off and begins hurriedly feeling for the gate.

"Stop, where are you off to?" says the stranger, clutching him by the arm. "Aie, aie, aie . . . what a fellow you are! How can you leave me all alone?"

"Let go!" cries the watchman, trying to pull his arm away.

"Sto-op! I bid you stop and you stop. Don't struggle, you dirty dog! If you want to stay among the living, stop and hold your tongue till I tell you. It's only that I don't care to spill blood or you would have been a dead man long ago, you scurvy rascal. . . Stop!"

The watchman's knees give way under him. In his terror he shuts his eyes, and trembling all over huddles close to the wall. He would like to call out, but he knows his cries would not reach any living thing. The stranger stands beside him and holds him by the arm. . . Three minutes pass in silence.

"One's in a fever, another's asleep, and the third is seeing pilgrims on their way," mutters the stranger. "Capital watchmen, they are worth their salary! Ye-es, brother, thieves have always been cleverer than watchmen! Stand still, don't stir. . ."

Five minutes, ten minutes pass in silence. All at once the wind brings the sound of a whistle.

"Well, now you can go," says the stranger, releasing the watchman's arm. "Go and thank God you are alive!"

The stranger gives a whistle too, runs away from the gate, and the watchman hears him leap over the ditch.

With a foreboding of something very dreadful in his heart, the watchman, still trembling with terror, opens the gate irresolutely and runs back with his eyes shut.

At the turning into the main avenue he hears hurried footsteps, and someone asks him, in a hissing voice: "Is that you, Timofey? Where is Mitka?"

And after running the whole length of the main avenue he notices a little dim light in the darkness. The nearer he gets to the light the more frightened he is and the stronger his foreboding of evil.

"It looks as though the light were in the church," he thinks. "And how can it have come there? Save me and have mercy on me, Queen of Heaven! And that it is."

The watchman stands for a minute before the broken window and looks with horror towards the altar. . . A little wax candle which the thieves had forgotten to put out flickers in the wind that bursts in at the window and throws dim red patches of light on the vestments flung about and a cupboard overturned on the floor, on numerous footprints near the high altar and the altar of offerings.

A little time passes and the howling wind sends floating over the churchyard the hurried uneven clangs of the alarm-bell. . .

THE CANTERVILLE GHOST

Oscar Wilde

Oscar Fingal O'Flahertie Wills Wilde (1854–1900) was born in Dublin. His father, Sir William Wilde, was a surgeon and a collector of Irish folk tales. His mother, Jane Francesca Elgee (Speranza), was a well-known poet. A brilliant dramatist, poet, short story writer, critic and novelist, Wilde's work is often overshadowed by his life. His relationship with Lord Alfred Douglas led to him being jailed for two years for gross indecency. He died destitute in Paris.

I

When Mr. Hiram B. Otis, the American Minister, bought Canterville Chase, every one told him he was doing a very foolish thing, as there was no doubt at all that the place was haunted. Indeed, Lord Canterville himself, who was a man of the most punctilious honour, had felt it his duty to mention the fact to Mr. Otis when they came to discuss terms.

"We have not cared to live in the place ourselves," said Lord Canterville, "since my grandaunt, the Dowager Duchess of Bolton, was frightened into a fit, from which she never really recovered, by two skeleton hands being placed on her shoulders as she was dressing for dinner, and I feel bound to tell you, Mr. Otis, that the ghost has been seen by several living members of my family, as well as by the rector of the parish, the Rev. Augustus Dampier, who is a Fellow of King's College, Cambridge. After the unfortunate accident to the Duchess, none of our younger servants would stay with us, and Lady Canterville often got very little sleep at night, in consequence of the mysterious noises that came from the corridor and the library."

"My Lord," answered the Minister, "I will take the furniture and the ghost at a valuation. I have come from a modern country, where we have everything that money can buy; and with all our spry young fellows painting the Old World red, and carrying off your best actors and prima-donnas, I reckon that if there were such a thing as a ghost in Europe, we'd have it at home in a very short time in one of our public museums, or on the road as a show."

"I fear that the ghost exists," said Lord Canterville, smiling, "though it may have resisted the overtures of your enterprising impresarios. It has been well known for three centuries, since 1584 in fact, and always makes its appearance before the death of any member of our family."

"Well, so does the family doctor for that matter, Lord Canterville. But there is no such thing, sir, as a ghost, and I guess the laws of Nature are not going to be suspended for the British aristocracy."

"You are certainly very natural in America," answered Lord Canterville, who did not quite understand Mr. Otis's last observation, "and if you don't mind a ghost in the house, it is all right. Only you must remember I warned you."

A few weeks after this, the purchase was concluded, and at the close of the season the Minister and his family went down to Canterville Chase. Mrs. Otis, who, as Miss Lucretia R. Tappan, of West 53d Street, had been a celebrated New York belle, was now a very handsome, middle-aged woman, with fine eyes, and a superb profile. Many American ladies on leaving their native land adopt an appearance of chronic ill-health, under the impression that it is a form of European refinement, but Mrs. Otis had never fallen into this error. She had a magnificent constitution, and a really wonderful amount of animal spirits. Indeed, in many respects, she was quite English, and was an excellent example of the fact that we have really everything in common with America nowadays, except, of course, language. Her eldest son, christened Washington by his parents in a moment of patriotism, which he never ceased to regret, was a fair-haired, rather good-looking young man, who had qualified himself for American diplomacy by leading the German at the Newport Casino for three successive seasons, and even in London was well known as an excellent dancer. Gardenias and the peerage were his only weaknesses. Otherwise he was extremely sensible. Miss Virginia E. Otis was a little girl of fifteen, lithe and lovely as a fawn, and with a fine freedom in her large blue eyes. She was a wonderful Amazon, and had once raced old Lord Bilton on her pony twice round the park, winning by a length and a half, just in front of the Achilles statue, to the huge delight of the young Duke of Cheshire, who proposed for her on the spot, and was sent back to Eton that very night by his guardians, in floods of tears. After Virginia came the twins, who were usually called "The Star and Stripes," as they were always getting swished. They were delightful boys, and, with the exception of the worthy Minister, the only true republicans of the family.

As Canterville Chase is seven miles from Ascot, the nearest railway station, Mr. Otis had telegraphed for a waggonette to meet them, and they started on their drive in high spirits. It was a lovely July evening, and the air was delicate with the scent of the pinewoods. Now and then they heard a wood-pigeon brooding over its own sweet voice, or saw, deep in the rustling fern, the burnished breast of the pheasant. Little squirrels peered at them from the beech-trees as they went by, and the rabbits scudded away through the brushwood and over the mossy knolls, with their white tails in the air. As they entered the avenue of Canterville Chase, however, the sky became suddenly overcast with clouds, a curious stillness seemed to hold the atmosphere, a great flight of rooks passed silently over their heads, and, before they reached the house, some big drops of rain had fallen.

Standing on the steps to receive them was an old woman, neatly dressed in black silk, with a white cap and apron. This was Mrs. Umney, the housekeeper, whom Mrs. Otis, at Lady Canterville's earnest request, had consented to keep in her former position. She made them each a low curtsey as they alighted, and said in a quaint, old-fashioned manner, "I bid you welcome to Canterville Chase." Following her, they passed through the fine Tudor hall into the library, a long, low room, panelled in black oak, at the end of which was a large stained glass window. Here they found tea laid out for them, and, after taking off their wraps, they sat down and began to look round, while Mrs. Umney waited on them.

Suddenly Mrs. Otis caught sight of a dull red stain on the floor just by the fireplace, and, quite unconscious of what it really signified, said to Mrs. Umney, "I am afraid something has been spilt there."

"Yes, madam," replied the old housekeeper in a low voice, "blood has been spilt on that spot."

"How horrid!" cried Mrs. Otis; "I don't at all care for blood-stains in a sitting-room. It must be removed at once."

The old woman smiled, and answered in the same low, mysterious voice, "It is the blood of Lady Eleanore de Canterville, who was murdered on that very spot by her own husband, Sir Simon de Canterville, in 1575. Sir Simon survived her nine years, and disappeared suddenly under very mysterious circumstances. His body has never been discovered, but his guilty spirit still haunts the Chase. The blood-stain has been much admired by tourists and others, and cannot be removed."

"That is all nonsense," cried Washington Otis; "Pinkerton's Champion Stain Remover and Paragon Detergent will clean it up in no time," and before the terrified housekeeper could interfere, he had fallen upon his knees, and was rapidly scouring the floor with a small stick of what looked like a black cosmetic. In a few moments no trace of the blood-stain could be seen.

"I knew Pinkerton would do it," he exclaimed, triumphantly, as he looked round at his admiring family; but no sooner had he said these words than a terrible flash of lightning lit up the sombre room, a fearful peal of thunder made them all start to their feet, and Mrs. Umney fainted.

"What a monstrous climate!" said the American Minister, calmly, as he lit a long cheroot. "I guess the old country is so overpopulated that they have not enough decent weather for everybody. I have always been of opinion that emigration is the only thing for England."

"My dear Hiram," cried Mrs. Otis, "what can we do with a woman who faints?"

"Charge it to her like breakages," answered the Minister; "she won't faint after that;" and in a few moments Mrs. Umney certainly came to. There was no doubt, however, that she was extremely upset, and she sternly warned Mr. Otis to beware of some trouble coming to the house.

"I have seen things with my own eyes, sir," she said, "that would make any Christian's hair stand on end, and many and many a night I have not closed my eyes in sleep for the awful things that are done here." Mr. Otis, however, and his wife warmly assured the honest soul that they were not afraid of ghosts, and, after invoking the blessings of Providence on her new master and mistress, and making arrangements for an increase of salary, the old housekeeper tottered off to her own room.

II

The storm raged fiercely all that night, but nothing of particular note occurred. The next morning, however, when they came down to breakfast, they found the terrible stain of blood once again on the floor. "I don't think it can be the fault of the Paragon Detergent," said Washington, "for I have tried it with everything. It must be the ghost." He accordingly rubbed out the stain a second time, but the second morning it appeared again. The third morning also it was there, though the library had been locked up at night by Mr. Otis himself, and the key carried up-stairs. The whole family were now quite interested; Mr. Otis began to suspect that he had been too dogmatic in his denial of the existence of ghosts, Mrs. Otis expressed her intention of joining the Psychical Society, and Washington prepared a long letter to Messrs. Myers and Podmore on the subject of the Permanence of Sanguineous Stains when connected with Crime. That night all doubts about the objective existence of phantasmata were removed forever.

The day had been warm and sunny; and, in the cool of the evening, the whole family went out to drive. They did not return home till nine o'clock, when they had a light supper. The conversation in no way turned upon ghosts, so there were not even those primary conditions of receptive expectations which so often precede the presentation of psychical phenomena. The subjects discussed, as I have since learned from Mr. Otis, were merely such as form the ordinary conversation of cultured Americans of the better class, such as the immense superiority of Miss Fanny Devonport over Sarah Bernhardt as an actress; the difficulty of obtaining green corn, buckwheat cakes, and hominy, even in the best English houses; the importance of Boston in the development of the world-soul; the advantages of the baggage-check system in railway travelling; and the sweetness of the New York accent as compared to the London drawl. No mention at all was made of the supernatural, nor was Sir Simon de Canterville alluded to in any way. At eleven o'clock the family retired, and by half-past all the lights were out. Some time after, Mr. Otis was awakened by a curious noise in the corridor, outside his room. It sounded like the clank of metal, and seemed to be coming nearer every moment. He got up at once, struck a match, and looked at the time. It was exactly one o'clock. He was quite calm, and felt his pulse, which was not at all feverish. The strange noise still continued, and with it he heard distinctly the sound of footsteps. He put on his slippers, took a small oblong phial out of his dressing-case, and opened the door. Right in front of him he saw, in the wan moonlight, an old man of terrible aspect. His eyes were as red burning coals; long grey hair fell over his shoulders in matted coils; his garments, which were of antique cut, were soiled and ragged, and from his wrists and ankles hung heavy manacles and rusty gyves.

"My dear sir," said Mr. Otis, "I really must insist on your oiling those chains, and have brought you for that purpose a small bottle of the Tammany Rising Sun Lubricator. It is said to be completely efficacious upon one application, and there are several testimonials to that effect on the wrapper from some of our most eminent native divines. I shall leave it here for you by the bedroom candles, and will be happy to supply you with more, should you require it." With these words the United States Minister laid the bottle down on a marble table, and, closing his door, retired to rest.

For a moment the Canterville ghost stood quite motionless in natural indignation; then, dashing the bottle violently upon the polished floor, he fled down the corridor, uttering hollow groans, and emitting a ghastly green light. Just, however, as he reached the top of the great oak staircase, a door was flung open, two little white-robed figures appeared, and a large pillow whizzed past his head! There was evidently no time to be lost, so, hastily adopting the Fourth dimension of Space as a means of escape, he vanished through the wainscoting, and the house became quite quiet.

On reaching a small secret chamber in the left wing, he leaned up against a moonbeam to recover his breath, and began to try and realize his position. Never, in a brilliant and uninterrupted career of three hundred years, had he been so grossly insulted. He thought of the Dowager Duchess, whom he had frightened into a fit as she stood before the glass in her lace and diamonds; of the four housemaids, who had gone into hysterics when he merely grinned at them through the curtains on one of the spare bedrooms; of the rector of the parish, whose candle he had blown out as he was coming late one night from the library, and who had been under the care of Sir William Gull ever since, a perfect martyr to nervous disorders; and of old Madame de Tremouillac, who, having wakened up one morning early and seen a skeleton seated in an armchair by the fire reading her diary, had been confined to her bed for six weeks with an attack of brain fever, and, on her recovery, had become reconciled to the Church, and broken off her connection with that notorious sceptic, Monsieur de Voltaire. He remembered the terrible night when the wicked Lord Canterville was found choking in his dressing-room, with the knave of diamonds half-way down his throat, and confessed, just before he died, that he had cheated Charles James Fox out of £50,000 at Crockford's by means of that very card, and swore that the ghost had made him swallow it. All his great achievements came back to him again, from the butler who had shot himself in the pantry because he had seen a green hand tapping at the window-pane, to the beautiful Lady Stutfield, who was always obliged to wear a black velvet band round her throat to hide the mark of five fingers burnt upon her white skin, and who drowned herself at last in the carp-pond at the end of the King's Walk.

With the enthusiastic egotism of the true artist, he went over his most cele-brated performances, and smiled bitterly to himself as he recalled to mind his last appearance as "Red Reuben, or the Strangled Babe," his début as "Guant Gibeon, the Blood-sucker of Bexley Moor," and the furore he had excited one lovely June evening by merely playing ninepins with his own bones upon the lawn-tennis ground. And after all this some wretched modern Americans were to come and offer him the Rising Sun Lubricator, and throw pillows at his head! It was quite unbearable. Besides, no ghost in history had ever been treated in this manner. Accordingly, he determined to have vengeance, and remained till day-light in an attitude of deep thought.

III

The next morning, when the Otis family met at breakfast, they discussed the ghost at some length. The United States Minister was naturally a little annoyed to find that his present had not been accepted. "I have no wish," he said, "to do the ghost any personal injury, and I must say that, considering the length of time he has been in the house, I don't think it is at all polite to throw pillows at him," – a very just remark, at which, I am sorry to say, the twins burst into shouts of laugh-ter. "Upon the other hand," he continued, "if he really declines to use the Rising

Sun Lubricator, we shall have to take his chains from him. It would be quite impossible to sleep, with such a noise going on outside the bedrooms."

For the rest of the week, however, they were undisturbed, the only thing that excited any attention being the continual renewal of the blood-stain on the library floor. This certainly was very strange, as the door was always locked at night by Mr. Otis, and the windows kept closely barred. The chameleon-like colour, also, of the stain excited a good deal of comment. Some mornings it was a dull (almost Indian) red, then it would be vermilion, then a rich purple, and once when they came down for family prayers, according to the simple rites of the Free American Reformed Episcopalian Church, they found it a bright emerald-green. These kaleidoscopic changes naturally amused the party very much, and bets on the subject were freely made every evening. The only person who did not enter into the joke was little Virginia, who, for some unexplained reason, was always a good deal distressed at the sight of the blood-stain, and very nearly cried the morning it was emerald-green.

The second appearance of the ghost was on Sunday night. Shortly after they had gone to bed they were suddenly alarmed by a fearful crash in the hall. Rushing down-stairs, they found that a large suit of old armour had become detached from its stand, and had fallen on the stone floor, while seated in a high-backed chair was the Canterville ghost, rubbing his knees with an expression of acute agony on his face. The twins, having brought their pea-shooters with them, at once discharged two pellets on him, with that accuracy of aim which can only be attained by long and careful practice on a writing-master, while the United States Minister covered him with his revolver, and called upon him, in accordance with Californian etiquette, to hold up his hands! The ghost started up with a wild shriek of rage, and swept through them like a mist, extinguishing Washington Otis's candle as he passed, and so leaving them all in total darkness. On reaching the top of the staircase he recovered himself, and determined to give his celebrated peal of demoniac laughter. This he had on more than one occasion found extremely useful. It was said to have turned Lord Raker's wig grey in a single night, and had certainly made three of Lady Canterville's French governesses give warning before their month was up. He accordingly laughed his most horrible laugh, till the old vaulted roof rang and rang again, but hardly had the fearful echo died away when a door opened, and Mrs. Otis came out in a light blue dressing-gown. "I am afraid you are far from well," she said, "and have brought you a bottle of Doctor Dobell's tincture. If it is indigestion, you will find it a most excellent remedy." The ghost glared at her in fury, and began at once to make preparations for turning himself into a large black dog, an accomplishment for which he was justly renowned, and to which the family doctor always attributed the permanent idiocy of Lord Canterville's uncle, the Hon. Thomas Horton. The sound of approaching footsteps, however, made him hesitate in his fell purpose, so he contented himself with becoming faintly phosphorescent, and vanished with a deep churchyard groan, just as the twins had come up to him.

On reaching his room he entirely broke down, and became a prey to the most violent agitation. The vulgarity of the twins, and the gross materialism of Mrs. Otis, were naturally extremely annoying, but what really distressed him most was that he had been unable to wear the suit of mail. He had hoped that even modern Americans would be thrilled by the sight of a Spectre in armour, if for no more sensible reason, at least out of respect for their natural poet Longfellow, over whose graceful and attractive poetry he himself had whiled away many a weary hour when the Cantervilles were up in town. Besides it was his own suit. He had worn it with great success at the Kenilworth tournament, and had been highly complimented on it by no less a person than the Virgin Queen herself. Yet when he had put it on, he had been completely overpowered by the weight of the huge breastplate and steel casque, and had fallen heavily on the stone pavement, barking both his knees severely, and bruising the knuckles of his right hand.

For some days after this he was extremely ill, and hardly stirred out of his room at all, except to keep the blood-stain in proper repair. However, by taking great care of himself, he recovered, and resolved to make a third attempt to frighten the United States Minister and his family. He selected Friday, August 17th, for his appearance, and spent most of that day in looking over his wardrobe, ultimately deciding in favour of a large slouched hat with a red feather, a winding-sheet frilled at the wrists and neck, and a rusty dagger. Towards evening a violent storm of rain came on, and the wind was so high that all the windows and doors in the old house shook and rattled. In fact, it was just such weather as he loved. His plan of action was this. He was to make his way quietly to Washington Otis's room, gibber at him from the foot of the bed, and stab himself three times in the throat to the sound of low music. He bore Washington a special grudge, being quite aware that it was he who was in the habit of removing the famous Canterville blood-stain by means of Pinkerton's Paragon Detergent. Having reduced the reckless and foolhardy youth to a condition of abject terror, he was then to proceed to the room occupied by the United States Minister and his wife, and there to place a clammy hand on Mrs. Otis's forehead, while he hissed into her trembling husband's ear the awful secrets of the charnel-house. With regard to little Virginia, he had not quite made up his mind. She had never insulted him in any way, and was pretty and gentle. A few hollow groans from the wardrobe, he thought, would be more than sufficient, or, if that failed to wake her, he might grabble at the counterpane with palsy-twitching fingers. As for the twins, he was quite determined to teach them a lesson. The first thing to be done was, of course, to sit upon their chests, so as to produce the stifling sensation of nightmare. Then, as their beds were quite close to each other, to stand between them in the form of a green, icy-cold corpse, till they became paralyzed with fear, and finally, to throw off the winding-sheet, and crawl round the room, with white, bleached bones and one rolling eyeball, in the character of "Dumb Daniel, or the Suicide's Skeleton," a rôle in which he had on more than one occasion produced a great effect, and which he considered quite equal to his famous part of "Martin the Maniac, or the Masked Mystery."

At half-past ten he heard the family going to bed. For some time he was disturbed by wild shrieks of laughter from the twins, who, with the light-hearted gaiety of schoolboys, were evidently amusing themselves before they retired to rest, but at a quarter-past eleven all was still, and, as midnight sounded, he sallied forth. The owl beat against the window-panes, the raven croaked from the old yew-tree, and the wind wandered moaning round the house like a lost soul; but the Otis family slept unconscious of their doom, and high above the rain and storm he could hear the steady snoring of the Minister for the United States. He stepped stealthily out of the wainscoting, with an evil smile on his cruel, wrinkled mouth, and the moon hid her face in a cloud as he stole past the great oriel window, where his own arms and those of his murdered wife were blazoned in azure and gold. On and on he glided, like an evil shadow, the very darkness seeming to loathe him as he passed. Once he thought he heard something call, and stopped; but it was only the baying of a dog from the Red Farm, and he went on, muttering strange sixteenth-century curses, and ever and anon brandishing the rusty dagger in the midnight air. Finally he reached the corner of the passage that led to luckless Washington's room. For a moment he paused there, the wind blowing his long grey locks about his head, and twisting into grotesque and fantastic folds the nameless horror of the dead man's shroud. Then the clock struck the quarter, and he felt the time was come. He chuckled to himself, and turned the corner; but no sooner had he done so than, with a piteous wail of terror, he fell back, and hid his blanched face in his long, bony hands. Right in front of him was standing a horrible spectre, motionless as a carven image, and monstrous as a madman's dream! Its head was bald and burnished; its face round, and fat, and white; and hideous laughter seemed to have writhed its features into an eternal grin. From the eyes streamed rays of scarlet light, the mouth was a wide well of fire, and a hideous garment, like to his own, swathed with its silent snows the Titan form. On its breast was a placard with strange writing in antique characters, some scroll of shame it seemed, some record of wild sins, some awful calendar of crime, and, with its right hand, it bore aloft a falchion of gleaming steel.

Never having seen a ghost before, he naturally was terribly frightened, and, after a second hasty glance at the awful phantom, he fled back to his room, tripping up in his long winding-sheet as he sped down the corridor, and finally dropping the rusty dagger into the Minister's jack-boots, where it was found in the morning by the butler. Once in the privacy of his own apartment, he flung himself down on a small pallet-bed, and hid his face under the clothes. After a time, however, the brave old Canterville spirit asserted itself, and he determined to go and speak to the other ghost as soon as it was daylight. Accordingly, just as the dawn was touching the hills with silver, he returned towards the spot where he had first laid eyes on the grisly phantom, feeling that, after all, two ghosts were better than one, and that, by the aid of his new friend, he might safely grapple with the twins. On reaching the spot, however, a terrible sight met his gaze. Something had evidently happened to the spectre, for the light had entirely faded from its hollow eyes, the gleaming falchion had fallen from its hand, and it was leaning up against the wall in a strained and uncomfortable attitude. He rushed forward and seized it in his arms, when, to his horror, the head slipped off and rolled on the floor, the body assumed a recumbent posture, and he found himself clasping a white dimity bed-curtain, with a sweeping-brush, a kitchen cleaver, and a hollow turnip lying at his feet! Unable to understand this curious transformation, he clutched the placard with feverish haste, and there, in the grey morning light, he read these fearful words:

YE OTIS GHOSTE
Ye Onlie True and Originale Spook,

Beware of Ye Imitationes.
All others are counterfeite.

The whole thing flashed across him. He had been tricked, foiled, and out-witted! The old Canterville look came into his eyes; he ground his toothless gums together; and, raising his withered hands high above his head, swore according to the picturesque phraseology of the antique school, that, when Chanticleer had sounded twice his merry horn, deeds of blood would be wrought, and murder walk abroad with silent feet.

Hardly had he finished this awful oath when, from the red-tiled roof of a distant homestead, a cock crew. He laughed a long, low, bitter laugh, and waited. Hour after hour he waited, but the cock, for some strange reason, did not crow again. Finally, at half-past seven, the arrival of the housemaids made him give up his fearful vigil, and he stalked back to his room, thinking of his vain oath and baffled purpose. There he consulted several books of ancient chivalry, of which he was exceedingly fond, and found that, on every occasion on which this oath had been used, Chanticleer had always crowed a second time. "Perdition seize the naughty fowl," he muttered, "I have seen the day when, with my stout spear, I would have run him through the gorge, and made him crow for me an "twere in death!" He then retired to a comfortable lead coffin, and stayed there till evening.

IV

The next day the ghost was very weak and tired. The terrible excitement of the last four weeks was beginning to have its effect. His nerves were completely shattered, and he started at the slightest noise. For five days he kept his room, and at last made up his mind to give up the point of the blood-stain on the library floor. If the Otis family did not want it, they clearly did not deserve it. They were evidently people on a low, material plane of existence, and quite incapable of appreciating the symbolic value of sensuous phenomena. The question of phantasmic apparitions, and the development of astral bodies, was of course quite a different matter, and really not under his control. It was his solemn duty to appear in the corridor once a week, and to gibber from the large oriel window on the first and third Wednesdays in every month, and he did not see how he could honourably escape from his obligations. It is quite true that his life had been very evil, but, upon the other hand, he was most conscientious in all things connected with the supernatural. For the next three Saturdays, accordingly, he traversed the corridor as usual between midnight and three o'clock, taking every possible precaution against being either heard or seen. He removed his boots, trod as lightly as possible on the old worm-eaten boards, wore a large black velvet cloak, and was careful to use the Rising Sun Lubricator for oiling his chains. I am bound to acknowledge that it was with a good deal of difficulty that he brought himself to adopt this last mode of protection. However, one night, while the family were at dinner, he slipped into Mr. Otis's bedroom and carried off the bottle. He felt a little humiliated at first, but afterwards was sensible enough to see that there was a great deal to be said for the invention, and, to a certain degree, it served his purpose. Still in spite of everything he was not left unmolested. Strings were continually being stretched across the corridor, over which he tripped in the dark, and on one occasion, while dressed for the part of "Black Isaac, or the Huntsman of Hogley Woods," he met with a severe fall, through treading on a butter-slide, which the twins had constructed from the entrance of the Tapestry Chamber to the top of the oak staircase. This last insult so enraged him, that he resolved to make one final effort to assert his dignity and social position, and determined to visit the insolent young Etonians the next night in his celebrated character of "Reckless Rupert, or the Headless Earl."

He had not appeared in this disguise for more than seventy years; in fact, not since he had so frightened pretty Lady Barbara Modish by means of it, that she suddenly broke off her engagement with the present Lord Canterville's grandfather, and ran away to Gretna Green with handsome Jack Castletown, declaring that nothing in the world would induce her to marry into a family that allowed such a horrible phantom to walk up and down the terrace at twilight. Poor Jack was afterwards shot in a duel by Lord Canterville on Wandsworth Common, and Lady Barbara died of a broken heart at Tunbridge Wells before the year was out, so, in every way, it had been a great success. It was, however an extremely difficult "make-up," if I may use such a theatrical expression in connection with one of the greatest mysteries of the supernatural, or, to employ a more scientific term, the higher-natural world, and it took him fully three hours to make his preparations. At last everything was ready, and he was very pleased with his appearance. The big leather riding-boots that went with the dress were just a little too large for him, and he could only find one of the two horse-pistols, but, on the whole, he was quite satisfied, and at a quarter-past one he glided out of the wainscoting and crept down the corridor. On reaching the room occupied by the twins, which I should mention was called the Blue Bed Chamber, on account of the colour of its hangings, he found the door just ajar. Wishing to make an effective entrance, he flung it wide open, when a heavy jug of water fell right down on him, wetting him to the skin, and just missing his left shoulder by a couple of inches. At the same moment he heard stifled shrieks of laughter proceeding from the four-post bed. The shock to his nervous system was so great that he fled back to his room as hard as he could go, and the next day he was laid up with a severe cold. The only thing that at all consoled him in the whole affair was the fact that he had not brought his head with him, for, had he done so, the consequences might have been very serious.

He now gave up all hope of ever frightening this rude American family, and contented himself, as a rule, with creeping about the passages in list slippers, with a thick red muffler round his throat for fear of draughts, and a small arquebuse, in case he should be attacked by the twins. The final blow he received occurred on the 19th of September. He had gone down-stairs to the great entrance-hall, feeling sure that there, at any rate, he would be quite unmolested, and was amusing himself by making satirical remarks on the large Saroni photographs of the United States Minister and his wife which had now taken the place of the Canterville family pictures. He was simply but neatly clad in a long shroud, spotted with churchyard mould, had tied up his jaw with a strip of yellow linen, and carried a small lantern and a sexton's spade. In fact, he was dressed for the character of "Jonas the Graveless, or the Corpse-Snatcher of Chertsey Barn," one of his most remarkable impersonations, and one which the Cantervilles had every reason to remember, as it was the real origin of their quarrel with their neighbour, Lord Rufford. It was about a quarter-past two o'clock in the morning, and, as far as he could ascertain, no one was stirring. As he was strolling towards the library, however, to see if there were any traces left of the blood-stain, suddenly there leaped out on him from a dark corner two figures, who waved their arms wildly above their heads, and shrieked out "BOO!" in his ear.

Seized with a panic, which, under the circumstances, was only natural, he rushed for the staircase, but found Washington Otis waiting for him there with the big garden-syringe, and being thus hemmed in by his enemies on every side, and driven almost to bay, he vanished into the great iron stove, which, fortunately for him, was not lit, and had to make his way home through the flues and chimneys, arriving at his own room in a terrible state of dirt, disorder, and despair.

After this he was not seen again on any nocturnal expedition. The twins lay in wait for him on several occasions, and strewed the passages with nutshells every night to the great annoyance of their parents and the servants, but it was of no avail. It was quite evident that his feelings were so wounded that he would not appear. Mr. Otis consequently resumed his great work on the history of the Democratic Party, on which he had been engaged for some years; Mrs. Otis organized a wonderful clam-bake, which amazed the whole county; the boys took to lacrosse euchre, poker, and other American national games, and Virginia rode about the lanes on her pony, accompanied by the young Duke of Cheshire, who had come to spend the last week of his holidays at Canterville Chase. It was generally assumed that the ghost had gone away, and, in fact, Mr. Otis wrote a letter to that effect to Lord Canterville, who, in reply, expressed his great pleasure at the news, and sent his best congratulations to the Minister's worthy wife.

The Otises, however, were deceived, for the ghost was still in the house, and though now almost an invalid, was by no means ready to let matters rest, particularly as he heard that among the guests was the young Duke of Cheshire, whose grand-uncle, Lord Francis Stilton, had once bet a hundred guineas with Colonel Carbury that he would play dice with the Canterville ghost, and was found the next morning lying on the floor of the card-room in such a helpless paralytic state that, though he lived on to a great age, he was never able to say anything again but "Double Sixes." The story was well known at the time, though, of course, out of respect to the feelings of the two noble families, every attempt was made to hush it up, and a full account of all the circumstances connected with it will be found in the third volume of Lord Tattle's Recollections of the Prince Regent and his Friends. The ghost, then, was naturally very anxious to show that he had not lost his influence over the Stiltons, with whom, indeed, he was distantly connected, his own first cousin having been married en secondes noces to the Sieur de Bulkeley, from whom, as every one knows, the Dukes of Cheshire are lineally descended. Accordingly, he made arrangements for appearing to Virginia's little lover in his celebrated impersonation of "The Vampire Monk, or the Bloodless Benedictine," a performance so horrible that when old Lady Startup saw it, which she did on one fatal New Year's Eve, in the year 1764, she went off into the most piercing shrieks, which culminated in violent apoplexy, and died in three days, after disinheriting the Cantervilles, who were her nearest relations, and leaving all her money to her London apothecary. At the last moment, however, his terror of the twins prevented his leaving his room, and the little Duke slept in peace under the great feathered canopy in the Royal Bedchamber, and dreamed of Virginia.

V

A few days after this, Virginia and her curly-haired cavalier went out riding on Brockley meadows, where she tore her habit so badly in getting through a hedge that, on their return home, she made up her mind to go up by the back staircase so as not to be seen. As she was running past the Tapestry Chamber, the door of which happened to be open, she fancied she saw some one inside, and thinking it was her mother's maid, who sometimes used to bring her work there, looked in to ask her to mend her habit. To her immense surprise, however, it was the Canterville Ghost himself! He was sitting by the window, watching the ruined gold of the yellowing trees fly through the air, and the red leaves dancing madly down the long avenue. His head was leaning on his hand, and his whole attitude was one of extreme depression. Indeed, so forlorn, and so much out of repair did he look, that little Virginia, whose first idea had been to run away and lock herself in her room, was filled with pity, and determined to try and comfort him. So light was her footfall, and so deep his melancholy, that he was not aware of her presence till she spoke to him.

"I am so sorry for you," she said, "but my brothers are going back to Eton to-morrow, and then, if you behave yourself, no one will annoy you."

"It is absurd asking me to behave myself," he answered, looking round in astonishment at the pretty little girl who had ventured to address him, "quite absurd. I must rattle my chains, and groan through keyholes, and walk about at night, if that is what you mean. It is my only reason for existing."

"It is no reason at all for existing, and you know you have been very wicked. Mrs. Umney told us, the first day we arrived here, that you had killed your wife."

"Well, I quite admit it," said the Ghost, petulantly, "but it was a purely family matter, and concerned no one else."

"It is very wrong to kill any one," said Virginia, who at times had a sweet puritan gravity, caught from some old New England ancestor.

"Oh, I hate the cheap severity of abstract ethics! My wife was very plain, never had my ruffs properly starched, and knew nothing about cookery. Why, there was a buck I had shot in Hogley Woods, a magnificent pricket, and do you know how she had it sent to table? However, it is no matter now, for it is all over, and I don't think it was very nice of her brothers to starve me to death, though I did kill her."

"Starve you to death? Oh, Mr. Ghost – I mean Sir Simon, are you hungry? I have a sandwich in my case. Would you like it?"

"No, thank you, I never eat anything now; but it is very kind of you, all the same, and you are much nicer than the rest of your horrid, rude, vulgar, dishonest family."

"Stop!" cried Virginia, stamping her foot, "it is you who are rude, and horrid, and vulgar, and as for dishonesty, you know you stole the paints out of my box to try and furbish up that ridiculous blood-stain in the library. First you took all my reds, including the vermilion, and I couldn't do any more sunsets, then you took the emerald-green and the chrome-yellow, and finally I had nothing left but indigo and Chinese white, and could only do moonlight scenes, which are always depressing to look at, and not at all easy to paint. I never told on you, though I was very much annoyed, and it was most ridiculous, the whole thing; for who ever heard of emerald-green blood?"

"Well, really," said the Ghost, rather meekly, "what was I to do? It is a very difficult thing to get real blood nowadays, and, as your brother began it all with his Paragon Detergent, I certainly saw no reason why I should not have your paints. As for colour, that is always a matter of taste: the Cantervilles have blue blood, for instance, the very bluest in England; but I know you Americans don't care for things of this kind."

"You know nothing about it, and the best thing you can do is to emigrate and improve your mind. My father will be only too happy to give you a free passage, and though there is a heavy duty on spirits of every kind, there will be no difficulty about the Custom House, as the officers are all Democrats. Once in New York, you are sure to be a great success. I know lots of people there who would give a hundred thousand dollars to have a grandfather, and much more than that to have a family ghost."

"I don't think I should like America."

"I suppose because we have no ruins and no curiosities," said Virginia, satirically.

"No ruins! no curiosities!" answered the Ghost; "you have your navy and your manners."

"Good evening; I will go and ask papa to get the twins an extra week's holiday."

"Please don't go, Miss Virginia," he cried; "I am so lonely and so unhappy, and I really don't know what to do. I want to go to sleep and I cannot."

"That's quite absurd! You have merely to go to bed and blow out the candle. It is very difficult sometimes to keep awake, especially at church, but there is no difficulty at all about sleeping. Why, even babies know how to do that, and they are not very clever."

"I have not slept for three hundred years," he said sadly, and Virginia's beautiful blue eyes opened in wonder; "for three hundred years I have not slept, and I am so tired."

Virginia grew quite grave, and her little lips trembled like rose-leaves. She came towards him, and kneeling down at his side, looked up into his old withered face.

"Poor, poor Ghost," she murmured; "have you no place where you can sleep?"

"Far away beyond the pine-woods," he answered, in a low, dreamy voice, "there is a little garden. There the grass grows long and deep, there are the great white stars of the hemlock flower, there the nightingale sings all night long. All night long he sings, and the cold crystal moon looks down, and the yew-tree spreads out its giant arms over the sleepers."

Virginia's eyes grew dim with tears, and she hid her face in her hands.

"You mean the Garden of Death," she whispered.

"Yes, death. Death must be so beautiful. To lie in the soft brown earth, with the grasses waving above one's head, and listen to silence. To have no yesterday, and no to-morrow. To forget time, to forget life, to be at peace. You can help me. You can open for me the portals of death's house, for love is always with you, and love is stronger than death is."

Virginia trembled, a cold shudder ran through her, and for a few moments there was silence. She felt as if she was in a terrible dream.

Then the ghost spoke again, and his voice sounded like the sighing of the wind. "Have you ever read the old prophecy on the library window?"

"Oh, often," cried the little girl, looking up; "I know it quite well. It is painted in curious black letters, and is difficult to read. There are only six lines:

> *When a golden girl can win*
> *Prayer from out the lips of sin,*
> *When the barren almond bears,*
> *And a little child gives away its tears,*
> *Then shall all the house be still*
> *And peace come to Canterville.*

But I don't know what they mean."

"They mean," he said, sadly, "that you must weep with me for my sins, because I have no tears, and pray with me for my soul, because I have no faith, and then, if you have always been sweet, and good, and gentle, the angel of death will have mercy on me. You will see fearful shapes in darkness, and wicked voices will whisper in your ear, but they will not harm you, for against the purity of a little child the powers of Hell cannot prevail."

Virginia made no answer, and the ghost wrung his hands in wild despair as he looked down at her bowed golden head. Suddenly she stood up, very pale, and with a strange light in her eyes. "I am not afraid," she said firmly, "and I will ask the angel to have mercy on you."

He rose from his seat with a faint cry of joy, and taking her hand bent over it with old-fashioned grace and kissed it. His fingers were as cold as ice, and his lips burned like fire, but Virginia did not falter, as he led her across the dusky room. On the faded green tapestry were broidered little huntsmen. They blew their tasselled horns and with their tiny hands waved to her to go back. "Go back! little Virginia," they cried, "go back!" but the ghost clutched her hand more tightly, and she shut her eyes against them. Horrible animals with lizard tails and goggle eyes blinked at her from the carven chimneypiece, and murmured, "Beware! little Virginia, beware! we may never see you again," but the Ghost glided on more swiftly, and Virginia did not listen. When they reached the end of the room he stopped, and muttered some words she could not understand. She opened her eyes, and saw the wall slowly fading away like a mist, and a great black cavern in front of her. A bitter cold wind swept round them, and she felt something pulling at her dress. "Quick, quick," cried the Ghost, "or it will be too late," and in a moment the wainscoting had closed behind them, and the Tapestry Chamber was empty.

VI

About ten minutes later, the bell rang for tea, and, as Virginia did not come down, Mrs. Otis sent up one of the footmen to tell her. After a little time he returned and said that he could not find Miss Virginia anywhere. As she was in the habit of going out to the garden every evening to get flowers for the dinner-table, Mrs. Otis was not at all alarmed at first, but when six o'clock struck, and Virginia did not appear, she became really agitated, and sent the boys out to look for her, while she herself and Mr. Otis searched every room in the house. At half-past six the boys came back and said that they could find no trace of their sister anywhere. They were all now in the greatest state of excitement, and did not know what to do, when Mr. Otis suddenly remembered that, some few days before, he had given a band of gipsies permission to camp in the park. He accordingly at once set off for Blackfell Hollow, where he knew they were, accompanied by his eldest son and two of the farm-servants. The little Duke of Cheshire, who was perfectly frantic with anxiety, begged hard to be allowed to go too, but Mr. Otis would not allow him, as he was afraid there might be a scuffle. On arriving at the spot, however, he found that the gipsies had gone, and it was evident that their departure had been rather sudden, as the fire was still burning, and some plates were lying on the grass. Having sent off Washington and the two men to scour the district, he ran home, and despatched telegrams to all the police inspectors in the county, telling them to look out for a little girl who had been kidnapped by tramps or gipsies. He then ordered his horse to be brought round, and, after insisting on his wife and the three boys sitting down to dinner, rode off down the Ascot road with a groom. He had hardly, however, gone a couple of miles, when he heard somebody galloping after him, and, looking round, saw the little Duke coming up on his pony, with his face very flushed, and no hat. "I'm awfully sorry, Mr. Otis," gasped out the boy, "but I can't eat any dinner as long as Virginia is lost. Please don't be angry with me; if you had let us be engaged last year, there would never have been all this trouble. You won't send me back, will you? I can't go! I won't go!"

The Minister could not help smiling at the handsome young scapegrace, and was a good deal touched at his devotion to Virginia, so leaning down from his horse, he patted him kindly on the shoulders, and said, "Well, Cecil, if you won't go back, I suppose you must come with me, but I must get you a hat at Ascot."

"Oh, bother my hat! I want Virginia!" cried the little Duke, laughing, and they galloped on to the railway station. There Mr. Otis inquired of the station-master if any one answering to the description of Virginia had been seen on the platform, but could get no news of her. The station-master, however, wired up and down the line, and assured him that a strict watch would be kept for her, and, after having bought a hat for the little Duke from a linen-draper, who was just putting up his shutters, Mr. Otis rode off to Bexley, a village about four miles away, which he was told was a well-known haunt of the gipsies, as there was a large common next to it. Here they roused up the rural policeman, but could get no information from him, and, after riding all over the common, they turned their horses' heads homewards, and reached the Chase about eleven o'clock, dead-tired and almost heart-broken. They found Washington and the twins waiting for them at the gate-house with lanterns, as the avenue was very dark. Not the slightest trace of Virginia had been discovered. The gipsies had been caught on Brockley meadows, but she was not with them, and they had explained their sudden departure by saying that they had mistaken the date of Chorton Fair, and had gone off in a hurry for fear they should be late. Indeed, they had been quite distressed at hearing of Virginia's disappearance, as they were very grateful to Mr. Otis for having allowed them to camp in his park, and four of their number had stayed behind to help in the search. The carp-pond had been dragged, and the whole Chase thoroughly gone over, but without any result. It was evident that, for that night at any rate, Virginia was lost to them; and it was in a state of the deepest depression that Mr. Otis and the boys walked up to the house, the groom following behind with the two horses and the pony. In the hall they found a group of frightened servants, and lying on a sofa in the library was poor Mrs. Otis, almost out of her mind with terror and anxiety, and having her forehead bathed with eau de cologne by the old housekeeper. Mr. Otis at once insisted on her having something to eat, and ordered up supper for the whole party. It was a melancholy meal, as hardly any one spoke, and even the twins were awestruck and subdued, as they were very fond of their sister. When they had finished, Mr. Otis, in spite of the entreaties of the little Duke, ordered them all to bed, saying that nothing more could be done that night, and that he would telegraph in the morning to Scotland Yard for some detectives to be sent down immediately. Just as they were passing out of the dining-room, midnight began to boom from the clock tower, and when the last stroke sounded they heard a crash and a sudden shrill cry; a dreadful peal of thunder shook the house, a strain of unearthly music floated through the air, a panel at the top of the staircase flew back with a loud noise, and out on the landing, looking very pale and white, with a little casket in her hand, stepped Virginia. In a moment they had all rushed up to her. Mrs. Otis clasped her passionately in her arms, the Duke smothered her with violent kisses, and the twins executed a wild war-dance round the group.

"Good heavens! child, where have you been?" said Mr. Otis, rather angrily, thinking that she had been playing some foolish trick on them. "Cecil and I have been riding all over the country looking for you, and your mother has been frightened to death. You must never play these practical jokes any more."

"Except on the Ghost! except on the Ghost!" shrieked the twins, as they capered about.

"My own darling, thank God you are found; you must never leave my side again," murmured Mrs. Otis, as she kissed the trembling child, and smoothed the tangled gold of her hair.

"Papa," said Virginia, quietly, "I have been with the Ghost. He is dead, and you must come and see him. He had been very wicked, but he was really sorry for all that he had done, and he gave me this box of beautiful jewels before he died."

The whole family gazed at her in mute amazement, but she was quite grave and serious; and, turning round, she led them through the opening in the wainscoting down a narrow secret corridor, Washington following with a lighted candle, which he had caught up from the table. Finally, they came to a great oak door, studded with rusty nails. When Virginia touched it, it swung back on its heavy hinges, and they found themselves in a little low room, with a vaulted ceiling, and one tiny grated window. Imbedded in the wall was a huge iron ring, and chained to it was a gaunt skeleton, that was stretched out at full length on the stone floor, and seemed to be trying to grasp with its long fleshless fingers an old-fashioned trencher and ewer, that were placed just out of its reach. The jug had evidently been once filled with water, as it was covered inside with green mould. There was nothing on the trencher but a pile of dust. Virginia knelt down beside the skeleton, and, folding her little hands together, began to pray silently, while the rest of the party looked on in wonder at the terrible tragedy whose secret was now disclosed to them.

"Hallo!" suddenly exclaimed one of the twins, who had been looking out of the window to try and discover in what wing of the house the room was situated. "Hallo! the old withered almond-tree has blossomed. I can see the flowers quite plainly in the moonlight."

"God has forgiven him," said Virginia, gravely, as she rose to her feet, and a beautiful light seemed to illumine her face.

"What an angel you are!" cried the young Duke, and he put his arm round her neck, and kissed her.

VII

Four days after these curious incidents, a funeral started from Canterville Chase at about eleven o'clock at night. The hearse was drawn by eight black horses, each of which carried on its head a great tuft of nodding ostrich-plumes, and the leaden coffin was covered by a rich purple pall, on which was embroidered in gold the Canterville coat-of-arms. By the side of the hearse and the coaches walked the servants with lighted torches, and the whole procession was wonderfully impressive. Lord Canterville was the chief mourner, having come up specially from Wales to attend the funeral, and sat in the first carriage along with little Virginia. Then came the United States Minister and his wife, then Washington and the three boys, and in the last carriage was Mrs. Umney. It was generally felt that, as she had been frightened by the ghost for more than fifty years of her life, she had a right to see the last of him. A deep grave had been dug in the corner of the churchyard, just under the old yew-tree, and the service was read in the most impressive manner by the Rev. Augustus Dampier. When the ceremony was over, the servants, according to an old custom observed in the Canterville family, extinguished their torches, and, as the coffin was being lowered into the grave, Virginia stepped forward, and laid on it a large cross made of white and pink almond-blossoms. As she did so, the moon came out from behind a cloud, and flooded with its silent silver the little churchyard, and from a distant copse a nightingale began to sing. She thought of the ghost's description of the Garden of Death, her eyes became dim with tears, and she hardly spoke a word during the drive home.

The next morning, before Lord Canterville went up to town, Mr. Otis had an interview with him on the subject of the jewels the ghost had given to Virginia. They were perfectly magnificent, especially a certain ruby necklace with old Venetian setting, which was really a superb specimen of sixteenth-century work, and their value was so great that Mr. Otis felt considerable scruples about allowing his daughter to accept them.

"My lord," he said, "I know that in this country mortmain is held to apply to trinkets as well as to land, and it is quite clear to me that these jewels are, or should be, heirlooms in your family. I must beg you, accordingly, to take them to London with you, and to regard them simply as a portion of your property which has been restored to you under certain strange conditions. As for my daughter, she is merely a child, and has as yet, I am glad to say, but little interest in such appurtenances of idle luxury. I am also informed by Mrs. Otis, who, I may say, is no mean authority upon Art, – having had the privilege of spending several winters in Boston when she was a girl, – that these gems are of great monetary worth, and if offered for sale would fetch a tall price. Under these circumstances, Lord Canterville, I feel sure that you will recognize how impossible it would be for me to allow them to remain in the possession of any member of my family; and, indeed, all such vain gauds and toys, however suitable or necessary to the dignity of the British aristocracy, would be completely out of place among those who have been brought up on the severe, and I believe immortal, principles of Republican simplicity. Perhaps I should mention that Virginia is very anxious that you should allow her to retain the box, as a memento of your unfortunate but misguided ancestor. As it is extremely old, and consequently a good deal out of repair, you may perhaps think fit to comply with her request. For my own part, I confess I am a good deal surprised to find a child of mine expressing sympathy with mediævalism in any form, and can only account for it by the fact that Virginia was born in one of your London suburbs shortly after Mrs. Otis had returned from a trip to Athens."

Lord Canterville listened very gravely to the worthy Minister's speech, pulling his grey moustache now and then to hide an involuntary smile, and when Mr. Otis had ended, he shook him cordially by the hand, and said: "My dear sir, your charming little daughter rendered my unlucky ancestor, Sir Simon, a very important service, and I and my family are much indebted to her for her marvellous courage and pluck. The jewels are clearly hers, and, egad, I believe that if I were heartless enough to take them from her, the wicked old fellow would be out of his grave in a fortnight, leading me the devil of a life. As for their being heirlooms, nothing is an heirloom that is not so mentioned in a will or legal document, and the existence of these jewels has been quite unknown. I assure you I have no more claim on them than your butler, and when Miss Virginia grows up, I dare say she will be pleased to have pretty things to wear. Besides, you forget, Mr. Otis, that you took the furniture and the ghost at a valuation, and anything that belonged to the ghost passed at once into your possession, as, whatever activity Sir Simon may have shown in the corridor at night, in point of law he was really dead, and you acquired his property by purchase."

Mr. Otis was a good deal distressed at Lord Canterville's refusal, and begged him to reconsider his decision, but the good-natured peer was quite firm, and finally induced the Minister to allow his daughter to retain the present the ghost had given her, and when, in the spring of 1890, the young Duchess of Cheshire was presented at the Queen's first drawing-room on the occasion of her marriage, her jewels were the universal theme of admiration. For Virginia received the coronet, which is the reward of all good little American girls, and was married to her boy-lover as soon as he came of age. They were both so charming, and they loved each other so much, that every one was delighted at the match, except the old Marchioness of Dumbleton, who had tried to catch the Duke for one of her seven unmarried daughters, and had given no less than three expensive dinner-parties for that purpose, and, strange to say, Mr. Otis himself. Mr. Otis was extremely fond of the young Duke personally, but, theoretically, he objected to titles, and, to use his own words, "was not without apprehension lest, amid the enervating influences of a pleasure-loving aristocracy, the true principles of Republican simplicity should be forgotten." His objections, however, were completely overruled, and I believe that when he walked up the aisle of St. George's, Hanover Square, with his daughter leaning on his arm, there was not a prouder man in the whole length and breadth of England.

The Duke and Duchess, after the honeymoon was over, went down to Canterville Chase, and on the day after their arrival they walked over in the afternoon to the lonely churchyard by the pine-woods. There had been a great deal of difficulty at first about the inscription on Sir Simon's tombstone, but finally it had been decided to engrave on it simply the initials of the old gentleman's name, and the verse from the library window. The Duchess had brought with her some lovely roses, which she strewed upon the grave, and after they had stood by it for some time they strolled into the ruined chancel of the old abbey. There the Duchess sat down on a fallen pillar, while her husband lay at her feet smoking a cigarette and looking up at her beautiful eyes. Suddenly he threw his cigarette away, took hold of her hand, and said to her, "Virginia, a wife should have no secrets from her husband."

"Dear Cecil! I have no secrets from you."

"Yes, you have," he answered, smiling, "you have never told me what happened to you when you were locked up with the ghost."

"I have never told any one, Cecil," said Virginia, gravely.

"I know that, but you might tell me."

"Please don't ask me, Cecil, I cannot tell you. Poor Sir Simon! I owe him a great deal. Yes, don't laugh, Cecil, I really do. He made me see what Life is, and what Death signifies, and why Love is stronger than both."

The Duke rose and kissed his wife lovingly.

"You can have your secret as long as I have your heart," he murmured.

"You have always had that, Cecil."

"And you will tell our children some day, won't you?"

Virginia blushed.

THE WITHERED ARM

Thomas Hardy

Thomas Hardy (1840–1928) was born into a working-class family in Higher Bockhampton, a village near Dorchester. His father was a master mason who played the fiddle for a local choir, his mother a devout Christian. Hardy left school at sixteen and qualified as an architect. His early poetry and novels were not well received, but with encouragement from George Meredith and Leslie Stephen (Virginia Woolf's father) he persisted and went on to become one of the most popular novelists of his generation.

I
A Lorn Milkmaid

It was an eighty-cow dairy, and the troop of milkers, regular and supernumerary, were all at work; for, though the time of year was as yet but early April, the feed lay entirely in water-meadows, and the cows were "in full pail". The hour was about six in the evening, and three-fourths of the large, red, rectangular animals having been finished off, there was opportunity for a little conversation.

"He do bring home his bride tomorrow, I hear. They've come as far as Anglebury today."

The voice seemed to proceed from the belly of the cow called Cherry, but the speaker was a milking-woman, whose face was buried in the flank of that motionless beast.

"Hav' anybody seen her?" said another.

There was a negative response from the first. "Though they say she's a rosy-cheeked, tisty-tosty little body enough," she added; and as the milkmaid spoke she turned her face so that she could glance past her cow's tall to the other side of the barton, where a thin, fading woman of thirty milked somewhat apart from the rest.

"Years younger than he, they say," continued the second, with also a glance of reflectiveness in the same direction.

"How old do you call him, then?"

"Thirty or so."

"More like forty," broke in an old milkman near, in a long white pinafore or "wropper", and with the brim of his hat tied down, so that he looked like a woman. "A was born before our Great Weir was builded, and I hadn't man's wages when I laved water there."

The discussion waxed so warm that the purr of the milk streams became jerky, till a voice from another cow's belly cried with authority, "Now then, what the Turk do it matter to us about Farmer Lodge's age, or Farmer Lodge's new mis'ess? I shall have to pay him nine pound a year for the rent of every one of these milchers, whatever his age or hers. Get on with your work, or "twill be dark afore we have done. The evening is pinking in a'ready." This speaker was the dairyman himself, by whom the milkmaids and men were employed.

Nothing more was said publicly about Farmer Lodge's wedding, but the first woman murmured under her cow to her next neighbour. "Tis hard for she," signifying the thin worn milkmaid aforesaid.

"O no," said the second. "He ha'n't spoke to Rhoda Brook for years."

When the milking was done they washed their pails and hung them on a many-forked stand made as usual of the peeled limb of an oak-tree, set upright in the earth, and resembling a colossal antlered horn. The majority then dispersed in various directions homeward. The thin woman who had not spoken was joined by a boy of twelve or thereabout, and the twain went away up the field also.

Their course lay apart from that of the others, to a lonely spot high above the water-meads, and not far from the border of Egdon Heath, whose dark countenance was visible in the distance as they drew nigh to their home.

"They've just been saying down in barton that your father brings his young wife home from Anglebury tomorrow," the woman observed. "I shall want to send you for a few things to market, and you'll be pretty sure to meet 'em."

"Yes, Mother," said the boy. "Is Father married then?"

"Yes . . . You can give her a look, and tell me what she's like, if you do see her."

"Yes, Mother."

"If she's dark or fair, and if she's tall – as tall as I. And if she seems like a woman who has ever worked for a living, or one that has been always well off, and has never done anything, and shows marks of the lady on her, as I expect she do."

"Yes."

They crept up the hill in the twilight and entered the cottage. It was built of mud-walls, the surface of which had been washed by many rains into channels and depressions that left none of the original flat face visible, while here and there in the thatch above a rafter showed like a bone protruding through the skin.

She was kneeling down in the chimney-corner, before two pieces of turf laid together with the heather inwards, blowing at the red-hot ashes with her breath till the turves flamed. The radiance lit her pale cheek, and made her dark eyes, that had once been handsome, seem handsome anew. "Yes," she resumed, "see if she is dark or fair, and if you can, notice if her hands be white; if not, see if they look as though she had ever done housework, or are milker's hands like mine."

The boy again promised, inattentively this time, his mother not observing that he was cutting a notch with his pocket-knife in the beech-backed chair.

II
The Young Wife

The road from Anglebury to Holmstoke is in general level, but there is one place where a sharp ascent breaks its monotony. Farmers homeward-hound from the former market-town, who trot all the rest of the way, walk their horses up this short incline.

The next evening while the sun was yet bright a handsome new gig, with a lemon-coloured body and red wheels, was spinning westward along the level highway at the heels of a powerful mare. The driver was a yeoman in the prime of life, cleanly shaven like an actor, his face being toned to that bluish-vermilion hue which so often graces a thriving farmer's features when returning home after successful dealings in the town. Beside him sat a woman, many years his junior – almost, indeed, a girl. Her face too was fresh in colour, but it was of a totally different quality – soft and evanescent, like the light under a heap of rose-petals.

Few people travelled this way, for it was not a main road; and the long white ribered and of gravel that stretched before them was empty, save of one small scarce-moving speck, which presently resolved itself into the figure of a boy, who was creeping on at a snail's pace, and continually looking behind him – the heavy bundle he carried being some excuse for, if not the reason of, his dilatoriness. When the bouncing gig-party slowed at the bottom of the incline above mentioned, the pedestrian was only a few yards in front. Supporting the large bundle by putting one hand on his hip, he turned and looked straight at the farmer's wife as though he would read her through and through, pacing along abreast of the horse.

The low sun was full in her face, rendering every feature, shade, and colour distinct, from the curve of her little nostril to the colour of her eyes. The farmer, though he seemed annoyed at the boy's persistent presence, did not order him to get out of the way; and thus the lad preceded them, his hard gaze never leaving her, till they reached the top of the ascent, when the farmer trotted on with relief in his lineaments having taken no outward notice of the boy whatever.

"How that poor lad stared at me!" said the young wife.

"Yes, dear; I saw that he did."

"He is one of the village, I suppose?"

"One of the neighbourhood. I think he lives with his mother a mile or two off."

"He knows who we are, no doubt?"

"O yes. You must expect to be stared at just at first, my pretty Gertrude."

"I do – though I think the poor boy may have looked at us in the hope we might relieve him of his heavy load, rather than from curiosity."

"O no," said her husband off-handedly. "These country lads will carry a hundredweight once they get it on their backs; besides his pack had more size than weight in it. Now, then, another mile and I shall be able to show you our house in the distance – if it is not too dark before we get there." The wheels spun round, and particles flew from their periphery as before, till a white house of ample dimensions revealed itself, with farm-buildings and ricks at the back.

Meanwhile the boy had quickened his pace, and turning up a by-lane some mile-and-a-half short of the white farmstead, ascended towards the leaner pastures, and so on to the cottage of his mother.

She had reached home after her day's milking at the outlying dairy, and was washing cabbage at the doorway in the declining light. "Hold up the net a moment," she said, without preface, as the boy came up.

He flung down his bundle, held the edge of the cabbage-net, and as she filled its meshes with the dripping leaves she went on, "Well, did you see her?"

"Yes; quite plain."

"Is she ladylike?"

"Yes; and more. A lady complete."

"Is she young?"

"Well, she's growed up, and her ways be quite a woman's."

"Of course. What colour is her hair and face?"

"Her hair is lightish, and her face as comely as a live doll's."

"Her eyes, then, are not dark like mine?"

"No – of a bluish turn, and her mouth is very nice and red; and when she smiles, her teeth show white."

"Is she tall?" said the woman sharply.

"I couldn't see. She was sitting down."

"Then do you go to Holmstoke church tomorrow morning: she's sure to be there. Go early and notice her walking in, and come home and tell me if she's taller than I."

"Very well, Mother. But why don't you go and see for yourself?"

"I go to see her! I wouldn't look up at her if she were to pass my window this instant. She was with Mr Lodge, of course. What did he say or do?"

"Just the same as usual."

"Took no notice of you?"

"None."

Next day the mother put a clean shirt on the boy, and started him off for Holmstoke church. He reached the ancient little pile when the door was just being opened, and he was the first to enter. Taking his seat by the font, he watched all the parishioners file in. The well-to-do Farmer Lodge came nearly last; and his young wife, who accompanied him, walked up the aisle with the shyness natural to a modest woman who had appeared thus for the first time. As all other eyes were fixed upon her, the youth's stare was not noticed now.

When he reached home his mother said, "Well?" before he had entered the room.

"She is not tall. She is rather short," he replied.

"Ah!" said his mother, with satisfaction.

"But she's very pretty – very. In fact, she's lovely." The youthful freshness of the yeoman's wife had evidently made an impression even on the somewhat hard nature of the boy.

"That's all I want to hear," said his mother quickly. "Now, spread the table-cloth. The hare you wired is very tender; but mind nobody catches you. You've never told me what sort of hands she had."

"I have never seen 'em. She never took off her gloves"

"What did she wear this morning?"

"A white bonnet and a silver-coloured gownd. It whewed and whistled so loud when it rubbed against the pews that the lady coloured up more than ever for very shame at the noise, and pulled it in to keep it from touching; but when she pushed into her seat, it whewed more than ever. Mr Lodge, he seemed pleased, and his waistcoat stuck out, and his great golden seals hung like a lord's; but she seemed to wish her noisy gownd anywhere but on her."

"Not she! However, that will do now."

These descriptions of the newly married couple were continued from time to time by the boy at his mother's request, after any chance encounter he had had with them. But Rhoda Brook, though she might easily have seen young Mrs Lodge for herself by walking a couple of miles, would never attempt an excursion towards the quarter where the farmhouse lay. Neither did she, at the daily milking in the dairyman's yard on Lodge's outlying second farm, ever speak on the subject of the recent marriage. The dairyman, who rented the cows of Lodge, and knew perfectly the tall milkmaid's history, with manly kindness always kept the gossip in the cow-barton from annoying Rhoda. But the atmosphere thereabout was full of the subject the first days of Mrs Lodge's arrival; and fom her boy's description and the casual words of the other milkers, Rhoda Brook could raise a mental image of the unconscious Mrs Lodge that was realistic as a photograph.

III
A Vision

One night, two or three weeks after the bridal return, when the boy had gone to bed, Rhoda sat a long time over the turf ashes that she had raked out in front of her to extinguish them. She contemplated so intently the new wife, as presented to her in her mind's eye over the embers, that she forgot the lapse of time. At last, wearied by her day's work, she too retired.

But the figure which had occupied her so much during this and the previous days was not to be banished at night. For the first time Gertrude Lodge "visited" the supplanted woman in her dreams. Rhoda Brook dreamed – since her assertion that she really saw, before falling asleep, was not to be believed – that the young wife, in the pale silk dress and white bonnet, but with features shockingly distorted, and wrinkled as by age, was sitting upon her chest as she lay. The pressure of Mrs Lodge's person grew heavier; the blue eyes peered cruelly into her face: and then the figure thrust forward its left hand mockingly, so as to make the wedding-ring it wore glitter in Rhoda's eyes. Maddened mentally, and nearly suffocated by pressure, the sleeper struggled; the incubus, still regarding her, withdrew to the foot of the bed, only, however, to come forward by degrees, resume her seat, and flash her left hand as before.

Gasping for breath, Rhoda, in a last desperate effort, swung out her right hand, seized the confronting spectre by its obtrusive left arm, and whirled it backward to the floor, starting up herself as she did so with a low cry.

"O, merciful heaven!" she cried, sitting on the edge of the bed in a cold sweat; "that was not a dream – she was here!"

She could feel her antagonist's arm within her grasp even now – the very flesh and hone of it, as it seemed. She looked on the floor whither she had whirled the spectre, but there was nothing to be seen.

Rhoda Brook slept no more that night, and when she went milking at the next dawn they noticed how pale and haggard she looked. The milk that she drew quivered into the pail; her hand had not calmed even yet. And still retained the feel of the arm. She came home to breakfast as wearily as if it had been suppertime.

"What was that noise in your chimmer, mother, last night?" said her son. "You fell off the bed, surely?"

"Did you hear anything fall? At what time?"

"Just when the clock struck two."

She could not explain, and when the meal was done went silently about her household works, the boy assisting her, for he hated going afield on the farms, and she indulged his reluctance. Between eleven and twelve the garden-gate clicked, and she lifted her eyes to the window. At the bottom of the garden, within the gate, stood the woman of her vision. Rhoda seemed transfixed.

"Ah, she said she would come!" exclaimed the boy, also observing her.

"Said so – when? How does she know us?"

"I have seen and spoken" to her. I talked to her yesterday."

"I told you," said the mother, flushing indignantly, "never to speak to anybody in that house, or go near the place."

"I did not speak to her till she spoke to me. And I did not go near the place. I met her in the road."

"What did you tell her?"

"Nothing. She said, "Are you the poor boy who had to bring the heavy load from market?" And she looked at my hoots, and said they would not keep my feet dry if it came on wet, because they were so cracked. I told her I lived with my mother, and we had enough to do to keep ourselves, and that's how it was; and she said then: "I'll come and bring you some better hoots, and see your mother." She gives away things to other folks in the meads besides us."

Mrs Lodge was by this time close to the door – not in her silk, as Rhoda had dreamt of in the bed-chamber, but in a morning hat, and gown of common light material, which became her better than silk. On her arm she carried a basket.

The impression remaining from the night's experience was still strong. Brook had almost expected to see the wrinkles, the scorn and the cruelty on her visitor's face. She would have escaped an interview, had escape been possible. There was, however, no backdoor to the cottage, and in an instant the boy had lifted the latch to Mrs Lodge's gentle knock.

"I see I have come to the right house," said she, glancing at the lad, and smiling. "But I was not sure till you opened the door."

The figure and action were those of the phantom; but her voice was so indescribably sweet, her glance so winning, her smile so tender, so unlike that of Rhoda's midnight visitant, that the latter could hardly believe the evidence of her senses. She was truly glad that she had not hidden away in sheer aversion, as she had been inclined to do. In her basket Mrs Lodge brought the pair of boots that she had promised to the boy, and other useful articles.

At these proofs of a kindly feeling towards her and hers Rhoda's heart reproached her bitterly. This innocent young thing should have her blessing and not her curse. When she left them a light seemed gone from the dwelling. Two days later she came again to know if the boots fitted; and less than a fortnight after paid Rhoda another call. On this occasion the boy was absent.

"I walk a good deal," said Mrs Lodge, "and your house is the nearest outside our own parish. I hope you are well. You don't look quite well."

Rhoda said she was well enough; and, indeed, though the paler of the two, there was more of the strength that endures in her well-defined features and large frame than in the soft-cheeked young woman before her. The conversation became quite confidential as regarded their powers and weaknesses; and when Mrs Lodge was leaving, Rhoda said, "I hope you will find this air agree with you, ma'am, and not suffer from the damp of the water-meads."

The younger one replied that there was not much doubt of her general health being usually good. "Though, now you remind me, she added, "I have one little ailment which puzzles me. It is nothing serious, but I cannot make it out."

She uncovered her left hand and arm; and their outline confronted Rhoda's gaze as the exact original of the limb she had beheld and seized in her dream. Upon the pink round surface of the arm were faint marks of an unhealthy colour, as if produced by a rough grasp. Rhoda's eyes became riveted on the discolorations; she fancied that she discerned in them the shape of her own four fingers.

"How did it happen?" she said mechanically.

"I cannot tell," replied Mrs Lodge, shaking her head. "One night when I was sound asleep, dreaming I was away in some strange place, a pain suddenly shot into my arm there, and was so keen as to awaken me. I must have struck it in the daytime, I suppose, though I don't remember doing so." She added, laughing, "I tell my dear husband that it looks just as if he had flown into a rage and struck me there. O, I daresay it will soon disappear."

"Ha, ha! Yes . . . On what night did it come?"

Mrs Lodge considered, and said it would be a fortnight ago on the morrow. "When I awoke I could not remember where I was," she added, "till the clock striking two reminded me."

She had named the night and hour of Rhoda's spectral encounter, and Brook felt like a guilty thing. The artless disclosure startled her; she did not reason on the freaks of coincidence; and all the scenery of that ghastly night returned with double vividness to her mind.

"O, can it be," she said to herself, when her visitor had departed, "that I exercise a malignant power over people against my own will?" She knew that she had been slyly called a witch since hey fall; but never having understood why that particular stigma had been attached to her, it had passed disregarded. Could this be the explanation, and had such things as this ever happened before?

IV
A Suggestion

The summer drew on, and Rhoda Brook almost dreaded to meet Mrs Lodge again, notwithstanding that her feeling for the young wife amounted well-nigh to affection. Something in her own individuality seemed to convict Rhoda of crime. Yet a fatality sometimes would direct the steps of the latter to the outskirts of Holmstoke whenever she left her house for any other purpose than her daily work; and hence it happened that their next encounter was out of doors. Rhoda could not avoid the subject which had so mystified her, and after the first few words she stammered, "I hope your – arm is well again, ma'm?" She had perceived with consternation that Gertrude Lodge carried her left arm stiffly.

"No; it not quite well. Indeed it is no better at all; it is rather worse. It pains me dreadfully sometimes."

"Perhaps you had better go to a doctor, ma'am."

She replied that she had already seen a doctor. Her husband had insisted upon her going to one. But the surgeon had not seemed to understand the afflicted limb at all; he had told her to bathe it in hot water, and she had bathed it, but the treatment had done no good.

"Will you let me see it?" said the milkwoman.

Mrs Lodge pushed up her sleeve and disclosed the place, which was a few inches above the wrist. As soon as Rhoda Brook saw it, she could hardly preserve her composure. There was nothing of the nature of a wound, but the arm at that point had a shrivelled look, and the outline of the four fingers appeared more distinct than at the former Moreover, she fancied that they were imprinted in precisely the relative position of her clutch upon the arm in the trance; the first linger towards Gertrude's wrist, and the fourth towards her elbow.

What the impress resembled seemed to have struck Gertrude herself since their last meeting. "It looks almost like finger marks," she said; adding with a faint laugh, "my husband says it is as if some witch, or the devil himself, had taken hold of me there, and blasted the flesh."

Rhoda shivered. "That's fancy," she said hurriedly. "I wouldn't mind it, if I were you."

"I shouldn't so much mind it," said the younger, with hesitation, "if – if I hadn't a notion that it makes my husband dislike me – no, love me less. Men think so much of personal appearance."

"Some do – he for one."

"Yes; and he was very proud of mine, at first."

"Keep your arm covered from his sight."

"Ah – he knows the disfigurement is there!" She tried to hide the tears that filled her eyes.

"Well, ma'am, I earnestly hope it will go away soon."

And so the milkwoman's mind was chained anew to the subject by a horrid sort of spell as she returned home. The sense of having been guilty of an act of malignity increased, affect as she might to ridicule her superstition. In her secret heart Rhoda did not altogether object to a slight diminution of her successor's beauty, by whatever means it had come about; but she did not wish to inflict upon her physical pain. For though this pretty young woman had rendered im-possible any reparation which Lodge might have made Rhoda for his past con-duct, everything like resentment at the unconscious usurpation had quite passed away from the elder's mind.

If the sweet and kindly Gertrude Lodge only knew of the dream-scene in the bed-chamber, what would she think? Not to inform her of it seemed treachery in the presence of her friendliness; but tell she could not of her own accord neither could she devise a remedy.

She mused upon the matter the greater part of the night; and the next day, after the morning milking, set out to obtain another glimpse of Gertrude Lodge if she could, being held to her by a gruesome fascination. By watching the house from a distance the milkmaid was presently able to discern the farmer's wife in a ride she was taking alone – probably to join her husband in some distant field. Mrs Lodge perceived her, and cantered in her direction.

"Good morning, Rhoda!" Gertrude said, when she had come up. "I was going to call."

Rhoda noticed that Mrs Lodge held the reins with some difficulty.

"I hope – the bad arm," said Rhoda.

"They tell me there is possibly one way by which I might be able to find out the cause, and so perhaps the cure of it," replied the other anxiously. "It is by going to some clever man over in Egdon Heath. They did not know if he was still alive – and I cannot remember his name at this moment; but they said that you knew more of his movements than anybody else hereabout, and could tell me if he were still to be consulted. Dear me what was his name? But you know."

"Not Conjuror Trendle?" said her thin companion, turning pale.

"Trendle – yes. Is he alive?"

"I believe so," said Rhoda, with reluctance.

"Why do you call him conjuror?"

"Well – they say – they used to say he was a – he had powers other folks have not."

"O, how could my people be so superstitious as to recommend a man of that sort! I thought they meant some medical man. I shall think no more of him."

Rhoda looked relieved, and Mrs Lodge rode on. The milkwoman had inwardly seen, from the moment she heard of her having been mentioned as a reference for this man, "that there must exist a sarcastic feeling among the work-folk that a sorceress would know the wbereabouts of the exorcist. They suspected her, then. A short time ago this" would have given no concern to a woman of her common sense. But she had a haunting reason to be superstitious now; and she had been seized with sudden dread that this Conjuror Trendle might name her as the malignant influence" which was blasting the fair person of Gertrude, and so lead her friend to hate her for ever, and to treat her as some fiend in human shape.

But all was not over. Two days after, a shadow intruded into the window-pattern thrown on Rhoda Brook's floor by the afternoon sun. The woman opened the door at once, almost breathlessly.

"Are you alone?" said Gertrude. She seemed to be no less harassed and anxious than Brook herself.

"Yes," said Rhoda.

"The place on my arm seems worse, and troubles me!" the young farmer's wife went OIL "It is so mysterious! I do hope it will not be an incurable wound. I have again been thinking of what they said about Conjuror Trendle. I don't really believe in such men, but I should not mind just visiting him, from curiosity – though on no account must my husband know. Is it far to where he lives?"

"Yes – five miles," said Rhoda backwardly. "In the heart of Egdon."

"Well, I should have to walk. Could not you go with me to show me the way – say tomorrow afternoon?"

"O, not I; that is—," the milkwoman murmured, with a start of dismay. Again the dread seized her that something to do with her fierce act in the dream might be revealed, and her character in the eyes of the most useful friend she had ever had be ruined irretrievably.

Mrs Lodge urged, and Rhoda finally assented, though with much misgiving.

Sad as the journey would be to her, she could not conscientiously stand in the way of a possible remedy for her patron's strange affliction. It was agreed that, to escape suspicion of their mystic intent, they should meet at the edge of the heath at the corner of a plantation which was visible from the spot where they now stood.

V
Conjuror Trendle

By the next afternoon Rhoda would have done anything to escape this inquiry. But she had promised to go. Moreover, there was a horrid fascination at times in becoming instrumental in throwing such possible light on her own character as would reveal her to be something greater in the occult world than she had ever herself suspected.

She started just before the time of day mentioned between them, and half an hour's brisk walking brought her to the south-eastern extension of the Egdon tract of country, where the fir plantation was. A slight figure, cloaked and veiled; was already there. Rhoda recognized, almost with a shudder, that Mrs Lodge bore her left arm in a sling.

They hardly spoke to each other, and immediately set out on their climb into the interior of this solemn, country, which stood high above the rich alluvial soil they had left half an hour before. It was a long walk; thick clouds made the at-mosphere dark, though it was as yet only early afternoon; and the wind howled dismally over the slopes of the heath – not improbably the same heath which had witnessed the agony of the Wessex King Ina, presented to after-ages as Lear. Gertrude Lodge talked most, Rhoda replying with monosyllabic preoccupation. She had a strange dislike to walking on the side of her companion where hung the afflicted arm, moving round to the other when inadvertently near it. Much heather had been brushed by their feet when they descended upon a cart-track, beside which stood the house of the man they sought.

He did not profess his remedial practices openly, or care anything about their continuance, his direct interests being those of a dealer in furze, turf, "sharp sand", and other local products. Indeed, he affected not to believe largely in his own powers, and when watts that had been shown him for cure miraculously disappeared – which it must be owned they infallibly did – he would say light-ly, "O, I only drink a glass of grog upon 'em at your expense – perhaps it's all chance", and immediately turn the subject.

He was at home when they arrived, having in fact seen them descending into his valley. He was a grey-bearded man, with a reddish face, and he looked singu-larly at Rhoda the first moment he beheld her. Mrs Lodge told him her errand; and then with words of self-disparagement he examined her arm.

"Medicine can't cure it," he said promptly. "'Tis the work of an enemy."

Rhoda shrank into herself, and drew back.

"An enemy? What enemy?" asked Mrs Lodge.

He shook his head. "That's best known to yourself," he said. "If you like, I can show the person to you, though I shall not myself know who it is. I can do no more; and don't wish to do that."

She pressed him; on which he told Rhoda to wait outside where she stood, and took Mrs Lodge into the room. It opened immediately from the door; and, as the latter remained ajar, Rhoda Brook could see the proceedings without taking part in them. He brought a tumbler from the dresser, nearly filled it with water, and fetching an egg, prepared it in some private way; after which he broke it on the edge of the glass, so that the white went in and the yolk remained. As it was getting gloomy, he took the glass and its contents to the window, and told Gertrude to watch the mixture closely. They leant over the table together, and the milkwoman could see the opaline hue of the egg-fluid changing form as it sank in the water, but she was not near enough to define the shape that it assumed.

"Do you catch the likeness of any face or figure as you look?" demanded the conjuror of the young woman.

She murmured a reply, in tones so low as to be inaudible to Rhoda, and continued to gaze intently into the glass. Rhoda turned, and walked a few steps away.

When Mrs Lodge came out, and her face was met by the light, it appeared exceedingly pale – as pale as Rhoda's – against the sad dun shades of the upland's garniture. Trendle shut the door behind her, and they at once started homeward together. But Rhoda perceived that her companion had quite changed.

"Did he charge much?" she asked tentatively.

"O no – nothing, He would not take a farthing," said Gertrude.

"And what did you see?" inquired Rhoda.

"Nothing I – care to speak of." The constraint in her manner was remarkable; her face,was so rigid as to wear an oldened aspect, faintly suggestive of the face in Rhoda's bed-chamber.

"Was it you who first proposed coming here?" Mrs Lodge suddenly inquired, after a long pause. "How very odd, if you did!"

"No. But I am not very sorry we have come, all things considered." She replied. For the first time a sense of triumph possessed her, and she did not altogether deplore that the young thing at her side should learn that their lives had been antagonized by other influences than their own.

The subject was no more alluded to during the long and dreary walk home. But in some way or other a story was whispered about the many-dairied lowland that winter that Mrs Lodge's gradual loss of the use of her left arm was owing to her being "overlooked" by Rhoda Brook. The latter kept her own counsel about the incubus, but her face grew sadder and thinner; and in the spring she and her boy disappeared from the neighbourhood of Holmstoke.

VI
A Second Attempt

Half a dozen years passed away and Mr and Mrs Lodge's married experience sank into prosiness, and worse. The farmer was usually gloomy and silent: the woman whom he had wooed for her grace and beauty was contorted and disfigured in the left limb; moreover, she had brought him no child, which rendered it likely that he would be the last of a family who had occupied that valley for some two hundred years. He thought of Rhoda Brook and her son; and feared this might be a judgement from heaven upon him.

The once blithe-hearted and enlightened Gertrude was changing into an irritable, superstitious woman, whose whole time was given to experimenting upon her ailment with every quack remedy she came across. She was honestly attached to her husband, and was ever secretly hoping against hope to win back his heart again by regaining some at least of her personal beauty. Hence it arose that her closet was lined with bottles, packets, and ointment-pots of every description – nay, bunches of mystic herbs, charms, and books of necromancy, which in her schoolgirl time she would have ridiculed as folly.

"Damned if you won't poison yourself with these apothecary messes and witch mixtures some time or other," said her husband, when his eye chanced to fall upon the multitudinous array.

She did not reply, but turned her sad, soft glance upon him in such heart-swollen reproach that he looked sorry for his words, and added, "I only meant it for your good, you know, Gertrude."

"I'll clear out the whole lot, and destroy them," said she huskily, "and try such remedies no more!"

"You want somebody to cheer you," he observed. "I once thought of adopting a boy; but he is too old now. And he is gone away I don't know where."

She guessed to whom he alluded; for, Rhoda Brook's story had in the course of years become known to her; though not a, word had ever passed between her husband and herself on the subject. Neither had she ever spoken to him of her visit to Conjuror Trendle, and of what was revealed to her, or she thought was revealed to her, by that solitary heathman.

She was now five-and-twenty; but she seemed older. "Six years of marriage, and only a few months of love," she sometimes whispered to herself. And then she thought of the apparent cause, and said, with a tragic glance at her withering limb, "If I could only be again as I was when he first saw me!"

She obediently destroyed her nostrums and charms; but there remained a hankering wish to try something else – some other sort of cure altogether. She had never revisited Trendle since she had been conducted to the house of the solitary by Rhoda against her will; but it now suddenly occurred to Gertrude that she would, in a last desperate effort at deliverance from this seeming curse, again seek out the man, if he yet lived. He was entitled to a certain credence, for the indistinct form he had raised in the glass had undoubtedly resembled the only woman in the world who – as she now knew, though not then – could have a reason for bearing her ill-will. The visit should be paid.

This time she went alone, though she nearly got lost on the heath, and roamed a considerable distance out of her way. Trendle's house was reached at last, however: he was not indoors, and instead of waiting at the cottage she went to where his bent figure was pointed out to her at work a long way off. Trendle remembered her, and laying down the handful of furze-roots which he was gathering and throwing into a heap, he offered to accompany her in the homeward direction, as the distance was considerable and the days were short. So they walked together, his head bowed nearly to the earth, and his form of a colour with it.

"You can send away warts and other excrescences, I know," she said; "why can't you send away this?" And the arm was uncovered.

"You think too much of my powers!" said Trendle; "and I am old and weak now, too. No, no; it is too much for me to attempt in my own person. What have ye tried?"

She named to him some of the hundred medicaments and counterspells which she had adopted from time to time. He shook his head.

"Some were good enough," he said approvingly; "but not many of them for such as this. This is of the nature of a blight, not of the nature of a wound; and if you ever do throw it off, it will be all at once."

"If I only could!"

"There is only one chance of doing it known to me. It has never failed in kindred afflictions – that I can declare. But it is hard to carry out, and especially for a woman."

"Tell me!" said she.

"You must touch with the limb the neck of a man who's been hanged."

She started a little at the image he had raised.

"Before he's cold – just after he's cut down," continued the conjuror impassively.

"How can that do good?"

It will turn the blood and change the constitution. But, as I say, to do it is hard. You must go to the jail when there's a hanging, and wait for him when he's brought off the gallows. Lots have done it, though perhaps not such pretty women as you. I used to send dozens for skin complaints. But that was in former times. The last I sent was in "13 – near twelve years ago."

He had no more to tell her; and, when he had put her into a straight track homeward, turned and left her, refusing all money as at first.

VII
A Ride

The communication sank deep into Gertrude's mind. Her nature was rather a timid one; and probably of all remedies that the white wizard could have suggested there was not one which would have filled her with so much aversion as this, not to speak of the immense obstacles in the way of its adoption.

Casterbridge, the county-town, was a dozen or fifteen miles off; and though in those days, when men were executed for horse-stealing, arson, and burglary, an assize seldom passed without a hanging, it was not likely that she could get access to the body of the criminal unaided. And the fear of her husband's anger made her reluctant to breathe a word of Trendle's suggestion to him or to anybody about him.

She did nothing for months, and patiently bore her disfigurement as before. But her woman's nature, craving for renewed love, through the medium of renewed beauty (she was but twenty-five), was ever stimulating her to try what, at any rate, could hardly do her any harm. "What came by a spell will go by a spell surely," she would say. Whenever her imagination pictured the act she shrank in terror from the possibility of it: then the words of the conjuror, "It will turn your blood", were seen to be capable of a scientific no less than ghastly interpretation; the mastering desire returned; and urged her on again.

There was at this time but one county paper, and that her husband only occasionally borrowed. But old-fashioned days had old-fashioned means, and news was extensively conveyed by word of mouth from market to market, or from fair to fair, so that, whenever such an event as an execution was about to take place, few within a radius of twenty miles were ignorant of the' coming sight; and, so far as Holmstoke was concerned, some enthusiasts had been known to walk all the way to Casterbridge and back in one day, solely to witness the spectacle. The next assizes were in March; and when Gertrude Lodge heard that they had been held, she inquired stealthily at the inn as to the result, as soon as she could find opportunity.

She was, however, too late. The time at which the sentences were to be carried out had arrived, and to make the journey and obtain permission at such short notice required at least her husband's assistance. She dared not tell him, for she had found by delicate experiment that these smouldering village beliefs made him furious if mentioned, partly because he half entertained them himself. It was therefore necessary to wait for another opportunity.

Her determination received a fillip from learning that two epileptic children had attended from this very village of Holmstoke many years before with beneficial results, though the experiment had been strongly condemned by the neighbouring clergy. April, May, June, passed; and it is no overstatement to say that by the end of the last-named month Gertrude well-nigh longed for the death of a fellow-creature. Instead of her formal prayers each night, her unconscious prayer was, "O Lord, hang some guilty or innocent person soon!"

This time she made earlier inquiries, and was altogether more systematic in her proceedings. Moreover the season was summer, between the haymaking and the harvest, and in the leisure thus afforded him her husband had been holiday-taking away from home.

The assizes were in July, and she went to the inn as before. There was to be one execution – only one – for arson.

Her greatest problem was not how to get to Casterbridge, but what means she should adopt for obtaining admission to the jail. Though access for such purposes had formerly never been denied, the custom had fallen into desuetude; and in contemplating her possible difficulties, she was again almost driven to fall back upon her husband. But, on sounding him about the assizes, he was so uncommunicative, so more than usually cold, that she did not proceed, and decided that whatever she did she would do alone.

Fortune, obdurate hitherto, showed her unexpected favour. On the Thursday before the Saturday fixed for the execution, Lodge remarked to her that he was going away from home for another day or two on business at a fair, and that he was sorry he could not take her with him.

She exhibited on this occasion so much readiness to stay at home that he looked at her in surprise. Time had been when she would have shown deep disappointment at the loss of such a jaunt. However, he lapsed into his usual taciturnity, and on the day named left Holmstoke.

It was now her turn. She at first had thought of driving, but on reflection held that driving would not do, since it would necessitate her keeping to the turnpike-road, and so increase by tenfold the risk of her ghastly errand being found out. She decided to ride, and avoid the beaten track, notwithstanding that in her husband's stables there was no animal just at present which by any stretch of imagination could be considered a lady's mount, in spite of his promise before marriage to always keep a mare for her. He had, however, many cart-horses, fine ones of their kind; and among the rest was a serviceable creature, an equine Amazon, with a back as broad as a sofa, on which Gertrude had occasionally taken an airing when unwell. This horse she chose.

On Friday afternoon one of the men brought it round. She was dressed, and before going down looked at her shrivelled arm. "Ah!" she said to it, "if it had not been for you this terrible ordeal would have been saved me!"

When strapping up the bundle in which she carried a few articles of clothing, she took occasion to say to the servant, "I take these in case I should not get back tonight from the person I am going to visit. Don't be alarmed if I am not in by ten, and close up the house as usual. I shall be home tomorrow for certain." She meant then to tell her husband privately: the deed accomplished was not like the deed projected. He would almost certainly forgive her.

And then the pretty palpitating Gertrude Lodge went from her husband's homestead; but though her goal was Casterbridge she did not take the direct route thither through Stickleford. Her cunning course at first was in precisely the opposite direction. As soon as she was out of sight, however, she turned to the left, by a road which led into Egdon, and on entering the heath wheeled round, and set out in the true course, due westerly. A more private way down the county could not be imagined; and as to direction, she had merely to keep her horse's head to a point a little to the right of the sun. She knew that she would light upon a furze-cutter or cottager of some sort from time to time, from whom she might correct her bearing.

Though the date was comparatively recent, Egdon was much less fragmentary in character than now. The attempts – successful and otherwise – at cultivation on the lower slopes, which intrude and break up the original heath Into small detached heaths, had not been carried far; Enclosure Acts had not taken effect, and the banks and fences which now exclude the cattle of those villagers who formerly enjoyed rights of commonage thereon, and the carts of those who had turbary privileges which kept them in firing all the year round, were not erected. Gertrude, therefore, rode along with no other obstacles than the prickly furze-bushes, the mats of heather, the white water-courses, and the natural steeps and declivities of the ground.

Her horse was sure, if heavy-footed and slow, and though a draught animal, was easy-paced; had it been otherwise, she was not a woman who could have ventured to ride over such a bit of country with a half-dead arm. It was therefore nearly eight o'clock when she drew rein to breathe her bearer on the last outlying high point of heath-land towards Casterbridge, previous to leaving Egdon for the cultivated valleys.

She halted before a pool called Rushy-pond, flanked by the ends of two hedges; a railing ran through the centre of the pond, dividing h in half. Over the railing she saw the low green country; over the green trees the roofs of the town; over the roofs a white flat façade, denoting the entrance to the county jail. On the roof of this front specks were moving about; they seemed to be workmen erecting something. Her flesh crept. She descended slowly, and was soon amid corn-fields and pastures In another half-hour, when it was almost dusk, Gertrude reached the White Hart, the first inn of the town on that side.

Little surprise was excited by her arrival; farmers' wives rode on horseback then more than they do now; though, for that matter, Mrs Lodge was not imagined to be a wife at all; the innkeeper supposed her some harum-skarum young woman who had come to attend "hang-fair" next day. Neither her husband nor herself ever dealt in Casterbridge market, so that she was unknown. While dismounting she beheld a crowd of boys standing at the door of a harness-maker's shop just above the inn, looking inside it with deep interest.

"What is going on there?" she asked of the ostler.

"Making the rope for tomorrow."

She throbbed responsively, and contracted her arm.

"Tis sold by the inch afterwards," the man continued. "I could get you a bit, miss, for nothing, if you'd like?"

She hastily repudiated any such wish, all the more from a curious creeping feeling that the condemned wretch's destiny was becoming interwoven with her own; and having engaged a room for the night, sat down to think.

Up to this time she had formed but the vaguest notions about her means of obtaining access to the prison. The words of the cunning-man returned to her mind. He had implied that she should use her beauty, impaired though it was, as a pass-key. In her inexperience she knew little about jail functionaries; she had heard of a high-sheriff and an under-sheriff, but dimly only. She knew, however, that there must be a hangman, and to the hangman she determined to apply.

VIII
A Water-side Hermit

At this date, and for several years after, there was a hangman to almost every jail. Gertrude found, on inquiry, that the Casterbridge official dwelt in a lonely cottage by a deep slow river flowing under the cliff on which the prison buildings were situate – the stream being the self-same one, though she did not know it, which watered the Stickleford and Holmstoke meads lower down in its course.

Having changed her dress, and before she had eaten or drunk – for she could not take her ease till she had ascertained some particulars – Gertrude pursued her way by a path along the water-side to the cottage indicated. Passing thus the outskirts of the jail, she discerned on the level roof over the gateway three rectangular lines against the sky, where the specks had been moving in her distant view; she recognized what the erection was, and passed quickly on. Another hundred yards brought her to the executioner's house, which a boy pointed out. It stood close to the same stream, and was hard by a weir, the waters of which emitted a steady roar.

While she stood hesitating the door opened, and an old man came forth shading a candle with one hand. Locking the door on the outside, he turned to a flight of wooden steps fixed against the end of the cottage, and began to ascend them, this being evidently the staircase to his bedroom. Gertrude hastened forward, but by the time she reached the foot of the ladder he was at the top. She called to him loudly enough to be heard above the roar of the weir; he looked down and said, "What d'ye want here?"

"To speak to you a minute."

The candle-light, such as it "was, fell upon her imploring, pale, upturned face, and Davies (as the hangman was called) backed down the ladder. "I was just going to bed," he said; "'Early to bed and early to rise', but I don't mind stopping a minute for such a one as you. Come into house." He reopened the door, and preceded her to the room within.

The implements of his daily work, which was that of a jobbing gardener, stood in a corner, and seeing probably that she looked rural, he said, "If you want me to undertake country work I can't come, for I never leave Caster-bridge for gentle nor simple – not I. My real calling is officer of justice," he added formally.

"Yes, yes! That's it. Tomorrow!"

"Ah! I thought so. Well, what's the matter about that? "Tis no use to come here about the knot – folks do come continually, but I tell 'em one knot is as merciful as another if ye keep it under the ear. Is the unfortunate man a relation; or, I should say, perhaps" (looking at her dress) "a person who's been in your employ?"

"No. What time is the execution?"

"The same as usual – twelve o'clock, or as soon after as the London mail-coach gets in. We always wait for that, in case of a reprieve."

"O – a reprieve – I hope not!" she said involuntarily.

"Well, – hee, hee! – as a matter of business, so do I! But still, if ever a young fellow deserved to be let off, this one does; only just turned eighteen," and only present by chance when the rick was fired. Howsomever, there's not much risk of that, as they are obliged to make an example of him, there having been so much destruction of property that way lately."

"I mean," she explained, "that I want to touch him for a charm, a cure of an affliction, by the advice of a man who has proved the virtue of the remedy."

"O yes, miss! Now I understand. I've had such people come in past years. But it didn't strike me that you looked of a sort to require blood-turning. What's the complaint? The wrong kind for this, I'll be bound."

"My arm." She reluctantly showed the withered skin.

"Ah! – 'tis all a-scram!" said the hangman, examining it.

"Yes," said she.

"Well," he continued, with interest, "that is the class o' subject, I'm bound to admit! I like the look of the wownd; it is as suitable for the cure as any I ever saw. "Twas a knowing-man that sent 'ee, whoever he was."

"You can contrive for me all that's necessary?" she said breathlessly.

"You should really have gone to the governor of the jail, and your doctor with 'ee, and given your name and address – that's how it used to be done, if I recollect. Still, perhaps, I can manage it for a trifling fee."

"O, thank you! I would rather do it this way, as I should like it kept private."

"Lover not to know, eh?"

"No – husband."

"Aha! Very well. I'll get 'ee a touch of the corpse."

"Where is it now?" she said, shuddering.

"It? – he, you mean; he's living yet. Just inside that little small winder up there in the glum." He signified the jail on the cliff above.

She thought of her husband and her friends. "Yes, of course," she said; "and how am I to proceed?"

He took her to the door. "Now, do you be waiting at the little wicket in the wall, that you'll find up there in the lane, not later than one o'clock. I will open it from the inside, as I shan't come home to dinner till he's cut down. Goodnight. Be punctual; and if you don't want anybody to know 'ee, wear a veil. Ah – once I had such a daughter as you!"

She went away, and climbed the path above, to assure herself that she would be able to find the wicket next day. Its outline was soon visible to her – a narrow opening in the outer wall of the prison precincts. The steep was so great that, having reached the wicket, she stopped a moment to breathe: and, looking back upon the water-side cot, saw the hangman again ascending his outdoor staircase. He entered the loft or chamber to which it led, and in a few minutes extinguished his light.

The town clock struck ten, and she returned to the White Hart as she had come.

IX
A Rencounter

It was one o'clock on Saturday. Gertrude Lodge, having been admitted to the jail as above described, was sitting in a waiting-room within the second gate, which stood under a classic archway of ashlar, then comparatively modern, and bearing the inscription, "COVNTY JAIL: 1793." This had been the façade she saw from the heath the day before. Near at hand was a passage to the roof on which the gallows stood.

The town was thronged, and the market suspended; but Gertrude had seen scarcely a soul. Having kept her room till the hour of the appointment, she had proceeded to the spot by a way which avoided the open space below the cliff where the spectators had gathered; but she could, even now, hear the multitudinous babble of their voices, out of which rose at intervals the hoarse croak of a single voice uttering the words, "Last dying speech and confession!" There had been no reprieve, and the execution was over; but the crowd still waited to see the body taken down.

Soon the persistent woman heard a trampling overhead, then a hand beckoned to her, and, following directions, she went out and crossed the inner paved court beyond the gate-house, her knees trembling so that she could scarcely walk. One of her arms was out of its sleeve, and only covered by her shawl.

On the spot at which she had now arrived were two trestles, and before she could think of their purpose she heard, heavy feet descending stairs somewhere at her back. Turn her head she would not, or could not, and, rigid in this position, she was conscious of a rough coffin' passing her borne by four men. It was open, and in it lay the body of a young man, wearing the smockfrock of a rustic, and fustian breeches. The corpse had been thrown into the coffin so hastily that the skirt of the smockfrock was hanging over. The burden was temporarily deposited on the trestles.

By this time the young woman's state was such that a grey mist seemed to float before her eyes, on account of which, and the veil she wore, she could scarcely discern anything: it was as though she had nearly died, but was held up by a sort of galvanism.

"Now!" said a voice close at hand, and she was just conscious that the word had been addressed to her.

By a last strenuous effort she advanced, at the same time hearing persons approaching behind her. She bared her poor curst arm; and Davies, uncovering the face of the corpse, took Gertrude's hand, and held it so that her arm lay across the dead man's neck, upon a line the colour of an unripe blackberry, which surrounded it.

Gertrude shrieked: "the turn o' the blood", predicted by the conjuror, had taken place. But at that moment a second shriek rent the air of the enclosure: it was not Gertrude's, and its effect upon her was to make her start round.

Immediately behind her stood Rhoda Brook, her face drawn, and her eyes red with weeping. Behind Rhoda stood Gertrude's own husband; his countenance lined, his eyes dim, but without a tear.

"D—n you! what are you doing here?" he said hoarsely.

"Hussy – to come between us and our child now!" cried Rhoda. "This is the meaning of what Satan showed me in the vision! You are like her at last!" And clutching the bare arm of the younger woman, she pulled her unresistingly back against the wall. Immediately Brook had loosened her hold the fragile young Gertrude slid down against the feet of her husband. When he lifted her up she was unconscious.

The mere sight of the twain had been enough to suggest to her that the dead young man was Rhoda's son. At that time the relatives of an executed convict had the privilege of claiming the body for burial, if they chose to do so; and it was for this purpose that Lodge was awaiting the inquest with Rhoda. He had been summoned by her as soon as the young man was taken in the crime, and at different times since; and he had attended in court during the trial. This was the "holiday" he had been indulging in of late. The two wretched parents had wished to avoid exposure; and hence had come themselves for the body, a wagon and sheet for its conveyance and covering being in waiting outside.

Gertrude's case was so serious that it was deemed advisable to call to her the surgeon who was at hand. She was taken out of the jail into the town; but she never reached home alive. Her delicate vitality, sapped perhaps by the paralysed arm, collapsed under the double shock that followed the severe strain, physical and mental, to which she had subjected herself during the previous twenty-four hours. Her blood had been "turned" indeed – too far. Her death took place in the town three days after.

Her husband was never seen in Casterbridge again; once only in the old market-place at Anglebury, which he had so much frequented, and very seldom in public anywhere Burdened at first with moodiness and remorse, he eventually changed for the better, and appeared as a chastened and thoughtful man. Soon after attending the funeral of his poor wife he took steps towards giving up the farms in Holmstoke and the adjoining parish, and, having sold every head of his stock, he went away to Port-Bredy, at the other end of the county, living there in solitary lodgings till his death two years later of a painless decline. It was then found that he had bequeathed the whole of his not inconsiderable property to a reformatory for boys, subject to the payment of a small annuity to Rhoda Brook, if she could be found to claim it.

For some time she could not be found; but eventually she reappeared in her old parish – absolutely refusing, however, to have anything to do with the provision made for her. Her monotonous milking at the dairy was resumed, and followed for many long years, till her form became bent, and her once abundant dark hair white and worn away at the forehead – perhaps by long pressure against the cows. Here, sometimes, those who knew her experiences would stand and observe her, and wonder what sombre thoughts were beating inside that impassive, wrinkled brow, to the rhythm of the alternating milk-streams.

MY OWN TRUE GHOST STORY

Rudyard Kipling

Rudyard Kipling (1865–1936) was born in Mumbai (then known as Bombay) to Anglo-Indian parents. His early childhood was idyllic, but in 1871 he was sent to England to be educated. These were not happy years for Kipling and he later credited his love of literature to an urge to escape his surroundings. In 1882 Kipling returned to India where he became a journalist. One of the most celebrated writers of his generation, Kipling's reputation is qualified by unease at his enthusiasm for imperialism.

As I came through the desert thus it was – As I came through the desert

– The City of Dreadful Night

Somewhere in the Other World, where there are books and pictures and plays and shop windows to look at, and thousands of men who spend their lives in building up all four, lives a gentleman who writes real stories about the real insides of people; and his name is Mr. Walter Besant. But he will insist upon treating his ghosts – he has published half a workshopful of them – with levity. He makes his ghost-seers talk familiarly, and, in some cases, flirt outrageously, with the phantoms. You may treat anything, from a Viceroy to a Vernacular Paper, with levity; but you must behave reverently toward a ghost, and particularly an Indian one.

There are, in this land, ghosts who take the form of fat, cold, pobby corpses, and hide in trees near the roadside till a traveler passes. Then they drop upon his neck and remain. There are also terrible ghosts of women who have died in child-bed. These wander along the pathways at dusk, or hide in the crops near a village, and call seductively. But to answer their call is death in this world and the next. Their feet are turned backward that all sober men may recognize them. There are ghosts of little children who have been thrown into wells. These haunt well curbs and the fringes of jungles, and wail under the stars, or catch women by the wrist and beg to be taken up and carried. These and the corpse ghosts, however, are only vernacular articles and do not attack Sahibs. No native ghost has yet been authentically reported to have frightened an Englishman; but many English ghosts have scared the life out of both white and black.

Nearly every other Station owns a ghost. There are said to be two at Simla, not counting the woman who blows the bellows at Syree dâk-bungalow on the

Old Road; Mussoorie has a house haunted of a very lively Thing; a White Lady is supposed to do night-watchman round a house in Lahore; Dalhousie says that one of her houses "repeats" on autumn evenings all the incidents of a horrible horse-and-precipice accident; Murree has a merry ghost, and, now that she has been swept by cholera, will have room for a sorrowful one; there are Officers' Quarters in Mian Mir whose doors open without reason, and whose furniture is guaranteed to creak, not with the heat of June but with the weight of Invisibles who come to lounge in the chairs; Peshawur possesses houses that none will willingly rent; and there is something – not fever – wrong with a big bungalow in Allahabad. The older Provinces simply bristle with haunted houses, and march phantom armies along their main thoroughfares.

Some of the dâk-bungalows on the Grand Trunk Road have handy little cemeteries in their compound – witnesses to the "changes and chances of this mortal life" in the days when men drove from Calcutta to the Northwest. These bungalows are objectionable places to put up in. They are generally very old, always dirty, while the *khansamah* is as ancient as the bungalow. He either chatters senilely, or falls into the long trances of age. In both moods he is useless. If you get angry with him, he refers to some Sahib dead and buried these thirty years, and says that when he was in that Sahib's service not a *khansamah* in the Province could touch him. Then he jabbers and mows and trembles and fidgets among the dishes, and you repent of your irritation.

In these dâk-bungalows, ghosts are most likely to be found, and when found, they should be made a note of. Not long ago it was my business to live in dâk-bungalows. I never inhabited the same house for three nights running, and grew to be learned in the breed. I lived in Government-built ones with red brick walls and rail ceilings, an inventory of the furniture posted in every room, and an excited snake at the threshold to give welcome. I lived in "converted" ones – old houses officiating as dâk-bungalows – where nothing was in its proper place and there wasn't even a fowl for dinner. I lived in second-hand palaces where the wind blew through open-work marble tracery just as uncomfortably as through a broken pane. I lived in dâk-bungalows where the last entry in the visitors' book was fifteen months old, and where they slashed off the curry-kid's head with a sword. It was my good luck to meet all sorts of men, from sober traveling missionaries and deserters flying from British Regiments, to drunken loafers who threw whisky bottles at all who passed; and my still greater good fortune just to escape a maternity case. Seeing that a fair proportion of the tragedy of our lives out here acted itself in dâk-bungalows, I wondered that I had met no ghosts. A ghost that would voluntarily hang about a dâk-bungalow would be mad of course; but so many men have died mad in dâk-bungalows that there must be a fair percentage of lunatic ghosts.

In due time I found my ghost, or ghosts rather, for there were two of them. Up till that hour I had sympathized with Mr. Besant's method of handling them, as shown in "The Strange Case of Mr. Lucraft and Other Stories." I am now in the Opposition.

We will call the bungalow Katmal dâk-bungalow. But *that* was the smallest part of the horror. A man with a sensitive hide has no right to sleep in dâk-bungalows. He should marry. Katmal dâk-bungalow was old and rotten and unrepaired. The floor was of worn brick, the walls were filthy, and the windows were nearly black with grime. It stood on a bypath largely used by native Sub-Deputy Assistants of all kinds, from Finance to Forests; but real Sahibs were rare. The *khansamah*, who was nearly bent double with old age, said so.

When I arrived, there was a fitful, undecided rain on the face of the land, accompanied by a restless wind, and every gust made a noise like the rattling of dry bones in the stiff toddy palms outside. The *khansamah* completely lost his head on my arrival. He had served a Sahib once. Did I know that Sahib? He gave me the name of a well-known man who has been buried for more than a quarter of a century, and showed me an ancient daguerreotype of that man in his prehistoric youth. I had seen a steel engraving of him at the head of a double volume of Memoirs a month before, and I felt ancient beyond telling.

The day shut in and the *khansamah* went to get me food. He did not go through the pretense of calling it "*khana*" – man's victuals. He said "*ratub*," and that means, among other things, "grub" – dog's rations. There was no insult in his choice of the term. He had forgotten the other word, I suppose.

While he was cutting up the dead bodies of animals, I settled myself down, after exploring the dâk-bungalow. There were three rooms, beside my own, which was a corner kennel, each giving into the other through dingy white doors fastened with long iron bars. The bungalow was a very solid one, but the partition walls of the rooms were almost jerry-built in their flimsiness. Every step or bang of a trunk echoed from my room down the other three, and every footfall came back tremulously from the far walls. For this reason I shut the door. There were no lamps – only candles in long glass shades. An oil wick was set in the bath-room.

For bleak, unadulterated misery that dâk-bungalow was the worst of the many that I had ever set foot in. There was no fireplace, and the windows would not open; so a brazier of charcoal would have been useless. The rain and the wind splashed and gurgled and moaned round the house, and the toddy palms rattled and roared. Half a dozen jackals went through the compound singing, and a hyena stood afar off and mocked them. A hyena would convince a Sadducee of the Resurrection of the Dead – the worst sort of Dead. Then came the *ratub* – a curious meal, half native and half English in composition – with the old *khansamah* babbling behind my chair about dead and gone English people, and the wind-blown candles playing shadow-bo-peep with the bed and the mosquito-curtains. It was just the sort of dinner and evening to make a man think of every single one of his past sins, and of all the others that he intended to commit if he lived.

Sleep, for several hundred reasons, was not easy. The lamp in the bath-room threw the most absurd shadows into the room, and the wind was beginning to talk nonsense.

Just when the reasons were drowsy with blood-sucking I heard the regular – "Let-us-take-and-heave-him-over" grunt of doolie-bearers in the compound. First one doolie came in, then a second, and then a third. I heard the doolies dumped on the ground, and the shutter in front of my door shook. "That's some one trying to come in," I said. But no one spoke, and I persuaded myself that it was the gusty wind. The shutter of the room next to mine was attacked, flung back, and the inner door opened. "That's some Sub-Deputy Assistant," I said, "and he has brought his friends with him. Now they'll talk and spit and smoke for an hour."

But there were no voices and no footsteps. No one was putting his luggage into the next room. The door shut, and I thanked Providence that I was to be left in peace. But I was curious to know where the doolies had gone. I got out of bed and looked into the darkness. There was never a sign of a doolie. Just as I was getting into bed again, I heard, in the next room, the sound that no man in his senses can possibly mistake – the whir of a billiard ball down the length of the slates when the striker is stringing for break. No other sound is like it. A minute afterwards there was another whir, and I got into bed. I was not frightened – indeed I was not. I was very curious to know what had become of the doolies. I jumped into bed for that reason.

Next minute I heard the double click of a cannon and my hair sat up. It is a mistake to say that hair stands up. The skin of the head tightens and you can feel a faint, prickly, bristling all over the scalp. That is the hair sitting up.

There was a whir and a click, and both sounds could only have been made by one thing – a billiard ball. I argued the matter out at great length with myself; and the more I argued the less probable it seemed that one bed, one table, and two chairs – all the furniture of the room next to mine – could so exactly duplicate the sounds of a game of billiards. After another cannon, a three-cushion one to judge by the whir, I argued no more. I had found my ghost and would have given worlds to have escaped from that dâk-bungalow. I listened, and with each listen the game grew clearer. There was whir on whir and click on click. Sometimes there was a double click and a whir and another click. Beyond any sort of doubt, people were playing billiards in the next room. And the next room was not big enough to hold a billiard table!

Between the pauses of the wind I heard the game go forward – stroke after stroke. I tried to believe that I could not hear voices; but that attempt was a failure.

Do you know what fear is? Not ordinary fear of insult, injury or death, but abject, quivering dread of something that you cannot see – fear that dries the inside of the mouth and half of the throat – fear that makes you sweat on the palms of the hands, and gulp in order to keep the uvula at work? This is a fine Fear – a great cowardice, and must be felt to be appreciated. The very improbability of billiards in a dâk-bungalow proved the reality of the thing. No man – drunk or sober – could imagine a game at billiards, or invent the spitting crack of a "screw-cannon."

A severe course of dâk-bungalows has this disadvantage – it breeds infinite credulity. If a man said to a confirmed dâk-bungalow-haunter: – "There is a corpse in the next room, and there's a mad girl in the next but one, and the woman and man on that camel have just eloped from a place sixty miles away," the hearer would not disbelieve because he would know that nothing is too wild, grotesque, or horrible to happen in a dâk-bungalow.

This credulity, unfortunately, extends to ghosts. A rational person fresh from his own house would have turned on his side and slept. I did not. So surely as I was given up as a bad carcass by the scores of things in the bed because the bulk of my blood was in my heart, so surely did I hear every stroke of a long game at billiards played in the echoing room behind the iron-barred door. My dominant fear was that the players might want a marker. It was an absurd fear; because creatures who could play in the dark would be above such superfluities. I only know that that was my terror; and it was real.

After a long, long while the game stopped, and the door banged. I slept because I was dead tired. Otherwise I should have preferred to have kept awake. Not for everything in Asia would I have dropped the door-bar and peered into the dark of the next room.

When the morning came, I considered that I had done well and wisely, and inquired for the means of departure.

"By the way, *khansamah*," I said, "what were those three doolies doing in my compound in the night?"

"There were no doolies," said the *khansamah*.

I went into the next room and the daylight streamed through the open door. I was immensely brave. I would, at that hour, have played Black Pool with the owner of the big Black Pool down below.

"Has this place always been a dâk-bungalow?" I asked.

"No," said the *khansamah*. "Ten or twenty years ago, I have forgotten how long, it was a billiard room."

"A how much?"

"A billiard room for the Sahibs who built the Railway. I was *khansamah* then in the big house where all the Railway-Sahibs lived, and I used to come across with brandy-*shrab*. These three rooms were all one, and they held a big table on which the Sahibs played every evening. But the Sahibs are all dead now, and the Railway runs, you say, nearly to Kabul."

"Do you remember anything about the Sahibs?"

"It is long ago, but I remember that one Sahib, a fat man and always angry, was playing here one night, and he said to me: – 'Mangal Khan, brandy-*pani do*,' and I filled the glass, and he bent over the table to strike, and his head fell lower and lower till it hit the table, and his spectacles came off, and when we – the Sahibs and I myself – ran to lift him. He was dead. I helped to carry him out. Aha, he was a strong Sahib! But he is dead and I, old Mangal Khan, am still living, by your favor."

That was more than enough! I had my ghost – a firsthand, authenticated article. I would write to the Society for Psychical Research – I would paralyze the Empire with the news! But I would, first of all, put eighty miles of assessed crop land between myself and that dâk-bungalow before nightfall. The Society might send their regular agent to investigate later on.

I went into my own room and prepared to pack after noting down the facts of the case. As I smoked I heard the game begin again, – with a miss in balk this time, for the whir was a short one.

The door was open and I could see into the room. *Click – click!* That was a cannon. I entered the room without fear, for there was sunlight within and a fresh breeze without. The unseen game was going on at a tremendous rate. And well it might, when a restless little rat was running to and fro inside the dingy ceiling-cloth, and a piece of loose window-sash was making fifty breaks off the window-bolt as it shook in the breeze!

Impossible to mistake the sound of billiard balls! Impossible to mistake the whir of a ball over the slate! But I was to be excused. Even when I shut my enlightened eyes the sound was marvelously like that of a fast game.

Entered angrily the faithful partner of my sorrows, Kadir Baksh.

"This bungalow is very bad and low-caste! No wonder the Presence was disturbed and is speckled. Three sets of doolie-bearers came to the bungalow late last night when I was sleeping outside, and said that it was their custom to rest in the rooms set apart for the English people! What honor has the *khansamah*? They tried to enter, but I told them to go. No wonder, if these *Oorias* have been here, that the Presence is sorely spotted. It is shame, and the work of a dirty man!"

Kadir Baksh did not say that he had taken from each gang two annas for rent in advance, and then, beyond my earshot, had beaten them with the big green umbrella whose use I could never before divine. But Kadir Baksh has no notions of morality.

There was an interview with the *khansamah*, but as he promptly lost his head, wrath gave place to pity, and pity led to a long conversation, in the course of which he put the fat Engineer-Sahib's tragic death in three separate stations – two of them fifty miles away. The third shift was to Calcutta, and there the Sahib died while driving a dogcart.

If I had encouraged him the *khansamah* would have wandered all through Bengal with his corpse.

I did not go away as soon as I intended. I stayed for the night, while the wind and the rat and the sash and the window-bolt played a ding-dong "hundred and fifty up." Then the wind ran out and the billiards stopped, and I felt that I had ruined my one genuine, hall-marked ghost story.

Had I only stopped at the proper time, I could have made *anything* out of it. That was the bitterest thought of all!

JOHN CHARRINGTON'S WEDDING

E. Nesbit

Edith Nesbit (1858–1924) was the author of classic fiction for children including her most famous, *The Railway Children*. Nesbit was a free thinker, an advocate of rational dress and a founder of the socialist organisation the Fabian Society, a precursor to the Labour Party. Her personal life was complicated by her husband Hubert Bland's affairs. She adopted two of his children by his mistress, who lived with them as their housekeeper. After Bland's death Nesbit married Thomas Tucker, a ship's engineer on the Woolwich Ferry.

No-one ever thought that May Foster would marry John Charrington; but he thought differently, and things which John Charrington intended should happen had a way of happening. He asked her to marry him before he went up to Oxford. She laughed and refused him. He asked her again next time he came home. Again she laughed, tossed her blonde head, and again refused him. A third time he asked her; she said it was becoming a confirmed habit, and laughed at him more than ever.

John was not the only man who wanted to marry her; she was the belle of our village, and we were all in love with her more or less; it was a sort of fashion, like heliotrope ties or Inverness capes. Therefore we were as much annoyed as surprised when John Charrington walked into our little local club – we held it in a loft over the saddler's, I remember – and invited us all to his wedding.

"Your wedding?"

"You don't mean it?"

"Who's the happy fair? When's it to be?"

John Charrington filled his pipe and lighted it before he replied. Then he said: "I'm sorry to deprive you fellows of your only joke, but Miss Foster and I are to be married in September."

"You don't mean it?"

"He's got the mitten again, and it's turned his head."

"No," I said, rising, "I see it's true. Lend me a pistol someone, or a first-class fare to the other end of Nowhere. Charrington has bewitched the only pretty girl in our twenty-mile radius. Was it mesmerism, or a love-potion, Jack?"

"Neither, sir, but a gift you'll never have – perseverance – and the best luck a man ever had in this world."

There was something in his voice that silenced me, and all chaff of the other fellows failed to draw him further.

The queer thing about it was that, when we congratulated Miss Foster, she blushed, and smiled, and dimpled, for all the world as though she were in love with him and had been in love with him all the time. Upon my word, I think she had. Women are strange creatures.

We were all asked to the wedding. In Brixham, everyone who was anybody knew everybody else who was anyone. My sisters were, I truly believe, more interested in the *trousseau* than the bride herself, and I was to be best man. The coming marriage was much canvassed at afternoon tea-tables, and at our little club over the saddler's; and the question was always asked: "Does she care for him?"

I used to ask that question myself in the early days of their engagement, but after a certain evening in August I never asked it again. I was coming home from the Club through the churchyard. Our church is on a thyme-grown hill, and the turf about it is so thick and soft that one's footsteps are noiseless.

I made no sound as I vaulted the low wall and threaded my way between the tombstones. It was at the same instant that I heard John Charrington's voice and saw her. May was sitting on a low, flat gravestone, her face turned towards the full splendour of the setting sun. Its expression ended, at once and for ever, any question of love for him; it was transfigured to a beauty I should not have believed possible, even to that beautiful little face.

John lay at her feet, and it was his voice that broke the stillness of the golden August evening.

"My dear, I believe I should come back from the dead, if you wanted me!"

I coughed at once to indicate my presence, and passed on into the shadow fully enlightened.

The wedding was to be early in September. Two days before, I had to run up to town on business. The train was late, of course, for we were on the South-Eastern, and as I stood grumbling with my watch in my hand, whom should I see but John Charrington and May Foster. They were walking up and down the unfrequented end of the platform, arm-in-arm, looking into each other's eyes, careless of the sympathetic interest of the porters.

Of course I knew better than to hesitate a moment before burying myself in the booking-office, and it was not till the train drew up at the platform that I obtrusively passed the pair with my Gladstone, and took the corner in a first-class smoking-carriage. I did this with as good an air of not seeing them as I could assume. I pride myself on my discretion, but if John were travelling alone, I wanted his company. I had it.

"Hullo, old man," came his cheery voice, as he swung his bag into my carriage, "here's luck. I was expecting a dull journey."

"Where are you off to?" I asked, discretion still bidding me turn my eyes away, though I saw, without looking, that hers were red-rimmed.

"To old Branbridge's," he answered, shutting the door, and leaning out for a last word with his sweetheart.

"Oh, I wish you wouldn't go, John," she was saying in a low, earnest voice. "I feel certain something will happen."

"Do you think I should let anything happen to keep me, and the day after tomorrow our wedding day?"

"Don't go," she answered, with a pleading intensity that would have sent my Gladstone on to the platform, and me after it. But she wasn't speaking to me. John Charrington was made differently – he rarely changed his opinion, never his resolutions.

He just touched the ungloved hands that lay on the carriage door.

"I must, May. The old boy has been awfully good to me, and now he's dying I must go and see him, but I shall come home in time – " The rest of the parting was lost in a whisper and in the rattling lurch of the starting train.

"You're sure to come?" she spoke, as the train moved.

"Nothing shall keep me," he answered, and we steamed out. After he had seen the last of the little figure on the platform, he leaned back in his corner and kept silence for a minute.

When he spoke it was to explain to me that his godfather, whose heir he was, lay dying at Peasemarsh Place, some fifty miles away, and he had sent for John, and John had felt bound to go.

"I shall be surely back tomorrow," he said, "or, if not, the day after, in heaps of time. Thank Heaven, one hasn't to get up in the middle of the night to get married nowadays."

"And suppose Mr Branbridge dies?"

"Alive or dead, I mean to be married on Thursday!" John answered, lighting a cigar and unfolding the *Times*.

At Peasemarsh station we said "goodbye", and he got out, and I saw him ride off. I went on to London, where I stayed the night.

When I got home the next afternoon, a very wet one, by the way, my sister greeted me with: "Where's Mr Charrington?"

"Goodness knows," I answered testily. Every man since Cain has resented that kind of question.

"I thought you might have heard from him," she went on, "as you give him away tomorrow."

"Isn't he back?" I asked, for I had confidently expected to find him at home.

"No, Geoffrey" – my sister always had a way of jumping to conclusions, especially such conclusions as were least favourable to her fellow-creatures – "he has not returned, and, what is more, you may depend upon it, he won't. You mark my words, there'll be no wedding tomorrow."

My sister Fanny has a power of annoying me which no other human being possesses.

"You mark my words," I retorted with asperity, "you had better give up making such a thundering idiot of yourself. There'll be more wedding tomorrow than ever you'll take first part in."

But though I could snarl confidently to my sister, I did not feel so comfortable when, late that night, I, standing on the doorstep of John's house, heard that he had not returned. I went home gloomily through the rain. Next morning brought a brilliant blue sky, gold sun, and all such softness of air and beauty of cloud as go to make up a perfect day. I woke with a vague feeling of having gone to bed anxious, and of being rather averse from facing that anxiety in the light of full wakefulness.

With my shaving-water came a letter from John which relieved my mind, and sent me up to the Fosters with a light heart.

May was in the garden. I saw her blue gown among the hollyhocks as the lodge gates swung to behind me. So I did not go up to the house, but turned aside down the turfed path.

"He's written to you too," she said, without preliminary greeting, when I reached her side.

"Yes, I'm to meet him at the station at three, and come straight on to the church."

Her face looked pale, but there was a brightness in her eyes and a softness about the mouth that spoke of renewed happiness.

"Mr Branbridge begged him so to stay another night that he had not the heart to refuse," she went on. "He is so kind, but . . . I wish he hadn't stayed."

I was at the station at half-past two. I felt rather annoyed with John. It seemed a sort of slight to the beautiful girl who loved him, that he should come, as it were out of breath, and with the dust of travel upon him, to take her hand, which some of us would have given the best years of our lives to take.

But when the three o'clock train glided in and glided out again, having brought no passengers to our little station, I was more than annoyed. There was no other train for thirty-five minutes; I calculated that, with much hurry, we might just get to the church in time for the ceremony; but, oh, what a fool to miss that first train! What other man would have done it?

That thirty-five minutes seemed a year, as I wandered round the station reading the advertisements and the time-tables and the company's bye-laws, and getting more and more angry with John Charrington. This confidence in his own power of getting everything he wanted the minute he wanted it, was leading him too far.

I hate waiting. Everyone hates waiting, but I believe I hate it more than anyone else does. The three-thirty-five was late too, of course.

I ground my pipe between my teeth and stamped with impatience as I watched the signals. Click. The signal went down. Five minutes later I flung myself into the carriage that I had brought for John.

"Drive to the church!" I said, as someone shut the door. "Mr Charrington hasn't come by this train."

Anxiety now replaced anger. What had become of this man? Could he have been taken suddenly ill? I had never known him have a day's illness in his life. And even so he might have telegraphed. Some awful accident must have happened to him. The thought that he had played her false never, no, not for a moment, entered my head. Yes, something terrible had happened to him, and on me lay the task of telling his bride. I almost wished the carriage would upset and break my head, so that someone else might tell her.

It was five minutes to four as we drew up at the churchyard. A double row of eager onlookers lined the path from lych-gate to porch. I sprang from the carriage and passed up between them. Our gardener had a good front place near the door. I stopped.

"Are they still waiting, Byles?" I asked, simply to gain time, for of course I knew they were, by the waiting crowd's attentive attitude.

"Waiting, sir? No, no, sir; why it must be over by now."

"Over! Then Mr Charrington's come?"

"To the minute, sir; must have missed you somehow, and I say, sir," lowering his voice, "I never see Mr John the least bit so afore, but my opinion is he's 'ad more than a drop; I wouldn't be going too far if I said he's been drinking pretty free. His clothes was all dusty and his face like a sheet. I tell you I didn't like the looks of him at all, and the folks inside are saying all sorts of things. You'll see, something's gone very wrong with Mr John, and he's tried liquor. He looked like a ghost, and he went in with his eyes straight before him, with never a look or a word for none of us; him that was always such a gentleman."

I had never heard Byles make so long a speech. The crowd in the churchyard were talking in whispers, and getting ready rice and slippers to throw at the bride and bridegroom. The ringers were ready with their hands on the ropes, to ring out the merry peal as the bride and bridegroom should come out.

A murmur from the church announced them; out they came. Byles was right. John Charrington did not look himself. There was dust on his coat, his hair was disarranged. He seemed to have been in some row, for there was a black mark above his eyebrow. He was deathly pale. But his pallor was not greater than that of the bride, who might have been carved in ivory – dress, veil, orange-blossoms, face and all.

As they passed out, the ringers stooped – there were six of them – and then, on the ears expecting the gay wedding peal, came the slow tolling of the passing bell.

A thrill of horror at so foolish a jest from the ringers passed through us all. But the ringers themselves dropped the ropes and fled like rabbits out into the sunlight. The bride shuddered, and grey shadows came about her mouth, but the bridegroom led her on down the path where the people stood with handfuls of rice; but the handfuls were never thrown, and the wedding bells never rang. In vain the ringers were urged to remedy their mistake; they protested, with many whispered expletives, that they had not rung that bell; that they would see themselves further before they'd ring anything more that day.

In a hush, like the hush in a chamber of death, the bridal pair passed into their carriage and its door slammed behind them.

Then the tongues were loosed. A babel of anger, wonder, conjecture from the guests and the spectators.

"If I'd seen his condition, sir," said old Foster to me as we drove off, "I would have stretched him on the floor of the church, sir, by Heaven I would, before I'd have let him marry my daughter!"

Then he put his head out of the window.

"Drive like hell," he cried to the coachman; "don't spare the horses."

We passed the bride's carriage. I forebore to look at it, and old Foster turned his head away and swore.

We stood in the hall doorway, in the blazing afternoon sun, and in about half a minute we heard wheels crunching the gravel. When the carriage stopped in front of the steps, old Foster and I ran down.

"Great Heaven, the carriage is empty! And yet – "

I had the door open in a minute, and this is what I saw –

No sign of John Charrington; and of May, his wife, only a huddled heap of white satin, lying half on the floor of the carriage and half on the seat.

"I drove straight here, sir," said the coachman, as the bride's father lifted her out, "and I'll swear no-one got out of the carriage."

We carried her into the house in her bridal dress, and drew back her veil. I saw her face. Shall I ever forget it? White, white, and drawn with agony and horror, bearing such a look of terror as I have never seen since, except in dreams. And her hair, her radiant blonde hair, I tell you it was white like snow.

As we stood, her father and I, half mad with the horror and mystery of it, a boy came up the avenue – a telegraph boy. They brought the orange envelope to me. I tore it open.

> John Charrington was thrown from the dog-cart on his way to the station at half-past one. Killed on the spot.
>
> Branbridge, Peasemarsh Place

And he was married to May Foster in our Parish Church at *half-past three*, in presence of half the parish!

"*I shall be married on Thursday dead or alive!*"

What had passed in that carriage on the homeward drive? No-one knows – no-one will ever know.

Before a week was over they laid her beside her husband in the churchyard where they had kept their love-trysts.

Thus is the story of John Charrington's wedding.

THRAWN JANET

Robert Louis Stevenson

Robert Louis Stevenson (1850–1894) is the author of *Treasure Island*, *The Strange Case of Dr Jekyll and Mr Hyde* and a swathe of novels, poetry, essays, short stories and travel writing. He was born in Edinburgh into a family of lighthouse engineers on his father's side, and lawyers and church ministers on his mother's. Stevenson made a stab at studying both engineering and law but was suited to neither. Plagued by ill-health from childhood, he was nevertheless an enthusiastic traveller. He was married to Fanny Osbourne and died in Samoa.

The Reverend Murdoch Soulis was long minister of the moorland parish of Balweary, in the vale of Dule. A severe, bleak-faced old man, dreadful to his hearers, he dwelt in the last years of his life, without relative or servant or any human company, in the small and lonely manse under the Hanging Shaw. In spite of the iron composure of his features, his eye was wild, scared, and uncertain; and when he dwelt, in private admonitions, on the future of the impenitent, it seemed as if his eye pierced through the storms of time to the terrors of eternity. Many young persons, coming to prepare themselves against the season of the Holy Communion, were dreadfully affected by his talk. He had a sermon on 1st Peter, v. and 8th, "The devil as a roaring lion," on the Sunday after every seventeenth of August, and he was accustomed to surpass himself upon that text both by the appalling nature of the matter and the terror of his bearing in the pulpit. The children were frightened into fits, and the old looked more than usually oracular, and were, all that day, full of those hints that Hamlet deprecated. The manse itself, where it stood by the water of Dule among some thick trees, with the Shaw overhanging it on the one side, and on the other many cold, moorish hill-tops rising toward the sky, had begun, at a very early period of Mr. Soulis's ministry, to be avoided in the dusk hours by all who valued themselves upon their prudence; and guidmen sitting at the clachan alehouse shook their heads together at the thought of passing late by that uncanny neighbourhood. There was one spot, to be more particular, which was regarded with especial awe. The manse stood between the highroad and the water of Dule with a gable to each; its back was toward the kirktown of Balweary, nearly half a mile away; in front of it, a bare garden, hedged with thorn, occupied the land between the river and the road. The house was two stories high, with two large rooms on each. It opened not directly on the garden, but on a causewayed path, or passage, giving on the road on the one hand, and closed on the other by the tall willows and elders that bordered on the stream. And it was this strip of causeway that enjoyed among the young parishioners of Balweary so infamous a reputation. The minister walked there often after dark, sometimes groaning aloud in the instancy of his unspoken prayers; and when he was from home, and the manse door was locked, the more daring schoolboys ventured, with beating hearts, to "follow my leader" across that legendary spot.

This atmosphere of terror, surrounding, as it did, a man of God of spotless character and orthodoxy, was a common cause of wonder and subject of inquiry among the few strangers who were led by chance or business into that unknown, outlying country. But many even of the people of the parish were ignorant of the strange events which had marked the first year of Mr. Soulis's ministrations; and among those who were better informed, some were naturally reticent, and others shy of that particular topic. Now and again, only, one of the older folk would warm into courage over his third tumbler, and recount the cause of the minister's strange and solitary life.

Fifty years syne, when Mr. Soulis cam' first into Ba'weary, he was still a young man – a callant, the folk said – fu' o' book learnin' and grand at the exposition, but, as was natural in sae young a man, wi' nae leevin' experience in religion. The younger sort were greatly taken wi' his gifts and his gab; but auld, concerned, serious men and women were moved even to prayer for the young man, whom they took to be a self-deceiver, and the parish that was like to be sae ill-supplied. It was before the days o' the moderates – weary fa' them; but ill things are like guid – they baith come bit by bit, a pickle at a time; and there were folk even then that said the Lord had left the college professors to their ain devices an' the lads that went to study wi' them wad hae done mair and better sittin' in a peat-bog, like their forbears of the persecution, wi' a Bible under their oxter and a speerit o' prayer in their heart. There was nae doubt, onyway, but that Mr. Soulis had been ower lang at the college. He was careful and troubled for mony things besides the ae thing needful. He had a feck o' books wi' him – mair than had ever been seen before in a' that presbytery; and a sair wark the carrier had wi' them, for they were a' like to have smoored in the Deil's Hag between this and Kilmackerlie. They were books o' divinity, to be sure, or so they ca'd them; but the serious were o' opinion there was little service for sae mony, when the hail o' God's Word would gang in the neuk of a plaid. Then he wad sit half the day and half the nicht forbye, which was scant decent – writin' nae less; and first, they were feared he wad read his sermons; and syne it proved he was writin' a book himsel', which was surely no fittin' for ane of his years and sma' experience.

Onyway it behoved him to get an auld, decent wife to keep the manse for him an' see to his bit denners; and he was recommended to an auld limmer – Janet M'Clour, they ca'ed her – and sae far left to himsel' as to be ower persuaded. There was mony advised him to the contrar, for Janet was mair than suspeckit by the best folk in Ba'weary. Lang or that, she had had a wean to a dragoon; she hadnae come forrit for maybe thretty year; and bairns had seen her mumblin' to hersel' up on Key's Loan in the gloamin', whilk was an unco time an' place for a God-fearin' woman. Howsoever, it was the laird himsel' that had first tauld the minister o' Janet; and in thae days he wad have gane a far gate to pleasure the laird. When folk tauld him that Janet was sib to the deil, it was a' superstition by his way of it; an' when they cast up the Bible to him an' the witch of Endor, he wad threep it doun their thrapples that thir days were a' gane by, and the deil was mercifully restrained.

Weel, when it got about the clachan that Janet M'Clour was to be servant at the manse, the folk were fair mad wi' her an' him thegether; and some o' the guidwives had nae better to dae than get round her door cheeks and chairge her wi' a' that was ken't again her, frae the sodger's bairn to John Tamson's twa kye. She was nae great speaker; folk usually let her gang her ain gate, an' she let them gang theirs, wi' neither Fair-gui-deen nor Fair-guid-day; but when she buckled to, she had a tongue to deave the miller. Up she got, an' there wasnae an auld story in Ba'weary but she gart somebody lowp for it that day; they couldnae say ae thing but she could say twa to it; till, at the hinder end, the guidwives up and claught hand of her, and clawed the coats aff her back, and pu'd her doun the clachan to the water o' Dule, to see if she were a witch or no, soum or droun. The carline skirled till ye could hear her at the Hangin' Shaw, and she focht like ten; there was mony a guidwife bure the mark of her neist day an' mony a lang day after; and just in the hettest o' the collieshangie, wha suld come up (for his sins) but the new minister.

"Women," said he (and he had a grand voice), "I charge you in the Lord's name to let her go."

Janet ran to him – she was fair wud wi' terror – an' clang to him, an' prayed him, for Christ's sake, save her frae the cummers; an' they, for their part, tauld him a' that was ken't, and maybe mair.

"Woman," says he to Janet, "is this true?"

"As the Lord sees me," says she, "as the Lord made me, no a word o't. Forbye the bairn," says she, "I've been a decent woman a' my days."

"Will you," says Mr. Soulis, "in the name of God, and before me, His unworthy minister, renounce the devil and his works?"

Weel, it wad appear that when he askit that, she gave a girn that fairly frichtit them that saw her, an' they could hear her teeth play dirl thegether in her chafts; but there was naething for it but the ae way or the ither; an' Janet lifted up her hand and renounced the deil before them a'.

"And now," says Mr. Soulis to the guidwives, "home with ye, one and all, and pray to God for His forgiveness."

And he gied Janet his arm, though she had little on her but a sark, and took her up the clachan to her ain door like a leddy of the land; an' her scrieghin, and laughin' as was a scandal to be heard.

There were mony grave folk lang ower their prayers that nicht; but when the morn cam' there was sic a fear fell upon a' Ba'weary that the bairns hid theirsels, and even the men folk stood and keekit frae their doors. For there was Janet comin' doun the clachan – her or her likeness, nane could tell – wi' her neck thrawn, and her held on ae side, like a body that has been hangit, and a grin on her face like an unstreakit corp. By an' by they got used wi' it, and even speered at her to ken what was wrang; but frae that day forth she couldnae speak like a Christian woman, but slavered and played click wi' her teeth like a pair o' shears; and frae that day forth the name o' God cam' never on her lips. Whiles she wad try to say it, but it michtnae be. Them that kenned best said least; but they never gied that Thing the name o' Janet M'Clour; for the auld Janet, by their way o't, was in muckle hell that day. But the minister was neither to haud nor to bind; he preached about naething but the folk's cruelty that had gi'en her a stroke of the palsy; he skelpt the bairns that meddled her; and he had her up to the manse that same nicht, and dwalled there a' his lane wi' her under the Hangin' Shaw.

Weel, time gaed by: and the idler sort commenced to think mair lichtly o' that black business. The minister was weel thocht o'; he was aye late at the writing, folk wad see his can'le doon by the Dule water after twal' at e'en; and he seemed pleased wi' himsel' and upsitten as at first, though a' body could see that he was dwining. As for Janet she cam' an' she gaed; if she didnae speak muckle afore, it was reason she should speak less then; she meddled naebody; but she was an eldritch thing to see, an' nane wad hae mistrysted wi' her for Ba'weary glebe.

About the end o' July there cam' a spell o' weather, the like o't never was in that countryside; it was lown an' het an' heartless; the herds couldnae win up the Black Hill, the bairns were ower weariet to play; an' yet it was gousty too, wi' claps o' het wund that rummled in the glens, and bits o' shouers that slockened naething. We aye thocht it but to thun'er on the morn; but the morn cam', an' the morn's morning, and it was aye the same uncanny weather, sair on folks and bestial. Of a' that were the waur, nane suffered like Mr. Soulis; he could neither sleep nor eat, he tauld his elders; an' when he wasnae writin' at his weary book, he wad be stravaguin' ower a' the countryside like a man possessed, when a' body else was blythe to keep caller ben the house.

Abune Hangin' Shaw, in the bield o' the Black Hill, there's a bit enclosed grund wi' an iron yett; and it seems, in the auld days, that was the kirkyaird o' Ba'weary, and consecrated by the Papists before the blessed licht shone upon the kingdom. It was a great howff, o' Mr. Soulis's onyway; there he would sit an' consider his sermons; and inded it's a bieldy bit. Weel, as he cam' ower the wast end o' the Black Hill, ae day, he saw first twa, an' syne fower, an' syne seeven corbie craws fleein' round an' round abune the auld kirkyaird. They flew laigh and heavy, an' squawked to ither as they gaed; and it was clear to Mr. Soulis that something had put them frae their ordinar. He wasnae easy fleyed, an' gaed straucht up to the wa's; and what suld he find there but a man, or the appearance of a man, sittin' in the inside upon a grave. He was of a great stature, an' black as hell, and his e'en were singular to see. Mr. Soulis had heard tell o' black men mony's the time; but there was something unco about this black man that daunted him. Het as he was, he took a kind o' cauld grue in the marrow o' his banes; but up he spak for a' that; an' says he: "My friend, are you a stranger in this place?" The black man answered never a word; he got upon his feet, an' begude to hirsle to the wa' on the far side; but he aye lookit at the minister; an' the minister stood an' lookit back; till a' in a meenute the black man was ower the wa' an' runnin' for the bield o' the trees. Mr. Soulis, he hardly kenned why, ran after him; but he was sair forjaskit wi' his walk an' the het, unhalsome weather; and rin as he likit, he got nae mair than a glisk o' the black man amang the birks, till he won doun to the foot o' the hillside, an' there he saw him ance mair, gaun, hap, step, an' lowp, ower Dule water to the manse.

Mr. Soulis wasnae weel pleased that this fearsome gangrel suld mak' sae free wi' Ba'weary manse; an' he ran the harder, an' wet shoon, ower the burn, an' up the walk; but the deil a black man was there to see. He stepped out upon the road, but there was naebody there; he gaed a' ower the gairden, but na, nae black man. At the binder end, and a bit feared as was but natural, he lifted the hasp and into the manse; and there was Janet M'Clour before his een, wi' her thrawn craig, and nane sae pleased to see him. And he aye minded sinsyne, when first he set his een upon her, he had the same cauld and deidly grue.

"Janet," says he, "have you seen a black man?"

"A black man!" quo' she. "Save us a'! Ye're no wise, minister. There's nae black man in a' Ba'weary."

But she didnae speak plain, ye maun understand; but yam-yammered, like a powny wi' the bit in its moo.

"Weel," says he, "Janet, if there was nae black man, I have spoken with the Accuser of the Brethren."

And he sat doun like ane wi' a fever, an' his teeth chittered in his heid.

"Hoots," says she, "think shame to yoursel', minister"; and gied him a drap brandy that she keept aye by her.

Syne Mr. Soulis gaed into his study amang a' his books. It's a lang, laigh, mirk chalmer, perishin' cauld in winter, an' no very dry even in the top o' the simmer, for the manse stands near the burn. Sae doun he sat, and thocht of a' that had come an' gane since he was in Ba'weary, an' his hame, an' the days when he was a bairn an' ran daffin' on the braes; and that black man aye ran in his held like the owercome of a sang. Aye the mair he thocht, the mair he thocht o' the black man. He tried the prayer, an' the words wouldnae come to him; an' he tried, they say, to write at his book, but he couldnae mak' nae mair o' that. There was whiles he thocht the black man was at his oxter, an' the swat stood upon him cauld as well-water; and there was other whiles, when he cam' to himsel' like a christened bairn and minded naething.

The upshot was that he gaed to the window an' stood glowrin' at Dule water. The trees are unco thick, an' the water lies deep an' black under the manse; and there was Janet washin' the cla'es wi' her coats kilted. She had her back to the minister, an' he, for his pairt, hardly kenned what he was lookin' at. Syne she turned round, an' shawed her face: Mr. Soulis had the same cauld grue as twice that day afore, an' it was borne in upon him what folk said, that Janet was deid lang syne, an' this was a bogle in her clay-cauld flesh. He drew back a pickle and he scanned her narrowly. She was tramp-trampin' in the cla'es, croonin' to hersel'; and eh! Gude guide us, but it was a fearsome face. Whiles she sang louder, but there was nae man born o' woman that could tell the words o' her sang; an' whiles she lookit side-lang doun, but there was naething there for her to look at. There gaed a scunner through the flesh upon his banes; and that was Heeven's advertisement. But Mr. Soulis just blamed himsel', he said, to think sae ill of a puir, auld afflicted wife that hadnae a freend forbye himsel'; an' he put up a bit prayer for him an' her, an' drank a little caller water – for his heart rose again the meat – an' gaed up to his naked bed in the gloaming.

That was a nicht that has never been forgotten in Ba'weary, the nicht o' the seeventeenth of August, seventeen hun'er' an' twal'. It had been het afore, as I hae said, but that nicht it was better than ever. The sun gaed doun amang un-co-lookin' clouds; it fell as mirk as the pit; no a star, no a breath o' wund; ye couldnae see your han' afore your face, and even the auld folk cuist the covers frae their beds and lay pechin' for their breath. Wi' a' that he had upon his mind, it was gey and unlikely Mr. Soulis wad get muckle sleep. He lay an' he tummled; the gude, caller bed that he got into brunt his very banes; whiles he slept, and whiles he waukened; whiles he heard the time o' nicht, and whiles a tyke yowlin' up the muir, as if somebody was deid; whiles he thocht he heard bogles claverin' in his lug, an' whiles he saw spunkies in the room. He behoved, he judged, to be sick; an' sick he was – little he jaloosed the sickness.

At the hinder end, he got a clearness in his mind, sat up in his sark on the bed-side, and fell thinkin' ance mair o' the black man an' Janet. He couldnae weel tell how – maybe it was the cauld to his feet – but it cam' in up upon him wi' a spate that there was some connection between thir twa, an' that either or baith o' them were bogles. And just at that moment, in Janet's room, which was neist to his, there cam' a stramp o' feet as if men were wars'lin', an' then a loud bang; an' then a wund gaed reishling round the fower quarters of the house; an' then a' was ance mair as seelent as the grave.

Mr. Soulis was feared for neither man nor deevil. He got his tinder-box, an' lit a can'le. He made three steps o't ower to Janet's door. It was on the hasp, an' he pushed it open, an' keeked bauldly in. It was a big room, as big as the minister's ain, a' plenished wi' grand, auld, solid gear, for he had nathing else. There was a fower-posted bed wi' auld tapestry; and a braw cabinet of aik, that was fu' o' the minister's divinity books, an' put there to be out o' the gate; an' a wheen duds o' Janet's lying here and there about the floor. But nae Janet could Mr. Soulis see; nor ony sign of a contention. In he gaed (an' there's few that wad ha'e followed him) an' lookit a' round, an' listened. But there was naethin' to be heard, neither inside the manse nor in a' Ba'weary parish, an' naethin' to be seen but the muckle shadows turnin' round the can'le. An' then, a' at ance, the minister's heart played dunt an' stood stock-still; an' a cauld wund blew amang the hairs o' his heid. Whaten a weary sicht was that for the puir man's een! For there was Janet hangin' frae a nail beside the auld aik cabinet: her heid aye lay on her shouther, her een were steeked, the tongue projeckit frae her mouth, and her heels were twa feet clear abune the floor.

"God forgive us all!" thocht Mr. Soulis, "poor Janet's dead."

He cam' a step nearer to the corp; an' then his heart fair whammled in his inside. For by what cantrip it wad ill-beseem a man to judge, she was hingin' frae a single nail an' by a single wursted thread for darnin' hose.

It's a awfu' thing to be your lane at nicht wi' siccan prodigies o' darkness; but Mr. Soulis was strong in the Lord. He turned an' gaed his ways oot o' that room, and lockit the door ahint him; and step by step, doon the stairs, as heavy as leed; and set doon the can'le on the table at the stairfoot. He couldnae pray, he couldnae think, he was dreepin' wi' caul' swat, an' naething could he hear but the dunt-dunt-duntin' o' his ain heart. He micht maybe have stood there an hour, or maybe twa, he minded sae little; when a' o' a sudden, he heard a laigh, uncanny steer up-stairs; a foot gaed to an' fro in the chalmer whaur the corp was hingin'; syne the door was opened, though he minded weel that he had lockit it; an' syne there was a step upon the landin', an' it seemed to him as if the corp was lookin' ower the rail and doun upon him whaur he stood.

He took up the can'le again (for he couldnae want the licht), and as saftly as ever he could, gaed straucht out o' the manse an' to the far end o' the causeway. It was aye pit-mirk; the flame o' th can'le, when he set it on the grund, brunt steedy an clear as in a room; naething moved, but the Dule water seepin' and sabbin' doon the glen, an' yon unhaly footstep that cam' ploddin' doun the stairs inside the manse. He kenned the foot ower weel, for it was Janet's; and at ilka step that cam' a wee thing nearer, the cauld got deeper in his vitals. He commended his soul to Him that made an' keepit him; "and O Lord," said he, "give me strength this night to war against the powers of evil."

By this time the foot was comin' through the passage for the door; he could hear a hand skirt alang the wa', as if the fearsome thing was feelin' for its way. The saughs tossed an' maned thegether, a long sigh cam' ower the hills, the flame o' the can'le was blawn aboot; an' there stood the corp of Thrawn Janet, wi' her grogram goun an' her black mutch, wi' the heid upon the shouther, an' the grin still upon the face o't – leevin', ye wad he said – deid, as Mr. Soulis weel kenned – upon the threshold o' the manse.

It's a strange thing that the saul of man should be that thirled into his perishable body; but the minister saw that, an' his heart didnae break.

She didnae stand there lang; she began to move again an' cam' slowly towards Mr. Soulis whaur he stood under the saughs. A' the life o' his body, a' the strength o' his speerit, were glowerin' frae his een. It seemed she was gaun to speak, but wanted words, an' made a sign wi' the left hand. There cam' a clap o' wund, like a cat's fuff; oot gaed the can'le, the saughs skrieghed like folk; an' Mr. Soulis keened that, live or die, this was the end o't.

"Witch, beldame, devil!" he cried, "I charge you, by the power of God, begone – if you be dead, to the grave – if you be damned, to hell."

An' at that moment the Lord's ain hand out o' the Heevens struck the Horror whaur it stood; the auld, deid, desecrated corp o' the witch-wife, sae lang keepit frae the grave and hirsled round by deils, lowed up like a brunstane spunk and fell in ashes to the grund; the thunder followed, peal on dirling peal, the rairing rain upon the back o' that; and Mr. Soulis lowped through the garden hedge, and ran, wi' skelloch upon skelloch, for the clachan.

That same mornin', John Christie saw the Black Man pass the Muckle Cairn as it was chappin' six; before eicht, he gaed by the change-house at Knockdow; an' no lang after, Sandy M'Lellan saw him gaun linkin' doun the braes frae Kilmackerlie. There's little doubt but it was him that dwalled se lang in Janet's body; but he was awa' at last; and sinsyne the deil has never fashed us in Ba'weary.

But it was a sair dispensation for the minister; lang, lang he lay ravin' in his bed; and frae that hour to this, he was the man ye ken the day.

THE YELLOW WALLPAPER

Charlotte Perkins Gilman

Charlotte Perkins Gilman (1860–1935) remains a celebrated American feminist. Despite being born into a well-connected New England family her early life was impoverished. She studied art, and in 1884 married artist Walter Stetson. Treatment for a bout of postpartum depression inspired *The Yellow Wallpaper*. The couple separated in 1888. She then married her first cousin George Houghton Gilman in 1900. Perkins Gilman committed suicide while suffering from inoperable breast cancer. Her suicide note stated that she 'chose chloroform over cancer'.

It is very seldom that mere ordinary people like John and myself secure ancestral halls for the summer.

A colonial mansion, a hereditary estate, I would say a haunted house, and reach the height of romantic felicity – but that would be asking too much of fate!

Still I will proudly declare that there is something queer about it.

Else, why should it be let so cheaply? And why have stood so long untenanted?

John laughs at me, of course, but one expects that in marriage.

John is practical in the extreme. He has no patience with faith, an intense horror of superstition, and he scoffs openly at any talk of things not to be felt and seen and put down in figures.

John is a physician, and *perhaps* – (I would not say it to a living soul, of course, but this is dead paper and a great relief to my mind) – *perhaps* that is one reason I do not get well faster.

You see he does not believe I am sick!

And what can one do?

If a physician of high standing, and one's own husband, assures friends and relatives that there is really nothing the matter with one but temporary nervous depression – a slight hysterical tendency – what is one to do?

My brother is also a physician, and also of high standing, and he says the same thing.

So I take phosphates or phosphites – whichever it is, and tonics, and journeys, and air, and exercise, and am absolutely forbidden to "work" until I am well again.

Personally, I disagree with their ideas.

Personally, I believe that congenial work, with excitement and change, would do me good.

But what is one to do?

I did write for a while in spite of them; but it DOES exhaust me a good deal – having to be so sly about it, or else meet with heavy opposition.

I sometimes fancy that in my condition if I had less opposition and more society and stimulus – but John says the very worst thing I can do is to think about my condition, and I confess it always makes me feel bad.

So I will let it alone and talk about the house.

The most beautiful place! It is quite alone, standing well back from the road, quite three miles from the village. It makes me think of English places that you read about, for there are hedges and walls and gates that lock, and lots of separate little houses for the gardeners and people.

There is a *delicious* garden! I never saw such a garden – large and shady, full of box-bordered paths, and lined with long grape-covered arbors with seats under them.

There were greenhouses, too, but they are all broken now.

There was some legal trouble, I believe, something about the heirs and coheirs; anyhow, the place has been empty for years.

That spoils my ghostliness, I am afraid, but I don't care – there is something strange about the house – I can feel it.

I even said so to John one moonlight evening, but he said what I felt was a *draught*, and shut the window.

I get unreasonably angry with John sometimes. I'm sure I never used to be so sensitive. I think it is due to this nervous condition.

But John says if I feel so, I shall neglect proper self-control; so I take pains to control myself – before him, at least, and that makes me very tired.

I don't like our room a bit. I wanted one downstairs that opened on the piazza and had roses all over the window, and such pretty old-fashioned chintz hangings! but John would not hear of it.

He said there was only one window and not room for two beds, and no near room for him if he took another.

He is very careful and loving, and hardly lets me stir without special direction.

I have a schedule prescription for each hour in the day; he takes all care from me, and so I feel basely ungrateful not to value it more.

He said we came here solely on my account, that I was to have perfect rest and all the air I could get. "Your exercise depends on your strength, my dear," said he, "and your food somewhat on your appetite; but air you can absorb all the time." So we took the nursery at the top of the house.

It is a big, airy room, the whole floor nearly, with windows that look all ways, and air and sunshine galore. It was nursery first and then playroom and gymnasium, I should judge; for the windows are barred for little children, and there are rings and things in the walls.

The paint and paper look as if a boys' school had used it. It is stripped off – the paper – in great patches all around the head of my bed, about as far as I can reach, and in a great place on the other side of the room low down. I never saw a worse paper in my life.

One of those sprawling flamboyant patterns committing every artistic sin.

It is dull enough to confuse the eye in following, pronounced enough to constantly irritate and provoke study, and when you follow the lame uncertain curves for a little distance they suddenly commit suicide – plunge off at outrageous angles, destroy themselves in unheard of contradictions. The color is repellent, almost revolting; a smouldering unclean yellow, strangely faded by the slow-turning sunlight.

It is a dull yet lurid orange in some places, a sickly sulphur tint in others.

No wonder the children hated it! I should hate it myself if I had to live in this room long.

There comes John, and I must put this away, – he hates to have me write a word.

We have been here two weeks, and I haven't felt like writing before, since that first day.

I am sitting by the window now, up in this atrocious nursery, and there is nothing to hinder my writing as much as I please, save lack of strength.

John is away all day, and even some nights when his cases are serious.

I am glad my case is not serious!

But these nervous troubles are dreadfully depressing.

John does not know how much I really suffer. He knows there is no *reason* to suffer, and that satisfies him.

Of course it is only nervousness. It does weigh on me so not to do my duty in any way!

I meant to be such a help to John, such a real rest and comfort, and here I am a comparative burden already!

Nobody would believe what an effort it is to do what little I am able, – to dress and entertain, and order things.

It is fortunate Mary is so good with the baby. Such a dear baby!

And yet I *cannot* be with him, it makes me so nervous.

I suppose John never was nervous in his life. He laughs at me so about this wall-paper!

At first he meant to repaper the room, but afterwards he said that I was letting it get the better of me, and that nothing was worse for a nervous patient than to give way to such fancies.

He said that after the wall-paper was changed it would be the heavy bedstead, and then the barred windows, and then that gate at the head of the stairs, and so on.

"You know the place is doing you good," he said, "and really, dear, I don't care to renovate the house just for a three months' rental."

"Then do let us go downstairs," I said, "there are such pretty rooms there."

Then he took me in his arms and called me a blessed little goose, and said he would go down to the cellar, if I wished, and have it whitewashed into the bargain.

But he is right enough about the beds and windows and things.

It is an airy and comfortable room as any one need wish, and, of course, I would not be so silly as to make him uncomfortable just for a whim.

I'm really getting quite fond of the big room, all but that horrid paper.

Out of one window I can see the garden, those mysterious deepshaded arbors, the riotous old-fashioned flowers, and bushes and gnarly trees.

Out of another I get a lovely view of the bay and a little private wharf belonging to the estate.

There is a beautiful shaded lane that runs down there from the house. I always fancy I see people walking in these numerous paths and arbors, but John has cautioned me not to give way to fancy in the least. He says that with my imaginative power and habit of story-making, a nervous weakness like mine is sure to lead to all manner of excited fancies, and that I ought to use my will and good sense to check the tendency. So I try.

I think sometimes that if I were only well enough to write a little it would relieve the press of ideas and rest me.

But I find I get pretty tired when I try.

It is so discouraging not to have any advice and companionship about my work. When I get really well, John says we will ask Cousin Henry and Julia down for a long visit; but he says he would as soon put fireworks in my pillow-case as to let me have those stimulating people about now.

I wish I could get well faster.

But I must not think about that. This paper looks to me as if it *knew* what a vicious influence it had!

There is a recurrent spot where the pattern lolls like a broken neck and two bulbous eyes stare at you upside down.

I get positively angry with the impertinence of it and the everlastingness. Up and down and sideways they crawl, and those absurd, unblinking eyes are everywhere. There is one place where two breadths didn't match, and the eyes go all up and down the line, one a little higher than the other.

I never saw so much expression in an inanimate thing before, and we all know how much expression they have! I used to lie awake as a child and get more entertainment and terror out of blank walls and plain furniture than most children could find in a toy store.

I remember what a kindly wink the knobs of our big, old bureau used to have, and there was one chair that always seemed like a strong friend.

I used to feel that if any of the other things looked too fierce I could always hop into that chair and be safe.

The furniture in this room is no worse than inharmonious, however, for we had to bring it all from downstairs. I suppose when this was used as a playroom they had to take the nursery things out, and no wonder! I never saw such ravages as the children have made here.

The wall-paper, as I said before, is torn off in spots, and it sticketh closer than a brother – they must have had perseverance as well as hatred.

Then the floor is scratched and gouged and splintered, the plaster itself is dug out here and there, and this great heavy bed which is all we found in the room, looks as if it had been through the wars.

But I don't mind it a bit – only the paper.

There comes John's sister. Such a dear girl as she is, and so careful of me! I must not let her find me writing.

She is a perfect and enthusiastic housekeeper, and hopes for no better profession. I verily believe she thinks it is the writing which made me sick!

But I can write when she is out, and see her a long way off from these windows.

There is one that commands the road, a lovely shaded winding road, and one that just looks off over the country. A lovely country, too, full of great elms and velvet meadows.

This wall-paper has a kind of sub-pattern in a different shade, a particularly irritating one, for you can only see it in certain lights, and not clearly then.

But in the places where it isn't faded and where the sun is just so – I can see a strange, provoking, formless sort of figure, that seems to skulk about behind that silly and conspicuous front design.

There's sister on the stairs!

Well, the Fourth of July is over! The people are gone and I am tired out. John thought it might do me good to see a little company, so we just had mother and Nellie and the children down for a week.

Of course I didn't do a thing. Jennie sees to everything now.

But it tired me all the same.

John says if I don't pick up faster he shall send me to Weir Mitchell in the fall.

But I don't want to go there at all. I had a friend who was in his hands once, and she says he is just like John and my brother, only more so!

Besides, it is such an undertaking to go so far.

I don't feel as if it was worth while to turn my hand over for anything, and I'm getting dreadfully fretful and querulous.

I cry at nothing, and cry most of the time.

Of course I don't when John is here, or anybody else, but when I am alone.

And I am alone a good deal just now. John is kept in town very often by serious cases, and Jennie is good and lets me alone when I want her to.

So I walk a little in the garden or down that lovely lane, sit on the porch under the roses, and lie down up here a good deal.

I'm getting really fond of the room in spite of the wall-paper. Perhaps *because* of the wall-paper.

It dwells in my mind so!

I lie here on this great immovable bed – it is nailed down, I believe – and follow that pattern about by the hour. It is as good as gymnastics, I assure you. I start, we'll say, at the bottom, down in the corner over there where it has not been touched, and I determine for the thousandth time that I *will* follow that pointless pattern to some sort of a conclusion.

I know a little of the principle of design, and I know this thing was not arranged on any laws of radiation, or alternation, or repetition, or symmetry, or anything else that I ever heard of.

It is repeated, of course, by the breadths, but not otherwise.

Looked at in one way each breadth stands alone, the bloated curves and flourishes – a kind of "debased Romanesque" with delirium tremens – go waddling up and down in isolated columns of fatuity.

But, on the other hand, they connect diagonally, and the sprawling outlines run off in great slanting waves of optic horror, like a lot of wallowing seaweeds in full chase.

The whole thing goes horizontally, too, at least it seems so, and I exhaust myself in trying to distinguish the order of its going in that direction.

They have used a horizontal breadth for a frieze, and that adds wonderfully to the confusion.

There is one end of the room where it is almost intact, and there, when the crosslights fade and the low sun shines directly upon it, I can almost fancy radiation after all, – the interminable grotesques seem to form around a common centre and rush off in headlong plunges of equal distraction.

It makes me tired to follow it. I will take a nap I guess.

I don't know why I should write this.

I don't want to.

I don't feel able.

And I know John would think it absurd. But I *must* say what I feel and think in some way – it is such a relief!

But the effort is getting to be greater than the relief.

Half the time now I am awfully lazy, and lie down ever so much.

John says I musn't lose my strength, and has me take cod liver oil and lots of tonics and things, to say nothing of ale and wine and rare meat.

Dear John! He loves me very dearly, and hates to have me sick. I tried to have a real earnest reasonable talk with him the other day, and tell him how I wish he would let me go and make a visit to Cousin Henry and Julia.

But he said I wasn't able to go, nor able to stand it after I got there; and I did not make out a very good case for myself, for I was crying before I had finished.

It is getting to be a great effort for me to think straight. Just this nervous weakness I suppose.

And dear John gathered me up in his arms, and just carried me upstairs and laid me on the bed, and sat by me and read to me till it tired my head.

He said I was his darling and his comfort and all he had, and that I must take care of myself for his sake, and keep well.

He says no one but myself can help me out of it, that I must use my will and self-control and not let any silly fancies run away with me.

There's one comfort, the baby is well and happy, and does not have to occupy this nursery with the horrid wall-paper.

If we had not used it, that blessed child would have! What a fortunate escape! Why, I wouldn't have a child of mine, an impressionable little thing, live in such a room for worlds.

I never thought of it before, but it is lucky that John kept me here after all, I can stand it so much easier than a baby, you see.

Of course I never mention it to them any more – I am too wise, – but I keep watch of it all the same.

There are things in that paper that nobody knows but me, or ever will.

Behind that outside pattern the dim shapes get clearer every day.

It is always the same shape, only very numerous.

And it is like a woman stooping down and creeping about behind that pattern. I don't like it a bit. I wonder – I begin to think – I wish John would take me away from here!

* * *

It is so hard to talk with John about my case, because he is so wise, and because he loves me so.

But I tried it last night.

It was moonlight. The moon shines in all around just as the sun does.

I hate to see it sometimes, it creeps so slowly, and always comes in by one window or another.

John was asleep and I hated to waken him, so I kept still and watched the moonlight on that undulating wall-paper till I felt creepy.

The faint figure behind seemed to shake the pattern, just as if she wanted to get out.

I got up softly and went to feel and see if the paper *did* move, and when I came back John was awake.

"What is it, little girl?" he said. "Don't go walking about like that – you'll get cold."

I though it was a good time to talk, so I told him that I really was not gaining here, and that I wished he would take me away.

"Why darling!" said he, "our lease will be up in three weeks, and I can't see how to leave before.

"The repairs are not done at home, and I cannot possibly leave town just now. Of course if you were in any danger, I could and would, but you really are better, dear, whether you can see it or not. I am a doctor, dear, and I know. You are gaining flesh and color, your appetite is better, I feel really much easier about you."

"I don't weigh a bit more," said I, "nor as much; and my appetite may be better in the evening when you are here, but it is worse in the morning when you are away!"

"Bless her little heart!" said he with a big hug, "she shall be as sick as she pleases! But now let's improve the shining hours by going to sleep, and talk about it in the morning!"

"And you won't go away?" I asked gloomily.

"Why, how can I, dear? It is only three weeks more and then we will take a nice little trip of a few days while Jennie is getting the house ready. Really dear you are better!"

"Better in body perhaps – " I began, and stopped short, for he sat up straight and looked at me with such a stern, reproachful look that I could not say another word.

"My darling," said he, "I beg of you, for my sake and for our child's sake, as well as for your own, that you will never for one instant let that idea enter your mind! There is nothing so dangerous, so fascinating, to a temperament like yours. It is a false and foolish fancy. Can you not trust me as a physician when I tell you so?"

So of course I said no more on that score, and we went to sleep before long. He thought I was asleep first, but I wasn't, and lay there for hours trying to decide whether that front pattern and the back pattern really did move together or separately.

On a pattern like this, by daylight, there is a lack of sequence, a defiance of law, that is a constant irritant to a normal mind.

The color is hideous enough, and unreliable enough, and infuriating enough, but the pattern is torturing.

You think you have mastered it, but just as you get well underway in following, it turns a back-somersault and there you are. It slaps you in the face, knocks you down, and tramples upon you. It is like a bad dream.

The outside pattern is a florid arabesque, reminding one of a fungus. If you can imagine a toadstool in joints, an interminable string of toadstools, budding and sprouting in endless convolutions – why, that is something like it.

That is, sometimes!

There is one marked peculiarity about this paper, a thing nobody seems to notice but myself, and that is that it changes as the light changes.

When the sun shoots in through the east window – I always watch for that first long, straight ray – it changes so quickly that I never can quite believe it.

That is why I watch it always.

By moonlight – the moon shines in all night when there is a moon – I wouldn't know it was the same paper.

At night in any kind of light, in twilight, candle light, lamplight, and worst of all by moonlight, it becomes bars! The outside pattern I mean, and the woman behind it is as plain as can be.

I didn't realize for a long time what the thing was that showed behind, that dim sub-pattern, but now I am quite sure it is a woman.

By daylight she is subdued, quiet. I fancy it is the pattern that keeps her so still. It is so puzzling. It keeps me quiet by the hour.

I lie down ever so much now. John says it is good for me, and to sleep all I can.

Indeed he started the habit by making me lie down for an hour after each meal.

It is a very bad habit I am convinced, for you see I don't sleep.

And that cultivates deceit, for I don't tell them I'm awake – O no!

The fact is I am getting a little afraid of John.

He seems very queer sometimes, and even Jennie has an inexplicable look.

It strikes me occasionally, just as a scientific hypothesis, – that perhaps it is the paper!

I have watched John when he did not know I was looking, and come into the room suddenly on the most innocent excuses, and I've caught him several times *looking at the paper*! And Jennie too. I caught Jennie with her hand on it once.

She didn't know I was in the room, and when I asked her in a quiet, a very quiet voice, with the most restrained manner possible, what she was doing with the paper – she turned around as if she had been caught stealing, and looked quite angry – asked me why I should frighten her so!

Then she said that the paper stained everything it touched, that she had found yellow smooches on all my clothes and John's, and she wished we would be more careful!

Did not that sound innocent? But I know she was studying that pattern, and I am determined that nobody shall find it out but myself!

Life is very much more exciting now than it used to be. You see I have something more to expect, to look forward to, to watch. I really do eat better, and am more quiet than I was.

John is so pleased to see me improve! He laughed a little the other day, and said I seemed to be flourishing in spite of my wall-paper.

I turned it off with a laugh. I had no intention of telling him it was *because* of the wall-paper – he would make fun of me. He might even want to take me away.

I don't want to leave now until I have found it out. There is a week more, and I think that will be enough.

I'm feeling ever so much better! I don't sleep much at night, for it is so interesting to watch developments; but I sleep a good deal in the daytime.

In the daytime it is tiresome and perplexing.

There are always new shoots on the fungus, and new shades of yellow all over it. I cannot keep count of them, though I have tried conscientiously.

It is the strangest yellow, that wall-paper! It makes me think of all the yellow things I ever saw – not beautiful ones like buttercups, but old foul, bad yellow things.

But there is something else about that paper – the smell! I noticed it the moment we came into the room, but with so much air and sun it was not bad. Now we have had a week of fog and rain, and whether the windows are open or not, the smell is here.

It creeps all over the house.

I find it hovering in the dining-room, skulking in the parlor, hiding in the hall, lying in wait for me on the stairs.

It gets into my hair.

Even when I go to ride, if I turn my head suddenly and surprise it – there is that smell!

Such a peculiar odor, too! I have spent hours in trying to analyze it, to find what it smelled like.

It is not bad – at first, and very gentle, but quite the subtlest, most enduring odor I ever met.

In this damp weather it is awful, I wake up in the night and find it hanging over me.

It used to disturb me at first. I thought seriously of burning the house – to reach the smell.

But now I am used to it. The only thing I can think of that it is like is the *colour* of the paper! A yellow smell.

There is a very funny mark on this wall, low down, near the mopboard. A streak that runs round the room. It goes behind every piece of furniture, except the bed, a long, straight, even *smooch*, as if it had been rubbed over and over.

I wonder how it was done and who did it, and what they did it for. Round and round and round – round and round and round – it makes me dizzy!

I really have discovered something at last.

Through watching so much at night, when it changes so, I have finally found out.

The front pattern *does* move – and no wonder! The woman behind shakes it!

Sometimes I think there are a great many women behind, and sometimes only one, and she crawls around fast, and her crawling shakes it all over.

Then in the very bright spots she keeps still, and in the very shady spots she just takes hold of the bars and shakes them hard.

And she is all the time trying to climb through. But nobody could climb through that pattern – it strangles so; I think that is why it has so many heads.

They get through, and then the pattern strangles them off and turns them upside down, and makes their eyes white!

If those heads were covered or taken off it would not be half so bad.

I think that woman gets out in the daytime!

And I'll tell you why – privately – I've seen her!

I can see her out of every one of my windows!

It is the same woman, I know, for she is always creeping, and most women do not creep by daylight.

I see her on that long road under the trees, creeping along, and when a carriage comes she hides under the blackberry vines.

I don't blame her a bit. It must be very humiliating to be caught creeping by daylight!

I always lock the door when I creep by daylight. I can't do it at night, for I know John would suspect something at once.

And John is so queer now, that I don't want to irritate him. I wish he would take another room! Besides, I don't want anybody to get that woman out at night but myself.

I often wonder if I could see her out of all the windows at once.

But, turn as fast as I can, I can only see out of one at one time.

And though I always see her, she MAY be able to creep faster than I can turn!

I have watched her sometimes away off in the open country, creeping as fast as a cloud shadow in a high wind.

If only that top pattern could be gotten off from the under one! I mean to try it, little by little.

I have found out another funny thing, but I shan't tell it this time! It does not do to trust people too much.

There are only two more days to get this paper off, and I believe John is beginning to notice. I don't like the look in his eyes.

And I heard him ask Jennie a lot of professional questions about me. She had a very good report to give.

She said I slept a good deal in the daytime.

John knows I don't sleep very well at night, for all I'm so quiet!

He asked me all sorts of questions, too, and pretended to be very loving and kind.

As if I couldn't see through him!

Still, I don't wonder he acts so, sleeping under this paper for three months.

It only interests me, but I feel sure John and Jennie are secretly affected by it.

Hurrah! This is the last day, but it is enough. John is to stay in town over night, and won't be out until this evening.

Jennie wanted to sleep with me – the sly thing! but I told her I should undoubtedly rest better for a night all alone.

That was clever, for really I wasn't alone a bit! As soon as it was moonlight and that poor thing began to crawl and shake the pattern, I got up and ran to help her.

I pulled and she shook, I shook and she pulled, and before morning we had peeled off yards of that paper.

A strip about as high as my head and half around the room.

And then when the sun came and that awful pattern began to laugh at me, I declared I would finish it to-day!

We go away to-morrow, and they are moving all my furniture down again to leave things as they were before.

Jennie looked at the wall in amazement, but I told her merrily that I did it out of pure spite at the vicious thing.

She laughed and said she wouldn't mind doing it herself, but I must not get tired.

How she betrayed herself that time!

But I am here, and no person touches this paper but me – not *alive*!

She tried to get me out of the room – it was too patent! But I said it was so quiet and empty and clean now that I believed I would lie down again and sleep all I could; and not to wake me even for dinner – I would call when I woke.

So now she is gone, and the servants are gone, and the things are gone, and there is nothing left but that great bedstead nailed down, with the canvas mattress we found on it.

We shall sleep downstairs to-night, and take the boat home to-morrow.

I quite enjoy the room, now it is bare again.

How those children did tear about here!

This bedstead is fairly gnawed!

But I must get to work.

I have locked the door and thrown the key down into the front path.

I don't want to go out, and I don't want to have anybody come in, till John comes.

I want to astonish him.

I've got a rope up here that even Jennie did not find. If that woman does get out, and tries to get away, I can tie her!

But I forgot I could not reach far without anything to stand on!

This bed will *not* move!

I tried to lift and push it until I was lame, and then I got so angry I bit off a little piece at one corner – but it hurt my teeth.

Then I peeled off all the paper I could reach standing on the floor. It sticks horribly and the pattern just enjoys it! All those strangled heads and bulbous eyes and waddling fungus growths just shriek with derision!

I am getting angry enough to do something desperate. To jump out of the window would be admirable exercise, but the bars are too strong even to try.

Besides I wouldn't do it. Of course not. I know well enough that a step like that is improper and might be misconstrued.

I don't like to *look* out of the windows even – there are so many of those creeping women, and they creep so fast.

I wonder if they all come out of that wall-paper as I did?

But I am securely fastened now by my well-hidden rope – you don't get *me* out in the road there! I suppose I shall have to get back behind the pattern when it comes night, and that is hard!

It is so pleasant to be out in this great room and creep around as I please!

I don't want to go outside. I won't, even if Jennie asks me to.

For outside you have to creep on the ground, and everything is green instead of yellow.

But here I can creep smoothly on the floor, and my shoulder just fits in that long smooch around the wall, so I cannot lose my way.

Why there's John at the door!

It is no use, young man, you can't open it!

How he does call and pound!

Now he's crying for an axe.

It would be a shame to break down that beautiful door!

"John dear!" said I in the gentlest voice, "the key is down by the front steps, under a plantain leaf!"

That silenced him for a few moments.

Then he said – very quietly indeed, "Open the door, my darling!"

"I can't," said I. "The key is down by the front door under a plantain leaf!"

And then I said it again, several times, very gently and slowly, and said it so often that he had to go and see, and he got it of course, and came in. He stopped short by the door.

"What is the matter?" he cried. "For God's sake, what are you doing!"

I kept on creeping just the same, but I looked at him over my shoulder.

"I've got out at last," said I, "in spite of you and Jane. And I've pulled off most of the paper, so you can't put me back!"

Now why should that man have fainted? But he did, and right across my path by the wall, so that I had to creep over him every time!

THE DANCING PARTNER

Jerome K. Jerome

Jerome Klapka Jerome (1859–1927) is best remembered for his comic novel *Three Men in a Boat*. Jerome left school at fourteen and worked various jobs, including office clerk, hack journalist and actor. He later claimed to have played 'every part in Hamlet except Ophelia'. Rejected by the British army as too old for active service in World War I, Jerome volunteered as an ambulance driver for the French Army.

"This story," commenced MacShaugnassy, "comes from Furtwangen, a small town in the Black Forest. There lived there a very wonderful old fellow named Nicholaus Geibel. His business was the making of mechanical toys, at which work he had acquired an almost European reputation. He made rabbits that would emerge from the heart of a cabbage, flop their ears, smooth their whiskers, and disappear again; cats that would wash their faces, and mew so naturally that dogs would mistake them for real cats and fly at them; dolls with phonographs concealed within them, that would raise their hats and say, 'Good morning; how do you do?' and some that would even sing a song.

"But, he was something more than a mere mechanic; he was an artist. His work was with him a hobby, almost a passion. His shop was filled with all manner of strange things that never would, or could, be sold – things he had made for the pure love of making them. He had contrived a mechanical donkey that would trot for two hours by means of stored electricity, and trot, too, much faster than the live article, and with less need for exertion on the part of the driver, a bird that would shoot up into the air, fly round and round in a circle, and drop to earth at the exact spot from where it started; a skeleton that, supported by an upright iron bar, would dance a hornpipe, a life-size lady doll that could play the fiddle, and a gentleman with a hollow inside who could smoke a pipe and drink more lager beer than any three average German students put together, which is saying much.

"Indeed, it was the belief of the town that old Geibel could make a man capable of doing everything that a respectable man need want to do. One day he made a man who did too much, and it came about in this way:

"Young Doctor Follen had a baby, and the baby had a birthday. Its first birthday put Doctor Follen's household into somewhat of a flurry, but on the occasion of its second birthday, Mrs Doctor Follen gave a ball in honour of the event. Old Geibel and his daughter Olga were among the guests.

"During the afternoon of the next day some three or four of Olga's bosom friends, who had also been present at the ball, dropped in to have a chat about it. They naturally fell to discussing the men, and to criticizing their dancing. Old Geibel was in the room, but he appeared to be absorbed in his newspaper, and the girls took no notice of him.

"'There seem to be fewer men who can dance at every ball you go to,' said one of the girls.

"'Yes, and don't the ones who can give themselves airs,' said another; 'they make quite a favor of asking you.'

"'And how stupidly they talk,' added a third. 'They always say exactly the same things: "How charming you are looking to-night." "Do you often go to Vienna? Oh, you should, it's delightful." "What a charming dress you have on." "What a warm day it has been." "Do you like Wagner?" I do wish they'd think of something new.'

"'Oh, I never mind how they talk,' said a forth. 'If a man dances well he may be a fool for all I care.'

"'He generally is,' slipped in a thin girl, rather spitefully.

"'I go to a ball to dance,' continued the previous speaker, not noticing the interruption. 'All I ask is that he shall hold me firmly, take me round steadily, and not get tired before I do.'

"'A clockwork figure would be the thing for you,' said the girl who had interrupted.

"'Bravo!' cried one of the others, clapping her hands, 'what a capital idea!'

"'What's a capital idea?' they asked.

"'Why, a clockwork dancer, or, better still, one that would go by electricity and never run down.'

"The girls took up the idea with enthusiasm.

"'Oh, what a lovely partner he would make,' said one; 'he would never kick you, or tread on your toes.'

"'Or tear your dress,' said another.

"'Or get out of step.'

"'Or get giddy and lean on you.'

"'And he would never want to mop his face with his handkerchief. I do hate to see a man do that after every dance.'

"'And wouldn't want to spend the whole evening in the supper-room.'

"'Why, with a phonograph inside him to grind out all the stock remarks, you would not be able to tell him from a real man,' said the girl who had first suggested the idea.

"'Oh yes, you would,' said the thin girl, 'he would be so much nicer.'

"Old Geibel had laid down his paper, and was listening with both his ears. On one of the girls glancing in his direction, however, he hurriedly hid himself again behind it.

"After the girls were gone, he went into his workshop, where Olga heard him walking up and down, and every now and then chuckling to himself; and that night he talked to her a good deal about dancing and dancing men – asked what dances were most popular – what steps were gone through, with many other questions bearing on the subject.

"Then for a couple of weeks he kept much to his factory, and was very thoughtful and busy, though prone at unexpected moments to break into a quiet low laugh, as if enjoying a joke that nobody else knew of.

"A month later another ball took place in Furtwangen. On this occasion it was given by old Wenzel, the wealthy timber merchant, to celebrate his niece's betrothal, and Geibel and his daughter were again among the invited.

"When the hour arrived to set out, Olga sought her father. Not finding him in the house, she tapped at the door of his workshop. He appeared in his shirt-sleeves, looking hot but radiant.

"'Don't wait for me,' he said, 'you go on, I'll follow you. I've got something to finish.'

"As she turned to obey he called after her, 'Tell them I'm going to bring a young man with me – such a nice young man, and an excellent dancer. All the girls will like him.' Then he laughed and closed the door.

"Her father generally kept his doings secret from everybody, but she had a pretty shrewd suspicion of what he had been planning, and so, to a certain extent, was able to prepare the guests for what was coming. Anticipation ran high, and the arrival of the famous mechanist was eagerly awaited.

"At length the sound of wheels was heard outside, followed by a great commotion in the passage, and old Wenzel himself, his jolly face red with excitement and suppressed laughter, burst into the room and announced in stentorian tones:

"'Herr Geibel – and a friend.'

"Herr Geibel and his 'friend' entered, greeted with shouts of laughter and applause, and advanced to the centre of the room.

"'Allow me, ladies and gentlemen,' said Herr Geibel, 'to introduce you to my friend, Lieutenant Fritz. Fritz, my dear fellow, bow to the ladies and gentlemen.'

"Geibel placed his hand encouragingly on Fritz's shoulder, and the Lieutenant bowed low, accompanying the action with a harsh clicking noise in his throat, unpleasantly suggestive of a death-rattle. But that was only a detail.

"'He walks a little stiffly' (old Geibel took his arm and walked him forward a few steps. He certainly did walk stiffly), 'but then, walking is not his forte. He is essentially a dancing man. I have only been able to teach him the waltz as yet, but at that he is faultless. Come, which of you ladies may I introduce him to as a partner? He keeps perfect time; he never gets tired; he won't kick you or tread on your dress; he will hold you as firmly as you like, and go as quickly or a slowly as you please; he never gets giddy; and he is full of conversation. Come, speak up for yourself, my boy.'

"The old gentleman twisted one of the buttons at the back of his coat, and immediately Fritz opened his mouth, and in thin tones that appeared to proceed from the back of his head, remarked suddenly, 'May I have the pleasure?' and then shut his mouth again with a snap.

"That Lieutenant Fritz had made a strong impression on the company was undoubted, yet none of the girls seemed inclined to dance with him. They looked askance at his waxen face, with its staring eyes and fixed smile, and shuddered. At last old Geibel came to the girl who had conceived the idea.

"'It is your own suggestion, carried out to the letter,' said Geibel, 'an electric dancer. You owe it to the gentleman to give him a trial.'

"She was a bright, saucy little girl, fond of a frolic. Her host added his entreaties, and she consented.

"Her Geibel fixed the figure to her. Its right arm was screwed round her waist, and held her firmly; its delicately jointed left hand was made to fasten upon her right. The old toymaker showed her how to regulate its speed, and how to stop it, and release herself.

"'It will take you round in a complete circle,' he explained; 'be careful that no one knocks against you, and alters its course.'

"The music struck up. Old Geibel put the current in motion, and Annette and her strange partner began to dance.

"For a while everyone stood watching them. The figure performed its purpose admirably. Keeping perfect time and step, and holding its little partner tight clasped in an unyielding embrace, it revolved steadily, pouring forth at the same time a constant flow of squeaky conversation, broken by brief intervals of grinding silence.

"'How charming you are looking tonight,' it remarked in its thin, far-away voice. 'What a lovely day it has been. Do you like dancing? How well our steps agree. You will give me another, won't you? Oh, don't be so cruel. What a charming gown you have on. Isn't waltzing delightful? I could go on dancing for ever – with you. Have you had supper?'

"As she grew more familiar with the uncanny creature, the girl's nervousness wore off, and she entered into the fun of the thing.

"'Oh, he's just lovely,' she cried, laughing; 'I could go on dancing with him all my life.'

"Couple after couple now joined them, and soon all the dancers in the room were whirling round behind them. Nicholaus Geibel stood looking on, beaming with childish delight at his success.

"Old Wenzel approached him, and whispered something in his ear. Geibel laughed and nodded, and the two worked their way quietly towards the door.

"'This is the young people's house to-night,' said Wenzel, as soon as they were outside; 'you and I will have a quiet pipe and glass of hock, over in the counting-house.'

"Meanwhile the dancing grew more fast and furious. Little Annette loosened the screw regulating her partner's rate of progress, and the figure flew round with her swifter and swifter. Couple after couple dropped out exhausted, but they only went the faster, till at length they remained dancing alone.

"Madder and madder became the waltz. The music lagged behind: the musicians, unable to keep pace, ceased, and sat staring. The younger guests applauded, but the older faces began to grow anxious.

"'Hadn't you better stop, dear,' said one of the women, 'you'll make yourself so tired.'

"But Annette did not answer.

"'I believe she's fainted,' cried out a girl who had caught sight of her face as it was swept by.

"One of the men sprang forward and clutched at the figure, but its impetus threw him down on to the floor, where its steel-cased feet laid bare his cheek. The thing evidently did not intend to part with its prize so easily.

"Had any one retained a cool head, the figure, one cannot help thinking, might easily have been stopped. Two or three men acting in concert might have lifted it bodily off the floor, or have jammed it into a corner. But few human heads are capable of remaining cool under excitement. Those who are not present think how stupid must have been those who were; those who are reflect afterwards how simple it would have been to do this, that, or the other, if only they had thought of it at the time.

"The women grew hysterical. The men shouted contradictory directions to one another. Two of them made a bungling rush at the figure, which had the end result of forcing it out of its orbit at the centre of the room, and sending it crashing against the walls and furniture. A stream of blood showed itself down the girl's white frock, and followed her along the floor. The affair was becoming horrible. The women rushed screaming from the room. The men followed them.

"One sensible suggestion was made: 'Find Geibel – fetch Geibel.'

"No one had noticed him leave the room, no one knew where he was. A party went in search of him. The others, too unnerved to go back into the ballroom, crowded outside the door and listened. They could hear the steady whir of the wheels upon the polished floor as the thing spun round and round; the dull thud as every now and again it dashed itself and its burden against some opposing object and ricocheted off in a new direction.

"And everlastingly it talked in that thin ghostly voice, repeating over and over the same formula: 'How charming you look to-night. What a lovely day it has been. Oh, don't be so cruel. I could go on dancing for ever – with you. Have you had supper?'

"Of course they sought Geibel everywhere but where he was. They looked in every room in the house, then they rushed off in a body to his own place, and spent precious minutes waking up his deaf old housekeeper. At last it occurred to one of the party that Wenzel was missing also, and then the idea of the counting-house across the yard presented itself to them, and there they found him.

"He rose up, very pale, and followed them; and he and old Wenzel forced their way through the crowd of guests gathered outside, and entered the room, and locked the door behind them.

"From within there came the muffled sound of low voices and quick steps, followed by a confused scuffling noise, then silence, then the low voices again.

"After a time the door opened, and those near it pressed forward to enter, but old Wenzel's broad head and shoulders barred the way.

"I want you – and you, Bekler,' he said, addressing a couple of the elder men. His voice was calm, but his face was deadly white. 'The rest of you, please go – get the women away as quickly as you can.'

"From that day old Nicholaus Geibel confined himself to the making of mechanical rabbits, and cats that mewed and washed their faces."

THE YELLOW SIGN

Robert W. Chambers

Robert William Chambers (1865–1933) was born in Brooklyn, New York. He began his professional life as a visual artist and studied at the École des Beaux-Arts and Académie Julian in Paris before focussing on writing. He wrote in several genres including horror, fantasy, science fiction, historical fiction and romance. Chambers is best known for his novel *The King in Yellow*. His weird tales influenced H.P. Lovecraft.

Let the red dawn surmise
What we shall do,
When this blue starlight dies
And all is through.

I

There are so many things which are impossible to explain! Why should certain chords in music make me think of the brown and golden tints of autumn foliage? Why should the Mass of Sainte Cécile bend my thoughts wandering among caverns whose walls blaze with ragged masses of virgin silver? What was it in the roar and turmoil of Broadway at six o'clock that flashed before my eyes the picture of a still Breton forest where sunlight filtered through spring foliage and Sylvia bent, half curiously, half tenderly, over a small green lizard, murmuring: "To think that this also is a little ward of God!"

When I first saw the watchman his back was toward me. I looked at him indifferently until he went into the church. I paid no more attention to him than I had to any other man who lounged through Washington Square that morning, and when I shut my window and turned back into my studio I had forgotten him. Late in the afternoon, the day being warm, I raised the window again and leaned out to get a sniff of air. A man was standing in the courtyard of the church, and I noticed him again with as little interest as I had that morning. I looked across the square to where the fountain was playing and then, with my mind filled with vague impressions of trees, asphalt drives, and the moving groups of nursemaids and holiday-makers, I started to walk back to my easel. As I turned, my listless glance included the man below in the churchyard. His face was toward me now, and with a perfectly involuntary movement I bent to see it. At the same moment he raised his head and looked at me. Instantly I thought of a coffin-worm. Whatever it was about the man that repelled me I did not know, but the impression of a plump white grave-worm was so intense and nauseating that I must have shown it in my expression, for he turned his puffy face away with a movement which made me think of a disturbed grub in a chestnut.

I went back to my easel and motioned the model to resume her pose. After working a while I was satisfied that I was spoiling what I had done as rapidly as possible, and I took up a palette knife and scraped the colour out again. The flesh tones were sallow and unhealthy, and I did not understand how I could have painted such sickly colour into a study which before that had glowed with healthy tones.

I looked at Tessie. She had not changed, and the clear flush of health dyed her neck and cheeks as I frowned.

"Is it something I've done?" she said.

"No, – I've made a mess of this arm, and for the life of me I can't see how I came to paint such mud as that into the canvas," I replied.

"Don't I pose well?" she insisted.

"Of course, perfectly."

"Then it's not my fault?"

"No. It's my own."

"I am very sorry," she said.

I told her she could rest while I applied rag and turpentine to the plague spot on my canvas, and she went off to smoke a cigarette and look over the illustrations in the *Courrier Français*.

I did not know whether it was something in the turpentine or a defect in the canvas, but the more I scrubbed the more that gangrene seemed to spread. I worked like a beaver to get it out, and yet the disease appeared to creep from limb to limb of the study before me. Alarmed, I strove to arrest it, but now the colour on the breast changed and the whole figure seemed to absorb the infection as a sponge soaks up water. Vigorously I plied palette-knife, turpentine, and scraper, thinking all the time what a *séance* I should hold with Duval who had sold me the canvas; but soon I noticed that it was not the canvas which was defective nor yet the colours of Edward. "It must be the turpentine," I thought angrily, "or else my eyes have become so blurred and confused by the afternoon light that I can't see straight." I called Tessie, the model. She came and leaned over my chair blowing rings of smoke into the air.

"What *have* you been doing to it?" she exclaimed

"Nothing," I growled, "it must be this turpentine!"

"What a horrible colour it is now," she continued. "Do you think my flesh resembles green cheese?"

"No, I don't," I said angrily; "did you ever know me to paint like that before?"

"No, indeed!"

"Well, then!"

"It must be the turpentine, or something," she admitted.

She slipped on a Japanese robe and walked to the window. I scraped and rubbed until I was tired, and finally picked up my brushes and hurled them through the canvas with a forcible expression, the tone alone of which reached Tessie's ears.

Nevertheless she promptly began: "That's it! Swear and act silly and ruin your brushes! You have been three weeks on that study, and now look! What's the good of ripping the canvas? What creatures artists are!"

I felt about as much ashamed as I usually did after such an outbreak, and I turned the ruined canvas to the wall. Tessie helped me clean my brushes, and then danced away to dress. From the screen she regaled me with bits of advice concerning whole or partial loss of temper, until, thinking, perhaps, I had been tormented sufficiently, she came out to implore me to button her waist where she could not reach it on the shoulder.

"Everything went wrong from the time you came back from the window and talked about that horrid-looking man you saw in the churchyard," she announced.

"Yes, he probably bewitched the picture," I said, yawning. I looked at my watch.

"It's after six, I know," said Tessie, adjusting her hat before the mirror.

"Yes," I replied, "I didn't mean to keep you so long." I leaned out of the window but recoiled with disgust, for the young man with the pasty face stood below in the churchyard. Tessie saw my gesture of disapproval and leaned from the window.

"Is that the man you don't like?" she whispered.

I nodded.

"I can't see his face, but he does look fat and soft. Some way or other," she continued, turning to look at me, "he reminds me of a dream, – an awful dream I once had. Or," she mused, looking down at her shapely shoes, "was it a dream after all?"

"How should I know?" I smiled.

Tessie smiled in reply.

"You were in it," she said, "so perhaps you might know something about it."

"Tessie! Tessie!" I protested, "don't you dare flatter by saying that you dream about me!"

"But I did," she insisted; "shall I tell you about it?"

"Go ahead," I replied, lighting a cigarette.

Tessie leaned back on the open window-sill and began very seriously.

"One night last winter I was lying in bed thinking about nothing at all in particular. I had been posing for you and I was tired out, yet it seemed impossible for me to sleep. I heard the bells in the city ring ten, eleven, and midnight. I must have fallen asleep about midnight because I don't remember hearing the bells after that. It seemed to me that I had scarcely closed my eyes when I dreamed that something impelled me to go to the window. I rose, and raising the sash leaned out. Twenty-fifth Street was deserted as far as I could see. I began to be afraid; everything outside seemed so – so black and uncomfortable. Then the sound of wheels in the distance came to my ears, and it seemed to me as though that was what I must wait for. Very slowly the wheels approached, and, finally, I could make out a vehicle moving along the street. It came nearer and nearer, and when it passed beneath my window I saw it was a hearse. Then, as I trembled with fear, the driver turned and looked straight at me. When I awoke I was standing by the open window shivering with cold, but the black-plumed hearse and the driver were gone. I dreamed this dream again in March last, and again awoke beside the open window. Last night the dream came again. You remember how it was raining; when I awoke, standing at the open window, my night-dress was soaked."

"But where did I come into the dream?" I asked.

"You – you were in the coffin; but you were not dead."

"In the coffin?"

"Yes."

"How did you know? Could you see me?"

"No; I only knew you were there."

"Had you been eating Welsh rarebits, or lobster salad?" I began, laughing, but the girl interrupted me with a frightened cry.

"Hello! What's up?" I said, as she shrank into the embrasure by the window.

"The – the man below in the churchyard; – he drove the hearse."

"Nonsense," I said, but Tessie's eyes were wide with terror. I went to the window and looked out. The man was gone. "Come, Tessie," I urged, "don't be foolish. You have posed too long; you are nervous."

"Do you think I could forget that face?" she murmured. "Three times I saw the hearse pass below my window, and every time the driver turned and looked up at me. Oh, his face was so white and – and soft? It looked dead – it looked as if it had been dead a long time."

I induced the girl to sit down and swallow a glass of Marsala. Then I sat down beside her, and tried to give her some advice.

"Look here, Tessie," I said, "you go to the country for a week or two, and you'll have no more dreams about hearses. You pose all day, and when night comes your nerves are upset. You can't keep this up. Then again, instead of going to bed when your day's work is done, you run off to picnics at Sulzer's Park, or go to the Eldorado or Coney Island, and when you come down here next morning you are fagged out. There was no real hearse. There was a soft-shell crab dream."

She smiled faintly.

"What about the man in the churchyard?"

"Oh, he's only an ordinary unhealthy, everyday creature."

"As true as my name is Tessie Reardon, I swear to you, Mr. Scott, that the face of the man below in the churchyard is the face of the man who drove the hearse!"

"What of it?" I said. "It's an honest trade."

"Then you think I *did* see the hearse?"

"Oh," I said diplomatically, "if you really did, it might not be unlikely that the man below drove it. There is nothing in that."

Tessie rose, unrolled her scented handkerchief, and taking a bit of gum from a knot in the hem, placed it in her mouth. Then drawing on her gloves she offered me her hand, with a frank, "Good-night, Mr. Scott," and walked out.

II

The next morning, Thomas, the bell-boy, brought me the *Herald* and a bit of news. The church next door had been sold. I thanked Heaven for it, not that being a Catholic I had any repugnance for the congregation next door, but because my nerves were shattered by a blatant exhorter, whose every word echoed through the aisle of the church as if it had been my own rooms, and who insisted on his r's with a nasal persistence which revolted my every instinct. Then, too, there was a fiend in human shape, an organist, who reeled off some of the grand old hymns with an interpretation of his own, and I longed for the blood of a creature who could play the doxology with an amendment of minor chords which one hears only in a quartet of very young undergraduates. I believe the minister was a good man, but when he bellowed: "And the Lorrrrd said unto Moses, the Lorrrd is a man of war; the Lorrrd is his name. My wrath shall wax hot and I will kill you with the sworrrrd!" I wondered how many centuries of purgatory it would take to atone for such a sin.

"Who bought the property?" I asked Thomas.

"Nobody that I knows, sir. They do say the gent wot owns this 'ere 'Amilton flats was lookin' at it. 'E might be a bildin' more studios."

I walked to the window. The young man with the unhealthy face stood by the churchyard gate, and at the mere sight of him the same overwhelming repugnance took possession of me.

"By the way, Thomas," I said, "who is that fellow down there?"

Thomas sniffed. "That there worm, sir? 'Es night-watchman of the church, sir. 'E maikes me tired a-sittin' out all night on them steps and lookin' at you insultin' like. I'd a punched 'is 'ed, sir – beg pardon, sir – "

"Go on, Thomas."

"One night a-comin' 'ome with Arry, the other English boy, I sees 'im a-sittin' there on them steps. We 'ad Molly and Jen with us, sir, the two girls on the tray service, an' 'e looks so insultin' at us that I up and sez: 'Wat you looking hat, you fat slug?' – beg pardon, sir, but that's 'ow I sez, sir. Then 'e don't say nothin' and I sez: 'Come out and I'll punch that puddin' 'ed.' Then I hopens the gate an' goes in, but 'e don't say nothin', only looks insultin' like. Then I 'its 'im one, but, ugh! 'is 'ed was that cold and mushy it ud sicken you to touch 'im."

"What did he do then?" I asked curiously.

" 'Im? Nawthin'."

"And you, Thomas?"

The young fellow flushed with embarrassment and smiled uneasily.

"Mr. Scott, sir, I ain't no coward, an' I can't make it out at all why I run. I was in the 5th Lawncers, sir, bugler at Tel-el-Kebir, an' was shot by the wells."

"You don't mean to say you ran away?"

"Yes, sir; I run."

"Why?"

"That's just what I want to know, sir. I grabbed Molly an' run, an' the rest was as frightened as I."

"But what were they frightened at?"

Thomas refused to answer for a while, but now my curiosity was aroused about the repulsive young man below and I pressed him. Three years' sojourn in America had not only modified Thomas's cockney dialect but had given him the American's fear of ridicule.

"You won't believe me, Mr. Scott, sir?"

"Yes, I will."

"You will lawf at me, sir?"

"Nonsense!"

He hesitated. "Well, sir, it's Gawd's truth that when I 'it 'im 'e grabbed me wrists, sir, and when I twisted 'is soft, mushy fist one of 'is fingers come off in me 'and."

The utter loathing and horror of Thomas' face must have been reflected in my own, for he added: "It's orful, an' now when I see 'im I just go away. 'E maikes me hill."

When Thomas had gone I went to the window. The man stood beside the church-railing with both hands on the gate, but I hastily retreated to my easel again, sickened and horrified, for I saw that the middle finger of his right hand was missing.

At nine o'clock Tessie appeared and vanished behind the screen with a merry "Good morning, Mr. Scott." When she had reappeared and taken her pose upon the model-stand I started a new canvas, much to her delight. She remained silent as long as I was on the drawing, but as soon as the scrape of the charcoal ceased and I took up my fixative she began to chatter.

"Oh, I had such a lovely time last night. We went to Tony Pastor's."

"Who are 'we'?" I demanded.

"Oh, Maggie, you know, Mr. Whyte's model, and Pinkie McCormick – we call her Pinkie because she's got that beautiful red hair you artists like so much – and Lizzie Burke."

I sent a shower of spray from the fixative over the canvas, and said: "Well, go on."

"We saw Kelly and Baby Barnes the skirt-dancer and – and all the rest. I made a mash."

"Then you have gone back on me, Tessie?"

She laughed and shook her head.

"He's Lizzie Burke's brother, Ed. He's a perfect gen'l'man."

I felt constrained to give her some parental advice concerning mashing, which she took with a bright smile.

"Oh, I can take care of a strange mash," she said, examining her chewing gum, "but Ed is different. Lizzie is my best friend."

Then she related how Ed had come back from the stocking mill in Lowell, Massachusetts, to find her and Lizzie grown up, and what an accomplished young man he was, and how he thought nothing of squandering half-a-dollar for ice-cream and oysters to celebrate his entry as clerk into the woollen department of Macy's. Before she finished I began to paint, and she resumed the pose, smiling and chattering like a sparrow. By noon I had the study fairly well rubbed in and Tessie came to look at it.

"That's better," she said.

I thought so too, and ate my lunch with a satisfied feeling that all was going well. Tessie spread her lunch on a drawing table opposite me and we drank our claret from the same bottle and lighted our cigarettes from the same match. I was very much attached to Tessie. I had watched her shoot up into a slender but exquisitely formed woman from a frail, awkward child. She had posed for me during the last three years, and among all my models she was my favourite. It would have troubled me very much indeed had she become "tough" or "fly," as the phrase goes, but I never noticed any deterioration of her manner, and felt at heart that she was all right. She and I never discussed morals at all, and I had no intention of doing so, partly because I had none myself, and partly because I knew she would do what she liked in spite of me. Still I did hope she would steer clear of complications, because I wished her well, and then also I had a selfish desire to retain the best model I had. I knew that mashing, as she termed it, had no significance with girls like Tessie, and that such things in America did not resemble in the least the same things in Paris. Yet, having lived with my eyes open, I also knew that somebody would take Tessie away some day, in one manner or another, and though I professed to myself that marriage was nonsense, I sincerely hoped that, in this case, there would be a priest at the end of the vista. I am a Catholic. When I listen to high mass, when I sign myself, I feel that everything, including myself, is more cheerful, and when I confess, it does me good. A man who lives as much alone as I do, must confess to somebody. Then, again, Sylvia was Catholic, and it was reason enough for me. But I was speaking of Tessie, which is very different. Tessie also was Catholic and much more devout than I, so, taking it all in all, I had little fear for my pretty model until she should fall in love. But *then* I knew that fate alone would decide her future for her, and I prayed inwardly that fate would keep her away from men like me and throw into her path nothing but Ed Burkes and Jimmy McCormicks, bless her sweet face!

Tessie sat blowing rings of smoke up to the ceiling and tinkling the ice in her tumbler.

"Do you know that I also had a dream last night?" I observed.

"Not about that man," she laughed.

"Exactly. A dream similar to yours, only much worse."

It was foolish and thoughtless of me to say this, but you know how little tact the average painter has. "I must have fallen asleep about ten o'clock," I continued, "and after a while I dreamt that I awoke. So plainly did I hear the midnight bells, the wind in the tree-branches, and the whistle of steamers from the bay, that even now I can scarcely believe I was not awake. I seemed to be lying in a box which had a glass cover. Dimly I saw the street lamps as I passed, for I must tell you, Tessie, the box in which I reclined appeared to lie in a cushioned wagon which jolted me over a stony pavement. After a while I became impatient and tried to move, but the box was too narrow. My hands were crossed on my breast, so I could not raise them to help myself. I listened and then tried to call. My voice was gone. I could hear the trample of the horses attached to the wagon, and even the breathing of the driver. Then another sound broke upon my ears like the raising of a window sash. I managed to turn my head a little, and found I could look, not only through the glass cover of my box, but also through the glass panes in the side of the covered vehicle. I saw houses, empty and silent, with neither light nor life about any of them excepting one. In that house a window was open on the first floor, and a figure all in white stood looking down into the street. It was you."

Tessie had turned her face away from me and leaned on the table with her elbow.

"I could see your face," I resumed, "and it seemed to me to be very sorrowful. Then we passed on and turned into a narrow black lane. Presently the horses stopped. I waited and waited, closing my eyes with fear and impatience, but all was silent as the grave. After what seemed to me hours, I began to feel uncomfortable. A sense that somebody was close to me made me unclose my eyes. Then I saw the white face of the hearse-driver looking at me through the coffin-lid – ”

A sob from Tessie interrupted me. She was trembling like a leaf. I saw I had made an ass of myself and attempted to repair the damage.

“Why, Tess,” I said, “I only told you this to show you what influence your story might have on another person’s dreams. You don’t suppose I really lay in a coffin, do you? What are you trembling for? Don’t you see that your dream and my unreasonable dislike for that inoffensive watchman of the church simply set my brain working as soon as I fell asleep?”

She laid her head between her arms, and sobbed as if her heart would break. What a precious triple donkey I had made of myself! But I was about to break my record. I went over and put my arm about her.

“Tessie dear, forgive me,” I said; “I had no business to frighten you with such nonsense. You are too sensible a girl, too good a Catholic to believe in dreams.”

Her hand tightened on mine and her head fell back upon my shoulder, but she still trembled and I petted her and comforted her.

“Come, Tess, open your eyes and smile.”

Her eyes opened with a slow languid movement and met mine, but their expression was so queer that I hastened to reassure her again.

“It’s all humbug, Tessie; you surely are not afraid that any harm will come to you because of that.”

“No,” she said, but her scarlet lips quivered.

“Then, what’s the matter? Are you afraid?”

“Yes. Not for myself.”

“For me, then?” I demanded gaily.

“For you,” she murmured in a voice almost inaudible. “I – I care for you.”

At first I started to laugh, but when I understood her, a shock passed through me, and I sat like one turned to stone. This was the crowning bit of idiocy I had committed. During the moment which elapsed between her reply and my answer I thought of a thousand responses to that innocent confession. I could pass it by with a laugh, I could misunderstand her and assure her as to my health, I could simply point out that it was impossible she could love me. But my reply was quicker than my thoughts, and I might think and think now when it was too late, for I had kissed her on the mouth.

That evening I took my usual walk in Washington Park, pondering over the occurrences of the day. I was thoroughly committed. There was no back out now, and I stared the future straight in the face. I was not good, not even scrupulous, but I had no idea of deceiving either myself or Tessie. The one passion of my life lay buried in the sunlit forests of Brittany. Was it buried for ever? Hope cried “No!” For three years I had been listening to the voice of Hope, and for three years I had waited for a footstep on my threshold. Had Sylvia forgotten? “No!” cried Hope.

I said that I was no good. That is true, but still I was not exactly a comic-opera villain. I had led an easy-going reckless life, taking what invited me of pleasure, deploring and sometimes bitterly regretting consequences. In one thing alone, except my painting, was I serious, and that was something which lay hidden if not lost in the Breton forests.

It was too late for me to regret what had occurred during the day. Whatever it had been, pity, a sudden tenderness for sorrow, or the more brutal instinct of gratified vanity, it was all the same now, and unless I wished to bruise an innocent heart, my path lay marked before me. The fire and strength, the depth of passion of a love which I had never even suspected, with all my imagined experience in the world, left me no alternative but to respond or send her away. Whether because I am so cowardly about giving pain to others, or whether it was that I have little of the gloomy Puritan in me, I do not know, but I shrank from disclaiming responsibility for that thoughtless kiss, and in fact had no time to do so before the gates of her heart opened and the flood poured forth. Others who habitually do their duty and find a sullen satisfaction in making themselves and everybody else unhappy, might have withstood it. I did not. I dared not. After the storm had abated I did tell her that she might better have loved Ed Burke and worn a plain gold ring, but she would not hear of it, and I thought perhaps as long as she had decided to love somebody she could not marry, it had better be me. I, at least, could treat her with an intelligent affection, and whenever she became tired of her infatuation she could go none the worse for it. For I was decided on that point, although I knew how hard it would be. I remembered the usual termination of Platonic liaisons, and thought how disgusted I had been whenever I heard of one. I knew I was undertaking a great deal for so unscrupulous a man as I was, and I dreamed the future, but never for one moment did I doubt that she was safe with me. Had it been anybody but Tessie I should not have bothered my head about scruples. For it did not occur to me to sacrifice Tessie as I would have sacrificed a woman of the world. I looked the future squarely in the face and saw the several probable endings to the affair. She would either tire of the whole thing, or become so unhappy that I should have either to marry her or go away. If I married her we would be unhappy. I with a wife unsuited to me, and she with a husband unsuitable for any woman. For my past life could scarcely entitle me to marry. If I went away she might either fall ill, recover, and marry some Eddie Burke, or she might recklessly or deliberately go and do something foolish. On the other hand, if she tired of me, then her whole life would be before her with beautiful vistas of Eddie Burkes and marriage rings and twins and Harlem flats and Heaven knows what. As I strolled along through the trees by the Washington Arch, I decided that she should find a substantial friend in me, anyway, and the future could take care of itself. Then I went into the house and put on my evening dress, for the little faintly-perfumed note on my dresser said, "Have a cab at the stage door at eleven," and the note was signed "Edith Carmichel, Metropolitan Theatre."

I took supper that night, or rather we took supper, Miss Carmichel and I, at Solari's, and the dawn was just beginning to gild the cross on the Memorial Church as I entered Washington Square after leaving Edith at the Brunswick. There was not a soul in the park as I passed along the trees and took the walk which leads from the Garibaldi statue to the Hamilton Apartment House, but as

I passed the churchyard I saw a figure sitting on the stone steps. In spite of myself a chill crept over me at the sight of the white puffy face, and I hastened to pass. Then he said something which might have been addressed to me or might merely have been a mutter to himself, but a sudden furious anger flamed up within me that such a creature should address me. For an instant I felt like wheeling about and smashing my stick over his head, but I walked on, and entering the Hamilton went to my apartment. For some time I tossed about the bed trying to get the sound of his voice out of my ears, but could not. It filled my head, that muttering sound, like thick oily smoke from a fat-rendering vat or an odour of noisome decay. And as I lay and tossed about, the voice in my ears seemed more distinct, and I began to understand the words he had muttered. They came to me slowly as if I had forgotten them, and at last I could make some sense out of the sounds. It was this:

"Have you found the Yellow Sign?"

"Have you found the Yellow Sign?"

"Have you found the Yellow Sign?"

I was furious. What did he mean by that? Then with a curse upon him and his I rolled over and went to sleep, but when I awoke later I looked pale and haggard, for I had dreamed the dream of the night before, and it troubled me more than I cared to think.

I dressed and went down into my studio. Tessie sat by the window, but as I came in she rose and put both arms around my neck for an innocent kiss. She looked so sweet and dainty that I kissed her again and then sat down before the easel.

"Hello! Where's the study I began yesterday?" I asked.

Tessie looked conscious, but did not answer. I began to hunt among the piles of canvases, saying, "Hurry up, Tess, and get ready; we must take advantage of the morning light."

When at last I gave up the search among the other canvases and turned to look around the room for the missing study I noticed Tessie standing by the screen with her clothes still on.

"What's the matter," I asked, "don't you feel well?"

"Yes."

"Then hurry."

"Do you want me to pose as – as I have always posed?"

Then I understood. Here was a new complication. I had lost, of course, the best nude model I had ever seen. I looked at Tessie. Her face was scarlet. Alas! Alas! We had eaten of the tree of knowledge, and Eden and native innocence were dreams of the past – I mean for her.

I suppose she noticed the disappointment on my face, for she said: "I will pose if you wish. The study is behind the screen here where I put it."

"No," I said, "we will begin something new;" and I went into my wardrobe and picked out a Moorish costume which fairly blazed with tinsel. It was a genuine costume, and Tessie retired to the screen with it enchanted. When she came forth again I was astonished. Her long black hair was bound above her forehead with a circlet of turquoises, and the ends, curled about her glittering girdle. Her feet were encased in the embroidered pointed slippers and the skirt of her costume, curiously wrought with arabesques in silver, fell to her ankles. The deep metallic blue vest embroidered with silver and the short Mauresque jacket spangled and sewn with turquoises became her wonderfully. She came up to me and held up her face smiling. I slipped my hand into my pocket, and drawing out a gold chain with a cross attached, dropped it over her head.

"It's yours, Tessie."

"Mine?" she faltered.

"Yours. Now go and pose," Then with a radiant smile she ran behind the screen and presently reappeared with a little box on which was written my name.

"I had intended to give it to you when I went home to-night," she said, "but I can't wait now."

I opened the box. On the pink cotton inside lay a clasp of black onyx, on which was inlaid a curious symbol or letter in gold. It was neither Arabic nor Chinese, nor, as I found afterwards, did it belong to any human script.

"It's all I had to give you for a keepsake," she said timidly.

I was annoyed, but I told her how much I should prize it, and promised to wear it always. She fastened it on my coat beneath the lapel.

"How foolish, Tess, to go and buy me such a beautiful thing as this," I said.

"I did not buy it," she laughed.

"Where did you get it?"

Then she told me how she had found it one day while coming from the Aquarium in the Battery, how she had advertised it and watched the papers, but at last gave up all hopes of finding the owner.

"That was last winter," she said, "the very day I had the first horrid dream about the hearse."

I remembered my dream of the previous night but said nothing, and presently my charcoal was flying over a new canvas, and Tessie stood motionless on the model-stand.

III

The day following was a disastrous one for me. While moving a framed canvas from one easel to another my foot slipped on the polished floor, and I fell heavily on both wrists. They were so badly sprained that it was useless to attempt to hold a brush, and I was obliged to wander about the studio, glaring at unfinished drawings and sketches, until despair seized me and I sat down to smoke and twiddle my thumbs with rage. The rain blew against the windows and rattled on the roof of the church, driving me into a nervous fit with its interminable patter. Tessie sat sewing by the window, and every now and then raised her head and looked at me with such innocent compassion that I began to feel ashamed of my irritation and looked about for something to occupy me. I had read all the papers and all the books in the library, but for the sake of something to do I went to the bookcases and shoved them open with my elbow. I knew every volume by its colour and examined them all, passing slowly around the library and whistling to keep up my spirits. I was turning to go into the dining-room when my eye fell upon a book bound in serpent skin, standing in a corner of the top shelf of the last bookcase. I did not remember it, and from the floor could not decipher the pale lettering on the back, so I went to the smoking-room and called Tessie. She came in from the studio and climbed up to reach the book.

"What is it?" I asked.

"*The King in Yellow.*"

I was dumfounded. Who had placed it there? How came it in my rooms? I had long ago decided that I should never open that book, and nothing on earth could have persuaded me to buy it. Fearful lest curiosity might tempt me to open it, I had never even looked at it in book-stores. If I ever had had any curiosity to read it, the awful tragedy of young Castaigne, whom I knew, prevented me from exploring its wicked pages. I had always refused to listen to any description of it, and indeed, nobody ever ventured to discuss the second part aloud, so I had absolutely no knowledge of what those leaves might reveal. I stared at the poisonous mottled binding as I would at a snake.

"Don't touch it, Tessie," I said; "come down."

Of course my admonition was enough to arouse her curiosity, and before I could prevent it she took the book and, laughing, danced off into the studio with it. I called to her, but she slipped away with a tormenting smile at my helpless hands, and I followed her with some impatience.

"Tessie!" I cried, entering the library, "listen, I am serious. Put that book away. I do not wish you to open it!" The library was empty. I went into both drawing-rooms, then into the bedrooms, laundry, kitchen, and finally returned to the library and began a systematic search. She had hidden herself so well that it was half-an-hour later when I discovered her crouching white and silent by the latticed window in the store-room above. At the first glance I saw she had been punished for her foolishness. *The King in Yellow* lay at her feet, but the book was open at the second part. I looked at Tessie and saw it was too late. She had opened *The King in Yellow.* Then I took her by the hand and led her into the studio. She seemed dazed, and when I told her to lie down on the sofa she obeyed me without a word. After a while she closed her eyes and her breathing became regular and deep, but I could not determine whether or not she slept. For a long while I sat silently beside her, but she neither stirred nor spoke, and at last I rose, and, entering the unused store-room, took the book in my least injured hand. It seemed heavy as lead, but I carried it into the studio again, and sitting down on the rug beside the sofa, opened it and read it through from beginning to end.

When, faint with excess of my emotions, I dropped the volume and leaned wearily back against the sofa, Tessie opened her eyes and looked at me. . .

We had been speaking for some time in a dull monotonous strain before I realised that we were discussing *The King in Yellow*. Oh the sin of writing such words – words which are clear as crystal, limpid and musical as bubbling springs, words which sparkle and glow like the poisoned diamonds of the Medicis! Oh the wickedness, the hopeless damnation of a soul who could fascinate and paralyze human creatures with such words, – words understood by the ignorant and wise alike, words which are more precious than jewels, more soothing than music, more awful than death!

We talked on, unmindful of the gathering shadows, and she was begging me to throw away the clasp of black onyx quaintly inlaid with what we now knew to be the Yellow Sign. I never shall know why I refused, though even at this hour, here in my bedroom as I write this confession, I should be glad to know *what* it was that prevented me from tearing the Yellow Sign from my breast and casting it into the fire. I am sure I wished to do so, and yet Tessie pleaded with me in vain. Night fell and the hours dragged on, but still we murmured to each other of the King and the Pallid Mask, and midnight sounded from the misty spires in the fog-wrapped city. We spoke of Hastur and of Cassilda, while outside the fog rolled against the blank window-panes as the cloud waves roll and break on the shores of Hali.

The house was very silent now, and not a sound came up from the misty streets. Tessie lay among the cushions, her face a grey blot in the gloom, but her hands were clasped in mine, and I knew that she knew and read my thoughts as I read hers, for we had understood the mystery of the Hyades and the Phantom of Truth was laid. Then as we answered each other, swiftly, silently, thought on thought, the shadows stirred in the gloom about us, and far in the distant streets we heard a sound. Nearer and nearer it came, the dull crunching of wheels, nearer and yet nearer, and now, outside before the door it ceased, and I dragged myself to the window and saw a black-plumed hearse. The gate below opened and shut, and I crept shaking to my door and bolted it, but I knew no bolts, no locks, could keep that creature out who was coming for the Yellow Sign. And now I heard him moving very softly along the hall. Now he was at the door, and the bolts rotted at his touch. Now he had entered. With eyes starting from my head I peered into the darkness, but when he came into the room I did not see him. It was only when I felt him envelop me in his cold soft grasp that I cried out and struggled with deadly fury, but my hands were useless and he tore the onyx clasp from my coat and struck me full in the face. Then, as I fell, I heard Tessie's soft cry and her spirit fled: and even while falling I longed to follow her, for I knew that the King in Yellow had opened his tattered mantle and there was only God to cry to now.

I could tell more, but I cannot see what help it will be to the world. As for me, I am past human help or hope. As I lie here, writing, careless even whether or not I die before I finish, I can see the doctor gathering up his powders and phials with a vague gesture to the good priest beside me, which I understand.

They will be very curious to know the tragedy – they of the outside world who write books and print millions of newspapers, but I shall write no more, and the father confessor will seal my last words with the seal of sanctity when his holy office is done. They of the outside world may send their creatures into wrecked homes and death-smitten firesides, and their newspapers will batten on blood and tears, but with me their spies must halt before the confessional. They know that Tessie is dead and that I am dying. They know how the people in the house, aroused by an infernal scream, rushed into my room and found one living and two dead, but they do not know what I shall tell them now; they do not know that the doctor said as he pointed to a horrible decomposed heap on the floor – the livid corpse of the watchman from the church: "I have no theory, no explanation. That man must have been dead for months!"

I think I am dying. I wish the priest would—

THE MONKEY'S PAW

W.W. Jacobs

William Wymark Jacobs (1863–1943) was born in Wapping. His father was a dockhand and wharf manager on the South Devon Wharf and many of Jacobs' stories involve humorous adventures of seafarers. *The Monkey's Paw* is his best-known story and has been adapted numerous times for radio, film and television.

I

Without, the night was cold and wet, but in the small parlour of Laburnam Villa the blinds were drawn and the fire burned brightly. Father and son were at chess, the former, who possessed ideas about the game involving radical changes, putting his king into such sharp and unnecessary perils that it even provoked comment from the white-haired old lady knitting placidly by the fire.

"Hark at the wind," said Mr. White, who, having seen a fatal mistake after it was too late, was amiably desirous of preventing his son from seeing it.

"I'm listening," said the latter, grimly surveying the board as he stretched out his hand. "Check."

"I should hardly think that he'd come to-night," said his father, with his hand poised over the board.

"Mate," replied the son.

"That's the worst of living so far out," bawled Mr. White, with sudden and unlooked-for violence; "of all the beastly, slushy, out-of-the-way places to live in, this is the worst. Path's a bog, and the road's a torrent. I don't know what people are thinking about. I suppose because only two houses in the road are let, they think it doesn't matter."

"Never mind, dear," said his wife, soothingly; "perhaps you'll win the next one."

Mr. White looked up sharply, just in time to intercept a knowing glance between mother and son. The words died away on his lips, and he hid a guilty grin in his thin grey beard.

"There he is," said Herbert White, as the gate banged to loudly and heavy footsteps came toward the door.

The old man rose with hospitable haste, and opening the door, was heard condoling with the new arrival. The new arrival also condoled with himself, so that Mrs. White said, "Tut, tut!" and coughed gently as her husband entered the room, followed by a tall, burly man, beady of eye and rubicund of visage.

"Sergeant-Major Morris," he said, introducing him.

The sergeant-major shook hands, and taking the proffered seat by the fire, watched contentedly while his host got out whiskey and tumblers and stood a small copper kettle on the fire.

At the third glass his eyes got brighter, and he began to talk, the little family circle regarding with eager interest this visitor from distant parts, as he squared his broad shoulders in the chair and spoke of wild scenes and doughty deeds; of wars and plagues and strange peoples.

"Twenty-one years of it," said Mr. White, nodding at his wife and son. "When he went away he was a slip of a youth in the warehouse. Now look at him."

"He don't look to have taken much harm," said Mrs. White, politely.

"I'd like to go to India myself," said the old man, "just to look round a bit, you know."

"Better where you are," said the sergeant-major, shaking his head. He put down the empty glass, and sighing softly, shook it again.

"I should like to see those old temples and fakirs and jugglers," said the old man. "What was that you started telling me the other day about a monkey's paw or something, Morris?"

"Nothing," said the soldier, hastily. "Leastways nothing worth hearing."

"Monkey's paw?" said Mrs. White, curiously.

"Well, it's just a bit of what you might call magic, perhaps," said the sergeant-major, offhandedly.

His three listeners leaned forward eagerly. The visitor absent-mindedly put his empty glass to his lips and then set it down again. His host filled it for him.

"To look at," said the sergeant-major, fumbling in his pocket, "it's just an ordinary little paw, dried to a mummy."

He took something out of his pocket and proffered it. Mrs. White drew back with a grimace, but her son, taking it, examined it curiously.

"And what is there special about it?" inquired Mr. White as he took it from his son, and having examined it, placed it upon the table.

"It had a spell put on it by an old fakir," said the sergeant-major, "a very holy man. He wanted to show that fate ruled people's lives, and that those who interfered with it did so to their sorrow. He put a spell on it so that three separate men could each have three wishes from it."

His manner was so impressive that his hearers were conscious that their light laughter jarred somewhat.

"Well, why don't you have three, sir?" said Herbert White, cleverly.

The soldier regarded him in the way that middle age is wont to regard presumptuous youth. "I have," he said, quietly, and his blotchy face whitened.

"And did you really have the three wishes granted?" asked Mrs. White.

"I did," said the sergeant-major, and his glass tapped against his strong teeth.

"And has anybody else wished?" persisted the old lady.

"The first man had his three wishes. Yes," was the reply; "I don't know what the first two were, but the third was for death. That's how I got the paw."

His tones were so grave that a hush fell upon the group.

"If you've had your three wishes, it's no good to you now, then, Morris," said the old man at last. "What do you keep it for?"

The soldier shook his head. "Fancy, I suppose," he said, slowly. "I did have some idea of selling it, but I don't think I will. It has caused enough mischief already. Besides, people won't buy. They think it's a fairy tale; some of them, and those who do think anything of it want to try it first and pay me afterward."

"If you could have another three wishes," said the old man, eyeing him keenly, "would you have them?"

"I don't know," said the other. "I don't know."

He took the paw, and dangling it between his forefinger and thumb, suddenly threw it upon the fire. White, with a slight cry, stooped down and snatched it off.

"Better let it burn," said the soldier, solemnly.

"If you don't want it, Morris," said the other, "give it to me."

"I won't," said his friend, doggedly. "I threw it on the fire. If you keep it, don't blame me for what happens. Pitch it on the fire again like a sensible man."

The other shook his head and examined his new possession closely. "How do you do it?" he inquired.

"Hold it up in your right hand and wish aloud," said the sergeant-major, "but I warn you of the consequences."

"Sounds like the *Arabian Nights*," said Mrs. White, as she rose and began to set the supper. "Don't you think you might wish for four pairs of hands for me?"

Her husband drew the talisman from pocket, and then all three burst into laughter as the sergeant-major, with a look of alarm on his face, caught him by the arm.

"If you must wish," he said, gruffly, "wish for something sensible."

Mr. White dropped it back in his pocket, and placing chairs, motioned his friend to the table. In the business of supper the talisman was partly forgotten, and afterward the three sat listening in an enthralled fashion to a second instalment of the soldier's adventures in India.

"If the tale about the monkey's paw is not more truthful than those he has been telling us," said Herbert, as the door closed behind their guest, just in time for him to catch the last train, "we sha'nt make much out of it."

"Did you give him anything for it, father?" inquired Mrs. White, regarding her husband closely.

"A trifle," said he, colouring slightly. "He didn't want it, but I made him take it. And he pressed me again to throw it away."

"Likely," said Herbert, with pretended horror. "Why, we're going to be rich, and famous and happy. Wish to be an emperor, father, to begin with; then you can't be henpecked."

He darted round the table, pursued by the maligned Mrs. White armed with an antimacassar.

Mr. White took the paw from his pocket and eyed it dubiously. "I don't know what to wish for, and that's a fact," he said, slowly. "It seems to me I've got all I want."

"If you only cleared the house, you'd be quite happy, wouldn't you?" said Herbert, with his hand on his shoulder. "Well, wish for two hundred pounds, then; that 'll just do it."

His father, smiling shamefacedly at his own credulity, held up the talisman, as his son, with a solemn face, somewhat marred by a wink at his mother, sat down at the piano and struck a few impressive chords.

"I wish for two hundred pounds," said the old man distinctly.

A fine crash from the piano greeted the words, interrupted by a shuddering cry from the old man. His wife and son ran toward him.

"It moved," he cried, with a glance of disgust at the object as it lay on the floor.

"As I wished, it twisted in my hand like a snake."

"Well, I don't see the money," said his son as he picked it up and placed it on the table, "and I bet I never shall."

"It must have been your fancy, father," said his wife, regarding him anxiously.

He shook his head. "Never mind, though; there's no harm done, but it gave me a shock all the same."

They sat down by the fire again while the two men finished their pipes. Outside, the wind was higher than ever, and the old man started nervously at the sound of a door banging upstairs. A silence unusual and depressing settled upon all three, which lasted until the old couple rose to retire for the night.

"I expect you'll find the cash tied up in a big bag in the middle of your bed," said Herbert, as he bade them good-night, "and something horrible squatting up on top of the wardrobe watching you as you pocket your ill-gotten gains."

He sat alone in the darkness, gazing at the dying fire, and seeing faces in it. The last face was so horrible and so simian that he gazed at it in amazement. It got so vivid that, with a little uneasy laugh, he felt on the table for a glass containing a little water to throw over it. His hand grasped the monkey's paw, and with a little shiver he wiped his hand on his coat and went up to bed.

II

In the brightness of the wintry sun next morning as it streamed over the breakfast table he laughed at his fears. There was an air of prosaic wholesomeness about the room which it had lacked on the previous night, and the dirty, shrivelled little paw was pitched on the sideboard with a carelessness which betokened no great belief in its virtues.

"I suppose all old soldiers are the same," said Mrs. White. "The idea of our listening to such nonsense! How could wishes be granted in these days? And if they could, how could two hundred pounds hurt you, father?"

"Might drop on his head from the sky," said the frivolous Herbert.

"Morris said the things happened so naturally," said his father, "that you might if you so wished attribute it to coincidence."

"Well, don't break into the money before I come back," said Herbert as he rose from the table. "I'm afraid it'll turn you into a mean, avaricious man, and we shall have to disown you."

His mother laughed, and following him to the door, watched him down the road; and returning to the breakfast table, was very happy at the expense of her husband's credulity. All of which did not prevent her from scurrying to the door at the postman's knock, nor prevent her from referring somewhat shortly to retired sergeant-majors of bibulous habits when she found that the post brought a tailor's bill.

"Herbert will have some more of his funny remarks, I expect, when he comes home," she said, as they sat at dinner.

"I dare say," said Mr. White, pouring himself out some beer; "but for all that, the thing moved in my hand; that I'll swear to."

"You thought it did," said the old lady soothingly.

"I say it did," replied the other. "There was no thought about it; I had just – What's the matter?"

His wife made no reply. She was watching the mysterious movements of a man outside, who, peering in an undecided fashion at the house, appeared to be trying to make up his mind to enter. In mental connexion with the two hundred pounds, she noticed that the stranger was well dressed, and wore a silk hat of glossy newness. Three times he paused at the gate, and then walked on again. The fourth time he stood with his hand upon it, and then with sudden resolution flung it open and walked up the path. Mrs. White at the same moment placed her hands behind her, and hurriedly unfastening the strings of her apron, put that useful article of apparel beneath the cushion of her chair.

She brought the stranger, who seemed ill at ease, into the room. He gazed at her furtively, and listened in a preoccupied fashion as the old lady apologized for the appearance of the room, and her husband's coat, a garment which he usually reserved for the garden. She then waited as patiently as her sex would permit, for him to broach his business, but he was at first strangely silent.

"I – was asked to call," he said at last, and stooped and picked a piece of cotton from his trousers. "I come from 'Maw and Meggins.'"

The old lady started. "Is anything the matter?" she asked, breathlessly. "Has anything happened to Herbert? What is it? What is it?"

Her husband interposed. "There, there, mother," he said, hastily. "Sit down, and don't jump to conclusions. You've not brought bad news, I'm sure, sir;" and he eyed the other wistfully.

"I'm sorry – " began the visitor.

"Is he hurt?" demanded the mother, wildly.

The visitor bowed in assent. "Badly hurt," he said, quietly, "but he is not in any pain."

"Oh, thank God!" said the old woman, clasping her hands. "Thank God for that! Thank – "

She broke off suddenly as the sinister meaning of the assurance dawned upon her and she saw the awful confirmation of her fears in the other's averted face. She caught her breath, and turning to her slower-witted husband, laid her trembling old hand upon his. There was a long silence.

"He was caught in the machinery," said the visitor at length in a low voice.

"Caught in the machinery," repeated Mr. White, in a dazed fashion, "yes."

He sat staring blankly out at the window, and taking his wife's hand between his own, pressed it as he had been wont to do in their old courting-days nearly forty years before.

"He was the only one left to us," he said, turning gently to the visitor. "It is hard."

The other coughed, and rising, walked slowly to the window. "The firm wished me to convey their sincere sympathy with you in your great loss," he said, without looking round. "I beg that you will understand I am only their servant and merely obeying orders."

There was no reply; the old woman's face was white, her eyes staring, and her breath inaudible; on the husband's face was a look such as his friend the sergeant might have carried into his first action.

"I was to say that 'Maw and Meggins' disclaim all responsibility," continued the other. "They admit no liability at all, but in consideration of your son's services, they wish to present you with a certain sum as compensation."

Mr. White dropped his wife's hand, and rising to his feet, gazed with a look of horror at his visitor. His dry lips shaped the words, "How much?"

"Two hundred pounds," was the answer.

Unconscious of his wife's shriek, the old man smiled faintly, put out his hands like a sightless man, and dropped, a senseless heap, to the floor.

III

In the huge new cemetery, some two miles distant, the old people buried their dead, and came back to a house steeped in shadow and silence. It was all over so quickly that at first they could hardly realize it, and remained in a state of expectation as though of something else to happen – something else which was to lighten this load, too heavy for old hearts to bear.

But the days passed, and expectation gave place to resignation – the hopeless resignation of the old, sometimes miscalled, apathy. Sometimes they hardly exchanged a word, for now they had nothing to talk about, and their days were long to weariness.

It was about a week after that the old man, waking suddenly in the night, stretched out his hand and found himself alone. The room was in darkness, and the sound of subdued weeping came from the window. He raised himself in bed and listened.

"Come back," he said, tenderly. "You will be cold."

"It is colder for my son," said the old woman, and wept afresh.

The sound of her sobs died away on his ears. The bed was warm, and his eyes heavy with sleep. He dozed fitfully, and then slept until a sudden wild cry from his wife awoke him with a start.

"The paw!" she cried wildly. "The monkey's paw!"

He started up in alarm. "Where? Where is it? What's the matter?"

She came stumbling across the room toward him. "I want it," she said, quietly. "You've not destroyed it?"

"It's in the parlour, on the bracket," he replied, marvelling. "Why?"

She cried and laughed together, and bending over, kissed his cheek.

"I only just thought of it," she said, hysterically. "Why didn't I think of it before? Why didn't you think of it?"

"Think of what?" he questioned.

"The other two wishes," she replied, rapidly. "We've only had one."

"Was not that enough?" he demanded, fiercely.

"No," she cried, triumphantly; "we'll have one more. Go down and get it quickly, and wish our boy alive again."

The man sat up in bed and flung the bedclothes from his quaking limbs. "Good God, you are mad!" he cried, aghast.

"Get it," she panted; "get it quickly, and wish – Oh, my boy, my boy!"

Her husband struck a match and lit the candle. "Get back to bed," he said, unsteadily. "You don't know what you are saying."

"We had the first wish granted," said the old woman, feverishly; "why not the second?"

"A coincidence," stammered the old man.

"Go and get it and wish," cried his wife, quivering with excitement.

The old man turned and regarded her, and his voice shook. "He has been dead ten days, and besides he – I would not tell you else, but – I could only recognize him by his clothing. If he was too terrible for you to see then, how now?"

"Bring him back," cried the old woman, and dragged him toward the door. "Do you think I fear the child I have nursed?"

He went down in the darkness, and felt his way to the parlour, and then to the mantelpiece. The talisman was in its place, and a horrible fear that the unspoken wish might bring his mutilated son before him ere he could escape from the room seized upon him, and he caught his breath as he found that he had lost the direction of the door. His brow cold with sweat, he felt his way round the table, and groped along the wall until he found himself in the small passage with the unwholesome thing in his hand.

Even his wife's face seemed changed as he entered the room. It was white and expectant, and to his fears seemed to have an unnatural look upon it. He was afraid of her.

"Wish!" she cried, in a strong voice.

"It is foolish and wicked," he faltered.

"Wish!" repeated his wife.

He raised his hand. "I wish my son alive again."

The talisman fell to the floor, and he regarded it fearfully. Then he sank trembling into a chair as the old woman, with burning eyes, walked to the window and raised the blind.

He sat until he was chilled with the cold, glancing occasionally at the figure of the old woman peering through the window. The candle-end, which had burned below the rim of the china candlestick, was throwing pulsating shadows on the ceiling and walls, until, with a flicker larger than the rest, it expired. The old man, with an unspeakable sense of relief at the failure of the talisman, crept back to his bed, and a minute or two afterward the old woman came silently and apathetically beside him.

Neither spoke, but lay silently listening to the ticking of the clock. A stair creaked, and a squeaky mouse scurried noisily through the wall. The darkness was oppressive, and after lying for some time screwing up his courage, he took the box of matches, and striking one, went downstairs for a candle.

At the foot of the stairs the match went out, and he paused to strike another; and at the same moment a knock, so quiet and stealthy as to be scarcely audible, sounded on the front door.

The matches fell from his hand and spilled in the passage. He stood motionless, his breath suspended until the knock was repeated. Then he turned and fled swiftly back to his room, and closed the door behind him. A third knock sounded through the house.

"*What's that?*" cried the old woman, starting up.

"A rat," said the old man in shaking tones – "a rat. It passed me on the stairs."

His wife sat up in bed listening. A loud knock resounded through the house.

"It's Herbert!" she screamed. "It's Herbert!"

She ran to the door, but her husband was before her, and catching her by the arm, held her tightly.

"What are you going to do?" he whispered hoarsely.

"It's my boy; it's Herbert!" she cried, struggling mechanically. "I forgot it was two miles away. What are you holding me for? Let go. I must open the door."

"For God's sake don't let it in," cried the old man, trembling.

"You're afraid of your own son," she cried, struggling. "Let me go. I'm coming, Herbert; I'm coming."

There was another knock, and another. The old woman with a sudden wrench broke free and ran from the room. Her husband followed to the landing, and called after her appealingly as she hurried downstairs. He heard the chain rattle back and the bottom bolt drawn slowly and stiffly from the socket. Then the old woman's voice, strained and panting.

"The bolt," she cried, loudly. "Come down. I can't reach it."

But her husband was on his hands and knees groping wildly on the floor in search of the paw. If he could only find it before the thing outside got in. A perfect fusillade of knocks reverberated through the house, and he heard the scraping of a chair as his wife put it down in the passage against the door. He heard the creaking of the bolt as it came slowly back, and at the same moment he found the monkey's paw, and frantically breathed his third and last wish.

The knocking ceased suddenly, although the echoes of it were still in the house. He heard the chair drawn back, and the door opened. A cold wind rushed up the staircase, and a long loud wail of disappointment and misery from his wife gave him courage to run down to her side, and then to the gate beyond. The street lamp flickering opposite shone on a quiet and deserted road.

ELIAS AND THE DRAUG

Jonas Lie

> Jonas Lie (1833–1908) was born in Eiker, near Drammen, in southern
> Norway. His family moved to the Arctic town of Tromsø when he was
> five years old. The Arctic's seasonal extremes – dreadful storms in winter,
> permanent daylight in summer – had a lasting influence on Lie's writing.
> He graduated in law in 1857 and practised in the town of Kongsvinger
> on the Swedish border. In 1874, he was granted an artist salary by the
> Norwegian Parliament.

On Kvalholmen down in Helgeland there once lived a poor fisherman, by name Elias, and his wife, Karen, who before her marriage had worked in the parsonage at Alstadhaug. They lived in a little hut, which they had built, and Elias hired out by the day in the Lofoten fisheries.

Kvalholmen was a lonely island, and there were signs at times that it was haunted. Sometimes when her husband was away from home, the good wife heard all sorts of unearthly noises and cries, which surely boded no good.

Each year there came a child; when they had been married seven years there were six children in the home. But they were both steady and hard working people, and by the time the last arrived, Elias had managed to put aside something and felt that he could afford a sixern, and thereafter do his Lofoten fishing as master in his own boat.

One day, as he was walking with a halibut harpoon in one hand, thinking about this, he suddenly came upon a huge seal, sunning itself in the lee of a rock near the shore, and apparently quite as much taken by surprise as he was.

Elias meanwhile was not slow. From the rocky ledge, on which he was standing, he plunged the long, heavy harpoon into its back just behind the neck. But then – oh, what a struggle! Instantly the seal reared itself up, stood erect on its tail, tall as the mast of a boat, and glowered at him with a pair of bloodshot eyes, at the same time showing its teeth in a grin so fiendish and venomous that Elias almost lost his wits from fright. Then suddenly it plunged into the sea and vanished in a spray of mingled blood and water.

That was the last Elias saw of it; but that very afternoon the harpoon, broken just below the iron barb, came drifting ashore near the boat landing not far from his house.

Elias had soon forgotten all about it. He bought his sixern that same autumn, and housed it in a little boat shed he had built during the summer.

One night, as he lay thinking about his new sixern, it occurred to him that perhaps, in order to safeguard it properly, he ought to put another shore on either side underneath it. He was so absurdly fond of the boat that he thought it only fun to get up and light his lantern and go down to look it over*

As he held up his lantern to see better, he suddenly glimpsed, on a tangle of nets in one corner, a face that resembled exactly the features of the seal. It grimaced for a moment angrily towards him and the light. Its mouth seemed to open wider and wider, and before he was aware of anything further, he saw a bulky man-form vanish out the door of the boat house, not so fast however but that he managed to make out, with the aid of his lantern, a long iron prong projecting from its back.

Elias now began to put two and two together. But even so he was more concerned for the safety of his boat than he was for his own life.

On the morning, early in January, when he set out for the fishing banks, with two men in the boat beside himself, he heard a voice call to him in the darkness from a skerry directly opposite the mouth of the cove. He thought that it laughed derisively.

"Better beware, Elias, when you get your fembøring!"

It was a long time, however, before Elias saw his way clear to get a fembøring – not until his eldest son was seventeen years old.

It was In the fall of the year that Ellas embarked with his whole family and went to Ranen to trade in his sixern for a fembøring. At home they left only a little Lapp girl, but newly confirmed, whom they had taken into their home some years before. There was one fembøring in particular which he had his eye on, a little four man boat, which the best shipwright thereabout had finished and tarred that very fall. For this boat he traded in his own sixern, paying the difference in coin.

Elias thereupon began to think of sailing home. He first stopped at the village store and laid in a supply for Christmas for himself and his family, among other things a little keg of brandy. It may be that, pleased as they were with the day's bargaining, both he and his wife had one drop too many before they left, and Bernt, their son, was given a taste too.

Whereupon they set sail for home in the new fembøring. Other ballast than himself, his wife and children, and his Christmas supplies he had none. His son Bernt sat at the stem; his wife, with the assistance of the second son, managed the halyard; Elias himself sat at the tiller, while the two younger sons, twelve and fourteen respectively, were to alternate at the bailing.

They had fifty odd miles of sea before them, and they had no sooner reached the open than it was apparent that the fembøring would be put to the test the very first time It was in use. A storm blew up before long, and soon white-crested waves began dashing themselves into spray. Then Ellas saw what kind of a boat he had. It rode the waves like a sea gull, without so much as taking in one single drop, and he was ready to swear that he would not even have to single-reef, as any ordinary fembøring would have been compelled to do in such weather.

As the day drew on, he noticed not far away another fembøring, completely manned, speeding along, just as he was then, with four reefs in the sail. It seemed to follow the same course, and he thought it strange that he had not noticed it before. It seemed to want to race with him, and when Elias realized this, he could not resist letting out a reef again.

So they raced along at a terrific speed past headlands and islands and skerries. To Elias it seemed that he had never before sailed so gloriously, and the femböring proved to be every whit that had been claimed – the best boat in Ranen.

Meanwhile the sea had risen, and already several huge waves had rolled over them, breaking against the stem up forward, where Bernt sat, and sweeping out to leeward near the stern.

Ever since dusk had settled over the sea, the other boat had kept very close to them, and they were now so near each other that they could have thrown a balling-dipper, one to the other, had they wished. And so they sailed on, side by side, all the evening, in an ever-increasing sea.

That last reef, Ellas began to think, ought really to be taken in again, but he was loath to give up the race, and made up his mind to wait as long as possible, until the other boat saw fit to reef in, for it was quite as hard pressed as he. And since they now had to fight both the cold and the wet, the brandy bottle was now and then brought forth and passed around.

The phosphorescent light, which played on the dark sea near his own boat, flashed eerily in the white crests around the stranger, which appeared to be plowing a furrow of light and throwing a fiery foam to either side. In the reflection of this light he could even distinguish the rope ends In the other boat. He could also make out the crew on board in their oilskin caps, but inasmuch as they were on the leeward side of him, they kept their backs turned and were almost hid behind the lofty gunwale, as it rose with the seas.

Of a sudden a gigantic breaker, whose white crest Elias had for some time seen in the darkness, crashed against the prow of the boat, where Bernt sat. For a moment the whole femböring seemed to come to a stop, the timbers creaked and jarred under the strain, and then the boat, which for half a second had balanced uncertainly, righted itself and sped forward, while the wave rolled out again to leeward.

All the while this was happening Elias thought he heard fiendish cries issuing from the other boat.

But when it was over, his wife, who sat at the halyard, cried out in a voice that cut him to the very soul, "My God, Elias, that sea took Marthe and Nils!"

These were their two youngest children, the former nine, the latter seven years old, who had been sitting forward close to Bernt.

"Hold fast to the halyard, Karen, or you may lose more!" was all that Elias answered.

It was necessary now to take in the fourth reef, and Elias had no sooner done so than he thought it advisable to reef in the fifth, for the sea was steadily rising. On the other hand, if he hoped to sail his boat clear of the ever mounting waves, he dared not lessen his sail more than was absolutely necessary.

It turned out, however, to be difficult going even with the sail thus diminished. The sea raged furiously, and deluged them with spray after spray. Finally Bernt and Anton, the next oldest, who had helped his mother at the halyard, had to take hold of the yardarm, something one resorts to only when a boat is hard pressed even with the last reef – in this case the fifth.

The rival boat, which in the meantime had disappeared from sight, bobbed up alongside them again with exactly the same amount of sail that he was carrying.

Elias now began rather to dislike the crew over there. The two men who stood holding the yardarm, and whose faces he could glimpse underneath their oilskin caps, appeared to him in the weird reflections from the spray more like specters than human beings. They spoke ne'er a word.

A little to leeward he spied the foaming ridge of another breaker rising before him in the dark, and he prepared himself to meet it. He turned the prow slantwise towards it, and let out as much sail as he dared, to give the boat speed enough to cleave its way through.

The sea struck them with the roar of a torrent. For a moment the boat again careened uncertainly. When it was all over, and the vessel had righted itself once more, his wife no longer sat at the halyard, nor was Anton at the yard-arm – they had both been washed asea.

This time, too, he thought he made out the same fiendish voices above the storm, but mingled with them he also heard his wife's agonizing cries as she called him by name. When he realized that she had been swept overboard, he muttered to himself, "In Jesus's name!" and said no more.

He felt vaguely that he would have preferred to follow her, but he realized at the same time that it was up to him to save the other three he had on board, Bernt and the two younger sons, the one twelve, the other fourteen, who for a while had been doing the bailing, but whom he had later placed in the stern behind him.

Bernt was now left to manage the yardarm alone, and the two, father and son, had to help each other as best they could. The tiller Elias did not dare let go; he held on to it with a hand of iron, long since numb from the strain.

After a while the companion boat bobbed up again; as before it had been momentarily lost to view. He now saw more clearly than before the bulky form that sat aft, much as he was sitting, and controlled the tiller. Projecting from his neck whenever he turned his back, just below the oilskin cap, Elias could clearly discern some four inches or so of an iron prong, which he had seen before.

At that he was convinced in his innermost soul of two things: One was that it was none other than the Draug himself who sat steering his half-boat alongside his and who had lured him on to destruction, and the other was that he was fated no doubt this night to sail the sea for the last time. For he who sees the Draug at sea Is a marked man. He said nothing to the others, in order not to discourage them, but he commended his soul in silence to the Lord.

He had found it necessary, during the last hours, to bear away from his course because of the storm, and when furthermore it took to snowing heavily, he realized that he would no doubt have to postpone any attempt to land until dawn.

Meanwhile they sailed on as before.

Now and again the boys aft complained of freezing, but there was nothing to do about that, wet as they were, and furthermore Elias sat preoccupied with his own thoughts.

He had been seized with an insatiable desire to avenge himself. What he would have liked to do, had he not had the lives of his three remaining children to safeguard, was suddenly to veer about in an attempt to ram and sink the cursed boat, which still as if to mock him ran ever alongside him, and whose fiendish purpose he now fully comprehended. If the halibut harpoon had once taken effect, why might not now a knife or a gaff do likewise? He felt he would willingly give his life to deal one good blow to this monster, who had so unmercifully robbed him of all that was dearest to him on earth, and who still seemed insatiate and demanded more.

About three or four o'clock in the morning they again spied rolling towards them in the darkness the white crest of a wave, so huge that Elias for a moment surely thought they were just off shore somewhere in the neighborhood of breakers. It was not long, however, before he understood that it really was only a colossal wave.

Then he thought he clearly heard some one laugh and cry out In the other boat.

"There goes your fembӧring, Elias!"

Elias, who foresaw the catastrophe, repeated loudly "In Jesus's name!" commanded his sons to hold fast, and told them if the boat went down to grasp the osier bands in the oarlocks, and not to let go till it had come afloat again. He let the elder of the two boys go forward to Bernt; the younger he kept close to himself, caressing his cheeks furtively once or twice, and assuring himself that the child had a tight hold.

The boat was literally buried beneath the towering comber, and was then pitched up on end, its stem high above the wave, before it finally went under. When it came afloat again, its keel now in the air, Elias, Bernt, and the twelve-year-old Martin appeared too, still clinging to the osier bands. But the third of the brothers had disappeared.

It was a matter of life and death now, first of all, to get the rigging cut away on one side, that they might be rid of the mast, which would otherwise rock the boat from beneath, and then to crawl up onto the hull and let the Imprisoned air out, which would otherwise have kept the boat too high afloat and prevented it riding the waves safely. After considerable difficulty they succeeded in so doing, and Elias, who had been the first to clamber up, assisted the other two to safety.

Thus they sat the long winter night through, desperately clinging with cramped hands and numb knees to the hull, as one wave after another swept over them..

After a few hours, Martin, whom the father had supported all this time as best he could, died of exhaustion and slipped into the sea.

They had several times attempted to call for help, but realizing that it was of no avail, they finally gave it up.

As the two, thus left alone, sat on the hull of the boat, Elias told Bernt he knew that he himself was fated soon to "follow mother" but he had a firm hope that Bernt would be saved in the end, if only he stuck it out like a man. And then he told him all about the Draug how he had wounded him in the neck with the halibut harpoon, and how the Draug was now taking his revenge and would surely not give in until they were quits.

It was towards nine o'clock in the morning before the day finally began to dawn. Elias then handed over to Bernt, who sat at his side, his silver watch with the brass chain, which he had broken in pulling it out from underneath his close-buttoned vests.

He still sat on a while longer, but as it grew lighter, Bernt saw that his father's face was ghastly pale. The hair on his head had parted in several places, as it often does just before death, and the skin on his hands was worn off from his efforts to hang on to the keel. Bernt realized that his father was near the end. He tried, as well as the pitching of the boat permitted, to edge over to him and support him. But when Elias noticed it, he waved him back.

"You stay where you are, Bernt, and hold fast! I'm going to mother! In Jesus's name!"

And so saying he threw himself backward down from the hull.

When the sea had got its own, it quieted down for a while, as every one knows who has straddled a hull. It became easier for Bernt to maintain his hold, and with the coming of daylight new hope kindled in him. The storm moderated, and in the full light of day he thought he recognized his surroundings – that he was, in fact, drifting directly off shore from his own home, Kvalholmen.

He began crying for help again, but he really had greater faith in a tide he knew bore landward, just beyond a projection of the island, which checked the fury of the sea.

He drifted nearer and nearer shore, and finally came so close to one of the skerries that the mast, which still floated alongside the boat, grated on the rocks with the rising and falling of the surf. Stiff as his muscles and joints were from his sitting so long and holding fast to the hull, he managed with a great effort to transfer himself to the skerry, after which he hauled in the mast and finally moored the femböring.

The little Lapp girl, who was home alone, for two whole hours thought she heard cries for help, and when they persisted she mounted the hilltop to look out to sea. There she saw Bernt on the skerry, and the upturned femböring beating up and down against it. She ran instantly down to the boat house, pushed out the old rowboat, and rowed It out to the skerry, hugging the shore round the island.

Bernt lay ill, under her care, the whole winter long, and did not take part in the fishing that year. People used to say that ever after he seemed now and again a little queer. To sea he would never go again; he had come to fear it.

He married the Lapp girl, and moved up to Malingen, where he broke new ground and cleared himself a home. There he is still living and doing well.

ANGELINE, *OR THE HAUNTED HOUSE*

Émile Zola

Born in Paris Émile Zola (1840–1902) is best known for his celebrated *Les Rougon-Macquart* series: twenty novels exploring the lives of an extended family during the second empire. An early exponent of naturalism, Zola believed that the novel is a result of experimentation and evidence gathering. The novelist 'collects the facts, sets the point of departure, establishes the solid ground on which the characters will walk and the phenomena be developed.' Émile Zola made a courageous intervention in the Dreyfus Affair with his essay, *J'Accuse.*

1

Nearly two years ago, I bicycling along a deserted road near Orgeval, just above Poissy, when the sudden appearance of an estate by the roadside surprised me so much that I jumped off my machine to get a better look at it. Under the November sky stood a brick house, of no great distinction, in the middle of a vast garden planted with ancient trees. The cold wind played havoc among the dead leaves. What made the place extraordinary and invested it with a wild atmosphere that gripped one's heart was the frightful state of decay into which it had fallen. Since one of the rain-beaten shutters that barred the garden had torn loose, as if to announce that the property was for sale, I yielded to a curiosity compounded of sorrow and uneasiness and entered the garden.

The house must have been uninhabited for perhaps thirty or forty years. The rigors of many winters had loosened the bricks from the cornices and over the moss-covered window-frames. Lizards passed across the facade like the first ripples of approaching disaster, furrowing the still solid but uncard-for structure. The flight of steps beyond was cleft by the frost and blocked with growths of nettles and brambles. It looked as if it led to death and desolation. But saddest of all were the curtainless windows, bare and misty, like blinded open eyes of a soulless body, some of them broken by little boys, and all revealing the mournful void within. The vast surrounding garden presented a scene of desolation. Its former flower bed could hardly be recognized beneath the mass of spreading weeds; its little walks had been devoured by voracious plants; its hedges were transformed into virgin forests; and the wild vegetation, suggesting a deserted cemetery, was shedding its last leaves under the damp shade of venerable trees, while the autumn wind wailed a sad lament.

Listening to the despairing cry that arose from all these objects, I lost the sense of my own existence and for some time my heart was troubled with a heavy fear, a growing distress, but an ardent compassion too, and I felt the need for understanding and sympathizing with all the misery and sorrow about me. When I finally decided to go, I perceived on the other side of the road, just where it forked, a kind of inn where one could get something to drink. I entered, determined to make the people who lived there talk to me.

I only found an old woman, who served me a glass of beer. She complained of the business on this out-of-the-way road along which scarcely two bicyclists passed each day. She told her own story in vague terms, saying that she was known as Mother Toussaint, that she had come from Vernon with her husband to take charge of this inn, that at first business had been fair, but that now things were going from bad to worse, and that she was a widow. But when she had unloosed this flood of words, and I began questioning her about the neighboring estate, she became circumspect and looked at me defiantly, as if she thought I wanted to wrest important secrets from her.

'Ah, yes, La Sauvagière; the haunted house, as they call it around here. I know nothing about it, sir. It was before my time, for I shall only have been here thirty years this coming Easter, and what happened there occurred at least forty years ago. When we came here the house was in almost the same state you see it in now. Summers and winters pass, but nothing moves except the falling stones.'

'But why don't they sell it,' I asked, 'since it is for sale?'

'Ah, why, why? How should I know? People say so many things.'

Somehow I finally inspired her with confidence, and then she burned with eagerness to tell me what people said. In the first place, she told me that no girl in the neighboring village dared to enter La Sauvagière after dark because rumor had it that a poor soul revisited the place at night. When I showed my astonishment that such a story could still be believed so near Paris, she shrugged her shoulders, and, though she at first tried to give the impression of being courageous, she eventually revealed her own unavowed terror.

'But you see, sir, there are certain facts. Why isn't it sold? I have seen people come who wanted to buy it, but they all went away quicker than they came, and not one of them has ever reappeared. One thing is certain – whoever risks visiting the house sees some extraordinary occurrences. Doors slam and then open noiselessly of their own accord, as if a terrible wind had blown them. Cries, groans, and sobs arise from the cellar, and if you insist on staying you hear a heart-rending voice continually crying "Angeline!" with such grief that your very bones freeze. I repeat that it is a proved fact – no one will tell you different.'

I confess that I began to get excited myself, and felt a cold chill running under my skin.

'And who is Angeline?'

Ah, sir, that would mean telling you everything. Anyway, I've told you all I know about it.'

However, she finally told me the whole story. Forty years ago, in 1858, when the Second Empire was at its height, a M. de G., who occupied a post in the Tuileries, lost his wife, by whom he had a ten-year-old daughter named Angeline, a miracle of beauty, and the living image of her mother. Two years later

M. de G. married again, taking as his second wife another celebrated beauty, the widow of a general. It was alleged that after the second marriage a terrible jealousy between Angeline and her stepmother cropped up. The girl's heart was broken to see her own mother so soon forgotten and so quickly replaced by this stranger. The wife was unbalanced by always having before her this living portrait of a woman whose memory she herself could never efface. La Sauvagière belonged to the new Mme. De G., and it was there, on seeing her husband passionately embrace his daughter one evening, that she jealously struck the child down. The poor little girl fell to the floor dead, her neck broken. What followed was terrible. To save the murderess the crazed father consented to bury the girl himself in the basement of the house. There the little body lay hidden for years, during which time they said she was visiting an aunt. Finally the howling of a dog who was scratching at the soil near where she was buried revealed the crime, but the authorities at the Tuileries suppressed it for fear of scandal. M. and Mme. De G. have died, but Angeline still comes back every night, answering the voice of lamentation that calls her from her mysterious hiding place in the dark beyond.

'Nobody had lied to me,' concluded Mother Toussaint. 'It is all as true as that two and two make four.'

I listened to her in amazement, astounded at her tale, yet enthralled by the violent and sombre weirdness of the drama. This M. de G. – I had often heard him mentioned, and I had the impression that he had remarried and that some family sorrow had soon afterward darkened his life. Was this true? What a tender, tragic story it was – one that aroused all the human passions, to the point of madness. A crime of passion of the most terrifying nature – a little girl, beautiful as the day, killed by her stepmother, and then buried in the corner of a cellar by the father who adored her. It was too full of emotion and horror to be ture. I decided to make some more inquiries and talk the matter over further. But then I asked myself: To what purpose? Why not carry this fearful tale in my mind with the fresh bloom of popular imagination still upon it?

As I got on my bicycle again I cast one last look on La Sauvagière. Nigh was falling, and the distressful house looked at me with its empty troubled windows like the eyes of death, while the autumn wind lamented in the ancient trees.

Why did this story lodge in my head until it became an obsession, a veritable torment? In vain I told myself that legends like this circulated all through the countryside, and that this one really held no direct interest for me. But, in spite of myself, the dead child haunted me – that delicious, tragic Angeline whom an imploring voice has summoned every night for forty years through empty rooms in an abandoned house.

During the first two months of the winter I undertook some research. Such a disappearance, though not important in itself, obviously contained enough dramatic interest to have been mentioned in the newspapers of the time. I went through the files as the Bibliothèque Nationale without discovering anything. Then I inquired among people who were employed at the Tuileries at the time, but not one of them could give me a clear reply, and many of them contradicted each other. I had just about abandoned all hope of finding the truth, though I was never free from torment at the thought of the mystery, when one morning good fortune started me down a new path.

Every two or three weeks I used to pay a visit of friendliness, tenderness, and admiration to the aged poet, V., who died last April almost seventy years old. For many years paralysis had nailed him to an armchair in his little study on the rue d'Assas, and his window looked out on the Luxembourg Gardens. There he was living a gentle life of dreams, having always dwelt in the world of imagination, where he had constructed for himself his own ideal palace in which he had loved and suffered far from the world of reality. Who does not recall his lovable face, his white hair, curly as a child's, his pale blue eyes that had preserved the innocence of youth? It could not be said of him that he always lied. The truth is that he invented unceasingly, and you could never tell just where reality ended and dreams began. He was a thoroughly charming old man, removed for a long time from active life, and his conversation often stirred me like a discreet and vague revelation of the unknown.

On this particular day I was sitting near the window in his narrow room that a warm fire always heated. Outside it was trebly cold. The Luxembourg Gardens were covered with a vast white expanse of immaculate snow. I don't know how I happened to mention the story of La Sauvagière, but it still preoccupied me. He listened with a tranquil smile behind which lurked a touch of sadness while I told him about the remarried father, the stepmother's jealousy of the little girl who was the image of the first wife, and finally about the burial in the cellar. Silence ensued as his pale gaze lost itself in the distant white immensity of the Luxembourg, while a shadow of dreams emanating from his person seemed to surround him with a quivering aura.

'I knew M. de G. intimately,' he remarked slowly. 'I knew his first wife, a woman of superhuman beauty; and I knew his second, a woman no less prodigiously endowed. I loved them both passionately, though I never said a word about it. I knew Angeline, and she was more beautiful still – men would have adored her on their knees. But things did not happen as you say.'

This stirred me profoundly. Had I at last found the unexpected truth of which I had despaired? Was I going oto know everything? At first I had no doubts whatever, and I said to him, 'Ah, my friend, what a service you will do me. At last my poor mind can be pacified. Speak quickly. Tell me everything.'

But he did not hear me, and his gaze was still lost in the distance. At length he spoke in a dreamy voice, as if he were himself creating the people and things he talked about.

'At the age of twelve Angeline possessed a soul in which all a woman's love had already flowered with transports of joy and sorrow. She in was who became wildly jealous of the new wife whom she was every day in her father's arms. She suffered as if from an act of frightful treason, for the new couple were not only insulting her mother, they were torturing her and tearing out her heart. Every night she heard her mother calling to her from her tomb, and one night, overcome by suffering and by the immensity of her love, this twelve-year-old girl plunged a knife into her own heart.'

I uttered a cry. 'Good Lord, is it possible!'

'What an unexpected horror it was the next day,' he continued without listening to me, 'when M. and Mme de G. found Angeline in her little bed with this knife buried to the hilt in her breast. They were on the point of departure for Italy, and there was no one in the house but an old servant who had brought up the child. Terrified that they might be accused of a crime, they called her to their aid and buried the little body under an orange tree in a corner of the greenhouse that stands behind their dwelling. There the remains were found when the old nurse told the story after the couple had died.'

Doubts assailed me, and I anxiously questioned him, asking whether he had not invented the tale.

'Do you, too, really believe,' I demanded, 'that Angeline can return every night in response to the heartrending cry of that mysterious voice?'

This time he looked at me, and once more broke into an indulgent smile.

'Return, my friend? Why, everyone returns. Why not allow the soul of that dear little dead girl to go on inhabiting the place where she loved and suffered? If you hear a voice calling out to her, it means that her life has not yet begun again; but it will begin again, you may be sure of that, for everything begins again, and nothing is lost, neither love nor beauty. Angeline! Angeline! And she will be born again among the sunshine and the flowers.'

This neither convinced nor calmed me. My old poet with the soul of a child had only brought me more trouble. Surely he was inventing, though, like all dreamers, perhaps he divined correctly.

'That's quite true, is it – all that you have told me?' I finally dared to ask him with a laugh. He too became gay.

'Why, of course it's true. Isn't the infinite always true?'

This was the last time I saw him, for I had to leave Paris shortly afterward. But I still remember him reflectively gazing upon the snow-covered Luxembourg, so tranquilly certain of his eternal dream, while for my part I was devoured by the eternal necessity of pinning down fugitive truth.

Eighteen months passed. I had had to travel, since great troubles and great joys had stirred my life. But invariably at certain times I would hear passing by me from afar the desolate cry of 'Angeline! Angeline!' And I would still tremble, assailed with doubt, tortured with necessity of knowing for sure. I could not forget, and uncertainty is my only hell.

I cannot say how it happened, but one beautiful June evening I found myself once more bicycling down the road past La Sauvagière. Had I actually wished to see it, or was it pure instinct that made me leave the main road? It was almost eight o'clock, but, since it was one of the longest days of the year, a triumphant sunset still blazed in a cloudless infinity of gold and azure. How light and delicious the air, what a sweet smell of trees and flowers, what tender gladness in the immense peace of the countryside.

Again, as on the first occasion, I was stupefied into leaping off my machine as I passed La Sauvagière. But I hesitated a minute. This was not the same piece of property. A lovely new garden glowed under the setting sun, the walls had ben rebuilt, and the house, which I could barely descry among the trees, seemed to have assumed the laughing gayety of youth. Was this the resurrection that my friend had announced? Had Angeline come to life in reply to the summons of that far-off voice?

I stood on the road, frozen with astonishment, until someone walking near me made me jump. It was Mother Toussaint, leading a cow from a neighboring pasture.

'Those people there weren't afraid,' I said, pointing to the house.

She recognized me, and stopped her animal.

'Ah, sir, there are people who would step on the toes of God Almighty. A year ago the present owner bought it; but he is a painter, – the painter B., – and, as you know, artists are capable of anything.'

As she led her cow away, she added over her shoulder, 'Well, we'll have to see how it turns out.'

This painter, the ingenious and delicate artist who had painted so many lovely Parisian ladies, I knew slightly. We used to shake hands whenever we met on the street, in the theatre, or at exhibitions. Suddenly I was seized by an irresistible desire to go in, to confess myself to him, and to beg him to tell me the truth about this Sauvagière place whose mystery had obsessed me. Without reasoning, without stopping to think of my dusty bicycling clothes that I had become accustomed to wearing everywhere, I wheeled my machine up to the mossy trunk of an old tree. In response to the clear ringing of a bell whose handle stuck out of the garden door, a servant appeared, to whom I gave my card, while he asked me to wait in the garden.

My surprise increased as I looked about me. The outside of the house had been repaired – no more lizards, no more loose bricks. The flight of steps, garnished with roses, had once more become a threshold of happy welcome. The living windows were laughing now, telling of happiness within behind their white curtains. The garden itself had been rid of its brambles and nettles, the flower bed had been reconstructed into a great odorous bouquet, and the old trees had been rejuvenated by the golden rain of the springtime sun.

When the servant appeared again he led me into a room, and told me that the gentleman of the house had gone to the near-by village, but that he would soon return. I would have waited for hours, and I kept my patience by looking over the room in which I found myself. It was luxuriously fitted out with thick carpets, cretonne portieres and hangings, a huge sofa, and deep armchairs. The tapestries were so ample that I was astonished at how quickly day disappeared. Soon night had almost entirely come. I do not know how long I had to wait, for I had been forgotten, and no one brought in a lamp. Seated here in the shadows, I set myself to living over again the whole tragic story, yielding to reverie. Had Angeline been murdered? Had she plunged a knife into her heart? And I confess that in this haunted house, now darkened once more, fear seized me – at first only lightly, to be sure, yet with a little tingle on the surface of my skin; but as time went on I was exasperated to find myself freezing from head to foot, and reduced to a state of real madness.

At first I seemed to hear vague noises somewhere. No doubt they came from the depths of the cellar – muffled cried, stifled sobs, the dull tread of a ghost. The noise mounted, drew nearer – the whole house seemed full of frightful distress. Suddenly, and with increasing volume, the terrible cry rang out, 'Angeline! Angeline! Angeline!' I thought I felt a cold breath passing across my face as a door opened sharply and Angeline entered. She walked across the room without seeing me, but I recognized her in the shaft of light that entered with her from the illuminated vestibule. This was indeed the little twelve-year-old dead girl, miraculously beautiful, her superb blonde hair flowing over her shoulders; and she was dressed in white – the pure white of the earth from which she arose every night. Silent and abstracted, she passed me and disappeared through another door as the cry rang out once more, further away this time, 'Angeline! Angeline! Angeline!' I stood rooted to the spot, my forehead damp with sweat, while every hair on my body vibrated with horror at this terrifying gust of mystery.

I believe that it was almost at this moment that the servant finally brought in the light and I was simultaneously conscious that the painter was there, shaking me by the hand and excusing himself for having made me wait so long. I had no false pride, and therefore told him the whole storty at once, as I had heard it. With what astonishment did he listen to me, and with what hearty peals of laughter did he hasten to reassure me.

'My dear fellow, you evidently do not know that I am the second Mme. de G.'s cousin. The poor woman! To accuse her of the murder of this child whom she loved and whose death she lamented as much as her husband did! The only true thing you have said is that the poor little girl lies dead here – not slain by her own hand (God forbid), but the victim of a sudden fever that struck her down like a thunderbolt. As a result the parents had a horror of this house, and would never come back to it – which explains why it remained uninhabited during their lifetime. After they died, interminable legal processes prevented its being sold promptly. I wanted it, however, and I waited many long years, and I can assure you that we have had no visitors from the other world.'

Still quaking a little, I babbled: 'But Angeline – I just saw her right there a minute ago. The terrible voice was calling her, and she walked right through this room.'

He opened the door himself and uttered the same cry, 'Angeline! Angeline! Angeline!'

The child returned, alive, vibrating with joy. It was she indeed, in her white dress, with her lovely blonde hair flowing over her shoulders, so beautiful, so radiant with hope, that she seemed to personify the whole springtime season and to give promise of love and a long, happy life.

The dear girl had returned – the dead child was born again in the new one. My old friend the poet had not lied: nothing is lost; everything begins again – beauty and love, both. Their mothers' voices call these little girls of yesterday, these lovers of tomorrow, and they return to life in sunshine and flowers. It was with this reawakened child that the house was haunted now, and today it had become young and happy again in the joy, at last rediscovered, of eternal life.

THE INEXPERIENCED GHOST

H.G. Wells

Herbert George Wells (1866–1946) was a prolific writer in many genres, but is best remembered today for his science fiction novels. The son of domestic servants, Wells worked as a teacher before finding success with his writing. He died of unspecified causes, having previously expressed the wish for his epitaph to read 'I told you so. You *damned* fools'.

The scene amidst which Clayton told his last story comes back very vividly to my mind. There he sat, for the greater part of the time, in the corner of the authentic settle by the spacious open fire, and Sanderson sat beside him smoking the Broseley clay that bore his name. There was Evans, and that marvel among actors, Wish, who is also a modest man. We had all come down to the Mermaid Club that Saturday morning, except Clayton, who had slept there overnight – which indeed gave him the opening of his story. We had golfed until golfing was invisible; we had dined, and we were in that mood of tranquil kindliness when men will suffer a story. When Clayton began to tell one, we naturally supposed he was lying. It may be that indeed he was lying – of that the reader will speedily be able to judge as well as I. He began, it is true, with an air of matter-of-fact anecdote, but that we thought was only the incurable artifice of the man

"I say!" he remarked, after a long consideration of the upward rain of sparks from the log that Sanderson had thumped, "you know I was alone here last night?"

"Except for the domestics," said Wish.

"Who sleep in the other wing," said Clayton. "Yes. Well—" He pulled at his cigar for some little time as though he still hesitated about his confidence. Then he said, quite quietly, "I caught a ghost!"

"Caught a ghost, did you?" said Sanderson. "Where is it?"

And Evans, who admires Clayton immensely and has been four weeks in America, shouted, "Caught a ghost, did you, Clayton? I'm glad of it! Tell us all about it right now."

Clayton said he would in a minute, and asked him to shut the door.

He looked apologetically at me. "There's no eavesdropping of course, but we don't want to upset our very excellent service with any rumours of ghosts in the place. There's too much shadow and oak panelling to trifle with that. And this, you know, wasn't a regular ghost. I don't think it will come again – ever."

"You mean to say you didn't keep it?" said Sanderson.

"I hadn't the heart to," said Clayton.

And Sanderson said he was surprised.

We laughed, and Clayton looked aggrieved. "I know," he said, with the flicker of a smile, "but the fact is it really was a ghost, and I'm as sure of it as I am that I am talking to you now. I'm not joking. I mean what I say."

Sanderson drew deeply at his pipe, with one reddish eye on Clayton, and then emitted a thin jet of smoke more eloquent than many words.

Clayton ignored the comment. "It is the strangest thing that has ever happened in my life. You know, I never believed in ghosts or anything of the sort, before, ever; and then, you know, I bag one in a corner; and the whole business is in my hands."

He meditated still more profoundly, and produced and began to pierce a second cigar with a curious little stabber he affected.

"You talked to it?" asked Wish.

"For the space, probably, of an hour."

"Chatty?" I said, joining the party of the sceptics.

"The poor devil was in trouble," said Clayton, bowed over his cigar-end and with the very faintest note of reproof.

"Sobbing?" some one asked.

Clayton heaved a realistic sigh at the memory. "Good Lord!" he said; "yes." And then, "Poor fellow! Yes."

"Where did you strike it?" asked Evans, in his best American accent.

"I never realised," said Clayton, ignoring him, "the poor sort of thing a ghost might be," and he hung us up again for a time, while he sought for matches in his pocket and lit and warmed to his cigar.

"I took an advantage," he reflected at last.

We were none of us in a hurry. "A character," he said, "remains just the same character for all that it's been disembodied. That's a thing we too often forget. People with a certain strength or fixity of purpose may have ghosts of a certain strength and fixity of purpose – most haunting ghosts, you know, must be as one-idea'd as monomaniacs and as obstinate as mules to come back again and again. This poor creature wasn't." He suddenly looked up rather queerly, and his eye went round the room. "I say it," he said, "in all kindliness, but that is the plain truth of the case. Even at the first glance he struck me as weak."

He punctuated with the help of his cigar.

"I came upon him, you know, in the long passage. His back was towards me and I saw him first. Right off I knew him for a ghost. He was transparent and whitish; clean through his chest I could see the glimmer of the little window at the end. And not only his physique but his attitude struck me as being weak. He looked, you know, as though he didn't know in the slightest whatever he meant to do. One hand was on the panelling and the other fluttered to his mouth. Like – so!"

"What sort of physique?" said Sanderson.

"Lean. You know that sort of young man's neck that has two great flutings down the back, here and here – so! And a little, meanish head with scrubby hair. And rather bad ears. Shoulders bad, narrower than the hips; turn-down collar, ready-made short jacket, trousers baggy and a little frayed at the heels. That's how he took me. I came very quietly up the staircase. I did not carry a light, you know--the candles are on the landing table and there is that lamp – and I was in my list slippers, and I saw him as I came up. I stopped dead at that – taking him in. I wasn't a bit afraid. I think that in most of these affairs one is never nearly so afraid or excited as one imagines one would be. I was surprised and interested. I thought, 'Good Lord! Here's a ghost at last! And I haven't believed for a moment in ghosts during the last five-and-twenty years.'"

"Um," said Wish.

"I suppose I wasn't on the landing a moment before he found out I was there. He turned on me sharply, and I saw the face of an immature young man, a weak nose, a scrubby little moustache, a feeble chin. So for an instant we stood – he looking over his shoulder at me and regarded one another. Then he seemed to remember his high calling. He turned round, drew himself up, projected his face, raised his arms, spread his hands in approved ghost fashion – came towards me. As he did so his little jaw dropped, and he emitted a faint, drawn-out 'Boo.' No, it wasn't – not a bit dreadful. I'd dined. I'd had a bottle of champagne, and being all alone, perhaps two or three – perhaps even four or five – whiskies, so I was as solid as rocks and no more frightened than if I'd been assailed by a frog. 'Boo!' I said. 'Nonsense. You don't belong to this place. What are you doing here?'

"I could see him wince. 'Boo-oo,' he said.

"'Boo – be hanged! Are you a member?' I said; and just to show I didn't care a pin for him I stepped through a corner of him and made to light my candle. 'Are you a member?' I repeated, looking at him sideways.

"He moved a little so as to stand clear of me, and his bearing became crest-fallen. 'No,' he said, in answer to the persistent interrogation of my eye; 'I'm not a member – I'm a ghost.'

"'Well, that doesn't give you the run of the Mermaid Club. Is there any one you want to see, or anything of that sort?' and doing it as steadily as possible for fear that he should mistake the carelessness of whisky for the distraction of fear, I got my candle alight. I turned on him, holding it. 'What are you doing here?' I said.

"He had dropped his hands and stopped his booing, and there he stood, abashed and awkward, the ghost of a weak, silly, aimless young man. 'I'm haunting,' he said.

"'You haven't any business to,' I said in a quiet voice.

"'I'm a ghost,' he said, as if in defence.

"'That may be, but you haven't any business to haunt here. This is a respectable private club; people often stop here with nursemaids and children, and, going about in the careless way you do, some poor little mite could easily come upon you and be scared out of her wits. I suppose you didn't think of that?'

"'No, sir,' he said, 'I didn't.'

"'You should have done. You haven't any claim on the place, have you? Weren't murdered here, or anything of that sort?'

"'None, sir; but I thought as it was old and oak-panelled—'

"'That's no excuse.' I regarded him firmly. 'Your coming here is a mistake,' I said, in a tone of friendly superiority. I feigned to see if I had my matches, and then looked up at him frankly. 'If I were you I wouldn't wait for cock-crow – I'd vanish right away.'

"He looked embarrassed. 'The fact is, sir—' he began.

"'I'd vanish,' I said, driving it home.

"'The fact is, sir, that – somehow – I can't.'

"'You can't?'

"'No, sir. There's something I've forgotten. I've been hanging about here since midnight last night, hiding in the cupboards of the empty bedrooms and things like that. I'm flurried. I've never come haunting before, and it seems to put me out.'

"'Put you out?'

"'Yes, sir. I've tried to do it several times, and it doesn't come off. There's some little thing has slipped me, and I can't get back.'

"That, you know, rather bowled me over. He looked at me in such an abject way that for the life of me I couldn't keep up quite the high, hectoring vein I had adopted. 'That's queer,' I said, and as I spoke I fancied I heard some one moving about down below. 'Come into my room and tell me more about it,' I said. 'I didn't, of course, understand this,' and I tried to take him by the arm. But, of course, you might as well have tried to take hold of a puff of smoke! I had forgotten my number, I think; anyhow, I remember going into several bedrooms – it was lucky I was the only soul in that wing – until I saw my traps. 'Here we are,' I said, and sat down in the arm-chair; 'sit down and tell me all about it. It seems to me you have got yourself into a jolly awkward position, old chap.'

"Well, he said he wouldn't sit down! He'd prefer to flit up and down the room if it was all the same to me. And so he did, and in a little while we were deep in a long and serious talk. And presently, you know, something of those whiskies and sodas evaporated out of me, and I began to realise just a little what a thundering rum and weird business it was that I was in. There he was, semi-transparent – the proper conventional phantom, and noiseless except for his ghost of a voice – flitting to and fro in that nice, clean, chintz-hung old bedroom. You could see the gleam of the copper candlesticks through him, and the lights on the brass fender, and the corners of the framed engravings on the wall, – and there he was telling me all about this wretched little life of his that had recently ended on earth. He hadn't a particularly honest face, you know, but being transparent, of course, he couldn't avoid telling the truth."

"Eh?" said Wish, suddenly sitting up in his chair.

"What?" said Clayton.

"Being transparent – couldn't avoid telling the truth – I don't see it," said Wish.

"I don't see it," said Clayton, with inimitable assurance. "But it is so, I can assure you nevertheless. I don't believe he got once a nail's breadth off the Bible truth. He told me how he had been killed – he went down into a London basement with a candle to look for a leakage of gas – and described himself as a senior English master in a London private school when that release occurred."

"Poor wretch!" said I.

"That's what I thought, and the more he talked the more I thought it. There he was, purposeless in life and purposeless out of it. He talked of his father and mother and his schoolmaster, and all who had ever been anything to him in the world, meanly. He had been too sensitive, too nervous; none of them had ever valued him properly or understood him, he said. He had never had a real friend in the world, I think; he had never had a success. He had shirked games and failed examinations. 'It's like that with some people,' he said; 'whenever I got into the examination-room or anywhere everything seemed to go.' Engaged to be married of course – to another over-sensitive person, I suppose – when the indiscretion with the gas escape ended his affairs. 'And where are you now?' I asked. 'Not in—?'

"He wasn't clear on that point at all. The impression he gave me was of a sort of vague, intermediate state, a special reserve for souls too non-existent for anything so positive as either sin or virtue. I don't know. He was much too ego-tistical and unobservant to give me any clear idea of the kind of place, kind of country, there is on the Other Side of Things. Wherever he was, he seems to have fallen in with a set of kindred spirits: ghosts of weak Cockney young men, who were on a footing of Christian names, and among these there was certainly a lot of talk about 'going haunting' and things like that. Yes – going haunting! They seemed to think 'haunting' a tremendous adventure, and most of them funked it all the time. And so primed, you know, he had come."

"But really!" said Wish to the fire.

"These are the impressions he gave me, anyhow," said Clayton, modestly. "I may, of course, have been in a rather uncritical state, but that was the sort of background he gave to himself. He kept flitting up and down, with his thin voice going talking, talking about his wretched self, and never a word of clear, firm statement from first to last. He was thinner and sillier and more pointless than if he had been real and alive. Only then, you know, he would not have been in my bedroom here – if he had been alive. I should have kicked him out."

"Of course," said Evans, "there are poor mortals like that."

"And there's just as much chance of their having ghosts as the rest of us," I admitted.

"What gave a sort of point to him, you know, was the fact that he did seem within limits to have found himself out. The mess he had made of haunting had depressed him terribly. He had been told it would be a 'lark'; he had come expecting it to be a 'lark,' and here it was, nothing but another failure added to his record! He proclaimed himself an utter out-and-out failure. He said, and I can quite believe it, that he had never tried to do anything all his life that he hadn't made a perfect mess of – and through all the wastes of eternity he never would. If he had had sympathy, perhaps—. He paused at that, and stood regard-ing me. He remarked that, strange as it might seem to me, nobody, not any one, ever, had given him the amount of sympathy I was doing now. I could see what he wanted straight away, and I determined to head him off at once. I may be a brute, you know, but being the Only Real Friend, the recipient of the confidences of one of these egotistical weaklings, ghost or body, is beyond my physical en-durance. I got up briskly. 'Don't you brood on these things too much,' I said. 'The thing you've got to do is to get out of this get out of this--sharp. You pull yourself together and try.' 'I can't,' he said. 'You try,' I said, and try he did."

"Try!" said Sanderson. "How?"

"Passes," said Clayton.

"Passes?"

"Complicated series of gestures and passes with the hands. That's how he had come in and that's how he had to get out again. Lord! what a business I had!"

"But how could any series of passes—?" I began.

"My dear man," said Clayton, turning on me and putting a great emphasis on certain words, "you want everything clear. I don't know how. All I know is that you do – that he did, anyhow, at least. After a fearful time, you know, he got his passes right and suddenly disappeared."

"Did you," said Sanderson, slowly, "observe the passes?"

"Yes," said Clayton, and seemed to think. "It was tremendously queer," he said. "There we were, I and this thin vague ghost, in that silent room, in this silent, empty inn, in this silent little Friday-night town. Not a sound except our voices and a faint panting he made when he swung. There was the bedroom candle, and one candle on the dressing- table alight, that was all – sometimes one or other would flare up into a tall, lean, astonished flame for a space. And queer things happened. 'I can't,' he said; 'I shall never—!' And suddenly he sat down on a little chair at the foot of the bed and began to sob and sob. Lord! what a harrowing, whimpering thing he seemed!

"'You pull yourself together,' I said, and tried to pat him on the back, and . . . my confounded hand went through him! By that time, you know, I wasn't nearly so massive as I had been on the landing. I got the queerness of it full. I remember snatching back my hand out of him, as it were, with a little thrill, and walking over to the dressing-table. 'You pull yourself together,' I said to him, 'and try.' And in order to encourage and help him I began to try as well."

"What!" said Sanderson, "the passes?"

"Yes, the passes."

"But—" I said, moved by an idea that eluded me for a space.

"This is interesting," said Sanderson, with his finger in his pipe- bowl. "You mean to say this ghost of yours gave away—"

"Did his level best to give away the whole confounded barrier? Yes."

"He didn't," said Wish; "he couldn't. Or you'd have gone there too."

"That's precisely it," I said, finding my elusive idea put into words for me.

"That is precisely it," said Clayton, with thoughtful eyes upon the fire.

For just a little while there was silence.

"And at last he did it?" said Sanderson.

"At last he did it. I had to keep him up to it hard, but he did it at last rather suddenly. He despaired, we had a scene, and then he got up abruptly and asked me to go through the whole performance, slowly, so that he might see. 'I believe,' he said, 'if I could see I should spot what was wrong at once.' And he did. 'I know,' he said. 'What do you know?' said I. 'I know,' he repeated. Then he said, peevishly, 'I can't do it if you look at me – I really can't; it's been that, partly, all along. I'm such a nervous fellow that you put me out.' Well, we had a bit of an argument. Naturally I wanted to see; but he was as obstinate as a mule, and suddenly I had come over as tired as a dog – he tired me out. 'All right,' I said, 'I won't look at you,' and turned towards the mirror, on the wardrobe, by the bed.

He started off very fast. I tried to follow him by looking in the looking-glass, to see just what it was had hung. Round went his arms and his hands, so, and so, and so, and then with a rush came to the last gesture of all – you stand erect and open out your arms – and so, don't you know, he stood. And then he didn't! He didn't! He wasn't! I wheeled round from the looking-glass to him. There was nothingl I was alone, with the flaring candles and a staggering mind. What had happened? Had anything happened? Had I been dreaming? . . . And then, with an absurd note of finality about it, the clock upon the landing discovered the moment was ripe for striking one. So! – Ping! And I was as grave and sober as a judge, with all my champagne and whisky gone into the vast serene. Feeling queer, you know – confoundedly queer! Queer! Good Lord!"

He regarded his cigar-ash for a moment. "That's all that happened," he said.

"And then you went to bed?" asked Evans.

"What else was there to do?"

I looked Wish in the eye. We wanted to scoff, and there was something, something perhaps in Clayton's voice and manner, that hampered our desire.

"And about these passes?" said Sanderson.

"I believe I could do them now."

"Oh!" said Sanderson, and produced a penknife and set himself to grub the dottel out of the bowl of his clay.

"Why don't you do them now?" said Sanderson, shutting his pen-knife with a click.

"That's what I'm going to do," said Clayton.

"They won't work," said Evans.

"If they do—" I suggested.

"You know, I'd rather you didn't," said Wish, stretching out his legs.

"Why?" asked Evans.

"I'd rather he didn't," said Wish.

"But he hasn't got 'em right," said Sanderson, plugging too much tobacco in his pipe.

"All the same, I'd rather he didn't," said Wish.

We argued with Wish. He said that for Clayton to go through those gestures was like mocking a serious matter. "But you don't believe—?" I said. Wish glanced at Clayton, who was staring into the fire, weighing something in his mind. "I do – more than half, anyhow, I do," said Wish.

"Clayton," said I, "you're too good a liar for us. Most of it was all right. But that disappearance . . . happened to be convincing. Tell us, it's a tale of cock and bull."

He stood up without heeding me, took the middle of the hearthrug, and faced me. For a moment he regarded his feet thoughtfully, and then for all the rest of the time his eyes were on the opposite wall, with an intent expression. He raised his two hands slowly to the level of his eyes and so began. . .

Now, Sanderson is a Freemason, a member of the lodge of the Four Kings, which devotes itself so ably to the study and elucidation of all the mysteries of Masonry past and present, and among the students of this lodge Sanderson is by no means the least. He followed Clayton's motions with a singular interest in his reddish eye. "That's not bad," he said, when it was done. "You really do, you know, put things together, Clayton, in a most amazing fashion. But there's one little detail out."

"I know," said Clayton. "I believe I could tell you which."

"Well?"

"This," said Clayton, and did a queer little twist and writhing and thrust of the hands.

"Yes."

"That, you know, was what he couldn't get right," said Clayton. "But how do you—?"

"Most of this business, and particularly how you invented it, I don't understand at all," said Sanderson, "but just that phase – I do." He reflected. "These happen to be a series of gestures – connected with a certain branch of esoteric Masonry. Probably you know. Or else – how?" He reflected still further. "I do not see I can do any harm in telling you just the proper twist. After all, if you know, you know; if you don't, you don't."

"I know nothing," said Clayton, "except what the poor devil let out last night."

"Well, anyhow," said Sanderson, and placed his churchwarden very carefully upon the shelf over the fireplace. Then very rapidly he gesticulated with his hands.

"So?" said Clayton, repeating.

"So," said Sanderson, and took his pipe in hand again.

"Ah, now," said Clayton, "I can do the whole thing – right."

He stood up before the waning fire and smiled at us all. But I think there was just a little hesitation in his smile. "If I begin—" he said.

"I wouldn't begin," said Wish.

"It's all right!" said Evans. "Matter is indestructible. You don't think any jiggery-pokery of this sort is going to snatch Clayton into the world of shades. Not it! You may try, Clayton, so far as I'm concerned, until your arms drop off at the wrists."

"I don't believe that," said Wish, and stood up and put his arm on Clayton's shoulder. "You've made me half believe in that story somehow, and I don't want to see the thing done!"

"Goodness!" said I, "here's Wish frightened!"

"I am," said Wish, with real or admirably feigned intensity. "I believe that if he goes through these motions right he'll go."

"He'll not do anything of the sort," I cried. "There's only one way out of this world for men, and Clayton is thirty years from that. Besides . . . And such a ghost! Do you think—?"

Wish interrupted me by moving. He walked out from among our chairs and stopped beside the tole and stood there. "Clayton," he said, "you're a fool."

Clayton, with a humorous light in his eyes, smiled back at him. "Wish," he said, "is right and all you others are wrong. I shall go. I shall get to the end of these passes, and as the last swish whistles through the air, Presto! – this hearthrug will be vacant, the room will be blank amazement, and a respectably dressed gentleman of fifteen stone will plump into the world of shades. I'm certain. So will you be. I decline to argue further. Let the thing be tried."

"No," said Wish, and made a step and ceased, and Clayton raised his hands once more to repeat the spirit's passing.

By that time, you know, we were all in a state of tension – largely because of the behaviour of Wish. We sat all of us with our eyes on Clayton – I, at least, with a sort of tight, stiff feeling about me as though from the back of my skull to the middle of my thighs my body had been changed to steel. And there, with a gravity that was imperturbably serene, Clayton bowed and swayed and waved his hands and arms before us. As he drew towards the end one piled up, one tingled in one's teeth. The last gesture, I have said, was to swing the arms out wide open, with the face held up. And when at last he swung out to this closing gesture I ceased even to breathe. It was ridiculous, of course, but you know that ghost-story feeling. It was after dinner, in a queer, old shadowy house. Would he, after all—?

There he stood for one stupendous moment, with his arms open and his upturned face, assured and bright, in the glare of the hanging lamp. We hung through that moment as if it were an age, and then came from all of us something that was half a sigh of infinite relief and half a reassuring "No!" For visibly – he wasn't going. It was all nonsense. He had told an idle story, and carried it almost to conviction, that was all! . . . And then in that moment the face of Clayton, changed.

It changed. It changed as a lit house changes when its lights are suddenly extinguished. His eyes were suddenly eyes that were fixed, his smile was frozen on his lips, and he stood there still. He stood there, very gently swaying.

That moment, too, was an age. And then, you know, chairs were scraping, things were falling, and we were all moving. His knees seemed to give, and he fell forward, and Evans rose and caught him in his arms. . .

It stunned us all. For a minute I suppose no one said a coherent thing. We believed it, yet could not believe it. . . I came out of a muddled stupefaction to find myself kneeling beside him, and his vest and shirt were torn open, and Sanderson's hand lay on his heart. . .

Well – the simple fact before us could very well wait our convenience; there was no hurry for us to comprehend. It lay there for an hour; it lies athwart my memory, black and amazing still, to this day. Clayton had, indeed, passed into the world that lies so near to, and so far from, our own, and he had gone thither by the only road that mortal man may take. But whether he did indeed pass there by that poor ghost's incantation, or whether he was stricken suddenly by apoplexy in the midst of an idle tale – as the coroner's jury would have us believe – is no matter for my judging; it is just one of those inexplicable riddles that must remain unsolved until the final solution of all things shall come. All I certainly know is that, in the very moment, in the very instant, of concluding those passes, he changed, and staggered, and fell down before us – dead!

THE WIND IN
THE ROSE-BUSH

Mary Wilkins Freeman

Mary Eleanor Wilkins Freeman (1852–1930) was born in Randolf, Massachusetts and was distantly related to Nathaniel Hawthorne. Her parents were orthodox Congregationalists and many of her stories reflect on puritan repression. Wilkins Freeman's work often grapples with themes of poverty and domestic servitude. Her best known novel is *Pembroke* (1894). She was one of the first women ever to be elected to the National Institute for Arts and Letters

Ford Village has no railroad station, being on the other side of the river from Porter's Falls, and accessible only by the ford which gives it its name, and a ferry line.

The ferry-boat was waiting when Rebecca Flint got off the train with her bag and lunch basket. When she and her small trunk were safely embarked she sat stiff and straight and calm in the ferry-boat as it shot swiftly and smoothly across stream. There was a horse attached to a light country wagon on board, and he pawed the deck uneasily. His owner stood near, with a wary eye upon him, although he was chewing, with as dully reflective an expression as a cow. Beside Rebecca sat a woman of about her own age, who kept looking at her with furtive curiosity; her husband, short and stout and saturnine, stood near her. Rebecca paid no attention to either of them. She was tall and spare and pale, the type of a spinster, yet with rudimentary lines and expressions of matronhood. She all unconsciously held her shawl, rolled up in a canvas bag, on her left hip, as if it had been a child. She wore a settled frown of dissent at life, but it was the frown of a mother who regarded life as a froward child, rather than as an overwhelming fate.

The other woman continued staring at her; she was mildly stupid, except for an over-developed curiosity which made her at times sharp beyond belief. Her eyes glittered, red spots came on her flaccid cheeks; she kept opening her mouth to speak, making little abortive motions. Finally she could endure it no longer; she nudged Rebecca boldly.

"A pleasant day," said she.

Rebecca looked at her and nodded coldly.

"Yes, very," she assented.

"Have you come far?"

"I have come from Michigan."

"Oh!" said the woman, with awe. "It's a long way," she remarked presently.

"Yes, it is," replied Rebecca, conclusively.

Still the other woman was not daunted; there was something which she determined to know, possibly roused thereto by a vague sense of incongruity in the other's appearance. "It's a long ways to come and leave a family," she remarked with painful slyness.

"I ain't got any family to leave," returned Rebecca shortly.

"Then you ain't—"

"No, I ain't."

"Oh!" said the woman.

Rebecca looked straight ahead at the race of the river.

It was a long ferry. Finally Rebecca herself waxed unexpectedly loquacious. She turned to the other woman and inquired if she knew John Dent's widow who lived in Ford Village. "Her husband died about three years ago," said she, by way of detail.

The woman started violently. She turned pale, then she flushed; she cast a strange glance at her husband, who was regarding both women with a sort of stolid keenness.

"Yes, I guess I do," faltered the woman finally.

"Well, his first wife was my sister," said Rebecca with the air of one imparting important intelligence.

"Was she?" responded the other woman feebly. She glanced at her husband with an expression of doubt and terror, and he shook his head forbiddingly.

"I'm going to see her, and take my niece Agnes home with me," said Rebecca.

Then the woman gave such a violent start that she noticed it.

"What is the matter?" she asked.

"Nothin', I guess," replied the woman, with eyes on her husband, who was slowly shaking his head, like a Chinese toy.

"Is my niece sick?" asked Rebecca with quick suspicion.

"No, she ain't sick," replied the woman with alacrity, then she caught her breath with a gasp.

"When did you see her?"

"Let me see; I ain't seen her for some little time," replied the woman. Then she caught her breath again.

"She ought to have grown up real pretty, if she takes after my sister. She was a real pretty woman," Rebecca said wistfully.

"Yes, I guess she did grow up pretty," replied the woman in a trembling voice.

"What kind of a woman is the second wife?"

The woman glanced at her husband's warning face. She continued to gaze at him while she replied in a choking voice to Rebecca:

"I – guess she's a nice woman," she replied. "I – don't know, I – guess so. I – don't see much of her."

"I felt kind of hurt that John married again so quick," said Rebecca; "but I suppose he wanted his house kept, and Agnes wanted care. I wasn't so situated that I could take her when her mother died. I had my own mother to care for, and I was school-teaching. Now mother has gone, and my uncle died six months ago and left me quite a little property, and I've given up my school, and

I've come for Agnes. I guess she'll be glad to go with me, though I suppose her stepmother is a good woman, and has always done for her."

The man's warning shake at his wife was fairly portentous.

"I guess so," said she.

"John always wrote that she was a beautiful woman," said Rebecca.

Then the ferry-boat grated on the shore.

John Dent's widow had sent a horse and wagon to meet her sister-in-law. When the woman and her husband went down the road, on which Rebecca in the wagon with her trunk soon passed them, she said reproachfully:

"Seems as if I'd ought to have told her, Thomas."

"Let her find it out herself," replied the man. "Don't you go to burnin' your fingers in other folks' puddin', Maria."

"Do you s'pose she'll see anything?" asked the woman with a spasmodic shudder and a terrified roll of her eyes.

"See!" returned her husband with stolid scorn. "Better be sure there's anything to see."

"Oh, Thomas, they say—"

"Lord, ain't you found out that what they say is mostly lies?"

"But if it should be true, and she's a nervous woman, she might be scared enough to lose her wits," said his wife, staring uneasily after Rebecca's erect figure in the wagon disappearing over the crest of the hilly road.

"Wits that so easy upset ain't worth much," declared the man. "You keep out of it, Maria."

Rebecca in the meantime rode on in the wagon, beside a flaxen-headed boy, who looked, to her understanding, not very bright. She asked him a question, and he paid no attention. She repeated it, and he responded with a bewildered and incoherent grunt. Then she let him alone, after making sure that he knew how to drive straight.

They had traveled about half a mile, passed the village square, and gone a short distance beyond, when the boy drew up with a sudden Whoa! before a very prosperous-looking house. It had been one of the aboriginal cottages of the vicinity, small and white, with a roof extending on one side over a piazza, and a tiny "L" jutting out in the rear, on the right hand. Now the cottage was transformed by dormer windows, a bay window on the piazzaless side, a carved railing down the front steps, and a modern hard-wood door.

"Is this John Dent's house?" asked Rebecca.

The boy was as sparing of speech as a philosopher. His only response was in flinging the reins over the horse's back, stretching out one foot to the shaft, and leaping out of the wagon, then going around to the rear for the trunk. Rebecca got out and went toward the house. Its white paint had a new gloss; its blinds were an immaculate apple green; the lawn was trimmed as smooth as velvet, and it was dotted with scrupulous groups of hydrangeas and cannas.

"I always understood that John Dent was well-to-do," Rebecca reflected comfortably. "I guess Agnes will have considerable. I've got enough, but it will come in handy for her schooling. She can have advantages."

The boy dragged the trunk up the fine gravel-walk, but before he reached the steps leading up to the piazza, for the house stood on a terrace, the front door opened and a fair, frizzled head of a very large and handsome woman appeared. She held up her black silk skirt, disclosing voluminous ruffles of starched embroidery, and waited for Rebecca. She smiled placidly, her pink, double-chinned face widened and dimpled, but her blue eyes were wary and calculating. She extended her hand as Rebecca climbed the steps.

"This is Miss Flint, I suppose," said she.

"Yes, ma'am," replied Rebecca, noticing with bewilderment a curious expression compounded of fear and defiance on the other's face.

"Your letter only arrived this morning," said Mrs. Dent, in a steady voice. Her great face was a uniform pink, and her china-blue eyes were at once aggressive and veiled with secrecy.

"Yes, I hardly thought you'd get my letter," replied Rebecca. "I felt as if I could not wait to hear from you before I came. I supposed you would be so situated that you could have me a little while without putting you out too much, from what John used to write me about his circumstances, and when I had that money so unexpected I felt as if I must come for Agnes. I suppose you will be willing to give her up. You know she's my own blood, and of course she's no relation to you, though you must have got attached to her. I know from her picture what a sweet girl she must be, and John always said she looked like her own mother, and Grace was a beautiful woman, if she was my sister."

Rebecca stopped and stared at the other woman in amazement and alarm. The great handsome blonde creature stood speechless, livid, gasping, with her hand to her heart, her lips parted in a horrible caricature of a smile.

"Are you sick!" cried Rebecca, drawing near. "Don't you want me to get you some water!"

Then Mrs. Dent recovered herself with a great effort. "It is nothing," she said. "I am subject to – spells. I am over it now. Won't you come in, Miss Flint?"

As she spoke, the beautiful deep-rose colour suffused her face, her blue eyes met her visitor's with the opaqueness of turquoise – with a revelation of blue, but a concealment of all behind.

Rebecca followed her hostess in, and the boy, who had waited quiescently, climbed the steps with the trunk. But before they entered the door a strange thing happened. On the upper terrace close to the piazza-post, grew a great rose-bush, and on it, late in the season though it was, one small red, perfect rose.

Rebecca looked at it, and the other woman extended her hand with a quick gesture. "Don't you pick that rose!" she brusquely cried.

Rebecca drew herself up with stiff dignity.

"I ain't in the habit of picking other folks' roses without leave," said she.

As Rebecca spoke she started violently, and lost sight of her resentment, for something singular happened. Suddenly the rose-bush was agitated violently as if by a gust of wind, yet it was a remarkably still day. Not a leaf of the hydrangea standing on the terrace close to the rose trembled.

"What on earth—" began Rebecca, then she stopped with a gasp at the sight of the other woman's face. Although a face, it gave somehow the impression of a desperately clutched hand of secrecy.

"Come in!" said she in a harsh voice, which seemed to come forth from her chest with no intervention of the organs of speech. "Come into the house. I'm getting cold out here."

"What makes that rose-bush blow so when their isn't any wind?" asked Rebecca, trembling with vague horror, yet resolute.

"I don't see as it is blowing," returned the woman calmly. And as she spoke, indeed, the bush was quiet.

"It was blowing," declared Rebecca.

"It isn't now," said Mrs. Dent. "I can't try to account for everything that blows out-of-doors. I have too much to do."

She spoke scornfully and confidently, with defiant, unflinching eyes, first on the bush, then on Rebecca, and led the way into the house.

"It looked queer," persisted Rebecca, but she followed, and also the boy with the trunk.

Rebecca entered an interior, prosperous, even elegant, according to her simple ideas. There were Brussels carpets, lace curtains, and plenty of brilliant upholstery and polished wood.

"You're real nicely situated," remarked Rebecca, after she had become a little accustomed to her new surroundings and the two women were seated at the tea-table.

Mrs. Dent stared with a hard complacency from behind her silver-plated service. "Yes, I be," said she.

"You got all the things new?" said Rebecca hesitatingly, with a jealous memory of her dead sister's bridal furnishings.

"Yes," said Mrs. Dent; "I was never one to want dead folks' things, and I had money enough of my own, so I wasn't beholden to John. I had the old duds put up at auction. They didn't bring much."

"I suppose you saved some for Agnes. She'll want some of her poor mother's things when she is grown up," said Rebecca with some indignation.

The defiant stare of Mrs. Dent's blue eyes waxed more intense. "There's a few things up garret," said she.

"She'll be likely to value them," remarked Rebecca. As she spoke she glanced at the window. "Isn't it most time for her to be coming home?" she asked.

"Most time," answered Mrs. Dent carelessly; "but when she gets over to Addie Slocum's she never knows when to come home."

"Is Addie Slocum her intimate friend?"

"Intimate as any."

"Maybe we can have her come out to see Agnes when she's living with me," said Rebecca wistfully. "I suppose she'll be likely to be homesick at first."

"Most likely," answered Mrs. Dent.

"Does she call you mother?" Rebecca asked.

"No, she calls me Aunt Emeline," replied the other woman shortly. "When did you say you were going home?"

"In about a week, I thought, if she can be ready to go so soon," answered Rebecca with a surprised look.

She reflected that she would not remain a day longer than she could help after such an inhospitable look and question.

"Oh, as far as that goes," said Mrs. Dent, "it wouldn't make any difference about her being ready. You could go home whenever you felt that you must, and she could come afterward."

"Alone?"

"Why not? She's a big girl now, and you don't have to change cars."

"My niece will go home when I do, and not travel alone; and if I can't wait here for her, in the house that used to be her mother's and my sister's home, I'll go and board somewhere," returned Rebecca with warmth.

"Oh, you can stay here as long as you want to. You're welcome," said Mrs. Dent.

Then Rebecca started. "There she is!" she declared in a trembling, exultant voice. Nobody knew how she longed to see the girl.

"She isn't as late as I thought she'd be," said Mrs. Dent, and again that curious, subtle change passed over her face, and again it settled into that stony impassiveness.

Rebecca stared at the door, waiting for it to open. "Where is she?" she asked presently.

"I guess she's stopped to take off her hat in the entry," suggested Mrs. Dent.

Rebecca waited. "Why don't she come? It can't take her all this time to take off her hat."

For answer Mrs. Dent rose with a stiff jerk and threw open the door.

"Agnes!" she called. "Agnes!" Then she turned and eyed Rebecca. "She ain't there."

"I saw her pass the window," said Rebecca in bewilderment.

"You must have been mistaken."

"I know I did," persisted Rebecca.

"You couldn't have."

"I did. I saw first a shadow go over the ceiling, then I saw her in the glass there" – she pointed to a mirror over the sideboard opposite – "and then the shadow passed the window."

"How did she look in the glass?"

"Little and light-haired, with the light hair kind of tossing over her forehead."

"You couldn't have seen her."

"Was that like Agnes?"

"Like enough; but of course you didn't see her. You've been thinking so much about her that you thought you did."

"You thought *you* did."

"I thought I saw a shadow pass the window, but I must have been mistaken. She didn't come in, or we would have seen her before now. I knew it was too early for her to get home from Addie Slocum's, anyhow."

When Rebecca went to bed Agnes had not returned. Rebecca had resolved that she would not retire until the girl came, but she was very tired, and she reasoned with herself that she was foolish. Besides, Mrs. Dent suggested that Agnes might go to the church social with Addie Slocum. When Rebecca suggested that she be sent for and told that her aunt had come, Mrs. Dent laughed meaningly.

"I guess you'll find out that a young girl ain't so ready to leave a sociable, where there's boys, to see her aunt," said she.

"She's too young," said Rebecca incredulously and indignantly.

"She's sixteen," replied Mrs. Dent; "and she's always been great for the boys."

"She's going to school four years after I get her before she thinks of boys," declared Rebecca.

"We'll see," laughed the other woman.

After Rebecca went to bed, she lay awake a long time listening for the sound of girlish laughter and a boy's voice under her window; then she fell asleep.

The next morning she was down early. Mrs. Dent, who kept no servants, was busily preparing breakfast.

"Don't Agnes help you about breakfast?" asked Rebecca.

"No, I let her lay," replied Mrs. Dent shortly.

"What time did she get home last night?"

"She didn't get home."

"What?"

"She didn't get home. She stayed with Addie. She often does."

"Without sending you word?"

"Oh, she knew I wouldn't worry."

"When will she be home?"

"Oh, I guess she'll be along pretty soon."

Rebecca was uneasy, but she tried to conceal it, for she knew of no good reason for uneasiness. What was there to occasion alarm in the fact of one young girl staying overnight with another? She could not eat much breakfast. Afterward she went out on the little piazza, although her hostess strove furtively to stop her.

"Why don't you go out back of the house? It's real pretty – a view over the river," she said.

"I guess I'll go out here," replied Rebecca. She had a purpose: to watch for the absent girl.

Presently Rebecca came hustling into the house through the sitting-room, into the kitchen where Mrs. Dent was cooking.

"That rose-bush!" she gasped.

Mrs. Dent turned and faced her.

"What of it?"

"It's a-blowing."

"What of it?"

"There isn't a mite of wind this morning."

Mrs. Dent turned with an inimitable toss of her fair head. "If you think I can spend my time puzzling over such nonsense as – " she began, but Rebecca interrupted her with a cry and a rush to the door.

"There she is now!" she cried. She flung the door wide open, and curiously enough a breeze came in and her own gray hair tossed, and a paper blew off the table to the floor with a loud rustle, but there was nobody in sight.

"There's nobody here," Rebecca said.

She looked blankly at the other woman, who brought her rolling-pin down on a slab of pie-crust with a thud.

"I didn't hear anybody," she said calmly.

"*I saw somebody pass that window!*"

"You were mistaken again."

"I *know* I saw somebody."

"You couldn't have. Please shut that door."

Rebecca shut the door. She sat down beside the window and looked out on the autumnal yard, with its little curve of footpath to the kitchen door.

"What smells so strong of roses in this room?" she said presently. She sniffed hard.

"I don't smell anything but these nutmegs."

"It is not nutmeg."

"I don't smell anything else."

"Where do you suppose Agnes is?"

"Oh, perhaps she has gone over the ferry to Porter's Falls with Addie. She often does. Addie's got an aunt over there, and Addie's got a cousin, a real pretty boy."

"You suppose she's gone over there?"

"Mebbe. I shouldn't wonder."

"When should she be home?"

"Oh, not before afternoon."

Rebecca waited with all the patience she could muster. She kept reassuring herself, telling herself that it was all natural, that the other woman could not help it, but she made up her mind that if Agnes did not return that afternoon she should be sent for.

When it was four o'clock she started up with resolution. She had been furtively watching the onyx clock on the sitting-room mantel; she had timed herself. She had said that if Agnes was not home by that time she should demand that she be sent for. She rose and stood before Mrs. Dent, who looked up coolly from her embroidery.

"I've waited just as long as I'm going to," she said. "I've come 'way from Michigan to see my own sister's daughter and take her home with me. I've been here ever since yesterday – twenty-four hours – and I haven't seen her. Now I'm going to. I want her sent for."

Mrs. Dent folded her embroidery and rose.

"Well, I don't blame you," she said. "It is high time she came home. I'll go right over and get her myself."

Rebecca heaved a sigh of relief. She hardly knew what she had suspected or feared, but she knew that her position had been one of antagonism if not accusation, and she was sensible of relief.

"I wish you would," she said gratefully, and went back to her chair, while Mrs. Dent got her shawl and her little white head-tie. "I wouldn't trouble you, but I do feel as if I couldn't wait any longer to see her," she remarked apologetically.

"Oh, it ain't any trouble at all," said Mrs. Dent as she went out. "I don't blame you; you have waited long enough."

Rebecca sat at the window watching breathlessly until Mrs. Dent came stepping through the yard alone. She ran to the door and saw, hardly noticing it this time, that the rose-bush was again violently agitated, yet with no wind evident elsewhere.

"Where is she?" she cried.

Mrs. Dent laughed with stiff lips as she came up the steps over the terrace. "Girls will be girls," said she. "She's gone with Addie to Lincoln. Addie's got an uncle who's conductor on the train, and lives there, and he got 'em passes, and they're goin' to stay to Addie's Aunt Margaret's a few days. Mrs. Slocum said Agnes didn't have time to come over and ask me before the train went, but she took it on herself to say it would be all right, and—"

"Why hadn't she been over to tell you?" Rebecca was angry, though not suspicious. She even saw no reason for her anger.

"Oh, she was putting up grapes. She was coming over just as soon as she got the black off her hands. She heard I had company, and her hands were a sight. She was holding them over sulphur matches."

"You say she's going to stay a few days?" repeated Rebecca dazedly.

"Yes; till Thursday, Mrs. Slocum said."

"How far is Lincoln from here?"

"About fifty miles. It'll be a real treat to her. Mrs. Slocum's sister is a real nice woman."

"It is goin' to make it pretty late about my goin' home."

"If you don't feel as if you could wait, I'll get her ready and send her on just as soon as I can," Mrs. Dent said sweetly.

"I'm going to wait," said Rebecca grimly.

The two women sat down again, and Mrs. Dent took up her embroidery.

"Is there any sewing I can do for her?" Rebecca asked finally in a desperate way. "If I can get her sewing along some—"

Mrs. Dent arose with alacrity and fetched a mass of white from the closet. "Here," she said, "if you want to sew the lace on this nightgown. I was going to put her to it, but she'll be glad enough to get rid of it. She ought to have this and one more before she goes. I don't like to send her away without some good underclothing."

Rebecca snatched at the little white garment and sewed feverishly.

That night she wakened from a deep sleep a little after midnight and lay a minute trying to collect her faculties and explain to herself what she was listening to. At last she discovered that it was the then popular strains of "The Maiden's Prayer" floating up through the floor from the piano in the sitting-room below. She jumped up, threw a shawl over her nightgown, and hurried downstairs trembling. There was nobody in the sitting-room; the piano was silent. She ran to Mrs. Dent's bedroom and called hysterically:

"Emeline! Emeline!"

"What is it?" asked Mrs. Dent's voice from the bed. The voice was stern, but had a note of consciousness in it.

"Who – who was that playing 'The Maiden's Prayer' in the sitting-room, on the piano?"

"I didn't hear anybody."

"There was some one."

"I didn't hear anything."

"I tell you there was some one. But – *there ain't anybody there.*"

"I didn't hear anything."

"I did – somebody playing 'The Maiden's Prayer' on the piano. Has Agnes got home? *I want to know.*"

"Of course Agnes hasn't got home," answered Mrs. Dent with rising inflection. "Be you gone crazy over that girl? The last boat from Porter's Falls was in before we went to bed. Of course she ain't come."

"I heard—"

"You were dreaming."

"I wasn't; I was broad awake."

Rebecca went back to her chamber and kept her lamp burning all night.

The next morning her eyes upon Mrs. Dent were wary and blazing with suppressed excitement. She kept opening her mouth as if to speak, then frowning, and setting her lips hard. After breakfast she went upstairs, and came down presently with her coat and bonnet.

"Now, Emeline," she said, "I want to know where the Slocums live."

Mrs. Dent gave a strange, long, half-lidded glance at her. She was finishing her coffee.

"Why?" she asked.

"I'm going over there and find out if they have heard anything from her daughter and Agnes since they went away. I don't like what I heard last night."

"You must have been dreaming."

"It don't make any odds whether I was or not. Does she play 'The Maiden's Prayer' on the piano? I want to know."

"What if she does? She plays it a little, I believe. I don't know. She don't half play it, anyhow; she ain't got an ear."

"That wasn't half played last night. I don't like such things happening. I ain't superstitious, but I don't like it. I'm going. Where do the Slocums live?"

"You go down the road over the bridge past the old grist mill, then you turn to the left; it's the only house for half a mile. You can't miss it. It has a barn with a ship in full sail on the cupola."

"Well, I'm going. I don't feel easy."

About two hours later Rebecca returned. There were red spots on her cheeks. She looked wild. "I've been there," she said, "and there isn't a soul at home. Something *has* happened."

"What has happened?"

"I don't know. Something. I had a warning last night. There wasn't a soul there. They've been sent for to Lincoln."

"Did you see anybody to ask?" asked Mrs. Dent with thinly concealed anxiety.

"I asked the woman that lives on the turn of the road. She's stone deaf. I suppose you know. She listened while I screamed at her to know where the Slocums were, and then she said, 'Mrs. Smith don't live here.' I didn't see anybody on the road, and that's the only house. What do you suppose it means?"

"I don't suppose it means much of anything," replied Mrs. Dent coolly. "Mr. Slocum is conductor on the railroad, and he'd be away anyway, and Mrs. Slocum often goes early when he does, to spend the day with her sister in Porter's Falls. She'd be more likely to go away than Addie."

"And you don't think anything has happened?" Rebecca asked with diminishing distrust before the reasonableness of it.

"Land, no!"

Rebecca went upstairs to lay aside her coat and bonnet. But she came hurrying back with them still on.

"Who's been in my room?" she gasped. Her face was pale as ashes.

Mrs. Dent also paled as she regarded her.

"What do you mean?" she asked slowly.

"I found when I went upstairs that – little nightgown of – Agnes's on – the bed, laid out. It was – *laid out*. The sleeves were folded across the bosom, and there was that little red rose between them. Emeline, what is it? Emeline, what's the matter? Oh!"

Mrs. Dent was struggling for breath in great, choking gasps. She clung to the back of a chair. Rebecca, trembling herself so she could scarcely keep on her feet, got her some water.

As soon as she recovered herself Mrs. Dent regarded her with eyes full of the strangest mixture of fear and horror and hostility.

"What do you mean talking so?" she said in a hard voice.

"It *is there*."

"Nonsense. You threw it down and it fell that way."

"It was folded in my bureau drawer."

"It couldn't have been."

"Who picked that red rose?"

"Look on the bush," Mrs. Dent replied shortly.

Rebecca looked at her; her mouth gaped. She hurried out of the room. When she came back her eyes seemed to protrude. (She had in the meantime hastened upstairs, and come down with tottering steps, clinging to the banisters.)

"Now I want to know what all this means?" she demanded.

"What what means?"

"The rose is on the bush, and it's gone from the bed in my room! Is this house haunted, or what?"

"I don't know anything about a house being haunted. I don't believe in such things. Be you crazy?" Mrs. Dent spoke with gathering force. The colour flashed back to her cheeks.

"No," said Rebecca shortly. "I ain't crazy yet, but I shall be if this keeps on much longer. I'm going to find out where that girl is before night."

Mrs. Dent eyed her.

"What be you going to do?"

"I'm going to Lincoln."

A faint triumphant smile overspread Mrs. Dent's large face.

"You can't," said she; "there ain't any train."

"No train?"

"No; there ain't any afternoon train from the Falls to Lincoln."

"Then I'm going over to the Slocums' again to-night."

However, Rebecca did not go; such a rain came up as deterred even her resolution, and she had only her best dresses with her. Then in the evening came the letter from the Michigan village which she had left nearly a week ago. It was from her cousin, a single woman, who had come to keep her house while she was away. It was a pleasant unexciting letter enough, all the first of it, and related mostly how she missed Rebecca; how she hoped she was having pleasant weather and kept her health; and how her friend, Mrs. Greenaway, had come to stay with her since she had felt lonesome the first night in the house; how she hoped Rebecca would have no objections to this, although nothing had been said about it, since she had not realized that she might be nervous alone. The cousin was painfully conscientious, hence the letter. Rebecca smiled in spite of her disturbed mind as she read it, then her eye caught the postscript. That was in a different hand, purporting to be written by the friend, Mrs. Hannah Greenaway, informing her that the cousin had fallen down the cellar stairs and broken her hip, and was in a dangerous condition, and begging Rebecca to return at once, as she herself was rheumatic and unable to nurse her properly, and no one else could be obtained.

Rebecca looked at Mrs. Dent, who had come to her room with the letter quite late; it was half-past nine, and she had gone upstairs for the night.

"Where did this come from?" she asked.

"Mr. Amblecrom brought it," she replied.

"Who's he?"

"The postmaster. He often brings the letters that come on the late mail. He knows I ain't anybody to send. He brought yours about your coming. He said he and his wife came over on the ferry-boat with you."

"I remember him," Rebecca replied shortly. "There's bad news in this letter."

Mrs. Dent's face took on an expression of serious inquiry.

"Yes, my Cousin Harriet has fallen down the cellar stairs – they were always dangerous – and she's broken her hip, and I've got to take the first train home to-morrow."

"You don't say so. I'm dreadfully sorry."

"No, you ain't sorry!" said Rebecca, with a look as if she leaped. "You're glad. I don't know why, but you're glad. You've wanted to get rid of me for some reason ever since I came. I don't know why. You're a strange woman. Now you've got your way, and I hope you're satisfied."

"How you talk."

Mrs. Dent spoke in a faintly injured voice, but there was a light in her eyes.

"I talk the way it is. Well, I'm going to-morrow morning, and I want you, just as soon as Agnes Dent comes home, to send her out to me. Don't you wait for anything. You pack what clothes she's got, and don't wait even to mend them, and you buy her ticket. I'll leave the money, and you send her along. She don't have to change cars. You start her off, when she gets home, on the next train!"

"Very well," replied the other woman. She had an expression of covert amusement.

"Mind you do it."

"Very well, Rebecca."

Rebecca started on her journey the next morning. When she arrived, two days later, she found her cousin in perfect health. She found, moreover, that the friend had not written the postscript in the cousin's letter. Rebecca would have returned to Ford Village the next morning, but the fatigue and nervous strain had been too much for her. She was not able to move from her bed. She had a species of low fever induced by anxiety and fatigue. But she could write, and she did, to the Slocums, and she received no answer. She also wrote to Mrs. Dent; she even sent numerous telegrams, with no response. Finally she wrote to the postmaster, and an answer arrived by the first possible mail. The letter was short, curt, and to the purpose. Mr. Amblecrom, the postmaster, was a man of few words, and especially wary as to his expressions in a letter.

"Dear madam," he wrote, "your favour rec'ed. No Slocums in Ford's Village. All dead. Addie ten years ago, her mother two years later, her father five. House vacant. Mrs. John Dent said to have neglected stepdaughter. Girl was sick. Medicine not given. Talk of taking action. Not enough evidence. House said to be haunted. Strange sights and sounds. Your niece, Agnes Dent, died a year ago, about this time.

"Yours truly,

"*Thomas Amblecrom.*"

A TRESS OF HAIR

Guy de Maupassant

Guy de Maupassant (1850–1893) grew up in Normandy. He was a protégé of Flaubert who introduced him to Émile Zola, Ivan Turgenev and Henry James. In 1868 he saved the poet Algernon Swinburne from drowning. Swinburne's collection of ghoulish objects made a great impression on Maupassant, especially the skinned hand of a parricide, which helped inspire his short story, *The Hand* (1875). Although often referred to as a naturalist, Maupassant resisted association with any particular school of writers.

The walls of the cell were bare and white washed. A narrow grated window, placed so high that one could not reach it, lighted this sinister little room. The mad inmate, seated on a straw chair, looked at us with a fixed, vacant and haunted expression. He was very thin, with hollow cheeks and hair almost white, which one guessed might have turned gray in a few months. His clothes appeared to be too large for his shrunken limbs, his sunken chest and empty paunch. One felt that this man's mind was destroyed, eaten by his thoughts, by one thought, just as a fruit is eaten by a worm. His craze, his idea was there in his brain, insistent, harassing, destructive. It wasted his frame little by little. It – the invisible, impalpable, intangible, immaterial idea – was mining his health, drinking his blood, snuffing out his life.

What a mystery was this man, being killed by an ideal! He aroused sorrow, fear and pity, this madman. What strange, tremendous and deadly thoughts dwelt within this forehead which they creased with deep wrinkles which were never still?

"He has terrible attacks of rage," said the doctor to me. "His is one of the most peculiar cases I have ever seen. He has seizures of erotic and macaberesque madness. He is a sort of necrophile. He has kept a journal in which he sets forth his disease with the utmost clearness. In it you can, as it were, put your finger on it. If it would interest you, you may go over this document."

I followed the doctor into his office, where he handed me this wretched man's diary, saying: "Read it and tell me what you think of it." I read as follows:

"Until the age of thirty-two I lived peacefully, without knowing love. Life appeared very simple, very pleasant and very easy. I was rich. I enjoyed so many things that I had no passion for anything in particular. It was good to be alive! I awoke happy every morning and did those things that pleased me during the day and went to bed at night contented, in the expectation of a peaceful tomorrow and a future without anxiety.

"I had had a few flirtations without my heart being touched by any true passion or wounded by any of the sensations of true love. It is good to live like that. It is better to love, but it is terrible. And yet those who love in the ordinary way must experience ardent happiness, though less than mine possibly, for love came to me in a remarkable manner.

"As I was wealthy, I bought all kinds of old furniture and old curiosities, and I often thought of the unknown hands that had touched these objects, of the eyes that had admired them, of the hearts that had loved them; for one does love things! I sometimes remained hours and hours looking at a little watch of the last century. It was so tiny, so pretty with its enamel and gold chasing. And it kept time as on the day when a woman first bought it, enraptured at owning this dainty trinket. It had not ceased to vibrate, to live its mechanical life, and it had kept up its regular tick-tock since the last century. Who had first worn it on her bosom amid the warmth of her clothing, the heart of the watch beating beside the heart of the woman? What hand had held it in its warm fingers, had turned it over and then wiped the enamelled shepherds on the case to remove the slight moisture from her fingers? What eyes had watched the hands on its ornamental face for the expected, the beloved, the sacred hour?

"How I wished I had known her, seen her, the woman who had selected this exquisite and rare object! She is dead! I am possessed with a longing for women of former days. I love, from afar, all those who have loved. The story of those dead and gone loves fills my heart with regrets. Oh, the beauty, the smiles, the youthful caresses, the hopes! Should not all that be eternal?

"How I have wept whole nights-thinking of those poor women of former days, so beautiful, so loving, so sweet, whose arms were extended in an embrace, and who now are dead! A kiss is immortal! It goes from lips to lips, from century to century, from age to age. Men receive them, give them and die.

"The past attracts me, the present terrifies me because the future means death. I regret all that has gone by. I mourn all who have lived; I should like to check time, to stop the clock. But time goes, it goes, it passes, it takes from me each second a little of myself for the annihilation of to-morrow. And I shall never live again.

"Farewell, ye women of yesterday. I love you!

"But I am not to be pitied. I found her, the one I was waiting for, and through her I enjoyed inestimable pleasure.

"I was sauntering in Paris on a bright, sunny morning, with a happy heart and a high step, looking in at the shop windows with the vague interest of an idler. All at once I noticed in the shop of a dealer in antiques a piece of Italian furniture of the seventeenth century. It was very handsome, very rare. I set it down as being the work of a Venetian artist named Vitelli, who was celebrated in his day.

"I went on my way.

"Why did the remembrance of that piece of furniture haunt me with such insistence that I retraced my steps? I again stopped before the shop, in order to take another look at it, and I felt that it tempted me.

"What a singular thing temptation is! One gazes at an object, and, little by little, it charms you, it disturbs you, it fills your thoughts as a woman's face might do. The enchantment of it penetrates your being, a strange enchantment of form, color and appearance of an inanimate object. And one loves it, one desires it, one wishes to have it. A longing to own it takes possession of you, gently at first, as though it were timid, but growing, becoming intense, irresistible.

"And the dealers seem to guess, from your ardent gaze, your secret and increasing longing.

"I bought this piece of furniture and had it sent home at once. I placed it in my room.

"Oh, I am sorry for those who do not know the honeymoon of the collector with the antique he has just purchased. One looks at it tenderly and passes one's hand over it as if it were human flesh; one comes back to it every moment, one is always thinking of it, wherever ore goes, whatever one does. The dear recollection of it pursues you in the street, in society, everywhere; and when you return home at night, before taking off your gloves or your hat; you go and look at it with the tenderness of a lover.

"Truly, for eight days I worshipped this piece of furniture. I opened its doors and pulled out the drawers every few moments. I handled it with rapture, with all the intense joy of possession.

"But one evening I surmised, while I was feeling the thickness of one of the panels, that there must be a secret drawer in it: My heart began to beat, and I spent the night trying to discover this secret cavity.

"I succeeded on the following day by driving a knife into a slit in the wood. A panel slid back and I saw, spread out on a piece of black velvet, a magnificent tress of hair.

"Yes, a woman's hair, an immense coil of fair hair, almost red, which must have been cut off close to the head, tied with a golden cord.

"I stood amazed, trembling, confused. An almost imperceptible perfume, so ancient that it seemed to be the spirit of a perfume, issued from this mysterious drawer and this remarkable relic.

"I lifted it gently, almost reverently, and took it out of its hiding place. It at once unwound in a golden shower that reached to the floor, dense but light; soft and gleaming like the tail of a comet.

"A strange emotion filled me. What was this? When, how, why had this hair been shut up in this drawer? What adventure, what tragedy did this souvenir conceal? Who had cut it off? A lover on a day of farewell, a husband on a day of revenge, or the one whose head it had graced on the day of despair?

"Was it as she was about to take the veil that they had cast thither that love dowry as a pledge to the world of the living? Was it when they were going to nail down the coffin of the beautiful young corpse that the one who had adored her had cut off her tresses, the only thing that he could retain of her, the only living part of her body that would not suffer decay, the only thing he could still love, and caress, and kiss in his paroxysms of grief?

"Was it not strange that this tress should have remained as it was in life, when not an atom of the body on which it grew was in existence?

"It fell over my fingers, tickled the skin with a singular caress, the caress of a dead woman. It affected me so that I felt as though I should weep.

"I held it in my hands for a long time, then it seemed as if it disturbed me, as though something of the soul had remained in it. And I put it back on the velvet, rusty from age, and pushed in the drawer, closed the doors of the antique cabinet and went out for a walk to meditate.

"I walked along, filled with sadness and also with unrest, that unrest that one feels when in love. I felt as though I must have lived before, as though I must have known this woman.

"And Villon's lines came to my mind like a sob:

> Tell me where, and in what place
> Is Flora, the beautiful Roman,
> Hipparchia and Thaïs
> Who was her cousin-german?
>
> Echo answers in the breeze
> O'er river and lake that blows,
> Their beauty was above all praise,
> But where are last year's snows?
>
> The queen, white as lilies,
> Who sang as sing the birds,
> Bertha Broadfoot, Beatrice, Alice,
> Ermengarde, princess of Maine,
> And Joan, the good Lorraine,
> Burned by the English at Rouen,
> Where are they, Virgin Queen?
> And where are last year's snows?

"When I got home again I felt an irresistible longing to see my singular treasure, and I took it out and, as I touched it, I felt a shiver go all through me.

"For some days, however, I was in my ordinary condition, although the thought of that tress of hair was always present to my mind.

"Whenever I came into the house I had to see it and take it in my hands. I turned the key of the cabinet with the same hesitation that one opens the door leading to one's beloved, for in my hands and my heart I felt a confused, singular, constant sensual longing to plunge my hands in the enchanting golden flood of those dead tresses.

"Then, after I had finished caressing it and had locked the cabinet I felt as if it were a living thing, shut up in there, imprisoned; and I longed to see it again. I felt again the imperious desire to take it in my hands, to touch it, to even feel uncomfortable at the cold, slippery, irritating, bewildering contact.

"I lived thus for a month or two, I forget how long. It obsessed me, haunted me. I was happy and tormented by turns, as when one falls in love, and after the first vows have been exchanged.

"I shut myself in the room with it to feel it on my skin, to bury my lips in it, to kiss it. I wound it round my face, covered my eyes with the golden flood so as to see the day gleam through its gold.

"I loved it! Yes, I loved it. I could not be without it nor pass an hour without looking at it.

"And I waited – I waited – for what? I do not know – For her!

"One night I woke up suddenly, feeling as though I were not alone in my room.

"I was alone, nevertheless, but I could not go to sleep again, and, as I was tossing about feverishly, I got up to look at the golden tress. It seemed softer than usual, more life-like. Do the dead come back? I almost lost consciousness as I kissed it. I took it back with me to bed and pressed it to my lips as if it were my sweetheart.

"Do the dead come back? She came back. Yes, I saw her; I held her in my arms, just as she was in life, tall, fair and round. She came back every evening – the dead woman, the beautiful, adorable, mysterious unknown.

"My happiness was so great that I could not conceal it. No lover ever tasted such intense, terrible enjoyment. I loved her so well that I could not be separated from her. I took her with me always and everywhere. I walked about the town with her as if she were my wife, and took her to the theatre, always to a private box. But they saw her – they guessed – they arrested me. They put me in prison like a criminal. They took her. Oh, misery!"

Here the manuscript stopped. And as I suddenly raised my astonished eyes to the doctor a terrific cry, a howl of impotent rage and of exasperated longing resounded through the asylum.

"Listen," said the doctor. "We have to douse the obscene madman with water five times a day. Sergeant Bertrand was the only one who was in love with the dead."

Filled with astonishment, horror and pity, I stammered out:

"But – that tress – did it really exist?"

The doctor rose, opened a cabinet full of phials and instruments and tossed over a long tress of fair hair which flew toward me like a golden bird.

I shivered at feeling its soft, light touch on my hands. And I sat there, my heart beating with disgust and desire, disgust as at the contact of anything accessory to a crime and desire as at the temptation of some infamous and mysterious thing.

The doctor said as he shrugged his shoulders:

"The mind of man is capable of anything."

"OH, WHISTLE, AND I'LL COME TO YOU, MY LAD"

M.R. James

Montague Rhodes James (1862–1936) grew up in Suffolk where his father was a clergyman. He became a distinguished medievalist scholar and taught at Cambridge and Eton. Despite being one of the first writers to locate ghost stories in the present day rather than a gothic past, James's stories often reflect his knowledge of medievalism. He has been credited as an influence by many writers including H.P. Lovecraft, Ruth Rendell and Stephen King.

"I suppose you will be getting away pretty soon, now Full Term is over, Professor," said a person not in the story to the Professor of Ontography, soon after they had sat down next to each other at a feast in the hospitable hall of St James's College.

The Professor was young, neat, and precise in speech.

"Yes," he said; "my friends have been making me take up golf this term, and I mean to go to the East Coast – in point of fact to Burnstow – (I dare say you know it) for a week or ten days, to improve my game. I hope to get off tomorrow."

"Oh, Parkins," said his neighbour on the other side, "if you are going to Burnstow, I wish you would look at the site of the Templars' preceptory, and let me know if you think it would be any good to have a dig there in the summer."

It was, as you might suppose, a person of antiquarian pursuits who said this, but, since he merely appears in this prologue, there is no need to give his entitlements.

"Certainly," said Parkins, the Professor: "if you will describe to me whereabouts the site is, I will do my best to give you an idea of the lie of the land when I get back; or I could write to you about it, if you would tell me where you are likely to be."

"Don't trouble to do that, thanks. It's only that I'm thinking of taking my family in that direction in the Long, and it occurred to me that, as very few of the English preceptories have ever been properly planned, I might have an opportunity of doing something useful on off-days."

The Professor rather sniffed at the idea that planning out a preceptory could be described as useful. His neighbour continued:

"The site – I doubt if there is anything showing above ground – must be down quite close to the beach now. The sea has encroached tremendously, as you know, all along that bit of coast. I should think, from the map, that it must be about three-quarters of a mile from the Globe Inn, at the north end of the town. Where are you going to stay?"

"Well, at the Globe Inn, as a matter of fact," said Parkins; "I have engaged a room there. I couldn't get in anywhere else; most of the lodging-houses are shut up in winter, it seems; and, as it is, they tell me that the only room of any size I can have is really a double-bedded one, and that they haven't a corner in which to store the other bed, and so on. But I must have a fairly large room, for I am taking some books down, and mean to do a bit of work; and though I don't quite fancy having an empty bed – not to speak of two – in what I may call for the time being my study, I suppose I can manage to rough it for the short time I shall be there."

"Do you call having an extra bed in your room roughing it, Parkins?" said a bluff person opposite. "Look here, I shall come down and occupy it for a bit; it'll be company for you."

The Professor quivered, but managed to laugh in a courteous manner.

"By all means, Rogers; there's nothing I should like better. But I'm afraid you would find it rather dull; you don't play golf, do you?"

"No, thank Heaven!" said rude Mr Rogers.

"Well, you see, when I'm not writing I shall most likely be out on the links, and that, as I say, would be rather dull for you, I'm afraid."

"Oh, I don't know! There's certain to be somebody I know in the place; but, of course, if you don't want me, speak the word, Parkins; I shan't be offended. Truth, as you always tell us, is never offensive."

Parkins was, indeed, scrupulously polite and strictly truthful. It is to be feared that Mr Rogers sometimes practised upon his knowledge of these characteristics. In Parkins's breast there was a conflict now raging, which for a moment or two did not allow him to answer. That interval being over, he said:

"Well, if you want the exact truth, Rogers, I was considering whether the room I speak of would really be large enough to accommodate us both comfortably; and also whether (mind, I shouldn't have said this if you hadn't pressed me) you would not constitute something in the nature of a hindrance to my work."

Rogers laughed loudly.

"Well done, Parkins!" he said. "It's all right. I promise not to interrupt your work; don't you disturb yourself about that. No, I won't come if you don't want me; but I thought I should do so nicely to keep the ghosts off." Here he might have been seen to wink and to nudge his next neighbour. Parkins might also have been seen to become pink. "I beg pardon, Parkins," Rogers continued; "I oughtn't to have said that. I forgot you didn't like levity on these topics."

"Well," Parkins said, "as you have mentioned the matter, I freely own that I do *not* like careless talk about what you call ghosts. A man in my position," he went on, raising his voice a little, "cannot, I find, be too careful about appearing to sanction the current beliefs on such subjects. As you know, Rogers, or as you ought to know; for I think I have never concealed my views – "

"No, you certainly have not, old man," put in Rogers *sotto voce*.

" – I hold that any semblance, any appearance of concession to the view that such things might exist is equivalent to a renunciation of all that I hold most sacred. But I'm afraid I have not succeeded in securing your attention."

"Your *undivided* attention, was what Dr Blimber actually *said*,"[1] Rogers interrupted, with every appearance of an earnest desire for accuracy. "But I beg your pardon, Parkins: I'm stopping you."

"No, not at all," said Parkins. "I don't remember Blimber; perhaps he was before my time. But I needn't go on. I'm sure you know what I mean."

"Yes, yes," said Rogers, rather hastily – "just so. We'll go into it fully at Burnstow, or somewhere."

In repeating the above dialogue I have tried to give the impression which it made on me, that Parkins was something of an old woman – rather henlike, perhaps, in his little ways; totally destitute, alas! of the sense of humour, but at the same time dauntless and sincere in his convictions, and a man deserving of the greatest respect. Whether or not the reader has gathered so much, that was the character which Parkins had.

On the following day Parkins did, as he had hoped, succeed in getting away from his college, and in arriving at Burnstow. He was made welcome at the Globe Inn, was safely installed in the large double-bedded room of which we have heard, and was able before retiring to rest to arrange his materials for work in apple-pie order upon a commodious table which occupied the outer end of the room, and was surrounded on three sides by windows looking out seaward; that is to say, the central window looked straight out to sea, and those on the left and right commanded prospects along the shore to the north and south respectively. On the south you saw the village of Burnstow. On the north no houses were to be seen, but only the beach and the low cliff backing it. Immediately in front was a strip – not considerable – of rough grass, dotted with old anchors, capstans, and so forth; then a broad path; then the beach. Whatever may have been the original distance between the Globe Inn and the sea, not more than sixty yards now separated them.

The rest of the population of the inn was, of course, a golfing one, and included few elements that call for a special description. The most conspicuous figure was, perhaps, that of an *ancien militaire*, secretary of a London club, and possessed of a voice of incredible strength, and of views of a pronouncedly Protestant type. These were apt to find utterance after his attendance upon the ministrations of the Vicar, an estimable man with inclinations towards a picturesque ritual, which he gallantly kept down as far as he could out of deference to East Anglian tradition.

Professor Parkins, one of whose principal characteristics was pluck, spent the greater part of the day following his arrival at Burnstow in what he had called improving his game, in company with this Colonel Wilson: and during the afternoon – whether the process of improvement were to blame or not, I am not sure – the Colonel's demeanour assumed a colouring so lurid that even Parkins jibbed at the thought of walking home with him from the links. He determined, after a short and furtive look at that bristling moustache and those incarnadined features, that it would be wiser to allow the influences of tea and tobacco to do

---

1 Mr Rogers was wrong, vide *Dombey and Son*, chapter xii.

what they could with the Colonel before the dinner-hour should render a meeting inevitable.

"I might walk home tonight along the beach," he reflected – "yes, and take a look – there will be light enough for that – at the ruins of which Disney was talking. I don't exactly know where they are, by the way; but I expect I can hardly help stumbling on them."

This he accomplished, I may say, in the most literal sense, for in picking his way from the links to the shingle beach his foot caught, partly in a gorse-root and partly in a biggish stone, and over he went. When he got up and surveyed his surroundings, he found himself in a patch of somewhat broken ground covered with small depressions and mounds. These latter, when he came to examine them, proved to be simply masses of flints embedded in mortar and grown over with turf. He must, he quite rightly concluded, be on the site of the preceptory he had promised to look at. It seemed not unlikely to reward the spade of the explorer; enough of the foundations was probably left at no great depth to throw a good deal of light on the general plan. He remembered vaguely that the Templars, to whom this site had belonged, were in the habit of building round churches, and he thought a particular series of the humps or mounds near him did appear to be arranged in something of a circular form. Few people can resist the temptation to try a little amateur research in a department quite outside their own, if only for the satisfaction of showing how successful they would have been had they only taken it up seriously. Our Professor, however, if he felt something of this mean desire, was also truly anxious to oblige Mr Disney. So he paced with care the circular area he had noticed, and wrote down its rough dimensions in his pocket-book. Then he proceeded to examine an oblong eminence which lay east of the centre of the circle, and seemed to his thinking likely to be the base of a platform or altar. At one end of it, the northern, a patch of the turf was gone – removed by some boy or other creature *ferae naturae*. It might, he thought, be as well to probe the soil here for evidences of masonry, and he took out his knife and began scraping away the earth. And now followed another little discovery: a portion of soil fell inward as he scraped, and disclosed a small cavity. He lighted one match after another to help him to see of what nature the hole was, but the wind was too strong for them all. By tapping and scratching the sides with his knife, however, he was able to make out that it must be an artificial hole in masonry. It was rectangular, and the sides, top, and bottom, if not actually plastered, were smooth and regular. Of course it was empty. No! As he withdrew the knife he heard a metallic clink, and when he introduced his hand it met with a cylindrical object lying on the floor of the hole. Naturally enough, he picked it up, and when he brought it into the light, now fast fading, he could see that it, too, was of man's making – a metal tube about four inches long, and evidently of some considerable age.

By the time Parkins had made sure that there was nothing else in this odd receptacle, it was too late and too dark for him to think of undertaking any further search. What he had done had proved so unexpectedly interesting that he determined to sacrifice a little more of the daylight on the morrow to archaeology. The object which he now had safe in his pocket was bound to be of some slight value at least, he felt sure.

Bleak and solemn was the view on which he took a last look before starting homeward. A faint yellow light in the west showed the links, on which a few figures moving towards the club-house were still visible, the squat martello tower, the lights of Aldsey village, the pale ribbon of sands intersected at intervals by black wooden groynings, the dim and murmuring sea. The wind was bitter from the north, but was at his back when he set out for the Globe. He quickly rattled and clashed through the shingle and gained the sand, upon which, but for the groynings which had to be got over every few yards, the going was both good and quiet. One last look behind, to measure the distance he had made since leaving the ruined Templars' church, showed him a prospect of company on his walk, in the shape of a rather indistinct personage, who seemed to be making great efforts to catch up with him, but made little, if any, progress. I mean that there was an appearance of running about his movements, but that the distance between him and Parkins did not seem materially to lessen. So, at least, Parkins thought, and decided that he almost certainly did not know him, and that it would be absurd to wait until he came up. For all that, company, he began to think, would really be very welcome on that lonely shore, if only you could choose your companion. In his unenlightened days he had read of meetings in such places which even now would hardly bear thinking of. He went on thinking of them, however, until he reached home, and particularly of one which catches most people's fancy at some time of their childhood. "Now I saw in my dream that Christian had gone but a very little way when he saw a foul fiend coming over the field to meet him." "What should I do now," he thought, "if I looked back and caught sight of a black figure sharply defined against the yellow sky, and saw that it had horns and wings? I wonder whether I should stand or run for it. Luckily, the gentleman behind is not of that kind, and he seems to be about as far off now as when I saw him first. Well, at this rate, he won't get his dinner as soon as I shall; and, dear me! it's within a quarter of an hour of the time now. I must run!"

Parkins had, in fact, very little time for dressing. When he met the Colonel at dinner, Peace – or as much of her as that gentleman could manage – reigned once more in the military bosom; nor was she put to flight in the hours of bridge that followed dinner, for Parkins was a more than respectable player. When, therefore, he retired towards twelve o'clock, he felt that he had spent his evening in quite a satisfactory way, and that, even for so long as a fortnight or three weeks, life at the Globe would be supportable under similar conditions – "especially," thought he, "if I go on improving my game."

As he went along the passages he met the boots of the Globe, who stopped and said:

"Beg your pardon, sir, but as I was abrushing your coat just now there was something fell out of the pocket. I put it on your chest of drawers, sir, in your room, sir – a piece of a pipe or somethink of that, sir. Thank you, sir. You'll find it on your chest of drawers, sir – yes, sir. Good night, sir."

The speech served to remind Parkins of his little discovery of that afternoon. It was with some considerable curiosity that he turned it over by the light of his candles. It was of bronze, he now saw, and was shaped very much after the manner of the modern dog-whistle; in fact it was – yes, certainly it was – actually no more nor less than a whistle. He put it to his lips, but it was quite full of a fine, caked-up sand or earth, which would not yield to knocking, but must be loosened with a knife. Tidy as ever in his habits, Parkins cleared out the earth on to a piece of paper, and took the latter to the window to empty it out. The night was clear and bright, as he saw when he had opened the casement, and he stopped for an instant to look at the sea and note a belated wanderer stationed on the shore in front of the inn. Then he shut the window, a little surprised at the late hours people kept at Burnstow, and took his whistle to the light again. Why, surely there were marks on it, and not merely marks, but letters! A very little rubbing rendered the deeply-cut inscription quite legible, but the Professor had to confess, after some earnest thought, that the meaning of it was as obscure to him as the writing on the wall to Belshazzar. There were legends both on the front and on the back of the whistle. The one read thus:

FLA

FUR   BIS

FLE

The other:

QUIS EST ISTE QUI VENIT

"I ought to be able to make it out," he thought; "but I suppose I am a little rusty in my Latin. When I come to think of it, I don't believe I even know the word for a whistle. The long one does seem simple enough. It ought to mean: 'Who is this who is coming?' Well, the best way to find out is evidently to whistle for him."

He blew tentatively and stopped suddenly, startled and yet pleased at the note he had elicited. It had a quality of infinite distance in it, and, soft as it was, he somehow felt it must be audible for miles round. It was a sound, too, that seemed to have the power (which many scents possess) of forming pictures in the brain. He saw quite clearly for a moment a vision of a wide, dark expanse at night, with a fresh wind blowing, and in the midst a lonely figure – how employed, he could not tell. Perhaps he would have seen more had not the picture been broken by the sudden surge of a gust of wind against his casement, so sudden that it made him look up, just in time to see the white glint of a seabird's wing somewhere outside the dark panes.

The sound of the whistle had so fascinated him that he could not help trying it once more, this time more boldly. The note was little, if at all, louder than before, and repetition broke the illusion – no picture followed, as he had half hoped it might. "But what is this? Goodness! what force the wind can get up in a few minutes! What a tremendous gust! There! I knew that window-fastening was no use! Ah! I thought so – both candles out. It is enough to tear the room to pieces."

The first thing was to get the window shut. While you might count twenty Parkins was struggling with the small casement, and felt almost as if he were pushing back a sturdy burglar, so strong was the pressure. It slackened all at once, and the window banged to and latched itself. Now to relight the candles and see what damage, if any, had been done. No, nothing seemed amiss; no glass even was broken in the casement. But the noise had evidently roused at least one member of the household: the Colonel was to be heard stumping in his stock-inged feet on the floor above, and growling. Quickly as it had risen, the wind did not fall at once. On it went, moaning and rushing past the house, at times rising to a cry so desolate that, as Parkins disinterestedly said, it might have made fanciful people feel quite uncomfortable; even the unimaginative, he thought after a quarter of an hour, might be happier without it.

Whether it was the wind, or the excitement of golf, or of the researches in the preceptory that kept Parkins awake, he was not sure. Awake he remained, in any case, long enough to fancy (as I am afraid I often do myself under such conditions) that he was the victim of all manner of fatal disorders: he would lie counting the beats of his heart, convinced that it was going to stop work every moment, and would entertain grave suspicions of his lungs, brain, liver, etc. – suspicions which he was sure would be dispelled by the return of daylight, but which until then refused to be put aside. He found a little vicarious comfort in the idea that someone else was in the same boat. A near neighbour (in the darkness it was not easy to tell his direction) was tossing and rustling in his bed, too.

The next stage was that Parkins shut his eyes and determined to give sleep every chance. Here again over-excitement asserted itself in another form – that of making pictures. Experto crede, pictures do come to the closed eyes of one trying to sleep, and are often so little to his taste that he must open his eyes and disperse them.

Parkins's experience on this occasion was a very distressing one. He found that the picture which presented itself to him was continuous. When he opened his eyes, of course, it went; but when he shut them once more it framed itself afresh, and acted itself out again, neither quicker nor slower than before. What he saw was this:

A long stretch of shore – shingle edged by sand, and intersected at short intervals with black groynes running down to the water – a scene, in fact, so like that of his afternoon's walk that, in the absence of any landmark, it could not be distinguished therefrom. The light was obscure, conveying an impression of gathering storm, late winter evening, and slight cold rain. On this bleak stage at first no actor was visible. Then, in the distance, a bobbing black object appeared; a moment more, and it was a man running, jumping, clambering over the groynes, and every few seconds looking eagerly back. The nearer he came the more obvious it was that he was not only anxious, but even terribly frightened, though his face was not to be distinguished. He was, moreover, almost at the end of his strength. On he came; each successive obstacle seemed to cause him more difficulty than the last. "Will he get over this next one?" thought Parkins; "it seems a little higher than the others." Yes; half climbing, half throwing himself, he did get over, and fell all in a heap on the other side (the side nearest to the spectator). There, as if really unable to get up again, he remained crouching under the groyne, looking up in an attitude of painful anxiety.

So far no cause whatever for the fear of the runner had been shown; but now there began to be seen, far up the shore, a little flicker of something light-coloured moving to and fro with great swiftness and irregularity. Rapidly growing larger, it, too, declared itself as a figure in pale, fluttering draperies, ill-defined. There was something about its motion which made Parkins very unwilling to see it at close quarters. It would stop, raise arms, bow itself towards the sand, then run stooping across the beach to the water-edge and back again; and then, rising upright, once more continue its course forward at a speed that was startling and terrifying. The moment came when the pursuer was hovering about from left to right only a few yards beyond the groyne where the runner lay in hiding. After two or three ineffectual castings hither and thither it came to a stop, stood upright, with arms raised high, and then darted straight forward towards the groyne.

It was at this point that Parkins always failed in his resolution to keep his eyes shut. With many misgivings as to incipient failure of eyesight, overworked brain, excessive smoking, and so on, he finally resigned himself to light his candle, get out a book, and pass the night waking, rather than be tormented by this persistent panorama, which he saw clearly enough could only be a morbid reflection of his walk and his thoughts on that very day.

The scraping of match on box and the glare of light must have startled some creatures of the night – rats or what not – which he heard scurry across the floor from the side of his bed with much rustling. Dear, dear! the match is out! Fool that it is! But the second one burnt better, and a candle and book were duly procured, over which Parkins pored till sleep of a wholesome kind came upon him, and that in no long space. For about the first time in his orderly and prudent life he forgot to blow out the candle, and when he was called next morning at eight there was still a flicker in the socket and a sad mess of guttered grease on the top of the little table.

After breakfast he was in his room, putting the finishing touches to his golfing costume – fortune had again allotted the Colonel to him for a partner – when one of the maids came in.

"Oh, if you please," she said, "would you like any extra blankets on your bed, sir?"

"Ah! thank you," said Parkins. "Yes, I think I should like one. It seems likely to turn rather colder."

In a very short time the maid was back with the blanket.

"Which bed should I put it on, sir?" she asked.

"What? Why, that one – the one I slept in last night," he said, pointing to it.

"Oh yes! I beg your pardon, sir, but you seemed to have tried both of "em; leastways, we had to make "em both up this morning."

"Really? How very absurd!" said Parkins. "I certainly never touched the other, except to lay some things on it. Did it actually seem to have been slept in?"

"Oh yes, sir!" said the maid. "Why, all the things was crumpled and throwed about all ways, if you'll excuse me, sir – quite as if anyone "adn't passed but a very poor night, sir."

"Dear me," said Parkins. "Well, I may have disordered it more than I thought when I unpacked my things. I'm very sorry to have given you the extra trouble, I'm sure. I expect a friend of mine soon, by the way – a gentleman from Cambridge – to come and occupy it for a night or two. That will be all right, I suppose, won't it?"

"Oh yes, to be sure, sir. Thank you, sir. It's no trouble, I'm sure," said the maid, and departed to giggle with her colleagues.

Parkins set forth, with a stern determination to improve his game.

I am glad to be able to report that he succeeded so far in this enterprise that the Colonel, who had been rather repining at the prospect of a second day's play in his company, became quite chatty as the morning advanced; and his voice boomed out over the flats, as certain also of our own minor poets have said, "like some great bourdon in a minster tower".

"Extraordinary wind, that, we had last night," he said. "In my old home we should have said someone had been whistling for it."

"Should you, indeed!" said Perkins. "Is there a superstition of that kind still current in your part of the country?"

"I don't know about superstition," said the Colonel. "They believe in it all over Denmark and Norway, as well as on the Yorkshire coast; and my experience is, mind you, that there's generally something at the bottom of what these country-folk hold to, and have held to for generations. But it's your drive" (or whatever it might have been: the golfing reader will have to imagine appropriate digressions at the proper intervals).

When conversation was resumed, Parkins said, with a slight hesitancy:

"A propos of what you were saying just now, Colonel, I think I ought to tell you that my own views on such subjects are very strong. I am, in fact, a convinced disbeliever in what is called the 'supernatural'."

"What!" said the Colonel, "do you mean to tell me you don't believe in second-sight, or ghosts, or anything of that kind?"

"In nothing whatever of that kind," returned Parkins firmly.

"Well," said the Colonel, "but it appears to me at that rate, sir, that you must be little better than a Sadducee."

Parkins was on the point of answering that, in his opinion, the Sadducees were the most sensible persons he had ever read of in the Old Testament; but feeling some doubt as to whether much mention of them was to be found in that work, he preferred to laugh the accusation off.

"Perhaps I am," he said; "but – Here, give me my cleek, boy! – Excuse me one moment, Colonel." A short interval. "Now, as to whistling for the wind, let me give you my theory about it. The laws which govern winds are really not at all perfectly known – to fisherfolk and such, of course, not known at all. A man or woman of eccentric habits, perhaps, or a stranger, is seen repeatedly on the beach at some unusual hour, and is heard whistling. Soon afterwards a violent wind rises; a man who could read the sky perfectly or who possessed a barometer could have foretold that it would. The simple people of a fishing-village have no barometers, and only a few rough rules for prophesying weather. What more natural than that the eccentric personage I postulated should be regarded as having raised the wind, or that he or she should clutch eagerly at the reputation of being able to do so? Now, take last night's wind: as it happens, I myself was whistling. I blew a whistle twice, and the wind seemed to come absolutely in answer to my call. If anyone had seen me – "

The audience had been a little restive under this harangue, and Parkins had, I fear, fallen somewhat into the tone of a lecturer; but at the last sentence the Colonel stopped.

"Whistling, were you?" he said. "And what sort of whistle did you use? Play this stroke first." Interval.

"About that whistle you were asking, Colonel. It's rather a curious one. I have it in my – No; I see I've left it in my room. As a matter of fact,

I found it yesterday."

And then Parkins narrated the manner of his discovery of the whistle, upon hearing which the Colonel grunted, and opined that, in Parkins's place, he should himself be careful about using a thing that had belonged to a set of Papists, of whom, speaking generally, it might be affirmed that you never knew what they might not have been up to. From this topic he diverged to the enormities of the Vicar, who had given notice on the previous Sunday that Friday would be the Feast of St Thomas the Apostle, and that there would be service at eleven o'clock in the church. This and other similar proceedings constituted in the Colonel's view a strong presumption that the Vicar was a concealed Papist, if not a Jesuit; and Parkins, who could not very readily follow the Colonel in this region, did not disagree with him. In fact, they got on so well together in the morning that there was not talk on either side of their separating after lunch.

Both continued to play well during the afternoon, or at least, well enough to make them forget everything else until the light began to fail them. Not until then did Parkins remember that he had meant to do some more investigating at the preceptory; but it was of no great importance, he reflected. One day was as good as another; he might as well go home with the Colonel.

As they turned the corner of the house, the Colonel was almost knocked down by a boy who rushed into him at the very top of his speed, and then, instead of running away, remained hanging on to him and panting. The first words of the warrior were naturally those of reproof and objurgation, but he very quickly discerned that the boy was almost speechless with fright. Inquiries were useless at first. When the boy got his breath he began to howl, and still clung to the Colonel's legs. He was at last detached, but continued to howl.

"What in the world is the matter with you? What have you been up to? What have you seen?" said the two men.

"Ow, I seen it wive at me out of the winder," wailed the boy, "and I don't like it."

"What window?" said the irritated Colonel. "Come pull yourself together, my boy."

"The front winder it was, at the 'otel," said the boy.

At this point Parkins was in favour of sending the boy home, but the Colonel refused; he wanted to get to the bottom of it, he said; it was most dangerous to give a boy such a fright as this one had had, and if it turned out that people had been playing jokes, they should suffer for it in some way. And by a series of questions he made out this story: The boy had been playing about on the grass in front of the Globe with some others; then they had gone home to their teas, and he was just going, when he happened to look up at the front winder and see it a-wiving at him. It seemed to be a figure of some sort, in white as far as he knew – couldn't see its face; but it wived at him, and it warn't a right thing – not to say not a right person. Was there a light in the room? No, he didn't think to look if there was a light. Which was the window? Was it the top one or the second one? The seckind one it was – the big winder what got two little uns at the sides.

"Very well, my boy," said the Colonel, after a few more questions. "You run away home now. I expect it was some person trying to give you a start. Another time, like a brave English boy, you just throw a stone – well, no, not that exactly, but you go and speak to the waiter, or to Mr Simpson, the landlord, and – yes – and say that I advised you to do so."

The boy's face expressed some of the doubt he felt as to the likelihood of Mr Simpson's lending a favourable ear to his complaint, but the Colonel did not appear to perceive this, and went on:

"And here's a sixpence – no, I see it's a shilling – and you be off home, and don't think any more about it."

The youth hurried off with agitated thanks, and the Colonel and Parkins went round to the front of the Globe and reconnoitred. There was only one window answering to the description they had been hearing.

"Well, that's curious," said Parkins; "it's evidently my window the lad was talking about. Will you come up for a moment, Colonel Wilson? We ought to be able to see if anyone has been taking liberties in my room."

They were soon in the passage, and Parkins made as if to open the door.

Then he stopped and felt in his pockets.

"This is more serious than I thought," was his next remark. "I remember now that before I started this morning I locked the door. It is locked now, and, what is more, here is the key." And he held it up. "Now," he went on, "if the servants are in the habit of going into one's room during the day when one is away, I can only say that – well, that I don't approve of it at all." Conscious of a somewhat weak climax, he busied himself in opening the door (which was indeed locked) and in lighting candles. "No," he said, "nothing seems disturbed."

"Except your bed," put in the Colonel.

"Excuse me, that isn't my bed," said Parkins. "I don't use that one. But it does look as if someone had been playing tricks with it."

It certainly did: the clothes were bundled up and twisted together in a most tortuous confusion. Parkins pondered.

"That must be it," he said at last. "I disordered the clothes last night in unpacking, and they haven't made it since. Perhaps they came in to make it, and that boy saw them through the window; and then they were called away and locked the door after them. Yes, I think that must be it."

"Well, ring and ask," said the Colonel, and this appealed to Parkins as practical.

The maid appeared, and, to make a long story short, deposed that she had made the bed in the morning when the gentleman was in the room, and hadn't been there since. No, she hadn't no other key. Mr Simpson, he kep' the keys; he'd be able to tell the gentleman if anyone had been up.

This was a puzzle. Investigation showed that nothing of value had been taken, and Parkins remembered the disposition of the small objects on tables and so forth well enough to be pretty sure that no pranks had been played with them. Mr and Mrs Simpson furthermore agreed that neither of them had given the duplicate key of the room to any person whatever during the day. Nor could Parkins, fair-minded man as he was, detect anything in the demeanour of master, mistress, or maid that indicated guilt. He was much more inclined to think that the boy had been imposing on the Colonel.

The latter was unwontedly silent and pensive at dinner and throughout the evening. When he bade goodnight to Parkins, he murmured in a gruff undertone:

"You know where I am if you want me during the night."

"Why, yes, thank you, Colonel Wilson, I think I do; but there isn't much prospect of my disturbing you, I hope. By the way," he added, "did I show you that old whistle I spoke of? I think not. Well, here it is."

The Colonel turned it over gingerly in the light of the candle.

"Can you make anything of the inscription?" asked Parkins, as he took it back.

"No, not in this light. What do you mean to do with it?"

"Oh, well, when I get back to Cambridge I shall submit it to some of the archaeologists there, and see what they think of it; and very likely, if they consider it worth having, I may present it to one of the museums."

"M!" said the Colonel. "Well, you may be right. All I know is that, if it were mine, I should chuck it straight into the sea. It's no use talking, I'm well aware, but I expect that with you it's a case of live and learn. I hope so, I'm sure, and I wish you a good night."

He turned away, leaving Parkins in act to speak at the bottom of the stair, and soon each was in his own bedroom.

By some unfortunate accident, there were neither blinds nor curtains to the windows of the Professor's room. The previous night he had thought little of this, but tonight there seemed every prospect of a bright moon rising to shine directly on his bed, and probably wake him later on. When he noticed this he was a good deal annoyed, but, with an ingenuity which I can only envy, he succeeded in rigging up, with the help of a railway-rug, some safety-pins, and a stick and umbrella, a screen which, if it only held together, would completely keep the moonlight off his bed. And shortly afterwards he was comfortably in that bed. When he had read a somewhat solid work long enough to produce a decided wish to sleep, he cast a drowsy glance round the room, blew out the candle, and fell back upon the pillow.

He must have slept soundly for an hour or more, when a sudden clatter shook him up in a most unwelcome manner. In a moment he realized what had happened: his carefully-constructed screen had given way, and a very bright frosty moon was shining directly on his face. This was highly annoying. Could he possibly get up and reconstruct the screen? or could he manage to sleep if he did not?

For some minutes he lay and pondered over all the possibilities; then he turned over sharply, and with his eyes open lay breathlessly listening. There had been a movement, he was sure, in the empty bed on the opposite side of the room. Tomorrow he would have it moved, for there must be rats or something playing about in it. It was quiet now. No! the commotion began again. There was a rustling and shaking: surely more than any rat could cause.

I can figure to myself something of the Professor's bewilderment and horror, for I have in a dream thirty years back seen the same thing happen; but the reader will hardly, perhaps, imagine how dreadful it was to him to see a figure suddenly sit up in what he had known was an empty bed. He was out of his own bed in one bound, and made a dash towards the window, where lay his only weapon, the stick with which he had propped his screen. This was, as it turned out, the worst thing he could have done, because the personage in the empty bed, with a sudden smooth motion, slipped from the bed and took up a position, with outspread arms, between the two beds, and in front of the door. Parkins watched it in a horrid perplexity. Somehow, the idea of getting past it and escaping through the door was intolerable to him; he could not have borne – he didn't know why – to touch it; and as for its touching him, he would sooner dash himself through the window than have that happen. It stood for the moment in a band of dark shadow, and he had not seen what its face was like. Now it began to move, in a stooping posture, and all at once the spectator realized, with some horror and some relief, that it must be blind, for it seemed to feel about it with its muffled arms in a groping and random fashion. Turning half away from him, it became suddenly conscious of the bed he had just left, and darted towards it, and bent and felt over the pillows in a way which made Parkins shudder as he had never in his life thought it possible. In a very few moments it seemed to know that the bed was empty, and then, moving forward into the area of light and facing the window, it showed for the first time what manner of thing it was.

Parkins, who very much dislikes being questioned about it, did once describe something of it in my hearing, and I gathered that what he chiefly remembers about it is a horrible, an intensely horrible, face of crumpled linen. What expression he read upon it he could not or would not tell, but that the fear of it went nigh to maddening him is certain.

But he was not at leisure to watch it for long. With formidable quickness it moved into the middle of the room, and, as it groped and waved, one corner of its draperies swept across Parkins's face. He could not, though he knew how perilous a sound was – he could not keep back a cry of disgust, and this gave the searcher an instant clue. It leapt towards him upon the instant, and the next moment he was half-way through the window backwards, uttering cry upon cry at the utmost pitch of his voice, and the linen face was thrust close into his own. At this, almost the last possible second, deliverance came, as you will have guessed: the Colonel burst the door open, and was just in time to see the dreadful group at the window. When he reached the figures only one was left. Parkins sank forward into the room in a faint, and before him on the floor lay a tumbled heap of bed-clothes.

Colonel Wilson asked no questions, but busied himself in keeping everyone else out of the room and in getting Parkins back to his bed; and himself, wrapped in a rug, occupied the other bed, for the rest of the night. Early on the next day Rogers arrived, more welcome than he would have been a day before, and the three of them held a very long consultation in the Professor's room. At the end of it the Colonel left the hotel door carrying a small object between his finger and thumb, which he cast as far into the sea as a very brawny arm could send it. Later on the smoke of a burning ascended from the back premises of the Globe.

Exactly what explanation was patched up for the staff and visitors at the hotel I must confess I do not recollect. The Professor was somehow cleared of the ready suspicion of delirium tremens, and the hotel of the reputation of a troubled house.

There is not much question as to what would have happened to Parkins if the Colonel had not intervened when he did. He would either have fallen out of the window or else lost his wits. But it is not so evident what more the creature that came in answer to the whistle could have done than frighten. There seemed to be absolutely nothing material about it save the bedclothes of which it had made itself a body. The Colonel, who remembered a not very dissimilar occurrence in India, was of the opinion that if Parkins had closed with it it could really have done very little, and that its one power was that of frightening. The whole thing, he said, served to confirm his opinion of the Church of Rome.

There is really nothing more to tell, but, as you may imagine, the Professor's views on certain points are less clear cut than they used to be. His nerves, too, have suffered: he cannot even now see a surplice hanging on a door quite un-moved, and the spectacle of a scarecrow in a field late on a winter afternoon has cost him more than one sleepless night.

THE READJUSTMENT

Mary Austin

Mary Hunter Austin (1868–1934) was an early feminist and supporter of Native American and Spanish-American rights. She was born in Carlinville, Illinois and at the age of five discovered an inner voice or spiritual centre that she referred to as 'I-Mary'. Her family moved to California in 1888 and settled in the San Joaquin Valley where Mary worked as a school teacher. She later moved to New Mexico. Her autobiography, *Earth Horizon*, was published in 1932.

Emma Jeffries had been dead and buried three days. The sister who had come to the funeral had taken Emma's child away with her, and the house was swept and aired; then, when it seemed there was least occasion for it, Emma came back. The neighbour woman who had nursed her was the first to know it. It was about seven of the evening, in a mellow gloom: the neighbour woman was sitting on her own stoop with her arms wrapped in her apron, and all at once she found herself going along the street under an urgent sense that Emma needed her. She was half–way down the block before she recollected that this was impossible, for Mrs. Jeffries was dead and buried; but as soon as she came opposite the house she was aware of what had happened. It was all open to the summer air; except that it was a little neater, not otherwise than the rest of the street. It was quite dark; but the presence of Emma Jeffries streamed from it and betrayed it more than a candle. It streamed out steadily across the garden, and even as it reached her, mixed with the smell of the damp mignonette, the neighbour woman owned to herself that she had always known Emma would come back.

"A sight stranger if she wouldn't," thought the woman who had nursed her. "She wasn't ever one to throw off things easily."

Emma Jeffries had taken death as she had taken everything in life, hard. She had met it with the same bright, surface competency that she had presented to the squalor of the encompassing desertness, to the insuperable commonness of Sim Jeffries, to the affliction of her crippled child; and the intensity of her word-less struggle against it had caught the attention of the townspeople and held it in a shocked curious awe. She was so long a–dying, lying there in that little low house, hearing the abhorred footsteps going about her rooms and the vulgar procedure of the community encroach upon her like the advances of the sand wastes on an unwatered field. For Emma had always wanted things different, wanted them with a fury of intentness that implied offensiveness in things as they were. And the townspeople had taken offence, the more so because she was not to be surprised in any inaptitude for their own kind of success. Do what you could, you could never catch Emma Jeffries in a wrapper after three o'clock in the afternoon. And she would never talk about the child – in a country where so little ever happened that even trouble was a godsend if it gave you something to talk about. It was reported that she did not even talk to Sim. But there the common resentment got back at her. If she had thought to effect anything with Sim Jeffries against the benumbing spirit of the place, the evasive hopefulness, the large sense of leisure that ungirt the loins, if she still hoped somehow to get away with him to some place for which by her dress, by her manner, she seemed forever and unassailably fit, it was foregone that nothing would come of it. They knew Sim Jeffries better than that. Yet so vivid had been the force of her wordless dissatisfaction that when the fever took her and she went down like a pasteboard figure in the damp, the wonder was that nothing toppled with her. And, as if she too had felt herself indispensable, Emma Jeffries had come back.

The neighbour woman crossed the street, and as she passed the far corner of the garden, Jeffries spoke to her. He had been standing, she did not know how long a time, behind the syringa-bush, and moved even with her along the fence until they came to the gate. She could see in the dusk that before speaking he wet his lips with his tongue.

"She's in there," he said, at last.

"Emma?"

He nodded. "I been sleeping at the store since – but I thought I'd be more comfortable – as soon as I opened the door, there she was."

"Did you see her?"

"No."

"How do you know, then?"

"Don't you know?"

The neighbour felt there was nothing to say to that.

"Come in," he whispered, huskily. They slipped by the rose-tree and the wistaria, and sat down on the porch at the side. A door swung inward behind them. They felt the Presence in the dusk beating like a pulse.

"What do you think she wants?" said Jeffries. "Do you reckon it's the boy?"

"Like enough."

"He's better off with his aunt. There was no one here to take care of him like his mother wanted." He raised his voice unconsciously with a note of justification, addressing the room behind.

"I am sending fifty dollars a month," he said; "he can go with the best of them."

He went on at length to explain all the advantage that was to come to the boy from living at Pasadena, and the neighbour woman bore him out in it.

"He was glad to go," urged Jeffries to the room. "He said it was what his mother would have wanted."

They were silent then a long time, while the Presence seemed to swell upon them and encroached upon the garden.

Finally, "I gave Ziegler the order for the monument yesterday," Jeffries threw out, appeasingly. "It's to cost three hundred and fifty."

The Presence stirred. The neighbour thought she could fairly see the controlled tolerance with which Emma Jeffries endured the evidence of Sim's ineptitude.

They sat on helplessly without talking after that until the woman's husband came to the fence and called her.

"Don't go," begged Sim.

"Hush," she said. "Do you want all the town to know? You had naught but good from Emma living, and no call to expect harm from her now. It's natural she should come back – if – if she was lonesome like – in – the place where she's gone to."

"Emma wouldn't come back to this place," Jeffries protested, "without she wanted something."

"Well, then, you've got to find out," said the neighbour woman.

All the next day she saw, whenever she passed the house, that Emma was still there. It was shut and barred, but the Presence lurked behind the folded blinds and fumbled at the doors. When it was night and the moths began in the columbine under the windows, it went out and walked in the garden.

Jeffries was waiting at the gate when the neighbour woman came. He sweated with helplessness in the warm dusk, and the Presence brooded upon them like an apprehension that grows by being entertained.

"She wants something," he appealed, "but I can't make out what. Emma knows she is welcome to everything I've got. Everybody knows I've been a good provider."

The neighbour woman remembered suddenly the only time she had ever drawn close to Emma Jeffries touching the child. They had sat up with it together all one night in some childish ailment, and she had ventured a question: "What does his father think?" And Emma had turned her a white, hard face of surpassing dreariness.

"I don't know," she admitted; "he never says."

"There's more than providing," suggested the neighbour woman.

"Yes. There's feeling . . . but she had enough to do to put up with me. I had no call to be troubling her with such." He left off to mop his forehead, and began again.

"Feelings!" he said; "there's times a man gets so wore out with feelings, he doesn't have them any more."

He talked, and presently it grew clear to the woman that he was voiding all the stuff of his life, as if he had sickened on it and was now done. It was a little soul knowing itself and not good to see. What was singular was that the Presence left off walking in the garden, came and caught like a gossamer on the ivy-tree, swayed by the breath of his broken sentences. He talked, and the neighbour woman saw him for once as he saw himself and Emma, snared and floundering in an inexplicable unhappiness. He had been disappointed too. She had never relished the man he was, and it made him ashamed. That was why he had never gone away, lest he should make her ashamed among her own kind. He was her husband, he could not help that though he was sorry for it. But he could keep the offence where least was made of it. And there was a child – she had wanted a child; but even then he had blundered – begotten a cripple upon her. He blamed himself utterly, searched out the roots of his youth for the answer to that, until the neighbour woman flinched to hear him. But the Presence stayed.

He had never talked to his wife about the child. How should he? There was the fact – the advertisement of his incompetence. And she had never talked to him. That was the one blessed and unassailable memory; that she had spread silence like a balm over his hurt. In return for it he had never gone away. He had resisted her that he might save her from showing among her own kind how poor a man he was. With every word of this ran the fact of his love for her – as he had loved her, with all the stripes of clean and uncleanness. He bared himself as a child without knowing; and the Presence stayed. The talk trailed off at last to the commonplaces of consolation between the retchings of his spirit. The Presence lessened and streamed toward them on the wind of the garden. When it touched them like the warm air of noon that lies sometimes in hollow places after night-fall, the neighbour woman rose and went away.

The next night she did not wait for him. When a rod outside the town – it was a very little one – the burrowing owls *whoo-whooed*, she hung up her apron and went to talk with Emma Jeffries. The Presence was there, drawn in, lying close. She found the key between the wistaria and the first pillar of the porch, but as soon as she opened the door she felt the chill that might be expected by one in-truding on Emma Jeffries in her own house.

"'The Lord is my shepherd!' " said the neighbour woman; it was the first religious phrase that occurred to her; then she said the whole of the psalm, and after that a hymn. She had come in through the door and stood with her back to it and her hand upon the knob. Everything was just as Mrs. Jeffries had left it, with the waiting air of a room kept for company.

"Em," she said, boldly, when the chill had abated a little before the sacred words – "Em Jeffries, I've got something to say to you. And you've got to hear," she added with firmness as the white curtains stirred duskily at the window. "You wouldn't be talked to about your troubles when . . . you were here before, and we humoured you. But now there is Sim to be thought of. I guess you heard what you came for last night, and got good of it. Maybe it would have been bet-ter if Sim had said things all along instead of hoarding them in his heart, but any way he has said them now. And what I want to say is, if you was staying on with the hope of hearing it again, you'd be making a mistake. You was an uncommon woman, Emma Jeffries, and there didn't none of us understand you very well, nor do you justice maybe; but Sim is only a common man, and I understand him because I'm that way myself. And if you think he'll be opening his heart to you every night, or be any different from what he's always been on account of what's happened, that's a mistake, too . . . and in a little while, if you stay, it will be as bad as it always was . . . men are like that . . . you'd better go now while there's understanding between you." She stood staring into the darkling room that seemed suddenly full of turbulence and denial. It seemed to beat upon her and take her breath, but she held on.

"You've got to go . . . Em . . . and I'm going to stay until you do." She said this with finality, and then began again.

"'The Lord is nigh unto them that are of a broken heart,' " and repeated the passage to the end. Then as the Presence sank before it, "You better go, Emma," persuasively, and again, after an interval:

"'He shall deliver thee in six troubles, yea, in seven shall no evil touch thee.' "

. . .The Presence gathered itself and was still. She could make out that it stood over against the opposite corner by the gilt easel with the crayon portrait of the child.

. . . "'For thou shalt forget thy misery. Thou shalt remember it as waters that are past,'" concluded the neighbour woman, as she heard Jeffries on the gravel outside. What the Presence had wrought upon him in the night was visible in his altered mien. He looked more than anything else to be in need of sleep. He had eaten his sorrow, and that was the end of it – as it is with men.

"I came to see if there was anything I could do for you," said the woman, neighbourly, with her hand upon the door.

"I don't know as there is," said he; "I'm much obliged, but I don't know as there is."

"You see," whispered the woman over her shoulder, "not even to me." She felt the tug of her heart as the Presence swept past her.

The neighbour went out after that and walked in the ragged street, past the school-house, across the creek below the town, out by the fields, over the head-gate, and back by the town again. It was full nine of the clock when she passed the Jeffries house. It looked, except for being a little neater, not other than the rest of the street. The door was open and the lamp was lit; she saw Jeffries black against it. He sat reading in a book, like a man at ease in his own house.

THE STRANGER

Ambrose Bierce

Ambrose Bierce (1842–1914) was born the tenth of thirteen children in a log cabin in south-western Ohio. His family moved west, and Bierce worked on an anti-slavery newspaper, *The Northern Indianan*, while he was still at school. He saw active service in the Union Army during the American Civil War. Bierce had a distinguished, occasionally controversial, career as a journalist. He disappeared somewhere in Mexico on a tour of civil war battlefields. His final letter closed, 'I leave here tomorrow for an unknown destination.'

A man stepped out of the darkness into the little illuminated circle about our failing campfire and seated himself upon a rock.

"You are not the first to explore this region," he said, gravely.

Nobody controverted his statement; he was himself proof of its truth, for he was not of our party and must have been somewhere near when we camped. Moreover, he must have companions not far away; it was not a place where one would be living or travelling alone. For more than a week we had seen, besides ourselves and our animals, only such living things as rattlesnakes and horned toads. In an Arizona desert one does not long coexist with only such creatures as these: one must have pack animals, supplies, arms – "an outfit." And all these imply comrades. It was perhaps a doubt as to what manner of men this unceremonious stranger's comrades might be, together with something in his words interpretable as a challenge, that caused every man of our half-dozen "gentlemen adventurers" to rise to a sitting posture and lay his hand upon a weapon – an act signifying, in that time and place, a policy of expectation. The stranger gave the matter no attention and began again to speak in the same deliberate, uninflected monotone in which he had delivered his first sentence: "Thirty years ago Ramon Gallegos, William Shaw, George W. Kent and Berry Davis, all of Tucson, crossed the Santa Catalina mountains and travelled due west, as nearly as the configuration of the country permitted. We were prospecting and it was our intention, if we found nothing, to push through to the Gila river at some point near Big Bend, where we understood there was a settlement. We had a good outfit but no guide – just Ramon Gallegos, William Shaw, George W. Kent and Berry Davis."

The man repeated the names slowly and distinctly, as if to fix them in the memories of his audience, every member of which was now attentively observing him, but with a slackened apprehension regarding his possible companions somewhere in the darkness that seemed to enclose us like a black wall; in the manner of this volunteer historian was no suggestion of an unfriendly purpose. His act was rather that of a harmless lunatic than an enemy. We were not so new to the country as not to know that the solitary life of many a plainsman had a tendency to develop eccentricities of conduct and character not always easily distinguishable from mental aberration. A man is like a tree: in a forest of his fellows he will grow as straight as his generic and individual nature permits; alone in the open, he yields to the deforming stresses and torsions that environ him. Some such thoughts were in my mind as I watched the man from the shadow of my hat, pulled low to shut out the firelight. A witless fellow, no doubt, but what could he be doing there in the heart of a desert?

Having undertaken to tell this story, I wish that I could describe the man's appearance; that would be a natural thing to do. Unfortunately, and somewhat strangely, I find myself unable to do so with any degree of confidence, for afterward no two of us agreed as to what he wore and how he looked; and when I try to set down my own impressions they elude me. Anyone can tell some kind of story; narration is one of the elemental powers of the race. But the talent for description is a gift.

Nobody having broken silence the visitor went on to say: "This country was not then what it is now. There was not a ranch between the Gila and the Gulf. There was a little game here and there in the mountains, and near the infrequent waterholes grass enough to keep our animals from starvation. If we should be so fortunate as to encounter no Indians we might get through. But within a week the purpose of the expedition had altered from discovery of wealth to preservation of life. We had gone too far to go back, for what was ahead could be no worse than what was behind; so we pushed on, riding by night to avoid Indians and the intolerable heat, and concealing ourselves by day as best we could. Sometimes, having exhausted our supply of wild meat and emptied our casks, we were days without food or drink; then a water-hole or a shallow pool in the bottom of an arroyo so restored our strength and sanity that we were able to shoot some of the wild animals that sought it also. Sometimes it was a bear, sometimes an antelope, a coyote, a cougar – that was as God pleased; all were food.

"One morning as we skirted a mountain range, seeking a practicable pass, we were attacked by a band of Apaches who had followed our trail up a gulch – it is not far from here. Knowing that they outnumbered us ten to one, they took none of their usual cowardly precautions, but dashed upon us at a gallop, firing and yelling. Fighting was out of the question: we urged our feeble animals up the gulch as far as there was footing for a hoof, then threw ourselves out of our saddles and took to the chaparral on one of the slopes, abandoning our entire outfit to the enemy. But we retained our rifles, every man – Ramon Gallegos, William Shaw, George W. Kent and Berry Davis."

"Same old crowd," said the humorist of our party. He was an Eastern man, unfamiliar with the decent observances of social intercourse. A gesture of disapproval from our leader silenced him and the stranger proceeded with his tale.

"The savages dismounted also, and some of them ran up the gulch beyond the point at which we had left it, cutting off further retreat in that direction and forcing us on up the side. Unfortunately the chaparral extended only a short distance up the slope, and as we came into the open ground above we took the fire of a dozen rifles; but Apaches shoot badly when in a hurry, and God so willed it that none of us fell. Twenty yards up the slope, beyond the edge of the brush, were vertical cliffs, in which, directly in front of us, was a narrow opening. Into that we ran, finding ourselves in a cavern about as large as an ordinary room in a house. Here for a time we were safe: a single man with a repeating rifle could defend the entrance against all the Apaches in the land. But against hunger and thirst we had no defence. Courage we still had, but hope was a memory.

"Not one of those Indians did we afterward see, but by the smoke and glare of their fires in the gulch we knew that by day and by night they watched with ready rifles in the edge of the bush – knew that if we made a sortie not a man of us would live to take three steps into the open. For three days, watching in turn, we held out before our suffering became insupportable. Then – it was the morning of the fourth day – Ramon Gallegos said: "'Señores, I know not well of the good God and what please him. I have live without religion, and I am not acquaint with that of you. Pardon, señores, if I shock you, but for me the time is come to beat the game of the Apache.'

"He knelt upon the rock floor of the cave and pressed his pistol against his temple. "Madre de Dios," he said, "comes now the soul of Ramon Gallegos."

"And so he left us – William Shaw, George W. Kent and Berry Davis.

"I was the leader: it was for me to speak.

"'He was a brave man,' I said – "he knew when to die, and how. It is foolish to go mad from thirst and fall by Apache bullets, or be skinned alive – it is in bad taste. Let us join Ramon Gallegos.'

"'That is right,' said William Shaw.

"'That is right,' said George W. Kent.

"I straightened the limbs of Ramon Gallegos and put a handkerchief over his face. Then William Shaw said: "I should like to look like that – a little while."

"And George W. Kent said that he felt that way, too.

"'It shall be so,' I said: "the red devils will wait a week. William Shaw and George W. Kent, draw and kneel."

"They did so and I stood before them.

"'Almighty God, our Father,' said I.

"'Almighty God, our Father,' said William Shaw.

"'Almighty God, our Father,' said George W. Kent.

"'Forgive us our sins,' said I.

"'Forgive us our sins,' said they.

"'And receive our souls.'

"'And receive our souls'

"'Amen!'

"'Amen!'

"I laid them beside Ramon Gallegos and covered their faces."

There was a quick commotion on the opposite side of the campfire: one of our party had sprung to his feet, pistol in hand.

"And you!" he shouted – "*You* dared to escape? – You dare to be alive? You cowardly hound, I'll send you to join them if I hang for it!"

But with the leap of a panther the captain was upon him, grasping his wrist. "Hold it in, Sam Yountsey, hold it in!"

We were now all upon our feet – except the stranger, who sat motionless and apparently inattentive. Someone seized Yountsey's other arm.

"Captain," I said, "there is something wrong here. This fellow is either a lunatic or merely a liar – just a plain, everyday liar whom Yountsey has no call to kill. If this man was of that party it had five members, one of whom – probably himself – he has not named."

"Yes," said the captain, releasing the insurgent, who sat down, "there is something – unusual. Years ago four dead bodies of white men, scalped and shamefully mutilated, were found about the mouth of that cave. They are buried there; I have seen the graves – we shall all see them tomorrow."

The stranger rose, standing tall in the light of the expiring fire, which in our breathless attention to his story we had neglected to keep going.

"There were four," he said – "Ramon Gallegos, William Shaw, George W. Kent and Berry Davis."

With this reiterated roll-call of the dead he walked into the darkness and we saw him no more.

At that moment one of our party, who had been on guard, strode in among us, rifle in hand and somewhat excited.

"Captain," he said, "for the last half-hour three men have been standing out there on the *mesa*." He pointed in the direction taken by the stranger. "I could see them distinctly, for the moon is up, but as they had no guns and I had them covered with mine I thought it was their move. They have made none, but, damn it! they have got on to my nerves."

"Go back to your post, and stay till you see them again," said the captain. "The rest of you lie down again, or I'll kick you all into the fire."

The sentinel obediently withdrew, swearing, and did not return. As we were arranging our blankets the fiery Yountsey said: "I beg your pardon, Captain, but who the devil do you take them to be?"

"Ramon Gallegos, William Shaw and George W. Kent."

"But how about Berry Davis? I ought to have shot him."

"Quite needless; you couldn't have made him any deader. Go to sleep.

THE ROCKER

Oliver Onions

Oliver Onions (1873–1961) was born in Bradford. He was a gifted illustrator who worked as a commercial artist during the Boer War and illustrated his early novels himself. Onions was married to the romantic novelist Berta Ruck, who found his name distasteful. In 1918 he changed it by deed poll to George Oliver, but continued to be published under his original name. His horror novella, *The Beckoning Fair One*, is considered a classic of the genre.

1

There was little need for the swart gipsies to explain, as they stood knee-deep in the snow round the bailiff of the Abbey Farm, what it was that had sent them. The unbroken whiteness of the uplands told that, and, even as they spoke, there came up the hill the dark figures of the farm men with shovels, on their way to dig out the sheep. In the summer, the bailiff would have been the first to call the gipsies vagabonds and roost-robbers; now . . . they had women with them too.

"The hares and foxes were down four days ago, and the liquid-manure pump's like a snowman," the bailiff said . . . "Yes, you can lie in the laithes and welcome – if you can find 'em. Maybe you'll help us find our sheep too – "

The gipsies had done so. Coming back again, they had had some ado to discover the spot where their three caravans made a hummock of white against a broken wall.

The women – they had four women with them – began that afternoon to weave the mats and baskets they hawked from door to door; and in the forenoon of the following day one of them, the black-haired, soft-voiced quean whom the bailiff had heard called Annabel, set her babe in the sling on her back, tucked a bundle of long cane-loops under her oxter, and trudged down between eight-foot walls of snow to the Abbey Farm. She stood in the latticed porch, dark and handsome against the whiteness, and then, advancing, put her head into the great hall-kitchen.

"Has the lady any chairs for the gipsy woman to mend?" she asked in a soft and insinuating voice . . .

They brought her the old chairs; she seated herself on a box in the porch; and there she wove the strips of cane in and out, securing each one with a little wooden peg and a tap of her hammer. The child remained in the sling at her back, taking the breast from time to time over her shoulder; and the silver wedding ring could be seen as she whipped the cane, back and forth.

As she worked, she cast curious glances into the old hall-kitchen. The snow outside cast a pallid, upward light on the heavy ceiling-beams; this was reflected in the polished stone floor; and the children, who at first had shyly stopped their play, seeing the strange woman in the porch – the nearest thing they had seen to gipsies before had been the old itinerant glazier with his frame of glass on his back – resumed it, but still eyed her from time to time. In the ancient walnut chair by the hearth sat the old, old lady who had told them to bring the chairs. Her hair, almost as white as the snow itself, was piled up on her head *à la Marquise*; she was knitting; but now and then she allowed the needle in the little wooden sheath at her waist to lie idle, closed her eyes, and rocked softly in the old walnut chair.

"Ask the woman who is mending the chairs whether she is warm enough there," the old lady said to one of the children; and the child went to the porch with the message.

"Thank you, little missie – thank you, lady dear – Annabel is quite warm," said the soft voice; and the child returned to the play.

It was a childish game of funerals at which the children played. The hand of Death, hovering over the dolls, had singled out Flora, the articulations of whose sawdust body were seams and whose boots were painted on her calves of fibrous plaster. For the greater solemnity, the children had made themselves sweeping trains of the garments of their elders, and those with cropped curls had draped their heads with shawls, the fringes of which they had combed out with their fingers to simulate hair – long hair, such as Sabrina, the eldest, had hanging so low down her back that she could almost sit on it. A cylindrical-bodied horse, convertible (when his flat head came out of its socket) into a locomotive, headed the sad *cortège*; then came the defunct Flora; then came Jack, the raffish sailor doll, with other dolls; and the children followed with hushed whisperings.

The youngest of the children passed the high-backed walnut chair in which the old lady sat. She stopped.

"Aunt Rachel – " she whispered, slowly and gravely opening very wide and closing very tight her eyes.

"Yes, dear?"

"Flora's dead!"

The old lady, when she smiled, did so less with her lips than with her faded cheeks. So sweet was her face that you could not help wondering, when you looked on it, how many men had also looked upon it and loved it. Somehow, you never wondered how many of them had been loved in return.

"I'm so sorry, dear," Aunt Rachel, who in reality was a great-aunt, said. "What did she die of this time?"

"She died of . . . Brown Titus . . . 'n now she's going to be buried in a grave as little as her bed."

"In a what, dear?"

"As little . . . dread . . . as little as my bed . . . you say it, Sabrina."

"She means, Aunt Rachel,

> Teach me to live that I may dread
> The Grave as little as my bed

Sabrina, the eldest, interpreted.

"Ah! . . . But won't you play at cheerful things, dears?"

"Yes, we will, presently, Aunt Rachel; gee up, horse! . . . Shall we go and ask the chair-woman if she's warm enough?"

"Do, dears."

Again the message was taken, and this time it seemed as if Annabel, the gipsy, was not warm enough, for she gathered up her loops of cane and brought the chair she was mending a little way into the hall-kitchen itself. She sat down on the square box they used to cover the sewing machine.

"Thank you, lady dear," she murmured, lifting her handsome almond eyes to Aunt Rachel. Aunt Rachel did not see the long, furtive, curious glance. Her own eyes were closed, as if she was tired; her cheeks were smiling; one of them had dropped a little to one shoulder, as it might have dropped had she held in her arms a babe; and she was rocking, softly, slowly, the rocker of the chair making a little regular noise on the polished floor.

The gipsy woman beckoned to one of the children.

"Tell the lady, when she wakes, that I will tack a strip of felt to the rocker, and then it will make no noise at all," said the low and wheedling voice; and the child retired again.

The interment of Flora proceeded . . .

An hour later Flora had taken up the burden of Life again. It was as Angela, the youngest, was chastising her for some offence, that Sabrina, the eldest, looked with wondering eyes on the babe in the gipsy's sling. She approached on tiptoe.

"May I look at it, please?" she asked timidly.

The gipsy set one shoulder forward, and Sabrina put the shawl gently aside, peering at the dusky brown morsel within.

"Sometime, perhaps – if I'm very careful – " Sabrina ventured diffidently, " – if I'm *very* careful – may I hold it?"

Before replying, the gipsy once more turned her almond eyes towards Aunt Rachel's chair. Aunt Rachel had been awakened for the conclusion of Flora's funeral, but her eyes were closed again now, and once more her cheek was dropped in that tender suggestive little gesture, and she rocked. But you could see that she was not properly asleep . . . It was, somehow, less to Sabrina, still peering at the babe in the sling, than to Aunt Rachel, apparently asleep, that the gipsy seemed to reply.

"You'll know some day, little missis, that a wean knows its own pair of arms," her seductive voice came.

And Aunt Rachel heard. She opened her eyes with a start. The little regular noise of the rocker ceased. She turned her head quickly; tremulously she began to knit again; and, as her eyes rested on the sidelong eyes of the gipsy woman, there was an expression in them that almost resembled fright.

2

They began to deck the great hall-kitchen for Christmas, but the snow still lay thick over hill and valley, and the gipsies' caravans remained by the broken wall where the drifts had overtaken them. Though all the chairs were mended, Annabel still came daily to the farm, sat on the box they used to cover the sewing machine, and wove mats. As she wove them, Aunt Rachel knitted, and from time to time fragments of talk passed between the two women. It was always the white-haired lady who spoke first, and Annabel made all sorts of salutes and obeisances with her eyes before replying.

"I have not seen your husband," Aunt Rachel said to Annabel one day. (The children at the other end of the apartment had converted a chest into an altar, and were solemnising the nuptials of the resurrected Flora and Jack, the raffish sailor-doll.)

Annabel made roving play with her eyes. "He is up at the caravans, lady dear," she replied. "Is there anything Annabel can bid him do?"

"Nothing, thank you," said Aunt Rachel.

For a minute the gipsy watched Aunt Rachel, and then she got up from the sewing machine box and crossed the floor. She leaned so close towards her that she had to put up a hand to steady the babe at her back.

"Lady dear," she murmured with irresistible softness, "your husband died, didn't he?"

On Aunt Rachel's finger was a ring, but it was not a wedding ring. It was a hoop of pearls.

"I have never had a husband," she said.

The gipsy glanced at the ring. "Then that is – ?"

"That is a betrothal ring," Aunt Rachel replied.

"Ah! . . ." said Annabel.

Then, after a minute, she drew still closer. Her eyes were fixed on Aunt Rachel's, and the insinuating voice was very low.

"Ah! . . . And did *it* die too, lady dear?"

Again came that quick, half-affrighted look into Aunt Rachel's face. Her eyes avoided those of the gipsy, sought them, and avoided them again.

"Did what die?" she asked slowly and guardedly . . .

The child at the gipsy's back did not need suck; nevertheless, Annabel's fingers worked at her bosom, and she moved the sling. As the child settled, Annabel gave Aunt Rachel a long look.

"Why do you rock?" she asked slowly.

Aunt Rachel was trembling. She did not reply. In a voice soft as sliding water the gipsy continued.

"Lady dear, we are a strange folk to you, and even among us there are those who shuffle the pack of cards and read the palm when silver has been put upon it, knowing nothing . . . But some of us *see* – some of us *see*."

It was more than a minute before Aunt Rachel spoke.

"You are a woman, and you have your babe at your breast now . . . Every woman sees the thing you speak of."

But the gipsy shook her head. "You speak of seeing with the heart. I speak of eyes – these eyes."

Again came a long pause. Aunt Rachel had given a little start, but had become quiet again. When at last she spoke it was in a voice scarcely audible.

"That cannot be. I know what you mean, but it cannot be . . . He died on the eve of his wedding. For my bridal clothes they made me black garments instead. It is long ago, and now I wear neither black nor white, but – " her hands made a gesture. Aunt Rachel always dressed as if to suit a sorrow that Time had deprived of bitterness, in such a tender and fleecy grey as one sees in the mists that lie like lawn over hedgerow and copse early of a midsummer's morning. "Therefore," she resumed, "your heart may see, but your eyes cannot see that which never was."

But there came a sudden note of masterfulness into the gipsy's voice.

"With my eyes – *these* eyes," she repeated, pointing to them.

Aunt Rachel kept her own eyes obstinately on her knitting needles. "None except I have seen it. It is not to be seen," she said.

The gipsy sat suddenly erect.

"It is not so. Keep still in your chair," she ordered, "and I will tell you when – "

It was a curious thing that followed. As if all the will went out of her, Aunt Rachel sat very still; and presently her hands fluttered and dropped. The gipsy sat with her own hands folded over the mat on her knees. Several minutes passed; then, slowly, once more that sweetest of smiles stole over Aunt Rachel's cheeks. Once more her head dropped. Her hands moved. Noiselessly on the rockers that the gipsy had padded with felt the chair began to rock. Annabel lifted one hand.

"*Dovo se li*" she said. "It is there."

Aunt Rachel did not appear to hear her. With that ineffable smile still on her face, she rocked . . .

Then, after some minutes, there crossed her face such a look as visits the face of one who, waking from sleep, strains his faculties to recapture some blissful and vanishing vision . . .

"*Jal* – it is gone," said the gipsy woman.

Aunt Rachel opened her eyes again. She repeated dully after Annabel: "It is gone."

"Ghosts," the gipsy whispered presently, "are of the dead. Therefore it must have lived."

But again Aunt Rachel shook her head. "It never lived."

"You were young, and beautiful? . . . "

Still the shake of the head. "He died on the eve of his wedding. They took my white garments away and gave me black ones. How then could it have lived?"

"Without the kiss, no . . . But sometimes a woman will lie through her life, and at the graveside still will lie . . . Tell me the truth."

But they were the same words that Aunt Rachel repeated: "He died on the eve of his wedding; they took away my wedding garments . . . " From her lips a lie could hardly issue. The gipsy"s face became grave . . .

She broke another long silence.

"I believe," she said at last. "It is a new kind – but no more wonderful than the other. The other I have seen, now I have seen this also. Tell me, does it come to any other chair?"

"It was his chair; he died in it," said Aunt Rachel.

"And you – shall you die in it?"

"As God wills."

"Has . . . *other life* . . . visited it long?"

"Many years; but it is always small; it never grows."

"To their mothers babes never grow. They remain ever babes . . . None other has ever seen it?"

"Except yourself, none. I sit here; presently it creeps into my arms; it is small and warm; I rock, and then . . . it goes."

"Would it come to another chair?"

"I cannot tell. I think not. It was his chair."

Annabel mused. At the other end of the room Flora was now bestowed on Jack, the disreputable sailor. The gipsy's eyes rested on the bridal party . . .

"Yet another might see it – "

"None has."

"No; but yet . . . The door does not always shut behind us suddenly. Perhaps one who has toddled but a step or two over the threshold might, by looking back, catch a glimpse . . . What is the name of the smallest one?"

"Angela."

"That means 'angel' . . . Look, the doll who died yesterday is now being married . . . It may be that Life has not yet sealed the little one's eyes. Will you let Annabel ask her if she sees what it is you hold in your arms?"

Again the voice was soft and wheedling . . .

"No, Annabel," said Aunt Rachel faintly.

"Will you rock again?"

Aunt Rachel made no reply.

"Rock . . . " urged the cajoling voice.

But Aunt Rachel only turned the betrothal ring on her finger. Over at the altar Jack was leering at his new-made bride, past decency; and little Angela held the wooden horse's head, which had parted from its body.

"Rock, and comfort yourself – " tempted the voice.

Then slowly Aunt Rachel rose from her chair.

"No, Annabel," she said gently. "You should not have spoken. When the snow melts you will go, and come no more; why then did you speak? It was mine. It was not meant to be seen by another. I no longer want it. Please go."

The swarthy woman turned her almond eyes on her once more.

"You cannot live without it," she said as she also rose . . .

And as Jack and his bride left the church on the reheaded horse, Aunt Rachel walked with hanging head from the apartment.

3

Thenceforward, as day followed day, Aunt Rachel rocked no more; and with the packing and partial melting of the snow the gipsies up at the caravans judged it time to be off about their business. It was on the morning of Christmas Eve that they came down in a body to the Abbey Farm to express their thanks to those who had befriended them; but the bailiff was not there. He and the farm men had ceased work, and were down at the church, practising the carols. Only Aunt Rachel sat, still and knitting, in the black walnut chair; and the children played on the floor.

A night in the toy-box had apparently bred discontent between Jack and Flora – or perhaps they sought to keep their countenances before the world; at any rate, they sat on opposite sides of the room, Jack keeping boon company with the lead soldiers, his spouse reposing, her lead-balanced eyes closed, in the broken clockwork motor-car. With the air of performing some vaguely momentous ritual, the children were kissing one another beneath the bunch of mistletoe that hung from the centre beam. In the intervals of kissing they told one another in whispers that Aunt Rachel was not very well, and Angela woke Flora to tell her that Aunt Rachel had Brown Titus also.

"Stay you here; I will give the lady dear our thanks," said Annabel to the group of gipsies gathered about the porch; and she entered the great hall-kitchen. She approached the chair in which Aunt Rachel sat.

There was obeisance in the bend of her body, but command in her long almond eyes, as she spoke.

"Lady dear, you must rock or you cannot live."

Aunt Rachel did not look up from her work.

"Rocking, I should not live long," she replied.

"We are leaving you."

"All leave me."

"Annabel fears she has taken away your comfort."

"Only for a little while. The door closes behind us, but it opens again."

"But for that little time, rock – "

Aunt Rachel shook her head.

"No. It is finished. Another has seen . . . Say goodbye to your companions; they are very welcome to what they have had; and God speed you."

"They thank you, lady dear . . . Will you not forget that Annabel saw, and rock?"

"No more."

Annabel stooped and kissed the hand that bore the betrothal hoop of pearls. The other hand Aunt Rachel placed for a moment upon the smoky head of the babe in the sling. It trembled as it rested there, but the tremor passed, and Annabel, turning once at the porch, gave her a last look. Then she departed with her companions.

That afternoon, Jack and Flora had shaken down to wedlock as married folk should, and sat together before the board spread with the dolls' tea-things. The pallid light in the great hall-kitchen faded; the candles were lighted; and then the children, first borrowing the stockings of their elders to hang at the bed's foot, were packed off early – for it was the custom to bring them down again at midnight for the carols. Aunt Rachel had their good-night kisses, not as she had them every night, but with the special ceremony of the mistletoe.

Other folk, grown folk, sat with Aunt Rachel that evening; but the old walnut chair did not move upon its rockers. There was merry talk, but Aunt Rachel took no part in it. The board was spread with ale and cheese and spiced loaf for the carol-singers; and the time drew near for their coming.

When at midnight, faintly on the air from the church below, there came the chiming of Christmas morning, all bestirred themselves.

"They'll be here in a few minutes," they said; "somebody go and bring the children down;" and within a very little while subdued noises were heard outside, and the lifting of the latch of the yard gate. The children were in their nightgowns, hardly fully awake; a low voice outside was heard giving orders; and then there arose on the night the carol.

"Hush!" they said to the wondering children; "listen! . . . "

It was the Cherry Tree Carol that rose outside, of how sweet Mary, the Queen of Galilee, besought Joseph to pluck the cherries for her Babe, and Joseph refused; and the voices of the singers, that had begun hesitatingly, grew strong and loud and free.

" . . . and Joseph wouldn't pluck the cherries," somebody was whispering to the tiny Angela . . .

> Mary said to Cherry Tree,
> "Bow down to my knee,
> That I may pluck cherries
> For my Babe and me."

the carollers sang; and "Now listen, darling", the one who held Angela murmured . . .

> The uppermost spray then
> Bowed down to her knee;
> "Thus you may see, Joseph,
> These cherries are for me."

> "O, eat your cherries, Mary,
> Give them your Babe now;
> O, eat your cherries, Mary,
> That grew upon the bough."

The little Angela, within the arms that held her, murmured, "It's the gipsies, isn't it, mother?"

"No, darling. The gipsies have gone. It's the carol-singers, singing because Jesus was born."

"But, mother . . . it *is* the gipsies, isn't it? . . . 'Cos look . . . "

"Look where?"

"At Aunt Rachel, mother . . . The gipsy woman wouldn't go without her little baby, would she?"

"No, she wouldn't do that."

"Then has she *lent* it to Aunt Rachel, like I lend my new toys sometimes?"

The mother glanced across at Aunt Rachel, and then gathered the night-gowned figure more closely.

"The darling's only half awake," she murmured . . . "Poor Aunt Rachel's sleepy too . . . "

Aunt Rachel, her head dropped, her hands lightly folded as if about some shape that none saw but herself, her face again ineffable with that sweet and peaceful smile, was once more rocking softly in her chair.

THE DOLL'S GHOST

F. Marion Crawford

Francis Marion Crawford (1854–1909) was born in Italy to American
parents. His father, a sculptor, died when Crawford was three years old
and his mother later remarried a painter. Crawford was an accomplished
linguist who mastered twenty languages and studied Sanskrit in India.
He died as a result of lung injuries incurred while undertaking research
into glass smelting for a novel

It was a terrible accident, and for one moment the splendid machinery of
Cranston House got out of gear and stood still. The butler emerged from the
retirement in which he spent his elegant leisure, two grooms of the chambers
appeared simultaneously from opposite directions, there were actually housemaids on the grand staircase, and those who remember the facts most exactly
assert that Mrs Pringle herself positively stood upon the landing. Mrs Pringle
was the housekeeper. As for the head nurse, the under nurse, and the nursery
maid, their feelings cannot be described. The head nurse laid one hand upon the
polished marble balustrade and stared stupidly before her, the under nurse stood
rigid and pale, leaning against the polished marble wall, and the nursery-maid
collapsed and sat down upon the polished marble step, just beyond the limits of
the velvet carpet, and frankly burst into tears.

The Lady Gwendolen Lancaster-Douglas-Scroop, youngest daughter of the
ninth Duke of Cranston, and aged six years and three months, picked herself up
quite alone, and sat down on the third step from the foot of the grand staircase
in Cranston House.

"Oh!" ejaculated the butler, and he disappeared again.

"Ah!" responded the grooms of the chambers, as they also went away.

"It's only that doll," Mrs Pringle was distinctly heard to say, in a tone of contempt.

The under nurse heard her say it. Then the three nurses gathered round Lady
Gwendolen and patted her, and gave her unhealthy things out of their pockets,
and hurried her out of Cranston House as fast as they could, lest it should be
found out upstairs that they had allowed the Lady Gwendolen Lancaster-Douglas-Scroop to tumble down the grand staircase with her doll in her arms. And as
the doll was badly broken, the nursery-maid carried it, with the pieces, wrapped
up in Lady Gwendolen's little cloak. It was not far to Hyde Park, and when they
had reached a quiet place they took means to find out that Lady Gwendolen
had no bruises. For the carpet was very thick and soft, and there was thick stuff
under it to make it softer.

Lady Gwendolen Douglas-Scroop sometimes yelled, but she never cried. It was because she had yelled that the nurse had allowed her to go downstairs alone with Nina, the doll, under one arm, while she steadied herself with her other hand on the balustrade, and trod upon the polished marble steps beyond the edge of the carpet. So she had fallen, and Nina had come to grief.

When the nurses were quite sure that she was not hurt, they unwrapped the doll and looked at her in her turn. She had been a very beautiful doll, very large, and fair, and healthy, with real yellow hair, and eyelids that would open and shut over very grown-up dark eyes. Moreover, when you moved her right arm up and down she said "Pa-pa," and when you moved the left she said "Ma-ma," very distinctly.

"I heard her say 'Pa' when she fell," said the under nurse, who heard everything. "But she ought to have said 'Pa-pa.'"

"That's because her arm went up when she hit the step," said the head nurse. "She'll say the other 'Pa' when I put it down again."

"Pa," said Nina, as her right arm was pushed down, and speaking through her broken face. It was cracked right across, from the upper corner of the forehead, with a hideous gash, through the nose and down to the little frilled collar of the pale green silk Mother Hubbard frock, and two little three-cornered pieces of porcelain had fallen out.

"I'm sure it's a wonder she can speak at all, being all smashed," said the under nurse.

"You'll have to take her to Mr Puckler," said her superior. "It's not far, and you'd better go at once."

Lady Gwendolen was occupied in digging a hole in the ground with a little spade, and paid no attention to the nurses.

"What are you doing?" enquired the nursery-maid, looking on.

"Nina's dead, and I'm diggin' her a grave," replied her ladyship thoughtfully.

"Oh, she'll come to life again all right," said the nursery-maid.

The under nurse wrapped Nina up again and departed. Fortunately a kind soldier, with very long legs and a very small cap, happened to be there; and as he had nothing to do, he offered to see the under nurse safely to Mr Puckler's and back.

Mr Bernard Puckler and his little daughter lived in a little house in a little alley, which led out off a quiet little street not very far from Belgrave Square. He was the great doll doctor, and his extensive practice lay in the most aristocratic quarter. He mended dolls of all sizes and ages, boy dolls and girl dolls, baby dolls in long clothes, and grown-up dolls in fashionable gowns, talking dolls and dumb dolls, those that shut their eyes when they lay down, and those whose eyes had to be shut for them by means of a mysterious wire. His daughter Else was only just over twelve years old, but she was already very clever at mending dolls' clothes, and at doing their hair, which is harder than you might think, though the dolls sit quite still while it is being done.

Mr Puckler had originally been a German, but he had dissolved his nationality in the ocean of London many years ago, like a great many foreigners. He still had one or two German friends, however, who came on Saturday evenings, and smoked with him and played picquet or "skat" with him for farthing points, and called him "Herr Doctor," which seemed to please Mr Puckler very much.

He looked older than he was, for his beard was rather long and ragged, his hair was grizzled and thin, and he wore horn-rimmed spectacles. As for Else, she was a thin, pale child, very quiet and neat, with dark eyes and brown hair that was plaited down her back and tied with a bit of black ribbon. She mended the dolls' clothes and took the dolls back to their homes when they were quite strong again.

The house was a little one, but too big for the two people who lived in it. There was a small sitting-room on the street, and the workshop was at the back, and there were three rooms upstairs. But the father and daughter lived most of their time in the workshop, because they were generally at work, even in the evenings.

Mr Puckler laid Nina on the table and looked at her a long time, till the tears began to fill his eyes behind the horn-rimmed spectacles. He was a very susceptible man, and he often fell in love with the dolls he mended, and found it hard to part with them when they had smiled at him for a few days. They were real little people to him, with characters and thoughts and feelings of their own, and he was very tender with them all. But some attracted him especially from the first, and when they were brought to him maimed and injured, their state seemed so pitiful to him that the tears came easily. You must remember that he had lived among dolls during a great part of his life, and understood them.

"How do you know that they feel nothing?" he went on to say to Else. "You must be gentle with them. It costs nothing to be kind to the little beings, and perhaps it makes a difference to them."

And Else understood him, because she was a child, and she knew that she was more to him than all the dolls.

He fell in love with Nina at first sight, perhaps because her beautiful brown glass eyes were something like Else's own, and he loved Else first and best, with all his heart. And, besides, it was a very sorrowful case. Nina had evidently not been long in the world, for her complexion was perfect, her hair was smooth where it should be smooth, and curly where it should be curly, and her silk clothes were perfectly new. But across her face was that frightful gash, like a sabre-cut, deep and shadowy within, but clean and sharp at the edges. When he tenderly pressed her head to close the gaping wound, the edges made a fine grating sound, that was painful to hear, and the lids of the dark eyes quivered and trembled as though Nina were suffering dreadfully.

"Poor Nina!" he exclaimed sorrowfully. "But I shall not hurt you much, though you will take a long time to get strong."

He always asked the names of the broken dolls when they were brought to him, and sometimes the people knew what the children called them, and told him. He liked "Nina" for a name. Altogether and in every way she pleased him more than any doll he had seen for many years, and he felt drawn to her, and made up his mind to make her perfectly strong and sound, no matter how much labour it might cost him.

Mr Puckler worked patiently a little at a time, and Else watched him. She could do nothing for poor Nina, whose clothes needed no mending. The longer the doll doctor worked, the more fond he became of the yellow hair and the beautiful brown glass eyes. He sometimes forgot all the other dolls that were waiting to be mended, lying side by side on a shelf, and sat for an hour gazing at Nina's face, while he racked his ingenuity for some new invention by which to hide even the smallest trace of the terrible accident.

She was wonderfully mended. Even he was obliged to admit that; but the scar was still visible to his keen eyes, a very fine line right across the face, downwards from right to left. Yet all the conditions had been most favourable for a cure, since the cement had set quite hard at the first attempt and the weather had been fine and dry, which makes a great difference in a dolls' hospital.

At last he knew that he could do no more, and the under nurse had already come twice to see whether the job was finished, as she coarsely expressed it.

"Nina is not quite strong yet," Mr Puckler had answered each time, for he could not make up his mind to face the parting.

And now he sat before the square deal table at which he worked, and Nina lay before him for the last time with a big brown paper box beside her. It stood there like her coffin, waiting for her, he thought. He must put her into it, and lay tissue paper over her dear face, and then put on the lid, and at the thought of tying the string his sight was dim with tears again. He was never to look into the glassy depths of the beautiful brown eyes any more, nor to hear the little wooden voice say "Pa-pa" and "Ma-ma." It was a very painful moment.

In the vain hope of gaining time before the separation, he took up the little sticky bottles of cement and glue and gum and colour, looking at each one in turn, and then at Nina's face. And all his small tools lay there, neatly arranged in a row, but he knew that he could not use them again for Nina. She was quite strong at last, and in a country where there should be no cruel children to hurt her she might live a hundred years, with only that almost imperceptible line across her face to tell of the fearful thing that had befallen her on the marble steps of Cranston House.

Suddenly Mr Puckler's heart was quite full, and he rose abruptly from his seat and turned away.

"Else," he said unsteadily, "you must do it for me. I cannot bear to see her go into the box."

So he went and stood at the window with his back turned, while Else did what he had not the heart to do.

"Is it done?" he asked, not turning round. "Then take her away, my dear. Put on your hat, and take her to Cranston House quickly, and when you are gone I will turn round."

Else was used to her father's queer ways with the dolls, and though she had never seen him so much moved by a parting, she was not much surprised.

"Come back quickly," he said, when he heard her hand on the latch. "It is growing late, and I should not send you at this hour. But I cannot bear to look forward to it any more."

When Else was gone, he left the window and sat down in his place before the table again, to wait for the child to come back. He touched the place where Nina had lain, very gently, and he recalled the softly tinted pink face, and the glass eyes, and the ringlets of yellow hair, till he could almost see them.

The evenings were long, for it was late in the spring. But it began to grow dark soon, and Mr Puckler wondered why Else did not come back. She had been gone an hour and a half, and that was much longer than he had expected, for it was barely half a mile from Belgrave Square to Cranston House. He reflected that the child might have been kept waiting, but as the twilight deepened he grew anxious, and walked up and down in the dim workshop, no longer thinking of Nina, but of Else, his own living child, whom he loved.

An undefinable, disquieting sensation came upon him by fine degrees, a chilliness and a faint stirring of his thin hair, joined with a wish to be in any company rather than to be alone much longer. It was the beginning of fear.

He told himself in strong German-English that he was a foolish old man, and he began to feel about for the matches in the dusk. He knew just where they should be, for he always kept them in the same place, close to the little tin box that held bits of sealing-wax of various colours, for some kinds of mending. But somehow he could not find the matches in the gloom.

Something had happened to Else, he was sure, and as his fear increased, he felt as though it might be allayed if he could get a light and see what time it was. Then he called himself a foolish old man again, and the sound of his own voice startled him in the dark. He could not find the matches.

The window was grey still; he might see what time it was if he went close to it, and he could go and get matches out of the cupboard afterwards. He stood back from the table, to get out of the way of the chair, and began to cross the board floor.

Something was following him in the dark. There was a small pattering, as of tiny feet upon the boards. He stopped and listened, and the roots of his hair tingled. It was nothing, and he was a foolish old man. He made two steps more, and he was sure that he heard the little pattering again. He turned his back to the window, leaning against the sash so that the panes began to crack, and he faced the dark. Everything was quite still, and it smelt of paste and cement and wood-filings as usual.

"Is that you, Else?" he asked, and he was surprised by the fear in his voice.

There was no answer in the room, and he held up his watch and tried to make out what time it was by the grey dusk that was just not darkness. So far as he could see, it was within two or three minutes of ten o'clock. He had been a long time alone. He was shocked, and frightened for Else, out in London, so late, and he almost ran across the room to the door. As he fumbled for the latch, he distinctly heard the running of the little feet after him.

"Mice!" he exclaimed feebly, just as he got the door open.

He shut it quickly behind him, and felt as though some cold thing had settled on his back and were writhing upon him. The passage was quite dark, but he found his hat and was out in the alley in a moment, breathing more freely, and surprised to find how much light there still was in the open air. He could see the pavement clearly under his feet, and far off in the street to which the alley led he could hear the laughter and calls of children, playing some game out of doors. He wondered how he could have been so nervous, and for an instant he thought of going back into the house to wait quietly for Else. But instantly he felt that nervous fright of something stealing over him again. In any case it was better to walk up to Cranston House and ask the servants about the child. One of the women had perhaps taken a fancy to her, and was even now giving her tea and cake.

He walked quickly to Belgrave Square, and then up the broad streets, listening as he went, whenever there was no other sound, for the tiny footsteps. But he heard nothing, and was laughing at himself when he rang the servants' bell at the big house. Of course, the child must be there.

The person who opened the door was quite an inferior person, for it was a back door, but affected the manners of the front, and stared at Mr Puckler superciliously under the strong light.

No little girl had been seen, and he knew "nothing about no dolls."

"She is my little girl," said Mr Puckler tremulously, for all his anxiety was returning tenfold, "and I am afraid something has happened."

The inferior person said rudely that "nothing could have happened to her in that house, because she had not been there, which was a jolly good reason why;" and Mr Puckler was obliged to admit that the man ought to know, as it was his business to keep the door and let people in. He wished to be allowed to speak to the under nurse, who knew him; but the man was ruder than ever, and finally shut the door in his face.

When the doll doctor was alone in the street, he steadied himself by the railing, for he felt as though he were breaking in two, just as some dolls break, in the middle of the backbone.

Presently he knew that he must be doing something to find Else, and that gave him strength. He began to walk as quickly as he could through the streets, following every highway and byway which his little girl might have taken on her errand. He also asked several policemen in vain if they had seen her, and most of them answered him kindly, for they saw that he was a sober man and in his right senses, and some of them had little girls of their own.

It was one o'clock in the morning when he went up to his own door again, worn out and hopeless and broken-hearted. As he turned the key in the lock, his heart stood still, for he knew that he was awake and not dreaming, and that he really heard those tiny footsteps pattering to meet him inside the house along the passage.

But he was too unhappy to be much frightened any more, and his heart went on again with a dull regular pain, that found its way all through him with every pulse. So he went in, and hung up his hat in the dark, and found the matches in the cupboard and the candlestick in its place in the corner.

Mr Puckler was so much overcome and so completely worn out that he sat down in his chair before the work-table and almost fainted, as his face dropped forward upon his folded hands. Beside him the solitary candle burned steadily with a low flame in the still warm air.

"Else! Else!" he moaned against his yellow knuckles. And that was all he could say, and it was no relief to him. On the contrary, the very sound of the name was a new and sharp pain that pierced his ears and his head and his very soul. For every time he repeated the name it meant that little Else was dead, somewhere out in the streets of London in the dark.

He was so terribly hurt that he did not even feel something pulling gently at the skirt of his old coat, so gently that it was like the nibbling of a tiny mouse. He might have thought that it was really a mouse if he had noticed it.

"Else! Else!" he groaned right against his hands.

Then a cool breath stirred his thin hair, and the low flame of the one candle dropped down almost to a mere spark, not flickering as though a draught were going to blow it out, but just dropping down as if it were tired out. Mr. Puckler felt his hands stiffening with fright under his face; and there was a faint rustling sound, like some small silk thing blown in a gentle breeze. He sat up straight, stark and scared, and a small wooden voice spoke in the stillness.

"Pa-pa," it said, with a break between the syllables.

Mr Puckler stood up in a single jump, and his chair fell over backwards with a smashing noise upon the wooden floor. The candle had almost gone out.

It was Nina's doll voice that had spoken, and he should have known it among the voices of a hundred other dolls. And yet there was something more in it, a little human ring, with a pitiful cry and a call for help, and the wail of a hurt child. Mr Puckler stood up, stark and stiff, and tried to look round, but at first he could not, for he seemed to be frozen from head to foot.

Then he made a great effort, and he raised one hand to each of his temples, and pressed his own head round as he would have turned a doll's. The candle was burning so low that it might as well have been out altogether, for any light it gave, and the room seemed quite dark at first. Then he saw something. He would not have believed that he could be more frightened than he had been just before that. But he was, and his knees shook, for he saw the doll standing in the middle of the floor, shining with a faint and ghostly radiance, her beautiful glassy brown eyes fixed on his. And across her face the very thin line of the break he had mended shone as though it were drawn in light with a fine point of white flame.

Yet there was something more in the eyes, too; there was something human, like Else's own, but as if only the doll saw him through them, and not Else. And there was enough of Else to bring back all his pain and to make him forget his fear.

"Else! My little Else!" he cried aloud.

The small ghost moved, and its doll-arm slowly rose and fell with a stiff, mechanical motion.

"Pa-pa," it said.

It seemed this time that there was even more of Else's tone echoing somewhere between the wooden notes that reached his ears so distinctly, and yet so far away. Else was calling him, he was sure.

His face was perfectly white in the gloom, but his knees did not shake any more, and he felt that he was less frightened.

"Yes, child! But where? Where?" he asked. "Where are you, Else?"

"Pa-pa!"

The syllables died away in the quiet room. There was a low rustling of silk, the glassy brown eyes turned slowly away, and Mr Puckler heard the pitter-patter of the small feet in the bronze kid slippers as the figure ran straight to the door. Then the candle burned high again, the room was full of light, and he was alone.

Mr Puckler passed his hand over his eyes and looked about him. He could see everything quite clearly, and he felt that he must have been dreaming, though he was standing instead of sitting down, as he should have been if he had just waked up. The candle burned brightly now. There were the dolls to be mended, lying in a row with their toes up. The third one had lost her right shoe, and Else was making one. He knew that, and he was certainly not dreaming now. He had not been dreaming when he had come in from his fruitless search and had heard the doll's footsteps running to the door. He had not fallen asleep in his chair. How could he possibly have fallen asleep when his heart was breaking? He had been awake all the time.

He steadied himself, set the fallen chair upon its legs, and said to himself again very emphatically that he was a foolish old man. He ought to be out in the streets looking for his child, asking questions, and enquiring at the police stations, where all accidents were reported as soon as they were known, or at the hospitals.

"Pa-pa!"

The longing, wailing, pitiful little wooden cry rang from the passage, outside the door, and Mr Puckler stood for an instant with white face, transfixed and rooted to the spot. A moment later his hand was on the latch. Then he was in the passage, with the light streaming from the open door behind him.

Quite at the other end he saw the little phantom shining clearly in the shadow, and the right hand seemed to beckon to him as the arm rose and fell once more. He knew all at once that it had not come to frighten him but to lead him, and when it disappeared, and he walked boldly towards the door, he knew that it was in the street outside, waiting for him. He forgot that he was tired and had eaten no supper, and had walked many miles, for a sudden hope ran through and through him, like a golden stream of life.

And sure enough, at the corner of the alley, and at the corner of the street, and out in Belgrave Square, he saw the small ghost flitting before him. Sometimes it was only a shadow, where there was other light, but then the glare of the lamps made a pale green sheen on its little Mother Hubbard frock of silk; and some-times, where the streets were dark and silent, the whole figure shone out brightly, with its yellow curls and rosy neck. It seemed to trot along like a tiny child, and Mr Puckler could almost hear the pattering of the bronze kid slippers on the pavement as it ran. But it went very fast, and he could only just keep up with it, tearing along with his hat on the back of his head and his thin hair blown by the night breeze, and his horn-rimmed spectacles firmly set upon his broad nose.

On and on he went, and he had no idea where he was. He did not even care, for he knew certainly that he was going the right way.

Then at last, in a wide, quiet street, he was standing before a big, sober-look-ing door that had two lamps on each side of it, and a polished brass bell-handle, which he pulled.

And just inside, when the door was opened, in the bright light, there was the little shadow, and the pale green sheen of the little silk dress, and once more the small cry came to his ears, less pitiful, more longing.

"Pa-pa!"

The shadow turned suddenly bright, and out of the brightness the beautiful brown glass eyes were turned up happily to his, while the rosy mouth smiled so divinely that the phantom doll looked almost like a little angel just then.

"A little girl was brought in soon after ten o'clock," said the quiet voice of the hospital doorkeeper. "I think they thought she was only stunned. She was holding a big brown-paper box against her, and they could not get it out of her arms. She had a long plait of brown hair that hung down as they carried her."

"She is my little girl," said Mr Puckler, but he hardly heard his own voice.

He leaned over Else's face in the gentle light of the children's ward, and when he had stood there a minute the beautiful brown eyes opened and looked up to his.

"Pa-pa!" cried Else, softly, "I knew you would come!"

Then Mr Puckler did not know what he did or said for a moment, and what he felt was worth all the fear and terror and despair that had almost killed him that night. But by and by Else was telling her story, and the nurse let her speak, for there were only two other children in the room, who were getting well and were sound asleep.

"They were big boys with bad faces," said Else, "and they tried to get Nina away from me, but I held on and fought as well as I could till one of them hit me with something, and I don't remember any more, for I tumbled down, and I suppose the boys ran away, and somebody found me there. But I'm afraid Nina is all smashed."

"Here is the box," said the nurse. "We could not take it out of her arms till she came to herself. Should you like to see if the doll is broken?"

And she undid the string cleverly, but Nina was all smashed to pieces. Only the gentle light of the children's ward made a pale green sheen in the folds of the little Mother Hubbard frock.

THE ROOM IN THE TOWER

E.F. Benson

Edward Frederic Benson (1867–1940) was born at Wellington College, Berkshire where his father was headmaster. He was educated at Marlborough College and King's College, Cambridge where he studied archaeology. Benson is best remembered for his *Mapp and Lucia* series, which has been adapted for radio and television. Several of the books are set in the fictional seaside town of Tilling, based on Rye on Sea, where Benson served as Mayor for three years.

It is probable that everybody who is at all a constant dreamer has had at least one experience of an event or a sequence of circumstances which have come to his mind in sleep being subsequently realized in the material world. But, in my opinion, so far from this being a strange thing, it would be far odder if this fulfilment did not occasionally happen, since our dreams are, as a rule, concerned with people whom we know and places with which we are familiar, such as might very naturally occur in the awake and daylit world. True, these dreams are often broken into by some absurd and fantastic incident, which puts them out of court in regard to their subsequent fulfilment, but on the mere calculation of chances, it does not appear in the least unlikely that a dream imagined by anyone who dreams constantly should occasionally come true. Not long ago, for instance, I experienced such a fulfilment of a dream which seems to me in no way remarkable and to have no kind of psychical significance. The manner of it was as follows.

A certain friend of mine, living abroad, is amiable enough to write to me about once in a fortnight. Thus, when fourteen days or thereabouts have elapsed since I last heard from him, my mind, probably, either consciously or subconsciously, is expectant of a letter from him. One night last week I dreamed that as I was going upstairs to dress for dinner I heard, as I often heard, the sound of the postman's knock on my front door, and diverted my direction downstairs instead. There, among other correspondence, was a letter from him. Thereafter the fantastic entered, for on opening it I found inside the ace of diamonds, and scribbled across it in his well-known handwriting, "I am sending you this for safe custody, as you know it is running an unreasonable risk to keep aces in Italy." The next evening I was just preparing to go upstairs to dress when I heard the postman's knock, and did precisely as I had done in my dream. There, among other letters, was one from my friend. Only it did not contain the ace of diamonds. Had it done so, I should have attached more weight to the matter, which, as it stands, seems to me a perfectly ordinary coincidence. No doubt I consciously or subconsciously expected a letter from him, and this suggested to me my dream. Similarly, the fact that my friend had not written to me for a fortnight suggested to him that he should do so. But occasionally it is not so easy to find such an explanation, and for the following story I can find no explanation at all. It came out of the dark, and into the dark it has gone again.

All my life I have been a habitual dreamer: the nights are few, that is to say, when I do not find on awaking in the morning that some mental experience has been mine, and sometimes, all night long, apparently, a series of the most dazzling adventures befall me. Almost without exception these adventures are pleasant, though often merely trivial. It is of an exception that I am going to speak.

It was when I was about sixteen that a certain dream first came to me, and this is how it befell. It opened with my being set down at the door of a big red-brick house, where, I understood, I was going to stay. The servant who opened the door told me that tea was going on in the garden, and led me through a low dark-panelled hall, with a large open fireplace, on to a cheerful green lawn set round with flower beds. There were grouped about the tea-table a small party of people, but they were all strangers to me except one, who was a school-fellow called Jack Stone, clearly the son of the house, and he introduced me to his mother and father and a couple of sisters. I was, I remember, somewhat astonished to find myself here, for the boy in question was scarcely known to me, and I rather disliked what I knew of him; moreover, he had left school nearly a year before. The afternoon was very hot, and an intolerable oppression reigned. On the far side of the lawn ran a red-brick wall, with an iron gate in its centre, outside which stood a walnut tree. We sat in the shadow of the house opposite a row of long windows, inside which I could see a table with cloth laid, glimmering with glass and silver. This garden front of the house was very long, and at one end of it stood a tower of three storeys, which looked to me much older than the rest of the building.

Before long, Mrs. Stone, who, like the rest of the party, had sat in absolute silence, said to me, "Jack will show you your room: I have given you the room in the tower."

Quite inexplicably my heart sank at her words. I felt as if I had known that I should have the room in the tower, and that it contained something dreadful and significant. Jack instantly got up, and I understood that I had to follow him. In silence we passed through the hall, and mounted a great oak staircase with many corners, and arrived at a small landing with two doors set in it. He pushed one of these open for me to enter, and without coming in himself, closed it behind me. Then I knew that my conjecture had been right: there was something awful in the room, and with the terror of nightmare growing swiftly and enveloping me, I awoke in a spasm of terror.

Now that dream or variations on it occurred to me intermittently for fifteen years. Most often it came in exactly this form, the arrival, the tea out on the lawn, the deadly silence succeeded by that one deadly sentence, the mounting with Jack Stone up to the room in the tower where horror dwelt, and it always came to a close in the nightmare of terror at that which was in the room, though I never saw what it was. At other times I experienced variations on this same theme. Occasionally, for instance, we would be sitting at dinner in the dining-room, into the windows of which I had looked on the first night when the dream of this house visited me, but wherever we were, there was the same silence, the same sense of dreadful oppression and foreboding. And the silence I knew would always be broken by Mrs. Stone saying to me, "Jack will show you your room: I have given you the room in the tower." Upon which (this was invariable) I had to follow him up the oak staircase with many corners, and enter the place that I dreaded more and more each time that I visited it in sleep. Or, again, I would find myself playing cards still in silence in a drawing-room lit with immense chandeliers, that gave a blinding illumination. What the game was I have no idea; what I remember, with a sense of miserable anticipation, was that soon Mrs. Stone would get up and say to me, "Jack will show you your room: I have given you the room in the tower." This drawing-room where we played cards was next to the dining-room, and, as I have said, was always brilliantly illuminated, whereas the rest of the house was full of dusk and shadows. And yet, how often, in spite of those bouquets of lights, have I not pored over the cards that were dealt to me, scarcely able for some reason to see them. Their designs, too, were strange: there were no red suits, but all were black, and among them there were certain cards which were black all over. I hated and dreaded those.

As this dream continued to recur, I got to know the greater part of the house. There was a smoking-room beyond the drawing-room, at the end of a passage with a green baize door. It was always very dark there, and as often as I went there I passed somebody whom I could not see in the doorway coming out. Curious developments, too, took place in the characters that peopled the dream as might happen to living persons. Mrs. Stone, for instance, who, when I first saw her, had been black haired, became grey, and instead of rising briskly, as she had done at first when she said, "Jack will show you your room: I have given you the room in the tower," got up very feebly, as if the strength was leaving her limbs. Jack also grew up, and became a rather ill-looking young man, with a brown moustache, while one of the sisters ceased to appear, and I understood she was married.

Then it so happened that I was not visited by this dream for six months or more, and I began to hope, in such inexplicable dread did I hold it, that it had passed away for good. But one night after this interval I again found myself being shown out onto the lawn for tea, and Mrs. Stone was not there, while the others were all dressed in black. At once I guessed the reason, and my heart leaped at the thought that perhaps this time I should not have to sleep in the room in the tower, and though we usually all sat in silence, on this occasion the sense of relief made me talk and laugh as I had never yet done. But even then matters were not altogether comfortable, for no one else spoke, but they all looked secretly at each other. And soon the foolish stream of my talk ran dry, and gradually an apprehension worse than anything I had previously known gained on me as the light slowly faded.

Suddenly a voice which I knew well broke the stillness, the voice of Mrs. Stone, saying, "Jack will show you your room: I have given you the room in the tower." It seemed to come from near the gate in the red-brick wall that bounded the lawn, and looking up, I saw that the grass outside was sown thick with gravestones. A curious greyish light shone from them, and I could read the lettering on the grave nearest me, and it was, "In evil memory of Julia Stone." And as usual Jack got up, and again I followed him through the hall and up the staircase with many corners. On this occasion it was darker than usual, and when I passed into the room in the tower I could only just see the furniture, the position of which was already familiar to me. Also there was a dreadful odour of decay in the room, and I woke screaming.

The dream, with such variations and developments as I have mentioned, went on at intervals for fifteen years. Sometimes I would dream it two or three nights in succession; once, as I have said, there was an intermission of six months, but taking a reasonable average, I should say that I dreamed it quite as often as once in a month. It had, as is plain, something of nightmare about it, since it always ended in the same appalling terror, which so far from getting less, seemed to me to gather fresh fear every time that I experienced it. There was, too, a strange and dreadful consistency about it. The characters in it, as I have mentioned, got regularly older, death and marriage visited this silent family, and I never in the dream, after Mrs. Stone had died, set eyes on her again. But it was always her voice that told me that the room in the tower was prepared for me, and whether we had tea out on the lawn, or the scene was laid in one of the rooms overlooking it, I could always see her gravestone standing just outside the iron gate. It was the same, too, with the married daughter; usually she was not present, but once or twice she returned again, in company with a man, whom I took to be her husband. He, too, like the rest of them, was always silent. But, owing to the constant repetition of the dream, I had ceased to attach, in my waking hours, any significance to it. I never met Jack Stone again during all those years, nor did I ever see a house that resembled this dark house of my dream. And then something happened.

I had been in London in this year, up till the end of the July, and during the first week in August went down to stay with a friend in a house he had taken for the summer months, in the Ashdown Forest district of Sussex. I left London early, for John Clinton was to meet me at Forest Row Station, and we were going to spend the day golfing, and go to his house in the evening. He had his motor with him, and we set off, about five in the afternoon, after a thoroughly delightful day, for the drive, the distance being some ten miles. As it was still so early we did not have tea at the clubhouse, but waited till we should get home. As we drove, the weather, which up till then had been, though hot, deliciously fresh, seemed to me to alter in quality, and become very stagnant and oppressive, and I felt that indefinable sense of ominous apprehension that I am accustomed to before thunder. John, however, did not share my views, attributing my loss of lightness to the fact that I had lost both my matches. Events proved, however, that I was right, though I do not think that the thunderstorm that broke that night was the sole cause of my depression.

Our way lay through deep high-banked lanes, and before we had gone very far I fell asleep, and was only awakened by the stopping of the motor. And with a sudden thrill, partly of fear but chiefly of curiosity, I found myself standing in the doorway of my house of dream. We went, I half wondering whether or not I was dreaming still, through a low oak-panelled hall, and out onto the lawn, where tea was laid in the shadow of the house. It was set in flower beds, a red-brick wall, with a gate in it, bounded one side, and out beyond that was a space of rough grass with a walnut-tree. The façade of the house was very long, and at one end stood a three-storied tower, markedly older than the rest.

Here for the moment all resemblance to the repeated dream ceased. There was no silent and somehow terrible family, but a large assembly of exceedingly cheerful persons, all of whom were known to me. And in spite of the horror with which the dream itself had always filled me, I felt nothing of it now that the scene of it was thus reproduced before me. But I felt the intensest curiosity as to what was going to happen.

Tea pursued its cheerful course, and before long Mrs. Clinton got up. And at that moment I think I knew what she was going to say. She spoke to me, and what she said was:

"Jack will show you your room: I have given you the room in the tower."

At that, for half a second, the horror of the dream took hold of me again. But it quickly passed, and again I felt nothing more than the most intense curiosity. It was not very long before it was amply satisfied.

John turned to me.

"Right up at the top of the house," he said, "but I think you'll be comfortable. We're absolutely full up. Would you like to go and see it now? By Jove, I believe that you are right, and that we are going to have a thunderstorm. How dark it has become."

I got up and followed him. We passed through the hall, and up the perfectly familiar staircase. Then he opened the door, and I went in. And at that moment sheer unreasoning terror again possessed me. I did not know for certain what I feared: I simply feared. Then like a sudden recollection, when one remembers a name which has long escaped the memory, I knew what I feared. I feared Mrs. Stone, whose grave with the sinister inscription, "In evil memory," I had so often seen in my dream, just beyond the lawn which lay below my window. And then once more the fear passed so completely that I wondered what there was to fear, and I found myself, sober and quiet and sane, in the room in the tower, the name of which I had so often heard in my dream, and the scene of which was so familiar.

I looked around it with a certain sense of proprietorship, and found that noth-ing had been changed from the dreaming nights in which I knew it so well. Just to the left of the door was the bed, lengthways along the wall, with the head of it in the angle. In a line with it was the fireplace and a small bookcase; opposite the door the outer wall was pierced by two lattice-paned windows, between which stood the dressing-table, while ranged along the fourth wall was the washing-stand and a big cupboard. My luggage had already been unpacked, for the furniture of dressing and undressing lay orderly on the wash-stand and toilet-table, while my dinner clothes were spread out on the coverlet of the bed. And then, with a sudden start of unexplained dismay, I saw that there were two rather conspicuous objects which I had not seen before in my dreams: one a life-sized oil-painting of Mrs. Stone, the other a black-and-white sketch of Jack Stone, representing him as he had appeared to me only a week before in the last of the series of these repeated dreams, a rather secret and evil-looking man of about thirty. His picture hung between the windows, looking straight across the room to the other portrait, which hung at the side of the bed. At that I looked next, and as I looked I felt once more the horror of nightmare seize me.

It represented Mrs. Stone as I had seen her last in my dreams: old and withered and white-haired. But in spite of the evident feebleness of body, a dreadful exuberance and vitality shone through the envelope of flesh, an exuberance wholly malign, a vitality that foamed and frothed with unimaginable evil. Evil beamed from the narrow, leering eyes; it laughed in the demon-like mouth. The whole face was instinct with some secret and appalling mirth; the hands, clasped together on the knee, seemed shaking with suppressed and nameless glee. Then I saw also that it was signed in the left-hand bottom corner, and wondering who the artist could be, I looked more closely, and read the inscription, "Julia Stone by Julia Stone."

There came a tap at the door, and John Clinton entered.

"Got everything you want?" he asked.

"Rather more than I want," said I, pointing to the picture.

He laughed.

"Hard-featured old lady," he said. "By herself, too, I remember. Anyhow she can't have flattered herself much."

"But don't you see?" said I. "It's scarcely a human face at all. It's the face of some witch, of some devil."

He looked at it more closely.

"Yes; it isn't very pleasant," he said. "Scarcely a bedside manner, eh? Yes; I can imagine getting the nightmare, if I went to sleep with that close by my bed. I'll have it taken down if you like."

"I really wish you would," I said.

He rang the bell, and with the help of a servant we detached the picture and carried it out onto the landing, and put it with its face to the wall.

"By Jove, the old lady is a weight," said John, mopping his forehead. "I wonder if she had something on her mind."

The extraordinary weight of the picture had struck me too. I was about to reply, when I caught sight of my own hand. There was blood on it, in considerable quantities, covering the whole palm.

"I've cut myself somehow," said I.

John gave a little startled exclamation.

"Why, I have too," he said.

Simultaneously the footman took out his handkerchief and wiped his hand with it. I saw that there was blood also on his handkerchief.

John and I went back into the tower room and washed the blood off; but neither on his hand nor on mine was there the slightest trace of a scratch or cut. It seemed to me that, having ascertained this, we both, by a sort of tacit consent, did not allude to it again. Something in my case had dimly occurred to me that I did not wish to think about. It was but a conjecture, but I fancied that I knew the same thing had occurred to him.

The heat and oppression of the air, for the storm we had expected was still undischarged, increased very much after dinner, and for some time most of the party, among whom were John Clinton and myself, sat outside on the path bounding the lawn, where we had had tea. The night was absolutely dark, and no twinkle of star or moon ray could penetrate the pall of cloud that overset the sky. By degrees our assembly thinned, the women went up to bed, men dispersed to the smoking- or billiard-room, and by eleven o'clock my host and I were the only two left. All the evening I thought that he had something on his mind, and as soon as we were alone he spoke.

"The man who helped us with the picture had blood on his hand, too, did you notice?" he said. "I asked him just now if he had cut himself, and he said he supposed he had, but that he could find no mark of it. Now where did that blood come from?"

By dint of telling myself that I was not going to think about it, I had succeeded in not doing so, and I did not want, especially just at bedtime, to be reminded of it.

"I don't know," said I, "and I don't really care so long as the picture of Mrs. Stone is not by my bed."

He got up.

"But it's odd," he said. "Ha! Now you'll see another odd thing."

A dog of his, an Irish terrier by breed, had come out of the house as we talked. The door behind us into the hall was open, and a bright oblong of light shone across the lawn to the iron gate which led on to the rough grass outside, where the walnut tree stood. I saw that the dog had all his hackles up, bristling with rage and fright; his lips were curled back from his teeth, as if he was ready to spring at something, and he was growling to himself. He took not the slightest notice of his master or me, but stiffly and tensely walked across the grass to the iron gate. There he stood for a moment, looking through the bars and still growling. Then of a sudden his courage seemed to desert him: he gave one long howl, and scuttled back to the house with a curious crouching sort of movement.

"He does that half a dozen times a day." said John. "He sees something which he both hates and fears."

I walked to the gate and looked over it. Something was moving on the grass outside, and soon a sound which I could not instantly identify came to my ears. Then I remembered what it was: it was the purring of a cat. I lit a match, and saw the purrer, a big blue Persian, walking round and round in a little circle just outside the gate, stepping high and ecstatically, with tail carried aloft like a banner. Its eyes were bright and shining, and every now and then it put its head down and sniffed at the grass.

I laughed.

"The end of that mystery, I am afraid." I said. "Here's a large cat having Walpurgis night all alone."

"Yes, that's Darius," said John. "He spends half the day and all night there. But that's not the end of the dog mystery, for Toby and he are the best of friends, but the beginning of the cat mystery. What's the cat doing there? And why is Darius pleased, while Toby is terror-stricken?"

At that moment I remembered the rather horrible detail of my dreams when I saw through the gate, just where the cat was now, the white tombstone with the sinister inscription. But before I could answer the rain began, as suddenly and heavily as if a tap had been turned on, and simultaneously the big cat squeezed through the bars of the gate, and came leaping across the lawn to the house for shelter. Then it sat in the doorway, looking out eagerly into the dark. It spat and struck at John with its paw, as he pushed it in, in order to close the door.

Somehow, with the portrait of Julia Stone in the passage outside, the room in the tower had absolutely no alarm for me, and as I went to bed, feeling very sleepy and heavy, I had nothing more than interest for the curious incident about our bleeding hands, and the conduct of the cat and dog. The last thing I looked at before I put out my light was the square empty space by my bed where the portrait had been. Here the paper was of its original full tint of dark red: over the rest of the walls it had faded. Then I blew out my candle and instantly fell asleep.

My awaking was equally instantaneous, and I sat bolt upright in bed under the impression that some bright light had been flashed in my face, though it was now absolutely pitch dark. I knew exactly where I was, in the room which I had dreaded in dreams, but no horror that I ever felt when asleep approached the fear that now invaded and froze my brain. Immediately after a peal of thunder crackled just above the house, but the probability that it was only a flash of lightning which awoke me gave no reassurance to my galloping heart. Something I knew was in the room with me, and instinctively I put out my right hand, which was nearest the wall, to keep it away. And my hand touched the edge of a picture-frame hanging close to me.

I sprang out of bed, upsetting the small table that stood by it, and I heard my watch, candle, and matches clatter onto the floor. But for the moment there was no need of light, for a blinding flash leaped out of the clouds, and showed me that by my bed again hung the picture of Mrs. Stone. And instantly the room went into blackness again. But in that flash I saw another thing also, namely a figure that leaned over the end of my bed, watching me. It was dressed in some close-clinging white garment, spotted and stained with mould, and the face was that of the portrait.

Overhead the thunder cracked and roared, and when it ceased and the deathly stillness succeeded, I heard the rustle of movement coming nearer me, and, more horrible yet, perceived an odour of corruption and decay. And then a hand was laid on the side of my neck, and close beside my ear I heard quick-taken, eager breathing. Yet I knew that this thing, though it could be perceived by touch, by smell, by eye and by ear, was still not of this earth, but something that had passed out of the body and had power to make itself manifest. Then a voice, already familiar to me, spoke.

"I knew you would come to the room in the tower," it said. "I have been long waiting for you. At last you have come. Tonight I shall feast; before long we will feast together."

And the quick breathing came closer to me; I could feel it on my neck.

At that the terror, which I think had paralyzed me for the moment, gave way to the wild instinct of self-preservation. I hit wildly with both arms, kicking out at the same moment, and heard a little animal-squeal, and something soft dropped with a thud beside me. I took a couple of steps forward, nearly tripping up over whatever it was that lay there, and by the merest good luck found the handle of the door. In another second I ran out on the landing, and had banged the door behind me. Almost at the same moment I heard a door open somewhere below, and John Clinton, candle in hand, came running upstairs.

"What is it?" he said. "I sleep just below you, and heard a noise as if – Good heavens, there's blood on your shoulder."

I stood there, so he told me afterwards, swaying from side to side, white as a sheet, with the mark on my shoulder as if a hand covered with blood had been laid there.

"It's in there," I said, pointing. "She, you know. The portrait is in there, too, hanging up on the place we took it from."

At that he laughed.

"My dear fellow, this is mere nightmare," he said.

He pushed by me, and opened the door, I standing there simply inert with terror, unable to stop him, unable to move.

"Phew! What an awful smell," he said.

Then there was silence; he had passed out of my sight behind the open door. Next moment he came out again, as white as myself, and instantly shut it.

"Yes, the portrait's there," he said, "and on the floor is a thing – a thing spotted with earth, like what they bury people in. Come away, quick, come away."

How I got downstairs I hardly know. An awful shuddering and nausea of the spirit rather than of the flesh had seized me, and more than once he had to place my feet upon the steps, while every now and then he cast glances of terror and apprehension up the stairs. But in time we came to his dressing-room on the floor below, and there I told him what I have here described.

The sequel can be made short; indeed, some of my readers have perhaps already guessed what it was, if they remember that inexplicable affair of the churchyard at West Fawley, some eight years ago, where an attempt was made three times to bury the body of a certain woman who had committed suicide. On each occasion the coffin was found in the course of a few days again protruding from the ground. After the third attempt, in order that the thing should not be talked about, the body was buried elsewhere in unconsecrated ground. Where it was buried was just outside the iron gate of the garden belonging to the house where this woman had lived. She had committed suicide in a room at the top of the tower in that house. Her name was Julia Stone.

Subsequently the body was again secretly dug up, and the coffin was found to be full of blood.

ON THE BRIGHTON ROAD

Richard Middleton

Richard Barham Middleton (1882–1911) was an English poet and author. He worked in London as a bank clerk. In order to overcome the boredom of his day job, he affected a bohemian life by night. Middleton suffered from severe depression, spending his last nine months in Brussels where he took his life, poisoning himself with chloroform.

Slowly the sun had climbed up the hard white downs, till it broke with little of the mysterious ritual of dawn upon a sparkling world of snow. There had been a hard frost during the night, and the birds, who hopped about here and there with scant tolerance of life, left no trace of their passage on the silver pavements. In places the sheltered caverns of the hedges broke the monotony of the whiteness that had fallen upon the coloured earth, and overhead the sky melted from orange to deep blue, from deep blue to a blue so pale that it suggested a thin paper screen rather than illimitable space. Across the level fields there came a cold, silent wind which blew a fine dust of snow from the trees, but hardly stirred the crested hedges. Once above the skyline, the sun seemed to climb more quickly, and as it rose higher it began to give out a heat that blended with the keenness of the wind.

It may have been this strange alternation of heat and cold that disturbed the tramp in his dreams, for he struggled for a moment with the snow that covered him, like a man who finds himself twisted uncomfortably in the bed-clothes, and then sat up with staring, questioning eyes. "Lord! I thought I was in bed," he said to himself as he took in the vacant landscape, "and all the while I was out here." He stretched his limbs, and, rising carefully to his feet, shook the snow off his body. As he did so the wind set him shivering, and he knew that his bed had been warm.

"Come, I feel pretty fit," he thought. "I suppose I am lucky to wake at all in this. Or unlucky – it isn't much of a business to come back to." He looked up and saw the downs shining against the blue, like the Alps on a picture-postcard. "That means another forty miles or so, I suppose," he continued grimly. "Lord knows what I did yesterday. Walked till I was done, and now I'm only about twelve miles from Brighton. Damn the snow, damn Brighton, damn everything!" The sun crept higher and higher, and he started walking patiently along the road with his back turned to the hills.

"Am I glad or sorry that it was only sleep that took me, glad or sorry, glad or sorry?" His thoughts seemed to arrange themselves in a metrical accompaniment to the steady thud of his footsteps, and he hardly sought an answer to his question. It was good enough to walk to.

Presently, when three milestones had loitered past, he overtook a boy who was stooping to light a cigarette. He wore no overcoat, and looked unspeakably fragile against the snow, "Are you on the road, guv'nor?" asked the boy huskily as he passed.

"I think I am," the tramp said.

"Oh! Then I'll come a bit of the way with you if you don't walk too fast. It's bit lonesome walking this time of day."

The tramp nodded his head, and the boy started limping along by his side.

"I'm eighteen," he said casually. "I bet you thought I was younger."

"Fifteen, I'd have said."

"You'd have backed a loser. Eighteen last August, and I've been on the road six years. I ran away from home five times when I was a little 'un, and the police took me back each time. Very good to me, the police was. Now I haven't got a home to run away from."

"Nor have I," the tramp said calmly.

"Oh, I can see what you are," the boy panted; "you're a gentleman come down. It's harder for you than for me." The tramp glanced at the limping, feeble figure and lessened his pace.

"I haven't been at it as long as you have," he admitted.

"No, I could tell that by the way you walk. You haven't got tired yet. Perhaps you expect something at the other end?"

The tramp reflected for a moment. "I don't know," he said bitterly, "I'm always expecting things."

"You'll grow out of that;" the boy commented. "It's warmer in London, but it's harder to come by grub. There isn't much in it really."

"Still, there's the chance of meeting somebody there who will understand—"

"Country people are better," the boy interrupted. "Last night I took a lease of a barn for nothing and slept with the cows, and this morning the farmer routed me out and gave me tea and toke because I was so little. Of course, I score there; but in London, soup on the Embankment at night, and all the rest of the time coppers moving you on."

"I dropped by the roadside last night and slept where I fell. It's a wonder I didn't die," the tramp said. The boy looked at him sharply.

"How did you know you didn't?" he said.

"I don't see it," the tramp said, after a pause.

"I tell you," the boy said hoarsely, "people like us can't get away from this sort of thing if we want to. Always hungry and thirsty and dog-tired and walking all the while. And yet if anyone offers me a nice home and work my stomach feels sick. Do I look strong? I know I'm little for my age, but I've been knocking about like this for six years, and do you think I'm not dead? I was drowned bathing at Margate, and I was killed by a gypsy with a spike; he knocked my head and yet I'm walking along here now, walking to London to walk away from it again, because I can't help it. Dead! I tell you we can't get away if we want to."

The boy broke off in a fit of coughing, and the tramp paused while he recovered.

"You'd better borrow my coat for a bit, Tommy," he said, "your cough's pretty bad."

"You go to hell!" the boy said fiercely, puffing at his cigarette; "I'm all right. I was telling you about the road. You haven't got down to it yet, but you'll find out presently. We're all dead, all of us who're on it, and we're all tired, yet somehow we can't leave it. There's nice smells in the summer, dust and hay and the wind smack in your face on a hot day – and it's nice waking up in the wet grass on a fine morning. I don't know, I don't know—" he lurched forward suddenly, and the tramp caught him in his arms.

"I'm sick," the boy whispered –"sick."

The tramp looked up and down the road, but he could see no houses or any sign of help. Yet even as he supported the boy doubtfully in the middle of the road a motor car suddenly flashed in the middle distance, and came smoothly through the snow.

"What's the trouble?" said the driver quietly as he pulled up. "I'm a doctor." He looked at the boy keenly and listened to his strained breathing.

"Pneumonia," he commented. "I'll give him a lift to the infirmary, and you, too, if you like."

The tramp thought of the workhouse and shook his head "I'd rather walk," he said.

The boy winked faintly as they lifted him into the car.

"I'll meet you beyond Reigate," he murmured to the tramp. "You'll see." And the car vanished along the white road.

All the morning the tramp splashed through the thawing snow, but at midday he begged some bread at a cottage door and crept into a lonely barn to eat it. It was warm in there, and after his meal he fell asleep among the hay. It was dark when he woke, and started trudging once more through the slushy roads.

Two miles beyond Reigate a figure, a fragile figure, slipped out of the darkness to meet him.

"On the road, guv'nor?" said a husky voice. "Then I'll come a bit of the way with you if you don't walk too fast. It's a bit lonesome walking this time of day."

"But the pneumonia!" cried the tramp, aghast.

"I died at Crawley this morning," said the boy.

HOW IT HAPPENED

Sir Arthur Conan Doyle

Sir Arthur Conan Doyle (1859–1930) was born in Edinburgh and is best remembered as the creator of the detective Sherlock Holmes. He studied medicine at Edinburgh University where one of his tutors, Dr Joseph Bell, helped to inspire the character of Holmes. In 1928, Conan Doyle helped free Oscar Slater, a German Jew wrongly convicted of murder. Doyle was a fervent believer in spiritualism. After his death his wife and various spiritualist groups claimed to have made contact with his spirit.

She was a writing medium. This is what she wrote:

I can remember some things upon that evening most distinctly, and others are like some vague, broken dreams. That is what makes it so difficult to tell a connected story. I have no idea now what it was that had taken me to London and brought me back so late. It just merges into all my other visits to London. But from the time that I got out at the little country station everything is extraordinarily clear. I can live it again – every instant of it.

I remember so well walking down the platform and looking at the illuminated clock at the end which told me that it was half-past eleven. I remember also my wondering whether I could get home before midnight. Then I remember the big motor, with its glaring headlights and glitter of polished brass, waiting for me outside. It was my new thirty-horse-power Robur, which had only been delivered that day. I remember also asking Perkins, my chauffeur, how she had gone, and his saying that he thought she was excellent.

"I'll try her myself," said I, and I climbed into the driver's seat.

"The gears are not the same," said he. "Perhaps, sir, I had better drive."

"No; I should like to try her," said I.

And so we started on the five-mile drive for home.

My old car had the gears as they used always to be in notches on a bar. In this car you passed the gear-lever through a gate to get on the higher ones. It was not difficult to master, and soon I thought that I understood it. It was foolish, no doubt, to begin to learn a new system in the dark, but one often does foolish things and one has not always to pay the full price for them. I got along very well until I came to Claystall Hill. It is one of the worst hills in England, a mile and a half long and one in six in places, with three fairly sharp curves. My park gate stands at the very foot of it upon the main London road.

We were just over the brow of this hill, where the grade is steepest; when the trouble began. I had been on the top speed and wanted to get her on the free; but she stuck between gears, and I had to get her back on the top again. By this time she was going at a great rate, so I clapped on both brakes, and one after the other they gave way. I didn't mind so much when I felt my footbrake snap, but when I put all my weight on my side-brake, and the lever clanged to its full limit without a catch, it brought a cold sweat out of me. By this time we were fairly tearing down the slope. The lights were brilliant, and I brought her round the first curve all right. Then we did the second one, though it was a close shave for the ditch. There was a mile of straight then with the third curve beneath it and after that the gate of the park. If I could shoot into that harbour all would be well, for the slope up to the house would bring her to a stand.

Perkins behaved splendidly. I should like that to be known. He was perfectly cool and alert. I had thought at the very beginning of taking the bank, and he read my intention.

"I wouldn't do it, sir," said he. "At this pace it must go over and we should have it on the top of us."

Of course he was right. He got to the electric switch and had it off, so we were in the free; but we were still running at a fearful pace. He laid his hands on the wheel.

"I'll keep her steady," said he, "if you care to jump and chance it. We can never get round that curve. Better jump, sir."

"No," said I; "I'll stick it out. You can jump if you like."

"I'll stick it with you, sir," said he.

If it had been the old car I should have jammed the gear-lever into the reverse and seen what would happen. I expect she would have stripped her gears or smashed up somehow, but it would have been a chance. As it was, I was helpless. Perkins tried to climb across, but you couldn't do it going at that pace. The wheels were whirring like a high wind and the big body creaking and groaning with the strain. But the lights were brilliant, and one could steer to an inch. I remember thinking what an awful and yet majestic sight we should appear to anyone who met us. It was a narrow road and we were just a great, roaring, golden death to anyone who came in our path.

We got round the corner with one wheel three feet high upon the bank. I thought we were surely over, but after staggering for a moment she righted and darted onwards. That was the third corner and the last one. There was only the park gate now. It was facing us but, as luck would have it, not facing us directly. It was about twenty yards to the left up the main road into which we ran. Perhaps I could have done it, but I expect that the steering-gear had been jarred when we ran on the bank. The wheel did not turn easily. We shot out of the lane. I saw the open gate on the left. I whirled round my wheel with all the strength of my wrists. Perkins and I threw our bodies across, and then the next instant, going at fifty miles an hour, my right wheel struck full on the right-hand pillar of my own gate. I heard the crash. I was conscious of flying through the air, and then – and then – !

When I became aware of my own existence once more I was among some brushwood in the shadow of the oaks upon the lodge side of the drive. A man was standing beside me. I imagined at first that it was Perkins, but when I looked again I saw that it was Stanley, a man whom I had known at college some years before, and for whom I had a really genuine affection. There was always something peculiarly sympathetic to me in Stanley's personality; and I was proud to think that I had some similar influence upon him. At the present moment I was surprised to see him, but I was like a man in a dream, giddy and shaken and quite prepared to take things as I found them without questioning them.

"What a smash!" I said. "Good Lord, what an awful smash!"

He nodded his head, and even in the gloom I could see that he was smiling the gentle, wistful smile which I connected with him.

I was quite unable to move. Indeed, I had not any desire to try to move. But my senses were exceedingly alert. I saw the wreck of the motor lit up by the moving lanterns. I saw the little group of people and heard the hushed voices. There were the lodge-keeper and his wife, and one or two more. They were taking no notice of me, but were very busy round the car. Then suddenly I heard a cry of pain.

"The weight is on him. Lift it easy," cried a voice.

"It's only my leg!" said another one, which I recognised as Perkins's. "Where's master?" he cried.

"Here I am," I answered, but they did not seem to hear me. They were all bending over something which lay in front of the car.

Stanley laid his hand upon my shoulder, and his touch was inexpressibly soothing. I felt light and happy, in spite of all.

"No pain, of course?" said he.

"None," said I.

"There never is," said he.

And then suddenly a wave of amazement passed over me. Stanley! Stanley! Why, Stanley had surely died of enteric at Bloemfontein in the Boer War!

"Stanley!" I cried, and the words seemed to choke my throat – "Stanley, you are dead."

THE BOWMEN

Arthur Machen

Arthur Machen (1863–1947) was born Arthur Llewelyn Jones, but adopted his wife's surname in order to inherit a legacy. He grew up in Gwent, and the landscape and folklore of his childhood were a continuing influence upon his fiction. Machen's life was shadowed by poverty. After failing to qualify for medical school he made his living as a journalist, publisher, tutor and actor. In 1943, in an attempt to ease Machen's financial difficulties, a group of writers launched a literary appeal for his eightieth birthday.

It was during the retreat of the eighty thousand, and the authority of the censorship is sufficient excuse for not being more explicit. But it was on the most awful day of that awful time, on the day when ruin and disaster came so near that their shadow fell over London far away; and, without any certain news, the hearts of men failed within them and grew faint; as if the agony of the army in the battlefield had entered into their souls.

On this dreadful day, then, when three hundred thousand men in arms with all their artillery swelled like a flood against the little English company, there was one point above all other points in our battle line that was for a time in awful danger, not merely of defeat, but of utter annihilation. With the permission of the censorship and of the military expert, this corner may, perhaps, be described as a salient, and if this angle were crushed and broken, then the English force as a whole would be shattered, the Allied left would be turned, and Sedan would inevitably follow.

All the morning the German guns had thundered and shrieked against this corner, and against the thousand or so of men who held it. The men joked at the shells, and found funny names for them, and had bets about them, and greeted them with scraps of music-hall songs. But the shells came on and burst, and tore good Englishmen limb from limb, and tore brother from brother, and as the heat of the day increased so did the fury of that terrific cannonade. There was no help, it seemed. The English artillery was good, but there was not nearly enough of it; it was being steadily battered into scrap iron.

There comes a moment in a storm at sea when people say to one another, "It is at its worst; it can blow no harder," and then there is a blast ten times more fierce than any before it. So it was in these British trenches.

There were no stouter hearts in the whole world than the hearts of these men; but even they were appalled as this seven-times-heated hell of the German cannonade fell upon them and overwhelmed them and destroyed them. And at this very moment they saw from their trenches that a tremendous host was moving against their lines. Five hundred of the thousand remained, and as far as they could see the German infantry was pressing on against them, column upon column, a grey world of men, ten thousand of them, as it appeared afterwards.

There was no hope at all. They shook hands, some of them. One man improvised a new version of the battle-song, "Good-bye, good-bye to Tipperary," ending with "And we shan't get there." And they all went on firing steadily. The officers pointed out that such an opportunity for high-class, fancy shooting might never occur again; the Germans dropped line after line; the Tipperary humorist asked: "What price Sidney Street?" And the few machine-guns did their best. But everybody knew it was of no use. The dead grey bodies lay in companies and battalions, as others came on and on and on, and they swarmed and stirred, and advanced from beyond and beyond.

"World without end. Amen," said one of the British soldiers with some irrelevance as he took aim and fired. And then he remembered – he says he cannot think why or wherefore – a queer vegetarian restaurant in London where he had once or twice eaten eccentric dishes of cutlets made of lentils and nuts that pretended to be steak. On all the plates in this restaurant there was printed a figure of St. George in blue, with the motto, *Adsit Anglis Sanctus Georgius* – May St. George be a present help to the English. This soldier happened to know Latin and other useless things, and now, as he fired at his man in the grey advancing mass – three hundred yards away – he uttered the pious vegetarian motto. He went on firing to the end, and at last Bill on his right had to clout him cheerfully over the head to make him stop, pointing out as he did so that the King's ammunition cost money and was not lightly to be wasted in drilling funny patterns into dead Germans.

For as the Latin scholar uttered his invocation he felt something between a shudder and an electric shock pass through his body. The roar of the battle died down in his ears to a gentle murmur; instead of it, he says, he heard a great voice and a shout louder than a thunder-peal crying, "Array, array, array!"

His heart grew hot as a burning coal, it grew cold as ice within him, as it seemed to him that a tumult of voices answered to his summons. He heard, or seemed to hear, thousands shouting: "St. George! St. George!"

"Ha! Messire, ha! sweet Saint, grant us good deliverance!"

"St. George for merry England!"

"Harow! Harow! Monseigneur St. George, succor us!"

"Ha! St. George! Ha! St. George! a long bow and a strong bow."

"Heaven's Knight, aid us!"

And as the soldier heard these voices he saw before him, beyond the trench, a long line of shapes, with a shining about them. They were like men who drew the bow, and with another shout, their cloud of arrows flew singing and tingling through the air towards the German hosts.

The other men in the trench were firing all the while. They had no hope; but they aimed just as if they had been shooting at Bisley.

Suddenly one of them lifted up his voice in the plainest English.

"Gawd help us!" he bellowed to the man next to him, "but we're blooming marvels! Look at those grey . . . gentlemen, look at them! D'ye see them? They're not going down in dozens nor in 'undreds; it's thousands, it is. Look! look! there's a regiment gone while I'm talking to ye."

"Shut it!" the other soldier bellowed, taking aim, "what are ye gassing about?"

But he gulped with astonishment even as he spoke, for, indeed, the grey men were falling by the thousands. The English could hear the guttural scream of the German officers, the crackle of their revolvers as they shot the reluctant; and still line after line crashed to the earth.

All the while the Latin-bred soldier heard the cry:

"Harow! Harow! Monseigneur, dear Saint, quick to our aid! St. George help us!"

"High Chevalier, defend us!"

The singing arrows fled so swift and thick that they darkened the air; the heathen horde melted from before them.

"More machine-guns!" Bill yelled to Tom.

"Don't hear them," Tom yelled back. "But, thank God, anyway; they've got it in the neck."

In fact, there were ten thousand dead German soldiers left before that salient of the English army, and consequently there was no Sedan. In Germany, a country ruled by scientific principles, the great general staff decided that the contemptible English must have employed shells containing an unknown gas of a poisonous nature, as no wounds were discernible on the bodies of the dead German soldiers. But the man who knew what nuts tasted like when they called themselves steak knew also that St. George had brought his Agincourt bowmen to help the English.

THE OPEN WINDOW

Saki

Saki (1870–1916), real name Hector Hugh Munro, was born in Burma where his father was Inspector-General of the Colonial Police. His mother died after being trampled by a runaway cow and Munro was sent home to be looked after by two aunts. Aunts often appear in his stories in unflattering lights. He joined the Burmese police force, but contracted malaria and was repatriated after eighteen months. Munro died at the battle of the Somme. His last words were, 'Put that damned cigarette out!'

"My aunt will be down presently, Mr. Nuttel," said a very self-possessed young lady of fifteen; "in the meantime you must try and put up with me."

Framton Nuttel endeavoured to say the correct something which should duly flatter the niece of the moment without unduly discounting the aunt that was to come. Privately he doubted more than ever whether these formal visits on a succession of total strangers would do much towards helping the nerve cure which he was supposed to be undergoing.

"I know how it will be," his sister had said when he was preparing to migrate to this rural retreat; "you will bury yourself down there and not speak to a living soul, and your nerves will be worse than ever from moping. I shall just give you letters of introduction to all the people I know there. Some of them, as far as I can remember, were quite nice."

Framton wondered whether Mrs. Sappleton, the lady to whom he was presenting one of the letters of introduction, came into the nice division.

"Do you know many of the people round here?" asked the niece, when she judged that they had had sufficient silent communion.

"Hardly a soul," said Framton. "My sister was staying here, at the rectory, you know, some four years ago, and she gave me letters of introduction to some of the people here."

He made the last statement in a tone of distinct regret.

"Then you know practically nothing about my aunt?" pursued the self-possessed young lady.

"Only her name and address," admitted the caller. He was wondering whether Mrs. Sappleton was in the married or widowed state. An undefinable something about the room seemed to suggest masculine habitation.

"Her great tragedy happened just three years ago," said the child; "that would be since your sister's time."

"Her tragedy?" asked Framton; somehow in this restful country spot tragedies seemed out of place.

"You may wonder why we keep that window wide open on an October afternoon," said the niece, indicating a large French window that opened on to a lawn.

"It is quite warm for the time of the year," said Framton; "but has that window got anything to do with the tragedy?"

"Out through that window, three years ago to a day, her husband and her two young brothers went off for their day's shooting. They never came back. In crossing the moor to their favourite snipe-shooting ground they were all three engulfed in a treacherous piece of bog. It had been that dreadful wet summer, you know, and places that were safe in other years gave way suddenly without warning. Their bodies were never recovered. That was the dreadful part of it." Here the child's voice lost its self-possessed note and became falteringly human. "Poor aunt always thinks that they will come back some day, they and the little brown spaniel that was lost with them, and walk in at that window just as they used to do. That is why the window is kept open every evening till it is quite dusk. Poor dear aunt, she has often told me how they went out, her husband with his white waterproof coat over his arm, and Ronnie, her youngest brother, singing 'Bertie, why do you bound?' as he always did to tease her, because she said it got on her nerves. Do you know, sometimes on still, quiet evenings like this, I almost get a creepy feeling that they will all walk in through that window – "

She broke off with a little shudder. It was a relief to Framton when the aunt bustled into the room with a whirl of apologies for being late in making her appearance.

"I hope Vera has been amusing you?" she said.

"She has been very interesting," said Framton.

"I hope you don't mind the open window," said Mrs. Sappleton briskly; "my husband and brothers will be home directly from shooting, and they always come in this way. They've been out for snipe in the marshes to-day, so they'll make a fine mess over my poor carpets. So like you men-folk, isn't it?"

She rattled on cheerfully about the shooting and the scarcity of birds, and the prospects for duck in the winter. To Framton it was all purely horrible. He made a desperate but only partially successful effort to turn the talk on to a less ghastly topic; he was conscious that his hostess was giving him only a fragment of her attention, and her eyes were constantly straying past him to the open window and the lawn beyond. It was certainly an unfortunate coincidence that he should have paid his visit on this tragic anniversary.

"The doctors agree in ordering me complete rest, an absence of mental excitement, and avoidance of anything in the nature of violent physical exercise," announced Framton, who laboured under the tolerably widespread delusion that total strangers and chance acquaintances are hungry for the least detail of one's ailments and infirmities, their cause and cure. "On the matter of diet they are not so much in agreement," he continued.

"No?" said Mrs. Sappleton, in a voice which only replaced a yawn at the last moment. Then she suddenly brightened into alert attention – but not to what Framton was saying.

"Here they are at last!" she cried. "Just in time for tea, and don't they look as if they were muddy up to the eyes!"

Framton shivered slightly and turned towards the niece with a look intended to convey sympathetic comprehension. The child was staring out through the open window with dazed horror in her eyes. In a chill shock of nameless fear Framton swung round in his seat and looked in the same direction.

In the deepening twilight three figures were walking across the lawn towards the window; they all carried guns under their arms, and one of them was additionally burdened with a white coat hung over his shoulders. A tired brown spaniel kept close at their heels. Noiselessly they neared the house, and then a hoarse young voice chanted out of the dusk: "I said, Bertie, why do you bound?"

Framton grabbed wildly at his stick and hat; the hall-door, the gravel-drive, and the front gate were dimly-noted stages in his headlong retreat. A cyclist coming along the road had to run into the hedge to avoid an imminent collision.

"Here we are, my dear," said the bearer of the white mackintosh, coming in through the window; "fairly muddy, but most of it's dry. Who was that who bolted out as we came up?"

"A most extraordinary man, a Mr. Nuttel," said Mrs. Sappleton; "could only talk about his illnesses, and dashed off without a word of good-bye or apology when you arrived. One would think he had seen a ghost."

"I expect it was the spaniel," said the niece calmly; "he told me he had a horror of dogs. He was once hunted into a cemetery somewhere on the banks of the Ganges by a pack of pariah dogs, and had to spend the night in a newly dug grave with the creatures snarling and grinning and foaming just above him. Enough to make anyone lose their nerve."

Romance at short notice was her speciality.

THE LADY'S MAID'S BELL

Edith Wharton

Edith Wharton (1862–1937) was the first woman to win a Pulitzer Prize. She was also nominated three times for the Nobel Prize for Literature. Wharton was born in New York, but much of her childhood was spent in Europe where her family travelled extensively. In 1913 she was divorced from her husband Edward Wharton, who had embezzled $50,000 of her trust fund. Wharton was a friend of Henry James, who she helped to support (without his knowledge) in his final years.

I

It was the autumn after I had the typhoid. I'd been three months in hospital, and when I came out I looked so weak and tottery that the two or three ladies I applied to were afraid to engage me. Most of my money was gone, and after I'd boarded for two months, hanging about the employment-agencies, and answering any advertisement that looked any way respectable, I pretty nearly lost heart, for fretting hadn't made me fatter, and I didn't see why my luck should ever turn. It did though – or I thought so at the time. A Mrs. Railton, a friend of the lady that first brought me out to the States, met me one day and stopped to speak to me: she was one that had always a friendly way with her. She asked me what ailed me to look so white, and when I told her, "Why, Hartley," says she, "I believe I've got the very place for you. Come in to-morrow and we'll talk about it."

The next day, when I called, she told me the lady she'd in mind was a niece of hers, a Mrs. Brympton, a youngish lady, but something of an invalid, who lived all the year round at her country-place on the Hudson, owing to not being able to stand the fatigue of town life.

"Now, Hartley," Mrs. Railton said, in that cheery way that always made me feel things must be going to take a turn for the better – "now understand me; it's not a cheerful place I'm sending you to. The house is big and gloomy; my niece is nervous, vaporish; her husband – well, he's generally away; and the two children are dead. A year ago, I would as soon have thought of shutting a rosy active girl like you into a vault; but you're not particularly brisk yourself just now, are you? and a quiet place, with country air and wholesome food and early hours, ought to be the very thing for you. Don't mistake me," she added, for I suppose I looked a trifle downcast; "you may find it dull, but you won't be unhappy. My niece is an angel. Her former maid, who died last spring, had been with her twenty years and worshipped the ground she walked on. She's a kind mistress to all, and where the mistress is kind, as you know, the servants are generally good-humored, so you'll probably get on well enough with the rest of the household. And you're the very woman I want for my niece: quiet, well-mannered, and educated above your station. You read aloud well, I think? That's a good thing; my niece likes to be read to. She wants a maid that can be something of a companion: her last was, and I can't say how she misses her. It's a lonely life. . .Well, have you decided?"

"Why, ma'am," I said, "I'm not afraid of solitude."

"Well, then, go; my niece will take you on my recommendation. I'll telegraph her at once and you can take the afternoon train. She has no one to wait on her at present, and I don't want you to lose any time."

I was ready enough to start, yet something in me hung back; and to gain time I asked, "And the gentleman, ma'am?"

"The gentleman's almost always away, I tell you," said Mrs. Ralston, quick-like – "and when he's there," says she suddenly, "you've only to keep out of his way."

I took the afternoon train and got out at D – station at about four o'clock. A groom in a dog-cart was waiting, and we drove off at a smart pace. It was a dull October day, with rain hanging close overhead, and by the time we turned into the Brympton Place woods the daylight was almost gone. The drive wound through the woods for a mile or two, and came out on a gravel court shut in with thickets of tall black-looking shrubs. There were no lights in the windows, and the house did look a bit gloomy.

I had asked no questions of the groom, for I never was one to get my notion of new masters from their other servants: I prefer to wait and see for myself. But I could tell by the look of everything that I had got into the right kind of house, and that things were done handsomely. A pleasant-faced cook met me at the back door and called the house-maid to show me up to my room. "You'll see madam later," she said. "Mrs. Brympton has a visitor."

I hadn't fancied Mrs. Brympton was a lady to have many visitors, and some-how the words cheered me. I followed the house-maid upstairs, and saw, through a door on the upper landing, that the main part of the house seemed well-fur-nished, with dark panelling and a number of old portraits. Another flight of stairs led us up to the servants' wing. It was almost dark now, and the house-maid excused herself for not having brought a light. "But there's matches in your room," she said, "and if you go careful you'll be all right. Mind the step at the end of the passage. Your room is just beyond."

I looked ahead as she spoke, and half-way down the passage, I saw a woman standing. She drew back into a doorway as we passed, and the house-maid didn't appear to notice her. She was a thin woman with a white face, and a darkish stuff gown and apron. I took her for the housekeeper and thought it odd that she didn't speak, but just gave me a long look as she went by. My room opened into a square hall at the end of the passage. Facing my door was another which stood open: the house-maid exclaimed when she saw it.

"There – Mrs. Blinder's left that door open again!" said she, closing it.

"Is Mrs. Blinder the housekeeper?"

"There's no housekeeper: Mrs. Blinder's the cook."

"And is that her room?"

"Laws, no," said the house-maid, cross-like. "That's nobody's room. It's empty, I mean, and the door hadn't ought to be open. Mrs. Brympton wants it kept locked."

She opened my door and led me into a neat room, nicely furnished, with a picture or two on the walls; and having lit a candle she took leave, telling me that the servants'-hall tea was at six, and that Mrs. Brympton would see me afterward.

I found them a pleasant-spoken set in the servants' hall, and by what they let fall I gathered that, as Mrs. Railton had said, Mrs. Brympton was the kindest of ladies; but I didn't take much notice of their talk, for I was watching to see the pale woman in the dark gown come in. She didn't show herself, however, and I wondered if she ate apart; but if she wasn't the housekeeper, why should she? Suddenly it struck me that she might be a trained nurse, and in that case her meals would of course be served in her room. If Mrs. Brympton was an invalid it was likely enough she had a nurse. The idea annoyed me, I own, for they're not always the easiest to get on with, and if I'd known, I shouldn't have taken the place. But there I was, and there was no use pulling a long face over it; and not being one to ask questions, I waited to see what would turn up.

When tea was over, the house-maid said to the footman: "Has Mr. Ranford gone?" and when he said yes, she told me to come up with her to Mrs. Brympton.

Mrs. Brympton was lying down in her bedroom. Her lounge stood near the fire and beside it was a shaded lamp. She was a delicate-looking lady, but when she smiled I felt there was nothing I wouldn't do for her. She spoke very pleasantly, in a low voice, asking me my name and age and so on, and if I had everything I wanted, and if I wasn't afraid of feeling lonely in the country.

"Not with you I wouldn't be, madam," I said, and the words surprised me when I'd spoken them, for I'm not an impulsive person; but it was just as if I'd thought aloud.

She seemed pleased at that, and said she hoped I'd continue in the same mind; then she gave me a few directions about her toilet, and said Agnes the house-maid would show me next morning where things were kept.

"I am tired to-night, and shall dine upstairs," she said. "Agnes will bring me my tray, that you may have time to unpack and settle yourself; and later you may come and undress me."

"Very well, ma'am," I said. "You'll ring, I suppose?"

I thought she looked odd.

"No – Agnes will fetch you," says she quickly, and took up her book again.

Well – that was certainly strange: a lady's maid having to be fetched by the house-maid whenever her lady wanted her! I wondered if there were no bells in the house; but the next day I satisfied myself that there was one in every room, and a special one ringing from my mistress's room to mine; and after that it did strike me as queer that, whenever Mrs. Brympton wanted anything, she rang for Agnes, who had to walk the whole length of the servants' wing to call me.

But that wasn't the only queer thing in the house. The very next day I found out that Mrs. Brympton had no nurse; and then I asked Agnes about the woman I had seen in the passage the afternoon before. Agnes said she had seen no one, and I saw that she thought I was dreaming. To be sure, it was dusk when we went down the passage, and she had excused herself for not bringing a light; but I had seen the woman plain enough to know her again if we should meet. I decided that she must have been a friend of the cook's, or of one of the other women-servants: perhaps she had come down from town for a night's visit, and the servants wanted it kept secret. Some ladies are very stiff about having their servants' friends in the house overnight. At any rate, I made up my mind to ask no more questions.

In a day or two, another odd thing happened. I was chatting one afternoon with Mrs. Blinder, who was a friendly disposed woman, and had been longer in the house than the other servants, and she asked me if I was quite comfortable and had everything I needed. I said I had no fault to find with my place or with my mistress, but I thought it odd that in so large a house there was no sewing-room for the lady's maid.

"Why," says she, "there is one; the room you're in is the old sewing-room."

"Oh," said I; "and where did the other lady's maid sleep?"

At that she grew confused, and said hurriedly that the servants' rooms had all been changed about last year, and she didn't rightly remember.

That struck me as peculiar, but I went on as if I hadn't noticed: "Well, there's a vacant room opposite mine, and I mean to ask Mrs. Brympton if I mayn't use that as a sewing-room."

To my astonishment, Mrs. Blinder went white, and gave my hand a kind of squeeze. "Don't do that, my dear," said she, trembling-like. "To tell you the truth, that was Emma Saxon's room, and my mistress has kept it closed ever since her death."

"And who was Emma Saxon?"

"Mrs. Brympton's former maid."

"The one that was with her so many years?" said I, remembering what Mrs. Railton had told me.

Mrs. Blinder nodded.

"What sort of woman was she?"

"No better walked the earth," said Mrs. Blinder. "My mistress loved her like a sister."

"But I mean – what did she look like?"

Mrs. Blinder got up and gave me a kind of angry stare. "I'm no great hand at describing," she said; "and I believe my pastry's rising." And she walked off into the kitchen and shut the door after her.

II

I had been near a week at Brympton before I saw my master. Word came that he was arriving one afternoon, and a change passed over the whole household. It was plain that nobody loved him below stairs. Mrs. Blinder took uncommon care with the dinner that night, but she snapped at the kitchen-maid in a way quite unusual with her; and Mr. Wace, the butler, a serious, slow-spoken man, went about his duties as if he'd been getting ready for a funeral. He was a great Bible-reader, Mr. Wace was, and had a beautiful assortment of texts at his command; but that day he used such dreadful language that I was about to leave the table, when he assured me it was all out of Isaiah; and I noticed that whenever the master came Mr. Wace took to the prophets.

About seven, Agnes called me to my mistress's room; and there I found Mr.

Brympton. He was standing on the hearth; a big fair bull-necked man, with a red face and little bad-tempered blue eyes: the kind of man a young simpleton might have thought handsome, and would have been like to pay dear for thinking it.

He swung about when I came in, and looked me over in a trice. I knew what the look meant, from having experienced it once or twice in my former places. Then he turned his back on me, and went on talking to his wife; and I knew what that meant, too. I was not the kind of morsel he was after. The typhoid had served me well enough in one way: it kept that kind of gentleman at arm's-length.

"This is my new maid, Hartley," says Mrs. Brympton in her kind voice; and he nodded and went on with what he was saying.

In a minute or two he went off, and left my mistress to dress for dinner, and I noticed as I waited on her that she was white, and chill to the touch.

Mr. Brympton took himself off the next morning, and the whole house drew a long breath when he drove away. As for my mistress, she put on her hat and furs (for it was a fine winter morning) and went out for a walk in the gardens, coming back quite fresh and rosy, so that for a minute, before her color faded, I could guess what a pretty young lady she must have been, and not so long ago, either.

She had met Mr. Ranford in the grounds, and the two came back together, I remember, smiling and talking as they walked along the terrace under my window. That was the first time I saw Mr. Ranford, though I had often heard his name mentioned in the hall. He was a neighbor, it appeared, living a mile or two beyond Brympton, at the end of the village; and as he was in the habit of spending his winters in the country he was almost the only company my mistress had at that season. He was a slight tall gentleman of about thirty, and I thought him rather melancholy-looking till I saw his smile, which had a kind of surprise in it, like the first warm day in spring. He was a great reader, I heard, like my mistress, and the two were forever borrowing books of one another, and sometimes (Mr. Wace told me) he would read aloud to Mrs. Brympton by the hour, in the big dark library where she sat in the winter afternoons. The servants all liked him, and perhaps that's more of a compliment than the masters suspect. He had a friendly word for every one of us, and we were all glad to think that Mrs. Brympton had a pleasant companionable gentleman like that to keep her company when the master was away. Mr. Ranford seemed on excellent terms with Mr. Brympton too; though I couldn't but wonder that two gentlemen so unlike each other should be so friendly. But then I knew how the real quality can keep their feelings to themselves.

As for Mr. Brympton, he came and went, never staying more than a day or two, cursing the dullness and the solitude, grumbling at everything, and (as I soon found out) drinking a deal more than was good for him. After Mrs. Brympton left the table he would sit half the night over the old Brympton port and madeira, and once, as I was leaving my mistress's room rather later than usual, I met him coming up the stairs in such a state that I turned sick to think of what some ladies have to endure and hold their tongues about.

The servants said very little about their master; but from what they let drop I could see it had been an unhappy match from the beginning. Mr. Brympton was coarse, loud and pleasure-loving; my mistress quiet, retiring, and perhaps a trifle cold. Not that she was not always pleasant-spoken to him: I thought her wonderfully forbearing; but to a gentleman as free as Mr. Brympton I daresay she seemed a little offish.

Well, things went on quietly for several weeks. My mistress was kind, my duties were light, and I got on well with the other servants. In short, I had nothing to complain of; yet there was always a weight on me. I can't say why it was so, but I know it was not the loneliness that I felt. I soon got used to that; and being still languid from the fever, I was thankful for the quiet and the good country air. Nevertheless, I was never quite easy in my mind. My mistress, knowing I had been ill, insisted that I should take my walk regular, and often invented errands for me: – a yard of ribbon to be fetched from the village, a letter posted, or a book returned to Mr. Ranford. As soon as I was out of doors my spirits rose, and I looked forward to my walks through the bare moist-smelling woods; but the moment I caught sight of the house again my heart dropped down like a stone in a well. It was not a gloomy house exactly, yet I never entered it but a feeling of gloom came over me.

Mrs. Brympton seldom went out in winter; only on the finest days did she walk an hour at noon on the south terrace. Excepting Mr. Ranford, we had no visitors but the doctor, who drove over from D – – about once a week. He sent for me once or twice to give me some trifling direction about my mistress, and though he never told me what her illness was, I thought, from a waxy look she had now and then of a morning, that it might be the heart that ailed her. The season was soft and unwholesome, and in January we had a long spell of rain. That was a sore trial to me, I own, for I couldn't go out, and sitting over my sewing all day, listening to the drip, drip of the eaves, I grew so nervous that the least sound made me jump. Somehow, the thought of that locked room across the passage began to weigh on me. Once or twice, in the long rainy nights, I fancied I heard noises there; but that was nonsense, of course, and the daylight drove such notions out of my head. Well, one morning Mrs. Brympton gave me quite a start of pleasure by telling me she wished me to go to town for some shopping. I hadn't known till then how low my spirits had fallen. I set off in high glee, and my first sight of the crowded streets and the cheerful-looking shops quite took me out of myself. Toward afternoon, however, the noise and confusion began to tire me, and I was actually looking forward to the quiet of Brympton, and thinking how I should enjoy the drive home through the dark woods, when I ran across an old acquaintance, a maid I had once been in service with. We had lost sight of each other for a number of years, and I had to stop and tell her what had happened to me in the interval. When I mentioned where I was living she rolled up her eyes and pulled a long face.

"What! The Mrs. Brympton that lives all the year at her place on the Hudson? My dear, you won't stay there three months."

"Oh, but I don't mind the country," says I, offended somehow at her tone. "Since the fever I'm glad to be quiet."

She shook her head. "It's not the country I'm thinking of. All I know is she's had four maids in the last six months, and the last one, who was a friend of mine, told me nobody could stay in the house."

"Did she say why?" I asked.

"No – she wouldn't give me her reason. But she says to me, Mrs. Ansey, she says, if ever a young woman as you know of thinks of going there, you tell her it's not worth while to unpack her boxes."

"Is she young and handsome?" said I, thinking of Mr. Brympton.

"Not her! She's the kind that mothers engage when they've gay young gentlemen at college."

Well, though I knew the woman was an idle gossip, the words stuck in my head, and my heart sank lower than ever as I drove up to Brympton in the dusk. There was something about the house – I was sure of it now. . .

When I went in to tea I heard that Mr. Brympton had arrived, and I saw at a glance that there had been a disturbance of some kind. Mrs. Blinder's hand shook so that she could hardly pour the tea, and Mr. Wace quoted the most dreadful texts full of brimstone. Nobody said a word to me then, but when I went up to my room Mrs. Blinder followed me.

"Oh, my dear," says she, taking my hand, "I'm so glad and thankful you've come back to us!"

That struck me, as you may imagine. "Why," said I, "did you think I was leaving for good?"

"No, no, to be sure," said she, a little confused, "but I can't a-bear to have madam left alone for a day even." She pressed my hand hard, and, "Oh, Miss Hartley," says she, "be good to your mistress, as you're a Christian woman." And with that she hurried away, and left me staring.

A moment later Agnes called me to Mrs. Brympton. Hearing Mr. Brympton's voice in her room, I went round by the dressing-room, thinking I would lay out her dinner-gown before going in. The dressing-room is a large room with a window over the portico that looks toward the gardens. Mr. Brympton's apartments are beyond. When I went in, the door into the bedroom was ajar, and I heard Mr. Brympton saying angrily: – "One would suppose he was the only person fit for you to talk to."

"I don't have many visitors in winter," Mrs. Brympton answered quietly.

"You have me!" he flung at her, sneering.

"You are here so seldom," said she.

"Well – whose fault is that? You make the place about as lively as a family vault –"

With that I rattled the toilet-things, to give my mistress warning and she rose and called me in.

The two dined alone, as usual, and I knew by Mr. Wace's manner at supper that things must be going badly. He quoted the prophets something terrible, and worked on the kitchen-maid so that she declared she wouldn't go down alone to put the cold meat in the ice-box. I felt nervous myself, and after I had put my mistress to bed I was half-tempted to go down again and persuade Mrs. Blinder to sit up awhile over a game of cards. But I heard her door closing for the night, and so I went on to my own room. The rain had begun again, and the drip, drip, drip seemed to be dropping into my brain. I lay awake listening to it, and turning over what my friend in town had said. What puzzled me was that it was always the maids who left. . .

After a while I slept; but suddenly a loud noise wakened me. My bell had rung. I sat up, terrified by the unusual sound, which seemed to go on jangling through the darkness. My hands shook so that I couldn't find the matches. At length I struck a light and jumped out of bed. I began to think I must have been dreaming; but I looked at the bell against the wall, and there was the little hammer still quivering.

I was just beginning to huddle on my clothes when I heard another sound. This time it was the door of the locked room opposite mine softly opening and closing. I heard the sound distinctly, and it frightened me so that I stood stock still. Then I heard a footstep hurrying down the passage toward the main house. The floor being carpeted, the sound was very faint, but I was quite sure it was a woman's step. I turned cold with the thought of it, and for a minute or two I dursn't breathe or move. Then I came to my senses.

"Alice Hartley," says I to myself, "someone left that room just now and ran down the passage ahead of you. The idea isn't pleasant, but you may as well face it. Your mistress has rung for you, and to answer her bell you've got to go the way that other woman has gone."

Well – I did it. I never walked faster in my life, yet I thought I should never get to the end of the passage or reach Mrs. Brympton's room. On the way I heard nothing and saw nothing: all was dark and quiet as the grave. When I reached my mistress's door the silence was so deep that I began to think I must be dreaming, and was half-minded to turn back. Then a panic seized me, and I knocked.

There was no answer, and I knocked again, loudly. To my astonishment the door was opened by Mr. Brympton. He started back when he saw me, and in the light of my candle his face looked red and savage.

"You!" he said, in a queer voice. "How many of you are there, in God's name?"

At that I felt the ground give under me; but I said to myself that he had been drinking, and answered as steadily as I could: "May I go in, sir? Mrs. Brympton has rung for me."

"You may all go in, for what I care," says he, and, pushing by me, walked down the hall to his own bedroom. I looked after him as he went, and to my surprise I saw that he walked as straight as a sober man.

I found my mistress lying very weak and still, but she forced a smile when she saw me, and signed to me to pour out some drops for her. After that she lay without speaking, her breath coming quick, and her eyes closed. Suddenly she groped out with her hand, and "Emma," says she, faintly.

"It's Hartley, madam," I said. "Do you want anything?"

She opened her eyes wide and gave me a startled look.

"I was dreaming," she said. "You may go, now, Hartley, and thank you kindly. I'm quite well again, you see." And she turned her face away from me.

III

There was no more sleep for me that night, and I was thankful when daylight came.

Soon afterward, Agnes called me to Mrs. Brympton. I was afraid she was ill again, for she seldom sent for me before nine, but I found her sitting up in bed, pale and drawn-looking, but quite herself.

"Hartley," says she quickly, "will you put on your things at once and go down to the village for me? I want this prescription made up –" here she hesitated a minute and blushed – "and I should like you to be back again before Mr. Brympton is up."

"Certainly, madam," I said.

"And – stay a moment –" she called me back as if an idea had just struck her – "while you're waiting for the mixture, you'll have time to go on to Mr. Ranford's with this note."

It was a two-mile walk to the village, and on my way I had time to turn things over in my mind. It struck me as peculiar that my mistress should wish the prescription made up without Mr. Brympton's knowledge; and, putting this together with the scene of the night before, and with much else that I had noticed and suspected, I began to wonder if the poor lady was weary of her life, and had come to the mad resolve of ending it. The idea took such hold on me that I reached the village on a run, and dropped breathless into a chair before the chemist's counter. The good man, who was just taking down his shutters, stared at me so hard that it brought me to myself.

"Mr. Limmel," I says, trying to speak indifferent, "will you run your eye over this, and tell me if it's quite right?"

He put on his spectacles and studied the prescription.

"Why, it's one of Dr. Walton's," says he. "What should be wrong with it?"

"Well – is it dangerous to take?"

"Dangerous – how do you mean?"

I could have shaken the man for his stupidity.

"I mean – if a person was to take too much of it – by mistake of course –" says I, my heart in my throat.

"Lord bless you, no. It's only lime-water. You might feed it to a baby by the bottleful."

I gave a great sigh of relief, and hurried on to Mr. Ranford's. But on the way another thought struck me. If there was nothing to conceal about my visit to the chemist's, was it my other errand that Mrs. Brympton wished me to keep private? Somehow, that thought frightened me worse than the other. Yet the two gentlemen seemed fast friends, and I would have staked my head on my mistress's goodness. I felt ashamed of my suspicions, and concluded that I was still disturbed by the strange events of the night. I left the note at Mr. Ranford's – and, hurrying back to Brympton, slipped in by a side door without being seen, as I thought.

An hour later, however, as I was carrying in my mistress's breakfast, I was stopped in the hall by Mr. Brympton.

"What were you doing out so early?" he says, looking hard at me.

"Early – me, sir?" I said, in a tremble.

"Come, come," he says, an angry red spot coming out on his forehead, "didn't I see you scuttling home through the shrubbery an hour or more ago?"

I'm a truthful woman by nature, but at that a lie popped out ready-made. "No, sir, you didn't," said I, and looked straight back at him.

He shrugged his shoulders and gave a sullen laugh. "I suppose you think I was drunk last night?" he asked suddenly.

"No, sir, I don't," I answered, this time truthfully enough.

He turned away with another shrug. "A pretty notion my servants have of me!" I heard him mutter as he walked off.

Not till I had settled down to my afternoon's sewing did I realize how the events of the night had shaken me. I couldn't pass that locked door without a shiver. I knew I had heard someone come out of it, and walk down the passage ahead of me. I thought of speaking to Mrs. Blinder or to Mr. Wace, the only two in the house who appeared to have an inkling of what was going on, but I had a feeling that if I questioned them they would deny everything, and that I might learn more by holding my tongue and keeping my eyes open. The idea of spending another night opposite the locked room sickened me, and once I was seized with the notion of packing my trunk and taking the first train to town; but it wasn't in me to throw over a kind mistress in that manner, and I tried to go on with my sewing as if nothing had happened.

I hadn't worked ten minutes before the sewing-machine broke down. It was one I had found in the house, a good machine, but a trifle out of order: Mrs. Blinder said it had never been used since Emma Saxon's death. I stopped to see what was wrong, and as I was working at the machine a drawer which I had never been able to open slid forward and a photograph fell out. I picked it up and sat looking at it in a maze. It was a woman's likeness, and I knew I had seen the face somewhere – the eyes had an asking look that I had felt on me before. And suddenly I remembered the pale woman in the passage.

I stood up, cold all over, and ran out of the room. My heart seemed to be thumping in the top of my head, and I felt as if I should never get away from the look in those eyes. I went straight to Mrs. Blinder. She was taking her afternoon nap, and sat up with a jump when I came in.

"Mrs. Blinder," said I, "who is that?" And I held out the photograph.

She rubbed her eyes and stared.

"Why, Emma Saxon," says she. "Where did you find it?"

I looked hard at her for a minute. "Mrs. Blinder," I said, "I've seen that face before."

Mrs. Blinder got up and walked over to the looking-glass. "Dear me! I must have been asleep," she says. "My front is all over one ear. And now do run along, Miss Hartley, dear, for I hear the clock striking four, and I must go down this very minute and put on the Virginia ham for Mr. Brympton's dinner."

IV

To all appearances, things went on as usual for a week or two. The only difference was that Mr. Brympton stayed on, instead of going off as he usually did, and that Mr. Ranford never showed himself. I heard Mr. Brympton remark on this one afternoon when he was sitting in my mistress's room before dinner.

"Where's Ranford?" says he. "He hasn't been near the house for a week. Does he keep away because I'm here?"

Mrs. Brympton spoke so low that I couldn't catch her answer.

"Well," he went on, "two's company and three's trumpery; I'm sorry to be in Ranford's way, and I suppose I shall have to take myself off again in a day or two and give him a show." And he laughed at his own joke.

The very next day, as it happened, Mr. Ranford called. The footman said the three were very merry over their tea in the library, and Mr. Brympton strolled down to the gate with Mr. Ranford when he left.

I have said that things went on as usual; and so they did with the rest of the household; but as for myself, I had never been the same since the night my bell had rung. Night after night I used to lie awake, listening for it to ring again, and for the door of the locked room to open stealthily. But the bell never rang, and I heard no sound across the passage. At last the silence began to be more dreadful to me than the most mysterious sounds. I felt that someone were cowering there, behind the locked door, watching and listening as I watched and listened, and I could almost have cried out, "Whoever you are, come out and let me see you face to face, but don't lurk there and spy on me in the darkness!"

Feeling as I did, you may wonder I didn't give warning. Once I very nearly did so; but at the last moment something held me back. Whether it was compassion for my mistress, who had grown more and more dependent on me, or unwillingness to try a new place, or some other feeling that I couldn't put a name to, I lingered on as if spell-bound, though every night was dreadful to me, and the days but little better.

For one thing, I didn't like Mrs. Brympton's looks. She had never been the same since that night, no more than I had. I thought she would brighten up after Mr. Brympton left, but though she seemed easier in her mind, her spirits didn't revive, nor her strength either. She had grown attached to me, and seemed to like to have me about; and Agnes told me one day that, since Emma Saxon's death, I was the only maid her mistress had taken to. This gave me a warm feeling for the poor lady, though after all there was little I could do to help her.

After Mr. Brympton's departure, Mr. Ranford took to coming again, though less often than formerly. I met him once or twice in the grounds, or in the village, and I couldn't but think there was a change in him too; but I set it down to my disordered fancy.

The weeks passed, and Mr. Brympton had now been a month absent. We heard he was cruising with a friend in the West Indies, and Mr. Wace said that was a long way off, but though you had the wings of a dove and went to the uttermost parts of the earth, you couldn't get away from the Almighty. Agnes said that as long as he stayed away from Brympton, the Almighty might have him and welcome; and this raised a laugh, though Mrs. Blinder tried to look shocked, and Mr. Wace said the bears would eat us.

We were all glad to hear that the West Indies were a long way off, and I remember that, in spite of Mr. Wace's solemn looks, we had a very merry dinner that day in the hall. I don't know if it was because of my being in better spirits, but I fancied Mrs. Brympton looked better too, and seemed more cheerful in her manner. She had been for a walk in the morning, and after luncheon she lay down in her room, and I read aloud to her. When she dismissed me I went to my own room feeling quite bright and happy, and for the first time in weeks walked past the locked door without thinking of it. As I sat down to my work I looked out and saw a few snow-flakes falling. The sight was pleasanter than the eternal rain, and I pictured to myself how pretty the bare gardens would look in their white mantle. It seemed to me as if the snow would cover up all the dreariness, indoors as well as out.

The fancy had hardly crossed my mind when I heard a step at my side. I looked up, thinking it was Agnes.

"Well, Agnes –" said I, and the words froze on my tongue; for there, in the door, stood Emma Saxon.

I don't know how long she stood there. I only know I couldn't stir or take my eyes from her. Afterward I was terribly frightened, but at the time it wasn't fear I felt, but something deeper and quieter. She looked at me long and long, and her face was just one dumb prayer to me – but how in the world was I to help her? Suddenly she turned, and I heard her walk down the passage. This time I wasn't afraid to follow – I felt that I must know what she wanted. I sprang up and ran out. She was at the other end of the passage, and I expected her to take the turn toward my mistress's room; but instead of that she pushed open the door that led to the backstairs. I followed her down the stairs, and across the passageway to the back door. The kitchen and hall were empty at that hour, the servants being off duty, except for the footman, who was in the pantry. At the door she stood still a moment, with another look at me; then she turned the handle, and stepped out. For a minute I hesitated. Where was she leading me to? The door had closed softly after her, and I opened it and looked out, half-expecting to find that she had disappeared. But I saw her a few yards off, hurrying across the court-yard to the path through the woods. Her figure looked black and lonely in the snow, and for a second my heart failed me and I thought of turning back. But all the while she was drawing me after her; and catching up an old shawl of Mrs. Blinder's I ran out into the open.

Emma Saxon was in the wood-path now. She walked on steadily, and I followed at the same pace, till we passed out of the gates and reached the high-road. Then she struck across the open fields to the village. By this time the ground was white, and as she climbed the slope of a bare hill ahead of me I noticed that she left no foot-prints behind her. At sight of that, my heart shrivelled up within me, and my knees were water. Somehow, it was worse here than indoors. She made the whole countryside seem lonely as the grave, with none but us two in it, and no help in the wide world.

Once I tried to go back; but she turned and looked at me, and it was as if she had dragged me with ropes. After that I followed her like a dog. We came to the village, and she led me through it, past the church and the blacksmith's shop, and down the lane to Mr. Ranford's. Mr. Ranford's house stands close to the road: a plain old-fashioned building, with a flagged path leading to the door between box-borders. The lane was deserted, and as I turned into it, I saw Emma Saxon pause under the old elm by the gate. And now another fear came over me. I saw that we had reached the end of our journey, and that it was my turn to act. All the way from Brympton I had been asking myself what she wanted of me, but I had followed in a trance, as it were, and not till I saw her stop at Mr. Ranford's gate did my brain begin to clear itself. It stood a little way off in the snow, my heart beating fit to strangle me, and my feet frozen to the ground; and she stood under the elm and watched me.

I knew well enough that she hadn't led me there for nothing. I felt there was something I ought to say or do – but how was I to guess what it was? I had never thought harm of my mistress and Mr. Ranford, but I was sure now that, from one cause or another, some dreadful thing hung over them. She knew what it was; she would tell me if she could; perhaps she would answer if I questioned her.

It turned me faint to think of speaking to her; but I plucked up heart and dragged myself across the few yards between us. As I did so, I heard the house-door open, and saw Mr. Ranford approaching. He looked handsome and cheerful, as my mistress had looked that morning, and at sight of him the blood began to flow again in my veins.

"Why, Hartley," said he, "what's the matter? I saw you coming down the lane just now, and came out to see if you had taken root in the snow." He stopped and stared at me. "What are you looking at?" he says.

I turned toward the elm as he spoke, and his eyes followed me; but there was no one there. The lane was empty as far as the eye could reach.

A sense of helplessness came over me. She was gone, and I had not been able to guess what she wanted. Her last look had pierced me to the marrow; and yet it had not told me! All at once, I felt more desolate than when she had stood there watching me. It seemed as if she had left me all alone to carry the weight of the secret I couldn't guess. The snow went round me in great circles, and the ground fell away from me. . . .

A drop of brandy and the warmth of Mr. Ranford's fire soon brought me to, and I insisted on being driven back at once to Brympton. It was nearly dark, and I was afraid my mistress might be wanting me. I explained to Mr. Ranford that I had been out for a walk and had been taken with a fit of giddiness as I passed his gate. This was true enough; yet I never felt more like a liar than when I said it.

When I dressed Mrs. Brympton for dinner she remarked on my pale looks and asked what ailed me. I told her I had a headache, and she said she would not require me again that evening, and advised me to go to bed.

It was a fact that I could scarcely keep on my feet; yet I had no fancy to spend a solitary evening in my room. I sat downstairs in the hall as long as I could hold my head up; but by nine I crept upstairs, too weary to care what happened if I could but get my head on a pillow. The rest of the household went to bed soon afterward; they kept early hours when the master was away, and before ten I heard Mrs. Blinder's door close, and Mr. Wace's soon after.

It was a very still night, earth and air all muffled in snow. Once in bed I felt easier, and lay quiet, listening to the strange noises that come out in a house after dark. Once I thought I heard a door open and close again below: it might have been the glass door that led to the gardens. I got up and peered out of the window; but it was in the dark of the moon, and nothing visible outside but the streaking of snow against the panes.

I went back to bed and must have dozed, for I jumped awake to the furious ringing of my bell. Before my head was clear I had sprung out of bed, and was dragging on my clothes. It is going to happen now, I heard myself saying; but what I meant I had no notion. My hands seemed to be covered with glue – I thought I should never get into my clothes. At last I opened my door and peered down the passage. As far as my candle-flame carried, I could see nothing unusual ahead of me. I hurried on, breathless; but as I pushed open the baize door leading to the main hall my heart stood still, for there at the head of the stairs was Emma Saxon, peering dreadfully down into the darkness.

For a second I couldn't stir; but my hand slipped from the door, and as it swung shut the figure vanished. At the same instant there came another sound from below stairs – a stealthy mysterious sound, as of a latch-key turning in the house-door. I ran to Mrs. Brympton's room and knocked.

There was no answer, and I knocked again. This time I heard some one moving in the room; the bolt slipped back and my mistress stood before me. To my surprise I saw that she had not undressed for the night. She gave me a startled look.

"What is this, Hartley?" she says in a whisper. "Are you ill? What are you doing here at this hour?"

"I am not ill, madam; but my bell rang."

At that she turned pale, and seemed about to fall.

"You are mistaken," she said harshly; "I didn't ring. You must have been dreaming." I had never heard her speak in such a tone. "Go back to bed," she said, closing the door on me.

But as she spoke I heard sounds again in the hall below: a man's step this time; and the truth leaped out on me.

"Madam," I said, pushing past her, "there is someone in the house –"

"Someone –?"

"Mr. Brympton, I think – I hear his step below –"

A dreadful look came over her, and without a word, she dropped flat at my feet. I fell on my knees and tried to lift her: by the way she breathed I saw it was no common faint. But as I raised her head there came quick steps on the stairs and across the hall: the door was flung open, and there stood Mr. Brympton, in his travelling-clothes, the snow dripping from him. He drew back with a start as he saw me kneeling by my mistress.

"What the devil is this?" he shouted. He was less high-colored than usual, and the red spot came out on his forehead.

"Mrs. Brympton has fainted, sir," said I.

He laughed unsteadily and pushed by me. "It's a pity she didn't choose a more convenient moment. I'm sorry to disturb her, but –"

I raised myself up, aghast at the man's action.

"Sir," said I, "are you mad? What are you doing?"

"Going to meet a friend," said he, and seemed to make for the dressing-room.

At that my heart turned over. I don't know what I thought or feared; but I sprang up and caught him by the sleeve.

"Sir, sir," said I, "for pity's sake look at your wife!"

He shook me off furiously.

"It seems that's done for me," says he, and caught hold of the dressing-room door.

At that moment I heard a slight noise inside. Slight as it was, he heard it too, and tore the door open; but as he did so he dropped back. On the threshold stood Emma Saxon. All was dark behind her, but I saw her plainly, and so did he. He threw up his hands as if to hide his face from her; and when I looked again she was gone.

He stood motionless, as if the strength had run out of him; and in the stillness my mistress suddenly raised herself, and opening her eyes fixed a look on him. Then she fell back, and I saw the death-flutter pass over her. . . .

We buried her on the third day, in a driving snow-storm. There were few people in the church, for it was bad weather to come from town, and I've a notion my mistress was one that hadn't many near friends. Mr. Ranford was among the last to come, just before they carried her up the aisle. He was in black, of course, being such a friend of the family, and I never saw a gentleman so pale. As he passed me, I noticed that he leaned a trifle on a stick he carried; and I fancy Mr. Brympton noticed it too, for the red spot came out sharp on his forehead, and all through the service he kept staring across the church at Mr. Ranford, instead of following the prayers as a mourner should.

When it was over and we went out to the graveyard, Mr. Ranford had disappeared, and as soon as my poor mistress's body was underground, Mr. Brympton jumped into the carriage nearest the gate and drove off without a word to any of us. I heard him call out, "To the station," and we servants went back alone to the house.

THE TERRIBLE OLD MAN

H.P. Lovecraft

Howard Phillips Lovecraft (1890–1937) was born and spent most of his life in Providence, Rhode Island. Lovecraft's father died in an asylum and his mother was also later institutionalised. A highly intelligent child, his formal education was disrupted by a series of nervous collapses. Lovecraft was best known to readers of American horror and pulp fiction during his lifetime. His critical reputation has grown posthumously, despite accusations of racism.

The inhabitants of Kingsport say and think many things about the Terrible Old Man which generally keep him safe from the attention of gentlemen like Mr. Ricci and his colleagues, despite the almost certain fact that he hides a fortune of indefinite magnitude somewhere about his musty and venerable abode. He is, in truth, a very strange person, believed to have been a captain of East India clipper ships in his day; so old that no one can remember when he was young, and so taciturn that few know his real name. Among the gnarled trees in the front yard of his aged and neglected place he maintains a strange collection of large stones, oddly grouped and painted so that they resemble the idols in some obscure Eastern temple. This collection frightens away most of the small boys who love to taunt the Terrible Old Man about his long white hair and beard, or to break the small – paned windows of his dwelling with wicked missiles; but there are other things which frighten the older and more curious folk who sometimes steal up to the house to peer in through the dusty panes. These folk say that on a table in a bare room on the ground floor are many peculiar bottles, in each a small piece of lead suspended pendulum-wise from a string. And they say that the Terrible Old Man talks to these bottles, addressing them by such names as Jack, Scar – Face, Long Tom, Spanish Joe, Peters, and Mate Ellis, and that whenever he speaks to a bottle the little lead pendulum within makes certain definite vibrations as if in answer.

Those who have watched the tall, lean, Terrible Old Man in these peculiar conversations, do not watch him again. But Angelo Ricci and Joe Czanek and Manuel Silva were not of Kingsport blood; they were of that new and heterogeneous alien stock which lies outside the charmed circle of New England life and traditions, and they saw in the Terrible Old Man merely a tottering, almost helpless grey-beard, who could not walk without the aid of his knotted cane, and whose thin, weak hands shook pitifully. They were really quite sorry in their way for the lonely, unpopular old fellow, whom everybody shunned, and at whom all the dogs barked singularly. But business is business, and to a robber whose soul is in his profession, there is a lure and a challenge about a very old and very feeble man who has no account at the bank, and who pays for his few necessities at the village store with Spanish gold and silver minted two centuries ago.

Messrs. Ricci, Czanek, and Silva selected the night of April 11th for their call. Mr. Ricci and Mr. Silva were to interview the poor old gentleman, whilst Mr. Czanek waited for them and their presumable metallic burden with a covered motor-car in Ship Street, by the gate in the tall rear wall of their host's grounds. Desire to avoid needless explanations in case of unexpected police intrusions prompted these plans for a quiet and unostentatious departure.

As prearranged, the three adventurers started out separately in order to prevent any evil-minded suspicions afterward. Messrs. Ricci and Silva met in Water Street by the old man's front gate, and although they did not like the way the moon shone down upon the painted stones through the budding branches of the gnarled trees, they had more important things to think about than mere idle superstition. They feared it might be unpleasant work making the Terrible Old Man loquacious concerning his hoarded gold and silver, for aged sea – captains are notably stubborn and perverse. Still, he was very old and very feeble, and there were two visitors. Messrs. Ricci and Silva were experienced in the art of making unwilling persons voluble, and the screams of a weak and exceptionally venerable man can be easily muffled. So they moved up to the one lighted window and heard the Terrible Old Man talking childishly to his bottles with pendulums. Then they donned masks and knocked politely at the weather-stained oaken door.

Waiting seemed very long to Mr. Czanek as he fidgeted restlessly in the covered motor-car by the Terrible Old Man's back gate in Ship Street. He was more than ordinarily tender-hearted, and he did not like the hideous screams he had heard in the ancient house just after the hour appointed for the deed. Had he not told his colleagues to be as gentle as possible with the pathetic old sea-captain? Very nervously he watched that narrow oaken gate in the high and ivy-clad stone wall. Frequently he consulted his watch, and wondered at the delay. Had the old man died before revealing where his treasure was hidden, and had a thorough search become necessary? Mr. Czanek did not like to wait so long in the dark in such a place. Then he sensed a soft tread or tapping on the walk inside the gate, heard a gentle fumbling at the rusty latch, and saw the narrow, heavy door swing inward. And in the pallid glow of the single dim street-lamp he strained his eyes to see what his colleagues had brought out of that sinister house which loomed so close behind. But when he looked, he did not see what he had expected; for his colleagues were not there at all, but only the Terrible Old Man leaning quietly on his knotted cane and smiling hideously. Mr. Czanek had never before noticed the colour of that man's eyes; now he saw that they were yellow.

Little things make considerable excitement in little towns, which is the reason that Kingsport people talked all that spring and summer about the three unidentifiable bodies, horribly slashed as with many cutlasses, and horribly mangled as by the tread of many cruel boot-heels, which the tide washed in. And some people even spoke of things as trivial as the deserted motor-car found in Ship Street, or certain especially inhuman cries, probably of a stray animal or migratory bird, heard in the night by wakeful citizens. But in this idle village gossip the Terrible Old Man took no interest at all. He was by nature reserved, and when one is aged and feeble, one's reserve is doubly strong. Besides, so ancient a sea-captain must have witnessed scores of things much more stirring in the far-off days of his unremembered youth.

THE GHOST

Richmal Crompton

Richmal Crompton Lamburn (1890–1969) was born in Bury, Lancashire. Her *William* stories, which starred a stoutly independent, naughty eleven-year-old, eclipsed her more serious novels, and Crompton was later to call the character 'my Frankenstein monster'. Crompton's non-gendered first name led many of her readers to assume she was a man. She taught classics, but in 1923 contracted poliomyelitis which resulted in a paralysed right leg and put an end to her teaching career. Crompton was a supporter of women's suffrage.

William lay on the floor of the barn, engrossed in a book. This was a rare thing with William. His bottle of lemonade lay untouched by his side, and he even forgot the half-eaten apple which reposed in his hand. His jaws were arrested midway in the act of munching.

"Our hero," he read, "was awakened about midnight by the sound of the rattling of chains. Raising himself on his arm he gazed into the darkness. About a foot from his bed he could discern a tall, white, faintly-gleaming figure and a ghostly arm which beckoned him."

William's hair stood on end.

"Crumbs!" he ejaculated.

"Nothing perturbed," he continued to read, "our hero rose and followed the spectre through the long winding passages of the old castle. Whenever he hesitated, a white, luminous arm, hung around with ghostly chains, beckoned him on."

"Gosh!" murmured the enthralled William. "I'd have bin scared!"

"At the panel in the wall the ghost stopped, and silently the panel slid aside, revealing a flight of stone steps. Down this went the apparition followed by our intrepid hero. There was a small stone chamber at the bottom, and into this the rays of moonlight poured, revealing a skeleton in a sitting attitude beside a chest of golden sovereigns. The gold gleamed in the moonlight."

"Golly!" gasped William, red with excitement.

"William!"

The cry came from somewhere in the sunny garden outside. William frowned sternly, took another bite of apple, and continued to read.

"Our hero gave a cry of astonishment."

"Yea, I'd have done that all right," agreed William.

"*William!*"

"Oh, shut *up*!" called William, irritably, thereby revealing his hiding-place. His grown-up sister, Ethel, appeared in the doorway.

"Mother wants you," she announced.

"Well, I can't come. I'm busy," said William, coldly, taking a draught of lemonade and returning to his book.

"Cousin Mildred's come," continued his sister.

William raised his freckled face from his book.

"Well, I can't help that, can I?" he said, with the air of one arguing patiently with a lunatic.

Ethel shrugged her shoulders and departed.

"He's reading some old book in the barn," he heard her announce, "and he says – "

Here he foresaw complications and hastily followed her.

"Well, I'm *comin'*, aren't I?" he said, "as fast as I can."

Cousin Mildred was sitting on the lawn. She was elderly and very thin and very tall, and she wore a curious, long, shapeless garment of green silk with a golden girdle.

"Dear child!" she murmured, taking the grimy hand that William held out to her in dignified silence.

He was cheered by the sight of tea and hot cakes.

Cousin Mildred ate little but talked much.

"I'm living in *hopes* of a psychic revelation, dear," she said to William's mother. "*In hopes!* I've heard of wonderful experiences, but so far none – alas! – have befallen me. Automatic writing I have tried, but any communication the spirits may have sent me that way remained illegible – quite illegible."

She sighed.

William eyed her with scorn while he consumed reckless quantities of hot cakes.

"I would *love* to have a psychic revelation," she sighed again.

"Yes, dear," murmured Mrs. Brown, mystified. "William, you've had enough."

"*Enough?*" said William, in surprise. "Why I've only had – " He decided hastily against exact statistics and in favour of vague generalities.

"I've only had hardly any," he said, aggrievedly.

"You've had *enough*, anyway," said Mrs. Brown firmly.

The martyr rose, pale but proud.

"Well, can I go then, if I can't have any more tea?"

"There's plenty of bread and butter."

"I don't want bread and butter," he said, scornfully.

"Dear child!" murmured Cousin Mildred, vaguely, as he departed.

He returned to the story and lemonade and apple, and stretched himself happily at full length in the shady barn.

"But the ghostly visitant seemed to be fading away, and with a soft sigh was gone. Our hero, with a start of surprise, realised that he was alone with the gold and the skeleton. For the first time he experienced a thrill of cold fear and slowly retreated up the stairs before the hollow and, as it seemed, vindictive stare of the grinning skeleton."

"I wonder wot he was grinnin' at?" said William.

"But to his horror the door was shut, the panel had slid back. He had no means of opening it. He was imprisoned on a remote part of the castle, where even the servants came but rarely, and at intervals of weeks. Would his fate be that of the man whose bones gleamed white in the moonlight?"

"Crumbs!" said William, earnestly.

Then a shadow fell upon the floor of the barn, and Cousin Mildred's voice greeted him.

"So you're here, dear? I'm just exploring your garden and thinking. I like to be alone. I see that you are the same, dear child!"

"I'm readin'," said William, with icy dignity.

"Dear boy! Won't you come and show me the garden and your favourite nooks and corners?"

William looked at her thin, vague, amiable face, and shut his book with a resigned sigh.

"All right," he said, laconically.

He conducted her in patient silence round the kitchen garden and the shrubbery. She looked sadly at the house, with its red brick, uncompromisingly-modern appearance.

"William, I wish your house was *old*," she said, sadly.

William resented any aspersions on his house from outsiders. Personally he considered newness in a house an attraction, but, if anyone wished for age, then old his house should be.

"*Old*!" he ejaculated. "Huh! I guess it's *old* enough."

"Oh, is it?" she said, delighted. "Restored recently, I suppose?"

"Umph," agreed William, nodding.

"Oh, I'm so glad. I may have some psychic revelation here, then?"

"Oh yes," said William, judicially. "I shouldn't wonder."

"William, have you ever had one?"

"Well," said William, guardedly, "I dunno."

His mysterious manner threw her into a transport.

"Of course not to anyone. But to *me* – I'm one of the sympathetic! To me you may speak freely, William."

William, feeling that his ignorance could no longer be hidden by words, maintained a discreet silence.

"To me it shall be sacred, William. I will tell no one – not even your parents. I believe that children see – clouds of glory and all that," vaguely. "With your unstained childish vision – "

"I'm eleven," put in William indignantly.

"You see things that to the wise are sealed. Some manifestation, some spirit, some ghostly visitant – "

"Oh," said William, suddenly enlightened, "you talkin' about *ghosts*?"

"Yes, ghosts, William."

Her air of deference flattered him. She evidently expected great things of him. Great things she should have. At the best of times with William imagination was stronger than cold facts.

He gave a short laugh.

"Oh, *ghosts*! Yes, I've seen some of 'em. I guess I *have*!"

Her face lit up.

"Will you tell me some of your experiences, William?" she said, humbly.

"Well," said William, loftily, "you won't go *talkin'* about it, will you?"

"Oh, *no*."

"Well, I've seen 'em, you know. Chains an' all. And skeletons. And ghostly arms beckonin' an' all that."

William was enjoying himself. He walked with a swagger. He almost believed what he said. She gasped.

"Oh, go on!" she said. "Tell me all."

He went on. He soared aloft on the wings of imagination, his hands in his pockets, his freckled face puckered up in frowning mental effort. He certainly enjoyed himself.

"If only some of it could happen to *me*," breathed his confidante. "Does it come to you at *nights*, William?"

"Yes," nodded William. "Nights mostly."

"I shall – watch to-night," said Cousin Mildred. "And you say the house is old?"

"Awful old," said William, reassuringly.

Her attitude to William was a relief to the rest of the family. Visitors sometimes objected to William.

"She seems to have almost taken to William," said his mother, with a note of unflattering incredulity in her voice.

William was pleased yet embarrassed by her attentions. It was a strange experience to him to be accepted by a grown-up as a fellow-being. She talked to him with interest and a certain humility, she bought him sweets and seemed pleased that he accepted them, she went for walks with him, and evidently took his constrained silence for the silence of depth and wisdom.

Beneath his embarrassment he was certainly pleased and flattered. She seemed to prefer his company to that of Ethel. That was one in the eye for Ethel. But he felt that something was expected from him in return for all this kindness and attention. William was a sportsman. He decided to supply it. He took a book of ghost stories from the juvenile library at school, and read them in the privacy of his room at night. Many were the thrilling adventures which he had to tell to Cousin Mildred in the morning. Cousin Mildred's bump of credulity was a large one. She supplied him with sweets on a generous scale. She listened to him with awe and wonder.

"William . . . you are one of the elect, the chosen," she said, "one of those whose spirits can break down the barrier between the unseen world and ours with ease." And always she sighed and stroked back her thin locks, sadly. "Oh, how I wish that some experience would happen to *me*!"

One morning, after the gift of an exceptionally large tin of toffee, William's noblest feelings were aroused. Manfully he decided that something *should* happen to her.

Cousin Mildred slept in the bedroom above William's. Descent from one window to the other was easy, but ascent was difficult. That night Cousin Mildred awoke suddenly as the clock struck twelve. There was no moon, and only dimly did she discern the white figure that stood in the light of the window. She sat up, quivering with eagerness. Her short, thin little pigtail, stuck out horizontally from her head. Her mouth was wide open.

"Oh!" she gasped.

The white figure moved a step forward and coughed nervously.

Cousin Mildred clasped her hands.

"Speak!" she said, in a tense whisper. "Oh, speak! Some message! Some revelation."

William was nonplussed. None of the ghosts he had read of had spoken. They had rattled and groaned and beckoned, but they had not spoken. He tried groaning and emitted a sound faintly reminiscent of a sea-sick voyager.

"Oh, *speak*!" pleaded Cousin Mildred.

Evidently speech was a necessary part of this performance. William wondered whether ghosts spoke English or a language of their own. He inclined to the latter view and nobly took the plunge.

"Honk. Yonk. Ponk," he said, firmly.

Cousin Mildred gasped in wonder.

"Oh, explain," she pleaded, ardently. "Explain in our poor human speech. Some message – "

William took fright. It was all turning out to be much more complicated than he had expected. He hastily passed through the room and out of the door, closing it noisily behind him. As he ran along the passage came a sound like a crash of thunder. Outside in the passage were Cousin Mildred's boots, William's father's boots, and William's brother's boots, and into these charged William in his headlong retreat. They slid noisily along the polished wooden surface of the floor, ricochetting into each other as they went. Doors opened suddenly and William's father collided with William's brother in the dark passage, where they wrestled fiercely before they discovered each other's identity.

"I heard that confounded noise and I came out – "

"So did I."

"Well, then, who *made* it?"

"Who did?"

"If it's that wretched boy up to any tricks again – "

William's father left the sentence unfinished, but went with determined tread towards his younger son's room. William was discovered, carefully spreading a sheet over his bed and smoothing it down.

Mr. Brown, roused from his placid slumbers, was a sight to make a brave man quail, but the glance that William turned upon him was guileless and sweet.

"Did you make that confounded row kicking boots about the passage?" spluttered the man of wrath.

"No, Father," said William, gently. "I've not bin kickin' no boots about."

"Were you down on the lower landing just now?" said Mr. Brown, with compressed fury.

William considered this question silently for a few seconds, then spoke up brightly and innocently.

"I dunno, Father. You see, some folks walk in their sleep and when they wake up they dunno where they've bin. Why, I've heard of a man walkin' down a fire escape in his sleep, and then he woke up and couldn't think how he'd got to be there where he was. You see, he didn't know he'd walked down all them steps sound asleep, and – "

"Be *quiet*," thundered his father. "What in the name of – what on earth are you doing making your bed in the middle of the night? Are you insane?"

William, perfectly composed, tucked in one end of his sheet.

"No Father, I'm not insane. My sheet just fell off me in the night and I got out to pick it up. I must of bin a bit restless, I suppose. Sheets come off easy when folks is restless in bed, and they don't know anythin' about it till they wake up jus' same as sleep walkin'. Why, I've heard of folks – "

"Be *quiet* – !"

At that moment William's mother arrived, placid as ever, in her dressing gown, carrying a candle.

"Look at him," said Mr. Brown, pointing at the meek-looking William.

"He plays Rugger up and down the passage with the boots all night and then he begins to make his bed. He's mad. He's – "

William turned his calm gaze upon him.

"*I* wasn't playin' Rugger with the boots, Father," he said, patiently.

Mrs. Brown laid her hand soothingly upon her husband's arm.

"You know, dear," she said, gently, "a house is always full of noises at night. Basket chairs creaking – "

Mr. Brown's face grew purple.

"*Basket chairs – !*" he exploded, violently, but allowed himself to be led unresisting from the room.

William finished his bed-making with his usual frown of concentration, then, lying down, fell at once into the deep sleep of childish innocence.

But Cousin Mildred was lying awake, a blissful smile upon her lips. She, too, was now one of the elect, the chosen. Her rather deaf ears had caught the sound of supernatural thunder as her ghostly visitant departed, and she had beamed with ecstatic joy.

"Honk," she murmured, dreamily. "Honk, Yonk, Ponk."

William felt rather tired the next evening. Cousin Mildred had departed leaving him a handsome present of a large box of chocolates. William had consumed these with undue haste in view of possible maternal interference. His broken night was telling upon his spirits. He felt distinctly depressed and saw the world through jaundiced eyes. He sat in the shrubbery, his chin in his hand, staring moodily at the adoring mongrel, Jumble.

"It's a rotten world," he said, gloomily. "I've took a lot of trouble over her and she goes and makes me feel sick with chocolates."

Jumble wagged his tail, sympathetically.

THE NATURE OF THE EVIDENCE

May Sinclair

Mary Amelia St Clair (1863–1946) was born in Rock Ferry, Cheshire. Her father, a wealthy Liverpool ship owner, went bankrupt, sank into alcoholism and died when Sinclair was still young. Her education was cut short when she was called home from her first year at Cheltenham Ladies College to help nurse her five brothers, four of whom died of congenital heart disease. Sinclair was active in the women's suffrage movement. Her interest in psychoanalysis and spiritualism were an influence on her fiction.

This is the story Marston told me. He didn't want to tell it. I had to tear it from him bit by bit. I've pieced the bits together in their time order, and explained things here and there, but the facts are the facts he gave me. There's nothing that I didn't get out of him somehow.

Out of *him* – you'll admit my source is unimpeachable. Edward Marston, the great K.C., and the author of an admirable work on "The Logic of Evidence". You should have read the chapters on "What Evidence Is and What It Is Not". You may say he lied; but if you knew Marston you'd know he wouldn't lie, for the simple reason that he's incapable of inventing anything. So that, if you ask me whether I believe this tale, all I can say is, I believe the things happened, because he said they happened and because they happened to him. As for what they *were* – well, I don't pretend to explain it, neither would he.

You know he was married twice. He adored his first wife, Rosamund, and Rosamund adored him. I suppose they were completely happy. She was fifteen years younger than he, and beautiful. I wish I could make you see how beautiful. Her eyes and mouth had the same sort of bow, full and wide-sweeping, and they stared out of her face with the same grave, contemplative innocence. Her mouth was finished off at each corner with the loveliest little moulding, rounded like the pistil of a flower. She wore her hair in a solid gold fringe over her forehead, like a child's, and a big coil at the back. When it was let down it hung in a heavy cable to her waist. Marston used to tease her about it. She had a trick of tossing back the rope in the night when it was hot under her, and it would fall smack across his face and hurt him.

There was a pathos about her that I can't describe – a curious, pure, sweet beauty, like a child's; perfect, and perfectly immature; so immature that you couldn't conceive its lasting – like that – any more than childhood lasts. Marston used to say it made him nervous. He was afraid of waking up in the morning and finding that it had changed in the night. And her beauty was so much a part of herself that you couldn't think of her without it. Somehow you felt that if it went she must go too.

Well, she went first.

For a year afterwards Marston existed dangerously, always on the edge of a breakdown. If he didn't go over altogether it was because his work saved him. He had no consoling theories. He was one of those bigoted materialists of the nineteenth-century type who believe that consciousness is a purely physiological function, and that when your body's dead, *you're* dead. He saw no reason to suppose the contrary. "When you consider," he used to say, "the nature of the evidence!"

It's as well to bear this in mind, so as to realise that he hadn't any bias or anticipation. Rosamund survived for him only in his memory. And in his memory he was still in love with her. At the same time he used to discuss quite cynically the chances of his marrying again.

It seems that in their honeymoon they had gone into that. Rosamund said she hated to think of his being lonely and miserable, supposing she died before he did. She would like him to marry again. If, she stipulated, he married the right woman.

He had put it to her: "And if I marry the wrong one?"

And she had said, That would be different. She couldn't bear that.

He remembered all this afterwards; but there was nothing in it to make him suppose, at the time, that she would take action.

We talked it over, he and I, one night.

"I suppose," he said, "I shall have to marry again. It's a physical necessity. But it won't be anything more. I shan't marry the sort of woman who'll expect anything more. I won't put another woman in Rosamund's place. There'll be no unfaithfulness about it."

And there wasn't. Soon after that first year he married Pauline Silver.

She was a daughter of old Justice Parker, who was a friend of Marston's people. He hadn't seen the girl till she came home from India after her divorce.

Yes, there'd been a divorce. Silver had behaved very decently. He'd let her bring it against *him*, to save her. But there were some queer stories going about. They didn't get round to Marston, because he was so mixed up with her people; and if they had he wouldn't have believed them. He'd made up his mind he'd marry Pauline the first minute he'd seen her. She was handsome; the hard, black, white and vermilion kind, with a little aristocratic nose and a lascivious mouth.

It was, as he had meant it to be, nothing but physical infatuation on both sides. No question of Pauline's taking Rosamund's place.

Marston had a big case on at the time.

They were in such a hurry that they couldn't wait till it was over; and as it kept him in London they agreed to put off their honeymoon till the autumn, and he took her straight to his own house in Curzon Street.

This, he admitted afterwards, was the part he hated. The Curzon Street house was associated with Rosamund; especially their bedroom – Rosamund's bedroom – and his library. The library was the room Rosamund liked best, because it was his room. She had her place in the corner by the hearth, and they were always alone there together in the evenings when his work was done; and when it wasn't done she would still sit with him, keeping quiet in her corner with a book.

Luckily for Marston, at the first sight of the library Pauline took a dislike to it.

I can hear her. "Br-rr-rh! There's something beastly about this room, Edward. I can't think how you can sit in it."

And Edward, a little caustic: "*You* needn't, if you don't like it."

"I certainly shan't."

She stood there – I can see her – on the hearthrug by Rosamund's chair, looking uncommonly handsome and lascivious. He was going to take her in his arms and kiss her vermilion mouth, when, he said, something stopped him. Stopped him clean, as if it had risen up and stopped between them. He supposed it was the memory of Rosamund, vivid in the place that had been hers.

You see it was just that place, of silent, intimate communion, that Pauline would never take. And the rich, coarse, contented creature didn't even want to take it. He saw that he would be left alone there, all right, with his memory.

But the bedroom was another matter. That, Pauline had made it understood from the beginning, she would have to have. Indeed, there was no other he could well have offered her. The drawing-room covered the whole of the first floor. The bedrooms above were cramped, and this one had been formed by throwing the two front rooms into one. It looked south, and the bathroom opened out of it at the back. Marston's small northern room had a door on the narrow landing at right angles to his wife's door. He could hardly expect her to sleep there, still less in any of the tight boxes on the top floor. He said he wished he had sold the Curzon Street house.

But Pauline was enchanted with the wide, three-windowed piece that was to be hers. It had been exquisitely furnished for poor little Rosamund: all seventeenth-century walnut wood, Bokhara rugs, thick silk curtains, deep blue with purple linings, and a big, rich bed covered with a purple counterpane embroidered in blue.

One thing Marston insisted on: that *he* should sleep on Rosamund's side of the bed, and Pauline in his own old place. He didn't want to see Pauline's body where Rosamund's had been. Of course he had to lie about it and pretend he had always slept on the side next the window.

I can see Pauline going about in that room, looking at everything; looking at herself, her black, white and vermilion, in the glass that had held Rosamund's pure rose and gold; opening the wardrobe where Rosamund's dresses used to hang, sniffing up the delicate, flower scent of Rosamund, not caring, covering it with her own thick trail.

And Marston (who cared abominably) – I can see him getting more miserable and at the same time more excited as the wedding evening went on. He took her to the play to fill up the time, or perhaps to get her out of Rosamund's rooms; God knows. I can see them sitting in the stalls, bored and restless, starting up and going out before the thing was half over, and coming back to that house in Curzon Street before eleven o'clock.

It wasn't much past eleven when he went to her room.

I told you her door was at right angles to his, and the landing was narrow, so that anybody standing by Pauline's door must have been seen the minute he opened his. He hadn't even to cross the landing to get to her.

Well, Marston swears that there was nothing there when he opened his own door; but when he came to Pauline's he saw Rosamund standing up before it; and, he said, "*She wouldn't let me in*."

Her arms were stretched out, barring the passage. Oh yes, he saw her face, Rosamund's face; I gathered that it was utterly sweet, and utterly inexorable. He couldn't pass her.

So he turned into his own room, backing, he says, so that he could keep looking at her. And when he stood on the threshold of his own door she wasn't there.

No, he wasn't frightened. He couldn't tell me what he felt; but he left his door open all night because he couldn't bear to shut it on her. And he made no other attempt to go in to Pauline; he was so convinced that the phantasm of Rosamund would come again and stop him.

I don't know what sort of excuse he made to Pauline the next morning. He said she was very stiff and sulky all day; and no wonder. He was still infatuated with her, and I don't think that the phantasm of Rosamund had put him off Pauline in the least. In fact, he persuaded himself that the thing was nothing but a hallucination, due, no doubt, to his excitement.

Anyhow, he didn't expect to see it at the door again the next night.

Yes. It was there. Only, this time, he said, it drew aside to let him pass. It smiled at him, as if it were saying, "Go in, if you must; you'll see what'll happen."

He had no sense that it had followed him into the room; he felt certain that, this time, it would let him be.

It was when he approached Pauline's bed, which had been Rosamund's bed, that she appeared again, standing between it and him, and stretching out her arms to keep him back.

All that Pauline could see was her bridegroom backing and backing, then standing there, fixed, and the look on his face. That in itself was enough to frighten her.

She said, "What's the matter with you, Edward?"

He didn't move.

"What are you standing there for? Why don't you come to bed?"

Then Marston seems to have lost his head and blurted it out: "I can't. I can't."

"Can't what?" said Pauline from the bed.

"Can't sleep with you. She won't let me."

"She?"

"Rosamund. My wife. She's there."

"What on earth are you talking about?"

"She's there, I tell you. She won't let me. She's pushing me back.".

He says Pauline must have thought he was drunk or something. Remember, she *saw* nothing but Edward, his face, and his mysterious attitude. He must have looked very drunk.

She sat up in bed, with her hard, black eyes blazing away at him, and told him to leave the room that minute. Which he did.

The next day she had it out with him. I gathered that she kept on talking about the "state" he was in.

"You came to my room, Edward, in a *disgraceful* state."

I suppose Marston said he was sorry, but he couldn't help it, he wasn't drunk. He stuck to it that Rosamund was there. He had seen her. And Pauline said, if he wasn't drunk then he must be mad, and he said meekly, "Perhaps I *am* mad."

That set her off, and she broke out in a fury. He was no more mad than she was; but he didn't care for her; he was making ridiculous excuses; shamming, to put her off. There was some other woman.

Marston asked her what on earth she supposed he'd married her for. Then she burst out crying and said she didn't know.

Then he seems to have made it up with Pauline. He managed to make her believe he wasn't lying, that he really had seen something, and between them they arrived at a rational explanation of the appearance. He had been overworking. Rosamund's phantasm was nothing but a hallucination of his exhausted brain.

This theory carried him on till bedtime. Then, he says, he began to wonder what would happen, what Rosamund's phantasm would do next. Each morning his passion for Pauline had come back again, increased by frustration, and it worked itself up *crescendo*, towards night. Supposing he *had* seen Rosamund. He might see her again. He had become suddenly subject to hallucinations. But as long as you *knew* you were hallucinated you were all right.

So what they agreed to do that night was by way of precaution, in case the thing came again. It might even be sufficient in itself to prevent his seeing anything.

Instead of going in to Pauline he was to get into the room before she did, and she was to come to him there. That, they said, would break the spell. To make him feel even safer he meant to be in bed before Pauline came.

Well, he got into the room all right.

It was when he tried to get into bed that – he saw her (I mean Rosamund).

She was lying there, in his place next the window, her own place, lying in her immature child-like beauty and sleeping, the firm full bow of her mouth softened by sleep. She was perfect in every detail, the lashes of her shut eyelids golden on her white cheeks, the solid gold of her square fringe shining, and the great braided golden rope of her hair flung back on the pillow.

He knelt down by the bed and pressed his forehead into the bedclothes, close to her side. He declared he could feel her breathe.

He stayed there for the twenty minutes Pauline took to undress and come to him. He says the minutes stretched out like hours. Pauline found him still kneeling with his face pressed into the bedclothes. When he got up he staggered.

She asked him what he was doing and why he wasn't in bed. And he said, "It's no use. I can't. I can't."

But somehow he couldn't tell her that Rosamund was there. Rosamund was too sacred; he couldn't talk about her. He only said: "You'd better sleep in my room tonight."

He was staring down at the place in the bed where he still saw Rosamund. Pauline couldn't have seen anything but the bedclothes, the sheet smoothed above an invisible breast, and the hollow in the pillow. She said she'd do nothing of the sort. She wasn't going to be frightened out of her own room. He could do as he liked.

He couldn't leave them there; he couldn't leave Pauline with Rosamund, and he couldn't leave Rosamund with Pauline. So he sat up in a chair with his back turned to the bed. No. He didn't make any attempt to go back. He says he knew she was still lying there, guarding his place, which was her place. The odd thing is that he wasn't in the least disturbed or frightened or surprised. He took the whole thing as a matter of course. And presently he dozed off into a sleep.

A scream woke him and the sound of a violent body leaping out of the bed and thudding on to its feet. He switched on the light and saw the bedclothes flung back and Pauline standing on the floor with her mouth open.

He went to her and held her. She was cold to the touch and shaking with terror, and her jaws dropped as if she was palsied.

She said, "Edward, there's something in the bed."

He glanced again at the bed. It was empty.

"There isn't," he said. "Look."

He stripped the bed to the foot-rail, so that she could see.

"There *was* something."

"Do you see it."

"No. I felt it."

She told him. First something had come swinging, smack across her face. A thick, heavy rope of woman's hair. It had waked her. Then she had put out her hands and felt the body. A woman's body, soft and horrible; her fingers had sunk in the shallow breasts. Then she had screamed and jumped.

And she couldn't stay in the room. The room, she said, was "beastly".

She slept in Marston's room, in his small single bed, and he sat up with her all night, on a chair.

She believed now that he had really seen something, and she remembered that the library was beastly, too. Haunted by something. She supposed that was what she had felt. Very well. Two rooms in the house were haunted; their bedroom and the library. They would just have to avoid those two rooms. She had made up her mind, you see, that it was nothing but a case of an ordinary haunted house; the sort of thing you're always hearing about and never believe in till it happens to yourself. Marston didn't like to point out to her that the house hadn't been haunted till she came into it.

The following night, the fourth night, she was to sleep in the spare room on the top floor, next to the servants, and Marston in his own room.

But Marston didn't sleep. He kept on wondering whether he would or would not go up to Pauline's room. That made him horribly restless, and instead of undressing and going to bed, he sat up on a chair with a book. He wasn't nervous; but he had a queer feeling that something was going to happen, and that he must be ready for it, and that he'd better be dressed.

It must have been soon after midnight when he heard the door knob turning very slowly and softly.

The door opened behind him and Pauline came in, moving without a sound, and stood before him. It gave him a shock; for he had been thinking of Rosamund, and when he heard the door knob turn it was the phantasm of

Rosamund that he expected to see coming in. He says, for the first minute, it was this appearance of Pauline that struck him as the uncanny and unnatural thing.

She had nothing, absolutely nothing on but a transparent white chiffony sort of dressing-gown. She was trying to undo it. He could see her hands shaking as her fingers fumbled with the fastenings.

He got up suddenly, and they just stood there before each other, saying nothing, staring at each other. He was fascinated by her, by the sheer glamour of her body, gleaming white through the thin stuff, and by the movement of her fingers. I think I've said she was a beautiful woman, and her beauty at that moment was overpowering.

And still he stared at her without saying anything. It sounds as if their silence lasted quite a long time, but in reality it couldn't have been more than some fraction of a second.

Then she began. "Oh, Edward, for God's sake *say* something. Oughtn't I to have come?"

And she went on without waiting for an answer. "Are you thinking of *her*? Because, if – if you are, I'm not going to let her drive you away from me . . . I'm not going to . . . She'll keep on coming as long as we don't – Can't you see that this is the way to stop it . . . ? When you take me in your arms."

She slipped off the loose sleeves of the chiffon thing and it fell to her feet. Marston says he heard a queer sound, something between a groan and a grunt, and was amazed to find that it came from himself.

He hadn't touched her yet – mind you, it went quicker than it takes to tell, it was still an affair of the fraction of a second – they were holding out their arms to each other, when the door opened again without a sound, and, without visible passage, the phantasm was there. It came incredibly fast, and thin at first, like a shaft of light sliding between them. It didn't do anything; there was no beating of hands, only, as it took on its full form, its perfect likeness of flesh and blood, it made its presence felt like a push, a force, driving them asunder.

Pauline hadn't seen it yet. She thought it was Marston who was beating her back. She cried out: "Oh, don't, don't push me away!" She stooped below the phantasm's guard and clung to his knees, writhing and crying. For a moment it was a struggle between her moving flesh and that still, supernatural being.

And in that moment Marston realised that he hated Pauline. She was fighting Rosamund with her gross flesh and blood, taking a mean advantage of her embodied state to beat down the heavenly, discarnate thing.

He called to her to let go.

"It's not I," he shouted. "Can't you *see* her?"

Then, suddenly, she saw, and let go, and dropped, crouching on the floor and trying to cover herself. This time she had given no cry.

The phantasm gave way; it moved slowly towards the door, and as it went it looked back over its shoulder at Marston, it trailed a hand, signalling to him to come.

He went out after it, hardly aware of Pauline's naked body that still writhed there, clutching at his feet as they passed, and drew itself after him, like a worm, like a beast, along the floor.

She must have got up at once and followed them out on to the landing; for, as he went down the stairs behind the phantasm, he could see Pauline's face, distorted with lust and terror, peering at them above the stairhead. She saw them descend the last flight, and cross the hall at the bottom and go into the library. The door shut behind them.

Something happened in there. Marston never told me precisely what it was, and I didn't ask him. Anyhow, that finished it.

The next day Pauline ran away to her own people. She couldn't stay in Marston's house because it was haunted by Rosamund, and he wouldn't leave it for the same reason.

And she never came back; for she was not only afraid of Rosamund, she was afraid of Marston. And if she *had* come it wouldn't have been any good. Marston was convinced that, as often as he attempted to get to Pauline, something would stop him. Pauline certainly felt that, if Rosamund were pushed to it, she might show herself in some still more sinister and terrifying form. She knew when she was beaten.

And there was more in it than that. I believe he tried to explain it to her; said he had married her on the assumption that Rosamund was dead, but that now he knew she was alive; she was, as he put it, "there". He tried to make her see that if he had Rosamund he couldn't have *her*. Rosamund's presence in the world annulled their contract.

You see I'm convinced that something *did* happen that night in the library. I say, he never told me precisely what it was, but he once let something out. We were discussing one of Pauline's love-affairs (after the separation she gave him endless grounds for divorce).

"Poor Pauline," he said, "she thinks she's so passionate."

"Well," I said, "wasn't she?"

Then he burst out. "No. She doesn't know what passion is. None of you know. You haven't the faintest conception. You'd have to get rid of your bodies first. *I* didn't know until –"

He stopped himself. I think he was going to say, "until Rosamund came back and showed me". For he leaned forward and whispered: "It isn't a localised affair at all . . . If you only knew –"

So I don't think it was just faithfulness to a revived memory. I take it there had been, behind that shut door, some experience, some terrible and exquisite contact. More penetrating than sight or touch. More – more extensive: passion at all points of being.

Perhaps the supreme moment of it, the ecstasy, only came when her phantasm had disappeared.

He couldn't go back to Pauline after *that*.

THE ROCKING-HORSE WINNER

D.H. Lawrence

David Herbert Lawrence (1885–1930) was born in Eastwood, Nottingham. His father was a miner, his mother a lace worker. Lawrence qualified as a teacher but left the profession in favour of becoming a full-time writer. His attitudes towards sex, equality, women and different ethnicities continue to make him a controversial figure. Penguin Books' publication of the unexpurgated edition of his novel, *Lady Chatterley's Lover*, in 1960 led to an obscenity trial. Lawrence died of tuberculosis. His remains are interred in Taos, New Mexico.

There was a woman who was beautiful, who started with all the advantages, yet she had no luck. She married for love, and the love turned to dust. She had bonny children, yet she felt they had been thrust upon her, and she could not love them. They looked at her coldly, as if they were finding fault with her. And hurriedly she felt she must cover up some fault in herself. Yet what it was that she must cover up she never knew. Nevertheless, when her children were present, she always felt the centre of her heart go hard. This troubled her, and in her manner she was all the more gentle and anxious for her children, as if she loved them very much. Only she herself knew that at the centre of her heart was a hard little place that could not feel love, no, not for anybody. Everybody else said of her: "She is such a good mother. She adores her children." Only she herself, and her children themselves, knew it was not so. They read it in each other's eyes.

There were a boy and two little girls. They lived in a pleasant house, with a garden, and they had discreet servants, and felt themselves superior to anyone in the neighbourhood.

Although they lived in style, they felt always an anxiety in the house. There was never enough money. The mother had a small income, and the father had a small income, but not nearly enough for the social position which they had to keep up. The father went into town to some office. But though he had good prospects, these prospects never materialised. There was always the grinding sense of the shortage of money, though the style was always kept up.

At last the mother said: "I will see if I can't make something." But she did not know where to begin. She racked her brains, and tried this thing and the other, but could not find anything successful. The failure made deep lines come into her face. Her children were growing up, they would have to go to school. There must be more money, there must be more money. The father, who was always very handsome and expensive in his tastes, seemed as if he never would be able to do anything worth doing. And the mother, who had a great belief in herself, did not succeed any better, and her tastes were just as expensive.

And so the house came to be haunted by the unspoken phrase: There must be more money! There must be more money! The children could hear it all the time though nobody said it aloud. They heard it at Christmas, when the expensive and splendid toys filled the nursery. Behind the shining modern rocking-horse, behind the smart doll's house, a voice would start whispering: "There must be more money! There must be more money!" And the children would stop playing, to listen for a moment. They would look into each other's eyes, to see if they had all heard. And each one saw in the eyes of the other two that they too had heard. "There must be more money! There must be more money!"

It came whispering from the springs of the still-swaying rocking-horse, and even the horse, bending his wooden, champing head, heard it. The big doll, sitting so pink and smirking in her new pram, could hear it quite plainly, and seemed to be smirking all the more self-consciously because of it. The foolish puppy, too, that took the place of the teddy-bear, he was looking so extraordinarily foolish for no other reason but that he heard the secret whisper all over the house: "There must be more money!"

Yet nobody ever said it aloud. The whisper was everywhere, and therefore no one spoke it. Just as no one ever says: "We are breathing!" in spite of the fact that breath is coming and going all the time.

"Mother," said the boy Paul one day, "why don't we keep a car of our own? Why do we always use uncle's, or else a taxi?"

"Because we're the poor members of the family," said the mother.

"But why are we, mother?"

"Well – I suppose," she said slowly and bitterly, "it's because your father has no luck."

The boy was silent for some time.

"Is luck money, mother?" he asked, rather timidly.

"No, Paul. Not quite. It's what causes you to have money."

"Oh!" said Paul vaguely. "I thought when Uncle Oscar said filthy lucker, it meant money."

"Filthy lucre does mean money," said the mother. "But it's lucre, not luck."

"Oh!" said the boy. "Then what is luck, mother?"

"It's what causes you to have money. If you're lucky you have money. That's why it's better to be born lucky than rich. If you're rich, you may lose your money. But if you're lucky, you will always get more money."

"Oh! Will you? And is father not lucky?"

"Very unlucky, I should say," she said bitterly.

The boy watched her with unsure eyes.

"Why?" he asked.

"I don't know. Nobody ever knows why one person is lucky and another unlucky."

"Don't they? Nobody at all? Does nobody know?"

"Perhaps God. But He never tells."

"He ought to, then. And are'nt you lucky either, mother?"

"I can't be, it I married an unlucky husband."

"But by yourself, aren't you?"

"I used to think I was, before I married. Now I think I am very unlucky indeed."

"Why?"

"Well – never mind! Perhaps I'm not really," she said.

The child looked at her to see if she meant it. But he saw, by the lines of her mouth, that she was only trying to hide something from him.

"Well, anyhow," he said stoutly, "I'm a lucky person."

"Why?" said his mother, with a sudden laugh.

He stared at her. He didn't even know why he had said it.

"God told me," he asserted, brazening it out.

"I hope He did, dear!", she said, again with a laugh, but rather bitter.

"He did, mother!"

"Excellent!" said the mother, using one of her husband's exclamations.

The boy saw she did not believe him; or rather, that she paid no attention to his assertion. This angered him somewhere, and made him want to compel her attention.

He went off by himself, vaguely, in a childish way, seeking for the clue to "luck". Absorbed, taking no heed of other people, he went about with a sort of stealth, seeking inwardly for luck. He wanted luck, he wanted it, he wanted it. When the two girls were playing dolls in the nursery, he would sit on his big rocking-horse, charging madly into space, with a frenzy that made the little girls peer at him uneasily. Wildly the horse careered, the waving dark hair of the boy tossed, his eyes had a strange glare in them. The little girls dared not speak to him.

When he had ridden to the end of his mad little journey, he climbed down and stood in front of his rocking-horse, staring fixedly into its lowered face. Its red mouth was slightly open, its big eye was wide and glassy-bright.

"Now!" he would silently command the snorting steed. "Now take me to where there is luck! Now take me!"

And he would slash the horse on the neck with the little whip he had asked Uncle Oscar for. He knew the horse could take him to where there was luck, if only he forced it. So he would mount again and start on his furious ride, hoping at last to get there.

"You'll break your horse, Paul!" said the nurse.

"He's always riding like that! I wish he'd leave off!" said his elder sister Joan.

But he only glared down on them in silence. Nurse gave him up. She could make nothing of him. Anyhow, he was growing beyond her.

One day his mother and his Uncle Oscar came in when he was on one of his furious rides. He did not speak to them.

"Hallo, you young jockey! Riding a winner?" said his uncle.

"Aren't you growing too big for a rocking-horse? You're not a very little boy any longer, you know," said his mother.

But Paul only gave a blue glare from his big, rather close-set eyes. He would speak to nobody when he was in full tilt. His mother watched him with an anxious expression on her face.

At last he suddenly stopped forcing his horse into the mechanical gallop and slid down.

"Well, I got there!" he announced fiercely, his blue eyes still flaring, and his sturdy long legs straddling apart.

"Where did you get to?" asked his mother.

"Where I wanted to go," he flared back at her.

"That's right, son!" said Uncle Oscar. "Don't you stop till you get there. What's the horse's name?"

"He doesn't have a name," said the boy.

"Get's on without all right?" asked the uncle.

"Well, he has different names. He was called Sansovino last week."

"Sansovino, eh? Won the Ascot. How did you know this name?"

"He always talks about horse-races with Bassett," said Joan.

The uncle was delighted to find that his small nephew was posted with all the racing news. Bassett, the young gardener, who had been wounded in the left foot in the war and had got his present job through Oscar Cresswell, whose batman he had been, was a perfect blade of the "turf". He lived in the racing events, and the small boy lived with him.

Oscar Cresswell got it all from Bassett.

"Master Paul comes and asks me, so I can't do more than tell him, sir," said Bassett, his face terribly serious, as if he were speaking of religious matters.

"And does he ever put anything on a horse he fancies?"

"Well – I don't want to give him away – he's a young sport, a fine sport, sir. Would you mind asking him himself? He sort of takes a pleasure in it, and perhaps he'd feel I was giving him away, sir, if you don't mind.

Bassett was serious as a church.

The uncle went back to his nephew and took him off for a ride in the car.

"Say, Paul, old man, do you ever put anything on a horse?" the uncle asked.

The boy watched the handsome man closely.

"Why, do you think I oughtn't to?" he parried.

"Not a bit of it! I thought perhaps you might give me a tip for the Lincoln."

The car sped on into the country, going down to Uncle Oscar's place in Hampshire.

"Honour bright?" said the nephew.

"Honour bright, son!" said the uncle.

"Well, then, Daffodil."

"Daffodil! I doubt it, sonny. What about Mirza?"

"I only know the winner," said the boy. "That's Daffodil."

"Daffodil, eh?"

There was a pause. Daffodil was an obscure horse comparatively.

"Uncle!"

"Yes, son?"

"You won't let it go any further, will you? I promised Bassett."

"Bassett be damned, old man! What's he got to do with it?"

"We're partners. We've been partners from the first. Uncle, he lent me my first five shillings, which I lost. I promised him, honour bright, it was only between me and him; only you gave me that ten-shilling note I started winning with, so I thought you were lucky. You won't let it go any further, will you?"

The boy gazed at his uncle from those big, hot, blue eyes, set rather close together. The uncle stirred and laughed uneasily.

"Right you are, son! I'll keep your tip private. How much are you putting on him?"

"All except twenty pounds," said the boy. "I keep that in reserve."

The uncle thought it a good joke.

"You keep twenty pounds in reserve, do you, you young romancer? What are you betting, then?"

"I'm betting three hundred," said the boy gravely. "But it's between you and me, Uncle Oscar! Honour bright?"

"It's between you and me all right, you young Nat Gould," he said, laughing. "But where's your three hundred?"

"Bassett keeps it for me. We're partners."

"You are, are you! And what is Bassett putting on Daffodil?"

"He won't go quite as high as I do, I expect. Perhaps he'll go a hundred and fifty."

"What, pennies?" laughed the uncle.

"Pounds," said the child, with a surprised look at his uncle. "Bassett keeps a bigger reserve than I do."

Between wonder and amusement Uncle Oscar was silent. He pursued the matter no further, but he determined to take his nephew with him to the Lincoln races.

"Now, son," he said, "I'm putting twenty on Mirza, and I'll put five on for you on any horse you fancy. What's your pick?"

"Daffodil, uncle."

"No, not the fiver on Daffodil!"

"I should if it was my own fiver," said the child.

"Good! Good! Right you are! A fiver for me and a fiver for you on Daffodil."

The child had never been to a race-meeting before, and his eyes were blue fire. He pursed his mouth tight and watched. A Frenchman just in front had put his money on Lancelot. Wild with excitement, he flayed his arms up and down, yelling "Lancelot! Lancelot!" in his French accent.

Daffodil came in first, Lancelot second, Mirza third. The child, flushed and with eyes blazing, was curiously serene. His uncle brought him four five-pound notes, four to one.

"What am I to do with these?" he cried, waving them before the boys eyes.

"I suppose we'll talk to Bassett," said the boy. "I expect I have fifteen hundred now; and twenty in reserve; and this twenty."

His uncle studied him for some moments.

"Look here, son!" he said. "You're not serious about Bassett and that fifteen hundred, are you?"

"Yes, I am. But it's between you and me, uncle. Honour bright?"

"Honour bright all right, son! But I must talk to Bassett."

"If you'd like to be a partner, uncle, with Bassett and me, we could all be partners. Only, you'd have to promise, honour bright, uncle, not to let it go beyond us three. Bassett and I are lucky, and you must be lucky, because it was your ten shillings I started winning with . . ."

Uncle Oscar took both Bassett and Paul into Richmond Park for an afternoon, and there they talked.

"It's like this, you see, sir," Bassett said. "Master Paul would get me talking about racing events, spinning yarns, you know, sir. And he was always keen on knowing if I'd made or if I'd lost. It's about a year since, now, that I put five shillings on Blush of Dawn for him: and we lost. Then the luck turned, with that ten shillings he had from you: that we put on Singhalese. And since that time, it's been pretty steady, all things considering. What do you say, Master Paul?"

"We're all right when we're sure," said Paul. "It's when we're not quite sure that we go down."

"Oh, but we're careful then," said Bassett.

"But when are you sure?" smiled Uncle Oscar.

"It's Master Paul, sir," said Bassett in a secret, religious voice. "It's as if he had it from heaven. Like Daffodil, now, for the Lincoln. That was as sure as eggs."

"Did you put anything on Daffodil?" asked Oscar Cresswell.

"Yes, sir, I made my bit."

"And my nephew?"

Bassett was obstinately silent, looking at Paul.

"I made twelve hundred, didn't I, Bassett? I told uncle I was putting three hundred on Daffodil."

"That's right," said Bassett, nodding.

"But where's the money?" asked the uncle.

"I keep it safe locked up, sir. Master Paul he can have it any minute he likes to ask for it."

"What, fifteen hundred pounds?"

"And twenty! And forty, that is, with the twenty he made on the course."

"It's amazing!" said the uncle.

"If Master Paul offers you to be partners, sir, I would, if I were you: if you'll excuse me," said Bassett.

Oscar Cresswell thought about it.

"I'll see the money," he said.

They drove home again, and, sure enough, Bassett came round to the garden-house with fifteen hundred pounds in notes. The twenty pounds reserve was left with Joe Glee, in the Turf Commission deposit.

"You see, it's all right, uncle, when I'm sure! Then we go strong, for all we're worth, don't we, Bassett?"

"We do that, Master Paul."

"And when are you sure?" said the uncle, laughing.

"Oh, well, sometimes I'm absolutely sure, like about Daffodil," said the boy; "and sometimes I have an idea; and sometimes I haven't even an idea, have I, Bassett? Then we're careful, because we mostly go down."

"You do, do you! And when you're sure, like about Daffodil, what makes you sure, sonny?"

"Oh, well, I don't know," said the boy uneasily. "I'm sure, you know, uncle; that's all."

"It's as if he had it from heaven, sir," Bassett reiterated.

"I should say so!" said the uncle.

But he became a partner. And when the Leger was coming on Paul was "sure" about Lively Spark, which was a quite inconsiderable horse. The boy insisted on putting a thousand on the horse, Bassett went for five hundred, and Oscar Cresswell two hundred. Lively Spark came in first, and the betting had been ten to one against him. Paul had made ten thousand.

"You see," he said. "I was absolutely sure of him."

Even Oscar Cresswell had cleared two thousand.

"Look here, son," he said, "this sort of thing makes me nervous."

"It needn't, uncle! Perhaps I shan't be sure again for a long time."

"But what are you going to do with your money?" asked the uncle.

"Of course," said the boy, "I started it for mother. She said she had no luck, because father is unlucky, so I thought if I was lucky, it might stop whispering."

"What might stop whispering?"

"Our house. I hate our house for whispering."

"What does it whisper?"

"Why – why" – the boy fidgeted – "why, I don't know. But it's always short of money, you know, uncle."

"I know it, son, I know it."

"You know people send mother writs, don't you, uncle?"

"I'm afraid I do," said the uncle.

"And then the house whispers, like people laughing at you behind your back. It's awful, that is! I thought if I was lucky -"

"You might stop it," added the uncle.

The boy watched him with big blue eyes, that had an uncanny cold fire in them, and he said never a word.

"Well, then!" said the uncle. "What are we doing?"

"I shouldn't like mother to know I was lucky," said the boy.

"Why not, son?"

"She'd stop me."

"I don't think she would."

"Oh!" – and the boy writhed in an odd way – "I don't want her to know, uncle."

"All right, son! We'll manage it without her knowing."

They managed it very easily. Paul, at the other's suggestion, handed over five thousand pounds to his uncle, who deposited it with the family lawyer, who was then to inform Paul's mother that a relative had put five thousand pounds into his hands, which sum was to be paid out a thousand pounds at a time, on the mother's birthday, for the next five years.

"So she'll have a birthday present of a thousand pounds for five successive years," said Uncle Oscar. "I hope it won't make it all the harder for her later."

Paul's mother had her birthday in November. The house had been 'whispering' worse than ever lately, and, even in spite of his luck, Paul could not bear up against it. He was very anxious to see the effect of the birthday letter, telling his mother about the thousand pounds.

When there were no visitors, Paul now took his meals with his parents, as he was beyond the nursery control. His mother went into town nearly every day. She had discovered that she had an odd knack of sketching furs and dress materials, so she worked secretly in the studio of a friend who was the chief "artist" for the leading drapers. She drew the figures of ladies in furs and ladies in silk and sequins for the newspaper advertisements. This young woman artist earned several thousand pounds a year, but Paul's mother only made several hundreds, and she was again dissatisfied. She so wanted to be first in something, and she did not succeed, even in making sketches for drapery advertisements.

She was down to breakfast on the morning of her birthday. Paul watched her face as she read her letters. He knew the lawyer's letter. As his mother read it, her face hardened and became more expressionless. Then a cold, determined look came on her mouth. She hid the letter under the pile of others, and said not a word about it.

"Didn't you have anything nice in the post for your birthday, mother?" said Paul.

"Quite moderately nice," she said, her voice cold and hard and absent.

She went away to town without saying more.

But in the afternoon Uncle Oscar appeared. He said Paul's mother had had a long interview with the lawyer, asking if the whole five thousand could not be advanced at once, as she was in debt.

"What do you think, uncle?" said the boy.

"I leave it to you, son."

"Oh, let her have it, then! We can get some more with the other," said the boy.

"A bird in the hand is worth two in the bush, laddie!" said Uncle Oscar.

"But I'm sure to know for the Grand National; or the Lincolnshire; or else the Derby. I'm sure to know for one of them," said Paul.

So Uncle Oscar signed the agreement, and Paul's mother touched the whole five thousand. Then something very curious happened. The voices in the house suddenly went mad, like a chorus of frogs on a spring evening. There were certain new furnishings, and Paul had a tutor. He was really going to Eton, his father's school, in the following autumn. There were flowers in the winter, and a blossoming of the luxury Paul's mother had been used to. And yet the voices in the house, behind the sprays of mimosa and almond-blossom, and from under the piles of iridescent cushions, simply trilled and screamed in a sort of ecstasy: "There must be more money! Oh-h-h; there must be more money. Oh, now, now-w! Now-w-w – there must be more money! – more than ever! More than ever!"

It frightened Paul terribly. He studied away at his Latin and Greek with his tutor. But his intense hours were spent with Bassett. The Grand National had gone by: he had not "known", and had lost a hundred pounds. Summer was at hand. He was in agony for the Lincoln. But even for the Lincoln he didn't "know", and he lost fifty pounds. He became wild-eyed and strange, as if something were going to explode in him.

"Let it alone, son! Don't you bother about it!" urged Uncle Oscar. But it was as if the boy couldn't really hear what his uncle was saying.

"I've got to know for the Derby! I've got to know for the Derby!" the child reiterated, his big blue eyes blazing with a sort of madness.

His mother noticed how overwrought he was.

"You'd better go to the seaside. Wouldn't you like to go now to the seaside, instead of waiting? I think you'd better," she said, looking down at him anxiously, her heart curiously heavy because of him.

But the child lifted his uncanny blue eyes.

"I couldn't possibly go before the Derby, mother!" he said. "I couldn't possibly!"

"Why not?" she said, her voice becoming heavy when she was opposed. "Why not? You can still go from the seaside to see the Derby with your Uncle Oscar, if that that's what you wish. No need for you to wait here. Besides, I think you care too much about these races. It's a bad sign. My family has been a gambling family, and you won't know till you grow up how much damage it has done. But it has done damage. I shall have to send Bassett away, and ask Uncle Oscar not to talk racing to you, unless you promise to be reasonable about it: go away to the seaside and forget it. You're all nerves!"

"I'll do what you like, mother, so long as you don't send me away till after the Derby," the boy said.

"Send you away from where? Just from this house?"

"Yes," he said, gazing at her.

"Why, you curious child, what makes you care about this house so much, suddenly? I never knew you loved it."

He gazed at her without speaking. He had a secret within a secret, something he had not divulged, even to Bassett or to his Uncle Oscar.

But his mother, after standing undecided and a little bit sullen for some moments, said: "Very well, then! Don't go to the seaside till after the Derby, if you don't wish it. But promise me you won't think so much about horse-racing and events as you call them!"

"Oh no," said the boy casually. "I won't think much about them, mother. You needn't worry. I wouldn't worry, mother, if I were you."

"If you were me and I were you," said his mother, "I wonder what we should do!"

"But you know you needn't worry, mother, don't you?" the boy repeated.

"I should be awfully glad to know it," she said wearily.

"Oh, well, you can, you know. I mean, you ought to know you needn't worry," he insisted.

"Ought I? Then I'll see about it," she said.

Paul's secret of secrets was his wooden horse, that which had no name. Since he was emancipated from a nurse and a nursery-governess, he had had his rocking-horse removed to his own bedroom at the top of the house.

"Surely you're too big for a rocking-horse!" his mother had remonstrated.

"Well, you see, mother, till I can have a real horse, I like to have some sort of animal about," had been his quaint answer.

"Do you feel he keeps you company?" she laughed.

"Oh yes! He's very good, he always keeps me company, when I'm there," said Paul.

So the horse, rather shabby, stood in an arrested prance in the boy's bedroom.

The Derby was drawing near, and the boy grew more and more tense. He hardly heard what was spoken to him, he was very frail, and his eyes were really uncanny. His mother had sudden strange seizures of uneasiness about him. Sometimes, for half an hour, she would feel a sudden anxiety about him that was almost anguish. She wanted to rush to him at once, and know he was safe.

Two nights before the Derby, she was at a big party in town, when one of her rushes of anxiety about her boy, her first-born, gripped her heart till she could hardly speak. She fought with the feeling, might and main, for she believed in common sense. But it was too strong. She had to leave the dance and go downstairs to telephone to the country. The children's nursery-governess was terribly surprised and startled at being rung up in the night.

"Are the children all right, Miss Wilmot?"

"Oh yes, they are quite all right."

"Master Paul? Is he all right?"

"He went to bed as right as a trivet. Shall I run up and look at him?"

"No," said Paul's mother reluctantly. "No! Don't trouble. It's all right. Don't sit up. We shall be home fairly soon." She did not want her son's privacy intruded upon.

"Very good," said the governess.

It was about one o'clock when Paul's mother and father drove up to their house. All was still. Paul's mother went to her room and slipped off her white fur cloak. She had told her maid not to wait up for her. She heard her husband downstairs, mixing a whisky and soda.

And then, because of the strange anxiety at her heart, she stole upstairs to her son's room. Noiselessly she went along the upper corridor. Was there a faint noise? What was it?

She stood, with arrested muscles, outside his door, listening. There was a strange, heavy, and yet not loud noise. Her heart stood still. It was a soundless noise, yet rushing and powerful. Something huge, in violent, hushed motion. What was it? What in God's name was it? She ought to know. She felt that she knew the noise. She knew what it was.

Yet she could not place it. She couldn't say what it was. And on and on it went, like a madness.

Softly, frozen with anxiety and fear, she turned the door-handle.

The room was dark. Yet in the space near the window, she heard and saw something plunging to and fro. She gazed in fear and amazement.

Then suddenly she switched on the light, and saw her son, in his green pyjamas, madly surging on the rocking-horse. The blaze of light suddenly lit him up, as he urged the wooden horse, and lit her up, as she stood, blonde, in her dress of pale green and crystal, in the doorway.

"Paul!" she cried. "Whatever are you doing?"

"It's Malabar!" he screamed in a powerful, strange voice. "It's Malabar!"

His eyes blazed at her for one strange and senseless second, as he ceased urging his wooden horse. Then he fell with a crash to the ground, and she, all her tormented motherhood flooding upon her, rushed to gather him up.

But he was unconscious, and unconscious he remained, with some brain-fever. He talked and tossed, and his mother sat stonily by his side.

"Malabar! It's Malabar! Bassett, Bassett, I know! It's Malabar!"

So the child cried, trying to get up and urge the rocking-horse that gave him his inspiration.

"What does he mean by Malabar?" asked the heart-frozen mother.

"I don't know," said the father stonily.

"What does he mean by Malabar?" she asked her brother Oscar.

"It's one of the horses running for the Derby," was the answer.

And, in spite of himself, Oscar Cresswell spoke to Bassett, and himself put a thousand on Malabar: at fourteen to one.

The third day of the illness was critical: they were waiting for a change. The boy, with his rather long, curly hair, was tossing ceaselessly on the pillow. He neither slept nor regained consciousness, and his eyes were like blue stones. His mother sat, feeling her heart had gone, turned actually into a stone.

In the evening Oscar Cresswell did not come, but Bassett sent a message, saying could he come up for one moment, just one moment? Paul's mother was very angry at the intrusion, but on second thoughts she agreed. The boy was the same. Perhaps Bassett might bring him to consciousness.

The gardener, a shortish fellow with a little brown moustache and sharp little brown eyes, tiptoed into the room, touched his imaginary cap to Paul's mother, and stole to the bedside, staring with glittering, smallish eyes at the tossing, dying child.

"Master Paul!" he whispered. "Master Paul! Malabar came in first all right, a clean win. I did as you told me. You've made over seventy thousand pounds, you have; you've got over eighty thousand. Malabar came in all right, Master Paul."

"Malabar! Malabar! Did I say Malabar, mother? Did I say Malabar? Do you think I'm lucky, mother? I knew Malabar, didn't I? Over eighty thousand pounds! I call that lucky, don't you, mother? Over eighty thousand pounds! I knew, didn't I know I knew? Malabar came in all right. If I ride my horse till I'm sure, then I tell you, Bassett, you can go as high as you like. Did you go for all you were worth, Bassett?"

"I went a thousand on it, Master Paul."

"I never told you, mother, that if I can ride my horse, and get there, then I'm absolutely sure – oh, absolutely! Mother, did I ever tell you? I am lucky!"

"No, you never did," said his mother.

But the boy died in the night.

And even as he lay dead, his mother heard her brother's voice saying to her, "My God, Hester, you're eighty-odd thousand to the good, and a poor devil of a son to the bad. But, poor devil, poor devil, he's best gone out of a life where he rides his rocking-horse to find a winner."

A HAUNTED HOUSE

Virginia Woolf

Virginia Woolf (1882–1941) was born into a large, prosperous, literary
London household. She married a fellow member of the Bloomsbury
group, the writer Leonard Woolf, with whom she founded the Hogarth
Press. The marriage was a happy one, but Woolf also had a relationship with Vita Sackville-West. Woolf's writings explore the parameters
of style and form in modern fiction. She suffered a series of breakdowns
and periods of depression and eventually ended her own life, drowning
herself in the river Ouse.

Whatever hour you woke there was a door shutting. From room to
room they went, hand in hand, lifting here, opening there, making
sure – a ghostly couple.
"Here we left it," she said. And he added, "Oh, but here too!" "It's upstairs,"
she murmured, "And in the garden," he whispered. "Quietly," they said, "or we
shall wake them."

But it wasn't that you woke us. Oh, no. "They're looking for it; they're drawing the curtain," one might say, and so read on a page or two. "Now they've
found it," one would be certain, stopping the pencil on the margin. And then,
tired of reading, one might rise and see for oneself, the house all empty, the doors
standing open, only the wood pigeons bubbling with content and the hum of
the threshing machine sounding from the farm. "What did I come in here for?
What did I want to find?" My hands were empty. "Perhaps it's upstairs then?"
The apples were in the loft. And so down again, the garden still as ever, only the
book had slipped into the grass.

But they had found it in the drawing-room. Not that one could ever see them.
The window-panes reflected apples, reflected roses; all the leaves were green in
the glass. If they moved in the drawing-room, the apple only turned its yellow
side. Yet, the moment after, if the door was opened, spread about the floor, hung
upon the walls, pendant from ceiling – what? My hands were empty. The shadow
of a thrush crossed the carpet; from the deepest wells of silence the wood pigeon
drew its bubble of sound. "Safe, safe, safe," the pulse of the house beat softly.
"The treasure buried; the room . . ." the pulse stopped short. Oh, was that the
buried treasure?

A moment later the light had faded. Out in the garden then? But the trees spun
darkness for a wandering beam of sun. So fine, so rare, coolly sunk beneath the
surface the beam I sought always burnt behind the glass. Death was the glass;
death was between us; coming to the woman first, hundreds of years ago, leaving

the house, sealing all the windows; the rooms were darkened. He left it, left her, went North, went East, saw the stars turned in the Southern sky; sought the house, found it dropped beneath the Downs. "Safe, safe, safe," the pulse of the house beat gladly. "The Treasure yours."

The wind roars up the avenue. Trees stoop and bend this way and that. Moonbeams splash and spill wildly in the rain. But the beam of the lamp falls straight from the window. The candle burns stiff and still. Wandering through the house, opening the windows, whispering not to wake us, the ghostly couple seek their joy.

"Here we slept," she says. And he adds, "Kisses without number." "Waking in the morning – " "Silver between the trees – " "Upstairs – " "In the garden – " "When summer came – " "In winter snowtime – " The doors go shutting far in the distance, gently knocking like the pulse of a heart.

Nearer they come; cease at the doorway. The wind falls, the rain slides silver down the glass. Our eyes darken; we hear no steps beside us; we see no lady spread her ghostly cloak. His hands shield the lantern. "Look," he breathes. "Sound asleep. Love upon their lips."

Stooping, holding their silver lamp above us, long they look and deeply. Long they pause. The wind drives straightly; the flame stoops slightly. Wild beams of moonlight cross both floor and wall, and, meeting, stain the faces bent; the faces pondering; the faces that search the sleepers and seek their hidden joy.

"Safe, safe, safe," the heart of the house beats proudly. "Long years – " he sighs. "Again you found me." "Here," she murmurs, "sleeping; in the garden reading; laughing, rolling apples in the loft. Here we left our treasure – " Stooping, their light lifts the lids upon my eyes. "Safe! safe! safe!" the pulse of the house beats wildly. Waking, I cry "Oh, is this *your* – buried treasure? The light in the heart."

HONEYSUCKLE COTTAGE

P.G. Wodehouse

Pelham Grenville Wodehouse's (1881–1975) father was a magistrate in Hong Kong. Wodehouse was educated in England at Dulwich College, a prominent public school. He worked at the London branch of the Hong Kong and Shanghai Bank before becoming a full-time writer. Wodehouse was in France when World War II broke out and made a series of ill-advised, but non-political, radio broadcasts for the Nazis which damaged his reputation. Wodehouse subsequently settled in America. He was knighted six weeks before his death.

Do you believe in ghosts? "asked Mr Mulliner abruptly.

I weighed the question thought- fully. I was a little surprised, for nothing in our previous conversation had suggested the topic.

"Well," I replied, "I don't like them, if that's what you mean. I was once butted by one as a child."

"Ghosts. Not goats."

"Oh, ghosts? Do I believe in ghosts?"

"Exactly."

"Well, yes – and no."

"Let me put it another way," said Mr Mulliner, patiently. "Do you believe in haunted houses? Do you believe that it is possible for a malign influence to envelop a place and work a spell on all who come within its radius?"

I hesitated.

"Well, no – and yes."

Mr Mulliner sighed a little. He seemed to be wondering if I was always as bright as this.

"Of course," I went on, "one has read stories. Henry James's *Turn of The Screw* . . ."

"I am not talking about fiction."

"Well, in real life – Well, look here, I once, as a matter of fact, did meet a man who knew a fellow . . ."

"My distant cousin James Rodman spent some weeks in a haunted house," said Mr Mulliner, who, if he has a fault, is not a very good listener. "It cost him five thousand pounds. That is to say, he sacrificed five thousand pounds by not remaining there. Did you ever", he asked, wandering, it seemed to me, from the subject, "hear of Leila J. Pinckney?"

Naturally I had heard of Leila J. Pinckney. Her death some years ago had diminished her vogue, but at one time it was impossible to pass a bookshop or a railway bookstall without seeing a long row of her novels. I had never myself actually read of them, but I knew that in her particular line of literature, the Squashily Sentimental, she had always been regarded by those entitled to judge as pre-eminent. The critics usually headed their reviews of her stories with the words:

ANOTHER PINCKNEY

or sometimes, more offensively:

ANOTHER PINCKNEY!!!

And once, dealing with, I think, *The Love Which Prevails*, the Literary expert of the *Scrutinizer* had compressed his entire critique into the single phrase "Oh, God!"

"Of course," I said. "But what about her?"

"She was James Rodman's aunt."

"Yes?"

"And when she died James found that she had left him five thousand pounds and the house in the country where she had lived for the last twenty years of her life."

"A very nice little legacy."

"Twenty years," repeated Mr Mulliner. "Grasp that, for it has a vital bearing on what follows. Twenty years, mind you, and Miss Pinckney turned out two novels and twelve short stories regularly every year, besides a monthly page of Advice to Young Girls in one of the magazines. That is to say, forty of her novels and no fewer than two hundred and forty of her short stories were written under the roof of Honeysuckle Cottage."

"A pretty name."

"A nasty, sloppy name," said Mr Mulliner severely, "which should have warned my distant cousin James from the start. Have you a pencil and a piece of paper?" He scribbled for a while, poring frowningly over columns of figures. "Yes," he said, looking up, "if my calculations are correct, Leila J. Pinckney wrote in all a matter of nine million one hundred and forty thousand words of glutinous sentimentality at Honey-suckle Cottage, and it was a condition of her will that James should reside there for six months in every year. Failing to do this, he was to forfeit the five thousand pounds."

"It must be great fun making a freak will," I mused. "I often wish I was rich enough to do it."

This was not a freak will. The conditions are perfectly understandable. James Rodman was a writer of sensational mystery stories, and his aunt Leila had always disapproved of his work. She was a great believer in the influence of environment, and the reason why she inserted that clause in her will was that she wished to compel James to move from London to the country. She considered that living in London hardened him and made his outlook on life sordid. She often asked him if he thought it quite nice to harp so much on sudden death and black-mailers with squints. Surely, she said, there were enough squinting black-mailers in the world without writing about them.

The fact that Literature meant such different things to these two had, I believe, caused something of a coolness between them, and James had never dreamed that he would be remembered in his aunt's will. For he had never concealed his opinion that Leila J. Pinckney's style of writing revolted him, however dear it might be to her enormous public. He held rigid views on the art of the novel, and always maintained that an artist with a true reverence for his craft should not descend to goo-ey love stories, but should stick austerely to revolvers, cries in the night, missing papers, mysterious Chinamen and dead bodies – with or without gash in throat. And not even the thought that his aunt had dandled him on her knee as a baby could induce him to stifle his literary conscience to the extent of pretending to enjoy her work. First, last and all the time, James Rodman had held the opinion – and voiced it fearlessly – that Leila J. Pinckney wrote bilge.

"It was a surprise to him, therefore, to find that he had been left this legacy. A pleasant surprise, of course. James was making quite a decent income out of the three novels and eighteen short stories which he produced annually, but an author can always find a use for five thousand pounds. And, as for the cottage, he had actually been looking about for a little place in the country at the very moment when he received the lawyer's letter. In less than a week he was installed at his new residence."

James's first impressions of Honeysuckle Cottage were, he tells me, wholly favourable. He was delighted with the place. It was a low, rambling, picturesque old house with funny little chimneys and a red roof, placed in the middle of the most charming country. With its oak beams, its trim garden, its trilling birds and its rose-hung porch, it was the ideal spot for a writer. It was just the sort of place, he reflected whimsically, which his aunt had loved to write about in her books. Even the apple-cheeked old house-keeper who attended to his needs might have stepped straight out of one of them.

It seemed to James that his lot had been cast in pleasant places. He had brought down his books, his pipes and his golf clubs, and was hard at work finishing the best thing he had ever done. *The Secret Nine* was the title of it; and on the beautiful summer afternoon on which this story opens he was in the study, hammering away at his typewriter, at peace with the world. The machine was running sweetly, the new tobacco he had bought the day before was proving admirable, and he was moving on all six cylinders to the end of a chapter.

He shoved in a fresh sheet of paper, chewed his pipe thoughtfully for a moment, then wrote rapidly:

For an instant Lester Gage thought that he must have been mistaken. Then the noise came again, faint but unmistakable – a soft scratching on the outer panel.

"His mouth set in a grim line. Silently, like a panther, he made one quick step to the desk", noiselessly opened a drawer, drew out his automatic. After that affair of the poisoned needle, he was taking no chances. Still in dead silence, he tiptoed to the door; then, flinging it suddenly open, he stood there, his weapon poised.

On the mat stood the most beautiful girl he had ever beheld. A veritable child of Faërie. She eyed him for a moment with a saucy smile; then with a pretty, roguish look of reproof shook a dainty forefinger at him.

"'I believe you've forgotten me, Mr. Gage !' she fluted with a mock severity which her eyes belied."

James stared at the paper dumbly. He was utterly perplexed. He had not had the slightest intention of writing anything like this. To begin with, it was a rule with him, and one which he never broke, to allow no girls to appear in his stories. Sinister landladies, yes, and naturally any amount of adventuresses with foreign accents, but never under any pretext what may be broadly described as girls. A detective story, he maintained, should have no heroine. Heroines only held up the action and tried to flirt with the hero when he should have been busy looking for clues, and then went and let the villain kidnap them by some childishly simple trick. In his writing, James was positively monastic.

And yet here was this creature with her saucy smile and her dainty forefinger horning in at the most important point in the story. It was uncanny.

He looked once more at his scenario. No, the scenario was all right.

In perfectly plain words it stated that what happened when the door opened was that a dying man fell in and after gasping, "The beetle! Tell Scotland Yard that the blue beetle is –" expired on the hearthrug, leaving Lester Gage not unnaturally somewhat mystified. Nothing whatever about any beautiful girls.

In a curious mood of irritation, James scratched out the offending passage, wrote in the necessary corrections and put the cover on the machine. It was at this point that he heard William whining.

The only blot on this paradise which James had so far been able to discover was the infernal dog, William. Belonging nominally to the gardener, on the very first morning he had adopted James by acclamation, and he maddened and infuriated James. He had a habit of coming and whining under the window when James was at work. The latter would ignore this as long as he could; then, when the thing became insupportable, would bound out of his chair, to see the animal standing on the gravel, gazing expectantly up at him with a stone in his mouth. WiUiam had a weak-minded passion for chasing stones; and on the first day James, in a rash spirit of camaraderie, had flung one for him. Since then James had thrown no more stones; but he had thrown any number of other solids, and the garden was Uttered with objects ranging from match boxes to a plaster statuette of the young Joseph prophesying before Pharaoh. And still Willam came and whined, an optimist to the last.

The whining, coming now at a moment when he felt irritable and unsettled, acted on James much as the scratching on the door had acted on Lester Gage. Silently, like a panther, he made one quick step to the mantelpiece, removed from it a china mug bearing the legend "A Present from Clacton-on-Sea", and crept to the window.

And as he did so a voice outside said: "Go away, sir, go away!" and there followed a short, high-pitched bark which was certainly not Williams'. William was a mixture of Airedale, setter, bull terrier, and mastiff; and when in vocal mood, favoured the mastiff side of his family.

James peered out. There on the porch stood a girl in blue. She held in her arms a small fluffy white dog, and she was endeavouring to foil the upward movement toward this of the blackguard William. William's mentality had been arrested some years before at the point where he imagined that everything in the world had been created for him to eat. A bone, a boot, a steak, the back wheel of a bicycle – it was all one to William. If it was there he tried to eat it.

He had even made a plucky attempt to devour the remains of the young Joseph prophesying before Pharaoh. And it was perfectly plain now that he regarded the curious wriggling object in the girl's arms purely in the light of a snack to keep body and soul together till dinner time.

"William!" bellowed James.

William looked courteously over his shoulder with eyes that beamed with the pure light of a life's devotion, wagged the whiplike tail which he had inherited from his bull terrier ancestor and resumed his intent scrutiny of the fluffy dog.

"Oh, please!" cried the girl. "This great rough dog is frightening poor Toto."

The man of letters and the man of action do not always go hand in hand, but practice had made James perfect in handling with swift efficiency any situation that involved William. A moment later that canine moron, having received the present from Clacton in the short ribs, was scuttling round the corner of the house, and James had jumped through the window and was facing the girl.

She was an extraordinarily pretty girl. Very sweet and fragile she looked as she stood there under the honeysuckle with the breeze ruffling a tendril of golden hair that strayed from beneath her coquettish little hat. Her eyes were very big and very blue, her rose-tinted face becomingly flushed. All wasted on James, though. He disliked all girls, and particularly the sweet, droopy type.

"Did you want to see somebody?" he asked stiffly.

"Just the house," said the girl, "if it wouldn't be giving any trouble. I do so want to see the room where Miss Pinckney wrote her books. This is where Leila J. Pinckney used to live, isn't it?"

"Yes; I am her nephew. My name is James Rodman."

"Mine is Rose Maynard."

James led the way into the house, and she stopped with a cry of delight on the threshold of the morning-room.

"Oh, how too perfect!" she cried. "So this was her study?"

"Yes."

"What a wonderful place it would be for you to think in if you were a writer too."

James held no high opinion of women's literary taste, but nevertheless he was conscious of an unpleasant shock.

"I am a writer," he said coldly. "I write detective stories."

"I–I'm afraid" – she blushed – "I'm afraid I don't often read detective stories."

"You no doubt prefer," said James, still more coldly, "the sort of thing my aunt used to write."

"Oh, I love her stories!" cried the girl, clasping her hands ecstatically. "Don't you?"

"I cannot say that I do."

"What?"

"They are pure apple sauce," said James sternly; "just nasty blobs of sentimentality, thoroughly untrue to life."

The girl stared.

"Why, that's just what's so wonderful about them, their trueness to life! You feel they might all have happened. I don't understand what you mean."

They were walking down the garden now. James held the gate open for her and she passed through into the road.

"Well, for one thing," he said, "I decline to believe that a marriage between two young people is invariably preceded by some violent and sensational experience in which they both share."

"Are you thinking of *Scent o' the Blossom*, where Edgar saves Maud from drowning?"

"I am thinking of every single one of my aunt's books."

He looked at her curiously. He had just got the solution of a mystery which had been puzzling him for some time. Almost from the moment he had set eyes on her she had seemed somehow strangely familiar. It now suddenly came to him why it was that he disliked her so much. "Do you know," he said, "you might be one of my aunt's heroines yourself? You're just the sort of girl she used to love to write about."

Her face lit up.

"Oh, do you really think so?" She hesitated. "Do you know what I have been feeling ever since I came here? I've been feeling that you are exactly like one of Miss Pickney's heroes."

"No, I say, really!" said James, revolted.

"Oh, but you are! When you jumped through that window it gave me quite a start. You were so exactly like Claude Masterson in *Heather o' the Hills*."

"I have not read *Heather o' the Hills*," said James, with a shudder.

"He was very strong and quiet, with deep, dark, sad eyes."

James did not explain that his eyes were sad because her society gave him a pain in the neck. He merely laughed scornfully.

"So now, I suppose," he said, "a car will come and knock you down and I shall carry you gently into the house and lay you – Look out!" he cried.

It was too late. She was lying in a little huddled heap at his feet. Round the corner a large automobile had come bowling, keeping with an almost affected precision to the wrong side of the road. It was now receding into the distance, the occupant of the tonneau, a stout red-faced gentleman in a fur coat, leaning out over the back. He had bared his head – not, one fears, as a pretty gesture of respect and regret, but because he was using his hat to hide the number plate.

The dog Toto was unfortunately uninjured.

James carried the girl gently into the house and laid her on the sofa in the morning-room. He rang the bell and the apple-cheeked housekeeper appeared.

"Send for the doctor," said James. "There has been an accident."

The housekeeper bent over the girl.

"Eh, dearie, dearie!" she said. "Bless her sweet pretty face!"

The gardener, he who technically owned William, was routed out from among the young lettuces and told to fetch Doctor Brady. He separated his bicycle from William, who was making a light meal off the left pedal, and departed on his mission. Doctor Brady arrived and in due course he made his report.

"No bones broken, but a number of nasty bruises. And, of course, the shock. She will have to stay here for some time, Rodman. Can't be moved."

"Stay here! But she can't! It isn't proper."

"Your housekeeper will act as a chaperon."

The doctor sighed. He was a stolid-looking man of middle age, with side whiskers.

"A beautiful girl, that Rodman," he said.

"I suppose so," said James.

"A sweet, beautiful girl. An elfin child."

"A what?" cried James, starting.

This imagery was very foreign to doctor Brady as he knew him. On the only previous occasion on which they had had any extended conversation, the doctor had talked exclusively about the effect of too much protein on the gastric juices.

"An elfin child; a tender, fairy creature. When I was looking at her just now, Rodman, I nearly broke down. Her little hand lay on the coverlet like some white lily floating on the surface of a still pool, and her dear, trusting eyes gazed up at me."

He pottered off down the garden, still babbling, and James stood staring after him blankly. And slowly, like some cloud athwart a summer sky, there crept over James's heart the chill shadow of a nameless fear.

It was about a week later that Mr Andrew McKinnon, the senior partner in the well-known firm of literary agents, McKinnon & Gooch, sat in his office in Chancery Lane, frowning thoughtfully over a telegram. He rang the bell.

"Ask Mr Gooch to step in here." He resumed his study of the telegram. "Oh, Gooch," he said when his partner appeared, "I've just had a curious wire from young Rodman. He seems to want to see me very urgently."

Mr Gooch read the telegram.

"Written under the influence of some strong mental excitement," he agreed. "I wonder why he doesn't come to the office if he wants to see you so badly."

"He's working very hard, finishing that novel for Prodder & Wiggs. Can't leave it, I suppose. Well, it's a nice day. If you will look after things here I think I'll motor down and let him give me lunch."

As Mr McKinnon's car reached the crossroads a mile from Honeysuckle Cottage, he was aware of a gesticulating figure by the hedge. He stopped the car.

"Morning, Rodman."

"Thank God you've come!" said James. It seemed to Mr McKinnon that the young man looked paler and thinner. "Would you mind walking the rest of the way? There's something I want to speak to you about."

Mr McKinnon alighted; and James, as he glanced at him, felt cheered and encouraged by the very sight of the man. The literary agent was a grim, hardbitten person, to whom, when he called at their offices to arrange terms, editors kept their faces turned so that they might at least retain their back collar studs. There was no sentiment in Andrew McKinnon. Editresses of society papers practiced their blandishments on him in vain, and many a publisher had waked screaming in the night, dreaming that he was signing a McKinnon contract.

"Well, Rodman," he said, "Prodder & Wiggs have agreed to our terms. I was writing to tell you so when your wire arrived. I had a lot of trouble with them, but it's fixed at 20 per cent, rising to 25, and two hundred pounds advance royalties on day of publication."

"Good!" said James absently. "Good! McKinnon, do you remember my aunt, Leila J. Pinkney?"

"Remember her? Why, I was her agent all her life."

"Of course. Then you know the sort of tripe she wrote."

"No author", said Mr McKinnon reprovingly, "who pulls down a steady twenty thousand pounds a year writes tripe."

"Well, anyway, you know her stuff."

"Who better?"

"When she died she left me five thousand pounds and her house, Honey-suckle Cottage. I'm living there now. McKinnon, do you believe in haunted houses?"

"No."

"Yet I tell you solemnly that Honeysuckle Cottage is haunted!"

"By your aunt?" said Mr McKinnon, surprised.

"By her influence. There's a malignant spell over the place; a sort of miasma of sentimentalism. Everybody who enters it succumbs."

"Tut-tut! You mustn't have these fancies."

"They aren't fancies."

"You are seriously meaning to tell me –"

"Well, how do you account for this? That book you were speaking about, which Prodder & Wiggs are to publish – *The Secret Nine*. Every time I sit down to write it a girl keeps trying to sneak in."

"Into the room?"

"Into the story."

"You don't want a love interest in your sort of book," said Mr McKinnon, shaking his head. "It delays the action."

"I know it does. And every day I have to keep shooing this infernal female out. An awful girl, McKinnon. A soppy soupy, treacly, drooping girl with a roguish smile. This morning she tried to butt in on the scene where Lester Gage is trapped in the den of the mysterious leper."

"No!"

"She did, I assure you. I had to rewrite three pages before I could get her out of it. And that's not the worst. Do you know, McKinnon, that at this moment I am actually living the plot of a typical Leila J. Pinckney novel in just the setting she always used! And I can see the happy ending coming nearer every day! A week ago a girl was knocked down by a car at my door and I've had to put her up, and every day I realise more clearly that sooner or later I shall ask her to marry me."

"Don't do it," said Mr McKinnon, a stout bachelor. "You're too young to marry."

"So was Methuselah," said James, a stouter. "But all the same I know I'm going to do it. It's the influence of this awful house weighing upon me. I feel like an eggshell in a maelstrom. I am being sucked on by a force too strong for me to resist. This morning I found myself kissing her dog!"

"No!"

"I did! And I loathe the little beast. Yesterday I got up at dawn and plucked a nosegay of flowers for her, wet with the dew."

"Rodman!"

"It's a fact. I laid them at her door and went downstairs kicking myself all the way. And there in the hall was the apple-cheeked housekeeper regarding me archly. If she didn't murmur 'Bless their sweet young hearts!' my ears deceive me."

"Why don't you pack up and leave?"

"If I do I lose the five thousand pounds."

"Ah!" said Mr McKinnon.

"I can understand what has happened. It's the same with all haunted houses. My aunt's subliminal ether vibrations have woven themselves into the texture of the place, creating an atmosphere which forces the ego of all who come in contact with it to attune themselves to it. It's either that or something to do with the fourth dimension."

Mr McKinnon laughed scornfully.

"Tut-tut!" he said again. "This is pure imagination. What has happened is that you've been working too hard. You'll see this precious atmosphere of yours will have no effect on me."

"That's exactly why I asked you to come down. I hoped you might break the spell."

"I will that," said Mr McKinnon jovially.

The fact that the literary agent spoke little at lunch caused James no apprehension. Mr McKinnon was ever a silent trencherman. From time to time James caught him stealing a glance at the girl, who was well enough to come down to meals now, limping pathetically; but he could read nothing in his face. And yet the mere look of his face was a consolation. It was so solid, so matter of fact, so exactly like an unemotional coconut.

"You've done me good," said James with a sigh of relief, as he escorted the agent down the garden to his car after lunch. "I felt all along that I could rely on your rugged common sense. The whole atmosphere of the place seems different now."

Mr McKinnon did not speak for a moment. He seemed to be plunged into thought.

"Rodman," he said, as he got into his car. "I've been thinking over that suggestion of yours of putting a love interest into *The Secret Nine*. I think you're wise. The story needs it. After all, what is there greater in the world than love? Love–love – aye, it's the sweetest word in the language. Put in a heroine and let her marry Lester Gage."

"If", said James grimly, "she does succeed in worming her way in she'll jolly well marry the mysterious leper. But look here, I don't understand –"

"It was seeing that girl that changed me," proceeded Mr McKinnon. And as James stared at him aghast, tears suddenly filled his hard-boiled eyes. He openly snuffled. "Aye, seeing her sitting there under the roses, with all that smell of honeysuckle and all. And the birdies singing so sweet in the garden and the sun lighting up her bonny face. The puir wee lass!" he muttered, dabbing at his eyes. "The puir bonny wee lass! Rodman," he said, his voice quivering, "I've decided that we're being hard on Prodder & Wiggs. Wiggs has had sickness in his home recently. We mustn't be hard on a man who's had sickness in his home, hey, laddie? No, no! I'm going to take back that contract and alter it to a flat 12 per cent and no advance royalties."

"What!"

"But you shan't lose by it, Rodman. No, no, you shan't lose by it, my many. I am going to waive my commission. The puir bonny wee lass!"

The car rolled off down the road. Mr McKinnon, seated in the back, was blowing his nose violently.

"This is the end!" said James.

It is necessary at this point to pause and examine James Rodman's position with an unbiased eye. The average man, unless he puts himself in James's place, will be unable to appreciate it. James, he will feel, was making a lot of fuss about nothing. Here he was, drawing daily closer and closer to a charming girl with big blue eyes, and surely rather to be envied than pitied.

But we must remember that James was one of Nature's bachelors. And no ordinary man, looking forward dreamily to a little home of his own with a loving wife putting out his slippers and changing the gramophone records, can realize the intensity of the instinct for self-preservation which animates Nature's bachelors in times of peril.

James Rodman had a congenital horror of matrimony. Though a young man, he had allowed himself to develop a great many habits, which were as the breath of life to him; and these habits, he knew instinctively, a wife would shoot to pieces within a week of the end of the honeymoon.

James liked to breakfast in bed; and, having breakfasted, to smoke in bed and knock the ashes out on the carpet. What wife would tolerate this practice?

James liked to pass his days in a tennis shirt, grey flannel trousers and slippers. What wife ever rests until she has inclosed her husband in a stiff collar, tight boots and a morning suit and taken him with her to *thés musicales*?

These and a thousand other thoughts of the same kind flashed through the unfortunate young man's mind as the days went by, and every day that passed seemed to draw him nearer to the brink of the chasm. Fate appeared to be taking a malicious pleasure in making things as difficult for him as possible. Now that the girl was well enough to leave her bed, she spent her time sitting in a chair on the sun-sprinkled porch, and James had to read to her – and poetry, at that; and not the jolly, wholesome sort of poetry the boys are turning out nowadays, either – good, honest stuff about sin and gas works and decaying corpses – but the old-fashioned kind with rhymes in it, dealing almost exclusively with love. The weather, moreover, continued superb. The honeysuckle cast its sweet scent on the gentle breeze; the roses over the porch stirred and nodded; the flowers in the garden were lovelier than ever; the birds sang their little throats sore. And every evening there was a magnificent sunset. It was almost as if Nature were doing it on purpose.

At last James intercepted Doctor Brady as he was leaving after one of his visits and put the thing to him squarely:

"When is that girl going?"

The doctor patted him on the arm.

"Not yet, Rodman." He said in a low, understanding voice. "No need to worry yourself about that. Mustn't be moved for days and days and days – I might almost say weeks and weeks and weeks."

"Weeks and weeks!" cried James.

"And weeks," said Doctor Brady. He prodded James roguishly in the abdomen. "Good luck to you, my boy, good luck to you," he said.

It was some small consolation to James that the mushy physician immediately afterward tripped over William on his way down the path, and broke his stethoscope. When a man is up against it like James every little helps.

He was walking dismally back to the house after this conversation when he was met by the apple-cheeked housekeeper.

"The little lady would like to speak to you, sir," said the apple-cheeked exhibit, rubbing her hands.

"Would she?" James said hollowly.

"So sweet and pretty she looks, sir – oh sir, you wouldn't believe! Like a blessed angel sitting there with her dear eyes all a-shining."

"Don't do it!" cried James with extraordinary vehemence. "Don't do it!"

He found the girl propped up on the cushions and thought once again how singularly he disliked her. And yet, even as he thought this, some force against which he had to fight madly was whispering to him: "Go to her and take that little hand! Breathe into that little ear the burning words that will make that little face turn away crimsoned with blushes!" He wiped a bead of perspiration from his forehead and sat down.

"Mrs Stick-in-the-Mud – what's her name? – says you want to see me."

The girl nodded.

"I've had a letter from Uncle Henry. I wrote to him as soon as I was better and told him what had happened, and he is coming here to-morrow morning."

"Uncle Henry?"

"That's what I call him, but he's really no relation. He is my guardian. He and Daddy were officers in the same regiment and when Daddy was killed, fighting on the Afghan frontier, he died in Uncle Henry's arms and with his last breath begged him to take care of me."

James started. A sudden wild hope had waked in his heart. Years ago, he remembered, he had read a book of his aunt's entitled *Rupert's Legacy*, and in that book –

"I'm engaged to marry him," said the girl quietly.

"Wow!" shouted James.

"What?" asked the girl, startled.

"Touch of cramp," said James. He was thrilling all over. That wild hope had been realized.

"It was Daddy's wish that we should marry," said the girl.

"And dashed sensible of him, too, dashed sensible," said James warmly.

"And yet," she went on, a little wistfully, "I sometimes wonder –"

"Don't!" said James. "Don't! You must respect Daddy's dying wish. There's nothing like Daddy's dying wish; you can't beat it. So he's coming here to-morrow, is he? Capital, capital! To lunch, I suppose? Excellent! I'll run down and tell Mrs. Who-is-it to lay in another chop."

It was with a gay and uplifted heart that James strolled the garden and smoked his pipe next morning. A great cloud seemed to have rolled itself away from him. Everything was for the best in the best of all possible worlds. He had finished *The Secret Nine* and shipped it off to Mr McKinnon, and now as he strolled there was shaping itself in his mind a corking plot about a man with only half a face who lived in a secret den and terrorized London with a series of shocking murders. And what made them so shocking was the fact that each of the victims, when discovered, was found to have only half a face too. The rest had been chipped off, presumably by some blunt instrument.

The thing was coming out magnificently, when suddenly his attention was diverted by a piercing scream. Out of the bushes fringing the river that ran beside the garden burst the apple-cheeked housekeeper.

"Oh, sir! Oh, sir! Oh, sir!"

"What is it?" demanded James irritably.

"Oh, sir! Oh, sir! Oh, sir!"

"Yes, and then what?"

"The little dog, sir! He's in the river!"

"Well, whistle him to come out."

"Oh, sir, do come quick! He'll be drowned!"

James followed her through the bushes, taking off his coat as he went. He was saying to himself: "I will not rescue this dog. I do not like the dog. It is high time he had a bath, and in any case it would be much simpler to stand on the bank and fish for him with a rake. Only an ass out of a Leila J. Pinckney book would dive into a beastly river to save –"

At this point he dived. Toto, alarmed by the splash, swam rapidly for the bank, but James was too quick for him. Grasping him firmly by the neck, he scrambled ashore and ran for the house, followed by the housekeeper.

The girl was seated on the porch. Over her there bent the tall soldierly figure of a man with keen eyes and greying hair. The housekeeper raced up.

"Oh, miss! Toto! In the river! He saved him! He plunged in and saved him!"

The girl drew a quick breath.

"Gallant, damme! By Jove! By gad! Yes, gallant, by George!" exclaimed the soldierly man.

The girl seemed to wake from a reverie.

"Uncle Henry, this is Mr Rodman. Mr Rodman, my guardian, Colonel Carteret."

"Proud to meet you, sir," said the colonel, his honest blue eyes glowing as he fingered his short crisp moustache. "As fine a thing as I ever heard of, damme!"

"Yes, you are brave – brave," the girl whispered.

"I am wet – wet," said James, and went upstairs to change his clothes.

When he came down for lunch he found to his relief that the girl had decided not to join them, and Colonel Carteret was silent and preoccupied. James, exerting himself in his capacity of host, tried him with the weather, golf, India, the Government, the high cost of living, first-class cricket, the modern dancing craze, and murderers he had met, but the other still preserved that strange, absent-minded silence. It was only when the meal was concluded and James had produced cigarettes that he came abruptly out of his trance.

"Rodman," he said, "I should like to speak to you."

"Yes?" said James, thinking it was about time.

"Rodman," said Colonel Carteret, "or rather, George – I may call you George?" he added, with a sort of wistful diffidence that had a singular charm.

"Certainly," replied James, "if you wish it. Though my name is James."

"James, eh? Well, well, it amounts to the same thing, eh, what, damme, by gad?" said the colonel with a momentary return of his bluff soldierly manner. "Well, then, James, I have something that I wish to say to you. Did Miss Maynard – did Rose happen to tell you anything about myself in – er – in connection with herself?"

"She mentioned that you and she were engaged to be married."

The colonel's tightly drawn lips quivered.

"No longer," he said.

"What?"

"No, John, my boy."

"James."

"No, James, my boy, no longer. While you were upstairs changing your clothes she told me – breaking down, poor child, as she spoke – that she wished our engagement to be at an end."

James half rose from the table, his cheeks blanched.

"You don't mean that!" he gasped.

Colonel Carteret nodded. He was staring out of the window, his fine eyes set in a look of pain.

"But this is nonsense!" cried James. "This is absurd! She – she mustn't be allowed to chop and change like this. I mean to say, it – it isn't fair –"

"Don't think of me, my boy."

"I'm not – I mean, did she give any reason?"

"Her eyes did."

"Her eyes did?"

"Her eyes, when she looked at you on the porch, as you stood there – young, heroic – having just saved the life of the dog she loves. It is you who have won that tender heart, my boy."

"Now listen," protested James, 'you aren't going to sit there and tell me that a girl falls in love with a man just because he saves her dog from drowning?"

"Why, surely," said Colonel Carteret, surprised. "What better reason could she have?" He sighed. "It is the old, old story, my boy. Youth to youth. I am an old man. I should have known – I should have foreseen – yes, youth to youth."

"You aren't a bit old."

"Yes, yes."

"No, no."

"Yes, yes."

"Don't keep on saying yes, yes!" cried James, clutching at his hair. "Besides, she wants a steady old buffer – a steady, sensible man of medium age – to look after her."

Colonel Carteret shook his head with a gentle smile.

"This is mere quixotry, my boy. It is splendid of you to take this attitude; but no, no."

"Yes, yes."

"No, no." He gripped James's hand for an instant, then rose and walked to the door. "That is all I wished to say, Tom."

"James."

"James. I just thought that you ought to know how matters stood. Go to her, my boy, go to her, and don't let any thought of an old man's broken dream keep you from pouring out what is in your heart. I am an old soldier, lad, an old soldier. I have learned to take the rough with the smooth. But I think – I think I will leave you now. I – I should – should like to be alone for a while. If you need me you will find me in the raspberry bushes.

He had scarcely gone when James also left the room. He took his hat and stick and walked blindly out of the garden, he knew not whither. His brain was numbed. Then, as his powers of reasoning returned, he told himself that he should have foreseen this ghastly thing. If there was one type of character over which Leila J. Pinckney had been wont to spread herself, it was the pathetic guardian who loves his ward but relinquishes her to the younger man. No wonder the girl had broken off the engagement. Any elderly guardian who allowed himself to come within a mile of Honeysuckle Cottage was simply asking for it. And then, as he turned to walk back, a sort of dull defiance gripped James. Why, he asked, should he be put upon in this manner? If the girl liked to throw over this man, why should he be the goat?

He saw his way clearly now. He just wouldn't do it, that was all. And if they didn't like it they could lump it.

Full of a new fortitude, he strode in at the gate. A Tall, soldierly figure emerged from the raspberry bushes and came to meet him.

"Well?" said Colonel Carteret.

"Well?" said James defiantly.

"Am I to congratulate you?"

James caught his keen blue eye and hesitated. It was not going to be so simple as he had supposed.

"Well – er –" he said.

Into the keen blue eyes there came a look that James had not seen there before. It was the stern hard look which, probably, had caused men to bestow upon this old soldier the name of Cold-Steel Carteret.

"You have not asked Rose to marry you?"

"Er – no; not yet."

The keen blue eyes grew keener and bluer.

"Rodman," said Colonel Carteret in a strange, quiet voice, "I have known that little girl since she was a tiny child. For years she has been all in all to me. Her father died in my arms and with his last breath bade me see that no harm came to his darling. I have nursed her through mumps, measles – aye, and chicken pox – and I live but for her happiness." He paused, with a significance that made James's toes curl. "Rodman," he said, "do you know what I would do to any man who trifled with that little girl's affections?" He reached in his hip pocket and an ugly-looking revolver glittered in the sunlight. "I would shoot him like a dog."

"Like a dog?" faltered James.

"Like a dog," said Colonel Carteret. He took James's arm and turned him towards the house. "She is on the porch. Go to her. And if –" He broke off. "But tut!" he said in a kindlier tone. "I am doing you an injustice, my boy. I know it."

"Oh, you are," said James fervently.

"Your heart is in the right place."

"Oh, absolutely," said James.

"The go to her, my boy. Later on you may have something to tell me. You will find me in the strawberry beds."

It was very cool and fragrant on the porch. Overhead, little breezes played and laughed among the roses. Somewhere in the distance sheep bells tinkled, and in the shrubbery a thrush was singing its evensong.

Seated in her chair behind a wicker table laden with tea things, Rose Maynard watched James as he shambled up the path.

"Tea's ready," she called gaily. "Where is Uncle Henry?" A look of pity and distress flitted for a moment over her flower-like face. "Oh, I – I forgot," she whispered.

"He's in the strawberry beds,' said James in a low voice.

She nodded unhappily.

"Of course, of course. Oh, why is life like this?" James heard her whisper.

He sat down. He looked at the girl. She was leaning back with closed eyes, and he thought he had never seen such a little squirt in his life. The idea of passing his remaining days in her society revolted him. He was stoutly opposed to the idea of marrying anyone; but if, as happens to the best of us, he ever were compelled to perform the wedding glide, he had always hoped it would be with some lady golf champion who would help him with his putting, and thus, by bringing his handicap down a notch or two, enable him to save something from the wreck, so to speak. But to link his lot with a girl who could tolerate the presence of the dog Toto; a girl who clasped her hands in pretty childish joy when she saw a nasturtium in bloom – it was too much. Nevertheless, he took her hand and began to speak.

'Miss Maynard – Rose –"

She opened her eyes and cast them down. A flush had come into her cheeks. The dog Toto at her side sat up and begged for cake, disregarded.

"Let me tell you a story. Once upon a time there was a lonely man who lived in a cottage all by himself –"

He stopped. Was it James Rodman who was talking this bilge?

"Yes?" whispered the girl.

" – but one day there came to him out of nowhere a little fairy princess. She – "

He stopped again, but this time not because of the sheer shame of listening to his own voice. What caused him to interrupt his tale was the fact that at this moment the tea table suddenly began to rise slowly in the air, tilting as it did so a considerable quantity of hot tea on to the knees of his trousers.

"Ouch!" cried James, leaping.

The table continued to rise, and then fell sideways, revealing the homely countenance of William, who, concealed by the cloth, had been taking a nap beneath it. He moved slowly forward, his eyes on Toto. For many a long day William had been desirous of putting to the test, once and for all, the problem of whether Toto was edible or not. Sometimes eh thought yes, at other times no. Now seemed an admirable opportunity for a definite decision. He advanced on the object of his experiment, making a low whistling noise through his nostrils, not unlike a boiling kettle. And Toto, after one long look of incredulous horror, tucked his shapely tail between his legs and, turning, raced for safety. He had laid a course in a bee line for the open garden gate, and William, shaking a dish of marmalade off his head a little petulantly, galloped ponderously after him. Rose Maynard staggered to her feet.

"Oh, save him!" she cried.

Without a word James added himself to the procession. His interest in Toto was but tepid. What he wanted was to get near enough to William to discuss with him that matter of the tea on his trousers. He reached the road and found that the order of the runners had not changed. For so small a dog Toto was moving magnificently. A cloud of dust rose as he skidded round the corner. William followed. James followed William.

And so they passed Farmer Birkett's barn, Farmer Giles's cow shed, the place where Farmer Willett's pigsty used to be before the big fire, and the Bunch of Grapes public house, Jno. Biggs propr., licensed to sell tobacco, wines and spirits. As it was they were turning down the lane that leads past Farmer Robinson's chicken run that Toto, thinking swiftly, bolted abruptly into a small drain-pipe.

"William!" roared James, coming up at a canter. He stopped to pluck a branch from the hedge and swooped darkly on.

William had been crouching before the pipe, making a noise like a bassoon into its interior; but now he rose and came beamingly to James. His eyes were aglow with chumminess and affection; and placing his forefeet on James's chest, he licked him three times on the face in rapid succession. And as he did so something seemed to snap in James. The scales seemed to fall from James's eyes. For the first time he saw William as he really was, the authentic type of dog that saves his master from a frightful peril. A wave of emotions wept over him.

"William!" he muttered. "William!"

William was making an early supper off a half brick he had found in the road. James stopped and patted him fondly.

"William," he whispered, "you knew when the time had come to change the conversation, didn't you, old boy!" He straightened himself. "Come William," he said. "Another four miles and we reach Meadowsweet Junction. Make it snappy and we shall just catch the up express, first stop London."

William looked up into his face and it seemed to James that he gave a brief nod of comprehension and approval. James turned. Through the trees to the east he could see the red roof of Honeysuckle Cottage, lurking like some evil dragon in ambush.

Then, together, man and dog passed silently into the sunset.

That (concluded Mr Mulliner) is the story of my distant cousin James Rodman. As to whether it is true, that, of course, is an open question. I, personally, am of opinion that it is. There is no doubt that James did go to live at Honeysuckle Cottage and, while there, underwent some experience which has left an ineradicable mark upon him. His eyes to-day have that unmistakable look which is to be seen only in the eyes of confirmed bachelors whose feet have been dragged to the very brink of the pit and who have gazed at close range into the naked face of matrimony.

And, if further proof be needed, there is William. He is now James's inseparable companion. Would any man be habitually seen with a dog like William unless he had some solid cause to be grateful to him – unless they were linked together by some deep and imperishable memory? I think not. Myself, when I observe William coming along the street, I cross the road and look into a shop window till he has passed. I am not a snob, but I dare not risk my position in Society by being seen talking to that curious compound.

Nor is the precaution an unnecessary one. There is about William a shameless absence of appreciation of class distinctions which recalls the worst excesses of the French Revolution. I have seen him with these eyes chivvy a Pomeranian belonging to a baroness in her own right from near the Achilles Statue to within a few yards of the Marble Arch.

And yet James walks daily with him in Piccadilly. It is surely significant.

THE SECOND DEATH

Graham Greene

Henry Graham Greene (1904–1991) was educated at Berkhamsted School where his father was headmaster. Greene was bullied at school, suffered a nervous collapse and took up Russian Roulette. He started writing while at Oxford University. The varied locations of Greene's novels reflect his extensive, international travels. His sister recruited him to MI6, where the double agent Kim Philby was his handler. Greene divided his novels into serious works and 'entertainments,' a distinction that became increasingly difficult as his career progressed.

She found me in the evening under trees that grew outside the village. I had never cared for her and would have hidden myself if I'd seen her coming. She was to blame, I'm certain, for her son's vices. If they were vices, but I'm very far from admitting that they were. At any rate he was generous, never mean, like others in the village I could mention if I chose.

I was staring hard at a leaf or she would never have found me. It was dangling from its twig, its stalk torn across by the wind or else by a stone one of the village children had flung. Only the green tough skin of the stalk held it there suspended. I was watching closely, because a caterpillar was crawling across the surface, making the leaf sway to and fro. The caterpillar was aiming at the twig, and I wondered whether it would reach it in safety or whether the leaf would fall with it into the water. There was a pool underneath the trees, and the water always appeared red, because of the heavy clay in the soil.

I never knew whether the caterpillar reached the twig, for, as I've said, the wretched woman found me. The first I knew of her coming was her voice just behind my ear.

"I've been looking in all the pubs for you," she said in her old shrill voice. It was typical of her to say "all the pubs" when there were only two in the place. She always wanted credit for trouble she hadn't really taken.

I was annoyed and I couldn't help speaking a little harshly. "You might have saved yourself the trouble," I said, "you should have known I wouldn't be in a pub on a fine night like this."

The old vixen became quite humble. She was always smooth enough when she wanted anything. "It's for my poor son," she said. That meant that he was ill. When he was well I never heard her say anything better than "that dratted boy." She'd make him be in the house by midnight every day of the week, as if there were any serious mischief a man could get up to in a little village like ours. Of course we soon found a way to cheat her, but it was the principle of the thing I objected to – a grown man of over thirty ordered about by his mother, just because she hadn't a husband to control. But when he was ill, though it might be with only a small chill, it was "my poor son."

"He's dying," she said, "and God knows what I shall do without him."

"Well, I don't see how I can help you," I said. I was angry, because he'd been dying once before and she'd done everything but actually bury him. I imagined it was the same sort of dying this time, the sort a man gets over. I'd seen him about the week before on his way up the hill to see the big-breasted girl at the farm. I'd watched him till he was like a little black dot, which stayed suddenly by a square grey box in a field. That was the barn where they used to meet. I've very good eyes and it amuses me to try how far and how clearly they can see. I met him again some time after midnight and helped him get into the house without his mother knowing, and he was well enough then – only a little sleepy and tired.

The old vixen was at it again. "He's been asking for you," she shrilled at me.

"If he's as ill as you make out," I said, "it would be better for him to ask for a doctor."

"Doctor's there, but he can't do anything." That startled me for a moment, I'll admit it, until I thought, "The old devil's malingering. He's got some plan or other." He was quite clever enough to cheat a doctor. I had seen him throw a fit that would have deceived Moses.

"For God's sake come," she said, "he seems frightened." Her voice broke quite genuinely, for I suppose in her way she was fond of him. I couldn't help pitying her a little, for I knew that he had never cared a mite for her and had never troubled to disguise the fact.

I left the trees and the red pool and the struggling caterpillar, for I knew that she would never leave me alone, now that her "poor boy" was asking for me. Yet a week ago there was nothing she wouldn't have done to keep us apart. She thought me responsible for his ways, as though any mortal man could have kept him off a likely woman when his appetite was up.

I think it must have been the first time I had entered their cottage by the front door since I came to the village ten years ago. I threw an amused glance at his window. I thought I could see the marks on the wall of the ladder we'd used the week before. We'd had a little difficulty in putting it straight, but his mother slept sound. He had brought the ladder down from the barn, and when he'd got safely in, I carried it up there again. But you could never trust his word. He'd lie to his best friend, and when I reached the barn I found the girl had gone. If he couldn't bribe you with his mother's money, he'd bribe you with other people's promises.

I began to feel uneasy directly I got inside the door. It was natural that the house should be quiet, for the pair of them never had any friends to stay, although the old woman had a sister-in-law living only a few miles away. But I didn't like the sound of the doctor's feet as he came downstairs to meet us. He'd twisted his face into a pious solemnity for our benefit, as though there was something holy about death, even about the death of my friend.

"He's conscious," he said, "but he's going. There's nothing I can do. If you want him to die in peace, better let his friend go along up. He's frightened about something."

The doctor was right. I could tell that as soon as I bent under the lintel and entered my friend's room. He was propped up on a pillow, and his eyes were on the door, waiting for me to come. They were very bright and frightened, and his hair lay across his forehead in sticky stripes. I'd never realized before what an ugly fellow he was. He had sly eyes that looked at you too much out of the corners, but when he was in ordinary health, they held a twinkle that made you forget the slyness. There was something pleasant and brazen in the twinkle, as much as to say "I know I'm sly and ugly. But what does that matter? I've got guts." It was that twinkle, I think, some women found attractive and stimulating. Now when the twinkle was gone, he looked a rogue and nothing else.

I thought it my duty to cheer him up, so I made a small joke out of the fact that he was alone in bed. He didn't seem to relish it, and I was beginning to fear that he too was taking a religious view of his death, when he told me to sit down, speaking quite sharply.

"I'm dying," he said, talking very fast, "and I want to ask you something. That doctor's no good – he'd think me delirious. I'm frightened, old man. I want to be reassured," and then after a long pause, "someone with common sense." He slipped a little farther down in his bed.

"I've only once been badly ill before," he said. "That was before you settled here. I wasn't much more than a boy. People tell me that I was even supposed to be dead. They were carrying me out to burial when a doctor stopped them just in time."

I'd heard plenty of cases like that, and I saw no reason why he should want to tell me about it. And then I thought I saw his point. His mother had not been too anxious once before to see if he were properly dead, though I had little doubt that she made a great show of grief – "My poor boy. I don't know what I shall do without him." And I'm certain that she believed herself then, as she believed herself now. She wasn't a murderess. She was only inclined to be premature.

"Look here, old man," I said, and I propped him a little higher on his pillow, "you needn't be frightened. You aren't going to die, and anyway I'd see that the doctor cut a vein or something before they moved you. But that's all morbid stuff. Why, I'd stake my shirt that you've got plenty more years in front of you. And plenty more girls too," I added to make him smile.

"Can't you cut out all that?" he said, and I knew then that he had turned religious. "Why," he said, "if I lived, I wouldn't touch another girl. I wouldn't, not one."

I tried not to smile at that, but it wasn't easy to keep a straight face. There's always something a bit funny about a sick man's morals. "Anyway," I said, "you needn't be frightened."

"It's not that," he said. "Old man, when I came round that other time, I thought that I'd been dead. It wasn't like sleep at all. Or rest in peace. There was someone there, all round me, who knew everything. Every girl I'd ever had. Even that young one who hadn't understood. It was before your time. She lived a mile down the road, where Rachel lives now, but she and her family went away afterwards. Even the money I'd taken from mother. I don't call that stealing. It's in the family. I never had a chance to explain. Even the thoughts I'd had. A man can't help his thoughts."

"A nightmare," I said.

"Yes, it must have been a dream, mustn't it? The sort of dream people do get when they are ill. And I saw what was coming to me too. I can't bear being hurt. It wasn't fair. And I wanted to faint and I couldn't, because I was dead."

"In the dream," I said. His fear made me nervous. "In the dream," I said again.

"Yes, it must have been a dream – mustn't it? – because I woke up. The curious thing was I felt quite well and strong. I got up and stood in the road, and a little farther down, kicking up the dust, was a small crowd, going off with a man – the doctor who had stopped them burying me."

"Well," I said.

"Old man," he said, "suppose it was true. Suppose I had been dead. I believed it then, you know, and so did my mother. But you can't trust her. I went straight for a couple of years. I thought it might be a sort of second chance. Then things got fogged and somehow . . . It didn't seem really possible. It's not possible. Of course it's not possible. You know it isn't, don't you?"

"Why no," I said. "Miracles of that sort don't happen nowadays. And anyway, they aren't likely to happen to you, are they? And here of all places under the sun."

"It would be so dreadful," he said, "if it had been true, and I'd got to go through all that again. You don't know what things were going to happen to me in that dream. And they'd be worse now." He stopped and then, after a moment, he added as though he were stating a fact, "When one's dead there's no unconsciousness any more for ever."

"Of course it was a dream," I said and squeezed his hand. He was frightening me with his fancies. I wished that he'd die quickly, so that I could get away from his sly, bloodshot and terrified eyes and see something cheerful and amusing, like the Rachel he had mentioned, who lived a mile down the road.

"Why," I said, "if there had been a man about working miracles like that, we should have heard of others, you many be sure. Even poked away in this god-forsaken spot," I said.

"There were some others," he said. "But the stories only went round among the poor, and they'll believe anything, won't they? There were lots of diseased and crippled they said he'd cured. And there was a man, who'd been born blind, and he came and just touched his eyelids and sight came to him. Those were all old wives' tales, weren't they?" he asked me, stammering with fear, and then lying suddenly still and bunched up at the side of the bed.

I began to say, "Of course they were all lies," but I stopped, because there was no need. All I could do was to go downstairs and tell his mother to come up and close his eyes. I wouldn't have touched them for all the money in the world. It was a long time since I'd thought of that day, ages and ages ago, when I felt a cold touch like spittle on my lids and opening my eyes had seen a man like a tree surrounded by other trees walking away.

A ROSE FOR EMILY

William Faulkner

William Cuthbert Faulkner (1897–1962) was born and spent most of his life in Mississippi. Much of his work explores the growth and decay of the American South. Faulkner entered the Canadian air force in 1918, but the war finished before he completed training. He won the Nobel Prize in Literature in 1949 and used part of his prize money to establish the PEN/Faulkner Award for Fiction.

I

When Miss Emily Grierson died, our whole town went to her funeral: the men through a sort of respectful affection for a fallen monument, the women mostly out of curiosity to see the inside of her house, which no one save an old man-servant – a combined gardener and cook – had seen in at least ten years.

It was a big, squarish frame house that had once been white, decorated with cupolas and spires and scrolled balconies in the heavily lightsome style of the seventies, set on what had once been our most select street. But garages and cotton gins had encroached and obliterated even the august names of that neighborhood; only Miss Emily's house was left, lifting its stubborn and coquettish decay above the cotton wagons and the gasoline pumps – an eyesore among eyesores. And now Miss Emily had gone to join the representatives of those august names where they lay in the cedar-bemused cemetery among the ranked and anonymous graves of Union and Confederate soldiers who fell at the battle of Jefferson.

Alive, Miss Emily had been a tradition, a duty, and a care; a sort of hereditary obligation upon the town, dating from that day in 1894 when Colonel Sartoris, the mayor – he who fathered the edict that no Negro woman should appear on the streets without an apron – remitted her taxes, the dispensation dating from the death of her father on into perpetuity. Not that Miss Emily would have accepted charity. Colonel Sartoris invented an involved tale to the effect that Miss Emily's father had loaned money to the town, which the town, as a matter of business, preferred this way of repaying. Only a man of Colonel Sartoris' generation and thought could have invented it, and only a woman could have believed it.

When the next generation, with its more modern ideas, became mayors and aldermen, this arrangement created some little dissatisfaction. On the first of the year they mailed her a tax notice. February came, and there was no reply. They wrote her a formal letter, asking her to call at the sheriff's office at her convenience. A week later the mayor wrote her himself, offering to call or to send his car for her, and received in reply a note on paper of an archaic shape, in a thin, flowing calligraphy in faded ink, to the effect that she no longer went out at all. The tax notice was also enclosed, without comment.

They called a special meeting of the Board of Aldermen. A deputation waited upon her, knocked at the door through which no visitor had passed since she ceased giving china-painting lessons eight or ten years earlier. They were admitted by the old Negro into a dim hall from which a stairway mounted into still more shadow. It smelled of dust and disuse – a close, dank smell. The Negro led them into the parlor. It was furnished in heavy, leather-covered furniture. When the Negro opened the blinds of one window, they could see that the leather was cracked; and when they sat down, a faint dust rose sluggishly about their thighs, spinning with slow motes in the single sun-ray. On a tarnished gilt easel before the fireplace stood a crayon portrait of Miss Emily's father.

They rose when she entered – a small, fat woman in black, with a thin gold chain descending to her waist and vanishing into her belt, leaning on an ebony cane with a tarnished gold head. Her skeleton was small and spare; perhaps that was why what would have been merely plumpness in another was obesity in her. She looked bloated, like a body long submerged in motionless water, and of that pallid hue. Her eyes, lost in the fatty ridges of her face, looked like two small pieces of coal pressed into a lump of dough as they moved from one face to another while the visitors stated their errand.

She did not ask them to sit. She just stood in the door and listened quietly until the spokesman came to a stumbling halt. Then they could hear the invisible watch ticking at the end of the gold chain.

Her voice was dry and cold. "I have no taxes in Jefferson. Colonel Sartoris explained it to me. Perhaps one of you can gain access to the city records and satisfy yourselves."

"But we have. We are the city authorities, Miss Emily. Didn't you get a notice from the sheriff, signed by him?"

"I received a paper, yes," Miss Emily said. "Perhaps he considers himself the sheriff . . . I have no taxes in Jefferson."

"But there is nothing on the books to show that, you see We must go by the –"

"See Colonel Sartoris. I have no taxes in Jefferson."

"But, Miss Emily—"

"See Colonel Sartoris." (Colonel Sartoris had been dead almost ten years.) "I have no taxes in Jefferson. Tobe!" The Negro appeared. "Show these gentlemen out."

II

So she vanquished them, horse and foot, just as she had vanquished their fathers thirty years before about the smell.

That was two years after her father's death and a short time after her sweetheart – the one we believed would marry her – had deserted her. After her father's death she went out very little; after her sweetheart went away, people hardly saw her at all. A few of the ladies had the temerity to call, but were not received, and the only sign of life about the place was the Negro man – a young man then – going in and out with a market basket.

"Just as if a man – any man – could keep a kitchen properly, "the ladies said; so they were not surprised when the smell developed. It was another link between the gross, teeming world and the high and mighty Griersons.

A neighbor, a woman, complained to the mayor, Judge Stevens, eighty years old.

"But what will you have me do about it, madam?" he said.

"Why, send her word to stop it," the woman said. "Isn't there a law?"

"I'm sure that won't be necessary," Judge Stevens said. "It's probably just a snake or a rat that nigger of hers killed in the yard. I'll speak to him about it."

The next day he received two more complaints, one from a man who came in diffident deprecation. "We really must do something about it, Judge. I'd be the last one in the world to bother Miss Emily, but we've got to do something." That night the Board of Aldermen met – three graybeards and one younger man, a member of the rising generation.

"It's simple enough," he said. "Send her word to have her place cleaned up. Give her a certain time to do it in, and if she don't. . ."

"Dammit, sir," Judge Stevens said, "will you accuse a lady to her face of smelling bad?"

So the next night, after midnight, four men crossed Miss Emily's lawn and slunk about the house like burglars, sniffing along the base of the brickwork and at the cellar openings while one of them performed a regular sowing motion with his hand out of a sack slung from his shoulder. They broke open the cellar door and sprinkled lime there, and in all the outbuildings. As they recrossed the lawn, a window that had been dark was lighted and Miss Emily sat in it, the light behind her, and her upright torso motionless as that of an idol. They crept quietly across the lawn and into the shadow of the locusts that lined the street. After a week or two the smell went away.

That was when people had begun to feel really sorry for her. People in our town, remembering how old lady Wyatt, her great-aunt, had gone completely crazy at last, believed that the Griersons held themselves a little too high for what they really were. None of the young men were quite good enough for Miss Emily and such. We had long thought of them as a tableau, Miss Emily a slender figure in white in the background, her father a spraddled silhouette in the foreground, his back to her and clutching a horsewhip, the two of them framed by the back-flung front door. So when she got to be thirty and was still single, we were not pleased exactly, but vindicated; even with insanity in the family she wouldn't have turned down all of her chances if they had really materialized.

When her father died, it got about that the house was all that was left to her; and in a way, people were glad. At last they could pity Miss Emily. Being left alone, and a pauper, she had become humanized. Now she too would know the old thrill and the old despair of a penny more or less.

The day after his death all the ladies prepared to call at the house and offer condolence and aid, as is our custom Miss Emily met them at the door, dressed as usual and with no trace of grief on her face. She told them that her father was not dead. She did that for three days, with the ministers calling on her, and the doctors, trying to persuade her to let them dispose of the body. Just as they were about to resort to law and force, she broke down, and they buried her father quickly.

We did not say she was crazy then. We believed she had to do that. We remembered all the young men her father had driven away, and we knew that with nothing left, she would have to cling to that which had robbed her, as people will.

III

She was sick for a long time. When we saw her again, her hair was cut short, making her look like a girl, with a vague resemblance to those angels in colored church windows – sort of tragic and serene.

The town had just let the contracts for paving the sidewalks, and in the summer after her father's death they began the work. The construction company came with niggers and mules and machinery, and a foreman named Homer Barron, a Yankee – a big, dark, ready man, with a big voice and eyes lighter than his face. The little boys would follow in groups to hear him cuss the niggers, and the niggers singing in time to the rise and fall of picks. Pretty soon he knew everybody in town. Whenever you heard a lot of laughing anywhere about the square, Homer Barron would be in the center of the group. Presently we began to see him and Miss Emily on Sunday afternoons driving in the yellow-wheeled buggy and the matched team of bays from the livery stable.

At first we were glad that Miss Emily would have an interest, because the ladies all said, "Of course a Grierson would not think seriously of a Northerner, a day laborer." But there were still others, older people, who said that even grief could not cause a real lady to forget *noblesse oblige* – without calling it *noblesse oblige*. They just said, "Poor Emily. Her kinsfolk should come to her." She had some kin in Alabama; but years ago her father had fallen out with them over the estate of old lady Wyatt, the crazy woman, and there was no communication between the two families. They had not even been represented at the funeral.

And as soon as the old people said, "Poor Emily," the whispering began. "Do you suppose it's really so?" they said to one another. "Of course it is. What else could . . ." This behind their hands; rustling of craned silk and satin behind jalousies closed upon the sun of Sunday afternoon as the thin, swift clop-clop-clop of the matched team passed: "Poor Emily."

She carried her head high enough – even when we believed that she was fallen. It was as if she demanded more than ever the recognition of her dignity as the last Grierson; as if it had wanted that touch of earthiness to reaffirm her imperviousness. Like when she bought the rat poison, the arsenic. That was over a year after they had begun to say "Poor Emily," and while the two female cousins were visiting her.

"I want some poison," she said to the druggist. She was over thirty then, still a slight woman, though thinner than usual, with cold, haughty black eyes in a face the flesh of which was strained across the temples and about the eye-sockets as you imagine a lighthouse-keeper's face ought to look. "I want some poison," she said.

"Yes, Miss Emily. What kind? For rats and such? I'd recom—"

"I want the best you have. I don't care what kind."

The druggist named several. "They'll kill anything up to an elephant. But what you want is—"

"Arsenic," Miss Emily said. "Is that a good one?"

"Is . . . arsenic? Yes, ma'am. But what you want—"

"I want arsenic."

The druggist looked down at her. She looked back at him, erect, her face like a strained flag. "Why, of course," the druggist said. "If that's what you want. But the law requires you to tell what you are going to use it for."

Miss Emily just stared at him, her head tilted back in order to look him eye for eye, until he looked away and went and got the arsenic and wrapped it up. The Negro delivery boy brought her the package; the druggist didn't come back. When she opened the package at home there was written on the box, under the skull and bones: "For rats."

IV

So the next day we all said, "She will kill herself"; and we said it would be the best thing. When she had first begun to be seen with Homer Barron, we had said, "She will marry him." Then we said, "She will persuade him yet," because Homer himself had remarked – he liked men, and it was known that he drank with the younger men in the Elks' Club – that he was not a marrying man. Later we said, "Poor Emily" behind the jalousies as they passed on Sunday afternoon in the glittering buggy, Miss Emily with her head high and Homer Barron with his hat cocked and a cigar in his teeth, reins and whip in a yellow glove.

Then some of the ladies began to say that it was a disgrace to the town and a bad example to the young people. The men did not want to interfere, but at last the ladies forced the Baptist minister – Miss Emily's people were Episcopal – to call upon her. He would never divulge what happened during that interview, but he refused to go back again. The next Sunday they again drove about the streets, and the following day the minister's wife wrote to Miss Emily's relations in Alabama.

So she had blood-kin under her roof again and we sat back to watch developments. At first nothing happened. Then we were sure that they were to be married. We learned that Miss Emily had been to the jeweler's and ordered a man's toilet set in silver, with the letters H. B. on each piece. Two days later we learned that she had bought a complete outfit of men's clothing, including a nightshirt, and we said, "They are married." We were really glad. We were glad because the two female cousins were even more Grierson than Miss Emily had ever been.

So we were not surprised when Homer Barron – the streets had been finished some time since – was gone. We were a little disappointed that there was not a public blowing-off, but we believed that he had gone on to prepare for Miss Emily's coming, or to give her a chance to get rid of the cousins. (By that time it was a cabal, and we were all Miss Emily's allies to help circumvent the cousins.) Sure enough, after another week they departed. And, as we had expected all along, within three days Homer Barron was back in town. A neighbor saw the Negro man admit him at the kitchen door at dusk one evening.

And that was the last we saw of Homer Barron. And of Miss Emily for some time. The Negro man went in and out with the market basket, but the front door remained closed. Now and then we would see her at a window for a moment, as the men did that night when they sprinkled the lime, but for almost six months she did not appear on the streets. Then we knew that this was to be expected too; as if that quality of her father which had thwarted her woman's life so many times had been too virulent and too furious to die.

When we next saw Miss Emily, she had grown fat and her hair was turning gray. During the next few years it grew grayer and grayer until it attained an even pepper-and-salt iron-gray, when it ceased turning. Up to the day of her death at seventy-four it was still that vigorous iron-gray, like the hair of an active man.

From that time on her front door remained closed, save for a period of six or seven years, when she was about forty, during which she gave lessons in china-painting. She fitted up a studio in one of the downstairs rooms, where the daughters and granddaughters of Colonel Sartoris' contemporaries were sent to her with the same regularity and in the same spirit that they were sent to church on Sundays with a twenty-five-cent piece for the collection plate. Meanwhile her taxes had been remitted.

Then the newer generation became the backbone and the spirit of the town, and the painting pupils grew up and fell away and did not send their children to her with boxes of color and tedious brushes and pictures cut from the ladies' magazines. The front door closed upon the last one and remained closed for good. When the town got free postal delivery, Miss Emily alone refused to let them fasten the metal numbers above her door and attach a mailbox to it. She would not listen to them.

Daily, monthly, yearly we watched the Negro grow grayer and more stooped, going in and out with the market basket. Each December we sent her a tax notice, which would be returned by the post office a week later, unclaimed. Now and then we would see her in one of the downstairs windows – she had evidently shut up the top floor of the house – like the carven torso of an idol in a niche, looking or not looking at us, we could never tell which. Thus she passed from generation to generation – dear, inescapable, impervious, tranquil, and perverse.

And so she died. Fell ill in the house filled with dust and shadows, with only a doddering Negro man to wait on her. We did not even know she was sick; we had long since given up trying to get any information from the Negro. He talked to no one, probably not even to her, for his voice had grown harsh and rusty, as if from disuse.

She died in one of the downstairs rooms, in a heavy walnut bed with a curtain, her gray head propped on a pillow yellow and moldy with age and lack of sunlight.

V

The Negro met the first of the ladies at the front door and let them in, with their hushed, sibilant voices and their quick, curious glances, and then he disappeared. He walked right through the house and out the back and was not seen again.

The two female cousins came at once. They held the funeral on the second day, with the town coming to look at Miss Emily beneath a mass of bought flowers, with the crayon face of her father musing profoundly above the bier and the ladies sibilant and macabre; and the very old men – some in their brushed Confederate uniforms – on the porch and the lawn, talking of Miss Emily as if she had been a contemporary of theirs, believing that they had danced with her and courted her perhaps, confusing time with its mathematical progression, as the old do, to whom all the past is not a diminishing road but, instead, a huge meadow which no winter ever quite touches, divided from them now by the narrow bottle-neck of the most recent decade of years.

Already we knew that there was one room in that region above stairs which no one had seen in forty years, and which would have to be forced. They waited until Miss Emily was decently in the ground before they opened it.

The violence of breaking down the door seemed to fill this room with pervading dust. A thin, acrid pall as of the tomb seemed to lie everywhere upon this room decked and furnished as for a bridal: upon the valance curtains of faded rose color, upon the rose-shaded lights, upon the dressing table, upon the delicate array of crystal and the man's toilet things backed with tarnished silver, silver so tarnished that the monogram was obscured. Among them lay a collar and tie, as if they had just been removed, which, lifted, left upon the surface a pale crescent in the dust. Upon a chair hung the suit, carefully folded; beneath it the two mute shoes and the discarded socks.

The man himself lay in the bed.

For a long while we just stood there, looking down at the profound and fleshless grin. The body had apparently once lain in the attitude of an embrace, but now the long sleep that outlasts love, that conquers even the grimace of love, had cuckolded him. What was left of him, rotted beneath what was left of the nightshirt, had become inextricable from the bed in which he lay; and upon him and upon the pillow beside him lay that even coating of the patient and biding dust.

Then we noticed that in the second pillow was the indentation of a head. One of us lifted something from it, and leaning forward, that faint and invisible dust dry and acrid in the nostrils, we saw a long strand of iron-gray hair.

THE HUNTER GRACCHUS

Franz Kafka

Franz Kafka (1883–1924) was born into a prosperous German-speaking Jewish family in Prague; at that time an anti-Semitic city. His father was a self-made businessman, his mother from a wealthy family. Kafka qualified as a lawyer. He found a post which allowed him to finish work at 2pm, leaving the rest of the day to write. Nevertheless tension between the need to make a living and his artistic desires, coupled with pressure from his father to conform, led to suicidal thoughts. He died of tuberculosis.

Two boys were sitting on the harbor wall playing with dice. A man was reading a newspaper on the steps of the monument, resting in the shadow of a hero who was flourishing his sword on high. A girl was filling her bucket at the fountain. A fruit-seller was lying beside his wares, gazing at the lake. Through the vacant window and door openings of a café one could see two men quite at the back drinking their wine. The proprietor was sitting at a table in front and dozing. A bark was silently making for the little harbor, as if borne by invisible means over the water. A man in a blue blouse climbed ashore and drew the rope through a ring. Behind the boatman two other men in dark coats with silver buttons carried a bier, on which, beneath a great flower-patterned fringed silk cloth a man was apparently lying.

Nobody on the quay troubled about the newcomers; even when they lowered the bier to wait for the boatman, who was still occupied with his rope, nobody went nearer, nobody asked them a question, nobody accorded them an inquisitive glance.

The pilot was still further detained by a woman who, a child at her breast, now appeared with loosened hair on the deck of the boat. Then he advanced and indicated a yellowish two-storied house that rose abruptly on the left near the water; the bearers took up their burden and bore it to the low but gracefully pillared door. A little boy opened a window just in time to see the party vanishing into the house, then hastily shut the window again. The door too was now shut; it was of black oak, and very strongly made. A flock of doves which had been flying around the belfry alighted in the street before the house. As if their food were stored within, they assembled in front of the door. One of them flew up to the first story and pecked at the window-pane. They were bright-hued, well-tended, lively birds. The woman on the boat flung grain to them in a wide sweep; they ate it up and flew across to the woman.

A man in a top hat tied with a band of black crêpe now descended one of the narrow and very steep lanes that led to the harbor. He glanced around vigilantly, everything seemed to distress him, his mouth twisted at the sight of some offal in a corner. Fruit skins were lying on the steps of the monument; he swept them off in passing with his stick. He rapped at the house door, at the same time taking his top hat from his head with his black-gloved hand. The door was opened at once, and some fifty little boys appeared in two rows in the long entry hall, and bowed to him.

The boatman descended the stairs, greeted the gentleman in black, conducted him up to the first story, led him around the bright and elegant loggia which encircled the courtyard, and both of them entered, while the boys pressed after them at a respectful distance, a cool spacious room looking toward the back, from whose window no habitation, but only a bare, blackish-gray rocky wall was to be seen. The bearers were busied in setting up and lighting several long candles at the head of the bier, yet these did not give light, but only disturbed the shadows which had been immobile till then, and made them flicker over the walls. The cloth covering the bier had been thrown back. Lying on it was a man with wildly matted hair, who looked somewhat like a hunter. He lay without motion and, it seemed, without breathing, his eyes closed; yet only his trappings indicated that this man was probably dead.

The gentleman stepped up to the bier, laid his hand on the brow of the man lying upon it, then kneeled down and prayed. The boatman made a sign to the bearers to leave the room; they went out, drove away the boys who had gathered outside, and shut the door. But even that did not seem to satisfy the gentleman, he glanced at the boatman; the boatman understood, and vanished through a side door into the next room. At once the man on the bier opened his eyes, turned his face painfully toward the gentleman, and said: "Who are you?" Without any mark of surprise the gentleman rose from his kneeling posture and answered: "The Burgomaster of Riva."

The man on the bier nodded, indicated a chair with a feeble movement of his arm, and said, after the Burgomaster had accepted his invitation: "I knew that, of course, Burgomaster, but in the first moments of returning consciousness I always forget, everything goes around before my eyes, and it is best to ask about anything even if I know. You too probably know that I am the Hunter Gracchus."

"Certainly," said the Burgomaster. "Your arrival was announced to me during the night. We had been asleep for a good while. Then toward midnight my wife cried: 'Salvatore' – that's my name – 'look at that dove at the window.' It was really a dove, but as big as a cock. It flew over me and said in my ear: 'Tomorrow the dead Hunter Gracchus is coming; receive him in the name of the city.' "

The Hunter nodded and licked his lips with the tip of his tongue: "Yes, the doves flew here before me. But do you believe, Burgomaster, that I shall remain in Riva?"

"I cannot say that yet," replied the Burgomaster. "Are you dead?"

"Yes," said the Hunter, "as you see. Many years ago, yes, it must be a great many years ago, I fell from a precipice in the Black Forest – that is in Germany – when I was hunting a chamois. Since then I have been dead."

"But you are alive too." said the Burgomaster.

"In a certain sense," said the Hunter, "in a certain sense I am alive too. My death ship lost its way; a wrong turn of the wheel, a moment's absence of mind on the pilot's part, the distraction of my lovely native country, I cannot tell what it was; I only know this, that I remained on earth and that ever since my ship has sailed earthly waters. So I, who asked for nothing better than to live among my mountains, travel after my death through all the lands of the earth."

"And you have no part in the other world?" asked the Burgomaster, knitting his brow.

"I am forever," replied the Hunter, "on the great stair that leads up to it. On that infinitely wide and spacious stair I clamber about, sometimes up, sometimes down, sometimes on the right, sometimes on the left, always in motion. The Hunter has been turned into a butterfly. Do not laugh."

"I am not laughing," said the Burgomaster in self-defense.

"That is very good of you," said the Hunter. "I am always in motion. But when I make a supreme flight and see the gate actually shining before me I awaken presently on my old ship, still stranded forlornly in some earthly sea or other. The fundamental error of my onetime death grins at me as I lie in my cabin. Julia, the wife of the pilot, knocks at the door and brings me on my bier the morning drink of the land whose coasts we chance to be passing. I lie on a wooden pallet, I wear – it cannot be a pleasure to look at me – a filthy winding sheet, my hair and beard, black tinged with gray, have grown together inextricably, my limbs are covered with a great flowered-patterned woman's shawl with long fringes. A sacramental candle stands at my head and lights me. On the wall opposite me is a little picture, evidently of a bushman who is aiming his spear at me and taking cover as best he can behind a beautifully painted shield. On shipboard one often comes across silly pictures, but that is the silliest of them all. Otherwise my wooden cage is quite empty. Through a hole in the side the warm airs of the southern night come in, and I hear the water slapping against the old boat.

"I have lain here ever since the time when, as the Hunter Gracchus living in the Black Forest, I followed a chamois and fell from a precipice. Everything happened in good order. I pursued, I fell, bled to death in a ravine, died, and this ship should have conveyed me to the next world. I can still remember how gladly I stretched myself out on this pallet for the first time. Never did the mountains listen to such songs from me as these shadowy walls did then.

"I had been glad to live and I was glad to die. Before I stepped aboard, I joyfully flung away my wretched load of ammunition, my knapsack, my hunting rifle that I had always been proud to carry, and I slipped into my winding sheet like a girl into her marriage dress. I lay and waited. Then came the mishap."

"A terrible fate," said the Burgomaster, raising his hand defensively. "And you bear no blame for it?"

"None," said the Hunter. "I was a hunter; was there any sin in that? I followed my calling as a hunter in the Black Forest, where there were still wolves in those days. I lay in ambush, shot, hit my mark, flayed the skins from my victims: was there any sin in that? My labors were blessed. 'The Great Hunter of the Black Forest' was the name I was given. Was there any sin in that?"

"I am not called upon to decide that," said the Burgomaster, "but to me also there seems to be no sin in such things. But then, whose is the guilt?"

"The boatman's," said the Hunter. "Nobody will read what I say here, no one will come to help me; even if all the people were commanded to help me, every door and window would remain shut, everybody would take to bed and draw the bed-clothes over his head, the whole earth would become an inn for the night. And there is sense in that, for nobody knows of me, and if anyone knew he would not know where I could be found, and if he knew where I could be found, he would not know how to deal with me, he would not know how to help me. The thought of helping me is an illness that has to be cured by taking to one's bed.

"I know that, and so I do not shout to summon help, even though at moments – when I lose control over myself, as I have done just now, for instance – I think seriously of it. But to drive out such thoughts I need only look around me and verify where I am, and – I can safely assert – have been for hundreds of years."

"Extraordinary," said the Burgomaster, "extraordinary. And now do you think of staying here in Riva with us?"

"I think not," said the Hunter with a smile, and, to excuse himself, he laid his hand on the Burgomaster's knee. "I am here, more than that I do not know, further than that I cannot go. My ship has no rudder, and it is driven by the wind that blows in the undermost regions of death."

HIGH WALKER AND BLOODY BONES

Zora Neale Hurston

Zora Neale Hurston (1891–1960) was one of the first African-American women to graduate from Barnard College in 1928. A talented novelist, short story writer, playwright and folklorist, Hurston studied anthropology at Columbia. Her use of idiomatic speech in her writing has attracted both praise and criticism. She suffered financial difficulties in later life and her remains lay in an unmarked grave in Florida until 1973, when it was located by the novelist Alice Walker, who erected a gravestone inscribed, 'A Genius of the South'.

This wuz uh man. His name was High Walker. He walked into a boneyard with skull-heads and other bones. So he would call them, "Rise up bloody bones and shake Yo'self." And de bones would rise up and come together, and shake theirselves and part and lay back down. Then he would say to hisself, "High Walker," and de bones would say "Be walkin'."

When he'd git off a little way he'd look back over his shoulder and shake hisself and say, "High Walker and bloody bones," and de bones would shake theirselves. Therefore he knowed he had power.

So uh man sold hisself to de high chief devil. He give 'im his whole soul and body tuh do ez he pleased wid it. He went out in uh drift uh woods and laid down flat on his back beyond all dese skull heads and bloody bones and said, "Go 'way Lawd, and come here Devil and do as you please wid me. Cause Ah want tuh do everything in de world dats wrong and never do nothing right."

And he dried up and died away on doin' wrong. His meat all left his bones and de bones all wuz separated.

And at dat time High Walker walked upon his skull head and kicked and kicked it on ahead of him a many and a many times and said tuh it, "Rise up and shake yo'self. High Walker is here."

Ole skull head wouldn't say nothin'. He looked back over his shoulder cause he heard some noises behind him and said, "Bloody bones you won't say nothin' yet. Rise tuh de power in de flesh."

Den de skull head said, "My mouf brought me here and if you don't mind, you'n will bring you here."

High Walker went on back to his white folks and told de white man dat a dry skull head wuz talkin' in de drift today. White man say he didn't believe it.

"Well, if you don't believe it, come go wid me and Ah'll prove it. And if it don't speak, you kin chop mah head off right where it at."

So de white man and High Walker went back in de drift tuh find dis ole skull head. So when he walked up tuh it, he begin tuh kick and kick de ole skull head, but it wouldn't say nothin'. High Walker looked at de white man and seen 'im whettin' his knife. Whettin' it hard and de sound of it said rick-de-rick, rick-de-rick, rick-de-rick! So High Walker kicked and kicked dat ole skull head and called it many and many uh time, but it never said nothin'. So de white man cut off High Walker's head.

And de ole dry skull head said, "See dat now! Ah told you dat mouf brought me here and if you didn't mind out it'd bring you here."

So de bloody bones riz up and shook they selves seben times and de white man got skeered and said, "What you mean by dis?"

De bloody bones say, "We got High Walker and we all bloody bones now in de drift together."

THE VEST

Dylan Thomas

Dylan Thomas (1914–1953) was born in Swansea. He attended Swansea Grammar School, where his father was a teacher. Thomas knew from an early age that he wanted to become a poet. He moved to London in 1934, the year his first collection was published. There he embraced the bohemian scene and met his future wife Caitlin Macnamara. Thomas's talent was recognised in his lifetime, but he was beset by financial difficulties, exacerbated by alcoholism. He died in New York while on a reading tour.

He rang the bell. There was no answer. She was out. He turned the key. The hall in the late afternoon light was full of shadows. They made one almost solid shape. He took off his hat and coat, looking sideways, so that he might not see the shape, at the light through the sitting-room door.

"Is anybody in?"

The shadows bewildered him. She would have swept them up as she swept the invading dust.

In the drawing-room the fire was low. He crossed over to it and sat down. His hands were cold. He needed the flames of the fire to light up the corners of the room. On the way home he had seen a dog run over by a motorcar. The sight of the blood had confused him. He had wanted to go down on his knees and finger the blood that made a round pool in the middle of the road. Someone had plucked at his sleeve, asking him if he was ill. He remembered that the sound and strength of his voice had drowned the first desire. He had walked away from the blood, with the stained wheels of the car and the soaking blackness under the bonnet going round and round before his eyes. He needed the warmth. The wind outside had cut between his fingers and thumbs.

She had left her sewing on the carpet near the coal-scuttle. She had been making a petticoat. He picked it up and touched it, feeling where her breasts would sit under the yellow cotton. That morning he had seen her head enveloped in a frock. He saw her, thin in her nakedness, as a bag of skin and henna drifting out of the light. He let the petticoat drop on to the floor again.

Why, he wondered, was there this image of the red and broken dog? It was the first time he had seen the brains of a living creature burst out of the skull. He had been sick at the last yelp and the sudden caving of the dog's chest. He could have killed and shouted, like a child cracking a blackbeetle between its fingers.

A thousand nights ago, she had lain by his side. In her arms, he thought of the bones of her arms. He lay quietly by her skeleton. But she rose next morning in the corrupted flesh.

When he hurt her, it was to hide his pain. When he struck her cheek until the skin blushed, it was to break the agony of his own head. She told him of her mother's death. Her mother had worn a mask to hide the illness at her face. He felt the locust of that illness on his own face, in the mouth and the fluttering eyelid.

The room was darkening. He was too tired to shovel the fire into life, and saw the last flame die. A new coldness blew in with the early night. He tasted the sickness of the death of the flame as it rose to the tip of his tongue, and swallowed it down. It ran around the pulse of the heart, and beat until it was the only sound. And all the pain of the damned. The pain of a man with a bottle breaking across his face, the pain of a cow with a calf dancing out of her, the pain of the dog, moved through him from his aching hair to the flogged soles of his feet.

His strength returned. He and the dripping calf, the man with the torn face, and the dog on giddy legs, rose up as one, in one red brain and body, challenging the beast in the air. He heard the challenge in his snapping thumb and finger, as she came in.

He saw that she was wearing her yellow hat and frock.

"Why are you sitting in the dark?" she said.

She went into the kitchen to light the stove. He stood up from his chair. Holding his hands out in front of him as though they were blind, he followed her. She had a box of matches in her hand. As she took out a dead match and rubbed it on the box, he closed the door behind him. "Take off your frock," he said.

She did not hear him, and smiled.

"Take off your frock," he said.

She stopped smiling, took out a live match and lit it.

"Take off your frock," he said.

He stepped towards her, his hands still blind. She bent over the stove. He blew the match out.

"What is it?" she said.

His lips moved, but he did not speak.

"Why?" she said.

He slapped her cheek quite lightly with his open hand.

"Take off your frock," he said.

He heard her frock rustle over her head, and her frightened sob as he touched her. Methodically his blind hands made her naked.

He walked out of the kitchen, and closed the door.

In the hall, the one married shadow had broken up. He could not see his own face in the mirror as he tied his scarf and stroked the brim of his hat. There were too many faces. Each had a section of his features, and each a stiffened lock of his hair. He pulled up the collar of his coat. It was a wet winter night. As he walked, he counted the lamps. He pushed a door open and stepped into the warmth. The room was empty. The woman behind the bar smiled as she rubbed two coins together. "It's a cold night," she said.

He drank up the whisky and went out.

He walked on through the increasing rain. He counted the lamps again, but they reached no number.

The corner bar was empty. He took his drink into the saloon, but the saloon was empty.

The Rising Sun was empty.

Outside, he heard no traffic. He remembered that he had seen nobody in the streets. He cried aloud in a panic of loneliness:

"Where are you, where are you?"

Then there was traffic, and the windows were blazing. He heard singing from the house on the corner.

The bar was crowded. Women were laughing and shouting. They spilt their drinks over their dresses and lifted their dresses up. Girls were dancing on the sawdust. A woman caught him by the arm, and rubbed his face on her sleeve, and took his hand in hers and put it on her throat. He could hear nothing but the voices of the laughing women and the shouting of the girls as they danced. Then the ungainly women from the seats and the corners rocked towards him. He saw that the room was full of women. Slowly, still laughing, they gathered close to him.

He whispered a word under his breath, and felt the old sickness turn sour in his belly. There was blood before his eyes.

Then he, too, burst into laughter. He stuck his hands deep in the pockets of his coat, and laughed into their faces.

His hand clutched around a softness in his pocket. He drew out his hand, the softness in it.

The laughter died. The room was still. Quiet and still, the women stood watching him.

He raised his hand up level with his eyes. It held a piece of soft cloth.

"Who'll buy a lady's vest," he said, "Going, going, ladies, who'll buy a lady's vest."

The meek and ordinary women in the bar stood still, their glasses in their hands, as he leant with his back to the counter and shouted with laughter and waved the bloody cloth in front of them.

A MAN FROM GLASGOW

W. Somerset Maugham

William Somerset Maugham (1874–1965) was born in Paris to English parents. He was orphaned at the age of ten and sent to live with a clergyman uncle and his wife in Kent. He worked briefly as an accounts clerk before qualifying as a doctor. Maugham acted as a secret agent in Russia during the revolution. He is best known for his semi-autobiographical novel, *Of Human Bondage*.

It is not often that anyone entering a great city for the first time has the luck to witness such an incident as engaged Shelley's attention when he drove into Naples. A youth ran out of a shop pursued by a man armed with a knife. The man overtook him and with one blow in the neck laid him dead on the road. Shelley had a tender heart. He didn't look upon it as a bit of local colour; he was seized with horror and indignation. But when he expressed his emotions to a Calabrian priest who was travelling with him, a fellow of gigantic strength and stature, the priest laughed heartily and attempted to quiz him. Shelley says he never felt such an inclination to beat anyone.

I have never seen anything so exciting as that, but the first time I went to Algeciras I had an experience that seemed to me far from ordinary. Algeciras was then an untidy, neglected town. I arrived somewhat late at night and went to an inn on the quay. It was rather shabby, but it had a fine view of Gibraltar, solid and matter–of–fact, across the bay. The moon was full. The office was on the first floor, and a slatternly maid, when I asked for a room, took me upstairs. The landlord was playing cards. He seemed little pleased to see me. He looked me up and down, curtly gave me a number, and then, taking no further notice of me, went on with his game. When the maid had shown me to my room I asked her what I could have to eat.

"What you like," she answered.

I knew well enough the unreality of the seeming profusion.

"What have you got in the house?"

"You can have eggs and ham."

The look of the hotel had led me to guess that I should get little else. The maid led me to a narrow room with whitewashed walls and a low ceiling in-which was a long table laid already for the next day's luncheon. With his back to the door sat a tall man, huddled over a *brasero*, the round brass dish of hot ashes which is erroneously supposed to give sufficient warmth for the temperate winter of Andalusia. I sat down at the table and waited for my scanty meal. I gave the stranger an idle glance. He was looking at me, but meeting my eyes he quickly turned away. I waited for my eggs. When at last the maid brought them he looked up again.

"I want you to wake me in time for the first boat," he said.

"*Si, señor.*"

His accent told me that English was his native tongue, and the breadth of his build, his strongly marked features, led me to suppose him a northerner. The hardy Scot is far more often found in Spain than the Englishman. Whether you go to the rich mines of Rio Tinto, or to the bodegas of Jerez, to Seville or to Cadiz, it is the leisurely speech of beyond the Tweed that you hear. You will meet Scotsmen in the olive groves of Carmona, on the railway between Algeciras and Bobadilla, and even in the remote cork woods of Merida.

I finished eating and went over to the dish of burning ashes. It was midwinter and the windy passage across the bay had chilled my blood. The man pushed his chair away as I drew mine forwards.

"Don't move," I said. "There's heaps of room for two."

I lit a cigar and offered one to him. In Spain the Havana from Gib is never unwelcome.

"I don't mind if I do," he said, stretching out his hand.

I recognised the singing speech of Glasgow. But the stranger was not talkative, and my efforts at conversation broke down before his monosyllables. We smoked in silence. He was even bigger than I had thought, with great broad shoulders and ungainly limbs; his face was sunburned, his hair short and grizzled. His features were hard; mouth, ears and nose were large and heavy and his skin much wrinkled. His blue eyes were pale. He was constantly pulling his ragged, grey moustache. It was a nervous gesture that I found faintly irritating. Presently I felt that he was looking at me, and the intensity of his stare grew so irksome that I glanced up expecting him, as before, to drop his eyes. He did, indeed, for a moment, but then raised them again. He inspected me from under his long, bushy eyebrows.

"Just come from Gib?" he asked suddenly.

"Yes."

"I'm going tomorrow – on my way home. Thank God."

He said the last two words so fiercely that I smiled.

"Don't you like Spain?"

"Oh, Spain's all right."

"Have you been here long?"

"Too long. Too long."

He spoke with a kind of gasp. I was surprised at the emotion my casual inquiry seemed to excite in him. He sprang to his feet and walked backwards and forwards. He stamped to and fro like a caged beast pushing aside a chair that stood in his way, and now and again repeated the words in a groan. "Too long. Too long." I sat still. I was embarrassed. To give myself countenance I stirred the *brasero* to bring the hotter ashes to the top, and he stood suddenly still, towering over me, as though my movement had brought back my existence to his notice. Then he sat down heavily in his chair.

"Do you think I'm queer?" he asked.

"Not more than most people," I smiled.

"You don't see anything strange in me?"

He leant forward as he spoke so that I might see him well.

"No."

"You'd say so if you did, wouldn't you?"

"I would."

I couldn't quite understand what all this meant. I wondered if he was drunk. For two or three minutes he didn't say anything and I had no wish to interrupt the silence.

"What's your name?" he asked suddenly. I told him.

"Mine's Robert Morrison."

"Scotch?"

"Glasgow. I've been in this blasted country for years. Got any baccy?"

I gave him my pouch and he filled his pipe. He lit it from a piece of burning charcoal.

"I can't stay any longer. I've stayed too long. Too long."

He had an impulse to jump up again and walk up and down, but he resisted it, clinging to his chair. I saw on his face the effort he was making. I judged that his restlessness was due to chronic alcoholism. I find drunks very boring, and I made up my mind to take an early opportunity of slipping off to bed.

"I've been managing some olive groves," he went on. "I'm here working for the Glasgow and South of Spain Olive Oil Company Limited."

"Oh, yes."

"We've got a new process for refining oil, you know. Properly treated, Spanish oil is every bit as good as Lucca. And we can sell it cheaper."

He spoke in a dry, matter–of–fact, business–like way. He chose his words with Scotch precision. He seemed perfectly sober.

"You know, Ecija is more or less the centre of the olive trade, and we had a Spaniard there to look after the business. But I found he was robbing us right and left, so I had to turn him out. I used to live in Seville; it was more convenient for shipping the oil. However, I found I couldn't get a trustworthy man to be at Ecija, so last year I went there myself. D'you know it?"

"No."

"The firm has got a big estate two miles from the town, just outside the village of San Lorenzo, and it's got a fine house on it. It's on the crest of a hill, rather pretty to look at, all white, you know, and straggling, with a couple of storks perched on the roof. No one lived there, and I thought it would save the rent of a place in town if I did."

"It must have been a bit lonely," I remarked.

"It was."

Robert Morrison smoked on for a minute or two in silence. I wondered whether there was any point in what he was telling me.

I looked at my watch.

"In a hurry?" he asked sharply.

"Not particularly. It's getting late."

"Well, what of it?"

"I suppose you didn't see many people?" I said, going back.

"Not many. I lived there with an old man and his wife who looked after me, and sometimes I used to go down to the village and play *tresillo* with Fernandez, the chemist, and one or two men who met at his shop. I used to shoot a bit and ride."

"It doesn't sound such a bad life to me."

I'd been there two years last spring. By God, I've never known such heat as we had in May. No one could do a thing. The labourers just lay about in the shade and slept. Sheep died and some of the animals went mad. Even the oxen couldn't work. They stood around with their backs all humped up and gasped for breath. That blasted sun beat down and the glare was so awful, you felt your eyes would shoot out of your head. The earth cracked and crumbled, and the crops frizzled. The olives went to rack and ruin. It was simply hell. One couldn't get a wink of sleep. I went from room to room, trying to get a breath of air. Of course I kept the windows shut and had the floors watered, but that didn't do any good. The nights were just as hot as the days. It was like living in an oven.

"At last I thought I'd have a bed made up for me downstairs on the north side of the house in a room that was never used because in ordinary weather it was damp. I had an idea that I might get a few hours' sleep there at all events. Anyhow it was worth trying. But it was no damned good; it was a washout. I turned and tossed and my bed was so hot that I couldn't stand it. I got up and opened the doors that led to the veranda and walked out. It was a glorious night. The moon was so bright that I swear you could read a book by it. Did I tell you the house was on the crest of a hill? I leant against the parapet and looked at the olive–trees. It was like the sea. I suppose that's what made me think of home. I thought of the cool breeze in the fir–trees and the racket of the streets in Glasgow. Believe it or not, I could smell them, and I could smell the sea. By God, I'd have given every bob I had in the world for an hour of that air. They say it's a foul climate in Glasgow. Don't you believe it. I like the rain and the grey sky and that yellow sea and the waves. I forgot that I was in Spain, in the middle of the olive country, and I opened my mouth and took a long breath as though I were breathing in the sea-fog.

"And then all of a sudden I heard a sound. It was a man's voice. Not loud, you know, low. It seemed to creep through the silence like – well, I don't know what it was like. It surprised me. I couldn't think who could be down there in the olives at that hour. It was past midnight. It was a chap laughing. A funny sort of laugh. I suppose you'd call it a chuckle. It seemed to crawl up the hill – disjointedly."

Morrison looked at me to see how I took the odd word he used to express a sensation that he didn't know how to describe.

I mean, it seemed to shoot up in little jerks, something like shooting stones out of a pail. I leant forward and stared. With the full moon it was almost as light as day, but I'm dashed if I could see a thing. The sound stopped, but I kept on looking at where it had come from in case somebody moved. And in a minute it started off again, but louder. You couldn't have called it a chuckle any more, it was a real belly laugh. It just rang through the night. I wondered it didn't wake my servants. It sounded like someone who was roaring drunk.

"Who's there?" I shouted.

The only answer I got was a roar of laughter. I don't mind telling you I was getting a bit annoyed. I had half a mind to go down and see what it was all about. I wasn't going to let some drunken swine kick up a row like that on my place in the middle of the night. And then suddenly there was a yell. By God, I was startled. Then cries. The man had laughed with a deep bass voice, but his cries were – shrill, like a pig having his throat cut.

"My God," I cried.

I jumped over the parapet and ran down towards the sound. I thought somebody was being killed. There was silence and then one piercing shriek. After that sobbing and moaning. I'll tell you what it sounded like, it sounded like someone at the point of death. There was a long groan and then nothing. Silence. I ran from place to place. I couldn't find anyone. At last I climbed the hill again and went back to my room.

You can imagine how much sleep I got that night. As soon as it was light, I looked out of the window in the direction from which the row had come and I was surprised to see a little white house in a sort of dale among the olives. The ground on that side didn't belong to us and I'd never been through it. I hardly ever went to that part of the house and so I'd never seen the house before. I asked José who lived there. He told me that a madman had inhabited it, with his brother and a servant.

"Oh, was that the explanation?" I said. "Not a very nice neighbour."

The Scot bent over quickly and seized my wrist. He thrust his face into mine and his eyes were starting out of his head with terror.

"The madman had been dead for twenty years," he whispered.

He let go my wrist and leant back in his chair panting.

"I went down to the house and walked all round it. The windows were barred and shuttered and the door was locked. I knocked. I shook the handle and rang the bell. I heard it tinkle, but no one came. It was a two-storey house and I looked up. The shutters were tight closed, and there wasn't a sign of life anywhere."

"Well, what sort of condition was the house in?" I asked.

"Oh, rotten. The whitewash had worn off the walls and there was practically no paint left on the door or the shutters. Some of the tiles off the roof were lying on the ground. They looked as though they'd been blown away in a gale."

"Queer," I said.

"I went to my friend Fernandez, the chemist, and he told me the same story as José. I asked about the madman and Fernandez said that no one ever saw him. He was more or less comatose ordinarily, but now and then he had an attack of acute mania and then he could be heard from ever so far laughing his head off and then crying. It used to scare people. He died in one of his attacks and his keepers cleared out at once. No one had ever dared to live in the house since.

"I didn't tell Fernandez what I'd heard. I thought he'd only laugh at me. I stayed up that night and kept watch. But nothing happened. There wasn't a sound. I waited about till dawn and then I went to bed."

"And you never heard anything more?"

"Not for a month. The drought continued and I went on sleeping in the lumber-room at the back. One night I was fast asleep, when something seemed to happen to me; I don't exactly know how to describe it, it was a funny feeling as though someone had given me a little nudge, to warn me, and suddenly I was wide awake. I lay there in my bed and then in the same way as before I heard a long, low gurgle, like a man enjoying an old joke. It came from away down in the valley and it got louder. It was a great bellow of laughter. I jumped out of bed and went to the window. My legs began to tremble. It was horrible to stand there and listen to the shouts of laughter that rang through the night. Then there was the pause, and after that a shriek of pain and that ghastly sobbing. It didn't sound human. I mean, you might have thought it was an animal being tortured. I don't mind telling you I was scared stiff. I couldn't have moved if I'd wanted to. After a time the sounds stopped, not suddenly, but dying away little by little. I strained my ears, but I couldn't hear a thing. I crept back to bed and hid my face.

I remembered then that Fernandez had told me that the madman's attacks only came at intervals. The rest of the time he was quite quiet. Apathetic, Fernandez said. I wondered if the fits of mania came regularly. I reckoned out how long it had been between the two attacks I'd heard. Twenty-eight days. It didn't take me long to put two and two together; it was quite obvious that it was the full moon that set him off. I'm not a nervous man really and I made up my mind to get to the bottom of it, so I looked out in the calendar which day the moon would be full next and that night I didn't go to bed. I cleaned my revolver and loaded it. I prepared a lantern and sat down on the parapet of my house to wait. I felt perfectly cool. To tell you the truth, I was rather pleased with myself because I didn't feel scared. There was a bit of a wind, and it whistled about the roof. It rustled over the leaves of the olive trees like waves shishing on the pebbles of the beach. The moon shone on the white walls of the house in the hollow. I felt particularly cheery.

At last I heard a little sound, the sound I knew, and I almost laughed. I was right; it was the full moon and the attacks came as regular as clockwork. That was all to the good. I threw myself over the wall into the olive grove and ran straight to the house. The chuckling grew louder as I came near. I got to the house and looked up. There was no light anywhere. I put my ears to the door and listened. I heard the madman simply laughing his bloody head off. I beat on the door with my fist and I pulled the bell. The sound of it seemed to amuse him. He roared with laughter. I knocked again, louder and louder, and the more I knocked the more he laughed. Then I shouted at the top of my voice.

"Open the blasted door, or I'll break it down."

I stepped back and kicked the latch with all my might. I flung myself at the door with the whole weight of my body. It cracked. Then I put all my strength into it and the damned thing smashed open.

I took the revolver out of my pocket and held my lantern in the other hand. The laughter sounded louder now that the door was opened. I stepped in. The stink nearly knocked me down. I mean, just think, the windows hadn't been opened for twenty years. The row was enough to raise the dead, but for a moment I didn't know where it was coming from. The walls seemed to throw the sound backwards and forwards. I pushed open a door by my side and went into a room. It was bare and white and there wasn't a stick of furniture in it. The sound was louder and I followed it. I went into another room, but there was nothing there. I opened a door and found myself at the foot of a staircase. The madman was laughing just over my head. I walked up, cautiously, you know, I wasn't taking any risks, and at the top of the stairs there was a passage.

I walked along it, throwing my light ahead of me, and I came to a room at the end. I stopped. He was in there. I was only separated from the sound by a thin door.

It was awful to hear it. A shiver passed through me and I cursed myself because I began to tremble. It wasn't like a human being at all. By Jove, I very nearly took to my heels and ran. I had to clench my teeth to force myself to stay. But I simply couldn't bring myself to turn the handle. And then the laughter was cut, cut with a knife you'd have said, and I heard a hiss of pain. I hadn't heard that before, it was too low to carry to my place, and then a gasp.

"Ay!" I heard the man speak in Spanish. "You're killing me. Take it away. O God, help me!"

He screamed. The brutes were torturing him. I flung open the door and burst in. The draught blew a shutter back and the moon streamed in so bright that it dimmed my lantern. In my ears, as clearly as I hear you speak and as close, I heard the wretched chap's groans. It was awful, moaning and sobbing, and frightful gasps. No one could survive that. He was at the point of death. I tell you I heard his broken, choking cries right in my ears. And the room was empty.

Robert Morrison sank back in his chair. That huge solid man had strangely the look of a lay figure in a studio. You felt that if you pushed him he would fall over in a heap on to the floor.

"And then?" I asked.

He took a rather dirty handkerchief out of his pocket and wiped his forehead.

I felt I didn't want to sleep in that room on the north side, so, heat or no heat, I moved back to my own quarters. Well, exactly four weeks later, about two in the morning, I was waked up by the madman's chuckle. It was almost at my elbow. I don't mind telling you that my nerve was a bit shaken by then, so next time the blighter was due to have an attack, next time the moon was full, I mean, I got Fernandez to come and spend the night with me. I didn't tell him anything. I kept him up playing cards till two in the morning, and then I heard it again. I asked him if he heard anything. "Nothing," he said. "There's somebody laughing," I said. "You're drunk, man," he said, and he began laughing too. That was too much. "Shut up, you fool," I said. The laughter grew louder and louder. I cried out. I tried to shut it out by putting my hands to my ears, but it wasn't a damned bit of good. I heard it and I heard the scream of pain. Fernandez thought I was mad. He didn't dare say so, because he knew I'd have killed him. He said he'd go to bed, and in the morning I found he'd slunk away. His bed hadn't been slept in. He'd taken himself off when he left me.

"After that I couldn't stop in Ecija. I put a factor there and went back to Seville. I felt myself pretty safe there, but as the time came near I began to get scared. Of course I told myself not to be a damned fool, but, you know, I damned well couldn't help myself. The fact is, I was afraid the sounds had followed me, and I knew if I heard them in Seville I'd go on hearing them all my life. I've got as much courage as any man, but damn it all, there are limits to everything. Flesh and blood couldn't stand it. I knew I'd go stark staring mad. I got in such a state that I began drinking, the suspense was so awful, and I used to lie awake counting the days. And at last I knew it'd come. And it came. I heard those sounds in Seville – sixty miles away from Ecija.'

I didn't know what to say. I was silent for a while.

"When did you hear the sounds last?' I asked.

"Four weeks ago."

I looked up quickly. I was startled.

"What d'you mean by that? It's not full moon tonight?"

He gave me a dark, angry look. He opened his mouth to speak and then stopped as though he couldn't. You would have said his vocal cords were paralysed, and it was with a strange croak that at last he answered.

"Yes, it is."

He stared at me and his pale blue eyes seemed to shine red. I have never seen in a man's face a look of such terror. He got up quickly and stalked out of the room, slamming the door behind him.

I must admit that I didn't sleep any too well that night myself.

THE DEMON LOVER

Elizabeth Bowen

Elizabeth Dorothea Cole Bowen (1899–1973) was born into an Anglo-Irish family in Dublin. Her father suffered a nervous breakdown when Bowen was around six, which triggered her lifelong stammer. Bowen's mother died when she was twelve, after which she was brought up by 'a committee of aunts'. She described her writing as, 'life with the lid on.' She was married to administrator Alan Cameron and had a thirty-two year love affair with a Canadian diplomat, Charles Ritchie.

Toward the end of her day in London Mrs. Drover went round to her shut-up house to look for several things she wanted to take away. Some belonged to herself, some to her family, who were by now used to their country life. It was late August; it had been a steamy, showery day: At the moment the trees down the pavement glittered in an escape of humid yellow afternoon sun. Against the next batch of clouds, already piling up ink-dark, broken chimneys and parapets stood out. In her once familiar street, as in any unused channel, an unfamiliar queerness had silted up; a cat wove itself in and out of railings, but no human eye watched Mrs. Drover's return. Shifting some parcels under her arm, she slowly forced round her latchkey in an unwilling lock, then gave the door, which had warped, a push with her knee. Dead air came out to meet her as she went in.

The staircase window having been boarded up, no light came down into the hall. But one door, she could just see, stood ajar, so she went quickly through into the room and unshuttered the big window in there. Now the prosaic woman, looking about her, was more perplexed than she knew by everything that she saw, by traces of her long former habit of life – the yellow smoke stain up the white marble mantelpiece, the ring left by a vase on the top of the escritoire; the bruise in the wallpaper where, on the door being thrown open widely, the china handle had always hit the wall. The piano, having gone away to be stored, had left what looked like claw marks on its part of the parquet. Though not much dust had seeped in, each object wore a film of another kind; and, the only ventilation being the chimney, the whole drawing room smelled of the cold hearth. Mrs. Drover put down her parcels on the escritoire and left the room to proceed upstairs; the things she wanted were in a bedroom chest.

She had been anxious to see how the house was – the part-time caretaker she shared with some neighbors was away this week on his holiday, known to be not yet back. At the best of times he did not look in often, and she was never sure that she trusted him. There were some cracks in the structure, left by the last bombing, on which she was anxious to keep an eye. Not that one could do anything –

A shaft of refracted daylight now lay across the hall. She stopped dead and stared at the hall table – on this lay a letter addressed to her.

She thought first – then the caretaker must be back. All the same, who, seeing the house shuttered, would have dropped a letter in at the box? It was not a circular, it was not a bill. And the post office redirected, to the address in the country, everything for her that came through the post. The caretaker (even if he were back) did not know she was due in London today – her call here had been planned to be a surprise – so his negligence in the manner of this letter, leaving it to wait in the dusk and the dust, annoyed her. Annoyed, she picked up the letter, which bore no stamp. But it cannot be important, or they would know . . . She took the letter rapidly upstairs with her, without a stop to look at the writing till she reached what had been her bedroom, where she let in light. The room looked over the garden and other gardens: The sun had gone in; as the clouds sharpened and lowered, the trees and rank lawns seemed already to smoke with dark. Her reluctance to look again at the letter came from the fact that she felt intruded upon – and by someone contemptuous of her ways. However, in the tenseness preceding the fall of rain she read it: It was a few lines.

Dear Kathleen: You will not have forgotten that today is our anniversary, and the day we said. The years have gone by at once slowly and fast. In view of the fact that nothing has changed, I shall rely upon you to keep your promise. I was sorry to see you leave London, but was satisfied that you would be back in time. You may expect me, therefore, at the hour arranged. Until then . . . K.

Mrs. Drover looked for the date: It was today's. She dropped the letter onto the bedsprings, then picked it up to see the writing again – her lips, beneath the remains of lipstick, beginning to go white. She felt so much the change in her own face that she went to the mirror, polished a clear patch in it, and looked at once urgently and stealthily in. She was confronted by a woman of forty-four, with eyes starting out under a hat brim that had been rather carelessly pulled down. She had not put on any more powder since she left the shop where she ate her solitary tea. The pearls her husband had given her on their marriage hung loose round her now rather thinner throat, slipping in the V of the pink wool jumper her sister knitted last autumn as they sat round the fire. Mrs. Drover's most normal expression was one of controlled worry, but of assent. Since the birth of the third of her little boys, attended by a quite serious illness, she had had an intermittent muscular flicker to the left of her mouth, but in spite of this she could always sustain a manner that was at once energetic and calm.

Turning from her own face as precipitately as she had gone to meet it, she went to the chest where the things were, unlocked it, threw up the lid, and knelt to search. But as rain began to come crashing down she could not keep from looking over her shoulder at the stripped bed on which the letter lay. Behind the blanket of rain the clock of the church that still stood struck six – with rapidly heightening apprehension she counted each of the slow strokes. "The hour arranged . . . My God," she said, "what hour? How should I . . . ? After twenty-five years . . ."

The young girl talking to the soldier in the garden had not ever completely seen his face. It was dark; they were saying goodbye under a tree. Now and then – for it felt, from not seeing him at this intense moment, as though she had never seen him at all – she verified his presence for these few moments longer by putting out a hand, which he each time pressed, without very much kindness, and painfully, on to one of the breast buttons of his uniform. That cut of the button on the palm of her hand was, principally, what she was to carry away. This was so near the end of a leave from France that she could only wish him already gone. It was August 1916. Being not kissed, being drawn away from and looked at intimidated Kathleen till she imagined spectral glitters in the place of his eyes. Turning away and looking back up the lawn she saw, through branches of trees, the drawing-room window alight: She caught a breath for the moment when she could go running back there into the safe arms of her mother and sister, and cry: "What shall I do, what shall I do? He has gone."

Hearing her catch her breath, her fiancé said, without feeling: "Cold?"

"You're going away such a long way."

"Not so far as you think."

"I don't understand?"

"You don't have to," he said. "You will. You know what we said."

"But that was – suppose you – I mean, suppose."

"I shall be with you," he said, "sooner or later. You won't forget that. You need do nothing but wait."

Only a little more than a minute later she was free to run up the silent lawn. Looking in through the window at her mother and sister, who did not for the moment perceive her, she already felt that unnatural promise drive down between her and the rest of all humankind. No other way of having given herself could have made her feel so apart, lost and forsworn. She could not have plighted a more sinister troth.

Kathleen behaved well when, some months later, her fiancé was reported missing, presumed killed. Her family not only supported her but were able to praise her courage without stint because they could not regret, as a husband for her, the man they knew almost nothing about. They hoped she would, in a year or two, console herself – and had it been only a question of consolation things might have gone much straighter ahead. But her trouble, behind just a little grief, was a complete dislocation from everything. She did not reject other lovers, for these failed to appear: For years she failed to attract men – and with the approach of her thirties she became natural enough to share her family's anxiousness on this score. She began to put herself out, to wonder; and at thirty-two she was very greatly relieved to find herself being courted by William Drover. She married him, and the two of them settled down in this quiet, arboreal part of Kensington: In this house the years piled up, her children were born, and they all lived till they were driven out by the bombs of the next war. Her movements as Mrs. Drover were circumscribed, and she dismissed any idea that they were still watched.

As things were – dead or living the letter writer sent her only a threat. Unable, for some minutes, to go on kneeling with her back exposed to the empty room, Mrs. Drover rose from the chest to sit on an upright chair whose back was firmly against the wall. The desuetude of her former bedroom, her married London home's whole air of being a cracked cup from which memory, with its reassuring power, had either evaporated or leaked away, made a crisis – and at just this crisis the letter writer had, knowledgeably, struck. The hollowness of the house this evening canceled years on years of voices, habits, and steps. Through the shut windows she only heard rain fall on the roofs around. To rally herself, she said she was in a mood – and for two or three seconds shutting her eyes, told herself that she had imagined the letter. But she opened them – there it lay on the bed.

On the supernatural side of the letter's entrance she was not permitting her mind to dwell. Who, in London, knew she meant to call at the house today? Evidently, however, this had been known. The caretaker, had he come back, had had no cause to expect her: He would have taken the letter in his pocket, to forward it, at his own time, through the post. There was no other sign that the caretaker had been in – but, if not? Letters dropped in at doors of deserted houses do not fly or walk to tables in halls. They do not sit on the dust of empty tables with the air of certainty that they will be found. There is needed some human hand – but nobody but the caretaker had a key. Under circumstances she did not care to consider, a house can be entered without a key. It was possible that she was not alone now. She might be being waited for, downstairs. Waited for – until when? Until "the hour arranged." At least that was not six o'clock: Six has struck.

She rose from the chair and went over and locked the door.

The thing was, to get out. To fly? No, not that: She had to catch her train. As a woman whose utter dependability was the keystone of her family life she was not willing to return to the country, to her husband, her little boys, and her sister, without the objects she had come up to fetch. Resuming work at the chest she set about making up a number of parcels in a rapid, fumbling-decisive way. These, with her shopping parcels, would be too much to carry; these meant a taxi – at the thought of the taxi her heart went up and her normal breathing resumed. I will ring up the taxi now; the taxi cannot come too soon: I shall hear the taxi out there running its engine, till I walk calmly down to it through the hall. I'll ring up – But no: the telephone is cut off . . . She tugged at a knot she had tied wrong.

The idea of flight . . . He was never kind to me, not really. I don't remember him kind at all. Mother said he never considered me. He was set on me, that was what it was – not love. Not love, not meaning a person well. What did he do, to make me promise like that? I can't remember – But she found that she could.

She remembered with such dreadful acuteness that the twenty-five years since then dissolved like smoke and she instinctively looked for the weal left by the button on the palm of her hand. She remembered not only all that he said and did but the complete suspension of her existence during that August week. I was not myself – they all told me so at the time. She remembered – but with one white burning blank as where acid has dropped on a photograph: Under no conditions could she remember his face.

So, wherever he may be waiting, I shall not know him. You have no time to run from a face you do not expect.

The thing was to get to the taxi before any clock struck what could be the hour. She would slip down the street and round the side of the square to where the square gave on the main road. She would return in the taxi, safe, to her own door, and bring the solid driver into the house with her to pick up the parcels from room to room. The idea of the taxi driver made her decisive, bold: She unlocked her door, went to the top of the staircase, and listened down.

She heard nothing – but while she was hearing nothing the passé air of the staircase was disturbed by a draft that traveled up to her face. It emanated from the basement: Down there a door or window was being opened by someone who chose this moment to leave the house.

The rain had stopped; the pavements steamily shone as Mrs. Drover let herself out by inches from her own front door into the empty street. The unoccupied houses opposite continued to meet her look with their damaged stare. Making toward the thoroughfare and the taxi, she tried not to keep looking behind. Indeed, the silence was so intense – one of those creeks of London silence exaggerated this summer by the damage of war – that no tread could have gained on hers unheard. Where her street debouched on the square where people went on living, she grew conscious of, and checked, her unnatural pace. Across the open end of the square two buses impassively passed each other: Women, a perambulator, cyclists, a man wheeling a barrow signalized, once again, the ordinary flow of life. At the square's most populous corner should be – and was – the short taxi rank. This evening, only one taxi – but this, although it presented its blank rump, appeared already to be alertly waiting for her. Indeed, without looking round the driver started his engine as she panted up from behind and put her hand on the door. As she did so, the clock struck seven. The taxi faced the main road: To make the trip back to her house it would have to turn – she had settled back on the seat and the taxi had turned before she, surprised by its knowing movement, recollected that she had not "said where." She leaned forward to scratch at the glass panel that divided the driver's head from her own.

The driver braked to what was almost a stop, turned round, and slid the glass panel back: The jolt of this flung Mrs. Drover forward till her face was almost into the glass. Through the aperture driver and passenger, not six inches between them, remained for an eternity eye to eye. Mrs. Drover's mouth hung open for some seconds before she could issue her first scream. After that she continued to scream freely and to beat with her gloved hands on the glass all round as the taxi, accelerating without mercy, made off with her into the hinterland of deserted streets.

MONEY FOR JAM

Sir Alec Guinness

Sir Alec Guinness (1914–2000) was one of the foremost actors of his
generation. His impressive range was reflected by performances in
Shakespearean plays, Ealing comedies and Hollywood blockbusters. In
the 1970s and 80s he won a new generation of fans as Obi-Wan Kenobi
in *Star Wars*, and as John le Carré's quiet spy George Smiley. Guinness
served in the Royal Navy Volunteer Reserve in World War II, during
which he commanded a landing craft taking part in the invasion of Sicily
and Elba.

The sun was hot and the foreign sea like plate-glass, the colour of pea-
cocks' tails. Little breezes played around a salt, low, bare, rocky Arca-
dia, and at noon, when we sailed, the day sang with prettiness. It was
like the sound of a flute. Or an oboe. Or was that the wind? The wind? No,
little breezes, pirouetting down from the north, a trifle cold, for they came
from high, snow-covered mountains. Even in retrospect the day held nothing
sinister, not until the sun went down. There was nothing that wasn't quite as it
ought to be. Yet this was the day dated 31 December, 1943. Curiously enough,
I still have my diary for that time, somewhat battered and stained, but legible,
and a proof to myself what life was like before the storm and what I was after
it. There is no entry under 31 December except a jotting in pencil, "St. Luke
12. And if he shall come in the second watch, or come in the third watch, and
find them so, blessed are those servants." Why does this fascinate? Then it is
blank for three days. Finally in ink, with a strange borrowed pen and writing
mine, but not like my own, are the words, "January 2. Not the second or third
watches. Unprepared in the morning, but resigned in the Dogs." For January
3 there is entered up, "We took the rings off Broadstairs' hand." After that I
didn't bother to keep a diary.

This was the situation. The enemy, thirty miles up the coast, also held all the opposite shore except the island of K. During the week ending 28 December they
had attacked and overrun the three large islands that are grouped round K. It was
apparent they would land on K. at any moment. They had complete air superiority
in that part of the world, and no Allied craft could sail in those waters except under cover of darkness. The idea was that the ninety-foot schooner, of which I was
captain, should run fifty tons of ammunition to the resistance group on K. and take
off as many women and children as possible. K., being the last link on the opposite

coast, must be saved at best, or turned into a battlefield at worst. Losing it was out of the question. It meant a trip of two hundred and twenty miles for us, there and back. The plans were hurried, but reasonably good and simple. We were to arrive at midnight and leave not later than 2 a.m. That would give us six hours of darkness at ten knots to get away from enemy reconnaissance planes. Everything had to be done in the dark, and if, by some misfortune, such as a breakdown or encountering an enemy vessel off the island, it would be imprudent for us to get away at the prescribed time, we were to find a small creek, run the schooner along-side rocks, disguise her with branches and camouflage netting and try our luck the following night. That is if we weren't spotted during the day. When loaded with the "ammo" the *Peter* – for that was her name – sat down squarely in the water.

"You know what to look for, don't you?" said the wiry little naval officer who brought me my sailing orders. "There's no moon, but if it's a clear night you should see the mountains of B. fine on your port bow by 22.00. Z. island is very low, but, as you can see on the chart, there's plenty of water round it. Keep as close inshore as possible in case of mines. When you come into the bay keep the guns closed up and slow down. And for God's sake tell the crew to keep their mouths shut. Silence is vital. When the chaps on K. spot you they will light a bonfire for ten minutes. If they light two bonfires or no bonfire, buzz off – it means we are too late. If it's all O.K. and they are ready for you, they'll swing a red lantern at the end of the jetty. There's a Major Backslide there, a drunken old so-and-so, but he knows his onions. He'll give you the latest dope which, inci-dentally, we'd like in the office when you get back. So long! It's money for jam."

"One moment," I said. "What other craft are out tonight?"

"Well, there's the usual patrol, but they won't touch you. Anything you see will be enemy. Except for twelve schooners, including *Mother of God, Topaz* and *Helena*, which are leaving here a few hours after you and working their way up the coast. Secret job. But you won't see them on the outward passage. Possibly coming back, though."

He went as briskly as he came, leaving my first lieutenant muttering "Money for jam!" Jimmy had an instinctive, and often unreasonable, dislike of the people who issued orders from offices. But really it wasn't a bad-looking little job, so long as the weather lasted. Never cared for the *Peter* when the sea got up. Always considered her top heavy.

So we sailed at noon on this cloudless day, hardly apprehensive, pleased to think we were on a mission of some small importance, but grumbling that it was going to mean New Year's Eve at sea. This annoyed the Scots lads in particular, but Taffey said "Think of the WOMEN we will be bringing back"; and the cox-swain said, "Got a tin of turkey and two of ham. Big eats!" Able Seaman Broad-stairs went down to the mess-deck, stripped, and vigorously applied hair-oil to his chest. "You'll never get it to grow by to-morrow night, son," grunted Stoker White, the oldest member of the crew. Broadstairs had a fine figure, and was a decent living kid, but he had no hair on his chest, which distressed him deeply. Whenever women were mentioned out came the violently-smelling hair-oil. Now he put it away and took to cleaning his silver signet rings with metal polish. He wore five of them and had a ring tattooed on the little finger of his left hand.

"Money for jam!" said Jimmy. "I could kick the tight little arse of that office boy!"

* * *

We sailed up the coast for ten miles, then pushed out to sea. I came off watch at tea-time and Jimmy took over. The crew consisted of the two of us and fourteen ratings, and we worked it watch and watch about, which is easy going on these short trips. Off watch in the daytime I usually sat in the cabin reading. Thinking to myself, I'm bound to be up all night, I turned in to get some early sleep after tea. The sun had grown dim, the bright blue sky was overcast with pale grey, and the sea was oily looking, shot with patches of dark satin-like water. No stars, tonight, I thought, and turned away from the scuttle and the light. A minute later Broadstairs entered the cabin to "darken ship." Very easily and swiftly I fell asleep. No dreams that I can remember. I slept for nearly two hours. When I woke it was with the strangest notion I have ever had in my life.

I am not a deeply religious man, and before the war was avowedly irreligious. I did not have convictions that could be called atheistic, but they were certainly agnostic. The war brought me back to an acceptance of the doctrines of the Church of England. I suppose I believe in ghosts. Certainly in good and evil spirits. But all that speculation had always seemed unimportant – chit-chat for a winter's evening at home, by a log fire, in the good old days of indifference. All thoughts of religious subjects, angelology, demons and what not were far from my mind that evening. I had no worries, other than the navigational one of successfully finding the island K.; and there was no obvious difficulty about that; I only call it "worry", because I have never sailed anywhere without wondering whether I would find the place. It is difficult to describe what happened to me at six o'clock that evening, yet I must attempt it, for on it hangs the whole significance of this experience from a personal point of view. It was as if – . It is impossible to state it simply enough and sound credible. It was as if – . I woke up with a start, the sweat pouring off me. I trembled. The cabin was filled with an evil presence and it was concentrated twelve or eighteen inches from my left ear. Fully awake, I heard with my ear, so it seemed to me, the word "TOMORROW." It was spoken clearly and quite loudly. Then the evil thing withdrew. Never have I felt so relieved at the departure of an unwanted guest as I was by that one. The electric light on the table, throwing its warm, yellow circle of light on the dark blue cloth, the books on the shelves, the luminous clock, the barometer, the coffee percolator, the chairs, a pair of sea-boots, an old sweater, an etching of New York on the bulkhead, all these things seemed so friendly and clinging, as if they had resented the intruder as much as myself. For there was no doubt of the meaning conveyed in that one word "Tomorrow". A whole sentence had been condensed, with evil intent, into that word. It had said, in fact, "Tomorrow you will die an unpleasant death." Now, death is a fearful thing, and often terrible, and much has been thought and written on the subject, but it has never preoccupied my mind. We are hedged in with platitudes about death . . . we must all die – that makes death seem easier and less important. The poems of Beddoes I have always found funny. Death held no special terrors for me, I'm convinced. But there was something in that evil experience which shook me. Not so much the personal, unpleasant message as the feeling that swept through me that this had been a devil's voice, and if the workings of this curious world were controlled by devils, then life was the most wretched affair, human kind the saddest creation, children merely sent into the world to mock a man with. This was diametrically opposed to what I had always believed to be true. To have trusted such a voice would have been to banish God and render Christ ridiculous. "If I am to die tomorrow," I said to myself, "why can I not be informed by an angel, or one of the fates, or the ghost of an angry saint, if I *must* be told supernaturally? Why must I be told by this evil, sneaking, contemptible thing?" That gave me hope, for there was something gossipy, hearsay and underhand about that voice. I went on to the bridge.

"Hullo," I said.

"Hullo," said Jimmy.

"What's the matter?" I asked. "You look white."

"Do I?" Jimmy gave a direction down the voice-pipe. "If I do it's because I feel a bit sick. Just had a bit of a scare. Don't know what it was. Got the creeps. But it's O.K. now."

I was silent for a moment and looked round the horizon. It was getting dark, and all land had disappeared.

"How's the barometer?" I asked.

"Steady."

The *Peter* was beginning to roll a little – not an unusual occurrence even in a calm sea. But I didn't like the soft sighing sound in the rigging. I do not think there is a more melancholy lonely sound in the world than that whine of wind on wires and ropes. Curious, but sometimes you hear it, and it makes you shiver, when you can hardly feel a breath of wind on your face. The air round the ship seemed quite gentle, but the sighing was there unmistakably. Then suddenly a hard, bleak puff of wind screamed down, turning the small black waves white, tugging at one's hair, the flag, sending doors banging, lifting the heavy canvas lashed over the hold, raising the sadness in the rigging to a screech, and passing as swiftly as it had come. Oh, that depressing sound, and the cold, leaden splash of the bow wave breaking on the night sea! I sent for a duffel coat and remained on the bridge.

At 20.30 the wind, such as it was, came from a north-westerly direction. Six minutes later it changed abruptly and increased. By a quarter to nine it was blowing gale force from the south. In this part of the world the dangerous winds are reputed to be the northerly ones, so I thought little of it. It was a nuisance and was going to mean a bad night unless it slackened. Almost perceptibly the waves increased in height from four or five feet to twelve. Within another half hour they were fifteen feet; that is, as high as the bridge. Coming right on the starboard beam, we rolled heavily.

"How's the barometer?"

"Dropped two points since six o'clock."

We altered course five degrees to starboard to make allowance for the beam sea. Jimmy turned in to get some sleep, but within half an hour was up again.

"It's a bastard, isn't it!" he said. He stood by me, and then added, "They are getting bigger, aren't they?" They certainly were getting bigger, and also increasingly difficult to see in the darkness. As he said it the signalman, whose cap had gone in the wind, but who continued to hold a hand to his head, as if to keep that in place, cried out, "Look at this one, sir! Bet it's twenty foot or more." The monster of a wave looked as if it might crush us, but the *Peter* lifted herself, swayed to an alarming angle, and rode lightly over. A motor mechanic, an ill-shaped little fellow from Glasgow, put his face up the companion-way. " 'Scuse me, sir, we going on?" "Yes, Mickey Mouse." Mickey Mouse whistled and slid down the steps.

At 23.00 we saw the black, low shape of Z. We were much closer than I had expected, and on the wrong side. So we altered course for a while and rode more easily with the sea astern. Z. having been put in its right place, we continued on our way. The spray, which was being whipped off the water, was getting hellish. Shortly before midnight we were in the narrow waters that divide K. from Z. Here, considering we were almost hemmed in by islands, we expected to find some abatement. There was none. The lightning broke out in a vivid pink flash and we saw clearly, for the first time, exactly how enormous the waves were. It seemed odd that they should race at this size into this almost protected area. What I had not realised was the deterioration of the weather outside the islands. Within the past half hour, on the weather side of Z., which was in fact offering us stout protection, had begun the greatest storm in living memory in these stormy parts. The *Peter* was increasingly difficult to handle, her bow continuously swinging away from the wind, and she wouldn't answer to the helm even when hard over. To turn her into those giant waves and that roaring wind we had to go full ahead on the engines, which nearly shook her to pieces, or play one engine off against the other, putting the outboard full ahead and the inboard half astern. The spray took the form of a rushing mist, which, seen in the lightning, had all the qualities of a nightmare. We wallowed down past K. bay. No bonfires. No red lanterns – though if they had lit twenty we should never have seen them. In any case, we could never have reached the jetty. The sea was tumbling from all sides, and I heard later the jetty had been carried away. Mercilessly our stern was lifted thirty feet in the air and then our bows, thirty feet in the air into this pink, hail-like mist, and then we were dropped with a sickening thud. To have used oil would have been sensible, but the movement of the ship was so violent it was impossible for a man to shift his position. To have gone on deck was certain death; where you were you stayed, holding on for very life.

We turned back. So far as any direction was possible we headed towards the south-west. I had no desire on arriving back at the far coast, to find myself on the wrong side of the front line of battle. The ship could not be steered in any sense of the word. All we could do was to try keep the heavy seas on the port bow. I must say the *Peter* rode them magnificently.

A few minutes after midnight there was a sound like a muffled pistol-shot heard above the deafening roar. I didn't see it go, but it was the wireless mast.

At about 2 A.M. there began a curious phenomenon. There were four of us on the bridge – Jimmy, the signalman Douglas, a lookout nicknamed Hopeless, and myself. We were all drenched to the skin and exhausted by the violence of our beating from the wind. We huddled together, clutching at the sides of the bridge. It was impossible to speak, for even if we bawled the wind, now tearing past us at a hundred miles an hour, laden with stinging salt water, wrenched the sound away from our lips and drowned it in a howl. But Hopeless managed, after a couple of attempts, to make some words heard. "CAN YOU SEE? IS – IT –

SPIRITS?" He was obviously upset about something. He couldn't let go to point, but it wasn't necessary, for we saw for ourselves. Creeping along the gunwale, starting from the bows, were ripples of bright blue light. In a minute they reached the bridge and crept under our fingers. Then the stump of the mast was ringed with blue – then every wire, every rope, all the edges of everything, including the hoods of our duffel coats, our finger-nails, the tops of our sea-boots. The light varied in thickness from the tenth of an inch to the breadth of a thumb, but all was of equal brilliance, a vivid blue, and seemed to move to and fro as if alive. For two hours we battled on, bristling with blue light, fascinated, entranced by its prettiness, and each of us hardly daring to wonder how the night would end. Before dawn the light receded.

The dawn came very late that morning. Jimmy managed to say "Happy New Year!" in my ear. The dawn was more terrible than the night, for the waves were thirty feet and over, and we could see each one completely and calculate its danger. They were a dirty yellow in colour, where they weren't white, as if they were scooping up the seabed. Some of them assumed fantastic toppling shapes, tapering up to narrow ribands of water through which we could see the wave behind; then the tops would be blown clean off, like eggs cut with a knife, and a solid mass of water would disappear in streaks in the air. Part of the port gunwale was smashed and washed away. At ten to eight we sighted a rocky island, tow hundred yards ahead. We saw it for the second we were balanced on top of a wave. We didn't get another opportunity, for it was hidden by walls of water. That island rises to twenty feet above sea level. It is about a quarter of a mile in circumference and uninhabited. From our perch on the top of the wave we saw the whole island was awash and at the northern end submerged. From that glimpse I was able to ascertain our position. We had been blown twenty-six miles north of our rough course during the night. I turned the ship head on into the sea. On a calm day the *Peter* could knock up fourteen knots. Her speed of advance into this sea, flat out, was half a knot.

Throughout the day we maintained the same speed – half a knot. The four of us clung together, in the same position we had been in all the time. I bawled down the voice-pipe to the coxswain, asking him if he was all right. "Fine!" came the reply, and I think I heard whistling. We all longed for something to drink, but it was out of the question. Every man in the ship was pinned to his position. How the lads in the engine-room, in that sickly smell of hot oil, stood it out I shall never know.

I cannot remember when we began to pray. When we realised, I think, that at this speed we had no hope of shelter that night, and a very good chance three or four times a minute of capsizing or being pounded to pieces. When we saw the rocky island awash, I was aware that Douglas, crouched against me, had released his hand for a moment to cross himself. That, I think, set us all – anyway, those of us on the bridge – saying the Our Father. We mingled our muttered prayers with attempts at rather bawdy music-hall songs, not in defiance of God, but to relieve our minds of the strain. By the afternoon our faces were sodden with water, puffy and raw. Our eyes were ghastly to look at and painful to keep open. One at a time we probably dropped asleep, to awake thirty seconds later wondering how many hours had gone by. So we stayed there, having no alternative.

445

SIR ALEC GUINNESS

At six o'clock I tried to sing "For those in peril on the sea" – and then it occurred to me to exorcise the ship. How silly and inexplicable that sounds! I am almost ashamed to write it. I wriggled round to face the after part of the ship, which included the cabin where I had experienced that evil thing. Jimmy and Douglas clasped me round the chest while I raised my right hand, making the sign of the cross. "In the name of Jesus Christ, leave us!" I said. Poor Hopeless! That depressed him more than anything. He began to cry.

The next morning we were weak and bitterly cold. The waves were of the same menacing height and ferocity, but the wind had dropped, probably to about eighty miles an hour. And we had lost our fear. We were all convinced we would die during the day. Shortly after noon we passed very close to the battered overturned hulk of a schooner. We could make out the name, *Topaz*. Subsequently we learnt that every one of those twelve that had sailed up the coast had been lost with all hands. On shore aircraft had been overturned by the wind on the airfields, gun emplacements on harbour walls had been washed away, with their gun crews, and in one well-protected harbour six sailors had been drowned. Giant waves rolled up the coast, in some cases running inland for two or three hundred yards.

Visibility was as bad as ever, but something about the sea suggested we were close to land. At 15.30 the engines, overheated, failed. We were drifting hopelessly. We were all resigned. The only anxiety of which I was conscious was the fact that Able Seaman Broadstairs couldn't swim. We all knew swimming would be of no help, but it seemed bad that he had never learnt to swim. I remember thinking, "I wish I couldn't swim, because that will make it worse. I shall struggle for life." It was on such lines that I tried to comfort myself about Broadstairs.

It began to get dusk. Jimmy said, "Christ! Not another night! I couldn't!" The waves were now of a tumbling, clumsy, falling-on-top-of-each-other nature. At 17.15 we grounded, twenty yards from a rocky beach. The sea was on the beam. "Abandon ship!" I yelled. One carley float was loosed by Hopeless. It somersaulted towards the shore before anyone could grab the line that held it. Then a gigantic wave, which made the others appear ripples, picked us up and carried us right inshore, flinging us on the rocks. We heard a splitting sound. The four of us on the bridge clambered down. The *Peter* was lying on her side, at an angle of thirty degrees, precariously balanced. She was still surrounded by heavy surf. It was then that Stoker White came out in his true colours. He girded himself with a rope and flung himself into the filthy yellow water. It looked suicidal – but he reached the shore and lay there – a large, fat, exhausted, panting creature – a link between us and safety. "Come on, you sons of she-devils!" he croaked. "Come on, sonny!". This last to Broadstairs. Broadstairs, grinning, caught hold of the rope and sprang from the ship's side. He slipped, fell, cracked his skull and broke his back. He didn't make any noise. The surf washed him away. The others wasted no time. One by one, orderly, silently, they got ashore. Jimmy was next to last. Then my turn came. I was scared, and put off the moment, though I knew to do so was taking a far greater risk than swinging on the rope. I crawled along to the cabin. Everything was broken, upside down, ruined – as if that evil presence had sought revenge on harmless, inanimate objects, the friendly possessions of a man. I have always had some decent books on board. I couldn't resist snatching one up from the deck, where it had fallen, splayed out. In drawing-room games of Desert Island Books I had always chosen the most rewarding to spend the rest of my life with – the Bible, Shakespeare, Dickens, Milton, and so on. I rejected them all at this moment and took a cheap thriller I hadn't read. That, and my diary. I stepped out on deck. The crew were all halloaing me. Managed the rope easily. So there we all were. That is, all of us except Broadstairs. We recovered his body next day, terribly battered. It was difficult getting the rings off his fingers. We sent them to his mother.

The *Peter* slipped on her side, rolled over, and split in two. We were five miles behind the Allied lines. Good.

One thing we all understood, each in his different way. Everyone of us had been purged of a pet vice or special fear.

IS THERE A LIFE BEYOND THE GRAVY?

Stevie Smith

> **Florence Margaret Smith** (1902–1971) was nicknamed Stevie after the jockey, Stevie Donoghue. Her father joined the merchant navy when Smith was four and soon after she was sent to a sanatorium to be treated for tuberculosis. It was during her stay there that she first contemplated suicide. After university she worked as a secretary. The 1950s were a difficult period for Smith, but she embraced – and was embraced by – the Beat culture of the 1960s. She was awarded the Queen's Gold Medal for Poetry in 1969.

It was a wonderfully sunny day; the willowherb waved in the ruins and the white fluff fell like snow. But alas – Celia glanced at the blue-faced clock in the Ministry tower – it was eleven o'clock.

She shook herself free of the rubble and stood up. The white earth fell from her hair and clothes.

"Are you all right?" said her cousin Casivalaunus, who was standing looking at her.

"Oh yes, thank you so much. Oh, hallo, Cas."

"Hallo, Celia. Well, I'll be off. See you at Uncle Heber's."

Celia took hold of her cousin's arm and hung on like grim death.

"You're sure you're all right?" said Cas, flicking at the white fluff with his service gloves. "I say, would you mind letting go of my arm?"

"So long, Cas."

"So long, Celia. You'll soon get accustomed to it."

He saluted, and walking quickly with elegant long strides made off down an avenue lined with broken pillars.

Celia leaped over the waterpipes that lay in the gutter and tore across the garden in the middle of the square. This was a short cut to the Ministry. She was already an hour late, but she thought it was a good thing to take the short cut, and very important to run.

"How do you do, Browser?" she called out, as she ran past the porter and up the stairs.

"Same as usual, miss," said the porter with a wink.

Well, it *was* much the same really; for one thing Celia had never in her life been early.

"You've never in your lifetime been early." Browser's parting shot (what a very carrying voice he had to be sure) followed her up the stairs and across the threshold of her room.

Tiny was standing over by the window squashing flies on the curtain.

"Hallo, Tiny."

"Hallo, Celia."

Celia flung her gloves into the wastepaper basket and put her hat on the statue of the Young Octavius. What a really fine room it was, she thought, so high and square, with such a beautiful moulded ceiling. But rather untidy. Celia sighed. She began to count up the number of things that would have to be put away one day, but not just now. Perhaps Tiny would put them away.

There was a leather revolver holster on the radiator, a set of tennis-balls on the table by the window, a tin, marked Harrogate Toffee, with some cartridges in it, a large feather duster and a jigsaw puzzle. On the floor lay a copy of Sir Sefton Choate's monograph *Across the Sinai Desert with the Children of Israel*, and sticking out of the tall bronze urn by the fireplace were a large landing-net and a couple of golf-clubs with broken sticks. A long thin climbing plant had managed to take root in the filing tray and was already half way up the wall.

Celia sighed again and closed her eyes. "Anything in today, Tiny, darling?"

"Just a telegram," said Tiny, and read it out:

"*To Criticisms Mainly Emanating Examerica He Anxiousest More Responsible Ministers Be Associated Cumhim But Sharpliest Protested Antisuggestion Camille Chautemps*" – wang wang, Tiny struck a note and intoned the rest of it – "*Quote Eye Appreciate Joke Buttwas He Who Signed Capitulation Abandoned Allies Sentenced Leaders Deathwards Unquote General DeGaulle Postremarking He Unthought Hed See Andre Maurois Again.*

"It is from our cousin," said Tiny. " 'Eye appreciate joke', I do not. Look," he pointed to the signature, *Casivalaunus*.

Tiny and Celia began to laugh their aggravating high-pitched laugh. This noise was very aggravating for Lord Loop – Augustus Loop – Tiny's brother, who occupied the adjoining room. He began to pound on the wall. Tiny turned quite pale. "Oh, lord, there goes Augustus," he said. He flicked at the papers on his desk and put a busy expression on his face.

"This cablegram," he said, "is dated 1942."

"I tell you what," said Celia, "I'll do the washing-up."

Celia had a large red Bristol glass tumbler, out of which she drank her morning milk. She was delighted with the appearance of this tumbler in the wash-basin and swam it round for some time, admiring the reflection. "But of course," she said, for she had acquired the habit of talking to herself, "it is to be seen at its best only with the white milk in it." There was also Tiny's old Spode cup and saucer to be washed – he had pinched this from Augustus – and a rather humdrum yellow jug that belonged to Sir Sefton. Celia suddenly remembered Sir Sefton and wondered if he was in yet. She was Sir Sefton's Personal Assistant. How grand that sounded! Personal Assistant to Sir Sefton Choate, Bt., MP, MIME – yes, he was a famous mining engineer, or had been, before "like the rest of us" he had been caught by the Ministry. Had he not written in his famous monograph on the Children of Israel, "It is probable, in this rich oil-bearing district, that Lot's wife was turned into a pillar of asphalt, not salt"?

From somewhere in the distance came the sound of a harp – the thin beautiful sound. That must be Jacky Sparrow in Publications. He was a graceful harpist. Celia remembered that she was lunching with Jacky today. She must hurry up and get on with the morning. The morning was like a beautiful coloured ball to be bounced and played with till the next thing came along to be done, and that was lunch-time.

Tiny came and banged on the door. "Hurry up, Celia! Crumbs, what ages you take. Sefton wants you."

"'Morning, Miss Phoze."

"'Morning, Sir Sefton."

"I had a rotten night last night," said the baronet. "I don't know. This way and that. Couldn't get a wink. Then I got up and sat on the side of the bath with my feet in hot water. No good. So I took a tablet. Thought it was Slumber-o, but must have got the wrong bottle. Turned it up next morning. D'you know what it was? Camomile. I was up all night."

Sir Sefton was sitting at his desk doing the *Morning Post* crossword puzzle.

"What's a difficult poem by Browning?"

"Paracelsus," said Celia, who was trying to write an article for the *Tribune* – where was that envelope with the figures on it? Was it two-thirds or two-fifths?

"*Eight* letters," said the baronet.

"Sordello."

"Hrrump, hrrump! Yes, that's it. Thank you very much, Miss Phoze . . . I don't think there's anything very much here." He began to rummage under his blotter, holding it up with one hand and paddling underneath with the other. "Oh, here's a note from the LCC. Let's see, March 1942? Well, it's answered itself by now." He went back to his puzzle.

"Where did the Kings of Israel reign?"

"Jerusalem," said Celia.

"Now now, it's not as easy as that."

"The Kings of Israel," said Celia, and began to stare round the room rather desperately. "I say, the charlady has left a packet of sandwiches in the curtain loop."

"Good heavens!" said Sir Sefton absentmindedly. "The Kings of Israel, the Kings of Israel?"

"Stead," said Sir Sefton. "I asked Jacky Sparrow about it, as a matter of fact; he's a dab at these things." He grinned delightedly. "'And Jeroboam reigned in his stead.' Smart, isn't it?" he said. "Well, well, Miss Phoze, I think I'll buzz off now. I'm going to this lecture on Oil Surrogates at the Institute. Thought I'd take Bozey with me – cheer him up you know – he's never been the same since his wife died. I said to him: 'Bozey, your good lady's gone, hasn't she? Very well, then, she's gone. No good moping, is there, we all have to go some time.'"

"Don't forget the hare," said Celia, as Sefton padded towards the door.

This was a large, dead animal, half wrapped in brown paper, that lay across the floor. Augustus had brought it up for Sefton from his farm (the beastly Augustus, thought Celia, for neither she nor Tiny could stand him). All the same, it was a fine animal, the hare, and stretched right across the room.

Sefton picked it up and went out rather burdened, with the creature trailing over one arm, and his umbrella on the other.

"God bless you," he said, with a happy smile. "God bless us all and the Pope of Rome."

There was a message from Jacky Sparrow on Celia's desk, to say that he would not be able to lunch as he had to rush off to the dentist's.

Celia and Tiny decided to have lunch in their room, and Celia went to get it from the canteen, because Mrs Bones always gave her more ice-cream than Tiny. Halfway through their picnic lunch, Augustus came into the room with a made-up boisterous expression on his face.

"Hallo, you two, pack up there; we're off to the countryside for an excursion."

Hand in hand Tiny and Celia went and stood in the garden of the square while Augustus went to get the car out. The garden now stretched for miles and was more full of flowers than it had been in the morning; indeed there was a rather alarming air of quickly growing vegetation.

"Perhaps we had better make a move," said Celia.

They walked together down a narrow pathway, between the giant blue flowers which grew and flowered high above their heads. Suddenly, coming round a hairy oriental poppy plant, they ran full tilt into Sir Sefton.

"Good heavens," he said, "I must hurry, or I shall be late for the meeting. I shall see you next week at the Ministry, Miss Phoze? Ah, howdedo, Loop? So long, all."

He went off in a fuss in the opposite direction.

"Next week?" said Tiny. "What can he be thinking of? – the poor old gentleman."

"Why, *this* week is the holidays, of course," said Celia. "We are going to stay with Uncle Heber."

"Oh yes," said Tiny, "I'd forgotten. How quickly the time comes round."

"Well, we'd better be getting on," said Celia, disengaging her foot from a young oak tree that was shooting up from a split acorn.

"But Augustus told us to wait for him."

"I don't care about Augustus," said Celia recklessly, and tossed back her fine dark hair. "After all, he can soon catch us up in his motor-car."

"Perhaps we had better keep to the pathway," said Tiny slyly.

The pretty grey grass was soft under their feet, but there was hardly room for the two of them to walk abreast.

"Yes, perhaps we had," said Celia, laughing. "It will save a lot of bother."

"Why, look," said Tiny, "here comes Jacky Sparrow."

Jacky came running along the narrow path towards them, jumping gracefully over the young shoots as he ran. He was carrying his harp in his outstretched arms.

"Hallo, hallo, hallo," he said, "can't stop, can't stop, can't stop. Sorry about the lunch, Celia; got to get me harp-string mended, got to catch the old chap before he lies down for the afternoon."

"Phew!" said Tiny, as Jacky disappeared from sight. "Everybody seems to be going in the opposite direction."

The vista now opened before them upon a slight decline. There was a fine white marble viaduct down below them to the right, and upon the viaduct was an old-fashioned train, with steam coming out of the coal-black engine and the fire stoked to flame upon the fender.

"Hurry, hurry, hurry," cried Tiny, catching Celia by the hand. "We have just time to take the train!"

The train was beginning to move as they tore up the steps and into the last carriage.

"Jolly good show," said Tiny; and then he said, "I hope Uncle Heber will be pleased to see us."

They both lay down on the carriage seat, and ate the sandwiches which Celia had brought with her from Sir Sefton's room.

The train was now running between high embankments. On the top of the embankment and down the side was the soft grass waving like beautiful hair; also on the top, against a Cambridge-blue sky, there were some poppies.

"Beautiful," said Tiny; "might be Norfolk."

"One always comes back to the British School," said Celia dreamily.

"What a dreamy girl you are," said Tiny.

The train, gathering speed at the bend, shot through an old-fashioned station. There were rounded Victorian window-panes in the waiting-room and a general air of coal, sea, soot and steamer oil.

"What station was that?" asked Celia.

"Looked like Dover," said Tiny.

"Can't be Dover," said Celia. "Dover isn't on the way to Uncle Heber's."

After another mile or so the train pulled up with a jerk and they sat up quickly to look out of the window. It was an enormous, long, busy station. People were hurrying down the platform towards the refreshment-room; soldiers, sailors and airmen stood about in groups drinking cups of tea from the trolleys.

"Just time to get dinner if you hurry," sang out a familiar voice, and there was Sir Sefton carrying a couple of bottles of hair-oil as well as the hare and the umbrella. "So long," he said, raising his hat to Celia and dropping one of the bottles, which smashed against the platform and released a beautiful odour. "So long, all, see you later."

"Must be Perth," said Tiny. He pulled the blind down with a snap, and pushed Celia on to the bunk.

Celia looked round the carriage, at the wash-basin, the lights just where you wanted them, the luggage-table, the many different sorts of racks, the air-conditioning control, the neat fawn blankets and clean pillow-cases.

"What a good thing we managed to get a sleeper," she said.

"I fancy we have to thank Sir Sefton for that."

"I think Sefton is simply ripping," said Celia.

"One of the best; jolly good show, sir," said Tiny.

"Can't be Perth," said Celia. "Perth isn't on the way to Uncle Heber's."

"We shall be in the mountains soon," said Tiny; "the mountain air is always so delicious. I trust that we shall catch a great many trout. It is a pity that we left the landing-net at home."

"Uncle Heber's country," said Celia, "is as flat as a pancake."

Tiny said, "We must continue steadfastly to look on the bright side of things," and promptly fell asleep.

There now came a great pounding at the door. It was Jacky Sparrow with his harp in his hand, and an inspector's cap on his head.

"All change, all change, all change," he cried out. Then he said, "So long, I simply must fly."

Celia and Tiny got the suitcases shut at last and tumbled out on to a grass-grown platform. There were a couple of donkeys grazing on the siding, but no people at all. The train gave a shiver and a backward slide, then it pulled itself together and rushed off, leaving a patch of black smoke hanging in mid-air. The smoke bellied out and hung, first black, then grey, then white, against a pale-blue sky.

"Thornton-le-Soke," read out Tiny from the station nameplate.

"You see," said Celia, "no mountains at all."

The station was set in a beautiful sunbaked plain under a wide skyline. The sea could be seen in the far distance, and a soft fresh wind blew inland over the samphire beds.

Tiny looked very happy. "We have arrived," he said. "It is curious, do you know I have not thought of Augustus for several moments?"

"I fancy," said Celia, "that Augustus has taken the wrong turning."

"Indeed?" said Tiny.

"Augustus was looking rather weird," said Celia in her dreamy way. "There he was, sitting high above the road in his old-fashioned motor-car, with his dust coat and his goggles, and the dust flying up behind the car and the chickens running away in front of it."

"Oh, did you see him?"

"Did *you*?"

"Yes, as a matter of fact I did see Augustus in his motor-car. I said nothing about it," said Tiny kindly, "because I did not wish to disturb you."

"Oh, not at all," said Celia; "thanks awfully all the same."

They now sat down on their suitcases like a couple of schoolchildren waiting to be fetched.

"Do you know who will fetch us, I think?" said Celia.

"It will be Uncle Heber for one."

"Uncle is an old and established person, he may not come, but if he comes there will also be another one, and that other one will be our cousin, Casivalaunus."

"Good heavens!" said Tiny. "He was seconded to Intelligence, was he not? I fancied he was in the mountains."

"You seem to have got the mountains on the brain."

Celia began to count the wooden palings opposite, counting aloud in German, "*Ein, zwei, drei, vier, fünf.*"

"Mark my words," said Tiny, "that car of Augustus's will *konk out* on the hills." He coughed. "If you will excuse the expression."

At this moment a long, thin person came in an elegant stroll along the platform towards them; he was wearing the uniform of a high-ranking British officer.

"There you are. What did I tell you?" said Celia. "It is Cas."

"I can't stand these clothes," said Cas. "You'll have to wait a minute while I change. Uncle's down below in the pony-trap. We drove it under the bridge, as Polly likes the shade. I'll just pop into the waiting-room, I won't be a tick."

"I do think our cousin has a vulgar parlance," said Tiny.

Celia tore down the station steps and climbed into the pony-trap beside Uncle Heber, and put her arms round him. Heber was wearing his shabby old clergy-man's clothes, a clerical grey ankle-length mackintosh and a shovel hat. He was crying quietly.

"We must get home quickly," he said. "I have set the supper table because it is Tuffie's night out, but there is much to do; we must hurry."

He pulled gently on the reins and Polly moved off at an amble, with the grass still sticking out of her mouth. Cas, in a light-green ski-jacket and flannel trousers, came running with Tiny. They caught hold of the trap and jumped in.

"All aboard," said Heber in a hollow voice.

As they drove the quiet country miles to the rectory, Celia began to sing, "Soft-ly, softly, softly, softly, The white snow fell."

"Now, Celia," said Cas, "we can do without that."

They were bowling along the sands by this time, bowling along the white sea sand down below the high-tide level where the sands were damp and firm. The sea crept out to the far horizon, where some dirty weather was blowing up; one could see the line of stormy white waves beyond the seawhorl worms, and the white bones and white seashells that lay in the hollow.

"There's some dirty weather coming," said Tiny.

"True, Tiny, true," said Cas.

"I hope we shan't be *kept in*," said Celia.

"I am sure we shall be able to *get out of the wind under the breakwater,* and that we shall be able to go for a *stretch, a blow, a turn, a tramp* and a *breather,*" said Cas, giving Tiny a sly pinch.

When they got to the rectory they had some sardines, some cheese, some bread, some margarine and some cocoa.

"There are some spring onions in the sideboard cupboard, if any person cares for such things," said Heber.

The dark fell suddenly upon them as they sat at supper, and the rainstorm slashed across the window-pane.

"Off to bed with you all," said Heber. "There are your candles, take them with you. You are sleeping in the three rooms on the first floor at the back of the house overlooking the beechwoods. The rooms are called Minnie, Yarrow and Florence. You, Celia, are in Minnie. The boys can take their choice."

"Oh, thank you, sir, thank you so much," said the boys.

"I must buzz off now," said Heber, "I have some business to attend to."

He took his white muffler from the chest in the hall where the surplices were kept and a horn lantern from the porch. "So long, all," he said.

Tiny looked rather frightened.

"He is certainly going to the church," said Celia.

They spoke in whispers together, and together went up the shallow treads of the staircase to bed.

Tiny pushed past Cas and went into the Florence room.

"Just what one might expect," muttered Cas furiously. "You know perfectly well, Tiny," he called through the door, "that I detest Yarrow." He turned to Celia. "I shall not be able to sleep a wink."

Tiny sat on the window-seat, crying. He leant far out into the night and his tears fell with a splash into the water-butt that was under the Florence window.

Then he got up and went into Celia's room. "I keep thinking of Augustus," he sobbed.

"Now, Tiny, now, Tiny," said Celia, "why do you do such a foolish thing?" But she was crying too.

"Then why are you crying, Celia?"

"Since I thought of Uncle going alone to the old, dark, cold church," said Celia, "I have had a feeling of disturbance."

"One must continue to look on the bright side of things," said Tiny.

As he spoke they heard the church bell tolling.

"It is tolling for the dead," said Celia.

She went and stood in the middle of the room with her fingers in her ears. Her white cotton nightdress flapped round her legs in the wind that blew in from the open window.

"Be sure Augustus will not come," she said. She stood quite still in a dull and violent stare. "Do you not remember," she said, "what Augustus did to Brendan Harper the poet?"

"No," said Tiny, cheering up a bit. "What was that?"

"If you do not remember, then I shall not tell you. All *that*," said Celia, "belongs to the dead past."

"To the *living* past," said Tiny, rather to himself.

"Augustus is an abject character," cried Celia, her voice rising to a high-pitched scream that quite drowned the wireless coming from Yarrow, where Cas sat sulking. "Do you suppose for a moment that our uncle would have such a person to darken the threshold?"

"Well, it is already rather dark," said Tiny. "I say, Cas has got the radio on, I do think he's the limit."

He began to pound on the wall.

"Starp that pounding!" yelled Cas.

"How vulgar he is," Tiny sniffed in a superior manner. "Well, so long, Celia, I'll be off."

The next morning, after a broken night, they assembled early for breakfast. Tuffie, who had spent her evening at the pictures, brought in a large jorum of porridge and set it in front of Heber, who was looking rather severe in a shiny black suit and a pair of black wool mittens. The three visitors lolled in their chairs waiting for the porridge to be served.

Heber looked severely at Celia. "Instead of lolling forever with your cousins in a negative mood, you should strive to improve. Do you all want to be sent back to school?" he inquired.

"Oh no, Uncle – oh no; oh, *rather* not!"

"Oh, Uncle," said Celia, "I will *try*."

Heber gave them an equivocal look and rapped the table with a small silver crucifix. "You will please stand," he said. And then he said, "For what we are about to receive."

Cas intoned "Et cetera" on a bell-like note, and they all sat down.

"What did you see last night, Tuffie?" inquired Celia politely.

"It was a lovely piece, duck," said Tuffie; "it was called Kingdom Kong."

"Thy kingdom kong," said Tiny with a giggle.

Cas kicked him under the table and turned to Heber.

"Who was it that arrived so late last night, sir, and was bedded down not without disturbance?"

Heber, who at Tiny's words had turned quite pale, spoke in a reedlike whisper.

"Sir Sefton Choate," he said, "has honoured us by an unexpected visit."

"My word!" said Tiny. "Not old Sefton? Well, I never!"

"Shut *up*, Tiny!" said Cas.

"You are so frivolous, Tiny," Celia sighed. "It is something one does not care to think about."

"Will he be making a long stay, sir, and where have you put him?"

"To the first part of the question, I do not know," said Heber in his ghostly voice. "To the second part, in Doom."

"Good heavens!" said Tiny, his mouth full of porridge. "Not in Doom?"

"And why not in Doom, pray?" said Heber. "Is not Doom our best bedroom, and does it not look out upon the cemetery?"

"It may be the best bedroom," said Tiny, with a wink at Celia, "and it may look out upon the cemetery, but the bed is pretty well untakable, sir, since Celia broke the springs last hols."

"Shut up, Tiny!" said Cas, but they all began to giggle furiously, stuffing their handkerchiefs into their mouths.

"Poor old chap," said Tiny, who was purple in the face by this time. "He won't get a wink."

"Not a wink, not a wink, not a tiddly-widdly wink," sang Celia, beating time with her porridge spoon.

They all joined in.

Celia said, "Mark my words, *he'll be up all night.*"

Heber rose to his feet like a lion in anger.

"It is Sunday today," he said, "you must all go to church."

"I make it Thursday," said Tiny. "What do you make it, Celia?"

Celia answered in German, with a strong North German accent, finishing up with her aggravating laugh: "*Bei mir ist's Montag um halb sechs.*"

"No, no," said Tiny, "it is Thursday." He smiled in an infatuated manner upon Celia and pointed to the lake that could just be seen from the kitchen window where they had set the table, "*C'est le lac de jeudi,*" he said, "for, you see, it is Thursday today."

Cas, who was getting rather restless, said, "Heads Sunday, tails Thursday." The coin came down heads.

"So long, Uncle," they said.

When they got to the church the service was already over, so they turned back along the grass path bordered with poplar trees. The weather had cleared again and it was hot and fine.

"I am afraid we shall not be able to get our church stamps for attendance," said Celia.

"I'm sorry about that," said Tiny.

"I thought our uncle's sermon was extremely to the point," said Cas.

"Quite affecting," said Celia.

"I always think that is one of his best sermons," said Tiny with a generous smile.

"I enjoyed the hymns so much," said Celia.

"I thought Mr Sparrow's voluntary on the harp was in excellent taste," said Cas. "Was I right in detecting a slight flaw in one of the strings?"

The white butterflies flew round their heads in the hot sunshine and the tall flowers, red, white and blue, waved against their shoulders as they walked along.

"Marguerites, cornflowers, poppies," drawled Celia, pressing the stalks in her hands.

"Don't pick the flowers, Celia," said Cas. "Do you wish to raise the devil?"

"How tall they grow," said Celia.

"Very fine," said Cas, with his eye still upon her.

"They would make a nice bouquet for the lunch-table," said Celia.

"Don't pick the flowers," said Cas and Tiny together, edging nearer to their cousin.

Celia now looked down at her clothes and found that she was dressed in a pink-and-white-striped sailor suit, white socks and black strapped pumps. She took off her hat to look at it and to ease the discomfort where the elastic was biting into her chin. It was a large floppy leghorn hat trimmed with cornflowers and daisies and a white satin bow.

"Do you realize, boys, that you are both wearing Eton suits?" she said, and took them by the hand.

"Why, look," said Tiny, as they came up the drive to the rectory, "there is old Sir Sefton standing in the doorway with our uncle."

"Howdedo, little girl?" said Sefton, pressing a bar of Fry's chocolate cream into Celia's hand. "We've put the hare in the fridge," he added in a confidential aside.

Celia shook hands with Sir Sefton, and gave a little nick of a curtsy.

"Celia has recently returned from her school in Potsdam," explained Cas, who was rather embarrassed by the curtsy.

"She has become quite Prussian," said Tiny.

Cas trod on his toe. "Shut up, Tiny," he said.

"Well, well, well, very nice, I'm sure," said Sir Sefton, who had not quite taken it in. He gave a large coloured ball to Tiny.

"I bought a model motor-car for you, my lad," he said, turning to Cas, "but it has not come yet."

"Oh, hurrah," said Cas. "Oh, thank you so much, sir."

"Are they going back to school after the holidays?" Sir Sefton inquired of Heber.

"Well," said Heber, "*that depends.*"

Cas and Tiny and Celia sat in the long, cool nursery.

"That depends . . ." said Tiny, with a rather fearful look at Celia. "Oh, Celia, I do hope we do not have to go back to school."

"Not likely," said Cas; "nothing more to learn."

"Cas is awfully smug," said Celia, putting her arms round Tiny, who was beginning to cry. "Cheer up, Tiny, you won't have Augustus, anyway."

"I was flogged twice through Homer at Eton," said Cas, with an ineffable smug smile.

Celia began to print a sentence in coloured chalks in her copy-book, there was a different chalk for each letter. Cas looked over her shoulder and read out what she had written: "Is there a life beyond the gravy?"

"It's an 'e'," he said, "not a 'y'."

At this moment there was a black shadow across the open window and a large, dark, fat boy fell into the room. He picked himself up and swaggered over to where Tiny was crouching beside Celia.

"I couldn't make anyone hear," he said.

Then he looked round the room with a sneering expression. "Crumbs," he said, "what a place, and what smudgy beasts you look! Why, Celia, the ink is all over your dress. There's no life here," he said; "you people simply don't know you're alive."

It was Augustus.

Cas came over to him and stood threatening him with the heavy ruler he had snatched from Celia's desk.

"*You* don't know you're dead," he said.

"It's better to know you're dead," said Tiny.

"Oh, much better," said Cas.

"There's no room here for anyone who doesn't know he's dead," said Celia.

They took hands and closed round Augustus, driving him back towards the window. He climbed on to the window-sill.

"We're all dead," cried the three children in a loud, shrill chorus that rose like the wail of a siren. "We're all dead, we've been dead *for ages*."

Tiny rushed forward, breaking hands with the others, and gave Augustus a great shove that sent him backwards out of the dark shadowed window.

"We rather like it," he said, as Augustus disappeared from view.

MARS IS HEAVEN

Ray Bradbury

Ray Bradbury (1920–2012) incorporated his childhood home of Waukegan, Illinois into some of his short stories and novels, where it symbolised a place of safety. He grew up during the depression, and was too poor to go to college, so educated himself via libraries. Bradbury's writing often contains a keen sense of social awareness. His best known novel, *Fahrenheit 451*, a dystopian depiction of a society where books are outlawed, can be interpreted as an allegory about McCarthyism.

The ship came down from space. It came from the stars and the black velocities, and the shining movements, and the silent gulfs of space. It was a new ship; it had fire in its body and men in its metal cells, and it moved with a clean silence, fiery and warm. In it were seventeen men, including a captain. The crowd at the Ohio field had shouted and waved their hands up into the sunlight, and the rocket had bloomed out great flowers of heat and color and run away into space on the *third* voyage to Mars!

Now it was decelerating with metal efficiency in the upper Martian atmospheres. It was still a thing of beauty and strength. It had moved in the midnight waters of space like a pale sea leviathan; it had passed the ancient Moon and thrown itself onward into one nothingness following another. The men within it had been battered, thrown about, sickened, made well again, each in his turn. One man had died, but now the remaining sixteen, with their eyes clear in their heads and their faces pressed to the thick glass ports, watched Mars swing up under them.

"Mars!" cried Navigator Lustig.

"Good old Mars!" said Samuel Hinkston, archaeologist.

"Well," said Captain John Black.

The rocket landed on a lawn of green grass. Outside, upon this lawn, stood an iron deer. Further up on the green stood a tall brown Victorian house, quiet in the sunlight, all covered with scrolls and rococo, its windows made of blue and pink and yellow and green colored glass. Upon the porch were hairy geraniums and an old swing which was hooked into the porch ceiling and which now swung back and forth, back and forth, in a little breeze. At the summit of the house was a cupola with diamond leaded-glass windows and a dunce-cap roof! Through the front window you could see a piece of music titled "Beautiful Ohio" sitting on the music rest.

Around the rocket in four directions spread the little town, green and motionless in the Martian spring. There were white houses and red brick ones, and tall elm trees blowing in the wind, and tall maples and horse chestnuts. And church steeples with golden bells silent in them.

The rocket men looked out and saw this. Then they looked at one another and then they looked out again. They held to each other's elbows, suddenly unable to breathe, it seemed. Their faces grew pale.

"I'll be damned," whispered Lustig, rubbing his face with his numb fingers. "I'll be damned."

"It just can't be," said Samuel Hinkston.

"Lord," said Captain John Black.

There was a call from the chemist. "Sir, the atmosphere is thin for breathing. But there's enough oxygen. It's safe."

"Then we'll go out," said Lustig.

"Hold on," said Captain John Black. "How do we know what this is?"

"It's a small town with thin but breathable air in it, sir."

"And it's a small town the like of Earth towns," said Hinkston, the archaeologist. "Incredible. It can't be, but it *is*."

Captain John Black looked at him idly. "Do you think that the civilizations of two planets can progress at the same rate and evolve in the same way, Hinkston?"

"I wouldn't have thought so, sir."

Captain Black stood by the port. "Look out there. The geraniums. A specialized plant. That specific variety has only been known on Earth for fifty years. Think of the thousands of years it takes to evolve plants. Then tell me if it is logical that the Martians should have: one, leaded-glass windows; two, cupolas; three, porch swings; four, an instrument that looks like a piano and probably *is* a piano; and five, if you look closely through this telescopic lens here, is it logical that a Martian composer would have published a piece of music titled, strangely enough, 'Beautiful Ohio'? All of which means that we have an Ohio River on Mars!"

"Captain Williams, of course!" cried Hinkston.

"What?"

"Captain Williams and his crew of three men! Or Nathaniel York and his partner. That would explain it!"

"That would explain absolutely nothing. As far as we've been able to figure, the York expedition exploded the day it reached Mars, killing York and his partner. As for Williams and his three men, their ship exploded the second day after their arrival. At least the pulsations from their radios ceased at that time, so we figure that if the men were alive after that they'd have contacted us. And anyway, the York expedition was only a year ago, while Captain Williams and his men landed here some time during last August. Theorizing that they are still alive, could they, even with the help of a brilliant Martian race, have built such a town as this and *aged* it in so short a time? Look at that town out there; why, it's been standing here for the last seventy years. Look at the wood on the porch newel; look at the trees, a century old, all of them! No, this isn't York's work or Williams'. It's something else. I don't like it. And I'm not leaving the ship until I know what it is."

"For that matter," said Lustig, nodding, "Williams and his men, as well as York, landed on the *opposite* side of Mars. We were very careful to land on *this* side."

"An excellent point. Just in case a hostile local tribe of Martians killed off York and Williams, we have instructions to land in a further region, to forestall a recurrence of such a disaster. So here we are, as far as we know, in a land that Williams and York never saw."

"Damn it," said Hinkston, "I want to get out into this town, sir, with your permission. It may be there *are* similar thought patterns, civilization graphs on every planet in our sun system. We may be on the threshold of the greatest psychological and metaphysical discovery of our age!"

"I'm willing to wait a moment," said Captain John Black.

"It may be, sir, that we're looking upon a phenomenon that, for the first time, would absolutely prove the existence of God, sir."

"There are many people who are of good faith without such proof, Mr. Hinkston."

"I'm one myself, sir. But certainly a town like this could not occur without divine intervention. The *detail*. It fills me with such feelings that I don't know whether to laugh or cry."

"Do neither, then, until we know what we're up against."

"Up against?" Lustig broke in. "Against nothing, Captain. It's a good, quiet green town, a lot like the old-fashioned one I was born in. I like the looks of it."

"When were you born, Lustig?"

"Nineteen fifty, sir."

"And you, Hinkston?"

"Nineteen fifty-five, sir. Grinnell, Iowa. And this looks like home to me."

"Hinkston, Lustig, I could be either of your fathers. I'm just eighty years old. Born in 1920 in Illinois, and through the grace of God and a science that, in the last fifty years, knows how to make *some* old men young again, here I am on Mars, not any more tired than the rest of you, but infinitely more suspicious. This town out here looks very peaceful and cool, and so much like Green Bluff, Illinois, that it frightens me. It's too *much* like Green Bluff." He turned to the radioman. "Radio Earth. Tell them we've landed. That's all. Tell them we'll radio a full report tomorrow."

"Yes, sir."

Captain Black looked out the rocket port with his face that should have been the face of a man eighty but seemed like the face of a man in his fortieth year. "Tell you what we'll do, Lustig; you and I and Hinkston'll look the town over. The other men'll stay aboard. If anything happens they can get the hell out. A loss of three men's better than a whole ship. If something bad happens, our crew can warn the next rocket. That's Captain Wilder's rocket, I think, due to be ready to take off next Christmas. If there's something hostile about Mars we certainly want the next rocket to be well armed."

"So are we. We've got a regular arsenal with us."

"Tell the men to stand by the guns then. Come on, Lustig, Hinkston."

The three men walked together down through the levels of the ship.

It was a beautiful spring day. A robin sat on a blossoming apple tree and sang continuously. Showers of petal snow sifted down when the wind touched the green branches, and the blossom scent drifted upon the air. Somewhere in the town someone was playing the piano and the music came and went, came and went, softly, drowsily. The song was "Beautiful Dreamer." Somewhere else a phonograph, scratchy and faded, was hissing out a record of "Roamin' in the Gloamin'," sung by Harry Lauder.

The three men stood outside the ship. They sucked and gasped at the thin, thin air and moved slowly so as not to tire themselves.

Now the phonograph record being played was:

Oh, give me a June night
The moonlight and you . . .

Lustig began to tremble. Samuel Hinkston did likewise.

The sky was serene and quiet, and somewhere a stream of water ran through the cool caverns and tree shadings of a ravine. Somewhere a horse and wagon trotted and rolled by, bumping.

"Sir," said Samuel Hinkston, "it must be, it *has* to be, that rocket travel to Mars began in the years before the First World War!"

"No."

"How else can you explain these houses, the iron deer, the pianos, the music?" Hinkston took the captain's elbow persuasively and looked into the captain's face. "Say that there were people in the year 1905 who hated war and got together with some scientists in secret and built a rocket and came out here to Mars –"

"No, no, Hinkston."

"Why not? The world was a different world in 1905; they could have kept it a secret much more easily."

"But a complex thing like a rocket, no, you couldn't keep it secret."

"And they came up here to live, and naturally the houses they built were similar to Earth houses because they brought the culture with them."

"And they've lived here all these years?" said the captain.

"In peace and quiet, yes. Maybe they made a few trips, enough to bring enough people here for one small town, and then stopped for fear of being discovered. That's why this town seems so old-fashioned. I don't see a thing, myself, older than the year 1927, do you? Or maybe, sir, rocket travel is older than we think. Perhaps it started in some part of the world centuries ago and was kept secret by the small number of men who came to Mars with only occasional visits to Earth over the centuries."

"You make it sound almost reasonable."

"It has to be. We've the proof here before us; all we have to do is find some people and verify it."

Their boots were deadened of all sound in the thick green grass. It smelled from a fresh mowing. In spite of himself, Captain John Black felt a great peace come over him. It had been thirty years since he had been in a small town, and the buzzing of spring bees on the air lulled and quieted him, and the fresh look of things was a balm to the soul.

They set foot upon the porch. Hollow echoes sounded from under the boards as they walked to the screen door. Inside they could see a bead curtain hung across the hall entry, and a crystal chandelier and a Maxfield Parrish painting framed on one wall over a comfortable Morris chair. The house smelled old, and of the attic, and infinitely comfortable. You could hear the tinkle of ice in a lemonade pitcher. In a distant kitchen, because of the heat of the day, someone was preparing a cold lunch. Someone was humming under her breath, high and sweet.

Captain John Black rang the bell.

Footsteps, dainty and thin, came along the hall, and a kind-faced lady of some forty years, dressed in the sort of dress you might expect in the year 1909, peered out at them.

"Can I help you?" she asked.

"Beg your pardon," said Captain Black uncertainly. "But we're looking for – that is, could you help us –" He stopped. She looked out at him with dark, wondering eyes.

"If you're selling something –" she began.

"No, wait!" he cried. "What town is this?"

She looked him up and down. "What do you mean, what town is it? How could you be in a town and not know the name?"

The captain looked as if he wanted to go sit under a shady apple tree. "We're strangers here. We want to know how this town got here and how you got here."

"Are you census takers?"

"No."

"Everyone knows," she said, "this town was built in 1868. Is this a game?"

"No, not a game!" cried the captain. "We're from Earth."

"Out of the *ground*, do you mean?" she wondered.

"No, we came from the third planet, Earth, in a ship. And we've landed here on the fourth planet, Mars –"

"This," explained the woman, as if she were addressing a child, "is Green Bluff, Illinois, on the continent of America, surrounded by the Atlantic and Pacific oceans, on a place called the world, or, sometimes, the Earth. Go away now. Good-by."

She trotted down the hall, running her fingers through the beaded curtains.

The three men looked at one another.

"Let's knock the screen door in," said Lustig.

"We can't do that. This is private property. Good God!"

They went to sit down on the porch step.

"Did it ever strike you, Hinkston, that perhaps we got ourselves somehow, in some way, off track, and by accident came back and landed on Earth?"

"How could we have done that?"

"I don't know, I don't know. Oh God, let me think."

Hinkston said, "But we checked every mile of the way. Our chronometers said so many miles. We went past the Moon and out into space, and here we are. I'm *positive* we're on Mars."

Lustig said, "But suppose, by accident, in space, in time, we got lost in the dimensions and landed on an Earth that is thirty or forty years ago."

"Oh, go away, Lustig!"

Lustig went to the door, rang the bell, and called into the cool dim rooms: "What year is this?"

"Nineteen twenty-six, of course," said the lady, sitting in a rocking chair, taking a sip of her lemonade.

"Did you hear that?" Lustig turned wildly to the others. "Nineteen twenty-six! We *have* gone back in time! This *is* Earth!"

Lustig sat down, and the three men let the wonder and terror of the thought afflict them. Their hands stirred fitfully on their knees. The captain said, "I didn't ask for a thing like this. It scares the hell out of me. How can a thing like this happen? I wish we'd brought Einstein with us."

"Will anyone in this town believe us?" said Hinkston. "Are we playing with something dangerous? Time, I mean. Shouldn't we just take off and go home?"

"No. Not until we try another house."

They walked three houses down to a little white cottage under an oak tree. "I like to be as logical as I can be," said the captain. "And I don't believe we've put our finger on it yet. Suppose, Hinkston, as you originally suggested, that rocket travel occurred years ago? And when the Earth people lived here a number of years they began to get homesick for Earth. First a mild neurosis about it, then a full-fledged psychosis. Then threatened insanity. What would you do as a psychiatrist if faced with such a problem?"

Hinkston thought. "Well, I think I'd rearrange the civilization on Mars so it resembled Earth more and more each day. If there was any way of reproducing every plant, every road, and every lake, and even an ocean, I'd do so. Then by some vast crowd hypnosis I'd convince everyone in a town this size that this really *was* Earth, not Mars at all."

"Good enough, Hinkston. I think we're on the right track now. That woman in that house back there just *thinks* she's living on Earth. It protects her sanity. She and all the others in this town are the patients of the greatest experiment in migration and hypnosis you will ever lay eyes on in your life."

"That's *it,* sir!" cried Lustig.

"Right!" said Hinkston.

"Well." The captain sighed. "Now we've got somewhere. I feel better. It's all a bit more logical. That talk about time and going back and forth and traveling through time turns my stomach upside down. But *this* way –" The captain smiled. "Well, well, it looks as if we'll be fairly popular here."

"Or will we?" said Lustig. "After all, like the Pilgrims, these people came here to escape Earth. Maybe they won't be too happy to see us. Maybe they'll try to drive us out or kill us."

"We have superior weapons. This next house now. Up we go."

But they had hardly crossed the lawn when Lustig stopped and looked off across the town, down the quiet, dreaming afternoon street. "Sir," he said.

"What is it, Lustig?"

"Oh, sir, *sir,* what I *see* –" said Lustig, and he began to cry. His fingers came up, twisting and shaking, and his face was all wonder and joy and incredulity. He sounded as if at any moment he might go quite insane with happiness. He looked down the street and began to run, stumbling awkwardly, falling, picking himself up, and running on. "Look, look!"

"Don't let him get away!" The captain broke into a run.

Now Lustig was running swiftly, shouting. He turned into a yard halfway down the shady street and leaped up upon the porch of a large green house with an iron rooster on the roof.

He was beating at the door, hollering and crying, when Hinkston and the captain ran up behind him. They were all gasping and wheezing, exhausted from their run in the thin air. "Grandma! Grandpa!" cried Lustig.

Two old people stood in the doorway.

"David!" their voices piped, and they rushed out to embrace and pat him on the back and move around him. "David, oh, David, it's been so many years! How you've grown, boy; how big you are, boy. Oh, David boy, how are you?"

"Grandma, Grandpa!" sobbed David Lustig. "You look fine, fine!" He held them, turned them, kissed them, hugged them, cried on them, held them out again, blinking at the little old people. The sun was in the sky, the wind blew, the grass was green, the screen door stood wide.

"Come in, boy, come in. There's iced tea for you, fresh, lots of it!"

"I've got friends here." Lustig turned and waved at the captain and Hinkston frantically, laughing. "Captain, come on up."

"Howdy," said the old people. "Come in. Any friends of David's are our friends too. Don't stand there!"

In the living room of the old house it was cool, and a grandfather clock ticked high and long and bronzed in one corner. There were soft pillows on large couches and walls filled with books and a rug cut in a thick rose pattern, and iced tea in the hand, sweating, and cool on the thirsty tongue.

"Here's to our health." Grandma tipped her glass to her porcelain teeth.

"How long you been here, Grandma?" said Lustig.

"Ever since we died," she said tartly.

"Ever since you what?" Captain John Black set down his glass.

"Oh yes." Lustig nodded. "They've been dead thirty years."

"And you sit there calmly!" shouted the captain.

"Tush." The old woman winked glitteringly. "Who are you to question what happens? Here we are. What's life, anyway? Who does what for why and where? All we know is here we are, alive again, and no questions asked. A second chance." She toddled over and held out her thin wrist. "Feel." The captain felt. "Solid, ain't it?" she asked. He nodded. "Well, then," she said triumphantly, "why go around questioning?"

"Well," said the captain, "it's simply that we never thought we'd find a thing like this on Mars."

"And now you've found it. I dare say there's lots on every planet that'll show you God's infinite ways."

"Is this Heaven?" asked Hinkston.

"Nonsense, no. It's a world and we get a second chance. Nobody told us why. But then nobody told us why we were on Earth, either. That other Earth, I mean. The one you came from. How do we know there wasn't *another* before *that* one?"

"A good question," said the captain.

Lustig kept smiling at his grandparents. "Gosh, it's good to see you. Gosh, it's good."

The captain stood up and slapped his hand on his leg in a casual fashion. "We've got to be going. Thank you for the drinks."

"You'll be back, of course," said the old people. "For supper tonight?"

"We'll try to make it, thanks. There's so much to be done. My men are waiting for me back at the rocket and –"

He stopped. He looked toward the door, startled.

Far away in the sunlight there was a sound of voices, a shouting and a great hello.

"What's that?" asked Hinkston.

"We'll soon find out." And Captain John Black was out the front door abruptly, running across the green lawn into the street of the Martian town.

He stood looking at the rocket. The ports were open and his crew was streaming out, waving their hands. A crowd of people had gathered, and in and through and among these people the members of the crew were hurrying, talking, laughing, shaking hands. People did little dances. People swarmed. The rocket lay empty and abandoned.

A brass band exploded in the sunlight, flinging off a gay tune from upraised tubas and trumpets. There was a bang of drums and a shrill of fifes. Little girls with golden hair jumped up and down. Little boys shouted, "Hooray!" Fat men passed around ten-cent cigars. The town mayor made a speech. Then each member of the crew, with a mother on one arm, a father or sister on the other, was spirited off down the street into little cottages or big mansions.

"Stop!" cried Captain Black.

The doors slammed shut.

The heat rose in the clear spring sky, and all was silent. The brass band banged off around a corner, leaving the rocket to shine and dazzle alone in the sunlight.

"Abandoned!" said the captain. "They abandoned the ship, they did! I'll have their skins, by God! They had orders!"

"Sir," said Lustig, "don't be too hard on them. Those were all old relatives and friends."

"That's no excuse!"

"Think how they felt, Captain, seeing familiar faces outside the ship!"

"They had their orders, damn it!"

"But how would you have felt, Captain?"

"I would have obeyed orders –" The captain's mouth remained open.

Striding along the sidewalk under the Martian sun, tall, smiling, eyes amazingly clear and blue, came a young man of some twenty-six years. "John!" the man called out, and broke into a trot.

"What?" Captain John Black swayed.

"John, you old son of a bitch!"

The man ran up and gripped his hand and slapped him on the back.

"It's you," said Captain Black.

"Of course, who'd you *think* it was?"

"Edward!" The captain appealed now to Lustig and Hinkston, holding the stranger's hand. "This is my brother Edward. Ed, meet my men, Lustig, Hinkston! My brother!"

They tugged at each other's hands and arms and then finally embraced. "Ed!" "John, you bum, you!" "You're looking fine, Ed, but, Ed, what *is* this? You haven't changed over the years. You died, I remember, when you were twenty-six and I was nineteen. Good God, so many years ago, and here you are and, Lord, what goes on?"

"Mom's waiting," said Edward Black, grinning.

"Mom?"

"And Dad too."

"Dad?" The captain almost fell as if he had been hit by a mighty weapon. He walked stiffly and without co-ordination. "Mom and Dad alive? Where?"

"At the old house on Oak Knoll Avenue."

"The old house." The captain stared in delighted amaze. "Did you hear that, Lustig, Hinkston?"

Hinkston was gone. He had seen his own house down the street and was running for it. Lustig was laughing. "You see, Captain, what happened to everyone on the rocket? They couldn't help themselves."

"Yes. Yes." The captain shut his eyes. "When I open my eyes you'll be gone." He blinked. "You're still there. God, Ed, but you look *fine*!"

"Come on, lunch's waiting. I told Mom."

Lustig said, "Sir, I'll be with my grandfolks if you need me."

"What? Oh, fine, Lustig. Later, then."

Edward seized his arm and marched him. "There's the house. Remember it?"

"Hell! Bet I can beat you to the front porch!"

They ran. The trees roared over Captain Black's head; the earth roared under his feet. He saw the golden figure of Edward Black pull ahead of him in the amazing dream of reality. He saw the house rush forward, the screen door swing wide. "Beat you!" cried Edward. "I'm an old man," panted the captain, "and you're still young. But then, you *always* beat me, I remember!"

In the doorway, Mom, pink, plump, and bright. Behind her, pepper-gray, Dad, his pipe in his hand.

"Mom, Dad!"

He ran up the steps like a child to meet them.

It was a fine long afternoon. They finished a late lunch and they sat in the parlor and he told them all about his rocket and they nodded and smiled upon him and Mother was just the same and Dad bit the end off a cigar and lighted it thoughtfully in his old fashion. There was a big turkey dinner at night and time flowing on. When the drumsticks were sucked clean and lay brittle upon the plates, the captain leaned back and exhaled his deep satisfaction. Night was in all the trees and coloring the sky, and the lamps were halos of pink light in the gentle house. From all the other houses down the street came sounds of music, pianos playing, doors slamming.

Mom put a record on the Victrola, and she and Captain John Black had a dance. She was wearing the same perfume he remembered from the summer when she and Dad had been killed in the train accident. She was very real in his arms as they danced lightly to the music. "It's not every day," she said, "you get a second chance to live."

"I'll wake in the morning," said the captain. "And I'll be in my rocket, in space, and all this will be gone."

"No, don't think that," she cried softly. "Don't question. God's good to us. Let's be happy."

"Sorry, Mom."

The record ended in a circular hissing.

"You're tired, Son." Dad pointed with his pipe. "Your old bedroom's waiting for you, brass bed and all."

"But I should report my men in."

"Why?"

"Why? Well, I don't know. No reason, I guess. No, none at all. They're all eating or in bed. A good night's sleep won't hurt them."

"Good night, Son." Mom kissed his cheek. "It's good to have you home."

"It's good to *be* home."

He left the land of cigar smoke and perfume and books and gentle light and ascended the stairs, talking, talking with Edward. Edward pushed a door open, and there was the yellow brass bed and the old semaphore banners from college and a very musty raccoon coat which he stroked with muted affection. "It's too much," said the captain. "I'm numb and I'm tired. Too much has happened today. I feel as if I'd been out in a pounding rain for forty-eight hours without an umbrella or a coat. I'm soaked to the skin with emotion."

Edward slapped wide the snowy linens and flounced the pillows. He slid the window up and let the night-blooming jasmine float in. There was moonlight and the sound of distant dancing and whispering.

"So this is Mars," said the captain, undressing.

"This is it." Edward undressed in idle, leisurely moves, drawing his shirt off over his head, revealing golden shoulders and the good muscular neck.

The lights were out; they were in bed, side by side, as in the days how many decades ago? The captain lolled and was nourished by the scent of jasmine pushing the lace curtains in upon the dark air of the room. Among the trees, upon a lawn, someone had cranked up a portable phonograph and now it was playing softly, "Always."

The thought of Marilyn came to his mind.

"Is Marilyn here?"

His brother, lying straight out in the moonlight from the window, waited and then said, "Yes. She's out of town. But she'll be here in the morning."

The captain shut his eyes. "I want to see Marilyn very much."

The room was square and quiet except for their breathing.

"Good night, Ed."

A pause. "Good night, John."

He lay peacefully, letting his thoughts float. For the first time the stress of the day was moved aside; he could think logically now. It had all been emotion. The bands playing, the familiar faces. But now . . .

How? he wondered. How was all this made? And why? For what purpose? Out of the goodness of some divine intervention? Was God, then, really that thoughtful of his children? How and why and what for?

He considered the various theories advanced in the first heat of the afternoon by Hinkston and Lustig. He let all kinds of new theories drop in lazy pebbles down through his mind, turning, throwing out dull flashes of light. Mom. Dad. Edward. Mars. Earth. Mars. Martians.

Who had lived here a thousand years ago on Mars? Martians? Or had this always been the way it was today?

Martians. He repeated the word idly, inwardly.

He laughed out loud almost. He had the most ridiculous theory quite suddenly. It gave him a kind of chill. It was really nothing to consider, of course. Highly improbable. Silly. Forget it. Ridiculous.

But, he thought, just *suppose* . . . Just suppose, now, that there were Martians living on Mars and they saw our ship coming and saw us inside our ship and hated us. Suppose, now, just for the hell of it, that they wanted to destroy us, as invaders, as unwanted ones, and they wanted to do it in a very clever way, so that we would be taken off guard. Well, what would the best weapon be that a Martian could use against Earth Men with atomic weapons?

The answer was interesting. Telepathy, hypnosis, memory, and imagination.

Suppose all of these houses aren't real at all, this bed not real, but only figments of my own imagination, given substance by telepathy and hypnosis through the Martians, thought Captain John Black. Suppose these houses are really some *other* shape, a Martian shape, but, by playing on my desires and wants, these Martians have made this seem like my old home town, my old house, to lull me out of my suspicions. What better way to fool a man, using his own mother and father as bait?

And this town, so old, from the year 1926, long before *any* of my men were born. From a year when I was six years old and there *were* records of Harry Lauder, and Maxfield Parrish paintings *still* hanging, and bead curtains, and "Beautiful Ohio," and turn-of-the-century architecture. What if the Martians took the memories of a town *exclusively* from *my* mind? They say childhood memories are the clearest. And after they built the town from *my* mind, they populated it with the most-loved people from all the minds of the people on the rocket!

And suppose those two people in the next room, asleep, are not my mother and father at all. But two Martians, incredibly brilliant, with the ability to keep me under this dreaming hypnosis all of the time.

And that brass band today? What a startlingly wonderful plan it would be. First, fool Lustig, then Hinkston, then gather a crowd; and all the men in the rocket, seeing mothers, aunts, uncles, sweethearts, dead ten, twenty years ago, naturally, disregarding orders, rush out and abandon ship. What more natural? What more unsuspecting? What more simple? A man doesn't ask too many questions when his mother is suddenly brought back to life; he's much too happy. And here we all are tonight, in various houses, in various beds, with no weapons to protect us, and the rocket lies in the moonlight, empty. And wouldn't it be horrible and terrifying to discover that all of this was part of some great clever plan by the Martians to divide and conquer us, and kill us? Sometime during the night, perhaps, my brother here on this bed will change form, melt, shift, and become another thing, a terrible thing, a Martian. It would be very simple for him just to turn over in bed and put a knife into my heart. And in all those other houses down the street, a dozen other brothers or fathers suddenly melting away and taking knives and doing things to the unsuspecting, sleeping men of Earth. . . .

His hands were shaking under the covers. His body was cold. Suddenly it was not a theory. Suddenly he was very afraid.

He lifted himself in bed and listened. The night was very quiet. The music had stopped. The wind had died. His brother lay sleeping beside him.

Carefully he lifted the covers, rolled them back. He slipped from bed and was walking softly across the room when his brother's voice said, "Where are you going?"

"What?"

His brother's voice was quite cold. "I said, where do you think you're going?"

"For a drink of water."

"But you're not thirsty."

"Yes, yes, I am."

"No, you're not."

Captain John Black broke and ran across the room. He screamed. He screamed twice.

He never reached the door.

In the morning the brass band played a mournful dirge. From every house in the street came little solemn processions bearing long boxes, and along the sun-filled street, weeping, came the grandmas and mothers and sisters and brothers and uncles and fathers, walking to the churchyard, where there were new holes freshly dug and new tombstones installed. Sixteen holes in all, and sixteen tombstones.

The mayor made a little sad speech, his face sometimes looking like the mayor, sometimes looking like something else.

Mother and Father Black were there, with Brother Edward, and they cried, their faces melting now from a familiar face into something else.

Grandpa and Grandma Lustig were there, weeping, their faces shifting like wax, shimmering as all things shimmer on a hot day.

The coffins were lowered. Someone murmured about "the unexpected and sudden deaths of sixteen fine men during the night –"

Earth pounded down on the coffin lids.

The brass band, playing "Columbia, the Gem of the Ocean," marched and slammed back into town, and everyone took the day off.

THE TOOTH

Shirley Jackson

Shirley Jackson (1916–1965) was born into a prosperous family in San Francisco. From an early age she felt herself at odds with her parents' bourgeois values. Jackson's mistrust of American society persisted. She wrote against bigotry and racism and her work often explores what lies beneath the surface. Jackson is best known for her short story, *The Lottery*, and the novel, *The Haunting of Hill House*. She was married to the literary critic, Stanley Edgar Hyman, a professor at Bennington College, Vermont.

The bus was waiting, panting heavily at the curb in front of the small bus station, its great blue-and-silver bulk glittering in the moonlight. There were only a few people interested in the bus, and at that time of night no one passing on the sidewalk: the one movie theatre in town had finished its show and closed its doors an hour before, and all the movie patrons had been to the drugstore for ice cream and gone on home; now the drugstore was closed and dark, another silent doorway in the long midnight street. The only town lights were the street lights, the lights in the all-night lunchstand across the street, and the one remaining counter lamp in the bus station where the girl sat in the ticket office with her hat and coat on, only waiting for the New York bus to leave before she went home to bed.

Standing on the sidewalk next to the open door of the bus, Clara Spencer held her husband's arm nervously. "I feel so funny," she said.

"Are you all right?" he asked. "Do you think I ought to go with you?"

"No, of course not," she said. "I'll be all right." It was hard for her to talk because of her swollen jaw; she kept a handkerchief pressed to her face and held hard to her husband. "Are you sure *you'll* be all right?" she asked. "I'll be back tomorrow night at the latest. Or else I'll call."

"Everything will be fine," he said heartily. "By tomorrow noon it'll all be gone. Tell the dentist if there's anything wrong I can come right down."

"I feel so funny," she said. "Light-headed, and sort of dizzy."

"That's because of the dope," he said. "All that codeine, and the whisky, and nothing to eat all day."

She giggled nervously. "I couldn't comb my hair, my hand shook so. I'm glad it's dark."

"Try to sleep in the bus," he said. "Did you take a sleeping pill?"

"Yes," she said. They were waiting for the bus driver to finish his cup of coffee in the lunchstand; they could see him through the glass window, sitting at the counter, taking his time. "I feel so *funny*," she said.

"You know, Clara," he made his voice very weighty, as though if he spoke more seriously his words would carry more conviction and be therefore more comforting, "you know, I'm glad you're going down to New York to have Zimmerman take care of this. I'd never forgive myself if it turned out to be something serious and I let you go to this butcher up here."

"It's just a *toothache*," Clara said uneasily, "nothing very serious about a *toothache*."

"You can't tell," he said. "It might be abscessed or something; I'm sure he'll have to pull it."

"Don't even talk like that," she said, and shivered.

"Well, it looks pretty bad," he said soberly, as before. "Your face so swollen, and all. Don't you worry."

"I'm not worrying," she said. "I just feel as if I were all tooth. Nothing else."

The bus driver got up from the stool and walked over to pay his check. Clara moved toward the bus, and her husband said, "Take your time, you've got plenty of time."

"I just feel funny," Clara said.

"Listen," her husband said, "that tooth's been bothering you off and on for years; at least six or seven times since I've known you you've had trouble with that tooth. It's about time something was done. You had a toothache on our honeymoon," he finished accusingly.

"Did I?" Clara said. "You know," she went on, and laughed, "I was in such a hurry I didn't dress properly. I have on old stockings and I just dumped everything into my good pocketbook."

"Are you sure you have enough money?" he said.

"Almost twenty-five dollars," Clara said. "I'll be home tomorrow."

"Wire if you need more," he said. The bus driver appeared in the doorway of the lunchroom. "Don't worry," he said.

"Listen," Clara said suddenly, "are you *sure* you'll be all right? Mrs. Lang will be over in the morning in time to make breakfast, and Johnny doesn't need to go to school if things are too mixed up."

"I know," he said.

"Mrs. Lang," she said, checking on her fingers. "I called Mrs. Lang, I left the grocery order on the kitchen table, you can have the cold tongue for lunch and in case I don't get back Mrs. Lang will give you dinner. The cleaner ought to come about four o'clock, I won't be back so give him your brown suit and it doesn't matter if you forget but be sure to empty the pockets."

"Wire if you need more money," he said. "Or call. I'll stay home tomorrow so you can call at home."

"Mrs. Lang will take care of the baby," she said.

"Or you can wire," he said.

The bus driver came across the street and stood by the entrance to the bus.

"Okay?" the bus driver said.

"Good-bye," Clara said to her husband.

"You'll feel all right tomorrow," her husband said. "It's only a toothache."

"I'm fine," Clara said. "Don't you worry." She got on the bus and then stopped, with the bus driver waiting behind her. "Milkman," she said to her husband. "Leave a note telling him we want eggs."

"I will," her husband said. "Good-bye."

"Good-bye," Clara said. She moved on into the bus and behind her the driver swung into his seat. The bus was nearly empty and she went far back and sat down at the window outside which her husband waited. "Good-bye," she said to him through the glass, "take care of yourself."

"Good-bye," he said, waving violently.

The bus stirred, groaned, and pulled itself forward. Clara turned her head to wave good-bye once more and then lay back against the heavy soft seat. Good Lord, she thought, what a thing to do! Outside, the familiar street slipped past, strange and dark and seen, unexpectedly, from the unique station of a person leaving town, going away on a bus. It isn't as though it's the first time I've ever been to New York, Clara thought indignantly, it's the whisky and the codeine and the sleeping pill and the toothache. She checked hastily to see if her codeine tablets were in her pocketbook; they had been standing, along with the aspirin and a glass of water, on the dining-room sideboard, but somewhere in the lunatic flight from her home she must have picked them up, because they were in her pocketbook now, along with the twenty-odd dollars and her compact and comb and lipstick. She could tell from the feel of the lipstick that she had brought the old, nearly finished one, not the new one that was a darker shade and had cost two-fifty. There was a run in her stocking and a hole in the toe that she never noticed at home wearing her old comfortable shoes, but which was now suddenly and disagreeably apparent inside her best walking shoes. Well, she thought, I can buy new stockings in New York tomorrow, after the tooth is fixed, after everything's all right. She put her tongue cautiously on the tooth and was rewarded with a split-second crash of pain.

The bus stopped at a red light and the driver got out of his seat and came back toward her. "Forgot to get your ticket before," he said.

"I guess I was a little rushed at the last minute," she said. She found the ticket in her coat pocket and gave it to him. "When do we get to New York?" she asked.

"Five-fifteen," he said. "Plenty of time for breakfast. One-way ticket?"

"I'm coming back by train," she said, without seeing why she had to tell him, except that it was late at night and people isolated together in some strange prison like a bus had to be more friendly and communicative than at other times.

"Me, I'm coming back by bus," he said, and they both laughed, she painfully because of her swollen face. When he went back to his seat far away at the front of the bus she lay back peacefully against the seat. She could feel the sleeping pill pulling at her; the throb of the toothache was distant now, and mingled with the movement of the bus, a steady beat like her heartbeat which she could hear louder and louder, going on through the night. She put her head back and her feet up, discreetly covered with her skirt, and fell asleep without saying good-bye to the town.

She opened her eyes once and they were moving almost silently through the darkness. Her tooth was pulsing steadily and she turned her cheek against the cool back of the seat in weary resignation. There was a thin line of lights along the ceiling of the bus and no other light. Far ahead of her in the bus she could see the other people sitting; the driver, so far away as to be only a tiny figure at the end of a telescope, was straight at the wheel, seemingly awake. She fell back into her fantastic sleep.

She woke up later because the bus had stopped, the end of that silent motion through the darkness so positive a shock that it woke her stunned, and it was a minute before the ache began again. People were moving along the aisle of the bus and the driver, turning around, said, "Fifteen minutes." She got up and followed everyone else out, all but her eyes still asleep, her feet moving without awareness. They were stopped beside an all-night restaurant, lonely and lighted on the vacant road. Inside, it was warm and busy and full of people. She saw a seat at the end of the counter and sat down, not aware that she had fallen asleep again when someone sat down next to her and touched her arm. When she looked around foggily he said, "Traveling far?"

"Yes," she said.

He was wearing a blue suit and he looked tall; she could not focus her eyes to see any more.

"You want coffee?" he asked.

She nodded and he pointed to the counter in front of her where a cup of coffee sat steaming.

"Drink it quickly," he said.

She sipped at it delicately; she may have put her face down and tasted it without lifting the cup. The strange man was talking.

"Even farther than Samarkand," he was saying, "and the waves ringing on the shore like bells."

"Okay, folks," the bus driver said, and she gulped quickly at the coffee, drank enough to get her back into the bus.

When she sat down in her seat again the strange man sat down beside her. It was so dark in the bus that the lights from the restaurant were unbearably glaring and she closed her eyes. When her eyes were shut, before she fell asleep, she was closed in alone with the toothache.

"The flutes play all night," the strange man said, "and the stars are as big as the moon and the moon is as big as a lake."

As the bus started up again they slipped back into the darkness and only the thin thread of lights along the ceiling of the bus held them together, brought the back of the bus where she sat along with the front of the bus where the driver sat and the people sitting there so far away from her. The lights tied them together and the strange man next to her was saying, "Nothing to do all day but lie under the trees."

Inside the bus, traveling on, she was nothing; she was passing the trees and the occasional sleeping houses, and she was in the bus but she was between here and there, joined tenuously to the bus driver by a thread of lights, being carried along without effort of her own.

"My name is Jim," the strange man said.

She was so deeply asleep that she stirred uneasily without knowledge, her forehead against the window, the darkness moving along beside her.

Then again that numbing shock, and, driven awake, she said, frightened, "What's happened?"

"It's all right," the strange man – Jim – said immediately. "Come along."

She followed him out of the bus, into the same restaurant, seemingly, but when she started to sit down at the same seat at the end of the counter he took her hand and led her to a table. "Go and wash your face," he said. "Come back here afterward."

She went into the ladies' room and there was a girl standing there powdering her nose. Without turning around the girl said, "Cost's a nickel. Leave the door fixed so's the next one won't have to pay."

The door was wedged so it would not close, with half a match folder in the lock. She left it the same way and went back to the table where Jim was sitting.

"What do you want?" she said, and he pointed to another cup of coffee and a sandwich. "Go ahead," he said.

While she was eating her sandwich she heard his voice, musical and soft, "And while we were sailing past the island we heard a voice calling us. . . ."

Back in the bus Jim said, "Put your head on my shoulder now, and go to sleep."

"I'm all right," she said.

"No," Jim said. "Before, your head was rattling against the window."

Once more she slept, and once more the bus stopped and she woke frightened, and Jim brought her again to a restaurant and more coffee. Her tooth came alive then, and with one hand pressing her cheek she searched through the pockets of her coat and then through her pocketbook until she found the little bottle of codeine pills and she took two while Jim watched her.

She was finishing her coffee when she heard the sound of the bus motor and she started up suddenly, hurrying, and with Jim holding her arm she fled back into the dark shelter of her seat. The bus was moving forward when she realized that she had left her bottle of codeine pills sitting on the table in the restaurant and now she was at the mercy of her tooth. For a minute she stared back at the lights of the restaurant through the bus window and then she put her head on Jim's shoulder and he was saying as she fell asleep, "The sand is so white it looks like snow, but it's hot, even at night it's hot under your feet."

Then they stopped for the last time, and Jim brought her out of the bus and they stood for a minute in New York together. A woman passing them in the station said to the man following her with suitcases, "We're just on time, it's five-fifteen."

"I'm going to the dentist," she said to Jim.

"I know," he said. "I'll watch out for you."

He went away, although she did not see him go. She thought to watch for his blue suit going through the door, but there was nothing.

I ought to have thanked him, she thought stupidly, and went slowly into the station restaurant, where she ordered coffee again. The counter man looked at her with the worn sympathy of one who has spent a long night watching people get off and on buses. "Sleepy?" he asked.

"Yes," she said.

She discovered after a while that the bus station joined Pennsylvania Terminal and she was able to get into the main waiting-room and find a seat on one of the benches by the time she fell asleep again.

Then someone shook her rudely by the shoulder and said, "What train you taking, lady, it's nearly seven." She sat up and saw her pocketbook on her lap, her feet neatly crossed, a clock glaring into her face. She said, "Thank you," and got up and walked blindly past the benches and got on to the escalator. Someone got on immediately behind her and touched her arm; she turned and it was Jim. "The grass is so green and so soft," he said, smiling, "and the water of the river is so cool."

She stared at him tiredly. When the escalator reached the top she stepped off and started to walk to the street she saw ahead. Jim came along beside her and his voice went on, "The sky is bluer than anything you've ever seen, and the songs. . . ."

She stepped quickly away from him and thought that people were looking at her as they passed. She stood on the corner waiting for the light to change and Jim came swiftly up to her and then away. "Look," he said as he passed, and he held out a handful of pearls.

Across the street there was a restaurant, just opening. She went in and sat down at a table, and a waitress was standing beside her frowning. "You was asleep," the waitress said accusingly.

"I'm very sorry," she said. It was morning. "Poached eggs and coffee, please."

It was a quarter to eight when she left the restaurant, and she thought, if I take a bus, and go straight downtown now, I can sit in the drugstore across the street from the dentist's office and have more coffee until about eight-thirty and then go into the dentist's when it opens and he can take me first.

The buses were beginning to fill up; she got into the first bus that came along and could not find a seat. She wanted to go to Twenty-third Street, and got a seat just as they were passing Twenty-sixth Street; when she woke she was so far downtown that it took her nearly half-an-hour to find a bus and get back to Twenty-third.

At the corner of Twenty-third Street, while she was waiting for the light to change, she was caught up in a crowd of people, and when they crossed the street and separated to go different directions someone fell into step beside her. For a minute she walked on without looking up, staring resentfully at the sidewalk, her tooth burning her, and then she looked up, but there was no blue suit among the people pressing by on either side.

When she turned into the office building where her dentist was, it was still very early morning. The doorman in the office building was freshly shaven and his hair was combed; he held the door open briskly, as at five o'clock he would be sluggish, his hair faintly out of place. She went in through the door with a feeling of achievement; she had come successfully from one place to another, and this was the end of her journey and her objective.

The clean white nurse sat at the desk in the office; her eyes took in the swollen cheek, the tired shoulders, and she said, "You poor thing, you look worn out."

"I have a toothache." The nurse half-smiled, as though she were still waiting for the day when someone would come in and say, "My feet hurt." She stood up into the professional sunlight. "Come right in," she said. "We won't make you wait."

There was sunlight on the headrest of the dentist's chair, on the round white table, on the drill bending its smooth chromium head. The dentist smiled with the same tolerance as the nurse; perhaps all human ailments were contained in the teeth, and he could fix them if people would only come to him in time. The nurse said smoothly, "I'll get her file, doctor. We thought we'd better bring her right in."

She felt, while they were taking an X-ray, that there was nothing in her head to stop the malicious eye of the camera, as though the camera would look through her and photograph the nails in the wall next to her, or the dentist's cuff buttons, or the small thin bones of the dentist's instruments; the dentist said, "Extraction," regretfully to the nurse, and the nurse said, "Yes, doctor, I'll call them right away."

Her tooth, which had brought her here unerringly, seemed now the only part of her to have any identity. It seemed to have had its picture taken without her; it was the important creature which must be recorded and examined and gratified; she was only its unwilling vehicle, and only as such was she of interest to the dentist and the nurse, only as the bearer of her tooth was she worth their immediate and practised attention. The dentist handed her a slip of paper with the picture of a full set of teeth drawn on it; her living tooth was checked with a black mark, and across the top of the paper was written "Lower molar; extraction."

"Take this slip," the dentist said, "and go right up to the address on this card; it's a surgeon dentist. They'll take care of you there."

"What will they do?" she said. Not the question she wanted to ask, not: What about me? or, How far down do the roots go?

"They'll take that tooth out," the dentist said testily, turning away. "Should have been done years ago."

I've stayed too long, she thought, he's tired of my tooth. She got up out of the dentist chair and said, "Thank you. Good-bye."

"Good-bye," the dentist said. At the last minute he smiled at her, showing her his full white teeth, all in perfect control.

"Are you all right? Does it bother you too much?" the nurse asked.

"I'm all right."

"I can give you some codeine tablets," the nurse said. "We'd rather you didn't take anything right now, of course, but I think I could let you have them if the tooth is really bad."

"No," she said, remembering her little bottle of codeine pills on the table of a restaurant between here and there. "No, it doesn't bother me too much."

"Well," the nurse said, "good luck."

She went down the stairs and out past the doorman; in the fifteen minutes she had been upstairs he had lost a little of his pristine morningness, and his bow was just a fraction smaller than before.

"Taxi?" he asked, and, remembering the bus down to Twenty-third Street, she said, "Yes."

Just as the doorman came back from the curb, bowing to the taxi he seemed to believe he had invented, she thought a hand waved to her from the crowd across the street.

She read the address on the card the dentist had given her and repeated it carefully to the taxi driver. With the card and the little slip of paper with "Lower molar" written on it and her tooth identified so clearly, she sat without moving, her hands still around the papers, her eyes almost closed. She thought she must have been asleep again when the taxi stopped suddenly, and the driver, reaching around to open the door, said, "Here we are, lady." He looked at her curiously.

"I'm going to have a tooth pulled," she said.

"Jesus," the taxi driver said. She paid him and he said, "Good luck," as he slammed the door.

This was a strange building, the entrance flanked by medical signs carved in stone; the doorman here was faintly professional, as though he were competent to prescribe if she did not care to go any farther. She went past him, going straight ahead until an elevator opened its door to her. In the elevator she showed the elevator man the card and he said, "Seventh floor."

She had to back up in the elevator for a nurse to wheel in an old lady in a wheel chair. The old lady was calm and restful, sitting there in the elevator with a rug over her knees; she said, "Nice day" to the elevator operator and he said, "Good to see the sun," and then the old lady lay back in her chair and the nurse straightened the rug around her knees and said, "Now we're not going to worry," and the old lady said irritably, "Who's worrying?"

They got out at the fourth floor. The elevator went on up and then the operator said, "Seven," and the elevator stopped and the door opened.

"Straight down the hall and to your left," the operator said.

There were closed doors on either side of the hall. Some of them said "DDS," some of them said "Clinic," some of them said "X-Ray." One of them, looking wholesome and friendly and somehow most comprehensible, said "Ladies." Then she turned to the left and found a door with the name on the card and she opened it and went in. There was a nurse sitting behind a glass window, almost as in a bank, and potted palms in tubs in the corners of the waiting room, and new magazines and comfortable chairs. The nurse behind the glass window said, "Yes?" as though you had overdrawn your account with the dentist and were two teeth in arrears.

She handed her slip of paper through the glass window and the nurse looked at it and said, "Lower molar, yes. They called about you. Will you come right in, please? Through the door to your left."

Into the vault? she almost said, and then silently opened the door and went in. Another nurse was waiting, and she smiled and turned, expecting to be followed, with no visible doubt about her right to lead.

There was another X-ray, and the nurse told another nurse: "Lower molar," and the other nurse said, "Come this way, please."

There were labyrinths and passages, seeming to lead into the heart of the office building, and she was put, finally, in a cubicle where there was a couch with a pillow and a wash-basin and a chair.

"Wait here," the nurse said. "Relax if you can."

"I'll probably go to sleep," she said.

"Fine," the nurse said. "You won't have to wait long."

She waited probably, for over an hour, although she spent the time half-sleeping, waking only when someone passed the door; occasionally the nurse looked in and smiled, once she said, "Won't have to wait much longer." Then, suddenly, the nurse was back, no longer smiling, no longer the good hostess, but efficient and hurried. "Come along," she said, and moved purposefully out of the little room into the hallways again.

Then, quickly, more quickly than she was able to see, she was sitting in the chair and there was a towel around her head and a towel under her chin and the nurse was leaning a hand on her shoulder.

"Will it hurt?" she asked.

"No," the nurse said, smiling. "You know it won't hurt, don't you?"

"Yes," she said.

The dentist came in and smiled down on her from over her head. "Well," he said.

"Will it hurt?" she said.

"Now," he said cheerfully, "we couldn't stay in business if we hurt people." All the time he talked he was busying himself with metal hidden under a towel, and great machinery being wheeled in almost silently behind her. "We couldn't stay in business at all," he said. "All you've got to worry about is telling us all your secrets while you're asleep. Want to watch out for that, you know. Lower molar?" he said to the nurse.

"Lower molar, doctor," she said.

Then they put the metal-tasting rubber mask over her face and the dentist said, "You know," two or three times absentmindedly while she could still see him over the mask. The nurse said "Relax your hands, dear," and after a long time she felt her fingers relaxing.

First of all things get so far away, she thought, remember this. And remember the metallic sound and taste of all of it. And the outrage.

And then the whirling music, the ringing confusedly loud music that went on and on, around and around, and she was running as fast as she could down a long horribly clear hallway with doors on both sides and at the end of the hallway was Jim, holding out his hands and laughing, and calling something she could never hear because of the loud music, and she was running and then she said, "I'm not afraid," and someone from the door next to her took her arm and pulled her through and the world widened alarmingly until it would never stop and then it stopped with the head of the dentist looking down at her and the window dropped into place in front of her and the nurse was holding her arm.

"Why did you pull me back?" she said, and her mouth was full of blood. "I wanted to go on."

"I didn't pull you," the nurse said, but the dentist said, "She's not out of it yet."

She began to cry without moving and felt the tears rolling down her face and the nurse wiped them off with a towel. There was no blood anywhere around except in her mouth; everything was as clean as before. The dentist was gone, suddenly, and the nurse put out her arm and helped her out of the chair. "Did I talk?" she asked suddenly, anxiously. "Did I say anything?"

"You said, 'I'm not afraid,' " the nurse said soothingly. "Just as you were coming out of it."

"No," she said, stopping to pull at the arm around her. "Did I *say* anything? Did I say where he is?"

"You didn't say *anything*," the nurse said. "The doctor was only teasing you."

"Where's my tooth?" she asked suddenly, and the nurse laughed and said, "All gone. Never bother you again."

She was back in the cubicle, and she lay down on the couch and cried, and the nurse brought her whisky in a paper cup and set it on the edge of the wash-basin.

"God has given me blood to drink," she said to the nurse, and the nurse said, "Don't rinse your mouth or it won't clot."

After a long time the nurse came back and said to her from the doorway, smiling, "I see you're awake again."

"Why?" she said.

"You've been asleep," the nurse said. "I didn't want to wake you."

She sat up; she was dizzy and it seemed that she had been in the cubicle all her life.

"Do you want to come along now?" the nurse said, all kindness again. She held out the same arm, strong enough to guide any wavering footstep; this time they went back through the long corridor to where the nurse sat behind the bank window.

"All through?" this nurse said brightly. "Sit down a minute, then." She indicated a chair next to the glass window, and turned away to write busily. "Do not rinse your mouth for two hours," she said, without turning around. "Take a laxative tonight, take two aspirin if there is any pain. If there is much pain or excessive bleeding, notify this office at once. All right?" she said, and smiled brightly again.

There was a new little slip of paper; this one said, "Extraction," and underneath, "Do not rinse mouth. Take mild laxative. Two aspirin for pain. If pain is excessive or any hemorrhage occurs, notify office."

"Good-bye," the nurse said pleasantly.

"Good-bye," she said.

With the little slip of paper in her hand, she went out through the glass door and, still almost asleep, turned the corner and started down the hall. When she opened her eyes a little and saw that it was a long hall with doorways on either side, she stopped and then saw the door marked "Ladies" and went in. Inside there was a vast room with windows and wicker chairs and glaring white tiles and glittering silver faucets; there were four or five women around the wash-basins, combing their hair, putting on lipstick. She went directly to the nearest of the three wash-basins, took a paper towel, dropped her pocketbook and the little slip of paper on the floor next to her, and fumbled with the faucets, soaking the towel until it was dripping. Then she slapped it against her face violently. Her eyes cleared and she felt fresher, so she soaked the paper again and rubbed her face with it. She felt out blindly for another paper towel, and the woman next to her handed her one, with a laugh she could hear, although she could not see for the water in her eyes. She heard one of the women say, "Where we going for lunch?" and another one say, "Just downstairs, prob'ly. Old fool says I gotta be back in half-an-hour."

Then she realized that at the wash-basin she was in the way of the women in a hurry so she dried her face quickly. It was when she stepped a little aside to let someone else get to the basin and stood up and glanced into the mirror that she realized with a slight stinging shock that she had no idea which face was hers.

She looked into the mirror as though into a group of strangers, all staring at her or around her; no one was familiar in the group, no one smiled at her or looked at her with recognition; you'd think my own face would know me, she thought, with a queer numbness in her throat. There was a creamy chinless face with bright blond hair, and a sharp-looking face under a red veiled hat, and a colorless anxious face with brown hair pulled straight back, and a square rosy face under a square haircut, and two or three more faces pushing close to the mirror, moving, regarding themselves. Perhaps it's not a mirror, she thought, maybe it's a window and I'm looking straight through at women washing on the other side. But there were women combing their hair and consulting the mirror; the group was on her side, and she thought, I hope I'm not the blonde, and lifted her hand and put it on her cheek.

She was the pale anxious one with the hair pulled back and when she realized it she was indignant and moved hurriedly back through the crowd of women, thinking, It isn't fair, why don't I have any color in my face? There were some pretty faces there, why didn't I take one of those? I didn't have time, she told herself sullenly, they didn't give me time to think, I could have had one of the nice faces, even the blonde would be better.

She backed up and sat down in one of the wicker chairs. It's mean, she was thinking. She put her hand up and felt her hair; it was loosened after her sleep but that was definitely the way she wore it, pulled straight back all around and fastened at the back of her neck with a wide tight barrette. Like a schoolgirl, she thought, only – remembering the pale face in the mirror – only I'm older than that. She unfastened the barrette with difficulty and brought it around where she could look at it. Her hair fell softly around her face; it was warm and reached to her shoulders. The barrette was silver; engraved on it was the name, "Clara."

"Clara," she said aloud. "*Clara?*" Two of the women leaving the room smiled back at her over their shoulders; almost all the women were leaving now, correctly combed and lipsticked, hurrying out talking together. In the space of a second, like birds leaving a tree, they all were gone and she sat alone in the room. She dropped the barrette into the ashstand next to her chair; the ashstand was deep and metal, and the barrette made a satisfactory clang falling down. Her hair down on her shoulders, she opened her pocketbook, and began to take things out, setting them on her lap as she did so. Handkerchief, plain, white, uninitialled. Compact, square and brown tortoise-shell plastic, with a powder compartment and a rouge compartment; the rouge compartment had obviously never been used, although the powder cake was half-gone. That's why I'm so pale, she thought, and set the compact down. Lipstick, a rose shade, almost finished. A comb, an opened package of cigarettes and a package of matches, a change purse, and a wallet. The change purse was red imitation leather with a zipper across the top; she opened it and dumped the money out into her hand. Nickels, dimes, pennies, a quarter. Ninety-seven cents. Can't go far on that, she thought, and opened the brown leather wallet; there was money in it but she looked first for papers and found nothing. The only thing in the wallet was money. She counted it; there were nineteen dollars. I can go a little farther on *that*, she thought.

There was nothing else in the pocketbook. No keys – shouldn't I have keys? she wondered – no papers, no address book, no identification. The pocketbook itself was imitation leather, light grey, and she looked down and discovered that she was wearing a dark grey flannel suit and a salmon pink blouse with a ruffle around the neck. Her shoes were black and stout with moderate heels and they had laces, one of which was untied. She was wearing beige stockings and there was a ragged tear in the right knee and a great ragged run going down her leg and ending in a hole in the toe which she could feel inside her shoe. She was wearing a pin on the lapel of her suit which, when she turned it around to look at it, was a blue plastic letter C. She took the pin off and dropped it into the ashstand, and it made a sort of clatter at the bottom, with a metallic clang when it landed on the barrette. Her hands were small, with stubby fingers and no nail polish; she wore a thin gold wedding ring on her left hand and no other jewelry.

Sitting alone in the ladies' room in the wicker chair, she thought, The least I can do is get rid of these stockings. Since no one was around she took off her shoes and stripped away the stockings with a feeling of relief when her toe was released from the hole. Hide them, she thought: the paper towel wastebasket. When she stood up she got a better sight of herself in the mirror; it was worse than she had thought: the grey suit bagged in the seat, her legs were bony, and her shoulders sagged. I look fifty, she thought; and then, consulting the face, but I can't be more than thirty. Her hair hung down untidily around the pale face and with sudden anger she fumbled in the pocketbook and found the lipstick; she drew an emphatic rosy mouth on the pale face, realizing as she did so that she was not very expert at it, and with the red mouth the face looking at her seemed somehow better to her, so she opened the compact and put on pink cheeks with the rouge. The cheeks were uneven and patent, and the red mouth glaring, but at least the face was no longer pale and anxious.

She put the stockings into the wastebasket and went barelegged out into the hall again, and purposefully to the elevator. The elevator operator said, "Down?" when he saw her and she stepped in and the elevator carried her silently downstairs. She went back past the grave professional doorman and out into the street where people were passing, and she stood in front of the building and waited. After a few minutes Jim came out of a crowd of people passing and came over to her and took her hand.

Somewhere between here and there was her bottle of codeine pills, upstairs on the floor of the ladies' room she had left a little slip of paper headed "Extraction"; seven floors below, oblivious of the people who stepped sharply along the sidewalk, not noticing their occasional curious glances, her hand in Jim's and her hair down on her shoulders, she ran barefoot through hot sand.

TWO IN ONE

Flann O'Brien

Flann O'Brien (1911–1966) is a pen name of Brian O'Nolan (Brian Ó'Nualláin), also known as Myles na Gopaleen (Myles na gCopaleen). O'Brien was born in Strabane, County Tyrone, Northern Ireland. His first language was Irish. In 1923, O'Brien's family moved to Dublin where he was educated at the Christian Brothers School, before going on to Dublin University. After graduating he joined the civil service where he worked for eighteen years. He is best remembered for his comic novels, *At Swim-Two-Birds* and *The Third Policeman*.

The story I have to tell is a strange one, perhaps unbelievable. I will try to set it down as simply as I can. I do not expect to be disturbed in my literary labours, for I am writing this in the condemned cell.

Let us say my name is Murphy. The unusual occurrence which led me here concerns my relations with another man whom we shall call Kelly. Both of us were taxidermists.

I will not attempt a treatise on what a taxidermist is. The word is ugly and inadequate. Certainly it does not convey to the layman that such an operator must combine the qualities of zoologist, naturalist, chemist, sculptor, artist, and carpenter. Who would blame such a person for showing some temperament now and again, as I did?

It is necessary, however, to say a brief word about this science. First, there is no such thing in modern practice as "stuffing" an animal. There is a record of stuffed gorillas having been in Carthage in the 5th century, and it is a fact that an Austrian prince, Siegmund Herberstein, had stuffed bison in the great hall of his castle in the 16th century – it was then the practice to draw the entrails of animals and to substitute spices and various preservative substances. There is a variety of methods in use to-day but, except in particular cases – snakes, for example, where preserving the translucency of the skin is a problem calling for special measures – the basis of all modern methods is simply this: you skin the animal very carefully according to a certain pattern, and you encase the skinless body in plaster of Paris. You bisect the plaster when cast providing yourself with two complementary moulds from which you can make a casting of the animal's body – there are several substances, all very light, from which such castings can be made. The next step, calling for infinite skill and patience, is to mount the skin on the casting of the body. That is all I need explain here, I think.

Kelly carried on a taxidermy business and I was his assistant. He was the boss – a swinish, overbearing mean boss, a bully, a sadist. He hated me, but enjoyed his hatred too much to sack me. He knew I had a real interest in the work, and a desire to broaden my experience. For that reason, he threw me all the common-place jobs that came in. If some old lady sent her favourite terrier to be done, that was me; foxes and cats and Shetland ponies and white rabbits – they were all strictly *my* department. I could do a perfect job on such animals in my sleep, and got to hate them. But if a crocodile came in, or a Great Borneo spider, or (as once happened) a giraffe – Kelly kept them all for himself. In the meantime he would treat my own painstaking work with sourness and sneers and complaints.

One day the atmosphere in the workshop had been even fouler than usual, with Kelly in a filthier temper than usual. I had spent the forenoon finishing a cat, and at about lunch-time put it on the shelf where he left completed orders.

I could nearly *hear* him glaring at it. Where was the tail? I told him there was no tail, that it was a Manx cat. How did I know it was a Manx cat, how did I know it was not an ordinary cat which had lost its tail in a motor accident or something? I got so mad that I permitted myself a disquisition on cats in general, mentioning the distinctions as between *Felis manul, Felis silvestris*, and *Felis lybica*, and on the unique structure of the Manx cat. His reply to that? He called me a slob. That was the sort of life *I* was having.

On this occasion something within me snapped. I was sure I could hear the snap. I had moved up to where he was to answer his last insult. The loathsome creature had his back to me, bending down to put on his bicycle clips. Just to my hand on the bench was one of the long, flat, steel instruments we use for certain operations with plaster. I picked it up and hit him a blow with it on the back of the head. He gave a cry and slumped forward. I hit him again. I rained blow after blow on him. Then I threw the tool away. I was upset. I went out into the yard and looked around. I remembered he had a weak heart. Was he dead? I remember adjusting the position of a barrel we had in the yard to catch rainwater, the only sort of water suitable for some of the mixtures we used. I found I was in a cold sweat but strangely calm. I went back into the workshop.

Kelly was just as I had left him. I could find no pulse. I rolled him over on his back and examined his eyes, for I have seen more lifeless eyes in my day than most people. Yes, there was no doubt: Kelly was dead. I had killed him. I was a murderer. I put on my coat and hat and left the place. I walked the streets for a while, trying to avoid panic, trying to think rationally. Inevitably, I was soon in a public house. I drank a lot of whiskey and finally went home to my digs. The next morning I was very sick indeed from this terrible mixture of drink and worry. Was the Kelly affair merely a fancy, a drunken fancy? No, there was no consolation in that sort of hope. He was dead all right.

It was as I lay in bed there, shaking, thinking, and smoking, that the mad idea came into my head. No doubt this sounds incredible, grotesque, even disgusting, but I decided I would treat Kelly the same as any other dead creature that found its way to the workshop.

Once one enters a climate of horror, distinction of degree as between one infamy and another seems slight, sometimes undetectable. That evening I went to the workshop and made my preparations. I worked steadily all next day. I will not appall the reader with gruesome detail. I need only say that I applied the general technique and flaying pattern appropriate to apes. The job took me four days at the end of which I had a perfect skin, face and all. I made the usual castings before committing the remains of, so to speak, the remains, to the furnace. My plan was to have Kelly on view asleep on a chair, for the benefit of anybody who might call. Reflection convinced me that this would be far too dangerous. I had to think again.

A further idea began to form. It was so macabre that it shocked even myself. For days I had been treating the inside of the skin with the usual preservatives – cellulose acetate and the like – thinking all the time. The new illumination came upon me like a thunderbolt. *I would don his skin and, when the need arose, BECOME Kelly!* His clothes fitted me. So would his skin. Why not?

Another day's agonised work went on various alterations and adjustments but that night I was able to look into a glass and see Kelly looking back at me, perfect in every detail except for the teeth and eyes, which had to be my own but which I knew other people would never notice.

Naturally I wore Kelly's clothes, and had no trouble in imitating his unpleasant voice and mannerisms. On the second day, having "dressed," so to speak, I went for a walk, receiving salutes from news-boys and other people who had known Kelly. And on the day after, I was foolhardy enough to visit Kelly's lodgings. Where on earth had I been, his landlady wanted to know. (She had noticed nothing.) What, I asked – had that fool Murphy not told her that I had to go to the country for a few days? No? I had told the good-for-nothing to convey the message.

I slept that night in Kelly's bed. I was a little worried about what the other landlady would think of my own absence. I decided not to remove Kelly's skin the first night I spent in his bed but to try to get the rest of my plan of campaign perfected and into sharper focus. I eventually decided that Kelly should announce to various people that he was going to a very good job in Canada, and that he had sold his business to his assistant Murphy. I would then burn the skin, I would own a business and – what is more stupid than vanity! – I could secretly flatter myself that I had committed the perfect crime.

Need I say that I had overlooked something?

The mummifying preparation with which I had dressed the inside of the skin was, of course, quite stable for the ordinary purposes of taxidermy. It had not occurred to me that a night in a warm bed would make it behave differently. The horrible truth dawned on me the next day when I reached the workshop and tried to take the skin off. *It wouldn't come off!* It had literally fused with my own! And in the days that followed, this process kept rapidly advancing. Kelly's skin got to live again, to breathe, to perspire.

Then followed more days of terrible tension. My own landlady called one day, inquiring about me of "Kelly." I told her I had been on the point of calling on *her* to find out where I was. She was disturbed about my disappearance – it was so unlike me – and said she thought she should inform the police. I thought it wise not to try to dissuade her. My disappearance would eventually come to be accepted, I thought. My Kelliness, so to speak, was permanent. It was horrible, but it was a choice of that or the scaffold.

I kept drinking a lot. One night, after many drinks, I went to the club for a game of snooker. This club was in fact one of the causes of Kelly's bitterness towards me. I had joined it without having been aware that Kelly was a member. His resentment was boundless. He thought I was watching him, and taking note of the attentions he paid the lady members.

On this occasion I nearly made a catastrophic mistake. It is a simple fact that I am a very good snooker player, easily the best in that club. As I was standing watching another game in progress awaiting my turn for the table, *I suddenly realised that Kelly did not play snooker at all!* For some moments, a cold sweat stood out on Kelly's brow at the narrowness of this escape. I went to the bar. There, a garrulous lady (who thinks her unsolicited conversation is a fair exchange for a drink) began talking to me. She remarked the long absence of my nice Mr. Murphy. She said he was missed a lot in the snooker room. I was hot and embarrassed and soon went home. To Kelly's place, of course.

Not embarrassment, but a real sense of danger, was to be my next portion in this adventure. One afternoon, two very casual strangers strolled into the workshop, saying they would like a little chat with me. Cigarettes were produced. Yes indeed, they were plain-clothes-men making a few routine inquiries. This man Murphy had been reported missing by several people. Any idea where he was? None at all. When had I last seen him? Did he seem upset or disturbed? No, but he was an impetuous type. I had recently reprimanded him for bad work. On similar other occasions he had threatened to leave and seek work in England. Had I been away for a few days myself? Yes, down in Cork for a few days. On business. Yes . . . yes . . . some people thinking of starting a natural museum down there, technical school people – that sort of thing.

The casual manner of these men worried me, but I was sure they did not suspect the truth and that they were genuinely interested in tracing Murphy. Still, I knew I was in danger, without knowing the exact nature of the threat I had to counter. Whiskey cheered me somewhat.

Then it happened. The two detectives came back accompanied by two other men in uniform. They showed me a search warrant. It was purely a formality; it had to be done in the case of all missing persons. They had already searched Murphy's digs and had found nothing of interest. They were very sorry for upsetting the place during my working hours.

A few days later the casual gentlemen called and put me under arrest for the wilful murder of Murphy, of myself. They proved the charge in due course with all sorts of painfully amassed evidence, including the remains of human bones in the furnace. I was sentenced to be hanged. Even if I could now prove that Murphy still lived by shedding the accursed skin, what help would that be? Where, they would ask, is Kelly?

This is my strange and tragic story. And I end it with the thought that if Kelly and I must each be either murderer or murdered, it is perhaps better to accept my present fate as philosophically as I can and be cherished in the public mind as the victim of this murderous monster, Kelly. He *was* a murderer, anyway.

SWADDLING CLOTHES

Yukio Mishima

Yukio Mishima (1925–1970) is the pen name of Kimitake Hiraoka who
was born in Tokyo. He escaped military service in World War II after
being misdiagnosed with tuberculosis. Mishima was detailed to work
in an aircraft factory which manufactured kamikaze planes. He subsequently produced an impressive body of work which included poetry,
short stories, novels, films, Kabuki plays and Noh dramas. Mishima
was also a model and bodybuilder. He embraced the ancient ideals of
Bushido and committed ritual suicide after leading a failed military coup.

He was always busy, Toshiko's husband. Even tonight he had to dash off
to an appointment, leaving her to go home alone by taxi. But what else
could a woman expect when she married an actor – an attractive one?
No doubt she had been foolish to hope that he would spend the evening with
her. And yet he must have known how she dreaded going back to their house,
unhomely with its Western-style furniture and with the bloodstains still showing
on the floor.

Toshiko had been oversensitive since girlhood: that was her nature. As the
result of constant worrying she never put on weight, and now, an adult woman,
she looked more like a transparent picture than a creature of flesh and blood.
Her delicacy of spirit was evident to her most casual acquaintance.

Earlier that evening, when she had joined her husband at a night club, she had
been shocked to find him entertaining friends with an account of "the incident."
Sitting there in his American-style suit, puffing at a cigarette, he had seemed to
her almost a stranger.

"It's a fantastic story," he was saying, gesturing flamboyantly as if in an attempt to outweigh the attractions of the dance band. "Here this new nurse for
our baby arrives from the employment agency, and the very first thing I notice
about her is her stomach. It's enormous – as if she had a pillow stuck under her
kimono! No wonder, I thought, for I soon saw that she could eat more than the
rest of us put together. She polished off the contents of our rice bin like that. . .
." He snapped his fingers. "'Gastric dilation' – that's how she explained her girth
and her appetite. Well, the day before yesterday we heard groans and moans
coming from the nursery. We rushed in and found her squatting on the floor,
holding her stomach in her two hands, and moaning like a cow. Next to her our
baby lay in his cot, scared out of his wits and crying at the top of his lungs. A
pretty scene, I can tell you!"

"So the cat was out of the bag?" suggested one of their friends, a film actor
like Toshiko's husband.

"Indeed it was! And it gave me the shock of my life. You see, I'd completely swallowed that story about 'gastric dilation.' Well, I didn't waste any time. I rescued our good rug from the floor and spread a blanket for her to lie on. The whole time the girl was yelling like a stuck pig. By the time the doctor from the maternity clinic arrived, the baby had already been born. But our sitting room was a pretty shambles!"

"Oh, that I'm sure of!" said another of their friends, and the whole company burst into laughter.

Toshiko was dumbfounded to hear her husband discussing the horrifying happening as though it were no more than an amusing incident which they chanced to have witnessed. She shut her eyes for a moment and all at once she saw the newborn baby lying before her: on the parquet floor the infant lay, and his frail body was wrapped in bloodstained newspapers.

Toshiko was sure that the doctor had done the whole thing out of spite. As if to emphasize his scorn for this mother who had given birth to a bastard under such sordid conditions, he had told his assistant to wrap the baby in some loose newspapers, rather than proper swaddling. This callous treatment of the newborn child had offended Toshiko. Overcoming her disgust at the entire scene, she had fetched a brand-new piece of flannel from her cupboard and, having swaddled the baby in it, had laid him carefully in an armchair.

This all had taken place in the evening after her husband had left the house. Toshiko had told him nothing of it, fearing that he would think her oversoft, oversentimental; yet the scene had engraved itself deeply in her mind. Tonight she sat silently thinking back on it, while the jazz orchestra brayed and her husband chatted cheerfully with his friends. She knew that she would never forget the sight of the baby, wrapped in stained newspapers and lying on the floor – it was a scene fit for a butchershop. Toshiko, whose own life had been spent in solid comfort, poignantly felt the wretchedness of the illegitimate baby.

I am the only person to have witnessed its shame, the thought occurred to her. The mother never saw her child lying there in its newspaper wrappings, and the baby itself of course didn't know. I alone shall have to preserve that terrible scene in my memory. When the baby grows up and wants to find out about his birth, there will be no one to tell him, so long as I preserve silence. How strange that I should have this feeling of guilt! After all, it was I who took him up from the floor, swathed him properly in flannel, and laid him down to sleep in the armchair.

They left the night club and Toshiko stepped into the taxi that her husband had called for her. "Take this lady to Ushigomé," he told the driver and shut the door from the outside. Toshiko gazed through the window at her husband's smiling face and noticed his strong, white teeth. Then she leaned back in the seat, oppressed by the knowledge that their life together was in some way too easy, too painless. It would have been difficult for her to put her thoughts into words. Through the rear window of the taxi she took a last look at her husband. He was striding along the street toward his Nash car, and soon the back of his rather garish tweed coat had blended with the figures of the passers-by.

The taxi drove off, passed down a street dotted with bars and then by a theatre, in front of which the throngs of people jostled each other on the pavement. Although the performance had only just ended, the lights had already been turned out and in the half dark outside it was depressingly obvious that the cherry blossoms decorating the front of the theatre were merely scraps of white paper.

Even if that baby should grow up in ignorance of the secret of his birth, he can never become a respectable citizen, reflected Toshiko, pursuing the same train of thoughts. Those soiled newspaper swaddling clothes will be the symbol of his entire life. But why should I keep worrying about him so much? Is it because I feel uneasy about the future of my own child? Say twenty years from now, when our boy will have grown up into a fine, carefully educated young man, one day by a quirk of fate he meets that other boy, who then will also have turned twenty. And say that the other boy, who has been sinned against, savagely stabs him with a knife. . .

It was a warm, overcast April night, but thoughts of the future made Toshiko feel cold and miserable. She shivered on the back seat of the car.

No, when the time comes I shall take my son's place, she told herself suddenly. Twenty years from now I shall be forty-three. I shall go to that young man and tell him straight out about everything – about his newspaper swaddling clothes, and about how I went and wrapped him in flannel.

The taxi ran along the dark wide road that was bordered by the park and by the Imperial Palace moat. In the distance Toshiko noticed the pinpricks of light which came from the blocks of tall office buildings.

Twenty years from now that wretched child will be in utter misery. He will be living a desolate, hopeless, poverty-stricken existence – a lonely rat. What else could happen to a baby who has had such a birth? He'll be wandering through the streets by himself, cursing his father, loathing his mother.

No doubt Toshiko derived a certain satisfaction from her somber thoughts: she tortured herself with them without cease. The taxi approached Hanzomon and drove past the compound of the British Embassy. At that point the famous rows of cherry trees were spread out before Toshiko in all their purity. On the spur of the moment she decided to go and view the blossoms by herself in the dark night. It was a strange decision for a timid and unadventurous young woman, but then she was in a strange state of mind and she dreaded the return home. That evening all sorts of unsettling fancies had burst open in her mind.

She crossed the wide street – a slim, solitary figure in the darkness. As a rule when she walked in the traffic Toshiko used to cling fearfully to her companion, but tonight she darted alone between the cars and a moment later had reached the long narrow park that borders the Palace moat. Chidorigafuchi, it is called – the Abyss of the Thousand Birds.

Tonight the whole park had become a grove of blossoming cherry trees. Under the calm cloudy sky the blossoms formed a mass of solid whiteness. The paper lanterns that hung from wires between the trees had been put out; in their place electric light bulbs, red, yellow, and green, shone dully beneath the blossoms. It was well past ten o'clock and most of the flower-viewers had gone home. As the occasional passers-by strolled through the park, they would automatically kick aside the empty bottles or crush the waste paper beneath their feet.

Newspapers, thought Toshiko, her mind going back once again to those happenings. Bloodstained newspapers. If a man were ever to hear of that piteous birth and know that it was he who had lain there, it would ruin his entire life. To think that I, a perfect stranger, should from now on have to keep such a secret – the secret of a man's whole existence. . . .

Lost in these thoughts, Toshiko walked on through the park. Most of the people still remaining there were quiet couples; no one paid her any attention. She noticed two people sitting on a stone bench beside the moat, not looking at the blossoms, but gazing silently at the water. Pitch black it was, and swathed in heavy shadows. Beyond the moat the somber forest of the Imperial Palace blocked her view. The trees reached up, to form a solid dark mass against the night sky. Toshiko walked slowly along the path beneath the blossoms hanging heavily overhead.

On a stone bench, slightly apart from the others, she noticed a pale object – not, as she had at first imagined, a pile of cherry blossoms, nor a garment forgotten by one of the visitors to the park. Only when she came closer did she see that it was a human form lying on the bench. Was it, she wondered, one of those miserable drunks often to be seen sleeping in public places? Obviously not, for the body had been systematically covered with newspapers, and it was the whiteness of those papers that had attracted Toshiko's attention. Standing by the bench, she gazed down at the sleeping figure.

It was a man in a brown jersey who lay there, curled up on layers of newspapers, other newspapers covering him. No doubt this had become his normal night residence now that spring had arrived. Toshiko gazed down at the man's dirty, unkempt hair, which in places had become hopelessly matted. As she observed the sleeping figure wrapped in its newspapers, she was inevitably reminded of the baby who had lain on the floor in its wretched swaddling clothes. The shoulder of the man's jersey rose and fell in the darkness in time with his heavy breathing.

It seemed to Toshiko that all her fears and premonitions had suddenly taken concrete form. In the darkness the man's pale forehead stood out, and it was a young forehead, though carved with the wrinkles of long poverty and hardship. His khaki trousers had been slightly pulled up; on his sockless feet he wore a pair of battered gym shoes. She could not see his face and suddenly had an overmastering desire to get one glimpse of it.

She walked to the head of the bench and looked down. The man's head was half buried in his arms, but Toshiko could see that he was surprisingly young. She noticed the thick eyebrows and the fine bridge of his nose. His slightly open mouth was alive with youth.

But Toshiko had approached too close. In the silent night the newspaper bedding rustled, and abruptly the man opened his eyes. Seeing the young woman standing directly beside him, he raised himself with a jerk, and his eyes lit up. A second later a powerful hand reached out and seized Toshiko by her slender wrist.

She did not feel in the least afraid and made no effort to free herself. In a flash the thought had struck her, Ah, so the twenty years have already gone by! The forest of the Imperial Palace was pitch dark and utterly silent.

HARRY

Rosemary Timperley

Rosemary Kenyon Timperley (1920–1988) was born in Crouch End, North London. Her father was an architect, her mother a teacher. After graduating from London University, Timperley taught English and History at South-East Essex Technical School. During World War II she volunteered at the Kensington Citizens Advice Bureau. In 1949 Timperley became a staff writer at *Reveille* where her duties involved editing the personal advice column. She is best remembered for her ghost stories, including *Harry*, which has been adapted for film several times.

Such ordinary things make me afraid. Sunshine. Sharp shadows on grass. White roses. Children with red hair. And the name – Harry. Such an ordinary name.

Yet the first time Christine mentioned the name, I felt a premonition of fear.

She was five years old, due to start school in three months' time. It was a hot, beautiful day and she was playing alone in the garden, as she often did. I saw her lying on her stomach in the grass, picking daisies and making daisy-chains with laborious pleasure. The sun burned on her pale red hair and made her skin look very white. Her big blue eyes were wide with concentration.

Suddenly she looked towards the bush of white roses, which cast its shadow over the grass, and smiled.

"Yes, I'm Christine," she said. She rose and walked slowly towards the bush, her little plump legs defenceless and endearing beneath the too short blue cotton skirt. She was growing fast.

"With my mummy and daddy," she said clearly. Then, after a pause, "Oh, but they *are* my mummy and daddy."

She was in the shadow of the bush now. It was as if she'd walked out of the world of light into darkness. Uneasy, without quite knowing why, I called her:

"Chris, what are you doing?"

"Nothing." The voice sounded too far away.

"Come indoors now. It's too hot for you out there."

"Not too hot."

"Come indoors, Chris."

She said: "I must go in now. Goodbye," then walked slowly towards the house.

"Chris, who were you talking to?"

"Harry," she said.

"Who's Harry?"

"Harry."

I couldn't get anything else out of her, so I just gave her some cake and milk and read to her until bedtime. As she listened, she stared out at the garden. Once she smiled and waved. It was a relief finally to tuck her up in bed and feel she was safe.

When Jim, my husband, came home I told him about the mysterious "Harry". He laughed.

"Oh, she's started that lark, has she?"

"What do you mean, Jim?"

"It's not so very rare for only children to have an imaginary companion. Some kids talk to their dolls. Chris has never been keen on her dolls. She hasn't any brothers or sisters. She hasn't any friends her own age. So she imagines someone."

"But why has she picked that particular name?"

He shrugged. "You know how kids pick things up. I don't know what you're worrying about, honestly I don't."

"Nor do I really. It's just that I feel extra responsible for her. More so than if I were her real mother."

"I know, but she's all right. Chris is fine. She's a pretty, healthy, intelligent little girl. A credit to you."

"And to you."

"In fact, we're thoroughly nice parents!"

"And so modest!"

We laughed together and he kissed me. I felt consoled.

Until next morning.

Again the sun shone brilliantly on the small, bright lawn and white roses. Christine was sitting on the grass, cross-legged, staring towards the rose bush, smiling.

"Hello," she said. "I hoped you'd come . . . Because I like you. How old are you? . . . I'm only five and a piece . . . I'm *not* a baby! I'm going to school soon and I shall have a new dress. A green one. Do you go to school? . . . What do you do then?" She was silent for a while, nodding, listening, absorbed.

I felt myself going cold as I stood there in the kitchen. "Don't be silly. Lots of children have an imaginary companion," I told myself desperately. "Just carry on as if nothing were happening. Don't listen. Don't be a fool."

But I called Chris in earlier than usual for her mid-morning milk.

"Your milk's ready, Chris. Come along."

"In a minute." This was a strange reply. Usually she rushed in eagerly for her milk and the special sandwich cream biscuits, over which she was a little gourmande.

"Come now, darling," I said.

"Can Harry come too?"

"No!" The cry burst from me harshly, surprising me.

"Goodbye, Harry. I'm sorry you can't come in but I've got to have my milk," Chris said, then ran towards the house.

"Why can't Harry have some milk too?" she challenged me.

"Who *is* Harry, darling?"

"Harry's my brother."

"But Chris, you haven't got a brother. Daddy and mummy have only got one child, one little girl, that's you. Harry can't be your brother."

"Harry's my brother. He says so." She bent over the glass of milk and emerged with a smeary top lip. Then she grabbed at the biscuits. At least "Harry" hadn't spoilt her appetite!

After she'd had her milk, I said, "We'll go shopping now, Chris. You'd like to come to the shops with me, wouldn't you?"

"I want to stay with Harry."

"Well you can't. You're coming with me."

"Can Harry come too?"

"No."

My hands were trembling as I put on my hat and gloves. It was chilly in the house nowadays, as if there were a cold shadow over it in spite of the sun outside. Chris came with me meekly enough, but as we walked down the street, she turned and waved.

I didn't mention any of this to Jim that night. I knew he'd only scoff as he'd done before. But when Christine's "Harry" fantasy went on day after day, it got more and more on my nerves. I came to hate and dread those long summer days. I longed for grey skies and rain. I longed for the white roses to wither and die. I trembled when I heard Christine's voice prattling away in the garden. She talked quite unrestrainedly to "Harry" now.

One Sunday, when Jim heard her at it, he said:

"I'll say one thing for imaginary companions, they help a child on with her talking. Chris is talking much more freely than she used to."

"With an accent," I blurted out.

"An accent?"

"A slight cockney accent."

"My dearest, every London child gets a slight cockney accent. It'll be much worse when she goes to school and meets lots of other kids."

"We don't talk cockney. Where does she get it from? Who can she be getting it from except Ha . . ." I couldn't say the name.

"The baker, the milkman, the dustman, the coalman, the window cleaner – want any more?"

"I suppose not." I laughed ruefully. Jim made me feel foolish.

"Anyway," said Jim, "*I* haven't noticed any cockney in her voice."

"There isn't when she talks to us. It's only when she's talking to – to him."

"To Harry. You know, I'm getting quite attached to young Harry. Wouldn't it be fun if one day we looked out and saw him?"

"Don't!" I cried. "Don't say that! It's my nightmare. My waking nightmare. Oh, Jim, I can't bear it much longer."

He looked astonished. "This Harry business is really getting you down, isn't it?"

"Of course it is! Day in, day out, I hear nothing but 'Harry this,' 'Harry that,' 'Harry says,' 'Harry thinks,' 'Can Harry have some?', 'Can Harry come too?' – it's all right for you out at the office all day, but I have to live with it: I'm – I'm afraid of it, Jim. It's so queer."

"Do you know what I think you should do to put your mind at rest?"

"What?"

"Take Chris along to see old Dr Webster tomorrow. Let him have a little talk with her."

"Do you think she's ill – in her mind?"

"Good heavens, no! But when we come across something that's a bit beyond us, it's as well to take professional advice."

Next day I took Chris to see Dr Webster. I left her in the waiting-room while I told him briefly about Harry. He nodded sympathetically, then said:

"It's a fairly unusual case, Mrs James, but by no means unique. I've had several cases of children's imaginary companions becoming so real to them that the parents got the jitters. I expect she's rather a lonely little girl, isn't she?"

"She doesn't know any other children. We're new to the neighbourhood, you see. But that will be put right when she starts school."

"And I think you'll find that when she goes to school and meets other children, these fantasies will disappear. You see, every child needs company of her own age, and if she doesn't get it, she invents it. Older people who are lonely talk to themselves. That doesn't mean that they're crazy, just that they need to talk to someone. A child is more practical. Seems silly to talk to oneself, she thinks, so she invents someone to talk to. I honestly don't think you've anything to worry about."

"That's what my husband says."

"I'm sure he does. Still, I'll have a chat with Christine as you've brought her. Leave us alone together."

I went to the waiting-room to fetch Chris. She was at the window. She said: "Harry's waiting."

"Where, Chris?" I said quietly, wanting suddenly to see with her eyes.

"There. By the rose bush."

The doctor had a bush of white roses in his garden.

"There's no one there," I said. Chris gave me a glance of unchildlike scorn. "Dr Webster wants to see you now, darling," I said shakily. "You remember him, don't you? He gave you sweets when you were getting better from chicken pox."

"Yes," she said and went willingly enough to the doctor's surgery. I waited restlessly. Faintly I heard their voices through the wall, heard the doctor's chuckle, Christine's high peal of laughter. She was talking away to the doctor in a way she didn't talk to me.

When they came out, he said: "Nothing wrong with her whatever. She's just an imaginative little monkey. A word of advice, Mrs James. Let her talk about Harry. Let her become accustomed to confiding in you. I gather you've shown some disapproval of this 'brother' of hers so she doesn't talk much to you about him. He makes wooden toys, doesn't he, Chris?"

"Yes, Harry makes wooden toys."

"And he can read and write, can't he?"

"And swim and climb trees and paint pictures. Harry can do everything. He's a wonderful brother." Her little face flushed with adoration.

The doctor patted me on the shoulder and said: "Harry sounds a very nice brother for her. He's even got red hair like you, Chris, hasn't he?"

"Harry's got red hair," said Chris proudly, "Redder than my hair. And he's nearly as tall as daddy only thinner. He's as tall as you, mummy. He's fourteen.

He says he's tall for his age. What *is* tall for his age?"

"Mummy will tell you about that as you walk home," said Dr Webster. "Now, goodbye, Mrs James. Don't worry. Just let her prattle. Goodbye, Chris. Give my love to Harry."

"He's there," said Chris, pointing to the doctor's garden. "He's been waiting for me."

Dr Webster laughed. "They're incorrigible, aren't they?" he said. "I knew one poor mother whose children invented a whole tribe of imaginary natives whose rituals and taboos ruled the household. Perhaps you're lucky, Mrs James!"

I tried to feel comforted by all this, but I wasn't. I hoped sincerely that when Chris started school this wretched Harry business would finish.

Chris ran ahead of me. She looked up as if at someone beside her. For a brief, dreadful second, I saw a shadow on the pavement alongside her own – a long, thin shadow – like a boy's shadow. Then it was gone. I ran to catch her up and held her hand tightly all the way home. Even in the comparative security of the house – the house so strangely cold in this hot weather – I never let her out of my sight. On the face of it she behaved no differently towards me, but in reality she was drifting away. The child in my house was becoming a stranger.

For the first time since Jim and I had adopted Chris, I wondered seriously: Who is she? Where does she come from? Who were her real parents? Who is this little loved stranger I've taken as a daughter? Who *is* Christine?

Another week passed. It was Harry, Harry all the time. The day before she was to start school, Chris said:

"Not going to school."

"You're going to school tomorrow, Chris. You're looking forward to it. You know you are. There'll be lots of other little girls and boys."

"Harry says he can't come too."

"You won't want Harry at school. He'll –" I tried hard to follow the doctor's advice and appear to believe in Harry – "He'll be too old. He'd feel silly among little boys and girls, a great lad of fourteen."

"I won't go to school without Harry. I want to be with Harry." She began to weep, loudly, painfully.

"Chris, stop this nonsense! Stop it!" I struck her sharply on the arm. Her crying ceased immediately. She stared at me, her blue eyes wide open and frighteningly cold. She gave me an adult stare that made me tremble. Then she said:

"You don't love me. Harry loves me. Harry wants me. He says I can go with him."

"I will not hear any more of this!" I shouted, hating the anger in my voice, hating myself for being angry at all with a little girl – *my* little girl – mine –

I went down on one knee and held out my arms.

"Chris, darling, come here."

She came, slowly. "I love you," I said. "I love you, Chris, and I'm real. School is real. Go to school to please me."

"Harry will go away if I do."

"You'll have other friends."

"I want Harry." Again the tears, wet against my shoulder now. I held her closely.

"You're tired, baby. Come to bed."

She slept with the tear stains still on her face.

It was still daylight. I went to the window to draw her curtains. Golden shadows and long strips of sunshine in the garden. Then, again like a dream, the long thin clear-cut shadow of a boy near the white roses. Like a mad woman I opened the window and shouted:

"Harry! Harry!"

I thought I saw a glimmer of red among the roses, like close red curls on a boy's head. Then there was nothing.

When I told Jim about Christine's emotional outburst he said: "Poor little kid. It's always a nervy business, starting school. She'll be all right once she gets there. You'll be hearing less about Harry too, as time goes on."

"Harry doesn't want her to go to school."

"Hey! You sound as if you believe in Harry yourself!"

"Sometimes I do."

"Believing in evil spirits in your old age?" he teased me. But his eyes were concerned. He thought I was going "round the bend" and small blame to him!

"I don't think Harry's evil," I said. "He's just a boy. A boy who doesn't exist, except for Christine. And who *is* Christine?"

"None of that!" said Jim sharply. "When we adopted Chris we decided she was to be our own child. No probing into the past. No wondering and worrying. No mysteries. Chris is as much ours as if she'd been born of our flesh. Who is Christine indeed! She's our daughter – and just you remember that!"

"Yes, Jim, you're right. Of course you're right."

He'd been so fierce about it that I didn't tell him what I planned to do the next day while Chris was at school.

Next morning Chris was silent and sulky. Jim joked with her and tried to cheer her, but all she would do was look out of the window and say: "Harry's gone."

"You won't need Harry now. You're going to school," said Jim.

Chris gave him that look of grown-up contempt she'd given me sometimes.

She and I didn't speak as I took her to school. I was almost in tears. Although I was glad for her to start school, I felt a sense of loss at parting with her. I suppose every mother feels that when she takes her ewe-lamb to school for the first time. It's the end of babyhood for the child, the beginning of life in reality, life with its cruelty, its strangeness, its barbarity. I kissed her goodbye at the gate and said:

"You'll be having dinner at school with the other children, Chris, and I'll call for you when school is over, at three o'clock."

"Yes, mummy." She held my hand tightly. Other nervous little children were arriving with equally nervous parents. A pleasant young teacher with fair hair and a white linen dress appeared at the gate. She gathered the new children towards her and led them away. She gave me a sympathetic smile as she passed and said: "We'll take good care of her."

I felt quite light-hearted as I walked away, knowing that Chris was safe and I didn't have to worry.

Now I started on my secret mission. I took a bus to town and went to the big, gaunt building I hadn't visited for over five years. Then, Jim and I had gone together. The top floor of the building belonged to the Greythorne Adoption Society. I climbed the four flights and knocked on the familiar door with its scratched paint. A secretary whose face I didn't know let me in.

"May I see Miss Cleaver? My name is Mrs James."

"Have you an appointment?"

"No, but it's very important."

"I'll see." The girl went out and returned a second later. "Miss Cleaver will see you, Mrs James."

Miss Cleaver, a tall, thin, grey haired woman with a charming smile, a plain, kindly face and a very wrinkled brow, rose to meet me. "Mrs James. How nice to see you again. How's Christine?"

"She's very well. Miss Cleaver, I'd better get straight to the point. I know you don't normally divulge the origin of a child to its adopters and vice versa, but I must know who Christine is."

"Sorry, Mrs James," she began, "our rules . . ."

"Please let me tell you the whole story, then you'll see I'm not just suffering from vulgar curiosity."

I told her about Harry.

When I'd finished, she said: "It's very queer. Very queer indeed. Mrs James, I'm going to break my rule for once. I'm going to tell you in strict confidence where Christine came from."

"She was born in a very poor part of London. There were four in the family, father, mother, son and Christine herself."

"Son?"

"Yes. He was fourteen when – when it happened."

"When what happened?"

"Let me start at the beginning. The parents hadn't really wanted Christine. The family lived in one room at the top of an old house which should have been condemned by the Sanitary Inspector in my opinion. It was difficult enough when there were only three of them, but with a baby as well life became a nightmare. The mother was a neurotic creature, slatternly, unhappy, too fat. After she'd had the baby she took no interest in it. The brother, however, adored the little girl from the start. He got into trouble for cutting school so he could look after her."

"The father had a steady job in a warehouse, not much money, but enough to keep them alive. Then he was sick for several weeks and lost his job. He was laid up in that messy room, ill, worrying, nagged by his wife, irked by the baby's crying and his son's eternal fussing over the child – I got all these details from neighbours afterwards, by the way. I was also told that he'd had a particularly bad time in the war and had been in a nerve hospital for several months before he was fit to come home at all after his demob. Suddenly it all proved too much for him."

"One morning, in the small hours, a woman in the ground floor room saw something fall past her window and heard a thud on the ground. She went out to look. The son of the family was there on the ground. Christine was in his arms. The boy's neck was broken. He was dead. Christine was blue in the face but still breathing faintly."

"The woman woke the household, sent for the police and the doctor, then they went to the top room. They had to break down the door, which was locked and sealed inside. An overpowering smell of gas greeted them, in spite of the open window."

"They found husband and wife dead in bed and a note from the husband saying:

"I can't go on. I am going to kill them all.
It's the only way."

"The police concluded that he'd sealed up door and windows and turned on the gas when his family were asleep, then lain beside his wife until he drifted into unconsciousness, and death. But the son must have wakened. Perhaps he struggled with the door but couldn't open it. He'd be too weak to shout. All he could do was pluck away the seals from the window, open it, and fling himself out, holding his adored little sister tightly in his arms."

"Why Christine herself wasn't gassed is rather a mystery. Perhaps her head was right under the bedclothes, pressed against her brother's chest – they always slept together. Anyway, the child was taken to hospital, then to the home where you and Mr James first saw her . . . and a lucky day that was for little Christine!"

"So her brother saved her life and died himself?" I said.

"Yes. He was a very brave young man."

"Perhaps he thought not so much of saving her as of keeping her with him. Oh dear! That sounds ungenerous. I didn't mean to be. Miss Cleaver, what was his name?"

"I'll have to look that up for you." She referred to one of her many files and said at last: "The family's name was Jones and the fourteen-year-old brother was called 'Harold'."

"And did he have red hair?" I murmured.

"That I don't know, Mrs James."

"But it's Harry. The boy was Harry. What does it mean? I can't understand it."

"It's not easy, but I think perhaps deep in her unconscious mind Christine has always remembered Harry, the companion of her babyhood. We don't think of children as having much memory, but there must be images of the past tucked away somewhere in their little heads. Christine doesn't *invent* this Harry. She *remembers* him. So clearly that she's almost brought him to life again. I know it sounds far-fetched, but the whole story is so odd that I can't think of any other explanation."

"May I have the address of the house where they lived?"

She was reluctant to give me this information, but I persuaded her and set out at last to find No. 13 Canver Row, where the man Jones had tried to kill himself and his whole family and almost succeeded.

The house seemed deserted. It was filthy and derelict. But one thing made me stare and stare. There was a tiny garden. A scatter of bright uneven grass splashed the bald brown patches of earth. But the little garden had one strange glory that none of the other houses in the poor sad street possessed – a bush of white roses. They bloomed gloriously. Their scent was overpowering.

I stood by the bush and stared up at the top window.

A voice startled me: "What are you doing here?"

It was an old woman, peering from the ground floor window.

"I thought the house was empty," I said.

"Should be. Been condemned. But they can't get me out. Nowhere else to go. Won't go. The others went quickly enough after it happened. No one else wants to come. They say the place is haunted. So it is. But what's the fuss about? Life and death. They're very close. You get to know that when you're old. Alive or dead. What's the difference?"

She looked at me with yellowish, bloodshot eyes and said: "I saw him fall past my window. That's where he fell. Among the roses. He still comes back. I see him. He won't go away until he gets her."

"Who – who are you talking about?"

"Harry Jones. Nice boy he was. Red hair. Very thin. Too determined though. Always got his own way. Loved Christine too much I thought. Died among the roses. Used to sit down here with her for hours, by the roses. Then died there. Or do people die? The church ought to give us an answer, but it doesn't. Not one you can believe. Go away, will you? This place isn't for you. It's for the dead who aren't dead, and the living who aren't alive. Am I alive or dead? You tell me. I don't know."

The crazy eyes staring at me beneath the matted white fringe of hair frightened me. Mad people are terrifying. One can pity them, but one is still afraid. I murmured:

"I'll go now. Goodbye," and tried to hurry across the hard hot pavements although my legs felt heavy and half-paralysed, as in a nightmare.

The sun blazed down on my head, but I was hardly aware of it. I lost all sense of time or place as I stumbled on.

Then I heard something that chilled my blood.

A clock struck three.

At three o'clock I was supposed to be at the school gates, waiting for Christine.

Where was I now? How near the school? What bus should I take?

I made frantic inquiries of passers-by, who looked at me fearfully, as I had looked at the old woman. They must have thought I was crazy.

At last I caught the right bus and, sick with dust, petrol fumes and fear, reached the school. I ran across the hot, empty playground. In a classroom, the young teacher in white was gathering her books together.

"I've come for Christine James. I'm her mother. I'm so sorry I'm late. Where is she?" I gasped.

"Christine James?" The girl frowned, then said brightly: "Oh, yes, I remember, the pretty little red-haired girl. That's all right, Mrs James. Her brother called for her. How alike they are, aren't they? And so devoted. It's rather sweet to see a boy of that age so fond of his baby sister. Has your husband got red hair, like the two children?"

"What did – her brother – say?" I asked faintly.

"He didn't say anything. When I spoke to him, he just smiled. They'll be home by now, I should think. I say, do you feel all right?"

"Yes, thank you. I must go home."

I ran all the way home through the burning streets.

"Chris! Christine, where are you? Chris! Chris!" Sometimes even now I hear my own voice of the past screaming through the cold house. "Christine! Chris!

Where are you? Answer me! Chrrriiiiiss!" Then: "Harry! Don't take her away! Come back! Harry! Harry!"

Demented, I rushed out into the garden. The sun struck me like a hot blade. The roses glared whitely. The air was so still I seemed to stand in timelessness, placelessness. For a moment, I seemed very near to Christine, although I couldn't see her. Then the roses danced before my eyes and turned red. The world turned red. Blood red. Wet red. I fell through redness to blackness to nothingness – to almost death.

For weeks I was in bed with sunstroke which turned to brain fever. During that time Jim and the police searched for Christine in vain. The futile search continued for months. The papers were full of the strange disappearance of the red-haired child. The teacher described the "brother" who had called for her. There were newspaper stories of kidnapping, baby-snatching, child-murders.

Then the sensation died down. Just another unsolved mystery in police files.

And only two people knew what had happened. An old crazed woman living in a derelict house, and myself.

Years have passed. But I walk in fear.

Such ordinary things make me afraid. Sunshine. Sharp shadows on grass. White roses. Children with red hair. And the name – Harry. Such an ordinary name!

THE GIRL I LEFT BEHIND ME

Muriel Spark

Muriel Spark (1918–2006) was born Muriel Sarah Camberg in Edinburgh, to a Jewish father and Presbyterian mother. Spark married Sydney Oswald Spark in Rhodesia (Zimbabwe). He was unstable and the marriage quickly ended. She worked in intelligence during World War II and afterwards pursued her writing. Her novels include *The Prime of Miss Jean Brodie* and *The Driver's Seat*. She left Britain in 1963. Spark received an OBE in 1967 and was made a DBE in 1993. She died in Italy.

It was just gone quarter past six when I left the office.

"Teedle-um-tum-tum" – there was the tune again, going round my head. Mr Letter had been whistling it all throughout the day between his noisy telephone calls and his dreamy sessions. Sometimes he whistled "Softly, Softly, Turn the Key", but usually it was "The Girl I Left Behind Me" rendered at a brisk hornpipe tempo.

I stood in the bus queue, tired out, and wondering how long I would endure Mark Letter (Screws & Nails) Ltd. Of course, after my long illness, it was experience. But Mr Letter and his tune, and his sudden moods of bounce, and his sudden lapses into lassitude, his sandy hair and little bad teeth, roused my resentment, especially when his tune barrelled round my head long after I had left the office; it was like taking Mr Letter home.

No one at the bus stop took any notice of me. Well, of course, why should they? I was not acquainted with anyone there, but that evening I felt particularly anonymous among the homegoers. Everyone looked right through me and even, it seemed, walked through me. Late autumn always sets my fancy towards sad ideas. The starlings were crowding in to roost on all the high cornices of the great office buildings. And I located, among the misty unease of my feelings, a very strong conviction that I had left something important behind me or some job incompleted at the office. Perhaps I had left the safe unlocked, or perhaps it was something quite trivial which nagged at me. I had half a mind to turn back, tired as I was, and reassure myself. But my bus came along and I piled in with the rest.

As usual, I did not get a seat. I clung to the handrail and allowed myself to be lurched back and forth against the other passengers. I stood on a man's foot, and said, "Oh, sorry." But he looked away without response, which depressed me. And more and more, I felt that I had left something of tremendous import at the office. "Teedle-um-tum-tum" – the tune was a background to my worry all the way home. I went over in my mind the day's business, for I thought, now, perhaps it was a letter which I should have written and posted on my way home.

That morning I had arrived at the office to find Mark Letter vigorously at work. By fits, he would occasionally turn up at eight in the morning, tear at the post and, by the time I arrived, he would have dispatched perhaps half a dozen needless telegrams; and before I could get my coat off, would deliver a whole day's instructions to me, rapidly fluttering his freckled hands in time with his chattering mouth. This habit used to jar me, and I found only one thing amusing about it; that was when he would say, as he gave instructions for dealing with each item, "Mark letter urgent." I thought that rather funny coming from Mark Letter, and I often thought of him, as he was in those moods, as Mark Letter Urgent.

As I swayed in the bus I recalled that morning's excess of energy on the part of Mark Letter Urgent. He had been more urgent than usual, so that I still felt put out by the urgency. I felt terribly old for my twenty-two years as I raked round my mind for some clue as to what I had left unfinished. Something had been left amiss; the further the bus carried me from the office, the more certain I became of it. Not that I took my job to heart very greatly, but Mr Letter's moods of bustle were infectious, and when they occurred I felt fussy for the rest of the day; and although I consoled myself that I would feel better when I got home, the worry would not leave me.

By noon, Mr Letter had calmed down a little, and for an hour before I went to lunch he strode round the office with his hands in his pockets, whistling between his seedy brown teeth that sailors' song "The Girl I Left Behind Me". I lurched with the bus as it chugged out the rhythm, "Teedle-um-tum-tum. Teedle-um . . ." Returning from lunch I had found silence, and wondered if Mr Letter was out, until I heard suddenly, from his tiny private office, his tune again, a low swift hum, trailing out towards the end. Then I knew that he had fallen into one of his afternoon daydreams.

I would sometimes come upon him in his little box of an office when these trances afflicted him. I would find him sitting in his swivel chair behind his desk. Usually he had taken off his coat and slung it across the back of his chair. His right elbow would be propped on the desk, supporting his chin, while from his left hand would dangle his tie. He would gaze at this tie; it was his main object of contemplation. That afternoon I had found him tie-gazing when I went into his room for some papers. He was gazing at it with parted lips so that I could see his small, separated discoloured teeth, no larger than a child's first teeth. Through them he whistled his tune. Yesterday, it had been "Softly, Softly, Turn the Key", but today it was the other.

I got off the bus at my usual stop, with my fare still in my hand. I almost threw the coins away, absentmindedly thinking they were the ticket, and when I noticed them I thought how nearly no one at all I was, since even the conductor had, in his rush, passed me by.

Mark Letter had remained in his dream for two and a half hours. What was it I had left unfinished? I could not for the life of me recall what he had said when at last he emerged from his office-box. Perhaps it was then I had made tea. Mr Letter always liked a cup when he was neither in his frenzy nor in his abstraction, but ordinary and talkative. He would speak of his hobby, fretwork. I do not think Mr Letter had any home life. At forty-six he was still unmarried, living alone in a house at Roehampton. As I walked up the lane to my lodgings I recollected that Mr Letter had come in for his tea with his tie still dangling from his hand, his throat white under the open-neck shirt, and his "Teedle-um-tum-tum" in his teeth.

At last I was home and my Yale in the lock. Softly, I said to myself, softly turn the key, and thank God I'm home. My landlady passed through the hall from kitchen to diningroom with a salt and pepper cruet in her crinkly hands. She had some new lodgers. "My guests", she always called them. The new guests took precedence over the old with my landlady. I felt desolate. I simply could not climb the stairs to my room to wash, and then descend to take brown soup with the new guests while my landlady fussed over them, ignoring me. I sat for a moment in the chair in the hall to collect my strength. A year's illness drains one, however young. Suddenly the repulsion of the brown soup and the anxiety about the office made me decide. I would not go upstairs to my room. I must return to the office to see what it was that I had overlooked.

"Teedle-um-tum-tum" – I told myself that I was giving way to neurosis. Many times I had laughed at my sister who, after she had gone to bed at night, would send her husband downstairs to make sure all the gas taps were turned off, all the doors locked, back and front. Very well, I was as silly as my sister, but I understood her obsession, and simply opened the door and slipped out of the house, tired as I was, making my weary way back to the bus stop, back to the office.

"Why should I do this for Mark Letter?" I demanded of myself. But really, I was not returning for his sake, it was for my own. I was doing this to get rid of the feeling of incompletion, and that song in my brain swimming round like a damned goldfish.

I wondered, as the bus took me back along the familiar route, what I would say if Mark Letter should still be at the office. He often worked late, or at least, stayed there late, doing I don't know what, for his screw and nail business did not call for long hours. It seemed to me he had an affection for those dingy premises. I was rather apprehensive lest I should find Mr Letter at the office, standing, just as I had last seen him, swinging his tie in his hand, beside my desk. I resolved that if I should find him there, I should say straight out that I had left something behind me.

A clock struck quarter past seven as I got off the bus. I realized that again I had not paid my fare. I looked at the money in my hand for a stupid second. Then I felt reckless. "Teedle-um-tum-tum" – I caught myself humming the tune as I walked quickly up the sad side street to our office. My heart knocked at my throat, for I was eager. Softly, softly, I said to myself as I turned the key of the outside door. Quickly, quickly, I ran up the stairs. Only outside the office door I halted, and while I found its key on my bunch it occurred to me how strangely my sister would think I was behaving.

I opened the door and my sadness left me at once. With a great joy I recognized what it was I had left behind me, my body lying strangled on the floor. I ran towards my body and embraced it like a lover.

POOR GIRL

Elizabeth Taylor

Elizabeth Taylor (1912–1975), née Coles, was born in Reading, Berkshire. Her novels and short stories are understated, witty examinations of middle-class English life and manners. She married John Taylor, the director of a sweet factory, and the couple had two children. Taylor wrote her first novel, *At Mrs Lippincote's* (1945) while her husband was serving in the RAF. She gave the impression of a life more domestic than literary, telling an interviewer that she worked her novels out, 'when I am doing the ironing'.

Miss Chasty's first pupil was a flirtatious little boy. At seven years, he was alarmingly precocious, and sometimes she thought that he despised his childhood, regarding it as a waiting time which he used only as a rehearsal for adult life. He was already more sophisticated than his young governess and disturbed her with his air of dalliance, the mockery with which he set about his lessons, the preposterous conversations he led her into, guiding her skilfully away from work, confusing her with bizarre conjectures and irreverent ideas, so that she would clasp her hands tightly under the plush table-cloth and pray that his father would not choose such a moment to observe her teaching, coming in abruptly as he sometimes did and signalling to her to continue the lesson.

At those times, his son's eyes were especially lively, fixed cruelly upon his governess as he listened, smiling faintly, to her faltering voice, measuring her timidity. He would answer her questions correctly, but significantly, as if he knew that by his aptitude he rescued her from dismissal. There were many governesses waiting employment, he implied – and this was so at the beginning of the century. He underlined her good fortune at having a pupil who could so easily learn, could display the results of her teaching to such an advantage for the benefit of the rather sombre, pompous figure seated at the window. When his father, apparently satisfied, had left them without a word, the boy's manner changed. He seemed fatigued and too absent-minded to reply to any more questions.

"Hilary!" she would say sharply. "Are you attending to me?" Her sharpness and her foolishness amused him, coming as he knew they did from the tension of the last ten minutes.

"Why, my dear girl, of course."

"You must address me by my name."

"Certainly, dear Florence."

"Miss Chasty."

His lips might shape the words, which he was too weary to say.

Sometimes, when she was correcting his sums, he would come round the table to stand beside her, leaning against her heavily, looking closely at her face, not at his book, breathing steadily down his nose so that tendrils of hair wavered on her neck and against her cheeks. His stillness, his concentration on her and his too heavy leaning, worried her. She felt something experimental in his attitude, as if he were not leaning against her at all, but against someone in the future. "He is only a baby," she reminded herself, but she would try to shift from him, feeling a vague distaste. She would blush, as if he were a grown man, and her heart could be heard beating quickly. He was aware of this and would take up the corrected book and move back to his place.

Once he proposed to her and she had the feeling that it was a proposal-rehearsal and that he was making use of her, as an actor might ask her to hear his lines.

"You must go on with your work" she said.

"I can shade in a map and talk as well."

"Then talk sensibly."

"You think I am too young, I daresay; but you could wait for me to grow up, I can do that quickly enough."

"You are far from grown-up at the moment."

"You only say these things because you think that governesses ought to. I suppose you don't know how governesses go on, because you have never been one until now, and you were too poor to have one of your own when you were young."

"That is impertinent, Hilary."

"You once told me your father couldn't afford one."

"Which is a different way of putting it."

"I shouldn't have thought they cost much." He had a way of just making a remark, of breathing it so gently that it was scarcely said, and might conveniently be ignored.

He was a dandified boy. His smooth hair was like a silk cap, combed straight from the crown to a level line above his topaz eyes. His sailor-suits were spotless. The usual boldness changed to an agonised fussiness if his serge sleeve brushed against chalk or if he should slip on the grassy terrace and stain his clothes with green. On their afternoon walks he took no risks and Florence, who had younger brothers, urged him in vain to climb a tree or jump across puddles. At first, she thought him intimidated by his mother or nurse; but soon she realised that his mother entirely indulged him and the nurse had her thoughts all bent upon the new baby; his fussiness was just another part of his grown-upness come too soon.

The house was comfortable, although to Florence rather too sealed-up and overheated after her own damp and draughty home. Her work was not hard and her loneliness only what she had expected. Cut off from the kitchen by her education, she lacked the feuds and camaraderie, gossip and cups of tea, which make life more interesting for the domestic staff. None of the maids – coming to light the lamp at dusk or laying the schoolroom-table for tea – ever presumed beyond a remark or two about the weather.

One late afternoon, she and Hilary returned from their walk and found the lamps already lit. Florence went to her room to tidy herself before tea. When she came down to the schoolroom, Hilary was already there, sitting on the window-seat and staring out over the park as his father did. The room was bright and warm and a maid had put a white cloth over the plush one and was beginning to lay the table.

The air was full of a heavy scent, dry and musky. To Florence, it smelt quite unlike the eau de cologne she sometimes sprinkled on her handkerchief, when she had a headache, and she disapproved so much that she returned the maid's greeting coldly and bade Hilary open the window.

"Open the window, dear girl?" he said. "We shall catch our very deaths."

"You will do as I ask and remember in future how to address me."

She was angry with the maid – who now seemed to her an immoral creature – and angry to be humiliated before her.

"But why?" asked Hilary.

"I don't approve of my schoolroom being turned into a scented bower." She kept her back to the room and was trembling, for she had never rebuked a servant before.

"I approve of it," Hilary said, sniffing loudly.

"I think it's lovely," the maid said. "I noticed it as soon as I opened the door."

"Is this some joke, Hilary?" Florence asked when the girl had gone.

"No. What?"

"This smell in the room?"

"No. You smell of it most, anyhow." He put his nose to her sleeve and breathed deeply.

It seemed to Florence that this was so, that her clothes had caught the perfume among the folds. She lifted her palms to her face, then went to the window and leant out into the air as far as she could.

"Shall I pour out the tea, dear girl?"

"Yes, please."

She took her place at the table abstractedly, and as she drank her tea she stared about the room, frowning. When Hilary's mother looked in, as she often did at this time, Florence stood up in a startled way.

"Good-evening, Mrs Wilson. Hilary, put a chair for your mamma."

"Don't let me disturb you."

Mrs Wilson sank into the rocking-chair by the fire and gently tipped to and fro.

"Have you finished your tea, darling boy?" she asked. "Are you going to read me a story from your book? Oh, there is Lady scratching at the door. Let her in for mamma."

Hilary opened the door and a bald old pug-dog with bloodshot eyes waddled in.

"Come, Lady! Beautiful one. Come to mistress! What is wrong with her, poor pet lamb?"

The bitch had stepped just inside the room and lifted her head and howled. "What has frightened her, then? Come, beauty! Coax her with a sponge-cake, Hilary."

She reached forward to the table to take the dish and doing so noticed Florence's empty tea-cup. On the rim was a crimson smear, like the imprint of a lip. She gave a sponge-finger to Hilary, who tried to quieten the pug, then she leaned back in her chair and studied Florence again as she had studied her when she engaged her a few weeks earlier. The girl's looks were appropriate enough, appropriate to a clergyman's daughter and a governess. Her square chin looked resolute, her green eyes innocent, her dress was modest and unbecoming. Yet Mrs Wilson could detect an excitability, even feverishness, which she had not noticed before and she wondered if she had mistaken guardedness for innocence and deceit for modesty.

She was reaching this conclusion – rocking back and forth – when she saw Florence's hand stretch out and turn the cup round in its saucer so that the red stain was out of sight.

"What is wrong with Lady?" Hilary asked, for the dog would not be pacified with sponge-fingers, but kept making barking advances farther into the room, then growling in retreat.

"Perhaps she is crying at the new moon," said Florence and she went to the window and drew back the curtain. As she moved, her skirts rustled. "If she has silk underwear as well!" Mrs Wilson thought. She had clearly heard the sound of taffetas, and she imagined the drab, shiny alpaca dress concealing frivolity and wantonness.

"Open the door, Hilary," she said. "I will take Lady away. Vernon shall give her a run in the park. I think a quiet read for Hilary and then an early bed-time, Miss Chasty. He looks pale this evening."

"Yes, Mrs Wilson." Florence stood respectfully by the table, hiding the cup.

"The hypocrisy!" Mrs Wilson thought and she trembled as she crossed the landing and went downstairs.

She hesitated to tell her husband of her uneasiness, knowing his susceptibilities to the kind of women whom his conscience taught him to deplore. Hidden below the apparent urbanity of their married life were old unhappinesses – little acts of treachery and disloyalty which pained her to remember, bruises upon her peace of mind and her pride: letters found, a pretty maid dismissed, an actress who had blackmailed him. As he read the Lesson in church, looking so perfectly upright and honourable a man, she sometimes thought of his escapades; but not with bitterness or cynicism, only with pain at her memories and a whisper of fear about the future. For some time she had been spared those whispers and had hoped that their marriage had at last achieved its calm. To speak of Florence as she must might both arouse his curiosity and revive the past. Nevertheless, she had her duty to her son to fulfil and her own anger to appease and she opened the library door very determinedly.

"Oliver, I am sorry to interrupt your work, but I must speak to you."

He put down the *Strand Magazine* quite happily, aware that she was not a sarcastic woman.

Oliver and his son were extraordinarily alike. "As soon as Hilary has grown a moustache we shall not know them apart," Mrs Wilson often said, and her husband liked this little joke which made him feel more youthful. He did not know that she added a silent prayer – "O God, please do not let him *be* like him, though."

"You seem troubled, Louise." His voice was rich and authoritative. He enjoyed setting to rights her little domestic flurries and waited indulgently to hear of some tradesman's misdemeanour or servant's laziness.

"Yes, I am troubled about Miss Chasty."

"Little Miss Mouse? I was rather troubled myself. I noticed two spelling faults in Hilary's botany essay, which she claimed to have corrected. I said nothing before the boy, but I shall acquaint her with it when the opportunity arises."

"Do you often go to the schoolroom, then?"

"From time to time. I like to be sure that our choice was wise."

"It was not. It was misguided and unwise."

"All young people seem slip-shod nowadays."

"She is more than slip-shod. I believe she should go. I think she is quite brazen. Oh, yes, I should have laughed at that myself if it had been said to me an hour ago, but I have just come from the schoolroom and it occurs to me that now she has settled down and feels more secure – since you pass over her mistakes – she is beginning to take advantage of your leniency and to show herself in her true colours. I felt a sinister atmosphere up there, and I am quite upset and exhausted by it. I went up to hear Hilary's reading. They were finishing tea and the room was full of the most over-powering scent, *her* scent. It was disgusting."

"Unpleasant?"

"No, not at all. But upsetting."

"Disturbing?"

She would not look at him or reply, hearing no more indulgence or condescension in his voice, but the quality of warming interest.

"And then I saw her teacup and there was a mark on it – a red smear where her lips had touched it. She did not know I saw it and as soon as she noticed it herself she turned it round, away from me. She is an immoral woman and she has come into our house to teach our son."

"I have never noticed a trace of artificiality in her looks. It seemed to me that she was rather colourless."

"She has been sly. This evening she looked quite different, quite flushed and excitable. I know that she had rouged her lips or painted them or whatever those women do." Her eyes filled with tears.

"I shall observe her for a day or two," Oliver said, trying to keep anticipation from his voice.

"I should like her to go at once."

"Never act rashly. She is entitled to a quarter's notice unless there is definite blame. We should make ourselves very foolish if you have been mistaken. Oh, I know that you are sure; but it has been known for you to misjudge others. I shall take stock of her and decide if she is unsuitable. She is still Miss Mouse to me and I cannot think otherwise until I see the evidence with my own eyes."

"There was something else as well," Mrs Wilson said wretchedly.

"And what was that?"

"I would rather not say." She had changed her mind about further accusations. Silk underwear would prove, she guessed, too inflammatory.

"I shall go up ostensibly to mention Hilary's spelling faults." He could not go fast enough and stood up at once.

"But Hilary is in bed."

"I could not mention the spelling faults if he were not."

"Shall I come with you?"

"My dear Louise, why should you? It would look very strange – a deputation about two spelling faults."

"Then don't be long, will you? I hope you won't be long."

He went to the schoolroom, but there was no one there. Hilary's story-book lay closed upon the table and Miss Chasty's sewing was folded neatly. As he was standing there looking about him and sniffing hard, a maid came in with a tray of crockery.

"Has Master Hilary gone to bed?" he asked, feeling rather foolish and confused.

The only scent in the air was a distinct smell – even a haze – of cigarette smoke.

"Yes, sir."

"And Miss Chasty – where is she?"

"She went to bed, too, sir."

"Is she unwell?"

"She spoke of a chronic head, sir."

The maid stacked the cups and saucers in the cupboard and went out. Nothing was wrong with the room apart from the smell of smoke and Mr Wilson went downstairs. His wife was waiting in the hall. She looked up expectantly, in some relief at seeing him so soon.

"Nothing," he said dramatically. "She has gone to bed with a headache. No wonder she looked feverish."

"You noticed the scent."

"There was none," he said. "No trace. Nothing. Just imagination, dear Louise. I thought that it must be so."

He went to the library and took up his magazine again, but he was too disturbed to read and thought with impatience of the following day.

Florence could not sleep. She had gone to her room, not with a headache but to escape conversations until she had faced the predicament alone. This she was doing, lying on the honeycomb quilt which, since maids do not wait on governesses, had not been turned down.

The schoolroom this evening seemed to have been wreathed about with a strange miasma; the innocent nature of the place polluted in a way that she could not understand or have explained. Something new, it seemed, had entered the room – the scent had clung about her clothes; the stained cup was her own cup, and her handkerchief with which she had rubbed it clean was still reddened; and finally, as she stared in the mirror, trying to reestablish her personality, the affected little laugh which startled her had come from herself. It had driven her from the room.

"I cannot explain the inexplicable," she thought wearily and began to prepare herself for bed. Home-sickness hit her like a blow on the head. "Whatever they do to me, I have always my home," she promised herself. But she could not think who "They" might be; for no one in this house had threatened her. Mrs Wilson had done no more than irritate her with her commonplace fussing over Hilary and her dog, and Florence was prepared to overcome much more than irritation. Mr Wilson's pomposity, his constant watch on her works, intimidated her, but she knew that all who must earn their living must have fears lest their work should not seem worth the wages. Hilary was easy to manage; she had quickly seen that she could always deflect him from rebelliousness by opening a new subject for conversation; any idea would be a counterattraction to naughtiness; he wanted her to sharpen his wits upon. "And is that all that teaching is, or should be?" she had wondered. The servants had been good to her, realising that she would demand nothing of them. She had suffered great loneliness, but had foreseen it as part of her position. Now she felt fear nudging it away. "I am not lonely any more," she thought. "I am not alone any more. And I have lost something." She said her prayers; then, sitting up in bed, kept the candle alight while she brushed her hair and read the Bible.

"Perhaps I have lost my reason," she suddenly thought, resting her finger on her place in the Psalms. She lifted her head and saw her shadow stretch up the powdery, rose-sprinkled wall. "How can I keep that secret?" she wondered. "When there is no one to help me do it? Only those who are watching to see it happen."

She was not afraid in her bedroom as she had been in the schoolroom, but her perplexed mind found no replies to its questions. She blew out the candle and tried to fall asleep, but lay and cried for a long time, and yearned to be at home again and comforted in her mother's arms.

In the morning she met kind enquiries. Nurse was so full of solicitude that Florence felt guilty. "I came up with a warm drink and put my head round the door but you were in the land of Nod so I drank it myself. I should take a grey powder; or I could mix you a gargle. There are a lot of throats about."

"I am quite better this morning," said Florence and she felt calmer as she sat down at the schoolroom-table with Hilary. "Yet, it was all true," her reason whispered. "The morning hasn't altered that."

"You have been crying," said Hilary. "Your eyes are red."

"Sometimes people's eyes are red from other causes – headaches and colds." She smiled brightly.

"And sometimes from crying, as I said. I should think usually from crying."

"Page fifty-one," she said, locking her hands together in her lap.

"Very well." He opened the book, pressed down the pages and lowered his nose to them, breathing the smell of print. "He is utterly sensuous," she thought. "He extracts every pleasure, every sensation, down to the most trivial."

They seemed imprisoned in the schoolroom, by the silence of the rest of the house and by the rain outside. Her calm began to break up into frustration and she put her hands behind her chair and pressed them against the hot mesh of the fireguard to steady herself. As she did so, she felt a curious derangement of both mind and body; of desire unsettling her once sluggish peaceful nature, desire horribly defined, though without direction.

"I have soon finished those," said Hilary, bringing his sums and placing them before her. She glanced at her palms which were criss-crossed deep with crimson where she had pressed them against the fireguard, then she took up her pen and dipped it into the red ink.

"Don't lean against me, Hilary," she said.

"I love the scent so much."

It had returned, musky, enveloping, varying as she moved.

She ticked the sums quickly, thinking that she would set Hilary more work and escape for a moment to calm herself – change her clothes or cleanse herself in the rain. Hearing Mr Wilson's footsteps along the passage, she knew that her escape was cut off and raised wild-looking eyes as he came in. He mistook panic for passion, thought that by opening the door suddenly he had caught her out and laid bare her secret, her pathetic adoration.

"Good morning," he said musically and made his way to the window-seat. "Don't let me disturb you." He said this without irony, although he thought: "So it is that way the wind blows! Poor creature!" He had never found it difficult to imagine women were in love with him.

"I will hear your verbs," Florence told Hilary, and opened the French Grammar as if she did not know them herself. Her eyes – from so much crying – were a pale and brilliant green, and as the scent drifted in Oliver's direction and he turned to her, she looked fully at him.

"Ah, the still waters!" he thought and stood up suddenly. "Ils vont," he corrected Hilary and touched his shoulder as he passed. "Are you attending to Miss Chasty?"

"Is she attending to me?" Hilary murmured. The risk was worth taking, for neither heard. His father appeared to be sleep-walking and Florence deliberately closed her eyes, as if looking down were not enough to blur the outlines of her desire.

"I find it difficult," Oliver said to his wife, "to reconcile your remarks about Miss Chasty with the young woman herself. I have just come from the schoolroom and she was engaged in nothing more immoral than teaching French verbs – that not very well incidentally."

"But can you explain what I have told you?"

"I can't do that," he said gaily. For who can explain a jealous woman's fancies? he implied.

He began to spend more time in the schoolroom; from surveillance, he said. Miss Chasty, though not outwardly of an amorous nature, was still not what he had at first supposed. A suppressed wantonness hovered beneath her primness. She was the ideal governess in his eye – irreproachable, yet not unapproachable. As she was so conveniently installed, he could take his time in divining the extent of her willingness; especially as he was growing older and the game was beginning to be worth more than the triumph of winning it. To his wife, he upheld Florence, saw nothing wrong save in her scholarship, which needed to be looked into – this, the explanation for his more frequent visits to the schoolroom. He laughed teasingly at Louise's fancies.

The schoolroom indeed became a focal point of the house – the stronghold of Mr Wilson's desire and his wife's jealousy.

"We are never alone," said Hilary. "Either Papa or Mamma is here. Perhaps they wonder if you are good enough for me."

"Hilary!" His father had heard the last sentence as he opened the door and the first as he hovered outside listening. "I doubt if my ears deceived me. You will go to your room while you think of a suitable apology and I think of an ample punishment."

"Shall I take my history book with me or shall I just waste time?"

"I have indicated how to spend your time."

"That won't take long enough," said Hilary beneath his breath as he closed the door.

"Meanwhile, I apologise for him," said his father. He did not go to his customary place by the window, but came to the hearth-rug where Florence stood behind her chair. "We have indulged him too much and he has been too much with adults. Have there been other occasions?"

"No, indeed, sir."

"You find him tractable?"

"Oh, yes."

"And are you happy in your position?"

"Yes."

As the dreaded, the now so familiar scent began to wreath about the room, she stepped back from him and began to speak rapidly, as urgently as if she were dying and must make some explanation while she could. "Perhaps, after all, Hilary is right and you do wonder about my competence – and if I can give him all he should have. Perhaps a man would teach him more. . . ."

She began to feel a curious infraction of the room and of her personality, seemed to lose the true Florence, and the room lightened as if the season had been changed.

"You are mistaken," he was saying. "Have I ever given you any hint that we were not satisfied?"

Her timidity had quite dissolved and he was shocked by the sudden boldness of her glance.

"I should rather give you a hint of how well pleased I am."

"Then why don't you?" she asked.

She leaned back against the chimney-piece and looped about her fingers a long necklace of glittering green beads. "Where did these come from?" she wondered. She could not remember ever having seen them before, but she could not pursue her bewilderment, for the necklace felt familiar to her hands, much more familiar than the rest of the room.

"When shall I?" he was insisting. "This evening, perhaps, when Hilary is in bed?"

"Then who is *he*, if Hilary is to be in bed?" she wondered. She glanced at him and smiled again. "You are extraordinarily alike," she said. "You and Hilary." "But Hilary is a little boy," she reminded herself. "It is silly to confuse the two."

"We must discuss Hilary's progress," he said, his voice so burdened with meaning that she began to laugh at him.

"Indeed we must," she agreed.

"Your necklace is the colour of your eyes." He took it from her fingers and leaned forward, as if to kiss her. Hearing footsteps in the passage she moved sharply aside, the necklace broke and the beads scattered over the floor.

"Why is Hilary in the garden at this hour?" Mrs Wilson asked. Her husband and the governess were on their knees, gathering up the beads.

"Miss Chasty's necklace broke," her husband said. She had heard that submissive tone before: his voice lacked authority only when he was caught out in some infidelity.

"I was asking about Hilary. I have just seen him running in the shrubbery without a coat."

"He was sent to his room for being impertinent to Miss Chasty."

"Please fetch him at once," Mrs Wilson told Florence. Her voice always gained in authority what her husband's lacked.

Florence hurried from the room, still holding a handful of beads. She felt badly shaken – as if she had been brought to the edge of some experience which had then retreated beyond her grasp.

"He was told to stay in his room," Mr Wilson said feebly.

"Why did her beads break?"

"She was fidgeting with them. I think she was nervous. I was making it rather apparent to her that I regarded Hilary's insubordination as proof of too much leniency on her part."

"I didn't know that she had such a necklace. It is the showiest trash I have ever seen."

"We cannot blame her for the cheapness of her trinkets. It is rather pathetic."

"There is nothing pathetic about her. We will continue this in the morning-room and they can continue their lessons, which are, after all, her reason for being here."

"Oh, they are gone," said Hilary. His cheeks were pink from the cold outside.

"Why did you not stay in your bedroom as you were told?"

"I had nothing to do. I thought of my apology before I got there. It was: "I am sorry, dear girl, that I spoke too near the point'."

"You could have spent longer and thought of a real apology."

"Look how long Papa spent and he did not even think of a punishment, which is a much easier thing."

Several times during the evening Mr Wilson said: "But you cannot dismiss a girl because her beads break."

"There have been other things and will be more," his wife replied.

So that there should not be more that evening, he did not move from the drawing-room where he sat watching her doing her wool-work. For the same reason, Florence left the schoolroom early. She went out and walked rather nervously in the park, feeling remorseful, astonished and upset.

"Did you mend your necklace?" Hilary asked her in the morning.

"I lost the beads."

"But my poor girl, they must be somewhere."

She thought: "There is no reason to suppose that I shall get back what I never had in the first place."

"Have you got a headache?"

"Yes. Go on with your work, Hilary."

"Is it from losing the beads?"

"No."

"Have you a great deal of jewellery I have not seen yet?"

She did not answer and he went on: "You still have your brooch with your grandmother's plaited hair in it. Was it cut off her head when she was dead."

"Your work, Hilary."

"I shudder to think of chopping it off a corpse. You could have some of my hair, now, while I am living." He fingered it with admiration, regarded a sum aloofly and jotted down his answer. "Could I cut some of yours?" he asked, bringing his book to be corrected. He whistled softly, close to her, and the tendrils of hair round her ears were gently blown about.

"It is ungentlemanly to whistle," she said.

"My sums are always right. It shows how I can chatter and subtract at the same time. Any governess would be annoyed by that. I suppose your brothers never whistle."

"Never."

"Are they to be clergymen like your father?"

"It is what we hope for one of them."

"I am to be a famous judge. When you read about me, will you say: "And to think I might have been his wife if I had not been so self-willed'?"

"No, but I hope that I shall feel proud that once I taught you."

"You sound doubtful."

He took his book back to the table. "We are having a quiet morning," he remarked. "No one has visited us. Poor Miss Chasty, it is a pity about the necklace," he murmured, as he took up his pencil again.

Evenings were dangerous to her. "He said he would come," she told herself, "and I allowed him to say so. On what compulsion did I?"

Fearfully, she spent her lonely hours out in the dark garden or in her cold and candle-lit bedroom. He was under his wife's vigilance and Florence did not know that he dared not leave the drawing-room. But the vigilance relaxed, as it does; his carelessness returned and steady rain and bitter cold drove Florence to warm her chilblains at the schoolroom fire.

Her relationship with Mrs Wilson had changed. A wary hostility took the place of meekness, and when Mrs Wilson came to the schoolroom at tea-times, Florence stood up defiantly and cast a look round the room as if to say: "Find what you can. There is nothing here." Mrs Wilson's suspicious ways increased her rebelliousness. "I have done nothing wrong," she told herself. But in her bedroom at night: "*I* have done nothing wrong," she would think.

"They have quite deserted us," Hilary said from time to time. "They have realised you are worth your weight in gold, dear girl; or perhaps I made it clear to my father that in this room he is an interloper."

"Hilary!"

"You want to put yourself in the right in case that door opens suddenly as it has been doing lately. There, you see! Good-evening, Mamma. I was just saying that I had scarcely seen you all day." He drew forward her chair and held the cushion behind her until she leaned back.

"I have been resting."

"Are you ill, Mamma?"

"I have a headache."

"I will stroke it for you, dear lady."

He stood behind her chair and began to smooth her forehead. "Or shall I read to you?" he asked, soon tiring of his task, "Or play the musical-box?"

"No, nothing more, thank you."

Mrs Wilson looked about her, at the tea-cups, then at Florence. Sometimes it seemed to her that her husband was right and that she was growing fanciful. The innocent appearance of the room lulled her and she closed her eyes for a while, rocking gently in her chair.

"I dozed off," she said when she awoke. The table was cleared and Florence and Hilary sat playing chess, whispering so that they should not disturb her.

"It made a domestic scene for us," said Hilary. "Often Miss Chasty and I feel that we are left too much in solitary bliss."

The two women smiled and Mrs Wilson shook her head. "You have too old a head on your shoulders," she said. "What will they say of you when you go to school?"

"What shall I say of *them*?" he asked bravely, but he lowered his eyes and kept them lowered. When his mother had gone, he asked Florence: "Did you go to school?"

"Yes."

"Were you unhappy there?"

"No, I was homesick at first."

"If I don't like it, there will be no point in my staying," he said hurriedly. "I can learn anywhere and I don't particularly want the corners knocked off, as my father once spoke of it. I shouldn't like to play cricket and all those childish games. Only to do boxing and draw blood," he added, with sudden bravado. He laughed excitedly and clenched his fists.

"You would never be good at boxing if you lost your temper."

"I suppose your brothers told you that. They don't sound very manly to me. They would be afraid of a good fight and the sight of blood, I daresay."

"Yes, I daresay. It is bedtime."

He was whipped up by the excitement he had created from his fears.

"Chess is a woman's game," he said and upset the board. He took the cushion from the rocking-chair and kicked it inexpertly across the room. "I should have thought the door would have opened then," he said. "But as my father doesn't appear to send me to my room, I will go there of my own accord. It wouldn't have been a punishment at bedtime in any case. When I am a judge I shall be better at punishments than he is."

When he had gone, Florence picked up the cushion and the chess-board. "I am no good at punishments either," she thought. She tidied the room, made up the fire, then sat down in the rocking-chair, thinking of all the lonely schoolroom evenings of her future. She bent her head over her needlework – the beaded sachet for her mother's birthday present. When she looked up she thought the lamp was smoking and she went to the table and turned down the wick. Then she noticed that the smoke was wreathing upwards from near the fireplace, forming rings which drifted towards the ceiling and were lost in a haze. She could hear a woman's voice humming softly and the floorboards creaked as if someone were treading up and down the room impatiently.

She felt in herself a sense of burning impatience and anticipation and watching the door opening found herself thinking: "If it is not he, I cannot bear it."

He closed the door quietly. "She has gone to bed," he said in a lowered voice. "For days I dared not come. She has watched me every moment. At last, this evening, she gave way to a headache. Were you expecting me?"

"Yes."

"And once I called you Miss Mouse! And you are still Miss Mouse when I see you about the garden, or at luncheon."

"In this room I can be by myself. It belongs to us."

"And not to Hilary as well – ever?" he asked her in amusement.

She gave him a quick and puzzled glance.

"Let no one intrude," he said hastily. "It is our room, just as you say."

She had turned the lamp too low and it began to splutter. "Firelight is good enough for us," he said, putting the light out altogether.

When he kissed her, she felt an enormous sense of disappointment, almost as if he were the wrong person embracing her in the dark. His arch masterfulness merely bored her. "A long wait for so little," she thought.

He, however, found her entirely seductive. She responded with a sensuous languor, unruffled and at ease like the most perfect hostess.

"Where did you practise this, Miss Mouse?" he asked her. But he did not wait for the reply, fancying that he heard a step on the landing. When his wife opened the door, he was trying desperately to light a taper at the fire. His hand was trembling, and when at last, in the terribly silent room, the flame crept up the spill it simply served to show up Florence's disarray, which, like a sleep-walker, she had not noticed or put right.

She did not see Hilary again, except as a blurred little figure at the schoolroom window – blurred because of her tear-swollen eyes.

She was driven away in the carriage, although Mr Wilson had suggested the station-fly. "Let us keep her disgrace and her tearfulness to ourselves," he begged, although he was exhausted by the repetitious burden of his wife's grief.

"*Her* disgrace!"

"My mistake, I have said, was in not taking your accusations about her seriously. I see now that I was in some way bewitched – yes, bewitched, is what it was – acting against my judgment; nay, my very nature. I am astonished that anyone so seemingly meek could have cast such a spell upon me."

Poor Florence turned her head aside as Williams, the coachman, came to fetch her little trunk and the basket-work holdall. Then she put on her cloak and prepared herself to go downstairs, fearful lest she should meet anyone on the way. Yet her thoughts were even more on her journey's end; for what, she wondered, could she tell her father and how expect him to understand what she could not understand herself?

Her head was bent as she crossed the landing and she hurried past the schoolroom door. At the turn of the staircase she pressed back against the wall to allow someone to pass. She heard laughter and then up the stairs came a young woman and a little girl. The child was clinging to the woman's arm and coaxing her, as sometimes Hilary had tried to coax Florence. "After lessons," the woman said firmly, but gaily. She looked ahead, smiling to herself. Her clothes were unlike anything that Florence had ever seen. Later, when she tried to describe them to her mother, she could only remember the shortness of a tunic which scarcely covered the knees, a hat like a helmet drawn down over eyes intensely green and matching a long necklace of glass beads which swung on her flat bosom. As she came up the stairs and drew near to Florence, she was humming softly against the child's pleading: silk rustled against her silken legs and all of the staircase, as Florence quickly descended, was full of fragrance.

In the darkness of the hall a man was watching the two go round the bend of the stairs. The woman must have looked back, for Florence saw him lift his hand in a secretive gesture of understanding.

"It is Hilary, not his father!" she thought. But the figure turned before she could be sure and went into the library.

Outside on the drive Williams was waiting with her luggage stowed away in the carriage. When she had settled herself, she looked up at the schoolroom window and saw Hilary standing there rather forlornly and she could almost imagine him saying: "My poor dear girl; so you were not good enough for me, after all?"

"When does the new governess arrive?" she asked Williams in a casual voice, that strove to conceal both pride and grief.

"There's nothing fixed as far as I have heard," he said.

They drove out into the lane.

"When will it be *her* time?" Florence wondered. "I am glad that I saw her before I left."

"We are sorry to see you going, Miss." He had heard that the maids were sorry, for she had given them no trouble.

"Thank you, Williams."

As they went on towards the station, she leaned back and looked at the familiar places where she had walked with Hilary. "I know what I shall tell my father now," she thought, and she felt peaceful and meek as though beginning to be convalescent after a long illness.

MEMORY OF A GIRL

Richard Brautigan

Richard Brautigan (1935–1984) was born in Tacoma, Washington. His parents separated before his birth. As a teenager Brautigan spent two months in Oregon State Hospital, where he was diagnosed with paranoid schizophrenia and given electroshock therapy. He moved to San Francisco, met many of the Beat writers and embraced counter culture. Brautigan is best known for his novel, *Trout Fishing in America*. He said of death, 'People wouldn't take life seriously if they didn't know it would turn dark on them.' Richard Brautigan committed suicide.

I cannot look at the Fireman's Fund Insurance Company building without thinking of her breasts. The building is at Presidio and California Streets in San Francisco. It is a red brick, blue and glass building that looks like a minor philosophy plopped right down on the site of what was once one of California's most famous cemeteries:

Laurel Hill Cemetery
1854–1946

Eleven United States Senators were buried there.

They, and everybody else were moved out years ago, but there are still some tall cypress trees standing beside the insurance company.

These trees once cast their shadows over graves. They were a part of daytime weeping and mourning, and night-time silence except for the wind.

I wonder if they ask themselves questions like: Where did everybody go who was dead? Where did they take them? And where are those who came here to visit them? Why were we left behind?

Perhaps these questions are too poetic. Maybe it would be best just to say: There are four trees standing beside an insurance company out in California.

BLACK-WHITE

Tove Jansson

Author and visual artist, **Tove Marika Jansson** (1914–2001) was born
in Finland. Her parents were the sculptor, Viktor Jansson, and the
illustrator and designer, Signe Hammarsten-Jansson. Tove Jansson is best
known for her creation of the Moomins, a family of trolls – tolerant creatures who love nature. Jansson turned to writing for adults in her fifties.
Her lifelong partner was the artist Tuulikki Pietilä. In 2014 Jansson was
honoured with a commemorative two euro coin marking the centenary
of her birth.

His wife's name was Stella, and she was an interior designer – Stella, his
beautiful star. Sometimes he tried to sketch her face, which was always
at rest, open and accessible, but he never succeeded. Her hands were
white and strong and she wore no rings. She worked quickly and without hesitation.

They lived in a house that Stella had designed, an enormous openwork of
glass and unpainted wood. The heavy planking had been chosen for its unusually
attractive grain and fastened with large brass screws. There were no unnecessary
objects to hide the structural materials. When dusk entered their rooms, it was
met with low, veiled lighting, while the glass walls reflected the night but held it
at a distance. They stepped out onto the terrace, and hidden spotlights came on
in the bushes. The darkness crept away, and they stood side by side, throwing no
shadows, and he thought, This is perfect. Nothing can change.

She never flirted. She looked straight at the person she was speaking to, and
when she undressed at night, she did it almost absentmindedly. The house was
like her, its eyes were wide open, and sometimes he worried that someone might
look in on them from the darkness. But the garden was surrounded by a wall,
and the gates were locked.

They often entertained. In the summer, they hung lanterns in the trees and
Stella's house resembled an illuminated seashell in the night. Happy people in
strong colors moved within this picture in groups or in twos and threes, some of
them inside the glass walls and some outside. It was a lovely pageant.

He was an illustrator. He worked mostly for magazines; now and then he did
a book jacket.

The only thing that bothered him was a mild but persistent pain in his back,
which may have resulted from the excessively low furniture. There was a large
black bearskin in front of the fireplace, and sometimes he wanted to lie on it with
outstretched arms and legs, bury his face in the fur and roll around like a dog

to rest his back. But he never did. The walls were glass, and there were no doors between the rooms.

The large table by the fireplace was also of glass. He was in the habit of laying out his drawings on it in order to show them to Stella before sending them on to the client. These moments meant a great deal to him.

Stella came and looked at his work. "It's good," she said. "Your use of line is perfect. All I'm missing is a dominant element."

"You mean it's too gray?" he said.

"Yes," she said. "It needs more white, more light."

They stood at the low table and he saw his drawings from a distance. They really were very gray.

"I think what it needs is black," he said. "But you need to look at them up close."

Afterward he thought for a long time about black as a focus. He was uneasy, and his back was worse.

The commission came in November. He went in to his wife and said, "Stella, I've been given a job that really intrigues me." He was happy, almost excited. Stella put down her pen and looked at him. She was always able to interrupt her work without annoyance.

"It's a terror anthology," he said. "Fifteen stories, with black-and-white illustrations and vignettes. I know I can do it. It suits me. It's my kind of thing, don't you think?"

"Absolutely," said his wife. "Are they in a rush?"

"Rush!" he burst out, and laughed. "This isn't some two-bit assignment, this is a serious piece of work. Full pages. They're giving me a couple of months." He rested his hands on her worktable and leaned forward. "Stella," he said gravely, "I'm going to use black as a dominant element. I'm going to do darkness. Gray, well, I'll only use gray when it's like holding your breath, like when you're waiting to be afraid."

She smiled. "It's so nice you've got something you find interesting."

The text arrived, and he lay down on his bed and read the first three stories, no more. He wanted to begin work believing that the best material would come further on and so retain his expectations as long as possible. The third story gave him an idea, and he sat down at the table and cut himself a piece of thick, chalk-white rag paper with an embossed maker's mark in the corner.

The house was quiet and they weren't expecting guests.

It had been very hard for him to get used to this paper because he couldn't forget how much it cost. Drawings on less expensive paper tended to be freer and better. But this time it was different. He loved the feel of the pen as it ran across the elegant surface in clean lines and at the same time he relished the barely discernible resistance that brought the lines to life.

It was midday. He closed the drapes, turned on the lamp, and began to work.

They ate dinner together, and he was very quiet. Stella asked no questions. Finally he said, "It's no good. There's too much light."

"But can't you close the drapes?"

"I did," he said. "But somehow it's still too light. It only gets gray, it doesn't get black!" He waited until the cook had finished serving and gone away. "There aren't any doors in this house," he burst out. "I can't close myself in!"

Stella stopped eating and looked at him. "You mean it's just not working," she said.

"No. All I get is gray."

"Then I think you should find another studio," said his wife. They went on eating, the tension gone. Over coffee she said, "My aunt's old house is standing empty. But I think there's still furniture in the little attic apartment. You could give it a try."

She called Jansson and asked him to put a heater in the attic room. Mrs. Jansson promised to leave food on the steps every day and to make sure the room was clean. Otherwise he'd have to keep house for himself and take a hot plate with him. It took only a few minutes to make all the arrangements.

When the bus appeared around the bend in the road, he turned earnestly to his wife. "Stella," he said. "It will only be for a couple of weeks, then I can finish up at home. I'm going to concentrate while I'm there. I won't be writing any letters, just working."

"Of course," said his wife. "Now take care of yourself. And call me from the general store if there's anything you need."

They kissed, and he climbed onto the bus. It was afternoon, and sleeting. Stella didn't wave, but she stood and watched until the bus was hidden by the trees. Then she closed the gate and walked back up to her house.

He recognized the bus stop and the evergreen hedge, but it had grown higher and grayer. He was also surprised that the hill was so steep. The road went straight up, bordered by a confused mass of withered undergrowth and cut by deep furrows where the rain had washed sand and gravel down the slope. The house clung tightly to the hill at an impossible angle just below the crown, and the house, the fence, the outbuildings, the fir trees, all of them seemed to be holding themselves upright with a terrible effort. He stopped at the steps and looked up at the façade. The house was very tall and narrow, and the windows looked like loopholes. The snow was melting, and in the silence he could hear nothing but water dripping in among the firs. He walked around to the back. At the rear of the house was a one-story kitchen that merged with the hill in a messy, ill-defined rampart of rubbish. Here in the shadow of the firs lay everything the old house had spit out in the course of its life, everything worn out and unnecessary, everything not to be seen. In the darkening winter evening, this landscape was utterly abandoned, a territory that had no meaning for anyone but him. He found it beautiful. Unhurriedly, he went into the house and up to the attic. He closed the door behind him. Jansson had been there with the heater, a glowing red rectangle over by the bed. He walked to the window and looked down the hill. It seemed to him that the house leaned outward, tired of clinging tightly to the slope. With great love and admiration, he thought of his wife, who had made it so easy for him to leave. He felt his darkness drawing closer.

After a long night without dreams, he set to work. He dipped his pen in the India ink and drew calmly – small, tight, skillful lines. But now he knew that gray is only the patient dusk that makes preparation for the night. He could wait. He was no longer working to make a picture but only in order to draw.

In the dusk he walked to the window and saw that the house was leaning outward. He wrote a letter.

Beloved Stella, the first full page is finished and I think it's good. It's warm here and very quiet. The Janssons had cleaned, and this afternoon they left a canister of food on the steps – lamb wrapped in cabbage, and milk. I make coffee on the hot plate. Don't worry about me, I'm getting along fine. I've been thinking about leaving the margins ragged – maybe I've been too conventional. Anyway, I was right that the dominant needs to be black. Thinking of you, a great deal.

He walked down to the general store and posted the letter after dark. The wind had come up a bit and the fir trees sighed as he walked home. The weather was still warm, snow was melting and running down the hill in furrows of sand and gravel. He had meant to write a longer, different letter.

The days passed quietly, and he worked steadily. The margins had grown fluid, and his pictures began in a vague and shadowy gray that felt its way inward, seeking darkness.

He had read the whole anthology and found it banal. There was only one story that was truly frightening. It placed its terror in full daylight in an ordinary room. But all the others gave him the opportunity to draw night or dusk. His vignettes were workmanlike depictions of the people and places the author and the reader would want to see. But they were uninteresting. Again and again he returned to his dark full pages. His back no longer ached.

It's the unexpressed that interests me, he thought. I've been drawing too explicitly; it's a mistake to clarify everything. He wrote to Stella.

> You know, I begin to think I've been depicting things for much too long. Now I'm trying to do something new that's all my own. It's much more important to suggest than to portray. I see my work as pieces of reality or unreality carved at random from a long and ineluctable course of events – the darkness I draw continues on endlessly. I cut across it with narrow and dangerous shafts of light . . . Stella, I'm not illustrating any longer. I'm making my own pictures, and they follow no text. Some day someone will explain them. Every time I finish a drawing, I go to the window and think about you.
>
> Your loving husband

He walked down to the general store and posted the letter. On his way home he ran into Jansson, who asked if there was a lot of water in the cellar.

"I haven't been in the cellar," he said.

"Maybe you could have a look," Jansson said. "What with all the rain we've had this year."

He unlocked the cellar and turned on the light. The bulb was mirrored in a motionless expanse of water, as shiny and black as oil. The cellar stairs descended into the water and vanished. He stood still and stared. The walls lay in deep shadow, hollowed out where pieces of the wall had collapsed, and the fallen pieces – lumps of stone and cement – lay half hidden under the water like swimming animals. It seemed to him that they swam backward, toward the angle where the cellar hallway turned and went farther in under the house. I must draw this house, he thought. Quickly. I need to hurry, while it lasts.

He drew the cellar. He drew the backyard, a chaos of carelessly discarded fragments, useless, coal black, and entirely anonymous in the snow. It was a picture of quiet, gloomy confusion. He drew the sitting room, he drew the veranda. Never before had he been so fully awake. His sleep was deep and easy, the way it had been as a boy. He woke instantaneously, without that half-conscious, uneasy borderland that breaks up sleep and poisons it. Sometimes he slept during the day and worked at night. He lived in a state of furious expectation. He finished one drawing after another. There were more than fifteen, many times more. He no longer bothered with the vignettes.

Stella, I'm drawing the sitting room. It's such a tired old room, completely empty. I draw nothing but the walls and floor, a worn plush carpet, and a wall panel with a repeating pattern. It's a picture of the footsteps that passed through the room, of the shadows that fell on the wall, of the words that still hang in the air – or maybe of the silence. All of that is still here, you see, and that's what I'm drawing. Every time I finish a drawing, I go to the window and think of you.

Stella, have you ever thought about the way wallpaper loosens and opens? It happens according to strict rules. No one can depict desolation who hasn't inhabited desolation and observed it very closely. Things condemned have a terrible beauty.

Stella, do you know what it feels like to see everything gray and cautious all your life and to always try to do your best but all you get is tired? And then suddenly you know, you know with absolute certainty. What are you doing right now? Are you working? Are you happy? Are you tired?

Yes, he thought. She's been working and she's a little tired. She's walking around in her house, getting undressed for the night. She's walking around turning off the lights, one by one, she's as white as blank paper, as white as the innocent challenge of the empty surface, and now she alone gives off light, Stella, my star.

He was almost certain that the house leaned outward. Through the window, he could see four steps but not the top one. He put sticks in the snow in order to measure the change in the house's angle of inclination. The water in the cellar did not rise. It didn't matter anyway. He had drawn both the cellar and the façade. He was now working exclusively on the ragged wallpaper in the sitting room. There was no mail. At times he was not certain which letters he had sent to his wife and which he had only imagined. She was farther away now, a picture, a faint pretty picture of a woman. At times, cool and naked, she moved through their large salon of white wood. He found it hard to remember her eyes.

Days and nights and many weeks went by. He worked the whole time. When a drawing was finished, he set it aside and forgot it, continuing at once with a new one, a new white paper, a blank white surface that offered the same challenge, the same limitless possibilities, and an absolute isolation from outside help. Each time he began to draw, he made sure that all the doors in the house were locked. It had begun to rain, but the rain didn't concern him. Nothing concerned him except the tenth story in the anthology. More and more, he thought about this one story, in which the author had subjected daylight to his terror and, against all the rules, enclosed it in an ordinary, pleasant room.

He came closer and closer to the tenth story. It was everywhere, and finally he decided to kill it by drawing. He took a fresh white paper and placed it on the table in front of him. He knew he had to make it visible, the only story in the whole anthology that was genuinely full of horror, and he knew he could illustrate it only one way – it was Stella's living room, her consummate room, where they lived their lives together. He was amazed but utterly certain. He walked around and lit the low lights, all of them, and the windows opened their eyes out toward the illuminated terrace. Beautiful, strange people moved slowly in groups of two or three, and he drew them all, calmly and surely, with small, gray, skillful lines. He drew the room, a terrifying room without doors, bulging with tension, the white walls shadowed with imperceptibly tiny cracks. He let them run on and widen. He drew them all. He saw that the window-wall's enormous sheet of glass was on the point of bursting from the pressure from within, and he began drawing it as fast as he could, and at the same time he saw the cleft that opened in the floor and it was black. He worked faster and faster, but before his pen could reach the darkness, the room he was drawing turned and crashed outward to its ruin.

THE MANGLER

Stephen King

Stephen Edwin King (b.1947) was born in Portland, Maine. He gained a BA in English from the University of Maine at Orono in 1970. King wrote his first novel, *Carrie*, while teaching English at the public high school in Hampden. The success of the book enabled him to become a full-time writer. He has written over fifty novels, seven non-fiction books and many short stories. His books have sold millions of copies and several have been adapted for television and cinema.

O fficer Hunton got to the laundry just as the ambulance was leaving – slowly, with no siren or flashing lights. Ominous. Inside, the office was stuffed with milling, silent people, some of them weeping. The plant itself was empty; the big automatic washers at the far end had not even been shut down. It made Hunton very wary. The crowd should be at the scene of the accident, not in the office. It was the way things worked – the human animal had a built-in urge to view the remains. A very bad one, then. Hunton felt his stomach tighten as it always did when the accident was very bad. Fourteen years of cleaning human litter from highways and streets and the sidewalks at the bases of very tall buildings had not been able to erase that little hitch in the belly, as if something evil had clotted there.

A man in a white shirt saw Hunton and walked towards him reluctantly. He was a buffalo of a man with head thrust forward between shoulders, nose and cheeks vein-broken either from high blood pressure or too many conversations with the brown bottle. He was trying to frame words, but after two tries Hunton cut him off briskly:

"Are you the owner? Mr Gartley?"

"No . . . no. I'm Stanner. The foreman. God, this –"

Hunton got out his notebook. "Please show me the scene of the accident, Mr Stanner, and tell me what happened."

Stanner seemed to grow even more white; the blotches on his nose and cheeks stood out like birthmarks. "D-do I have to?"

Hunton raised his eyebrows. "I'm afraid you do. The call I got said it was serious."

"Serious –" Stanner seemed to be battling with his gorge; for a moment his Adam's apple went up and down like a monkey on a stick. "Mrs Frawley is dead. Jesus, I wish Bill Garley *was* here."

"What happened?"

Stanner said, "You better come over here."

He led Hunton past a row of hand presses, a shirt-folding unit, and then stopped by a laundry-marking machine. He passed a shaky hand across his forehead. "You'll have to go over by yourself, Officer. I can't look at it again. It makes me . . . I can't. I'm sorry."

Hunton walked around the marking machine with a mild feeling of contempt for the man. They run a loose shop, cut corners, run live steam through home-welded pipes, they work with dangerous cleaning chemicals without the proper protection, and finally, someone gets hurt. Or gets dead. Then they can't look. They can't –

Hunton saw it.

The machine was still running. No one had shut it off. The machine he later came to know intimately: the Hadley-Watson Model-6 Speed Ironer and Folder. A long and clumsy name. The people who worked here in the steam and the wet had a better name for it. The mangler.

Hunton took a long, frozen look, and then he performed a first in his fourteen years as a law-enforcement officer: he turned around, put a convulsive hand to his mouth, and threw up.

"You didn't eat much," Jackson said.

The women were inside, doing dishes and talking babies while John Hunton and Mark Jackson sat in lawn chairs near the aromatic barbecue. Hunton smiled slightly at the understatement. He had eaten nothing.

"There was a bad one today," he said. "The worst."

"Car crash?"

"No. Industrial."

"Messy?"

Hunton did not reply immediately, but his face made an involuntary, writhing grimace. He got a beer out of the cooler between them, opened it, and emptied half of it. "I suppose you college profs don't know anything about industrial laundries?"

Jackson chuckled. "This one does. I spent a summer working in one as an undergraduate."

"Then you know the machine they call the speed ironer?"

Jackson nodded. "Sure. They run damp flatwork through them, mostly sheets and linen. A big, long machine."

"That's it," Hunton said. "A woman named Adelle Frawley got caught in it at the Blue Ribbon Laundry crosstown. It sucked her right in."

Jackson looked suddenly ill. "But . . . that can't happen, Johnny. There's a safety bar. If one of the women feeding the machine accidentally gets a hand under it, the bar snaps up and stops the machine. At least that's how I remember it."

Hunton nodded. "It's a state law. But it happened."

Hunton closed his eyes and in the darkness he could see the Hadley-Watson speed ironer again, as it had been that afternoon. It formed a long, rectangular box in shape, thirty feet by six. At the feeder end, a moving canvas belt moved under the safety bar, up at a slight angle, and then down. The belt carried the damp-dried, wrinkled sheets in continuous cycle over and under sixteen huge revolving cylinders that made up the main body of the machine. Over eight and under eight, pressed between them like thin ham between layers of superheated bread. Steam heat in the cylinders could be adjusted up to 300 degrees for maximum drying. The pressure on the sheets that rode the moving canvas belt was set at 800 pounds per square foot to get out every wrinkle.

And Mrs Frawley, somehow, had been caught and dragged in. The steel, asbestos-jacketed pressing cylinders had been as red as barn paint, and the rising steam from the machine had carried the sickening stench of hot blood. Bits of her white blouse and blue slacks, even ripped segments of her bra and panties, had been torn free and ejected from the machine's far end thirty feet down, the bigger sections of cloth folded with grotesque and blood-stained neatness by the automatic folder. But not even that was the worst.

"It tried to fold everything," he said to Jackson, tasting bile in his throat. "But a person isn't a sheet, Mark. What I saw . . . what was left of her . . ." Like Stanner, the hapless foreman, he could not finish. "They took her out in a basket," he said softly.

Jackson whistled. "Who's going to get it in the neck? The laundry or the state inspectors?"

"Don't know yet," Hunton said. The malign image still hung behind his eyes, the image of the mangler wheezing and thumping and hissing, blood dripping down the green sides of the long cabinet in runnels, the burning *stink* of her . . . "It depends on who okayed that goddamn safety bar and under what circumstances."

"If it's the management, can they wiggle out of it?"

Hunton smiled without humour. "The woman died, Mark. If Gartley and Stanner were cutting corners on the speed ironer's maintenance, they'll go to jail. No matter who they know on the City Council."

"Do you think they were cutting corners?"

Hunton thought of the Blue Ribbon Laundry, badly lighted, floors wet and slippery, some of the machines incredibly ancient and creaking. "I think it's likely," he said quietly.

They got up to go in the house together. "Tell me how it comes out, Johnny," Jackson said. "I'm interested."

Hunton was wrong about the mangler; it was clean as a whistle.

Six state inspectors went over it before the inquest, piece by piece. The net result was absolutely nothing. The inquest verdict was death by misadventure.

Hunton, dumbfounded, cornered Roger Martin, one of the inspectors, after the hearing. Martin was a tall drink of water with glasses as thick as the bottoms of shot glasses. He fidgeted with a ball-point pen under Hunton's questions.

"Nothing? Absolutely nothing doing with the machine?"

"Nothing," Martin said. "Of course, the safety bar was the guts of the matter. It's in perfect working order. You heard that Mrs Gillian testify. Mrs Frawley must have pushed her hand too far. No one saw that; they were watching their own work. She started screaming. Her hand was gone already, and the machine was taking her arm. They tried to pull her out instead of shutting it down – pure panic. Another woman, Mrs Keene, said she *did* try to shut it off, but it's a fair assumption that she hit the start button rather than the stop in the confusion. By then it was too late."

"Then the safety bar malfunctioned," Hunton said flatly. "Unless she put her hand over it rather than under?"

"You can't. There's a stainless-steel facing above the safety bar. And the bar itself didn't malfunction. It's circuited into the machine itself. If the safety bar goes on the blink, the machine shuts down."

"Then how did it happen, for Christ's sake?"

"We don't know. My colleagues and I are of the opinion that the only way the speed ironer could have killed Mrs Frawley was for her to have fallen into it from above. And she had both feet on the floor when it happened. A dozen witnesses can testify to that."

"You're describing an impossible accident," Hunton said.

"No. Only one we don't understand." He paused, hesitated, and then said: "I will tell you one thing, Hunton, since you seem to have taken this case to heart. If you mention it to anyone else, I'll deny I said it. But I didn't like that machine. It seemed . . . almost to be mocking us. I've inspected over a dozen speed ironers in the last five years on a regular basis. Some of them are in such bad shape that I wouldn't have a dog unleashed around them – the state law is lamentably lax. But they were only machines for all that. But this one . . . it's a spook. I don't know why, but it is. I think if I'd found one thing, even a technicality, that was off whack, I would have ordered it shut down. Crazy, huh?"

"I felt the same way," Hunton said.

"Let me tell you about something that happened two years ago in Milton," the inspector said. He took off his glasses and began to polish them slowly on his vest. "Fella had parked an old ice-box out in his backyard. The woman who called us said her dog had been caught in it and suffocated. We got the state policeman in the area to inform him it had to go to the town dump. Nice enough fella, sorry about the dog. He loaded it into his pickup and took it to the dump the next morning. That afternoon a woman in the neighbourhood reported her son missing."

"God," Hunton said.

"The icebox was at the dump and the kid was in it, dead. A smart kid, according to the mother. She said he'd no more play in an empty icebox than he would take a ride with a strange man. Well, he did. We wrote it off. Case closed?"

"I guess," Hunton said.

"No. The dump caretaker went out next day to take the door off the thing. City Ordinance No. 58 on the maintenance of public dumping places." Martin looked at him expressionlessly. "He found six dead birds inside. Gulls, sparrows, a robin. And he said the door closed on his arm while he was brushing them out. Gave him a hell of a jump. The mangler at the Blue Ribbon strikes me like that, Hunton. I don't like it."

They looked at each other wordlessly in the empty inquest chamber, some six city blocks from where the Hadley-Watson Model-6 Speed Ironer and Folder sat in the busy laundry, steaming and fuming over its sheets. The case was driven out of his mind in the space of a week by the press of more prosaic police work. It was only brought back when he and his wife dropped over to Mark Jackson's house for an evening of bid whist and beer.

Jackson greeted him with: "Have you ever wondered if that laundry machine you told me about is haunted, Johnny?"

Hunton blinked, at a loss. "What?"

"The speed ironer at the Blue Ribbon Laundry, I guess you didn't catch the squeal this time."

"What squeal?" Hunton asked, interested.

Jackson passed him the evening paper and pointed to an item at the bottom of page two. The story said that a steam line had let go on the large speed ironer at the Blue Ribbon Laundry, burning three of the six women working at the feeder end. The accident had occurred at 3.45 p.m. and was attributed to a rise in steam pressure from the laundry's boiler. One of the women, Mrs Annette Gillian, had been held at City Receiving Hospital with second-degree burns.

"Funny coincidence," he said, but the memory of Inspector Martin's words in the empty inquest chamber suddenly recurred: *It's a spook . . .* And the story about the dog and the boy and the birds caught in the discarded refrigerator.

He played cards very badly that night.

Mrs Gillian was propped up in bed reading *Screen Secrets* when Hunton came into the four-bed hospital room. A large bandage blanketed one arm and the side of her neck. The room's other occupant, a young woman with a pallid face, was sleeping.

Mrs Gillian blinked at the blue uniform and then smiled tentatively. "If it was for Mrs Cherinikov, you'll have to come back later. They just gave her medication."

"No, it's for you, Mrs Gillian." Her smile faded a little. "I'm here unofficially – which means I'm curious about the accident at the laundry. John Hunton." He held out his hand.

It was the right move. Mrs Gillian's smile became brilliant and she took his grip awkwardly with her unburnt hand. "Anything I can tell you, Mr Hunton. God, I thought my Andy was in trouble at school again."

"What happened?"

"We was running sheets and the ironer just blew up – or it seemed that way. I was thinking about going home an' getting off my dogs when there's this great big bang, like a bomb. Steam is everywhere and this hissing noise . . . awful." Her smile trembled on the verge of extinction. "It was like the ironer was breathing. Like a dragon, it was. And Alberta – that's Alberta Keene – shouted that something was exploding and everyone was running and screaming and Ginny Jason started yelling she was burnt. I started to run away and I fell down. I didn't know I got it worst until then. God forbid it was no worse than it was. That live steam is three hundred degrees."

"The paper said a steam line let go. What does that mean?"

"The overhead pipe comes down into this kinda flexible line that feeds the machine. George – Mr Stanner – said there must have been a surge from the boiler or something. The line split wide open."

Hunton could think of nothing else to ask. He was making ready to leave when she said reflectively:

"We never used to have these things on that machine. Only lately. The steam line breaking. That awful, awful accident with Mrs Frawley, God rest her. And little things. Like the day Essie got her dress caught in one of the drive chains. That could have been dangerous if she hadn't ripped it right out. Bolts and things fall off. Oh, Herb Diment – he's the laundry repairman – has had an awful time with it. Sheets get caught in the folder. George says that's because they're using too much bleach in the washers, but it never used to happen. Now the girls hate to work on it. Essie even says there are still little bits of Adelle Frawley caught in it and it's sacrilege or something. Like it had a curse. It's been that way ever since Sherry cut her hand on one of the clamps."

"Sherry?" Hunton asked.

"Sherry Ouelett. Pretty little thing, just out of high school. Good worker. But clumsy sometimes. You know how young girls are."

"She cut her hand on something?"

"Nothing strange about *that*. There are clamps to tighten down the feeder belt, see. Sherry was adjusting them so we could do a heavier load and probably dreaming about some boy. She cut her finger and bled all over everything." Mrs Gillian looked puzzled. "It wasn't until after that the bolts started falling off. Adelle was . . . you know . . . about a week later. As if the machine had tasted blood and found it liked it. Don't women get funny ideas sometimes, Officer Hinton?"

"Hunton," he said absently, looking over her head and into space.

Ironically, he had met Mark Jackson in a washateria in the block that separated their houses, and it was there that the cop and the English professor still had their most interesting conversations.

Now they sat side by side in bland plastic chairs, their clothes going round and round behind the glass portholes of the coin-op washers. Jackson's paperback copy of Milton's collected works lay neglected beside him while he listened to Hunton tell Mrs Gillian's story.

When Hunton had finished, Jackson said, "I asked you once if you thought the mangler might be haunted. I was only half joking. I'll ask you again now."

"No," Hunton said uneasily. "Don't be stupid."

Jackson watched the turning clothes reflectively. "Haunted is a bad word. Let's say possessed. There are almost as many spells for casting demons in as there are for casting them out. Frazier's *Golden Bough* is replete with them. Druidic and Aztec lore contain others. Even older ones, back to Egypt. Almost all of them can be reduced to startlingly common denominators. The most common, of course, is the blood of a virgin." He looked at Hunton, "Mrs Gillian said the trouble started after this Sherry Ouelette accidentally cut herself."

"Oh, come on," Hunton said.

"You have to admit she sounds just the type," Jackson said.

"I'll run right over to her house," Hunton said with a small smile. "I can see it. "Miss Ouelette, I'm Officer John Hunton. I'm investigating an ironer with a bad case of demon possession and would like to know if you're a virgin." Do you think I'd get a chance to say goodbye to Sandra and the kids before they carted me off to the booby hatch?"

"I'd be willing to bet you'll end up saying something just like that," Jackson said without smiling. "I'm serious, Johnny. That machine scares the hell out of me and I've never seen it."

"For the sake of conversation," Hunton said, "what are some of the other so-called common denominators?"

Jackson shrugged. "Hard to say without study. Most Anglo-Saxon hex formulas specify graveyard dirt or the eye of a toad. European spells often mention the hand of glory, which can be interpreted as the actual hand of a dead man or one of the hallucinogenics used in connection with the Witches' Sabbath – usually belladonna or a psilocybin derivative. There could be others."

"And you think all those things got into the Blue Ribbon ironer? Christ, Mark, I'll bet there isn't any belladonna within a five-hundred-mile radius. Or do you think someone whacked off their Uncle Fred's hand and dropped it in the folder?"

"If seven hundred monkeys typed for seven hundred years –"

"One of them would turn out the works of Shakespeare," Hunton finished sourly. "Go to hell. Your turn to go across to the drugstore and get some dimes for the dryers."

It was very funny how George Stanner lost his arm in the mangler.

Seven o'clock Monday morning the laundry was deserted except for Stanner and Herb Diment, the maintenance man. They were performing the twice-yearly function of greasing the mangler's bearings before the laundry's regular day began at seven-thirty. Diment was at the far end, greasing the four secondaries and thinking of how unpleasant this machine made him feel lately, when the mangler suddenly roared into life.

He had been holding up four of the canvas exit belts to get at the motor beneath and suddenly the belts were running in his hands, ripping the flesh off his palms, dragging him along.

He pulled free with a convulsive jerk seconds before the belts would have carried his hands into the folder.

"What the Christ, George!" he yelled. "Shut the frigging thing *off*"

George Stanner began to scream.

It was a high, wailing, blood-maddened sound that filled the laundry, echoing off the steel faces of the washers, the grinning mouths of the steam presses, the vacant eyes of the industrial dryers. Stanner drew in a great, whooping gasp of air and screamed again: "*Oh God of Christ I'm caught I'M CAUGHT –*"

The rollers began to produce rising steam. The folder gnashed and thumped. Bearings and motors seemed to cry out with a hidden life of their own.

Diment raced to the other end of the machine.

The first roller was already going a sinister red. Diment made a moaning, gobbling noise in his throat. The mangler howled and thumped and hissed.

A deaf observer might have thought at first that Stanner was merely bent over the machine at an odd angle. Then even a deaf man would have seen the pallid, eye-bulging rictus of his face, mouth twisted open in a continuous scream. The arm was disappearing under the safety bar and beneath the first roller; the fabric of his shirt had torn away at the shoulder seam and his upper arm bulged grotesquely as the blood was pushed steadily backwards.

"Turn if off!" Stanner screamed. There was a snap as his elbow broke.

Diment thumbed the off button.

The mangler continued to hum and growl and turn.

Unbelieving, he slammed the button again and again – nothing. The skin of

Stanner's arm had grown shiny and taut. Soon it would split with the pressure the roll was putting on it; and still he was conscious and screaming. Diment had a nightmare cartoon image of a man flattened by a steamroller, leaving only a shadow.

"Fuses –" Stanner screeched. His head was being pulled down, down, as he was dragged forward.

Diment whirled and ran to the boiler room, Stanner's screams chasing him like lunatic ghosts. The mixed stench of blood and steam rose in the air.

On the left wall were three heavy grey boxes containing all the fuses for the laundry's electricity. Diment yanked them open and began to pull the long, cylindrical fuses like a crazy man, throwing them back over his shoulders. The overhead lights went out; then the air compressor; then the boiler itself, with a huge dying whine.

And still the mangler turned. Stanner's screams had been reduced to bubbly moans.

Diment's eye happened on the fire axe in its glassed-in box. He grabbed it with a small, gagging whimper and ran back. Stanner's arm was gone almost to the shoulder. Within seconds his bent and straining neck would be snapped against the safety bar.

"I can't," Diment blubbered, holding the axe. "Jesus, George, I can't, I can't, I –"

The machine was an abattoir now. The folder spat out pieces of shirt sleeve, scraps of flesh, a finger. Stanner gave a huge, whooping scream and Diment swung the axe up and brought it down in the laundry's shadowy lightlessness. Twice. Again.

Stanner fell away, unconscious and blue, blood jetting from the stump just below the shoulder. The mangler sucked what was left into itself . . . and shut down.

Weeping, Diment pulled his belt out of its loops and began to make a tourniquet.

Hunton was talking on the phone with Roger Martin, the inspector. Jackson watched him while he patiently rolled a ball back and forth for three-year-old Patty Hunton to chase.

"He pulled *all* the fuses?" Hunton was asking. "And the off button just didn't function, huh? . . . Has the ironer been shut down? . . . Good. Great. Huh? . . . No, not official." Hunton frowned, then looked sideways at Jackson. "Are you still reminded of that refrigerator, Roger? . . . Yes. Me too, Goodbye."

He hung up and looked at Jackson. "Let's go see the girl, Mark."

She had her own apartment (the hesitant yet proprietary way she showed them in after Hunton had flashed his buzzer made him suspect that she hadn't had it long), and she sat uncomfortably across from them in the carefully decorated, postage-stamp living room.

"I'm Officer Hunton and this is my associate, Mr Jackson. It's about the accident at the laundry." He felt hugely uncomfortable with this dark, shyly pretty girl.

"Awful," Sherry Ouelette murmured. "It's the only place I've ever worked. Mr Gartley is my uncle. I liked it because it let me have this place and my own friends. But now . . . it's so *spooky.*"

"The State Board of Safety has shut the ironer down pending a full investigation," Hunton said. "Did you know that?"

"Sure," She sighed restlessly. "I don't know what I'm going to do –"

"Miss Ouelette," Jackson interrupted, "you had an accident with the ironer, didn't you? Cut your hand on a clamp, I believe?"

"Yes, I cut my finger." Suddenly her face clouded. "That was the first thing." She looked at them woefully. "Sometimes I feel like the girls don't like me so much any more . . . as if I were to blame."

"I have to ask you a hard question," Jackson said slowly. "A question you won't like. It seems absurdly personal and off the subject, but I can only tell you it is not. Your answers won't ever be marked down in a file or record."

She looked frightened. "D-did I do something?"

Jackson smiled and shook his head; she melted. *Thank God for Mark*, Hunton thought.

"I'll add this, though: the answer may help you keep your nice little flat here, get your job back, and make things at the laundry the way they were before."

"I'd answer anything to have that," she said.

"Sherry, are you a virgin?"

She looked utterly flabbergasted, utterly shocked, as if a priest had given communion and then slapped her. Then she lifted her head, made a gesture at her neat efficiency apartment, as if asking them how they could believe it might be a place of assignation.

"I'm saving myself for my husband," she said simply.

Hunton and Jackson looked calmly at each other, and in that tick of a second, Hunton knew that it was all true: a devil had taken over the inanimate steel and cogs and gears of the mangler and had turned it into something with its own life.

"Thank you," Jackson said quietly.

"What now?" Hunton asked bleakly as they rode back. "Find a priest to exorcise it?"

Jackson snorted. "You'd go a far piece to find one that wouldn't hand you a few tracts to read while he phoned the booby hatch. It has to be our play, Johnny."

"Can we do it?"

"Maybe. The problem is this: We know something is in the mangler. We don't know *what*." Hunton felt cold, as if touched by a fleshless finger. "There are a great many demons. Is the one we're dealing with in the circle of Bubastis or Pan? Baal? Or the Christian deity we call Satan? We don't know. If the demon had been deliberately cast, we would have a better chance. But this seems to be a case of random possession."

Jackson ran his fingers through his hair. "The blood of a virgin, yes. But that narrows it down hardly at all. We have to be sure, very sure."

"Why?" Hunton asked bluntly. "Why not just get a bunch of exorcism formulas together and try them out?"

Jackson's face went cold. "This isn't cops "n" robbers, Johnny. For Christ's sake, don't think it is. The rite of exorcism is horribly dangerous. It's like controlled nuclear fission, in a way. We could make a mistake and destroy ourselves. The demon is caught in that piece of machinery. But give it a chance and –"

"It could get out?"

"It would love to get out," Jackson said grimly. "And it likes to kill."

When Jackson came over the following evening, Hunton had sent his wife and daughter to a movie. They had the living room to themselves, and for this Hunton was relieved. He could still barely believe what he had become involved in.

"I cancelled my classes," Jackson said, "and spent the day with some of the most god-awful books you can imagine. This afternoon I fed over thirty recipes for calling demons into the tech computer. I've got a number of common elements. Surprisingly few."

He showed Hunton the list: blood of a virgin, graveyard dirt, hand of glory, bat's blood, night moss, horse's hoof, eye of toad.

There were others, all marked secondary.

"Horse's hoof," Hunton said thoughtfully. "Funny –"

"Very common. In fact –"

"Could these things – any of them – be interpreted loosely?" Hunton interrupted.

"If lichens picked at night could be substituted for night moss, for instance?"

"Yes."

"It's very likely," Jackson said. "Magical formulas are often ambiguous and elastic. The black arts have always allowed plenty of room for creativity."

"Substitute Jell-O for horse's hoof," Hunton said. "Very popular in bag lunches. I noticed a little container of it sitting under the ironer's sheet platform on the day the Frawley woman died. Gelatine is made from horses' hooves."

Jackson nodded. "Anything else?"

"Bat's blood . . . well, it's a big place. Lots of unlighted nooks and crannies. Bats seem likely, although I doubt if the management would admit to it. One could conceivably have been trapped in the mangler."

Jackson tipped his head back and knuckled bloodshot eyes. "It fits . . . it all fits."

"It does?"

"Yes. We can safely rule out the hand of glory, I think. Certainly no one dropped a hand into the ironer *before* Mrs Frawley's death, and belladonna is definitely not indigenous to the area."

"Graveyard dirt?"

"What do you think?"

"It would have to be a hell of a coincidence," Hunton said. "Nearest cemetery is Pleasant Hill, and that's five miles from the Blue Ribbon."

"Okay," Jackson said. "I got the computer operator – who thought I was getting ready for Halloween – to run a positive breakdown of all the primary and secondary elements on the list. Every possible combination. I threw out some two dozen which were completely meaningless. The others fall into fairly clear-cut categories. The elements we've isolated are in one of those."

"What is it?"

Jackson grinned. "An easy one. The mythos centres in South America with branches in the Caribbean. Related to voodoo. The literature I've got looks on the deities as strictly bush league, compared to some of the real heavies, like Saddath or He-Who-Cannot-Be-Named. The thing in that machine is going to slink away like the neighbourhood bully."

"How do we do it?"

"Holy water and a smidgen of the Holy Eucharist ought to do it. And we can read some of the Leviticus to it. Strictly Christian white magic."

"You're sure it's not worse?"

"Don't see how it can be," Jackson said pensively. "I don't mind telling you I was worried about that hand of glory. That's very black juju. Strong magic."

"Holy water wouldn't stop it?"

"A demon called up in conjunction with the hand of glory could eat a stack of Bibles for breakfast. We would be in bad trouble messing with something like that at all. Better to pull the goddamn thing apart."

"Well, are you completely sure –"

"No, but fairly sure. It all fits too well."

"When?"

"The sooner, the better," Jackson said. "How do we get in? Break a window?"

Hunton smiled, reached into his pocket, and dangled a key in front of Jackson's nose.

"Where'd you get that? Gartley?"

"No," Hunton said. "From a state inspector named Martin."

"He knows what we're doing?"

"I think he suspects. He told me a funny story a couple of weeks ago."

"About the mangler?"

"No," Hunton said. "About a refrigerator. Come on."

Adelle Frawley was dead; sewed together by a patient undertaker, she lay in her coffin. Yet something of her spirit perhaps remained in the machine, and if it did, it cried out. She would have known, could have warned them. She had been prone to indigestion, and for this common ailment she had taken a common stomach tablet called E-Z Gel, purchasable over the counter of any drugstore for seventy-nine cents. The side panel holds a printed warning: People with glaucoma must not take E-Z Gel, because the active ingredient causes an aggravation of that condition. Unfortunately, Adelle Frawley did not have that condition. She might have remembered the day, shortly before Sherry Ouelette cut her hand, that she had dropped a full box of E-Z Gel tablets into the mangler by accident. But she was dead, unaware that the active ingredient which soothed her heartburn was a chemical derivative of belladonna, known quaintly in some European countries as the hand of glory.

There was a sudden ghastly burping noise in the spectral silence of the Blue Ribbon Laundry – a bat fluttered madly for its hole in the insulation above the dryers where it had roosted, wrapping wings around its blind face.

It was a noise almost like a chuckle.

The mangler began to run with a sudden, lurching grind – belts hurrying through the darkness, cogs meeting and meshing and grinding, heavy pulverizing rollers rotating on and on.

It was ready for them.

When Hunton pulled into the parking lot it was shortly after midnight and the moon was hidden behind a raft of moving clouds. He jammed on the brakes and switched off the lights in the same motion; Jackson's forehead almost slammed against the padded dash.

He switched off the ignition and the steady thump-hiss-thump became louder. "It's the mangler," he said slowly. "It's the mangler. Running by itself. In the middle of the night."

They sat for a moment in silence, feeling the fear crawl up their legs.

Hunton said, "All right. Let's do it."

They got out and walked to the building, the sound of the mangler growing louder. As Hunton put the key into the lock of the service door, he thought that the machine *did* sound alive – as if it were breathing in great hot gasps and speaking to itself in hissing, sardonic whispers.

"All of a sudden I'm glad I'm with a cop," Jackson said. He shifted the brown bag he held from one arm to the other. Inside was a small jelly jar filled with holy water wrapped in waxed paper, and a Gideon Bible.

They stepped inside and Hunton snapped up the light switches by the door. The fluorescents flickered into cold life. At the same instant the mangler shut off.

A membrane of steam hung over its rollers. It waited for them in its new ominous silence.

"God, it's an ugly thing," Jackson whispered.

"Come on," Hunton said. "Before we lose our nerve."

They walked over to it. The safety bar was in its down position over the belt which fed the machine.

Hunton put out a hand. "Close enough, Mark. Give me the stuff and tell me what to do."

"But –"

"No argument."

Jackson handed him the bag and Hunton put it on the sheet table in front of the machine. He gave Jackson the Bible.

"I'm going to read," Jackson said. "When I point at you, sprinkle the holy water on the machine with your fingers. You say: In the name of the Father, and of the Son, and of the Holy Ghost, get thee from this place, thou unclean. Got it?"

"Yes."

"The second time I point, break the wafer and repeat the incantation again."

"How will we know if it's working?"

"You'll know. The thing is apt to break every window in the place getting out. If it doesn't work the first time, we keep doing it until it does."

"I'm scared green," Hunton said.

"As a matter of fact, so am I."

"If we're wrong about the hand of glory –"

"We're not," Jackson said. "Here we go."

He began. His voice filled the empty laundry with spectral echoes. "Turnest not thou aside to idols, nor make molten gods for yourself. I am the Lord thy God . . ." The words fell like stones into a silence that had suddenly become filled with a creeping, tomblike cold. The mangler remained still and silent under the flourescents, and to Hunton it still seemed to grin.

". . . and the land will vomit you out for having defiled it, as it vomited out nations before you." Jackson looked up, his face strained, and pointed.

Hunton sprinkled holy water across the feeder belt.

There was a sudden, gnashing scream of tortured metal. Smoke rose from the canvas belts where the holy water had touched and took on writhing, red-tinged shapes. The mangler suddenly jerked into life.

"We've got it!" Jackson cried above the rising clamour. "It's on the run!"

He began to read again, his voice rising over the sound of the machinery. He pointed to Hunton again, and Hunton sprinkled some of the host. As he did so he was suddenly swept with a bone-freezing terror, a sudden vivid feeling that it had gone wrong, that the machine had called their bluff – and was the stronger.

Jackson's voice was still rising, approaching climax.

Sparks began to jump across the arc between the main motor and the secondary; the smell of ozone filled the air, like the copper smell of hot blood. Now the main motor was smoking; the mangler was running at an insane, blurred speed; a finger touched to the central belt would have caused the whole body to be hauled in and turned to a bloody rag in the space of five seconds. The concrete beneath their feet trembled and thrummed.

A main bearing blew with a searing flash of purple light, filling the chill air with the smell of thunderstorms, and still the mangler ran, faster and faster, belts and rollers and cogs moving at a speed that made them seem to blend and merge, change, melt, transmute –

Hunton, who had been standing almost hypnotized, suddenly took a step backwards. "Get away!" he screamed over the blaring racket.

"We've almost got it!" Jackson yelled back. "Why –"

There was a sudden indescribable ripping noise and a fissure in the concrete floor suddenly raced towards them and past, widening. Chips of ancient cement flew up in a starburst.

Jackson looked at the mangler and screamed.

It was trying to pull itself out of the concrete, like a dinosaur trying to escape a tar pit. And it wasn't precisely an ironer any more. It was still changing, melting. The 550-volt cable fell, spitting blue fire, into the rollers and was chewed away. For a moment two fireballs glared at them like lambent eyes, eyes filled with a great and cold hunger.

Another fault line tore open. The mangler leaned towards them, within an ace of being free of the concrete moorings that held it. It leered at them; the safety bar had slammed up and what Hunton saw was a gaping, hungry mouth filled with steam.

They turned to run and another fissure opened at their feet. Behind them, a great screaming roar as the thing came free. Hunton leaped over, but Jackson stumbled and fell sprawling.

Hunton turned to help and a huge, amorphous shadow fell over him, blocking the fluorescents.

It stood over Jackson, who lay on his back, staring up in a silent rictus of terror – the perfect sacrifice. Hunton had only a confused impression of something black and moving that bulked to a tremendous height above them both, something with glaring electric eyes the size of footballs, an open mouth with a moving canvas tongue.

He ran: Jackson's dying scream followed him.

When Roger Martin finally got out of bed to answer the doorbell, he was still only a third awake; but when Hunton reeled in, shock slapped him fully into the world with a rough hand.

Hunton's eyes bulged madly from his head, and his hands were claws as he scratched at the front of Martin's robe. There was a small oozing cut on his cheek and his face was splashed with dirty grey specks of powdered cement.

His hair had gone dead white.

"Help me . . . for Jesus' sake, help me. Mark is dead. Jackson is dead."

"Slow down," Martin said. "Come in the living room."

Hunton followed him, making a thick whining noise in this throat, like a dog.

Martin poured him a two-ounce knock of Jim Beam and Hunton held the glass in both hands, downing the raw liquor in a choked gulp. The glass fell unheeded to the carpet and his hands, like wandering ghosts, sought Martin's lapels again.

"The mangler killed Mark Jackson. It . . . it . . . oh God, it might get out! We can't let it get out! We can't . . . we . . . oh –" He began to scream, a crazy, whooping sound that rose and fell in jagged cycles.

Martin tried to hand him another drink but Hunton knocked it aside. "We have to burn it," he said. "Burn it before it can get out. Oh, what if it gets out? Oh Jesus, what if –" His eyes suddenly flickered, glazed, rolled up to show the whites, and he fell to the carpet in a stonelike faint.

Mrs Martin was in the doorway, clutching her robe to her throat. "Who is he, Rog? Is he crazy? I thought –" She shuddered.

"I don't think he's crazy." She was suddenly frightened by the sick shadow of fear on her husband's face. "God, I hope he came quick enough."

He turned to the telephone, picked up the receiver, froze.

There was a faint, swelling noise from the east of the house, the way that Hunton had come. A steady, grinding clatter, growing louder. The living-room window stood half open and now Martin caught a dark smell on the breeze. An odour of ozone . . . or blood.

He stood with his hand on the useless telephone as it grew louder, louder, gnashing and fuming, something in the streets that was hot and steaming. The blood stench filled the room.

His hand dropped from the telephone.

It was already out.

THE DEAD ASTRONAUT

J.G. Ballard

James Graham Ballard (1930–2009) was a master of dystopian fiction. He was born in Shanghai where his father was managing director of a printing company. His family were interred by the Japanese during World War II. The experience formed the basis of his semi-autobiographical novel, *Empire of the Sun*. Ballard's wife Mary died suddenly in 1964, after which Ballard raised their three children alone. He credited domesticity in Shepperton as one of the forces that enabled him to write. He refused a CBE in 2003.

Cape Kennedy has gone now, its gantries rising from the deserted dunes. Sand has come in across the Banana River, filling the creeks and turning the old space complex into a wilderness of swamps and broken concrete. In the summer, hunters build their blinds in the wrecked staff-cars; but by early November, when Judith and I arrived, the entire area was abandoned. Beyond Cocoa Beach, where I stopped the car, the ruined motels were half hidden in the saw grass. The launching towers rose into the evening air like the rusting ciphers of some forgotten algebra of the sky.

"The perimeter fence is half a mile ahead," I said. "We'll wait here until it's dark. Do you feel better now?"

Judith was staring at an immense funnel of cerise cloud that seemed to draw the day with it below the horizon, taking the light from her faded blonde hair. The previous afternoon, in the hotel in Tampa, she had fallen ill briefly with some unspecified complaint.

"What about the money?" she asked. "They may want more, now that we're here."

"Five thousand dollars? Ample, Judith. These relic hunters are a dying breed – few people are interested in Cape Kennedy any longer. What's the matter?"

Her thin fingers were fretting at the collar of her suede jacket. "I . . . it's just that perhaps I should have worn black."

"Why? Judith, this isn't a funeral. For heaven's sake, Robert died twenty years ago. I know all he meant to us, but . . ."

Judith was staring at the debris of tyres and abandoned cars, her pale eyes becalmed in her drawn face. "Philip, don't you understand, he's coming back now. Someone's got to be here. The memorial service over the radio was a horrible travesty – my God, that priest would have had a shock if Robert had talked back to him. There ought to be a full-scale committee, not just you and I and these empty nightclubs."

In a firmer voice, I said: "Judith, there would be a committee – *if* we told the NASA Foundation what we know. The remains would be interred in the NASA vault at Arlington, there'd be a band – even the President might be there. There's still time."

I waited for her to reply, but she was watching the gantries fade into the night sky. Fifteen years ago, when the dead astronaut orbiting the earth in his burned-out capsule had been forgotten, Judith had constituted herself a memorial committee of one. Perhaps, in a few days, when she finally held the last relics of Robert Hamilton's body in her own hands, she would come to terms with her obsession.

"Philip, over there! Is that –"

High in the western sky, between the constellations Cepheus and Cassiopeia, a point of white light moved towards us, like a lost star searching for its zodiac. Within a few minutes, it passed overhead, its faint beacon setting behind the cirrus over the sea.

"It's all right, Judith." I showed her the trajectory timetables pencilled into my diary. "The relic hunters read these orbits off the sky better than any computer. They must have been watching the pathways for years."

"Who was it?"

"A Russian woman pilot – Valentina Prokrovna. She was sent up from a site near the Urals twenty-five years ago to work on a television relay system."

"Television? I hope they enjoyed the programme."

This callous remark, uttered by Judith as she stepped from the car, made me realize once again her special motives for coming to Cape Kennedy. I watched the capsule of the dead woman disappear over the dark Atlantic stream, as always moved by the tragic but serene spectacle of one of these ghostly voyagers coming back after so many years from the tideways of space. All I knew of this dead Russian was her code name: Seagull. Yet, for some reason, I was glad to be there as she came down. Judith, on the other hand, felt nothing of this. During all the years she had sat in the garden in the cold evenings, too tired to bring herself to bed, she had been sustained by her concern for one only of the twelve dead astronauts orbiting the night sky.

As she waited, her back to the sea, I drove the car into the garage of an abandoned nightclub fifty yards from the road. From the trunk I took out two suitcases. One, a light travel-case, contained clothes for Judith and myself. The other, fitted with a foil inlay, reinforcing straps and a second handle, was empty.

We set off north towards the perimeter fence, like two late visitors arriving at a resort abandoned years earlier.

It was twenty years now since the last rockets had left their launching platforms at Cape Kennedy. At the time, NASA had already moved Judith and me – I was a senior flight-programmer – to the great new Planetary Space Complex in New Mexico. Shortly after our arrival, we had met one of the trainee astronauts, Robert Hamilton. After two decades, all I could remember of this over-polite but sharp-eyed young man was his albino skin, so like Judith's pale eyes and opal hair, the same cold gene that crossed them both with its arctic pallor. We had been close friends for barely six weeks. Judith's infatuation was one of those confused sexual impulses that well-brought-up young women express in their own naive way; and as I watched them swim and play tennis together, I felt not so much resentful as concerned to sustain the whole passing illusion for her.

A year later, Robert Hamilton was dead. He had returned to Cape Kennedy for the last military flights before the launching grounds were closed. Three hours after lift-off, a freak meteorite collision ruptured his oxygen support system. He had lived on in his suit for another five hours. Although calm at first, his last radio transmissions were an incoherent babble Judith and I had never been allowed to hear.

A dozen astronauts had died in orbital accidents, their capsules left to revolve through the night sky like the stars of a new constellation; and at first, Judith had shown little response. Later, after her miscarriage, the figure of this dead astronaut circling the sky above us re-emerged in her mind as an obsession with time. For hours, she would stare at the bedroom clock, as if waiting for something to happen.

Five years later, after I resigned from NASA, we made our first trip to Cape Kennedy. A few military units still guarded the derelict gantries, but already the former launching site was being used as a satellite graveyard. As the dead capsules lost orbital velocity, they homed on to the master radio beacon. As well as the American vehicles, Russian and French satellites in the joint Euro-American space projects were brought down here, the burned-out hulks of the capsules exploding across the cracked concrete.

Already, too, the relic hunters were at Cape Kennedy, scouring the burning saw grass for instrument panels and flying suits and – most valuable of all – the mummified corpses of the dead astronauts.

These blackened fragments of collar-bone and shin, kneecap and rib, were the unique relics of the space age, as treasured as the saintly bones of medieval shrines. After the first fatal accident in space, public outcry demanded that these orbiting biers be brought down to earth. Unfortunately, when a returning moon rocket crashed into the Kalahari Desert, aboriginal tribesmen broke into the vehicle. Believing the crew to be dead gods, they cut off the eight hands and vanished into the bush. It had taken two years to track them down. From then on, the capsules were left in orbit to burn out on re-entry.

Whatever remains survived the crash landings in the satellite graveyard were scavenged by the relic hunters of Cape Kennedy. This band of nomads had lived for years in the wrecked cars and motels, stealing their icons under the feet of the wardens who patrolled the concrete decks. In early October, when a former NASA colleague told me that Robert Hamilton's satellite was becoming unstable, I drove down to Tampa and began to inquire about the purchase price of Robert's mortal remains. Five thousand dollars was a small price to pay for laying his ghost to rest in Judith's mind.

Eight hundred yards from the road, we crossed the perimeter fence. Crushed by the dunes, long sections of the twenty-foot-high palisade had collapsed, the saw grass growing through the steel mesh. Below us, the boundary road passed a derelict guardhouse and divided into two paved tracks. As we waited at this rendezvous, the headlamps of the wardens' half-tracks flared across the gantries near the beach.

Five minutes later, a small dark-faced man climbed from the rear seat of a car buried in the sand fifty yards away. Head down, he scuttled over to us.

"Mr and Mrs Groves?" After a pause to peer into our faces, he introduced himself tersely: "Quinton. Sam Quinton."

As he shook hands, his clawlike fingers examined the bones of my wrist and forearm. His sharp nose made circles in the air. He had the eyes of a nervous bird, forever searching the dunes and the grass. An Army webbing belt hung around his patched black denims. He moved his hands restlessly in the air, as if conducting a chamber ensemble hidden behind the sand hills, and I noticed his badly scarred palms. Huge weals formed pale stars in the darkness.

For a moment, he seemed disappointed by us, almost reluctant to move on. Then he set off at a brisk pace across the dunes, now and then leaving us to blunder about helplessly. Half an hour later, when we entered a shallow basin near a farm of alkali-settling beds, Judith and I were exhausted, dragging the suitcases over the broken tyres and barbed wire.

A group of cabins had been dismantled from their original sites along the beach and re-erected in the basin. Isolated rooms tilted on the sloping sand, mantelpieces and flowered paper decorating the outer walls.

The basin was full of salvaged space material: sections of capsules, heat shields, antennas and parachute canisters. Near the dented hull of a weather satellite, two sallow-faced men in sheepskin jackets sat on a car seat. The older wore a frayed Air Force cap over his eyes. With his scarred hands, he was polishing the steel visor of a space helmet. The other, a young man with a faint beard hiding his mouth, watched us approach with the detached and neutral gaze of an undertaker.

We entered the largest of the cabins, two rooms taken off the rear of a beach-house. Quinton lit a paraffin lamp. He pointed around the dingy interior. "You'll be . . . comfortable," he said without conviction. As Judith stared at him with unconcealed distaste, he added pointedly: "We don't get many visitors."

I put the suitcases on the metal bed. Judith walked into the kitchen and Quinton began to open the empty case.

"It's in here?"

I took the two packets of $100 bills from my jacket. When I had handed them to him, I said: "The suitcase is for the . . . remains. Is it big enough?"

Quinton peered at me through the ruby light, as if baffled by our presence there. "You could have spared yourself the trouble. They've been up there a long time, Mr Groves. After the impact" – for some reason, he cast a lewd eye in Judith's direction – "there might be enough for a chess set."

When he had gone, I went into the kitchen. Judith stood by the stove hands on a carton of canned food. She was staring through the window at the metal salvage, refuse of the sky that still carried Robert Hamilton in its rusty centrifuge. For a moment, I had the feeling that the entire landscape of the earth was covered with rubbish and that here, at Cape Kennedy, we had found its source.

I held her shoulders. "Judith, is there any point in this? Why don't we go back to Tampa? I could drive here in ten days' time when it's all over–"

She turned from me, her hands rubbing the suede where I had marked it. "Philip, I want to be here – no matter how unpleasant. Can't you understand?"

At midnight, when I finished making a small meal for us, she was standing on the concrete wall of the settling tank. The three relic hunters sitting on their car seats watched her without moving, scarred hands like flames in the darkness.

At three o'clock that morning, as we lay awake on the narrow bed, Valentina Prokrovna came down from the sky. Enthroned on a bier of burning aluminium three hundred yards wide, she soared past on her final orbit. When I went out into the night air, the relic hunters had gone. From the rim of the settling tank, I watched them race away among the dunes, leaping like hares over the tyres and wire.

I went back to the cabin. "Judith, she's coming down. Do you want to watch?"

Her blonde hair tied within a white towel, Judith lay on the bed, staring at the cracked plasterboard ceiling. Shortly after four o'clock, as I sat beside her, a phosphorescent light filled the hollow. There was the distant sound of explosions, muffled by the high wall of the dunes. Lights flared, followed by the noise of engines and sirens.

At dawn the relic hunters returned, hands wrapped in makeshift bandages, dragging their booty with them.

After this melancholy rehearsal, Judith entered a period of sudden and unexpected activity. As if preparing the cabin for some visitor, she rehung the curtains and swept out the two rooms with meticulous care, even bringing herself to ask Quinton for a bottle of cleanser. For hours she sat at the dressing table, brushing and shaping her hair, trying out first one style and then another. I watched her feel the hollows of her cheeks, searching for the contours of a face that had vanished twenty years ago. As she spoke about Robert Hamilton, she almost seemed worried that she would appear old to him. At other times, she referred to Robert as if he were a child, the son she and I had never been able to conceive since her miscarriage. These different roles followed one another like scenes in some private psychodrama. However, without knowing it, for years Judith and I had used Robert Hamilton for our own reasons. Waiting for him to land, and well aware that after this Judith would have no one to turn to except myself, I said nothing.

Meanwhile, the relic hunters worked on the fragments of Valentina Prokrovna's capsule: the blistered heat shield, the chassis of the radio-telemetry unit and several cans of film that recorded her collision and act of death (these, if still intact, would fetch the highest prices, films of horrific and dreamlike violence played in the underground cinemas of Los Angeles, London and Moscow). Passing the next cabin, I saw a tattered silver space-suit spread-eagled on two automobile seats. Quinton and the relic hunters knelt beside it, their arms deep inside the legs and sleeves, gazing at me with the rapt and sensitive eyes of jewellers.

An hour before dawn, I was awakened by the sound of engines along the beach. In the darkness, the three relic hunters crouched by the settling tank, their pinched faces lit by the headlamps. A long convoy of trucks and half-tracks was moving into the launching ground. Soldiers jumped down from the tailboards, unloading tents and supplies.

"What are they doing?" I asked Quinton. "Are they looking for us?"

The old man cupped a scarred hand over his eyes. "It's the Army," he said uncertainly. "Manoeuvres, maybe. They haven't been here before like this."

"What about Hamilton?" I gripped his bony arm. "Are you sure –"

He pushed me away with a show of nervous temper. "We'll get him first. Don't worry, he'll be coming sooner than they think."

Two nights later, as Quinton prophesied, Robert Hamilton began his final descent. From the dunes near the settling tanks, we watched him emerge from the stars on his last run. Reflected in the windows of the buried cars, a thousand images of the capsule flared in the saw grass around us. Behind the satellite, a wide fan of silver spray opened in a phantom wake.

In the Army encampment by the gantries, there was a surge of activity. A blaze of headlamps crossed the concrete lanes. Since the arrival of these military units, it had become plain to me, if not to Quinton, that far from being on manoeuvres, they were preparing for the landing of Robert Hamilton's capsule. A dozen half-tracks had been churning around the dunes, setting fire to the abandoned cabins and crushing the old car bodies. Platoons of soldiers were repairing the perimeter fence and replacing the sections of metalled road that the relic hunters had dismantled.

Shortly after midnight, at an elevation of forty-two degrees in the north-west, betwen Lyra and Hercules, Robert Hamilton appeared for the last time. As Judith stood up and shouted into the night air, an immense blade of light cleft the sky. The expanding corona sped towards us like a gigantic signal flare, illuminating every fragment of the landscape.

"Mrs Groves!" Quinton darted after Judith and pulled her down into the grass as she ran towards the approaching satellite. Three hundred yards away, the silhouette of a half-track stood out on an isolated dune, its feeble spotlights drowned by the glare.

With a low metallic sigh, the burning capsule of the dead astronaut soared over our heads, the vaporizing metal pouring from its hull. A few seconds later, as I shielded my eyes, an explosion of detonating sand rose from the ground behind me. A curtain of dust lifted into the darkening air like a vast spectre of powdered bone. The sounds of the impact rolled across the dunes. Near the launching gantries, fires flickered where fragments of the capsule had landed. A pall of phosphorescing gas hung in the air, particles within it beading and winking.

Judith had gone, running after the relic hunters through the swerving spotlights. When I caught up with them, the last fires of the explosion were dying among the gantries. The capsule had landed near the old Atlas launching pads, forming a shallow crater fifty yards in diameter. The slopes were scattered with glowing particles, sparkling like fading eyes. Judith ran distraughtly up and down, searching the fragments of smouldering metal.

Someone struck my shoulder. Quinton and his men, hot ash on their scarred hands, ran past like a troop of madmen, eyes wild in the crazed night. As we darted away through the flaring spotlights, I looked back at the beach. The gantries were enveloped in a pale-silver sheen that hovered there, and then moved away like a dying wraith over the sea.

* * *

At dawn, as the engines growled among the dunes, we collected the last remains of Robert Hamilton. The old man came into our cabin. As Judith watched from the kitchen, drying her hands on a towel, he gave me a cardboard shoe-box.

I held the box in my hands. "Is this all you could get?"

"It's all there was. Look at them, if you want."

"That's all right. We'll be leaving in half an hour."

He shook his head. "Not now. They're all around. If you move, they'll find us."

He waited for me to open the shoe-box, then grimaced and went out into the pale light.

We stayed for another four days, as the Army patrols searched the surrounding dunes. Day and night, the half-tracks lumbered among the wrecked cars and cabins. Once, as I watched with Quinton from a fallen water tower, a half-track and two jeeps came within four hundred yards of the basin, held back only by the stench from the settling beds and the cracked concrete causeways.

During this time, Judith sat in the cabin, the shoe-box on her lap. She said nothing to me, as if she had lost all interest in me and the salvage-filled hollow at Cape Kennedy. Mechanically, she combed her hair, making and remaking her face.

On the second day, I came in after helping Quinton bury the cabins to their windows in the sand. Judith was standing by the table.

The shoe-box was open. In the centre of the table lay a pile of charred sticks, as if she had tried to light a small fire. Then I realized what was there. As she stirred the ash with her fingers, grey flakes fell from the joints, revealing the bony points of a clutch of ribs, a right hand and shoulder blade.

She looked at me with puzzled eyes. "They're black," she said.

Holding her in my arms, I lay with her on the bed. A loudspeaker reverberated among the dunes, fragments of the amplified commands drumming at the panes.

When they moved away, Judith said: "We can go now."

"In a little while, when it's clear. What about these?"

"Bury them. Anywhere, it doesn't matter." She seemed calm at last, giving me a brief smile, as if to agree that this grim charade was at last over.

Yet, when I had packed the bones into the shoe-box, scraping up Robert Hamilton's ash with a dessert spoon, she kept it with her, carrying it into the kitchen while she prepared our meals.

It was on the third day that we fell ill.

After a long, noise-filled night, I found Judith sitting in front of the mirror, combing thick clumps of hair from her scalp. Her mouth was open, as if her lips were stained with acid. As she dusted the loose hair from her lap, I was struck by the leprous whiteness of her face.

Standing up with an effort, I walked listlessly into the kitchen and stared at the saucepan of cold coffee. A sense of indefinable exhaustion had come over me, as if the bones in my body had softened and lost their rigidity. On the lapels of my jacket, loose hair lay like spinning waste.

"Philip . . ." Judith swayed towards me. "Do you feel – What is it?"

"The water." I poured the coffee into the sink and massaged my throat. "It must be fouled."

"Can we leave?" She put a hand up to her forehead. Her brittle nails brought down a handful of frayed ash hair. "Philip, for God's sake – I'm losing all my hair!"

Neither of us was able to eat. After forcing myself through a few slices of cold meat, I went out and vomited behind the cabin.

Quinton and his men were crouched by the wall of the settling tank. As I walked towards them, steadying myself against the hull of the weather satellite, Quinton came down. When I told him that the water supplies were contaminated, he stared at me with his hard bird's eyes.

Half an hour later, they were gone.

The next day, our last there, we were worse. Judith lay on the bed, shivering in her jacket, the shoe-box held in one hand. I spent hours searching for fresh water in the cabins. Exhausted, I could barely cross the sandy basin. The Army patrols were closer. By now, I could hear the hard gear-changes of the half-tracks. The sounds from the loudspeakers drummed like fists on my head.

Then, as I looked down at Judith from the cabin doorway, a few words stuck for a moment in my mind.

". . . *contaminated area . . . evacuate . . . radioactive. . .*"

I walked forward and pulled the box from Judith's hands.

"Philip . . ." She looked up at me weakly. "Give it back to me."

Her face was a puffy mask. On her wrists, white flecks were forming. Her left hand reached towards me like the claw of a cadaver.

I shook the box with blunted anger. The bones rattled inside. "For God's sake, it's *this*! Don't you see – why we're ill?"

"Philip – where are the others? The old man. Get them to help you."

"They've gone. They went yesterday, I told you." I let the box fall on to the table. The lid broke off, spilling the ribs tied together like a bundle of firewood. "Quinton knew what was happening – why the Army is here. They're trying to warn us."

"What do you mean?" Judith sat up, the focus of her eyes sustained only by a continuous effort. "Don't let them take Robert. Bury him here somewhere. We'll come back later."

"Judith!" I bent over the bed and shouted hoarsely at her. "Don't you realize – there was a *bomb* on board! Robert Hamilton was carrying an atomic weapon!" I pulled back the curtains from the window. "My God, what a joke. For twenty years, I put up with him because I couldn't ever be really sure . . ."

"Philip . . ."

"Don't worry, I used him – thinking about him was the only thing that kept us going. And all the time, he was waiting up there to pay us back!"

There was a rumble of exhaust outside. A half-track with red crosses on its doors and hood had reached the edge of the basin. Two men in vinyl suits jumped down, counters raised in front of them.

"Judith, before we go, tell me . . . I never asked you –"

Judith was sitting up, touching the hair on her pillow. One half of her scalp was almost bald. She stared at her weak hands with their silvering skin. On her face was an expression I had never seen before, the dumb anger of betrayal.

As she looked at me, and at the bones scattered across the table, I knew my answer.

RANDAL

Robert Nye

Robert Nye (b.1939) left school at the age of sixteen. He continued to educate himself in English literature while working various jobs including reporter, milkman and market gardener. Nye was poetry critic at *The Times* from 1971 to 1976, after which he became head book reviewer at *The Scotsman*. A poet and novelist, his awards include the Guardian Fiction Prize (1976) and the Cholmondeley Award (2007). Robert Nye lives near Cork in Ireland. He is a Fellow of the Royal Society of Literature.

She didn't blame Randal for leaving his. Day in, day out, boiled bacon. Sundays should be different. Sundays should be butcher's meat. But the world wasn't like that any more.

"I'm cold," she said.

The clocks in the cottage were striking two. There was a grandfather clock in the front parlour and a marble clock on the mantelpiece in the kitchen where they sat eating. The grandfather clock had a strong steady tick, while the marble clock sounded fussy and overwound. Striking the hour, the grandfather clock sounded a stroke before the marble clock, so that the effect was of a slightly hysterical echo. It was as if the marble clock was repeating what the grandfather clock had just said, but distorting it in the process.

"Cold, cold," said Madge.

Her sister Iseabal was staring at her. Her sister Iseabal had picked up the china teapot and was silently holding it out. She sat straightbacked in her straightbacked chair.

Madge coughed, then had to push her spectacles back to rest on the thin bridge of her nose. She lifted up her cup and saucer. Iseabal poured her a cup of tea. Madge did not take milk or sugar. She sipped the hot tea, but it scarcely warmed her.

"Those clocks are fast again," said Iseabal.

Madge bit her lip. "I put them right with my own hand," she said.

"They're old," said Iseabal. "Listen to this one. It's got a hiccup in it." She stirred three spoons of sugar into her tea. "As for the grandfather," she said, "I think it's in its second childhood."

The cottage kitchen was very small. There were three chairs at the kitchen table. Sitting there, you could reach out in any direction and almost touch a wall. All the walls were covered with the same rose-patterned wallpaper.

Madge reached out now and touched the marble clock affectionately. "Remember Gregor MacGregor?" she said.

Iseabal sighed. "What should I want to remember him for?"

"Gregor MacGregor was wicked," Madge said, stroking the face of the marble clock. "He carried hay on a Sunday. Drunk as a faucet he was, most of the time. And when he wasn't drunk he was hogging." Her plump round cheeks dimpled above a sentimental smile. "He'd promise you anything," she went on, "but you'd never get it. He'd promise you the sea, he would; he'd promise you the sea, and the mountain. Anything that wasn't his to give. His promise was like the froth on the water. And cunning. 'The fox knows well, where the geese dwell!' He wouldn't just steal your eggs. Or your hen. Not Gregor MacGregor. Ambitious, he was. Steal your eggs *and* your hen. That was Gregor."

Her sister Iseabal was making her fingers crack by clasping her bony hands together. Madge acknowledged by the merest pause the unease which this noise betokened. Then she went on:

"Steal eggs and hen and tip his cap and tell you he was doing you a favour. What good it ever did him I don't know. If you ask me he was more than half-daft. Never satisfied, Gregor MacGregor. In winter it was August, August, August he'd be talking of. In summer he was all for Christmas. You never know where you are with a man like that."

Iseabal sniffed, and brushed back a wisp of her iron-grey hair. "A pity he never used his teeth to stop his tongue," she said.

There were three plates on the kitchen table. Two of the plates on the kitchen table were empty. Madge shivered and coughed and pushed her empty plate aside with a trembling thumb. Then she stood up and went to the little window over the sink.

"Remember when Parlan caught him out over the white goat?" she said. "He was that angry, Parlan, he hit him with a big stick, and Gregor fell in the cesspit." She chuckled to herself at the memory. "So Gregor takes a chicken in a sack," she murmured, watching her breath cloud the cold window pane, "and he climbs up on Parlan's roof and drops that chicken down the chimney just when Parlan's daughter had the plum jam stewing on the fire. A chicken squawking round the kitchen all covered in hot plum jam! It took them weeks to scrub it off the ceiling. And, as if that wasn't sufficient, Gregor went and wrote a poem about Parlan and every verse ending with 'I trust he finds thorns in his porridge', and the funny thing was, when Parlan read the poem – "

"That's enough," said Iseabal sharply. "I don't want to hear another word about Gregor MacGregor. He's dead."

The word hung in the thin air of the kitchen like an icicle.

"Quick to the feast," said Madge, "quick to the grave."

Iseabal was making her fingers crack again. "He was dead before he died," she said. "Dead, who is not in God. Dead then. Dead now."

Madge pressed her lips lightly to the cold glass. "He was so small," she said.

Iseabal stood up from the table and pushed back her chair. "We'll have that nice bath after we've washed up," Iseabal said. "A proper Sunday bath."

"I'm cold," said Madge. She coughed. "Remember the bad winter?" she said. "When all the swedes and mangolds got frozen and Randal ran out of hay after the summer being so wet, and the sheep were dying and their fleeces all stiff and stuck to the ground, and some of them with their legs broken, coming into the house for a bit of potato peelings, anything, and then the snow so deep it was high over the hedge there."

Iseabal leaned on her outspread fingers. The nails showed purple with the weight, but the tips were white. "That bath," she said. "Do you hear me?"

"I hear you," Madge said. She did not turn away from the window. Her forehead was resting against the pane. "I was here in the kitchen washing up," she said, "and the egg wouldn't come off the eggcups no matter how hot the water, and me scratching away with the scourer, it just wouldn't come off, and I heard this bleating, and I had to scrape the ice off the catch before I could get the window open, and the glass itself all over coated with frost so you couldn't see through it. And when I got the window open, there was this lamb by the drain, and the drain frozen solid, and the lamb bleating and bleating, just born, not long born, the night before perhaps it was, and it was all red and wet and smudgy one side of its head." She turned away from the window and faced her sister Iseabal. "A crow had picked its eye out," she said.

The sisters looked at each other calmly for a moment. Then:

"That's enough," said Iseabal. "We'll wash up first."

Madge nodded and went back to the table and put her cup and saucer on her plate. She reached across and gathered up the others. She said, "Can't say I blame Randal for leaving that boiled bacon. Too salty."

"A matter of taste," said Iseabal.

Carrying the cups and plates towards the sink, Madge stopped to look out of the window again. "It's snowing," she said, in a cheerful voice.

Her sister was just behind her. "Nice," her sister was saying. "Like those streaks in Randal's hair."

Madge watched the snow stream and make brief flowers on the pane. She coughed. "It was red as fire once," she said. She put the plates and cups and knives and forks into the low sink. Her sister had taken the black pan of water from the grate and now it was being held out towards her with the long handle wrapped in Iseabal's apron. Madge poured the water into the sink and rolled the sleeves of her dress and started washing up.

"Did you say red?" said Iseabal.

"No," Madge said.

"Did you say Randal's hair was *red*?"

"No," Madge said.

"You did," said her sister.

"I didn't," Madge said. "Are you going to dry?"

"Red, you said."

"Black," Madge said, looking at her hands working in the water. "Black."

"Yes, but you said red," said Iseabal. "You said it was red."

Madge scrubbed at the bacon marks with a piece of wire wool. "Look," she said, "what are we arguing for? I know the colour of my brother's hair."

"I should think so," said Iseabal. "Black."

"As the crow," Madge said.

The cat purred on the hearth.

Iseabal polished the plates fiercely with a thin cloth. "A streak of white about the temples makes a man distinguished," Iseabal said. "But it wouldn't if his hair was red."

"No," said Madge.

"Never trust a man with red hair," her sister said. "Black hair is straightforward hair. Randal's hair is good black."

"I know it," said Madge wearily. "Didn't I say so? Don't I keep on saying so?"

Iseabal smiled at her own reflection in a spoon. Then she turned aside to hang up their cups on the hooks in the dresser.

"What can Randal be thinking of you?" Iseabal said softly.

Madge did not look at her. Instead, she turned right round and said in a bold voice, "What *do* you think of me, Randal?"

Iseabal reached out her finger and made a cup swing. The marble clock ticked fussily. Iseabal nodded her head.

"What did he say?" Madge asked at last.

Iseabal smiled. "You heard him," she said.

"I didn't quite catch it."

"What's the matter with you," said Iseabal, "that you don't hear your own flesh and blood when he speaks to you?"

Madge pushed her glasses up her nose. She said nothing. She returned her attention to the sink.

"Ashamed of her?" said Iseabal. "Yes, I am too."

Madge poked at the crockery in the water. "He didn't say that," she said. Her voice was a whisper.

"That's what he said," said Iseabal.

"I don't believe it," Madge muttered.

Iseabal shrugged, putting away the knives. "You have little faith," she said.

"No," said Madge savagely. "He didn't say that. He didn't." Iseabal wiped her fingers on the towel that hung from a nail beside the sink. "He speaks his mind straight," she said, and sniffed.

Madge pulled out the plug. The water ran away with a choking sound.

"I'll get the bath in from the outhouse," Madge said, in a voice that sought to please two people.

"Fine," her sister said. "You go ahead, dear."

Madge slipped on her coat and went out of the door. The snow was flying up the hill. The sky looked like a bad egg, full of it. She pulled up her collar and hurried across the yard. The tin bath made a jagged black mark, revealing the gravel under the snow, as she dragged it back to the cottage from the outhouse.

Madge came in coughing with the cold. "Give me a hand," she said. "You know it's heavy."

She had her back towards her sister, dragging the bath, so she could not see what was happening in the room.

When Madge turned round she saw that her sister had her finger to her lips. Iseabal was kneeling in front of the easy chair. "Randal's fallen asleep," she whispered.

"So I see," said Madge.

"Well," she went on, after a moment's silence, "shall I fetch it?"

"No," Iseabal said, "I will," and she went out smiling, on tip-toes.

Madge pulled the curtains shut as softly as she could. The little rings made a rushing noise. She looked round nervously. The light from the grate was almost golden with the curtains drawn.

The cat twitched in a bad dream, or as its heart missed a beat.

Madge slipped off her coat and dragged the bath in front of the fire without making a sound. Then she picked up the scuttle in her arms, and set it down beside the bath. She knelt. She took sticks and papers and pieces of coal from the scuttle and began arranging them inside the bath. She worked neatly, making a pattern.

Her sister Iseabal came back in with snow across her hair. She carried a green can in each hand.

"There," Iseabal said, putting the cans down beside the bath. "Good. You put the sticks and papers in."

"And some bits of coal," Madge said.

Iseabal smiled. "Isn't that a waste?"

"You never know," Madge said.

Her sister shrugged, accepting, and unscrewed the top of one of the green cans. She poured a thin stream into the bath.

"More than that," Madge said.

"It's plenty," said Iseabal.

"Let me do it," Madge said, standing up.

She took the can from her sister and walked right round the bath, pouring freely as she went. When she reached the spot where she had started, she stopped, nodded to her sister, and went round once more, still pouring.

"That will do," Iseabal said.

"Yes," said Madge. "That will do."

She set down the empty can and they stood looking at each other. Iseabal shook the snow from her grey hair with an almost flirtatious gesture, and smiled. Iseabal's fingers came up to touch the smile on her own face as if to make sure it was there. After that they avoided each other's eyes.

Madge undressed quickly. Half-turned away from the chair, she held out her hand and her sister took it. Iseabal's hand was hot. Madge helped her sister into the bath. Iseabal knelt down.

"Go on," Iseabal said.

Madge picked up the other green can and unscrewed the top. She poured half of the contents over her sister without looking at her. She could hear it trickling down.

"It's stinky," Iseabal said.

"Well," said Madge, "what do you expect it to be?"

"I'm not complaining," said Iseabal.

Madge nodded. She climbed into the bath and handed her sister the can. She knelt down facing Iseabal, but with her glasses off and her eyes shut. She felt the liquid pouring over her.

Madge tilted up her face. "Plenty in my hair," she said, and some ran into her mouth.

Madge coughed.

"Sorry," said her sister.

"Never mind," said Madge.

In the dark, with her eyes tight shut, Madge could hear the marble clock ticking. She waited. "Go on then," she said at last.

"I thought you had them," Iseabal said.

Madge opened her eyes. For the first time since taking off their clothes, they looked at each other. Iseabal was smiling. "There's a box in the knife drawer," Iseabal said. "Or we could use a taper."

"That would not be right," Madge said. She climbed out of the bath, groped around on the floor until she found her glasses, put them on, and went to the dresser. The matchbox was wrapped in a table napkin, beside the cheese grater. Madge unfolded the napkin and put the matchbox on the table. She refolded the napkin and replaced it in the drawer. Then she shut the drawer. She picked up the matchbox from the table and went back to the bath.

Madge removed her spectacles and knelt down once more facing her sister. She clasped the matchbox in her right hand. Its edge was sharp against her palm.

"Randal's still asleep," said Iseabal.

"Of course," said Madge.

She looked into her sister's eyes but she could only see herself reflected there. The firelight flickered across Iseabal's proud face.

"Shall I say a prayer?" Madge asked.

"Can you remember one?" said her sister.

"No," Madge admitted. "I can't."

The two clocks struck the half hour, with the grandfather as usual a heart-beat in front.

"The devil," said Iseabal.

"Never mind," Madge said.

The fire crackled in the grate.

"Mercy on us," said Iseabal.

"Amen," Madge said.

The cat looked up at them with bright unwondering eyes, then put its head back between its black and white paws.

"I never did like that graveyard," said Iseabal.

Madge nodded absent-mindedly, giving her sister the box of matches into her hand. Then she said, as an afterthought, catching at Iseabal's wrist, "But I don't think *you* should strike the match."

"Why not?" said Iseabal.

"I just don't think you should," Madge said.

Iseabal smiled. "All right," she said. "You do it. You and your remembering. But you were always the strong one, really."

"No doubt," said Madge. "But I don't think I should do it either."

Iseabal smiled. "Who then?" she said.

"Who?" said Madge. "You know who."

"Randal," said Iseabal softly.

"Randal," Madge said in a great voice.

They both shut their eyes. There came the sound of the striking of a match against the matchbox. At first it would not light. The match had to scrape against the box twice without success. The third time it lit.

THE VINEGAR MOTHER

Ruth Rendell

Ruth Barbara Rendell (1930–2015), née Grasemann, was born in London and grew up in South Woodford, Essex. She worked as a reporter for the *Chigwell Times*, before marrying journalist Donald Rendell. Rendell's first six novels were rejected by publishers, but in 1964, *From Doon with Death*, featuring Inspector Wexford, was accepted. She went on to publish twenty Wexford novels and over fifty other books. Ruth Rendell also wrote under the name Barbara Vine. She was a member of the House of Lords.

All this happened when I was eleven.

Mop Felton was at school with me and she was supposed to be my friend. I say "supposed to be" because she was one of those close friends all little girls seem to have yet don't very much like. I had never liked Mop. I knew it then just as I know it now, but she was my friend because she lived in the next street, was the same age, in the same form, and because my parents, though not particularly intimate with the Feltons, would have it so.

Mop was a nervous, strained, dramatic creature, in some ways old for her age and in others very young. Hindsight tells me that she had no self-confidence but much self-esteem. She was an only child who flew into noisy rages or silent huffs when teased. She was tall and very skinny and dark, and it wasn't her hair, thin and lank, which accounted for her nickname. Her proper name was Alicia. I don't know why we called her Mop, and if now I see in it some obscure allusion to mopping and mowing (a Shakespearean description which might have been associated with her) or in the monosyllable the hint of a witch's familiar (again, not inept) I am attributing to us an intellectual sophistication which we didn't possess.

We were gluttons for nicknames. Perhaps all schoolgirls are. But there was neither subtlety nor finesse in our selection. Margaret myself, I was dubbed Margarine. Rhoda Joseph, owing to some gagging and embarrassment during a public recitation of Wordsworth, was for ever after Lucy; Elizabeth Goodwin Goat because this epithet had once been applied to her by higher authority on the hockey field. Our nicknames were not exclusive, being readily interchangeable with our true christian names at will. We never used them in the presence of parent or teacher and they, if they had known of them, would not have deigned use them to us. It was, therefore, all the more astonishing to hear them from the lips of Mr Felton, the oldest and richest of any of our fathers.

Coming home from work into a room where Mop and I were: "How's my old Mopsy, then?" he would say, and to me, "Well, it's jolly old Margarine!"

I used to giggle, as I always did when confronted by something mildly embarrassing that I didn't understand. I was an observant child but not sensitive. Children, in any case, are little given to empathy. I can't recall that I ever pitied Mop for having a father who, though over fifty, pretended too often to be her contemporary. But I found it satisfactory that my own father, at her entry, would look up vaguely from his book and mutter, "Hallo – er, Alicia, isn't it?"

The Feltons were on a slightly higher social plane than we, a fact I did know and accepted without question and without resentment. Their house was bigger, each parent possessed a car, they ate dinner in the evenings. Mr Felton used to give Mop half a glass of sherry to drink.

"I don't want you growing up ignorant of wine," he would say.

And if I were present I would get the sherry too. I suppose it was Manzanilla, for it was very dry and pale yellow, the colour of the stone in a ring Mrs Felton wore and which entirely hid her wedding ring.

They had a cottage in the country where they went at the weekends and sometimes for the summer holidays. Once they took me there for a day. And the summer after my eleventh birthday, Mr Felton said:

"Why don't you take old Margarine with you for the holidays?"

It seems strange now that I should have wanted to go. I had a very happy childhood, a calm, unthinking, unchanging relationship with my parents and my brothers. I liked Rhoda and Elizabeth far more than I liked Mop, whose rages and fantasies and sulks annoyed me, and I disliked Mrs Felton more than any grown-up I knew. Yet I did want to go very much. The truth was that even then I had begun to develop my passion for houses, the passion that has led me to become a designer of them, and one day in that cottage had been enough to make me love it. All my life had been spent in a semi-detached villa, circa 1935, in a London suburb. The Feltons' cottage, which had the pretentious (not to me, then) name of Sanctuary, was four hundred years old, thatched, half-timbered, of wattle and daub construction, a calendar-maker's dream, a chocolate box artist's ideal. I wanted to sleep within those ancient walls, tread upon floors that had been there before the Armada came, press my face against glass panes that had reflected a ruff or a Puritan's starched collar.

My mother put up a little opposition. She liked me to know Mop, she also perhaps liked me to be associated with the Feltons' social *cachet*, but I had noticed before that she didn't much like me to be in the care of Mrs Felton.

"And Mr Felton will only be there at the weekends," she said.

"If Margaret doesn't like it," said my father, "she can write home and get us to send her a telegram saying you've broken your leg."

"Thanks very much," said my mother. "I wish you wouldn't teach the children habits of deception."

But in the end she agreed. If I were unhappy, I was to phone from the call-box in the village and then they would write and say my grandmother wanted me to go and stay with her. Which, apparently, was not teaching me habits of deception.

In the event, I wasn't at all unhappy, and it was to be a while before I was even disquieted. There was plenty to do. It was fruit-growing country, and Mop and

I picked fruit for Mr Gould, the farmer. We got paid for this, which Mrs Felton seemed to think *infra dig*. She didn't associate with the farmers or the agricultural workers. Her greatest friend was a certain Lady Elsworthy, an old woman whose title (I later learned she was the widow of a Civil Service knight) placed her in my estimation in the forefront of the aristocracy. I was stricken dumb whenever she and her son were at Sanctuary and much preferred the company of our nearest neighbour, a Mrs Potter, who was perhaps gratified to meet a juvenile enthusiast of architecture. Anyway, she secured for me the *entrée* to the Hall, a William and Mary mansion, through whose vast chambers I walked hand in hand with her, awed and wondering and very well content.

Sanctuary had a small parlour, a large dining-living room, a kitchen and a bathroom on the ground floor and two bedrooms upstairs. The ceilings were low and sloping and so excessively beamed, some of the beams being carved, that were I to see it now I would probably think it vulgar, though knowing it authentic. I am sure that nowadays I would think the Feltons' furniture vulgar, for their wealth, such as it was, didn't run to the purchasing of true antiques. Instead, they had those piecrust tables and rent tables and little escritoires which, cunningly chipped and scratched in the right places, inlaid with convincingly scuffed and dimly gilded leather, maroon, olive or amber, had been manufactured at a factory in Romford.

I knew this because Mr Felton, down for the weekend, would announce it to whomsoever might be present.

"And how old do you suppose that is, Lady Elsworthy?" he would say, fingering one of those deceitful little tables as he placed on it her glass of citrine-coloured sherry. "A hundred and fifty years? Two hundred?"

Of course she didn't know or was too well-bred to say.

"One year's your answer! Factory-made last year and I defy anyone but an expert to tell the difference."

Then Mop would have her half-glass of sherry and I mine while the adults watched us for the signs of intoxication they seemed to find so amusing in the young and so disgraceful in the old. And then dinner with red or white wine, but none for us this time. They always had wine, even when, as was often the case, the meal was only sandwiches or bits of cold stuff on toast. Mr Felton used to bring it down with him on Saturdays, a dozen bottles sometimes in a cardboard case. I wonder if it was good French wine or sour cheap stuff from Algeria that my father called plonk. Whatever Mr Felton's indulgence with the sherry had taught me, it was not to lose my ignorance of wine.

But wine plays a part in this story, an important part. For as she sipped the dark red stuff in her glass, blood-black with – or am I imagining this? – a blacker scaling of lees in its depths, Lady Elsworthy said:

"Even if you're only a moderate wine-drinker, my dear, you ought, you really ought, to have a vinegar mother."

On this occasion I wasn't the only person present to giggle. There were cries of "A *what*?" and some laughter, and then Lady Elsworthy began an explanation of what a vinegar mother was, a culture of acetobacter that would convert wine into vinegar. Her son, whom the adults called Peter, supplied the technical details and the Potters asked questions and from time to time someone would say, "A vinegar mother! What a name!" I wasn't much interested and I wandered off into the garden where, after a few minutes, Mop joined me. She was, as usual, carrying a book but instead of sitting down, opening the book and excluding me, which was her custom, she stood staring into the distance of the Stour Valley and the Weeping Hills – I think she leant against a tree – and her face had on it that protuberant-featured expression which heralded one of her rages. I asked her what was the matter.

"I've been sick."

I knew she hadn't been, but I asked her why.

"That horrible old woman and that horrible thing she was talking about, like a bit of liver in a bottle, she said." Her mouth trembled. "Why does she call it a vinegar *mother?*"

"I don't know," I said. "Perhaps because mothers make children and it makes vinegar."

That only seemed to make her angrier and she kicked at the tree.

"Shall we go down to the pond or are you going to read?" I said.

But Mop didn't answer me so I went down to the pond alone and watched the bats that flitted against a pale green sky. Mop had gone up to our bedroom. She was in bed reading when I got back. No reader myself, I remember the books she liked and remember too that my mother thought she ought not to be allowed to read them. That night it was Lefanu's *Uncle Silas* which engrossed her. She had just finished Dr James's *Ghost Stories of an Antiquary*. I don't believe, at that time, I saw any connection between her literary tastes and her reaction to the vinegar mother, nor did I attribute this latter to anything lacking in her relationship with her own mother. I couldn't have done so, I was much too young. I hadn't, anyway, been affected by the conversation at supper and I went to bed with no uneasy forebodings about what was to come.

In the morning when Mop and I came back from church – we were sent there, I now think, from a desire on the part of Mr and Mrs Felton to impress the neighbours rather than out of vicarious piety – we found the Elsworthys once more at Sanctuary. Lady Elsworthy and her son and Mrs Felton were all peering into a round glass vessel with a stoppered mouth in which was some brown liquid with a curd floating on it. This curd did look quite a lot like a slice of liver.

"It's alive," said Mop. "It's a sort of animal."

Lady Elsworthy told her not to be a little fool and Mrs Felton laughed. I thought my mother would have been angry if a visitor to our house had told me not to be a fool, and I also thought Mop was really going to be sick this time.

"We don't have to have it, do we?" she said.

"Of course we're going to have it," said Mrs Felton. "How dare you speak like that when Lady Elsworthy has been kind enough to give it to me! Now we shall never have to buy nasty shop vinegar again."

"Vinegar doesn't cost much," said Mop.

"Isn't that just like a child! Money grows on trees as far as she's concerned."

Then Lady Elsworthy started giving instructions for the maintenance of the thing. It must be kept in a warm atmosphere. "Not out in your chilly kitchen, my dear." It was to be fed with wine, the dregs of each bottle they consumed.

"But not white wine. You tell her why not, Peter, you know I'm no good at the scientific stuff. It must never be touched with a knife or metal spoon."

"If metal touches it," said Peter Elsworthy, "It will shrivel and die. In some ways, you see, it's a tender plant."

Mop had banged out of the room. Lady Elsworthy was once more bent over her gift, holding the vessel and placing it in a suitable position where it was neither too light nor too cold. From the garden I could hear the drone of the lawn mower, plied by Mr Felton. Those other two had moved a little away from the window, away from the broad shaft of sunshine in which we had found them bathed. As Peter Elsworthy spoke of the tender plant, I saw his eyes meet Mrs Felton's and there passed between them a glance, mysterious, beyond my comprehension, years away from anything I knew. His face became soft and strange. I wanted to giggle as I sometimes giggled in the cinema, but I knew better than to do so there, and I went away and giggled by myself in the garden, saying, "Soppy, soppy!" and kicking at a stone.

But I wasn't alone. Mr Felton came pushing the lawn mower up behind me. He used to sweat in the heat and his face was red and wet like the middle of a joint of beef when the brown part had been carved off. A grandfather rather than a father, I thought him.

"What's soppy, my old Margarine? Mind out of my way or I'll cut your tail off."

It was August and the season had begun, so on Sunday afternoons he would take the shotgun he kept hanging in the kitchen and go out after rabbits. I believe he did this less from a desire to eat rabbit flesh than from a need to keep in with the Elsworthys who shot every unprotected thing that flew or scuttled. But he was a poor shot and I used to feel relieved when he came back empty-handed. On Sunday evenings he drove away to London.

"Poor old Daddy back to the grindstone," he would say. "Take care of yourself, my old Mop." And to me, with wit, "Don't melt away in all this sunshine, Margarine."

That Sunday Mrs Felton made him promise to bring a dozen more bottles of wine when he returned the following weekend.

"Reinforcements for my vinegar mother."

"It's stupid wasting wine to make it into vinegar," said Mop. I wondered why she used to hover so nervously about her parents at this leave-taking time, watching them both, her fists clenched. Now I know it was because, although she was rude to them and seemed not to care for them, she longed desperately to see them exchange some demonstration of affection greater than Mrs Felton's apathetic lifting of her cheek and the hungry peck Mr Felton deposited upon it. But she waited in vain, and when the car had gone would burst into a seemingly inexplicable display of ill temper or sulks.

So another week began, a week in which our habits, until then routine and placid, were to change.

Like a proper writer, a professional, I have hinted at Mrs Felton and, I hope, whetted appetites, but I have delayed till now giving any description of her. But having announced her entry through the mouths of my characters (as in all the best plays) I shall delay no more. The stage is ready for her and she shall enter it, in her robes and with her trumpets.

She was a tall thin woman and her skin was as brown as a pale Indian's. I thought her old and very ugly, and I couldn't understand a remark of my mother's that I had overheard to the effect that Mrs Felton was "quite beautiful if you liked that gypsy look". I suppose she was about thirty-seven or thirty-eight. Her hair was black and frizzy, like a bush of heather singed by fire, and it grew so low on her forehead that her black brows sprang up to meet it, leaving only an inch or so of skin between. She had a big mouth with brown thick lips she never painted and enormous eyes whose whites were like wet eggshells.

In the country she wore slacks and a shirt. She made some of her own clothes and those she made were dramatic. I remember a hooded cloak she had of brown hessian and a long evening gown of embroidered linen. At that time women seldom wore cloaks or long dresses, either for evening or day. She chain-smoked and her fingers were yellow with nicotine.

Me she almost entirely ignored. I was fed and made to wash properly and told to change my clothes and not allowed to be out after dark. But apart from this she hardly spoke to me. I think she had a ferocious dislike of children, for Mop fared very little better than I did. Mrs Felton was one of those women who fall into the habit of only addressing their children to scold them. However presentable Mop might make herself, however concentratedly good on occasion her behaviour – for I believe she made great efforts – Mrs Felton couldn't bring herself to praise. Or if she could, there would always be the sting in the tail, the "Well, but look at your nails!" or "It's very nice but do you have to pick this moment?" And Mop's name on her tongue – as if specifically chosen to this end – rang with a sour slither, a little green snake slipping from its hole, as the liquid and the sibilant scathed out, "Alicia!"

But at the beginning of that third week a slight change came upon her. She was not so much nicer or kinder as more vague, more nervously abstracted. Mop's peccadilloes passed unnoticed and I, if late for a meal, received no venomous glance. It was on the Tuesday evening that the first wine bottle appeared at our supper table.

We ate this meal, cold usually but more than a bread and butter tea, at half-past seven or eight in the evening, and after it we were sent to bed. There had never before been the suggestion that we should take wine with it. Even at the weekends we were never given wine, apart from our tiny glasses of educative sherry. But that night at sunset – I remember the room all orange and quiet and warm – Mrs Felton brought to the table a bottle of red wine instead of the teapot and the lemon barley water, and set out three glasses.

"I don't like wine," said Mop.

"Yes, you do. You like sherry."

"I don't like that dark red stuff. It tastes bitter. Daddy won't let me have wine."

"Then we won't tell Daddy. If it's bitter you can put sugar in it. My God, any other child would think it was in heaven getting wine for supper. You don't know when you're well off and you never have. You've no appreciation."

"I suppose you want us to drink it so you can have the leftovers for your horrible vinegar thing," said Mop.

"It's not horrible and don't you dare to speak to me like that," said Mrs Felton, but there was something like relief in her voice. Can I remember that? Did I truly observe *that*? No. It is now that I know it, now when all the years have passed, and year by year has come more understanding. Then, I heard no relief. I saw no baser motive in Mrs Felton's insistence. I took it for granted, absurd and somehow an inversion of the proper course of things though it seemed, that we were to drink an expensive substance in order that the remains of it might be converted into a cheap substance. But childhood is a looking-glass country where so often one is obliged to believe six impossible things before breakfast.

I drank my wine and, grudgingly, Mop drank two full glasses into which she had stirred sugar. Most of the rest was consumed by Mrs Felton who then poured the dregs into the glass vessel for the refreshment of the vinegar mother. I don't think I had ever drunk or even tasted table wine before. It went to my head, and as soon as I was in bed at nine o'clock I fell into a profound thick sleep.

But Mop was asleep before me. She had lurched into bed without washing and I heard her heavy breathing while I was pulling on my nightdress. This was unusual. Mop wasn't exactly an insomniac but, for a child, she was a bad sleeper. Most evenings as I was passing into those soft clouds of sleep, into a delightful drowsiness that at any moment would be closed off by total oblivion, I would hear her toss and turn in bed or even get up and move about the room. I knew, too, that sometimes she went downstairs for a glass of water or perhaps just for her mother's company, for on the mornings after such excursions Mrs Felton would take her to task over breakfast, scathingly demanding of invisible hearers why she should have been cursed with such a restless nervy child who, even as a baby, had never slept a peaceful night through.

On the Tuesday night, however, she had no difficulty in falling asleep. It was later, in the depths of the night (as she told me in the morning) that she had awakened and lain wakeful for hours, or so she said. She had heard the church clock chime two and three; her head had ached and she had had a curious trembling in her limbs. But, as far as I know, she said nothing of this to her mother, and her headache must have passed by the middle of the morning. For, when I left the house at ten to go with Mrs Potter to an auction that was being held in some neighbouring mansion, she was lying on a blanket on the front lawn, reading the book Mr Felton had brought down for her at the weekend: *Fifty Haunted Houses*. And she was still reading it, was deep in *The Mezzotint* or some horror of Blackwood's, when I got back at one.

It must have been that day, too, when she began to get what I should now call obsessional about the vinegar mother. Several times, three or four times certainly, when I went into the dining room, I found her standing by the Romford factory antique on which Lady Elsworthy's present stood gazing, with the fascination of someone who views an encapsulated reptile, at the culture within. It was not to me in any way noisome or sinister, nor was it even particularly novel. I had seen a dish of stewed fruit forgotten and allowed to ferment in my grandmother's larder, and apart from the fungus on that being pale green, there was little difference between it and this crust of bacteria. Mop's face, so repelled yet so compelled, made me giggle. A mistake, this, for she turned on me, lashing out with a thin wiry arm.

"Shut up, shut up! I hate you."

But she had calmed and was speaking to me again by suppertime. We sat on the wall above the road and watched Mr Gould's Herefords driven from their pasture up the lane home to the farm. Swallows perched on the telephone wires like taut strings of black and white beads. The sky was lemony-green and greater birds flew homeward across it.

"I'd like to put a spoon in it," said Mop, "and then I'd see it shrivel up and die."

"She'd know," I said.

"Who's she?"

"Your mother, of course." I was surprised at the question when the answer was so obvious. "Who else?"

"I don't know."

"It's only an old fungus," I said. "It isn't hurting you."

"Alicia! Aleeciah!" A sharp liquid cry, the sound of a sight, and the sight wine or vinegar flung in a curving jet.

"Come on, Margarine," said Mop. "Supper's ready."

We were given no wine that night, but on the next a bottle and the glasses once more appeared. The meal was a heavier one than usual, meat pie with potatoes as well as salad. Perhaps the wine was sweet this time or of a finer vintage, for it tasted good to me and I drank two glasses. It never occurred to me to wonder what my parents, moderate and very nearly abstemious, would have thought of this corruption of their daughter. Of course it didn't. To a child grown-ups are omniscient and all-wise. Much as I disliked Mrs Felton, I never supposed she could wish to harm me or be indifferent as to whether or not I were harmed.

Mop, too, obeyed and drank. This time there was no demur from her. Probably she was once again trying methods of ingratiation. We went to bed at nine and I think Mop went to sleep before me. I slept heavily as usual, but I was aware of some disturbance in the night, of having been briefly awakened and spoken to. I remembered this, though not much more for a while, when I finally woke in the morning. It was about seven, a pearly morning of birdsong, and Mop was sitting on the window seat in her nightdress.

She looked awful, as if she had got a bad cold coming or had just been sick.

"I tried to wake you up in the night," she said.

"I thought you had," I said. "Did you have a dream?"

She shook her head. "I woke up and I heard the clock strike one and then I heard footsteps on the path down there."

"In this garden, d'you mean?" I said. "Going or coming?"

"I don't know," she said oddly. "They must have been coming."

"It was a burglar," I said. "We ought to go down and see if things have been stolen."

"It wasn't a burglar." Mop was getting angry with me and her face was blotchy. "I did go down. I lay awake for a bit and I didn't hear any more, but I couldn't go back to sleep and I wanted a drink of water. So I went down."

"Well, go on," I said.

But Mop couldn't go on. And even I, insensitive and unsympathetic to her as I was, could see she had been badly frightened, was still frightened, and then I remembered what had wakened me in the night, exactly what had happened. I remembered being brought to brief consciousness by the choking gasps of someone who is screaming in her sleep. Mop had screamed herself awake and the words she had spoken to me had been, "The vinegar mother! The vinegar mother!"

"You had a nightmare," I said.

"Oh, shut up," said Mop. "You never listen. I shan't ever tell you anything again."

But later in the day she did tell me. I think that by this time she had got it into some sort of proportion, although she was still very frightened when she got to the climax of what she insisted couldn't have been a dream. She had, she said, gone downstairs about half an hour after she heard the footsteps in the garden. She hadn't put a light on as the moon was bright. The dining room door was partly open, and when she looked inside she saw a hooded figure crouched in a chair by the window. The figure was all in brown, and Mop said she saw the hood slide back and disclose its face. The thing that had made her scream and scream was this face which wasn't a face at all, but a shapeless mass of liver.

"You dreamed it," I said. "You must have. You were in bed when you screamed, so you must have been dreaming."

"I did go down," Mop insisted.

"Maybe you did," I said, "but the other bit was a dream. Your mother would have come if she'd heard you screaming downstairs."

No more was said about the dream or whatever it was after that, and on Saturday Mr Felton arrived and took us to the Young Farmers' Show at Marks Tey. He brought me my parents' love and the news that my eldest brother had passed his exam and got seven O Levels, and I was happy. He went shooting with Peter Elsworthy on Sunday afternoon, and Peter came back with him and promised to drive me and Mop and Mrs Felton to the seaside for the day on Tuesday.

It was a beautiful day that Tuesday, perhaps the best of all the days at Sanctuary, and I who, on the morning after Mop's dream, had begun to wonder about making that deceitful phone call from the village, felt I could happily remain till term began. We took a picnic lunch and swam in the wide shallow sea. Mrs Felton wore a proper dress of blue and white cotton which made her brown skin look like a tan, and had smoothed down her hair, and smiled and was gracious and once called Mop dear. Suddenly I liked Peter Elsworthy. I suppose I had one of those infatuations for him that are fused in young girls by a kind smile, one sentence spoken as to a contemporary, one casual touch of the hand. On that sunny beach I was moved towards him by inexplicable feelings, moved into a passion the sight of him had never before inspired, and which was to die as quickly as it had been born when the sun had gone, the sea was left behind, and he was once more Mrs Felton's friend in the front seats of the car.

I had followed him about that day like a little dog, and perhaps it was my unconcealed devotion that drove him to leave us at our gate and refuse even to come in and view the progress of the vinegar mother. His excuse was that he had to accompany his mother to an aunt's for dinner. Mrs Felton sulked ferociously after he had gone and we got a supper of runny scrambled eggs and lemon barley water.

On the following night there appeared on our table a bottle of claret. The phone rang while we were eating, and while Mrs Felton was away answering it I took the daring step of pouring my wine into the vinegar mother.

"I shall tell her," said Mop.

"I don't care," I said. "I can't drink it, nasty, sour, horrible stuff."

"You shouldn't call my father's wine horrible when you're a guest," said Mop, but she didn't tell Mrs Felton. I think she would have poured her own to follow mine except that she was afraid the level in the vessel would rise too much, or was it that by then nothing would have induced her to come within feet of the culture?

I didn't need wine to make me sleep, but if I had taken it I might have slept more heavily. A thin moonlight was in the room when I woke up to see Mop's bed empty. Mop was standing by the door, holding it half-open, and she was trembling. It was a bit eerie in there with Mop's long shadow jumping about against the zig-zag beams on the wall. But I couldn't hear a sound.

"What's the matter now?" I said.

"There's someone down there."

"How d'you know? Is there a light on?"

"I heard glass," she said.

How can you hear glass? But I knew what she meant and I didn't much like it. I got up and went over to the doorway and looked down the stairs. There was light coming from under the dining room door, a white glow that could have been from the moon or from the oil lamp they sometimes used. Then I too heard glass, a chatter of glass against glass and a thin trickling sound.

Mop said in a breathy hysterical voice, "Suppose she goes about in the night to every place where they've got one? She goes about and watches over them and makes it happen. She's down there now doing it. Listen!"

Glass against glass . . .

"That's crazy," I said. "It's those books you read."

She didn't say anything. We closed the door and lay in our beds with the bed-lamp on. The light made it better. We heard the clock strike twelve. I said "Can we go to sleep now?" And when Mop nodded I put out the light.

The moon had gone away, covered perhaps by clouds. Into the black silence came a curious drawn-out cry. I know now what it was, but no child of eleven could know. I was only aware then that it was no cry of grief or pain or terror, but of triumph, of something at last attained; yet it was at the same time unhuman, utterly outside the bounds of human restraint.

Mop began to scream.

I had the light on and was jumping up and down on my bed, shouting to her to stop, when the door was flung open and Mrs Felton came in, her hair a wild heathery mass, a dressing gown of quilted silk, black-blood colour, wrapped round her and tied at the waist with savagery. Rage and violence were what I expected. But Mrs Felton said nothing. She did what I had never seen her do, had never supposed anything would make her do. She caught Mop in an embrace and hugged her, rocking her back and forth. They were both crying, swaying on the bed and crying. I heard footsteps on the garden path, soft, stealthy, finally fading away.

Mop said nothing at all about it to me the next day. She withdrew into her books and sulks. I believe now that the isolated demonstration of affection she had received from her mother in the night led her to hope more might follow. But Mrs Felton had become weirdly reserved, as if in some sort of long dream. I noticed with giggly embarrassment that she hardly seemed to see Mop hanging about her, looking into her face, trying to get her attention. When Mop gave up at last and took refuge in the garden with Dr James on demons, Mrs Felton lay on the dining room sofa, smoking and staring at the ceiling. I went in once to fetch my cardigan – for Mrs Potter was taking me to the medieval town at Lavenham for the afternoon – and she was still lying there, smiling strangely to herself, her long brown hands playing with her necklace of reddish-brown beads.

She went off for a walk by herself on Friday afternoon and she was gone for hours. It was very hot, too hot to be in a garden with only thin apple tree shade. I was sitting at the dining room table, working on a scrapbook of country house pictures Mrs Potter had got me to make, and Mop was reading, when the phone rang. Mop answered it, but from the room where I was, across the passage, I could hear Mr Felton's hearty bray.

"How's life treating you, my old Mop?"

I heard it all, how he was coming down that night instead of in the morning and would be here by midnight. She might pass the message on to her mother, but not to worry as he had his own key. And his kind regards to jolly old Margarine if she hadn't, by this time, melted away into a little puddle!

Mrs Felton came back at five in Peter Elsworthy's car. There were leaves in her hair and bits of grass on the back of her skirt. They pored over the vinegar mother, moving it back into a cool dark corner, and enthusing over the colour of the liquor under the floating liver-like mass.

"A tender plant that mustn't get overheated," said Peter Elsworthy, picking a leaf out of Mrs Felton's hair and laughing. I wondered why I had ever liked him or thought him kind.

Mop and I were given *rosé* with our supper out of a dumpy little bottle with a picture of cloisters on its label. By now Mrs Felton must have learned that I didn't need wine to make me sleep, so she didn't insist on my having more than one glass. The vinegar mother's vessel was three-quarters full.

I was in bed and Mop nearly undressed when I remembered about her father's message.

"I forgot to tell her," said Mop, yawning and heavy-eyed.

"You could go down and tell her now."

"She'd be cross. Besides, he's got his key."

"You don't like going down in the dark by yourself," I said. Mop didn't answer. She got into bed and pulled the sheet over her head.

We never spoke to each other again.

She didn't return to school that term, and at the end of it my mother told me she wasn't coming back. I never learned what happened to her. The last – almost the last – I remember of her was her thin sallow face that lately had always looked bewildered, and the dark circles round her old woman's eyes. I remember the books on the bedside table: *Fifty Haunted Houses*, the *Works of Sheridan Lefanu*, *The Best of Montague Rhodes James*. The pale lacquering of moonlight in that room with its beams and its slanted ceiling. The silence of night in an old and haunted countryside. Wine breath in my throat and wine weariness bringing heavy sleep . . .

Out of that thick slumber I was awakened by two sharp explosions and the sound of breaking glass. Mop had gone from the bedroom before I was out of bed, scarcely aware of where I was, my head swimming. Somewhere downstairs Mop was screaming. I went down. The whole house, the house called Sanctuary, was bright with lights. I opened the dining room door.

Mr Felton was leaning against the table, the shotgun still in his hand. I think he was crying. I don't remember much blood, only the brown dead nakedness of Mrs Felton spread on the floor with Peter Elsworthy bent over her, holding his wounded arm. And the smell of gunpowder like fireworks and the stronger sickening stench of vinegar everywhere, and broken glass in shards, and Mop screaming, plunging a knife again and again into a thick slimy liver mass on the carpet.

I USED TO LIVE HERE ONCE

Jean Rhys

Jean Rhys (1890–1979) was born in Dominica. She went to England at the age of sixteen and, after dropping out of the Royal Academy of Dramatic Art, became a chorus girl. Her early novels draw on her bohemian life in London and Europe and a series of ill-starred relationships. *Wide Sargasso Sea*, a novel featuring the first Mrs Rochester, *Jane Eyre's* mad woman in the attic, was published in 1966 after a period of literary obscurity.

She was standing by the river looking at the stepping stones and remembering each one. There was the round unsteady stone, the pointed one, the flat one in the middle – the safe stone where you could stand and look round. The next wasn't so safe for when the river was full the water flowed over it and even when it showed dry it was slippery. But after that it was easy and soon she was standing on the other side.

The road was much wider than it used to be but the work had been done carelessly. The felled trees had not been cleared away and the bushes looked trampled. Yet it was the same road and she walked along feeling extraordinarily happy.

It was a fine day, a blue day. The only thing was that the sky had a glassy look that she didn't remember. That was the only word she could think of. Glassy. She turned the corner, saw that what had been the old pavé had been taken up, and there too the road was much wider, but it had the same unfinished look.

She came to the worn stone steps that led up to the house and her heart began to beat. The screw pine was gone, so was the mock summer house called the ajoupa, but the clove tree was still there and at the top of the steps the rough lawn stretched away, just as she remembered it. She stopped and looked towards the house that had been added to and painted white. It was strange to see a car standing in front of it.

There were two children under the big mango tree, a boy and a little girl, and she waved to them and called "Hello" but they didn't answer her or turn their heads. Very fair children, as Europeans born in the West Indies so often are: as if the white blood is asserting itself against all odds.

The grass was yellow in the hot sunlight as she walked towards them. When she was quite close she called again, shyly: "Hello." Then, "I used to live here once," she said.

Still they didn't answer. When she said for the third time "Hello" she was quite near them. Her arms went out instinctively with the longing to touch them.

It was the boy who turned. His grey eyes looked straight into hers. His expression didn't change. He said: "Hasn't it gone cold all of a sudden. D'you notice? Let's go in." "Yes, let's," said the girl.

Her arms fell to her sides as she watched them running across the grass to the house. That was the first time she knew.

THE DEATH OF PEGGY MEEHAN

William Trevor

William Trevor Cox (b.1928) was born in County Cork, Ireland. His
father was a bank manager who frequently moved branches, and Trevor
had attended thirteen different schools by the age of thirteen. He read
history at Trinity College, Dublin, after which he became a teacher in
Northern Ireland and then England. Later he worked as a copywriter
before becoming a full-time writer in 1965. Trevor's awards include the
Bob Hughes Lifetime Achievement Award in Irish Literature. He lives in
Devon with his wife, Jane Ryan.

Like all children, I led a double life. There was the ordinariness of dressing in
the morning, putting on shoes and combing hair, stirring a spoon through
porridge I didn't want, and going at ten to nine to the nuns' elementary
school. And there was a world in which only the events I wished for happened,
where boredom was not permitted and of which I was both God and King.

In my ordinary life I was the only child of parents who years before my birth
had given up hope of ever having me. I remember them best as being different
from other parents: they were elderly, it seemed to me, two greyly fussing people
with grey hair and faces, in grey clothes, with spectacles. "Oh, no, no," they murmured regularly, rejecting on my behalf an invitation to tea or to play with some
other child. They feared on my behalf the rain and the sea, and walls that might
be walked along, and grass because grass was always damp. They rarely missed
a service at the Church of the Holy Redeemer.

In the town where we lived, a seaside town thirty miles from Cork, my father
was employed as a senior clerk in the offices of Cosgriff and McLoughlin, Solic-
itors and Commissioners for Oaths. With him on one side of me and my mother
on the other, we walked up and down the brief promenade in winter, while the
seagulls shrieked and my father worried in case it was going to rain. We never
went for walks through fields or through the heathery wastelands that sloped
gently upwards behind the town, or by the river where people said Sir Walter
Ralegh had fished. In summer, when the visitors from Cork came, my mother
didn't like to let me near the sands because the sands, she said, were full of fleas.
In summer we didn't walk on the promenade but out along the main Cork road
instead, past a house that appeared to me to move. It disappeared for several
minutes as we approached it, a trick of nature, I afterwards discovered, caused
by the undulations of the landscape. Every July, for a fortnight, we went to stay

in Montenotte, high up above Cork city, in a boarding-house run by my mother's sister, my Aunt Isabella. She, too, had a grey look about her and was religious.

It was here, in my Aunt Isabella's Montenotte boarding-house, that this story begins: in the summer of 1936, when I was seven. It was a much larger house than the one we lived in ourselves, which was small and narrow and in a terrace. My Aunt Isabella's was rather grand in its way, a dark place with little unexpected half-landings, and badly lit corridors. It smelt of floor polish and of a mustiness that I have since associated with the religious life, a smell of old cassocks. Everywhere there were statues of the Virgin, and votive lights and black-framed pictures of the Holy Child. The residents were all priests, old and middle-aged and young, eleven of them usually, which was all the house would hold. A few were always away on their holidays when we stayed there in the summer.

In the summer of 1936 we left our own house in the usual way, my father fastening all the windows and the front and back doors and then examining the house from the outside to make sure he'd done the fastening and the locking properly. We walked to the railway station, each of us carrying something, my mother a brown cardboard suitcase and my father a larger one of the same kind. I carried the sandwiches we were to have on the train, and a flask of carefully made tea and three apples, all packed into a sixpenny fish basket.

In the house in Montenotte my Aunt Isabella told us that Canon McGrath and Father Quinn were on holiday, one in Tralee, the other in Galway. She led us to their rooms, Canon McGrath's for my father and Father Quinn's for my mother and myself. The familiar trestle-bed was erected at the foot of the bed in my mother's room. During the course of the year a curate called Father Lalor had repaired it, my aunt said, after it had been used by Canon McGrath's brother from America, who'd proved too much for the canvas.

"Ah, aren't you looking well, Mr Mahon!" the red-faced and jolly Father Smith said to my father in the dining-room that evening. "And isn't our friend here getting big for himself?" He laughed loudly, gripping a portion of the back of my neck between a finger and a thumb. Did I know my catechism? he asked me. Was I being good with the nuns in the elementary school? "Are you in health yourself, Mrs Mahon?" he inquired of my mother.

My mother said she was, and the red-faced priest went to join the other priests at the main dining-table. He left behind him a smell that was different from the smell of the house, and I noticed that he had difficulty in pulling the chair out from the table when he was about to sit down. He had to be assisted in this by a new young curate, a Father Parsloe. Father Smith had been drinking stout again, I said to myself.

Sometimes in my aunt's house there was nothing to do except to watch and to listen. Father Smith used to drink too much stout; Father Magennis, who was so thin you could hardly bear to look at him and whose flesh was the colour of whitewash, was not long for this world; Father Riordon would be a bishop if only he could have tidied himself up a bit; Canon McGrath had once refused to baptize a child; young Father Lalor was going places. For hours on end my Aunt Isabella would murmur to my parents about the priests, telling about the fate of one who had left the boarding-house during the year or supplying background information about a new one. My parents, so faultlessly regular in their church attendance and interested in all religious matters, were naturally pleased to listen. God and the organization of His Church were far more important than my father's duties in Cosgriff and McLoughlin, or my mother's housework, or my own desire to go walking through the heathery wastelands that sloped gently upwards behind our town. God and the priests in my Aunt Isabella's house, and the nuns of the convent elementary school and the priests of the Church of the Holy Redeemer, were at the centre of everything. "Maybe it'll appeal to our friend," Father Smith had once said in the dining-room, and I knew that he meant that maybe one day I might be attracted towards the priesthood. My parents had not said anything in reply, but as we ate our tea of sausages and potato-cakes I could feel them thinking that nothing would please them better.

Every year when we stayed with my aunt there was an afternoon when I was left in charge of whichever priests happened to be in, while my parents and my aunt made the journey across the city to visit my father's brother, who was a priest himself. There was some difficulty about bringing me: I had apparently gone to my uncle's house as a baby, when my presence had upset him. Years later I overheard my mother whispering to Father Riordon about this, suggesting – or so it seemed – that my father had once been intent on the priestly life but had at the last moment withdrawn. That he should afterwards have fathered a child was apparently an offence to his brother's feeling of propriety. I had the impression that my uncle was a severe man, who looked severely on my father and my mother and my Aunt Isabella on these visits, and was respected by them for being as he was. All three came back subdued, and that night my mother always prayed for much longer by the side of her bed.

"Father Parsloe's going to take you for a walk," my Aunt Isabella said on the morning of the 1936 visit. "He wants to get to know you."

You walked all the way down from Montenotte, past the docks, over the river and into the city. The first few times it could have been interesting, but after that it was worse than walking on the concrete promenade at home. I'd have far preferred to have played by myself in my aunt's overgrown back garden, pretending to be grown up, talking to myself in a secret way, having wicked thoughts. At home and in my aunt's garden I became a man my father had read about in a newspaper and whom, he'd said, we must all pray for, a thief who broke the windows of jewellers' shops and lifted out watches and rings. I became Father Smith, drinking too much stout and missing the steps of the stairs. I became Father Magennis and would lie on the weeds at the bottom of the garden or under a table, confessing to gruesome crimes at the moment of death. In my mind I mocked the holiness of my parents and imitated their voices; I mocked the holiness of my Aunt Isabella; I talked back to my parents in a way I never would; I laughed and said disgraceful things about God and the religious life. Blasphemy was exciting.

"Are you ready so?" Father Parsloe asked when my parents and my aunt had left for the visit to my uncle. "Will we take a bus?"

"A bus?"

"Down to the town."

I'd never in my life done that before. The buses were for going longer distances in. It seemed extraordinary not to walk, the whole point of a walk was to walk.

"I haven't any money for the bus," I said, and Father Parsloe laughed. On the upper deck he lit a cigarette. He was a slight young man, by far the youngest of the priests in my aunt's house, with reddish hair and a face that seemed to be on a slant. "Will we have tea in Thompson's?" he said. "Would that be a good thing to do?"

We had tea in Thompson's café, with buns and cakes and huge meringues such as I'd never tasted before. Father Parsloe smoked fourteen cigarettes and drank all the tea himself. I had three bottles of fizzy orangeade. "Will we go to the pictures?" Father Parsloe said when he'd paid the bill at the cash desk. "Will we chance the Pavilion?"

I had never, of course, been to the pictures before. My mother said that the Star Picture House, which was the only one in our town, was full of fleas.

"One and a half," Father Parsloe said at the cash desk in the Pavilion and we were led away into the darkness. THE END it announced on the screen, and when I saw it I thought we were too late. "Ah, aren't we in lovely time?" Father Parsloe said.

I didn't understand the film. It was about grown-ups kissing one another, and about an earthquake, and then a motor-car accident in which a woman who'd been kissed a lot was killed. The man who'd kissed her was married to another woman, and when the film ended he was sitting in a room with his wife, looking at her. She kept saying it was all right.

"God, wasn't that great?" Father Parsloe said as we stood in the lavatory of the Pavilion, the kind of lavatory where you stand up, like I'd never been in before. "Wasn't it a good story?"

All the way back to Montenotte I kept remembering it. I kept seeing the face of the woman who'd been killed, and all the bodies lying on the streets after the earthquake, and the man at the end, sitting in a room with his wife. The swaying of the bus made me feel queasy because of the meringues and the orangeade, but I didn't care.

"Did you enjoy the afternoon?" Father Parsloe asked, and I told him I'd never enjoyed anything better. I asked him if the pictures were always as good. He assured me they were.

My parents, however, didn't seem pleased. My father got hold of a *Cork Examiner* and looked up the film that was on at the Pavilion and reported that it wasn't suitable for a child. My mother gave me a bath and examined my clothes for fleas. When Father Parsloe winked at me in the dining-room my parents pretended not to notice him.

That night my mother prayed for her extra long period, after the visit to my uncle. I lay in the dimly lit room, aware that she was kneeling there, but thinking of the film and the way the people had kissed, not like my parents ever kissed. At the convent elementary school there were girls in the higher classes who were pretty, far prettier than my mother. There was one called Claire, with fair hair and a softly freckled face, and another called Peggy Meehan, who was younger and black-haired. I had picked them out because they had spoken to me, asking me my name. I thought them very nice.

I opened my eyes and saw that my mother was rising from her knees. She stood for a moment at the edge of her bed, not smiling, her lips still moving, continuing her prayer. Then she got into bed and put out the light.

I listened to her breathing and heard it become the breathing which people have when they're asleep, but I couldn't sleep myself. I lay there, still remembering the film and remembering being in Thompson's and seeing Father Parsloe lighting one cigarette after another. For some reason, I began to imagine that I was in Thompson's with Father Parsloe and the two girls from the convent, and that we all went off to the Pavilion together, swinging along the street. "Ah, isn't this the life for us?" Father Parsloe said as he led us into the darkness, and I told the girls I'd been to the Pavilion before and they said they never had.

I heard eleven o'clock chiming from a nearby church. I heard a stumbling on the stairs and then the laughter of Father Smith, and Father Riordon telling him to be quiet. I heard twelve chiming and half past twelve, and a quarter to one, and one.

After that I didn't want to sleep. I was standing in a classroom of the convent and Claire was smiling at me. It was nice being with her. I felt warm all over, and happy.

And then I was walking on the sands with Peggy Meehan. We ran, playing a game she'd made up, and then we walked again. She asked if I'd like to go on a picnic with her, next week perhaps.

I didn't know what to do. I wanted one of the girls to be my friend. I wanted to love one of them, like the people had loved in the film. I wanted to kiss one and be with one, just the two of us. In the darkness of the bedroom they both seemed close and real, closer than my mother, even though I could hear my mother breathing. "Come on," Peggy Meehan whispered, and then Claire whispered also, saying we'd always be best friends, saying we might run away. It was all wrong that there were two of them, yet both vividly remained. "Tuesday," Peggy Meehan said. "We'll have the picnic on Tuesday."

Her father drove us in his car, away from the town, out beyond the heathery wastelands, towards a hillside that was even nicer. But a door of the car, the back door against which Peggy Meehan was leaning, suddenly gave way. On the dust of the road she was as dead as the woman in the film.

"Poor Peggy," Claire said at some later time, even though she hadn't known Peggy Meehan very well. "Poor little Peggy." And then she smiled and took my hand and we walked together through the heathery wastelands, in love with one another.

A few days later we left my Aunt Isabella's house in Montenotte and returned on the train to our seaside town. And a week after that a new term began at the convent elementary school. Peggy Meehan was dead, the Reverend Mother told us, all of us assembled together. She added that there was diphtheria in the town.

I didn't think about it at first; and I didn't connect the reality of the death with a fantasy that had been caused by my first visit to a cinema. Some part of my mind may passingly have paused over the coincidence, but that was all. There was the visit to the Pavilion itself to talk about in the convent, and the description of the film, and Father Parsloe's conversation and the way he'd smoked fourteen cigarettes in Thompson's. Diphtheria was a terrible disease, my mother said when I told her, and naturally we must all pray for the soul of poor Peggy Meehan.

But as weeks and months went by, I found myself increasingly remembering the story I had told myself on the night of the film, and remembering particularly how Peggy Meehan had fallen from the car, and how she'd looked when she was dead. I said to myself that that had been my wickedest thought, worse than my blasphemies and yet somehow part of them. At night I lay in bed, unable to sleep, trying hopelessly to pray for forgiveness. But no forgiveness came, for there was no respite to the images that recurred, her face in life and then in death, like the face of the woman in the film.

A year later, while lying awake in the same room in my aunt's boardinghouse, I saw her. In the darkness there was a sudden patch of light and in the centre of it she was wearing a sailor-suit that I remembered. Her black plaits hung down her back. She smiled at me and went away. I knew instinctively then, as I watched her and after she'd gone, that the fantasy and the reality were part and parcel: I had caused this death to occur.

Looking back on it now, I can see, of course, that that feeling was a childish one. It was a childish fear, a superstition that occurring to an adult would cause only a shiver of horror. But, as a child, with no one to consult about the matter, I lived with the thought that my will was more potent than I knew. In stories I had learnt of witches and spells and evil spirits, and power locked up in people. In my games I had wickedly denied the religious life, and goodness, and holiness. In my games I had mocked Father Smith, I had pretended that the dying Father Magennis was a criminal. I had pretended to be a criminal myself, a man who broke jewellers' windows. I had imitated my parents when it said you should honour your father and your mother. I had mocked the holiness of my Aunt Isabella. I had murdered Peggy Meehan because there wasn't room for her in the story I was telling myself. I was possessed and evil: the nuns had told us about people being like that.

I thought at first I might seek advice from Father Parsloe. I thought of asking him if he remembered the day we'd gone on our outing, and then telling him how, in a story I was telling myself, I'd caused Peggy Meehan to be killed in a car accident like the woman in the film, and how she'd died in reality, of diphtheria. But Father Parsloe had an impatient kind of look about him this year, as if he had worries of his own. So I didn't tell him and I didn't tell anyone. I hoped that when we returned to our own house at the end of the stay in Montenotte I wouldn't see her again, but the very first day we were back I saw her at four o'clock in the afternoon, in the kitchen.

After that she came irregularly, sometimes not for a month and once not for a year. She continued to appear in the same sudden way but in different clothes, and growing up as I was growing up. Once, after I'd left the convent and gone on to the Christian Brother's, she appeared in the classroom, smiling near the blackboard.

She never spoke. Whether she appeared on the promenade or at school or in my aunt's house or our house, close to me or at a distance, she communicated only with her smile and with her eyes: I was possessed of the Devil, she came herself from God. In her eyes and her smile there was that simple message, a message which said also that my thoughts were always wicked, that I had never believed properly in God or the Virgin or Jesus who died for us.

I tried to pray. Like my mother, kneeling beside my bed. Like my aunt and her houseful of priests. Like the nuns and Christian Brothers, and other boys and girls of the town. But prayer would not come to me, and I realized that it never had. I had always pretended, going down on my knees at Mass, laughing and blaspheming in my mind. I hated the very thought of prayer. I hated my parents in an unnatural manner, and my Aunt Isabella and the priests in her house. But the dead Peggy Meehan fresh from God's heaven, was all forgiveness in her patch of light, smiling to rid me of my evil spirit.

She was there at my mother's funeral, and later at my father's. Claire, whom I had destroyed her for, married a man employed in the courthouse and became a Mrs Madden, prematurely fat. I naturally didn't marry anyone myself.

I am forty-six years old now and I live alone in the same seaside town. No one in the town knows why I am solitary. No one could guess that I have lived with a child's passionate companionship for half a lifetime. Being no longer a child, I naturally no longer believe that I was responsible for the death. In my passing, careless fantasy I wished for it and she, already dead, picked up my living thoughts. I should not have wished for it because in middle age she is a beautiful creature now, more beautiful by far than fat Mrs Madden.

And that is all there is. At forty-six I walk alone on the brief promenade, or by the edge of the sea or on the road to Cork, where the moving house is. I work, as my father worked, in the offices of Cosgriff and McLoughlin. I cook my own food. I sleep alone in a bed that has an iron bedstead. On Sundays I go hypocritically to Mass in the Church of the Holy Redeemer; I go to Confession and do not properly confess; I go to Men's Confraternity, and to Communion. And all the time she is there, appearing in her patch of light to remind me that she never leaves me. And all the time, on my knees at Mass, or receiving the Body and the Blood, or in my iron bed, I desire her. In the offices of Cosgriff and McLoughlin I dream of her nakedness. When we are old I shall desire her, too, with my shrunken, evil body.

In the town I am a solitary, peculiar man. I have been rendered so, people probably say, by my cloistered upbringing, and probably add that such an upbringing would naturally cultivate a morbid imagination. That may be so, and it doesn't really matter how things have come about. All I know is that she is more real for me than anything else is in this seaside town or beyond it. I live for her, living hopelessly, for I know I can never possess her as I wish to. I have a carnal desire for a shadow, which in turn is His mockery of me: His fitting punishment for my wickedest thought of all.

A BEAUTIFUL CHILD

Truman Capote

Truman Capote (1924–1984) was born Truman Persons in New Orleans, to a salesman father and a teenage mother. His parents divorced when he was a toddler and he lived with relatives in Alabama for several years before his mother returned for him. It was a lonely childhood, but in Alabama, Capote met his lifelong friend, the writer Harper Lee. Capote is best known for his novel *Breakfast at Tiffany's* and the genre redefining *In Cold Blood*. He was openly homosexual at a time of great prejudice.

Time: 28 April 1955.
    Scene: The chapel of the Universal Funeral Home at Lexington Avenue and Fifty-second Street, New York City. An interesting galaxy packs the pews: celebrities, for the most part, from an international arena of theater, films, literature, all present in tribute to Constance Collier, the English-born actress who had died the previous day at the age of seventy-five.

Born in 1880, Miss Collier had begun her career as a music-hall Gaiety Girl, graduated from that to become one of England's principal Shakespearean actresses (and the longtime fiancée of Sir Max Beerbohm, whom she never married, and perhaps for that reason was the inspiration for the mischievously unobtainable heroine in Sir Max's novel *Zuleika Dobson*). Eventually she emigrated to the United States, where she established herself as a considerable figure on the New York stage as well as in Hollywood films. During the last decades of her life she lived in New York, where she practiced as a drama coach of unique caliber; she accepted only professionals as students, and usually only professionals who were already "stars" – Katharine Hepburn was a permanent pupil; another Hepburn, Audrey, was also a Collier protégée, as were Vivien Leigh and, for a few months prior to her death, a neophyte Miss Collier referred to as "my special problem," Marilyn Monroe.

Marilyn Monroe, whom I'd met through John Huston when he was directing her in her first speaking role in *The Asphalt jungle*, had come under Miss Collier's wing at my suggestion. I had known Miss Collier perhaps a half-dozen years, and admired her as a woman of true stature, physically, emotionally, creatively; and, for all her commanding manner, her grand cathedral voice, as an adorable person, mildly wicked but exceedingly warm, dignified yet *gemütlich*. I loved to go to the frequent small lunch parties she gave in her dark Victorian studio in mid-Manhattan; she had a barrel of yarns to tell about her adventures as a leading lady opposite Sir Beerbohm Tree and the great French actor

Coquelin, her involvements with Oscar Wilde, the youthful Chaplin, and Garbo in the silent Swede's formative days. Indeed she was a delight, as was her devoted secretary and companion, Phyllis Wilbourn, a quietly twinkling maiden lady who, after her employer's demise, became, and has remained, the companion of Katharine Hepburn. Miss Collier introduced me to many people who became friends: the Lunts, the Oliviers, and especially Aldous Huxley. But it was I who introduced her to Marilyn Monroe, and at first it was not an acquaintance she was too keen to acquire: her eyesight was faulty, she had seen none of Marilyn's movies, and really knew nothing about her except that she was some sort of platinum sex-explosion who had achieved global notoriety; in short, she seemed hardly suitable clay for Miss Collier's stern classic shaping. But I thought they might make a stimulating combination.

They did. "Oh yes," Miss Collier reported to me, "there is something there. She is a beautiful child. I don't mean that in the obvious way – the perhaps too obvious way. I don't think she's an actress at all, not in any traditional sense. What she has – this presence, this luminosity, this flickering intelligence – could never surface on the stage. It's so fragile and subtle, it can only be caught by the camera. It's like a hummingbird in flight: only a camera can freeze the poetry of it. But anyone who thinks this girl is simply another Harlow or harlot or whatever is *mad*. Speaking of mad, that's what we've been working on together: Ophelia. I suppose people would chuckle at the notion, but really, she could be the most exquisite Ophelia. I was talking to Greta last week, and I told her about Marilyn's Ophelia, and Greta said yes, she could believe that because she had seen two of her films, very bad and vulgar stuff, but nevertheless she had glimpsed Marilyn's possibilities. Actually, Greta has an amusing idea. You know that she wants to make a film of *Dorian Gray*? With her playing Dorian, of course. Well, she said she would like to have Marilyn opposite her as one of the girls Dorian seduces and destroys. Greta! So unused! Such a gift – and rather like Marilyn's, if you consider it. Of course, Greta is a consummate artist, an artist of the utmost control. This beautiful child is without any concept of discipline or sacrifice. Somehow I don't think she'll make old bones. Absurd of me to say, but somehow I feel she'll go young. I hope, I really pray, that she survives long enough to free the strange lovely talent that's wandering through her like a jailed spirit."

But now Miss Collier had died, and here I was loitering in the vestibule of the Universal Chapel waiting for Marilyn; we had talked on the telephone the evening before, and agreed to sit together at the services, which were scheduled to start at noon. She was now a half-hour late; she was *always* late, but I'd thought just for once! For God's sake, goddamnit! Then suddenly there she was, and I didn't recognize her until she said . . .

MARILYN: Oh, baby, I'm so sorry. But see, I got all made up, and then I decided maybe I shouldn't wear eyelashes or lipstick or anything, so then I had to wash all that off, and I couldn't imagine what to wear . . .

> (What she had imagined to wear would have been appropriate for the abbess of a nunnery in private audience with the Pope. Her hair was entirely concealed by a black chiffon scarf; her black dress was loose and long and

looked somehow borrowed; black silk stockings dulled the blond sheen of her slender legs. An abbess, one can be certain, would not have donned the vaguely erotic black high-heeled shoes she had chosen, or the owlish black sunglasses that dramatized the vanillapallor of her dairy-fresh skin.)

TC: You look fine.

MARILYN (gnawing an already chewed-to-the-nub thumbnail): Are you sure? I mean, I'm so jumpy. Where's the john? If I could just pop in there for a minute –

TC: And pop a pill? No! Shhh. That's Cyril Ritchard's voice: he's started the eulogy.

(Tiptoeing, we entered the crowded chapel and wedged ourselves into a narrow space in the last row. Cyril Ritchard finished; he was followed by Cathleen Nesbitt, a lifelong colleague of Miss Collier's, and finally Brian Aherne addressed the mourners. Through it all, my date periodically removed her spectacles to scoop up tears bubbling from her blue-gray eyes. I'd sometimes seen her without make-up, but today she presented a new visual experience, a face I'd not observed before, and at first I couldn't perceive why this should be. Ah! It was because of the obscuring head scarf. With her tresses invisible, and her complexion cleared of all cosmetics, she looked twelve years old, a pubescent virgin who has just been admitted to an orphanage and is grieving over her plight. At last the ceremony ended, and the congregation began to disperse.)

MARILYN: Please, let's sit here. Let's wait till everyone's left.

TC: Why?

MARILYN: I don't want to have to talk to anybody. I never know what to say.

TC: Then you sit here, and I'll wait outside. I've got to have a cigarette.

MARILYN: You can't leave me alone! My God! Smoke here.

TC: *Here?* In the chapel?

MARILYN: Why not? What do you want to smoke? A reefer?

TC: Very funny. Come on, let's go.

MARILYN: Please. There's a lot of shutterbugs downstairs. And I certainly don't want them taking my picture looking like this.

TC: I can't blame you for that.

MARILYN: You said I looked fine.

TC: You do. Just perfect – if you were playing the Bride of Frankenstein.

MARILYN: Now you're laughing at me.

TC: Do I look like I'm laughing?

MARILYN: You're laughing inside. And that's the worst kind of laugh. (Frowning; nibbling thumbnail) Actually, I could've worn make-up. I see all these other people are wearing make-up.

TC: I am. Globs.

MARILYN: Seriously, though. It's my hair. I need color. And I didn't have time to get any. It was all so unexpected, Miss Collier dying and all. See?

(She lifted her kerchief slightly to display a fringe of darkness where her hair parted.)

TC: Poor innocent me. And all this time I thought you were a bona-fide blonde.

MARILYN: I am. But nobody's *that* natural. And incidentally, fuck you.

TC: Okay, everybody's cleared out. So up, up.

MARILYN: Those photographers are still down there. I know it.

TC: If they didn't recognize you coming in, they won't recognize you going out.

MARILYN: One of them did. But I'd slipped through the door before he started yelling.

TC: I'm sure there's a back entrance. We can go that way.

MARILYN: I don't want to see any corpses.

TC: Why would we?

MARILYN: This is a funeral parlor. They must keep them somewhere. That's all I need today, to wander into a room full of corpses. Be patient. I'll take us somewhere and treat us to a bottle of bubbly.

(So we sat and talked and Marilyn said: "I hate funerals. I'm glad I won't have to go to my own. Only, I don't want a funeral – just my ashes cast on waves by one of my kids, if I ever have any. I wouldn't have come today except Miss Collier cared about me, my welfare, and she was just like a granny, a tough old granny, but she taught me a lot. She taught me how to breathe. I've put it to good use, too, and I don't mean just acting. There *are* other times when breathing is a problem. But when I first heard about it, Miss Collier cooling, the first thing I thought was: Oh, gosh, what's going to happen to Phyllis?! Her whole life was Miss Collier. But I hear she's going to live with Miss Hepburn. Lucky Phyllis; she's going to have fun now. I'd change places with her pronto. Miss Hepburn is a terrific lady, no shit. I wish she was my friend. So I could call her up sometimes and . . . well, I don't know, just call her up."

We talked about how much we liked New York and loathed Los Angeles ("Even though I was born there, I still can't think of one good thing to say about it. If I close my eyes, and picture L.A., all I see is one big varicose vein"); we talked about actors and acting ("Everybody says I can't act. They said the same thing about Elizabeth Taylor. And they were wrong. She was great in *A Place in the Sun*. I'll never get the right part, anything I really want. My looks are against me. They're too specific"); we talked some more about Elizabeth Taylor, and she wanted to know if I knew her, and I said yes, and she said well, what is she like, what is she *really* like, and I said well, she's a little bit like you, she wears her heart on her sleeve and talks salty, and Marilyn said fuck you and said well, if somebody asked me what Marilyn Monroe was like, what was Marilyn Monroe *really* like, what would I say, and I said I'd have to think about that.)

TC: Now do you think we can get the hell out of here? You promised me champagne, remember?

MARILYN: I remember. But I don't have any money.

TC: You're always late and you never have any money. By any chance are you under the delusion that you're Queen Elizabeth?

MARILYN: Who?

TC: Queen Elizabeth. The Queen of England.

MARILYN (frowning): What's that cunt got to do with it?

TC: Queen Elizabeth never carries money either. She's not allowed to. Filthy lucre must not stain the royal palm. It's a law or something.

MARILYN: I wish they'd pass a law like that for me.

TC: Keep going the way you are and maybe they will.

MARILYN: Well, gosh. How does she pay for anything? Like when she goes shopping.

TC: Her lady-in-waiting trots along with a bag full of farthings.

MARILYN: You know what? I'll bet she gets everything free. In return for endorsements.

TC: Very possible. I wouldn't be a bit surprised. By Appointment to Her Majesty. Corgi dogs. All those Fortnum & Mason goodies. Pot. Condoms.

MARILYN: What would she want with condoms?

TC: Not her, dopey. For that chump who walks two steps behind. Prince Philip.

MARILYN: Him. Oh, yeah. He's cute. He looks like he might have a nice prick. Did I ever tell you about the time I saw Errol Flynn whip out his prick and play the piano with it? Oh well, it was a hundred years ago, I'd just got into modeling, and I went to this half-ass party, and Errol Flynn, so pleased with himself, he was there and he took out his prick and played the piano with it. Thumped the keys. He played *You Are My Sunshine*. Christ! Everybody says Milton Berle has the biggest schlong in Hollywood. But who *cares*? Look, don't you have *any* money?

TC: Maybe about fifty bucks.

MARILYN: Well, that ought to buy us some bubbly.

(Outside, Lexington Avenue was empty of all but harmless pedestrians. It was around two, and as nice an April afternoon as one could wish: ideal strolling weather. So we moseyed toward Third Avenue. A few gawkers spun their heads, not because they recognized Marilyn as *the* Marilyn, but because of her funeral finery; she giggled her special little giggle, a sound as tempting as the jingling bells on a Good Humor wagon, and said: "Maybe I should always dress this way. Real anonymous."

As we neared P. J. Clarke's saloon, I suggested P.J.'s might be a good place to refresh ourselves, but she vetoed that: "It's full of those advertising creeps. And that bitch Dorothy Kilgallen, she's always in there getting bombed. What is it with these micks? The way they booze, they're worse than Indians."

I felt called upon to defend Kilgallen, who was a friend, somewhat, and I allowed as to how she could upon occasion be a clever funny woman. She said: "Be that as it may, she's written some bitchy stuff about me. But all those cunts hate me. Hedda. Louella. I know you're supposed to get used to it, but I just can't. It really hurts. What did I ever do to those hags? The only one who writes a decent word about me is Sidney Skolsky. But he's a guy. The guys treat me okay. Just like maybe I was a human person. At least they give me the benefit of the doubt. And Bob Thomas is a gentleman. And Jack O'Brian."

We looked in the windows of antique shops; one contained a tray of old rings, and Marilyn said: "That's pretty. The garnet with the seed pearls. I wish I could wear rings, but I hate people to notice my hands. They're too fat. Elizabeth Taylor has fat hands. But with those eyes, who's looking at her hands? I like to dance naked in front of mirrors and watch my titties jump around. There's nothing wrong with them. But I wish my hands weren't so fat."

Another window displayed a handsome grandfather clock, which prompted her to observe: "I've never had a home. Not a real one with all my own furniture. But if I ever get married again, and make a lot of money, I'm going to hire a couple of trucks and ride down Third Avenue buying every damn kind of crazy thing. I'm going to get a dozen grandfather clocks and line them all up in one room and have them all ticking away at the same time. That would be real homey, don't you think?")

MARILYN: Hey! Across the street!

TC: What?

MARILYN: See the sign with the palm? That must be a fortune-telling parlor.

TC: Are you in the mood for that?

MARILYN: Well, let's take a look.

(It was not an inviting establishment. Through a smeared window we could discern a barren room with a skinny, hairy gypsy lady seated in a canvas chair under a hellfire-red ceiling lamp that shed a torturous glow; she was knitting a pair of baby-booties, and did not return our stares. Nevertheless, Marilyn started to go in, then changed her mind.)

MARILYN: Sometimes I want to know what's going to happen. Then I think it's better not to. There's two things I'd like to know, though. One is whether I'm going to lose weight.

TC: And the other?

MARILYN: That's a secret.

TC: Now, now. We can't have secrets today. Today is a day of sorrow, and sorrowers share their innermost thoughts.

MARILYN: Well, it's a man. There's something I'd like to know. But that's all I'm going to tell. It really *is* a secret.

(And I thought: That's what you think; I'll get it out of you.)

TC: I'm ready to buy that champagne.

(We wound up on Second Avenue in a gaudily decorated deserted Chinese restaurant. But it did have a well-stocked bar, and we ordered a bottle of Mumm's; it arrived unchilled, and without a bucket, so we drank it out of tall glasses with ice cubes.)

MARILYN: This is fun. Kind of like being on location – if you like location. Which I most certainly don't. *Niagara.* That stinker. Yuk.

TC: So let's hear about your secret lover.

MARILYN: (Silence)

TC: (Silence)

MARILYN: (Giggles)

TC: (Silence)

MARILYN: You know so many women. Who's the most attractive woman you know?

TC: No contest. Barbara Paley. Hands down.

MARILYN (frowning): Is that the one they call "Babe"? She sure doesn't look like any Babe to me. I've seen her in *Vogue* and all. She's so elegant. Lovely. Just looking at her pictures makes me feel like pig-slop.

TC: She might be amused to hear that. She's very jealous of you.

MARILYN: Jealous of *me?* Now there you go again, laughing.

TC: Not at all. She *is* jealous.

MARILYN: But why?

TC: Because one of the columnists, Kilgallen I think, ran a blind item that said something like: "Rumor hath it that Mrs. DiMaggio rendezvoused with television's toppest tycoon and it wasn't to discuss business." Well, she read the item and she believes it.

MARILYN: Believes *what?*

TC: That her husband is having an affair with you. William S. Paley. TV's toppest tycoon. He's partial to shapely blondes. Brunettes, too.

MARILYN: But that's batty. I've never met the guy.

TC: Ah, come on. You can level with me. This secret lover of yours – it's William S. Paley, *n'est-ce pas?*

MARILYN: No! It's a writer. He's a writer.

TC: That's more like it. Now we're getting somewhere. So your lover is a writer. Must be a real hack, or you wouldn't be ashamed to tell me his name.

MARILYN (furious, frantic): What does the "S" stand for?

TC: "S." What "S"?

MARILYN: The "S" in William S. Paley.

TC: Oh, *that* "S." It doesn't stand for anything. He sort of tossed it in there for appearance sake.

MARILYN: It's just an initial with no name behind it? My goodness. Mr. Paley must be a little insecure.

TC: He twitches a lot. But let's get back to our mysterious scribe.

MARILYN: Stop it! You don't understand. I have so much to lose.

TC: Waiter, we'll have another Mumm's, please.

MARILYN: Are you trying to loosen my tongue?

TC: Yes. Tell you what. We'll make an exchange. I'll tell you a story, and if you think it's interesting, then perhaps we can discuss your writer friend.

MARILYN (tempted, but reluctant): What's your story about?

TC: Errol Flynn.

MARILYN: (Silence)

TC: (Silence)

MARILYN (hating herself): Well, go on.

TC: Remember what you were saying about Errol? How pleased he was with his prick? I can vouch for that. We once spent a cozy evening together. If you follow me.

MARILYN: You're making this up. You're trying to trick me.

TC: Scout's honor. I'm dealing from a clean deck. (Silence; but I can see that she's hooked, so after lighting a cigarette . . .) Well, this happened when I was eighteen. Nineteen. It was during the war. The winter of 1943. That night Carol Marcus or maybe she was already Carol Saroyan, was giving a party for her best friend, Gloria Vanderbilt. She gave it in her mother's apartment on Park Avenue. Big party. About fifty people. Around midnight Errol Flynn rolls in with his alter ego, a swashbuckling playboy named Freddie McEvoy. They were both pretty loaded. Anyway, Errol started yakking with me, and he was bright, we were making each other laugh, and suddenly he said he wanted to go to El Morocco, and did I want to go with him and his buddy McEvoy. I said okay, but then McEvoy didn't want to leave the party and all those debutantes, so in the end Errol and I left alone. Only we didn't go to El Morocco. We took a taxi down to Gramercy Park, where I had a little one-room apartment. He stayed until noon the next day.

MARILYN: And how would you rate it? On a scale of one to ten.

TC: Frankly, if it hadn't been Errol Flynn, I don't think I would have remembered it.

MARILYN: That's not much of a story. Not worth mine – not by a long shot.

TC: Waiter, where is our champagne? You've got two thirsty people here.

MARILYN: And it's not as if you'd told me anything new. I've always known Errol zigzagged. I have a masseur, he's practically my sister, and he was Tyrone Power's masseur, and he told me all about the thing Errol and Ty Power had going. No, you'll have to do better than that.

TC: You drive a hard bargain.

MARILYN: I'm listening. So let's hear your best experience. Along those lines.

TC: The best? The most memorable? Suppose you answer the question first.

MARILYN: And *I* drive hard bargains! Ha! (Swallowing champagne) Joe's not bad. He can hit home runs. If that's all it takes, we'd still be married. I still love him, though. He's genuine.

TC: Husbands don't count. Not in this game.

MARILYN (nibbling nail; really thinking): Well, I met a man, he's related to Gary Cooper somehow. A stockbroker, and nothing much to look at – sixty-five, and he wears those very thick glasses. Thick as jellyfish. I can't say what it was, but –

TC: You can stop right there. I've heard all about him from other girls. That old swordsman really scoots around. His name is Paul Shields. He's Rocky Cooper's stepfather. He's supposed to be sensational.

MARILYN: He is. Okay, smart-ass. Your turn.

TC: Forget it. I don't have to tell you damn nothing. Because I know who your masked marvel is: Arthur Miller. (She lowered her black glasses: Oh boy, if looks could kill, wow!) I guessed as soon as you said he was a writer.

MARILYN (stammering): But how? I mean, nobody . . . I mean, hardly anybody –

TC: At least three, maybe four years ago Irving Drutman –

MARILYN: Irving *who*?

TC: Drutman. He's a writer on the *Herald Tribune*. He told me you were fooling around with Arthur Miller. Had a hang-up on him. I was too much of a gentleman to mention it before.

MARILYN: Gentleman! You bastard. (Stammering again, but dark glasses in place) You don't understand. That was long ago. That ended. But this is new. It's all different now, and –

TC: Just don't forget to invite me to the wedding.

MARILYN: If you talk about this, I'll murder you. I'll have you bumped off. I know a couple of men who'd gladly do me the favor.

TC: I don't question that for an instant.

(At last the waiter returned with the second bottle.)

MARILYN: Tell him to take it back. I don't want any. I want to get the hell out of here.

TC: Sorry if I've upset you.

MARILYN: I'm not upset.

(But she was. While I paid the check, she left for the powder room, and I wished I had a book to read: her visits to powder rooms sometimes lasted as long as an elephant's pregnancy. Idly, as time ticked by, I wondered if she was popping uppers or downers. Downers, no doubt. There was a newspaper on the bar, and I picked it up; it was written in Chinese. After twenty minutes had passed, I decided to investigate. Maybe she'd popped a lethal dose, or even cut her wrists. I found the ladies' room, and knocked on the door. She said: "Come in." Inside, she was confronting a dimly lit mirror. I said: "What are you doing?" She said: "Looking at Her." In fact, she was coloring her lips with ruby lipstick. Also, she had removed the somber head scarf and combed out her glossy fine-as-cotton-candy hair.)

MARILYN: I hope you have enough money left.

TC: That depends. Not enough to buy pearls, if that's your idea of making amends.

MARILYN: (giggling, returned to good spirits. I decided I wouldn't mention Arthur Miller again): No. Only enough for a long taxi ride.

TC: Where are we going – Hollywood?

MARILYN: Hell, no. A place I like. You'll find out when we get there.

(I didn't have to wait that long, for as soon as we had flagged a taxi, I heard her instruct the cabby to drive to the South Street Pier, and I thought: Isn't that where one takes the ferry to Staten Island? And my next conjecture was: She's swallowed pills on top of that champagne and now she's off her rocker.)

TC: I hope we're not going on any boat rides. I didn't pack my Dramamine.

MARILYN: (happy, giggling): Just the pier.

TC: May I ask why?

MARILYN: I like it there. It smells foreign, and I can feed the sea gulls.

TC: With what? You haven't anything to feed them.

MARILYN: Yes, I do. My purse is full of fortune cookies. I swiped them from that restaurant.

TC (kidding her): Uh-huh. While you were in the john I cracked one open. The slip inside was a dirty joke.

MARILYN: Gosh. Dirty fortune cookies?

TC: I'm sure the gulls won't mind.

(Our route carried us through the Bowery. Tiny pawnshops and blood-donor stations and dormitories with fifty-cent cots and tiny grim hotels with dollar beds and bars for whites, bars for blacks, everywhere bums, bums, young, far from young, ancient, bums squatting curbside, squatting amid shattered glass and pukey debris, bums slanting in doorways and huddled like penguins at street corners. Once, when we paused for a red light, a purple-nosed scarecrow weaved toward us and began swabbing the taxi's windshield with a wet rag clutched in a shaking hand. Our protesting driver shouted Italian obscenities.)

MARILYN: What is it? What's happening?

TC: He wants a tip for cleaning the window.

MARILYN (shielding her face with her purse): How horrible! I can't stand it. Give him something. Hurry. Please!

(But the taxi had already zoomed ahead, damn near knocking down the old lush. Marilyn was crying.)

I'm sick.

TC: You want to go home?

MARILYN: Everything's ruined.

TC: I'll take you home.

MARILYN: Give me a minute. I'll be okay.

> (Thus we traveled on to South Street, and indeed the sight of a ferry moored there, with the Brooklyn skyline across the water and careening, cavorting sea gulls white against a marine horizon streaked with thin fleecy clouds fragile as lace – this tableau soon soothed her soul.
>
> As we got out of the taxi we saw a man with a chow on a leash, a prospective passenger, walking toward the ferry, and as we passed them, my companion stopped to pat the dog's head.)

THE MAN (firm, but not unfriendly): You shouldn't touch strange dogs. Especially chows. They might bite you.

MARILYN: Dogs never bite me. Just humans. What's his name?

THE MAN: Fu Manchu.

MARILYN (giggling): Oh, just like the movie. That's cute.

THE MAN: What's yours?

MARILYN: My name? Marilyn.

THE MAN: That's what I thought. My wife will never believe me. Can I have your autograph?

> (He produced a business card and a pen; using her purse to write on, she wrote: *God Bless You – Marilyn Monroe*.)

MARILYN: Thank you.

THE MAN: Thank *you*. Wait'll I show this back at the office.

> (We continued to the edge of the pier, and listened to the water sloshing against it.)

MARILYN: I used to ask for autographs. Sometimes I still do. Last year Clark Gable was sitting next to me in Chasen's, and I asked him to sign my napkin.

> (Leaning against a mooring stanchion, she presented a profile: Galatea surveying unconquered distances. Breezes fluffed her hair, and her head turned toward me with an ethereal ease, as though a breeze had swiveled it.)

TC: So when do we feed the birds? I'm hungry, too. It's late, and we never had lunch.

MARILYN: Remember, I said if anybody ever asked you what I was like, what Marilyn Monroe was *really* like – well, how would you answer them? (Her tone was teaseful, mocking, yet earnest, too: she wanted an honest reply) I bet you'd tell them I was a slob. A banana split.

TC: Of course. But I'd also say . . .

> (The light was leaving. She seemed to fade with it, blend with the sky and clouds, recede beyond them. I wanted to lift my voice louder than the sea gulls' cries and call her back: Marilyn! Marilyn, why did everything have to turn out the way it did? Why does life have to be so fucking rotten?)

TC: I'd say . . .

MARILYN: I can't hear you.

TC: I'd say you are a beautiful child.

FLEUR

Louise Erdrich

Karen Louise Erdrich (b.1954) is of Native American and European-American heritage and is an enrolled member of the Turtle Mountain Chippewa tribe. She was born in Little Falls, Minnesota and grew up on a reservation in Wahpeton, North Dakota. Erdrich joined Dartmouth College's first co-educational class in 1972, and later gained an MA in Creative Writing from Johns Hopkins University. Her awards include the National Book Award for Fiction. She received an honorary Doctorate of Letters from Dartmouth College in 2009.

The first time she drowned in the cold and glassy waters of Lake Turcot, Fleur Pillager was only a girl. Two men saw the boat tip, saw her struggle in the waves. They rowed over to the place she went down, and jumped in. When they dragged her over the gunwales, she was cold to the touch and stiff, so they slapped her face, shook her by the heels, worked her arms back and forth, and pounded her back until she coughed up lake water. She shivered all over like a dog, then took a breath. But it wasn't long afterward that those two men disappeared. The first wandered off, and the other, Jean Hat, got himself run over by a cart.

It went to show, my grandma said. It figured to her, all right. By saving Fleur Pillager, those two men had lost themselves.

The next time she fell in the lake, Fleur Pillager was twenty years old and no one touched her. She washed onshore, her skin a dull dead gray, but when George Many Women bent to look closer, he saw her chest move. Then her eyes spun open, sharp black riprock, and she looked at him. "You'll take my place," she hissed. Everybody scattered and left her there, so no one knows how she dragged herself home. Soon after that we noticed Many Women changed, grew afraid, wouldn't leave his house, and would not be forced to go near water. For his caution, he lived until the day that his sons brought him a new tin bathtub. Then the first time he used the tub he slipped, got knocked out, and breathed water while his wife stood in the other room frying breakfast.

Men stayed clear of Fleur Pillager after the second drowning. Even though she was good-looking, nobody dared to court her because it was clear that Misshepeshu, the waterman, the monster, wanted her for himself. He's a devil, that one, love-hungry with desire and maddened for the touch of young girls, the strong and daring especially, the ones like Fleur.

Our mothers warn us that we'll think he's handsome, for he appears with green eyes, copper skin, a mouth tender as a child's. But if you fall into his arms, he sprouts horns, fangs, claws, fins. His feet are joined as one and his skin, brass scales, rings to the touch. You're fascinated, cannot move. He casts a shell necklace at your feet, weeps gleaming chips that harden into mica on your breasts. He holds you under. Then he takes the body of a lion or a fat brown worm. He's made of gold. He's made of beach moss. He's a thing of dry foam, a thing of death by drowning, the death a Chippewa cannot survive.

Unless you are Fleur Pillager. We all knew she couldn't swim. After the first time, we thought she'd never go back to Lake Turcot. We thought she'd keep to herself, live quiet, stop killing men off by drowning in the lake. After the first time, we thought she'd keep the good ways. But then, after the second drowning, we knew that we were dealing with something much more serious. She was haywire, out of control. She messed with evil, laughed at the old women's advice, and dressed like a man. She got herself into some half-forgotten medicine, studied ways we shouldn't talk about. Some say she kept the finger of a child in her pocket and a powder of unborn rabbits in a leather thong around her neck. She laid the heart of an owl on her tongue so she could see at night, and went out, hunting, not even in her own body. We know for sure because the next morning, in the snow or dust, we followed the tracks of her bare feet and saw where they changed, where the claws sprang out, the pad broadened and pressed into the dirt. By night we heard her chuffing cough, the bear cough. By day her silence and the wide grin she threw to bring down our guard made us frightened. Some thought that Fleur Pillager should be driven off the reservation, but not a single person who spoke like this had the nerve. And finally, when people were just about to get together and throw her out, she left on her own and didn't come back all summer. That's what this story is about.

During that summer, when she lived a few miles south in Argus, things happened. She almost destroyed that town.

When she got down to Argus in the year of 1920, it was just a small grid of six streets on either side of the railroad depot. There were two elevators, one central, the other a few miles west. Two stores competed for the trade of the three hundred citizens, and three churches quarreled with one another for their souls. There was a frame building for Lutherans, a heavy brick one for Episcopalians, and a long narrow shingled Catholic church. This last had a tall slender steeple, twice as high as any building or tree.

No doubt, across the low, flat wheat, watching from the road as she came near Argus on foot, Fleur saw that steeple rise, a shadow thin as a needle. Maybe in that raw space it drew her the way a lone tree draws lightning. Maybe, in the end, the Catholics are to blame. For if she hadn't seen that sign of pride, that slim prayer, that marker, maybe she would have kept walking.

But Fleur Pillager turned, and the first place she went once she came into town was to the back door of the priest's residence attached to the landmark church. She didn't go there for a handout, although she got that, but to ask for work. She got that too, or the town got her. It's hard to tell which came out worse, her or the men or the town, although the upshot of it all was that Fleur lived.

The four men who worked at the butcher's had carved up about a thousand carcasses between them, maybe half of that steers and the other half pigs, sheep, and game animals like deer, elk, and bear. That's not even mentioning the chickens, which were beyond counting. Pete Kozka owned the place, and employed Lily Veddar, Tor Grunewald, and my stepfather, Dutch James, who had brought my mother down from the reservation the year before she disappointed him by dying. Dutch took me out of school to take her place. I kept house half the time and worked the other in the butcher shop, sweeping floors, putting sawdust down, running a hambone across the street to a customer's bean pot or a package of sausage to the corner. I was a good one to have around because until they needed me, I was invisible. I blended into the stained brown walls, a skinny, big-nosed girl with staring eyes. Because I could fade into a corner or squeeze beneath a shelf, I knew everything, what the men said when no one was around, and what they did to Fleur.

Kozka's Meats served farmers for a fifty-mile area, both to slaughter, for it had a stock pen and chute, and to cure the meat by smoking it or spicing it in sausage. The storage locker was a marvel, made of many thicknesses of brick, earth insulation, and Minnesota timber, lined inside with sawdust and vast blocks of ice cut from Lake Turcot, hauled down from home each winter by horse and sledge.

A ramshackle board building, part slaughterhouse, part store, was fixed to the low, thick square of the lockers. That's where Fleur worked. Kozka hired her for her strength. She could lift a haunch or carry a pole of sausages without stumbling, and she soon learned cutting from Pete's wife, a string-thin blonde who chain-smoked and handled the razor-sharp knives with nerveless precision, slicing close to her stained fingers. Fleur and Fritzie Kozka worked afternoons, wrapping their cuts in paper, and Fleur hauled the packages to the lockers. The meat was left outside the heavy oak doors that were only opened at 5:00 each afternoon, before the men ate supper.

Sometimes Dutch, Tor, and Lily ate at the lockers, and when they did I stayed too, cleaned floors, restoked the fires in the front smokehouses, while the men sat around the squat cast-iron stove spearing slats of herring onto hardtack bread. They played long games of poker or cribbage on a board made from the planed end of a salt crate. They talked and I listened, although there wasn't much to hear since almost nothing ever happened in Argus. Tor was married, Dutch had lost my mother, and Lily read circulars. They mainly discussed about the auctions to come, equipment, or women.

Every so often, Pete Kozka came out front to make a whist, leaving Fritzie to smoke cigarettes and fry raised doughnuts in the back room. He sat and played a few rounds but kept his thoughts to himself. Fritzie did not tolerate him talking behind her back, and the one book he read was the New Testament. If he said something, it concerned weather or a surplus of sheep stomachs, a ham that smoked green or the markets for corn and wheat. He had a good-luck talisman, the opal-white lens of a cow's eye. Playing cards, he rubbed it between his fingers. That soft sound and the slap of cards was about the only conversation.

Fleur finally gave them a subject.

Her cheeks were wide and flat, her hands large, chapped, muscular. Fleur's shoulders were broad as beams, her hips fishlike, slippery, narrow. An old green dress clung to her waist, worn thin where she sat. Her braids were thick like the tails of animals, and swung against her when she moved, deliberately, slowly in her work, held in and half-tamed, but only half. I could tell, but the others never saw. They never looked into her sly brown eyes or noticed her teeth, strong and curved and very white. Her legs were bare, and since she padded around in beadwork moccasins they never saw that her fifth toes were missing. They never knew she'd drowned. They were blinded, they were stupid, they only saw her in the flesh.

And yet it wasn't just that she was a Chippewa, or even that she was a woman, it wasn't that she was good-looking or even that she was alone that made their brains hum. It was how she played cards.

Women didn't usually play with men, so the evening that Fleur drew a chair up to the men's table without being so much as asked, there was a shock of surprise.

"What's this," said Lily. He was fat, with a snake's cold pale eyes and precious skin, smooth and lily-white, which is how he got his name. Lily had a dog, a stumpy mean little bull of a thing with a belly drum-tight from eating pork rinds. The dog liked to play cards just like Lily, and straddled his barrel thighs through games of stud, rum poker, vingt-un. The dog snapped at Fleur's arm that first night, but cringed back, its snarl frozen, when she took her place.

"I thought," she said, her voice soft and stroking, "you might deal me in."

There was a space between the heavy bin of spiced flour and the wall where I just fit. I hunkered down there, kept my eyes open, saw her black hair swing over the chair, her feet solid on the wood floor. I couldn't see up on the table where the cards slapped down, so after they were deep in their game I raised myself up in the shadows, and crouched on a sill of wood.

I watched Fleur's hands stack and ruffle, divide the cards, spill them to each player in a blur, rake them up and shuffle again. Tor, short and scrappy, shut one eye and squinted the other at Fleur. Dutch screwed his lips around a wet cigar.

"Gotta see a man," he mumbled, getting up to go out back to the privy. The others broke, put their cards down, and Fleur sat alone in the lamplight that glowed in a sheen across the push of her breasts. I watched her closely, then she paid me a beam of notice for the first time. She turned, looked straight at me, and grinned the white wolf grin a Pillager turns on its victims, except that she wasn't after me.

"Pauline there," she said, "how much money you got?"

We'd all been paid for the week that day. Eight cents was in my pocket.

"Stake me," she said, holding out her long fingers. I put the coins in her palm and then I melted back to nothing, part of the walls and tables. It was a long time before I understood that the men would not have seen me no matter what I did, how I moved. I wasn't anything like Fleur. My dress hung loose and my back was already curved, an old woman's. Work had roughened me, reading made my eyes sore, caring for my mother before she died had hardened my face. I was not much to look at, so they never saw me.

When the men came back and sat around the table, they had drawn together. They shot each other small glances, stuck their tongues in their cheeks, burst out laughing at odd moments, to rattle Fleur. But she never minded. They played their vingt-un, staying even as Fleur slowly gained. Those pennies I had given her drew nickels and attracted dimes until there was a small pile in front of her.

Then she hooked them with five-card draw, nothing wild. She dealt, discarded, drew, and then she sighed and her cards gave a little shiver. Tor's eye gleamed, and Dutch straightened in his seat.

"I'll pay to see that hand," said Lily Veddar.

Fleur showed, and she had nothing there, nothing at all.

Tor's thin smile cracked open, and he threw his hand in too.

"Well, we know one thing," he said, leaning back in his chair, "the squaw can't bluff."

With that I lowered myself into a mound of swept sawdust and slept. I woke up during the night, but none of them had moved yet, so I couldn't either. Still later, the men must have gone out again, or Fritzie come out to break the game, because I was lifted, soothed, cradled in a woman's arms and rocked so quiet that I kept my eyes shut while Fleur rolled me into a closet of grimy ledgers, oiled paper, balls of string, and thick files that fit beneath me like a mattress.

The game went on after work the next evening. I got my eight cents back five times over, and Fleur kept the rest of the dollar she'd won for a stake. This time they didn't play so late, but they played regular, and then kept going at it night after night. They played poker now, or variations, for one week straight, and each time Fleur won exactly one dollar, no more and no less, too consistent for luck.

By this time, Lily and the other men were so lit with suspense that they got Pete to join the game with them. They concentrated, the fat dog sitting tense in Lily Veddar's lap, Tor suspicious, Dutch stroking his huge square brow, Pete steady. It wasn't that Fleur won that hooked them in so, because she lost hands too. It was rather that she never had a freak hand or even anything above a straight. She only took on her low cards, which didn't sit right. By chance, Fleur should have gotten a full or flush by now. The irritating thing was she beat with pairs and never bluffed, because she couldn't, and still she ended up each night with exactly one dollar. Lily couldn't believe, first of all, that a woman could be smart enough to play cards, but even if she was, that she would then be stupid enough to cheat for a dollar a night. By day I watched him turn the problem over, his hard white face dull, small fingers probing at his knuckles, until he finally thought he had Fleur figured out as a bit-time player, caution her game. Raising the stakes would throw her.

More than anything now, he wanted Fleur to come away with something but a dollar. Two bits less or ten more, the sum didn't matter, just so he broke her streak.

Night after night she played, won her dollar, and left to stay in a place that just Fritzie and I knew about. Fleur bathed in the slaughtering tub, then slept in the unused brick smokehouse behind the lockers, a windowless place tarred on the inside with scorched fats. When I brushed against her skin I noticed that she smelled of the walls, rich and woody, slightly burnt. Since that night she put me in the closet I was no longer afraid of her, but followed her close, stayed with her, became her moving shadow that the men never noticed, the shadow that could have saved her.

August, the month that bears fruit, closed around the shop, and Pete and Fritzie left for Minnesota to escape the heat. Night by night, running, Fleur had won thirty dollars, but only Pete's presence had kept Lily at bay. But Pete was gone now, and one payday, with the heat so bad no one could move but Fleur, the men sat and played and waited while she finished work. The cards sweat, limp in their fingers, the table was slick with grease, and even the walls were warm to the touch. The air was motionless. Fleur was in the next room boiling heads.

Her green dress, drenched, wrapped her like a transparent sheet. A skin of lakeweed. Black snarls of veining clung to her arms. Her braids were loose, half-unraveled, tied behind her neck in a thick loop. She stood in steam, turning skulls through a vat with a wooden paddle. When scraps boiled to the surface, she bent with a round tin sieve and scooped them out. She'd filled two dishpans.

"Ain't that enough now?" called Lily. "We're waiting." The stump of a dog trembled in his lap, alive with rage. It never smelled me or noticed me above Fleur's smoky skin. The air was heavy in my corner, and pressed me down. Fleur sat with them.

"Now what do you say?" Lily asked the dog. It barked. That was the signal for the real game to start.

"Let's up the ante," said Lily, who had been stalking this night all month. He had a roll of money in his pocket. Fleur had five bills in her dress. The men had each saved their full pay.

"Ante a dollar then," said Fleur, and pitched hers in. She lost, but they let her scrape along, cent by cent. And then she won some. She played unevenly, as if chance was all she had. She reeled them in. The game went on. The dog was stiff now, poised on Lily's knees, a ball of vicious muscle with its yellow eyes slit in concentration. It gave advice, seemed to sniff the lay of Fleur's cards, twitched and nudged. Fleur was up, then down, saved by a scratch. Tor dealt seven cards, three down. The pot grew, round by round, until it held all the money. Nobody folded. Then it all rode on one last card and they went silent. Fleur picked hers up and blew a long breath. The heat lowered like a bell. Her card shook, but she stayed in.

Lily smiled and took the dog's head tenderly between his palms.

"Say, Fatso," he said, crooning the words, "you reckon that girl's bluffing?"

The dog whined and Lily laughed. "Me too," he said, "let's show." He swept his bills and coins into the pot and then they turned their cards over.

Lily looked once, looked again, then he squeezed the dog up like a fist of dough and slammed it on the table.

Fleur threw her arms out and drew the money over, grinning that same wolf grin that she'd used on me, the grin that had them. She jammed the bills in her dress, scooped the coins up in waxed white paper that she tied with string.

"Let's go another round," said Lily, his voice choked with burrs. But Fleur opened her mouth and yawned, then walked out back to gather slops for the one big hog that was waiting in the stock pen to be killed.

The men sat still as rocks, their hands spread on the oiled wood table. Dutch had chewed his cigar to damp shreds, Tor's eye was dull. Lily's gaze was the only one to follow Fleur. I didn't move. I felt them gathering, saw my stepfather's veins, the ones in his forehead that stood out in anger. The dog had rolled off the table and curled in a knot below the counter, where none of the men could touch it.

Lily rose and stepped out back to the closet of ledgers where Pete kept his private stock. He brought back a bottle, uncorked and tipped it between his fingers. The lump in his throat moved, then he passed it on. They drank, quickly felt the whiskey's fire, and planned with their eyes things they couldn't say out loud.

When they left, I followed. I hid out back in the clutter of broken boards and chicken crates beside the stock pen, where they waited. Fleur could not be seen at first, and then the moon broke and showed her, slipping cautiously along the rough board chute with a bucket in her hand. Her hair fell, wild and coarse, to her waist, and her dress was a floating patch in the dark. She made a pig-calling sound, rang the tin pail lightly against the wood, froze suspiciously. But too late. In the sound of the ring Lily moved, fat and nimble, stepped right behind Fleur and put out his creamy hands. At his first touch, she whirled and doused him with the bucket of sour slops. He pushed her against the big fence and the package of coins split, went clinking and jumping, winked against the wood. Fleur rolled over once and vanished in the yard.

The moon fell behind a curtain of ragged clouds, and Lily followed into the dark muck. But he tripped, pitched over the huge flank of the pig, who lay mired to the snout, heavily snoring. I sprang out of the weeds and climbed the side of the pen, stuck like glue. I saw the sow rise to her neat, knobby knees, gain her balance, and sway, curious, as Lily stumbled forward. Fleur had backed into the angle of rough wood just beyond, and when Lily tried to jostle past, the sow tipped up on her hind legs and struck, quick and hard as a snake. She plunged her head into Lily's thick side and snatched a mouthful of his shirt. She lunged again, caught him lower, so that he grunted in pained surprise. He seemed to ponder, breathing deep. Then he launched his huge body in a swimmer's dive.

The sow screamed as his body smacked over hers. She rolled, striking out with her knife-sharp hooves, and Lily gathered himself upon her, took her foot-long face by the ears and scraped her snout and cheeks against the trestles of the pen. He hurled the sow's tight skull against an iron post, but instead of knocking her dead, he merely woke her from her dream.

She reared, shrieked, drew him with her so that they posed standing upright. They bowed jerkily to each other, as if to begin. Then his arms swung and flailed. She sank her black fangs into his shoulder, clasping him, dancing him forward and backward through the pen. Their steps picked up pace, went wild. The two dipped as one, box-stepped, tripped each other. She ran her split foot through his hair. He grabbed her kinked tail. They went down and came up, the same shape and then the same color, until the men couldn't tell one from the other in that light and Fleur was able to launch herself over the gates, swing down, hit gravel.

The men saw, yelled, and chased her at a dead run to the smokehouse. And Lily too, once the sow gave up in disgust and freed him. That is where I should have gone to Fleur, saved her, thrown myself on Dutch. But I went stiff with fear and couldn't unlatch myself from the trestles or move at all. I closed my eyes and put my head in my arms, tried to hide, so there is nothing to describe but what I couldn't block out. Fleur's hoarse breath, so loud it filled me, her cry in the old language, and my name repeated over and over among the words.

The heat was still dense the next morning when I came back to work. Fleur was gone but the men were there, slack-faced, hung over. Lily was paler and softer than ever, as if his flesh had steamed on his bones. They smoked, took pulls off a bottle. It wasn't noon yet. I worked awhile, waiting shop and sharpening steel. But I was sick, I was smothered, I was sweating so hard that my hands slipped on the knives, and I wiped my fingers clean of the greasy touch of the customers' coins. Lily opened his mouth and roared once, not in anger. There was no meaning to the sound. His boxer dog, sprawled limp beside his foot, never lifted its head. Nor did the other men.

They didn't notice when I stepped outside, hoping for a clear breath. And then I forgot them because I knew that we were all balanced, ready to tip, to fly, to be crushed as soon as the weather broke. The sky was so low that I felt the weight of it like a yoke. Clouds hung down, witch teats, a tornado's green-brown cones, and as I watched one flicked out and became a delicate probing thumb. Even as I picked up my heels and ran back inside, the wind blew suddenly, cold, and then came rain.

Inside, the men had disappeared already and the whole place was trembling as if a huge hand was pinched at the rafters, shaking it. I ran straight through, screaming for Dutch or for any of them, and then I stopped at the heavy doors of the lockers, where they had surely taken shelter. I stood there a moment. Everything went still. Then I heard a cry building in the wind, faint at first, a whistle and then a shrill scream that tore through the walls and gathered around me, spoke plain so I understood that I should move, put my arms out, and slam down the great iron bar that fit across the hasp and lock.

Outside, the wind was stronger, like a hand held against me. I struggled forward. The bushes tossed, the awnings flapped off storefronts, the rails of porches rattled. The odd cloud became a fat snout that nosed along the earth and sniffled, jabbed, picked at things, sucked them up, blew them apart, rooted around as if it was following a certain scent, then stopped behind me at the butcher shop and bored down like a drill.

I went flying, landed somewhere in a ball. When I opened my eyes and looked, stranger things were happening.

A herd of cattle flew through the air like giant birds, dropping dung, their mouths opened in stunned bellows. A candle, still lighted, blew past, and tables, napkins, garden tools, a whole school of drifting eyeglasses, jackets on hangers, hams, a checkerboard, a lampshade, and at last the sow from behind the lockers, on the run, her hooves a blur, set free, swooping, diving, screaming as everything in Argus fell apart and got turned upside down, smashed, and thoroughly wrecked.

Days passed before the town went looking for the men. They were bachelors, after all, except for Tor, whose wife had suffered a blow to the head that made her forgetful. Everyone was occupied with digging out, in high relief because even though the Catholic steeple had been torn off like a peaked cap and sent across five fields, those huddled in the cellar were unhurt. Walls had fallen, windows were demolished, but the stores were intact and so were the bankers and shop owners who had taken refuge in their safes or beneath their cash registers. It was a fair-minded disaster, no one could be said to have suffered much more than the next, at least not until Fritzie and Pete came home.

Of all the businesses in Argus, Kozka's Meats had suffered worst. The boards of the front building had been split to kindling, piled in a huge pyramid, and the shop equipment was blasted far and wide. Pete paced off the distance the iron bathtub had been flung – a hundred feet. The glass candy case went fifty, and landed without so much as a cracked pane. There were other surprises as well, for the back rooms where Fritzie and Pete lived were undisturbed. Fritzie said the dust still coated her china figures, and upon her kitchen table, in the ashtray, perched the last cigarette she'd put out in haste. She lit it up and finished it, looking through the window. From there, she could see that the old smokehouse Fleur had slept in was crushed to a reddish sand and the stockpens were completely torn apart, the rails stacked helter-skelter. Fritzie asked for Fleur. People shrugged. Then she asked about the others and, suddenly, the town understood that three men were missing.

There was a rally of help, a gathering of shovels and volunteers. We passed boards from hand to hand, stacked them, uncovered what lay beneath the pile of jagged splinters. The lockers, full of the meat that was Pete and Fritzie's investment, slowly came into sight, still intact. When enough room was made for a man to stand on the roof, there were calls, a general urge to hack through and see what lay below. But Fritzie shouted that she wouldn't allow it because the meat would spoil. And so the work continued, board by board, until at last the heavy oak doors of the freezer were revealed and people pressed to the entry. Everyone wanted to be the first, but since it was my stepfather lost, I was let go in when Pete and Fritzie wedged through into the sudden icy air.

Pete scraped a match on his boot, lit the lamp Fritzie held, and then the three of us stood still in its circle. Light glared off the skinned and hanging carcasses, the crates of wrapped sausages, the bright and cloudy blocks of lake ice, pure as winter. The cold bit into us, pleasant at first, then numbing. We must have stood there a couple of minutes before we saw the men, or more rightly, the humps of fur, the iced and shaggy hides they wore, the bearskins they had taken down and wrapped around themselves. We stepped closer and tilted the lantern beneath the flaps of fur into their faces. The dog was there, perched among them, heavy as a doorstop. The three had hunched around a barrel where the game was still laid out, and a dead lantern and an empty bottle, too. But they had thrown down their last hands and hunkered tight, clutching one another, knuckles raw from beating at the door they had also attacked with hooks. Frost stars gleamed off their eyelashes and the stubble of their beards. Their faces were set in concentration, mouths open as if to speak some careful thought, some agreement they'd come to in each other's arms.

Power travels in the bloodlines, handed out before birth. It comes down through the hands, which in the Pillagers were strong and knotted, big, spidery, and rough, with sensitive fingertips good at dealing cards. It comes through the eyes, too, belligerent, darkest brown, the eyes of those in the bear clan, impolite as they gaze directly at a person.

In my dreams, I look straight back at Fleur, at the men. I am no longer the watcher on the dark sill, the skinny girl.

The blood draws us back, as if it runs through a vein of earth. I've come home and, except for talking to my cousins, live a quiet life. Fleur lives quiet too, down on Lake Turcot with her boat. Some say she's married to the waterman, Misshepeshu, or that she's living in shame with white men or windigos, or that she's killed them all. I'm about the only one here who ever goes to visit her. Last winter, I went to help out in her cabin when she bore the child, whose green eyes and skin the color of an old penny made more talk, as no one could decide if the child was mixed blood or what, fathered in a smokehouse, or by a man with brass scales, or by the lake. The girl is bold, smiling in her sleep, as if she knows what people wonder, as if she hears the old men talk, turning the story over. It comes up different every time and has no ending, no beginning. They get the middle wrong too. They only know that they don't know anything.

THE LIVES OF THE DEAD

Tim O'Brien

Tim O'Brien (b.1946) was born in Minnesota. His father was an insurance salesman, his mother a primary school teacher. He graduated from Macalester College in 1968 with a BA in political science and was immediately drafted into the US army. O'Brien fought in the Vietnam War from 1969 to 1970, despite being opposed to it, and won a Purple Heart. After being demobbed he studied at Harvard and then joined the *Washington Post*. O'Brien's experiences in Vietnam inform his memoirs and fiction.

But this too is true: stories can save us. I'm forty-three years old, and a writer now, and even still, right here, I keep dreaming Linda alive. And Ted Lavender, too, and Kiowa, and Curt Lemon, and a slim young man I killed, and an old man sprawled beside a pigpen, and several others whose bodies I once lifted and dumped into a truck. They're all dead. But in a story, which is a kind of dreaming, the dead sometimes smile and sit up and return to the world.

Start here: a body without a name. On an afternoon in 1969 the platoon took sniper fire from a filthy little village along the South China Sea. It lasted only a minute or two, and nobody was hurt, but even so Lieutenant Jimmy Cross got on the radio and ordered up an air strike. For the next half hour we watched the place burn. It was a cool bright morning, like early autumn, and the jets were glossy black against the sky. When it ended, we formed into a loose line and swept east through the village. It was all wreckage. I remember the smell of burnt straw; I remember broken fences and heaps of stone and brick and pottery. The place was deserted – no people, no animals – and the only confirmed kill was an old man who lay face-up near a pigpen at the center of the village. His right arm was gone. At his face there were already many flies and gnats.

Dave Jensen went over and shook the old man's hand. "How-dee-doo," he said.

One by one the others did it too. They didn't disturb the body, they just grabbed the old man's hand and offered a few words and moved away.

Rat Kiley bent over the corpse. "Gimme five," he said. "A real honor."

"Pleased as punch," said Henry Dobbins.

I was brand-new to the war. It was my fourth day; I hadn't yet developed a sense of humor. Right away, as if I'd swallowed something, I felt a moist sickness rise up in my throat. I sat down beside the pigpen, closed my eyes, put my head between my knees.

After a moment Dave Jensen touched my shoulder.

"Be polite now," he said. "Go introduce yourself. Nothing to be afraid about, just a nice old man. Show a little respect for your elders."

"No way."

"Maybe it's too real for you?"

"That's right," I said. "Way too real."

Jensen kept after me, but I didn't go near the body. I didn't even look at it except by accident. For the rest of the day there was still that sickness inside me, but it wasn't the old man's corpse so much, it was the awesome act of greeting the dead. At one point, I remember, they sat the body up against a fence. They crossed his legs and talked to him. "The guest of honor," Mitchell Sanders said, and he placed a can of orange slices in the old man's lap. "Vitamin C," he said gently. "A guy's health, that's the most important thing."

They proposed toasts. They lifted their canteens and drank to the old man's family and ancestors, his many grandchildren, his newfound life after death. It was more than mockery. There was a formality to it, like a funeral without the sadness.

Dave Jensen flicked his eyes at me.

"Hey, O'Brien," he said, "you got a toast in mind? Never too late for manners."

I found things to do with my hands. I looked away and tried not to think.

Late in the afternoon, just before dusk, Kiowa came up and asked if he could sit at my foxhole for a minute. He offered me a Christmas cookie from a batch his father had sent him. It was February now, but the cookies tasted fine.

For a few moments Kiowa watched the sky.

"You did a good thing today," he said. "That shaking hands crap, it isn't decent. The guys'll hassle you for a while – especially Jensen – but just keep saying no. Should've done it myself. Takes guts, I know that."

"It wasn't guts. I was scared."

Kiowa shrugged. "Same difference."

"No, I couldn't *do* it. A mental block or something. . . I don't know, just creepy."

"Well, you're new here. You'll get used to it." He paused for a second, studying the green and red sprinkles on a cookie. "Today – I guess this was your first look at a real body?"

I shook my head. All day long I'd been picturing Linda's face, the way she smiled.

"It sounds funny," I said, "but that poor old man, he reminds me of. . .I mean, there's this girl I used to know. I took her to the movies once. My first date."

Kiowa looked at me for a long while. Then he leaned back and smiled.

"Man," he said, "that's a bad date."

Linda was nine then, as I was, but we were in love. It was real. When I write about her now, three decades later, it's tempting to dismiss it as a crush, an infatuation of childhood, but I know for a fact that what we felt for each other was as deep and rich as love can ever get. It had all the shadings and complexities of mature adult love, and maybe more, because there were not yet words for it, and because it was not yet fixed to comparisons or chronologies or the ways by which adults measure such things.

I just loved her.

She had poise and great dignity. Her eyes, I remember, were deep brown like her hair, and she was slender and very quiet and fragile-looking.

Even then, at nine years old, I wanted to live inside her body. I wanted to melt into her bones - *that* kind of love.

And so in the spring of 1956, when we were in the fourth grade, I took her out on the first real date of my life – a double date, actually, with my mother and father. Though I can't remember the exact sequence, my mother had somehow arranged it with Linda's parents, and on that damp spring night my dad did the driving while Linda and I sat in the back seat and stared out opposite windows, both of us trying to pretend it was nothing special. For me, though, it was very special. Down inside I had important things to tell her, big profound things, but I couldn't make any words come out. I had trouble breathing. Now and then I'd glance over at her, thinking how beautiful she was: her white skin and those dark brown eyes and the way she always smiled at the world – always, it seemed – as if her face had been designed that way. The smile never went away. That night, I remember, she wore a new red cap, which seemed to me very stylish and sophisticated, very unusual. It was a stocking cap, basically, except the tapered part at the top seemed extra long, almost too long, like a tail growing out of the back of her head. It made me think of the caps that Santa's elves wear, the same shape and color, the same fuzzy white tassel at the tip.

Sitting there in the back seat, I wanted to find some way to let her know how I felt, a compliment of some sort, but all I could manage was a stupid comment about the cap. "Jeez," I must've said, "what a *cap*."

Linda smiled at the window – she knew what I meant – but my mother turned and gave me a hard look. It surprised me. It was as if I'd brought up some horrible secret.

For the rest of the ride I kept my mouth shut. We parked in front of the Ben Franklin store and walked up Main Street toward the State Theater. My parents went first, side by side, and then Linda in her new red cap, and then me tailing along ten or twenty steps behind. I was nine years old; I didn't yet have the gift for small talk. Now and then my mother glanced back, making little motions with her hand to speed me up.

At the ticket booth, I remember, Linda stood off to one side. I moved over to the concession area, studying the candy, and both of us were very careful to avoid the awkwardness of eye contact. Which was how we knew about being in love. It was pure knowing. Neither of us, I suppose, would've thought to use that word, love, but by the fact of not looking at each other, and not talking, we understood with a clarity beyond language that we were sharing something huge and permanent.

Behind me, in the theater, I heard cartoon music.

"Hey, step it up," I said. I almost had the courage to look at her. "You want popcorn or *what*?"

The thing about a story is that you dream it as you tell it, hoping that others might then dream along with you, and in this way memory and imagination and language combine to make spirits in the head. There is the illusion of alive-ness. In Vietnam, for instance, Ted Lavender had a habit of popping four or five tranquilizers every morning. It was his way of coping, just dealing with the realities, and the drugs helped to ease him through the days. I remember how peaceful his eyes were. Even in bad situations he had a soft, dreamy expression on his face, which was what he wanted, a kind of escape. "How's the war to-day?" somebody would ask, and Ted Lavender would give a little smile to the sky and say, "Mellow – a nice smooth war today." And then in April he was shot in the head outside the village of Than Khe. Kiowa and I and a couple of others were ordered to prepare his body for the dustoff. I remember squatting down, not wanting to look but then looking. Lavender's left cheekbone was gone. There was a swollen blackness around his eye. Quickly, trying not to feel anything, we went through the kid's pockets. I remember wishing I had gloves. It wasn't the blood I hated; it was the deadness. We put his personal effects in a plastic bag and tied the bag to his arm. We stripped off the canteens and ammo, all the heavy stuff, and wrapped him up in his own poncho and carried him out to a dry paddy and laid him down.

For a while nobody said much. Then Mitchell Sanders laughed and looked over at the green plastic poncho.

"Hey, Lavender," he said, "how's the war today?"

There was a short quiet.

"Mellow," somebody said.

"Well, that's good," Sanders murmured, "that's real, real good. Stay cool now."

"Hey, no sweat, I'm mellow."

"Just ease on back, then. Don't need no pills. We got this incredible chopper on call, this once in a lifetime mind-trip."

"Oh, yeah – mellow!"

Mitchell Sanders smiled. "There it is, my man, this chopper gonna take you up high and cool. Gonna relax you. Gonna alter your whole perspective on this sorry, sorry shit."

We could almost see Ted Lavender's dreamy blue eyes. We could amost hear him.

"Roger that," somebody said. "I'm ready to fly."

There was the sound of the wind, the sound of birds and the quiet afternoon, which was the world we were in.

That's what a story does. The bodies are animated. You make the dead talk. They sometimes say things like, "Roger that." Or they say, "Timmy, stop crying," which is what Linda said to me after she was dead.

Even now I can see her walking down the aisle of the old State Theater in Wor-thington, Minnesota. I can see her face in profile beside me, the cheeks softly lighted by coming attractions.

The move that night was *The Man Who Never Was*. I remember the plot clearly, or at least the premise, because the main character was a corpse. That fact alone, I know, deeply impressed me. It was a World War Two film: the Allies devise a scheme to mislead Germany about the site of the upcoming landings in Europe. They get their hands on a body – a British soldier, I believe; they dress him up in an officer's uniform, plant fake documents in his pockets, then dump him in the sea and let the currents wash him onto a Nazi beach. The Germans find the documents; the deception wins the war. Even now, I can remember the awful splash as that corpse fell into the sea. I remember glancing over at Linda, thinking it might be too much for her, but in the dim gray light she seemed to be smiling at the screen. There were little crinkles at her eyes, her lips open and gently curving at the corners. I couldn't understand it. There was nothing to smile at. Once or twice, in fact, I had to close my eyes, but it didn't help much. Even then I kept seeing the soldier's body tumbling toward the water, splashing down hard, how inert and heavy it was, how completely dead.

It was a relief when the movie finally ended.

Afterward, we drove out to the Dairy Queen at the edge of town. The night had a quilted, weighted-down quality, as if somehow burdened, and all around us the Minnesota prairies reached out in long repetitive waves of corn and soybeans, everything flat, everything the same. I remember eating ice cream in the back seat of the Buick, and a long blank drive in the dark, and then pulling up in front of Linda's house. Things must've been said, but it's all gone now except for a few last images. I remember walking her to the front door. I remember the brass porch light with its fierce yellow glow, my own feet, the juniper bushes along the front steps, the wet grass, Linda close beside me. We were in love. Nine years old, yes, but it was real love, and now we were alone on those front steps. Finally we looked at each other.

"Bye," I said.

Linda nodded and said, "Bye."

Over the next few weeks Linda wore her new red cap to school every day. She never took it off, not even in the classroom, and so it was inevitable that she took some teasing about it. Most of it came from a kid named Nick Veenhof. Out on the playground, during recess, Nick would creep up behind her and make a grab for the cap, almost yanking it off, then scampering away. It went on like that for weeks: the girls giggling, the guys egging him on. Naturally I wanted to do something about it, but it just wasn't possible. I had my reputation to think about. I had my pride. And there was also the problem of Nick Veenhof. So I stood off to the side, just a spectator, wishing I could do things I couldn't do. I watched Linda clamp down the cap with the palm of her hand, holding it there, smiling over in Nick's direction as if none of it really mattered.

For me, though, it did matter. It still does. I should've stepped in; fourth grade is no excuse. Besides, it doesn't get easier with time, and twelve years later, when Vietnam presented much harder choices, some practice at being brave might've helped a little.

Also, too, I might've stopped what happened next. Maybe not, but at least it's possible.

Most of the details I've forgotten, or maybe blocked out, but I know it was an afternoon in late spring, and we were taking a spelling test, and halfway into it Nick Veenhof held up his hand and asked to use the pencil sharpener. Right away the kids laughed. No doubt he'd broken the pencil on purpose, but it wasn't something you could prove, and so the teacher nodded and told him to hustle it up. Which was a mistake. Out of nowhere Nick developed a terrible limp. He moved in slow motion, dragging himself up to the pencil sharpener and carefully slipping in his pencil and then grinding away forever. At the time, I suppose, it was funny. But on the way back to his seat Nick took a short detour. He squeezed between two desks, turned sharply right, and moved up the aisle toward Linda.

I saw him grin at one of his pals. In a way, I already knew what was coming.

As he passed Linda's desk, he dropped the pencil and squatted down to get it. When he came up, his left hand slipped behind her back. There was a half-second hesitation. Maybe he was trying to stop himself; maybe then, just briefly, he felt some small approximation of guilt. But it wasn't enough. He took hold of the white tassel, stood up, and gently lifted off her cap.

Somebody must've laughed. I remember a short, tinny echo. I remember Nick Veenhof trying to smile. Somewhere behind me, a girl said, "Uh," or a sound like that.

Linda didn't move.

Even now, when I think back on it, I can still see the glossy whiteness of her scalp. She wasn't bald. Not quite. Not completely. There were some tufts of hair, little patches of grayish brown fuzz. But what I saw then, and keep seeing now, is all that whiteness. A smooth, pale, translucent white. I could see the bones and veins; I could se the exact structure of her skull. There was a large Band-Aid at the back of her head, a row of black stitches, a piece of gauze taped above her left ear.

Nick Veenhof took a step backward. He was still smiling, but the smile was doing strange things.

The whole time Linda stared straight ahead, her eyes looked on the blackboard, her hands loosely folded at her lap. She didn't say anything. After a time, though, she turned and looked at me across the room. It lasted only a moment, but I had the feeling that a whole conversation was happening between us. *Well?* she was saying, and I was saying, *Sure, okay.*

Later on, she cried for a while. The teacher helped her put the cap back on, then we finished the spelling test and did some fingerpainting, and after school that day Nick Veenhof and I walked her home.

It's now 1990. I'm forty-three years old, which would've seemed impossible to a fourth grader, and yet when I look at photographs of myself as I was in 1956, I realize that in the important ways I haven't changed at all. I was Timmy then; now I'm Tim. But the essence remains the same. I'm not fooled by the baggy pants or the crew cut or the happy smile – I know my own eyes – and there is no doubt that the Timmy smiling at the camera is the Tim I am now. Inside the body, or beyond the body, there is something absolute and unchanging. The human life is all one thing, like a blade tracing loops on ice; a little kid, a twenty-three-year old infantry sergeant, a middle-aged writer knowing guilt and sorrow.

And as a writer now, I want to save Linda's life. Not her body – her life.

She died, of course. Nine years old and she died. It was a brain tumor. She lived through the summer and into the first part of September, and then she was dead.

But in a story I can steal her soul. I can revive, at least briefly, that which is absolute and unchanging. In a story, miracles can happen. Linda can smile and sit up. She can reach out, touch my wrist, and say, "Timmy, stop crying."

I needed that kind of miracle. At some point I had come to understand that Linda was sick, maybe even dying, but I loved her and just couldn't accept it. In the middle of the summer, I remember, my mother tried to explain to me about brain tumors. Now and then, she said, bad things start growing inside us. Sometimes you can cut them out and other times you can't, and for Linda it was one of the times when you can't.

I thought about it for several days. "All right," I finally said. "So will she get better now?"

"Well, no," my mother said, "I don't think so." She stared at a spot behind my shoulder. "Sometimes people don't ever get better. They die sometimes."

I shook my head.

"Not Linda," I said.

But on a September afternoon, during noon recess, Nick Veenhof came up to me on the school playground. "Your girlfriend," he said, "she kicked the bucket."

At first I didn't understand.

"She's dead," he said. "My mom told me at lunchtime. No lie, she actually kicked the goddang *bucket*."

All I could do was nod. Somehow it didn't quite register. I turned away, glanced down at my hands for a second, then walked home without telling anyone.

It was a little after one o'clock, I remember, and the house was empty.

I drank some chocolate milk and then lay down on the sofa in the living room, not really sad, just floating, trying to imagine what it was to be dead. Nothing much came to me. I remember closing my eyes and whispering her name, almost begging, trying to make her come back. "Linda," I said, "please." And then I concentrated. I willed her alive. It was a dream, I suppose, or a daydream, but I made it happen. I saw her coming down the middle of Main Street, all alone. It was nearly dark and the street was deserted, no cars or people, and Linda wore a pink dress and shiny black shoes. All her hair had grown back. The scars and stitches were gone. In the dream, if that's what it was, she was playing a game of some sort, laughing and running up the empty street, kicking a big aluminum water bucket.

Right then I started to cry. After a moment Linda stopped and carried her water bucket over to the curb and asked why I was so sad.

"Well, God," I said, "you're dead."

Linda nodded at me. She was standing under a yellow streetlight. A nine-year-old girl, just a kid, and yet there was something ageless in her eyes – not a child, not an adult – just a bright ongoing everness, that same pinprick of absolute lasting light that I see today in my own eyes as Timmy smiles at Tim from the graying photographs of that time.

"Dead," I said.

Linda smiled. It was a secret smile, as if she knew things nobody could ever know, and she reached out and touched my wrist and said, "Timmy, stop crying. It doesn't *matter*."

In Vietnam, too, we had ways of making the dead seem not quite so dead.

Shaking hands, that was one way. By slighting death, by acting, we pretended it was not the terrible thing it was. By our language, which was both hard and wistful, we transformed the bodies into piles of waste. Thus, when someone got killed, as Curt Lemon did, his body was not really a body, but rather one small bit of waste in the midst of a much wider wastage. I learned that words make a difference. It's easier to cope with a kicked bucket than a corpse; if it isn't human, it doesn't matter much if it's dead. And so a VC nurse, fried by napalm, was a crispy critter. A Vietnamese baby, which lay nearby, was a roasted peanut. "Just a crunchie munchie," Rat Kiley said as he stepped over the baby.

We kept the dead alive with stories. When Ted Lavender was shot in the head, the men talked about how they'd never seen him so mellow, how tranquil he was, how it wasn't the bullet but the tranquilizers that blew his mind. He wasn't dead, just laid-back. There were Christians among us, like Kiowa, who believed in the New Testament stories of life after death. Other stories were passed down like legends from old-timer to newcomer. Mostly, though, we had to make up our own. Often they were exaggerated, or blatant lies, but it was a way of bringing body and soul back together, or a way of making new bodies for the souls to inhabit. There was a story, for instance, about how Curt Lemon had gone trick-or-treating on Halloween. A dark, spooky night, and so Lemon put on a ghost mask and painted up his body all different colors and crept across a paddy to a sleeping village – almost stark naked, the story went, just boots and balls and an M-16 – and in the dark Lemon went from hootch to hootch – ringing doorbells, he called it – and a few hours later, when he slipped back into the perimeter, he had a whole sackful of goodies to share with his pals: candles and joss sticks and a pair of black pajamas and statuettes of the smiling Buddha. That was the story, anyway. Other versions were much more elaborate, full of descriptions and scraps of dialogue. Rat Kiley liked to spice it up with extra details. "See, what happens is, it's like four in the morning, and Lemon sneaks into a hootch with that weird ghost mask on. Everybody's asleep, right? So he wakes up this cute little mama-san. Tickles her foot. 'Hey, Mama-san,' he goes, real soft like. 'Hey, Mama-san – trick or treat!' Should've seen her *face*. About freaks. I mean, there's this buck naked ghost standing there, and he's got this M-16 up against her ear and he whispers, 'Hey, Mama-san, trick or fuckin' treat!' Then he takes off her pj's. Strips her right down. Sticks the pajamas in his sack and tucks her into bed and heads for the next hootch."

Pausing a moment, Rat Kiley would grin and shake his head. "Honest to God," he'd murmur. "Trick or treat. Lemon – there's one class act."

To listen to the story, especially as Rat Kiley told it, you'd never know that Curt Lemon was dead. He was still out there in the dark, naked and painted up, trick-or-treating, sliding from hootch to hootch in that crazy white ghost mask. But he was dead.

In September, the day after Linda died, I asked my father to take me down to Benson's Funeral Home to view the body. I was a fifth grader then; I was curious. On the drive downtown my father kept his eyes straight ahead. At one point, I remember, he made a scratchy sound in his throat. It took him a long time to light up a cigarette.

"Timmy," he said, "you're sure about this?"

I nodded at him. Down inside, of course, I wasn't sure, and yet I had to see her one more time. What I needed, I suppose, was some sort of final confirmation, something to carry with me after she was gone.

When we parked in front of the funeral home, my father turned and looked at me. "If this bothers you," he said, "just say the word. We'll make a quick get-away. Fair enough?"

"Okay," I said.

"Or if you start to feel sick or anything—"

"I *won't*," I told him.

Inside, the first thing I noticed was the smell, thick and sweet, like something sprayed out of a can. The viewing room was empty except for Linda and my father and me. I felt a rush of panic as we walked up the aisle. The smell made me dizzy. I tried to fight it off, slowing down a little, taking short, shallow breaths through my mouth. But at the same time I felt a funny excitement. Anticipation, in a way – the same awkward feeling when I walked up the sidewalk to ring her doorbell on our first date. I wanted to impress her. I wanted something to happen between us, a secret signal of some sort. The room was dimly lighted, almost dark, but at the far end of the aisle Linda's white casket was illuminated by a row of spotlights up in the ceiling. Everything was quiet. My father put his hand on my shoulder, whispered something, and backed off. After a moment I edged forward a few steps, pushing up on my toes for a better look.

It didn't seem real. A mistake, I thought. The girl lying in the white casket wasn't Linda. There was a resemblance, maybe, but where Linda had always been very slender and fragile-looking, almost skinny, the body in that casket was fat and swollen. For a second I wondered if somebody had made a terrible blunder. A technical mistake: like they'd pumped her too full of formaldehyde or embalming fluid or whatever they used. Her arms and face were bloated. The skin at her cheeks was stretched out tight like the rubber skin on a balloon just before it pops open. Even her fingers seemed puffy. I turned and glanced behind me, where my father stood, thinking that maybe it was a joke – hoping it was a joke- almost believing that Linda would jump out from behind one of the curtains and laugh and yell out my name.

But she didn't. The room was silent. When I looked back at the casket, I felt dizzy again. In my heart, I'm sure, I knew this was Linda, but even so I couldn't find much to recognize. I tried to pretend she was taking a nap, her hands folded at her stomach, just sleeping away the afternoon. Except she didn't *look* asleep. She looked dead. She looked heavy and totally dead.

I remember closing my eyes. After a while my father stepped up beside me.

"Come on now," he said. "Let's go get some ice cream."

In the months after Ted Lavender died, there were many other bodies. I never shook hands – not that – but one afternoon I climbed a tree and threw down what was left of Curt Lemon. I watched my friend Kiowa sink into the muck along the Song Tra Bong. And in early July, after a battle in the mountains, I was assigned to a six-man detail to police up the enemy KIAs. There were twenty-seven bodies altogether, and parts of several others. The dead were everywhere. Some lay in piles. Some lay alone. One, I remember, seemed to kneel. Another was bent from the waist over a small boulder, the top of his head on the ground, his arms rigid, the eyes squinting in concentration as if he were about to perform a handstand or somersault. It was my worst day at the war. For three hours we carried the bodies down the mountain to a clearing alongside a narrow dirt road. We had lunch there, then a truck pulled up, and we worked in two-man teams to load the truck. I remember swinging the bodies up. Mitchell Sanders took a man's feet, I took the arms, and we counted to three, working up momentum, and then we tossed the body high and watched it bounce and come to rest among the other bodies. The dead had been dead for more than a day. They were all badly bloated. Their clothing was stretched tight like sausage skins, and when we picked them up, some made sharp burping sounds as the gases were released. They were heavy. Their feet were bluish green and cold. The smell was terrible. At one point Mitchell Sanders looked at me and said, "Hey, man, I just realized something."

"What?"

He wiped his eyes and spoke very quietly, as if awed by his own wisdom.

"Death sucks," he said.

Lying in bed at night, I made up elaborate stories to bring Linda alive in my sleep. I invented my own dreams. It sounds impossible, I know, but I did it. I'd picture somebody's birthday party – a crowded room, I'd think, and a big chocolate cake with pink candles – and then soon I'd be dreaming it, and after a while Linda would show up, as I knew she would, and in the dream we'd look at each other and not talk much, because we were shy, but then later I'd walk her home and we'd sit on her front steps and stare at the dark and just be together.

She'd say amazing things sometimes. "Once you're alive," she'd say, "you can't ever be dead."

Or she'd say: "Do I *look* dead?"

It was a kind of self-hypnosis. Partly willpower, partly faith, which is how stories arrive.

But back then it felt like a miracle. My dreams had become a secret meeting place, and in the weeks after she died I couldn't wait to fall asleep at night. I began going to bed earlier and earlier, sometimes even in bright daylight. My mother, I remember, finally asked about it at breakfast one morning. "Timmy, what's *wrong*?" she said, but all I could do was shrug and say, "Nothing. I just need sleep, that's all." I didn't dare tell the truth. It was embarrassing, I suppose, but it was also a precious secret, like a magic trick, where if I tried to explain it, or even talk about it, the thrill and mystery would be gone. I didn't want to lose Linda.

She was dead. I understood that. After all, I'd seen her body, and yet even a nine-year-old I had begun to practice the magic of stories. Some I just dreamed up. Others I wrote down – the scenes and dialogue. And at night time I'd slide into sleep knowing that Linda would be there waiting for me. Once, I remember, we went ice skating late at night, tracing loops and circles under yellow floodlights. Later we sat by a wood stove in the warming house, all alone, and after a while I asked her what it was like to be dead. Apparently Linda thought it was a silly question. She smiled and said, "Do I *look* dead?"

I told her no, she looked terrific. I waited a moment, then asked again, and

Linda made a soft little sigh. I could smell our wool mittens drying on the stove.

For a few seconds she was quiet.

"Well, right now," she said, "I'm *not* dead. But when I am, it's like. . . I don't know, I guess it's like being inside a book that nobody's reading."

"A book?" I said.

"An old one. It's up on a library shelf, so you're safe and everything, but the book hasn't been checked out for a long, long time. All you can do is wait. Just hope somebody'll pick it up and start reading."

Linda smiled at me.

"Anyhow, it's not so bad," she said. "I mean, when you're dead, you just have to be yourself." She stood up and put on her red stocking cap. "This is stupid. Let's go skate some more."

So I followed her down to the frozen pond. It was late, and nobody else was there, and we held hands and skated almost all night under the yellow lights.

And then it becomes 1990. I'm forty-three years old, and a writer now, still dreaming Linda alive in exactly the same way. She's not the embodied Linda; she's mostly made up, with a new identity and a new name, like the man who never was. Her real name doesn't matter. She was nine years old. I loved her and then she died. And yet right here, in the spell of memory and imagination, I can still see her as if through ice, as if I'm gazing into some other world, a place where there are no brain tumors and no funeral homes, where there are no bodies at all. I can see Kiowa, too, and Ted Lavender and Curt Lemon, and sometimes I can even see Timmy skating with Linda under the yellow floodlights. I'm young and happy. I'll never die. I'm skimming across the surface of my own history, moving fast, riding the melt beneath the blades, doing loops and spins, and when I take a high leap into the dark and come down thirty years later, I realize it is as Tim trying to save Timmy's life with a story.

OFF-BROADWAY: 1971

Jewelle Gomez

Writer and activist **Jewelle Gomez** (b.1948) was born and brought up in Boston, Massachusetts. Gomez has been active in the civil rights movement and in campaigns against racism, sexism, apartheid and the Vietnam War, among others. She is the author of several books, including *The Gilda Stories,* which have won two Lambda Literary Awards. Gomez said of Gilda, 'She experiences life as a black woman, but she has privilege as a vampire . . .' Gomez is married to Dr Dianne Abbe Sabin.

Gilda hooked the weighty ring of keys back onto her belt loop and hung the padlocks from her pocket. Their metallic jangle reminded her of the sound of Savannah's West Indian bangle bracelets as she tapped on the beauty shop door. But that was many years ago. Savannah had opened her own beauty shop in Mississippi, and when Gilda last heard from her, Savannah's hair no longer needed to be bleached white. Gilda reached up, pulling down the ponderous metal gate that protected the theater in a fluid motion.

"Let me help with that."

Only mildly surprised to hear Julius' voice, Gilda did not turn.

"Thanks," she said softly, and continued tugging the rusted metal grill. He smiled when it clanged to the ground. Gilda tossed him one of the padlocks, and they knelt to secure the gate. His back was schoolmaster straight as he struggled with the stiff, old locks. She liked him: he was an efficient company manager who had a feel for what would and would not work for a small group with little money. He didn't treat the actors like self-indulgent children nor the technicians like a nuisance.

"All set. Now how about a drink?" Julius said, breaking into Gilda's thoughts.

"Why didn't you go along with the others?"

"It didn't seem right, leaving the stage manager here alone to lock up while we were celebrating a snap first run-through that couldn't have happened without you."

Amusement sparkled in her face as she looked up into his dark brown eyes. He was fairer skinned than she, a slight sprinkling of freckles crossing his nose that matched the brownish-red color of his close-cut nappy hair. The streetlight glinted on the small sapphire shining in his left ear. His shoulders were broad, his waist slim. With his full lips and polished smile he looked more like an actor than an administrator. They walked across 23rd Street to Sixth Avenue and stood on the corner while Julius waited for Gilda to answer his invitation.

"Let's walk a bit," she said. Then, after a block, "There's a cafe just opened on Cornelia Street."

They were silent most of the way. The waning moon cast a soft yellow light over midnight. Gilda was grateful to be moving after sitting in the tiny lighting booth for three hours during the rehearsal. She savored the feel of the night air on her face and smiled at being alive – still. The shine in Julius' eyes rivaled the other light as he took her arm.

Once they were seated in the restaurant he felt familiar, as Aurelia had, and Gilda relaxed into the comfort. He ordered a cappuccino before saying, "Tell me something."

"Yes, what?"

"Anything. Like where you're from. What you want to do. How'd we end up working our asses off for this little white theater company when we're supposed to be about nation-building?" He laughed wryly at the wilted sound of the rhetoric.

"In my father's house there are many mansions."

"Oh god, a Baptist!"

The young, white waiter didn't bother to look at them as he delivered their order. He sniffed sharply at the sound of their laughter, then turned on his heel, looking like an eager actor. It was amazing to Gilda how they all seemed to struggle to achieve the same trim body, coiffured hair, and characterless movement, yet still hoped to be different from each other. Since her arrival in the City she had watched them auditioning for each of the three shows she'd worked on – young, stunning, transitory good looks full of edgy ambition. They, more than anyone else, reminded her of the difference between herself and mortals.

She almost laughed when she thought of that word – *mortals*. It had taken many years before she was able to make the distinction in her thoughts, and the demarcation still felt fussy at times, not quite uncrossable.

"I was hoping for something a little more specific."

"What's to know?" came her sharp response. "I come from a small town in Mississippi no one has ever heard of and doesn't even exist anymore. Not even as a bus stop. I love the theater. I write songs. The world is the world. That's why we're here. When we get tired of it, we'll do something else."

"That cuts the conversation, doesn't it."

Gilda immediately regretted being so abrupt. But looking across the table she found it hard to really see him. His separateness as mortal felt like an impenetrable curtain between them, one she wished didn't exist.

"Not really, it's only the variations that make the human story interesting, right?" She strained across the table trying to reignite his enthusiasm. "I mean, it's the same ones over and over again. But the specifics are what make Baldwin different from Hemingway or Shakespeare or Hansberry. Why do you feel uncomfortable being with a white company?" she asked with genuine curiosity.

"I made all the sit-ins for the movement. While I was in college, protest was practically a credit course! Suddenly I look up and find all my dashikis folded at the bottom of a trunk and I'm helping to manage money for a group of middle-class white kids who want to play theater."

Gilda sensed there was more, so she let the rattling noises of other customers fill the air as Julius shifted in his seat, uncomfortable with the casual way white patrons coming in tried to size them up. Dangerous? Noisy? Exotic?

"I decided to leave off reading the papers 'til the end of the day. I get so P.O.'d I can't get my feet under me, you know? And then I go there and I like it – the work, most of the folks. But shit, man . . ."

Gilda understood: Attica filled the headlines. She, too, tried to push the news of death out of her mind. She'd seen the pictures of inmates killing and being killed, lined up in the prison yard, and the image was always the same as her memories of the slave quarters: dark men with eyes full of submission and rage. Their bodies plumped with bullets were the same ashen color as those fallen beside the trees to which they had been tied as punishment. She understood his restless anxiety.

"I know people from other companies, black companies. The New Lafayette folks are still around."

"Whoa! You know the New Lafayette?" he asked incredulously.

"Of course. They were the reason I first came to the City. I thought those guys were going to change the world. The rituals, the spirit. They held black life in their hands; they reached inside me in a way. . ."

Julius was eager to pursue. "Did you see *To Raise the Dead and* –"

"*Foretell the Future!*" Gilda broke in and they finished in unison, excited by their memories.

"So what happened to those guys?" Julius continued. "I mean, not all of them could be dying to go to Hollywood. It's like they just evaporated."

"They wanted to work like everybody else, I suppose. And white people stopped feeling guilty and donating money. Most of the men we marched with ran out of liberation ideas. They had a big dream about black men being free, but that's as far as it went. They really didn't have a full vision – you know, women being free, Puerto Ricans being free, homosexuals being free. So things kind of folded in on top of themselves."

"Shit, who the hell's got time for all that . . ."

"Ask the folks you don't hang out with after run-throughs who's got time for all that. You think these companies breeze through life on righteousness? I had a friend, a brilliant woman who devoted her life to a little black company, doing the scut work, the kind that's just got to get done and nobody's willing to pay for it. She figured the brothers would be ready when nation time came. She worked like crazy: grant applications, giving advice backstage when directors got stuck, and housecleaning when they said they were too busy to get to the theater on time. But when nation time came she might as well have been wearing a sheet! Grant money went to every brother in the place but not to her. A row of cotton is a row of cotton, so if you think she felt any different from how you feel, you haven't really been thinking." Gilda was surprised at the depth of her own feelings, about the disappointment she had seen on the faces of black women over the years.

"Damn, hold up. I get it. I ain't hardly trying to say that."

Gilda didn't really hear Julius. She struggled to keep herself from slipping backward into the past. The hot rows, their leafy stalks licking at her legs, the heavy sun overhead. Her sisters moved quickly down the rows, making it into a game. She tried to keep up but never could. And the first time she fell into the dirt, face down, almost smothering, she waited for the lash she was accustomed to hearing around her. But her sister's hand had lifted her effortlessly and dragged her along as if she were just another burden like the sack of white cotton.

Looking into Julius' eyes Gilda remembered he could not see these things, and her words felt too sharp. She didn't want to go back into the past; it was too far away, and they were all dead now.

"As long as you, me, and Irene stick with this company it won't just be a group of white kids playing games. Irene is supposed to direct a play next season," Gilda added.

"Yeah, I know. I guess I wasn't prepared. Fisk is a far throw from Manhattan and I miss it. You know how it is, you fall into a groove and the roll is long."

"You better catch a new groove!" She thought for a moment she had been too sharp again.

But then he laughed and said, "Power to the people!" and the past was in its proper place.

"I suppose you want to go somewhere they can pay you a living wage. A bourgeois wage. What do you want to do with all this experience?"

"Right now I want to just hang with you." Gilda looked at Julius, taking in all that made him who he was. There was a calm assurance in his manner. Also a tentative nature about him that could be read as aloofness. His eyes told her he was lonely in the City. Being with her now was something he had wanted for a long while. And something else she couldn't yet decipher.

"Julius, I don't think it would work. I like you, but let's not ruin a good friendship."

She saw pain flicker across his face for an instant before evaporating. Gilda hated the way men shifted gears to protect themselves from humiliation.

"Hey, it was just an idea," he said as if she'd just turned down tickets to a basketball game. He started to pick up his cup, but Gilda held his eyes, probing to see exactly what he felt. The camouflage and subterfuge were sometimes too exhausting for her.

Her gaze caught him up short and revealed his sadness. She saw how alone he really was. His parents were dead; he had no close relatives. Having nothing to keep him in the South, he had come to New York City. Gilda was the first person he'd reached out to in the two years since his arrival. In spite of his cynicism about working with a white theater company, Julius was eager, just as Aurelia had been. He sustained a vision of the world made better in part by his efforts and those of people he respected. Gilda shuffled back through her memories of his interactions with the company, the director and actors. She recalled his swift expertise and grace. He was young yet not easily intimidated. His sense of self was strong, but for the moment he was adrift, needing a friend more than a lover.

She slipped back, releasing the gentle hold she'd had on him and letting him regather his thoughts, then said, "I've got a great and longtime friend who owns a bar in Soho. Will you go with me sometime? We can collect old actor stories and drink fine wine. You tell me your problems, I'll tell you mine."

"Did you know it, you're a poet?" Julius responded with a wide smile, as eager as Gilda not to lose the friendship they were building.

She said good night to him on the corner of Seventh Avenue and Christopher

Street. Gilda walked north to her small garden apartment in Chelsea, wondering how Julius had survived the harshness of the city. The relationship he fantasized between them could never be, yet his loneliness drew her. It mirrored Aurelia's melancholy in some ways, but was more profound; somehow it suited him in spite of his struggle against it.

As she got to her door she put Julius out of her thoughts. She resisted the confusion he stirred in her, deciding he was best considered when she was among friends. Once out of her workshirt and square-cut painter's pants, she curled up in the large overstuffed armchair that sat in her small living room. Heavy velvet curtains shut out the drafts and what light there was outside. She pulled out her old copy of the *Tao Te Ching*. Lao-Tsu's laconic writings lay gracefully before her. She took comfort in knowing that she could read the calligraphy characters as easily now as did contemporaries of Confucius in the sixth century B.C. The pen strokes were warm and familiar: *The nameless is the beginning of heaven and earth. The named is the mother of ten thousand things.*

The delicate figures did not soothe her restlessness. She looked at the clock: it was only 2:00 A.M. Gilda did not have to be at the theater again until six in the evening; the hours yawned before her. So much time. She considered dressing once more and going over to Sorel's club. There were sure to be a couple of her friends there about this time, others like herself who slept through the day and lived at night. The disparate, tiny group who formed a makeshift family were always there.

But she had little patience for idle conversation and was uncertain whether she was ready to discuss her feelings with Anthony and Sorel. The urge to simply escape, to leave and forget the world here for a while, hovered over her. But the play was opening in a couple of weeks. She couldn't go away for at least two months.

She expelled a sharp breath of frustration. How good it would feel to go to San Francisco, she thought. She missed walking the streets of the city, feeling its age and newness, the history curled around her there. It was as far into the past as she ever ventured. And there was an ease among the people. One that Sorel, during his decade here, had not yet been successful in transplanting to the east.

Here she felt smothered by ambition. Recognizing the absence of that in Julius made Gilda smile. She closed the book and went out into the postage-stamp garden. Because most of the businesses closed up shop at dinnertime, and there were few habitable apartment buildings, the area was quiet at night. Gilda's tenement, owned by her holding company, in turn owned by her investment company, was similiar to those around it, except the heat and hot water always worked and the sidewalk was clean. It contained a mix of Americana: Francisco, a Dominican cab driver; Danny, an Irish man who had been the building's superintendent for fifteen years, his wife Tillie, and their stream of grandchildren; Rodney, the black actor who went off to his job at the Transit Authority every morning and returned in the evening with his dance bag over his shoulder; and Marcie, a young Puerto Rican who lived just above Gilda. He was the only actual friend she had in the building. Marcie had invited her up a couple of times and she'd accepted without thinking twice. When she sat on his studio couch, enveloped in the Indian bedspread and fluffy pillows, she realized how difficult his charade was. During the day he was Marc at his job at the telephone company. He had been one of the first male operators and wore it like a badge of honor. But what he wore best were sable eyelashes and capri pants.

"I'm a free man. What I wear is my business!" she heard him shout after slamming his door behind a quickly departing relative. He and Gilda had been on good terms ever since then.

Except for his younger sister who slipped downtown to visit him on holidays, his family had generally stopped speaking to him years before. Gilda knew he welcomed neighborly intimacy as much as she did.

Gilda gazed up at the stars and then turned to look at Marcie's window. The shades were drawn, but she could see a glimmer of red light underneath. He must have company, she thought, and dropped the idea of visiting him. He always went out by himself at the beginning of the evening but inevitably had someone with him when he returned home. In the morning, by choice, he was usually alone again. They had spent many mornings together over the coffee whose aroma enticed Gilda even though she never drank it.

She considered Marcie for a long time when thinking who might want to join her in her life. He was strong, directed, devoted. But Gilda saw him, like Aurelia, too tied to the life of the present. His world was now, not the expanse of time between now and the future. She tried to envision Julius against such a horizon.

Gilda felt impatient with her self-indulgence. Either use the time or leave it alone, she demanded of herself. She couldn't understand why Julius upset her so much. It was certainly not the first time a man had propositioned her. She passed off their suggestions so easily, though, that they usually never remembered they had made them. What was upsetting her then? Gilda found her comfort with women. That was just the way it was. Julius was full of the manufactured responses that men somehow inherit from their dead mothers and fathers. Damn! He still reached out to her through the night air.

Gilda went back inside and slipped into her jeans and T-shirt. She pulled a sweater over her head, relocked her front door, and started walking south. She was seated in Sorel's rear booth before she realized she was going there. Anthony stood formally beside the table looking much as he had when they first met – somewhat pale, wiry, his large hands preternaturally still at his sides. He looked like a student, yet Gilda felt as if she had returned home to her teacher.

"I'm afraid you've arrived much before Sorel. He will not be back with us for a week, perhaps two."

"I know, Anthony. I just wanted to be here. To see you."

"Splendid. May I bring you a bottle then? Sorel has been hoarding things for you to try since you've not been to visit us in so long."

"Only if you'll sit with me for a while."

Anthony nodded, then turned to the tall door at the back of the pub where Sorel kept his personal favorites stored. As often happened Gilda was comforted by the ease with which Anthony, Sorel, and she had become accustomed to the new manners the world had to offer.

In many ways the mores of this time were much more complex, obscure – there was a great deal of room for surprise. She looked around her. Here she was not an object of curiosity as she had been long ago. Some of those present she knew and nodded to; but they, sensing her desire to be alone with Anthony, remained at their own tables. The sound of the room was much softer than the one in which she first sat with Sorel. Few mortals came here, and there was no gambling room – only a long bar, a few booths, and a billiard table. The bartender raised his glass in her direction, and she smiled in easy camaraderie. Anthony returned and opened a bottle of wine, a burgundy, and described how Sorel had expanded his wine holdings in that region.

"What, no champagne tonight?"

"I've tried to make Sorel understand it's an overrated drink. For years he's humored me, but still he loves those bubbles. I, myself, prefer a hearty drink that stays with you through the chill of night." With that Anthony poured the dark red wine into wide-mouthed glasses, then sat across from Gilda in the high-backed booth.

They sipped silently, with Anthony only muttering a small sound of appreciation. Gilda spoke before she knew exactly what was going to be said, in much the same way as she had unwittingly discovered herself in front of the club. "I have a friend, a young man, I think I'd like to bring with me to Sorel's homecoming gathering."

Anthony did not rush in with words but waited for Gilda to continue. She reached across the table and poured more wine for them both.

"I really look forward to Sorel's report from New Zealand. I expect he and Bird have caused quite a stir among the landowners there. I wish Bird were returning with him. Anyway, my friend is a young man a bit at odds with himself right now, but I would really like you to meet him." Her voice trailed off to a whisper. Then she said, "And I'm afraid. I can't have another loss like Aurelia or Eleanor."

Anthony reached across the polished wood of the table and rubbed one finger across Gilda's hand, whose fingers were wound tightly around the bowl of her glass.

"And this friend has a name?"

"Julius."

"He takes a place in your heart?"

"As a friend, yes. I feel none of the overwhelming rush of desire that blurred my vision with Eleanor. Nor much of the foreboding that stifled me with Aurelia. But I'm still uncertain. It would be so easy to make a mistake, to cause such horror. I won't do that." She could feel the fear rise in her throat and knew that Anthony sensed it.

"Did you know that before the end, Eleanor came to see Sorel almost every evening? It was quite sweet, actually. She would sit at his table after you moved east and simply look out with him at the many people who visited the salon. They spoke often of her childhood when they first met. And he talked with her of Europe. She developed a consuming desire to visit just from those conversations. It seemed a refreshing change had set in, for a few years at least. Sorel thought she was trying to find peace. Your stay with us forced her to face something none of us had been able to. Her creation was a mistake, and she continued to contribute to the bitterness that surrounded her. She took no responsibility for her life. I think Eleanor came to see what a waste that was. Sorel was really very happy to spend that time with her."

"Yet she took the true death."

"Yes, but not, I think, because of any mistake in judgment on Sorel's part. But rather on her own. She knew she had done a foolish thing with Samuel and his wife. She had set something in motion that would haunt her always, and Samuel would never relent as long as he lived. Her decision to take the true death was a decision not to destroy him. She said as much before it was done. She asked of you on occasion," Anthony finished in a soft voice.

Gilda felt a nervous chill slip down her back. She took a large sip from the glass of wine. "But Sorel has been devastated by her death. How can you speak of it so simply? I'm sure he's not feeling the easy relief you seem to think."

"I don't presume any easy relief. Sorel has his grief, as do we all. But he'll not be ended by it. He can live with his mistakes in judgment. If you're not willing to take that chance, then you must reconsider how you will spend the coming years."

After a while he spoke again. "I imagine you feel some degree of disloyalty to Bird in your desire to bring one among us. This is unnecessary. I'm sure Bird would say the same thing to you if you gave her a chance."

"You may be right. I still feel stuck, as if I were part of a wheel spinning in place. Knowing the right thing to do. . ."

"Stop trying to make the perfect move; trust your instincts more. You've been through quite a bit in the past years. I'm sure you're as good a student as you've always been."

"I can't be a student for all my time!"

"We are students for all our time if we're lucky enough to know it. But that doesn't mean you wait for Bird to grant you some dispensation before you really live. She can be mother, father, sister, lover – but she cannot create the family for you. You are part of our family and you will create others to be a part of it. This is no one's mission but your own."

"When she came to me in Boston I believed she would stay."

"Even when she said she would not?"

"Yes."

"You think of it as running away from you. For her it may simply have been running to other things that are most important. You were on your own, your world set. For Bird the world is travel, pulling together the strands of knowledge about her nation, other people from whom she's been separated. You are a part of her life, but Woodard's is gone; it will never be again."

"That day in the farmhouse, when I lay in the bed waiting for Bird to come back from Woodard's, my greatest fear was that she would decide not to complete the process, that she'd leave me to the mortal life. I was certain I'd never learn to live in the world I'd come to know. It was the most fear I had ever experienced, apart from the constancy of terror that was plantation life."

"But she didn't. She knew this life was one in which you would excel, she knew you'd learn to be. . .as we are, a living history. You don't need Bird at your side to be this. You need only look forward, just as you did the day you decided to escape the plantation."

Gilda didn't respond. Anthony went on as if she had.

"Since there's no overwhelming reason not to, why not bring this Julius to

Sorel's welcome-home party. You're bound to see more clearly after drinking that silly champagne all evening." The smile gleaming on Anthony's face made Gilda laugh. They didn't speak of Julius anymore as they sipped the wine. Gilda left through the heavy oak door.

She walked east enjoying the coolness of the night air as it invited the morning. When she stood in front of Julius' apartment she looked up at the ancient building adorned with peeling fire escapes. East First Street was almost deserted, and the streetlamps glared and sparkled on the broken glass in the gutters. A *walk-up, no doubt*, she thought.

Gilda easily coaxed the ineffectual lock open and entered his apartment. It was clean and orderly despite the crumbling state of the building. His desk was covered with neat stacks of papers, and books stood lined up in rows. Julius, lying naked under a blanket on a mattress on the floor, shifted uneasily in his sleep. Looking down at him it was easy to see what a child he was. The beard that grew in during the night was soft on his chin, and the whiteness of his teeth was inviting under his partially opened lips. His reverie was of her as she entered the dream.

She glanced at a family snapshot that sat framed beside the bed and at the large posters of Angela Davis, Ché Guevera, and Malcolm X that hung on the walls. She pulled the covers from Julius' body. He stirred, opened his eyes, and she caught him in a gaze he couldn't break.

"The dream doesn't have to end," she said softly, then lay down beside him, touching her fingers to his skin as lightly as the years touched her unlined face. She held him in her arms and kissed his full lips, listening to his satisfied murmurs. His eyes closed again, convinced this was a dream. She ran her hands across his body making his flesh tingle. Julius held her tightly, his lips seeking hers. His body responded as a man's, and she lay across his lean thighs and chest providing a comforting sensation. Her hands were as hypnotic as her eyes. As the moment approached when his mind provided the gratification his body hungered for, she sliced across the flesh of his neck with her fingernail and watched the blood ease slowly to the surface.

She pressed her lips eagerly to the wound and drew the life from him as his body exploded with the joy of his imagination. She listened inside of him and was surprised to see the image of the snapshot that sat atop the stack of books beside his bed. She stopped as she felt his pulse weaken, held her hand on his chest, and lifted herself away from his body to ease his breathing. He relaxed into satisfaction. She spoke soft, hypnotic words in his ear until his breathing became regular.

"Good-bye, sweet baby," she whispered.

Gilda was back on the street in only a few moments and inside her apartment so quickly it felt as if she had never left. She slipped out of her clothes and took a quick shower. The running water made her slightly uncomfortable even though she'd lined the walls with the Mississippi earth she carried everywhere with her. The towel felt good against her skin, and she had no regrets. He would wake in the morning satisfied, as would she, and both could still be separate.

She pulled the silk comforter over her naked body; the earth lining the bed frame beneath her felt cool and familiar. Gilda tried to remember what her family had been like. She was Tack's child. She knew that wasn't her father's real name but one they called him because he was so good with horses. He worked in the tack house and had been sold away before she was born. Her mother's face was the only one she remembered clearly. Everyone said that, unlike her nine sisters, Gilda resembled her mother. She had been rather tall, her smooth dark-brown skin topped by a full head of thick hair she was endlessly trying to manage so it would not be an embarrassment to the mistress. She worked inside the house, unusual for a woman of her deep color. Her skills with herbs, in addition to her cooking, made them reluctant to lose her to the fields and the sun.

Instead she died from the influenza she caught taking care of one of the endless white women who got sick. Knowing she was now just another slave, likely to be sold away, Gilda had run. She wasn't sure what *sold away* meant except that she would disappear like her father had. She regretted leaving her sisters but knew it would only be a matter of time before they'd be sold away too. That had been so long ago.

Gilda remained as determined to survive now as she had then. She knew about the empires of black people in Mali and Ghana, and although there didn't seem to be much hope at the moment, she would wait and work and move around the world toward the future. As she looked in the mirror, seeing her mother's eyes staring back out at her was comforting. Bird's presence in her walk, the sound of Bernice's laughter in her own, all made the connection to life less tenuous. Finding those she loved within herself eased the passage of time.

Life was indeed interminable. The inattention of her contemporaries to some mortal questions, like race, didn't suit her. She didn't believe a past could, or should, be so easily discarded. Her connection to the daylight world came from her blackness. The memories of her master's lash as well as her mother's face, legends of the Middle Passage, lynchings she had not been able to prevent, images of black women bent over scouring brushes – all fueled her ambition. She had been attacked more than once by men determined that she die, but of course she had not. She felt their hatred as personally as any mortal. The energy of the struggles of those times sustained her, somehow.

Gilda tried to rest now. This was not really sleep, not until that final time when the earth or sea would close around her and the fragments of her body.

She wondered why Julius had no brothers or sisters. Why he'd been left so unequivocally alone in the world. The movements of the sixties had fueled Julius' vision of the future, too, but to Gilda, George Jackson's death this past September signaled the end of that era. Angela was somewhere out there alone now with a cause but no community. The horror of slavery appeared to reap endless returns.

Gilda recognized her repeated attempts to grasp what the right step might be. Her need to shrug off human entrapments was strong, but her bond with the past life was deeper. She shoved the thoughts out of her mind, burying the turmoil they caused by promising herself a trip to the West Coast no matter how she managed it.

The darkness of her room was complete. No shadows played behind the locked door. Everything was still above her as she lay in her restless tomb. *To die but not to perish is to be eternally present.* The words of the *Tao* played in her mind, lulling her into sleep. She succumbed to the silence of dawn while the world around her prepared to awaken.

* * *

During a break in rehearsal, one week before the play's opening night, Gilda ran through the words to a song she was writing at the same time as she scanned the production book checking the light and sound cues. She glanced down at the cast milling around restlessly as the director worked to reblock an actor's movement. The route from one chair to another became everyone's focus as they weighed what effect the minute changes would have on their positions. The play was a political polemic full of naive hope and loud music, not unlike many others that were playing the off-Broadway boards at the time.

Denise, the dance captain, was a brilliant dancer and charismatic singer. David, the second male lead, was a born comedian. But the play itself was just a sketch.

The director had been invited by the company partly because of the name he had made directing a popular antiwar musical, and also because word was out that he was in emotional trouble. He had been replaced on a Broadway-bound production the year before. Those were just the qualities that made him irresistible to this anarchistic little group. Gilda sensed him flounder for a second under the pressure to make a quick, clean decision about the moves.

She called out from the booth, "Excuse me, Charles, but Equity rules say they have a break about now."

There was laughter in her voice. They all knew times when they'd worked hours on end, eating hurriedly only when their characters were not required on stage.

Charles was grateful for the interruption and replied, "Well, if we must bow to the tyranny of the masses, I'll spring for coffee." Someone took orders for the run to the deli, Gilda untangled her legs from the wires, and Sonia, who worked the sound, climbed down from the booth. Julius stood at the bottom of the ladder, a tentative smile on his face.

"You going out for something to eat?"

"No, I want to talk to Charles about the blocking problem."

"How about later after the rehearsal?"

"Not tonight, Julius, rain check." Gilda walked away, cautiously ignoring the look of disappointment on his face.

That night, after the gate had been drawn, Gilda headed downtown, enjoying the brisk air and trying to wipe the memory of Julius' face from her mind. She crossed 14th and walked until coming to West Street. Men's bars studded the neighborhood, sleazy landmarks in the crumbling dock area. Gilda rarely ventured to this part of the City. Its aura of danger – the excitement and pain – was not usually appealing to her. She crossed under the West Side Highway to the piers where young men, most trimly bearded, paraded to entice other men. There was danger in taking blood here: the men's bodies were frequently saturated with drugs and alchohol, and Gilda didn't know with what or how much. But tonight, danger was all that would satisfy her.

She walked stiff and wide-legged with her hands in her pockets so that no one would notice her womanhood. She passed a middle-aged white man who hurried toward the street, tucking in his blue button-down shirt and closing a vest over his slightly bulging belly. He looked backward over his shoulder quickly, as if the man who had just given him pleasure would leap on his back to destroy him at any moment. Gilda saw the young man with curly hair leaning against the pilings, rinsing his mouth with beer from a bottle, then spitting into the Hudson. He poured some beer on his hands, wiped them on his denims, and started toward the street. Almost without hesitation he popped a pill into his mouth, washing it down with the last of the beer. The bottle crashed into the abandoned warehouse building behind him.

As the glass tinkled among the other broken bottles, he noticed Gilda coming toward him. He walked a little taller, eager to check out the new figure. Just as he realized she was a woman, Gilda caught him with her eyes. No, tonight was not a night of love. It was a night of feeding.

Gilda held him in her gaze and wiped his mind clear. His eyes opened wide, unseeing, as she pushed him backward into the shadows of the shell-shocked warehouse. She turned his face to the wall, pulling the jacket away from his back and neck with an easy rip. She pressed his body hard against the rough building and sliced open the skin on his neck. He moaned slightly as he felt the pressure against his body. Gilda took his blood easily, barely thinking of what might be in his mind. A small thing, actually. He wanted to visit a friend who was sick but somehow never found the motivation. He felt guilty. Gilda took her share of the blood, and by the time she released him, his resolve to make the visit was firm. The drug that diluted his blood pulsed through Gilda's veins, light exploded in her head, and her breathing raced dangerously. She didn't care. She just wanted to forget her own indecision and the boy who sold his body on a crumbling dock.

She pulled back and held her hand over the wound. Her eyes were out of focus and her hand leaden with what she was sure were depressants. Reaching into the front pocket of his jeans she found a slender ampule. His breathing was shallow and didn't improve, so she flipped off its cap and passed the popper quickly beneath his nose. His heart rate quickened, and soon his pulse rose. His body stiffened in its struggle to consciousness. She threw the container over her shoulder into the river and left him there, against the building, clinging to life with tenacity. Gilda ran quickly, even though the drug made her feel stiff and uncertain.

Once free of the area she walked more slowly, looking at the people on the street and enjoying the movement of the lights. She could hear sounds coming from the buildings around her as if they were programmed through a stereo in her ear. The music from a penthouse above was as clear as the clink of dishes in the storefront diner. She arrived home, took a shower, and tried to wash away the smell of the city.

Gilda sat outside in the back, watching the stars and listening to the music from Marcie's place, where tonight a blue light glowed. That meant he had more than one guest with him. She heard the laughter and salsa floating down. Gilda wondered if the boy on the dock came home to friends such as these – unexpected and challenging. She watched the stars until they faded and dawn started to take over the sky.

The show opened a week later. So few things went wrong that Charles was triumphant and the cast confident they would run forever. At the cast party they milled around Charles' West 97th Street apartment, reliving special moments, releasing the tension that had been stored for weeks. Gilda sat at a narrow counter watching the young faces. She was pleased with the show – it made a statement and showed off good talent. The group sat stroking each other's egos for getting this far. Critics would be coming in three days, so the edge was not completely off, but they were good and they knew it. Julius came around to the back of the counter and offered to pour her a drink. Gilda declined and turned back to the rest of the group. Night sparkled outside the large uncurtained windows as Julius stood sipping from a large glass of scotch.

"Drinking alcohol is not good for you," Gilda teased with a little smile. He ignored the remark, and they were silent again. Then Julius said, "I had a dream about you the other night. You came to my pad and woke me up to make love to me. I was. . .well. . .happy. But then you left and I couldn't breathe. I thought I was dying. I couldn't wake myself up and kept calling you, begging you not to leave me there, dying, but I couldn't get the words out."

Gilda sat very still staring past Julius at the photograph of Greta Garbo on the wall behind him. When she caught his eyes they were pinpoints of curiosity. She looked around the room feeling him holding on to her.

"I know you're trying to keep from getting into something with me. I'm not a complete fool, sisterlove. You made yourself pretty clear. But I've got to let you know how it is for me. I can't imagine life without you somewhere near me. If it's as a friend and not a lover, then let it be that. Just don't ice me out."

Gilda watched him sip from his glass. "Are you so alone in the world that you need to settle?"

"I'm not settling. My mother used to say that one good friend is worth a thousand. . .well you know. I don't want to lose our friendship when the show's over or the company's gone or I find another job."

"You don't understand what it means to be my friend."

"Maybe not, but give me a chance to deal with it. Nothing I do in this business or my career means anything if I spend my life alone. You don't understand that, do you?"

For a moment Gilda heard Skip's voice that evening in the Cape Cod cottage when he assured them he wasn't using drugs, that he had nothing to apologize for. His voice and Julius' became one in their urgency.

"I understand being alone better than you can ever imagine. I've learned to appreciate being alone and how to choose one's companions carefully." Her words made Julius' brown skin flush pink, showing up the dark freckles.

The life I offer is not for you. I feel for you as I would if I had a brother I loved. Trust that no matter where you are in this world if you ever need my help, it is only for you to ask and I will be at your side. In that we will never be separate.

With these words, Gilda remembered the last time she made this promise. The forlorn acceptance that had shone in Aurelia's eyes was all Gilda had asked for. Julius couldn't offer such acquiescence, but surprised at the outpouring, tears welled in his eyes. He blinked to hold them back, then looked quickly about the room.

No one hears. The words are for you alone, Gilda said.

It was then Julius realized that her lips had not moved. He had heard her clearly nonetheless. She slid from the bar stool and walked toward Charles, standing alone near the table laden with bread and cheese. She made her good-byes quickly, then left, eager to be rid of the brightly lit room and Julius' need.

As Gilda walked toward Broadway she knew that if it were possible for her to cry, she would be doing so now. She turned downtown looking forward to the distracting sights between the Upper West Side and Chelsea. At 96th Street she was fascinated by the glare of the Red Apple supermarket and the newsstand bursting with publications. Couples speaking in the frenzied Spanish of the City congregated in front of the dance hall located above the heavily shuttered jewelry store. The Riviera and Riverside movie theaters were the only things that stood silent at this intersection.

She didn't stop at 95th Street, only glanced up at the dark marquee of the Thalia. The ubiquitous *Jules et Jim* was playing. Gilda wondered idly how many times she'd seen it. It was on the bill with *Ship of Fools*. It must be Oskar Werner week, she thought, just as Julius stopped beside her, short of breath. He stood in her path, blocking light from the corner liquor store.

"You understand me so well. . .feel so much for me, but you walk away. I can't accept it," Julius said, not entirely certain now that he'd heard her earlier words.

"You have no choice," Gilda said, her anxiety making her impatient. He grabbed her arm. "Please." The word was simple and plaintive. His hand on her arm was strong and urgent, but she broke his grip with little effort.

"Why can't it be different? How do you know?" His voice was childlike as he faced this complete unknown. The strength in it demanded that she answer honestly.

"Don't interfere with me. It's my decision. That's all I have to say to you!" Her eyes and her voice were mesmerizing. She left him standing puzzled and hurt on the corner as she made her way to Riverside Drive. She walked hurriedly downtown, her pace so quick that those nearby never saw her.

She rushed into her apartment, locked the door, and went out to the backyard, turning for solace to the endless, familiar stars. They were friends that had lasted through time with her. The window opened behind her, and Marcie called down from his apartment.

"Hey girl, what the hell you doin' out there? Come on up and get a drink."

"No, thanks. I've had enough for tonight. You having a party?"

"Naw, those punks left already. I'm just watching the late movie. You wanna watch some TV?"

Gilda walked over to the second floor window so she wouldn't have to shout. "No, I'm going to relax for a while. Opening nights are always like the end of a race."

"Was it good?"

"Yes," Gilda responded, letting her pleasure surface. "When you want to see it I'll reserve a couple of comps for you."

Marcie's brown eyes sparkled.

"Hey, hey yeah, how about Saturday? Can we come on Saturday?"

"Sure, I'll leave two tickets for you at the box."

"Yeah, girl, I'll dress up real sharp, you know! Let it all hang out!"

"You'll like the show, too. Just don't bring any stuffy types, you know. . .politics. . ."

"Honey, I got principles. I got to know how you vote before you take off your coat!"

As Marcie closed his window and went back to the television Gilda marveled at the clarity of his world. She had never met anyone quite as satisfied as Marcie was with the decisions he made in life. Gilda went back inside and settled down with a book, certain that rest would completely elude her.

On the night of Sorel's welcome-home party, Gilda took a change of clothes to the theater. She was getting rid of her sweaty jeans and T-shirt in the women's room after the show when she heard Julius call her name outside the door.

"Well, I've got you cornered in there. Everyone's just about gone so no one can rescue you. I'm here to invite you out to a night of frantic disco and assorted other depravities, sisterlove."

His youthful fear was barely concealed behind his bravado. Gilda said nothing and continued to change her clothes, packing her work outfit in a plastic bag to be stowed in the lighting booth.

She opened the bathroom door wearing a mauve jersey blouse and matching pants, soft leather boots, and a hint of lipstick.

"Aw, shit!" was all Julius could manage to say.

"Is that a critical opinion or are you waiting to get in here?" Gilda said with a smile.

"I guess you've already got a date," Julius said, realizing that he'd never seen Gilda wearing anything other than her work clothes.

"In fact I'm going to a party for a dear and old friend of mine," Gilda responded. Having made and remade her mind over the past week a number of times, she finally decided to simply wait and see what the evening brought. There had been no time to speak with Julius during the show, and so she left herself open to whatever happened. She was happy he had sought her out.

"I was going to ask if you'd like to come along. Hang out for a while. It's a rather old crowd, a kind of a white crowd, so there won't be much discoing. But I would love you to meet Sorel and Anthony."

The confusion was swept from Julius' face by a smile. "Right on! I'm down. But do I need to change? I probably should."

"You look fine. You always dress like you're ready to meet somebody's parents anyway."

She let Julius climb up the ladder and toss her bag of clothes into the lighting booth before they pulled down the heavy gate and put on the padlocks. They flagged a taxi and were climbing out in front of Sorel's pub before Gilda really had a chance to think about her decision – or if she had made one. It had been over a year since she last saw Sorel. He'd spent most of the time in New Zealand and she'd been working with the theater. She had avoided talking to him, afraid to hear anything more about Eleanor's death, afraid she would feel, in some part, to blame. Julius grasped her arm gently.

"Are you O.K.?"

"I'm fine. I just realized what a long day this has been. But everything is everything," she said laughing, using a phrase tossed around at the theater. A few minutes later Gilda pushed the heavy oak door open. People looked up as they entered. She heard Sorel's exclamation above everyone's and saw him pull away from his circle of friends. He looked the same, his large body dressed in impeccably tailored clothes, soft, colorful shoes, his eyes sparkling like the champagne he liked so much.

"Ah, my child, we've been waiting."

"Some of us work, you know, at jobs, not globe-hopping." She fell into his arms laughing as he encircled her.

"You call that a job, scampering around on ladders all day and singing all night? You just neglect me because I'm old!"

"Careful how you abuse me; I've brought my boss along to set you straight." Julius grinned and tried not to look embarrassed.

He experienced the slight discomfort he felt when in a room filled almost entirely with white people. Without looking around he could feel their appraisal. He held onto Gilda's hand even as Sorel began pulling her into the room. Julius felt a moment of sharp panic as her hand left his and he stood alone. The others continued to look him over, and some were smiling. He still couldn't quell the cold chill that flooded him. He felt a little dizzy, overwhelmed, but by what he could not tell. Julius jumped at the hand on his arm.

"Come, sit at Sorel's table. Gilda will want to make a proper introduction." He looked down to see a large, pale hand guiding him effortlessly into the room. Anthony tried to soothe Julius' thoughts with his own when he sensed the boy's discomfort.

Once seated beside Gilda he felt less unnerved, especially when she turned her smile on him and introduced him to Sorel and Anthony.

"I'm pleased to meet you. Until today I haven't met any of Gilda's friends, so this is a real treat."

"We're more like family after all this time," Sorel said before turning to Anthony. "Will you bring up that bottle I put to chill earlier?"

Anthony turned away from the table, and Sorel laughed raucously. "He thought my trip might quench my thirst for champagne – he knows nothing of obsession!"

Those around him laughed and turned to their own conversations. When Anthony reappeared Sorel continued. "We, too, have met few of Gilda's recent friends. Let's have a toast. To the family of friends we gather about us. May we live and love eternally!"

He raised his fresh glass toward Julius who took a tall, fluted glass offered by Anthony. The entire room joined in the toast, and the din of conversation rose and fell casually.

"Sorel and Anthony have been my teachers in many things," Gilda said, looking at Julius with an impish glance. Here among these people he thought she seemed younger, almost like a student. The space between them appeared to lessen.

"And you've been ours. Have you ever been to San Francisco, Julius?" Sorel asked.

"No, I just about made it up here to New York. I'm still a country boy."

"Let me tell you of a country!" Sorel responded.

With that began a round of stories about his trip to New Zealand that lasted into the early morning hours. Julius was amazed at the capacity Sorel and Gilda showed for champagne. He stopped drinking sometime after 2:00 A.M. They had both continued and were somehow still coherent. Just before dawn Julius noticed that most of the patrons had departed and the bartender and Anthony had cleaned away the glasses.

"We better be off, my sweet," Gilda said to Julius. He warmed at her affectionate touch and rose from the booth.

"Maybe we could get you to come uptown and see our show," Julius proffered shyly. "It's just an off-Broadway showcase, but we worked pretty hard."

"Do you hear that, Anthony? Shall we get out our theater capes and venture north?" Anthony gave only a brief smile.

"Of course we shall! The cauldron of experimentation, doing away with musty conventions – you name the night and we'll be front row center to shout bravo."

"Please come next weekend, then," Julius responded.

Gilda felt awkward at never having invited Sorel and Anthony herself. It seemed so natural when Julius did it, yet she had never considered letting these worlds intersect, until tonight.

They said their good-byes and stepped out into the deserted street. Julius was about to suggest that they walk west to a street where a cab was more likely to be cruising when one pulled up in front of them, as if summoned. Gilda slipped inside and was quiet on their short ride uptown. She kissed Julius lightly on the cheek when they arrived at his building. He got out and leaned down into the window before the cab could move.

"Thanks for letting me meet your friends. It means a lot to me that you did that. They've got a real family feel, you know?"

"Yes, I guess Anthony and Sorel have been family for me here."

"And this Bird he was talking about. She sounds like a real deal. Like landowners down under may never recover!" Julius laughed with a purity of spirit that thrilled Gilda. "When she lands on these shores again the U.S. government is in deep stew."

Gilda laughed loudly. Through his eyes Gilda saw Bird as the hero her own curiosity made her.

"Catch you later, sisterlove." He tapped the cab, signaling it to pull off, and turned back toward his door.

The next day at the theater a box was delivered for Gilda. When she opened it she found a note from Sorel apologizing for not giving it to her at the party. Nestled in soft tissue paper was a large, flat rock. And in a separately wrapped package there was a note from Bird and an ancient, carved arrowhead. Gilda ran her hands over the cool stone in the privacy of the bathroom and put the letter from Bird in her pocket to be read later at home.

Gilda opened Bird's letter while sitting in the armchair that night. It was a single page crammed with tight script that described where Bird had been living.

The final paragraph turned abruptly:

I suppose you've considered bringing someone into our life. I, too, have thought of this but don't think I'll ever learn to settle down long enough to teach someone in the same way as you've been taught. Sorel and Anthony have been good and constant, but I do worry about you. You must make roots for yourself, for you are my roots. I will be listening for your thoughts and planning to see you before too much time has passed.

Gilda wondered how much of her thinking had aleady found its way to Bird over the past months. She walked outside to the backyard and paced for a minute or two. Marcie's windows were completely dark, and the alley surrounding the yard seemed quiet for a change. She looked up again at the stars, remembering Bird telling her that the stars would be their link. Wherever they were in the world they would look up at the same stars.

Gilda went back inside the apartment, then left through the front door, moving quickly to the Lower East Side. When she let herself into Julius' apartment she discovered he was not there. She sat quietly on the bed and waited. It was almost 1:00 A.M. when he came home. His eyes were gleaming as if he'd had a bit to drink, but he did not move like he was drunk. Gilda remained silent as he took off his leather jacket and laid his briefcase on the desk. Gilda was sitting on the mattress, her eyes closed as if in meditation when he entered the bedroom. Julius wasn't sure he really saw her.

He noted that the curtains were all drawn in the room and that a curious quiet hovered over everything. His confusion kept him from speaking. He stood numbly at the foot of the bed, looking down as she opened her eyes and spoke.

"I don't want to trick you, Julius. Or seduce you. I want you to see the family I bring you into. It's a family that I've belonged to for more than one hundred years, yet I've been alone, too." He felt the gentle pressure of her mind. His guard relaxed, and what she said felt both alien and natural.

"I need an ally, a brother. If you want it, life can be yours, and we will be sister and brother throughout time. Our love will outlast the tears, the plays, the lights, these old buildings. What you must sacrifice may be too much, but once done it is final."

"You're talking some other language."

"Yes, I am," she peered into his eyes, making his mind let go of the world around them. He became open to the words and could understand without her speaking aloud.

He said, "I want to be with you. That's all that's important to me."

"That will not be enough. I'm not offering some melodramatic romance where the audience sighs sweetly at the final curtain."

"I know that."

"But you can't really know, no one can, until it's done. Until it's too late. It is commitment as you've always fantasized it – in college dormitories when you talked of revolution, in the theater when they speak of changing the world. The reality of it can never be as one imagines."

Julius looked both excited and afraid, but the solemnity of Gilda's words were ameliorated by the kind love he saw in her eyes. She both warned and entreated him at the same time. "I offer you the capacity to live on until you decide it is over. There are many who would love you in those years. I am only one," she said in the kindest of voices as she closed her eyes.

Julius knelt on the bed and looked around at the faces on the walls. He took in the books and other little things that identified this as his room. The picture of his mother and father as they had been when first married stood beside his bed as it had all of his life. He had tried to project himself into that photograph so many times since their deaths to recapture the comfort of their love.

Gilda listened patiently to his thoughts and let them evoke the sadness that still rushed in when she thought of those she had once loved who were now dead. She opened her eyes and her arms; Julius lay in them like a child. She ran her fingers gently over his face and neck, enjoying the softness of his skin, smiling at the freckles that marked his nose and cheeks. He raised his hand to her head and thrust his fingers into the short, nappy hair that framed her face, pulling her face down to his. She encircled him with her arms, kissing his eyes and nose. She felt his pulse begin to race as she passed her hand over his chest.

She pressed her lips to his in a gesture that was full of the excitement she'd held inside herself for so long. It was a kiss both passionate and chaste, leaving Julius feeling like a child in her arms, yet still a man. When she sliced the flesh on his neck, he opened his eyes in shock but did not try to pull away. His body trembled, then lay still, as the life drained from him into her. Gilda stopped, bit her own tongue, and kissed him hard, breaking the skin inside his lip. She thrust her tongue into his mouth.

He took back his blood, now mixed with hers, gagging on its sweet texture. Gilda pulled back again – two times more – to draw the blood from the wound in his neck. Each time she took him closer to the edge of life, letting Julius feel that perimeter and the abyss beyond it. She drew out his life and waited for him to make a sign of protest. If he did she would leave him to his life and wipe these moments from his mind. But he only opened wider for her. His eyes lost their focus, and his body was limp. Gilda pulled her shirt from her chest and sliced an opening below her breast. She pressed Julius to her, waiting to feel the power of his mouth taking in the life she offered.

He began to suck at the blood insistently, finally understanding the power that moved between them. Electricity surged through him. His head pounded, blocking out all thought until he heard Gilda speaking inside of him.

And what do you leave in exchange? This is your first lesson. You must never take your share of the blood without leaving something of use behind.

Gilda felt his moment of confusion. He'd been lost in the blood and didn't yet understand their way. She repeated her question and was immediately flooded with the sense of well-being only a child can feel when lying in the arms of its parent. She opened her eyes and looked up at the snapshot of Julius' mother, feeling the complete joy he had felt as a child. He left this most exquisite feeling with her, his gift as he pulled back from Gilda's breast. She closed her eyes in joy and held his hand to his wound, letting him help heal it.

She touched her reddened lips to the bridge of his nose and his forehead as she murmured words too soft for anyone in the world to hear. Her thoughts silenced him when he started to speak. *Sleep, there is much to be done tomorrow.*

With her back against a thin pillow she held him until he slept comfortably. Inside his dreams she planted calming thoughts that would hold him in peaceful sleep until she returned. She let herself out, looking up only briefly at his shrouded windows before making her way back to her own apartment. Her mind raced trying to organize the things that had to be done.

She removed two large duffels from her closet. She changed into her boots lined with her native soil and the cloak Sorel had had woven for her by the seamstress who created her new wardrobe years before. It was rare for her to actually spend so much full daylight time out-of-doors. Regular errands that required little effort weren't uncommon, but this trip would use all of Gilda's resources. Deciding not to wait for a taxi, Gilda started for the airport on foot. She could be in Virginia by noon, fill the bags with his Virginia earth, and be back in time for the half-hour call at the theater. As she moved quickly through the City, past the tunnel, the factories, the cemeteries, and shipping firms, she tried to keep her mind only on her destination, but a myriad of thoughts rumbled around inside her with the noise and disturbance of the planes roaring overhead.

She tried to remember her own response to the truth of the choice she had made and to imagine how Julius would react. No matter what he'd said about friendship there might be little solace once he really understood what world he now belonged to. She was taking him away from the life he knew, and she could not provide solid answers to what this life would be.

Words from the *Tao* came to her: *Give up sainthood, renounce wisdom. . .* The airline terminals were just ahead. The simple truth was that it was done.

They would be each other's family now. It's more important to see the simplicity. She could only hope her judgment had been correct – that it was a good choice for Julius as well. She closed the door to doubt and began to anticipate the night when she would have Julius to show the world to. They would care for each other until they returned to the source, the stillness and the movement that is the way of nature. There would be no sad past between them as there still remained with Bird. When they were ready to travel separately they would be certain it was the natural time for that to happen and not filled with shadowy anger or fear.

Her Mississippi soil lay comfortably inside her shoes, protecting her from the weakening properties of daylight. She hummed a soft tune to herself, one her mother had sung while preparing poultices and compounds for the mistress' perpetual headaches. Gilda smiled remembering her mother's dark face and began to laugh to herself as she settled in the plane. She imagined what kind of companion Julius would be – his enthusiasm and idealism just the thing she needed to face eternity. She looked below at the thousands of tiny lights that sparkled in the receding city and remembered the first time she had seen a city shine with electricity. The lights were such a gaudy imitation of the stars. Gilda strained her neck to see out the window through the clouds. But dawn was upon the City, and the stars had moved on. She wondered if Bird was also looking up at them now. She pulled down the window shade and put her head back, listening.

After a moment she heard Bird whispering in her ear. It was a soft murmur of comfort, not words, but sounds meant to elicit ease. Gilda relaxed and sent out her message: *We've finally delivered a brother for me.*

DEATH BY LANDSCAPE

Margaret Atwood

Margaret Atwood (b.1939) was born in Ottawa and grew up in northern
Ontario, Quebec and Toronto. She attended the University of Toronto,
Radcliffe College and Harvard University. Atwood has published over
forty volumes of poetry, children's literature, fiction, and non-fiction. She
is also the author of fourteen novels. Atwood won the 2000 Booker Prize
and the 2001 Dashiell Hammett Prize from the International Association
of Crime Writers for *The Blind Assassin*. She lives in Toronto with her
partner, the writer Graeme Gibson.

Now that the boys are grown up and Rob is dead, Lois has moved to a
condominium apartment in one of the newer waterfront developments.
She is relieved not to have to worry about the lawn, or about the ivy
pushing its muscular little suckers into the brickwork, or the squirrels gnawing
their way into the attic and eating the insulation off the wiring, or about strange
noises. This building has a security system, and the only plant life is in pots in
the solarium.

Lois is glad she's been able to find an apartment big enough for her pictures.
They are more crowded together than they were in the house, but this arrangement gives the walls a European look: blocks of pictures, above and beside one
another, rather than one over the chesterfield, one over the fireplace, one in the
front hall, in the old acceptable manner of sprinkling art around so it does not
get too intrusive. This way has more of an impact. You know it's not supposed
to be furniture.

None of the pictures is very large, which doesn't mean they aren't valuable.
They are paintings, or sketches and drawings, by artists who were not nearly
as well known when Lois began to buy them as they are now. Their work later
turned up on stamps, or as silk-screen reproductions hung in the principals'
offices of high schools, or as jigsaw puzzles, or on beautifully printed calendars
sent out by corporations as Christmas gifts, to their less important clients. These
artists painted mostly in the twenties and thirties and forties; they painted landscapes. Lois has two Tom Thomsons, three A. Y. Jacksons, a Lawren Harris. She
has an Arthur Lismer, she has a J. E. H. MacDonald. She has a David Milne. They
are pictures of convoluted tree trunks on an island of pink wave-smoothed stone,
with more islands behind; of a lake with rough, bright, sparsely wooded cliffs;
of a vivid river shore with a tangle of bush and two beached canoes, one red,
one grey; of a yellow autumn woods with the ice-blue gleam of a pond half-seen
through the interlaced branches.

It was Lois who'd chosen them. Rob had no interest in art, although he could see the necessity of having something on the walls. He left all the decorating decisions to her, while providing the money, of course. Because of this collection of hers, Lois's friends – especially the men – have given her the reputation of having a good nose for art investments.

But this is not why she bought the pictures, way back then. She bought them because she wanted them. She wanted something that was in them, although she could not have said at the time what it was. It was not peace: she does not find them peaceful in the least. Looking at them fills her with a wordless unease. Despite the fact that there are no people in them or even animals, it's as if there is something, or someone, looking back out.

When she was thirteen, Lois went on a canoe trip. She'd only been on overnights before. This was to be a long one, into the trackless wilderness, as Cappie put it. It was Lois's first canoe trip, and her last.

Cappie was the head of the summer camp to which Lois had been sent ever since she was nine. Camp Manitou, it was called; it was one of the better ones, for girls, though not the best. Girls of her age whose parents could afford it were routinely packed off to such camps, which bore a generic resemblance to one another. They favoured Indian names and had hearty, energetic leaders, who were called Cappie or Skip or Scottie. At these camps you learned to swim well and sail, and paddle a canoe, and perhaps ride a horse or play tennis. When you weren't doing these things you could do Arts and Crafts and turn out dingy, lumpish clay ashtrays for your mother – mothers smoked more, then – or bracelets made of coloured braided string.

Cheerfulness was required at all times, even at breakfast. Loud shouting and the banging of spoons on the tables were allowed, and even encouraged, at ritual intervals. Chocolate bars were rationed, to control tooth decay and pimples. At night, after supper, in the dining hall or outside around a mosquito-infested campfire ring for special treats, there were singsongs. Lois can still remember all the words to "My Darling Clementine," and to "My Bonnie Lies Over the Ocean," with acting-out gestures: a rippling of the hands for "the ocean," two hands together under the cheek for "lies." She will never be able to forget them, which is a sad thought.

Lois thinks she can recognize women who went to these camps, and were good at it. They have a hardness to their handshakes, even now; a way of standing, legs planted firmly and farther apart than usual; a way of sizing you up, to see if you'd be any good in a canoe – the front, not the back. They themselves would be in the back. They would call it the stern.

She knows that such camps still exist, although Camp Manitou does not. They are one of the few things that haven't changed much. They now offer copper enamelling, and functionless pieces of stained glass baked in electric ovens, though judging from the productions of her friends' grandchildren the artistic standards had not improved.

To Lois, encountering it in the first year after the war, Camp Manitou seemed ancient. Its log-sided buildings with the white cement in between the half-logs, its flagpole ringed with whitewashed stones, its weathered grey dock jutting out into Lake Prospect, with its woven rope bumpers and its rusty rings for tying up, its prim round flowerbed of petunias near the office door, must surely have been there always. In truth it dated only from the first decade of the century; it had been founded by Cappie's parents, who'd thought of camping as bracing to the character, like cold showers, and had been passed along to her as an inheritance, and an obligation.

Lois realized, later, that it must have been a struggle for Cappie to keep Camp Manitou going, during the Depression and then the war, when money did not flow freely. If it had been a camp for the very rich, instead of the merely well off, there would have been fewer problems. But there must have been enough Old Girls, ones with daughters, to keep the thing in operation, though not entirely shipshape: furniture was battered, painted trim was peeling, roofs leaked. There were dim photographs of these Old Girls dotted around the dining hall, wearing ample woollen bathing suits and showing their fat, dimpled legs, or standing, arms twined, in odd tennis outfits with baggy skirts.

In the dining hall, over the stone fireplace that was never used, there was a huge moulting stuffed moose head, which looked somehow carnivorous. It was a sort of mascot; its name was Monty Manitou. The older campers spread the story that it was haunted, and came to life in the dark, when the feeble and undependable lights had been turned off or, due to yet another generator failure, had gone out. Lois was afraid of it at first, but not after she got used to it.

Cappie was the same: you had to get used to her. Possibly she was forty, or thirty-five, or fifty. She had fawn-coloured hair that looked as if it was cut with a bowl. Her head jutted forward, jiggling like a chicken's as she strode around the camp, clutching notebooks and checking things off in them. She was like their minister in church: both of them smiled a lot and were anxious because they wanted things to go well; they both had the same overwashed skins and stringy necks. But all this disappeared when Cappie was leading a singsong, or otherwise leading. Then she was happy, sure of herself, her plain face almost luminous. She wanted to cause joy. At these times she was loved, at others merely trusted.

There were many things Lois didn't like about Camp Manitou, at first. She hated the noisy chaos and spoon-banging of the dining hall, the rowdy singsongs at which you were expected to yell in order to show that you were enjoying yourself. Hers was not a household that encouraged yelling. She hated the necessity of having to write dutiful letters to her parents claiming she was having fun. She could not complain, because camp cost so much money.

She didn't much like having to undress in a roomful of other girls, even in the dim light, although nobody paid any attention, or sleeping in a cabin with seven other girls, some of whom snored because they had adenoids or colds, some of whom had nightmares, or wet their beds and cried about it. Bottom bunks made her feel closed in, and she was afraid of falling out of top ones; she was afraid of heights. She got homesick, and suspected her parents of having a better time when she wasn't there than when she was, although her mother wrote to her every week saying how much they missed her. All this was when she was nine. By the time she was thirteen she liked it. She was an old hand by then.

* * *

Lucy was her best friend at camp. Lois had other friends in winter, when there was school and itchy woollen clothing and darkness in the afternoons, but Lucy was her summer friend.

She turned up the second year, when Lois was ten, and a Bluejay. (Chicka-dees, Bluejays, Ravens, and Kingfishers – these were the names Camp Manitou assigned to the different age groups, a sort of totemic clan system. In those days, thinks Lois, it was birds for girls, animals for boys: wolves, and so forth. Though some animals and birds were suitable and some were not. Never vultures, for instance; never skunks, or rats.)

Lois helped Lucy to unpack her tin trunk and place the folded clothes on the wooden shelves, and to make up her bed. She put her in the top bunk right above her, where she could keep an eye on her. Already she knew that Lucy was an ex-ception, to a good many rules; already she felt proprietorial.

Lucy was from the United States, where the comic books came from, and the movies. She wasn't from New York or Hollywood or Buffalo, the only American cities Lois knew the names of, but from Chicago. Her house was on the lake shore and had gates to it, and grounds. They had a maid, all of the time. Lois's family only had a cleaning lady twice a week.

The only reason Lucy was being sent to *this* camp (she cast a look of minor scorn around the cabin, diminishing it and also offending Lois, while at the same time daunting her) was that her mother had been a camper here. Her mother had been a Canadian once, but had married her father, who had a patch over one eye, like a pirate. She showed Lois the picture of him in her wallet. He got the patch in the war. "Shrapnel," said Lucy. Lois, who was unsure about shrapnel, was so impressed she could only grunt. Her own two-eyed, unwounded father was tame by comparison.

"My father plays golf," she ventured at last.

"*Everyone* plays golf," said Lucy. "My *mother* plays golf."

Lois's mother did not. Lois took Lucy to see the outhouses and the swimming dock and the dining hall with Monty Manitou's baleful head, knowing in ad-vance they would not measure up.

This was a bad beginning; but Lucy was good-natured, and accepted Camp Manitou with the same casual shrug with which she seemed to accept everything. She would make the best of it, without letting Lois forget that this was what she was doing.

However, there were things Lois knew that Lucy did not. Lucy scratched the tops off all her mosquito bites and had to be taken to the infirmary to be daubed with Ozonol. She took her T-shirt off while sailing, and although the counsellor spotted her after a while and made her put it back on, she burnt spectacularly, bright red, with the X of her bathing-suit straps standing out in alarming white; she let Lois peel the sheets of whispery-thin burned skin off her shoulders. When they sang "Alouette" around the campfire, she did not know any of the French words. The difference was that Lucy did not care about the things she didn't know, whereas Lois did.

During the next winter, and subsequent winters, Lucy and Lois wrote to each other. They were both only children, at a time when this was thought to be a disadvantage, so in their letters they pretended to be sisters, or even twins. Lois had to strain a little over this, because Lucy was so blonde, with translucent skin and large blue eyes like a doll's, and Lois was nothing out of the ordinary – just a tallish, thinnish, brownish person with freckles. They signed their letters LL, with the L's entwined together like the monograms on a towel. (Lois and Lucy, thinks Lois. How our names date us. Lois Lane, Superman's girlfriend, enterprising female reporter; "I Love Lucy." Now we are obsolete, and it's little Jennifers, little Emilys, little Alexandras and Carolines and Tiffanys.)

They were more effusive in their letters than they ever were in person. They bordered their pages with X's and O's, but when they met again in the summers it was always a shock. They had changed so much, or Lucy had. It was like watching someone grow up in jolts. At first it would be hard to think up things to say.

But Lucy always had a surprise or two, something to show, some marvel to reveal. The first year she had a picture of herself in a tutu, her hair in a ballerina's knot on the top of her head; she pirouetted around the swimming dock, to show Lois how it was done, and almost fell off. The next year she had given that up and was taking horseback riding. (Camp Manitou did not have horses.) The next year her mother and father had been divorced, and she had a new stepfather, one with both eyes, and a new house, although the maid was the same. The next year, when they had graduated from Bluejays and entered Ravens, she got her period, right in the first week of camp. The two of them snitched some matches from their counsellor, who smoked illegally, and made a small fire out behind the farthest outhouse, at dusk, using their flashlights. They could set all kinds of fires by now; they had learned how in Campcraft. On this fire they burned one of Lucy's used sanitary napkins. Lois is not sure why they did this, or whose idea it was. But she can remember the feeling of deep satisfaction it gave her as the white fluff singed and the blood sizzled, as if some wordless ritual had been fulfilled.

They did not get caught, but then they rarely got caught at any of their camp transgressions. Lucy has such large eyes, and was such an accomplished liar.

This year Lucy is different again: slower, more languorous. She is no longer interested in sneaking around after dark, purloining cigarettes from the counsellor, dealing in black-market candy bars. She is pensive, and hard to wake in the mornings. She doesn't like her stepfather, but she doesn't want to live with her real father either, who has a new wife. She thinks her mother may be having a love affair with a doctor; she doesn't know for sure, but she's seen them smooching in his car, out on the driveway, when her stepfather wasn't there. It serves him right. She hates her private school. She has a boyfriend, who is sixteen and works as a gardener's assistant. This is how she met him: in the garden. She describes to Lois what it is like when he kisses her – rubbery at first, but then your knees go limp. She has been forbidden to see him, and threatened with boarding school. She wants to run away from home.

Lois has little to offer in return. Her own life is placid and satisfactory, but there is nothing much that can be said about happiness. "You're so lucky," Lucy tells her, a little smugly. She might as well say *boring* because this is how it makes Lois feel.

* * *

Lucy is apathetic about the canoe trip, so Lois has to disguise her own excitement. The evening before they are to leave, she slouches into the campfire ring as if coerced, and sits down with a sigh of endurance, just as Lucy does.

Every canoe trip that went out of camp was given a special send off by Cappie and the section leader and counsellors, with the whole section in attendance. Cappie painted three streaks of red across each of her cheeks with a lipstick. They looked like three-fingered claw marks. She put a blue circle on her forehead with fountain-pen ink, and tied a twisted bandana around her head and stuck a row of frazzle-ended feathers around it, and wrapped herself in a red-and-black Hudson's Bay blanket. The counsellors, also in blankets but with only two streaks of red, beat on tom-toms made of round wooden cheese boxes with leather stretched over the top and nailed in place. Cappie was Chief Cappeosota. They all had to say "How!" when she walked into the circle and stood there with one hand raised.

Looking back on this, Lois finds it disquieting. She knows too much about Indians: this is why. She knows, for instance, that they should not even be called Indians, and that they have enough worries without other people taking their names and dressing up as them. It has all been a form of stealing.

But she remembers, too, that she was once ignorant of this. Once she loved the campfire, the flickering of light on the ring of faces, the sound of the fake tom-toms, heavy and fast like a sacred heartbeat; she loved Cappie in a red blanket and feathers, solemn, as a chief should be, raising her hand and saying, "Greetings, my Ravens." It was not funny, it was not making fun. She wanted to be an Indian. She wanted to be adventurous and pure, and aboriginal.

"You go on big water," says Cappie. This is her idea – all their ideas – of how Indians talk. "You go where no man has ever trod. You go many moons." This is not true. They are only going for a week, not many moons. The canoe route is clearly marked, they have gone over it on a map, and there are prepared campsites with names which are used year after year. But when Cappie says this – and despite the way Lucy rolls her eyes – Lois can feel the water stretching out, with the shores twisting away on either side, immense and a little frightening.

"You bring back much wampum," says Cappie. "Do good in war, my braves, and capture many scalps." This is another of her pretences: that they are boys, and bloodthirsty. But such a game cannot be played by substituting the word "squaw." It would not work at all.

Each of them has to stand up and step forward and have a red line drawn across her cheeks by Cappie. She tells them they must follow in the paths of their ancestors (who most certainly, thinks Lois, looking out the window of her apartment and remembering the family stash of daguerreo-types and sepia-coloured portraits of her mother's dressing table, the stiff-shirted, black-coated, grim-faced men and the beflounced women with their severe hair and their corseted respectability, would never have considered heading off onto an open lake, in a canoe, just for fun).

At the end of the ceremony they all stood and held hands around the circle, and sang taps. This did not sound very Indian, thinks Lois. It sounded like a bugle call at a military post, in a movie. But Cappie was never one to be much concerned with consistency, or with archaeology.

* * *

After breakfast they next morning they set out from the main dock, in four canoes, three in each. The lipstick stripes have not come off completely, and still show faintly pink, like healing burns. They wear their white denim sailing hats, because of the sun, and thin-striped T-shirts, and pale baggy shorts with the cuffs rolled up. The middle one kneels, propping her rear end against the rolled sleeping bags. The counsellors going with them are Pat and Kip. Kip is no-nonsense; Pat is easier to wheedle, or fool.

There are white puffy clouds and a small breeze. Glints come from the little waves. Lois is in the bow of Kip's canoe. She still can't do a J-stroke very well, and she will have to be in the bow or the middle for the whole trip. Lucy is behind her; her own J-stroke is even worse. She splashes Lois with her paddle, quiet a big splash.

"I'll get you back," says Lois.

"There was a stable fly on your shoulder," Lucy says.

Lois turns to look at her, to see if she's grinning. They're in the habit of splashing each other. Back there, the camp has vanished behind the first long point of rock and rough trees. Lois feels as if an invisible rope has broken. They're floating free, on their own, cut loose. Beneath the canoe the lake goes down, deeper and colder than it was a minute before.

"No horsing around in the canoe," says Kip. She's rolled her T-shirt sleeves up to the shoulder; her arms are brown and sinewy, her jaw determined, her stroke perfect. She looks as if she knows exactly what she is doing.

The four canoes keep close together. They sing, raucously and with defiance; they sing "The Quartermaster's Store," and "Clementine," and "Alouette." It is more like bellowing than singing.

After that the wind grows stronger, blowing slantwise against the bows, and they have to put all their energy into shoving themselves through the water.

Was there anything important, anything that would provide some sort of reason or clue to what happened next? Lois can remember everything, every detail; but it does her no good.

They stopped at noon for a swim and lunch, and went on in the afternoon. At last they reached Little Birch, which was the first campsite for overnight. Lois and Lucy made the fire, while the others pitched the heavy canvas tents. The fireplace was already there, flat stones piled into a U. A burned tin can and a beer bottle had been left in it. Their fire went out, and they had to restart it. "Hustle your bustle," said Kip. "We're starving."

The sun went down, and in the pink sunset light they brushed their teeth and spat the toothpaste froth into the lake. Kip and Pat put all the food that wasn't in cans into a packsack and slung it into a tree, in case of bears.

Lois and Lucy weren't sleeping in a tent. They'd begged to be allowed to sleep out; that way they could talk without the others hearing. If it rained, they told Kip, they promised not to crawl dripping into the tent over everyone's legs: they would get under the canoes. So they were out on the point.

Lois tried to get comfortable inside her sleeping bag, which smelled of musty storage and of earlier campers, a stale salty sweetness. She curled herself up, with her sweater rolled up under her head for a pillow and her flashlight inside her sleeping bag so it wouldn't roll away. The muscles of her sore arms were making small pings, like rubber bands breaking.

Beside her Lucy was rustling around. Lois could see the glimmering oval of her white face.

"I've got a rock poking into my back," said Lucy.

"So do I," said Lois. "You want to go into the tent?" She herself didn't, but it was right to ask.

"No," said Lucy. She subsided into her sleeping bag. After a moment she said, "It would be nice not to go back."

"To camp?" said Lois.

"To Chicago," said Lucy. "I hate it there."

"What about your boyfriend?" said Lois. Lucy didn't answer. She was either asleep or pretending to be.

There was a moon, and a movement in the trees. In the sky there were stars, layers of stars that went down and down. Kip said that when the stars were bright like that instead of hazy it meant bad weather later on. Out on the lake there were two loons, calling to each other in their insane, mournful voices. At the time it did not sound like grief. It was just background.

The lake in the morning was flat calm. They skimmed along over the glassy surface, leaving V-shaped trails behind them; it felt like flying. As the sun rose higher it got hot, almost too hot. There were stable flies in the canoes, landing on a bare arm or leg for a quick sting. Lois hoped for wind.

They stopped for lunch at the next of the named campsites, Lookout Point. It was called this because, although the site itself was down near the water on a flat shelf of rock, there was a sheer cliff nearby and a trail that led up to the top. The top was the lookout, although what you were supposed to see from there was not clear. Kip said it was just a view.

Lois and Lucy decided to make the climb anyway. They didn't want to hang around waiting for lunch. It wasn't their turn to cook, though they hadn't avoided much by not doing it, because cooking lunch was no big deal, it was just unwrapping the cheese and getting out the bread and peanut butter, but Pat and Kip always had to do their woodsy act and boil up a billy tin for their own tea.

They told Kip where they were going. You had to tell Kip where you were going, even if it was only a little way into the woods to get dry twigs for kindling. You could never go anywhere without a buddy.

"Sure," said Kip, who was crouching over the fire, feeding driftwood into it. "Fifteen minutes to lunch."

"Where are they off to?" said Pat. She was bringing their billy tin of water from the lake.

"Lookout," said Kip.

"Be careful," said Pat. She said it as an afterthought, because it was what she always said.

"They're old hands," Kip said.

Lois looks at her watch: it's ten to twelve. She is the watch-minder; Lucy is careless of time. They walk up the path, which is dry earth and rocks, big round-ed pinky-grey boulders or split-open ones with jagged edges. Spindly balsam and spruce trees grow to either side, the lake is blue fragments to the left. The sun is right overhead; there are no shadows anywhere. The heat comes up at them as well as down. The forest is dry and crackly.

It isn't far, but it's a steep climb and they're sweating when they reach the top. They wipe their faces with their bare arms, sit gingerly down on a scorching-hot rock, five feet from the edge but too close for Lois. It's a lookout all right, a sheer drop to the lake and a long view over the water, back the way they've come. It's amazing to Lois that they've travelled so far, over all that water, with nothing to propel them but their own arms. It makes her feel strong. There are all kinds of things she is capable of doing.

"It would be quite a dive off here," says Lucy.

"You'd have to be nuts," says Lois.

"Why?" says Lucy. "It's really deep. It goes straight down." She stands up and takes a step nearer the edge. Lois gets a stab in her midriff, the kind she gets when a car goes too fast over a bump. "Don't," she says.

"Don't what?" says Lucy, glancing around at her mischievously. She knows how Lois feels about heights. But she turns back. "I really have to pee," she says.

"You have toilet paper?" says Lois, who is never without it. She digs in her shorts pocket.

"Thanks," says Lucy.

They are both adept at peeing in the woods: doing it fast so the mosquitos don't get you, the underwear pulled up between the knees, the squat with the feet apart so you don't wet your legs, facing downhill. The exposed feeling of your bum, as if someone is looking at you from behind. The etiquette when you're with someone is not to look. Lois stands up and starts to walk back down the path, to be out of sight.

"Wait for me?" says Lucy.

Lois climbed down, over and around the boulders, until she could not see Lucy; she waited. She could hear the voices of the others, talking and laughing, down near the shore. One voice was yelling, "Ants! Ants!" Someone must have sat on an ant hill. Off to the side, in the woods, a raven was croaking, a hoarse single note.

She looked at her watch: it was noon. This is when she heard the shout.

She has gone over and over it in her mind since, so many times that the first, real shout has been obliterated, like a footprint trampled by other footprints. But she is sure (she is almost positive, she is nearly certain) that it was not a shout of fear. Not a scream. More like a cry of surprise, cut off too soon. Short, like a dog's bark.

"Lucy?" Lois said. Then she called "Lucy!" By now she was clambering back up, over the stones of the path. Lucy was not up there. Or she was not in sight.

Stop fooling around," Lois said. "It's lunch-time." But Lucy did not rise from behind a rock or step out, smiling, from behind a tree. The sunlight was all around; the rocks looked white. "This isn't funny!" Lois said, and it wasn't, panic was rising in her, the panic of a small child who does not know where the bigger ones are hidden. She could hear her own heart. She looked quickly around; she lay down on the ground and looked over the edge of the cliff. It made her feel cold. There was nothing.

She went back down the path, stumbling; she was breathing too quickly; she was too frightened to cry. She felt terrible – guilty and dismayed, as if she had done something very bad, by mistake. Something that could never be repaired. "Lucy's gone," she told Kip.

Kip looked up from the fire, annoyed. The water in the billy can was boiling. "What do you mean, gone?" she said. "Where did she go?"

"I don't know," said Lois. "She's just gone."

No one had heard the shout, but then no one had heard Lois calling, either. They had been talking among themselves, by the water.

Kip and Pat went up to the lookout and searched and called, and blew their whistles. Nothing answered.

Then they came back down, and Lois had to tell exactly what had happened. The other girls all sat in a circle and listened to her. Nobody said anything. They all looked frightened, especially Pat and Kip. They were the leaders. You did not just lose a camper like this, for no reason at all.

"Why did you leave her alone?" said Kip.

"I was just down the path," said Lois. "I told you. She had to go to the bathroom." She did not say pee in front of people older than herself.

Kip looked disgusted.

"Maybe she just walked off into the woods and got turned around," said one of the girls.

"Maybe she's doing it on purpose," said another.

Nobody believed either of these theories

They took the canoes and searched around the base of the cliff, and peered down into the water. But there had been no sound of falling rock, there had been no splash. There was no clue, nothing at all. Lucy had simply vanished.

That was the end of the canoe trip. It took them the same two days to go back that it had taken coming in, even though they were short a paddler. They did not sing,

After that, the police went in a motorboat, with dogs; they were the Mounties and the dogs were German shepherds, trained to follow trails in the woods. But it had rained since, and they could find nothing.

Lois is sitting in Cappie's office. Her face is bloated with crying, she's seen that in the mirror. By now she feels numbed; she feels as if she's been drowned. She can't stay here. It has been too much of a shock. Tomorrow her parents are coming to take her away. Several of the girls who were on the canoe trip are also being collected. The others will have to stay, because their parents are in Europe, or cannot be reached.

Cappie is grim. They've tried to hush it up, but of course everyone in camp knows. Soon the papers will know too. You can't keep it quiet, but what can be said? What can be said that makes any sense? "Girl vanishes in broad daylight, without a trace." It can't be believed. Other things, worse things, will be suspected. Negligence, at the very least. But they have always taken such care. Bad luck will gather around Camp Manitou like a fog; parents will avoid it, in favour of other, luckier places. Lois can see Cappie thinking all this, even through her numbness. It's what anyone would think.

Lois sits on the hard wooden chair in Cappie's office, beside the old wooden desk, over which hangs the thumb-tacked bulletin board of normal camp routine, and gazes at Cappie through her puffy eyelids. Cappie is now smiling what is supposed to be a reassuring smile. Her manner is too casual; she's after something. Lois has seen this look on Cappie's face when she's been sniffing out contraband chocolate bars, hunting down those rumoured to have snuck out of their cabins at night.

"Tell me again," says Cappie, "from the beginning."

Lois has told her story so many times by now, to Pat and Kip, to Cappie, to the police, that she knows it word for word. She knows it, but she no longer believes it. It has become a story. "I told you," she said. "She wanted to go to the bathroom. I gave her my toilet paper. I went down the path, I waited for her. I heard this kind of shout . . . "

"Yes," says Cappie, smiling confidingly, "but before that. What did you say to one another?"

Lois thinks. Nobody has asked her this before. "She said you could dive off there. She said it went straight down."

"And what did you say?"

"I said you'd have to be nuts."

"Were you mad at Lucy?" says Cappie, in an encouraging voice.

"No," says Lois. "Why would I be mad at Lucy? I wasn't ever mad at Lucy." She feels like crying again. The times when she has in fact been mad at Lucy have been erased already. Lucy was always perfect.

"Sometimes we're angry when we don't know we're angry," says Cappie, as if to herself. "Sometimes we might do a thing without meaning to, or without knowing what will happen. We lose our tempers."

Lois is only thirteen, but it doesn't take long to figure out that Cappie is not including herself in any of this. By *we* she means Lois. She is accusing Lois of pushing Lucy off the cliff. The unfairness of this hits her like a slap. "I didn't!" she says.

"Didn't what?" says Cappie softly. "Didn't what, Lois?"

Lois does the worst thing, she begins to cry. Cappie gives her a look like a pounce. She's got what she wanted.

Later, when she was grown up, Lois was able to understand what this interview had been about. She could see Cappie's desperation, her need for a story, a real story with a reason in it; anything but the senseless vacancy Lucy had left for her to deal with. Cappie wanted Lois to supply the reason, to be the reason. It wasn't even for the newspapers or the parents, because she could never make such an accusation without proof. It was for herself: something to explain the loss of Camp Manitou and of all she had worked for, the years of entertaining spoiled children and buttering up parents and making a fool of herself with feathers stuck in her hair. Camp Manitou was in fact lost. It did not survive.

Lois worked all this out, twenty years later. But it was far too late. It was too late even ten minutes afterwards, when she'd left Cappie's office and was walking slowly back to her cabin to pack. Lucy's clothes were still there, folded on the shelves, as if waiting. She felt the other girls in the cabin watching her with speculation in their eyes. *Could she have done it? She must have done it.* For the rest of her life, she has caught people watching her in this way.

Maybe they weren't thinking this. Maybe they were merely sorry for her. But she felt she had been tried and sentenced, and this is what has stayed with her: the knowledge that she had been singled out, condemned for something that was not her fault.

Lois sits in the living room of her apartment, drinking a cup of tea. Through the knee-to-ceiling window she has a wide view of Lake Ontario, with its skin of wrinkled blue-grey light, and of the willows of Centre Island shaken by a wind, which is silent at this distance, and on this side of the glass. When there isn't too much pollution she can see the far shore, the foreign shore; though today it is obscured.

Possibly she could go out, go downstairs, do some shopping; there isn't much in the refrigerator. The boys say she doesn't get out enough. But she isn't hungry, and moving, stirring from this space, is increasingly an effort.

She can hardly remember, now, having her two boys in the hospital, nursing them as babies; she can hardly remember getting married, or what Rob looked like. Even at the time she never felt she was paying full attention. She was tired a lot, as if she was living not one life but two: her own, and another, shadowy life that hovered around her and would not let itself be realized – the life of what would have happened if Lucy had not stepped sideways, and disappeared from time.

She would never go up north, to Rob's family cottage or to any place with wild lakes and wild trees and the calls of loons. She would never go anywhere near. Still, it was as if she was always listening for another voice, the voice of a person who should have been there but was not. An echo.

While Rob was alive, when the boys were growing up, she could pretend she didn't hear it, this empty space in sound. But now there is nothing much left to distract her.

She turns away from the window and looks at her pictures. There is the pinkish island, in the lake, with the intertwisted trees. It's the same landscape they paddled through, that distant summer. She's seen travelogues of this country, aerial photographs; it looks different from above, bigger, more hopeless: lake after lake, random blue puddles in dark green bush, the trees like bristles.

How could you ever find anything there, once it was lost? Maybe if they cut it all down, drained it all away, they might find Lucy's bones, some time, wherever they are hidden. A few bones, some buttons, the buckle from her shorts.

But a dead person is a body; a body occupies space, it exists somewhere. You can see it; you put it in a box and bury it in the ground, and then it's a box in the ground. But Lucy is not in a box, or in the ground. Because she is nowhere definite, she could be anywhere.

And these paintings are not landscape paintings. Because there aren't any landscapes up there, not in the old, tidy European sense, with a gentle hill, a curving river, a cottage, a mountain in the background, a golden evening sky. Instead there's a tangle, a receding maze, in which you can become lost almost as soon as you step off the path. There are no backgrounds in any of these paintings, no vistas; only a great deal of foreground that goes back and back, endlessly, involving you in its twists and turns of tree and branch and rock. No matter how far back in you go, there will be more. And the trees themselves are hardly trees; they are currents of energy, charged with violent colour.

Who knows how many trees there were on the cliff just before Lucy disappeared? Who counted? Maybe there was one more, afterwards.

Lois sits in her chair and does not move. Her hand with the cup is raised halfway to her mouth. She hears something, almost hears it: a shout of recognition, or of joy.

She looks at the paintings, she looks into them. Every one of them is a picture of Lucy. You can't see her exactly, but she's there, in behind the pink stone island or the one behind that. In the picture of the cliff she is hidden by the clutch of fallen rocks towards the bottom, in the one of the river shore she is crouching beneath the overturned canoe. In the yellow autumn woods she's behind the tree that cannot be seen because of the other trees, over beside the blue sliver of pond; but if you walked into the picture and found the tree, it would be the wrong one, because the right one would be further on.

Everyone has to be somewhere, and this is where Lucy is. She is in Lois's apartment, in the holes that open inwards on the wall, not like windows but like doors. She is here. She is entirely alive.

ASHPUTTLE *OR* THE MOTHER'S GHOST

Angela Carter

Angela Carter (1940–1992) was born Angela Olive Stalker in Eastbourne, Sussex. She was evacuated to her grandmother's house in Yorkshire during World War II and subsequently lived in Balham in London. Carter studied English literature at Bristol University. She is the author of nine novels and four collections of stories. Carter's awards include a Somerset Maugham Award, which enabled her to live in Tokyo for two years. She taught part-time on the Writing MA at the University of East Anglia from 1984–1987.

I
The Mutilated Girls

But although you could easily take the story away from Ashputtle and centre it on the mutilated sisters – indeed, it would be easy to think of it as a story about cutting bits off women, so that they *will fit in*, some sort of circumcision-like ritual chop, nevertheless, the story always begins not with Ashputtle or her stepsisters but with Ashputtle's mother, as though it is really always the story of her mother even if, at the beginning of the story, the mother herself is just about to exit the narrative because she is at death's door: "A rich man's wife fell sick, and, feeling that her end was near, she called her only daughter to her bedside."

Note the absence of the husband/father. Although the woman is defined by her relation to him ("a rich man's wife") the daughter is unambiguously hers, as if hers alone, and the entire drama concerns only women, takes place almost exclusively among women, is a fight between two groups of women – in the right-hand corner, Ashputtle and her mother; in the left-hand corner, the stepmother and *her* daughters, of whom the father is unacknowledged but all the same is predicated by both textual and biological necessity.

In the drama between two female families in opposition to one another because of their rivalry over men (husband/father, husband/son), the men seem no more than passive victims of their fancy, yet their significance is absolute because it is ("a rich man", "a king's son") economic.

Ashputtle's father, the old man, is the first object of their desire and their dissension; the stepmother snatches him from the dead mother before her corpse is cold, as soon as her grip loosens. Then there is the young man, the potential bridegroom, the hypothetical son-in-law, for whose possession the mothers fight, using their daughters as instruments of war or as surrogates in the business of mating.

If the men, and the bank balances for which they stand, are the passive victims of the two grown women, then the girls, all three, are animated solely by the wills of their mothers, Even if Ashputtle's mother dies at the beginning of the story, her status as one of the dead only makes her position more authoritative. The mother's ghost dominates the narrative and is, in a real sense, the motive centre, the event that makes all the other events happen.

On her death bed, the mother assures the daughter: "I shall always look after you and always be with you." The story tells you how she does it.

At this point, when her mother makes her promise, Ashputtle is nameless. She is her mother's daughter. That is all we know. It is the stepmother who names her Ashputtle, as a joke, and, in doing so, wipes out her real name, whatever that is, banishes her from the family, exiles her from the shared table to the lonely hearth among the cinders, removes her contingent but honourable status as daughter and gives her, instead, the contingent but disreputable status of servant.

Her mother told Ashputtle she would always look after her, but then she died and the father married again and gave Ashputtle an imitation mother with daughters of her own whom she loves with the same fierce passion as Ashputtle's mother did and still, posthumously, does, as we shall find out.

With the second marriage comes the vexed question: who shall be the daughters of the house? Mine! declares the stepmother and sets the freshly named, non-daughter Ashputtle to sweep and scrub and sleep on the hearth while her daughters lie between clean sheets in Ashputtle's bed. Ashputtle, no longer known as the daughter of her mother, nor of her father either, goes by a dry, dirty, cindery nickname for everything has turned to dust and ashes.

Meanwhile, the false mother sleeps on the bed where the real mother died and is, presumably, pleasured by the husband/father in that bed, unless there is no pleasure in it for her. We are not told what the husband/ father does as regards domestic or marital function, but we can surely make the assumption that he and the stepmother share a bed, because that is what married people do.

And what can the real mother/wife do about it? Burn as she might with love, anger and jealousy, she is dead and buried.

The father, in this story, is a mystery to me. Is he so besotted with his new wife that he cannot see how his daughter is soiled with kitchen refuse and filthy from her ashy bed and always hard at work? If he sensed there was a drama in hand, he was content to leave the entire production to the women for, absent as he might be, always remember that it is in *his* house where Ashputtle sleeps on the cinders, and he is the invisible link that binds both sets of mothers and daughters in their violent equation. He is the unmoved mover, the unseen organising principle, like God, and, like God, up he pops in person, one fine day, to introduce the essential plot device.

Besides, without the absent father there would be no story because there would have been no conflict.

If they had been able to put aside their differences and discuss everything amicably, they'd have combined to expel the father. Then all the women could have slept in one bed. If they'd kept the father on, he could have done the housework.

This is the essential plot device introduced by the father: he says, "I am about to take a business trip. What presents would my three girls like me to bring back for them?"

Note that: his *three* girls.

It occurs to me that perhaps the stepmother's daughters were really, all the time, his own daughters, just as much his own daughters as Ashputtle, his "natural" daughters, as they say, as though there is something inherently unnatural about legitimacy. *That* would realign the forces in the story. It would make his connivance with the ascendancy of the other girls more plausible. It would make the speedy marriage, the stepmother's hostility, more probable.

But it would also transform the story into something else, because it would provide motivation, and so on; it would mean I'd have to provide a past for all these people, that I would have to equip them with three dimensions, with tastes and memories, and I would have to think of things for them to eat and wear and say. It would transform "Ashputtle" from the bare necessity of fairy tale, with its characteristic copula formula, "and then", to the emotional and technical complexity of bourgeois realism. They would have to learn to think. Everything would change.

I will stick with what I know.

What presents do his three girls want?

"Bring me a silk dress," said his eldest girl. "Bring me a string of pearls," said the middle one. What about the third one, the forgotten one, called out of the kitchen on a charitable impulse and drying her hands, raw with housework, on her apron, bringing with her the smell of old fire?

"Bring me the first branch that knocks against your hat on the way home," said Ashputtle.

Why did she ask for that? Did she make an informed guess at how little he valued her? Or had a dream told her to use this random formula of unacknowledged desire, to allow blind chance to choose her present for her? Unless it was her mother's ghost, awake and restlessly looking for a way home, that came into the girl's mouth and spoke the request for her.

He brought her back a hazel twig. She planted it on her mother's grave and watered it with tears. It grew into a hazel tree. When Ashputtle came out to weep upon her mother's grave, the turtle dove crooned: "I'll never leave you, I'll always protect you."

Then Ashputtle knew that the turtle dove was her mother's ghost and she herself was still her mother's daughter, and although she had wept and wailed and longed to have her mother back again, now her heart sank a little to find out that her mother, though dead, was no longer gone and henceforward she must do her mother's bidding.

Came the time for that curious fair they used to hold in that country, when all the resident virgins went to dance in front of the king's son so that he could pick out the girl he wanted to marry.

The turtle dove was mad for that, for her daughter to marry the prince. You might have thought her own experience of marriage might have taught her to be wary, but no, needs must, what else is a girl to do? The turtle dove was mad for her daughter to marry so she flew in and picked up the new silk dress with her beak, dragged it to the open window, threw it down to Ashputtle. She did the same with the string of pearls. Ashputtle had a good wash under the pump in the yard, put on her stolen finery and crept out the back way, secretly, to the dancing grounds, but the stepsisters had to stay home and sulk because they had nothing to wear.

The turtle dove stayed close to Ashputtle, pecking her ears to make her dance vivaciously, so that the prince would see her, so that the prince would love her, so that he would follow her and find the clue of the fallen slipper, for the story is not complete without the ritual humiliation of the other woman and the mutilation of her daughters.

The search for the foot that fits the slipper is essential to the enactment of this ritual humiliation.

The other woman wants that young man desperately. She would do anything to catch him. Not losing a daughter, but gaining a son. She wants a son so badly she is prepared to cripple her daughters. She takes up a carving knife and chops off her elder daughter's big toe, so that her foot will fit the little shoe.

Imagine.

Brandishing the carving knife, the woman bears down on her child, who is as distraught as if she had not been a girl but a boy and the old woman was after a more essential portion than a toe. "No!" she screams. "Mother! No! Not the knife! No!" But off it comes, all the same, and she throws it in the fire, among the ashes, where Ashputtle finds it, wonders at it, and feels both awe and fear at the phenomenon of mother love.

Mother love, which winds about these daughters like a shroud.

The prince saw nothing familiar in the face of the tearful young woman, one shoe off, one shoe on, displayed to him in triumph by her mother, but he said: "I promised I would marry whoever the shoe fitted so I will marry you," and they rode off together.

The turtle dove came flying round and did not croon or coo to the bridal pair but sang a horrid song: "Look! Look! There's blood in the shoe!"

The prince returned the ersatz ex-fiancee at once, angry at the trick, but the stepmother hastily lopped off her other daughter's heel and pushed *that* poor foot into the bloody shoe as soon as it was vacant so, nothing for it, a man of his word, the prince helped up the new girl and once again he rode away.

Back came the nagging turtle dove: "Look!" And, sure enough, the shoe was full of blood again.

"Let Ashputtle try," said the eager turtle dove.

So now Ashputtle must put her foot into the hideous receptacle, this open wound, still slick and warm as it is, for nothing in any of the many texts of this tale suggests the prince washed the shoe out between the fittings. It was an ordeal in itself to put a naked foot into the bloody shoe, but her mother, the turtle dove, urged her to do so in a soft, cooing croon that could not be denied.

If she does not plunge without revulsion into this open wound, she won't be fit to marry.

That is the song of the turtle dove, while the other mad mother stood impotently by.

Ashputtle's foot, the size of the bound foot of a Chinese woman, a stump. Almost an amputee already, she put her tiny foot in it.

"Look! Look!" cried the turtle dove in triumph, even while the bird betrayed its ghostly nature by becoming progressively more and more immaterial as

Ashputtle stood up in the shoe and commenced to walk around. Squelch, went the stump of the foot in the shoe. Squelch.

"Look!" sang out the turtle dove. "Her foot fits the shoe like a corpse fits the coffin!

"See how well I look after you, my darling!"

II
The Burned Child

A burned child lived in the ashes. No, not really burned – more charred, a little bit charred, like a stick half-burned and picked off the fire. She looked like charcoal and ashes because she lived in the ashes since her mother died and the hot ashes burned her so she was scabbed and scarred. The burned child lived on the hearth, covered in ashes, as if she were still mourning.

After her mother died and was buried, her father forgot the mother and forgot the child and married the woman who used to rake the ashes, and that was why the child lived in the unraked ashes, and there was nobody to brush her hair, so it stuck out like a mat, nor to wipe the dirt off her scabbed face, and she had no heart to do it for herself, but she raked the ashes and slept beside the little cat and got the burned bits from the bottom of the pot to eat, scraping them out, squatting on the floor, by herself in front of the fire, not as if she were human, because she was still mourning.

Her mother was dead and buried, but felt perfect exquisite pain of love when she looked up through the earth and saw the burned child covered in ashes.

"Milk the cow, burned child, and bring back all the milk," said the stepmother, who used to rake the ashes and milk the cow, once upon a time, but the burned child did all that, now.

The ghost of the mother went into the cow.

"Drink milk, grow fat," said the mother's ghost.

The burned child pulled on the udder and drank enough milk before she took the bucket back and nobody saw, and time passed, she drank milk every day, she grew fat, she grew breasts, she grew up.

There was a man the stepmother wanted and she asked him into the kitchen to get his dinner, but she made the burned child cook it, although the stepmother did all the cooking before. After the burned child cooked the dinner the stepmother sent her off to milk the cow.

"I want that man for myself," said the burned child to the cow.

The cow let down more milk, and more, and more, enough for the girl to have a drink and wash her face and wash her hands. When she washed her face, she washed the scabs off and now she was not burned at all, but the cow was empty.

"Give your own milk, next time," said the ghost of the mother inside the cow. "You've milked me dry."

The little cat came by. The ghost of the mother went into the cat.

"Your hair wants doing," said the cat. "Lie down."

The little cat unpicked her raggy lugs with its clever paws until the burned child's hair hung down nicely, but it had been so snagged and tangled that the cat's claws were all pulled out before it was finished.

"Comb your own hair, next time," said the cat. "You've maimed me."

The burned child was clean and combed, but stark naked.

There was a bird sitting in the apple tree. The ghost of the mother left the cat and went into the bird. The bird struck its own breast with its beak. Blood poured down on to the burned child under the tree. It ran over her shoulders and covered her front and covered her back. When the bird had no more blood, the burned child got a red silk dress.

"Make your own dress, next time," said the bird. "I"m through with that bloody business."

The burned child went into the kitchen to show herself to the man. She was not burned any more, but lovely. The man left off looking at the stepmother and looked at the girl.

"Come home with me and let your stepmother stay and rake the ashes," he said to her and off they went. He gave her a house and money. She did all right.

"Now I can go to sleep," said the ghost of the mother. "Now everything is all right."

III
Travelling Clothes

The stepmother took the red-hot poker and burned the orphan's face with it because she had not raked the ashes. The girl went to her mother's grave. In the earth her mother said: "It must be raining. Or else it is snowing. Unless there is a heavy dew tonight."

"It isn't raining, it isn't snowing, it's too early for the dew. My tears are falling on your grave, mother."

The dead woman waited until night came. Then she climbed out and went to the house. The stepmother slept on a feather bed, but the burned child slept on the hearth among the ashes. When the dead woman kissed her, the scar vanished. The girl woke up. The dead woman gave her a red dress.

"I had it when I was your age."

The girl put the red dress on. The dead woman took worms from her eyesockets; they turned into jewels. The girl put on a diamond ring.

"I had it when I was your age."

They went together to the grave.

"Step into my coffin."

"No," said the girl. She shuddered.

"I stepped into *my* mother's coffin when I was your age."

The girl stepped into the coffin although she thought it would be the death of her. It turned into a coach and horses. The horses stamped, eager to be gone.

"Go and seek your fortune, darling."

THE GOURMET

Kazuo Ishiguro

Kazuo Ishiguro (b.1954) Kazuo Ishiguro was born in Nagasaki, Japan. His family came to Britain in 1960. He read English and Philosophy at the University of Kent. Ishiguro has worked as a grouse-beater at Balmoral, a community worker in Glasgow and a residential social worker in London. He studied Creative Writing at the University of East Anglia, where he was mentored by Angela Carter. Ishiguro won the Booker Prize in 1989 for *The Remains of the Day*. He lives in London.

1. A CHURCH IN A LONDON STREET. 1904. NIGHT.
    A large church set back from the street. A horse-drawn carriage stands outside.
    Close shot: a wooden plaque on church gate reading:

    I was hungered and ye gave me meat
    I was thirsty and ye gave me drink
    I was a stranger and ye took me in.

    Matthew 25:35

2. CHURCH CRYPT. NIGHT.
    Point of view: unseen protagonists as they search around the darkened crypt with a lantern. The lantern reveals ragged men heaped one on another, sleeping in whatever posture the conditions allow. A chorus of snores.

3. CHURCH. NIGHT.
    Viewed from the pulpit. Shadows. We see the empty pews by the moonlight coming through the windows.
    Breathing is heard. At first barely discernible, it grows clearer: the sounds of two men in physical exertion. Their shapes emerge from the shadows, coming slowly towards us down a side aisle: two men dressed in cloaks and hats. They are carrying something heavy between them.
    We hear whispering again, sinister, the words barely discernible.

    WHISPER 1: Perhaps over there. [*Heavy breath*.] Over towards that door.
    WHISPER 2: Yes, yes. [*Heavy breath*.] We'll take it through to the vestry.
    WHISPER 1: Just a little further now. As you say, the vestry.

4. VESTRY. DOORWAY TO BACK ROOM.
    The vestry is a small bare room, which we see by the moonlight through a

window. At the moment, we are interested only in the doorway which leads through to a back room. This doorway has no door – it is black and ominous, like the gateway to another world.

Meanwhile, the whispers continue.

WHISPER 1: Yes, indeed, you're quite correct. We should cut it along this piece . . .
WHISPER 2: Yes, yes. [*Heavy breath*.] We'll take it through to the vestry.
WHISPER 1: Just a little further now. As you say, the vestry.

5. CHURCH. NIGHT.
Long shot: the Church. We are zooming in slowly. Sound of horse hooves in the distance.

6. VESTRY. DOORWAY TO BACK ROOM.
Still moving in on the black doorway. The whispers continue.

WHISPER 1: Yes, yes. I think that direction.
WHISPER 2: You think we should cut it along here?
WHISPER 1: Yes, indeed, along that strip there. As you say.

We have now come right up to the doorway, but there is utter blackness across the threshold.

We then move down slowly, in time to see a thin line of blood run out from the blackness towards us along the vestry floor.

7. AIRPORT RUNWAY. DAY. 1985.
Jet-liner coming into land.

8. ROOF. CAR PARK OF AIRPORT TERMINAL. DAY.
Carter stands at the edge of the roof, watching the landing.

Carter, mid-twenties, slim, dapperly dressed in chauffeur's uniform. Even if he were not wearing dark glasses and his cap pulled down low, his face would probably reveal little emotion; as it is, there is something sinister and assassin-like about him.

He looks at his watch, then back out towards the runway. Evidently, this is the plane he has been waiting for. He walks off out of shot with an almost deliberate lack of hurry.

9. CARRIAGEWAY. DAY.
Rolls Royce in motion.

10. CAR.
Carter is driving. He continues to wear his dark glasses, as he will do throughout the film.

Manley Kingston is in the back seat, preoccupied with something on his lap.

Manley is in his fifties; large, formidable British upper-class presence. He wears a habitual expression of disdain and boredom, but there is also a maverick streak in his face – a hint of the decadent or criminal.

Close up: photograph of church in Manley's hand. The church is the one we saw in scene one. The photograph has emerged from an attaché case on Manley's lap.

On Manley: studying the photograph as though to commit its details to memory.

Close up: open attaché case into which Manley returns the photograph amid other documents. Evidently, he only happened across it while searching for something else, and he now continues through the contents of his case. We glimpse two sketch plans (of the church) and three mortis keys on a ring. Each has a large tag; one is marked 'vestry'. Manley's hand moves these aside as he continues to search. Carter continues to drive silently, while Manley remains preoccupied with the attaché case.

In the ensuing exchange, there is just a hint of malice and sarcasm in Carter's voice – but no more than a hint, and Manley is too preoccupied to notice. Carter has a London working-class accent.

CARTER: Weather nice in Brazil, was it, Sir?
MANLEY: [*Not looking up from his case.*] Paraguay. [*Pause.*]
CARTER: Beg your pardon. Sir?
MANLEY: Paraguay. I've just come from Paraguay.
CARTER: Sorry, sir. Madam told me you were in Brazil.
MANLEY: I suppose I was. I became tired of the place.

Manley has found what he was looking for – an address card. He leans forward and holds it out for Carter.

MANLEY: We're going to drop in at this address on our way home, if you will, Carson.

Carter takes the card without turning, glances at it and puts it on the dashboard. Manley settles back in his seat and gazes out of the window, a preoccupied look still on his face.

CARTER: Carter, Sir.
MANLEY: What?
CARTER: Name's *Carter*, Sir.
MANLEY: [*Turning back to window, impatiently.*] Oh yes, yes.

Move in on Carter's face. It is impossible to tell what is going on behind his glasses.

11. LONDON.
A series of shots of the Rolls's journey into London.

12. DR GROSVENOR'S HOUSE. DAY.

Rolls halts in front of a very expensive house. Manley gets out, studying an address card. He waves carelessly towards the car, then walks to the house.

13. DR GROSVENOR'S ENTRANCE HALL.
A hum of conversation coming from within the house. The doorbell rings.

The figure of Watkins as yet not clearly seen comes into shot and opens the door. Manley is on the doorstep.

WATKINS: [*Off: cheerfully.*] Good afternoon, Sir.
MANLEY: Ah. My name is Manley Kingston. Dr Grosvenor is expecting me.
WATKINS: Come in, Mr Kingston. [*Following Manley's gaze.*] Oh, we're having a little reception. Eduardo Perez is in London, and he wished to premiere some of his new dishes.
MANLEY: [*Distracted*] Is that so?

Manley goes on looking through into the inner room. Watkins, who should really be leading him in, is delaying doing so to savour these few moments with a celebrity. He beams admiringly at Manley. Manley begins to move further into the house.

MANLEY: Dr Grosvenor about?
WATKINS: [*Suddenly remembering himself.*] Why yes, of course. Let me get you a drink, Mr Kingston, then I'll go and find him.

14. DR GROSVENOR'S HOUSE. RECEPTION ROOM.
An elegant, spacious room of a private house, large enough to hold comfortably the twenty or so guests present. The guests are middle-aged to elderly, formally dressed, men far outnumbering women. This could be a gathering of university professors or classical music critics. They stand conversing in groups of three and four, holding wine glasses.

Watkins is leading Manley across the room towards the wine. Two male guests break off talking as Watkins and Manley come past them. They steal interested glances at Manley, looking him up and down, then stare after him, somewhat disapprovingly. We can hear amid the general hubbub the following exchange, taking place elsewhere in the room:

MALE VOICE 1: But I do think I agree with you on the whole. You have a genuine point there. That whole generation, their central themes were far too centred on protein. Far too centred on protein . . . [*Then in lowered voice.*] I say, look, I believe that's Manley Kingston. That fellow there . . .

15. RECEPTION ROOM. ONE CORNER.
Watkins and Manley have reached the table with the wine. Watkins hands Manley a glass.

WATKINS: I'll go and find Dr Grosvenor. Won't be a moment, Mr Kingston.

Watkins goes out of shot. Manley turns to the table with a preoccupied air. His back is to the camera and the rest of the room.

Meanwhile, amid the general hubbub, we hear:

MALE VOICE 2: Not at all, not at all, don't get me wrong. I'm very fond of de Montière's work. He does have a splendid sensitivity towards textures. But don't you find his soufflés in particular a little – incoherent?

Two guests we have not yet seen have come up to Manley. These are Proterston, a grey distinguished-looking man, and a Japanese, Takeda. Initially, it is not clear if they have come simply to replenish drinks, or if their interest is in Manley.

Manley remains with his back turned. Proterston attempts to catch Manley's attention. Meanwhile, Takeda is staring at Manley as though he is an exhibit in a museum.

FEMALE VOICE: But I suppose one can't help getting the feeling de Montière achieved his best work in the mid-sixties. I suppose there I do have to agree with you . . . [*Fades into general hum of conversation.*]
PROTERSTON: [*Finally deciding on the direct approach.*] Excuse me, it's Mr Manley Kingston, isn't it?

Manley turns, startled out of his thoughts. He has not touched his wine. Proterston smiles genially. Takeda continues to stare.

MANLEY: Er – yes. Indeed.
PROTERSTON: This is a genuine pleasure. My name is Proterston.

Proterston clearly hopes Manley will recognize the name.

MANLEY: [*No sense of recognition.*] Oh really?
PROTERSTON: [*Gives small self-conscious laugh.*] As a matter of fact, I published an article about you quite recently, Mr Kingston. In *Gourmet Academica*, the spring issue. I thought perhaps you might have come across it.
MANLEY: [*With little interest.*] I'm afraid I didn't.

Manley now becomes aware of Takeda staring up at him. Manley looks down at him with distaste.

PROTERSTON: Oh – er – this is Mr Takeda.
TAKEDA: [*Heavy accent.*] Great honour. [*He continues to stare at Manley without offering his hand.*] Great honour. Manley Kingston. Great great honour.
PROTERSTON: I should point out, Mr Kingston, my article was entirely in support of your – er – approach. I'd been an admirer of yours for some time

and thought, well, in my own small way, I should add my voice to the ranks of your supporters.

Manley is searching the room for Watkins.

MANLEY: Very grateful. I'll keep a look out for it.

Takeda now speaks a great torrent of words in his native tongue. He addresses Proterston while gesturing dramatically towards Manley. Proterston nods throughout. Manley continues to look over at some point behind the camera.

PROTERSTON: Mr Takeda was wondering what had brought you over to London. He was wondering if in fact you had a specific project in mind – here in London?

Clearly, Proterston is himself very eager to know the answer. But Manley has been signalled to from across the room. He puts down his glass and starts to move off. He remembers Proterston and Takeda at the last moment.

MANLEY: Oh, excuse me. Delighted.

16. RECEPTION ROOM.
Manley moves through the guests towards Watkins, who is standing near some double doors. Watkins, smiling eagerly, has his arm raised in preparation for ushering Manley through the doors.

17. DR GROSVENOR'S HOUSE. HALLWAY.
Manley comes through doors held open by Watkins and they move towards the stairs.

18. DR GROSVENOR'S STUDY. EARLY EVENING.
Dr Grosvenor likes to work in a darkened atmosphere. Perhaps this is why he has drawn the blinds, although it is not yet dark outside. The source of light is a powerful desk lamp.

The room is used for consultative purposes as well as for its owner's private study. A client's chair faces Dr Grosvenor's desk. Behind the desk, bookshelves. The books we can see are about food; not cookery books, but serious studies with titles like *Eating Rituals of the Aborigines in the Nineteenth Century, Protein and Culture, The Evolution of the Carnivore*.

Dr Grosvenor, fifty-five, elegant, assured, but also with an air of depravity; he may be a wealthy doctor in private practice who performs shady operations.

MANLEY: You mentioned in your letter, Doctor, you were having difficulty obtaining one of the solutions I requested . . .
DR GROSVENOR: [*Cutting in.*] Oh no, no. A very minor problem. I have everything you asked for.

MANLEY: Ah.

DR GROSVENOR: And may I say, Mr Kingston, I'm very happy to be of assistance to you. An honour.

MANLEY: Mmm.

DR GROSVENOR: [*A small laugh.*] Forgive me, I suppose you must be getting rather impatient.

He opens a drawer in his desk. Before removing anything, he looks teasingly at Manley.

DR GROSVENOR: [*Continuing.*] You look rather like a hunter, Mr Kingston, just before his big kill.

He smiles and produces an attaché case. He puts it on the desk, opens the lid, then turns it towards Manley.

DR GROSVENOR: [*Continuing.*] I think you'll find everything in order.

MANLEY: Ah.

Manley leans forward hungrily.

Over the shoulder: the attaché case contains papers and documents packed in an orderly manner, uppermost of which is a large photograph of the church we saw in scene one. The case also contains a small metal box.

Manley adjusts the desk-lamp and begins to examine the contents. Dr Grosvenor leans back and smiles.

DR GROSVENOR: Would I be correct in supposing, Mr Kingston, that tonight's adventure, if successful, would even by your standards constitute something of a remarkable feat? A – shall we say – crowning achievement?

MANLEY: [*Absorbed with the attaché case.*] Indeed, indeed.

Dr Grosvenor watches Manley for a few beats, smiling.

DR GROSVENOR: Your career has interested me for some time, Mr Kingston.

Pause. Manley remains absorbed and does not respond.

DR GROSVENOR: I've come to love and enjoy dishes which the average European would feel nauseous just to look at. But let me say, Mr Kingston, I have no hesitation in admitting I have not come anywhere near your level of er – enterprise.

MANLEY: [*Not listening; still absorbed.*] Mmmm.

Dr Grosvenor goes on watching Manley, smiling silently, for another beat or two.

DR GROSVENOR: You know, Mr Kingston, I have little time for those who attempt to denigrate your name . . .

Close up: attaché case. As Dr Grosvenor continues, we watch Manley's hands sorting through the contents.

Manley's hands move to the metal box. Inside, the box is antiseptically packed with test-tubes, packets and containers. Meanwhile, Dr Grosvenor is enjoying his own lecture.

DR GROSVENOR: [*Continuing.*] You see, I've always found something noble about your career. Noble in the most fundamental sense. In the primitive world, man was obliged to go out into an unknown wilderness and discover food. He was unbound then by prejudices about what did and did not comprise the edible. He tried anything he could get his hands on. You, Mr Kingston, are one of the few in modern times worthy of our great pioneers in taste. The rest of us, even someone like myself, we're akin to the women-folk who waited in the caves worrying about how to cook what the hunters brought back . . .

Dr Grosvenor is interrupted by Manley snapping shut the lid of the attaché case.

MANLEY: I am most indebted to you, Dr Grosvenor.
DR GROSVENOR: Not at all. A pleasure.

Manley gets to his feet, holding the case. He moves towards the door.

MANLEY: I'll be on my way.

Dr Grosvenor rises to show Manley out.

DR GROSVENOR: You're extremely welcome, Mr Kingston, to remain a while and sample Señor Perez's new offerings. He'll be presenting his dishes in twenty minutes.
MANLEY: [*With haughty disdain.*] So kind, no thank you.
DR GROSVENOR: You're familiar with Señor Perez's work?
MANLEY: [*Shaking his head; he has long been above such things.*] Mmmm.
DR GROSVENOR: A very interesting talent. Personally, I find his preparations suffer from certain unnecessarily *romantic* effects. But really, overall, a very interesting talent. In his native Central America, he's regarded as something of a revolutionary. You're sure you won't stay? [*But he laughs before Manley has time to respond.*] But of course, you have other plans.
MANLEY: Quite.

19. CAR. DAY.
Carter is in the front seat of the stationary Rolls, eating a take-away ham-

burger. He chews slowly and deliberately, as though he is chewing over some deep plot. He glances outside, and something makes him stop chewing. Then he puts away his unfinished burger, carefully re-packing it in its napkins and cardboard.

20. DR GROSVENOR'S HOUSE. DAY.

The Rolls has remained where we last saw it.

What Carter has seen is Manley emerging from the house and coming towards the car, attaché case in hand. Carter gets out of the car and opens the back door for Manley. Manley gets in. Rolls drives off.

21. BEDROOM. DAY.

Manley is sitting on the edge of a double bed, dressed in a safari jacket. What resembles items of kitchenware dangle from his belt. He is examining something on the bed, which means his back is turned to his wife, Winnie, kneeling on the carpet by the bed. She is fastening a small saucepan to Manley's belt.

Winnie, forty-seven, is a small, stay-at-home woman; not the type to have affairs during her husband's prolonged absences. Her nervous manner in the ensuing scene arises not from any fear of Manley, but because she is in awe of him. Her bedroom would normally be tidy, comfortable and conservative. But for the moment, spread all over the bed are "tools" which look vaguely surgical, vaguely like more kitchenware; also, an open suitcase from which the "tools" have originated, a small camping stove, a bulky net. On the floor nearby – though we need not see this for the moment – is a large empty duffle bag.

Throughout the ensuing dialogue, Manley remains preoccupied with these items – concerned there is nothing omitted and that all is in working order.

Winnie finishes fastening the saucepan. She now begins to tie a wok on to Manley's back. Her task is not facilitated by Manley, who – oblivious to Winnie – is constantly moving. This infuriating charade continues throughout the following dialogue. But Winnie, for her part, displays not a hint of impatience.

WINNIE: Was the trip to Iceland useful at all?
MANLEY: Mmm? Oh . . . I didn't go. Nothing very interesting up there any more.
WINNIE: What a pity. Mr Knutsen would have been so disappointed.
MANLEY: Knutsen? Oh yes.

Then Manley turns slightly towards Winnie, thus sabotaging her wok-tying.

WINNIE: [*An embarrassed smile.*] You wrote to me last time you were in Iceland. You told me all about Mr Knutsen. And about his most interesting oven.
MANLEY: [*Preoccupied again.*] Mmm.

WINNIE: [*Fondly.*] Two years ago now. 1984.
MANLEY: Mmm.

Manley begins to load the various items into his duffle bag, giving each item a final check before packing it. Meanwhile, Winnie continues her attempts to secure the wok on to Manley's back.

MANLEY: I suppose . . . [*He turns slightly, again sabotaging the wok-tying.*] you're curious as to where I'm going tonight.
WINNIE: [*Laughs.*] I know you don't like me to pry.
MANLEY: [*Preoccupied with packing again.*] Mmm.

Winnie finally succeeds in securing the wok.

WINNIE: There!

Another angle: Manley stands up and surveys the room to check he has not forgotten anything. He picks up his duffle bag, which is now very full.

MANLEY: [*Looking around the room a last time.*] Hmm. Should be everything.

Winnie, too, glances concernedly around the room. Manley turns to exit.

22. MANLEY'S MANSION BLOCK.
Carter is waiting, leaning against the Rolls, eating his hamburger in the slow deliberate manner we saw before. As he does so he is looking at the front of the Kingstons' mansion block.
Point of view: Carter. Move slowly up and across the obviously expensive and ornate archway around the Kingstons' front door. Resume on Carter: chewing his hamburger slowly as though chewing over the details of the archway. His face, as usual, gives little away.

23. HALL.
Manley begins to put his coat on. This presents difficulties on account of the dangling objects about his person. As he moves to the door Winnie comes into the hall. She moves to follow him and we hear the front door slam off screen. Hold on Winnie, devoid of expression.

24. MANLEY'S MANSION BLOCK.
Manley comes down the front path towards the Rolls, still parked as we last saw it. He is carrying his duffle bag and is still struggling a little with his coat. Carter holds the door open for Manley.

25. A STREET. NORTH OF WEST END.
Rolls Royce moving through the street.

26. CAR.
Carter is at the wheel. Manley is in the back seat, looking out of the side window, deep in thought.

27. ANTE-ROOM IN SOUTH AMERICA. NIGHT.
    Close shot: Rossi.

28. CAR. DAY.
    On Manley: deep in thought.

    MANLEY: You know, Carson, I've been working on this project now for nine years.

    On Carter.

    CARTER: Carter, Sir. [*Pause.*] Name's Carter, Sir.

    On Manley: still lost in thought, no sign of his having heard Carter. Move in on Manley's face – car drives into a tunnel.

29. ANTE-ROOM IN SOUTH AMERICA. NIGHT.
    Close shot: Rossi.
    MANLEY: [*Voice over.*] Mmm. Three times before, I've tried and failed. But this time, I've covered every eventuality.

30. CAR.
    Close shot: Manley still lost in thought.

    MANLEY: Trial and error, Carson. Persevere and it's bound to come right in the end.

    On Carter: who does not react at all.

    MANLEY: Nine years . . .

31. ROOM IN SOUTH AMERICA. NIGHT.

    MANLEY: Nine years since I met Rossi.

    Background music begins. A room with four men and two beautiful women.
    Background music gets louder and continues through the following series of shots. The shots are silent – we hear no sound other than the music.
    The door: which is chained and bolted. This is the object of the men's stares; evidently, someone has knocked. A servant in breeches, about forty, comes into shot. He looks through a peep-hole, says something through the door and waits apprehensively. Then, satisfied, he unchains and unbolts the door, lets in Rossi, and quickly shuts the door again. Rossi is over seventy, a white-haired man in a white suit. He could be a scientist. He surveys the room with a calm, amused expression.
    Point of view: Rossi. The room suggests money and decadence – like a back room of a brothel or casino. Five male guests are sitting around the room. Four of these – all aged forty-five or over – are of Latin origin. They look like men accustomed to power, but at the moment, they are smoking as though to relieve nervousness. They look furtively towards the camera. A guilty thrill hovers around them, as though a drug- or sex-orgy is about to take place.

Rossi's gaze settles on a fifth guest: this is Manley sitting apart, looking bored. Manley is fanning himself with a hat.

An electric fan: in motion on a chest of drawers.

A large joint of meat: being brought in on a platter and placed at a low table at the centre of the guests. The meat is not readily identifiable.

Latin man: looks at the meat like a Catholic boy looking at his first naked woman – shock, fascination, fear, embarrassment.

Faces around the table: display unconvincing attempts to conceal nervousness and excitement. Grins exchanged as though for reassurance. Manley, by contrast, is eating without the least self-consciousness. Again, he looks over to Rossi. Rossi too is an old hand. He wears a similar bored look.

The joint: being carved. Soft, pinkish, bloody.

Faces eating the meat, chewing and tasting with fascinated deliberation. Guilt, pleasure, nervousness.

Manley eats without the least self-consciousness. He looks over to Rossi, who returns a look as though to say: "What a bore."

32. ANTE-CHAMBER. NIGHT.

Background music fades. Sound of insects and birds fade in.

Manley is looking out of the window, smoking a cigar. He looks sulky. Rossi is standing in the room behind him, also smoking. He has just been trying to make some point to Manley. The door into the next room is ajar, through which can be heard sounds of merry-making – tension-relieving after the eating of the meat. Laughter and shouting continue in the background throughout the ensuing dialogue, but never so loud as to interrupt the speakers.

ROSSI: [*With an Italian accent.*] You look offended, Mr Kingston. [*He smiles reconcilingly.*] Please. I didn't mean to imply you are not a man of great achievements. Of course you are. And I am very sincere, when I ask you to see me as your father-figure. You see, Mr Kingston . . . [*Lowers voice.*] I am now old. I have a bad heart. I will not live much longer.

Manley turns to Rossi. He looks vaguely interested, but not at all sympathetic. He says nothing.

ROSSI: No need for sympathies, Mr Kingston. I have no desire to live much longer. I have done everything there is to do. My tongue has tasted everything on this earth. [*Pauses. Then with meaning.*] Even once, something that was *not* of this earth.

Rossi smiles conceitedly. Manley's curiosity has been aroused. He takes the cigar from his mouth and turns to Rossi.

MANLEY: Not of this earth?

ROSSI: You see, Mr Kingston, I am your true father. And you are my true son.

I wish you to be the heir to my greatest accomplishment. This is why I tell you this. Yes. I have tasted that which is not of this earth. I have eaten a ghost.

Manley is stunned. He is at once inspired and humiliated. He asks the following question despite himself.

MANLEY: What – er – did it taste like?
ROSSI: [*Laughs triumphantly.*] I wonder how many in the world have had the privilege of hearing such a question from your lips, Mr Kingston.

Manley is now really put out. He turns to leave.

MANLEY: Quite, quite.

ROSSI: [*Becoming suddenly serious.*] Mr Kingston, please.

Rossi ushers Manley to come back. Manley hesitates.

ROSSI: Don't mix with those nonentities. I wish to help you. You are my natural heir.

Manley comes back and stares again out of the window. He puts his cigar in his mouth and avoids looking at Rossi. Rossi too looks out at the view. He draws deeply on his cigar.

ROSSI: The process by which one consumes a ghost is not a simple one. I devoted many years research to the task. I am willing, Mr Kingston, to pass to you – and you only – the fruits of my labour. I ask only in return that you acknowledge me, in the years to come – in your *great* years – as your mentor. You are interested, are you not, Mr Kingston?

A confident glint is in Rossi's eye. He has Manley hooked.

ROSSI: Good. Come to my apartment tomorrow and we will discuss this further. [*With a smile, Rossi starts to leave. Then turns.*] As for your – er – question, the taste is exquisite. [*He gestures with his hands.*] Like nothing on earth.

33. CENTRAL LONDON. NIGHT.
Rolls Royce in motion. Background music ends.

34. CAR. NIGHT.
On Manley: now very alert, leaning forward to see up ahead.

MANLEY: That's it there, Carson. Slow down.

35. STREET OUTSIDE CHURCH. NIGHT.

Point of view: Manley from car. A dingy back street. Derelict houses and graffitied walls. Up ahead is the church we first saw in 1904 (scene one). Outside it, along the church wall, is a queue of men.

Reverse angle: Manley through the window of the approaching car. The car has slowed right down. Manley is looking out intently.

Point of view: Manley from car. We are passing the church gate. At its centre is a wooden plaque. This is not the same plaque we saw in scene one – the design and translation are modern.

> I was hungry and you gave me food
> I was thirsty and you gave me drink
> I was a stranger and you welcomed me.
>
> Matthew 25:35

36. CAR. NIGHT.

Manley is looking intently out of his window.

37. STREET OUTSIDE CHURCH. NIGHT.

Point of view: Manley from car. We are now moving along the queue of homeless men – about twenty in number. Some lean against the wall, some crouch, others sit on the pavement.

There are only men here, because the church takes in only men. Otherwise, a mixed crowd – multi-racial, all ages. Only a few of them are "traditional" tramps; most are losing a battle to maintain a conventional "respectable" appearance. A significant number of teenagers. Their faces are bored and weary. They look towards the passing Rolls without surprise and with little interest.

MANLEY: Drive on a little, Carson. Round that corner there.

Close shot: Carter, whose face gives away nothing. *Another angle*: Rolls moving past queue of men.

38. CUL-DE-SAC. NIGHT.

Dingy ground covered with rubbish. The car comes into shot as it rounds the corner into the cul-de-sac. It halts.

Carter gets out and comes round to open the door for Manley, but Manley has already opened the door himself before Carter can do so.

Manley struggles out, with his big coat, holding his duffle bag. Indeed, he is not unlike a stereotype tramp.

MANLEY: Be here at five tomorrow morning, will you, Carson?

Manley turns and sets off towards the corner, hoisting his bag on his shoulder. He raises his hand without looking round.

On Carter: his face impassive as ever.

39. STREET OUTSIDE CHURCH. NIGHT.

Manley walks purposefully towards the queue of men.

Another angle on a section of the queue: Manley comes into shot. He walks past the queuing men, completely ignoring them. He goes out of shot, leaving us to favour the men in the queue. The men in shot glance neutrally after Manley. He is of no special interest to them.

A few further angles on men in the queue: there is little conversation; most have arrived singly and do not have the will to strike up new acquaintances. Many look exhausted – they have been walking around aimlessly all day – and some look ill. There is a self-consciousness here, such as one may find in a dole queue.

40. FRONT OF THE CHURCH GATE.

Two or three men at the head of the queue are in shot, leaning against the gate.

Manley comes striding into shot. He tries to open the gate, which is locked. He pushes at it.

MAN IN QUEUE: There *is* a queue, mate.
MANLEY: [*Turning.*] What?
MAN IN QUEUE: Queue. [*He nods in the direction of the queue.*]

Manley looks towards the queue, then again at the locked gate. He is very put out.

MANLEY: Mmm.

Grudgingly, Manley strides off towards the back of the queue and out of shot.

41. STREET OUTSIDE CHURCH. NIGHT.

Manley is walking back towards the end of the queue. He ignores the men.

42. PAVEMENT.

David, the last man in the queue, is sitting on the pavement, his back against the church wall.

David, thirty, wears a corduroy jacket and a shirt – which appear for the moment to be in reasonable condition – and ill-fitting trousers with wide flares. Like others in the queue, he looks bored and tired. To a large extent, he is affecting these looks to disguise his feeling uncomfortable and undignified.

Manley comes into shot and takes his place in the queue beside David. Manley shuffles discontentedly, then looks worriedly at the length of the queue ahead.

David observes Manley. In the ensuing dialogue, David speaks with a nonchalance which is not quite convincing.

DAVID: Don't worry, we'll be alright.
MANLEY: [*Noticing him for the first time.*] What?

DAVID: The first fifty always get in.

MANLEY: Oh. Oh yes. [*A quick glance down the queue.*] But *when* do we get in? I was given to believe the place opened at eight.

DAVID: Supposed to. Never does these days though. Not enough people to run the place any more.

MANLEY: Mmmm. I didn't reckon on standing in a queue.

DAVID: Gets longer every night. Here's a few more.

43. STREET.

Point of view: Manley and David. From the direction Manley originally came, two more men are coming down the street to join the queue.

44. PAVEMENT. NIGHT.

Manley and David are both sitting on the ground, gazing emptily ahead of them. During the ensuing dialogue more men join the queue and Manley keeps looking anxiously at the queue in front of him.

DAVID: Get around much, do you?

MANLEY: What?

DAVID: You travel around much.

MANLEY: Oh – yes. I suppose I do. Thousands of miles each year.

DAVID: [*Nodding in weary sympathy.*] Yeah. Same here. [*Pause.*] Just the last few weeks, I've been up to Manchester, come back down here, up to Scunthorpe. Get fed up after a while. [*Pause.*]

You're *from* London, are you?

MANLEY: [*He has not been listening.*] What?

DAVID: You were born here. In London.

MANLEY: Oh – yes. Yes. I don't stay here much though. [*With disparagement.*] A city like this has little to offer someone like me.

DAVID: [*Nodding sympathetically again.*] Yeah. Hopeless. Just as bad everywhere else in the bloody country. If not worse. So what you doing back in London then?

MANLEY: [*Shrugs.*] Usual reason I go anywhere. Hunger.

DAVID: Yeah well. You got to eat.

MANLEY: [*Looking away again.*] Hunger. The lengths I've gone to satisfy it. Yet it always returns.

DAVID: I know what you mean. One point last week, I actually started looking in the bins. [*Laughs.*] Really.

MANLEY: [*A tired shrug.*] It's an old game, but always worth trying. I often recommend it.

DAVID: Surprising what you find if you bother to look.

MANLEY: An interesting process takes place inside a refuse bin. A kind of stewing pot of randomness. The chance factor often produces recipes far beyond the capabilities of ordinary imaginations.

For the first time, the thought crosses David's mind that Manley may be a little eccentric. He decides to agree anyway.

DAVID: Yeah, I suppose so. No good being proud and starving to death. Still, you'll get a decent supper tonight.

Manley turns slowly and looks at David as though for the first time.

MANLEY: How do you know that?

DAVID: Well, that's what you're waiting here for, isn't it?
MANLEY: But how the devil did *you* get to hear of it?
DAVID: [*Shrugs defensively.*] Known about it for ages.
MANLEY: You've what?
DAVID: Got it from an advice centre. Off Piccadilly Circus.
MANLEY: [*Outraged.*] Piccadilly Circus? [*Then realizing his mistake.*] Ah. Ah yes. [*Turning away again.*] No doubt, no doubt.

45. STREET OUTSIDE CHURCH.
Long shot: the queue along the wall.

46. IN FRONT OF THE CHURCH GATE.
Sounds of the gate being unlocked from the inside. It opens.

47. CHURCH COURTYARD.
The men are moving in line to some point around the side of the church building. The main doors of the church remain closed.

48. CHURCH. BACK LOBBY.
The men are filing in from outside, crossing the small lobby and going further inside the church through another door.
    There is occasional conversation, but no more than might be expected in a bus queue. When people talk, their voices tend to be lowered self-consciously.
    Manley and David go by in the procession. David shuffles along, looking only ahead of him. Manley is looking around with careful interest.

49. STAIRCASE DOWN TO THE CRYPT.
The procession files down an old stone staircase. Very much a feeling of going underground.

50. CHURCH CRYPT.
A catering trolley is being wheeled along. On the trolley are a large soup canister, a bakery tray loaded with an assortment of rolls, two ladles, a few "towers" of polyester beakers.
    We do not see clearly the surroundings through which the trolley is being pushed, but from the dim artificial light, we get an impression we are down near the basement of the building. The trolley stops momentarily. Widening, we see this is due to some double doors which are presently closed. Volunteer 1, a young woman in shirt and jeans, comes into shot to hold open one of the doors. As we follow the trolley through the doorway, Volunteer 2, a young man, comes into view. It is he who is pushing the trolley. We follow

the volunteers and the trolley into the church crypt.

The crypt is the same large basement room we saw in scene two. If space alone were the criterion, this room would be adequate shelter for the fifty or so men now present. However, there is a comfortless, airless feeling about the place. There are now mattresses spread on the floor beside the walls, but otherwise there has been little visible change since 1904. Lighting is by spotlights, which create heavy shadows.

The men have been sitting on the mattresses conversing much more than they did in the queue outside. As the trolley comes in, there is an oddly quiet, but immediate response; the men rise and move towards the centre of the room where the trolley is expected to halt. No one pushes or comes rushing; there is, nevertheless, an urgency in their manner.

51. CRYPT. A CORNER.

Over the shoulder: a sketch plan of the church, which we glimpsed in the attaché case.

Another angle: Manley is seated on a mattress, back to the wall, studying the sketch plan. He is ignoring the arrival of the trolley.

Beside him, David is crouching on his heels. He looks anxiously in the direction of the food, then hesitantly at Manley. Shadows moving around them suggest they are among the last to get up.

DAVID: I thought you were hungry.
MANLEY: What? Oh . . . No, no. I'm going to dine later.
DAVID: There won't be any left later.

But Manley is absorbed in his sketch plan. He looks at it intently, frowns, then cranes his neck trying to see something on the other side of the room.

David shrugs, gets to his feet and goes out of shot.

52. CRYPT. A CORNER.

Manley is still sitting by the wall, studying his plan.

53. CRYPT.

At the trolley, the two volunteers are as busy as ever.

Then – a series of shots around the room of the men eating.

Some of the men, not far from the trolley, are eating standing up. Others eat sitting on their mattresses, backs against a wall. Not only the environment, but the means by which they are obliged to eat makes the whole procedure appear rather disgusting. The men "drink" the beans from the beaker, then chew, taking an occasional bite from a roll. Some eat hungrily. Others appear to be eating only because they know they should, without really caring if they do or not. Many look mentally and physically exhausted. Meanwhile, the buzz of conversation continues. Above which we hear:

VOLUNTEER 1: [*Off: calling in background.*] Don't bung your cups on the ground, please. We'll come round with a bag in a minute. Don't bung them on the ground, you've got to sleep here, remember.

One young man stares into his beaker, not eating.

 An older man is making a particular mess of his supper. The beans are running down his chin, but he chews on regardless.

54. CRYPT.
The lights have been turned off, but there is still light coming in from some-where, enabling us to make out the shapes of the fifty or so men huddled or lying asleep.

 A grotesque chorus of snores.

55. CRYPT. IN FRONT OF THE DOUBLE DOORS.
The snores continue.

 One of the double doors opens. Manley enters. He comes in backwards, preoccupied with something outside the doors. His duffle bag is on his shoulder.

 He closes the door quietly and turns. He is holding his sketch-plan. He brings this close to his face in the bad light, lowers it again, then looks about him with a perturbed air.

56. CRYPT.
A slow pan across sleeping, snoring shapes.

57. CRYPT. A CORNER. NIGHT.
Close shot: David, asleep on his side. A hand comes into shot and shakes David's shoulder. David starts awake – the reflex of someone used to sleep-ing in places where he fears discovery. He looks up.

 Point of view: David. Manley's face is looking down at him. There is something alarming about Manley's face seen in these circumstances.

MANLEY: [*Whispering; he is now more animated than we have yet seen him.*] I need your assistance.
DAVID: What's the matter?
MANLEY: [*Holding up the sketch-plan.*] My information has not proved to be as accurate as I had a right to expect. Do you know the geography of this building?
DAVID: [*Props himself up on to his elbows and looks past Manley as though for some explanation.*] What? What you up to?
MANLEY: I wish to reach the vestry. I need first to get up to the main church.
DAVID: [*Pointing.*] Well, you can go up through . . . [*He breaks off.*] Look, what you up to?
MANLEY: I am hungry. I wish to dine. Perhaps you'd be so good as to indicate to me how to get to the main church.
DAVID: Well, no wonder you're hungry. You should have ate when you had the chance. What's all this about the vestry anyhow?
MANLEY: [*Becoming impatient.*] I expect to find my dinner there.
DAVID: You reckon?
MANLEY: To *that* extent, my information should prove reliable. Now, if you'd be so good as to assist me. I'm *very* hungry.

DAVID: Should have eaten when I told you to.

David turns over to go back to sleep. But he remembers the times *he* has been hungry. Almost immediately, he looks up again at Manley, sighs and begins to get up.

DAVID: There won't be anything left anyway.

58. STAIRCASE.
David and Manley are climbing the staircase we came down earlier. We cannot see much in the darkness, but we hear Manley's heavy breathing. This may well be due to physical effort, but it also sounds like mounting excitement.

59. TOP OF STAIRCASE.
The better light shows us that Manley is still carrying his duffle bag.

DAVID: [*Low voice.*] You'll know better next time. Stomach's *always* going to catch up with you.

Manley, breathing heavily, consults his sketch map.

MANLEY: Mmmm.

Manley starts to go in one direction. David touches his arm and leads in the opposite direction.

DAVID: This way.

60. CHURCH.
Viewed from the pulpit. Many shadows. We see the pews, etc., by the moonlight coming through the windows.
   In a shot strongly reminiscent of scene three, we first hear Manley's breathing, then gradually make out the figures of Manley and David. We hear, in lowered voices:

DAVID: [*Voice-over.*] They catch us doing this, we'll get banned from this place. [*Then a new thought.*] Anyway, it'll all be locked up.
MANLEY: [*Voice-over.*] I have all the appropriate keys.
DAVID: [*Voice-over.*] God. How d'you get those?

61. IN FRONT OF THE VESTRY DOOR.
Close up: Manley's hands sorting through a bunch of mortis keys. These keys all have large tags – these are the same we glimpsed in scene ten.
   Wider angle: Manley selects a key and fits it to the vestry door. Meanwhile, David stands beside him, casting nervous glances all around the church.

MANLEY: [*As key turns.*] Ah.

Manley opens the door. David looks quickly at the doorway, then throws more furtive glances around the church.

DAVID: Well, enjoy yourself.

David begins to move off. Manley grasps his arm – but not aggressively. It could almost be an insistent hospitality.

MANLEY: You're very welcome to join me. In fact, I suspect I'll need further assistance. Please.

Manley ushers a reluctant David into the vestry.

62. VESTRY.

David looks about him. Manley comes in behind him. He shuts and *locks* the door. David does not see this. Manley also surveys the vestry.

 Point of view: Manley and David: A small bare room as in scene four. Light from outside illuminates the doorway through to the back room. Now, as in 1904, the doorway has no door. It is black and ominous, like the gateway to another world.

DAVID: [*Trying to hide nervousness.*] Well, I can't see any food. Anyway, I've had my supper.

David turns and goes to the vestry door, and finds it locked. He tries a few more times to open it. His manner reveals how desperate he is to get out of the vestry. He turns and looks back at Manley.

 Manley, all the while, has been looking around the room with interest, not bothering with David's efforts to get out.

DAVID: You've locked it.

Manley puts down his duffle bag, then takes off his coat, revealing his safari costume with dangling pans, spoons, etc. He drops the coat on the floor.

 David watches for a beat, then looks towards the doorway to the back room.

DAVID: [*Sounding casual.*] Er – I'll take a look what's in here.

David sneaks past Manley towards the black doorway. Manley is too preoccupied with his unpacking to look up at David.

 On black doorway: David hesitates at the threshold, trying to see into the blackness. He gives a quick glance towards Manley, then vanishes through the doorway.

 On Manley: who looks up and watches the doorway as though for confirmation of something he knows will happen.

 On black doorway: hold on the doorway for an ominously long time –

long enough so that we expect a scream or something from within.

Then David appears in the doorway. He looks utterly drained.

MANLEY: [*Smiling.*] Well? What did you find in there?

DAVID: [*Shocked.*] There's nothing there. Completely black. [*He manages a nervous laugh.*] I thought for a minute I wouldn't get back out.

MANLEY: Now, my friend, why don't you help me instead of wandering around like that. There's a good fellow.

Manley is holding out his hand invitingly towards the floor.

Another angle: in the half-light, we make out an array of objects Manley has laid out on the floor. These are basically the objects we saw in scene twenty-two: the stove, the various metallic utensils, the net, jars and containers – and Dr Grosvenor's box.

On David: the experience in the back room has shaken him. He seems to have lost the will to offer any resistance. He looks meekly at the equipment. Then, as though suddenly remembering, he looks nervously back to the black doorway and takes a step away from it. *Dissolve to*:

63. VESTRY.

Close shot: a candle burning on a saucer on the floor.

Another angle: Manley is shifting about studying something on the floor around the black doorway. We cannot yet see what it is he is studying. He crouches, moves around to get another perspective, like a golfer assessing a crucial putt.

David is standing behind him, leaning against a wall. He is clutching his jacket protectively to himself.

MANLEY: Mmm.

Manley crouches again to scrutinize the unseen objects on the floor. Clearly, he is unhappy about something.

Manley straightens, then without taking his eyes from the floor, gestures towards David.

MANLEY: Your jacket. That will do.

DAVID: What?

MANLEY: [*Gesturing more impatiently; eyes still fixed on the floor.*] Give me your jacket.

David is still clutching his jacket to himself.

DAVID: Rather not, if it's all right with you. I need this jacket.

MANLEY: [*Impatient.*] You'll get it back, man. Now this is important. Your jacket.

Manley goes on studying the floor, a hand held out in full expectation of being handed the jacket.

David looks about him, then reluctantly begins to take off his jacket. At one point, he hesitates, then continues. The reason for his hesitation is that there is a big hole in his shirt, previously hidden by the jacket. He tries to make the hole less conspicuous by hiding it under an arm.

Manley takes the jacket from David without looking at him and continues to shift and assess, holding the jacket open before him.

DAVID: Look – er – I need that jacket. It's not going to get . . .
MANLEY: [*Cutting in.*] You'll get it back. Now, kindly allow me a few moments of silence. The most *precise* calculations are essential here.

David looks on, worried for his jacket.

64. VESTRY. LATER.

Close shot: the rip on David's shirt. David is fingering it self-consciously, as though somehow it can be folded away.

Widen to find Manley and David sitting on the floor, backs against the wall, facing the black doorway. The candle is on the floor in front of them. Manley is not expecting the ghost to appear quite yet. Nevertheless, his eyes are fixed on the doorway. He wears a brooding look. David is also looking at the doorway. His posture suggests he is trying to maximize the distance between himself and the doorway.

On the black doorway: hold on the doorway for a beat. Then moving down, we see something has happened to the floor in front of the threshold. A line of what appears to be pieces of bread forms a semi-circle around the doorway. Within the semi-circle, the floor is covered with white powder, dotted with what looks like olives. In a central position, David's jacket is laid out, arms outstretched.

On Manley and David: David gives a start at Manley's voice, though it is not loud.

MANLEY: Very well. I will tell you.
DAVID: What's that?
MANLEY: One night in nineteen hundred and four, a pauper was murdered. In *there*.

David follows Manley's gaze.

On the black doorway: we close in slowly over the following exchange.

DAVID: [*Voice-over.*] Why?
MANLEY: [*Voice-over.*] What?
DAVID: [*Voice-over.*] Why was he murdered?
MANLEY: [*Voice-over: he considers this an irrelevant diversion.*] Oh . . . some human organs were needed for research purposes, some such thing. In any case, he was brought up here and killed through *there*. Eighty years ago.

MANLEY: [*Continuing; teasing David into the conclusion.*] On this very night.

DAVID: I get it. We're waiting for his ghost to appear.

MANLEY: Very good. And I am informed it is a very reliable ghost, as ghosts go. [*A pause.*]

DAVID: And you're going to . . .

MANLEY: Precisely.

On the black doorway.

MANLEY: [*Voice-over continuing.*] And I am now *quite* hungry.

65. VESTRY. AN HOUR LATER.

Close shot: the rip on David's shirt. Now, it is being allowed to hang open. Widen to reveal David, sitting as before, back against the wall. He no longer looks frightened; he seems resigned, past caring.

Pan slowly until close on Manley, sitting beside David. He now looks much more hungry and impatient. He is hunched forward, breathing heavily, his gaze fixed on the doorway. He looks lecherous.

Another angle: Manley suddenly lurches forward, looking intently ahead. David does not react, but goes on staring blankly in front of him. This is because Manley has lurched forward numerous times before during the past hour. Manley relaxes and settles back.

MANLEY: Hmm. I thought I saw something move again.

DAVID: [*Emotionlessly.*] I'm the ghost around here. It's me.

MANLEY: Now, you're quite clear what you are to do? It's absolutely imperative everything is timed precisely.

DAVID: [*Staring blankly ahead.*] I'm the ghost around here. Could vanish tonight, nobody would notice.

MANLEY: Sssh!

Manley lurches forward.

On the black doorway: hold for a few beats. Nothing happens.

On Manley and David: Manley is settling back again. David is still gazing blankly ahead.

MANLEY: Mmm.

66. CHURCH.

Point of view: unidentified presence which is moving up the side aisle of the church. It then seeks out the vestry door.

67. VESTRY.

Close shot: Manley's face igniting with excitement.

MANLEY: [*Hissing.*] There!

Manley rises to his feet, his eyes never leaving the doorway. We see his net is grasped in his hands. David, as though awakened from a dream, starts, then also hurries to his feet.

MANLEY: [*Off; hissing.*] This time definitely! Something moved. Prepare yourself.

Hold on the doorway: there is a movement amid the darkness, which we cannot identify. Then a tramp appears in the doorway. His coat and body become visible, then his face. This is an "old-fashioned" tramp, with a big raggy coat. He is middle-aged, small, with a friendly, cheeky face. There is absolutely nothing eerie about him. The tramp rubs his eyes, as though he has just been awakened, then grins sheepishly.

TRAMP: Evening.

On Manley and David: both staring at the tramp in some confusion. Manley's net is poised in one hand.

TRAMP: What's going on here then? What's all this? [*He prods with his foot the powder on the floor.*] Spilt something here, have you?
MANLEY: Leave that alone!
TRAMP: [*Looking offended.*] Don't know who are you are, mate, but you won't catch much with that there. After butterflies, go back to Hampstead Heath.
MANLEY: [*Lowering his net, outraged.*] What are *you* doing here?
TRAMP: What am I doing here? I might ask you geezers the same question. I always sleep here. I clean the floors for the old reverend and he lets me stay in here. Can't sleep down there with all that snoring and God knows what else going on. Still, don't know how you geezers got to come up here.
MANLEY: We happen to be awaiting a highly important event. And you, my man, are *in the way*.
TRAMP: [*Shrugs.*] Pardon me, mate. But I tell you there's nothing much in there. If there is, I never noticed it.

As he says this, the tramp turns and looks into the black doorway. Hold on the tramp, his back turned to camera.

MANLEY: Well, I assure you something is very likely to materialize, and I would ask you kindly to remove yourself from that vicinity.

The tramp does not respond. His back has not moved since he turned. Hold a further beat, then zoom in quickly as the tramp begins to turn back towards camera. For a fleeting moment, we glimpse the tramp's face, which has changed. It is the face of a dead man – staring, horror-struck, blood on the lips. We only catch this fleetingly, because we immediately cut to: Manley and David, utterly shocked. Manley comes to his senses first.

MANLEY: The flame, quick! Quick, man, quick!

Another angle: something causes a ring of flames to burst around the doorway. The figure of the tramp remains as still as a statue, caught half-turned, looking over his shoulder. We cannot see the face through the flames.

Point of view: Ghost. Through the flames, David is frantically throwing some powder from a bowl towards the camera. His urgency owes more to some illogical sense of self-defence than to enthusiasm for Manley's cause.

Manley is unfurling his net. Taking deliberate aim, he throws it. The net covers the camera, and the screen goes black.

68. VESTRY/BACKROOM. A HALF-HOUR LATER.
Fade in: the vestry is empty. The net, and David's jacket, lie on the floor at the doorway to the back room. The flames have gone and there is no sign of fire-damage.

There is now light coming from within the back room. We move in slowly through the doorway to discover: Manley sitting on a small stool, hunched over his stove, cooking something in his wok. The flame of the stove appears to be our only source of light. It is not strong enough to show us details of the back room. However:

David is caught within the glow of the stove. He is propped against a wall. He is staring towards Manley.

Close-up: Manley's face. Impatient and lecherous, looking down at what he is cooking. He smiles in anticipation.

Manley puts spices into the wok. Hissing and sizzling sounds issue from the wok. We do not yet see the contents of the wok.

David, eyes blank, is still staring towards Manley.

69. CENTRAL LONDON. VERY EARLY MORNING.
Charing Cross and Trafalgar Square. The city has not yet awoken.

70. BACK ALLEY NEAR CHARING CROSS. VERY EARLY MORNING.
Garbage and old newspapers on the ground. A row of dustbins line the alley. At the far end, an old man is looking through a bin for food. He holds a plastic carrier bag into which he puts anything edible. We watch him going from bin to bin, coming towards us up the alley.

Manley appears in the foreground of our shot. He now has his overcoat on again. He is staggering. He halts and leans against a wall, turning to camera as he does so. Manley looks very ill. He is clutching his stomach and breathing heavily. Manley turns and vomits into the nearest dust-bin. Meanwhile, the old man, searching a few bins away, has his back towards Manley and is thus unaware of Manley's vomiting. Manley finishes vomiting, turns towards us and staggers away out of shot. The old man finishes with his bin and turns to the next in line. One glance tells him this is empty. His next bin is the one Manley has vomited into. The old man comes walking up the alley towards us, holding open his carrier bag expectantly. Just as he is about to peer into the bin, we cut to:

71. THE UNDERPASS OF A BRIDGE. VERY EARLY MORNING.

About fifteen men are sheltering on the pavement beneath the bridge. There are signs here of permanent encampment; empty bottles, blankets, newspapers and cardboard boxes marking out "places". Around half the men are in sitting positions, propped up by the wall – either because they are awake, or because they sleep in this position.

Manley's figure appears at the far end of the underpass and comes staggering towards us. The men pay little attention to him. Manley stops halfway down the underpass, leaning against the wall to regain his breath.

Another angle: just where Manley has halted, one homeless man is sitting on the ground. He is around forty. He wears a suit but no tie. His clothes are now stained and creased, but conceivably, in these same clothes several months ago, this man may have sold insurance. The homeless man looks up sympathetically at Manley and indicates the space next to him. There is a "seat" of flattened cardboard.

HOMELESS MAN: Sit down. Take a rest.
MANLEY: Mmm.

Manley sits down, still short of breath. He looks broodingly into the space ahead of him. The homeless man fixes Manley with a friendly smile. Manley ignores him for a while, but the homeless man continues smiling. Manley gives the homeless man a quick glance, then looks beyond his companion, down the underpass.

On Manley and homeless man: Manley rubs his stomach slowly and gazes broodingly into space once more.

HOMELESS MAN: Overdid it, did we?
MANLEY: What?
HOMELESS MAN: Bit too much of the old . . . [*Makes a drinking gesture.*]

Manley looks at the homeless man with disdain. Then with dignity:

MANLEY: I was hungry. I ate. Now I am sick.
HOMELESS MAN: [*Shrugs.*] Right, right. See what you mean.
MANLEY: You see what I mean? I very much doubt that. How could *you* ever understand the kind of hunger I suffer?
HOMELESS MAN: Well. We all get hungry, don't we?

Manley gives the homeless man another disparaging look.

MANLEY: You have no idea what *real* hunger is.

Homeless man shrugs. Manley continues to look broodingly into space, slowly rubbing his stomach.

72. THE UNDERPASS. EARLY MORNING. A LITTLE LATER.

A Rolls Royce appears at the far end of the underpass and comes slowly past the homeless people.

73. CAR. EARLY MORNING.

Carter, driving, is watching the pavement. He has been searching for some time. His gaze fixes on Manley and the barest hint of a smile crosses his face. He brings the car to a halt, then for a beat or two, remains in his seat, gazing out towards Manley.

74. THE UNDERPASS.

The Rolls has stopped in front of Manley and the homeless man. Manley looks moodily up at the car, but makes no move to stand up. Carter comes out, unhurrying. He makes no move to assist Manley to his feet; instead, he opens the back door and stands holding it open. Manley rises to his feet tiredly. Carter continues to hold the door open, making no effort to assist the struggling Manley as he climbs into the car. *On homeless man*: there is no surprise on his face. Few things surprise him. He watches with the same friendly smile.

Sounds of doors slamming.

Another angle: the Rolls starts up. It moves past the rest of the homeless people and out of shot.

75. A LONDON STREET.

The Rolls moves along a deserted street.

76. CAR.

During the following speech, Manley continues to look tiredly out of the window. Although he ostensibly addresses Carter, he is really just thinking aloud and thus does not notice anything amiss in Carter's silence.

MANLEY: [*Without triumph.*] You may like to know, Carson. I achieved what I set out to do last night.

Carter shows no reaction.

MANLEY: Not quite as extraordinary as one may have expected. [*Pause.*] A disappointment all in all. Perhaps I'll take a trip up to Iceland again. [*Pause.*] Mmm. So dreary, Carson. [*Pause*] Life gets so dreary once you've tasted its more obvious offerings.

Manley continues to gaze out of the window, lost in his thoughts.

77. BACK ROOM/VESTRY. VERY EARLY MORNING.

Close shot: David. Asleep propped up against the wall, then he starts awake. He looks around then relaxes. The back room is small and stark, a kind of storeroom for odd bits of church junk. Although we need not notice this yet, there is an old full-length mirror propped against one wall. On the floor are the remains of Manley's presence. It looks much like any untidily abandoned camp-site. The wok sits crookedly on the gas stove. Spoons, spatulas, an empty plate, jars and packets lie strewn around. Manley's stool has keeled over.

David is behaving much like someone waking after a heavy drinking binge. He sighs heavily and rubs the back of his neck. He suddenly remembers the rip in his shirt and examines it as though in hope that it may have healed overnight. He rises to his feet tiredly. He continues to finger the rip in a preoccupied way, while his eyes search the room for something.

Point of view: David.

The wok with three or four pieces of meat still stuck to the edges. With a tired curiosity, he goes to the wok and crouches down by it.

David reaches down and picks off a piece of meat from the wok. He holds it gingerly, as one might a slug. He brings it cautiously to his face. The smell – powerful and awful – hits him. He grimaces and flings the piece of meat away. Then he sighs again and stares emptily in front of him. Still fingering the rip in his shirt, David goes to the doorway. He continues to glance about him in search of something. Through the doorway, we can see to the vestry door, which is now slightly ajar. We move down to the floor around the back room doorway, to discover the object of David's search – his jacket. It lies amid white powdery ash.

David picks up his jacket, brushes as much ash off as possible, then puts it on. There is a large hole burnt around the shoulder. David notices this with dismay. He fingers the hole in his jacket, then his attention is caught by something in the back room. He returns into the back room, holding the burn in his jacket as though it is a wound.

What David has seen is the full-length mirror, left abandoned against a wall. He stands in front of it, then takes his hand away from the burn in his jacket. He looks at his appearance with an empty expression. Then he sighs, shrugs and turns away, once again rubbing the back of his neck.

78. CENTRAL LONDON. EARLY MORNING.
Rolls moving through morning streets.

PROLOGUE, 1963

Tananarive Due

Tananarive Due (b.1966) was born in Tallahassee, Florida, to civil rights activist, Patricia Stephens Due and civil rights lawyer, John D. Due Jr. She worked on the *Miami Herald* while writing her first novel, *The Between* (1995). She has published over a dozen books and now teaches on the creative writing MFA program at Antioch University, Los Angeles. Due lives in Southern California with her husband, the writer Steven Barnes, and their son.

Hilton was seven when his grandmother died, and it was a bad time. But it was worse when she died again.

Hilton called her Nana, but her real name was Eunice Kelly. She raised Hilton by herself in rural Florida, in Belle Glade, which was forty miles from Palm Beach's rich white folks who lived like characters in a storybook. They shared a two-room house with a rusty tin roof on a road named for Frederick Douglass. The road wasn't paved, and the stones hurt Hilton's tender feet whenever he walked barefoot. Douglass Road was bounded by tomato fields behind an old barbed wire fence Nana told him never to touch because he might get something she called tetanus, and they couldn't afford a doctor. Hilton knew they were poor, but he never felt deprived because he had everything he wanted. Even as young as he was, Hilton understood the difference.

Nana had been a migrant worker for years, so she had muscles like a man on her shoulders and forearms. Nana always saved her money, and she played the organ for pay at the church the monied blacks attended across town, so she hadn't harvested sugarcane or picked string beans alongside the Puerto Ricans and Jamaicans in a long time.

Hilton worshipped her. She was his whole world. He didn't know anything about his parents except that they were gone, and he didn't miss them. He didn't think it was fair to his friends that they had mamas and daddies instead of Nana.

Nana always said she didn't intend for Hilton to end up in the fields, that there were bigger things in store for him, so she sent him to school instead. She'd taught him to read before he ever walked through the doorway of the colored school a half mile away. And it was when he came home from school on a hot May afternoon that his life was changed forever.

He found Nana sprawled across her clean-swept kitchen floor, eyes closed, a white scarf wrapped around her head. She wasn't moving, and not a sound came from her. Hilton didn't panic just yet because Nana was old and sometimes fainted from heat when she tried to act younger, so he knelt beside her and shook her, calling her name. That worked by itself sometimes. Otherwise, he'd need to find her salts. But when he touched her forearm, he drew his hand away with a cry. Even with the humidity in the little house and the steam from pots boiling over on top of the stove, their lids bouncing like angry demons, Nana's flesh felt as cold as just-drawn well water. As cold as December. He'd never touched a person who felt that way, and even as a child he knew only dead people turned cold like that.

Hilton stumbled to his feet and ran crying outside to find a grown-up who could help. He was only half seeing because of his tears, banging on door after door on Douglass Road, yelling through the screens, and finding no one home. After each door, his sobs rose higher and his throat closed up a little more tightly until he could barely breathe. It was as though everyone were simply gone now, and no one was left but him. He felt like he'd tried a hundred houses, and all he'd found was barking dogs. The barking and running made him feel dizzy. He could hardly catch his breath any more, like he would die himself.

In truth, there were only six houses on Douglass Road. The last belonged to Zeke Higgs, a Korean War veteran angry with middle age, angry with white folks, and whom no child with sense would bother on any other day because he kept a switch by his door. Zeke appeared like a shadow behind his screen when Hilton came pounding and crying, "Nana's dead. Come help Nana." Zeke scooped Hilton under his arm and ran to the house.

When he got home, Hilton's childhood flew from him. Nana was no longer lying lifeless on the kitchen floor. She was standing over the kitchen stove, stirring pots, and the first thing she said was: "I wondered where you'd run off to, boy." She looked at Zeke's face and nodded at him, then she fixed her eyes on Hilton. "I'm 'fraid Nana's made a mess of supper, Hilton. Just a mess."

"You all right, Mrs. Kelly?" Zeke asked, studying her face. Hilton did the same. She was perspiring, and her cheeks were redder than usual underneath her thin cocoa-colored skin.

"Just fine. May have had a fainting spell is all. I hope Hilton didn't send you into a fright."

Zeke mumbled something about how it wasn't a bother, although he was annoyed. Hilton barely noticed Zeke slip back out of the house because his eyes were on Nana. His tiny hand still tingled from the memory of the cold flesh he'd touched, as unhuman as meat from the butcher. Nana's smiles and gentle manner frightened him in a way he didn't understand. He stood watching her, his tears still flowing.

Nana glanced at him several times over her shoulder while she tried to scrape burned stew from the bottom of her good iron saucepan. The scraping sounded grating and insistent to Hilton. For the first time in his life, Hilton wondered if Nana might ever do anything to try to hurt him.

Finally, Nana said, "You go on out of the way now, Hilton. Supper's late today. Don't give me that face now, pumpkin. Nana's not going to leave you."

Hilton wanted to take Nana's fingers and squeeze them, to see if the cold was still there, but she hadn't reached out to him and he wouldn't dare touch her if she did. Hilton felt something had changed, maybe forever. He went outside to play with a three-wheeled wagon he'd found, but he wasn't really playing. He was sitting on the front stoop, rocking the wagon back and forth in front of him, but he barely knew where he was or what he was doing. And, as he'd sensed, things were different after that day he found Nana on the kitchen floor: She began to wake up crying out from bad dreams. He watched her get out of bed for a glass of water in the moonlight, her nightgown so soaked with sweat he could see all the lines of her body as though she wore no clothes. Many nights Hilton went to sleep alone because Nana would stay up humming and writing hymns on the porch. She said she did this because she couldn't sleep. Hilton knew the truth, that she didn't want to. Maybe she had met the boogeyman.

It was fine with Hilton to be alone, because it was hard for him to sleep with Nana there. Her sleep breathing sounded different to him, the breaths longer and drawn farther and farther apart until he was sure the next one wasn't coming, but it always did. Once, he counted a minute between her breaths. He tried to hold his own breath that long, but he couldn't.

Nana was confused all the time now. She would get cross with him more easily than before, and she'd smack his backside for no good reason. One day Hilton was smacked when he didn't bring home cubes of sugar he knew she had never asked him to bring.

This went on for nearly a year, and Hilton began to hate her. He was afraid of her for reasons he didn't know or want to know. She'd never hurt him, not really, and on the rare occasions he touched her now her skin felt warm, but his memory of that day in the kitchen was too strong.

All of this changed the day Hilton took his first ride on a Greyhound, sitting at the back, of course, when Nana and their Belle Glade cousins took him to Miami for the Kelly-James family reunion. Twice before, Nana had stayed home and his women cousins drove him to the reunions to meet his kin, but she decided to go this year. The smells coming from Nana's picnic basket and the wonder of the flat, endless Florida landscape through the bus window were enough to make Hilton forget his fear.

The reunion was at Virginia Key Beach, and Hilton had never seen anyplace like it. This was a beach in Miami for only colored people, and folks of all shapes and shades had flocked there that day. Hilton had become a good swimmer in canals near Nana's house in Belle Glade, but he'd never seen so much sand and the trees and a green ocean stretching to forever. He'd always been told the ocean was blue, so the sparkling green ribbons of current were a wonder to him. Anything could happen on a day like today.

No one warned Hilton about the undertow, and he wouldn't have understood if they had, but Nana did tell him he could only go in the water if he didn't go far; this would have been enough if Hilton had minded like he should have. Nana, who was helping the ladies set up picnic tables, pointed to the orange buoy floating out in the water and said he could go only halfway there. And Hilton said "Yes, Nana" and ran splashing into the water knowing that he would go exactly where he wanted because in the water he would be free.

He swam easily past the midway point to the buoy, and he could see from here that it was cracked and the glowing paint was old. He wanted to get a closer look at it, maybe grab it and tread water and gaze back at all those brown bodies on the sand. And it was here that he met up with the undertow.

It was friendly at first. He felt as though the water had closed a grip around his tiny kicking legs and dunked him beneath the surface like a doughnut then spat him back up a few feet from where he started. Hilton coughed and smiled, splashing with his arms. He didn't know the water could do that by itself. It was like taking a ride.

The buoy was now farther than it was before the ocean played with him. It was off to his left now when it had been straight ahead. As Hilton waited to see if he could feel those swirling currents beneath him again, he heard splinters of Nana's voice in the wind, calling from the beach: "Hilton, you get back here, boy! You hear me? Get back here."

So the ocean was not free after all, Hilton realized. He'd better do as he was told, or he wouldn't get any coconut cake or peach cobbler, if it wasn't too late for that already. He began sure strokes back toward the shore.

The current still wanted to play, and this time it was angry Hilton was trying to leave so soon. He felt the cold grip seize his waist and hold his legs still. He was so started he gasped a big breath of air, just in time to be plunged into the belly of the ocean, tumbled upside down and then up again, with water pounding all around his ears in a roar. Hilton tried to kick and stroke, but he didn't know which way was up or down and all he could see was the water all around him specked with the tiny ocean life. Even in his panic, Hilton knew not to open his mouth, but his lungs were starting to hurt and the tumbling was never-ending. Hilton believed he was being swept to the very bottom of the ocean, or out to sea as far as the ship he'd seen passing earlier. Frantically, he flailed his arms.

He didn't hear Nana shout out from where she stood at the shore, but he'd hear the story told many times later. There was no lifeguard that day, but there were plenty of Kelly and James men who followed Nana, who stripped herself of her dress and ran into the water. The woman hadn't been swimming in years, but her limbs didn't fail her this one time she needed to glide across the water. The men followed the old woman into the sea.

Hilton felt he couldn't hold his breath anymore, and the water mocked him all around. It filled his ears, his nose, and finally his mouth, and his muscles began to fail him. It was then, just as he believed his entire fifty-pound body would fill with water, that he felt an arm around his waist. He fought the arm at first, thinking it was another current, but the grip was firm and pulled him up, up, up, until he could see light and Nana's weary, determined face. That was all he saw, because he went limp then.

He would hear the rest from others who told him in gentle ways about Chariots to the Everlasting and that sort of thing. One of the James men had been swimming closely behind Nana, and she passed Hilton to his arms. Then she simply stopped swimming, they said. Said maybe she just gave out. Nana's head began to sink below the water, and just as one of the Kelly men reached to try to take her arm, the current she'd pulled Hilton from took her instead. The man carrying Hilton could only swim against it with all his might toward the shore. Many people almost drowned that day.

When Hilton's senses came back to him and he was lying on the beach, caked in gritty sand, all that was left of Nana was her good flowered dress, damp and crumpled at the water's edge.

So what the gifted old folks, the seers, often say is true:

Sometimes the dead go unburied.

NOBODY KNOWS MY NAME

Joyce Carol Oates

Joyce Carol Oates (b.1938) was born in Lockport, New York and was raised on her grandparents' farm in Erie County. She began her education in a one-room schoolhouse, was the first in her family to graduate high school, and is a graduate of Syracuse University and the University of Wisconsin. Oates has published over seventy books and has been awarded numerous accolades for her work. She is Professor of Creative Writing at Princeton University.

She was a precocious child, aged nine. She understood that there was danger even before she saw the cat with thistledown gray fur like breath, staring at her, eyes tawny-golden and unperturbed, out of the bed of crimson peonies.

It was summer. Baby's first summer they spoke of it. At Lake St. Cloud in the Adirondack Mountains in the summer house with the dark shingles and field-stone fireplaces and the wide second-floor veranda that, when you stepped out on it, seemed to float in the air, unattached to anything. At Lake St. Cloud neighbors' houses were hardly visible through the trees, and she liked that. Ghost houses they were, and their inhabitants. Only voices carried sometimes, or radio music, from somewhere along the lakeshore a dog's barking in the early morning, but cats make no sound – that was one of the special things about them. The first time she'd seen the thistledown gray cat she'd been too surprised to call to it, the cat had stared at her and she had stared at the cat, and it seemed to her that the cat had recognized her, or in any case it had moved its mouth in a silent miming of speech – not a "meow" as in a silly cartoon but a human word. But in the next instant the cat had disappeared so she'd stood alone on the terrace feeling the sudden loss like breath sucked out of her and when Mommy came outside carrying the baby, the pretty candy cane towel flung over her shoulder to protect it from the baby's drool, she hadn't heard Mommy speaking to her at first because she was listening so hard to something else. Mommy repeated what she'd said, "Jessica – ? Look who's here."

Jessica. That was the word, the name, the thistledown gray cat had mimed.

Back home, in the city, all the houses on Prospect Street which was their street were exposed, like in glossy advertisements. The houses were large and made of brick or stone and their lawns were large and carefully tended and never hidden from one another, never secret as at Lake St. Cloud. Their neighbors knew their names and were always calling out hello to Jessica even when they could tell she was looking away from them, thinking *I don't see anybody, they can't see me* but always there was the intrusion and backyards too ran together separated only by flower beds or hedges you could look over. Jessica loved the summer house that used to be Grandma's before she died and went away and left it to them though she was never certain it was *real* or only something she'd dreamt. She had trouble sometimes remembering what *real* was and what *dream* was and whether they could ever be the same or were always different. It was important to know because if she confused the two Mommy might notice, and question her, and once Daddy couldn't help laughing at her in front of company, she'd been chattering excitedly in that way of a shy child suddenly feverish to talk telling of how the roof of the house could be lifted and you could climb out using the clouds as stairs. Daddy interrupted to tell her no, no Jessie sweetheart that's just a dream, laughing at the stricken look in her eyes so she went mute as if he'd slapped her and backed away and ran out of the room to hide. And tore at her thumbnail with her teeth to punish herself.

Afterward Daddy came to her and squatted in front of her to look level in her eyes saying he was sorry he'd laughed at her and he hoped she wasn't mad at Daddy, it's just she's so *cute*, her eyes so *blue*, did she forgive Daddy? and she nodded yes her eyes filling with tears of hurt and rage and in her heart *No! no! no!* but Daddy didn't hear, and kissed her like always.

That was a long time ago. She'd only been in preschool then. A baby herself, so silly. No wonder they laughed at her.

The terrible worry was, for a while, they might not be driving up to Lake St. Cloud this summer.

It was like floating – just the name. Lake St. Cloud. And clouds reflected in the lake, moving across the ripply surface of the water. It was *up* to Lake St. Cloud in the Adirondacks when you looked at the map of New York State and it was *up* when Daddy drove, into the foothills and into the mountains on curving, sometimes twisting roads. She could feel the journey *up* and there was no sensation so strange and so wonderful.

Will we be going to the lake? Jessica did not dare ask Mommy or Daddy because to ask such a question was to articulate the very fear the question was meant to deny. And there was the terror, too, that the summer house was after all not *real* but only Jessica's *dream* because she wanted it so badly.

Back before Baby was born, in spring. Weighing only five pounds eleven ounces. Back before the "C-section" she heard them speak of so many times over the telephone, reporting to friends and relatives. "C-section" – she saw floating geometrical figures, octagons, hexagons, as in one of Daddy's architectural magazines, and Baby was in one of these, and had to be sawed out. The saw was a special one, Jessica knew, a surgeon's instrument. Mommy had wanted "natural labor" but it was to be "C-section" and Baby was to blame, but nobody spoke of it. There should have been resentment of Baby, and anger and disgust, for all these months Jessica was *good* and Baby-to-be *bad*. And nobody seemed to know, or to care. *Will we be going to the lake this year? Do you still love me?* – Jessica did not dare ask for fear of being told.

This was the year, the year of Mommy's swelling belly, when Jessica came to know many things without knowing how she knew. The more she was not told, the more she understood. She was a grave, small-boned child with pearly blue eyes and a delicate oval of a face like a ceramic doll's face and she had a habit of which all adults disapproved of biting her thumbnail until it bled or even sucking at her thumb if she believed she was unobserved but most of all she had the power to make herself invisible sometimes watching and listening and hearing more than was said. The times that Mommy was unwell that winter, and the dark circles beneath her eyes, and her beautiful chestnut hair brushed limp behind her ears, and her breath panting from the stairs, or just walking across a room. From the waist up Mommy was still Mommy but from the waist down, where Jessica did not like to look, the thing that was Baby-to-be, Baby-Sister-to-be, had swollen up grotesquely inside her so her belly was in danger of bursting. And Mommy might be reading to Jessica or helping with her bath when suddenly the pain would hit, Baby kicked hard, so hard Jessica could feel it too, and the warm color draining from Mommy's face, and the hot tears flooding her eyes. And Mommy would kiss Jessica hurriedly, and go away. And if Daddy was home she would call for him in that special voice meaning she was trying to keep calm. Daddy would say *Darling, you're all right, it's fine, I'm sure it's fine*, helping Mommy to sit somewhere comfortable, or lie down with her legs raised; or to make her way slow as an elderly woman down the hall to the bathroom. That was why Mommy laughed so much, and was so breathless, or began to cry suddenly. *These hormones!* she'd laugh. *Or, I'm too old! We waited too long! I'm almost forty! God help me, I want this baby so badly!* and Daddy would be comforting, mildly chiding, he was accustomed to handling Mommy in her moods, *Shhh! What kind of silly talk is that? Do you want to scare Jessie, do you want to scare* me? And though Jessica might be asleep in her room in her bed she would hear, and she would know, and in the morning she would remember as if what was *real* was also *dream*, with the secret power of *dream* to give you knowledge others did not know you possessed.

But Baby was born, and given a name: ____. Which Jessica whispered but, in her heart, did not *say*.

Baby was born in the hospital, sawed out of the C-section as planned. Jessica was brought to see Mommy and Baby _____ and the surprise of seeing them *the two of them so together* Mommy so tired-looking and so happy, and Baby that had been an *it*, that ugly swelling in Mommy's belly, was painful as an electric shock – swift-shooting through Jessica, even as Daddy held her perched on his knee beside Mommy's bed, it left no trace. *Jessie, darling – see who's here? Your baby sister _____ isn't she beautiful? Look at her tiny toes, her eyes, look at her hair that's the color of yours, isn't she beautiful?* and Jessica's eyes blinked only once or twice and with her parched lips she was able to speak, to respond as they wanted her to respond, like being called upon in school when her thoughts were in pieces like a shattered mirror but she gave no sign, she had the power, you must tell adults only what they want you to tell them so they will love you.

So Baby was born, and all the fears were groundless. And Baby was brought back in triumph to the house on Prospect Street flooded with flowers where there was a nursery repainted and decorated specially for her. And eight weeks later Baby was taken in the car up to Lake St. Cloud, for Mommy was strong enough now, and Baby was gaining weight so even the pediatrician was impressed, already able to focus her eyes, and smile, or seem to smile, and gape her toothless little mouth in wonderment hearing her name _____! _____! _____! so tirelessly uttered by adults. For everybody adored Baby, whose very poop was delightful to them. For everybody was astonished at Baby, who had only to blink and drool and gurgle and squawk red-faced moving her bowels inside her diaper or, in her battery-operated baby swing, fall abruptly asleep as if hypnotized – *isn't she beautiful! isn't she a love!* And to Jessica was put the question again, again, again *Aren't you lucky to have a baby sister?* and Jessica knew the answer that must be given, and given with a smile, a quick shy smile and a nod. For everybody brought presents for Baby, where once they had brought presents for another baby. (Except, as Jessica learned, overhearing Mommy talking with a woman friend, there were many more presents for Baby than there had been for Jessica. Mommy admitted to her friend there were really *too* many, she felt guilty, now they were well-to-do and not scrimping and saving as when Jessica was born, *now* they were deluged with baby things, almost three hundred presents! – she'd be writing thank-you notes for a solid year.)

At Lake St. Cloud, Jessica thought, it will be different.

At Lake St. Cloud, Baby won't matter so much.

But she was wrong: immediately she knew she was wrong, and wanting to come here was maybe a mistake. For never before had the big old summer house been so *busy.* And so *noisy.* Baby was colicky sometimes, and cried and cried and cried through the night, and certain special rooms like the first-floor sunroom that was so beautiful, all latticed windows overlooking the lake, were given over to Baby and soon took on Baby's smell. And sometimes the upstairs veranda where pine siskins, tame little birds, fluttered about the trees, making their sweet questioning cries – given over to Baby. The white wicker bassinet that was a family heirloom, pink and white satin ribbons threaded through the wicker, the gauzy lace veil drawn across sometimes to shield Baby's delicate face from the sun; the changing table heaped with disposable diapers; the baby blankets, baby booties, baby panties, baby pajamas, baby bibs, baby sweaters, baby rattles, mobiles, stuffed toys – everywhere. Because of Baby, more visitors, including distant aunts and uncles and cousins Jessica did not know, came to Lake St. Cloud than ever before; and always the question put to Jessica was *Aren't you lucky to have a baby sister? a beautiful baby sister?* These visitors Jessica dreaded more than she'd dreaded visitors in the city for they were intruding now in this special house, this house Jessica had thought would be as it had always been, before Baby, or any thought of Baby. Yet even here Baby was the center of all happiness, and the center of all attention. As if a radiant light shone out of Baby's round blue eyes which everybody *except Jessica* could see.

(Or were they just pretending? – with adults, so much was phony and outright lying, but you dared not ask. For then they would *know* that you *know*. And they would cease to love you.)

This secret, Jessica meant to tell the thistledown gray cat with the fur like breath but she saw in the cat's calm measuring unperturbed gaze that the cat already knew. He knew more than Jessica for he was older than Jessica, and had been here, at Lake St. Cloud, long before she was born. She'd thought him a neighbor's cat but really he was a wild cat belonging to nobody – *I am who I am, nobody knows my name.* Yet he was well fed, for he was a hunter. His eyes tawny-gold capable of seeing in the dark as no human being's eyes could. Beautiful with his filmy gray fur threaded just perceptibly with white, and his clean white bib, white paws and tail tip. He was a long-hair, part Persian, fur thicker and fuller than the fur of any cat Jessica had ever seen before. You could see he was strong-muscled in his shoulders and thighs, and of course he was unpredictable in his movements – one moment it seemed he was about to trot to Jessica's outstretched hand to take a piece of breakfast bacon from her, and allow her to pet him, as she pleaded, "Kitty-kitty-kitty! Oh kitty – " and the next moment he'd vanished into the shrubbery behind the peony bushes, as if he'd never been there at all. A faint thrashing in his wake, and then nothing.

Tearing at her thumbnail with her teeth to draw blood, to punish herself. For she was such a silly child, such an ugly stupid left-behind child, even the thistledown gray cat despised her.

Daddy was in the city one week from Monday till Thursday and when he telephoned to speak to Mommy, and to speak babytalk to Baby, Jessica ran away to hide. Later Mommy scolded her, "Where were you? – Daddy wanted to say hello," and Jessica said, eyes widened in disappointment, "Mommy, I was here all along." And burst into tears.

The thistledown gray cat, leaping to catch a dragonfly and swallowing it in mid-air.

The thistledown gray cat, leaping to catch a pine siskin, tearing at its feathers with his teeth, devouring it at the edge of the clearing.

The thistledown gray cat, leaping from a pine bough to the railing of the veranda, walking tail erect along the railing in the direction of Baby sleeping in her bassinet. And where is Mommy?

I am who am, nobody knows my name.

Jessica was wakened from sleep in the cool pine-smelling dark in this room she didn't recognize at first by something brushing against her face, a ticklish sensation in her lips and nostrils, and her heart pounding in fear – but fear for what, for what had been threatening to suck her breath away and smother her, what was it, who was it, she did not know.

It had crouched on her chest, too. Heavy, furry-warm. Its calm gold-glowing eyes. Kiss? Kiss-kiss? Kissy-kiss, Baby? – except *she was not Baby*. Never Baby!

* * *

It was July, and the crimson peonies were gone, and there were fewer visitors now. Baby had had a fever for a day and a night, and Baby had somehow (how? during the night?) scratched herself beneath the left eye with her own tiny finger-nail, and Mommy was terribly upset, and had to be restrained from driving Baby ninety miles to a special baby doctor in Lake Placid. Daddy kissed Mommy and Baby both and chided Mommy for being too excitable, for God's sake honey get hold of yourself, this is nothing, you know this is nothing, we've been through this once already, haven't we? – and Mommy tried to keep her voice calm saying, Yes but every baby is different, and I'm different now, I'm more in love with _____ than ever with Jessie, God help me I think that's so. And Daddy sighed and said, Well I guess I am, too, it's maybe that we're more mature now and we know how precarious life is and we know we're not going to live forever the way it used to seem, only ten years ago we *were* young, and through several thicknesses of walls – at night, in the summer house above the lake, voices carried as they did not in the city – Jessica sucked on her thumb, and listened; and what she did not hear, she dreamt.

For that was the power of the night, where the thistledown gray cat stalked his prey, that you could dream what was real – and it *was* real, because you dreamt it.

Always, since Mommy was first unwell last winter, and Baby-to-be was making her belly swell, Jessica had understood that there was danger. That was why Mommy walked so carefully, and that was why Mommy stopped drinking even white wine which she loved with dinner, and that was why no visitors to the house, not even Uncle Albie who was everybody's favorite, and a chain-smoker, were allowed to smoke on the premises. Never again! And there was a danger of cold drafts even in the summer – Baby was susceptible to respiratory infections, even now she'd more than doubled her weight. And there was a danger of some-body, a friend or relative, eager to hold Baby, but not knowing to steady Baby's head and neck, which were weak. (After twelve weeks, Jessica had yet to hold her baby sister in her arms. She was shy, she was fearful. *No thank you, Mommy,* she'd said quietly. Not even seated close beside Mommy so the three of them could cuddle on a cozy, rainy day, in front of the fireplace, not even with Mom-my guiding Jessica's hands – *No thank you, Mommy.*) And if Mommy ate even a little of a food wrong for Baby, for instance lettuce, Baby became querulous and twitchy after nursing from gas sucked with Mommy's milk and cried through the night. *Yet nobody was angry with Baby.*

And everybody was angry with Jessica when, one night at dinner, Baby in her bassinet beside Mommy, gasping and kicking and crying, Jessica suddenly spat out her food on her plate and clamped her hands over her ears and ran out of the dining room as Mommy and Daddy and the weekend house guests stared after her.

And there came Daddy's voice, "Jessie? – come back here – "

And there came Mommy's voice, choked with hurt, "Jessica! – that's *rude* – "

* * *

That night the thistledown gray cat climbed onto her window-sill, eyes gleaming out of the shadows. She lay very still in bed frightened *Don't suck my breath away! don't!* and after a long pause she heard a low hoarse-vibrating sound, a comforting sound like sleep, and it was the thistledown gray cat purring. So she knew she was safe, and she knew she would sleep. And she did.

Waking in the morning to Mommy's screams. Screaming and screaming her voice rising like something scrambling up the side of a wall. Screaming except now awake Jessica was hearing jays' cries close outside her window in the pines where there was a colony of jays and where if something disturbed them they shrieked and flew in quick darting swoops flapping their wings to protect themselves and their young.

The thistledown gray cat trotting behind the house, tail stiffly erect, head high, a struggling blue-feathered bird gripped between his strong jaws.

All this time there was one thing Jessica did not think about, ever. It made her stomach tilt and lurch and brought a taste of bright hot bile into her mouth so *she did not think about it ever.*

Nor did she look at Mommy's breasts inside her loose-fitting shirts and tunics. Breasts filled with warm milk bulging like balloons. *Nursing* it was called, but Jessica did not think of it. It was the reason Mommy could never be away from Baby for more than an hour – in fact, Mommy loved Baby so, she could never be away from Baby for more than a few minutes. When it was time, when Baby began to fret and cry, Mommy excused herself a pride and elation showing in her face and tenderly she carried Baby away, to Baby's room where she shut the door behind them. Jessica ran out of the house, grinding her fists into her tight-closed eyes even as she ran stumbling, sick with shame. *I did not do that, ever. I was not a baby, ever.*

And there was another thing Jessica learned. She believed it was a trick of the thistledown gray cat, a secret wisdom imparted to her. Suddenly one day she realized that, in the midst of witnesses, even Mommy who was so sharp-eyed, she could "look at" Baby with wide-open eyes yet not "see" Baby – where Baby was, in her bassinet, or in her perambulator or swing, or cradled in Mommy's or Daddy's arms, *there was an emptiness.*

Just as she was able calmly to hear Baby's name _____ and even speak that name _____ if required yet not acknowledge it in her innermost heart.

She understood then that Baby would be going away soon. For, when Grandma took sick and was hospitalized, Grandma who was Daddy's mother and who had once owned the summer place at Lake St. Cloud, though Jessica had loved the old woman she'd been nervous and shy around her once she'd begun to smell that orangish-sweet smell lifting from Grandma's shrunken body. And sometimes looking at Grandma she would narrow her eyes so where Grandma was there was a figure blurred as in a dream and after a while an emptiness. She'd been a little girl then, four years old. She'd whispered in Mommy's ear,

"Where is Grandma going?" and Mommy told her to hush, just hush, Mommy had seemed upset at the question so Jessica knew not to ask it again, nor to ask it of Daddy. She hadn't known if she was scared of the emptiness where Grandma was or whether she was restless having to pretend there was anything there in the hospital bed, anything that had to do with *her*.

Now the thistledown gray cat leapt nightly to her windowsill where the window was open. With a swipe of his white paw he'd knocked the screen inward so now he pushed his way inside, his tawny eyes glowing like coins and his guttural mew like a human query, teasing – *Who? You?* And the deep vibrating purr out of his throat that sounded like laughter as he leapt silently to the foot of Jessica's bed and trotted forward as she stared in astonishment to press his muzzle – his muzzle that was warm and sticky with the blood of prey only just killed and devoured in the woods – against her face! *I am who I am, nobody knows my name.* The thistledown gray cat held her down, heavy on her chest. She tried to throw him off, but could not. She was trying to scream, no she was laughing helplessly – the stiff whiskers tickled so. "Mommy! Daddy – " she tried to draw breath to scream but could not, for the giant cat, his muzzle pressed against her mouth, sucked her breath from her.

I am who I am, nobody knows my name, nobody can stop me.

It was a cool sky-blue morning in the mountains. At this hour, seven-twenty, Lake St. Cloud was clear and empty, no sailboats and no swimmers and the child was barefoot in shorts and T-shirt at the edge of the dock when they called to her from the kitchen door and at first she didn't seem to hear then turned slowly and came back to the house and seeing the queer, pinched look in her face they asked her was she feeling unwell? – was something wrong? Her eyes were a translucent pearly blue that did not seem like the eyes of a child. There were faint, bruised indentations in the skin beneath the eyes. Mommy who was holding Baby in the crook of an arm stooped awkwardly to brush Jessica's uncombed hair from her forehead which felt cool, waxy. Daddy who was brewing coffee asked her with a smiling frown if she'd been having bad dreams again? – she'd had upsetting dreams as a small child and she'd been brought in to sleep with Mommy and Daddy then, between them in the big bed where she'd been safe. But carefully she told them no, no she wasn't sick, she was fine. She just woke up early, that was all. Daddy asked her if Baby's crying in the middle of the night had disturbed her and she said no she didn't hear any crying and again Daddy said if she had bad dreams she should tell them and she said, in her grave, careful voice, "If I had some dreams, I don't remember them." She smiled then, not at Daddy, or at Mommy, a look of quick contempt. "I'm too old for *that*."

Mommy said, "No one's too old for nightmares, honey." Mommy laughed sadly and leaned to kiss Jessica's cheek but already Baby was stirring and fretting and Jessica drew away. She wasn't going to be trapped by Mommy's tricks, or Daddy's. Ever again.

This is how it happened, when it happened.

On the upstairs veranda in gusts of sunshine amid the smell of pine needles and the quick sweet cries of pine siskins Mommy was talking with a woman friend on the cellular phone, and Baby who had just nursed was asleep in her heirloom bassinet with the fluttering satin ribbons, and Jessica who was restless this afternoon leaned over the railing with Daddy's binoculars staring at the glassy lake – the farther shore, where what appeared to the naked eye as mere dots of light were transformed into tiny human figures – a flock of mallards in an inlet at the edge of their property – the tangled grasses and underbrush beyond the peony bed where she'd seen something move. Mommy murmured, "Oh, damn! – this connection!" and told Jessica she was going to continue her conversation downstairs, on another phone, she'd be gone only a few minutes, would Jessica look after Baby? And Jessica shrugged and said yes of course. Mommy who was barefoot in a loose summer shift with a dipping neckline that made Jessica's eyes pinch peered into Baby's bassinet checking to see Baby *was* deeply asleep, and Mommy hurried downstairs, and Jessica turned back to the binoculars, which were heavy in her hands, and made her wrists ache unless she rested them on the railing. She was dreamy counting the sailboats on the lake, there were five of them within her range of vision, it made her feel bad because it was after Fourth of July now and Daddy kept promising he'd get the sailboat fixed up and take her out, always in previous summers Daddy had sailed by now though as he said he wasn't much of a sailor, he required perfect weather and today had been perfect all day – balmy, fragrant, gusts of wind but not too much wind – but Daddy was in the city at his office today, wouldn't be back till tomorrow evening – and Jessica was brooding, gnawing at her lower lip recalling now there was Baby, Mommy probably wouldn't go with them in the boat anyway, all that was changed. And would never be the same again. And Jessica saw the movements of quick-flitting birds in the pine boughs, and a blurred shape gray like vapor leaping past her field of vision, was it a bird? an owl? she was trying to locate it in the pine boughs which were so eerily magnified, every twig, every needle, every insect enlarged and seemingly only an inch from her eyes, when she realized she'd been hearing a strange, unnerving noise, a gurgling, gasping noise, and a rhythmic creaking of wood, and in astonishment she turned to see, less than three yards behind her, the thistledown gray cat hunched inside the bassinet, on Baby's tiny chest, pressing its muzzle against Baby's mouth . . .

The bassinet rocked with the cat's weight and the rough kneading motions of his paws. Jessica whispered, "No! – oh, no – " and the binoculars slipped from her fingers. As if this were a dream, her legs and arms were paralyzed. The giant cat, fierce-eyed, its filmy gray fur lifting light as milkweed silk, its white-tipped plume of a tail erect, paid her not the slightest heed as he sucked vigorously at the baby's mouth, kneading and clawing at his small prey who was thrashing for life, you would not think an infant of only three months could so struggle, tiny arms and legs flailing, face mottled red, but the thistledown cat was stronger, much stronger, and could not be deflected from his purpose – *to suck away Baby's breath, to suffocate, to smother with his muzzle.*

For the longest time Jessica could not move – this is what she would say, confess, afterward. And by the time she ran to the bassinet, clapping her hands to scare the cat away, Baby had ceased struggling, her face still flushed but rapidly draining of color, like a wax doll's face, and her round blue eyes were livid with tears, unfocused, staring sightless past Jessica's head.

Jessica screamed, "Mommy!"

Taking hold of her baby sister's small shoulders to shake her back into life, the first time Jessica had ever really touched her baby sister she loved so, but there was no life in the baby – it was too late. Crying, screaming, "Mommy! Mommy! Mommy!"

And that was how Mommy found Jessica – leaning over the bassinet, shaking the dead infant like a rag doll. Her father's binoculars, both lenses shattered, lay on the veranda floor at her feet.

TERMINUS

Hilary Mantel

Hilary Mantel (b.1952) was born in Glossop, Derbyshire and studied at the London School of Economics and the University of Sheffield. Mantel spent the late 1970s and early 1980s in Botswana and Saudi Arabia. Her awards include the Costa Book Award and the Orange Prize. She is a Dame of the British Empire and the first woman to be awarded the Booker Prize twice. Her novel, *Wolf Hall*, has sold over 800,000 copies in the UK.

On January 9th, shortly after eleven on a dark sleety morning, I saw my dead father on a train pulling out of Clapham Junction, bound for Waterloo.

I glanced away, not recognising him at once. We were on parallel tracks. When I looked back, the train had picked up speed, and carried him away.

My mind at once moved ahead, to the concourse at Waterloo Station, and the meeting which I felt sure must occur. The train on which he was travelling was one of the old six-seater-carriage-and-corridor type, its windows near-opaque with the winter's accumulation, and a decade of grime plastered to its metal. I wondered where he'd come from: Windsor? Ascot? You'll understand that I travel in the region a good deal, and one gets to know the rolling stock.

There were no lights in the carriage he had chosen. (The bulbs are often stolen or vandalised.) His face had an unpleasant tinge; his eyes were deeply shadowed, and his expression was thoughtful, almost morose.

At last released by the green signal, my own train began to draw forward. Its pace was stately and I thought that he must have a good seven minutes on me, certainly more than five.

As soon as I saw him, sitting sad but upright in that opposite carriage, my mind went back to the occasion when . . . to the occasion when . . . But no. It did not go back. I tried, but I could not find an occasion. Even when I scrubbed the recesses of my brain, I could not scour one out. I should like to be rich in anecdote. Fertile to invent. But there's no occasion, only the knowledge that a certain number of years have passed.

When we disembarked the platform was slick with cold, sliding underfoot. The bomb warnings were pasted up everywhere, also the beggar warnings, and posters saying take care not to slip or trip, which are insulting to the public, as few people would do it if they could help it: only some perhaps, a few attention-seekers. An arbitrary decision had placed a man to take tickets, so that was fumbling, and further delay. I was irritated by this; I wanted to get on with the whole business, whatever the business was going to be.

It came to me that he had looked younger, as though death had moved him back a stage. There had been in his expression, melancholy though it was, something purposive; and I was sure of this, that his journey was not random. And so it was this perception, rather than any past experience – is experience always past? – that made me think he might linger for a rendezvous, that moving towards me and then away, on his Basingstoke train or perhaps from as far as Southampton, he might make time for a meeting with me.

I tell you this: if you are minded to unite at Waterloo Station, lay your plans well and in advance. Formalise in writing, for extra caution. I stood still, a stone in the rude stream, as the travellers crashed and surged around me. Where might he go? What might he want? (I had not known, God help me, that the dead were loose.) A cup of coffee? A glance at the rack of best-selling paperbacks? An item from Boots the Chemist, a cold cure, a bottle of some aromatic oil?

Something small and hard, that was inside my chest, that was my heart, drew smaller then. I had no idea what he would want. The limitless possibilities that London affords . . . if he should bypass me and find his way in to the city . . . but even then, among the limitless possibilities, I could not think of a single thing that he might want.

So I hunted for him, peeping into W.H. Smith and the Costa Coffee boutique. My mind tried to provide occasions to which it could go back, but none occurred. I coveted something sweet, a glass of hot chocolate to warm my hands, an Italian wafer dusted with cocoa powder. But my mind was cold and my intention urgent.

It struck me that he might be leaving for the Continent. He could take the train from here to Europe, and how would I follow? I wondered what documents he would be likely to need, and whether he bore currency. Are dispensations different? As ghosts, can they pass the ports? I thought of a court of shadow ambassadors, with shadow portfolios tucked within their silks.

There is a rhythm – and you know this – to which people move in any great public space. There is a certain speed which is no one's decision, but which is set going every day, soon after dawn. Break the rhythm and you'll rue it, for you'll be kicked and elbows will collide. Brutal British mutter of sorry, oh sorry – except often travellers are too angry I find for common politeness, hesitate too long or limp and you will be knocked out of the way. It occurred to me for the first time that this rhythm is a mystery indeed, controlled not by the railways or the citizens but by a higher power: that it is an aid to dissimulation, a guide to those who would otherwise not know how to act.

For how many of all these surging thousands are solid, and how many of these assumptions are tricks of the light? How many, I ask you, are connected at all points, how many are utterly and convincingly in the state they purport to be: which is, alive? That lost, objectless, sallow man, a foreigner with his bag on his back; that woman whose starved face recalls a plague-pit victim? Those dwellers in the brown houses of Wandsworth, those denizens of balcony flats and walkways; those grumbling commuters gathered for Virginia Water, those whose homes perch on embankments, or whose roofs glossy with rain fly away from the traveller's window? How many?

For distinguish me, will you? Distinguish me "the distinguished thing". Render me the texture of flesh. Pick me what it is, in the timbre of the voice, that marks out the living from the dead. Show me a bone that you know to be a living bone. Flourish it, will you? Find one, and show me.

Moving on, I stared over the chill cabinet with its embalmed meals for travellers. I caught a glimpse of a sleeve, of an overcoat which I thought might be familiar, and my narrow heart skipped sideways. But then the man turned, and his face was sodden with stupidity, and he was someone else, and less than I required him to be.

Not many places were left. I looked at the pizza stand but I did not think he would eat in a public place, and not anything foreign. (Again my mind darted forward to the Gare du Nord and the chances of catching up.) The bureau de change I'd already checked, and had scooped aside the curtain of the photograph booth, which seemed empty at the time but I had thought it might be a trick or a test.

So nowhere then. Dwelling again on his expression – and you will remember I saw it only for a moment, and in shadows – I discerned something that I did not see at first. It seemed, almost, that his look was turning inward. There was a remoteness, a wish for privacy: as if he were the warden of his own identity.

Suddenly – the thought born in a second – I understood: he is travelling *incognito*. Shame and rage then made me lean back against plate glass, against front window of bookshop; aware that my own image swims behind me, and that my ghost, in its winter cloak, is forced into the glass, forced there and fixed for any passer to stare at, living or dead, as long as I have not strength or power to move. My morning's experience, till then unprocessed and scantily observed, now arrived inside me. I had raised my eyes, I had lifted my gaze, I had with naked curiosity looked into the carriage on the parallel track, and by indecent coincidence I had happened to see a thing I should never have seen.

It seemed urgent now to go into the city and to my meeting. I gathered my cloak about me, my customary suit of solemn black. I looked in my bag to pat that all my papers were in order. I went to a stall and handed over a pound coin, for which I was given a pack of paper handkerchiefs in a plastic sheath as thin as skin, and using my nails I tore it till the membrane parted, and the paper itself was under my hand: it was a provision, in case of unseemly tears. Though paper reassures me, its touch. It's what you respect.

This is a bleak winter. Even old people admit it is more frigid than the usual, and it is known that as you stand in the taxi queue the four winds sting your eyes. I am on my way to a chilly room, where men who might have been my father but more fond will resolve some resolutions, transact some transactions, agree on the minutes: I notice how easily, in most cases, committees agree the minutes, but when we are singular and living our separate lives we dispute – don't we? – each second we believe we own. It's not generally agreed, it's not much appreciated, that people are divided by all sorts of things, and that, frankly, death is the least of them. When lights are blossoming out across the boulevards and parks, and the town assumes its Victorian *sagesse*, I shall be moving on again. I see that both the living and the dead commute, riding their familiar trains. I am not, as you will have gathered, a person who needs false excitement, or simulated innovation. I am willing, though, to tear up the timetable and take some new routes; and I know I shall find, at some unlikely terminus, a hand that is meant to rest in mine.

THE SPECIALIST'S HAT

Kelly Link

Kelly Link (b.1969) was born in Miami, Florida. She is a graduate of Columbia University and the MFA program of UNC Greensboro. She is co-founder of Small Beer Press and the author of four collections of short stories, *Stranger Things Happen*, *Magic for Beginners*, *Pretty Monsters*, and *Get in Trouble*. Link lives with her husband and daughter in Northampton, Massachusetts.

"When you're Dead," Samantha says, "you don't have to brush your teeth. . ."

"When you're Dead," Claire says, "you live in a box, and it's always dark, but you're not ever afraid."

Claire and Samantha are identical twins. Their combined age is twenty years, four months, and six days. Claire is better at being Dead than Samantha.

The babysitter yawns, covering up her mouth with a long white hand. "I said to brush your teeth and that it's time for bed," she says. She sits cross-legged on the flowered bedspread between them. She has been teaching them a card game called Pounce, which involves three decks of cards, one for each of them. Samantha's deck is missing the Jack of Spades and the Two of Hearts, and Claire keeps on cheating. The babysitter wins anyway. There are still flecks of dried shaving cream and toilet paper on her arms. It is hard to tell how old she is – at first they thought she must be a grownup, but now she hardly looks older than they. Samantha has forgotten the babysitter's name.

Claire's face is stubborn. "When you're Dead," she says, "you stay up all night long."

"When you're dead," the babysitter snaps, "it's always very cold and damp, and you have to be very, very quiet or else the Specialist will get you."

"This house is haunted," Claire says.

"I know it is," the babysitter says. "I used to live here."

> *Something is creeping up the stairs,*
> *Something is standing outside the door,*
> *Something is sobbing, sobbing in the dark;*
> *Something is sighing across the floor.*

Claire and Samantha are spending the summer with their father, in the house called Eight Chimneys. Their mother is dead. She has been dead for exactly 282 days.

Their father is writing a history of Eight Chimneys, and of the poet, Charles

Cheatham Rash, who lived here at the turn of the century, and who ran away to sea when he was thirteen, and returned when he was thirty-eight. He married, fathered a child, wrote three volumes of bad, obscure poetry, and an even worse and more obscure novel, *The One Who Is Watching Me Through the Window,* before disappearing again in 1907, this time for good. Samantha and Claire's father says that some of the poetry is actually quite readable, and at least the novel isn't very long.

When Samantha asked him why he was writing about Rash, he replied that no one else had, and why didn't she and Samantha go play outside. When she pointed out that she was Samantha, he just scowled and said how could he be expected to tell them apart when they both wore blue jeans and flannel shirts, and why couldn't one of them dress all in green and the other pink?

Claire and Samantha prefer to play inside. Eight Chimneys is as big as a castle, but dustier and darker than Samantha imagines a castle would be. There are more sofas, more china shepherdesses with chipped fingers, fewer suits of armor. No moat.

The house is open to the public, and, during the day, people – families – driving along the Blue Ridge Parkway will stop to tour the grounds and the first story; the third story belongs to Claire and Samantha. Sometimes they play explorers, and sometimes they follow the caretaker as he gives tours to visitors. After a few weeks, they have memorized his lecture, and they mouth it along with him. They help him sell postcards and copies of Rash's poetry to the tourist families who come into the little gift shop. When the mothers smile at them, and say how sweet they are, they stare back and don't say anything at all. The dim light in the house makes the mothers look pale and flickery and tired. They leave Eight Chimneys, mothers and families, looking not quite as real as they did before they paid their admissions, and of course Claire and Samantha will never see them again, so maybe they aren't real. Better to stay inside the house, they want to tell the families, and if you must leave, then go straight to your cars.

The caretaker says the woods aren't safe.

Their father stays in the library on the second story all morning, typing, and in the afternoon he takes long walks. He takes his pocket recorder along with him, and a hip flask of Old Kentucky, but not Samantha and Claire.

The caretaker of Eight Chimneys is Mr. Coeslak. His left leg is noticeably shorter than his right. Short black hairs grow out of his ears and his nostrils, and there is no hair at all on top of his head, but he's given Samantha and Claire permission to explore the whole of the house. It was Mr. Coeslak who told them that there are copperheads in the woods, and that the house is haunted. He says they are all, ghosts and snakes, a pretty badtempered lot, and Samantha and Claire should stick to the marked trails, and stay out of the attic.

Mr. Coeslak can tell the twins apart, even if their father can't; Claire's eyes are grey, like a cat's fur, he says, but Samantha's are *gray,* like the ocean when it has been raining.

Samantha and Claire went walking in the woods on the second day that they were at Eight Chimneys. They saw something. Samantha thought it was a woman, but Claire said it was a snake. The staircase that goes up to the attic has been locked. They peeked through the keyhole, but it was too dark to see anything.

And so he had a wife, and they say she was real pretty. There was another man who wanted to go with her, and first she wouldn't, because she was afraid of her husband, and then she did. Her husband found out, and they say he killed a snake and got some of this snake's blood and put it in some whiskey and gave it to her. He had learned this from an island man who had been on a ship with him. And in about six months snakes created in her and they got between her meat and the skin. And they say you could just see them running up and down her legs. They say she was just hollow to the top of her body, and it kept on like that till she died. Now my daddy said he saw it.

– An Oral History of Eight Chimneys

Eight Chimneys is over two hundred years old. It is named for the eight chimneys which are each big enough that Samantha and Claire can both fit in one fireplace. The chimneys are red brick, and on each floor there are eight fireplaces, making a total of twenty-four. Samantha imagines the chimney stacks stretching like stout red tree trunks, all the way up through the slate roof of the house. Beside each fireplace is a heavy black firedog, and a set of wrought iron pokers shaped like snakes. Claire and Samantha pretend to duel with the snake-pokers before the fireplace in their bedroom on the third floor. Wind rises up the back of the chimney. When they stick their faces in, they can feel the air rushing damply upward, like a river. The flue smells old and sooty and wet, like stones from a river.

Their bedroom was once the nursery. They sleep together in a poster bed which resembles a ship with four masts. It smells of mothballs, and Claire kicks in her sleep. Charles Cheatham Rash slept here when he was a little boy, and also his daughter. She disappeared when her father did. It might have been gambling debts. They may have moved to New Orleans. She was fourteen years old, Mr. Coeslak said. What was her name, Claire asked. What happened to her mother, Samantha wanted to know. Mr. Coeslak closed his eyes in an almost wink. Mrs. Rash had died the year before her husband and daughter disappeared, he said, of a mysterious wasting disease. He can't remember the name of the poor little girl, he said.

Eight Chimneys has exactly one hundred windows, all still with the original wavery panes of handblown glass. With so many windows, Samantha thinks, Eight Chimneys should always be full of light, but instead the trees press close against the house, so that the rooms on the first and second story – even the third-story rooms – are green and dim, as if Samantha and Claire are living deep under the sea. This is the light that makes the tourists into ghosts. In the morning, and again towards evening, a fog settles in around the house. Sometimes it is grey like Claire's eyes, and sometimes it is gray, like Samantha's.

I met a woman in the wood,
Her lips were two red snakes.
She smiled at me, her eyes lewd
And burning like a fire.

A few nights ago, the wind was sighing in the nursery chimney. Their father had already tucked them in, and turned off the light. Claire dared Samantha to stick her head into the fireplace, in the dark, and so she did. The cold wet air licked at her face, and it almost sounded like voices talking low, muttering. She couldn't quite make out what they were saying.

Their father has mostly ignored Claire and Samantha since they arrived at Eight Chimneys. He never mentions their mother. One evening they heard him shouting in the library, and when they came downstairs, there was a large sticky stain on the desk, where a glass of whiskey had been knocked over. It was looking at me, he said, through the window. It had orange eyes.

Samantha and Claire refrained from pointing out that the library is on the second story.

At night, their father's breath has been sweet from drinking, and he is spending more and more time in the woods, and less in the library. At dinner, usually hot dogs and baked beans from a can, which they eat off of paper plates in the first floor dining room, beneath the Austrian chandelier (which has exactly 632 leaded crystals shaped like teardrops), their father recites the poetry of Charles Cheatham Rash, which neither Samantha nor Claire cares for.

He has been reading the ship diaries which Rash kept, and he says that he has discovered proof in them that Rash's most famous poem, "The Specialist's Hat," is not a poem at all, and in any case, Rash didn't write it. It is something that one of the men on the whaler used to say, to conjure up a whale. Rash simply copied it down and stuck an end on it and said it was his.

The man was from Mulatuppu, which is a place neither Samantha nor Claire has ever heard of. Their father says that the man was supposed to be some sort of magician, but he drowned shortly before Rash came back to Eight Chimneys. Their father says that the other sailors wanted to throw the magician's chest overboard, but Rash persuaded them to let him keep it until he could be put ashore, with the chest, off the coast of North Carolina.

> *The specialist's hat makes a noise like an agouti;*
> *The specialist's hat makes a noise like a collared peccary;*
> *The specialist's hat makes a noise like a white-lipped peccary;*
> *The specialist's hat makes a noise like a tapir;*
> *The specialist's hat makes a noise like a rabbit;*
> *The specialist's hat makes a noise like a squirrel;*
> *The specialist's hat makes a noise like a curassow;*
> *The specialist's hat moans like a whale in the water;*
> *The specialist's hat moans like the wind in my wife's hair;*
> *The specialist's hat makes a noise like a snake;*
> *I have hung the hat of the specialist upon my wall.*

The reason that Claire and Samantha have a babysitter is that their father met a woman in the woods. He is going to see her tonight, and they are going to have a picnic supper and look at the stars. This is the time of year when the Perseids can be seen, falling across the sky on clear nights. Their father said that he has been walking with the woman every afternoon. She is a distant relation of Rash, and besides, he said, he needs a night off, and some grownup conversation.

Mr. Coeslak won't stay in the house after dark, but he agreed to find someone to look after Samantha and Claire. Then their father couldn't find Mr. Coeslak, but the babysitter showed up precisely at seven o'clock. The babysitter, whose name neither twin quite caught, wears a blue cotton dress with short floaty sleeves. Both Samantha and Claire think she is pretty in an old-fashioned sort of way.

They were in the library with their father, looking up Mulatuppu in the red leather atlas, when she arrived. She didn't knock on the front door, she simply walked in, and up the stairs, as if she knew where to find them.

Their father kissed them goodbye, a hasty smack, told them to be good and he would take them into town on the weekend to see the Disney film. They went to the window to watch as he walked out of the house and into the woods. Already it was getting dark, and there were fireflies, tiny yellow-hot sparks in the air. When their father had quite disappeared into the trees, they turned around and stared at the babysitter instead. She raised one eyebrow. "Well," she said. "What sort of games do you like to play?"

> *Widdershins around the chimneys,*
> *Once, twice, again.*
> *The spokes click like a clock on the bicycle;*
> *They tick down the days of the life of a man.*

First they played Go Fish, and then they played Crazy Eights, and then they made the babysitter into a mummy by putting shaving cream from their father's bathroom on her arms and legs, and wrapping her in toilet paper. She is the best babysitter they have ever had.

At nine-thirty, she tried to put them to bed. Neither Claire nor Samantha wanted to go to bed, so they began to play the Dead game. The Dead game is a let's pretend that they have been playing every day for 274 days now, but never in front of their father or any other adult. When they are Dead, they are allowed to do anything they want to. They can even fly, by jumping off the nursery beds, and just waving their arms. Someday this will work, if they practice hard enough.

The Dead game has three rules.

One. Numbers are significant. The twins keep a list of important numbers in a green address book that belonged to their mother. Mr. Coeslak's tour has been a good source of significant amounts and tallies: they are writing a tragical history of numbers.

Two. The twins don't play the Dead game in front of grownups. They have been summing up the babysitter, and have decided that she doesn't count. They tell her the rules.

Three is the best and most important rule. When you are Dead, you don't have to be afraid of anything. Samantha and Claire aren't sure who the Specialist is, but they aren't afraid of him.

To become Dead, they hold their breath while counting to 35, which is as high as their mother got, not counting a few days.

"You never lived here," Claire says. "Mr. Coeslak lives here."

"Not at night," says the babysitter. "This was my bedroom when I was little."

"Really?" Samantha says. Claire says, "Prove it."

The babysitter gives Samantha and Claire a look, as if she is measuring them: how old; how smart; how brave; how tall. Then she nods. The wind is in the flue, and in the dim nursery light they can see the little strands of fog seeping out of the fireplace. "Go stand in the chimney," she instructs them. "Stick your hand as far up as you can, and there is a little hole on the left side, with a key in it."

Samantha looks at Claire, who says, "Go ahead." Claire is fifteen minutes and some few uncounted seconds older than Samantha, and therefore gets to tell Samantha what to do. Samantha remembers the muttering voices, and then reminds herself that she is Dead. She goes over to the fireplace and ducks inside.

When Samantha stands up in the chimney, she can only see the very edge of the room. She can see the fringe of the mothy blue rug, and one bed leg, and beside it, Claire's foot, swinging back and forth like a metronome. Claire's shoelace has come undone, and there is a Band-Aid on her ankle. It all looks very pleasant and peaceful from inside the chimney, like a dream, and for a moment, she almost wishes she didn't have to be Dead. But it's safer, really.

She sticks her left hand up as far as she can reach, trailing it along the crumbly wall, until she feels an indentation. She thinks about spiders and severed fingers, and rusty razorblades, and then she reaches inside. She keeps her eyes lowered, focused on the corner of the room, and Claire's twitchy foot.

Inside the hole, there is a tiny cold key, its teeth facing outward. She pulls it out, and ducks back into the room. "She wasn't lying," she tells Claire.

"Of course I wasn't lying," the babysitter says. "When you're Dead, you're not allowed to tell lies."

"Unless you want to," Claire says.

> Dreary and dreadful beats the sea at the shore.
> Ghastly and dripping is the mist at my door.
> The clock in the hall is chiming one, two, three, four.
> The morning comes not, no, never, no more.

Samantha and Claire have gone to camp for three weeks every summer since they were seven. This year their father didn't ask them if they wanted to go back, and after discussing it, they decided that it was just as well. They didn't want to have to explain to all their friends how they were half-orphans now. They are used to being envied, because they are identical twins. They don't want to be pitiful.

It has not even been a year, but Samantha realizes that she is forgetting what her mother looked like. Not her mother's face so much as the way she smelled, which was something like dry hay, and something like Chanel No. 5, and like something else too. She can't remember whether her mother had gray eyes, like her, or grey eyes, like Claire. She doesn't dream about her mother anymore, but she does dream about Prince Charming, a bay whom she once rode in the horse show at her camp. In the dream, Prince Charming did not smell like a horse at all. He smelled like Chanel No. 5. When she is Dead, she can have all the horses she wants, and they all smell like Chanel No. 5.

* * *

"Where does the key go to?" Samantha says.

The babysitter holds out her hand. "To the attic. You don't really need it, but taking the stairs is easier than the chimney. At least the first time."

"Aren't you going to make us go to bed?" Claire says.

The babysitter ignores Claire. "My father used to lock me in the attic when I was little, but I didn't mind. There was a bicycle up there and I used to ride it around and around the chimneys until my mother let me out again. Do you know how to ride a bicycle?"

"Of course," Claire says.

"If you ride fast enough, the Specialist can't catch you."

"What's the Specialist?" Samantha says. Bicycles are okay, but horses can go faster.

"The Specialist wears a hat," say the babysitter. "The hat makes noises."

She doesn't say anything else.

> When you're dead, the grass is greener
> Over your grave. The wind is keener.
> Your eyes sink in, your flesh decays. You
> Grow accustomed to slowness; expect delays.

The attic is somehow bigger and lonelier than Samantha and Claire thought it would be. The babysitter's key opens the locked door at the end of the hallway, revealing a narrow set of stairs. She waves them ahead and upwards.

It isn't as dark in the attic as they had imagined. The oaks that block the light and make the first three stories so dim and green and mysterious during the day, don't reach all the way up. Extravagant moonlight, dusty and pale, streams in the angled dormer windows. It lights the length of the attic, which is wide enough to hold a softball game in, and lined with trunks where Samantha imagines people could sit, could be hiding and watching. The ceiling slopes down, impaled upon the eight thick-waisted chimney stacks. The chimneys seem too alive, somehow, to be contained in this empty, neglected place; they thrust almost angrily through the roof and attic floor. In the moonlight, they look like they are breathing. "They're so beautiful," she says.

"Which chimney is the nursery chimney?" Claire says.

The babysitter points to the nearest righthand stack. "That one," she says. "It runs up through the ballroom on the first floor, the library, the nursery."

Hanging from a nail on the nursery chimney is a long, black object. It looks lumpy and heavy, as if it were full of things. The babysitter takes it down, twirls it on her finger. There are holes in the black thing, and it whistles mournfully as she spins it. "The Specialist's hat," she says.

"That doesn't look like a hat," says Claire. "It doesn't look like anything at all." She goes to look through the boxes and trunks that are stacked against the far wall.

"It's a special hat," the babysitter says. "It's not supposed to look like anything. But it can sound like anything you can imagine. My father made it."

"Our father writes books," Samantha says.

"My father did too." The babysitter hangs the hat back on the nail. It curls blackly against the chimney. Samantha stares at it. It nickers at her. "He was a bad poet, but he was worse at magic."

Last summer, Samantha wished more than anything that she could have a horse. She thought she would have given up anything for one – even being a twin was not as good as having a horse. She still doesn't have a horse, but she doesn't have a mother either, and she can't help wondering if it's her fault. The hat nickers again, or maybe it is the wind in the chimney.

"What happened to him?" Claire asks.

"After he made the hat, the Specialist came and took him away. I hid in the nursery chimney while it was looking for him, and it didn't find me."

"Weren't you scared?"

There is a clattering, shivering, clicking noise. Claire has found the babysitter's bike and is dragging it towards them by the handlebars. The babysitter shrugs. "Rule number three," she says.

Claire snatches the hat off the nail. "I'm the Specialist!" she says, putting the hat on her head. It falls over her eyes, the floppy shapeless brim sewn with little asymmetrical buttons that flash and catch at the moonlight like teeth. Samantha looks again, and sees that they are teeth. Without counting, she suddenly knows that there are exactly fifty-two teeth on the hat, and that they are the teeth of agoutis, of curassows, of white-lipped peccaries, and of the wife of Charles Cheatham Rash. The chimneys are moaning, and Claire's voice booms hollowly beneath the hat. "Run away, or I'll catch you and eat you!"

Samantha and the babysitter run away, laughing, as Claire mounts the rusty, noisy bicycle and pedals madly after them. She rings the bicycle bell as she rides, and the Specialist's hat bobs up and down on her head. It spits like a cat. The bell is shrill and thin, and the bike wails and shrieks. It leans first towards the right, and then to the left. Claire's knobby knees stick out on either side like makeshift counterweights.

Claire weaves in and out between the chimneys, chasing Samantha and the babysitter. Samantha is slow, turning to look behind. As Claire approaches, she keeps one hand on the handlebars, and stretches the other hand out towards Samantha. Just as she is about to grab Samantha, the babysitter turns back and plucks the hat off Claire's head.

"Shit!" the babysitter says, and drops it. There is a drop of blood forming on the fleshy part of the babysitter's hand, black in the moonlight, where the Specialist's hat has bitten her.

Claire dismounts, giggling. Samantha watches as the Specialist's hat rolls away. It gathers speed, veering across the attic floor, and disappears, thumping down the stairs. "Go get it," Claire says. "You can be the Specialist this time."

"No," the babysitter says, sucking at her palm. "It's time for bed."

When they go down the stairs, there is no sign of the Specialist's hat. They brush their teeth, climb into the ship-bed, and pull the covers up to their necks. The babysitter sits between their feet. "When you're Dead," Samantha says, "do you still get tired and have to go to sleep? Do you have dreams?"

"When you're Dead," the babysitter says, "everything's a lot easier. You don't have to do anything that you don't want to. You don't have to have a name, you don't have to remember. You don't even have to breathe."

She shows them exactly what she means.

When she has time to think about it (and now she has all the time in the world to think), Samantha realizes, with a small pang, that she is now stuck, indefinitely between ten and eleven years old, stuck with Claire and the babysitter. She considers this. The number 10 is pleasing and round, like a beach ball, but all in all, it hasn't been an easy year. She wonders what 11 would have been like. Sharper, like needles, maybe. She has chosen to be Dead instead. She hopes that she's made the right decision. She wonders if her mother would have decided to be Dead, instead of dead, if she could have.

Last year, they were learning fractions in school when her mother died. Fractions remind Samantha of herds of wild horses, piebalds and pintos and palominos. There are so many of them, and they are, well, fractious and unruly. Just when you think you have one under control, it throws up its head and tosses you off. Claire's favorite number is 4, which she says is a tall, skinny boy. Samantha doesn't care for boys that much. She likes numbers. Take the number 8, for instance, which can be more than one thing at once. Looked at one way, 8 looks like a bent woman with curvy hair. But if you lay it down on its side, it looks like a snake curled with its tail in its mouth. This is sort of like the difference between being Dead and being dead. Maybe when Samantha is tired of one, she will try the other.

On the lawn, under the oak trees, she hears someone calling her name. Samantha climbs out of bed and goes to the nursery window. She looks out through the wavy glass. It's Mr. Coeslak. "Samantha, Claire!" he calls up to her. "Are you all right? Is your father there?" Samantha can almost see the moonlight shining through him. "They're always locking me in the tool room. Goddamn spooky things," he says. "Are you there, Samantha? Claire? Girls?"

The babysitter comes and stands beside Samantha. The babysitter puts her finger to her lip. Claire's eyes glitter at them from the dark bed. Samantha doesn't say anything, but she waves at Mr. Coeslak. The babysitter waves too. Maybe he can see them waving, because after a little while, he stops shouting and goes away. "Be careful," the babysitter says. "*He'll* be coming soon. It will be coming soon."

She takes Samantha's hand, and leads her back to the bed, where Claire is waiting. They sit and wait. Time passes, but they don't get tired, they don't get any older.

Who's there?
Just air.

The front door opens on the first floor, and Samantha, Claire, and the babysitter can hear someone creeping, creeping up the stairs. "Be quiet," the babysitter says. "It's the Specialist."

Samantha and Claire are quiet. The nursery is dark and the wind crackles like a fire in the fireplace.

"Claire, Samantha, Samantha, Claire?" The Specialist's voice is blurry and wet. It sounds like their father's voice, but that's because the hat can imitate any noise, any voice. "Are you still awake?"

"Quick," the babysitter says. "It's time to go up to the attic and hide."

Claire and Samantha slip out from under the covers and dress quickly and silently. They follow her. Without speech, without breathing, she pulls them into the safety of the chimney. It is too dark to see, but they understand the babysitter perfectly when she mouths the word, *Up*. She goes first, so they can see where the fingerholds are, the bricks that jut out for their feet. Then Claire. Samantha watches her sister's foot ascend like smoke, the shoelace still untied.

"Claire? Samantha? Goddammit, you're scaring me. Where are you?" The Specialist is standing just outside the half-open door. "Samantha? I think I've been bitten by something. I think I've been bitten by a goddamn snake." Samantha hesitates for only a second. Then she is climbing up, up, up the nursery chimney.

STIGMATA

Phyllis Alesia Perry

Phyllis Alesia Perry (b.1961) was born in Atlanta, Georgia. She grew up in Tuskegee, Alabama and graduated from the University of Alabama in 1982. Perry worked as an editor for the *Alabama Journal* and is a recipient of the Pulitzer Prize. She lives in Atlanta and has published two novels, *Stigmata* – from which this is an extract – and *A Sunday in June*.

Ruth knows first.

We sit in the old apple tree behind Aunt Eva's house in Johnson creek, having just delivered several basketfuls of apples to Aunt Eva. She watches us from the back porch where she peels some for canning.

My fantastic out-of-body story has my cousin sitting still as stone, her cheek against the rough bark of an upward-reaching branch. Funny, she doesn't look the least bit shocked, and she presses for details.

"Damn," she murmurs. "You did it again."

"Again?"

"Ah, I remember it well," she says, mockingly putting her hand to her chin and looking skyward. "Nineteen-seventy-seven, wasn't it? You called me by someone else's name, fell off the bed and stared in space for a couple of days. I wrote about it in my diary."

"But I never told you . . ."

"You never told me what you saw, Lizzie. But you called me Joy. Ancestor of ours, right? So's Grace. Why are these people trying to talk to you?"

"You make it sound like ordinary conversation."

"Well, I know it ain't that. But some kind of communication between then and now is going on here. I mean, is there funk after death?"

I roll my eyes.

"Was there something familiar about the house you were in, about the room?" she asks.

"Yeah, I told you. But I can't tell you where I'd seen it." I look off over the top of the house, the church, and towards the cemetery where Grace lay. "Maybe I was in Grace's house, you know, that old empty place back up in the woods where we used to play. But it wasn't anything like you'd remember, Ruth. It was . . . it was home, with furniture and rugs on the floor. It was like remembering, but more. I saw what she was seeing. I saw . . . man! I saw Mother as a little girl. When I woke up, or came to, or whatever, it didn't feel like a dream. Felt like I'd stepped out of one room and into another."

"You said you weren't asleep. Both times you winked out and then back?"

"But I had to be asleep, Ruth, right?" She is taking me far too seriously, frightening me.

"I don't know. Maybe Grace was trying to tell you something. And Bessie."

"Damn, girl. This ain't no *Twilight Zone* thing."

"No, much better." She grins. "The real stuff always is. So what else?"

"Well, I am kinda achy when I wink back in. Sore. Some places feel almost raw. But after a few hours I'm OK."

"Ooooh. Physical manifestations. Did you do something in the other times that hurt you? That could be proof that you really went."

"No." I look down at Aunt Eva, who has stopped peeling and now stares at us, not moving. She can't hear us, can she?

"Where are the pains?"

"My wrists and ankles and back. Stinging."

"Lemme see." She holds out her hands and I give her mine. Turning them over, she examines the wrists. "I don't see anything," she says, putting her fingers against my right arm. Then she is still. She puts her hands around my wrists and lets out a small gasp, dropping them as if they are hot.

"What? What?" I search her face, and her eyes are clouded.

"I felt something," she whispers.

"No shit. What?"

"Pain." Ruth closes her eyes. "Just for a second. Pain."

"What kind of pain? I don't feel anything, at least not now."

"But . . . oh Jesus, it's there! Just under your skin."

"Ruth." I touch her hand and she flinches. "What am I gonna do?"

"I don't know. But Lizzie . . ."

"Yes?"

"There's more coming. Coming fast." She keeps her eyes closed. Her lips tremble.

"Ruth . . . you can feel that?"

She nods.

"How?"

Ruth opens her eyes and says, "How is it that you can step into the life of a woman who died before you were born?"

"There is no answer to that," I say.

We stay at Aunt Eva's that weekend. We had driven down from Tuskegee in Ruth's new car after classes Friday to help with the apples and to taste the first pies, and had planned to go back that evening to catch a party on campus.

But after we climb down from the tree, we decide to stay. We call our mothers, who are playing cards with two other ladies at my house in Tuskegee. I imagine my father safety cocooned behind the door of his study, sipping and reading. Nothing can get me to go home and disturb such domesticity tonight.

"Can you touch me now?" I ask Ruth after dinner, after Aunt Eva is in bed and we sprawl on the front steps. She reaches out a hand and takes mine tensely, sliding her palms over the wrist and forearm. After a few seconds, I feel her relax.

"It's OK," she says, taking her hand back nevertheless.

We're sick, I think, as Ruth swats a lightning bug. *Very sick.*

That night I wake because the night chill has crept into my heart. I open my eyes and I'm standing upright under the night sky. My bare toes dig little depressions into the dirt road just beyond Aunt Eva's front porch, where I can sense, rather than see, Ruth standing, watching. Her long frame sways toward me.

Sleepwalking. That's a new twist. Can't remember the dream that brought me out here. Can't move until I remember what I'm supposed to remember. It just feels so good to be out, but I can't move to what waits for me.

Closing my eyes, I try to remember. That pain is back, especially along the wrists. I rub them. I'm being pulled, but I can't go where they want me to go. Not there.

Ruth's eerie pitter-patter follows me, down the road a bit past Son Jackson's house, and then a turn right to the pasture that runs all the way down to the little river we call Johnson Creek. Our white nightgrowns fly out from our legs, making us winged spirits, and Son Jackson's cows, standing still as stone a moment before, turn their long heads to look.

I stop and close my eyes. Salty air saps the moisture from my lips. Why am I here and why can't I go home, when I know my mother waits for me?

The ground slowly rolls under my feet. I smell – taste – sweat and blood and months of misery. The scent knocks me dizzy for a moment and I stumble forward. Then I am pulled, jerked. I open my eyes, but there is a void in front of me. Light, gray and weak, filters in slowly from the left side of my vision, and I see the deck, the water beyond and the line of dark bodies going jerkily forward into the ghost-land. Each bent back ahead of me is familiar.

A gurgling sob reaches me. Mine. I'd been steadily shuffling forward, but I can't go any farther.

The rail is under my palm, the weight of another person dangles from my wrist. The bottom of my foot scrapes the top of the rail; I try to ignore the sound of the chain dragging along the wooden deck. Trying to stand on the rail, I expect to be jerked back at any moment. I crouch there for what seems to be an eternity. The man attached to my wrist whispers to me urgently in some strange tongue. When I turn to look at him there is some slow-crackling fire in his stare. I am to go, his eyes say, and he'll go with me.

So I throw my leg over the other side, but I feel myself being pulled. . . .

I hit the water with a hard thud, rolling over and scraping my forehead on something – is it the side of the boat? I touch bottom and the water is pitch-dark; no sunlight. Where is the sun?

A hand grabs me and my head breaks the surface. But I'm not sure I want to open my mouth to breathe.

"Dammit!" Ruth says, her voice coming from far away, but her fingers biting into my arm. "Help me – at least a little here, Lizzie! You're like a damn rock!" she drags me through the water crossways to the current; it tugs gently but insistently on my limbs.

I drift into that now-familiar sensation of disorientation; my mind crawls down a long hallway. I now Ruth is there, but when I look into her face, I see someone else. A dark girl in African clothes, silent but with eyes that speak of horrible things. She and I seem to walk back and forth, holding on to each other.

Cold water slaps my face as I stumble and fall.

"Lizzie," I hear Ruth half-growl, half-moan. "Lizzie, don't blink out on me now!"

Hands in my armpits haul me upright again and I stand face-to-face with Ruth, chest-deep in the cold, tumbling flow of Johnson Creek. If Ruth looks that frightened, I wonder how I look. The African girl is gone. The ship deck is gone. Involuntarily, I touch my arms under the water, but I already know there are no chains.

"Lizzie . . ." Ruth strokes my forehead and then stares at the smear of blood and water on her fingers.

"Your head," she says. "You're bloody. Let's get the hell outta this water!"

We wade through to the shallows. Ruth scolds. I can think of no response to her mumbling, frightened questions.

The creek isn't very wide, but it's sort of deep in the middle. If I had dived over in the shallows, where the rocks ruled, that likely would have been the end of my story.

Over my shoulder, I see the thin-railed small-plank bridge that spans the stream. Luckily, I'd gone over in the deepest part with water to cushion the fall. Still – I touch a hand to my head as Ruth drags me by the arm to the bank – I hit something. Is that why I feel so fuzzy?

Despite the warmth of the night, we shiver violently as we stumble to shore, and we don't break stride until we are climbing Aunt Eva's porch steps.

Inside, Ruth almost tears the soaking nightgown off me, still whispering urgent questions at me as I stand there naked, hair dripping and on its way back to wherever hair goes, back to damn Africa, I guess. She searches for something dry. I can't answer her questions. I don't know what to say. Cursing, she wraps me in a sheet and slips away down the hall.

OK, OK, OK, I think, clutching the sheet closer. *Ayo-Bessie. Grace. Y'all just trying to confuse me.* Grace always speaks loudly, her memories hissing insistently inside my head. And behind her are the dream-like tangles of Ayo's life. More distant but also more painful. I shiver, wanting it all to go away immediately, but I still see the burning eyes of the man on the ship's deck, lit up with some fever.

"Lizzie," says Ruth, slipping back into the room and closing the door, "you got to say something to me so that I know you're doing all right here." She is still soaking wet. She drops a dry gown, one of Aunt Eva's, over my head.

"Lizzie?!" she grabs my arm, and we both gasp. A searing pain passes through my body, radiating from the wrist she has in her hand. Her eyes widen and she looks otherworldly, her body rigid with pain, her hair hanging limply against her chin, and the wet gown still glued to her body.

"Let go of me," I manage to choke out. "Please. It hurts."

But she hesitates, as if it is difficult to move. Finally she reaches up with her other hand and pries her own fingers from around my flesh. I slump, suddenly so tired, staring at the red, round marks on my wrists.

I watch her wearily take off the wet gown and put on another. She sits on the edge of the bed and begins drying her hair with a towel. She tosses me another dry towel and slips under the covers.

"Go to bed before you die shivering there, Lizzie," she says. "But don't touch me."

I turn off the light. Ruth breathes heavily beside me in the bed we share, and

I try to scoot my body as close to the wall as possible.

"Don't tell the doctor," she says.

"What?" I turn my head to look at her, trying to see her face in the dark. I only discern the faint outlines of her cheek, her nose, her ear.

"I wouldn't tell your father or Sarah about what happened tonight if I were you," Ruth says.

"I wasn't going to."

"Good idea." Ruth turns her back towards me, and I sink down in the bed. I am afraid to sleep, since the line between dreaming and waking has become hard to see with the naked eye.

THE HANGING GIRL

Ali Smith

Novelist and short story writer, **Ali Smith** (b.1962) was born in Inverness. She graduated from the University of Aberdeen and studied for a PhD at the University of Cambridge. Smith lectured in English at the University of Strathclyde before becoming a full-time writer. Her awards include the Whitbread Novel Award, the Scottish Arts Council Book of the Year Award and the Bailey's Women's Prize for Fiction. Ali Smith lives in Cambridge with her partner Sarah Wood.

They're going to hang me.

I don't think they will blindfold me. The sun on the snow. What a day, a beautiful spring day. Smell of sawn wood. One of the men is holding the ropes. Not men, boys. Another hits at my feet with his gloves and shouts something over his shoulder. I think they think I am too near the edge. They don't want me to hang myself. Clean wood underfoot. I think everyone from the house is already dead. They are doing this to other people too. I don't recognize any of them. My wrists have made the ends of my sweater loose and round and the cold air gets in. I haven't changed my clothes for six days. The rope round my wrists is hairy. Not too tight. Just tight enough. The boy who tied them was kind. They've made signs to hang round our necks. The signs have two languages on them. What I can read says we have been made an example of. Spring is coming. When they took me out there were chickens pecking in the snow where the snow is thinner, and there is a crow somewhere in the trees, the noise of a crow. The way crows build their nests, balanced on nothing, on the holes between branches.

A man is pulling pointed legs out from beneath a camera. I don't know what type of camera it is. It's a film camera. This will be filmed. People have sat down on the chairs to watch. Something is going to start soon. A man just got up and gave his chair to a lady. They are having a conversation. She's looking at the sky and nodding. The man with the greatcoat has stopped in front of me. His head comes up to my stomach. He's standing on something. I can't see what it is. I can't see his face. There's snow on the brim of his hat. It hasn't snowed for days. He must have come through trees. He is sliding the knot round away from my chin. The knot makes his hand in its glove look small. He has moved to the woman next to me. I think I can get myself to the edge again. The camera has started making a noise. Careful. Careful.

Here I go here I go here I go again the big number one more time ladies and gentlemen put your hands together please for this little lady a singer a swinger in the performance of a lifetime (music applause) start spreading the noose

I'm leaving today slow slow build it build it up blast it out thank you thank you ladiesan-gentlemen I'm a little hoarse forgive me my throat's a little tight for it today but a very warm welcome to the show I'm your (g)host for this evening morning afternoon evening morning afternoon and I just know we're going to have a really great time together why did the chicken cross the road? well wouldn't you if someone wanted to wring your neck? (groans of laughter) why couldn't they hang the insolent girl? because she had such a – yes – brass neck (laughter and clapping) no no please no time for that a lot to get through no time to hang about (laughter) yes! please! madam! thank you! but to be serious just for a moment – only for a moment sir don't look so worried! – in all seriousness remember (dim lights to spot and cue grave music) *nothing* that you will see tonight is faked *nothing* that will pass before your eyes here is fabricated in any way *no* tricks of the light no tricks of the lens this death is pure live entertainment and I swear it will really happen right before your eyes over and over and over again for over and over amen boys girls ladies gentlemen thank you I appreciate it I do and now (drumroll) the moment we're waiting for . . . today's victim on . . . *This Is My Death* – yes it's you yes this time you now from nowhere you get more much more than you bargained for me you get me scrawny broken albatross to hang round your neck in one lunge I'm off the scaffold and into your head surprise! and swinging gaudy bauble on a tree coo-ee hello it's me hung by my thread first my face before the rope then my face tight pinched constipated those tight lines are my eyes and mouth halfway through the slow snap in two ah then my eyes rolled to heaven a blank thank you thank you ladies and gents ghastly I know so nice to meet you to make your acquaintance nice knowing you pity it was so short but no more time oh well never mind see you later alligator goodnight Irene I'll see you in your dreams.

My head at its broken angle. My eyes gone. The creak of the rope on the beam above.

Please, you boys in the front row. Please. No filming up my skirt.

Anyone like to see it one more time? Push button one for yes, button two for no.

Pauline went to the doctor's. I've got aches and pains all over, she said. I feel dizzy and light-headed. My stomach's sore after I eat. My skin feels sensitive like I've got flu, and I'm having delusions.

Delusions, the doctor said.

I keep imagining there's somebody behind me, but the thing is, there's nobody there, Pauline said.

Somebody behind you, the doctor said. He clicked the mouse on his computer.

Following me, Pauline said. All the time. Wherever I go. But every time I look round, whoever it is is gone.

Mm, the doctor said. Interesting.

It's very disconcerting, Pauline said. Actually it's getting to be a bit of a pain in the neck.

Where exactly in the neck? the doctor asked.

Not just the neck, all over really, Pauline said. Can you give me an antibiotic?

The doctor printed out a prescription. Take the whole course, he said. I think the unspecific aches will clear up. It's probably what we call a rota bug. You need some indigestion tablets for the stomach. You might find it cheaper to ask at Boots for their own name brand, they're just as good. As for the other, I'll refer you to our counsellor.

Thanks, Pauline said.

It took three months for Pauline's referral. By the time she was sitting in one of the plush armchairs on the other side of the desk from the counsellor she had lost a substantial amount of weight, there were black circles round her eyes, and her hair had outgrown the style it was supposed to have.

It's a woman, she whispered, a woman or a girl, I can't tell which. I can only just catch her, and only sometimes, in the corner of my eye. I'm pretty sure she's here now. I don't really like talking about her in the third person. It seems rude.

Behind the counsellor's head there was a poster of the Munch painting of the screaming person on the bridge. Above the face was the word DEPRESSION and a question mark, in shimmery out-of-focus letters.

The piece of plastic on her desk said that the counsellor's name was Mrs Jane Figgis. Mrs Figgis looked tired. She wrote down Pauline's name. Now then, she said. Pauline. We've got a six-week block of meetings, Pauline, and I'm hoping you will be able to make it here to the office at this time every week for the next five weeks not including today.

I will, Pauline said.

Including this week, that makes six weeks in all, Mrs Figgis said. Now. If you feel like you're going to be unable to keep to this arrangement, for any reason at all, for instance if you're ill, or you have another appointment somewhere else, or you just don't feel like coming, if you could telephone reception and explain that you can't comply with our schedule on that particular week.

Yes of course, Pauline said, but I'm always available on Thursday mornings, Thursday's fine for me.

Because if you cancel, Pauline, you see, you must understand. Whether you choose to or you have to forego one of our scheduled meetings, regardless of reasons I'm afraid, you'll lose that meeting altogether. I just have to make that clear, and I hope it isn't a problem for you, Mrs Figgis said.

No, no problem at all, I understand, Pauline said. She signalled with her eyes to the armchair on the left of her. She's here now, she said. I think she's in that chair there.

Yes, the counsellor said. She wrote something down and looked at her watch. Tell me about yourself, she said. Let's start with your childhood.

It's nothing to do with my childhood. When I try to picture it, the entity called childhood, it repeats on me, rich and well-meaning as a glass of milk and I know that it was a time of effortless seasons, fanning down one after the other like the pages of a book slow-riffled by the thumb of some blithe, indolent hand.

My name is Pauline Gaitskill. I was born in July 1966. I work for Hummings Mints; I design the combinations of sugar, flavouring and chemicals to make the insides of the Hummings range chewy and harmless. I've been doing this for the six years since I left college. I'm solely responsible for several things: Hummings Chewy Spearmints, Hummings Chewy Peppermints and Hummings

Chewy Strongmints. At the moment I am working on a potential new project, Hummings Chewy Traditional Olde English Mints.

Recently something has changed for me. It is possible, I suppose, that it's been changed for longer, that I just didn't notice, but I've been aware of it since the first week of November last year.

I remember because that night we had friends over; we had stripped our front and back rooms and we were celebrating our new polished wood floor. Our friends brought some dope, which made us hilarious and we were lolling and giggling round the aftermath of supper. The table was strewn with our leftovers. Someone had left the television on in the adjoining room, a programme where some elderly people were talking about their lives, and every so often, I remember, there would be film of mounds of dead bodies from all over the world over the century, over the lifetimes of the old people. The thing I remember is that every time any one of us caught sight of these dead bodies in the other room we would all end up destroyed, in helpless laughter.

Mike is my partner. He makes toothpaste dispensers; we're perfectly suited. That night he was telling Roger and Liz about something he'd read in the Sunday paper, where the last words of pilots in planes about to crash were recorded, and were usually oh fuck or oh shit or oh Christ. Then we all joined in making up people's famous last words. Marc Bolan: at least I went out on a smash hit. Marie-Antoinette: did you have to take so much off? I only wanted a trim. (I thought that one up.) Liz had one about Princess Diana, I don't remember. I remember we had a long and detailed argument about whether famous last words were valid after or before the death, and we eventually decided that they'd have to be said before to count, since you couldn't really say anything after you were dead, and then we went round the table and each of us had to think of one. Look how close I can get to the edge of this cli-i-i-i-. Do you think we should be driving quite so fa–. Don't worry, it's perfectly sa–. Liz had one which was the same each time with different endings. Why are you coming towards me in that threatening way with such a big sharp kitchen kni–, that tennis ra–, hypodermic syri–, sawn-off sho–. There were people lining up in black and white on television, about to be shot or hung. I pretended to be one of them. I said: I really wish this was just a game of famous last wo–. I got the biggest laugh. We were laughing our heads off.

The next day my head felt all light. The next day was the first day I had an inkling that something might actually be wrong.

The waiting room was full of people waiting to talk to counsellors. Pauline stood at the receptionist's desk until the receptionist looked up from her screen.

I won't be coming to my appointment next week, Pauline said. Or the week after that, or, I'm afraid, the week after that. And I won't be able to come next month at all. I'm very busy next month.

The receptionist clicked up the first of Pauline's appointments and began deleting the letters of her name. Pauline pushed through the heavy swing doors. She paused to hold the door open. She didn't want it to swing back and hit whoever was at her heels.

Pretty blonde Pauline turning heads in the sun of a June afternoon. Blonde and wide-eyed like a girl from an old-fashioned hairspray commercial, frowning slightly, quite attractively, as if concentrating; looking all the better for being a little too gaunt; her long hair shimmering and the sight of her sending a pleasant shiver over the surfaces of the hearts of passers-by as she walked down the street.

Pauline stopped suddenly, very suddenly turned round.

Nearly, she said in a whisper. Nearly caught you.

Pauline talking to the ghost as she walked, but quietly so nobody would think her deranged, humming what she said into a singsong so anybody would think her just strolling along, singing a song. Me and my sha-dow, strolling down the a-ven-ue, me and my sha-dow. I know you're there. What do you want. I know you want something. What do you want from me. She smiled back at a man who was smiling at her from behind his fruit stall.

Day-dreaming, darling?

Yes, I suppose I am, she said.

Can I do you anything today, love?

Not today, thanks.

Pauline went into an empty church, sat down at the back.

Is this right? she said under her breath. Is this any good?

The church was shockingly cold. Pauline sat in a pew then lay down on her back. She looked up at the rafters. A medieval-looking man hung carved into the wall. He had his arm round the shoulder of another man most of whose face had been chiselled off, and he was holding open the wound in his own side so the man with no face could put his fingers into it. The face that remained was patient, indifferent. Pauline sneezed, and heard the sneeze repeat itself in the church a fraction of a second after it had left her nose.

Bless me, she said.

Less me, the echo said.

She lay as flat as she could. She crushed out the space between her back and the wood she was lying on.

Nothing there, she said.

Air, the echo said.

I give up. I'm going mad. I am, Pauline said.

Vup. Ad. Am, the echo said.

Out on the street heat haze or car haze hung at the traffic lights. Pauline crossed the road to the fruit stall and bought eight oranges from the man.

Got a cold? the man said.

Vitamins, Pauline said.

At the newsagent's she bought a newspaper and a bottle of water. When she came out she saw the girl hanging from a lamppost. She watched her, cut down, fall through the air and crumple on to the ground.

The bottle smashed open on the pavement. The oranges rolled into the road. A boy stopped his bike and picked up what he could as the cars roared past. He held out his arms full of oranges to the woman standing with her mouth open, broken glass round her feet and water seeping into the cracks in the concrete. A mother tugged on a small child's hand, told her to come away.

Are you in pain? Pauline said.

Eh? the boy holding the oranges said. You all right? All right then?

The women watching from the pelican crossing decided between them that she was drunk.

Your poor head. Is it heavy? Pauline said.

The water was evaporating already on the pavement. The boy put the oranges down, stepped back.

She draped the hanged girl's arms round her shoulders, hoisted her on to her back. The girl's head swung down, loose, hung round Pauline's neck. Pauline held it in her bare hands.

I think we are friends now. She is much less shy than she was to start with, and I have invited her to stay for as long as she wants. She is staying in the guest room. I have been trying to explain to Mike, but he just refuses to see it.

She has an endless appetite for television. She lies on the couch with her head propped on the arm of it and watches tv like a sick child. (Actually I think she only is about twelve, or thirteen at the most.) She loves quizzes, game shows, shows where people sing. She particularly seems to love old musicals. She watched the whole of *Oliver!* and I could tell, she was moved, especially when Nancy gets killed.

She becomes quite agitated if anything serious is on. Mike gets very angry and we have had several arguments, the last and most furious so far over a documentary film of some Canadian loggers taking chainsaws to trees. But she didn't want to see it and I will not have her suffer. Anyway Mike didn't really want to watch it; he's never wanted to watch such things before. He was just trying to prove a point.

For someone with such bad co-ordination she gets around pretty well. She likes to hang herself from things all over the house. She's tried out all the light fittings in all the rooms. She likes the upstairs banister rail; she enjoys the drop in the landing. Last night she hung on the wall like a picture. I think she was trying to make me laugh.

It is exciting having a friend again. Mike is a little resentful, which is unreasonable. It's not as if we skulk in corners and discuss him or anything. It's not as if we talk at all. I don't believe she understands English, even if she could talk. I sing to her sometimes; it's a universal language. I show her words in the paper and try to explain them until she looks bored. We have a book of photographs of wild flowers. She is always signalling to me to find the pictures of the small pink ones, field bindweed, and the small blue ones, forget-me-not.

The way her eyes are set up beneath the lids makes her look cynical, and once you get to know her she's not like that at all. She hangs off the tree at the bottom of the lawn and birds swoop round her, rest on her shoulders or the side of her head. One day I lay on the grass and she lay beside me; we stayed there all afternoon and all evening, until it got dark. She wanted to watch the things coming out of the ground.

I would like to remove what's left of the rope. It looks heavy and uncomfortable; it must rub. But when I showed her the knife – it's too thick for scissors – she flew off up the stairs in a panic and hung from the light in the back bedroom and wouldn't come down. I heard her thump back on to the carpet well after I went to bed.

I wonder what her name is. I have no idea how to find out. I tell her, to comfort her, because she must need comfort, that there's nothing so strange or different about it, that she's missing nothing, that it's the same for everyone; every one of us falling through air with one end of the rope attached to our birthdates till the rope pulls tight. Some people just have less far to fall, I say.

But she looks at me with her white eyes, her head hanging like an empty ventriloquist's dummy, and I know what the look means. Some people are pushed. Some people aren't given enough rope. You can't know what it was like.

True. I don't know. I have no idea what it was like.

I can make a good guess as to where she is now. In her favourite place, doing her favourite thing, swinging beneath my kitchen clock pretending to be the pendulum.

Pauline stopped going in to work. Mike found out when Pauline's boss called his office to ask if she was any better. He drove home in the middle of the day and found her lying on her back on the lawn, staring at the sky with her hair in the soil beneath the rose bush.

That night in bed he put his head on her arm.

Love, he said. Baffling, all this. Really it is.

No, Pauline said. Baffling is where they hang you by the foot; they used to do it in parts of Europe and in Scotland, it's a symbolic sacrifice, like putting you in the stocks. They did it to people who owed money or to perpetrators of mild forms of treason. It's not the same thing at all.

Mike sat up, took Pauline by an earnest hand, made his face earnest. Tell me it again, he said. I'm trying to understand. In your dreams, and in your head –

– uh huh, in my dreams, if you like, Pauline said

– you've got this pretty girl always going to her death, Mike said.

A pretty girl going to her death, Pauline said. Does the prettiness make a difference?

Of course, Mike said. He smiled. I'd think it'd be much harder to watch a pretty girl having to die, he said.

Pretty, Pauline said. Well, it's hard to tell. She's beautiful, of course. But it's not what you'd call a pretty sight. But yes, I suppose she was once pretty. Or she might have been, if she'd had the chance. Anyway, she's a friend. Friends are always pretty, even if they're not.

Pauline stared at the wall. Mike lay back and watched her stare into space. He thought about the three thin pretty girls from the American sitcom about friends, and then he imagined them on their way to die. He made up various possible deaths for them. Then he replaced them with some of the prettier girls from work.

Christ, he said.

He turned over so Pauline wouldn't sense his erection, closed his eyes and shook his head sharply, pictured himself instead, driving along the motorway under turn-off signs and signs flashing warnings about fog, driving fast along boring country lanes and slowing as he came into a village, past a sign about old people crossing, a sign about a hump-backed bridge, a narrowing of the road, a sharp bend, a sign saying keep your distance.

I don't know what to do, Mike told Roger at lunch. I'm at the end of my tether. She won't go to work. She won't answer the phone. She won't come out, not even down to the pub for a quick drink. She sits in the house all day in a room with the curtains closed, or on the kitchen floor with her legs crossed leaning against the fridge, or she shuts herself in the bathroom and talks to herself. She won't talk to me. She watches rubbish all the time on tv. Her work phoned me; they can't sign her off sick without a sick note and she won't go to the doctor, she keeps saying she's better. But she lies in bed all day and won't get up. She's hardly eating. I've bought her presents. They make no difference.

Yeah, Roger said. Liz says she can't get her to speak to her. She says it's as if she's a different person. She thinks she needs therapy.

She's been, Mike said. She won't go back. The therapist told her it was displaced guilt.

What's this? Maggie said across the table. What's this about guilt? Somebody's guilty of something around here and I don't know about it?

Mike bristled. He didn't want anyone else listening in.

Pauline says it's a load of rot, he said to Roger. She says there's nothing displaced about it and the sooner we all realize it, the better.

Yeah, right, Roger said. He frowned. Guilty of what? he said. He hadn't really been listening, and didn't want Mike to realize. He began wondering whether Pauline was having an affair after all, like Liz thought. (He and Liz had been discussing it. In fact they had had rather a nice time discussing it, and had gone out for a meal specifically to do so, and had spent more time talking to each other because of it than they had for quite a long time, and afterwards they had been exceptionally close and had had some very good sex.)

Well, you know, Mike said. Like when. Like this thing that happened about a month ago, I was reading this piece out of the paper about soldiers taking an amateur video of each other pretending to be shooting people in the mouth and raping people, and the paper had got hold of the videotape and now the soldiers were in trouble. I mean, it isn't even a *real* bad thing, but she went running crying out of the room. I mean, it was only them having a laugh. I told her. Terrible things happen all the time. You can't be this sensitive, you just can't.

No, Maggie said, you can't, can you? When Dave and I were in Washington we went to the museum they've got about the holocaust, you know? It's an amazing building. But it's so depressing, and it's really tiring.

Liz's father, Roger said, used to do this thing. He used to take pictures of gravestones all the time. Liz has all these photos of her and her mother and sisters on days out in cemeteries. Her father used to make them go because it was easy to park and you could always find somewhere to sit. Weird. I mean, sick.

Spooky, Maggie said looking at Mike.

Right, Mike said. He was sweating. He held his arms close in to his sides, in case there were patches showing under them. He looked at his plate, at what looked like gristle on his fork. Last night he had woken in the middle of the night from the same dream, the recurring dream, where his parents appeared to him smiling, vibrantly alive.

He glanced at Maggie, across from him, all sympathetic face. He could feel Roger looking at him, paused over his pudding, waiting to hear more, to find out what the trouble was. He looked at the clock. Lunch hour was almost up and he'd eaten hardly any lunch.

Inside his mouth he could feel his tongue, rooted to him like a thick-stemmed plant. It was moving. It touched against the soft flesh of the walls of his mouth.

You can hang a work of art. You can hang a whole exhibition of works of art. You hang meat until it properly matures, and a jury or a parliament can be hung.

You can hang on somebody, on his or her every word, and something can hang on, depend on, something or someone else. Clothes can hang well on you. Something can hang over you. There's the other kind of hangover. There's hang out and hang dog and get the hang of. Hang back. Hanging garden. Hang together. Hang down your head, hang fire, hanger on and hang on (as in, wait a minute). Hang in the balance. Well-hung. Hang-up (psychological), and hang up (telephone).

I have started to make lists of these into a kind of mantra to try to interest her, even if only subconsciously, in all the other possible meanings. It is the least I can do.

I touch my neck, apply different pressures to the cords of my muscles. It amazes me how tough and sensitive they are. I speak while I'm doing it, and hear how the pressure changes the sound that comes out.

I carry her up the stairs. I put her down on the bathroom stool, run the water, swirl the hot and the cold together. I dry my hands and undress her, as gently as I can because she is always sore. Then I lift her up and slide her into the water and she rests her head on the side of the bath. I soap her all over. Her feet, between her toes, up her calves and thighs and between them, up her taut back and down her front, between her ungrown breasts, under her arms, round and under the rope. I squeeze the flannel out over her head and wash off anything left of the soap. Then I wrap her in the bathtowel that's been warming on the radiator. I dry her all over. I dry between her toes and behind her knees with talcum powder. I towel her hair and comb it out. I carry her on my back into the bedroom, and then I tuck her into the bed. Until she is asleep, I lie next to her above the covers. She likes me to breathe with her. When she is asleep I slip off the bed, switch the light out and close the door over. I leave the landing light on. She is afraid of the dark.

On the nights when she can't sleep, I sit with her. I look into her white-charred eyes. I let her put her cold hand on my heart.

It is the very least I can do.

Pauline jumped off the garage roof and broke her leg when she landed. The bone came right out through the skin.

A neighbour called both the paramedics and the police for good measure. The policeman arrived first.

I can't help you, love, he told Pauline. I'm the reporting officer. Even if you were on fire, even if you were bleeding to death right here in front of me on the lawn, I'd not be able to do anything. It's my duty only to report what happens here until the emergency services come.

Pauline lay on the grass with her leg jutted up. Tears streamed across her face and she was laughing. The policeman looked at her teeth. He thought what a fine mouth she had, and how very good-looking she was. He turned his back, one foot swivelling in the flower-bed, opened his book and wrote it down. Upon my arrival the young woman was hysterical, and was quite unable to assess her own position.

Mike was round at Maggie's. He had been walking back and fore outside her house, and now he was sitting on her couch holding a large whisky. Maggie was saying all the right things; all the useful, surprisingly comforting things. But none of us can do anything about it, she said. We'd all like to, but we can't. However much we'd like to, it's just not possible. Some things are out of our control. We have to survive. She needs help, Michael, professional help, the kind of help you and I just can't give her.

Mike liked it that Maggie called him Michael. It somehow made things feel new, and possible.

Where's Dave? he said.

Not here, Maggie said.

Mike's head and throat felt tight, as if he were about to cry. Maggie, I'm scared, he said.

Don't be, Maggie said. Don't be scared.

She was behind him, and she leaned forward and brushed her hand across the back of his neck, and where her hand touched him his hair stood on end.

She took me to a slightly higher place so we could see better.

She brought her friends. They crowded in to see, all their grey forms in a mass upon the lawn, they overfilled the garden and the other back gardens and crammed into the lanes, spilling across the road and down the road. Some of them sitting for a better view up on top of parked cars and sheds and other roofs, all of them spreading down the streets and drives and round the cul de sacs, pushing into the waste lots and the fields and the outskirts, lining the roads and the motorway further than the eye, a great greyed carpet studded with lost things, and there was only one thing left for me to do. The silence like a cheer going up, roaring round my head when, flung into the air, diving like a bad swimmer into it, I went over the edge.

For a moment she held me, lightened, delighted. Then she hovered above me like a piece of litter caught up in a crosswind.

For a moment, it's true, I was falling free, suspended by nothing.

Christ but something's really aching somewhere.

God, though, what a beautiful day.

TEMPORAL ANOMALY

Kate Atkinson

Kate Atkinson (b.1951) was born in York and lives in Edinburgh. She studied English at the University of Dundee and later taught in the city. Atkinson's novels include *Life After Life*, *Started Early*, *Took My Dog* and *Case Histories*. Her books often explore the difficult stuff of life; incest, murder, divorce and betrayal. They are also characterised by humour and a belief in the essential goodness of humanity. Atkinson was awarded an MBE in the Queen's 2011 Birthday Honours, for services to literature.

Marianne was thinking about lemons when she died. More specifically, she was thinking about the lemons she had brought back from the Amalfi coast many weeks ago and which were now quietly decaying at the bottom of her fridge. It was raining, hard Scottish rain, and everyone was driving too fast, including Marianne, because no one wanted to be on the M9 in the rain, in the gloaming light.

Marianne wondered if the lemons were still good enough to cook with. Perhaps she could make a lemon meringue pie. She'd never made one but that didn't mean she couldn't. Marianne imagined how surprised her husband and son would be if she presented them with a lemon meringue pie for supper. She imagined herself walking into the dining room, bearing the pie aloft like a smiling, old-fashioned wife, like her own mother.

She had bought the lemons from a stall by the side of the road, when they were driving back to their hotel in Ravello. That was the day they had taken the boat trip to Capri. It had been very hot and all three of them had been irritable because Capri had turned out not to be what they had expected. It was full of expensive designer boutiques and rude Italians and all the cafés were busy. When Marianne saw the stall with the lemons she made Robert stop the car and he cursed her because he said it was too dangerous to stop and she said he was too cautious and he said that she was irresponsible and she said that was unfair and all the time Liam had played Donkey Kong on his Game Boy in the back of their rented Fiat Brava and said nothing.

The old woman in charge of the stall filled a plastic carrier bag with the lemons without saying a word and gave Marianne a scornful look as if she had nothing but contempt for tourists, especially the ones who wanted her lemons.

Marianne took the plastic bag on the plane home as hand-luggage, stuffing the lemons into the overhead locker on their scheduled flight out of Naples, and when she opened the locker again on the runway at Edinburgh airport she was hit by their lemony fragrance – sharp and sweet at the same time – which reminded her of the lemon soaps she used to get in her Christmas stocking. When Robert saw the plastic bag he said, "You'll never do anything with them," and he had been right. But now she could surprise him, and it would remind him of the sunshine, like a gift. Or, of course, it might remind him of the road between Positano and Ravello and the heat and her crankiness and the arguments which hadn't gone away but were only waiting for the right time to resurface.

The car was buffeted by wind and the weather report on Forth FM said that the road bridge was closed to high-sided vehicles. Marianne wondered if she had a recipe for lemon meringue pie. She could phone her mother and ask her to read one out to her from one of her many cookery books. She fumbled for her mobile in her handbag on the back seat of her car – Robert always yelled at her if he saw her do that – and speed-dialled her mother's number. Her mother sounded distracted when she answered, as if she'd already put Marianne out of her thoughts even though it was less than an hour since they'd kissed goodbye.

"Have you got a good recipe for lemon meringue pie?" Marianne asked but then she never caught her mother's answer because a darkness, like a great pair of black wings, covered her car and she could no longer hear her mother or the car engine or the rain or Forth FM on the radio, only the deafening sound of Hades' chariot wheels as he overtook her on the inside lane, so close that she could smell the rank sweat on the flanks of his horses and the stench of his breath like rotten mushrooms. And then Hades leant out of his chariot and punched a hole in the windscreen of her Audi and Marianne thought, "This is really going to hurt."

Marianne could see a fire engine making its way along the hard shoulder of the motorway, its blue lights sparkling in the dark. She had never noticed before that the blue lights on emergency vehicles were the colour of sapphires. Good Indian sapphires. Her father had been a jeweller and when she visited his shop he would take out the little drawers from the mahogany cabinet in which he kept his cut gems, graded and sorted by size and type, and show her the jewels, like tiny stars, resting on velvet cushions that were blacker than the night. Blacker than Hades' horses.

The traffic was tailed back on the eastbound carriageway for as far as Marianne could see – which was quite a long way, because she was suspended some twenty feet in the air. The Audi was slewed across the road, surrounded by more flashing sapphire lights. Broken glass glistened around it like carelessly scattered diamonds. An ambulance was parked with its doors open while the paramedics knelt on the road, treating the accident victim. A traffic police car and two big police Honda 1100s formed a barricade around the paramedics. The police themselves stood around, looking on, like a reluctant audience. The fluorescent yellow of their jackets, slick with rain, was brighter than a million lemons in the darkness.

A gust of wind caught Marianne and she drifted closer to the accident. She wasn't surprised to see herself down there, broken and crazed with blood, as the paramedics stuck tubes and needles into her and spoke in low professional tones to each other. Marianne supposed she was hovering (literally, it seemed) between life and death, her soul waiting to fly away while her body clung to the earth. You heard about it all the time. Near-death experiences. One of the paramedics was attaching defibrillator pads to Marianne's chest. She wondered if she would feel it when they shocked her. She wished she could tell the paramedics and the police how grateful she was for what they were doing for her, how kind they were. Especially as she looked like such a hopeless case from up here.

There was no sign, she noticed, of a tunnel or of a white light, no glimpse of the Elysian Fields. Her father didn't appear to be waiting for her on the other side, nor was Buster, the little Westie she had loved so much as a child. Marianne thought that perhaps it wouldn't be so bad leaving this life behind if she could have Buster back in the next.

On the opposite carriageway of the M9, the cars crawled past, their brake lights forming a slow-moving chain of glittering rubies. Marianne could see the pale now, although her watch still said ten past five. Marianne was sure that every single last cell in her body was bruised. A petrol tanker sped by, oblivious to her, followed by the M9 Express bus. She wondered if she should try to flag a vehicle down, or would it cause another accident? One was surely enough for a lifetime. A huge articulated lorry with "Tesco" written on the side caused a wake of diesel-scented air that made her feel sick. Marianne wondered if it was on its way to the Tesco in Colinton where she did her shopping. She had always hated shopping, but now she would have very much liked to be wandering along the brightly lit aisles, choosing between iceberg and cos, Persil Non-Bio and Fairy.

Now that she had been brought back to life, nothing would be hateful any more, not now that she understood about the days being precious. She had heard about that too, those people who had come back from the shores of Acheron and found their attitude to life transformed so that they cherished even the wind and the rain and each and every painful, stumbling step made along the hard shoulder of the M9. The neon oasis of the Little Chef on the bypass, ablaze with lights in the dark, was as beautiful as a newly found constellation in the night sky.

Inside the Little Chef it was warm and smelt of old fat and cheap coffee and Marianne would never have believed how comforting those scents could be. Before. Before she died.

The Little Chef's other customers ignored her – a whey-faced teenage motorcyclist, two tired truckers, an argumentative couple and two young girls who didn't look old enough to drive. Out of everyone in the place, it was Marianne who looked least likely to be the person involved in a car crash.

A sullen-looking girl with bad skin was guarding the food under the heat lamps. She was eating a Mars Bar and reading a celebrity magazine that had Romney Wright pouting on the cover. According to her name badge, the girl was called Faith. Was she really called Faith or was it some kind of metaphysical statement? In Marianne's avant-garde hairdresser's, they had words sandblasted on the mirrors – "Serenity", "Confidence", "Compassion" – as if they were promoting Zen Buddhism instead of ridiculously overpriced cut-and-blow-drys. Marianne wondered if Faith's badge was a sign of some kind. She wondered if now that she had been saved from death she would see signs everywhere.

"Excuse me," Marianne said. Faith ignored her. "Excuse me, Faith?" Faith finished her Mars Bar and yawned. Marianne leant over the metal troughs of chips and beans and fried fish and tugged at the sleeve of Faith's nylon uniform. She pulled Faith's hair, she pinched her skin, but Marianne may as well have been a breath on the air for all the notice Faith took of her. Marianne tried to accost the other customers, with much the same effect – no one could see her.

She went into the ladies' toilets to check her reflection in the mirror – to check if she had a reflection in the mirror – and was relieved to find that she had. What she saw wasn't good. Her clothes were torn and filthy, she was covered in oil and bruises, her hair was matted with blood and what she very much hoped wasn't brain matter (it was going to take more than serenity and compassion to fix that), and she had a tremendous gash across her forehead which was in urgent need of stitches. Marianne was mortified. It was no wonder no one wanted to speak to her. She picked a piece of road out of her chin and rearranged her hair to cover some of the skull fracture.

Was she dead? She didn't look dead. She didn't feel dead. She felt fucking awful but she didn't feel dead. And if she was dead then she would be a ghost but she couldn't do any of the things ghosts were supposed to be able to do – she couldn't float, she couldn't pass through doors and walls, she was cold and hungry and tired (so tired), and still seemed to be subject to all the same rules of the phenomenal world as before. If she was dead then it seemed a lot like being alive, although worse, admittedly. And surely the astral plane wasn't going to turn out to be a Little Chef?

Marianne went to look for a phone. She didn't have her handbag any more but she had a twenty-pence piece in her coat pocket. She dropped the coin in the slot and dialled home. Robert answered, "Hello?" sounding abrupt and tired. Marianne thought he must be going mad with worry. "It's me, Robert," she said, surprised at how much her voice was trembling, "it's Marianne," and she waited for the relief and the tears but all he kept saying was "Hello? Hello? Is someone there?" then she heard that funny little noise he made when he was annoyed and the line went dead. Marianne tried to get her coin back but she couldn't. This really wasn't good at all.

Apart from a little speeding – and how she regretted that now – Marianne had previously been a law-abiding person, certainly the most law-abiding lawyer that she knew, but given her current invisibility and her dreadful hunger, she thought she was more than justified in stealing food from under Faith's blackhead-encumbered nose, loading up a plate with chips, beans and sausages – she couldn't remember the last time she ate sausages – and washing them down with a can of Irn-Bru. She liked the Irn-Bru a lot and wondered why she'd never allowed Liam to drink it. She would in future. If there was a future.

Marianne walked the four miles home from the Little Chef. When she got in the house she crawled up the stairs on her hands and knees and went straight to Liam's room. She turned on the lamp by his bed and looked at her son. His eyelids were blue in sleep and his skin had a faint opalescent sheen of perspiration. He was in the last days of his childhood, she could smell it like a sour trace on his breath. She kissed him softly on his cheek and then she turned off the lamp, lay down on the bed and curled herself like an overcoat around her son. It turned out that love was everything, after all.

In the morning she would wake up and everything would be all right. (How many times in her life had she told herself that?) She would wake and hear Robert moving about the house. His morning routine never changed – there would be the sound of running water, the kettle banging onto the hob, Radio Scotland's "Good Morning, Scotland" suddenly blaring in the kitchen and, just as she did every morning, Marianne would say to her son, "Good morning, sleepyhead." And life would go on.

Marianne woke up. For a moment she thought she had had a dreadful nightmare that had been forgotten on waking but then she remembered the car crash. She ached so much she could hardly move her limbs. Liam slept on peacefully beside her. The house was quiet and Marianne wondered what time it was. Then she heard footsteps on the stairs and the bedroom door opened and Robert entered the room. Marianne couldn't remember when she had been so pleased to see Robert, not for years certainly.

She strained into a sitting position. Her mouth was so dry and ashy that she could hardly speak. "Robert," she croaked. "I'm all right." Robert sat on the edge of the bed. He looked dreadful, his skin grey, his eyes bloodshot and baggy. "I'm all right," Marianne repeated. Robert shook Liam gently awake.

"Liam," Robert said, his face crumpling in a way that made Marianne worry for him, "Liam, something very bad has happened. To Mum. A very bad thing."

* * *

Marianne thought fondly of the Little Chef on the bypass. It was the last place she had visited in the outside world. For six months now she had been housebound. Presumably, she had come back to say goodbye because that was what the newly dead did – they came back to say goodbye to their loved ones – and somehow or other she had got stuck here. Before she was dead, Marianne would never have used the term "loved ones", but six months of watching *Oprah* and *Trisha* and *Sally Jesse Raphael* had softened her vocabulary.

It was only television that gave her life (if you could call it that) any structure. She was glad that Robert had installed cable after she died. Now she had a narrative thread to guide her through the long, empty days. She could watch *Crossroads, The Bold and the Beautiful* as well as *Classic Green Acres*, which was currently running episodes from twenty years ago when Veronica Steer was still married to Jackson Todd and Gig Alexander still had hair. The characters on *Green Acres* were almost as real as Marianne's own family. In fact, she saw more of them than she did her own family. Robert and Liam never seemed to be home any more. Liam went somewhere after school, although she didn't know where because he never talked about it, and as for Robert, he was always late home and when he came in he smelt of alcohol and cigarettes and guilt.

After the initial grief and despair Marianne had been shocked at how quickly her husband and her son had returned to the rhythm of their lives. Liam still cried himself to sleep sometimes – Marianne had to go and hide in the airing cupboard with her hands over her ears because she couldn't bear it – but apart from that, they hardly ever talked about her. Sometimes Liam said, "Mum would have liked this" or "Mum used to do this", but then he would fall silent and stare into space and she could see him thinking how strange it was that she had disappeared so completely from his life and it seemed such a dreadful shame that she couldn't tell him that she was still there, that it was beginning to look as though she was going to be there for ever. She should have hung on to that last coin, the twenty-pence piece she'd used to phone Robert from the Little Chef – what if that had been her fare for the last ferry of all?

Marianne didn't know if she had been buried or cremated but she had known on which day her funeral took place because Robert and Liam returned home in the middle of the afternoon looking pale and numb. Robert was wearing the black tie he brought out only for funerals, and they both carried the sickly scent of lilies on their clothes. Marianne thought it would have been nice if they had brought people back to the house. She would have especially liked to see her mother. Marianne hoped they made her look pretty in her coffin. Marianne hoped that a lot of lovely things were said about her at her funeral. She wished she could have gone but there was some kind of invisible barrier, like a force field, that prevented her leaving the house.

The existence of this force field was the only evidence that there might possibly be someone in charge (but who?) in the afterlife. Although you could hardly call it an afterlife. It was more like a greyish half-life, a kind of uninspiring limbo. Wasn't it the Plain of Asphodel in the Underworld where people went tediously through the motions of their lives without pleasure or pain? She wished she'd paid more attention in Classical Studies. Or in Religious Studies, or indeed anything that might have provided some clues to being the living dead. She supposed she might be a zombie, but were zombies invisible? She was fairly sure she wasn't a vampire – apart from having no desire whatsoever to drink blood (although a good rare steak would have been welcome) – because she knew a lot about vampires now, thanks to *Buffy*. But what was she? There were more unanswered questions now than there had been when she was alive. Had she entered into a parallel existence of some kind? Or perhaps she would eventually come back, possibly as a completely different person, like Temple Bain, daughter of Digby Craddock, the shepherd on *Green Acres*.

Marianne lifted her feet so that Ella could hoover beneath them. Ella had been Marianne's cleaner, two days a week, for three years, and all Marianne's suspicions about how little work Ella did proved to be well-founded. The kettle was on before she even took her coat off and for the first hour of the day she sat with her feet up watching *Lorraine*, smoking cigarette after cigarette and drinking the cheap instant coffee that Robert bought nowadays instead of the expensive Italian roast that Marianne used to get in Valvona and Crolla.

Ella finished her cursory hoovering and sagged down onto the sofa next to Marianne and lit a cigarette. No wonder the place had always reeked of air freshener on the days Ella was in. Marianne sneaked one of Ella's cigarettes when she wasn't looking. She felt she had every reason to take up smoking and no reason not to. The bad-for-your-health argument really didn't apply any more.

Ella was wearing a pair of Marianne's trousers – black Warehouse – far too good for doing housework in. Marianne had been taking a nap in the conservatory the day they got rid of her clothes, and by the time she realized her entire wardrobe was leaving the house in black bin liners, Robert and Ella had already loaded up the boot of the car and left her with nothing but the jeans and sweater she'd been wearing. Robert must have offered Ella the pick of Marianne's wardrobe as every time she appeared now she was wearing something that had once belonged to Marianne (and still did as far as Marianne was concerned). And it wasn't just her clothes that had been disposed of, everything had gone – makeup, perfume, every last hair-clip, as if Robert couldn't wait to eliminate her from the house.

It was just as well that on the day they disposed of her worldly goods Marianne had been wearing all her jewellery (there was undoubtedly a certain freedom in being dead), including the good pieces her father had given her over the years. Now, of course, she had to keep on wearing them in case they were got rid of. It was easy to feel overdressed when you were slumped in front of *Countdown* in a garnet choker and diamond earrings, not to mention her bridal tiara, which her father had had specially commissioned out of blue topazes and fresh-water pearls. She'd noticed her first grey hairs when she put the tiara on. She was sure they hadn't been there before. It seemed particularly unfair that she was both dead and getting older.

If she combed her hair forward and positioned the tiara just right she could almost hide the ugly scar on her forehead. She had stitched up all her wounds with the only thread she could find in the house (she had never been a needle-woman), which unfortunately was black, so that now she gave the impression of being hand-made.

Where was her mother? Why hadn't she been the one who had sorted out her clothes and why did she never come to the house to see Liam? What if something had happened to her as well? What if she had fallen down dead from shock when she heard about Marianne's death? She wished she could speak to her mother about all the puzzling ontological questions raised on a daily basis when you were dead. She wished she could speak to anyone about anything.

On *Star Trek: Voyager* things weren't going well (they rarely did). The shields were down, the plasma manifolds were malfunctioning and the warp drive was offline. *Voyager* was lost in space, seventy thousand light years from home. Marianne knew the feeling. She worked her way through a bag of Monster Munch and a can of Fanta. This was the best time of day because soon Liam would come home and flop down on the sofa and surf mindlessly through every channel. Sometimes Marianne managed to arrange her body so that he unwittingly put his head on her shoulder or lap and those moments almost made her feel alive.

Captain Kathryn Janeway was trying to stop *Voyager* being pulled into some kind of rift in the space–time continuum, "a quantum singularity". Marianne wondered if there was such a thing or if the writers had made it up. Real or not, she knew what would happen to the crew of *Voyager* if they couldn't avoid the rift – they would find themselves in a temporal anomaly. They always did. It happened to Buffy a lot as well. Once you were in a temporal anomaly everything was topsy-turvy – you would find yourself moving backwards (or forwards or sidewards) in time, or there would be a parallel universe where two of you existed, or you might even be dead and come back to life. Did the people who made television programmes know something about the physics of time that other people hadn't noticed? Marianne had a suspicion that if she studied television carefully she might find the key to her own dilemma – only last week, for example, Captain Janeway had watched her own funeral (which on a starship, of course, meant that you floated off into endless, soundless space). And poor Buffy was two months in her grave before she came back from the dead. Marianne had been dead six months now but there might still be hope for her.

She discovered half a pomegranate that Liam had left lying on the coffee table and picked at the seeds with a pin. She hadn't started decomposing – the grey hairs hardly counted. It would be easy enough for her to start again where she had left off. Indeed, recently, she had begun to feel quite cheerful again, as if the greyness of her existence was lightening, as if winter was finally turning into spring.

Voyager had escaped the temporal anomaly and Captain Janeway ordered Lieutenant Paris to set a course for home. Marianne heard the front door open and bang shut carelessly. Liam burst into the room, discarding his school bag and jacket on the floor. He flung himself on the sofa and turned to Marianne and said, "Hi, Mum, what's for tea?" and – just like that, no reason, no explanation – she had her life back, day after day as precious and as delicate as a rope of pearls.

* * *

Marianne was on her way to see her mother. She still didn't understand where her mother had been while she was dead and her mother was reluctant to discuss it saying it was better to let sleeping dogs lie, which seemed almost wilfully enigmatic to Marianne. Marianne had been back in the land of the living for six months, six months of summer. On the telephone lines she could see swallows gathered like musical notes. The summer was over, but there would be more. There were always more summers, even when you were no longer there to see them. That was a thought you had to hold on to.

And today they would sit in her mother's garden, which was a miracle for this dreich part of the hemisphere – a cornucopia of lettuce and beetroot and onions, of sweet peas and honeysuckle and roses, strawberries and raspberries and blackcurrants, pears and plums and apples. Marianne wondered what had happened to her Amalfi lemons in the fridge – she had never come across them during the time she was dead – but just then the sky darkened and Marianne heard the sound of horses' hooves and she looked in the rear-view mirror and thought, "Oh no, not again."

THE MIRROR

Haruki Murakami

Haruki Murakami (b.1949) was born in Kyoto, Japan. He studied theatre arts at Waseda University. In 1974 he opened a jazz bar, Peter Cat, which he ran until the publication of his first novel enabled him to become a full-time writer. His books have been translated into fifty languages. Nine novels, four short story collections and two works of non-fiction are currently available in English translation. He has translated several American writers, including Truman Capote and Tim O'Brien, into Japanese.

All the stories you've been telling tonight seem to fall into two categories. There's the type where you have the world of the living on one side, the world of death on the other, and some force that allows a crossing-over from one side to the other. This would include ghosts and the like. The second type involves paranormal abilities, premonitions, the ability to predict the future. All of your stories belong to one of these two groups.

In fact, your experiences tend to fall almost totally under one of these categories or the other. What I mean is, people who see ghosts just see ghosts and never have premonitions. And those who have premonitions don't see ghosts. I don't know why, but there would appear to be some individual predilection for one or the other. At least that's the impression I get.

Of course some people don't fall into either category. Me, for instance. In my thirty-odd years I've never once seen a ghost, never once had a premonition or prophetic dream. There was one time I was in a lift with a couple of friends and they swore they saw a ghost riding with us, but I didn't see a thing. They claimed there was a woman in a grey suit standing right next to me, but there wasn't any woman with us, at least not as far as I could make out. The three of us were the only ones in the lift. No kidding. And these two friends weren't the type to play tricks on me. The whole thing was really weird, but the fact remains that I've still never seen a ghost.

But there was one time – just the one time – when I had an experience that scared me out of my wits. This happened more than ten years ago, and I've never told anybody about it. I was afraid to even talk about it. I felt that if I did, it might happen all over again, so I've never brought it up. But tonight each of you has related his own frightening experience, and as the host I can't very well call it a night without contributing something of my own. So I've decided to come right out and tell you the story. Here goes.

* * *

I graduated from high school at the end of the 1960s, just as the student movement was in full swing. I was part of the hippie generation, and refused to go to university. Instead, I wandered all over Japan working at various manual labouring jobs. I was convinced that was the most righteous way to live. Young and impetuous, I suppose you'd call me. Looking back on it now, though, I think I had a pretty amusing life back then. Whether that was the right choice or not, if I had it to do over again, I'm pretty sure I would.

In the autumn of my second year of roaming all over the country, I got a job for a couple of months as a nightwatchman at a high school. This was a school in a tiny town in Niigata Prefecture. I'd got pretty worn out working over the summer and wanted to take it easy for a while. Being a nightwatchman isn't exactly rocket science. During the day I slept in the caretaker's office, and at night all I had to do was go twice around the whole school making sure everything was OK. The rest of the time I listened to records in the music room, read books in the library, played basketball by myself in the gym. Being alone all night in a school isn't so bad, really. Was I afraid? Not at all. When you're eighteen or nineteen, nothing gets to you.

I don't imagine any of you have ever worked as a nightwatchman, so maybe I should explain the duties. You're supposed to make two rounds each night, at 9 p.m. and 3 a.m. That's the schedule. The school was a fairly new three-storey concrete building, with eighteen to twenty classrooms. Not an especially large school as these things go. In addition to the classrooms you had a music room, a home economics room, an art studio, a science lab, a staff office and the headmaster's office. Plus a separate cafeteria; swimming pool, gym and theatre. My job was to make a quick check of all of these.

As I made my rounds, I worked through a twenty-point checklist. I'd make a tick next to each one – staff office, *tick*, science lab, *tick* . . . I suppose I could have just stayed in bed in the caretaker's room, where I slept, and ticked these off without going to the trouble of actually walking around. But I wasn't such a casual sort of fellow. It didn't take much time to make the rounds, and besides, if someone broke in while I was sleeping, I'd be the one who'd get attacked.

Anyway, there I was each night at nine and three, making my rounds, a torch in my left hand, a wooden kendo sword in my right. I'd practised kendo in school and felt pretty confident of my ability to fend off anyone. If an attacker was an amateur, and even if he had a real sword with him, that wouldn't have frightened me. I was young, remember. If it happened now, I'd run like hell.

Anyhow, this took place on a windy night at the beginning of October. Actually it was rather steamy for the time of year. A swarm of mosquitoes buzzed around in the evening, and I remember burning a couple of mosquito-repellent coils to keep the little buggers at bay. The wind was noisy. The gate to the swimming pool was broken and the wind made the gate slap open and shut. I thought of fixing it, but it was too dark out, so it kept banging all night.

My 9 p.m. round went by fine, all twenty items on my list neatly ticked off. All the doors were locked, everything in its proper place. Nothing out of the ordinary. I went back to the caretaker's room, set my alarm for three, and fell fast asleep.

When the alarm went off at three, though, I woke up feeling strange. I can't explain it, but I just felt different. I didn't feel like getting up – it was as though something was suppressing my will to get out of bed. I'm the type who usually leaps right out of bed, so I couldn't understand it. I had to force myself to get out of bed and prepare to make my rounds. The gate to the pool was still making its rhythmic banging, but it sounded different from before. Something's definitely weird, I thought, reluctant to get going. But I made up my mind I had to do my job, no matter what. If you duck doing your duty once, you'll duck out again and again, and I didn't want to fall into that. So I picked up my torch and wooden sword and off I went.

It was an altogether odd night. The wind grew stronger as the night went on, the air more humid. My skin started itching and I couldn't focus. I decided to go round the gym, theatre and pool first. Everything checked out OK. The gate to the pool banged away in the wind like some crazy person who alternately shakes his head and nods. There was no order to it. First a couple of nods – yes, yes – then no, no, no . . . It's an odd thing to compare it to, I know, but that's what it felt like.

Inside the school building it was situation normal. I looked around and ticked off the points on my list. Nothing out of the ordinary had happened, despite the strange feeling I'd had. Relieved, I started back to the caretaker's room. The last place on my checklist was the boiler room next to the cafeteria on the east side of the building, the opposite side from the caretaker's room. This meant I had to walk down the long hallway on the first floor on my way back. It was pitch black. On nights when the moon was out, there was a little light in the hallway, but when there wasn't, you couldn't see a thing. I had to shine my torch ahead of me to see where I was going. This particular night, a typhoon was not too far off, so there was no moon at all. Occasionally there'd be a break in the clouds, but then it plunged into darkness again.

I walked faster than usual down the hallway, the rubber soles of my basketball shoes squeaking against the linoleum floor. It was a green linoleum floor, the colour of a hazy bed of moss. I can picture it even now.

The entrance to the school was halfway down the hallway, and as I passed it I thought, *What the – ?* I thought I'd seen something in the dark. I broke out in a sweat. Taking a firmer grip on the sword handle, I turned towards what I saw. I shined my torch at the wall next to the shelf for storing shoes.

And there I was. A mirror, in other words. It was just my reflection in a mirror. There wasn't a mirror there the night before, so they must have put one in between then and now. Oh boy, was I startled. It was a long, full-length mirror. Relieved that it was just me in a mirror, I felt a bit stupid for having been so surprised. So that's all it is, I told myself. How dumb. I put my torch down, took a cigarette from my pocket and lit it. As I took a puff, I glanced at myself in the mirror. A faint street light from outside shone in through the window, reaching the mirror. From behind me, the swimming pool gate was banging in the wind.

After a couple of puffs, I suddenly noticed something odd. My reflection in the mirror wasn't me. It looked exactly like me on the outside, but it definitely was not me. No, that's not it. It *was* me, of course, but *another* me. Another me that never should have been. I don't know how to put it. It's hard to explain what it felt like.

The one thing I did understand was that this other figure loathed me. Inside it was a hatred like an iceberg floating in a dark sea. The kind of hatred that no one could ever diminish.

I stood there for a while, dumbfounded. My cigarette slipped from between my fingers and fell to the floor. The cigarette in the mirror fell to the floor, too. We stood there, staring at each other. I felt as if I was bound hand and foot, and couldn't move.

Finally his hand moved, the fingertips of his right hand touching his chin, and then slowly, like an insect, crept up his face. I suddenly realised I was doing the same thing. As though I were the reflection of what was in the mirror and he was trying to take control of me.

Wrenching out my last ounce of strength I roared out a growl, and the bonds that held me rooted to the spot broke. I raised my kendo sword and smashed it down on the mirror as hard as I could. I heard glass shattering but didn't look back as I raced back to my room. Once inside, I hurriedly locked the door and leapt under the covers. I was worried about the cigarette I'd dropped to the floor, but there was no way I was going back. The wind was howling the whole time, and the gate to the pool continued to make a racket until dawn. Yes, yes, no, yes, no, no, no . . .

I'm sure you've already guessed the ending to my story. There never was any mirror.

When the sun came up, the typhoon had already passed. The wind had died down and it was a sunny day. I went over to the entrance. The cigarette butt I'd tossed away was there, as was my wooden sword. But no mirror. There never had been any mirror there.

What I saw wasn't a ghost. It was simply – myself. I can never forget how terrified I was that night, and whenever I remember it, this thought always springs to mind: that the most frightening thing in the world is our own self. What do you think?

You may have noticed that I don't have a single mirror here in my house. Learning to shave without one was no easy feat, believe me.

THE STRANGERS

Lydia Davis

Lydia Davis (b.1947) was born in Northampton, Massachusetts and studied at Barnard College. She is the author of one novel and seven story collections. Davis has also translated French novels into English, including Marcel Proust's *Swann's Way* (2003). She was named a Chevalier of the Order of the Arts and Letters by the French government. Lydia Davis was the winner of the 2013 Man Booker International Prize. She is a professor of creative writing at the University at Albany.

My grandmother and I live among strangers. The house does not seem big enough to hold all the people who keep appearing in it at different times. They sit down to dinner as though they had been expected – and indeed there is always a place laid for them – or come into the drawing room out of the cold, rubbing their hands and exclaiming over the weather, settle by the fire and take up a book I had not noticed before, continuing to read from a place they had marked with a worn paper bookmark. As would be quite natural, some of them are bright and agreeable, while others are unpleasant – peevish or sly. I form immediate friendships with some – we understand each other perfectly from the moment we meet – and look forward to seeing them again at breakfast. But when I go down to breakfast they are not there; often I never see them again. All this is very unsettling. My grandmother and I never mention this coming and going of strangers in the house. But I watch her delicate pink face as she enters the dining room leaning on her cane and stops in surprise – she moves so slowly that this is barely perceptible. A young man rises from his place, clutching his napkin at his belt, and goes to help her into her chair. She adjusts to his presence with a nervous smile and a gracious nod, though I know she is as dismayed as I am that he was not here this morning and will not be here tomorrow and yet behaves as though this were all very natural. But often enough, of course, the person at the table is not a polite young man but a thin spinster who eats silently and quickly and leaves before we are done, or an old woman who scowls at the rest of us and spits the skin of her baked apple onto the edge of her plate. There is nothing we can do about this. How can we get rid of people we never invited who leave of their own accord anyway, sooner or later? Though we are of different generations, we were both brought up never to ask questions and only to smile at things we did not understand.

THE SAGEBRUSH KID

Annie Proulx

Annie Proulx (b.1935) was born in Norwich, Connecticut, where her
mother's ancestors had lived since 1635. Proulx's father was in the textile
trade and her family moved frequently. She attended Colby College,
Maine and studied history at the University of Vermont before becoming
a journalist. Proulx is the author of eight books. Her awards include
a Pulitzer Prize and a PEN/Faulkner award. Annie Proulx was in her
mid-fifties when her first collection of short stories, *Heart Songs* (1988),
was published. She lives in Wyoming.

Those who think the Bermuda Triangle disappearances of planes, boats,
long-distance swimmers and floating beach balls a unique phenomenon
do not know of the inexplicable vanishings along the Red Desert section
of Ben Holladay's stagecoach route in the days when Wyoming was a territory.

Historians have it that just after the Civil War Holladay petitioned the U.S.
Postal Service, major source of the stage line's income, to let him shift the route
fifty miles south to the Overland Trail. He claimed that the northern California –
Oregon-Mormon Trail had recently come to feature ferocious and unstoppable
Indian attacks that endangered the lives of drivers, passengers, telegraph operators
at the stage stops, smiths, hostlers and cooks at the swing stations; even the horses
and the expensive red and black Concord coaches (though most of them were actually Red Rupert mud wagons). Along with smoking letters outlining murderous
Indian attacks he sent Washington detailed lists of goods and equipment damaged
or lost – a Sharp's rifle, flour, horses, harness, doors, fifteen tons of hay, oxen,
mules, bulls, grain burned, corn stolen, furniture abused, the station itself along
with barn, sheds, telegraph office burned, crockery smashed, windows ditto. No
matter that the rifle had been left propped against a privy, had been knocked to
the ground by the wind and buried in sand before the owner exited the structure,
or that the dishes had disintegrated in a whoop-up shooting contest, or that the
stagecoach damage resulted from shivering passengers building a fire inside the
stage with the bundles of government documents the coach carried. He knew his
bureaucracy. The Washington post office officials, alarmed at the bloodcurdling
news, agreed to the route change, saving the Stagecoach King a great deal of money, important at that time while he, privy to insider information, laid his plans
to sell the stage line the moment the Union Pacific gathered enough shovels and
Irishmen to start construction on the transcontinental railroad.

Yet the Indian attack Holladay so gruesomely described was nothing more
than a failed Sioux war party, the battle ruined when only one side turned up.

The annoyed Indians, to reap something from the trip, gathered up a coil of copper wire lying on the ground under a telegraph pole where it had been left by a wire stringer eager to get to the saloon. They carted it back to camp, fashioned it into bracelets and necklaces. After a few days of wearing the bijoux, most of the war party broke out in severe rashes, an affliction that persisted until a medicine man, R. Singh, whose presence among the Sioux cannot be detailed here, divined the evil nature of the talking wire and caused the remainder of the coil and all the bracelets and earbobs to be buried. Shortly thereafter, but in no apparent way connected to the route change or the copper wire incident, travelers began to disappear in the vicinity of the Sandy Skull station.

The stationmaster at Sandy Skull was Bill Fur, assisted by his wife, Mizpah. In a shack to one side a telegraph operator banged his message key. The Furs had been married seven years but had no children, a situation in those fecund days that caused them both grief Mizpah was a little cracked on the subject and traded one of Bill's good shirts to a passing emigrant wagon for a baby pig, which she dressed in swaddling clothes and fed from a nipple-fitted bottle that had once contained Wilfee's Equine Liniment & Spanish Pain Destroyer but now held milk from the Furs' unhappy cow – an object of attention from range bulls, rustlers and roundup cowboys, who spent much of her time hiding in a nearby cave. The piglet one day tripped over the hem of the swaddling dress and was carried off by a golden eagle. Mrs. Fur, bereft, traded another of her husband's shirts to a passing emigrant wagon for a chicken. She did not make the swaddling gown mistake twice, but fitted the chicken with a light leather jerkin and a tiny bonnet. The bonnet acted as blinders and the unfortunate poult never saw the coyote that seized her within the hour.

Mizpah Fur, heartbroken and suffering from loneliness, next fixed her attention on an inanimate clump of sagebrush that at twilight took on the appearance of a child reaching upward as if piteously begging to be lifted from the ground. This sagebrush became the lonely woman's passion. It seemed to her to have an enchanting fragrance reminiscent of pine forests and lemon zest. She surreptitiously brought it a daily dipper of water (mixed with milk) and took pleasure in its growth response, ignoring the fine cactus needles that pierced her worn moccasins with every trip to the beloved *Atriplex*. At first her husband watched from afar, muttering sarcastically, then himself succumbed to the illusion, pulling up all grass and encroaching plants that might steal sustenance from the favored herb. Mizpah tied a red sash around the sagebrush's middle. It seemed more than ever a child stretching its arms up, even when the sun leached the wind-fringed sash to pink and then dirty white.

Time passed, and the sagebrush, nurtured and cosseted as neither piglet nor chicken nor few human infants had ever been – for Mizpah had taken to mixing gravy and meat juice with its water – grew tremendously. At twilight it now looked like a big man hoisting his hands into the air at the command to stick em up. It sparkled festively in winter snow. Travelers noted it as the biggest sagebrush in the lonely stretch of desert between Medicine Bow and Sandy Skull station. It became a landmark for deserting soldiers. Bill Fur, clutching the handle of a potato hoe, hit on the right name when he announced that he guessed he would go out and clear cactus away from the vicinity of their Sagebrush Kid.

About the time that Bill Fur planed a smooth path to and around the Sagebrush Kid, range horses became scarce in the vicinity of the station. The Furs and local ranchers had always been able to gather wild mustangs, and through a few sessions with steel bolts tied to their forelocks, well-planned beatings with a two-by-four and merciless first rides by some youthful buster whose spine hadn't yet been compressed into a solid rod, the horses were deemed ready-broke to haul stagecoaches or carry riders. Now the mustangs seemed to have moved to some other range. Bill Fur blamed it on the drought which had been bad.

"Found a water hole somewheres else," he said.

A party of emigrants camped overnight near the station, and at dawn the captain pounded on the Furs' door demanding to know where their oxen were.

"Want a git started," he said, a man almost invisible under a flop-rimmed hat, cracked spectacles, full beard and a mustache the size of a dead squirrel. His hand was deep in his coat pocket, a bad sign, thought Bill Fur who had seen a few coat-pocket corpses.

"I ain't seen your oxes," he said. "This here's a horse-change station," and he pointed to the corral where two dozen broomtails stood soaking up the early sun. "We don't have no truck with oxes."

"Them was fine spotted oxen, all six matched," said the captain in a dangerous, low voice.

Bill Fur, curious now, walked with the bearded man to the place the oxen had been turned out the night before. Hoofprints showed where the animals had ranged around eating the sparse bunchgrass. They cast wide and far but could not pick up the oxen trail as the powdery dust changed to bare rock that took no tracks. Later that week the disgruntled emigrant party was forced to buy a mixed lot of oxen from the sutler at Fort Halleck, a businessman who made a practice of buying up worn-out stock for a song, nursing them back to health and then selling them for an opera to those in need.

"Indans probly got your beasts," said the sutler. "They'll bresh out the tracks with a sage branch so's you'd never know but that they growed wings and flapped south."

The telegraph operator at the station made a point of keeping the Sabbath. After his dinner of sage grouse with rose-haw jelly, he strolled out for an afternoon constitutional and never returned to his key. This was serious, and by Wednesday Bill Fur had had to ride into Rawlins and ask for a replacement for "the biblethumpin, damn old goggle-eyed snappin turtle who run off" The replacement, plucked from a Front Street saloon, was a tough drunk who lit his morning fires with pages from the former operator's bible and ate one pronghorn a week, scorching the meat in a never-washed skillet.

"Leave me have them bones," said Mizpah, who had taken to burying meat scraps and gnawed ribs in the soil near the Sagebrush Kid.

"Help yourself," he said, scraping gristle and hocks onto the newspaper that served as his tablecloth and rolling it up. "Goin a make soup stock, eh?"

Two soldiers from Fort Halleck dined with the Furs and at nightfall slept out in the sagebrush. In the morning their empty bedrolls, partly drifted with fine sand, lay flat, the men's saddles at the heads for pillows, their horse tack looped on the sage. The soldiers themselves were gone, apparently deserters who had taken leave bareback. The wind had erased all signs of their passage. Mizpah Fur made use of the bedrolls, converting them into stylish quilts by appliquéing a pleasing pattern of black stripes and yellow circles onto the coarse fabric.

It may have been a trick of the light or the poor quality window glass, as wavery and distorting as tears, but Mizpah, sloshing her dishrag over the plates and gazing out, thought she saw the sagebrush's arms not raised up but akimbo, as though holding a water divining rod. Worried that some rambunctious buck trying his antlers had broken the branches, she stepped to the door to get a clear look. The arms were upright again and tossing in the wind.

Dr. Frill of Rawlins, on a solitary hunting trip, paused long enough to share a glass of bourbon and the latest town news with Mr. Fur. A week later a group of the doctor's scowling friends rode out inquiring of the medico's whereabouts. Word was getting around that the Sandy Skull station was not the best place to spend the night, and suspicion was gathering around Bill and Mizpah Fur. It would not be the first time a stationmaster had taken advantage of a remote posting. The Furs were watched for signs of opulence. Nothing of Dr. Frill was ever found, although a hat, stuck in the mud of a playa three miles east, might have been his.

A small group of Sioux, including R. Singh, on their way to the Fort Halleck sutler's store to swap hides for tobacco, hung around for an hour one late afternoon asking for coffee and bread which Mizpah supplied. In the early evening as the dusk thickened they resumed their journey. Only Singh made it to the fort, but the shaken Calcutta native could summon neither Sioux nor American nor his native tongue to his lips. He bought two twists of tobacco and through the fluid expression of sign language tagged a spot with a Mormon freight group headed for Salt Lake City.

A dozen outlaws rode past Sandy Skull station on their way to Powder Springs for a big gang hooraw to feature a turkey pull, fried turkey and pies of various flavors as well as the usual floozy contingent and uncountable bottles of Young Possum and other liquids pleasing to men who rode hard and fast on dusty trails. They amused themselves with target practice on the big sagebrush, trying to shoot off its waving arms. Five of them never got past Sandy Skull station. When the Furs, who had been away for the day visiting the Clug ranch, came home they saw the Sagebrush Kid maimed, only one arm, but that still bravely raised as though hailing them. The telegraph operator came out of his shack and said that the outlaws had done the deed and that he had chosen not to confront them, but to bide his time and get revenge later, for he too had developed a proprietorial interest in the Sagebrush Kid. Around that time he put in a request for a transfer to Denver or San Francisco.

Everything changed when the Union Pacific Railroad pushed through, killing off the stagecoach business. Most of the stage station structures disappeared, carted away bodily by ranchers needing outbuildings. Bill and Mizpah Fur were forced to abandon the Sandy Skull station. After tearful farewells to the Sagebrush Kid they moved to Montana, adopted orphan cowboys and ran a boardinghouse.

The decades passed and the Sagebrush Kid continued to grow, though slowly.

The old stage road filled in with drift sand and greasewood. A generation later a section of the coast-to-coast Lincoln Highway rolled past. An occasional motorist, mistaking the Sagebrush Kid for a distant shade tree, sometimes approached, swinging a picnic basket. Eventually an interstate highway swallowed the old road and truckers used the towering Sagebrush Kid in the distance as a marker to tell them they were halfway across the state. Although its foliage remained luxuriant and its size enormous, the Kid seemed to stop growing during the interstate era.

Mineral booms and busts surged through Wyoming without affecting the extraordinary shrub in its remote location of difficult access until BelAmerCan Energy, a multinational methane extraction company, found promising indications of gas in the area, applied for and got permits and began drilling. The promise was realized. They were above a vast deposit of coal gas. Workers from out of state rushed to the bonanza. A pipeline had to go in and more workers came. The housing shortage forced men to sleep four to a bed in shifts at the dingy motels forty miles north.

To ease the housing difficulties, the company built a man-camp out in the sagebrush. The entrance road ran close to the Sagebrush Kid. Despite the Kid's size, because it was just a sagebrush, it went unnoticed. There were millions of sagebrush plants – some large, some small. Beside it was a convenient pull-out. The man-camp was a large gaunt building that seemed to erupt from the sand. The cubicles and communal shower rooms, stairs, the beds, the few doors were metal. A spartan kitchen staffed by Mrs. Quirt, the elderly wife of a retired rancher, specialized in bacon, fried eggs, boiled potatoes, store-bought bread and jam and occasionally a stewed chicken. The boss believed the dreary sagebrush steppe and the monotonous diet were responsible for wholesale worker desertion. The head office let him hire a new cook, an ex-driller with a meth habit whose cuisine revolved around canned beans and pickles.

After three weeks Mrs. Quirt was reinstated, presented with a cookbook and a request to try something new. It was a disastrous order. She lit on complex recipes for boeuf bourguignonne, parsnip gnocchi, bananas stuffed with shallots, kale meatballs with veal ice cream. When the necessary ingredients were lacking she did what she had always done on the ranch – substituted what was on hand, as bacon, jam, eggs. After a strange repast featuring canned clams, strawberry Jell-O and stale bread, many men went outside to heave it up in the sage. Not all of them came back and it was generally believed they had hiked forty miles to the hot-bed motel town.

The head office, seeing production, income and profits slump because they could not keep workers on, hired a cook who had worked for an Italian restaurant. The food improved dramatically, but there was still an exodus. The cook ordered exotic ingredients that were delivered by a huge Speedy Food truck. After the driver delivered the cases of sauce and mushrooms, he parked in the shade of the big sagebrush to eat his noontime bologna sandwich, read a chapter of *Ambush on the Pecos Trail* and take a short nap. Three drillers coming in from the day shift noticed the truck idling in the shade. They noticed it again the next morning on the way to the rig. A refrigerator truck, it was still running. A call came three days later from the company asking if their driver had been there.

The news that the truck was still in the sagebrush brought state troopers. After noticing spots of blood on the seat and signs of a struggle (a dusty boot print on the inside of the windshield), they began stringing crime-scene tape around the truck and the sagebrush.

"Kellogg, get done with the tape and get out here," called a sergeant to the laggard trooper behind the sagebrush. The thick branches and foliage hid him from view and the tape trailed limply on the ground. Kellogg did not answer. The sergeant walked around to the back of the sagebrush. There was no one there.

"Goddamn it, Kellogg, quit horsin around." He ran to the front of the truck, bent and looked beneath it. He straightened, shaded his eyes and squinted into the shimmering heat. The other two troopers, Bridle and Gloat, stood slack-jawed near their patrol car.

"You see where Kellogg went?"

"Maybe back up to the man-camp? Make a phone call or whatever?"

But Kellogg was not at the man-camp, had not been there.

"Where the hell did he go? *Kellogg!!!*"

Again they all searched the area around the truck, working out farther into the sage, then back toward the truck again. Once more Bridle checked beneath the truck, and this time he saw something lying against the back inner tire. He pulled it out.

"Sergeant Sparkler, I found this." He held out a tiny scrap of torn fabric that perfectly matched his own brown uniform. "I didn't see it before because it's the same color as the dirt." Something brushed the back of his neck and he jumped, slapping it away.

"Damn big sagebrush," he said, looking at it. Deep in the branches he saw a tiny gleam and the letters "OGG."

"Jim, his nameplate's in there!" Sparkler and Gloat came in close, peering into the shadowy interior of the gnarled sagebrush giant. Sergeant Sparkler reached for the metal name tag.

The botanist sprayed insect repellent on his ears, neck and hair. The little black mosquitoes fountained up as he walked toward the tall sagebrush in the distance. It looked as large as a tree and towered over the ocean of lesser sage. Beyond it the abandoned man-camp shimmered in the heat, its window frames warped and crooked. His heart rate increased. Years before he had scoffed at the efforts of botanical explorers searching for the tallest coast red-wood, or the tallest tree in the New Guinea jungle, but at the same time he began looking at sagebrush with the idea of privately tagging the tallest. He had measured some huge specimens of basin big sagebrush near the Killpecker dunes and recorded their heights in the same kind of little black notebook used by Ernest Heming-way and Bruce Chatwin. The tallest reached seven feet six inches. The monster before him certainly beat that by at least a foot.

As he came closer he saw that the ground around it was clear of other plants. He had only a six-foot folding rule in his backpack, and as he held it up against the huge plant it extended less than half its height. He marked the six-foot level with his eye. He had to move in close to get the next measurement.

"I'm guessing thirteen feet," he said to the folding rule, placing one hand on a muscular and strangely warm branch.

The Sagebrush Kid stands out there still. There are no gas pads, no compression stations near it. No road leads to it. Birds do not sit on its branches. The man-camp, like the old stage station, has disappeared. At sunset the great sagebrush holds its arms up against the red sky. Anyone looking in the right direction can see it.

THE WHITE COT

Jackie Kay

Jackie Kay (b.1961) is a poet, playwright, novelist and short story writer. She was born in Edinburgh to a Scottish mother and a Nigerian father. Kay was adopted at birth and the experience of growing up in a white family inspired her first poetry collection, *The Adoption Papers* (1991). Her work often explores themes of race, identity and sexuality. Jackie Kay lives in Manchester and is Professor of Creative Writing at Newcastle University. In 2006, she was awarded an MBE for services to literature.

It is seldom that Sam and I get away. Sam works long hours and is reluctant to take time off. This time, I think it was obvious I needed a break. I'd been feeling a little down, crying at the slightest thing, and had said often, I think I'm going through the change. I hadn't actually stopped my monthlies, but they were becoming very sporadic.

We arrived at the house around eight in the evening. There was still light in the sky, a brooding light expecting rain. We drove down a long tree-lined driveway to find our cottage at the bottom on the left. Sam unlocked the front door into a large kitchen. At first the house was a disappointment; it struck us as soul-less. "Don't worry," Sam said. "As soon as we've unpacked our things and hung them up, and got our books out, it will feel like ours." I hoped so. Rented houses often seemed as if they were never truly inhabited. You were too aware of the people who had cleared away all signs of themselves, as if they had never been here at all. There was a feeling of people vanishing that hung in the grotesque decor of the place. Each room was decorated with such purpose that it all felt unreal. I couldn't imagine the mind of the person who had gone from innocent room to innocent room creating such strangeness.

"Which room shall we pick for our bedroom?" Sam shouted from the top of the stairs. "Come here and help me choose?" I climbed the stairs slowly, heavily. Why did I think that coming away would make things better? There was a bedroom with pink and yellow wallpaper with a very strong geometric design. "That wallpaper would drive me mad," I said to Sam. "Look, the view from this window is lovely," Sam said. I looked out; ahead of me was a path, a path that somebody had cut through the long, long grass. The wild grass was full of buttercups and cow parsley and tiny purple flowers: the path cut stretched into the distance and curved towards the east. I could imagine myself walking down it, away into the distance and disappearing off the face of the earth. "No, not this room," I said to Sam. "You choose then, Dionne. I don't mind which room we have. But don't take all day. It's late."

The walls of the bedroom downstairs were painted a deep red. "Very sexy!" Sam said, walking into the room. In the corner of the room was an empty cot, an old-fashioned one that had a lace awning over the top like a sun roof. The paint on the bars was scratched a little. The curtains were tied at the sides; it was like a mini-four-poster bed. Inside, there were two soft blankets neatly folded into squares. One was baby blue with a sandy coloured teddy bear stitched in relief. One was pink with a fat white rabbit. There was a tiny white pillow, a white towelling fitted sheet on the mattress and a minute lacy duvet. In the opposite corner of the room was a rocking horse. "Odd combination," Sam said. "We could move the horse out into the kitchen, but we couldn't move the cot."

"Well, it's this one or the one upstairs," Sam said and I nodded. I felt like I couldn't speak. Sam went out to the car and brought in our case. "Why don't you put your feet up and I'll unpack for both of us?" I went into the living room, painted bright yellow and with table lamps covered with feathers. I couldn't shift the uneasy feeling. I sat down on the armchair, cream with red and grey flowers, and then stood up again. I went into the kitchen: yellow painted cupboards, pale blue painted Welsh dresser, black and white floor, navy blue and red small tiles. I stood staring, then put the kettle on. It sounded unnaturally loud. It seemed to go on and on and on, bubbling away furiously before boiling. I could see the water through a window in the kettle splattering against it like rain. I made us both a cup of tea and returned to the living room and sat down. Sam came through and laughed at the expression on my face. "Don't look so miserable, you're on holiday! Shall we have a leaf through these leaflets and plan our days?" "Let's leave it until tomorrow," I said. "Let's not make plans."

That night I got into the side of the bed near the window. Sam was already in bed on the other side, book in hand. No matter which house we sleep in, we always choose the same side of the bed; Sam has the left and I have the right. "You were ages," Sam said, putting the book down, and curling into me, turning off the bedside lamp. I lay facing out. I lay for the longest time with my eyes open and at some point in the night I felt as if someone had entered the room and gently closed my eyes, tiny fingers, pushing down the lids, pulling the covers over me. I woke up, disorientated with a dull ache in my abdomen. The space next to me was empty. I looked at my phone. It was already ten o'clock. I didn't feel as if I'd been asleep, I felt as if I'd tossed and turned the whole night long, throwing the covers off, putting them back on. At one point in the night, I'd sat bolt upright, drenched in sweat, and full of dread.

Sam had the boiled eggs on; the coffee that we'd brought ourselves, ground with our own grinder, was already bubbling away in our coffeepot. The smell of fresh ground beans was in the air. The half-cut grapefruits were on the table, glasses of orange juice and a jar of our favourite vintage marmalade. There was even warmed milk in the microwave and it was sitting in a jug, painted with cherries and green apples. "Once you've had your breakfast, you'll feel better. There's nothing like boiling an egg in a place to make it feel your own." Sam had set the timer on the BlackBerry to get the eggs done to perfection. Sam liked eggs very runny and I liked mine just as they were about to go hard. "It's one thing we are all allowed to be fussy about, eggs," Sam was often saying. "That and how we like our tea; any other fussiness is just neurotic." The first time this made me laugh, but when it kept being repeated, I wondered what it was really about. Did Sam think I was over-fussy, neurotic?

I sat down at the table and tapped on the shell of my brown egg. I picked the pieces of shell off the top and then broke in. Sam had already been out and got a newspaper. "Want a bit of the paper?" "No, thanks," I said. "You should take an interest in what's going on in the world, bloody hell; what a mess they've made of Manchester!"

"I've told you," I said. "I can't read any more. The words just swim in front of me."

"You should go and get your eyes checked out, then," Sam said. "Often prescriptions change in middle age." Sam's glasses were tilted on the end of her nose. "Your glasses aren't right for your eyes," I said. "Or you wouldn't be peering over them!"

"At least I can still read," Sam said and returned to dipping her slice of toast into her queasily runny egg. "I don't know how you can eat your egg that runny," I said. "Leave me and my egg alone," she said, and shook the newspaper out to find the article she had just been reading. "Clegg is a pain in the arse; he's duped the lot of us." Sam sat reading the paper, eating her egg, slurping her coffee. Her thick black hair was a little tousled. She seemed quite content. She looked as if there was nothing the matter at all. I managed to finish my egg and spread some marmalade on a slice of toast and stare into space for quite some time before Sam said, "Do you want to go for a walk?"

She took my arm firmly and we went out through the pale blue wooden door at the bottom of the garden. We crossed the narrow country road and climbed a wall that had two wooden steps jutting out of it. Then we walked the path that we could see from the bedroom window. At one point we got to a place that we couldn't see from the window, beyond the curve of the path, and I felt like we were suddenly free. "It's as if that house has eyes," I said to Sam, "and now that we are out of its sight-line, I feel suddenly better! Let's stay away. Let's not go back there." "You are joking, aren't you?" Sam said. "You get more and more bonkers every day. I didn't have all this with the menopause you know. I never even noticed it."

"Well, you were one of the lucky ones," I said. "You got away with it. I feel as if I've been stolen and some other woman has been put in my place. I just feel so anxious all the time, like I'm on the edge of something." "You'll be fine," she said as I smiled grimly. "Well, try and enjoy yourself, why don't you?" Sam said, irritated. "I mean I've taken all this time off. I've booked us a holiday house . . ."

"It's not work that you're missing," I said.

"What are you talking about?" Sam said.

"You know what I'm talking about," I said.

"Oh, here we go! I give up. If you want to see things that are not there, that is your choice," Sam said. "I'll tell you one thing. I'll give you top marks for imagination."

She walked ahead on the path, big angry strides. I just stood on the spot staring after her, until she came back for me. I looped my arm through her arm. "I'm sorry," I said, close to tears. "You seem so distant, half the time. I just keep thinking there is someone, even though of course I know there isn't."

"You like saying it though, don't you? You like bringing it up. It's not funny any more, that one."

"I know," I said, "So – what you're saying is there isn't anyone else?" I was half-joking, but Sam took me seriously.

"No, there isn't anyone else," she said, and patted my arm. She stopped on the path and turned round and hugged me and kissed my lips, softly. "I just wish I'd had a baby," I blurted out. Sam pulled back. "What?" Sam said. "Where did that come from?"

"I can't stop thinking what my life would have been like if I'd had my daughter. Do you remember what I wanted to call her?" Sam shook her head, sadly. "Don't go down this path," she said, "are you deliberately trying to ruin our holiday?"

I wanted her to listen, that's all I wanted. "Here I am going through this mid-life Hell, and I've got nothing to show for it. You knew I wanted a baby."

"Dionne! What's going on? Why are you bringing all that up? That was years ago," Sam said. "Let's go back to the house! I knew we shouldn't have chosen that room! Even for me, there's something creepy about an empty cot!"

"What do you mean, *even for me*, like you're the reasonable one?"

"I mean, I'm not the one who wanted a baby. Don't read something into everything! We're on holiday! We're supposed to be relaxing." Sam took my arm again along the last of the path. We came to the bit where we had to climb over the wall. Sam went first, and then turned around to help me. I lifted my leg over and climbed down the wooden step.

"You were the one who chose the house!" I said to her and the thought startled me. "You were the one who looked at the rooms on the Internet. You knew what was in each room."

Sam gave me a look that was half fear and half something I couldn't name. "I don't know what to do," she said. "I just don't know what to do."

We walked back to the house. I'd taken my arm back. The sun was actually out and the sky was really blue with low-lying white clouds, sweet and innocent like a child's drawing. "What kind of mother do you think you would have been?" Sam said and her voice was low, and she said the words very slowly with a space between each word: "What kind of mother do you think you would have been?" I said nothing. I walked behind her dragging my feet and she kept turning to stare. She looked unhappy; the optimism of the morning had already been knocked out of her. "Hurry up," she said. "Why do you have to make everything miserable, even a walk in the sunshine?" When we got back to the cottage, Sam unlocked the door, got in a fluster about which key unlocked which bit of the door, finally got us in, and went to the bathroom and slammed the bathroom door shut. I think she cried in there, but when she's like that it's best to leave her alone.

I go and lie down in the bedroom. The more I look at the cot in the room, the more it disturbs me. I start to try and move it across the floor, to see if it will move out of the room altogether and into the other room. But it won't move. It's too solid. "What are you doing?" Sam says, coming into the room, red-eyed. "I was just trying to see if this would move!" "Why?" she says. "You were the one that picked this room. Do you want to move rooms?" she says. "We'll change rooms if that will help?" Her voice sounds gentle now; she is trying to make things better. Maybe she regrets her question; I don't know. "No, that would just be silly," I say. "I'll be fine when I feel rested. I'm just not sleeping; it doesn't matter where I sleep with all these hot flushes in the night. I throw the covers off and then throw them back on." "Tell me about it," Sam says laughing. "I might have to go and sleep in the other room tonight. You were so restless last night; I hardly got any sleep either. I think we're both a bit tetchy today. Shall we start again, darling?" Sam hugs me in a half-hearted sort of a way, as if she must make the best of things.

All day it has felt like I've been waiting for the night, even though the night and the thought of the night frighten me, I've waited for it just the same. When Sam said she would sleep in the other room, I felt a little hurt, then liberated. It is when I am just about to have that sensation of somebody coming and shutting my eyelids with their tiny fingers that I hear it, the sound of the cot rocking back and forth, back and forth. It's a creaking sound. I don't dare move because I want it to go on. I want to hear it. Then, ever so softly and quite far away, I hear a baby's gurgle and the sound of chimes, wind chimes. And a strange little laugh, a merry little baby's laugh, a frothy high chuckle, delighted and surprised. I get up and walk to the cot. There's nothing there. There is nothing there, nothing there at all. I creep back to my bed and listen carefully as if my life depended on every single sound. Upstairs, I can hear Sam pad around. It is late for her to be up. I look at my phone, which suddenly lights up. It is two in the morning. A bit later, I don't know the time, I'm sure I hear the front door open.

When I wake in the morning the cot is empty and the blue and pink blankets are folded neatly in a square. I'm grateful for the daylight because for a minute I assume that with it comes normalcy, sanity. I've upset myself thinking of the baby girl I longed for those years ago. I even had a name for her, Lottie, and a middle name, Daphne. Lottie Daphne Drake. I could picture her. I still can picture her: a head of floppy dark-brown curls, dark eyes, soft skin, tiny little feet; tiny hands. A sunny disposition, Lottie had, always gurgling and giggling, curious about everything. And she would have been very quick to learn to say Mama. I thought about her so deeply that I conceived her in my mind. It was a mistake for me to ever name her. I imagined my mornings and nights, my days and evenings, my life; I imagined my life lit up by her life, my daughter's. I imagined how she, little Lottie, would have changed my life. I pictured her so vividly I almost feel that what I went through was like a miscarriage; something I can never get Sam to understand.

"Morning," I say to Sam, and she looks at me a little warily. "Sleep well?" "The minute my head hit the pillow," Sam says. "Out like a light." I wonder if this is really the truth, but I don't ask her. I don't dare say, "Is that really the truth?"

"I'd quite like to catch up with my old school friend I was telling you about. She's not far from here." I say.

"I don't think you're up to seeing friends," Sam says. "You're acting weird with me, what do you think you'll be like with people you hardly see?" "I'm making an effort," I say. "You told me I should make an effort." "Not that kind of effort!" Sam says and laughs to herself, incredulously, a little snort of a laugh.

That day, Sam took me for a drive in the country and I stared out the window. It might yet be all right between us; I might just be going through this change which friends have told me has made them depressed or anxious, paranoid even. "If only I'd had a baby," I said to Sam in the car, "then it would feel worthwhile. I wouldn't mind the hot flushes or the depression if I had a daughter now, a twenty year old daughter or a twenty year old son. Was it that you were jealous of Paul? Is that what it was?" Sam ignored me as if I hadn't spoken and we drove through the beautiful Somerset countryside in silence.

In the cottage that night, Sam made us dinner, spaghetti Bolognese, and opened a bottle of Chianti. She lit a candle. She said, "Look Dionne, darling, the past is past. We can't do anything about it. I would have loved it if we had had a child together, you know that."

"A child *together* is what you wanted! You would have liked to have been able to make me pregnant!"

"I would have. Is that a terrible thing?"

"But you couldn't!"

"Thanks for that! Is that my fault?"

"You wouldn't agree to me getting pregnant twenty years ago when there was still time!"

"That is not true and you know it is not true," Sam said, "I was happy for you to try with Paul. It was you who didn't want Paul coming between us, not me. Why do you go over the past and distort things?"

"It's not what I remember. *You* didn't want him coming between us!"

"Well, he's come between us and he isn't even here," Sam said.

That night Sam looked over at me sitting in the armchair. "Dee?" she said. "Come and have a cuddle." And I went to her and all the things in my head went quiet for a bit.

"Shall I come in and sleep with you tonight?"

I said yes. I said yes because I wanted her to hear it, to feel it. Sam got into bed with her book and read for a bit and then put the light off. I lay very still waiting for the sounds to start, the wind chimes; the far away baby's gurgle, the sound of the empty cot rocking back and forth, back and forth. I must have fallen asleep. I woke up to the sound of a car in the drive, and then I drifted off again. It was some way into the night before I heard it. I got up and looked in the cot and there was nothing there except the blue blanket had been unwrapped and was not now folded into a square. I shook Sam awake. "Sam, there is somebody else here," I said. "Sam!" She woke up and rubbed her eyes. "What now?" she said. "What is it?" She got up and looked in the cot. "I've seen it all now," she said. "You moved that earlier today, didn't you, and now you're pretending somebody else has done it?"

"I didn't touch it," I said. "I swear I didn't touch it. I swear on my own life."

"Well, I bloody well didn't touch it," Sam said. But there was something in her voice, a belligerence, something a little odd. "Only you know what you are capable of," I said and climbed back into bed, and put out my bedside light. I squeezed my eyes shut and lay still waiting to see what she would do next when she thought I had fallen asleep. I had terrible pains in my stomach. After years of being regular as clockwork, it was now difficult to predict.

It must have been sometime later; perhaps two or even three hours later, when I saw Sam tiptoe to the cot. She stood looking over it for quite a while. Then she left the room. Not long after that I heard the sound of the wind chimes and the baby gurgling and I sat bolt upright. I was clammy with fear. Not just a hot flush but the sweat of sheer terror. I got out of bed and crept across the floor as quietly as I could. I peered into the cot. The pink blanket was now unfolded and lying on top of the blue one and the cot was rocking, back and forth, back and forth, with some momentum, and Sam was nowhere in the room. I put my hand to the side of the cot to still it, to stop the rocking and when I looked inside again I saw that the blankets had rolled up into the shape of a small baby and I touched the back and said, there, there. Sam came down the stairs and stood beside me in the semi-dark. She touched my back. She whispered, "Back to your bed, darling, it's very late."

The next day, Sam drove me into Bath and we had a bowl of soup in a delicatessen and bought some things for supper, some cheeses, some olives, some salami and bread. "You look pale," Sam said over lunch, sipping her strong coffee. "I so wanted this break to do you good."

"It is doing me good," I said and I meant it. I couldn't wait for the night. I'd started not to dread it but to anticipate it, to look forward to it. There was nothing to be frightened of. In the evening we watched a film; a favourite of ours, *An Imitation of Life*. We both wept, as usual, at the end. And again Sam said, "If you don't mind, my love, I'm going to have to sleep in the other room again. I find all your night-time restlessness a bit exhausting. I'll be back to work soon and I won't feel rested at all."

"I don't mind," I said. "More room for me to stretch out." That night I didn't lie down. I lay sitting up in bed. I felt a loose feeling and then a letting go. When I got up, the bed sheets were soaked in blood. So much blood, I stared at it appalled as if it was the scene a crime I had committed and couldn't remember. I pulled the sheet off and padded into the bathroom in the dark. I put the sodden sheet in the sink and rinsed it over and over again with cold water. The blood stain wouldn't budge. I found some bleach under the sink and put some of that in. Then I took the whole dripping sheet into the kitchen and put it in the washing machine. I went about the house quietly looking for the airing cupboard trying to remember where I'd seen spare sheets. Finally, I found a fresh one in the bathroom cupboard upstairs. I could hear voices in the other bedroom. I could hear laughing and giggling.

I went downstairs to my bedroom again, and switched on the bedside lamp. I couldn't stop crying. I'd lost so much blood, I felt weak. I tried to put the fresh sheet on. It seemed the most difficult task; every time I got it on one corner, it popped off the other. I stared at the cot. The folded blankets were not folded and the little pillow was curled up under them in the shape of a baby. Up the stairs the wind chimes started and the faint sound of the baby's gurgle, then the giggle, then the cot started rocking again, back and forth, and back and forth. I got up and pulled the rocking horse against the door. I pulled two chairs into the room and put them against the door too. I lifted her out of the cot and rocked her in my arms. I started singing softly at first, *Summer time and the living is easy, fish are jumping and the cotton is high. Your daddy's rich and your momma's good-looking, so hush little baby, don't you cry*. There was a pounding on the door. "Dionne! Open the door! Open the door now!" "I can't, darling," I whispered. "I'm needed here." Sam pushed against the door and knocked over the horse and the chairs. She stared at me. She said, "What on earth are you playing at?" "What are *you* playing at?" I said. "Well, it's all out now. And I'm getting out. We're going to live on our own, aren't we?" I said to the baby. Sam stared at me and looked as if she was going to faint. "You're looking very pale," I said to Sam.

BELONGING

Ben Okri

Ben Okri (b.1959) was born in Minna, northern Nigeria not long before the official end of British colonial rule. After a short spell in London where his father studied law, Okri and his family returned to Nigeria in 1968, where he grew up in the shadow of the Nigeria-Biafra War. He left school at fourteen and published his first book at the age of nineteen. Okri's publications include eight novels and several collections of poetry, short stories and essays. His work has been translated into over twenty languages.

I had gone into a house by accident or maybe not. Originally I was searching for Margaret House, a mansion block. Anyway I went into this flat and the man of the house took me for his in-law, whom he had never met, or had met once before, a long time ago. He began saying things to me confidentially, telling me how he disapproved of some acquaintance, and how we should do this that or other, and how my wife did or didn't do what she was supposed to do, and he bared his heart and said many intimate things.

I watched him. When the misunderstanding began I tried to correct his error, but he seemed so keen to believe who I was and he was so absent-minded and yet single-minded in his rattling on that I didn't get a moment to correct his mistaking me for someone else.

Besides, I found I rather began to enjoy it. I enjoyed being someone else. It was fascinating. It was quite a delight suddenly finding myself part of a ready-made family, finding myself belonging. The thrill of belonging was wonderful.

The flat was cluttered with items of a rich family life. It was obviously a large extended family. The man who was addressing me was making food for a feast, adding ingredients for a cake, mixing condiments for a sauce, and it all smelt good. The enveloping party and family mood quite intoxicated me.

I began to think that maybe I was the man he took me for. And that if he saw me as another then maybe I *was* that other. Maybe I'd just woken from a dream into a reality in which I was who he thought I was, and that my old identity belonged to the dream. But as I toyed with this notion there was a growing sense in me that any minute the real person that was expected would turn up. Or, if not, that the wife of the real person would turn up, and would not recognise me.

The fear increased in me. Any minute now I would be unmasked. What would I do then? I felt awful. I dreaded it. I hadn't got myself into this deliberately. I hadn't even spoken a word during the whole time I was in that room, being mistaken for someone else. I wanted to belong. I wanted to belong there. A sentence of unmasking, like death, hung over me. I waited, and listened to the man of the house talking, as time ticked away, bringing closer my inevitable disgrace.

Before I had strayed into that flat I had been going to meet a relation, my last living relation. It was, it seemed, the last stop for me in the world. I had nowhere else to go. Now I had this family, with food and a festival atmosphere promised. And yet . . .

And then, as I stood there, the door behind me opened. A black, Arabic, pock-marked, elderly gentleman came into the room, and I knew instantly that this was the man I had been mistaken for. He had the quiet and unmistakable author-ity of being who he was, the real in-law. And my first shock was that I looked nothing like him at all. I was younger, fresher, better-looking. I had vigour and freedom. I wasn't trapped by tradition. I was lithe. I could go any which way. I had many futures open to me. This man seemed weighed down. There was an air about him of one whose roads were closed, whose future was determined, whose roles were fixed. He was, in the worst sense of the word, middle-aged; with no freedom, even to think independent thoughts. All this I sensed in a flash, but realised fully only afterwards. But I was profoundly shocked to have been mistaken for this man.

At the very moment the in-law entered the flat, the man of the house, who'd mistaken me in the first place, looked up, saw the real in-law, and knew him to be the one. I think he recognised him. How unobservant can people be! Anyway, at that instant he turned to me and, in outrage, said:

"And who are you?"

I think events swam before my eyes after that. My unmasking was very pub-lic. Suddenly people appeared from thin air, and were told in loud voices about my impersonation of the in-law. There were vigorous comments and curses and stares of amazement. People glared at me as though I were a monstrous criminal. Women regarded me darkly from behind veils. I feared for my life. Soon I was out in the street, surrounded by a crowd, by the community of an extended fam-ily. I was holding out a map and was saying:

"It was a mistake. I was looking for Margaret House, or Margaret Court."

During the whole commotion I saw the name of the place I'd been looking for on the next building. I bore their outrage and their loud comments silently. Then after a while I set off for the building next door, my original destination. But the man of the house, who'd mistaken me for the in-law, said:

"Don't go there. You don't want to go there."

Then I looked towards Margaret House. I looked at the grounds. I saw people milling about, in aimless circles. They twitched, moved listlessly, or erratically. They were dark forms, in dark overcoats, and their bodies were all shadows, as if they were in Hades. They moved as if they had invisible lead weights on their feet. They seemed to have no sense of anything. The courtyard was of concrete, but their collective presence made it look dark and sinister and touched with unpredictable danger. There was the merest hint that they were mad . . .

I started to go in that direction, but, after the man of the house spoke, I stopped. I could feel the disturbed wind from the people milling about in an evil shade, in the courtyard of Margaret House. Then I changed direction, and went back towards the crowd, then out to the street, towards a life of my own.

DINNER OF THE DEAD ALUMNI

Adam Marek

Adam Marek's (b.1974) short stories have appeared on BBC Radio 4 Extra, and in many magazines and anthologies, including *Prospect*, *The Sunday Times Magazine* and *The Best British Short Stories* 2011 and 2013. He has published two short story collections, *The Stone Thrower* and *Instruction Manual for Swallowing*. Marek was awarded the 2011 Arts Foundation Short Story Fellowship and was shortlisted for both the inaugural Sunday Times EFG Short Story Award and the Edge Hill Short Story Prize.

Today the streets of Cambridge are crawling with dead alumni. Their ghosts perch on punts, trailing their fingers through the green weed without raising a ripple. They fly round Trinity College's Great Court, performing the 367m run before even the tenth of the twenty-four chimes. They cheer themselves, but their cheers reach no corporeal ears. The dead waft through the Grand Arcade, raising goosebumps on the fresh navels of girls texting outside Topshop. They hover at the doorway of the Apple store, whooping every time a fresh burst of radio waves casts them across the concourse and dashes their weightless bodies on the ground.

Preston cannot see them, but ever since he and Yolanda arrived with their twin girls, he has been aware of something funky in the air.

Static discharges from the ghosts of Trinity College have horripilated every hair on his body, and it is these upright antennae that have made him as sensitive as a flytrap. This hypersensitivity allows Preston to notice, for the first time, the unearthly magnetism of Kelly from all the way across the Apple store.

Something about Kelly wakes up his belly button. It blinks and blinks as if this is the first girl it has ever seen. Preston knows her name is Kelly because that is what it says on her badge. Her job title though, two point sizes smaller, defies both his eyes and his belly button. To all seeing parts of his body, she is just Kelly, dark curls tumbling at her neck, wearing a helter-skelter of candy stripes. Preston falls all the way down her and leaves his breath at the top.

When she puts down the iPhone and leaves the shop, Preston cannot help but follow.

Yes, Preston is married. Yes, he has twin girls. Here they all are, coming out of the Grand Arcade public toilets, stopping to watch the teenage boy with the bright orange hair run at the wall, bound up its surface, and then flip himself over. The rubber soles of his Converse boots slap the pavement with a sound that knocks olives from ciabattas. Even the ghosts stop to watch the boy. Here is an amazed Bertrand Russell with his arms folded across his chest.

The twins, Libby and Daniela, are lively now they've peed. Their fingers are still wet from washing, pulling at the ties of Yolanda's top, snapping threads, until Yolanda smacks the back of their hands and begs them to leave her alone for just one moment.

The girls have dried ice cream around their mouths. There is something porcine in the flair of their nostrils. These are identical twins. If they were even a little different, they would not draw stares the way they do. Yolanda tries to ignore the people who are so fascinated by her uncanny younglings. She holds their hands high enough to prevent mischief and marches them through the arcade towards the Apple store.

Today, the Master of Trinity College has invoked the memory of the dead. It is 350 years since the college's greatest alumnus, Isaac Newton, first attended the college, and it is 100 years since Ludwig Wittgenstein first came to the campus. A moment in time worthy of marking. Living alumni from around the world have come to Cambridge to celebrate, elbow to elbow with the dead.

In the chapel, delighted tourists startle Newton's statue with their camera flashes. One Vietnamese lady is so excited, she feels herself re-made by Trinity's architecture. Something of its grandeur has straightened her spine. She pokes her enormous glasses hard against her face. Now Cambridge is inside her, proud and worthy. Its lawns lay down for her. This is where she will send the children she has yet to conceive, *if* they don't get into Hogwarts.

All around Cambridge, in halls and houses, blue gowns are pulled over heads. Trinity's wizards group together where they find each other on the streets. A magical fraternity, for whom Wordsworth's "Loquacious clock" speaks, so special even the sun has got its hat on.

In Trinity College Hall, high up in the rafters, a wooden mallard listens to the sounds of cutlery being placed far below, and to the percussion of crockery rolling like spun pennies at each of the guests' places.

Distracted like this, the duck does not notice AA Milne and Jawaharlal Nehru behind it whispering to each other and giggling, wondering if, between them, they can conjure enough solidity in their fingertips to break this bird's inertia.

We must feel sorry for this mallard, who has been moved from rafter to rafter by ingenious pranksters for decades. Who has watched bread broken by England's best minds from vertiginous heights, while not one crumb has ever been cast in its direction.

Kelly moves fast in heels, even over cobbles. Preston weaves around the tourists, keeping her candy stripes in sight. To understand why he chases her vapour trail like this, you must know about a girlfriend Preston had when he was sixteen. She told him something that would haunt him for ever.

Her name was Annabel, and she was a violent kisser who left his lips swollen and tender and tasting of cherry Chapstick. He cannot think about her without hearing the sound of incisors clashing. She told him that for every person, there is a partner so perfect that if you touch them, you'll both orgasm immediately.

Preston had many questions about Annabel's myth, such as, would orgasm occur *every* time these two people touched each other? If, say, the magic happened in a train carriage where the two people were standing, and the rocking of the train was knocking them together again and again, would they come repeatedly? Was the effect expendable? Annabel had only a surface knowledge of this phenomenon and was unable to answer his questions.

He and Annabel did not share this magical property. They worked each other sore to reach such climaxes. But this idea stayed with him, fascinated him, throughout his life. The assessment of girls for this property was simple and discreet and he conducted it frequently. Obsessively. He did it in pubs, in queues at the cinema, at the supermarket, never finding her.

His relationships were always short. To him, they could only be temporary because despite their individual merits, what was the point in being with anyone but his absolute perfect match?

It sounded to Preston like a most inconvenient gift, and yet he yearned for it. An orgasm that one did not have to work for, that came unsolicited at some unsuspecting moment, would surely be the most wondrous of all.

Throughout Preston's thirty-two years, he had sloughed the beliefs of his youth, leaving the most outrageous first. He skipped over Santa and crunched fairies and were-wolves beneath his boots when he was still wearing size 4s. He stomped on people who could move objects with their minds and did not look back.

But this one belief, in the spontaneous orgasm of two people perfectly attuned to each other, stayed with him. It had been so appealing to his 16-year-old mind, and it was so impossible to disprove by scientific study, that he clung to it. The last piece of magic on Earth. And today, the day that Trinity's dead walk the streets of Cambridge, he feels more certainly than ever before that he has found his orgasmic twin.

Already the blood has rushed from his head into the divining rod which he follows through the market square crowds, past stalls of ostrich meat and novelty Obama t-shirts and Jamaican patties, so enchanted that he ignores the rational part of his mind that reminds him about Yolanda.

Yolanda arrives at the Apple shop. She scans the top of people's heads, because Preston is taller than most men, but he is not there. She moves around the big tables, and pulls the twins' hands away from the laptops, and tells the sales assistants with their weird hair and their informality that she needs no help. Maybe Preston has stooped to look at goodies he cannot afford. She moves through the whole shop twice, and then scans heads again, but he is not there.

Outside the shop, while she takes out her phone and dials Preston's number, Libby and Daniela point amazedly at the ghosts, who are leaning into the wind of radio-waves pouring from the shop. The ghosts stretch their arms wide, their eyes closed with delight.

Galumphing down Trinity Street comes the ghost of Aleister Crowley, class of

1898, horny as a dunnock. How desperately he needs something, anything, to make naked magic with. But everywhere he looks, every phantasmic face to which he raises a cheeky eyebrow turns away. Where are all the lady-ghosts? And where are all the adventurous men? These ghosts are shameful in their conventionality.

Aleister bites at the air, bites ineffectually at the necks of the living, until, finally, a pair of luminous eyes meets his – another dead alumnus who has awoken from his sleep engorged, causing Aleister's ectoplasm to bubble.

These ghosts have no need for propriety. The last time either of them loved another like this it was illegal, but watch them now set upon each other's mouths with ravenous joy. Fingers groping through layers of refracted light. They drop to the ground, and there, at five-thirty on a Saturday afternoon in June, being walked through by students and tourists and terriers, they satiate each other.

Preston is startled by the vibration of his phone in his pocket, and then a second later, the ring begins – the opening beats of Michael Jackson's "Billy Jean". He takes the phone out, and on the screen is a photo of Yolanda he took last Christmas. She is poking her tongue out.

He lets the phone ring until his voicemail answers, and then he puts it back in his pocket. He will call her in a few minutes once he has decided how to explain that he has to catch up with this girl, lay his hand upon her, to test whether his instincts are correct, that this is the one person on the planet for whom he is specifically made. Surely a demonstration of two people enjoying simultaneous orgasm from one touch alone would negate the need for explanations and excuses? No one bound by mere marital and coincidental attachment could argue with something as miraculous as that.

But now . . . where is she? From the mouth of Rose Crescent, a tour group in matching purple jumpers has poured into Trinity Street, closing the gaps between bodies through which he was navigating, and despite his height, he has lost her.

Preston tries to push through the people like he is a ghost, like he will not bounce off them, but bounce off them he does, and soon, alerted by the angry grunts of people knocked aside, the crowd moves to let him through. To Preston, this almost biblical division of shoppers is another clear sign. The path is so clear that he is able to run, staring into every shop window for a second to see if she has gone inside. Every moment that he does not find her makes it more likely that he will never see her again.

Behind the college, on the river, a raft of punts nods into the weed as each of the students steps upon it. They take hands and help each other onto this buoyant stage, excited because this is the first time they have ever done it. On the banks, students and fellows and parents sit on tartan blankets popping corks and gouging stalks from the hearts of strawberries.

And here too there are ghosts, the angle of the sun turning their blue to gold. They watch the students and ache to feel once more the giddy thrill of an unsteady platform beneath their feet, the simple joy of something that confounds the senses.

Guys in gowns thrust poles deep into the Cam and guide the raft out to the middle. The singers arrange themselves by voice and height as they have rehearsed, and grin because these sensations are still novel.

When they are in position, they wait for a certain stillness that is imperceptible from the bank, and then they open their mouths.

The pink bellows that cradle their lungs push out something so sweet it causes champagne pourers to overfill their glasses, and even the dead to weep.

This sound is trampled in the marketplace, where Yolanda kneels before her girls. They have been fighting over Libby's Sea Monkeys keyring – a mini-aquarium the size of a child's fist filled with overfed brine shrimp.

Yolanda holds Daniela's forearm out to show Libby the deep red crescents which fit Libby's fingernails like a glass slipper.

It terrifies Yolanda that they fight like this. When the girls first became aware of each other, before they could even sit up, they would use their chubby little arms like clubs against each other, they would kick with their sticky feet, and they bit before they even had teeth. On their third birthday, Yolanda found Daniela crouched over Libby pressing a cushion onto her face.

Yolanda had suggested to Preston that they take the girls somewhere, to see someone, but he had been adamant that this is how kids behave. Every time the twins fight, Yolanda thinks about the barn owl chicks she saw on *Springwatch*, all hatched a week apart, of different sizes, like Matryoshka dolls, and how they did fit inside one another, because the largest chick ate the others alive. It tipped its head all the way back, shuddering with the effort of swallowing something only one size smaller than itself.

Yolanda calls Preston again, and again gets no answer. Behind her lips, her vitriol is rehearsing.

Mummy, Libby says, where are all those blue people going?

What blue people? Yolanda says.

And then Libby bolts, her greasy little fingers slipping easily out of Yolanda's hand.

Yolanda yells her name and runs after her as fast as Daniela's feet can keep up, but Libby whips round the knees of people in the market. Yolanda unpacks the voice she only uses at home when the curtains are closed, a full-force roar that reconfigures her face and terrifies the shoppers around her. When this sound hits one old dear, she falls into a display of honeydew melons, and they tumble together, bashed knees, bruised melons and a broken wrist. Yolanda picks up Daniela and runs after Libby whose white dress appears only every few seconds as gaps open up between people. Squeezed tight against Yolanda's chest as she runs, Daniela's feet jiggle above the street, whizzing past paper bags and wristwatches. Her chin is knocked by her mother's shoulder and her teeth slam together on her lip. As blood wells up through the split, she starts to howl.

Preston's ankle is throbbing. Weakened by a tennis injury, it cannot cope with these cobbles, but he pushes on. He would run on bloodied stumps if he had to.

Every one of his senses is tuned to the wavelength of red and white candy stripes and he scans the windows of Strada and Heffers and the Royal Bank of Scotland as he charges past. His body flushes with pleasure chemicals as he sees the briefest flash of candy-stripe fabric going through the Great Gate of Trinity College.

On the river, the choir has reached crescendo, their voices threaded together and cast over the bank-side audience, captivating them so deeply that even their breath needs permission.

The sound draws the dead from all over Cambridge. It awakens late risers from their beds – beds which have collapsed around their sleepers, so long have they slept.

The porters wearing their practised faces do not stop porting, but lift up the edges of their bowler hats to trap inside some of the music for later, when they can enjoy it in bare feet, patrolling their rooms with their belts unbuckled.

In the kitchens, the singing is barely audible amongst the sound of wooden spoons in pans, knives on chopping boards, bubbles struggling against glass lids. But it causes the crystal glasses to ring most eerily. It drives the ghost of Byron's bear crazy. Watch it gambol through the dining room, shaking its blue-bloodied muzzle, loping through the completed silver service. Not even the flames atop the candelabra notice it pass.

On the river, the last note pulls behind it a silence so deep and terrifying that every hand feels compelled to fill this void with the most reassuring applause it can muster.

At the Great Gate, Preston queues among the gowned fellows, his extraordinary height allowing him to see over the top of their heads into the Great Court, but his candy-striped girl has vanished.

He lets his phone ring until it tires in his pocket. He still does not have an explanation for Yolanda.

When he looks at his watch, he causes everyone around him to look at their watches, and this need to know the time flows out from him in a great concentric wave, compelling everyone at that very moment to know the time. As if in answer, the clock above the Great Court chimes the hour twice over. It is six o'clock.

At the mouth of the Great Gate, beneath Henry VIII brandishing his wooden chair-leg, Preston notices for the first time that he is the only one in the queue not wearing a gown and the only one not carrying an invitation card.

On King's Parade, everyone stops to look at their watches together, and in this moment of stillness, they stare at Yolanda running. She is an impressive sight, her plaited ponytail slapping at her back. The cords in her neck come out to amplify her voice as she yells Libby's name. Her flip-flops slap the paving, ticking out the double chimes of Trinity's clock. And over her shoulder, Daniela, hypnotised by shaking, clings to her mother's chest, watching the amazed faces recede behind her.

Ahead of them, Libby chases the ghosts.

Now they have all arrived at the college, the living and the dead. The ghosts need no invitation, and melt through the queue like it's not there, melt through Preston, who is shuffling forward in the procession. He watches each person in front showing their invite to the porter. This porter looks like he is immune to bargaining. He has a big-chested solidity and eyes that have no whites. His mouth does not reciprocate smiles.

Preston apologizes as he cuts sideways through the crowd, towards a group of four younger men in gowns. One of them has some kind of colourful juggling equipment, and the others are gathered around him, examining it. Their conversation stops as he approaches, and their mouths open slightly when they appreciate his size. Preston hunches in the way that he does.

I've forgotten my invite, he says. And my gown. I'll give you two hundred quid for a loan of one of yours.

I don't get undressed for less than five hundred, the juggler-boy says laughing outrageously at himself. And I don't think it would fit you anyway. The laughter of the other boys spills all over the pavement, splashes against Preston who stands as still as a lighthouse, his face ignited. He retreats back into the queue, a full head taller than anyone else.

On the ground, Aleister Crowley's mouth is at the neck of his man, whispering incantations over his neon moles. This couple is insensible of footsteps and the heavy pendulums of carrier bags. Aleister's spell unwraps itself, a mischievous gift, something from the other side, loosening the screws of gravity.

Preston's fantastic height has caught the attention of the porter at the gate. Preston has seen him note the pink collar of his shirt – so alien among the starched-white-on-navy of the fellows' uniforms. Far ahead, through the arches of the fountain, climbing the stone steps to the Hall, is the candy-striped woman. She is now wearing a gown, and the fabric swishes about her, revealing slivers of her wonderful stripes.

Now the queue has narrowed at the mouth of the entrance. There are only three people ahead of Preston. Fear floods his system with something radioactive, something that burns at his joints. Fear of being turned away, and fear of never knowing whether this woman was the one.

The fear turns to energy and energy turns to action. To the amusement of the fellows around him, Preston steps straight over the barrier and runs.

The porter calls out stop. Gives chase. Other porters come. Other men in gowns pursue him. But Preston is a daddy long-legs, each of his strides covering three of a normal man's. He pounds across the lawn, past the fountain. Those behind him cannot keep up, and those ahead of him stand aside for fear of the violent strength such a giant could command.

For the second time today, a path clears for Preston.

He leaps up the stone steps in a single bound, into the corridor, past the ghosts of Newton and John Dryden and Francis Bacon who stand before their portraits imitating their own expressions.

He ducks low through the entrance to the Hall, and two hundred faces all turn towards him.

Trinity Street is awash with gowns and chatter, and in this confusion, Yolanda has lost sight of Libby. She imagines someone, some dribbling, broken-toothed paedophile putting pawprints on her white dress and over her mouth. Faced with this terrifying vision she stops and gathers up everything she has inside her. Her yell is so fierce it moves through the crowd like a shockwave. Ankles, unbolted by Aleister Crowley's tongue, betray their owners. Yolanda's ululation fells everyone. Every knee, every hip, every elbow and every shoulder on Trinity

Street, in one great wave hits the pavement. There is a collective groan as the force of the fall pushes air from the lungs of more than three hundred people.

At the end of her scream, Yolanda's teeth sing like a tuning fork.

Before the fallen pick themselves up, while they are too shocked to even apologise to those they have scratched and groped as they fell, the only person standing is Libby, and an orchard of ghosts who stand rooted to the stones, staring at Yolanda. The force of her howl against their backs was a delicious sensation worth all of those numb decades.

Amongst them, Libby is staring at her smashed keyring aquarium, crying.

In the rafters, the mallard watches the colossus step into the room, and is suddenly airborne. Its wings are moulded firmly to its sides and all attempts to flap are futile. It watches the room turn around it, sees far above, its former perch and behind it, AA Milne and Jawaharlal Nehru high-fiving each other in delight. And then it crashes to the ground.

This isn't how Preston wanted this moment to be.

Standing in the middle of Trinity's fellows, ten feet tall and clutching a Waterstone's bag, sweaty from the pursuit, he scans the room and finds his girl. The timing of the duck's fall is so precise that there is a common misperception that he has knocked his head against the rafters and dislodged it.

The porters have waited moments while they gathered together in enough numbers to tackle this monster. Eight of them move in on him. Preston sees the girl, sitting on a bench close-by. One leg is crossed over the other, revealing a bare knee so smooth that his gaze can't settle upon it without sliding down her shin.

His insides are a-shiver. Closing the gap between himself and Kelly in two great strides, he takes in all of her. He can imagine the weight of her curls against his face, the plush smothering smack of her lips.

She recoils as he approaches, sliding her bottom along the bench, but already he is there. For the first time he is able to read the rest of her name badge: Dr Kelly Campbell, Dept of Physics.

It will all make sense in a moment, he tries to say, but he is panting and his words come out all mashed into one. He could never have imagined that this moment of revelation, which should be spectacular for them both, would have happened with an audience. But somehow it is fitting.

Preston reaches out and wraps his long fingers around Kelly's wrist. She tries to pull away, and even stands up, but it is too late. The magic is already happening.

The sensation begins simultaneously in Preston's balls and his feet, rocketing through his insides, hormonal fireworks fizzing against the underside of muscles and curling round bones, making his titanic cartilage groan with pleasure.

He is compelled to close his eyes, to fully savour the fanfare that is boiling in his underpants, but he does not. Something is wrong.

Kelly is still trying to wrestle free from his grip. Her face shows no sign of supernatural ecstasy. Only horror.

Preston is coming alone.

It is too late to stop. Even if he let go of her now. His insides are on fire and the fire will not stop until he is all ashes. He has never felt an orgasm like this before. Hidden fuses throughout his systems flare and blow. Cells chime against cells. The pleasure is uncontainable, and his terror makes it even sweeter. Terror because now he sees all around him the blue faces of Trinity's past. Lights obscure his vision. His knees crumple. He is unmade.

Even knelt like this before Kelly, he is still taller than her. And her expression is one of revulsion.

Porters have his collar, have his arms, grab his fingers and force them to relinquish Kelly. Yank him backwards with such velocity he is forced to run on his heels. Men and women gather round Kelly, healing her with their murmurs, and block her from Preston's view.

As the orgasm, the most tremendous orgasm in the universe, subsides, a sense of abjection washes in to fill the space it has left.

The porters drag Preston down the stone steps, across the lawn, to the front gate where queuing fellows still wait. For the third time today, the crowd divides to allow him through.

When Yolanda reaches Libby, the shoppers have stood up and are brushing themselves down, looking around to see what has happened. Maybe they suspect a bomb has gone off. But as soon as the first person has resumed shopping, the others follow, and within seconds, it's as if Yolanda's utterance never existed.

Libby is on her knees, sobbing, picking up the fractured pieces of her Sea Monkeys keyring from the ground. In between cobbles, the little brine shrimp twitch their tails, their segmented legs working the meniscus of their spilled environment.

Yolanda sets Daniela down on the ground. And now that the adrenaline is retreating back into the caves of her body, she feels all the muscles she has pulled in her pursuit. Something holding her spine straight has snapped. Something in her thigh is burning. She is conceiving Libby's punishment when among the crowd of strangers she sees Preston. His walk is weird and hobbled.

I'm sorry, he says.

Yolanda starts in with the where have you beens and I've been going crazy I've just had to chase our daughter through the street do you have any idea what . . . and then she stops because Preston is wearing a familiar expression which she can't quite place.

I don't feel so good, he says.

Why are you walking funny? What the hell happened to you?

Preston needs time to concoct an explanation. I'm okay, he says. Let's just go home.

But this is not acceptable to Yolanda, and she shifts tack on the questions and suggests scenarios to Preston to which he must reply yes or no. Have you been attacked? Have you had an aneurysm? This method of elimination is unlikely to reveal the exact circumstances which have led Preston to be standing here, concealing a sticky patch of semen from the world with a carrier bag, but Yolanda is relentless.

In the Hall, Preston's fingerprints have faded from Kelly's arm. The mallard has been set upon the head table beside a basket of rolls. The gravy is thickening in the pot. The singers are back on the bank. Byron's bear is cavorting unseen in the river. Aleister and his mate lay on their backs looking up through the people at the blushing sky. They are breathless. The master of Trinity tings his glass three times with a teaspoon. This dinner of the dead alumni has begun most memorably.

SAD, DARK THING

Michael Marshall Smith

Michael Marshall Smith (b.1965) was born in Knutsford, Cheshire. He lived in Illinois, Florida, South Africa and Australia before his family settled back in England in 1973. Marshall Smith studied Philosophy and Social and Political Science at Cambridge, where he joined the Cambridge Footlights. He has published five novels as Michael Marshall Smith and seven under the name of Michael Marshall. He lives in Santa Cruz, California with his wife and son.

A imless. A short, simple word. It means "without aim", where "aim" derives from the idea of calculation with a view to action. Without purpose or direction, therefore, without a considered goal or future that you can see. People mainly use the word in a blunt, softened fashion. They walk "aimlessly" down a street, not sure whether to have a coffee or if they should they check out the new magazines in the bookstore or maybe sit on that bench and watch the world go by. It's not a big deal, this aimlessness. It's a temporary state and often comes with a side order of ease. An hour without something hanging over you, with no great need to do or achieve anything in particular? In this world of busy lives and do-this and do-that, it sounds pretty good.

But being wholly without purpose? With no direction home? That is not such a good deal. Being truly aimless is like being dead. It may even be the same thing, or worse. It is the aimless who find the wrong roads, and go down them, simply because they have nowhere else to go.

Miller usually found himself driving on Saturday afternoons. He could make the morning go away by staying in bed an extra half-hour, tidying away stray emails, spending time on the deck, looking out over the forest with a magazine or the iPad and a succession of coffees. He made the coffees in a machine that sat on the kitchen counter and cost nearly eight hundred dollars. It made a very good cup of coffee. It should. It had cost nearly eight hundred dollars.

By noon a combination of caffeine and other factors would mean that he wasn't very hungry. He would go back indoors nonetheless, and put together a plate from the fridge. The ingredients would be things he'd gathered from delis up in San Francisco during the week, or else from the New Leaf markets in Santa Cruz or Felton as he returned home on Friday afternoon. The idea was that this would constitute a treat, and remind him of the good things in life. That was the idea. He would also pour some juice into one of the only two glasses in the cabinet that got any use. The other was his scotch glass, the one with the faded white logo on it, but that only came out in the evenings. He was very firm about that.

He would bring the plate and glass back out and eat at the table which stood further along the deck from the chair in which he'd spent most of the morning. By then the sun would have moved around, and the table got shade, which he preferred when he was eating. The change in position was also supposed to make it feel like he was doing something different to what he'd done all morning, though it did not, especially. He was still a man sitting in silence on a raised deck, within view of many trees, eating expensive foods that tasted like cardboard.

Afterward he took the plate indoors and washed it in the sink. He had a dish-washer, naturally. Dishwashers are there to save time. He washed the plate and silverware by hand, watching the water swirl away and then drying everything and putting it to one side. He was down a wife, and a child, now living three hundred miles away. He was short on women and children, therefore, but in their place, from the hollows they had left behind, he had time. Time crawled in an endless parade of minutes from between those cracks, arriving like an army of little black ants, crawling up over his skin, up his face, and into his mouth, ears and eyes.

So why not wash the plate. And the knife, and the fork, and the glass. Hold back the ants, for a few minutes, at least.

He never left the house with a goal. On those afternoons he was, truly, aimless. From where the house stood, high in the Santa Cruz mountains, he could have reached a number of diverting places within an hour or two. San Jose. Saratoga. Los Gatos. Santa Cruz itself, then south to Monterey, Carmel and Big Sur. Even way down to Los Angeles, if he felt like making a weekend of it.

And then what?

Instead he simply drove.

There are only so many major routes you can take through the area's moun-tains and redwood forests. Highways 17 and 9, or the road out over to Bonny Doon, Route 1 north or south. Of these, only 17 is of any real size. In between the main thoroughfares, however, there are other options. Roads that don't do much except connect one minor two-lane highway to another. Roads that used to count for something before modern alternatives came along to supplant or supersede or negate them.

Side roads, old roads, forgotten roads.

Usually there wasn't much to see down these last roads. Stretches of forest, maybe a stream, eventually a house, well back from the road. Rural, mountain-ous backwoods where the tree and poison oak reigned supreme. Chains across tracks which led down or up into the woods, some gentle inclines, others pretty steep, meandering off toward some house which stood even further from the through-lines, back in a twenty- or fifty-acre lot. Every now and then you'd pass one of the area's very few tourist traps, like the "Mystery Spot", an old-fashioned affair which claimed to honour a site of "Unfathomable Weirdness" but in fact paid cheerful homage to geometry, and to man's willingness to be deceived.

He'd seen all of these long ago. The local attractions with his wife and child, the shadowed roads and tracks on his own solitary excursions over the last few months. At least, you might have thought he would have seen them all. Every Saturday he drove, however, and every time he found a road he had never seen before.

Today the road was off Branciforte Drive, the long, old highway which heads off through largely uncolonised regions of the mountains and forests to the southeast of Scott's Valley. As he drove north along it, mind elsewhere and nowhere, he noticed a turning. A glance in the rearview mirror showed no one behind and so he slowed to peer along the turn.

A two-lane road, overhung with tall trees, including some redwoods. It gave no indication of leading anywhere at all.

Fine by him.

He made the turn and drove on. The trees were tall and thick, cutting off much of the light from above. The road passed smoothly up and down, riding the natural contours, curving abruptly once in a while to avoid the trunk of an especially big tree or to skirt a small canyon carved out over millennia by some small and bloody-minded stream. There were no houses or other signs of habitation. Could be public land, he was beginning to think, though he didn't recall there being any around here and hadn't seen any indication of a park boundary, and then he saw a sign by the road up ahead.

STOP

That's all it said. Despite himself, he found he was doing just that, pulling over toward it. When the car was stationary, he looked at the sign curiously. It had been hand-lettered, some time ago, in black marker on a panel cut from a cardboard box and nailed to a tree.

He looked back the way he'd come, and then up the road once more. He saw no traffic in either direction, and also no indication of why the sign would be here. Sure, the road curved again about forty yards ahead, but no more markedly than it had ten or fifteen times since he'd left Branciforte Drive. There had been no warning signs on those bends. If you simply wanted to people to observe the speed limit then you'd be more likely to advise them to "Slow", and anyway it didn't look at all like an official sign.

Then he realised that, further on, there was in fact a turning off the road.

He took his foot off the brake and let the car roll forward down the slope, crunching over twigs and gravel. A driveway, it looked like, though a long one, bending off into the trees. Single lane, roughly made up. Maybe five yards down it was another sign, evidently the work of the same craftsman as the previous.

TOURISTS WELCOME

He grunted, in something like a laugh. If you had yourself some kind of attraction, of course tourists were welcome. What would be the point otherwise? It was a strange way of putting it.

An odd way of advertising it, too. No indication of what was in store or why a busy family should turn off what was already a pretty minor road and head off into the woods. No lure except those two words.

They were working on him, though, he had to admit. He eased his foot gently back on the gas and carefully directed the car along the track, between the trees.

* * *

After about a quarter of a mile he saw a building ahead. A couple of them, in fact, arranged in a loose compound. One a ramshackle two-storey farmhouse, the other a disused barn. There was also something that was or had been a garage, with a broken-down truck/tractor parked diagonally in front of it. It was parked insofar as it was not moving, at least, not in the sense that whoever had last driven the thing had made any effort, when abandoning it, to align its form with anything. The surfaces of the vehicle were dusty and rusted and liberally covered in old leaves and specks of bark. A wooden crate, about four feet square, stood rotting in the back. The near front tyre was flat.

The track ended in a widened parking area, big enough for four or five cars. It was empty. There was no sign of life at all, in fact, but something – he wasn't sure what – said this habitation was a going concern, rather than collection of ruins that someone had walked away from at some point in the last few years.

Nailed to a tree in front of the main house, was another cardboard sign.

WELCOME

He parked, turned off the engine, and got out. It was very quiet. It usually is in those mountains, when you're away from the road. Sometimes you'll hear the faint roar of an airplane, way up above, but apart from that it's just the occasional tweet of some winged creature or an indistinct rustle as something small and furry or scaly makes its way through the bushes.

He stood for a few minutes, flapping his hand to discourage a noisy fly which appeared from nowhere, bothered his face, and then zipped chaotically off.

Eventually he called out. "Hello?"

You'd think that – on what was evidently a very slow day for this attraction, whatever it was – the sound of an arriving vehicle would have someone bustling into sight, eager to make a few bucks, to pitch their wares. He stood a few minutes more, however, without seeing or hearing any sign of life. It figured. Aimless people find aimless things, and it didn't seem like much was going to happen here. You find what you're looking for, and he hadn't been looking for anything at all.

He turned back toward the car, aware that he wasn't even feeling disappointment. He hadn't expected much, and that's exactly what he'd got.

As he held up his hand to press the button to unlock the doors, however, he heard a creaking sound.

He turned back to see there was now a man on the tilting porch that ran along half of the front of the wooden house. He was dressed in canvas jeans and a vest that had probably once been white. The man had probably once been clean, too, though he looked now like he'd spent most of the morning trying to fix the underside of a car. Perhaps he had.

"What you want?"

His voice was flat and unwelcoming. He looked to be in his mid to late fifties. Hair once black was now half grey, and also none too clean. He did not look like he'd been either expecting or desirous of company.

"What have you got?"

The man on the porch leant on the rail and kept looking at him, but said nothing.

"It says 'Tourists Welcome'," Miller said, when it became clear the local had nothing to offer. "I'm not feeling especially welcome, to be honest."

The man on the porch looked weary. "Christ. The boy was supposed to take down those damned signs. They still up?"

"Yes."

"Even the one out on the road, says 'Stop'?"

"Yes," Miller said. "Otherwise I wouldn't have stopped."

The other man swore and shook his head. "Told the boy weeks ago. Told him I don't know how many times."

Miller frowned. "You don't notice, when you drive in and out? That the signs are still there?"

"Haven't been to town in a while."

"Well, look. I turned down your road because it looked like there was something to see."

"Nope. Doesn't say anything like that."

"It's implied, though, wouldn't you say?"

The man lifted his chin a little. "You a lawyer?"

"No. I'm a businessman. With time on my hands. Is there something to see here, or not?"

After a moment the man on the porch straightened, and came walking down the steps.

"One dollar," he said. "As you're here."

"For what? The parking?"

The man stared at him as if he was crazy. "No. To see."

"One dollar?" It seemed inconceivable that in this day and age there would be anything under the sun for a dollar, especially if it was trying to present as something worth experiencing. "Really?"

"That's cheap," the man said, misunderstanding.

"It is what it is," Miller said, getting his wallet out and pulling a dollar bill from it.

The other man laughed, a short, sour sound. "You got that right."

After he'd taken the dollar and stuffed it into one of the pockets of his jeans, the man walked away. Miller took this to mean that he should follow, and so he did. It looked for a moment as if they were headed toward the house, but then the path – such as it was – took an abrupt right onto a course that led them between the house and the tilting barn. The house was large and gabled, and must once have been quite something. Lord knows what it was doing out here, lost by itself in a patch of forest that had never been near a major road or town or anyplace else that people with money might wish to be. Its glory days were long behind it, anyway. Looking up at it, you'd give it about another five years standing, unless someone got onto rebuilding or at least shoring it right away.

The man led the way through slender trunks into an area around the back of the barn. Though the land in front of the house and around the side had barely been what you'd think of as tamed, here the forest abruptly came into its own. Trees of significant size shot up all around, looking – as redwoods do – like they'd been there since the dawn of time. A sharp, rocky incline led down toward a stream about thirty yards away. The stream was perhaps eight feet across, with steep sides. A rickety bridge of old, grey wood lay across it. The man led him to the near side of this, and then stopped.

"What?"

"This is it."

Miller looked again at the bridge. "A dollar, to look at a bridge some guy threw up fifty years ago?" Suddenly it wasn't seeming so dumb a pricing system after all.

The man handed him a small, tarnished key, and raised his other arm to point. Between the trees on the other side of the creek was a small hut.

"It's in there."

"What is?"

The man shrugged. "A sad, dark thing."

The water which trickled below the bridge smelt fresh and clean. Miller got a better look at the hut, shed, whatever, when he reached the other side. It was about half the size of a log cabin, but made of grey, battered planks instead of logs. The patterns of lichen over the sides and the moss-covered roof said it been here, and in this form, for a good long time – far longer than the house, most likely. Could be an original settler's cabin, the home of whichever long-ago pioneer had first arrived here, driven west by hope or desperation. It looked about contemporary with the rickety bridge, certainly.

There was a small padlock on the door.

He looked back.

The other man was still standing at the fat end of the bridge, looking up at the canopy of leaves above. It wasn't clear what he'd be looking at, but it didn't seem like he was waiting for the right moment to rush over, bang the other guy on the head, and steal his wallet. If he'd wanted to do that he could have done it back up at the house. There was no sign of anyone else around – this boy he'd mentioned, for example – and he looked like he was waiting patiently for the conclusion of whatever needed to happen for him to have earned his dollar.

Miller turned back and fitted the key in the lock. It was stiff, but it turned. He opened the door. Inside was total dark. He hesitated, looked back across the bridge, but the man had gone.

He opened the door further, and stepped inside.

The interior of the cabin was cooler than it had been outside, but also stuffy. There was a faint smell. Not a bad smell, particularly. It was like old, damp leaves. It was like the back of a closet where you store things you do not need. It was like a corner of the attic of a house not much loved, in the night, after rain.

The only light was that which managed to get past him from the door behind. The cabin had no windows, or if it had, they had been covered over. The door he'd entered by was right at one end of the building, which meant the rest of the interior led ahead. It could only have been ten, twelve feet. It seemed longer, because it was so dark. The man stood there, not sure what happened next.

The door slowly swung closed behind him, not all the way, but leaving a gap of a couple of inches. No-one came and shut it on him or turned the lock or started hollering about he'd have to pay a thousand bucks to get back out again. The man waited.

In a while, there was a quiet sound.

It was a rustling. Not quite a shuffling. A sense of something moving a little at the far end, turning away from the wall, perhaps. Just after the sound, there was a low waft of a new odour, as if the movement had caused something to change its relationship to the environment, as if a body long held curled or crouched in a particular shape or position had realigned enough for hidden sweat to be released into the unmoving air.

Miller froze.

In all his life, he'd never felt the hairs on the back of his neck rise. You read about it, hear about it. You knew they were supposed to do it, but he'd never felt it, not his own hairs, on his own neck. They did it then, though, and the peculiar thing was that he was not afraid, or not only that.

He was in there with something, that was for certain. It was not a known thing, either. It was . . . he didn't know. He wasn't sure. He just knew that there was something over there in the darkness. Something about the size of a man, he thought, maybe a little smaller.

He wasn't sure it was male, though. Something said to him it was female. He couldn't imagine where this impression might be coming from, as he couldn't see it and he couldn't hear anything, either – after the initial movement, it had been still. There was just something in the air that told him things about it, that said underneath the shadows it wrapped around itself like a pair of dark angel's wings, it knew despair, bitter madness and melancholy better even than he did. He knew that beneath those shadows it was naked, and not male.

He knew also that it was this, and not fear, that was making his breathing come ragged and forced.

He stayed in there with it for half an hour, doing nothing, just listening, staring into the darkness but not seeing anything. That's how long it seemed like it had been, anyway, when he eventually emerged back into the forest. It was hard to tell.

He closed the cabin door behind him but he did not lock it, because he saw that the man was back, standing once more at the far end of the bridge. Miller clasped the key firmly in his fist and walked over toward him.

"How much?" he said.

"For what? You already paid."

"No," Miller said. "I want to buy it."

It was eight by the time Miller got back to his house. He didn't know how that could be unless he'd spent longer in the cabin than he realised. It didn't matter a whole lot, and in fact there were good things about it. The light had begun to fade. In twenty minutes it would be gone entirely. He spent those minutes sitting in the front seat of the car, waiting for darkness, his mind as close to a comfortable blank as it had been in a long time.

When it was finally dark he got out the car and went over to the house. He dealt with the security system, opened the front door and left it hanging open.

He walked back to the vehicle and went around to the trunk. He rested his hand on the metal there for a moment, and it felt cold. He unlocked the back and turned away, not fast but naturally, and walked toward the set of wooden steps which led to the smaller of the two raised decks. He walked up them and stood there for a few minutes, looking out into the dark stand of trees, and then turned and headed back down the steps toward the car.

The trunk was empty now, and so he shut it, and walked slowly toward the open door of his house, and went inside, and shut and locked that door behind him too.

It was night, and it was dark, and they were both inside and that felt right.

He poured a small scotch in a large glass. He took it out through the sliding glass doors to the chair on the main deck where he'd spent the morning, and sat there cradling the drink, taking a sip once in a while. He found himself remembering, as he often did at this time, the first time he'd met his wife. He'd been living down on East Cliff then, in a house which was much smaller that this one but only a couple of minutes' walk from the beach. Late one Saturday afternoon, bored and restless, he'd taken a walk to the Crow's Nest, the big restaurant that was the only place to eat or drink along that stretch. He'd bought a similar scotch at the upstairs bar and taken it out onto the balcony to watch the sun go down over the harbour. After a while he noticed that, amongst the family groups of sunburned tourists and knots of tattooed locals there was a woman sitting at a table by herself, She had a tall glass of beer and seemed to be doing the same thing he was, and he wondered why. Not why she was doing that, but why he was – why they both were. He did not know then, and he did not know now, why people sit and look out into the distance by themselves, or what they hope to see.

After a couple more drinks he went over and introduced himself. Her name was Catherine and she worked at the university. They got married eighteen months later and though by then – his business having taken off in the meantime – he could have afforded anywhere in town, they hired out the Crow's Nest and had the wedding party there. A year after that their daughter was born and they called her Matilde, after Catherine's mother, who was French. Business was still good and they moved out of his place on East Cliff and into the big house he had built in the mountains and for seven years all was good, and then, for some reason, it was no longer good any more. He didn't think it had been his fault, though it could have been. He didn't think it was her fault either, though that too was possible. It had simply stopped working. They'd been two people, and then one, but then two again, facing different ways. There had been a view to share together, then there was not, and if you look with only one eye then there is no depth of field. There had been no infidelity. In some ways that might have been easier. It would have been something to react to, to blame, to hide behind. Far worse, in fact, to sit on opposite sides of the breakfast table and wonder who the other person was, and why they were there, and when they would go.

Six months later, she did. Matilde went with her, of course. He didn't think there was much more that could be said or understood on the subject. When first he'd sat out on this deck alone, trying to work it all through in his head, the recounting could take hours. As time went on, the story seemed to get shorter and shorter. As they said around these parts, it is what it is.

Or it was what it was.

Time passed and then it was late. The scotch was long gone but he didn't feel the desire for any more. He took the glass indoors and washed it at the sink, putting it on the draining board next to the plate and the knife and the fork from lunch. No lights were on. He hadn't bothered to flick any switches when he came in, and – having sat for so long out on the deck – his eyes were accustomed, and he felt no need to turn any on now.

He dried his hands on a cloth and walked around the house, aimlessly at first. He had done this many times in the last few months, hearing echoes. When he got to the area which had been Catherine's study, he stopped. There was nothing left in the space now bar the empty desk and the empty bookshelves. He could tell that the chair had been moved, however. He didn't recall precisely how it had been, or when he'd last listlessly walked this way, but he knew that it had been moved, somehow.

He went back to walking, and eventually fetched up outside the room that had been Matilde's. The door was slightly ajar. The space beyond was dark.

He could feel a warmth coming out of it, though, and heard a sound in there, something quiet, and he turned and walked slowly away.

He took a shower in the dark. Afterward he padded back to the kitchen in his bare feet and a gown and picked his scotch glass up from the draining board. Even after many, many trips through the dishwasher you could see the ghost of the restaurant logo that had once been stamped on it, the remains of a mast and a crow's nest. Catherine had slipped it into her purse one long-ago night, without him knowing about it, and then given the glass to him as an anniversary present. How did a person who would do that change into the person now living half the state away? He didn't know, any more than he knew why he had so little to say on the phone to his daughter, or why people sat and looked at views, or why they drove to nowhere on Saturday afternoons. Our heads turn and point at things. Light comes into our eyes. Words come out of our mouths.

And then? And so?

Carefully, he brought the edge of the glass down upon the edge of the counter. It broke pretty much as he'd hoped it would, the base remaining in one piece, the sides shattering into several jagged points.

He padded back through into the bedroom, put the broken glass on the nightstand, took off the robe, and lay back on the bed. That's how they'd always done it, when they'd wanted to signal that tonight didn't have to just be about going to sleep. Under the covers with a book, then probably not tonight, Josephine. Naked and on top, on the other hand . . .

A shorthand. A shared language. There is little sadder, however, than a tongue for which only one speaker remains. He closed his eyes, and after a while, for the first time since he'd stood stunned in the driveway and watched his family leave, he cried.

Afterward he lay and waited.

She came in the night.

Three days later, in the late afternoon, a battered truck pulled down into the driveway and parked alongside the car that was there. It was the first time the truck had been on the road in nearly two years, and the driver left the engine running when he got out because he wasn't all that sure it would start up again. The patched front tyre was holding up, though, for now.

He went around the back and opened up the wooden crate, propping the flap with a stick. Then he walked over to the big front door and rang on the bell. Waited a while, and did it again. No answer. Of course.

He rubbed his face in his hands, wearily, took a step back. The door looked solid. No way a kick would get it open. He looked around and saw the steps up to the side deck.

When he got around to the back of the house he picked up the chair that sat by itself, hefted it to judge the weight, and threw it through the big glass door. When he'd satisfied himself that the hole in the smashed glass was big enough, he walked back along the deck and around the front and then up the driveway to stand on the road for a while, out of view of the house.

He smoked a cigarette, and then another to be sure, and when he came back down the driveway he was relived to see that the flap on the crate on the back of his truck was now closed.

He climbed into the cab and sat a moment, looking at the big house. Then he put the truck into reverse, got back up to the highway, and drove slowly home.

When he made the turn into his own drive later, he saw the STOP sign was still there. Didn't matter how many times he told the boy, the sign was still there.

He drove along the track to the house, parked the truck. He opened the crate without looking at it, and went inside.

Later, sitting on his porch in the darkness, he listened to the sound of the wind moving through the tops of the trees all around. He drank a warm beer, and then another. He looked at the grime on his hands. He wondered what it was that made some people catch sight of the sign, what it was in their eyes, what it was in the way they looked, that made them see. He wondered how the man in the big house had done it, and hoped he had not suffered much. He wondered why he had never attempted the same thing. He wondered why it was only on nights like these that he was able to remember that his boy had been dead twenty years.

Finally he went indoors and lay in bed staring at the ceiling. He did this every night, even though there was never anything there to see: nothing unless it is that sad, dark thing that eventually takes us in its arms and makes us sleep.

GUESTS

Joanne Rush

Joanne Rush (b.1983) holds a PhD from Cambridge University in Renaissance literature. She now lives in London, where she divides her time between writing and teaching. She travels often to the Balkans, and recently worked in Mostar for a theatre company, Youth Bridge Global, as assistant director of a multilingual *Twelfth Night*. Her current project – a novel about modern Bosnia – combines her interests in the aftermath of war and the power of theatre.

They say February is the best month to step on a mine. If it is under enough snow it may not detonate. The snow begins in December, like the first gospel; by February it is several feet deep. It is a matter of record that, on Candlemas night in 1994, a group of women from the village of Lisac, in flight from Mladić's army, crossed the mined snowfields to safety. They did not speak, or they spoke only in whispers. They held the barbed wire apart for each other. Then did they run or crawl or dance, knowing that at any moment the solid ground might buck them into quick oblivion, the snow convert to flames?

It is the first of June, 2011. My husband will be glad the snow is gone, despite the increased risk of being blown up: he found the Bosnian winter very cold. He said so last Christmas, in a rare phone call. He didn't mention Bosnia openly, of course, because the British government has no official presence there. Each time he phones he tells me not to worry. He says he's not in danger, but I know this to be untrue. There are no exact maps of the minefields in Bosnia. Even now, sixteen years after the war ended, a donkey sometimes loses its life; or a child, or a spy.

I met my husband when I was nineteen years old. I had come up to Cambridge from a village in Warwickshire to study Computer Sciences. He had come up from Victoria City, Hong Kong, for the same reason. In Cambridge it is called coming up even if you come down. We were called compscis. Only students of unfashionable subjects were given abbreviations: as well as compscis, there were natscis (Natural Scientists) and asnacs (an acronym for Anglo-Saxon, Norse, and Celtic). When I got to know my husband, he would say these all sounded like animals that hadn't made it onto the ark.

Getting to know him didn't happen at once. There were lots of other compscis, most of them dishearteningly loud, and for a while we hovered shyly on opposite edges of this crowd. We finally met on the last Tuesday of Michaelmas term, in the café of the William Gates building. I often ate lunch there; he rarely did, but the kitchen on his college staircase had been declared unsafe. I found this out because he was behind me in the queue for jacket potatoes. One of the first things I noticed about him was that he breathed in, almost inaudibly, before each sentence: a slight inverted gasp which gave a feeling of urgency to his utterances. I also noticed that his elbows stuck out slightly, and that he had very fine black hair, like a mole.

He asked permission to sit beside me, and conscientiously tucked his elbows in. Then, impelled by the dual forces of hunger and loneliness, he plunged into his potato and his life story. His name was Jon. His mother was English, his father Chinese; he had arrived in Cambridge – which was very beautiful, but the cyclists were suicidal and everyone was on drugs – after a twelve hour flight to Heathrow, eight weeks ago, and he was still living out of a single suitcase; he had sent his other possessions ahead "by sheep", and they were yet to turn up, though he had called the lost property line "a tousand times".

In the weeks to come, I would grow to love the crisp Cantonese consonants that occasionally snuck into his English sentences, and his unsteady phonemes. Already I was entranced by his suitcases, voyaging from Hong Kong to Cambridge by sheep.

What followed our first, word- and potato-filled encounter, was an almost entirely non-verbal companionship. Then as now, Jon preferred computer languages to human ones, and most of the time I found this restful, but it did make things harder when we were apart. He particularly disliked telephones. So what stands out most brightly in my memory of the summer at the end of our first year, when I returned unwillingly to my parents in Warwickshire, and he went home to Hong Kong, is the day he sent me a postcard of Victoria Harbour with two lists on the back:

Things we like
1. *Quiet*
2. *King's College Chapel*
3. *Different sides of the bed*

Things we dislike
1. *Bicycles on pavements*
2. *Weed*
3. *Crowds*

Beside the second list was a pencil sketch of an ark, in which were two blobs. In case I should mistake these for his still lost suitcases, or even the miscreant sheep, he had printed below them: COMPSCIS.

"What do you feel about mmharriage?" Jon asked me, at the beginning of our fourth year in Cambridge. (He doesn't stutter, but with certain English words he sometimes fumbles a catch.)

We planned a very modest ceremony. His parents couldn't come – they didn't like flying – but mine were there: my father gruff, my mother querulous. She had already made plain her feelings about my mmharriage to "a half yellow man".

"Of course I'm not racist, dear," she said, a number of times. "It just that he's so quiet. Don't you want someone more like us?"

1. *Quiet*, I thought. 2. *King's College Chapel*. 3. *Different sides of the bed.*

Things did get more complicated later on, but I never doubted the soundness of this basis for love.

Jon's supervisor took him aside a few weeks before we graduated. She had been asked to recommend someone for a job at GCHQ. "Legalised hacking," she called it: exactly the sort of thing he'd be good at. I was already planning to set up as a freelance web designer, and neither of us wanted to face London. So we moved to Cheltenham Spa.

Our shabby third-storey flat was not a castle, unless of the air. It had white stuccoed ceilings, quietly peeling, and few comforts at first beyond a second-hand dinner table and a very low futon bed. Nevertheless we were happy there.

For two years Jon was deskbound in Cheltenham. But twelve months ago he was invited to a meeting about an important operation, co-run with the Americans, which needed someone in precisely his field of expertise. If he agreed, he'd be stationed at an old British military base in Bosnia. They couldn't say exactly how long for. My husband is a man of principle: he does things he doesn't want to do because he feels he should. I've got fewer principles: I just hoped it wouldn't take long.

Jon left for Bosnia in June 2010. That summer I kept myself busy, working from home. My job meant I spent a lot of time on the phone, explaining to clients the difference between mythology and technology, turning their dreams and visions into navigable sites – I'm not an imaginative person, but I'm good at detail. I got through one day at a time.

At the end of our street was a coffee shop, which was Polish and sold astonishing cakes. When the flat felt too empty I worked there instead. The waitress wore a black panelled apron with DONT ASK written across it in wobbly white velcro letters, or sometimes ASK ME L8R. "Wait one minute," she said. "*Sernik* arrives from kitchen." This was often the closest I got to a real conversation all day.

When I wasn't working, I went for long walks. Sometimes I walked past GCHQ, that vast blister of glass and concrete on the edge of the A40. I'd been told it had a street inside, and a computer room the size of the Royal Albert Hall. Jon's face appeared in there each day, pixelated, on a plasma screen. "Good morning, Cheltenham," he said. "See and hear you fine." Then he vanished, replaced by a man in Beirut or Kabul.

Autumn came, then winter. The waitress in the Polish café said I was looking peaky, a word she'd recently learnt. I stopped going there so often: I didn't like people fretting. But I still took long walks, sometimes right up into the Cotswolds. On these walks I allowed myself to picture Jon. I did this cautiously, small bits at a time. His hands. The blurred edge of his jaw. Never whole.

I spent Christmas alone, after some deliberation. In the morning I ate half a croissant and started crying. The tears took a long time to stop. At four o'clock Jon phoned. "Happy Christmas," he said. He sounded far away. He asked me how I was, and I told him I was fine. "It's very cold here," he said. We talked for a stilted quarter of an hour. He said, "Take care of yourself. I love you." Then he added quickly, "Listen, I may be onto something. I can't explain on the phone, but it might mean I'm back soon."

"I hope so," I said. I put the receiver down, expecting to feel happy. But instead I felt more sad. My husband didn't know that leaving someone could not be put right simply by coming back to them. Delicacy, filaments, were beyond him. He had strong hands, but that meant his forte was lifting heavy objects: small things slipped through his fingers, fragile things cracked in his grip.

When Christmas was over, I had a stroke of luck. A maritime museum in the south of England commissioned me to design a website. Charles, the man I spoke to on the phone, said they didn't want to use templates: everything must be bespoke. It was a challenging project; it would take three or four months to complete. I was anxious to begin.

A few days after that I ran out of milk, and popped into town for more. When I got back, there was a diminutive old lady in a headscarf standing in my kitchen, grinding coffee in a brass mill. At her elbow was a small copper jug. "*Dobro jutro,*" she said. Her smile was animated, but she was clearly dead.

Over the weeks that followed, unaccommodated ghosts filled the flat. The oldest arrived first, shapeless, clutching suitcases. They came from Mostar, Sarajevo, Banjaluka, from eighteen years ago. They had walked past engines blown out of vehicles and the half-cremated remains of other human beings, they had fallen over cliffs, stepped on mines, and been shot with guns – in the eye neatly once or the back many times. They had borne most, without a doubt, so it was not up to me to question where they chose to put it down.

It was a busy time for me. Charles phoned several times a week to discuss my progress, which was never fast enough for his taste. But it was nice to have company when I finished work in the evenings, and mostly the ghosts were no bother, though sometimes they moved things and it took me a while to find them. When I walked past they reached out to touch me. Their hands grazed my shoulder, tugged on my hair. None of this was malicious: all they wanted was my attention.

At first their conversations were unintelligible to me, like the lyrics of music that is playing in another room. But over time the words separated out and acquired meaning.

When they perceived this, the *gosti* – ghosts, guests-became more demanding. They needed paprika, they needed clean towels. They needed someone to listen to them, and who else was there?

In spring more ghosts arrived: mostly men. They appeared to be waiting for something, and to ease this process they got hold of my husband's single malt whisky. They also smoked constantly, dropping the butts on the carpet. I don't mean to be rude, but it wouldn't have killed them to use an ash tray.

As the flat filled up, it was the living room that attracted the greatest number of ghosts. The fumes from home-grown Bosnian tobacco mixed with the earthy smell of American cigarettes accepted as bribes or bought on the black market: Smokin Joes and Camel Reds were passed across my coffee table by card-playing Muslim soldiers whose fingers were stained pollen-yellow with nicotine. '*Čmaru jedan*,' they muttered. '*Baja pojela ti jaja.*' You arsehole. I hope a bug eats your balls. When they were winning, they switched to old battle songs. 'The scent of lilies fills the meadow,' they hummed under their breath. On the other side of the room a dead Serb glared.

One of the ghosts, a young boy, stood apart by the TV. My attention was drawn to him because of his wing-like elbows, which reminded me of Jon. He was clutching a bass guitar, although his hands had been destroyed by a shell.

'That one is my grandson.'

It was the old woman with the coffee pot, the one from the first day; she'd walked through the wall beside me. I wished they wouldn't do that: it left marks.

'He's a good boy, but I don't like his music – all that banging and shouting. You want a little coffee? Yes you have time. Sit here next to me.'

'Tchk! Look at this. My doctor calls them liver spots. I said to him Doctor, it looks to me like I'm going mouldy. He gives me cream for them but I don't like to use it, Allah never meant for us to cure old age.'

'Now Tarik, that grandson of mine, he's a Muslim but you wouldn't know it. I've seen him drinking šlivovica, he even eats sausage rolls. Well like his daddy he was raised in Sarajevo so it's not surprising. Young people there just glue their eyes to the West, it's always been that way. Tarik's in a rock band with three older boys I don't like much. They call themselves *Histerija*, and worship some London noiseniks by name of Led Zep Lin. The only time I went to one of their concerts I had to put my hands over my ears. '*Ja sam budućnost*,' they kept on shouting. Such nonsense. I think all the jiggling about was meant to be dancing, but it looked more like some kind of fit.

'Just a few weeks after that the siege started. You know, every morning of my life I'd woken up to the tram bells, but on that day they stopped dead and didn't ring again for three years. It seemed like everything stopped, even gravity. Snipers were killing people in the streets, and by the time anyone dared go out for the bodies they'd got stiff. I'll never forget how the arms stuck out and the heads twisted sideways instead of flopping. Or the shelling either: it was like that rock concert all over again.'

'My husband, may Allah rest him, left the house each evening to stand on the street with other Sarajevan men and talk. Those poor men looked worse than the dead and no wonder: they'd eaten bread made of oats, then of the stalks of hazel bushes, then of ground apple skins. They said the West had forgotten us, but it's my opinion the West never knew we existed. Of course Tarik listened to them. He knew he was a Muslim by then, surely enough: he thought he'd grow up into arms. But I sent him out to buy beans the day the mortar hit Markale market in February '94, and sixty-eight people died. That shell blew off both his poor hands, though what killed him was the fragment that got buried in his skull.'

Tarik stood in the corner of my living room, clutching his guitar. 'I am the future,' he whispered. Angry chords curled around him. '*Ja sam budućnost.*'

'Motherfucking Chetnik!'

"Sisterfucking Turk!"

The coffee table across the room from us collapsed, and playing cards swooped through the air like startled birds. Two red-faced men in black leather jackets squared up to each other: the glaring Serb had tripped over a card player's foot. I thought they were going to fight, but the card player's friends grabbed him by the shoulders and the Serb allowed himself to be shunted back to our side of the room, grumbling loudly and cracking his knuckle-tattoos into his palms.

Such eruptions were frequent, especially at first. "You did this," the ghosts accused each other. "You did that." But their voices were tired: it was hard for them to remember which flag to kiss and which to burn. The elderly ghosts were happier recalling their vegetable gardens than their disputes; they sat together to drink šlivovica and reminisce. And the soldiers from different armies exchanged cigarettes more often than blows. So in my living room Bosnian Muslims, Catholics, Orthodox Christians and Sephardic Jews gathered and pooled like drops of water.

In March or April – I'm not sure which – Charles began to call more persistently, wanting to know when the website would be finished. "Is something wrong?" he said. Eventually I took the phone off the hook.

I barely left the flat, even to buy food. Instead I ate what the ghosts cooked. They filled my kitchen with the smell of lamb frying in garlic and paprika; then they got distracted, by an argument about politics or ingredients, and burnt the bottoms of my pans. I did sometimes go out, to get things they had forgotten: tomatoes, an egg. But those times were getting rarer. The light was too bright, the people too solid; their voices reached me from a long way away, like sounds heard underwater. I preferred to devote myself to the ghosts: their recipes and whims, their stories.

So I was there when Lejla walked in. Though barely more than a child, she was visibly pregnant. She leant against the living room wall, just inside the threshold, holding her heavy belly in her hands.

"Pass that cushion, dear? *Ouf*, that's better. At my age a body has too many bones and they all get closer to the surface."

It was Tarik's grandmother again, clutching her eternal coffee pot. "That poor child," she said. "She's a Croat, see the dinky gold cross? It's a wonder she held onto it. I've just this minute been chatting to a woman who was locked up with her in Banjaluka. She's making chicken liver pilaf if you want some later."

This was Lejla's story, as told to me by Tarik's grandmother, who heard it from the ghost in my kitchen, who saw it with her own eyes.

She was a nice girl from a good Croat family, who didn't decide to get out of the newly declared Republic of Serbia quickly enough. So she was separated from them and held in a makeshift prison camp next to the police station.

At night there were rapes. Guards with flashlights, or just torches made of lighted paper, searched for anyone who was young and female.

They used a knife to cut her dress open. Then they raped her many times in one night. She was thirteen years old. When she became pregnant they continued to rape her nightly.

Eventually they put her in a train waggon meant for cattle but crowded with

Croat women and girls. The train travelled south to the foot of Vlašić mountain. When it ran out of track, buses took them the rest of the way up. Lejla joined an interminable line of people: heads down, shuffling, sometimes stumbling, but moving slowly towards free Bosnia, or so they hoped. The road cut into the side of the mountain was narrow, and there were corpses on the rocks below. At some point in the night she tripped and joined them.

In my living room, she – Lejla – listened shyly to the music that came from Tarik, the handless guitar-playing boy. She moved towards him so slowly she did not seem to be moving at all. But she was.

"Jimmy Page," she said quietly.

He frowned. "John Paul Jones." He had a memorable voice for a boy: gravelly, smoke-scarred.

"Is he better?"

"I prefer bass guitar."

"I do too."

It wasn't long before the Muslim boy with the shell-broken hands was deep in conversation with the raped Croat girl.

She did tell him some of what had happened to her. Shutting her eyes, touching the raised bumps of the wallpaper with one hand. But mostly they talked about rock music. He was enthusiastic about the electric guitar of Plavi Orkestar; she giggled. "They dance like chickens," she said. "They hug turkeys in their videos." She mentioned the plangent music of Crvena Jabuka; he thought it was wet. "You may discord," he said politely. But she did not discord with him, not at all.

I watched her a lot, I admit. She was so young. I worried about how she would cope with motherhood: how could a child look after a child? Sometimes I forgot that they were both already dead.

I stopped work on the maritime museum's website. When I was not watching Lejla and Tarik, I went into the kitchen and helped the older ghosts cook: I peeled their potatoes, I rubbed flour and lard together to make pastry. Or I sat at the breakfast bar and listened to them talk. All the ghosts were keenly interested in the search for General Mladić, the Bosnian-born Serb who had led an army through their country; most of them were angry at how long it was taking.

"He's in Serbia."

"He's not in Serbia at all, he's in Montenegro."

"He's escaped Europe altogether by now."

"That butchering peasant."

"What occupies him these days?"

"He used to keep bees."

"No doubt he still jeers at his goats."

"The ones he named Major and Mitterand and Kohl?"

"Yes, after those Western politicians he so despised."

"His health too must be much on his mind."

"He's old by now."

"So would I be, but for him."

"So would we all be."

At first the ghosts were easily distracted from the manhunt. They compared the size of their gardens, or the size of the peppers they had grown in their gardens. They had aimed to sit on a porch swing through summer evenings, but into their modest ambitions had blundered Mladić. He had shelled their houses and mined their vegetable patches. He had said: "I shall be vindicated by history." They were his dead.

Then, last Thursday, I came downstairs to find all the ghosts clustered round the television, jostling each other for the best view. As I watched, the screen fizzed and spat, and my husband appeared. It was definitely him: his pointy elbows, moley hair. The ghosts nudged me slyly, but then the picture flickered and Jon was replaced by a man with a polka-dot tie and greased-back hair. "Kruno Standeker, the journalist," Tarik's grandmother whispered to me. "He was killed by a road mine near Mostar seventeen years ago."

"Ratko Mladić," intoned Standeker, "was born in Bosnia in 1942. He went to military school in Serbia and entered the Yugoslav army, rising to the rank of Colonel General. When Bosnia declared independence in 1992, he blockaded the city of Sarajevo and shelled it for four years. In 1994, he allegedly ordered the genocide of over eight thousand Muslims in Srebrenica."

The screen filled with soundless black-and-white footage. The war was over, and Mladić – ears sticking out beneath his peaked cap – was retreating to Serbia, where he lived in army barracks, going openly to football matches and horse races. Then the political atmosphere turned against him and he was on the run in Han Pijesak and New Belgrade, moving every two or three weeks between housing estates whose walls were covered with spray-paint vampires and signatures like coils of barbed wire. Serbia put a price on his head; international arrest warrants were drawn up. He left the overpopulated cities and went to live in the country, in a village of plum tree orchards and pepper fields, in a farmhouse made from clay bricks. He had mistaken boredom for safety; he thought no one would look for him there. Even so, he went out only at night. It was as if he had become one of the graffiti vampires from the housing estate walls, as if light petrified him.

For as long as he could remember, Mladić had been a skilful chess player, winning games across the length and breadth of Bosnia: in prison camps, at military headquarters, on the front lines. Now he sat before the chessboard, hour after hour, while an invisible foreigner, a man with electronic eyes and ears, chased his pieces across the black and white squares.

Mladić lived, fortified by obscurity, with cousin Branko, his Glorious Defender: his castle, of course. But most of his pawns – the army, the police, the secret services – had already been taken, the treacherous bastards, they'd gone over to the other side. And now his queen was under threat, his wife Bosiljka suddenly detained and questioned; harassed, beset, while he, helpless, fumed. Even his son – his slick-wheeled, Dacia-driving knight – was closely watched: it was too dangerous to see him much.

The screen spurted into Technicolor, revealing a woman sitting upright at a virtual desk. "DAWN RAID," she reported, and the ghosts inhaled a collective gasp. They'd been channel-surfing since the news broke – they knew the story off by heart, in all its permutations – but this was their favourite part. "MEN

IN MASKS MOVE IN," they mouthed in perfect synchronicity with the woman on the screen, working their mandibles hard. Ten plain-clothed policemen or twenty special officers, armed or unarmed, depending which broadcaster you picked. Mladić was on his way to the garden for a pre-dawn stroll, or he was sitting in his front room wearing a tracksuit. He was handcuffed or he was not handcuffed; he was made to sit in the yard or he was taken into the house. He definitely offered his captors some home-made plum brandy. "Checkmate," he conceded politely. "Which one of you is the foreigner?"

I started to understand.

"High-tech surveillance and tracking techniques were behind this operation," the reporter was saying primly. "The British and American intelligence services have been formally thanked for their assistance. Also Bakir Izetbegović, the Muslim member of Bosnia's tripartite presidency, has announced that the arrest was completed with the support of Bosnian security agencies."

Was *that* what my husband had been doing? Hunting down the butcher of Srebrenica, bringing the man who called himself God to justice for crimes against humanity? Of course – it must be. Why else would the ghosts have come here?

All day long my guests were jubilant: they twittered and squeaked. They wanted a banquet, a celebration: they wanted, when it came down to it, a wake. Most of them also wanted to keep watching television, so although I'd have liked to see if Jon reappeared, I offered to help in the kitchen.

The first thing we made was *bosanski lonac*, as this would take five hours to cook. We layered chunks of lamb and potato with vegetables including cabbage and peppers, added garlic cloves and chopped parsley, seasoned it generously, and poured white wine and stock over the top. I turned on the gas and brought the oven up to temperature, then placed the stew carefully on the bottom shelf.

The ghosts showed me how to make *sarmas* while the stew was cooking, rolling grape leaves around tiny portions of rice and meat. Once or twice someone opened the oven, and the kitchen filled with the warm, heavy smell of lamb and the floury sourness of half-cooked potatoes. Whenever that happened, cigarette-smoking soldiers appeared in the kitchen to ask how long it would be. The cooks shooed them out. They made *baklava* ahead of time: spreading honey onto filo pastry and adding rosewater to crushed pistachio nuts. The air filled with a back-of-the-throat sweetness and another smell I couldn't identify, which made me uneasy.

I went into the living room to get away from this smell, and also to check what was happening on the news. It's a good thing I did, because soon after that there was an almighty crack as the oven exploded in the kitchen. I remember being lifted off the ground by the force of the explosion, and the sound of glass smashing; then nothing until the siren-scream and epileptic blue lights of the ambulance.

So that's it. I am in bed in a private room in Gloucestershire Royal Hospital. I have concussion and two broken ribs, and the doctors put me on a drip when I first came in because I was badly emaciated. They said that firemen had been over the wreckage of my kitchen and found nothing but a few pieces of an empty pot in the oven; they suggested I had barely eaten for weeks or months. I know they wanted me to concede that I let the gas build up to dangerous levels on purpose, triggering the explosion in a cry for help. But I survived because I was in the living room not the kitchen, and gas doesn't explode by itself. It must have been a spark from one of the soldiers' cigarettes: they kept looking in the oven to see if the stew was done.

When I pointed this out to the doctors, they said it might help if I wrote down what I remembered of the last few months. I've been happy while doing this. The ghosts were always telling me their stories, so I think it is what they would have wanted, too.

And now I'm told my husband will be coming back from Bosnia soon. One thing is certain: Jon won't see the funny side of me being the one to get blown up. When he goes away he says *be safe*, by which he means *safer than normal*, because if something happens to me he won't be here.

THE FESTIVAL OF THE IMMORTALS

Helen Simpson

Helen Simpson (b.1959) was born in Bristol. She has published five collections of short stories, including *In-Flight Entertainment* (2010). Simpson read English at Oxford University, where she wrote a thesis on Restoration farce. She then worked for five years as a staff writer at *Vogue* before becoming a freelance writer. Her awards include the E.M. Forster Award (2002) and The Society of Authors Travelling Scholarship (2006). Simpson lives in London and is a Fellow of the Royal Society of Literature.

The Daniel Defoe event had just been cancelled, and as a consequence of this the queue for the tea tent was stretching half way round the meadow. Towards the back, shivering slightly this damp October morning, were two women who looked to be somewhere in the early November of their lives.

"Excuse me, but are you going to the next talk?" one of them asked the other, waving a festival brochure at a late lost wasp.

"Who, me?" replied the woman. "Yes. Yes, I am. It's Charlotte Brontë reading from Villette, I believe."

"Hmm, I hope they keep the actual reading element to a minimum," said the first, wrinkling her nose. "Don't you? I can read Villette any time."

"Good to hear it in her own voice, though," suggested the other.

"Oh I don't know," said the first. "I think that can be overdone. Some curiosity value, of course, but half the time an actor would read it better. No, I want to know what she's like. That difficult father. Terribly short-sighted. Extremely short full stop. The life must shed light on the work, don't you think. What's the matter, have I got a smudge on my face or something?"

"It's not . . . ?" said the other, gazing at her wide-eyed. "It's not Viv Armstrong is it?"

"Yes," said Viv Armstrong, for that was indeed her name. "But I'm afraid I don't . . ."

"Phyllis!" beamed the other. "Phyllis Goodwin. The ATS, remember? Bryanston Square? Staining our legs brown with cold tea and drawing on the seams with an eyebrow pencil?"

"Fuzzy!" exclaimed Viv at last. "Fuzzy Goodwin!"

"Nobody's called me that for over fifty years," said Phyllis. "It was when you wrinkled your nose in that particular way, that's when I knew it was you."

The rest of their time in the queue flew by. Before they knew it they were carrying tea and carrot cake over to a table beneath the rustling amber branches of an ancient beech tree.

"I'm seventy-eight and I'm still walking up volcanoes," Viv continued, as they settled themselves. "I don't get to the top any more but I still go up them. I'm off to Guatemala next week."

Eager, impulsive, slapdash, Phyllis remembered. Rule-breaking. Artless. Full of energy. In some ways, of course, she must have changed, but just now, she appeared exactly, comically, as she always had been, in her essence if not in her flesh. Although even here, physically, her smile was the same, the set of her shoulders, the sharpness of nose and eyes.

"The first time I saw you, we were in the canteen," said Phyllis. "You were reading The Waves and I thought, ah, a kindred spirit. I was carrying a steamed treacle pudding and I sat down beside you."

That's right, thought Viv, Fuzzy had had a sweet tooth-look at the size she was now. She'd had long yellow hair, too, just like Veronica Lake, but now it was short and white.

"I still do dip into The Waves every so often," she said aloud. "It's as good as having a house by the sea, don't you think? Especially as you get older. Oh, I wonder if she's on later, Virginia, I'd love to go to one of her readings."

Viv knew many writers intimately thanks to modern biographers, but she was only really on first name terms with members of the Bloomsbury group.

"Unfortunately not," said Phyllis. "That's a cast iron rule of this festival, a writer can only appear if they're out of copyright, and Virginia isn't out of it for another five years".

"But she must be, surely," said Viv. "Isn't copyright fifty years?"

"Well it was, until recently," said Phyllis. "And Virginia was out of it by the early nineties, I happen to know because I was at one of her readings here. Oh, she was wonderful. What a talker! She kept the whole marquee in stitches – spellbound – rocking with laughter. But then they changed the copyright law, something to do with the EU, and now it's life plus seventy years, and she went back in again. So she won't be allowed to return until 2011 at the earliest. Very galling as we might not still be here by then."

"Oh I don't know," said Viv. "Aren't you being rather gloomy? Seventy-eight isn't that old."

"It is quite old, though," said Phyllis doubtfully.

"Well I suppose so. But it's not old old," said Viv. "It's not ninety. Come on, now, Fuzzy, we've got some catching up to do."

In the next few minutes they attempted to condense the last half-century into digestible morsels for each other. Viv had put in a year at teacher training college then found teaching posts through Gabbitas-Thring, while Phyllis had taken a secretarial course at Pitman's College in Bloomsbury followed by a cost accounting job at the Kodak factory where she lived, totting up columns of figures in a large ledger at a slanting desk. At some point between the Olympics being held at White City and the year of the Festival of Britain, they had met their respective husbands.

"All this is such outside stuff, though," said Phyllis obscurely. She was supposed to be writing her memoirs, spurred on by a local Life-writing course, but had been dismayed at her attempts so far, so matter-of-fact and chirpy and boring.

They ploughed on. Viv had settled just inside the M25, before it was there, of course, while Phyllis lived just outside it. They had had three children each, and now had seven grandchildren between them.

"Two girls and a boy," said Viv. "One's in computers, one's a physiotherapist and one has yet to find his feet. He's forty-eight."

"Oh," said Phyllis. "Well I had the other combination, two boys and a girl. Ned's an animal feed operator but his real love is Heavy Metal, much good it's done him. Peter's an accountant – no, I keep forgetting, they don't call them accountants any more. They're financial consultants now."

"Like refuse collectors. 'My old man's a dustman.' Remember that?" said Viv. "Then there was 'My old man said follow the van, and don't dilly-dally on the way.' My mother used to sing that. I divorced my old man, by the way, sometime back in the seventies."

"I'm sorry," said Phyllis.

"Don't be silly," said Viv. "I've realised I'm a natural chopper and changer. Or rather, I start off enthusiastic and then spot the feet of clay. It's a regular pattern. I did eventually find the love of my life, when I was in my sixties, but he died. What about your daughter, though? Didn't you mention a daughter?"

"Yes," said Phyllis, blinking. "Sarah. She went into the book business. In fact, she's the one who dreamed up the idea behind this festival, and now she runs it. Artistic Director of the Festival of Immortals, that's her title."

"Good Lord," said Viv. "The opportunities there are for girls these days!"

" It's a full-time year-round job as you can imagine," said Phyllis, gaining confidence. "She spent months this year trying to persuade Shakespeare to run a workshop but the most she could get him to do was half-promise to give a masterclass in the sonnet. He's supposed to be arriving by helicopter at four this afternoon but it's always touch and go with him, she says, it's impossible to pin him down."

"Good Lord", said Viv again, and listened enthralled as Phyllis told her anecdotes from previous years, the time Rabbie Burns had kept an adoring female audience waiting 40 minutes and had eventually been tracked down to the stationery cupboard deep in congress or whatever he called it with Sarah's young assistant Sophie. Then there was the awful day Sarah had introduced a reading as being from The Floss on the Mill and George Eliot had looked so reproachful, even more so than usual, but Sarah did tend to reverse her words when flustered, it wasn't intentional. Every year Alexander Pope roared up in a fantastic high-powered low-slung sportscar, always a new one, always the latest model. Everybody looked forward to that. Jane Austen could be very sarcastic in interviews if you asked her a question she didn't like, she'd said something very rude to Sarah last year, very cutting, when Sarah had questioned her on what effect she thought being fostered by a wet-nurse had had on her. Because of course that was what people were interested in now, that sort of detail, there was no getting away from it.

Last year had been really fascinating, if a bit morbid, they'd taken illness as their theme – Fanny Burney on the mastectomy she'd undergone without anaesthetic, Emily Brontë giving a riveting description of the time she was bitten by a rabid dog and how she'd gone straight back home and heated up a fire iron and used it herself to cauterise her arm. Emily had been very good in the big round table discussion, too, the one called "TB and Me," very frank. People had got the wrong idea about her, Sarah said, she wasn't unfriendly, just rather shy; she was lovely when you got to know her.

"They've done well, our children, when you think of it," commented Viv. "But then, there was no reason for them not to. First-generation university."

Phyllis had tried to describe in her memoir how angry and sad she had been at having to leave school at fourteen; how she'd just missed the 1944 Education Act with its free secondary schooling for everyone. Books had been beyond her parents' budget, but with the advent of paperbacks as she reached her teens she had become a reader. Why couldn't she find a way to make this sound interesting?

"Penny for your thoughts, Fuzzy," said Viv.

"Viv," said Phyllis, "Would you mind not calling me that? I never did like that name and it's one of the things I'm pleased to have left in the past."

"Oh!" said Viv. "Right you are."

"Because names do label you," said Phyllis. "I mean, Phyllis certainly dates me."

"I was called Violet until I left home," confessed Viv. "Then I changed to Viv and started a new life."

"I always assumed Viv was short for Vivien," said Phyllis. " Like Vivien Leigh. I saw Gone with the Wind five times. Such a shame about her and Laurence Olivier."

"Laurence Olivier as Heathcliff!" exclaimed Viv. "Mr Darcy. Henry V. Henry V! That was my first proper Shakespeare, that film."

"Mine too," confessed Phyllis. "Then later I was reading 'The Whitsun Weddings', – I'd been married myself for a while – and I came to the last verse and there it was, that shower of arrows fired by the English bowmen, just like in the film. The arrows were the new lives of the young married couples on the train and it made me cry, it made me really depressed, that poem."

"Not what you'd call a family man, Philip Larkin," said Viv.

"Not really," said Phyllis. "You know, thinking about it, the only time I stopped reading altogether was when they were babies. Three under five. I couldn't do that again."

"I did keep reading," said Viv. "But there were quite a few accidents. And I was always a Smash potato sort of housewife, if I'm honest."

"I wish I had been," said Phyllis enviously.

She cast her mind back to all that; the hours standing over the twin tub, the one hundred ways with mince, nagging the children to clean out the guinea pig cage, collecting her repeat prescription for Valium. That time too she had tried to record in her memoir, but it had been even more impossible to describe than the days of her girlhood.

"It's not in the books we've read, is it, how things have been for us," said Viv. "There's only Mrs Ramsay, really, and she's hardly typical."

"I've been bound by domestic ties," said Phyllis. "But I'm still a feminist."

"Are you?" said Viv, impressed.

"Well I do think women should have the vote so yes, I suppose I am. Because a lot of people don't really, underneath, think women should have the vote, you know."

"I had noticed," said Viv.

"It's taken me so long to notice how the world works that I think I should be allowed extra time," said Phyllis.

At this point she decided to confide in Viv about her struggles in Life writing. For instance, all she could remember about her grandmother was that she was famous for having once thrown a snowball into a fried fish shop; but was that the sort of thing that was worth remembering? Another problem was, just as you didn't talk about yourself in the same way you talked about others, so you couldn't write about yourself from the outside either. Not really. Which reminded her, there had been such a fascinating event here last year, Sarah had been interviewing Thomas Hardy and it had come out that he'd written his own biography, in the third person, and got his wife Florence to pretend that she'd written it! He'd made her promise to bring it out as her own work after he'd died. The audience had been quite indignant, but, as he told Sarah, he didn't want to be summed up by anybody else, he didn't want to be cut and dried and skewered on a spit. How would you like it, he'd asked Sarah and she'd had to agree she wouldn't. This year she, Sarah, had taken care to give him a less contentious subject altogether – he was appearing tomorrow with Coleridge and Katherine Mansfield at an event called The Notebook Habit.

"Yes," said Viv, " I've got a ticket for that."

This whole business of misrepresentation was one of Sarah's main bugbears at the Festival, Phyllis continued. She found it very difficult knowing how to handle the hecklers. Ottoline Morrell, for example, turned up at any event where DH Lawrence was appearing, carrying on about Women in Love, how she wasn't Hermione Roddice, how she'd never have thrown a paperweight at anyone, how dare he and all the rest of it. Sarah had had to organise discreet security guards because of incidents like that. The thing was, people minded about posterity. They minded about how they would be remembered.

"Not me," said Viv.

"Really?" said Phyllis.

"I'm more than what's happened to me or where I've been," said Viv. "I know that and I don't care what other people think. I can't be read like a book. And I'm not dead yet, so I can't be summed up or sum myself up. Things might change."

"Goodness," said Phyllis, amazed.

"Call no man happy until he is dead," shrugged Viv, glancing at her watch. "And now it's time for Charlotte Brontë. I had planned to question her about those missing letters to Constantin Heger, but I don't want Sarah's security guards after me."

The two women started to get up, brushing cake crumbs from their skirts and assembling bags and brochures.

"Look, there's Sarah now," said Phyllis, pointing towards the marquee.

Linking arms, they began to make their way across the meadow to where the next queue was forming.

"And look, that must be Charlotte Brontë with her, in the bonnet," Viv indicated. "See, I was right! She is short."

GRANDPA'S GHOST

Fay Weldon

Fay Weldon (b.1931) was brought up in New Zealand and returned to Britain when she was ten. She read Economics and Psychology at the University of St Andrews. Weldon worked briefly for the Foreign Office and as a journalist. She also had a successful career as an advertising copywriter before becoming a full-time writer. Weldon has published thirty-four novels, five short story collections and numerous plays for stage, television and radio. She lives in London. Her memoir, *Auto Da Fay*, was published in 2002.

I t's been such a horrible year," said Marta to Griff. "Do we have to have a party?"

"It hasn't been too bad," said Griff, who was the cheerful one. "Nobody's died, nobody's been ill, we own the roof over our heads and we've paid the gas bill. Isn't that worth celebrating?"

"I just want to cry," said Marta. She was 38, past the age when actresses get work easily, and she'd been "resting" for a full 18 months. She felt discarded and unlucky. Griff worked in IT at the town hall.

Right now they had a hard time making ends meet. They had two children: Bernard and Meryl, 12 and 10. Bernard hated his school, Meryl loved hers. But then Meryl had her mother's looks.

As her maternal grandmother Emma said, "The prettier you are, the easier your life." Grandpa Paul had never said anything nice in his life; now he haunted the house at 12, Chicklade Grove where they lived. Or so Meryl swore.

"Grandpa again," she'd say when the cat was sick in her shoe, or Bernard broke his hockey stick, or when Marta left the bathroom tap on and the ceiling came down, or someone's football came through the kitchen window, or the postman put next door's letters through their door.

"Oh please don't," her mother would beg. "Grandpa's dead and buried and out of the way."

"No he isn't," Meryl would say. "He's in the corner of the cellar stairs pretending to be a blanket and saying, 'Heh, heh, heh,' when you go down to read the gas. It's why you can't get a job. It's why no one buys the house."

Which was nonsense of course, and who believed in ghosts in this day and age? Marta's dad hadn't even died at No 12, but in a hospice five miles away. Emma, her mum, had died two years before him, patient and good, worn out from putting up with Paul's meanness, his shouting and his jeering "heh, heh, hehs".

It wasn't as if anyone went down into the dark, dank cellar if they could help it. Why would they? Only Griff sometimes, to check the meter, and the would-be buyers who came, saw and went away. They'd already dropped the price by £30,000. A whole year and it hadn't sold.

"A party, a party!" the children begged. "On New Year's Eve!"

"We've nothing to celebrate," said Marta. "And we can't afford it."

But Griff was adamant. True, funds were tight because the unexpected kept happening: the drains had blocked, a tree had fallen through next door's roof and Griff had broken a leg trying to move it – but he refused to be downhearted.

"If you've had a run of bad luck," he said, "all you can do is gather friends round and drink to a better future. So let's do it!"

Reluctantly, Marta started ringing round. It was amazing what a lot of people responded, even at such short notice. Next door asked if they could bring a friend who was staying, a Trinidadian Glaswegian – a very special man. "Fine by us," said Griff, "he can do the first footing. We're all on the fair side."

"Eh?" asked next door.

"Scottish New Year legend has it that the first one over the threshold brings good luck if he's dark, bad luck if he's fair. We're in need of a dark-haired person."

"Ah," said next door. "You're on!"

The party was to be on Tuesday night. On the Monday, Griff went out into the cold to bring home the special offer on Strongbow and Stella, prosecco for the ladies plus two bottles of own-brand vintage champers at £15.99 for midnight. The fridge was full of mince pies baked by Meryl, so Marta would have to take the champagne to the cellar to keep it cold.

No one liked the cellar stairs, especially now Meryl had started telling everyone that her grandfather was living down there, a ghost disguised as an old blanket, and the cause of all the accidents.

"Poor old Grandpa Paul," said Meryl. "He gets the blame for everything."

"No, I do," said Bernard. Marta had just shouted at him for trying to chop down the For Sale sign.

Marta switched on the new EU long-life low-wattage bulb. She hadn't been to the cellar for ages. The bulb cast a gloomy light on the discarded possessions of the decades – old sewing machines, bicycles, car batteries, leather suitcases – when she heard it.

"Plumbing?" she said aloud.

"Heh, heh, heh."

That noise again. Spooky. On the corner where the stairs turned, there was a pile of old clothes, or blankets or something – or someone, leaning against the wall. She switched on her torch to brave a closer look – and a pair of glittering eyes shot open. "Heh, heh, heh" again.

The eyes had a cartoonish quality; the "heh, heh, heh" was the jeering half-giggle that her father would make when her mother said something stupid. Or was it coming from Marta herself?

She retreated backwards up the stairs as fast as she could, dropped the torch, tripped and fell a good 10 steps, taking with her the plastic bag that held the vintage fizz.

"You're lucky you didn't break your wrist," said Griff. "I wish you'd be more careful!" They were in the hospital. But once all the blood, pain and fear had passed, Marta ended up with no more than a bad sprain and a stitch or two where broken glass had gone through the plastic bag.

"Not Mum's fault, Dad," said Meryl. "Just Grandpa again. It's his house."

"Not any more," said Marta. "It's mine. I deserve it."

She'd had a long, hard journey with her father. He'd first barred her from his door when she was 16 and went to drama school against his wishes. Emma had had to sneak out to visit her own daughter.

"You have to forgive him," her mother had said. "He's only trying to bring you to your senses. He'll calm down." Paul had, and Marta had been allowed back in. But when, after college, she and Griff had moved in together, Paul would make his displeasure clear by going to the pub whenever they came round, even after Bernard was born.

"Little brat," Paul had called him. Then when baby Meryl was coming along and Griff and Marta thought it was time to get married, Paul wouldn't go to the wedding.

"Have some mercy," her mother said. "Your father can hardly walk you down the aisle when you're seven months pregnant. Can't you make do with a register office?"

But Marta couldn't: she wanted a white wedding in a church with her father to give her away. It didn't happen. Then, four years later, Emma got a brain tumour – probably from secondary smoking, the doctor said – and Marta blamed her father.

Indeed, she'd burst into tears at the funeral and spoken the truth in front of everyone: "If it wasn't for you, Dad, she'd still be alive. You killed her."

After that, father and daughter didn't speak. It wasn't that Marta didn't try. She sent cards and made phone calls, but they were never returned. And when the old man fell ill with lung cancer and she'd gone to visit him at the hospice, he'd refused to see her. He'd asked the nurse to send her away. Marta was dreadfully hurt. Then when he died she'd refused to go to his funeral.

"Marta!" Griff had been shocked. "But he's your father!"

"He disowned me," she said. "So I disown him. Anyway I hate funerals and I have an audition."

Griff took Meryl and Bernard to the funeral, and Marta stayed home. No one was more surprised than Marta when the will was read and he'd left her the family home: five bedrooms, one bathroom, large garden. They were thrilled to be able to move out of their rented flat and join the property-owning classes.

But what a poisoned chalice! Inheritance tax, new roof, community charge, utility bills – it was impossible. They would downsize: No 12 went on the market, but no one would buy.

At the party, Marta had her arm in a sling and found herself telling her misfortunes to the Trinidadian Glaswegian, who was a very handsome man with soft, intelligent eyes. She even told him how her dead father was sitting on the cellar stairs cursing her. But then she had had quite a lot of prosecco.

"I don't suppose he's cursing you," said the Trinidadian from Glasgow. "He's just sitting on your cellar stairs because you didn't go to his funeral – and he's unburied in your heart."

"Don't be silly!" said Marta, shocked. Whose side was this guy on?

"And you're so guilty," went on the Trinidadian, "that you made yourself fall down those stairs. No such thing as an accident." Marta bristled.

"What did your mother die of?" he asked.

"A brain tumour," she said.

Her eyes were smarting.

"Nothing at all to do with secondary smoking," he observed. "Poor man! Burying his wife and you accusing him of murder in front of everyone!"

"But they were always quarrelling." It began to sound a little feeble.

"Husband and wives always are," said the man from Trinidad. "Doesn't mean they don't love each other." Now Marta was sniffling.

"He turned me away from the hospice."

"He loved you. He wanted you to remember him in his prime."

"Total nonsense," she said. "I'll remember him as a ghost on the stairs who can't even die. Miserable old sod." But now she was crying, great big gulps. People were looking.

"Family is family," he said. "You quarrel and you make up, but not going to a funeral is just not what you do. He was right about not being an actress. You didn't make a go of it, did you? And as for having a white wedding, come on! You were a mother, not a virgin."

"Oh stop, stop!" she cried.

"You'd better go down and say you're sorry," he said. So she did.

She shone the torch into the pile of rags and the eyes glittered back.

"I'm really sorry, Dad," she said. "It's just so easy to blame others."

It wasn't a ghost, it was a pile of old blankets and coats. She turned off the torch and the eyes became buttons.

"Heh, heh," coughed the boiler, or whatever it was. She shook out a blanket and a cloud of tiny moths fluttered away. That was odd: it wasn't the time of year for moths. When she went upstairs, the Glaswegian said, "Has he gone?"

"I think so," she said. Midnight struck. Everyone toasted the New Year and sang Auld Lang Syne.

"Just as well," he said. He went out the front door and came back in, first footing, and handed Griff a piece of coal. Ritual satisfied. Everyone cheered.

In the morning he came round and offered to buy the house. No agent's fees needed. He was the father of six and needed a large house in London. It would suit him just fine.

"I told you it was Grandpa, Mum," said Meryl.

GHOST

James Robertson

James Robertson (b.1958) is a poet, novelist, short story writer and editor who writes for children and adults, in English and in Scots. He was born in Kent and grew up in Scotland. Robertson studied history at Edinburgh University. He was first Writer in Residence for the Scottish Parliament (2004). James Robertson's novels include *The Testament of Gideon Mack*, *And The Land Lay Still* and *The Professor of Truth*.

Another time – any number of other times – she might turn around and nothing would be there. Nothing would have happened. Because that was the thing, it was always over, she never quite saw *it*. What she saw was the ripple, the vibration, the aftermath. And this was why the experience was never complete. She understood this. She was an unreliable witness, because what she saw was not what she saw but a visual echo of what she *might* have seen.

She looked through the dining-room window and it was as if a gust of wind, on a day entirely still, had waltzed across the grass and flowerbeds. Along the route of the old brick path that had been there before they redesigned the garden. No cat or bird moved like that. And no gust of wind either, because there was a gauzy kind of shade to it, and a shape. And *waltz* wasn't right after all, for something so straight, so pedestrian.

She thought, *Did I ever see her when the brick path was still in place?* And that was odd, because until that moment she'd never thought of it as female, but there it was: *her*.

She thought, *A day does not exist unless we say so, and even when we say so it requires collective will and individual imagination to sustain its existence. The next day, it's gone. You cannot capture time and hold it. A date in a diary proves nothing.*

She thought, *I will go to my grave believing that I saw whatever it was I saw.* She was quite shocked at this betrayal of her own scepticism, this undoing of reason, but not as much as she might have been. Because it was not the first time.

She didn't have a "gift'. She absolutely didn't believe that about herself. It wasn't about her, it was about the garden, and who had been there before.

One year in every four, she thought, *there is a day after this one that does not exist in the other years. We accept that: it's an invention.* But this was different: a real, unreal thing that had happened, somehow, just before she, somehow, witnessed it.

EXTENDED COPYRIGHT